the ANGEL

Also by CARLA NEGGERS

ABANDON
CUT AND RUN
THE WIDOW
BREAKWATER
DARK SKY
THE RAPIDS
NIGHT'S LANDING
COLD RIDGE
ON THE EDGE
"Shelter Island"
THE HARBOR
STONEBROOK COTTAGE
THE CABIN
THE CARRIAGE HOUSE
THE WATERFALL
ON FIRE
KISS THE MOON
CLAIM THE CROWN

CARLA NEGGERS

the ANGEL

MIRA®

MIRA

ISBN-13: 978-0-7783-2483-6
ISBN-10:   0-7783-2483-4

THE ANGEL

www.MIRABooks.com

Printed in U.S.A.

First Printing: May 2008
10 9 8 7 6 5 4 3 2 1

To Kate and Conor

ACKNOWLEDGMENTS

To Brendan Gunning for all the wonderful Irish and Irish-American stories, and to Myles Heffernan, Paul Hudson, Jamie Carr and Christine Wenger for sharing your knowledge and expertise.

To Sarah Gallick for the help with Irish saints and for sending me early excerpts from *The Big Book of Women Saints*.

To my daughter, Kate Jewell, and my son-in-law, Conor Hansen, for getting us all to southwest Ireland. Conor, I'll never forget standing in the stone house where your great-grandfather was born, or meeting your cousins on the Beara Peninsula.

To Don Lucey for the insight into Irish music and all the great recommendations.

To my agent, Margaret Ruley, and to my editor, Margaret Marbury, for the unwavering patience and support, and to the rest of the fabulous team in New York and Toronto— Donna Hayes, Craig Swinwood, Loriana Sacilotto, Dianne Moggy, Katherine Orr, Marleah Stout, Heather Foy, Michelle Renaud, Stacy Widdrington, Margie Miller, Adam Wilson and everyone who makes MIRA Books such an incredible pleasure to work with.

And to Joe Jewell, my husband, for all the great times in Boston, "our" city, and to Zack Jewell, my son...yes, another trip to Ireland is in the works. Can't wait!

Carla Neggers
P.O. Box 826
Quechee, VT 05059
www.carlaneggers.com

~ *Prologue*

South Boston, Massachusetts
2:00 p.m., EDT
July 12, Thirty Years Ago

A scrap of yellow crime scene tape bobbed in the rising tide of Boston Harbor where the brutalized body of nineteen-year-old Deirdre McCarthy had washed ashore. Bob O'Reilly couldn't take his eyes off it.

Neither could Patsy McCarthy, Deirdre's mother, who stood next to him in the hot summer sun. Coming out here was her idea. Bob didn't want to, but he didn't know what else to do. He couldn't let her go alone.

"Deirdre was an angel."

"She was, Mrs. McCarthy. Deirdre was the best."

Ninety degrees outside, and Patsy shivered in her pastel blue polyester sweater. She'd lost weight in the three weeks since Deirdre hadn't come home after her shift as a nurse's aide. At first the police had believed she was just another South Boston girl who'd gone wrong. Patsy kept at them. Not Deirdre.

She disappeared on the night of the summer solstice. The longest day of the year.

Appropriate, somehow, Bob thought.

Patsy's eyes, as clear and as blue as the afternoon sky, lifted to the horizon, as if she were trying to see the island of her birth, as if Ireland could bring her the comfort and strength she needed to get through her ordeal. She'd left the southwest Irish coast forty years ago at the age of nine and hadn't been back since. She loved to tell stories about her Irish childhood, how she was born in a one-room cottage with no plumbing, no central heat—not even an outhouse—and how she'd learned to bake her famous brown bread on an open fire.

Bob wondered how she'd tell this story. The story of her daughter's kidnapping, rape, torture and murder.

The police hadn't released details, but Bob, the son of a Boston cop, had heard rumors of unspeakable acts of violence and depravity. He was twenty and planned on becoming a detective, and one day he would have to wade through such details himself. He hoped the victim would never be someone he knew. He and Deirdre had learned to roller-skate together, had given each other their first kiss, just to see what it was like.

"I heard the cry of a banshee all last night," Patsy said quietly. "I can't say I do or don't believe in fairies, but I heard what I heard. I knew we'd find Deirdre this morning."

The fine hairs stood on the back of Bob's neck. A retired firefighter walking his golden retriever at sunrise had come upon Deirdre's body. The police had come and gone, working with a grim efficiency, given Boston's skyrocketing homicide rate. Now they had another killer to hunt.

With the city behind them and the boats out on the water and planes taking off from Logan Airport, Bob still could hear the lapping of the tide on the sand. He'd never felt so damn helpless and alone.

"Deirdre Ita McCarthy." Patsy crossed her arms on her chest as if she were cold. "It's the name of an Irish saint, you know. Saint Ita was born Deirdre and took the name Ita when she made her vows. Ita means 'thirsting for divine love.'"

Patsy was deeply religious, but Bob had stopped attending mass regularly when he was sixteen and his mother said it was up to him to go or not go. He knew he'd go back to church for Deirdre's funeral.

"I've never been good at keeping track of the saints." He tried to smile. "Even the Irish ones."

"Saint Patrick, Saint Brigid and Saint Ita are early Celtic saints. Saint Ita had the gift of prophecy. Angels visited her throughout her life. Do you believe in angels, Bob?"

"I've never thought about it."

"I do," she whispered. "I believe in angels."

It wouldn't strike Patsy as particularly contradictory to say in one breath she'd heard a banshee—a solitary fairy—and in another that she believed in angels. If her beliefs brought her comfort, Bob didn't care. He didn't know what to tell her about banshees or angels or anything else. Her husband had died of a heart attack four years ago. Now this. "The police will find who took Deirdre from us."

"No. They won't. They can't." Patsy shifted her gaze back to the crime scene tape floating in the water. "The police are only human after all."

"They won't rest until they catch whoever did this."

"It was the devil who took Deirdre. It wasn't a man."

"Doesn't matter. If the police have to go to hell to find and arrest the devil, that's what they'll do. If I have to do it myself, I will."

"No—no, Bob. Deirdre wouldn't have you sacrifice your soul. She's with her sister angels now. She's at peace."

Bob suddenly realized Patsy meant the devil literally. He pictured

Deirdre with her blond hair and blue eyes, her translucent skin and innocent smile. She was as good as good ever was. She wouldn't have stood a chance with someone who meant her harm. Devil or no devil.

He'd miss her. He'd miss her for as long as he lived.

He pushed back his emotions. It was something he'd need to learn to do if he was going to be a detective and catch people the likes of whoever had killed Deirdre.

"We don't want this cretin to hurt someone else."

"No, we don't." Patsy turned from the water. "But there are other ways to fight the devil."

Two hours later, Bob found his sister, Eileen, reciting the rosary on a bench in the shade of a sprawling oak on the Boston College campus, where she had a summer work-study job at the library.

"I didn't know you still had rosary beads," he said.

"I didn't, either. I found them in my jewelry box this morning." She spoke in a near whisper as she held a single ivory-colored bead between her thumb and forefinger. "I haven't said the rosary in ages. I thought I might not remember, but it came right back to me."

Bob sat next to her. His sister was the smart one in the family. She'd returned two days ago from a summer study program in Dublin. No one had called to tell her Deirdre had gone missing. What could Eileen do from Ireland? Why spoil her time there, when they all hoped Deirdre would turn up, safe and sound?

When news of the discovery of Deirdre's body reached the O'Reilly household that morning, Eileen pretended nothing had happened and left for work.

"I've just come from the waterfront with Mrs. McCarthy," Bob said.

Eileen tensed, as if his words were a blow, and he didn't go on. Her hair was more dirty blond than red like his, and she had more freckles. She'd never thought she was all that attractive, but she'd always been hard on herself—his sister had no limit to her personal list of faults big and small.

"There's nothing the police can do now." Eileen lifted her eyes from her rosary beads and shifted her gaze to her older brother. "Is there?"

"They can find Deirdre's killer. They can stop him from killing again."

"They can't undo what happened."

His sister's left hand trembled, but her right hand, which held her rosary beads, was steady. Bob noticed how pale she was, as if she'd been sick. His smart, driven sister had so many plans for her life, but coming back home from Ireland to Deirdre's disappearance had thrown Eileen right back into the world she was trying to exit.

And now Deirdre was dead.

Eileen's fingers automatically moved to the next bead, and he saw her lips move as she silently recited the Hail, Mary.

He waited for her to finish the entire rosary and return her beads to their navy velvet pouch. She clutched it in her hand and leaned back against the bench.

They both watched a squirrel run up a maple tree.

Without looking at her brother, Eileen said, "I'm pregnant."

Of all the things Bob had anticipated she might say when she'd finished praying, he hadn't imagined that one. Their parents would be shocked. *He* was shocked. She didn't have a boyfriend that he knew about.

He fought an urge to run away. Get out of Boston, away from the aftermath of Deirdre's death, from what was to come with his sister. It all flashed in his mind—Patsy grieving next door, the police hunting for Deirdre's killer, Eileen getting bigger, trying to figure out what to do with the baby.

The baby's father. Who the hell was he?

Bob curled his hands into tight fists. He was young. He didn't have to stay in Boston and deal with all these problems. He could go anywhere. He could be a detective in New York or Miami or Seattle.

Hawaii, he thought. He could move to Honolulu.

"How far along are you?" he asked.

"Not far. I haven't had the test yet, but I know."

"Eileen…" Bob looked at his younger sister, but she didn't meet his eyes. "What happened in Ireland?"

But she jumped to her feet and walked quickly toward the ivy-covered building where she worked, and he didn't follow her.

A week later, a series of calls into the Boston Police Department alerted them to a man who had just leaped from a boat into Boston Harbor.

He was in flames when he hit the water.

By the time a passing pleasure boat reached him, he was dead.

Within hours, the dead man was identified as Stuart Fuller, a twenty-four-year-old road worker who rented an attic apartment three blocks from the house where Deirdre McCarthy lived with her mother. Police discovered overwhelming evidence that tied him to Deirdre's murder.

They had their devil.

The autopsy on Fuller determined that he'd drowned, but his burns would have killed him if he hadn't gone into the water.

That evening, Bob found Patsy on her back porch with about twenty small angel figurines lined up on the top of the wide wooden railing. Despite the summer heat, she wore a pink polyester sweater, as if she expected never to be warm again.

"Deirdre collected angels," Patsy said.

"I know. It made it easy to buy her presents." Bob pointed at a colorful glass angel he'd found for her on a high school trip to Cape Cod. "I got her that one for her sixteenth birthday."

"It's beautiful, Bob."

His throat tightened. "Mrs. McCarthy——"

"The police were here this morning. They told me about Stuart Fuller. They asked me if I knew him."

"Did you?"

"Not that I recall. I suppose I could have seen him in the neighborhood." She narrowed her eyes slightly. "At church, perhaps. The devil is always drawn to good."

Bob watched her use a damp cloth to clean a delicate white porcelain angel holding a small Irish harp. It was one of the more valuable figurines in Deirdre's collection and one of her favorites. She'd loved all kinds of angels—it didn't matter if they were cheap, cheesy, expensive, ethnic. She used to tell Bob she wanted to buy a glass curio cabinet in which to display them.

"Patsy…do you know anything about Fuller's death?"

She seemed not to hear him. "I have a story I want to tell you."

Bob didn't have the patience for one of her stories right now. "Which one?"

"One you've never heard before." She held up the cleaned figurine to the light. "My grandfather first told it to me as a child in Ireland. Oh, he was a wonderful storyteller."

"I'm sure he was, but——"

"It's a story about three brothers who get into a battle with fairies over an ancient stone angel." Patsy's eyes sparked, and for a moment, she seemed almost happy. "It was one of Deirdre's favorites."

"Then it can't be depressing. Deirdre didn't like depressing stories."

"She didn't, did she? Come, Bob. I'll make tea and heat up some brown bread for you. It's my mother's recipe. I made it fresh this morning. My father used to say my mother made the best brown bread in all of West Cork."

Bob had no choice but to follow Patsy into her small kitchen and help her set out the tea and the warm, dense bread. How many times had he and Eileen and Deirdre sat here, listening to Patsy tell old Irish stories?

She joined him at the table, her cheeks flushed as she buttered a small piece of bread. "Once upon a time," she said, laying on her Irish accent, "there were three brothers who lived on the southwest coast of Ireland—a farmer, a hermit monk and a ne'er-do-well, who was, of course, everyone's favorite…"

Bob drank the tea, ate the bread and pushed back tears for the friend he'd lost as he listened to Patsy's story.

~Chapter 1

Near Mount Monadnock
Southern New Hampshire
4:00 p.m., EDT
June 17, Present Day

Keira Sullivan swiped at a mosquito and wondered if its Irish cousins would be as persistent. She'd find out soon enough, she thought as she walked along the trail to her mother's cabin in the southern New Hampshire woods. She'd be on a plane to Ireland tomorrow night, off to the southwest Irish coast to research an old story of mischief, magic and an ancient stone angel.

In the meantime, she had to get this visit behind her and attend a reception tonight in Boston. But she couldn't wait to be tucked in her rented Irish cottage, alone with her art supplies, her laptop, her camera and her walking shoes.

For the next six weeks, she'd be free to think, dream, draw, paint, explore and, perhaps, make peace with her past.

More accurately, with her mother's past.

The cabin came into view, nestled on an evergreen-blanketed hill above a stream. Keira could hear the water tumbling over rocks and feel it cooling the humid late spring air. Birds twittered and fluttered nearby—chickadees, probably. Her mother would have given all the birds on her hillside names.

The mosquito followed Keira the last few yards up the path. It had found her at the dead-end dirt road where she'd left her car and stayed with her throughout the long trek through the woods. She was less than two hours from Boston, but she might as well have been on another planet as she sweated in the June heat, her blond hair coming out of its pins, her legs spattered with mud. She wished instead of shorts she'd worn long pants, in case her solo mosquito summoned reinforcements.

She stood on the flat, gray rock that served as a step to the cabin's back entrance. Her mother had built the cabin herself, using local lumber, refusing help from family and friends. She'd hired out, reluctantly, only what she couldn't manage on her own.

There was no central heat, no plumbing, no electricity. She had no telephone, no radio, no television—no mail delivery, even. And forget about a car.

On frigid New England winter nights, life had to get downright unbearable, if not dangerous, but Keira knew her mother would never complain. She had chosen the simple, rugged existence of a religious ascetic. No one had thrust it upon her.

Keira peered through the screen door, grateful that her mother's stripped-down lifestyle didn't prohibit the use of screens. The pesky mosquito could stay outside.

"Hello—it's me, Mum. Keira."

As if her mother had other children. As if she might have forgotten her only daughter's name since chucking the outside world. Keira had last visited her mother several weeks ago but hadn't stayed long. Then again, they hadn't spent much time together in the past few years, never mind the past eighteen months when she'd first announced her intention to pursue this new commitment.

Her mother had always been religious, which Keira respected, but this, she thought as she swiped again at her mosquito—this isolated hermit's life just wasn't right.

"Keira!" her mother called, sounding cheerful. "Come in, come in. I'm here in the front room. Leave your shoes on the step, won't you?"

Keira kicked off her hiking shoes and entered the kitchen—or what passed for one. It consisted of a few rustic cupboards and basic supplies that her mother had scavenged at yard sales for her austere life. Her priest had talked her into a gas-powered refrigerator. He was working on talking her into a gas-powered stove and basic plumbing—even just a single cold-water faucet—but she was resisting. Except for the coldest days, she said, she could manage to fetch her own water from the nearby spring.

Winning an argument with Eileen O'Reilly Sullivan had never been an easy task.

Keira crossed the rough pine-board floor into the cabin's main living area. Her mother, dressed in a flowing top and elastic-waist pants, got up from a high stool at a big hunk of birch board set on trestles that served as her worktable. Her graying hair was blunt cut, reminding Keira of a nun, but although her mother had turned to a religious life, she'd taken no vows.

"It's so good to see you, Keira."

"You, too." Keira meant it, but if she wanted to see her mother, she had to come out here—her mother wouldn't come to her in Boston. "The place looks great. Nice and cozy."

"It's home."

Her mother sat back on her work stool. Behind her, a picture window overlooked an evergreen-covered hillside that dropped down to a stream. Keira appreciated the view, but, as much as she needed solitude herself at times, she couldn't imagine living out here.

A nearby hemlock swayed in a gust of wind, sending a warm breeze through the tiny cabin. Except for a wooden crucifix, the barn-board walls of the main room were unadorned. Besides the worktable and stool, the only other furnishings were an iron bed with a thin mattress, a rocking chair and a narrow chest of drawers. Not only was the small, efficient cast-iron woodstove the sole source of heat, it was also where her mother did any cooking. She chopped the wood for the stove herself.

The land on which the cabin was built was owned by a South Boston couple whose country home was through the woods, in the opposite direction of the path Keira had just used. She considered them complicit in her mother's withdrawal from the world—from her own family. They'd let her choose the spot for her cabin and then stood back, neutral, until she'd finally moved in last summer.

A year out here, Keira thought. *A year, and she looks as content as ever.*

"It really is so good to see you, sweetheart," her mother said quietly.

"I didn't mean to interrupt your work."

"Oh, don't worry about that."

A large sheet of inexpensive sketch paper was spread out on her worktable. Before retreating to the woods, she'd owned an art supply store in the southern New Hampshire town where she'd moved as a young widow with a small daughter. Over the years, she'd become adept at calligraphy and the tricky art of gilding, supplementing her income by restoring gilt picture frames and mirrors and creating elaborate wedding and birth announcements. Now she was applying her skills to the almost-forgotten art of producing an illuminated manuscript. The same couple who'd let her build on their land had found someone willing to pay her to illustrate an original manuscript of select Bible passages. Other than requesting an Irish Celtic sensibility and choosing the passages, the client left her alone.

It was painstaking work—deliberate, skilled, imaginative. She had her supplies at arm's reach. Brushes, pens, inks, paints, calligraphy nibs, gilding tips, a gilding cushion, polishing cloths and burnishers.

"You're working on your own Book of Kells," Keira said with a smile.

Her mother shook her head. "The Book of Kells is a masterpiece. It's been described as the work of angels. I'm a mere human."

Another wind gust shook the trees outside on the hill. Storms were brewing, a cold front about to move in and blow out the humidity that had settled over New England during the past week. Keira wanted to get back to her car before the rain started.

"Did you see the Book of Kells when you were in Ireland in college?"

"I did." Her mother's tone was distant, controlled. She shifted her gaze to the blank, pure white paper on her desk, as if envisioning the intricate, thousand-year-old illuminated manuscript. "I'll never forget it. What I'm doing is quite different. Much simpler."

"It'll be wonderful."

"Thank you. The Book of Kells consists mainly of the four Gospels, but I was asked to start with the fall of Adam and Eve." Her mother's eyes, a striking shade of cornflower blue, shone with sudden humor. "I haven't settled on the right serpent."

Keira noticed a series of small pencil sketches taped to the birch board. "Those are some pretty wild serpents. It doesn't get to you, being up here all alone drawing pictures of bad-assed snakes and bolts of lightning?"

Her mother laughed. "No bolts of lightning, I'm afraid. Although..." She thought a moment. "I don't know, Keira, you could be onto something. A bright, organic bolt of lightning in the Garden of Eden could work, don't you think?"

Keira could feel the tension easing out of her. She'd moved to Boston in January after a brief stint in San Diego and had trekked up here on snowshoes, hoping just to find her mother alive and reasonably sane. But her mother had been warm and toasty, a pot of chili bubbling on her woodstove, content with her rigid routines of prayer and work. Keira had thought living closer would mean they'd see more of each other. It hadn't. She could have stayed in San Diego or moved to Miami or Tahiti or Mozambique—or Ireland, she thought. The land of her ancestors.

The land of her father.

Maybe.

Her mother's sociability didn't last, and the humor in her eyes died almost immediately. A studied blankness—a sense of peace, she would no doubt say—brought a neutrality to her expression. She seemed to take a conscious step back from her engagement with the world. In this case, the world as represented by her daughter.

Keira tried not to be offended. "I came to say goodbye for a few weeks. I leave for Ireland tomorrow night for six weeks."

"Six weeks? Isn't that a long time?"

"I'm doing something different this trip." Keira hesitated, then said, "I'm renting a cottage on the southwest coast. The Beara Peninsula."

Her mother gazed out at her wooded hillside. A second screen door opened onto another rock step and a small yard where she'd planted a vegetable garden, fencing it off to keep out deer and who knew what other animals.

Finally, she let out a breath. "Always so restless."

True enough, Keira thought. As a child, she'd roamed the woods with a sketch pad and colored pencils. In college, she'd snapped up every opportunity to go places—backpacking with friends out West, jumping on a lobster boat with a short-lived boyfriend, spending a summer in Paris on a shoestring. After college, she'd tried several careers before falling back on what she loved most—drawing, painting, folklore. She'd managed to combine them into a successful career, becoming known for her illustrations of classic poems and folktales. That her work was portable, allowing her to indulge her sense of adventure, was another plus.

"When I was here last," she said, "I told you about a project I'm involved with—I'm working with an Irish professor who's putting together a conference on Irish folklore next spring. It'll be in two parts, one in Boston and one in Cork."

"I remember," her mother said.

"One of the emphases will be on twentieth-century immigrants to America. I've been working that angle, and I ended up deciding to put together and illustrate a collection specifically of their stories. I have a wonderful one Gran told me before she died. She was from West Cork—"

"I know she was. Keira…" Her mother's eyes were pained.

"What's wrong? I've been to Ireland before. Not the Beara Peninsula, but—Mum, are you afraid I'm going to run into my father?"

"Your father was John Michael Sullivan."

But Keira was referring to her biological father. Her mother had returned home from a summer study program in Ireland at nineteen, pregnant with Keira. When Keira was a year old, her mother had married John Sullivan, a South Boston electrician ten years her senior. He was killed in a car accident two years later, and his widow and adopted daughter had moved out of Boston and started a new life.

Keira had no clear memory of him, but when she looked at pictures of him, she felt an overwhelming sense of affection, gratitude and grief, as if some part of her did remember him. Her mother never discussed that one trip to Ireland thirty years ago. For all Keira knew, her biological father could have been a Swedish tourist or another American student.

She debated a moment, then said, "A woman on your old street in South Boston heard about the folklore project and got in touch with me. She told me this incredible story about three Irish brothers who fight with each other and fairies over an ancient stone angel—"

"Patsy McCarthy," her mother said in a toneless voice.

"That's right. She says she told you this story, too, before your trip to Ireland. The brothers believe the statue is of one of the angels said to visit Saint Ita during her lifetime. The fairies believe it's not an angel at all but actually one of their own who's been turned to stone. There's more to it—it's quite a tale."

"Mrs. McCarthy told a lot of stories."

"Her grandfather heard this one when he worked in the copper mines on the Beara Peninsula and told it to Patsy when she was a little girl in Ireland. The village where the brothers lived isn't named, but there are enough details—"

"To pinpoint it. Yes, I know."

"And the spot where the hermit monk brother lived. You could make a stab at finding it, at least, if you know the story." Keira waited, but when her mother didn't respond, continued. "Patsy told me you were determined to find the village and look for the hermit monk's hut on your trip to Ireland before I was born."

"She's a gifted storyteller."

"Yes, she is."

Her mother lifted a small, filmy sheet of gold leaf to the light streaming in through the window. The use of gold—real gold—was what distinguished a true illuminated manuscript, but Keira knew it was far too soon for her mother to apply gold to her work-in-progress.

"Do you know the difference between sin and evil, Keira?"

Keira didn't want to talk about sin and evil. She wanted to talk about Patsy's old story and magic, mischief and fairies. "It's not something I think much about."

"Adam and Eve sinned." Her mother turned the gold leaf so that it gleamed in the late-afternoon light. "They wanted to please God, but they succumbed to temptation. They regretted their disobedience. They took no delight in what they did."

"In other words, they sinned."

"Yes, but the serpent is a different case altogether. He delights in his wrongdoing. He exults in thwarting God. He sees himself as the antithesis of God. Unlike Adam and Eve, the serpent didn't commit a sin in the Garden of Eden. The serpent chose evil."

"Honestly, Mum, I don't know how you can stand to think about this stuff out here by yourself."

She set the thin gold leaf on the pure white paper. Keira knew from experience that the gold leaf was difficult to work with but re-silient, able to withstand considerable manipulation without breaking into pieces. Applied properly, it looked like solid gold, not just a whisper of gold.

"We all sin, Keira," her mother said without a hint of a smile, "but we're not all evil. The devil understands that. Evil is a particular dispensation of the soul."

"Does this have anything to do with Ireland? With what happened there when you—"

"No. It has nothing at all to do with Ireland." She took a breath. "So, how's your work?"

Keira stifled her irritation at the abrupt change of subject. It felt like a dismissal and probably was, but she reminded herself that she hadn't come out to the woods to judge her mother, or even for information. She'd come simply to say goodbye before flying out of Boston tomorrow night.

"My work's going great right now, thanks." Why go into detail when that world no longer interested or concerned her mother?

"That's good to hear. Thank you for stopping by." She got to her feet and hugged Keira goodbye. "Live your life, sweetheart. Don't get too caught up in all these crazy old stories. And please don't worry about me out here. I'm fine."

On her way back through the woods, Keira resisted the urge to look over her shoulder for the devil and serpents. Instead, she remembered herself as a child, and how her mother would sing her Irish songs and read her stories. Every kind of story—stories about fairies and wizards and giants, about hobbits and elves and dark lords, princes and princesses, witches, goblins, cobblers, explorers and adventurers.

How could such a fun-loving, sociable woman end up alone out here?

But Keira had to admit there had been hints of what was to come—that she'd seen glimpses in her mother of a mysterious sadness and private guilt, of a longing for a peace that she knew could never really be hers in this life.

Her mother insisted she hadn't withdrawn from the world or rejected her family but rather had embraced her religious beliefs in a personal and profound way. She viewed herself as participating in a centuries-old monastic tradition.

That was no doubt true, but Keira didn't believe her mother's retreat to her isolated cabin was rooted entirely in her faith. As she'd listened to Patsy McCarthy tell her old story, Keira had begun to wonder if her mother's trip to Ireland thirty years ago had somehow set into motion her eventual turn to the life of a religious hermit.

Another mosquito—or maybe the same one—found Keira, buzzing in her ear and jerking her back to the here and now, to her own life. She swiped at the mosquito as she plunged down the narrow trail through the woods to the dead-end dirt road where she'd parked.

The story of the three Irish brothers, the fairies and the stone angel wasn't about a pot of gold at the end of the rainbow. Ultimately, Keira thought, it was about the push-pull of family ties and the deep, human yearning for a connection with others, for happiness and good fortune.

Mostly, it was just a damn good yarn—a mesmerizing story that Keira could illustrate and tell on the pages of her new book.

"They say the stone angel lies buried to this day in the old ruin of the hermit monk's hut."

Maybe, maybe not. Patsy McCarthy, and her grandfather before her, easily could have exaggerated and embellished the story over the years. It didn't matter. Keira was hooked, and she couldn't wait to be on her way to Ireland.

In the meantime, she had to get back to Boston in time for a reception and a silent auction to benefit the Boston-Cork folklore project that had brought her to Patsy's South Boston kitchen in the first place.

She glanced back into the woods, wishing her mother could be at the reception tonight. "Not just for my sake, Mum," Keira whispered. "For your own."

⌒ Chapter 2

Boston Public Garden
Boston, Massachusetts
7:00 p.m., EDT
June 17

Victor Sarakis didn't let the heavy downpour stop him.

He couldn't.

He had to warn Keira Sullivan.

Rain spattered on the asphalt walks of the Public Garden, a Victorian oasis in the heart of Boston. He picked up his pace, wishing he'd remembered to bring an umbrella or even a hooded jacket, but he didn't have far to go. Once through the Public Garden, he had only to cross Charles Street and make his way up Beacon Street to an address just below the gold-domed Massachusetts State House.

He could do it. He *had* to do it.

The gray, muted light and startling amount of rain darkened his mood and further fueled his sense of urgency.

"Keira can't go to Ireland."

He was surprised he spoke out loud. He was aware that many

people didn't consider him entirely normal, but he'd never been one to talk to himself.

"She can't look for the stone angel."

Drenched to the bone as he was, he'd look like a madman when he arrived at the elegant house where the benefit auction that Keira was attending tonight was being held. He couldn't let that deter him. He had to get her to hear him out.

He had to tell her what she was up against.

What was after her.

Evil.

Pure evil.

Not mental illness, not sin—evil.

Victor had to warn her in person. He couldn't call the authorities and leave it to them. What proof did he have? What evidence? He'd sound like a lunatic.

Just stop Keira from going to Ireland. Then he could decide how to approach the police. What to tell them.

"Victor."

His name seemed to be carried on the wind.

The warm, heavy rain streamed down his face and back, poured into his shoes. He slowed his pace.

"Victor."

He realized now that he hadn't imagined the voice.

His gaze fell on the Public Garden's shallow pond, rain pelting into its gray water. The famous swan boats were tied up for the evening. With the fierce storms, the Public Garden was virtually empty of people.

No witnesses.

Victor broke into an outright run, even as he debated his options. He could continue on the walkways to Charles Street, or he could charge through the pond's shallow water, try to escape that way.

But already he knew there'd be no escape.

"Victor."

His gait faltered. He couldn't run fast enough. He wasn't athletic, but that didn't matter.

He couldn't outrun such evil.

He couldn't outrun one of the devil's own.

No one could.

~ Chapter 3

Beacon Hill
Boston, Massachusetts
8:30 p.m., EDT
June 17

Not for the first time in his life, Simon Cahill found himself in an argument with an unrelenting snob, this time in Boston, but he could as easily have been in New York, San Francisco, London or Paris. He'd been to all of them. He enjoyed a good argument—especially with someone as obnoxious and pretentious as Lloyd Adler.

Adler looked to be in his early forties and wore jeans and a rumpled black linen sport coat with a white T-shirt, his graying hair pulled back in a short ponytail. He gestured across the crowded, elegant Beacon Hill drawing room toward a watercolor painting of an Irish stone cottage. "Keira Sullivan is more Tasha Tudor and Beatrix Potter than Picasso, wouldn't you agree, Simon?"

Probably, but Simon didn't care. The artist in question was supposed to have made her appearance by now. Adler had griped about that, too, but her tardiness hadn't seemed to stop people from bidding on the two paintings she'd donated to tonight's auction. The second was of a fairy or elf or some damn thing in a magical glen. Proceeds would go to support a scholarly conference on Irish and Irish-American folklore to be held next spring in Boston and Cork, Ireland.

In addition to being a popular illustrator, Keira Sullivan was also a folklorist.

Simon hadn't taken a close look at either of her donated paintings. A week ago, he'd been in Armenia searching for survivors of a moderate but damaging earthquake. Over a hundred people had died. Men, women, children.

Mostly children.

But now he was in a suit—an expensive one—and drinking champagne in the first-floor chandeliered drawing room of an elegant early nineteenth-century brick house overlooking Boston Common. He figured he deserved to be mistaken for an art snob.

"Beatrix Potter's the artist who drew Peter Rabbit, right?"

"Yes, of course."

Simon swallowed more of his champagne. It wasn't bad, but he wasn't a snob about champagne, either. He liked what he liked and didn't worry about the rest. He didn't mind if other people fussed over what they were drinking—he just minded if they were a pain in the ass about it. "When I was a kid, my mother decorated my room with cross-stitched scenes of Peter and his buddies."

"I beg your pardon?"

"Cross-stitch. You know—you count these threads and—" Simon stopped, deliberately, and shrugged. He knew he didn't look like the kind of guy who'd had Beatrix Potter rabbits on his wall as a kid, but he was telling the truth. "Now that I'm thinking about it, I wonder what happened to my little rabbits."

Adler frowned, then chuckled. "That's very funny," he said, as if he couldn't believe Simon was serious. "Keira Sullivan is good at what she does, obviously, but I hate to see her work overshadow several quite interesting pieces here tonight. A shame, really."

Simon looked at Adler, who suddenly went red and bolted into the crowd, mumbling that he needed to say hello to someone.

A lot of his arguments ended that way, Simon thought as he finished off his champagne, got rid of his empty glass and grabbed a full one from another tray. The event was catered, and most of the guests were dressed up and having a good time. From what he'd heard, they included a wide range of people—academics, graduate students, artists, musicians, folklorists, benefactors, a couple of priests and a handful of politicians and rich art collectors.

And at least two cops, but Simon steered clear of them.

"Lloyd Adler's not that easy to scare off," Owen Garrison said, shaking his head as he joined Simon. Owen was lean and good-looking, but all the Garrisons were. Simon was built like a bull. No other way to say it.

"I'm on good behavior tonight." He grinned, cheekily putting out his pinkie finger as he sipped his fresh champagne. Owen just rolled his eyes. Simon decided he'd probably had enough to drink and set the glass on a side table. Too much bubbly and he'd start a fight. "I didn't say a word."

"You didn't have to," Owen said. "One look, and he scurried."

"No way. I'm charming. Everyone says so."

"Not everyone."

Probably true, but Simon did tend to get along with people. He was at the reception as a favor to Owen, whose family, not coincidentally, owned the house where it was taking place. The Garrisons were an old-money family who'd left Boston for Texas after the death of Owen's sister, Dorothy, at fourteen. It was a hellish story.

Just eleven himself at the time, Owen had watched her fall off a cliff and drown near the Garrison summer home in Maine. There was nothing he could have done to save her.

Simon suspected the trauma of that day was the central reason Owen had founded Fast Rescue, an international search-and-rescue organization. It was based in Austin and operated on mostly private funds to perform its central mission to put expert volunteer teams in place within twenty-four hours of a disaster—man-made or natural—anywhere in the world.

Simon had become a Fast Rescue volunteer eighteen months ago, a decision that was complicating his life more than it should have, and not, he thought, because the Armenian mission had fallen at a particularly awkward time for him.

Owen, a top search-and-rescue expert himself, was wearing an expensive suit, too, but he still looked somewhat out of place in the house his great-grandfather had bought a century ago. The decor was in shades of cream and sage green, apparently Dorothy Garrison's favorite colors. The first floor was reserved for meetings and func-tions, but the second and third floors comprised the offices for the foundation named in Dorothy's honor and dedicated to projects her family believed would have been of particular interest to her.

Owen glanced toward the door to the house's main entry. "Still no sign of Keira Sullivan. Her uncle's getting impatient."

Her uncle was Bob O'Reilly, her mother's older brother and one of the two cops there tonight Simon was avoiding. Owen's fiancée, Abigail Browning, was the other one. She and O'Reilly were both detectives with the Boston Police Department. O'Reilly was a beefy, freckle-faced redhead with a couple decades on the job. Abigail was in her early thirties, slim and dark-haired, a rising star in the Homicide Unit.

She was also the daughter of John March, the director of the Federal Bureau of Investigation and the reason Simon's association with Fast Rescue had become complicated. He used to work for March. Sort of still did.

He'd decided to avoid Abigail and O'Reilly because both of them would have a nose for liars.

"Any reason to worry about your missing artist?" he asked Owen.

"Not at this point. It's pouring rain, and the Red Sox are in town— rained out by now, I'm sure. I imagine traffic's a nightmare."

"Can you call her?"

"She doesn't own a cell phone. No phone upstairs in her apart- ment, either."

"Why not?"

"Just the way she is."

A flake, Simon thought. He'd learned, not that he was interested, that Keira was renting a one-bedroom apartment on the top floor of the Garrison house until she figured out whether she wanted to stay in Boston. He understood wanting to keep moving—he lived on a boat himself and not by accident.

"Abigail's bidding on one of Keira's pieces," Owen said.

"The fairies or the Irish cottage?"

"The cottage, I think."

They were imaginative, cheerful pieces. Keira had a flare for cap- turing and creating a mood—a part-real, part-imagined place where people wanted to be. Her work wasn't sentimental, but it wasn't edgy and self-involved, either. Simon didn't have much use for a painting of fairies or an Irish cottage in his life. No house to hang it in, for one thing.

Irish music kicked up, and he noticed an ensemble of young mu- sicians in the far corner, obviously enjoying themselves on their mix of traditional instruments. He picked out a tin whistle, Irish harp, bodhran, mandolin, fiddle and guitar.

Not bad, Simon thought. But then, he liked Irish music.

"The girl on the harp is Fiona O'Reilly," Owen said. "Bob's oldest daughter."

Simon wasn't sure he wanted to know any more about Owen's friends in Boston, especially ones in, or related to, people in law enforcement. It was all too tricky. Too damn dangerous. But here he was, playing with fire.

Owen's gaze drifted back to his fiancée, who wore a simple black dress and was laughing and half dancing to the spirited music. Abigail caught his eye and waved, her smile broadening. They were working on setting a date for their wedding. Whenever it was, Simon planned to be out of the country.

"You can't tell her about me, Owen."

"I know." He broke his eye contact with Abigail and sighed at Simon. "She'll find out you're not just another Fast Rescue volunteer on her own. One way or the other, she'll figure out your relationship with her father—she'll figure out that I knew and didn't tell her. Then she'll hang us both by our thumbs."

"We'll deserve it, but you still can't tell her. My association with March is classified. We shouldn't even be talking about it now."

Owen gave a curt nod.

Simon felt a measure of sympathy for his friend. "I'm sorry I put you in this position."

"You didn't. It just happened."

"I should have lied."

"You did lie. You just didn't get away with it."

The song ended, and the band transitioned right into the "The Rising of the Moon," a song Simon knew well enough from his days in Dublin pubs to hum. But he didn't hum, because if he'd been mistaken for an art critic—or at least an art snob—already tonight, next he'd be mistaken for a music critic. Then he'd have to rethink his entire approach to his life, or at least start a brawl.

"In some ways," he said, "my lie was more true than the truth."

Owen grabbed a glass of champagne. "Only you could come up with a statement like that, Simon."

"There are facts, and there's truth. They're not always the same thing."

A whirl of movement by the entry drew Simon's attention, and he gave up on trying to explain himself.

A woman stood in the doorway, soaking wet, water dripping off the ends of her long, blond hair.

"The missing artist, I presume."

Even as he spoke, Simon saw that something was wrong. He heard Owen's breath catch and knew he saw it, too. The woman—she had to be Keira Sullivan—was unnaturally pale and unsteady on her feet, her eyes wide as she seemed to search the crowd for someone.

Simon surged forward, Owen right with him, and they reached her just as she rallied, straightening her spine and pushing a sopping lock of hair out of her face. She was dressed for the woods, but even as obviously shaken as she was, she had a pretty, fairy-princess look about her with her black-lashed blue eyes and flaxen hair that was half pinned up, half hanging almost to her elbows.

She was slim and fine-boned, and whatever had just happened, Simon knew it hadn't been good.

"There's a body," she said tightly. "A man. Dead."

That Simon hadn't expected.

Owen touched her wrist. "Where, Keira?"

"The Public Garden—he drowned, I think."

Simon was familiar enough with Boston to know the Public Garden was just down Beacon Street. "Are the police there?" he asked.

She nodded. "I called 911. Two Boston University students found him—the body. We all got caught in the rain, but they were ahead of me and saw him before I did. He was in the pond. They pulled him out. They're just kids. They were so upset. But there was nothing anyone could do at that point." Despite her distress, she was composed, focused. Her eyes narrowed. "My uncle's here, isn't he?"

"Yes," Simon said, but he wasn't sure she heard him.

He noticed Detectives Browning and O'Reilly working their way to Keira from different parts of the room, their intense expressions indicating they'd already found out about the body through other means. They'd have pagers, cell phones.

The well-dressed crowd and the lively Irish music—the laughter and the tinkle of champagne glasses—were a contrast to stoic, drenched Keira Sullivan and her stark report of a dead man.

Abigail got there first. "Keira," she said crisply but not without sympathy. "I just heard about what happened. Let's go into the foyer where it's quiet, okay?"

Keira didn't budge. "I didn't see anything or the patrol officers on the scene wouldn't have let me go." She wasn't combative, just firm, stubborn. "I'm not a witness, Abigail."

Abigail didn't argue, but she didn't have to because Keira suddenly whipped around, water flying out of her hair, and shot back into the foyer, out of sight of onlookers in the drawing room. Simon knew better than to butt in, but he figured she wanted to avoid her uncle, who was about two seconds from getting through the last knot of people.

Simon wished he still had his champagne. "I wonder who the dead guy is."

Owen stiffened. "Simon—"

"I'm just saying."

But Owen didn't have a chance to respond before Detective O'Reilly arrived, his hard-set jaw suggesting he wasn't pleased with the turn the evening had taken. "Where's Keira?"

"Talking to Abigail," Owen said quickly, as if he didn't want to give Simon a chance to open his mouth.

O'Reilly gave the unoccupied doorway a searing look. "She's okay?"

"Remarkably so," Owen said. "She's not the one who actually found the body."

"She called it in." Obviously, that was plenty for O'Reilly not to like. He sucked in a breath. "How the hell does a grown man drown in the Public Garden pond? It's about two feet deep. It's not even a real pond."

Good question, but Simon didn't go near it. He wasn't on O'Reilly's radar, and he preferred to keep it that way.

The senior detective glanced back toward his daughter, Fiona, the harpist. She and her ensemble were taking a break. "I need to go with Abigail, see what this is all about," O'Reilly said, addressing Owen. "You'll make sure Fiona stays here until I know what's going on?"

"Sure."

"And Keira. Keep her here, too."

Owen looked surprised at the request. "Bob, she's old enough—"

"Yeah, whatever. Just don't let her go traipsing back down to the Public Garden and getting into the middle of things. She's like that. Always has been."

"There's no reason to think the drowning was anything but an accident, is there?"

"Not at this point," O'Reilly said without elaboration and stalked into the foyer.

Simon didn't mind being a fly on the wall for a change. "Does the uncle get along with his daughter and niece?"

"They get along fine," Owen said, "but Bob sometimes forgets that Keira is ten years older than Fiona. For that matter, he forgets Fiona's nineteen. They're a complicated family."

"All families are complicated, even the good ones." Simon moved closer to the foyer doorway just as Keira started up the stairs barefoot, wet socks and shoes in one hand. She was prettier than he'd expected. Drop-you-in-your-tracks pretty, really. He noticed her uncle scowling at her from the bottom of the stairs and grinned, turning back to Owen. "Maybe especially the good ones."

Ten seconds later, the two BPD detectives left.

The Irish ensemble started up again, playing a quieter tune.

Owen headed for Fiona O'Reilly, who cast a worried look in his direction. She had freckles, but otherwise didn't resemble her father as far as Simon could see. Her long hair had reddish tints but really was almost as blond as her cousin's, and she was a lot better looking than her father.

People in the crowd seemed unaware of the drama over by the door. Caterers brought out trays of hot hors d'oeuvres. Mini spinach quiches, some little flaky buttery things oozing cheese, stuffed mushrooms, skewered strips of marinated chicken. Simon wasn't hungry. He noticed Lloyd Adler pontificating to an older couple who looked as if they thought he was a pretentious ass, too.

Simon went in the opposite direction of Adler and made his way to the back wall where Keira's two donated watercolors were on display.

He decided to bid on the one with the cottage, just to give himself something to do.

It was a white stone cottage set against a background of wildflowers, green pastures and ocean that wasn't in any part of Ireland that he had ever visited. He supposed that was part of the point—to create a place of imagination and dreams. A beautiful, bucolic place. A place not entirely of this world.

At least not the world in which he lived and worked.

Simon settled on a number and put in his bid, one that virtually assured him of ending up with the painting. He could give it to Abigail and Owen as a wedding present. Even if he didn't plan to go to the wedding, he could give them a present.

He acknowledged an itch to head down to the Public Garden with the BPD detectives, but he let it go. He'd seen enough dead bodies, enough to last him for a long time. A lifetime, even. Except he knew there would be more. There always were.

Instead, he decided to find another glass of champagne, maybe grab a couple of the chicken skewers and wait for a dry, calmer Keira Sullivan to make her appearance.

⌒ Chapter 4

Beacon Hill
Boston, Massachusetts
8:45 p.m., EDT
June 17

Keira peeled off her hiking shorts and added them to the wet heap on the bathroom floor of her attic apartment. Her hands shook as she splashed herself with cold water and tried not to think about the dead man and the expressions of the two students as they'd frantically checked him for a pulse, uncertain of their actions, desperate to do the right thing even as they were repulsed by the idea of touching a corpse.

"The poor man," she said to her reflection. "I wonder who he is." She saw herself wince, and whispered, *"Was."*

She towel-dried her hair as best she could, expecting a twig or a dead mosquito to fall out, a souvenir from her earlier hike to her mother's. None did, and she combed out the tangles and pinned it up. She'd been looking forward to tonight's auction and reception, but her visit with her mother and then the awful scene in the Public

Garden had sucked all the excitement out of her. She just wanted to get the evening over with and be on her way to Ireland.

But for Ireland, she wouldn't have even been in the Public Garden tonight. She'd dropped her car off with a friend in Back Bay to look after for the next six weeks and ran into the students dragging the man out of the pond on her way to the Garrison house. As she'd raced up Beacon Street after the police had arrived, she couldn't shake the notion that her mother's talk about sin and evil had put her in the Public Garden at exactly the wrong moment.

But that was unfair, Keira thought, and as she returned to her bedroom, she found herself wishing she could call her mother and tell her what had happened.

Everything changes.

She dug through her small closet, pulling out a long, summery skirt and top. The apartment was no more permanent than anywhere else she'd lived, but she liked the space—the efficient, downsize appliances, the light, the view of the Common. It wasn't on the grand scale as the rest of the house, but it had charm and character and worked just fine for now. Compared to her mother's cabin, Keira thought, her apartment was a palace.

In five minutes, she had wriggled into her outfit, put on a bit of makeup and was rushing back down the stairs again. Two deep breaths, and she entered the drawing room. Her cousin Fiona's ensemble was playing a jaunty tune that didn't fit Keira's mood, but she tried to appreciate it nonetheless.

Owen immediately fell in alongside her, and she smiled at him. "I'm okay," she said before he could ask.

"Good."

He had a way about him that helped center people. Keira could imagine how reassuring his presence would be to a trapped earthquake victim. "Who was the man I saw you with earlier?" she asked. "Big guy. Another BPD type?"

She thought Owen checked a grin, but he wasn't always easy to read. "You must mean Simon Cahill. He's a volunteer with Fast Rescue."

"From Boston?"

"From wherever he happens to be at the moment." Owen smiled as he grabbed a glass of champagne from a caterer's tray and handed it to her. "A little like you in that regard. I don't know what happened to him. He was here two seconds ago."

Just as well he'd taken off, Keira thought. She'd spotted him at the height of her distress, and if Owen was a steadying presence, Simon Cahill, she thought, was the opposite. Even in those few seconds of contact, she'd felt probed and exposed, as if he'd assumed she had something to hide and was trying to see right through her.

She thanked Owen for the champagne and eased into the crowd, realizing her hair was still damp from the downpour. For the most part, people she greeted seemed unaware of her earlier arrival, which spared her having to explain.

Colm Dermott, a wiry, energetic Irishman, approached her with his usual broad smile. She'd met him two years ago on a trip to Ireland, where he was a highly respected professor of anthropology at University College Cork. He'd arrived in Boston in April after cobbling together grants to put together the Boston-Cork conference and had immediately recruited Keira to help.

"The auction's going well." He seemed genuinely excited. "You must be eager to go off tomorrow."

"I'm packed and ready to go," she said.

"Ah, you'll have a grand time."

She'd given Colm a copy of the video recording she'd made of

Patsy McCarthy telling her story, but hadn't told him about her mother and her long-ago trip to Ireland.

They chatted a bit more, but Keira couldn't relax. Finally, Colm sighed at her. "Is something wrong, Keira?"

She took a too-big gulp of champagne. "It's been a strange day."

Before she could explain further, her emotional younger cousin burst through the crowd, her blue eyes shining with both excitement and revulsion. "Keira, are you okay?" Fiona asked. "Owen just told me about the man you found drowned. I wondered why Dad and Abigail left so fast."

Colm looked shocked. "I had no idea. Keira, what happened? No wonder you're distracted."

She quickly explained, both Colm and Fiona listening intently. "It wasn't a pleasant scene. I wish I could have arrived sooner, but it might not have made any difference. He could have had a heart attack or a stroke, and that's why he ended up in the water."

"Do you know who he was?" Colm asked.

Keira shook her head. "No idea."

"I hope he wasn't murdered," Fiona said abruptly.

"I hope not, too," Keira said, reminding herself that her cousin was the daughter of an experienced homicide detective. "The police are there in full force, at least."

Owen returned and spoke to Fiona. "I just talked to your father. He's going to be a while and asked me to give you a ride back to your apartment—"

"I can take the subway."

"Not an option."

Fiona rolled her eyes. "My dad worries too much."

But she seemed to know better than to argue with Owen. She and some friends were subletting an apartment for the summer that her father considered a rathole, on a bad street, too far from the subway and too big a leap for a daughter just a year out of high school. Keira had stayed out of that particular discussion.

"I'll water your plants while you're in Ireland," Fiona said, giving a quick grin. "Maybe I'll talk Dad into buying me a ticket to Ireland for a week. You and I could visit pubs and listen to Irish music."

"That'd be fun," Keira said.

"It would be, wouldn't it? Right now I guess I should go pack up."

"I'm sorry I didn't get to hear more of your band."

"They were fantastic," Colm interjected.

Fiona beamed and headed across the room with Owen.

Colm turned back to Keira with a smile. "Fiona's more like her father than she thinks, isn't she?" But he didn't wait for an answer, his smile fading as he continued. "If there's anything I can do, you know how to reach me."

"I appreciate that. Thanks, Colm."

He rushed off to speak to someone else, and Keira found herself another glass of champagne. As she took a sip, feeling calmer, she noticed small, white-haired Patsy McCarthy in the foyer.

Keira immediately moved toward her. "Patsy—please, come in. I'm so glad you could make it."

"Thank you for inviting me." Within seconds of meeting almost a month ago, Patsy had dispensed with any formalities and insisted Keira call her by her first name. She nodded back toward the door. "I thought it'd never stop raining."

"I know what you mean. It was quite a downpour."

With a sudden move, Patsy clutched Keira's hand. "I wanted to see you before you left for Ireland. You're going to look for the stone angel, aren't you?"

"I'll be in the village that undoubtedly inspired the story—"

"You'll be there on the summer solstice. Look for the angel then."

The summer solstice played a key role in the story. "I'll do my best."

"The Good People want to find the stone angel as much as you do. The fairies, I mean. The angel's been missing for so long, but they won't have forgotten it. If you're clever, you can let them help you." Patsy dropped Keira's hand and straightened her spine. "I'm not saying I believe in fairies myself, of course."

Keira didn't tackle the older woman's ambivalence. "If they believe the angel's one of their own turned to stone and want it for themselves, why would they help me?"

"That's why you must be clever. Don't let them know they're helping you."

"I'll try to be very clever, then."

"The brothers will be looking for the angel, in their own way. They and the fairies all want the tug-of-war over it to resume. It's meant to resume." Patsy tightened her grip on Keira's hand. "If you find the angel, you must leave it out in the open. In the summer sun. It'll get to where it belongs. Don't let it go to a museum."

"I promise, Patsy," Keira said, surprised by the older woman's intensity. "I'll look for the angel on the summer solstice, then, I'll be clever and if I find the angel, I'll leave it out in the sun—assuming that's up to me. The Irish might have other ideas."

Patsy seemed satisfied and, looking more relaxed, released Keira's hand and eyed a near-empty tray of chocolate-dipped strawberries.

Keira smiled. "Help yourself. Would you like to take a look around?"

"I would, indeed," Patsy said, lifting a fat strawberry onto a cocktail napkin. "I have every one of your books, you know. Do you think you'll illustrate my story one day?"

"I'd love to."

"That'd be something. It's a good story, isn't it?"

"It's a wonderful story."

Patsy smiled suddenly, her eyes lighting up. "Irish brothers, an angel and fairies. All the best stories have fairies, don't you think?"

"I love stories with fairies."

With Keira at her side, Patsy ate her strawberry and moved from artwork to artwork, as if she were in a museum, gasping when she came to Keira's two paintings. "Oh, Keira. My dear Keira. Your paintings are even more incredible in real life." She paused, clearly overcome by emotion. "This is the Ireland I remember."

Whether it was an accurate statement or one colored by time and sentiment, Keira appreciated Patsy's response. "It means a lot to me that you like my work."

When Patsy finished her tour of the drawing room, she took another chocolate-covered strawberry and started for the foyer. "Can I see you back home?" Keira asked.

Patsy shook her head. "My parish priest drove me. Father Palermo. Like the city in Sicily. He couldn't find a parking space, so he's driving around until I finish up. Did you know that my church is named after Saint Ita?"

Keira smiled. "The Irish saint in your story."

"It's strange how life works sometimes, isn't it?"

They walked outside together. A simple black sedan waited at the curb. A handsome, dark-haired man in a priest's black suit and white clerical collar got out and looked across the car's shiny roof. "Are you ready, Mrs. McCarthy, or shall I drive around the Common one more time? I don't want to rush you."

"I'm all set. This is the artist I told you about, Father. Keira Sullivan."

"Ah. Miss Sullivan. I've heard so much about you."

Keira couldn't read his tone, but Patsy added politely, "Keira, I'd like you to meet Father Michael Palermo."

He tilted his head back slightly, as if appraising her. "Mrs. McCarthy tells me you're collecting stories from twentieth-century Irish immigrants."

"That's right. She's been very generous with her time."

Patsy waved a hand in dismissal. "I'm just an old woman with an ear for a good story."

Father Palermo kept his gaze on Keira. "Your mother grew up a couple doors down from Mrs. McCarthy."

"Two," Keira said without elaboration. "A pleasure to meet you, Father."

"Likewise."

He climbed back in behind the wheel, and Patsy got into the passenger seat and smiled at Keira. "Give my love to Ireland," she said with a wink.

After they left, Keira lingered on the sidewalk. The wind had picked up, but after the heat and humidity of recent days, she appreciated the drier conditions that came with the gusts. The puddles that had formed in dips in the sidewalk would be dry by morning.

"So you're off to Ireland in search of angels and fairies." Simon Cahill grinned at her as he leaned against the black iron railing to the steps of the Garrison house. "Do you believe in fairies?"

"That's not what's important in my work."

"Ah, I see. That's a dodge, but whatever. Keira, right?"

"That's right—and you're Simon. Owen's friend. I didn't realize you were still here."

"I have to pay for my painting."

"Your painting?"

"Your watercolor of the Irish cottage. I couldn't resist."

"You bid on my painting? Why?"

He shrugged. "Why not?"

Keira didn't answer. He was obviously a man who could charm his way into or out of anything. And he made her uncomfortable— no, not uncomfortable…self-conscious. Aware. Maybe it was because he was the first person she'd spotted when she'd arrived from the Public Garden. Some kind of weird imprinting that was inevitable, unavoidable.

Finally, she said, "You don't care about a painting of an Irish cottage."

"I care. I just didn't bid on it for myself. Abigail wanted it, but she was going to lose out. I decided it'd be a nice wedding present for her and Owen. He'll like it because she likes it." The corners of Simon's mouth twitched with amusement. "Don't frown. He thinks you're good, too."

Not only, Keira thought, was Simon dangerously charming, but he was also observant. And frank. "Thank you for bidding on the painting. The proceeds from the auction will be put to good use. You're not from around here, are you?"

"Not really."

"Then where do you live?"

"Direct, aren't you? I have a boat. It's at a pier in East Boston at the moment, but it's only been there since yesterday. Before that, it was in Maine. I met Owen and some other Fast Rescue people at his place on Mount Desert Island after our mission to Armenia."

Keira had read about the devastating earthquake. "That must have been tough."

"It was." He didn't elaborate. "I was in London when it happened. I go back tomorrow."

"What's in London?"

"The queen. Castles. Good restaurants."

The man had an appealing sense of humor, and, in spite of the tension of the past few hours, Keira felt herself relaxing. "Very funny. I meant what's in London for you?"

"I'm visiting a friend. What about Ireland? What's there for you, besides angels and fairies?"

Answers, she thought, but she shrugged. "I guess I'll find out."

His eyes narrowed on her, and she noticed they were a vivid, rich shade of green. "Up for a bit of adventure, are you?"

"I suppose I am."

"Have a good trip, then."

He ambled off down Beacon Street. When she returned to the drawing room, Keira checked with Colm. "How much did my cottage painting go for?"

"Ten thousand."

She couldn't hide her surprise. "Dollars?"

"Yes, dollars, Keira. It was four times the highest bid. Simon Cahill bought it. Do you know him?"

"No, I just met him tonight. What about you?"

"I talked with him for all of thirty seconds. Well, he must want to support the conference."

"He must. I'm grateful for his generosity."

"As am I," Colm said.

Keira said good-night and headed for the stairs up to her apartment, amazed at how Simon had managed to get under her skin in such a short time.

It had to be because of the intensity of the past few hours. What on earth did they have in common?

She'd be back to normal by morning, finishing up her packing and heading to the airport by evening. At least she wasn't going to Ireland by way of London; there was no risk they'd be sitting next to each other on the same flight.

It was a long way across the Atlantic.

~ Chapter 5

Abigail Browning paced on the sidewalk along the edge of the man-made pond where the two college students had discovered the body of Victor Sarakis, a fifty-year-old resident of Cambridge who apparently, even according to the initial take of the medical examiner, had drowned in about two feet of water.

Normally, Abigail found the Public Garden a soothing, pleasant place to be, with its graceful Victorian walks and statues, its formal flower beds and labeled trees, its mini suspension bridge over the curving pond. Technically, it was a botanical garden—a refuge in the heart of the city of Boston.

Tonight, it was the scene of a bizarre, as yet unexplained death. Police lights and the garden's own Victorian-looking lamps illuminated the scene as detectives, patrol officers, crime scene technicians and reporters did their work. By tomorrow morning, there would be virtually no sign of what had gone on here tonight. The swan boats, a popular Public Garden attraction for over a century, could resume their graceful tour of the shallow water.

Abigail stopped pacing, grateful, at least, that she'd worn a pantsuit and flats to tonight's reception. Trees, flowers and grass were still dripping from the downpour. Most likely, it had been raining, and raining hard, when Victor Sarakis ended up in the water. The medical examiner had already removed the body for an autopsy. Anything was possible. Heart attack, stroke, an unfortunate slip in the heavy rain.

Pushed, tripped, hit on the back of the head.

Abigail wasn't ready to jump to any conclusions.

She glanced sideways at Bob O'Reilly, who'd decided, on his own, to interview the two students. Reinterview, Abigail thought, irritated. The responding officers had talked to the students. She'd talked to them. Now Bob was talking to them. For no good reason, either, except that he was a senior detective with decades of experience on her and presumably knew what he was doing. But she wished he'd go back up to Beacon Street and listen to his daughter play Irish music.

The students—summer engineering students from the Midwest—looked worn out. They could have gone back to their dorm a long time ago—they just didn't.

They'd told Bob the same story, about cutting through the Public Garden from a bookstore on Newbury Street, hoping to beat the storm and get to a friend's apartment on Cambridge Street. When the skies opened up on them, they debated going back to the bookstore or pushing on to their friend's place.

Then they'd spotted a body in the pond.

"You could tell he was dead by looking at him?" Bob gave them one of his trademark skeptical snorts. "How?"

"I don't know," the thinner of the two students said. He had a scraggly beard and was shivering as his wet clothes dried in the breeze. "It was obvious."

"He didn't look like he'd been in the water that long," his friend said. He was meatier, and he'd gotten just as wet, but he wasn't shivering.

"Long enough," Bob said.

The students didn't respond.

"You didn't see him before you noticed him in the pond?" Bob asked.

They shook their heads. They'd answered the same question before, maybe twice already. Abigail knew she'd asked it.

Bob gave them a thoughtful look. "How do you like BU?"

The skinny student didn't hide his surprise—and maybe a touch of annoyance—at the personal question as well as his friend did. "What?"

"My daughter goes there. Music major."

"We don't know any music majors," the meaty kid said quickly.

Abigail bit her tongue at the exchange, but Bob didn't mention Fiona by name and finally told the students to go on back to their dorms. This time, they didn't hesitate.

Bob turned to her. His red hair had frizzed up in the humidity and rain, and his freckles stood out on his pale skin. "You look like you want to smack me."

"It's a thought."

He obviously didn't care. She'd never met anyone with a thicker hide. She owned a triple-decker in Jamaica Plain, a Boston neighborhood, with him and a third detective, an arrangement that for the most part worked out well, but tonight, for the first time, she could see the potential for complications.

"Press is all over this one," Bob said, nodding to a camera crew. "Some rich guy from Cambridge tripping on his shoelaces and drowning in the Public Garden swan pond."

"We don't know he's rich, and, actually, it's called the lagoon."

"Lagoon? Lagoon reminds me of *Gilligan's Island*. Why don't they just call it a pond?"

"Maybe it's a Victorian thing." Abigail ran both her hands through her short, dark curls, noticing wet spots where water had dropped onto her head from leaves of the nearby shade trees. "And Mr. Sarakis was wearing loafers. No laces to trip over."

"Figure of speech."

Abigail said nothing.

"This is a straightforward death investigation, Abigail. Guy running in the rain slips or trips and goes flying, hits his head on the concrete, falls into the drink and drowns. A freak accident."

"A good detective doesn't let assumptions drive conclusions," she said, adding with just a touch of sarcasm, "I wonder who gave me that advice when I decided to become a detective?"

"Don't give me a hard time. I'm not in the mood."

She didn't blame him for wanting Victor Sarakis's death to be an accident, considering his niece was the one who'd called 911.

Abigail kept her mouth shut. Normally she would appreciate Bob's insight, his questions. He'd been in Boston law enforcement through some of its most difficult crime years. He wasn't bitter and burnt-out so much as cynical. He'd seen it all, he liked to say, and not much of it had been good. But she didn't want him around right now. It wasn't just because of Keira's involvement with the case, either.

"Never mind my bad mood," he said. "You've been prickly for days."

"So?"

He didn't answer, and she felt him studying her in the same way he had when they'd first met eight years ago. He hadn't believed she'd make a good police officer, much less a good homicide detective. She'd won him over slowly, despite what he considered a lot of baggage. Her father was the FBI director, a liability from Bob O'Reilly's perspective because it brought attention to her. By itself, it was enough for him to rule her out as police officer material. But that wasn't all. She'd quit law school after her husband was murdered four days into their Maine honeymoon, a case that had remained unresolved for seven years, until a break last summer.

Finally, she knew how Chris—her first love—had died, and who had killed him. For seven years, it was all she'd wanted in life. Answers. Justice. The lifting of the burden of not knowing what had happened that awful day.

But the break in the case had changed her life in a way she hadn't anticipated. During her hunt for her husband's killer last summer, she'd also opened herself up to falling in love again.

She could feel Bob's eyes on her and brought herself back to the present. "There's no evidence of foul play," he said.

Abigail chose her words carefully. "So far, no, there isn't."

"He had his wallet in his back pocket."

Indeed, the wallet had made identifying Victor Sarakis easy because it came complete with his driver's license, ATM card, credit cards, insurance cards, bookstore frequent-buyer card and seventy-seven dollars in cash. No loose change, unless it had fallen out of his pants into the water or grass. If it had, the crime scene guys would find it.

But Abigail knew Bob had raised the point about the wallet because it played into his desire for Sarakis's death to be an accident.

"What do you suppose he was doing out here in the rain?" she asked, knowing Bob wouldn't like the question but refusing to let him bulldoze her.

"Movie, play, Starbucks. It's Boston in June. He could have been doing a million different things."

"He's from Cambridge."

"A lot of people from Cambridge cross the river for a night on the town."

She knew that and wasn't sure why she'd brought it up, except that Victor Sarakis didn't strike her as a night-on-the-town sort. He wore expensive, if traditional, clothes—khakis, polo shirt and loafers. No socks. She hadn't found a receipt from a nearby restaurant or shop or ticket stubs in his pockets. Patrol officers were at his house in Cambridge attempting to notify next of kin, but, so far, no one was home.

"Keira arrived at the party late. I wonder—"

"Don't even go there." Bob's tone had sharpened. "You have no cause to push this thing."

Abigail wasn't intimidated. "A dead man. That's cause enough."

He tilted his head back slightly in that way she knew so well. It said that he knew she was deliberately pushing his buttons, that he wasn't saying anything now because he was going to give her a chance to dig a deeper hole for herself.

So she did. "I wonder if Victor Sarakis was on his way to the auction. Maybe he was going to bid on one of Keira's paintings."

Bob rocked back on his heels. He and Abigail had worked together a long time, and she knew her comment would set him off. He could be volatile, or he could be patient. The choice depended on what he wanted, what tactic he thought would work to his best advantage. He wasn't unemotional. He just had his emotions under tight wraps.

As far as Abigail could see, Bob had never known what to make of his niece. At almost thirty, Keira was a successful illustrator and folklorist, but with no roots, no sense of place. She'd been on the move since high school. Bob, on the other hand, had never lived anywhere but Boston.

"I doubt it was the only event on Beacon Hill tonight, but go ahead,

Abigail," he said. "Check the guest list. Knock on every door within ten blocks of here. It's not like you have anything else to do, right?"

She had a full caseload. Every detective in the department did. But she shrugged. "I'm trying to remember how I heard about the auction. I don't remember getting an actual invitation. I think it was just an announcement." She sighed. She didn't know why she was antagonizing Bob. "Forget it. I'm getting ahead of myself."

He seemed to soften slightly, but that could be a tactic, too. "It's the time of year. Summer solstice is getting close. It's worse than a full moon. Too damn much sun, I swear. Brings out the weirdos."

Abigail couldn't resist a smile. "Bob, nobody says weirdos anymore."

He grinned at her. "I do."

"What's with you and the summer solstice?"

"Nothing." He yawned—deliberately, Abigail thought—and did a couple of shoulder rolls, as if he needed to loosen up. "I should get back. When you see Owen, thank him for giving Fiona a ride home for me."

"Sure, Bob. I'm sorry Keira got here when she did. It's not an easy thing, coming upon a body."

"Fiona wants to spend a week in Ireland with Keira visiting pubs and playing music. Can you imagine the two of them?" He wrinkled up his face and blew out a breath. "Fiona keeps telling me I worry too much. Maybe I do. I don't even like her taking the subway alone, never mind getting on a plane to Ireland by herself."

"She takes the subway all the time. She's a music student. She's got lessons, ensemble practice."

"Plays the freaking harp. You believe I have a daughter majoring in harp?" He rubbed the back of his neck as if he were in pain. "And I have a niece who paints pictures of fairies and wildflowers and collects loony stories people tell by the fire."

"They're both incredibly talented, and Keira's successful in a highly competitive business. Plus, they both get along with you, which is saying something."

Bob let his hand drop to his side. "Wait'll you have kids."

His words were like a gut punch, and Abigail looked away quickly, muttering a good-night and making a beeline for the crime scene guys, thinking of something she could ask them. Anything. Didn't matter what. She didn't want Bob to see her expression, to wonder what demons were haunting her now.

This was private, damn it. Personal. Up to her and her alone to figure out.

Kids.

She pictured herself with a big belly, Owen with a toddler on his shoulders—the three of them in the Public Garden on a beautiful June day. But it was a fantasy. Reality was so much more complicated. She and Owen weren't even married yet, and babies would change her life, change his life.

Abigail turned her attention back to the pond. What *had* brought Victor Sarakis to Boston tonight? Never mind her mood or Bob's mood, it was a question that needed an answer.

She spotted a crime scene guy she recognized. What was his name? She couldn't remember. He was new. Really young. Grew up on a tough street in Roxbury.

"Malcolm," she whispered, then raised her voice, calling to him. "Malcolm—hang on a second."

"Yes, Detective?"

She glanced back at Bob, who pointed a finger at her and shook it— his way of telling her he knew what she was up to and would be watching.

Malcolm frowned at her. Abigail pointed to the sidewalk. "I just want to make sure we get photos of any cracks in the walks that could trip a guy running in the rain."

"Of course. No problem."

"Thanks."

Bob continued across the picturesque mini suspension bridge over the pond. With a sigh of relief, Abigail studied the spot where Victor Sarakis had come to the end of his life. There was no fence on this section of the pond. If he'd tripped—or whatever—on the opposite bank, the knee-high cable fence could have broken his fall, perhaps kept him from drowning. But the water was so shallow—he must have been unconscious, otherwise why didn't he just get up?

The autopsy would tell her more, but she had to agree with Bob and the medical examiner that Victor Sarakis's untimely death was likely an accident.

In the meantime, she had work to do, and a long night ahead of her.

She touched her cell phone, but decided—no. Owen already knew she had a case and would be back to her place late. He had an early start in the morning for a Fast Rescue meeting in Austin. He was always on the go—Austin, Boston, his place in Maine, disaster sites and training facilities all over the world.

Let him get to bed, Abigail thought, and not worry about her. She wouldn't want him to hear anything in her voice that would tell him she was gnawing on a worry, a problem. Because he'd ask her to explain, and she wasn't sure she could. Whatever was going on with her wasn't about him. It was about her.

And in those long years after Chris's death, she'd grown accustomed to working out her issues on her own.

She wondered if Victor Sarakis had left behind any children, but pushed the thought out of her mind as she joined Malcolm in looking for cracks in the walks.

⌒ Chapter 6

FBI Director John March greeted Simon with a curt handshake in an ultraprivate VIP lounge at Boston's Logan Airport. March had flown up from Washington, D.C., that morning specifically for this meeting. He had an entourage of hulking FBI special agents and staffers with him, but they stayed out in the hall.

He was in his midfifties and trim, and although his hair was iron-gray, its curls reminded Simon of March's daughter, Abigail. But March wouldn't be seeing her today. He wouldn't risk it. Simon knew it wasn't just that March was protecting a classified mission. He didn't want to have to explain his complicated history with the Cahills to a daughter—a cop daughter, no less—who knew nothing about it. It didn't have to be a secret. It just was one.

"Some days, Simon," the FBI director said, "I wish you'd decided to become a plumber."

"If it's any consolation, some days I wish I had, too." Simon had been fourteen, crying over his father's casket at a proper Irish wake in the heart of Georgetown when he'd first met March. "At least when you're a plumber and you're knee-deep in crap, no one tries to convince you it's gravy."

"I've put you in a difficult position."

"I put myself there. You're just capitalizing on it. That's your job. I'm not holding it against you."

"My daughter will." March's tone didn't change from its unemotional, careful professionalism. "I've kept too many secrets from her as it is."

Simon thought he detected a note of regret in the older man's tone, but maybe not. Simon didn't have the details, but apparently John March had known more about the circumstances surrounding the murder of his daughter's first husband, an FBI special agent, than he'd let on. Nothing that would have led to his killer any sooner. But Abigail didn't necessarily see it that way.

"Comes with the territory," Simon said without much sympathy.

He hadn't asked for March's help all those years ago, when the then FBI special agent was wracked with grief and guilt after failing to stop the execution of Brendan Cahill, a DEA agent and friend, in Colombia. But there was nothing March could have done. The killers had videotaped themselves. The video showed them tying up Simon's father. Blindfolding him. Firing two bullets into his forehead. Simon had seen the tape. For years, he thought he'd stumbled onto it—that he'd been clever, outwitting the brilliant, powerful John March. He was over that illusion now. March had arranged for Simon to find the tape and see his father's murder.

Instead of feeling angry, bitter and betrayed, Simon had felt understood. March had known that once Brendan Cahill's young son had realized the tape existed, he'd find a way to see it.

What Simon hadn't realized, until recently, was that March had never mentioned him or his father to his daughter. Not once in twenty years.

He was a hard man to figure out.

March stayed on his feet. "I've told you as much as I know about what comes next."

Simon doubted that, but he shrugged. "Great. I'll be in London cooling my heels."

"We've got him, Simon. We've got Estabrook, thanks to you."

With a little luck, the "thanks to you" part would stay between Simon and March, but Simon had learned not to count on luck. "I'll feel better when he's in custody."

"Understood."

Simon could sense March's awkwardness. Ordinarily he would keep his focus on the big picture and not concern himself with what a mission meant for Simon personally. But this mission was different. Eighteen months ago, Simon had left the FBI and started a new life—volunteering for Fast Rescue, making a living helping businesses and individuals plan for disasters. It wasn't a bad life. He had a good reputation, a decent income and the kind of freedom he'd never had as a federal agent.

Enter Norman Estabrook.

To the public, Estabrook was a thrill-seeking billionaire hedge fund entrepreneur into extreme mountain climbing, high-risk ballooning, kayaking down remote, snake-infested rivers—whatever gave him an adrenaline rush. To a tight inner circle of trusted associates, he was also at the center of a network that dealt in illegal drugs and laundered cash for some very nasty people. Estabrook didn't need the money, obviously, and he sure as hell didn't care about advancing any particular cause. He liked the action. He liked thwarting authority.

In particular, Norman Estabrook liked thwarting John March.

Simon was in the perfect position to infiltrate Estabrook's network, and that was what he'd done. He'd known from the beginning if Norman Estabrook was arrested as a major-league criminal—which he would be—and Simon's role as an undercover federal agent remained a secret, his name would still be associated with Estabrook and his criminal network. Who'd hire him for anything, never mind trust him with their lives?

If he was exposed as an FBI agent, there went that career, too.

Either way, Estabrook would want him dead.

But Simon figured those were the breaks in his line of work. He stayed on his feet and noticed March did, too, the comforts of the lounge immaterial to either of them. They'd simply needed a private place to meet.

Simon grinned at the no-nonsense FBI director. "If this blows up in my face, I can always become a plumber."

"You could do worse," March said.

"Estabrook didn't make a fortune by being stupid."

"You've done your part, Simon. You provided what we needed to unravel this bastard's network. He's a bad actor, and so is the company he keeps." March gave a thin smile. "Excluding you, of course."

"Of course."

"There's nothing more you can do right now. Estabrook's at his ranch in Montana, and he thinks you're visiting a friend and recuperating from the Armenia mission."

Simon shrugged. "I tend to get into brawls when I'm at a loose end."

"You're not at a loose end. You're in wait mode."

"Same thing."

"If there's another disaster—"

"I wouldn't wish a disaster on anyone just to give me something to do. Owen's trying to get me to get involved with Fast Rescue training. Makes my eyes roll back in my head, thinking about training people to do what I already know how to do."

March looked down, and Simon could have sworn he saw him smile. "Just do what a disaster consultant and search-and-rescue specialist would do between jobs, and you'll be fine."

"Will Davenport's putting me up in London."

"Ah. Sir Davenport. Or is it Lord Davenport?"

"One or the other. Both. Hell, I don't know."

March's eyes didn't change. Nor did his mouth. Nothing, but Simon detected a change nonetheless. Will Davenport was a wealthy Brit who believed he owed Simon his life. Maybe he did, but Simon wasn't keeping score. Apparently Will also had a history—a less favorable one—with the FBI director. Simon didn't know what it was and wasn't sure he wanted to.

"I take it Davenport is unaware of your reasons for going to London."

It was a statement, but Simon responded. "If he is, he's keeping it to himself."

"That'd be a first," March said, making a move for the door. "Simon, we've got Estabrook, and we'll blow open his network and save lives. A lot of lives. You know that, don't you?"

"I do, sir. I also know Abigail's eventually going to find out my history with you—"

"Not your problem."

It wasn't that March had acted as something of a surrogate father to Simon for the past twenty years that would get to Abigail. It was that she'd never known. At first, Simon was too caught up in his own anger and grief even to notice that March never took him to meet his family. He'd show up at Simon's ball games—a few times at the police station, after Simon got into fights—and stay in touch with the occasional phone call. When Simon headed off to the University of Massachusetts, March paid him a couple of visits each semester, taking him out for pizza, checking in with him about grades. March never suggested the FBI as a career. He wasn't director in those days, and when Simon decided to apply to the academy, he never discussed the idea with him.

March opened the door. "Stay in touch," he said.

"I will. By the way, do you know Keira Sullivan?"

"We've met. Very pretty—talented artist."

"She found a dead guy in the Public Garden last night."

"That was her?"

Simon didn't know why he'd brought her up. "She's heading to Ireland tonight to research some story about Irish brothers, fairies and a stone angel. I don't know. I could forget Will and go chase fairies in the Irish hills—" But he stopped, noticing a change in March's expression. "Something wrong?"

"I'm just preoccupied with this Estabrook thing." He seemed to manufacture a smile. "Keira Sullivan's a temptation you don't need right now, wouldn't you say?"

Simon didn't answer, and March left, shutting the door sharply behind him as he went out into the hall.

With a groan of pure frustration, Simon plopped down on a plush chair and lifted his feet onto a coffee table. He noticed a copy of the morning *Boston Globe* on the table. On the front page was a grainy black-and-white shot of the man who'd drowned in the Public Garden. Well off, middle-aged, no wife or children. The BPD Homicide Unit was investigating, but there was no indication of foul play.

Simon pictured Keira Sullivan bursting into the Beacon Hill house last night after she'd called 911. Pale, soaked, dressed like a lumberjack. Twenty minutes later, she'd floated back into the drawing room looking like a willowy Irish fairy princess herself. He admitted he was intrigued, but March had a point. Without even trying, Simon could think of about a thousand reasons why he shouldn't waste his time indulging in fantasies about Keira Sullivan. Artist, folklorist, flake. BPD detective's niece. Off to Ireland.

She was also friends with Owen Garrison, who was already keeping what he knew about Simon from Abigail and didn't need to worry about lying to Keira, too.

Simon dropped his feet back to the lounge floor.

Who was he kidding? He *was* indulging in fantasies about Keira Sullivan.

Just as well he had the trip to London. Best to find some water and a candy bar for his flight.

As he exited the lounge, he envisioned—as if it were right in front of him—the painting of the Irish cottage he'd bought at last night's auction. It was as if he was there, in Keira's world, and he imagined her with brush in hand, her pale blond hair pulled back, her blue eyes focused on where the next dab of paint would go.

Simon heaved a cathartic sigh. "Get a grip," he muttered.

The hall was empty of FBI agents. His flight would be boarding soon.

He went in search of a candy bar.

~Chapter 7

Beara Peninsula, Southwest Ireland
6:30 p.m., IST
June 20

On her second night in Ireland, Keira indulged in a "toasted special"—a grilled ham, cheese, tomato and red onion sandwich—and a mug of coffee liberally laced with some Irish whiskey. She hadn't specified a brand. She'd told Eddie O'Shea, the owner of the only pub in the tiny Beara Peninsula village where she was to spend the next six weeks, that she wanted whiskey, whiskey from Ireland. Otherwise, she didn't care.

"Another coffee?" Eddie asked her. He was a sandy-haired, slight man with a quick wit and a friendly nature that seemed tailor-made for his work.

"No, thank you." Keira heard the touch of Boston in her voice, a surprise to her given her wandering lifestyle. She picked up a triangle of her sandwich, melted cheese oozing from the toasted white bread, a bit of onion curling into a charred sliver of ham. Less than two days on the southwest coast of Ireland, and she was settling in fine and looking forward to her stay there. "If I had more coffee, I'd have more whiskey, and then I'd be in a fix."

Eddie eyed her with what she could only describe as skeptical amusement. "You're not driving."

"I plan to take a walk." She picked up her mug, the coffee still very hot, and let it warm her hands. "I love these long June days. Tomorrow's the summer solstice. You never know what mischief you might encounter this time of year."

"Off to dance with fairies and engage in a bit of magic, are you? Well, be careful, or you'll be mistaken for a fairy princess yourself."

"Do you believe in the Good People, then, Eddie?" she asked with a smile.

"I'm not a superstitious man."

She hadn't told him Patsy's story. Investigating a tale of Irish brothers, fairies and a stone angel, Keira had decided, required a clear-but-not-too-clear head. She wanted to be gutsy but not reckless, determined but not insane. She hoped the combination of whiskey and caffeine would do the trick.

Eddie moved off with a tray of drinks, delivering them to a knot of men gathered in a semicircle of spindly chairs in front of a small television. She'd learned they were local farmers and fishermen who'd known each other all their lives. They'd arrived at the pub one by one over the past hour to watch a hurling match and argue good-naturedly among themselves. If they'd been arguing about fairies, magic, ancient rituals and ancient stories told by the fire—that, Keira thought, would have compelled her to eavesdrop, perhaps even to join them. She didn't know much about hurling, except that it was fast, rough and immensely popular with Eddie O'Shea and his friends.

She'd had dinner at the pub last night, too. She'd hit it off with Eddie right away. Nonetheless, she was keenly aware that the locals were beginning to construct a story about her and her presence in their village. She supposed she'd helped by dropping an odd tidbit here and there—not fiction so much as not the whole truth. She'd never once lied to any of them.

They believed she'd come to Ireland in the typical Irish-American search for her roots and herself, and she supposed, in a way, she had.

She left a few euros on the wooden bar and took her coffee with her as she stepped outside into what was, truly, one of the finer evenings of this and her two previous visits to Ireland. A good beginning to her stay, she thought. She could feel her jet lag easing, the tension of her last hours in Boston finally losing its grip on her.

A man in a threadbare tweed jacket, wool pants, an Irish wool cap and mud-encrusted wellies sat at a picnic table next to the pub's entrance. He faced the street, smoking a cigarette. He looked up at Keira with eyes as clear and true a blue as she'd ever seen. His skin was weather-beaten, laced with deep wrinkles. He had short, straight gray hair. He could have been sixty or eighty—or a hundred-and-eighty, she thought. He had a timeless quality to him.

He said something in Irish that didn't include one of the fifty or so words she knew. Her mother spoke Irish—or used to. "I'm sorry—"

"Enjoy your walk, Keira Sullivan." He blew out a cloud of cigarette smoke and gave just the slightest of smiles. "I know you. Ah, yes. I know you well."

She was so stunned, she jumped back, stumbling and nearly spilling coffee down her front.

When she righted herself, coffee intact, the man was gone.

Where had he slipped off to so fast?

Keira peered up the quiet, narrow village street, lined with brightly colored stucco houses. The vivid blue, fuchsia, green, yellow and red could light up even the gloomiest Irish weather. Baskets of lavender and dark pink geraniums hung from lampposts. A few cars were parked along the sides of the road, but there was no traffic. Except for a single dog barking toward the water and the occasional hoots from the men in the pub, the street was quiet.

Keira debated going back into the pub to see if the man was there, or asking Eddie O'Shea if he'd seen him, but as much as she and Eddie had hit it off, she'd known him less than two days and didn't want to stir up any further gossip.

Maybe the mysterious man had overindulged in Guinness and was staggering up a nearby lane, or he lived in one of the houses on the main street and simply had gone home.

Maybe he'd decided to have a little fun with the American tourist.

She couldn't read anything into what the man—a perfect stranger—had said.

Keira took his spot at the picnic table, and as she sipped her coffee, lukewarm now, she noticed there wasn't even a hint of cigarette smoke in the pleasant evening air.

After she left the pub, Keira shoved her hands into the pockets of a traditional Irish wool knit sweater she'd bought in Kenmare, a pretty village famous for its shops and restaurants. It was located farther up Kenmare Bay, which separated the Beara and the Iveragh peninsulas, two of the five fingers of land in southwest Ireland that jutted out into the stormy Atlantic Ocean.

She turned onto a bucolic lane that ran parallel to the village's protected harbor, gray and still now at low tide, and across the bay, the jagged silhouette of the MacGillicuddy Reeks of the Iveragh Peninsula were outlined against the muted sky. Off to her right, the rugged, barren mountains of the sparsely populated Beara Peninsula rose up sharply, with tufts of milky clouds, or fog, maybe, sinking into rocky crevices.

Keira could hear the distant bleating of the sheep that dotted the hills.

The ancient stone walls along the lane were overgrown with masses of pink roses and wildflowers—blue, purple and yellow thistles, pink foxglove, various drifts and spikes of white flowers.

And holly, Keira saw with a smile, lots of it. By tradition, cutting down a holly tree was bad luck.

There were tall rhododendrons and the occasional pop of a bright fuchsia that had long ago escaped cultivation. The southwest Irish climate, warmed by the Gulf Stream, was mild year-round, hospitable to subtropical plants in spite of fierce gales.

Her rented cottage was just up ahead, a traditional structure of gray stone that, to her relief, was charming and perfect for her stay. Keira made a mental note to send a postcard to Colm Dermott thanking him for his help in finding it.

She hugged her sweater closer to her and pushed back any thoughts that might entice her to duck into her cottage and pour herself another whiskey and put on music, then tuck herself among her warm blankets and sketch pretty pictures of Irish scenery. It was tempting just to forget her mission.

After another thirty yards, she turned onto a dirt track that wound through the middle of a rock-strewn pasture, marked off with barbed wire and rising sharply. She'd walked up this way yesterday to get a feel for her surroundings. She was surprised at how well they corresponded to the details in Patsy's story.

Sheep grazed far up into the hills, part of the Slieve Miskish Mountains that ran down the lower spine of the peninsula to the Atlantic and the now-defunct copper mines, where Patsy's grandfather had worked.

The track leveled off briefly, and Keira heard a grunt nearby.

A cow. It's only a damn cow.

Then came a shriek of laughter, and a woman's voice. "Oh, no! Look—I stepped in it!"

A man chuckled. "Apparently cows don't care about prehistoric ruins."

The couple climbed over a barbed-wire fence onto the track. They were obviously American, the slight breeze catching the ends of their graying hair as they checked their scuffed walking shoes for cow manure. The woman smiled at Keira. "I suppose if one's going to traipse through a cow pasture, one should expect cow patties. Are you going out to the stone circle?"

"Not tonight," Keira said.

She'd checked out the stone circle yesterday after her arrival. It was one of over a hundred of the mysterious megalithic structures in County Cork, a particularly good example because it was relatively large and missing just one of its eleven stones. Getting to it required climbing over fences and navigating cows, rutted ground, rocks and manure.

The woman gave up on her shoe. "It's incredible—and to see it this time of year..." She beamed, obviously delighted with her adventure. "Such a thrill. We half hoped we'd run into fairies dancing."

Her companion sighed. "*You* hoped we'd see fairies."

She rolled her eyes with amusement and addressed Keira. "My husband has no sense of romance." She gestured broadly toward the harbor and village below. "We're staying in Kenmare. You're American, too?"

"I'm from Boston—I'm renting a cottage here," Keira said, leaving her explanation at that.

"Lovely. Well, enjoy your walk."

"Mind the cow flops if you go in the pasture," her husband said.

Keira wished the couple a good-night, and as they ambled down the gravel track, she felt more relaxed. It wasn't as remote out here as it seemed. She'd come prepared. She had food, water, a flashlight, a first-aid kit and a whistle for emergencies.

"You'll be in Ireland on the summer solstice. Look for the angel then."

The summer solstice wasn't until tomorrow, but Keira figured she'd have a good look around tonight, get the lay of the land. With a little luck, maybe Patsy's story would lead her straight to the hermit monk's hut.

Regardless, it was a beautiful evening, and Keira was enjoying herself on her first full day of what promised to be a perfect six weeks in Ireland.

~Chapter 8

Abigail parked her unmarked BPD car on a quiet street off Memorial Drive lined with mature trees and stately homes. Very Cambridge. Victor Sarakis's house was a traditional Colonial with gray-painted shingles and black shutters. He was relatively wealthy, she'd discovered, and also something of an eccentric.

She turned the engine off and scowled at Bob O'Reilly next to her. He'd jumped into the passenger seat at BPD headquarters a half second before she could hit the locks and take off without him. He was getting on her nerves, but wasn't everyone? "Shouldn't you be pushing papers somewhere?"

He opened his door and glanced over at her. "What did you do, sit there stewing all this time and thinking up that one?"

"No, it just popped out."

"Good. I'll pretend it didn't."

Abigail didn't respond. She knew he objected to her coming out to Cambridge. He had good reason. The medical examiner had determined that Victor Sarakis had drowned. There was no indication of foul play, a contributing natural cause or the involvement of alcohol or drugs, illegal or otherwise. A full autopsy report, with the results of more tests, was in the works, but everything still pointed to a bizarre accident. From past death investigations, Abigail knew it was entirely possible they'd never figure out the exact sequence of events that had led to Sarakis's death.

Bob had already made clear he didn't care what the exact sequence of events was. He wanted Abigail to focus on clear-cut homicide cases. She didn't report to him, but he'd been charged with improving BPD's percentage of solved versus unsolved homicide cases after a withering series of pieces in the media and figured that gave him license to get in anyone's and everyone's face, including hers.

Abigail had hoped to get to Cambridge and back without Bob ever knowing, but that hadn't worked out. A middle-aged man in apparent good health drowning in two feet of water was provocative—worth a bit of follow-up, at least in her judgment. Bob was free to disagree, provided he stayed out of her way.

She got out of the car, shutting her door with more force than was necessary. It was hot—too hot for June. Tomorrow it'd rain, and then she'd be griping about that. Given her mood, she had to admit that Owen had picked the perfect time for a quick trip to Fast Rescue's Austin headquarters.

She went around the front of the car to the sidewalk. Tom Yarborough, her partner for the past six months, shared Bob's opinion of the Sarakis drowning but hadn't made a stink when she'd said she wanted to head out here on her own.

Bob motioned for her to go ahead of him up Sarakis's front walk. "It's your investigation," he said.

Ignoring his sarcasm, Abigail took in her surroundings. The brick walkway was chipped. The front door needed a fresh coat of its dark green paint. The iron railing was loose on the steps. She had no cause to look into Sarakis's finances yet, but she wondered if eccentricity explained the run-down condition of his place. Everything sagged or was in need of scraping, paint, a good carpenter. A termite inspection wouldn't hurt, either.

She took note of the full attic, one-story sunroom and attached two-car garage. "What do you think, Bob—five, six bedrooms?"

"At least, except they won't all be bedrooms. No wife, no kids. Retired at fifty. He'll have a library, a game room, a dead-animal room—you know, to display stuffed birds and deer heads."

"Think he was a hunter?"

"Didn't have to be."

From her years working with Bob, Abigail knew he wasn't being literal. He was sizing up Victor Sarakis as a moderately wealthy, eccentric loner who probably had serious amateur interests—ones that probably didn't include gardening, she thought as she noted the dandelions, crabgrass and bare spots that dominated the small front lawn. His was definitely the ugly duckling house on the street.

She rang the doorbell, the faint sound of a ding inside the house telling her it worked.

"Tomorrow's the summer solstice," Bob said next to her, as if that explained an unusual death in the Boston Public Garden.

Abigail glanced back at him. "Don't start that again. The summer solstice is a happy time. Lots of sun, flowers, bonfires, dancing."

"Too much daylight, people go nuts. They can't take it. Brings out the worst in them."

She had no idea if he was serious.

"I know what's eating me," he said simply. "The summer solstice, and my crazy niece chasing fairies in Ireland. You, though. What's going on with you?"

"What's going on is that I'm trying to do my job, and you're here interfering."

"That's not what's going on. You're used to me interfering. You know you don't have to be here. You're letting a straightforward death investigation consume you."

"What was Sarakis doing that close to the water? It must have been raining when he ended up in the lagoon." She knew she'd said lagoon instead of pond just to get on Bob's nerves. He deserved it. "You'd think he'd have stuck to the walks and gotten to shelter as fast as possible."

"Maybe he was feeding the pigeons."

Just as she reached for the bell again, the door opened. A trim man with close-cropped graying hair stood on the threshold, looking tired, grim. He wore neatly pressed slacks and a loose-fitting silky sweater. From his expression, Abigail guessed he already knew who they were, but she showed him her badge and introduced herself and Bob.

"I'm Jay Augustine, Victor's brother-in-law." He stood back, opening the door wider. "Please, come in."

"I'm sorry for your loss, Mr. Augustine," Abigail said.

"Thank you." He waited for her and Bob to enter the foyer, then shut the door. "Why don't we talk in the sunroom—"

"That'd be fine," Abigail said.

He led them down a center hall. From what she could see, the interior of the house was immaculate and tastefully decorated, a decided contrast to the ratty exterior. They went through an elegant dining room into a small, adjoining room with windows on three sides and French doors that opened onto a brick terrace. Abigail noticed Bob was paying attention, taking in every detail—habit from years on the job, she thought, if not any real interest in her case.

Jay Augustine stood in the middle of the sunroom as if he didn't know what else to do with himself. "Victor spent a great deal of time in here. It's the only casual room in the house. He—" Augustine's voice cracked, and he paused, clearing his throat. "Every room in the house is crammed with his various collections. Except this one. Funnily enough, he spent most of his time in here."

"What did he collect?" Abigail asked.

"My brother-in-law had many interests and the time and money to indulge them. He went all over the world. My wife and I are dealers in fine art and antiques, but Victor bought most of the pieces you see here on his travels. He lived a full life, Detective Browning. That's at least some consolation."

Abigail didn't respond.

"Well." Augustine took in a breath. "You're homicide detectives, aren't you?"

She nodded. "It's routine to conduct an investigation when—"

"When a man trips and falls in the Boston Public Garden?"

She noted the slightest edge to his tone. "Where do you and your wife live, Mr. Augustine?"

"We have a home in Newton. Our showroom is in Boston, on Clarendon Street."

"When did you last see your brother-in-law?"

"I stopped by two weeks ago. Charlotte—that's my wife—was with me, but I can't speak for her. She may have seen Victor since then. They were close, but they didn't live in each other's pockets."

Bob walked over to the French doors and looked out at the terrace, as run-down as the front of the house. "Where's Mrs. Augustine now?" he asked.

"In Boston at our showroom," Jay said. "It's quiet there. Most of our business is done by appointment. She's having a difficult time. Victor was such a vital presence in our lives. I actually met Charlotte through him. We've only been married two years... I'd located an Italian Renaissance tapestry Victor had been looking for. He was different, as you can see for yourselves, but he was a good man."

"Where were you the night your brother-in-law died?" Abigail asked.

"In New York on business. Charlotte was at home." He swallowed visibly, then nodded to the terrace. "Victor had been talking about hiring a yard service and getting repairs done on the house. He'd had complaints from neighbors. He wasn't angry. He was aware that he was oblivious to things like peeling paint, chipped shutters and weeds. He just didn't care, provided the house was keeping out the elements and his collections were protected."

Bob started to pace, a sign he was getting impatient. Abigail moved back toward the dining room, noticed a knee-high wooden elephant, ornate silver, an array of Asian masks, a huge, colorfully painted bowl in the middle of the table. She'd never been one for a lot of antiques and collectibles around her.

"My wife and I are busy, Detective," Jay Augustine said behind her. "We had no warning—we're dealing with our shock as best we can. I could take the time to show you around, but I don't see what point it would serve."

At that point, neither did Abigail. Augustine ducked past her, and she and Bob followed him back out to the hall.

"What do you and your wife do now?" Bob asked.

Jay seemed surprised by the question. "Now? Oh, you mean with this house and Victor's collections. He left a will, thank heaven. Charlotte is meeting with the attorney tomorrow."

Bob bent over slightly and peered at a parade of statues of giraffes on a console. "Guess he collected giraffes, huh? Is your wife his sole next of kin?"

"Yes. Victor never married."

"Did he keep good records of what he owned?"

"Not particularly."

"He have anything a museum might want?"

Augustine inhaled through his nose, as if to rein in his impatience. "Potentially a considerable amount of what Victor collected would interest a museum—and Charlotte and me, too, if that's what you're going to ask next."

Bob didn't respond. Abigail knew he didn't care if he was getting on Augustine's nerves. "Did your brother-in-law spell out what he wanted done with his collections?"

"He left those decisions to my wife. To be quite frank, I'm saddened but not surprised that Victor died the way he did. He was very absentminded. He often lost track of where he was and what he was doing. You're wasting your time, Detective Browning. I'm sure the citizens of Boston have more urgent things for you to do than to investigate an accidental drowning."

"Again, I'm sorry for your loss," she said.

"No, you're not," he snapped, walking briskly up the hall.

As they came to the foyer, Abigail noticed that the pocket doors to a room on her right had popped open a few inches. Just inside was a bronze statue with horns, bulging eyes and a forked tongue.

It was a five-foot-tall statue of the devil.

"Mind if we take a peek in here?" she asked mildly.

Jay regarded her impassively. "As you wish, Detective."

Using two fingers, Bob slid open the pocket doors and gave a low whistle as he and Abigail entered the wood-paneled room. The devil statue was frightening, but it wasn't alone. The walls and the furnishings—large oak library-style tables, smaller side tables, open and glass-fronted bookcases—were jam-packed with items that all appeared to involve, in some way, the devil.

"Ol' Scratch lives," Bob said.

"Victor was a gifted amateur scholar and independent thinker," Jay Augustine said, not defensively.

Abigail noted a stack of books on a small table that all appeared to be about hell, damnation, devils or evil. "Where did he get this stuff?" she asked.

"Various places," Jay said. "Victor was obsessive once he sunk his teeth into something. About three years go he developed an interest in evil, hell and the devil. He considered it no more unusual than someone else's interest in goblins and trolls."

"I like flowers myself," Abigail said.

"Not everything in here is an original." Jay nodded toward a disturbing painting on the front wall of naked men suffering in a fiery hell. "That Bosch, for instance, is a copy. You know Bosch, don't you?"

"I don't," Bob said blandly.

"Hieronymus Bosch was a Dutch painter in the Middle Ages known for his vivid depictions of hell and damnation. He had a fervent belief in the fundamental evil of man. In his world—depicted brilliantly in his work—man was redeemable only by faith in God."

"Doesn't look as if anyone got redeemed in this painting," Abigail said.

"It's called *Hell*. Appropriate, don't you think? It's one in a series of four paintings Bosch did in the late fifteenth century. The others are *Ascent of the Blessed, Terrestrial Paradise* and *The Fall of the Damned*."

"Sounds as if you know something about this collection yourself," Abigail said.

Augustine shrugged. "Charlotte and I saw the originals on a trip to Italy last summer. We helped Victor find a painter to do this copy."

This obviously struck a nerve with Bob. "What for?"

"He wanted it."

Bob moved closer to the painting. "Kind of looks like Mordor in the *Lord of the Rings* movies, doesn't it? I haven't read the books. My daughters have—I got through *The Hobbit,* and that was it for me."

By habit and conviction, Abigail knew, he never used the names of any of his three daughters—Fiona, Madeleine and Jayne. At nineteen, Fiona was the eldest and more or less on her own, but Madeleine and Jayne were just fourteen and eleven. They lived with their mother in Lexington, close enough to visit their father regularly. They were good kids and got along with him, not always an easy task.

But Abigail didn't want to think about kids right now.

She wandered through the room. Sarakis's devil collection included paintings, drawings, illustrations, ceramics, books—and movies, she noted with surprise, from Vincent Price to *The Omen* and *Beetlejuice.*

"This shit gives me the willies," Bob blurted.

Abigail nodded to a locked door at the far end of the room. "What's in there?"

"That's Victor's climate-controlled room," Jay said with a slight, irritated sigh. "It maintains precise temperature and humidity conditions that certain items require for preservation. It's quite small and cramped, Detective."

A noise out in the hall drew their attention back toward the pocket doors.

A bushy-haired man—no more than twenty-five—stood in the doorway in a Harvard T-shirt and baggy shorts. "I thought that was a cop car out front."

Augustine seemed to welcome the intrusion. "Liam, it's good to see you. Detectives, this is Liam Butler, Victor's personal assistant."

"That sounds lofty," Liam said, his cheerfulness incongruous given all the images of hell and damnation around him. "I did scut work for Victor in exchange for a small salary and a suite upstairs. I'm a graduate student at Harvard. Political science— I don't know anything about art or collectibles. This was the perfect job. Flexible hours, decent pay, independence. It's been great." He gave a small moan, ran a hand through his hair. "I still can't believe he's gone."

"How did you come to know Mr. Sarakis?" Abigail asked.

"He and my father worked together—a brokerage firm in Boston. My father's at the Chicago office. He's still slogging away. Victor retired about six months ago." Liam seemed eager to talk. "He had me help sort through and catalog his collections. He's got things stashed all over the house. I swear we're going to find an Egyptian mummy stuffed under one of the beds."

"It's all a legal matter now that Victor's dead," Jay said stiffly.

Abigail looked for a reaction from Liam, but he didn't even seem to notice Jay had spoken. "How long did you work for Mr. Sarakis?" she asked.

"Eighteen months. I'm going to miss this job."

"What will you do now?"

He blew out a breath, shaking his head. "Stay here as long as I can, then find a new place. I can move in with some friends, maybe. Rents are expensive around here, but I saved some cash, thanks to Victor."

"Victor always spoke highly of Liam," Jay said.

Bob eased over to a black-wire sculpture of a particularly vile-looking devil. "Looks like a twisted great blue heron to me. So is Victor's sister into the devil and evil?"

Augustine tensed visibly. "I'm sure that Charlotte will be happy to answer any legitimate questions you have, Detective O'Reilly."

Bob shrugged. "Good."

Abigail noticed Liam backing out into the hall at the testy exchange. "Did you see Mr. Sarakis the day he died?" she asked.

"Just at breakfast. I spent most of the day helping a friend study for her orals—well, not study so much as deal with the pressure."

"What was Mr. Sarakis's state of mind that morning?"

"Preoccupied. That wasn't unusual, though. He was always chewing on some idea, some interest. He was a brilliant, inquisitive man, Detective." Liam choked up a moment. "A gentle soul—a true Renaissance man."

"He was also a little strange," Bob interjected.

"Yeah. So what?" There was no defensiveness or irritation in Liam's tone. He seemed to be asking a genuine question, trying to understand what Victor Sarakis's eccentricities could possibly have had to do with his death.

A fair point, Abigail thought. "What problem was he 'chewing' on?" she asked.

"I don't know. He didn't say, and I didn't ask. It wasn't a big deal. He'd often lose himself in his thoughts. Don't get me wrong. He was a great guy. But you can look around here and see why he retired at fifty, can't you?"

She could, indeed. "Do you know why he went to Boston the night he died?"

"Nope," Liam said without hesitation. "Look, I wish I could help, but I don't know what Victor was doing in Boston or why he drowned. I'm sorry it happened, that's all. If you have more questions, ask away. It'd be good to get all this over with. Otherwise, I'd just as soon go up to my room."

"Go ahead," Bob said. "We'll be in touch if we have further questions."

With a look of relief, Liam departed, disappearing up the stairs as Abigail joined Bob in the hall.

Jay stepped past them into the foyer and pulled open the creaky front door. "I appreciate your thoroughness, but if there's no reason to believe Victor's death wasn't simply an unfortunate accident— well, I think you know what I'm saying."

No fishing expedition, Abigail thought. No assuming Sarakis's unusual interests had a role in his death. A wealthy eccentric with a fascination with the devil drowning in two feet of water—reporters would love that one. The Augustines, who had a business to protect, would understandably want to avoid triggering a media sensation.

She and Bob walked back across the weedy yard to her car. The shade had kept the interior reasonably cool, and she rolled down a window, letting in the warm air.

"Okay," Bob said, "so the devil stuff's weird."

"Something's not right about this man's death, Bob."

"Maybe so. Brief Cambridge PD. Keep digging." He added sardonically, "Of course, that's not an order, since you don't report to me—"

"I appreciate the green light."

"Yellow light. Not green."

Abigail stuck the key in the ignition. Some days, there was no pleasing Bob O'Reilly.

Chapter 9

Beara Peninsula, Southwest Ireland
8:00 p.m., IST
June 21, The Summer Solstice

Keira climbed over a barbed-wire fence—her third fence crossing of the evening—and dropped to the soft, thick grass on the other side, its ankle height suggesting that no cows or sheep fed out here. As far as she could tell, nearly every square inch of the virtually treeless hills around her was marked off for grazing. Sheep, being more nimble than cows, could navigate the rock outcroppings and steep terrain higher up in the mountains.

She hoisted her backpack onto one shoulder. Once again, she'd come prepared, even if it meant a heavy pack. Last night's hike had confirmed more details in Patsy's story and narrowed down the possibilities of where the hermit monk's hut might have been—or might yet still be. Tonight, Keira hoped either to find it or to settle on a spot that would work for the illustrations she had in mind.

With plenty of light left in the long June dusk, she'd be back in her cottage, tucked into her bed, before she needed to resort to her flashlight. The open landscape helped her feel less isolated, less as if she was a little out of her mind, heading off into the Irish hills in search of evidence that an old story told to her in a South Boston kitchen wasn't pure fiction.

She pictured Patsy McCarthy with her wisps of white hair, her bright eyes sparkling as she told the old story.

"The monk, who was a kind and generous man, lived a simple life of prayer in a stone hut he'd built with his own hands by the spring in the rock-strewn hills above the harbor..."

Keira smiled as she took a moment to regain her bearings. She was still in open pasture, above a stream that had carved a dip in the general upward slope of the hills. She'd left the dirt track a while back. A sharp barb had cut through her pants into her thigh on that first fence-crossing, but she'd bit back a curse of pain, not wanting to alert the bull referred to in the Beware Of Bull sign tacked onto a post just before a small wooden bridge over the stream. The land was owned by Eddie O'Shea's brother Aidan, who had given her permission to go exploring. She'd passed a modern barn and his scatter of well-used farm equipment along the track, but they were out of sight now.

She made her way down the hill, the barren rocks and grass giving way to the trees and undergrowth that flourished along the banks of the stream, the ground wetter now, mushier, the air cooler. All she had to do was climb up the hill and she'd be back out in the open again.

Had her mother come out here on the summer solstice thirty years ago?

"Every year on the summer solstice, the mischief would begin anew."

The stream was one of the distinctive landmarks in the story. The stone circle, the harbor, the position and the shape of the hills—they had all helped pinpoint the village and confirm that the story, however much of it was myth, referred to a real place.

"The monk had no help from his brothers in building his little hut by the spring. He used his own hands, carrying stones up from the village. He didn't mind. He'd always preferred his own company. His solitary life suited him."

Keira crept along the bank of the stream, dodging tree branches, pushing her way through tangles of vines and holly, the lush vegetation creating shifting shadows and a very different mood than out in the pasture. She picked up her pace, wondering how long to give her search tonight.

But even as she formed the thought, she stopped abruptly, half in disbelief.

She was standing at the base of the remains of what appeared to be an old hut built into the hillside, just as Patsy McCarthy had described, its gray stone visible here and there under a cloak of wild-growing ivy.

Containing her excitement, Keira skirted a large oak tree for a closer look at the ruin.

She could make out a front wall, the remnants of a chimney and a doorway—the door itself probably had been appropriated for another use decades ago. What must have been a thatched roof was gone, replaced now with a natural canopy of vines and debris. She couldn't estimate the structure's age with any accuracy, but she could always ask Eddie O'Shea to put her in touch with someone local who might know. Colm Dermott, a respected scholar, would certainly help.

Abandoned buildings weren't unusual in southwest Ireland, particularly hard hit by the famine years and subsequent mass emigration, but this one fired Keira's imagination. The monk in Patsy's story— or perhaps a monk upon whom he'd been based—could actually have lived here, in this tiny ruin on the hillside above the stream.

"Never mind that the monk was content in his isolation, his brothers thought he needed company—needed them, in fact. They had other ideas about his life."

Keira could hear the gurgling of the stream directly behind her and, in the distance, sheep bleating at irregular intervals, comforting sounds for their familiarity, their normalcy. Whoever had lived out here clearly had maintained a simple existence. It didn't have to be Patsy's monk. For all Keira knew, Patsy's father, or his father, could have wandered out here and decided to add the ruin to their story of the three brothers and make a good story better.

"It wasn't just his brothers with other ideas, either. Oh, no."

Patsy had hesitated at that point in her telling, her reluctance to admit she believed in fairies palpable.

"It was the monk who first discovered the angel, in the ashes by the fire on the evening of the spring equinox. At first, he thought his brothers had put it there. More of their mischief."

Keira heard a rustling sound nearby and sucked in a breath as she looked around her.

Just above her on the hillside, a large black dog paused in front of a hawthorn, drooling, snarling at her.

"Easy, poochie," she said in a low voice. She'd never been particularly good with dogs, and this was no friendly Irish sheepdog. "Easy, now."

The dog growled, his short black hair standing on end on his upper spine.

Keira put some firmness into her tone. "You just stop. There's no need to growl at me."

Panting now, the dog edged down the hill toward her.

She'd prepared for everything, she thought, except mean dogs.

Mud, fallen leaves, ivy, stone and a half-dead tree partially obstructed the door's opening, but she pushed aside a tangle of muck and greenery and slipped inside, hoping the dog wouldn't try to follow her. She reached into her backpack for her emergency whistle. If nothing else, it might scare off the dog should he go on the offensive.

She heard another growl, a sharp yip and more rustling of brush. Then, nothing.

Assuming the dog ran off, Keira eased her backpack off her shoulder and set it on the mud floor as she surveyed her surroundings. The hut was very small, with a tiny window opening high up on the far end, above a mostly intact loft, and another window opening over the doorway—the only entrance, as far as she could see. The main wooden support beam above her looked to be holding firm, but rafters had caved in on each other, fallen leaves, branches and ivy forming their own organic roof. On the wall opposite the loft stood a largely intact chimney constructed of more gray stone.

"The monk had never seen such a thing in all his life as the stone angel. She was so beautiful, he sat by the fire and stared at her for hours."

As Keira's eyes adjusted to the semidarkness inside the hut, she got out her water bottle and plastic bag of snacks—a couple of energy bars, nuts, an apple. She tried to imagine the reclusive monk in Patsy's story, going with the idea that he had existed and had lived here. What would he have look liked? What would his life on this hillside have entailed? It would have been rough, no doubt, dominated by the necessities of getting food and water, staying warm, maintaining even a modest level of hygiene.

In some ways, Keira thought, it would have been similar to her mother's lifestyle in the woods.

Patsy was a mesmerizing storyteller, taking Keira through every twist and turn as the brothers tried to figure out how the stone angel had come to them and what it meant. They all agreed the angel was a harbinger of good fortune. The monk brother believed Saint Ita herself had sent the angel to turn him and his brothers more deeply to lives of prayer, charity and simplicity as a means of bringing them good spiritual fortune. The farmer brother believed the angel would bring the good fortune of a bountiful harvest and productive cows and sheep.

The ne'er-do-well brother, of course, had another idea altogether and believed the angel was meant to help him and his brothers—the entire village, in fact—turn a profit so they could open their own pub.

All three brothers were convinced the angel had Saint Ita's gift of prophecy.

They were still arguing about their predictions three months later—on the night of the summer solstice—when fairies appeared and plucked the angel from the monk's hearth.

Keira smiled, remembering the glee with which Patsy had told that part of the story.

The monk took the theft as a test of his faith and mettle and resolved to get the angel back. For the next three months, he chased the fairies through the hills, until, on the night of the autumnal equinox, the stone angel appeared again on his hearth.

He kept its return a secret from his brothers. When the winter solstice came and went without a visit from the fairies, the monk thought he'd won the contest of wills, that he was right in his interpretation of the meaning of the angel and all would be well.

But his brothers eventually discovered his deception and accused him of lying and hypocrisy.

They continued arguing, but without animosity—arguing was a way of life for them. It was what they were used to, it was what they loved about each other. A good fight offered them a way to be together.

On the next summer solstice, the fairies again came for the angel.

Then on the autumn equinox, the angel reappeared on the hearth.

On it went, the monk arguing with his two brothers and chasing the fairies, the angel disappearing and reappearing on the equinox or the solstice.

In her elaborate telling of the story, Patsy had used just the right descriptive detail, the well-timed pause, the perfect tone to convey frustration, amusement, a sense of mischief. She'd teared up at the ending, when, one day, the angel simply disappeared from the hills for good. No one had it—not the fairies, not the brothers.

Staying close to the hut's doorway, Keira sipped her water and let the memory of Patsy's voice quiet her mind. She could smell the mud and the pungency of the vines and decaying leaves around her in the hut, feel the dampness, making it easy to imagine the monk's excitement at finding a beautiful stone angel on his hearth.

It would be there…by the fire…

"Keira."

She went still, her water bottle suspended in midair.

Was it the wind, or had she just heard someone whisper her name?

Then came a creak, a groan of what sounded like a tree being uprooted—and then the sharp scrape of rock against rock. Dirt and ivy loosened overhead, and decaying leaves and twigs fell onto the mud floor.

Keira lunged for the door, but didn't get far as several rafters collapsed onto each other, sending dirt and debris down in front of her. She heard stones tumbling on the chimney side of the ruin.

No time.

She had to take cover *now*.

She about-faced and dove under the loft, scrambling into the far corner of the hut, dropping her water bottle and emergency rations into the mud as she covered her head with her arms.

After a few seconds, the rocks and debris stopped falling. Keira held her breath, not daring to move or utter a sound. She waited. A minute passed. Two minutes.

Nothing.

Hoping the worst was over, she lowered her arms from her head and, still not making a sound, peered through the dust to assess her situation.

Who was out there? Who had whispered her name?

She could make out the half-crumbled fireplace and…something. She squinted, blinked, squinted again.

A small stone statue stood in the rubble in front of the fireplace.

An angel.

On the hearth.

Suspicious that her imagination, fueled by adrenaline, had conjured up Patsy's mythical stone angel, Keira expected she'd blink once more and it'd disappear, turn out to be just more ordinary rock.

But it didn't disappear. She could see wings, a beautiful, delicately featured face and, in the angel's arms, a small Celtic harp.

The three brothers in Patsy's story all agreed they'd heard the angel playing a harp.

Saint Ita had lived in Ireland in the sixth century, but there was no way for Keira to tell if the angel was fourteen-hundred or a hundred years old—or if it'd been bought off a garden-store shelf that morning and popped in here as a summer solstice prank. Maybe she wasn't the only one in the area familiar with the story. At this point, she thought, anything was possible.

Just as she proceeded to get a closer look, she heard a loud snap and tucked herself into a tight ball as more of the ruin caved in. Even with her face pressed up against her knees, she could taste dirt and dust from the collapsing stones and mortar. If her side of the old hut gave way, she was doomed.

But she knew it wouldn't.

It just won't, she thought, surprised by her sense of certainty.

Keira remained in her tucked-in position until all she could hear were the gentle sounds of the stream and the breeze blowing through the trees just outside.

She didn't know how long she waited—at least an hour—but when she was as sure as she could be that the hut had collapsed as much as it was going to, she raised her head and coughed in the settling dust as she took in her situation.

A massive pile of stone and debris had fallen just beyond her free space under the loft, blocking her route to the door. She wouldn't be going out the way she'd come in, but that left few options. There was no rear exit, and the tiny windows were too far up for her to reach without a ladder.

Keira picked up her water bottle and her bag of snacks out of the mud, grimacing when she realized that her backpack was buried somewhere in the rubble.

Even with the long Irish June days, it would be fully dark in a few hours.

She didn't need more time to digest her situation. It was obvious to her.

She was trapped.

⌒ Chapter 10

London, England
5:00 p.m., BST
June 22

Simon took his cell phone to a quieter corner of the bustling London hotel bar and asked Owen Garrison to repeat what he'd just said. Something about an artist who'd turned up missing in Ireland.

Keira Sullivan.

The flaxen-haired fairy princess with a penchant for trouble.

"You met her the other night in Boston," Owen said.

"I remember." Simon pictured her floating into the drawing room in her long skirt. "She was off to Ireland to look into an old story. What's going on?"

"She was supposed to call her uncle this morning from the pub in the village where she's rented a cottage. When he didn't hear from her, he checked with the pub. The barman said he'd expected her to stop in last night, but she didn't, and no one's seen her today. She doesn't have a cell phone, and there's no phone at the cottage she rented."

Simon felt the muscles in the back of his neck tighten. "Why doesn't her uncle ask someone from the pub to go knock on her door?"

"He did. She wasn't there. Her rented car's in the driveway."

"She's an adult. She's in Ireland on her own. How do we know she didn't just jump on the bus and go to Dublin for a few days?"

"We don't. Bob's not panicking, but he's got this thing about the summer solstice. It's bad luck for his family or something. I know it's a lot to ask as a favor, but if you're at a loose end and could take a look, you'd have a cop in Boston in your debt."

"Always a good idea."

"I've e-mailed you a file on Keira. Link to her Web site, directions to her cottage."

Simon was more accustomed to diving into rescue missions following major disasters, not tracking down some flaky creative type who'd taken off into the Irish countryside. As attractive as this one was.

"All right. I'll see what I can do." He started to hang up, but added, "I haven't rescued a damsel in distress in a while."

"Bob said for me to tell you Keira's also a dead shot with a Glock."

"Is she now?" It was obviously a warning from the uncle for Simon to behave, but he was more amused than intimidated. "Even better. And she's pretty."

"Alas," Owen said, "that she is."

Simon also knew—as Owen and Bob O'Reilly would also know—that if something had gone wrong and Keira was in trouble, the sooner they got started looking for her, the better her odds of surviving.

After he disconnected, Simon returned to his stool at the bar next to his latest partner in debate, a London banker he'd just met, also friends with Will Davenport. The banker had ordered another martini and seemed ready to settle in for an evening of putting an upstart American in his place. He was Simon's age but dressed as if he'd just stepped from tea with Edward VIII. If not for the hotel's dress code, Simon would have been in jeans. Instead, he'd opted for black slacks and a charcoal pullover that barely passed muster.

"Sorry, mate," he told the banker. "Duty calls."

"The fake English accent is annoying, Simon."

"That's the idea."

Simon headed up the elevator to the elegant suite where he was supposed to be keeping a low profile while the FBI and other law enforcement entities went after Norman Estabrook and his pals.

Would John March consider taking off to Ireland to check on an artist late for a call to her cop uncle a way of keeping a low profile?

Probably not, Simon thought, turning on his laptop and opening up his e-mail.

"Whoa."

Having met Keira Sullivan, he'd expected pretty, but in the publicity shot on her Web site, she was smiling, with flowers—pink roses and something purple and frothy—in her shining flaxen hair. She had gorgeous, black-lashed blue eyes, and she wore a dark green velvet dress that gave her the look of an elf princess out of Tolkien—one with a very nice cleavage. He couldn't help but notice, although the flowers in her hair had momentarily distracted him.

"Now that can't be a good sign," he muttered, clicking the link to her bio.

She was born in South Boston and raised in southern New Hampshire, but she'd lived all over the place since—New York, Nashville, Sedona, San Diego. She supported herself, apparently, with her increasingly popular illustrations of classic poems and folktales, but she also had an academic background in folklore.

No mention of a husband or kids.

Simon dialed the number for Will's assistant, Josie Goodwin.

Josie, who was particular about people, liked Simon because he'd saved Will's life. At least to hear Will tell it. That particular rescue hadn't been an easy one, Simon remembered. Just him, a rope and an ax. He'd pulled Will out of a bombed-out cave in Afghanistan. Will had never explained what he was doing there, and Simon had never asked. Nor had Simon explained his own presence.

He hadn't seen Will yet this trip. Supposedly, he was extending a stay in Scotland to go fishing. But he'd told friends he was in Scotland fishing when he was lying half-dead in the rubble of an Afghan cave.

That was two years ago, before Simon had met Owen Garrison or had even heard of Fast Rescue and its teams of highly trained volunteers.

"I need to get to southwest Ireland," he told Josie.

"When?"

"Now."

"Ah. You do love to present a challenge." A keyboard clicked in the background. "I can arrange for a flight into Kerry tonight, but you'll have to hurry. I'll need to have a car pick you up in ten minutes."

"I'll be ready." He smiled into the phone. "Thanks, Moneypenny."

"Fancy yourself a James Bond, do you? More of a Hulk, I think, or perhaps a Conan the Barbarian." She clicked more keys. "But let me arrange for the car, and you go pack."

"I owe you—"

"No," she said, serious now, "you don't."

Ten minutes later, he was downstairs, his car waiting. He'd be at Keira Sullivan's cottage in a few hours.

Then what?

He had no idea, but in his world, a fascination with Irish stories, fairies and magic didn't bode well.

⌒ *Chapter 11*

Keira bit into the last of her three energy bars. It was oatmeal raisin and not half-bad, although she'd begun to fantasize about warm rhubarb crumble at Eddie O'Shea's pub. She'd been trapped in her Irish ruin for almost twenty-four hours. She was uncomfortable, dirty and hungry, but as dank and unpleasant as it was in her intact corner under the loft, she was strangely unafraid. She was unhurt, reasonably dry and safe, and she still had food and water. She also had a solid plan for getting out. It was just taking longer to execute than she wanted it to.

Smoky light filtered through the cracks in the cloak of ivy and debris above the rubble beyond the low ceiling of the loft. The half moon had helped last night, but she had to hurry if she didn't want to spend another night in there. Her flashlight was in her buried backpack, along with the rest of her emergency supplies.

"No more breaks," she said aloud, pushing up the sleeves of her sweater as she stood up.

In ducking into the ruin to escape the dog, she must have dislodged a rock or tree root—or even just the ground—and started a chain reaction. Rafters, mud, mortar and stone had fallen between her and the fireplace, blocking any hope of getting out through the door. She didn't dare fool with that mess. She wasn't an engineer— she couldn't take the chance of collapsing the rest of the ruin around her.

That meant that her only practical route of escape was up.

The distance between her and the loft was too great for her just to step on a rock or jump up. She'd had to build a ladder. In principle, it sounded simple. In practice—it was anything but. Safety and stability were serious concerns, and the task of finding good "steps" for her makeshift ladder and setting them in place took time, energy, muscle and a certain tolerance for bruises, scrapes and wrecked knuckles and fingernails. As impatient as Keira was to get out, she forced herself not to rush and risk injury.

The bottom "rung" was a large, relatively flat rock. No problem there. Two smaller rocks that she'd exhumed from the rubble provided the next steps up. Again, no problem. Then came a hunk of wood—part of an old rafter, she assumed. It was an iffier prospect than the rocks, but she thought it would work reasonably well.

But she still lacked a few feet, and she was eyeing a sapling out toward the main area of freshly fallen rubble, wondering if she could figure out a way to make it work to bridge the gap between her top step and the edge of the loft.

She noticed a fat, black slug oozing along the mud floor and grimaced. She'd seen her first slug at daylight, and her first spider about an hour later. Now that she knew she had company, she couldn't bear the thought of being trapped in her cell-like free space for another night. She had about six square feet to work in. There were no bathroom facilities, but she could make do. It was the slugs, spiders and darkness that got to her. She wanted out.

Her ladder would work. She knew it would. The plan was to be free by nightfall and off to the pub before anyone missed her. She'd need to call her uncle as soon as possible, but it was a workday for him—surely he was too busy to have noticed his grown niece in Ireland hadn't called that morning, as promised.

Bypassing the slug, Keira reached for the sapling. Her emergency whistle was somewhere in the mud and muck, but she wasn't sure she'd have bothered with it, anyway. She much preferred to get out of here on her own and go about her business. Let everyone think she'd gone off gallery hopping in Kenmare and be none the wiser. She'd left a note in her cottage detailing her route in case of mishap, but obviously no one had become sufficiently concerned about her absence to check on her. She'd have heard a search party out on the hills.

Just as well no one was coming to her rescue, she thought, pulling on the sapling carefully, dislodging it an inch at a time. At the first sign of falling rock and debris, she'd duck back into her corner.

She couldn't see the stone angel from her position under the loft—let alone reach it—but once she was free, she'd investigate from outside the ruin. Had the cave-in crushed the angel?

Or had the fairies come for it?

Keira smiled at the thought. Another hour—two hours at most—and she'd be free.

~ *Chapter 12*

Beara Peninsula, Southwest Ireland
8:00 p.m., IST
June 22

Turn onto lane just past pub.

Look for pink roses and a small traditional stone cottage on right.

Owen's directions to Keira Sullivan's rented cottage were minimal, but as he drove into her tiny village on Kenmare Bay, Simon had no reason to believe they were inadequate. Josie Goodwin had arranged a sporty car for him at the Kerry County airport, but he'd paid for it himself. He'd only go so far in accommodating her boss's need to repay Simon for saving his life. Simon wasn't nearly as wealthy as Will Davenport, but he wasn't a pauper, either.

This was a personal favor to Owen, not Fast Rescue business.

Simon had spent a fair amount of time in Ireland, for both business and pleasure, and enjoyed the narrow, twisting roads out to the Beara Peninsula. He recalled someone telling him that birds from North America would occasionally cross the Atlantic by mistake and end up crash-landing on Dursey Island at the tip of the Beara. Having himself occasionally ended up in foreign lands he hadn't realized he'd set out for, Simon could well imagine the lost birds suddenly finding themselves in an Irish sheep pasture instead of on a Brooklyn street.

With only one pub in the village where Keira had set up house-keeping, the lane was easy to find.

Simon slowed as he came to a small, picture-perfect traditional stone cottage with masses of pink roses and wildflowers. It had to be Keira's rental. He pulled into a dirt driveway behind a parked Micra—presumably her rental—and got out, pausing a moment to get a feel for the place. A fine mist had left water droplets on the grass and flowers. The air was cooler, windier down the peninsula.

The cottage was unlit. As he approached the front door, he saw no sign of anyone home. Just in case, he knocked loudly. "Keira? It's Simon Cahill."

He waited, but the silence continued.

The door was unlocked. Now here, he thought, was a problem.

But it wasn't much of a lock, and an intruder could have gotten inside easily. Still, an unlocked door was an invitation to trouble. He pushed open the door and flipped on a light switch along the inside wall.

An overhead light glowed on the vibrant yellow painted walls of a single main room that combined the living and kitchen areas. Probably helped on dark and dreary days, Simon thought, noting the comfortable furnishings—overstuffed sofa and chair covered in bright flowers, side tables stacked with books, a sturdy-looking pine table with two pine chairs. The table was spread with colored pencils, oil pastels, sharpeners, erasers, pads and sheets of sketch paper.

He opened a medium-size sketchbook, expecting pretty, whim-sical scenes of bucolic Ireland. Instead, he found three dark, atmos-pheric sketches of what he supposed was, or at least was inspired by, the rugged local scenery.

As he started to shut the sketchbook, Simon noticed a tiny, cheerful red gnome sitting on a fence post in the top drawing. He had to smile. This was a touch of the quirky, fair-haired Keira he'd expected to find.

He checked the kitchen. The electric kettle was unplugged, cold and empty. There were no dirty dishes in the sink. No food left out. He opened up the small fridge—no clues there, either. She had a stash of butter, cheese, bread, milk, coffee, half a cucumber, carrots, two apples.

He looked for a note detailing her whereabouts, but found none.

Helping himself to one of the apples, Simon headed for the bedroom. More vibrant paint—fuchsia this time. A double bed, its flowered duvet neatly pulled up over the pillows. Inside the closet were a couple of blouses and one skirt on hangers, a well-worn brocade satchel suitcase, a pair of sport sandals on the floor and a robe—white, silky—on a hook. He supposed his missing illustrator could have another suitcase, a smaller one for quick side trips. But why leave behind her robe?

He pulled open the drawers of the tall pine chest. More clothes, sturdy stuff for hikes in the countryside.

"Well, Keira, where are you?"

Simon gazed out the window at the beautiful, remote landscape. She could have taken the bus to Dublin for a few days, or she could have headed out into the hills for a ramble and slid off a cliff into the Atlantic. Who the hell knew?

Stifling his annoyance at her poor planning, he flipped through a stack of receipts and brochures on top of the dresser. He didn't find any type of note or letter or even doodle indicating where she was— nothing that would help him locate her.

He headed back outside, grabbing his rain jacket out of his car—

one didn't travel to Ireland without rain gear—and ambled off down the lane in the moonlight. Keira had picked herself a spot right out of an Irish fairytale, that was for certain.

The village pub was lit up and lively with food, drink and conversation among a mix of tourists and locals.

Simon eased onto a barstool and ordered coffee. It was getting dark on the peninsula, and he needed to keep a clear head. "My name's Simon Cahill," he told the sandy-haired barman. "I'm trying to locate Keira Sullivan."

The barman—presumably the Eddie O'Shea who'd spoken to her uncle—tilted his head back and eyed Simon with open suspicion. "You've come all the way from America?"

"London." Simon didn't object to O'Shea's obvious protectiveness. "Keira's uncle asked me to look in on her through a mutual friend. You talked to the uncle earlier. Boston detective."

"His name?"

"Bob O'Reilly. To be honest, I don't know him well."

O'Shea seemed satisfied. "Keira sat right where you are two nights ago."

"Did she say she was going anywhere?"

"She said she was looking forward to the summer solstice."

Simon recalled overhearing the old woman in Boston mentioning the summer solstice. It had something to do with her story about the angel, the brothers, the fairies. He wished he'd done a more thorough job of eavesdropping on what all she and Keira had said to each other.

O'Shea filled a coffee press with fresh grounds and hot water and set it and a mug on the bar, then pulled a pitcher of cream from a small refrigerator and plopped it next to the coffee. "Keira likes to roam about the countryside."

Simon pushed down the press, then poured the coffee. It smelled kick-ass strong, and he added as much cream as he could without overflowing the mug. "Has she ruffled any local feathers?"

"Not that I would know. She's only been here a short time, but I can see she's one who goes her own way."

"She left her cottage unlocked."

"Now, why would you care about that? Think someone around here would rob her?"

"You never know."

Eddie O'Shea grew red in the face. "*I* know."

Simon was neither embarrassed nor offended by the barman's strong reaction. "Any idea where she is?"

"There's no telling."

"She give you any hints?"

Calmer now, O'Shea shook his head. "She likes to pull my leg about fairies and leprechauns. I told her I've no use for that nonsense."

"Would you say she's careful, takes normal precautions?"

"I suppose that depends on what you'd call normal, wouldn't it, Mr. Cahill? It's the wet and the cold and the rock I worry about. One slip." O'Shea snapped his fingers. "That'd do it."

It would, indeed, Simon thought.

"I have to say..." O'Shea grabbed Simon's coffee press and set it on the work counter behind him. "Never mind."

Simon waited a moment, but when the barman didn't go on, he nudged. "What were you going to say, Mr. O'Shea?"

"I don't recall telling you my name."

Simon recognized that he was being tested and decided not to play games with the man. "You didn't. You told Keira's uncle in Boston."

O'Shea sighed, less confrontational. "Keira had something on her mind. She didn't tell me any details, and I didn't ask." He snatched up a white cloth and mopped the spotless, gleaming bar. "For all I know, she's off to kiss the Blarney Stone or some damn thing."

"If necessary, can you help me pull together a search team at first light?"

"I can."

Simon drank a bit more of his coffee and started to pay for it, but O'Shea waved off any money. "Thanks," Simon said quietly, sensing the man's worry. "I'll see what I can find out."

So far, it was proving to be a cheap trip to Ireland. He headed outside, debating his options. He assumed everyone else in the pub had eavesdropped on his conversation with O'Shea and would have volunteered information on Keira if they had any.

Simon noticed a man in simple farmer's clothes smoking a cigarette at a picnic table by the pub entrance. "Your girlie's stirring up things best left alone." His eyes were a piercing shade of blue, and his voice was steady, sober. "There are good spirits and evil spirits. Best to leave all of them be."

"Did Keira talk about these spirits?"

The man smiled a little. "You have the look of an Irishman."

That was all he had to say. He took one last drag on his cigarette, then got up and headed down the quiet street. Simon started to call after him, but before he could get a word out, the man had disappeared into the mist.

As Simon walked back along the quiet lane, fog swept down from the hills, adding to the moodiness and the sense of remoteness of the place. Obviously, his AWOL artist wasn't a fainthearted type, but he had to admit he understood the draw of being out here alone.

And it was the land of her ancestors and his, which had its own appeal—as well as its own dangers. Easy to get caught up in the romance of a place and think one was safe, protected.

Lights in bungalows along the lane and down toward the harbor suggested life in the little village—families gathered in front of the television, getting cleaned up for the next day, settling in for the night. Simon had seldom known such normalcy himself.

When he returned to Keira's rented cottage, he flipped through another sketchbook, pausing at a hasty-looking pencil drawing of a winding stream amid thick trees and lush undergrowth.

A real place, or a product of her obviously vivid imagination?

Simon turned to the next page. The stream again—this time, curling under a small wooden bridge on a dirt track running through open, rocky pasture.

He tore off the page, folded it and shoved it into his jacket pocket.

If the stream, the dirt track, the fence and the bridge existed, then Keira had drawn enough detail for him to find them—and, with any luck, her.

~ Chapter 13

Beacon Hill
Boston, Massachusetts
4:00 p.m., EDT
June 22

Abigail joined Bob O'Reilly on the front steps of the Garrison house while Fiona and her friends practiced in the drawing room. "They're on their millionth run-through of 'Boil the Breakfast Early,'" Bob said. "One more time, and my fillings are going to start falling out."

"I don't know Irish music that well, but I like that song," Abigail said.

"It's a happy tune, at least. The sad ones make me want to drive straight to the shooting range."

"Ever take music lessons as a kid?"

"Fiddle. Hated it."

"Irish dancing?" she asked.

"I'm taking the Fifth on that one."

"I don't know, Bob, I can see you as this little redheaded kid step dancing—"

"I'm armed, Abigail."

She leaned against the stair railing, feeling the heat and humidity building back in after a couple of dry days. "Any word from Simon?"

Bob shook his head. "You think I'm overreacting."

"I didn't say that."

"Any other time of year—any other place—" He broke off. "Keira's never lived a simple life. A dead man in the Public Garden the other night, and now this."

"Did you check with the Irish police? Any accident reports, unidentified—"

"No. I haven't checked. I'm not going to. She's fine."

Abigail wasn't sure what to say. "I imagine you'll hear something from Simon soon. Owen says he's one of Fast Rescue's best, and he's a disaster-preparedness consultant."

Bob grunted. "Keira's a damn disaster all by herself."

"You don't mean that, Bob. You're just worried."

Abigail tensed, noticing Charlotte Augustine walking up Beacon Street, clutching a book in one hand.

"What?" Bob asked.

"Never mind. Maybe you should go inside and see Fiona."

He followed her gaze to Charlotte. "Who's that?"

"Victor Sarakis's sister. Look, let me deal with her—"

"What's she doing here?"

"I don't know, Bob," Abigail said testily. "Will you just go inside and—"

"Nope. They're playing a dirge now. I'm in a bad enough mood." He nodded toward the street. "Go ahead. Pretend I'm not here."

She didn't argue with him, just descended the stairs and intercepted Charlotte. "Mrs. Augustine, what can I do for you?"

She was in her late forties, trim and average-looking except for badly dyed red-brown hair. She wore a crisp, conservative navy skirt

suit that Abigail figured had to be hot for late June. They'd met yesterday at her and her husband's house in Newton. It had been a short
visit. Abigail still had nothing but gut instinct to indicate Victor
Sarakis's death wasn't an accident. She'd left her card for Charlotte—
which didn't include the address for the Garrison house.

"I don't mean to intrude, Detective Browning, but I thought I
might find you here. I was at our showroom, trying to work. It's difficult…" Her voice faltered. "I can't get over what happened."

Bob descended two steps. "Did Detective Browning ask you to
meet her here?"

"Oh, no. No, no." Charlotte's faced reddened. "I just remembered
reading about her husband's murder last summer and that he was
connected to the Dorothy Garrison Foundation."

"Her husband wasn't killed last summer. Abigail figured out who
killed him last summer. He wasn't connected to the foundation,
either. The man she's—"

"It doesn't matter," Abigail said, jumping in before Bob explained
her whole life to this woman.

Charlotte thrust the book she was carrying at Abigail. "Here's the
history of Satan I mentioned yesterday."

Abigail took it from her. "Thanks." It was a weighty, musty tome.
She glanced at the title. Sure, enough. *A History of the Devil* was emblazoned on the cover in academic-looking type.

Bob leaned over her. "Not exactly light reading, is it?"

"It's a thorough but basic history," Charlotte said. "Victor—I can't
explain why he was so fascinated by the subject. He's the one who
gave me the book."

"Birthday present?" Bob asked, neutral.

"No. I think he just wanted me to understand his interest. He liked
to remind me that the devil is a single entity. People tend to forget

there's only one Satan. One devil. We think of him in multiples these days, though, don't we? He's become generic—a cliché."

"I suppose you're right," Abigail said. "Mrs. Augustine, do you believe your brother's obsession with the devil played a role in his death?"

Charlotte seemed hardly to hear the question. "I don't know what to believe," she said. "You're a homicide detective. Do you consider most murders the devil's work?"

"I don't," Bob interjected.

"It doesn't matter what we think," Abigail said. "Is that what your brother believed?"

"He never said."

"When was the last time—"

"The last time we discussed the devil?" Charlotte gave a bitter laugh. "It's all we ever talked about. Tell me, if God is all-powerful, why not rid us of Satan? Why not just defeat the devil and free us all of his influence?"

"Or she," Bob said. "The devil could be a she, right?"

Charlotte didn't even crack a smile. "The devil is God's enemy, but he's our enemy, too. Mankind's enemy. He tempts, lures, cajoles, tricks. He takes many forms in order to do his evil. He's always on the search for new minions—fresh and able diabolical followers."

Bob rubbed the side of his mouth with one finger. "That's in the book, right?"

She didn't seem to hear him. "If God can't defeat Satan, how can we mere humans hope to?" She smiled suddenly, as if she'd just realized she was starting to sound like a nut. "I hope you find the book instructive, Detective Browning."

Abigail gave her a tight smile. "I'm sure I will."

"I don't really believe there's a connection between my brother's interest in evil and his death. I just—I don't know. I suppose I'm hoping the book will give you a better appreciation of Victor's interests the way it did me."

"I understand, Mrs. Augustine."

She seemed relieved, smiling again as she nodded toward the drawing room. "The music's wonderful. Irish, isn't it?"

Bob bristled visibly. "I don't know much about music."

"Of course," Charlotte mumbled. "Well, I should be going. Thank you for your time."

Abigail watched her for a moment before turning back to Bob. "I didn't tell her to come here."

"Good thing we were here. I wouldn't want her dropping off a devil book with Fiona. You know, Abigail, it's easier for someone with an anonymous life to be a detective."

She had to admit that lately her life had been anything but anonymous. With her father's high-profile job, it never had been, but people were used to it. They'd already factored in that she was the daughter of the current FBI director. But her husband's shocking death—and the discovery of his murderer last summer—had kept Abigail in the news. Falling for a Garrison and the founder of Fast Rescue had only added to the complications of her life.

Bob sighed at her book. "When the nuns started in on hell, damnation and the devil in catechism class, I'd sneak out to the drugstore and buy comics. You know, good guys, bad guys. Bad guys lose. Good guys win. Simple."

"Nothing about Victor Sarakis strikes me as simple."

"I've been at this job for a lot of years, and I've never once run into a murder committed by the devil. They've all been committed by human beings. Our job is to figure out which human beings. Period, end of story."

Fiona O'Reilly, in skinny jeans and a baggy Irish rugby shirt, appeared in the doorway behind him. "Dad?"

He turned sharply. "Hey, kid. You guys finished?"

"We're taking a ten-minute break. Dad—who was that?"

"Just a woman who wanted to give Abigail a book."

But Abigail saw that Fiona was pale, even scared. "Fiona, do you know her?"

"No! I just—with your work and all...I was curious. Dad, you don't have to wait for me if there's something you need to do."

Abigail kept the front cover of the book out of Fiona's line of sight, but she hadn't checked the back cover. For all she knew, it was decorated in the flames of hell and red, fork-tongued devils.

One devil, she reminded herself. *The rest would be his minions.*

"There's nothing I need to do," Bob told his daughter. But he eyed her a moment, then said, "Fi, what's up?"

She peered past him at the street. "Did she know the man who drowned?"

"He was her brother," Abigail said.

Bob shot her a look, but Fiona gulped in a breath. "Did he have anything to do with the old woman and the priest who were here?"

"Fiona," her father said. "What old woman and priest?"

His daughter's eyes flickered on him, and color rose in her cheeks. "Nothing. Never mind. I forgot you and Abigail weren't here. You didn't see them—"

Abigail started up the steps. "Fiona, it's okay. You can tell us. If it's nothing, it's nothing. If it's something, we need to know."

"It's nothing—my mistake. Honestly."

She wasn't lying, Abigail decided, but she wasn't telling all she knew, either. Bob had to see it, too. But he said, "Come on, Fi, let's go inside. You and your friends can play a tune and I'll see if I can remember how to dance to it."

Abigail reined in her impatience. "Bob—"

He glared at her over her shoulder. "Go home, Abigail. Read about the devil." Then he gave her a strained grin. "No way am I dancing an Irish jig in front of you."

"If Fiona—"

"Leave my daughter to me."

Abigail sighed, nodding. She saw the worry etched in his face and decided not to push him. "All right. Let me know if you hear from Simon, and I'll do the same."

He didn't respond. As Fiona started back into the elegant house, she turned and glanced down the street, her face pale again, but she said nothing and neither did Abigail.

By the time she was unlocking her car door, she could hear Irish music again and almost peeked into the windows, just to see if Bob O'Reilly was dancing.

Chapter 14

Keira heard a rustling sound outside the ruin and went still, her upper body on the loft, her hands gripping rafters and ivy. Her feet were balanced precariously on the length of branch she'd propped at the top of her makeshift ladder.

The black dog? A stray sheep?

Whoever had whispered her name last night?

"Keira!"

She was so startled, she nearly lost her footing. This wasn't a creepy whisper—someone was obviously out looking for her.

Eddie O'Shea?

"Keira Sullivan—are you out here?"

Not Eddie. A man, though, but obviously an American, his voice steady, confident—and familiar, somehow.

Her makeshift ladder teetered under her. It was just a matter of time—minutes, probably—before it gave way. When it did, she wanted to be safe on the loft, not hanging by her fingernails.

"It's Simon. Simon Cahill."

Keira lost her grip for a split second, catching herself and hanging on as she swore under her breath. Of all people. She wasn't so far gone as to have conjured up a search-and-rescue expert, but did it have to be this one?

"We met the other night in Boston."

Oh, indeed.

His presence meant that her uncle, for whom she'd long been a mystery if not a disappointment, had immediately kicked into worry mode after she'd missed her call to him. He must have gotten in touch with Owen, who in turn had gotten in touch with Simon in London.

But Keira tried to stick to the practicalities of her situation. Simon was a big guy. He knew how to pull people out of rubble. It would be dark soon. And it would be rude and ungrateful to let him wander past her when he'd taken the trouble—for whatever reason—to come out here to look for her.

Never mind any potential gloating on his part or stubborn pride on hers. She could use his help.

"I'm here!" she called. "By the stream—there's a stone ruin…"

"Got it. What's your situation?"

"There was a cave-in, and I got trapped in here. I'm not injured—I'm about to climb out through the loft."

"Have you had food and water?"

"Yes. I'm doing fine."

"Then let's get you out of there." He sounded controlled, capable—and very close now, somewhere on the back side of the hut. "Tell me where you are."

She explained her position. "There's just one door and it's blocked—"

"So I see. How the hell did that happen?"

"Beats me." She didn't want to get into Patsy's story, the black dog, the voice, the angel—the fairies.

She heard a creak and a thud, and in the next second, the ivy and muck a few feet above her gave way, creating a larger opening. Smoky light poured in.

Simon peered down at Keira. "How'd you get up there?" he asked.

"I built a ladder."

"Resourceful."

"I don't know if you can see, but I'm trying to scoot onto a loft. I'm not sure how stable it is."

"Then why don't I pull you out and we call it a night? I'd rather not have to come down there. The place looks as if it has rats."

"No rats. Just spiders and slugs."

"I don't mind spiders, but I'd rather deal with rats than slugs."

Keira guessed that he was deliberately trying to calm her nerves. She started to edge farther onto the loft, but she felt the branch lurch to one side under her. "I feel like Winnie the Pooh stuck in the entrance to the cave. He couldn't go forward, and he couldn't go backward. But if I can just—"

"Hold on, okay? I'm dropping a rope down to you. I want you to grab it and hang on, then tie it around your waist. Can you do that?"

"Happily."

"It's not perfect, but it's the best I can do, unless you want to wait for the local fire department—"

"I don't want to wait."

She could feel his smile more than see it. "I didn't think so."

Simon lowered the rope through the opening, and she caught it, her hands weak and scraped from the hours of hauling, pulling, lifting and digging. "There's a window—if I can reach it, I can crawl out that way."

"Not unless you really are a fairy princess and can change into a bird or a bat. It's too small, probably smaller than you realize from your position."

"I could climb up the rafters—"

"One thing at a time, Keira."

She hung on to the rope. She didn't know how she could tie it around her without further destabilizing the ladder and decided not to risk it. "How did you secure this rope? You're not just holding on to it, are you? I don't want you to hurt your back."

He laughed. "No worries."

This was his show, she thought. Between his succinct, efficient directions and her urgent desire to get out of there, she managed to creep farther up onto the loft.

The ladder started collapsing, and before Keira could react, Simon reached one arm down through the opening and hauled her up and out onto the back wall of the hut, grabbing her around the middle before her momentum took her straight over the edge. Although the hut was wedged into the hill, there was still a drop to the ground.

Simon was solid muscle, a big, broad-shouldered, bruiser of a man. She didn't have to do a thing except breathe.

"Okay?" he asked.

She balanced next to him on ivy and old stone and mortar. "Yes, thanks."

"Hang on one sec, and I'll help you get down from here."

Keira welcomed the feel of the breeze on her face, and she looked at Simon with his thick black hair, his green eyes—a clear, mesmerizing green, she thought. She'd noticed he was good-looking in

Boston, but now, at dusk on a long June day, out on the southwest coast of Ireland, she was struck by how sexy he was. Being close to him was enough to make her throat catch.

He looked totally relaxed, as if he'd just wandered up from the village pub.

She quickly thrust the rope at him. "I can jump," she said.

He shook his head. "I don't advise it—"

But she was already springing off the wall, and if he could have stopped her, he didn't. She bent her knees and landed on her feet, letting herself drop onto her forearms into the tall grass at the base of an oak tree.

She leaped to her feet, brushing herself off as she grinned up at Simon. "It's good to be free."

"Lucky you didn't land on a rock."

"I suppose I am."

He hopped down next to her, without having to drop down onto all fours to break his fall. "Where did you learn how to land like that?"

"Police academy."

He shook his head. "I'm not even going to ask."

"One of my false starts in life. Thank you," she added. "I appreciate the backup."

"Backup?" He seemed amused, but he gave her a quick, professional appraisal. "Should I check you over for injuries—"

"I'm not hurt." Keira imagined his big hands on her and felt a rush of heat, but attributed it to relief and adrenaline and changed the subject. "Did you have any trouble finding me? My directions were okay?"

"What directions?"

"In the note I left at my cottage. I assume you went there first."

"I didn't see a note."

"No? It was on the counter. Maybe the wind blew it onto the floor. How did you find me, then?"

"I used your drawings."

She digested the notion of him going through her sketchbooks, but decided that, given the circumstances, she had no complaints.

"I found the rope and a flashlight in the kitchen," he said.

"You're good at pulling people out of messes, aren't you?"

"First time I've come to the rescue of an American in Ireland."

He wasn't making fun of her, she realized, dusting herself off and wondering just how awful she looked. Filthy hair and nails and scraped knuckles. She could imagine her face—dirty, smudged, probably pale—and she ached, as much from the tension of her ordeal as hauling rocks and crawling around in the ruin.

"What happened?" Simon asked quietly.

The ruin looked downright eerie in the gathering darkness, and Keira didn't know how she could accurately explain the past twenty-four hours to this feet-flat-on-the-floor man.

"I'm not sure, exactly," she said.

He eyed her, and she could sense his questions, his doubts about her judgment, but he picked up his rope, slung it over his shoulder and didn't press her to explain. "You've had a hell of a time." He nodded up the stream toward open pasture. "Let's get you back to your cottage."

"One quick thing first."

Without waiting for his response, Keira pushed through the tall grass down the slope, then carefully approached the front of the hut. As she'd suspected, the half-dead tree had fallen across the open doorway, either because of the cave-in or the cause of it.

Simon stood next to her and toed a sprawling branch of the tree, its sparse leaves withered. "This tree looks as if it could have given way at any time. Any wind last night?"

"Not really, no."

"You can see the ground's eroded under this corner of the ruin. When the tree fell, it probably triggered this entire section to give way. Lucky the whole thing didn't just come down on top of you."

"I was never afraid," Keira said. "At least not after the first hour."

"Adrenaline'll do that."

"It wasn't just adrenaline."

"Ah. Fairies?"

She was almost relieved at his cheerful jibe, because it meant he was no longer keeping an eye on her for signs of injury or mental distress. But she didn't respond as she leaned over the fallen tree and tried to peer into the hut.

"I want to check on something," she said, half to herself, then glanced back at Simon. "Can I borrow your flashlight? Mine's in there with my backpack."

He handed over a small flashlight. "Don't push your luck. I can't save you from a rock falling on your head."

"If a rock falls on my head, it'll be my own fault."

"Only I'll be the one explaining it to your cop uncle back in Boston."

A fair point, but Keira had no intention of going back to her cottage until she checked the fireplace for the angel. She grabbed a small branch of the tree and pulled it away from the door's opening. "I think I can see what I need to without actually having to crawl back in there."

"There's a reason I didn't try to rescue you this way."

"Yes, because I was inside and you didn't want to make my situation worse. But I'm not inside anymore. As a matter of fact, I was about to get out on my own when you arrived." She smiled at him, hoping she came across at least reasonably sane. "I'm not going to quibble, but 'rescue' isn't the word I'd use."

"What word would you use?"

"I don't know. I'll have to think about it. Are you going to help me?"

He pointed to the hut. "What's in there, Keira?"

She didn't answer right away. She didn't know what to make of this man; even less, her reaction to him. But she'd slept only fitfully last night, and she hadn't had enough to eat or drink, especially given the amount of hard physical labor she'd performed. Her judgment could be off. She knew he was a volunteer with Fast Rescue, but that meant he could be anything. A firefighter, a paramedic, an engineer. He had an easy manner about him, but she wasn't fooled—he was intense, alert and obviously very good at search-and-rescue. He deserved at least an honest response, even if it was incomplete.

"I'm not sure," she said finally. "Let's just say that I saw something I want to have another look at."

She tried to pull back the branch far enough to allow her to shine the flashlight into the ruin, but realized she wasn't going to manage on her own. She'd need three hands, or at least more energy. "Could you help?"

He sighed. "All right." He eased in behind her. "But if I decide the structure's too unstable, that's it. We're done, and we head back to your cottage."

"Fair enough."

He took hold of a larger, thicker branch and lifted it, creating enough of an opening for Keira to squeeze between the branch and the trunk. She planted her middle on the rough bark and switched on the flashlight, directing its beam into the ruin. But it didn't reach the fireplace, and she had to lean farther in over the tree.

As she did so, she was aware that Simon had a perfect view of her butt.

"Why did you come out here alone?" he asked.

She wrestled her way another few inches over the tree trunk. "Why did you?"

"I had to rescue a pretty damsel in distress."

There was no condemnation in his tone. Not a lot of amusement, either. He sounded as if he was simply stating what he regarded as a fact. But Keira didn't feel like a damsel in distress, and pretty? Not tonight.

"I had something I needed to do," she said. "I took sensible precautions in case I got lost or injured." She scooted forward another inch. Any farther, and she'd go right over the branch and headfirst into the ruin again. "I brought an emergency whistle with me."

"Did you use it?"

"No. It ended up..." But she didn't continue. She went still, her beam of light hitting what looked to be part of the fireplace. "Hold on."

Gingerly edging forward, Keira tried to direct the light toward the hearth where she'd seen the angel. She felt Simon's hand on her hip, steadying her, but pretended it was her imagination. She didn't need any distractions.

The smell of the mud inside the ruin, the taste of it, the thought of slugs and spiders, and the feel of the cool, rough stone against her free hand brought her back to the first moments of the collapse. But she didn't stay there, refused to.

She steadied the flashlight and moved forward another few inches, until just her upper thighs were on the tree trunk. Simon's grip on her tightened.

"Keira," he said, his tone itself a warning.

"One sec."

She squinted at the remains of the fireplace and hearth, picturing the hermit monk out here alone on just such a night, sitting in front of a peat fire, waiting for the fairies as he contemplated the mysteries of the stone angel.

Keira moved the flashlight up and down the fireplace. Maybe the upheaval of the stone and mud and mortar—of trees and ivy and dead leaves—had thrown her off and she had the wrong spot. She'd been inside when she'd spotted the angel, and she was coming at it now from a different angle. She'd only had a few minutes inside the ruin before it had started crashing down on her.

On her third sweep with the flashlight, she was convinced she had the right spot. There was no need to squirm all the way inside for a closer inspection.

It wouldn't change the simple fact that nothing was there.

The stone angel had vanished.

If, Keira thought, it had ever been there.

But it had, and as she withdrew, backing up over the tree trunk and under the branch, she pictured its simple, stunning beauty. She hadn't imagined the statue.

Simon kept his hand on her hip until she was clear of the tree and back up on her feet. He narrowed those amazing green eyes on her. But she saw him tense. "Stand still."

The sharpness of his tone made her heart jump. She followed his gaze to her middle and saw what was wrong.

She was covered in blood.

It was smeared from her breasts to her waist. She could feel it now, more sticky than wet, and she gasped in shock. "Simon—I don't— I can't…breathe…"

"Did you cut yourself?"

"I'm okay." She gripped his arm above his elbow, forcing herself to get her emotions under control. "I'm not hurt."

"Keira—"

"It's not my blood."

Chapter 15

Beara Peninsula, Southwest Ireland
10:00 p.m., IST
June 22

Sheep's blood.

Keira tilted her head back and let the hot water of her cottage shower flow through her hair and down her back, her skin red from where she'd scrubbed the blood and mud off her. She'd used a citrus bath gel and shampoo. She breathed in the tangy scent and turned off the water, reaching for a towel as she stepped out of the shower.

She'd resisted the impulse to strip off her clothes after seeing the blood. Simon had remained crisply efficient, showing little reaction when he discovered entrails and bits of sheep's wool in the undergrowth on the chimney side of the hut. Keira had checked out the grisly scene herself and promptly vomited in the grass.

She wasn't embarrassed. Simon had more experience with such sights.

It was getting dark when they headed back to her cottage. She'd broken into a run and made a beeline for the bedroom, grabbing fresh clothes, then for the shower.

All she'd thought about was getting clean.

She wrapped her towel around her and took another for her hair, drying it as best she could and pulling it back into a loose ponytail. She got dressed, welcoming the feel of her clean, dry jeans and sweater.

When she returned to the kitchen, her good-looking rescuer glanced up from his inspection of the side door. "This door's locked. Front door isn't."

"I locked both doors, or at least I tried to. They're not great locks. Maybe the front-door lock popped open."

"Where's your key?"

"In my backpack in the ruin. There's a spare— I'll get it." She pulled open a utility closet off the kitchen and grabbed a key from a hook above the washer. "There's no sign anyone broke in here. Maybe my note just blew under the refrigerator."

He shrugged. "We could check."

She gave him a cool look. "You don't believe I wrote a note, do you?"

"You've just been through a trauma, Keira. Telling yourself you wrote a note describing your location helped you get through it. There's nothing wrong with that."

"I wrote the note with my favorite drawing pencil. I sketched a little shamrock on the bottom for fun."

He was undeterred. "In your head, you did."

"I also locked both doors."

He stood back from the side door. "All right. First things first. You're done in. Why don't I cook you up something? Toast, eggs—"

"We can get to the pub before it closes. I want lights, people." She took a breath. "And warm rhubarb crumble. All last night, all day today...I kept thinking about warm rhubarb crumble."

"Then let's go see if Eddie O'Shea has some."

As they headed out to the lane, Simon asked if she wanted him to drive her to the pub, but she shook her head. She preferred walking. It was just after sunset on the long June day, the night not yet fully dark. And it was so quiet, she thought. There was barely any wind, and she could hear only the distant bleating of sheep far up in the hills, nothing from the sheep and cows in the pens close by the lane.

Keira wasn't fooled by his silence as he walked beside her. "I know you must have a lot of questions," she said.

"They can wait."

When they reached the pub, he settled at a table with three local men chatting among themselves. They seemed surprised, but when he called for a round of drinks, they warmed right up to him.

Keira eased onto a high stool at the bar. Eddie O'Shea shook his head at her. "You got yourself into a fix, didn't you?"

"I did, indeed," she said. "Please tell me you have rhubarb crumble, Eddie."

"Fresh this afternoon."

"Perfect. And a shot of Irish whiskey. You pick the brand."

He splashed whiskey in a glass and set it in front of her. "Are you going to tell me what happened?"

"I had a mishap in an old ruin up in the hills above my cottage." She drank some of her whiskey. It burned all the way down, but she welcomed it, nonetheless. "I'm sorry if I worried anyone."

"You're safe. That's what matters."

Behind her, Simon adopted a remarkably natural Irish accent and made an inflammatory comment about Irish weather. The men roared, and the good-natured fight was on. He could get away with anything, Keira decided. He was charming and convivial, a hale-and-hearty type who fit right in with the Irishmen. They all sat with their arms crossed on their chests, legs stretched out, comfortable with each other as they laughed and argued.

If it'd been a group of Wall Street investment bankers he had to drink with, Keira had the feeling Simon would have fit in with them, too. He wasn't a chameleon so much as a man at ease with himself.

Eddie placed a plate of steaming crumble on the bar and grinned at her. "Wouldn't have been near as good if one of us'd come to your rescue, now, would it?"

She felt herself blush and tried to blame the whiskey. "I appreciate Simon's help, but I was about to get out of there on my own when he turned up."

"Ha. So you say."

She dipped her spoon into melting vanilla ice cream mixed with the sweet-sour rhubarb crumble and felt her exhaustion, her hunger. Her head spun with images of the past twenty-four hours. She saw Eddie's gaze fix on her scraped knuckles, his frown as he returned to his work.

"Do you know anyone around here who owns a black dog?" she asked.

He had his back to her as he got beer glasses down from a shelf. "What kind of black dog?"

"I don't know. A dog…that's black."

"Short hair, long hair, big dog, little dog?"

"Maybe like a black lab, but not quite that big. A mutt."

He turned back to her and started filling the glasses with beer from a tap. "You're describing half the dogs I shoo out of here every morning and every night."

"What about creepy, scary, mean black dogs?"

"That would be my mother-in-law's dog." His eyes sparked with humor as he set a full glass on a tray. "Or maybe it's my mother-in-law herself."

One of the men at the table hooted at him. "You don't have a mother-in-law, you lying snake."

Eddie nodded to the man, also blue-eyed, sandy-haired and wiry. "That, my dear Keira, is my worthless brother Patrick."

She'd met Aidan O'Shea, the third O'Shea brother, briefly upon her arrival on the Beara Peninsula—he owned the cottage she'd rented as well as the pasture where she'd come upon the ruin. She wondered if any of them would know anything about a bloody, dead sheep. But she didn't ask. She didn't want to think about the sheep right now.

"Deep down, Eddie," she said, taking another bite of crumble, "you believe in fairies, don't you?"

Instead of answering, he moved off to the table with the tray of beers. But as he unloaded them, he gave Keira a sideways glower, which told her that he'd at least heard the question.

As she finished her rhubarb crumble and concentrated on her whiskey, Simon joined her at the bar, remaining on his feet. "I ran into a man outside on the picnic table earlier," he said, addressing Eddie. "Older guy in a wool vest and wellies—right off an Irish postcard. Smoking a cigarette. Did you see him?"

Eddie slipped back behind the bar and grabbed a cleaning cloth. "An old man, you say?"

"He was there one minute and off into the mist the next."

"Is that so, now?" Eddie mopped up a tiny spill. "I must have missed him."

Keira finished her whiskey, remembering her strange encounter two nights ago. It had to be the same man.

Simon stood back from the bar. "That's the way it's going to be, is it?"

Eddie shrugged. "That's the way."

Keira started to speak, but Simon had pulled out his wallet, obviously preparing to pay for the drinks and her crumble. Eddie put up a hand and shook his head. "On the house."

"Thank you," Keira mumbled, her head spinning now with fatigue, sugar and alcohol. As she eased off the stool, it occurred to her she didn't know where Simon planned to spend the night. "We can go. I'm sure you'll want to get back to Cork or Kenmare or wherever you're staying—"

"I'm not going anywhere tonight."

The men at the table all looked at the two Americans—expectant, eager for a sparring match, their eyes twinkling with amusement. Keira figured they'd side with Simon. She couldn't have picked a more appealing rescuer, nor could she blame him and his new Irish friends if they thought her flighty, eccentric and reckless for having ended up trapped in an Irish ruin for the past twenty-four hours.

"Let's go," Simon said quietly.

Eddie slung his cleaning cloth over his shoulder. "Stay safe, Keira," he said.

She nodded. "Thanks."

When she stepped outside, she shivered and tightened her sweater around her in a chilly wind kicking up off the Kenmare. "There's something about this place…" She smelled the lavender in the baskets hanging on the lampposts that lined the quiet street. "It's like a part of my soul is here. I can't explain it."

"You don't have to," Simon said next to her.

She abandoned the thought. She wasn't even sure where it had come from—the whiskey, probably. "If I hadn't told my uncle I'd call this morning, no one would have been the wiser—"

"You have people who care about you enough to worry. Don't be too hard on yourself, Keira. You're only human." Simon grinned back at her. "Well. I think you're only human. Could be you're a fairy princess after all."

"A shape-shifter," she said, starting up the street toward the lane. "At any moment, I might just change into a lizard or a snake—"

"Not a snake. Not while we're in Ireland."

She realized she was as comfortable with him as the men at the pub had been. He rescued people from dire situations, but she wouldn't say he was chivalrous. That suited her; natural charm she could handle—any forced gallantry would just make her feel hemmed in and needy.

"Cold?" he asked her.

"Not really."

"Keira...I'm staying with you tonight. Word of your ordeal is going to spread, and given what you do for a living, and how damn pretty you are, who knows what kind of nutcase it'll bring to your doorstep."

"Probably none at all."

"Well," he said, leaning in closer to her, "you can't always count on your magic and fairies, now, can you?"

"A little brute strength does come in handy on occasion."

He smiled. "And charm."

"Telling me I'm too stupid to live isn't charming."

"Honesty has its place. You're worn out, Keira, and you need to rest. But I want to know what happened up at that ruin. You were up there because of the story that old woman in Boston told you, weren't you?"

She nodded. "It's a wonderful story, Simon. It has mischief, magic, fairies, Irish brothers." She shivered in the wind as they turned onto the lane. "It's not a dark, tragic story."

"Do people around here know it?"

"I haven't had a chance to find out. I asked Colm Dermott about it.

He was at the reception in Boston, too. He's an expert in Irish folklore, but he's never heard the story or any recognizable version of it."

Simon slung a big arm over her shoulders. "I'd love to hear this magical story of yours."

"There's no way I can tell it the way Patsy does. I've only known her a few weeks, but my mother and my uncle grew up a couple doors down from her in South Boston. She's a natural storyteller."

"How does it start?"

"With three Irish brothers—a farmer, a hermit monk and a ne'er-do-well."

Keira went on from there, telling the story in truncated form as she and Simon continued along the dark, quiet lane.

When she finished, he dropped his arm from her shoulder. "You love this stuff, don't you?"

"I do. Normally I don't care about the literal truth of a story. That's not the point. But this one…" She looked up at the sprinkle of stars against the blackening sky. "I thought it'd be fun to see if I could find the hermit monk's hut—to see what happened there on the night of the summer solstice."

"So you think the fairies toppled that ruin onto your head?"

"I don't know." But she thought a moment, remembered the eerie whisper of her name and shook her head. "No. I do know. Whether they were there or not isn't for me to say, but—it wasn't fairies that caused the cave-in, Simon."

Keira could feel his eyes on her and took note of his sudden reserve. There was none of his boisterous charm now. He plucked a pink blossom from the massive rosebush that tumbled over the ancient wall in front of her cottage. "Keira…"

"I ducked into the ruin to get away from a dog," she said. "There was this voice. This whisper."

He eased the rose blossom into her hair, then ran one finger along her jaw. "Tell me."

She slowed her pace and told him about last night—about finding the old stone hut, running into the dog, hearing the voice just before the cave-in.

And the angel. Keira told him about that, too.

As she walked up her cottage driveway, she was aware of Simon watching her, studying her, and she turned to him. "You're thinking what I saw was just a hunk of rock that I mistook for the stone angel in the story. And the dog—that it was an ordinary sheepdog, not some big, menacing dog—" She paused, cold now in the wind. "And the whisper was the evening breeze."

"You're imaginative, and you've experienced a trauma. You're also exhausted and spinning on sugar and alcohol."

"But did I get it right about what you're thinking?"

He approached her, snatched the flower just as it fell from behind her ear. "I'm not that good with flowers. I probably should have checked this one for bugs, huh?"

"Simon…"

"You had a close call out here."

"I've had close calls at home."

"Let's see how things look in the morning. I don't like the sheep's blood and entrails. Did you hear anything that in retrospect—"

"Was a sheep in the throes of death? No. I didn't."

He nodded without comment.

"Maybe what happened had nothing to do with me or Patsy's story."

"Do you believe that?"

"It doesn't matter what I believe. What matters are the facts." She gave a mock shudder and tried to laugh. "Now I sound like my uncle."

"At least you don't look like him."

"We have the same eyes," she said.

"The same color, maybe. Ah, Keira, Keira," Simon said in his exaggerated, fake Irish accent. "You're gutsy. I'll say that for you."

She couldn't help but smile as she unlocked the side door and slipped into her cottage. She looked back at him. "You can come in. I'm not going to make you sleep in your car, and I can tell you're not going anywhere. You can have my bed." She waved a hand toward the living room. "I'll sleep out here on the couch."

Simon entered the kitchen, locking the door behind him. "No, you won't."

"You deserve a good night's sleep after charging to my rescue, and I'll fit on the couch better than you would. I'm beat, Simon. Nothing's going to keep me awake. I just want to curl up under a stack of blankets—"

"I can sleep next to you in your bed without getting personal." He winked, giving her the slightest smile. "I'm disciplined."

She stared at him. "You're serious!"

"You should have thought of the consequences before you took off into the hills."

"I did think of them. And you've no room to talk. You went looking for me by yourself. You're unfamiliar with the area."

"Rocks, grass, sheep. What else is there to know?"

"There's a mean bull—"

He laughed. "I always make allowances for mean bulls. Plus, I had Owen waiting to hear from me, and I had a working cell phone—and I was prepared."

"You had a rope and a flashlight. That's not prepared."

"I had a jackknife, too."

He was irreverent, confident but not quite cocky—a man most anyone would find hard to stay mad at for long. Keira appreciated his straightforward opinion of her escapade. She hated being coddled. But she wasn't ready to give in. "If you're in my bed with me, I'll never get any sleep."

She winced at how her words sounded and, suddenly feeling hot, ran into the bedroom, whisked an extra blanket off the foot of the bed, then headed back into the living room.

Simon, merrily whistling some Irish tune, retreated to the bathroom.

She dropped onto the couch and pulled the blanket up over her front. She didn't have the energy to go back for a pillow.

She really did need a bed.

"This is insane," she muttered, dragging the blanket with her back into the bedroom.

Skipping her usual nightgown, she changed into sweatpants and a T-shirt and climbed into the bed, pulling the duvet up to her chin. As a volunteer for Fast Rescue, Simon would be accustomed to rough conditions. A too-short couch wouldn't be a problem for him.

She heard the shower.

No. Don't picture him naked...

She just wanted to close her eyes and go to sleep and forget the past twenty-four hours until morning. With a good night's sleep, she'd be rested enough to climb back up the dirt track, over the fences and through the steep pasture in order to check out the ruin in daylight.

But she was still wide awake when the shower stopped, and Simon walked into the bedroom wearing a Guinness T-shirt and shorts. He smelled not of her citrus bath gel but the plain soap that had come with the cottage. She noticed the thick muscles in his legs and arms and thought of his hand on her hip while she'd wormed her way into the hut's entrance to check on the stone angel.

He yanked back the duvet on the opposite side of the bed and climbed in. "Cozy," he said, pulling the duvet over him. "I figure if you didn't really want me here, you'd have stretched out in the middle and not left any room."

"I'd never get any sleep on the couch." She scooted another two inches toward the edge of the bed. "Pretend there's an invisible electric fence between us."

He adjusted his pillow. "Will do."

"Black dogs often appear in stories as supernatural shape-shifters."

"You might not want to think about that right now."

"Their purpose can be for good or for evil," she said.

"Why don't you picture that painting of yours I bid on in Boston?"

She shut her eyes. "It's a half real, half imagined place," she said. "The dog was real. I didn't imagine him."

"Maybe not." Simon's voice was surprisingly close, gentle. "Get some sleep, Keira."

"You, too."

"I will as soon as you stop talking about shape-shifting black dogs."

She smiled. "Sweet dreams."

"Yeah. Sweet dreams."

⌒Chapter 16

South Boston, Massachusetts
8:00 p.m., EDT
June 22

Bob O'Reilly rang the doorbell to Patsy McCarthy's single-family house on the tidy South Boston street where he and his sister had grown up. He'd made a practice of not dwelling on Deirdre's murder thirty years ago, but he thought of her now, running out onto the street as a young teenager, always more attractive than she'd realized. He'd never met anyone like her.

It was hot and late, and he didn't want to be here.

But Patsy opened the door, and when she saw him, she put her hand to her mouth and gave a small gasp. "Nothing's happened—"

"No," he said. "Everything's fine."

"You've got that cop look of yours." She relaxed slightly, dropping her hand back to her side. "I remember when you were a little boy, and you'd come here with that same look on your face. Your mother and I knew you'd become a police officer."

"Mrs. McCarthy, what did you tell Keira?"

"What do you mean?"

"You went to see her the other night—the night before she left for Ireland."

Patsy opened the door wider and stepped out onto the stoop, pulling her sweater more tightly, despite the heat. Bob could see into her front hall, where she had a wall covered with postcards of Ireland and stickers of shamrocks and leprechaun hats. It'd been that way forever. She never went anywhere herself, but she'd ask people she knew to send her postcards from their trips. Even back when Eileen took off to study in Ireland at nineteen, Patsy had asked her to send postcards for her wall.

"I didn't tell Keira about Deirdre," she said, her expression hardening. "If that's what you're asking."

Bob didn't mince words. "It is."

"It's not my place to tell her."

He heard that subtext—that it was his place to tell his niece, and presumably his three daughters, about his murdered childhood neighbor. But he didn't go there. "What did you tell her, then?"

"Old family stories."

"The one about the Irish brothers and the stone angel?"

Her mood seemed to lighten. "You remember it?"

"Sure. Yeah, of course. Patsy, you know you've opened up a can of worms telling Keira that story. Telling her that her mother looked for the village where it was set when she went to Ireland before Keira was born."

"Oh, Bob." Patsy waved her bony fingers at him. "So what if I did? Maybe Keira will be the one to find the angel. Wouldn't that be something?"

Bob gave an inward groan. Yeah, hell, he thought, it'd be something. After he'd dragged out of Fiona what she'd overheard Patsy telling Keira at the Garrison house, he'd known what to expect, but the confirmation hit him in the gut. His sister had gone off in search of that stupid angel thirty years ago. He didn't know the details— Eileen had never told him—but he'd long suspected that little adventure of hers had everything to do with how she'd come home from Ireland pregnant.

No question, Keira was retracing her mother's footsteps. Bob didn't want to think about what would have happened if Simon Cahill hadn't pulled her out of that ruin when he did.

Not that Bob was all that sure about Cahill. Big brute of a guy, good-looking, charming.

Bob ground his teeth together. All three of his daughters looked up to Keira. He loved her to death, but having her right there in Boston was a lot different than having her in San Diego or the other places she'd lived in the past few years. Fiona already was bugging him about going on adventures of her own.

"Bob?"

"It's okay, Patsy," he said. "You haven't done anything wrong. When did you and Keira hook up?"

"It's been a couple of months. I have all her books. She's so talented, Bob, isn't she?"

"That she is. Did she get in touch with you or you with her?"

"I e-mailed her. I'm handy with a computer, I'll have you know. I heard about the Irish project and went to her Web site—"

"How'd you hear about the project?"

"Billie and Jeanette Murphy told me about it. You remember them, don't you, Bob?"

Bob nodded. They were a few years ahead of him in school, and they'd made a fortune in Boston real estate. They lived in a high-priced waterfront condominium that was technically in South

Boston, although not exactly part of the old neighborhood, and they owned the land on which his sister had built her cabin.

"Who else did you tell that story to?" he asked Patsy.

"I've told it for years to anyone and everyone. Why shouldn't I?"

"Didn't say you shouldn't."

"Then what's wrong with you? Why are you here?"

He sighed. "Keira ran into a little trouble in Ireland. She's fine— I just let myself get worked up over it. Because of Eileen, I guess. That summer."

Patsy clutched his hand, digging her bony fingers into his palm. "You're sure Keira's all right?"

"I'm sure. Don't worry, okay? She's got someone with her."

"I told her three or four stories my grandfather used to tell me. Keira seemed to enjoy them, but she especially liked the one about the three brothers. It was Deirdre's favorite, too. She wanted Eileen to look for the stone angel when she was in Ireland. Bob, you remember how excited Deirdre was about Eileen's trip, don't you?"

He pried Patsy's small hand from his and squeezed it gently, then kissed her on the cheek. "I remember every minute I spent with Deirdre. She was the best. You okay? Anything you're not telling me?"

"You're a good boy, Bob. You always have been."

It wasn't a direct answer. "Nah. I'm not that good." He tried to relax but couldn't, and he slipped one of his cards into her palm. "You hold on to that. It's got all my phone numbers on it. If you think of anything you want to tell me—anything unusual happens—you call. Better safe than sorry, right?"

She nodded.

But he knew he didn't have her full trust. He hadn't kept up with her the way he probably should have, but he'd known her forever and felt her restraint, her resistance. "Patsy…"

"I'll call you if I think of anything else," she said, then smiled, letting go of his hand. "Don't worry so much."

He grinned at her. "Now you sound like one of my ex-wives. It's good to see you, Patsy. The priest from your church drove you to see Keira? I don't know him."

"He's been at Saint Ita's for a little more than a year. Father Palermo. He came up with the idea to have a church bazaar with an angel theme. I brought in my entire angel collection to display. We had such a wonderful time."

He heard her native Ireland in her voice now. "Sorry I missed it."

She gave him an impish grin. "No, you're not."

"I should come by more often."

"You should."

"You can tell me that story again. It's perfect for Keira's new book."

"I think so, too. That would be wonderful, wouldn't it?" She looked happier, more at ease. "I'm so glad to see you, Bob. Come back soon."

"I will." He started down the steps, then turned and pointed at her. "You'll call, right? Anytime. I'm available 24/7."

She rolled her eyes. "You really do worry too much."

He probably did, Bob thought, returning to his car, unable to shake his uneasiness. He wanted to blame the summer solstice and his general pessimism, but he knew that wasn't all—it was the body in the Public Garden, the dead man's devil room and now Keira's mess in Ireland.

And Fiona. His daughter hadn't told him everything, either.

He debated trying again with Patsy, but he knew it wouldn't do him any good. She was a sweet soul, but she was also stubborn and secretive. In her own way, she was hard as nails. He remembered taking her out to the waterfront where Deirdre's body had washed ashore and how she'd talked about ways to fight the devil. If anyone could do it, it was Patsy McCarthy.

* * *

After Bob left, Patsy changed into her housecoat and slippers and poured herself just the tiniest bit of Irish whiskey to take with her into the dining room. She knew she'd have a hard time sleeping tonight. She was accustomed to keeping her own company, and she wasn't afraid in her own house—that wasn't it, she thought as she stood in front of the curio cabinet where she kept the best of Deirdre's angels.

You should have invited Bob in for tea.

He'd have come—she could tell he suspected she hadn't told him everything that was on her mind. He'd have used tea as a way to get her to open up to him, and she wasn't going to.

She sat at the table, sipping her whiskey and gazing at the angels.

Finally, she started up to bed, but a noise drew her into the kitchen. She flipped on her back-porch light, hoping it was a cat in her wind chimes. She had only the one set left. She used to have a half dozen, but one of her neighbors, a young hotel events coordinator who'd "discovered" the east side of South Boston and moved next door, had complained about them. Patsy would never have said a word over such a thing herself. Her neighbor had no such compunctions and had demanded that even this last set of chimes go, too. Off to a white-elephant sale with it, the woman had suggested.

"If there's not an ordinance against wind chimes," she'd said, "there should be."

How could someone deny an old woman the pleasure of one lonely set of wind chimes?

Patsy used to know all her neighbors, but maybe it was just as well she didn't even know this one's name. She'd told Patsy she was attracted to their street for its proximity to downtown Boston and the waterfront. No mention of family, friends, anything of the sort. She talked about "gentrification," a word Patsy loathed.

"No gentry here," she muttered, peering out her kitchen window.

If it was a cat in her wind chimes, she resolved not to take her irritation out on an innocent animal. That would be wrong, although she had no doubt her neighbor wouldn't resist if similarly provoked.

How different it was now from when Deirdre was growing up and would bring her friends to the house. Patsy had loved baking for them, telling them stories. She'd hoped to have five or six children, but it hadn't worked out that way. She'd had just Deirdre.

Patsy opened the back door, comfortable in her slippers and cotton housecoat. But she didn't see a cat, and her wind chimes were quiet in the still, humid air.

She paused, frowning. Did she hear music now?

"Oh, my goodness," she whispered. "I do!"

It wasn't her wind chimes, either, or her imagination. She wasn't losing her mind. No—it was music she heard, sweet, mournful music. She didn't recognize the melody, but it had an Irish sound. Where was it coming from?

Was it a tipsy neighbor, humming as he staggered home after over imbibing at a nearby pub?

Kids?

The music stopped. The wind chimes stirred, clinking pleasantly in the summer night. Patsy didn't know what had started them dancing. There was no breeze that she could feel.

As she turned to check the wind chimes, she saw a stone statue of an angel standing on the broad porch railing.

She grabbed the front of her housecoat with one hand, as a way to steady herself, and stepped out onto the porch, thinking maybe she'd drunk more whiskey than she'd realized. But she could see the statue clearly—it was definitely an angel, about two feet tall and constructed of gray stone, with wings, an Irish harp in one arm and a face that was so loving and peaceful, Patsy thought of her daughter.

How did the statue get here? Was it a gift for her collection?

She reached for the back of a metal porch chair. Surely the music hadn't come from this captivating statue. It couldn't have, unless it was some kind of elaborate music box.

Had someone left it as a prank, then?

Real angels, Patsy remembered, appeared before those who were worthy.

I'm not worthy.

They also fought demons.

I'm a sinner…I'm not a demon.

And this was a statue—a beautiful statue. It wasn't a real angel.

She'd call Bob. She'd ask him to come back here. She'd tell him everything. All she knew, all she suspected.

She left the angel on the porch and returned to her kitchen, locking the door behind her.

"Patsy…"

The voice came from the dining room.

"Patricia Brigid McCarthy…"

Whoever was whispering her name was with her in the house. Patsy reached for Bob's card on the counter, but she knew she was too late. There was no more time.

The devil had come for her.

As she dove for her telephone, she began to pray.

~Chapter 17

Beara Peninsula, Southwest Ireland
5:30 a.m., IST
June 23

Keira flopped an arm down on Simon's stomach in her sleep. He was wide awake and had been for some time. So much, he thought, for her invisible electric fence. Not that he minded. He felt her warmth next to him. The early-morning sunlight streaming in through the window landed on his bedmate's long, pale hair and fair, smooth skin, and he figured if someone saw her lying here there'd be a new story to tell by the fire.

But she was in a troubled sleep, moaning to herself, thrashing. He felt her entire body tense, and she made a fist, clutching his T-shirt and a good hunk of flesh. Her nails were cut short, and there were nicks and scrapes on her knuckles and wrist from the hours she'd spent trapped. It was a strong hand, and yet delicate, and Simon imagined her slender fingers skimming over him.

Just kill me now.

He wondered how much Keira hadn't told him about her trip to Ireland.

She was self-sufficient and obviously not one to panic, but he wouldn't be surprised if she'd come out to the southwest coast of Ireland thinking fairies would protect her. Who knew, maybe they had kept her safe in that ruin. From the outside, it looked as if no one could have lived through the cave-in, but not only did Keira live, she'd come through her ordeal relatively unscathed.

Simon had to admit that if he hadn't come along, she probably would have managed to climb out of there on her own. But he wasn't sure what she'd have done if he hadn't been there when she'd stood up, covered in blood.

She cried out in her sleep and dug her fingers into his chest. He felt her knee coming at him but deflected the blow, just as her other hand went for his head.

Time to wake her up. In the close quarters his work often required, he had witnessed his share of teammates having nightmares. Usually he'd just toss his watch or a water bottle at the person and say, "Hey, pal, wake up. You're having a nightmare." But he was reluctant to be that perfunctory with Keira, not so much because he wanted to be gentle with her—he wanted her to be gentle with *him*. They were in the same bed, and she was in good shape. One well-placed blow would ruin his day.

And they were in a tricky mustn't-touch situation that another well-placed blow could make even trickier.

He placed his hand on hers—the one that had a grip on his shirt and some skin and hair he wanted to keep. "Keira."

She bolted upright, holding on to his hand, clearly not awake. She was breathing hard, close to the point of hyperventilating, and looked repulsed and terrified, haunted by whatever images were assaulting her in her sleep.

"Keira, you're having a nightmare."

Her eyes focused on him, widened, and she dropped his hand and rolled back to her side of the bed. Simon didn't know what had her more distressed—her nightmare, or waking up half on top of him.

"I was…" She raked a hand through her hair and inched a bit farther from him. "Spiders and slugs were crawling on me."

Simon leaned back against his pillows. "Nasty."

She blew out a breath, shivering. "It was awful."

"Nightmares are normal after a trauma."

She lifted her gaze to the window. The shade was up, and the lace curtains were pulled back, providing a view of a small sheep pen across the yard. "Do you have nightmares?" she asked without looking at him.

"Sometimes."

"Your work with Fast Rescue—"

"I've had a lot of training to help me learn to process what I experience. There's no training for what you went through in that ruin."

Her very blue eyes shifted to him. "Did I hurt you?"

"Not at all." He grinned at her. "It's not a bad way to wake up, as a matter of fact. If I'd stayed in London, I'd have woken up in a big, elegant, empty bed. This is cozy, the two of us—"

"I'll go into the other room. You can go back to sleep."

"I'm good. Wide awake." He threw off the duvet and got up. "Take your time. I'll make coffee."

"That'd be great. I'm still—" She waved her hand. "I'm still fighting off spiders and slugs."

Her hair was tangled, and her shirt was askew. Now that she was safe, Simon knew, her mind—consciously or subconsciously—could indulge in the fear, revulsion, claustrophobia and whatever other emotions it hadn't let her access during the hours she was trapped.

And he'd be a slug himself if he took advantage of her waking up from a stress-induced nightmare.

He retreated to the kitchen and filled the electric kettle with water, turned it on and headed for the bathroom, changing into jeans and a sweater. His own hair was a mess. He wet his hands and ran them over his head, gave up and went back into the kitchen. He heaped grounds into a coffee press and poured on what looked like the right amount of water.

While the coffee steeped, he got down two mugs, and he imagined being here with Keira on an ordinary morning, making coffee, planning their day. He wouldn't have jumped right out of bed after she'd clawed at him while having a nightmare, that was for damn sure.

Simon indulged in those images for about five seconds before he pushed them far to the back of his mind, filled his mug with the strong, steaming coffee and headed outside. A dozen or so sheep stirred in the pasture on the other side of the fence. The sun dipped in and out of gray clouds, and the air was brisk, scented with roses, the damp grass and, he swore, the sea.

Keira joined him with her mug of coffee, and he nodded to the dramatic hills that swept up into the heart of the peninsula. "It's beautiful country, but six weeks is a long time to be out here alone."

"I have a lot of work to do—and exploring," she said with an unembarrassed smile. "I won't be alone the entire time. I have friends from San Diego who're vacationing in Ireland in a few weeks and plan to stop by, and Colm Dermott will be here in late July with his family. And being on my own gives me a chance to get to know some of the local people."

Simon eyed her. "Keira, I've called the Irish police to come have a look at the ruin. They're on their way."

"When did you call?"

"Early. You were still dreaming about slugs and spiders."

"I suppose it makes sense, bringing in the police." But she quickly sipped her coffee and winced. "Strong, isn't it?"

"I just eyeballed the measurements."

"It's good—thank you."

She'd put on jeans and an oversize rugby shirt and combed the tangles out of her hair, but Simon had to admit his heart had skipped a few beats at the sight of her. He figured half the men she met probably fell a little in love with her within seconds of setting eyes on her. So why the hell wasn't she here with a man? He considered the prudence of asking her, then figured why not, "No boyfriend to take off with to Ireland?"

She didn't avert her eyes from him even a millimeter. "No. As I said, I plan to get a lot of work done while I'm here."

"A man would just get in the way?"

"That's not what I said."

She walked over to the fence and cupped her mug in both hands as she sipped her coffee and stared out at the pasture. Simon watched her, aware that she wasn't fully there with him. She was either still in her nightmare or, more likely, back in the ruin. He stayed quiet, giving her time, recognizing that he wanted to dive into whatever world she was trapped in and rescue her. Slay her demons, if need be. It was kind of mad, but he'd be dishonest if he didn't acknowledge the protective impulse, understand it for what it was. But Keira was a woman who went her own way, not out of defiance so much as disposition. It was just who she was.

His father had been like that, and he'd ended up dead.

She took her coffee down the driveway to the roses and mishmash of wildflowers. Across the lane and down the hill, the harbor glistened in the early morning sun. She seemed to soak in the scenery, the life and movement of the new day. She had an unpretentiousness and clarity about her that Simon could appreciate, and hell if he didn't want to scoop her up and carry her back inside for the rest of the day. Let the weather turn bad. What would they care?

"I don't really know you at all," she said abruptly, then turned to him.

Not a subject he wanted to get into. "What's to know?"

"You're a volunteer with Fast Rescue. Unless you're independently wealthy, that must mean you have a job. What do you do that you can drop everything to respond to a disaster anywhere in the world, live on a boat, go off to London—"

"I have my own business." It was true, as far as it went. "I work with various corporations and individuals on disaster preparedness and response planning. I also do some training. Some guide work."

"Guide work?"

He leveled his gaze on her. "If an artistic type wants to search for a mysterious ruin on a remote Irish peninsula on the night of the summer solstice, I can get her there and back safely."

"It wasn't night. Sunset isn't until ten o'clock here in June."

"Let's leave out night, then. Keira, you haven't told me everything about why you're here—"

"How did you end up as a Fast Rescue volunteer?"

He sighed. Obviously, she intended for them to do this her way. "A friend of a friend put me in touch with Owen."

But it wasn't that simple. That friend was John March, who'd put Simon in touch with Owen eighteen months ago simply because Fast Rescue needed search-and-rescue experts, and Simon, in the middle of sorting out what was supposed to be his post-FBI life, was one. At the time, March knew Owen only as the Maine summer neighbor of March's murdered FBI agent son-in-law. Owen hadn't yet fallen for Abigail, Chris Browning's widow, March's daughter.

By then, Simon was back in the FBI fold, working undercover and going after Norman Estabrook. Owen, who was thorough and protective of Fast Rescue and had extensive contacts of his own, figured out Simon's personal history with March, his undercover status, that his mission likely involved Norman Estabrook.

With the imminent takedown of Estabrook and the dismantling of his network, Owen was left in the unenviable position of not being able to tell the woman he loved what he knew about Simon, her father, their friendship. That information was all on a need-to-know basis, and Abigail didn't need to know.

Neither, Simon thought, did Keira Sullivan.

A brown cow meandered up to the fence in the enclosure across the lane. Simon walked over to her and patted her. She pushed her head against his hand, obviously enjoying the attention. "So, Miss Cow, what did you see the other day? Did you see Keira here go off into the hills? Did you see someone sneak into her cottage and steal her note?" He lowered his ear to the cow, pretending he was listening to what she had to say. "Ah. Fairies. I see. It was the summer solstice, and you saw fairies dancing." He glanced back at Keira. "Don't you wish cows could talk?"

"All right, all right." Keira laughed, dumping out the last of her coffee into the grass. "Let's go meet the guards."

~ Chapter 18

Beara Peninsula, Southwest Ireland
6:30 a.m., IST
June 23

Coffee and sunlight had Keira feeling more like herself as she tried to keep up with Simon as they crossed the open pasture in the general direction of the ruin. "Slow down," she said. "I'm tall, but your lope is still my run, and I can't keep up with you, especially after my nightmare from hell."

He glanced sideways at her, the wind catching the ends of his black hair. "I thought my coffee would put some zip in your step."

"It did. I'd be crawling otherwise."

Threatening clouds pushed down onto the hills. The wind was picking up, but Keira welcomed the brisk air and hoped it would help clear her head, stop her from thinking about waking up from her nightmare and finding herself more or less in Simon's arms. Common sense warned her not to get too caught up in her physical attraction to him. He'd be on his way back to London soon. He lived a very different life from hers, and even if a one-night stand would have been fun, she wasn't the type and never had been.

When they came to another fence, Simon hopped over it, then turned and offered her a hand. She took it, resisted the impulse just to jump into his arms. But he caught her around the middle and lifted her down to the ground, giving her a quick, irreverent smile. "You were about to land in sheep manure."

She glanced down, and sure enough, he wasn't kidding. "I see that your search-and-rescue skills are highly adaptable."

"Helps to know I'm dealing with someone who doesn't look over her shoulder for trouble."

Simon started down the hill to the muddy, thick undergrowth along the stream. Keira matched his pace, not letting him get too far ahead of her. "I'm not paranoid. I'm not going to sit home because something bad might happen if I go out."

"I can see that." He came to the stream and pushed back the low branch of an oak that dipped almost down to the water. "If the angel wasn't just another hunk of Irish rock, how did it get onto the hearth? Why hasn't anyone around here found it and sold it to a museum or put it on eBay by now?"

"I don't know."

"More important, where did it go?"

Keira shivered, wishing she'd worn a coat instead of just throwing a sweater on over her rugby shirt. "I don't know that, either."

Instead of putting her on the defensive, his questions—fired at her ever since they'd started the hike back up to the ruin—had helped her to focus on the specifics of her ordeal and remember them with greater clarity.

"Tell me about the fairies in this story," he said, thrashing along the edge of the stream. "Are we talking about a solitary fairy—a banshee or a leprechaun or something—or a fairy troop?"

"You know Irish folklore?"

"Not much. Enough to ask you a question."

"And to spark a good argument in an Irish pub, I imagine. It's a fairy troop, at least according to Patsy. They're determined and relentless. They believe they're entitled to the statue—"

"Because they insist it's one of their own who's been turned to stone."

Keira smiled. "So you were paying attention last night."

He winked at her. "Hard to resist a magical story told on a dark Irish night."

"It's easy to see out here how Ireland's strong oral tradition took root, isn't it? In any case, the fairies won't take no for an answer. They want the statue back."

"Patsy McCarthy obviously believes the statue exists, or at least wants to believe it." Simon pushed back another low-hanging branch along the stream. "I didn't overhear everything she said to you, but I gather she's with the brothers and thinks the angel can bring good fortune."

"She asked me to look for it on the summer solstice," Keira said.

"Because of the story itself—the angel first appears on the hearth on the night of the summer solstice. Someone else familiar with the story would know that."

"And therefore could have picked the same night as I did to be out here."

Just ahead, Keira spotted the ivy-enshrouded ruin through the trees, the cave-in making it easier not to miss. She stifled a sudden sense of dread, noticing that Simon hadn't slackened his pace at all.

But he paused just then and glanced back at her. "You okay?"

She nodded, ignoring a tightening in her throat and chest. *Concentrate on figuring this thing out.* "I've been thinking," she said, continuing on up the hill. "And I suspect the collapse itself might have exposed the angel. What if it was buried in the ruin?"

"Then the question is what caused the cave-in at that precise moment?"

"Someone poking around the same as me. But," she said, standing just below the tree that had fallen across the ruin's only door, "why leave me out here trapped inside the rubble?"

Simon's eyes darkened. "Good question. Have you told the story to anyone besides Professor Dermott?"

She shook her head. "I can't speak for Patsy, though."

"Who all knows you were coming out here to research an Irish story?"

"I've made no secret of it, but I haven't given the details to many people. The location of my cottage, for instance. I'm aware I'm here on my own."

As she tried to get a better look at a heap of rubble, Keira almost stepped on a tuft of sheep's wool in the tall grass. She repressed a sudden wave of the revulsion she'd felt last night when she'd realized she was covered in blood.

"Keira?"

"Just getting my bearings," she said, choking back the memory.

Simon eased closer to her, coming within an inch of his arm brushing against hers. "Do you remember any details now that you're back here?"

With her back to the ruin, Keira looked at the stream, sunlight and shade dancing on the clear, shallow water. "It's an enchanting spot, isn't it?" But when he didn't answer, she turned again, squinting at the dead tree, the partially-collapsed chimney. "I didn't sneak out here—I wasn't singing or anything, but I wasn't worried about anyone hearing me, either. Once I saw the dog, I was preoccupied with him. I certainly made enough noise if someone else was out here and didn't want to be seen. As for the sheep…" She grimaced. "It wasn't an act of nature that killed that poor animal."

"We don't have enough to go on to say for sure. Let's let the police get out here and see what they say."

She stared at the remains of the tiny hut. "It wasn't my imagination that started this place collapsing on top of me."

"No, it was probably your crawling around in an unstable structure without the proper knowledge or equipment." Simon's tone was more matter of fact than critical. "You were worried about the dog and not paying attention."

"That doesn't explain the angel. Maybe someone purposely started the cave-in to trap me, then figured I was dead or at least incapacitated and stole the angel. If it's an authentic early Celtic statue, it's valuable."

"And if it's solid rock, it's also heavy."

"It's only about two feet tall. I doubt it's that heavy."

"So this 'someone,' whoever it is, crawls into the hut after it collapsed, grabs the angel and—"

Keira shook her head. "Not *after* the cave-in, while it was happening. I saw the angel during a brief lull in the collapse. After it started up again, I couldn't see much—I was huddled under the loft trying to keep rocks and rafters from falling on my head. Someone could have grabbed the angel and crawled out in the middle of the action."

"Risky," Simon commented.

"Opportunistic, too." She gestured to the tree blocking the door. "I'll bet he—or she—toppled the tree, deliberately or accidentally, on the way out, then headed for my cottage and stole my note to delay my rescue or the discovery of my body."

"Any candidates?"

"No."

She was aware of Simon watching her and turned toward him, noticing that his eyes were as green as the vegetation on their lush hillside. She felt a drop of rain on her hair. The wind was picking up. She could hear it howling up on the exposed hills. The police would be here soon, and she'd have to go through it all again—why she'd come out here, what had happened, every detail of the past two days.

Her gaze fell on a smear of dried blood in the disturbed ground by the fallen tree, and she turned abruptly and ran, thrashing up the hillside through the mass of trees and undergrowth. She came to a barbed-wire fence, barely breaking her stride as she clambered over it.

The wind was fierce out in the open. She could hear sheep bleating nearby, and as she stood on a rock jutting out of the ground, she could see the harbor far below, fishing boats, a pricey-looking sailboat. Crossing her arms in a gust of wind, she squinted out at the jagged MacGillicuddy Reeks across the bay, soon, no doubt, to be consumed in gray clouds and fog.

Simon stood next to her. "We'll wait here for the guards," he said calmly.

The Garda, Keira thought. The Irish police. "A Garda Siochana,"she said, half to herself. "I'm butchering the pronunciation, but it means Guardians of the Peace. I like that."

"Keira…"

"I'm okay. I had a mini panic attack." She stepped off her rock, wishing again for warmer attire. "I have to go back to Boston. At least for a few days. I want to check with Patsy to make sure she didn't leave out a part of the story that might help me make sense of what happened here, and I want to talk to Colm Dermott. I can't—" She broke off, then resumed. "I have to figure out what happened at that ruin, Simon. I can't stay here for six more weeks without knowing."

"All right. I'll get you back to Boston. Today, if you'd like."

She nodded. "I would. Thank you. I'm not as rested today as I'd hoped I'd be."

Her fatigue wasn't just due to the aftereffects of her experience in the ruin or her nightmare. It was also due to her night in bed with him, waking up in his arms—even if she'd been clawing imagined slugs and spiders off him. She'd come within a split second of asking him to make love to her.

Another reason, she thought, to head to Boston.

Simon took a breath. "Hell, Keira."

She didn't know whether she made the first move or he did, but suddenly she was in his arms. His mouth found hers, and she let go of all her tension and threw her arms around his neck, deepening their kiss. She loved the taste of him, the feel of his hard body against hers, the warmth of him in the cold, damp wind.

He lifted her off her feet. The hem of her shirt rode up, and he spread his hands on the bare skin of her lower back, sending a jolt of pure desire straight through her. She pressed herself into him, was sure she heard him give a moan of a yearning as wild and uncontrolled as her own.

A gust of wind blew down from the hills, and more sprinkles fell, the combination of the cold air and water with the heat of their kiss setting every nerve in her body on fire. Sensations coursed through her. She'd never responded to anyone the way she did Simon. She wanted to run her hands through his hair, taste every part of him, feel him inside her. And it wasn't just adrenaline, or being out on an Irish hill—she'd had a strong reaction to him the moment she'd spotted him in Boston.

"I'd love to go back to the cottage," she said between kisses. "A storm's brewing. We could forget all this mess…"

But even as she spoke, he was lowering her back onto the cool, damp ground, and she steadied herself and caught her breath as she adjusted her shirt and looked out across the barren landscape.

Just as well they'd stopped when they did, Keira thought, because now she could see two men walking toward the ruin.

"The guards have arrived," Simon said with a hint of amusement.

"In the nick of time, wouldn't you say?"

"Hardly." And, as if to make his point, he gave her a fast, fierce kiss. "We'll pick up where we left off another time. We're not finished."

Keira didn't respond, just ran toward the two Irish police officers and waved to them, hoping they'd have answers. Perhaps they'd tell her they'd just arrested someone who'd been out killing sheep and terrorizing tourists.

But she knew that was unlikely, because the answers weren't in Ireland.

They were in Boston.

～Chapter 19

Using a screwdriver she'd borrowed from Bob O'Reilly, Abigail opened a gallon can of blue paint she'd put on newspaper in her bedroom. A grainy black-and-white picture of Victor Sarakis stared up at her, as if to remind her that the investigation into his death was not yet finished.

She tried to focus on the paint. "Do you like the color?" she asked Owen, who watched her from the doorway.

"It's a nice shade."

He didn't give a damn about paint. She knew he didn't, but she still had to ask. She wanted him to like it, to have some role—however small—in its selection. He'd arrived back in Boston last night from Austin. Her gaze drifted to the double bed—anything larger wouldn't fit in the tiny room. She hadn't bothered to make it. The sheets were tangled from their lovemaking.

"If you want a different color," she said, "now's the time to speak up."

"Blue's good. I can help—"

"It's so small in here, we'd just bump into each other and get paint all over everything." She lifted off the lid, set it on Victor's face and put down the screwdriver, picking up the wood stirrer that came with the paint. "I'm not kicking you out."

"I know you're not."

Did he? She wasn't sure anymore. "I'm preoccupied with a case." She dipped the stick into the paint and smiled, or tried to. "I've got the devil on my mind."

She'd been reading Charlotte Augustine's book on the history of the devil last night when Owen had arrived. "It's your day off," he said. "You could sit in a lounge chair, drink wine and read Jane Austen."

"Sounds tempting." There were a thousand things she could do besides paint the bedroom.

"Simon's on his way back here with Keira," Owen said.

"Bob told me when I went out for the paper. He's been beside himself. I guess I don't blame him. It's weird, Keira coming on the body in the Public Garden and now this mess in Ireland." Abigail shoved the stick into the paint. "I don't like coincidences."

"Is there any reason to think the two are connected?"

"No."

When she didn't go on, Owen drew himself up straight from the door frame. "There are a couple of things I need do at the foundation. Nothing important. Fiona O'Reilly and her friends are coming back to practice. If you want to, stop by later." He smiled. "We can dance an Irish jig."

Abigail felt a little of the tension go out of her. "Do you know how?"

"No, but maybe Bob could teach us."

"That I'd like to see."

She stirred the paint. It was such a great color. She'd picked it out while Owen was out of town. He could afford decorators, but she couldn't, not on a detective's salary. And she didn't want to. She'd had visions of redecorating the bedroom together, but it wasn't working out that way.

Without looking at him, she continued. "Bob's annoyed with me. I sat outside last night reading a history of Satan while I waited for you. The man who drowned the other night was obsessed with devil imagery."

"Bob thinks you're wasting your time?"

"I'm bucking him and everyone else I work with. We're all under pressure to improve our percentage of solved cases, and this one—it's not even a case at this point, really. The preliminary work's done. I should wait for the full autopsy report. It could be a couple more weeks."

"You think you should wait, or everyone else thinks you should?"

"Both." She lifted the stirring stick out of the paint and scraped the excess off on the edge of the can. "Something's not right about this man's death, Owen."

"In other words, as the lead detective, you don't believe waiting for the autopsy report is in the best interests of your investigation."

"That's a better way to put it than to tell me I'm just being difficult." She looked up at him from her paint can. "I love you, Owen. You know that, don't you?"

"Never a doubt. Abigail—"

She jumped in before he could finish. "The color will darken when it dries."

"It'll be perfect. But you're not going to paint today, are you?"

She rolled back onto her heels, not responding right away. One of the many things she loved about him was his insight—she didn't have to constantly explain herself. "I haven't decided. I admit I'm preoccupied. I can't shake this Sarakis thing. I keep thinking I'm missing something, and someone's going to end up hurt if I don't figure out what."

"Do what you have to do today, Abigail."

"We're grilling tonight. Keira and Simon will be here by then, won't they?"

Owen nodded. "I'm picking them up at the airport."

"I don't like this, Owen. I'm glad to know the Irish police are investigating. What if some nut followed Keira to Ireland and tried to kill her? It could all be a bizarre mix of accident, coincidence and her imagination. But I'd want to know more if I were an Irish detective."

"You want to know more as a Boston detective."

She sighed. "I guess I do. Can't help it."

"Simon's on the case. He's got contacts even I don't know about." Owen stepped into the room and kissed her softly. "You know you could paint this room chartreuse for all I care, don't you? I'm not looking at the walls when I'm in here."

She laughed. "I should call that bluff and exchange my pretty blue for a really ugly chartreuse and see how you like it."

He left, and thirty seconds later, Abigail did exactly as he predicted and gave up on painting. She placed the top back on the can, tapped it down tight and got to her feet, part of her wishing he'd kicked over the paint can and swept her off to the beach for the day. They could be in southern Maine in less than two hours, depending on traffic.

Getting out of her way, going off to Beacon Hill, had nothing to do with painting the bedroom or her preoccupation with the drowning in the Public Garden. Owen was simply giving her room to figure out what was going on with her.

And wasn't that part of why she'd fallen in love with him?

She headed through her small, IKEA-decorated kitchen out to the backyard. Hers was the first-floor and the smallest of the three apartments in the Jamaica Plain triple-decker she'd bought with Bob and Scoop Wisdom, an internal affairs detective. Abigail had heard Scoop leave early for work and thought Bob had gone off, too, but she found him out back drinking coffee and cleaning the grill.

"I just saw Owen," Bob said. "Why aren't you with him?"

"I'm painting the bedroom."

"No, you're not. You're messing with that accidental drowning."

She knew he'd said "accidental" deliberately to get under her skin. "You know damn well it hasn't been determined—"

"Officially it hasn't." He dug his grill scraper into a baked-on hunk of black gunk. "I don't know what's going on with you and Owen, but you two need to talk before someone besides me notices it's affecting your work."

"Nothing's going on with Owen and me, and my work's fine. Since when are you the relationship expert, anyway?"

He ignored her, flipping the black glob onto a paper towel. He wore shorts, a Red Sox T-shirt and sports sandals—not an outfit he'd wear to work. "Take it from someone whose had two marriages go sour on him. It's worse when you're lying in bed alone again, and you know you should have just let it out, talked. Maybe it would have helped save things, maybe it wouldn't have, but you'd know you'd done everything you could."

Abigail didn't want to talk to him about relationships. "You're not going in today?"

"Nope. Abigail, you need to listen to me." He pointed his grill-cleaning brush at her. "You were on your own for seven years. You spent those years focused on becoming a detective and finding your husband's killer."

"I lived my life, Bob," she said quietly, knowing he wasn't going to quit until she said something.

"Yeah, but your life revolved around finding Chris's killer.

Everything else came second. You know it did. You got your answers last summer, but you didn't have a chance to absorb them before you and Owen fell like bags of rocks for each other." Bob attacked the grill again. "I don't think you know if you want to stay a detective."

"That's insane. What else would I do?"

"Wrong question. Ask yourself if being a detective matters to you today as much as it did last summer before you got that tip that sent you to Maine."

To Mount Desert Island, she thought, where her husband had been born and raised. Where he'd died on his honeymoon, on the rocky coastline between his childhood home and Owen's summer home. Chris's killer had lain in wait for him, shot him, left him to die. Owen found his dead friend the next morning. Now, eight years later, Abigail had what people called—awkwardly, inadequately—closure.

"I'm not asking myself anything," she told Bob.

"Then you've been hanging around me too long. This job doesn't make it easy to talk. We get used to just not going there. To bottling it up." He managed a grudging grin. "Only, I'm not that deep. Nothing to bottle up."

"Owen and I are fine," Abigail said, feeling her prickliness return. "I'm almost finished with the book Charlotte Augustine loaned me. You know, Lucifer is a fallen angel."

Bob glared at her. "So?"

"Keira went to Ireland to investigate an old story about a stone angel twenty-four hours after finding Victor Sarakis—"

"You want to jerk my chain, fine," Bob said, dropping his wire brush onto the grill. "But you just remember. I'm a senior detective who can kick your ass from here to Bunker Hill if you don't straighten out."

Abigail didn't back down. "My gut tells me there's a connection between Victor Sarakis's death and what happened to Keira in Ireland. Your gut would, too, if you weren't emotionally involved."

She knew questioning his judgment and instincts—telling him outright that he was, in fact, emotionally involved in her case—would set him off, and it did. He glared at her, his entire face turning red. "I'm getting you pulled off this investigation."

"Just try it. See what I do."

He turned purple, swore under his breath and thundered up the outside stairs to his third-floor apartment.

Abigail exhaled, feeling lousy. Bob was her friend, and he'd had a rough couple of days. She had no business baiting him that way.

She debated following him upstairs to apologize, but rejected the idea. They'd just end up in a bigger fight.

Neither one of them could get along with anyone these days.

She went back inside, grabbed her car keys and headed out.

Jay and Charlotte Augustine's Back Bay showroom was located above an upscale health club with lots of sweating, intense, skinny people on treadmills, stair-climbers, elliptical machines, exercise balls. The treadmills had their own televisions, and most of the machines were placed in front of tall windows that overlooked the street. Abigail used the BPD gym. It wasn't bad, but it was perfunctory.

She took a claustrophobic little elevator up to the renovated brick building's third floor. It let her out into a reception area that consisted of an oak rolltop desk, an unoccupied ergonomic swivel chair and a library table that held a telephone, computer and crates of manila files. Behind the desk was a floor-to-ceiling partition and a locked door that, presumably, led to the main room.

The door opened, and Liam Butler, Victor Sarakis's graduate

student assistant, poked his head out. "Hey, Detective," he said. "I thought I heard the elevator. What's up?"

"I wanted to stop by and thank Mrs. Augustine for a book she gave me."

"I know the one—I suggested it. Fascinating, isn't it? Believe it or not, there are entire college courses on the devil. Victor could have taught one—he was that knowledgeable on the subject."

"What about you?"

"I'm not that wild about it, to be honest. I had nightmares when I first started working for him, but I got over my resistance after a while. Victor understood. He said it was natural to be reluctant to confront evil, even on an intellectual basis. Part of the deal, really."

"A defense mechanism," Abigail said casually, then nodded to the open door. "Mind if I have a look in there?"

"If I said no, you'd need a warrant, right?"

"If you said no, I'd leave."

"Gee, don't tempt me. But it'd be provocative, wouldn't it? If I just told you to get lost?"

She didn't answer. She'd need more time with Liam Butler, she decided, to have a better sense of him. The outfit he had on looked like the same one he'd worn the other day, but she couldn't tell for sure. His hair was greasier—she doubted he'd showered. She didn't know if that was the norm for him or if the sudden death of his landlord, friend and employer had yanked him out of his routines. He seemed as easygoing as he had been at their first encounter with Jay Augustine in Victor's devil room. Abigail knew from personal as well as professional experience that not everyone handled loss in the same way. From what she'd seen so far, Liam's behavior—even tweaking her over a search warrant—wasn't entirely out of the ordinary.

"I have a key, in case you're wondering," he said. "I check on the place when Jay and Charlotte are out of town—once or twice a week, at most."

"They don't have employees?"

"Sometimes they hire a tempt to sit at the front desk, but that's only if paying customers are coming by and they need the extra help. They don't keep regular hours. Most of the people who come here have appointments."

"Do the Augustines know you're here now?"

He shrugged. "I don't know. I haven't seen them. I guess we're all still trying to get our heads around what's happened." He held open the door and motioned with one arm. "Care to have a look around? I was only joking around about the warrant. No one's got anything to hide, Detective."

Abigail entered a room that looked as if it took up all or most of the third floor of the narrow building. Larger items—furniture, statues, trunks—were arranged on the floor in what looked to be an orderly fashion. She peeked at deep shelves filled with colorful pottery vases, small statues of animals and naked warriors, an ornately carved box and an ancient-looking bronze falcon.

"Jay and Charlotte keep good records," Liam said. "They know everything in here, right down to the mice turds."

Abigail smiled at his infectious humor. "Do they have a specialty?"

"They have to be pragmatic, but they'd deal exclusively in Classical and early Medieval works if they could."

"European?"

"Ideally, I guess."

She wandered between stacks of wooden crates. "Give me some examples."

"I don't know—I have a hard enough time keeping track of

Victor's collections. Jay and Charlotte don't keep their really good stuff here. I know that much. A lot of it's museum quality, and they just don't have that level of security in this showroom. Their most valuable items are specially handled and go right from the seller to the buyer. They're known for being knowledgeable and trustworthy."

"Do they do a good business?"

"They make most of their money on a handful of deals a year—according to Victor, at least."

Abigail had no reason to doubt Liam's information. "The history I read says that anthropomorphic images of Satan didn't take hold until around the sixth century. Would the Augustines be interested—"

"They aren't into the devil the way Victor was. Most of their customers aren't, either."

"So a Medieval statue of Lucifer wouldn't interest them?"

"I doubt it, but I guess it'd depend. There are alternative religious subjects—happier ones. They deal in a lot of jewelry and household items." Liam gave an irreverent grin. "You'd be surprised how popular chamber pots are."

Abigail heard the elevator open.

"Oops," Liam said. "Guess you're caught. The pesky detective returns with more questions."

She ignored him, and he followed her back out to the reception area.

Both Augustines looked startled to see her, but Jay recovered first, greeting Abigail politely. "Detective Browning, it's good to see you. What can we do for you?"

She didn't give him a direct answer. "It's an interesting business you have. Do you deal in Irish-Celtic pieces?"

"When we can get them," Charlotte said, obviously awkward.

Abigail doubted Charlotte had told her husband about giving the detective investigating her brother's death a book on the devil.

Clearly, it would be simpler for the Augustines if Victor's death were ruled an accident.

"Any Celtic work is in high demand," her husband added.

Abigail didn't pursue the subject and guiltily wondered if she would have if Bob had been with her. "Could Mr. Sarakis have stopped by here——"

"The night he died?" Charlotte asked, gulping in a breath. "No, I don't think so."

"Did he have his own key?" Abigail asked.

Liam shook his head. "Not on him. I had it."

Jay sat at the rolltop desk and spun the chair around, turning on the computer. "Anything else, Detective? Please feel free to look around as much as you'd like, but if you don't mind, we have work to do."

"I'm done for now."

"Where's your partner?" Charlotte asked.

Jay tapped the computer keyboard. "She's here on her own," he said, giving Abigail a cool look. "Aren't you, Detective?"

She didn't answer. "If you think of anything else, you know how to reach me."

When she headed back down the elevator, Abigail checked with the health club to ask a few questions. The manager wasn't in, but she left her card with a skinny kid at the front desk. "Please ask him to call me." She pointed to the computer. "Do people who use the club sign in and out?"

"Just in," he said.

"You keep the records?"

"Uh-huh. They're all on computer."

"Do the Augustines belong to the club?"

The kid nodded. "Mrs. Augustine comes in more than her

husband. When he does, though—man, he goes at it like you wouldn't believe. Uses every machine in here."

Abigail couldn't help but smile. "Thanks for your help."

"You bet."

As she left, he gave her a little salute. She laughed and headed out to her car, realizing she'd just accomplished exactly nothing. She drove the few blocks to Beacon Street and parked in front of the Garrison house. When she opened her car door, she heard Irish music and remembered it was her day off. She didn't have to be talking about devils and Medieval art and health club procedures. She could be dancing with Owen, even if neither of them could dance.

Before she could get out of her car, her cell phone rang, and a man with a heavy Irish accent identified himself as Seamus Harrigan, a detective with the Irish Garda. "I'm returning your call, Detective Browning. What can I do for you?"

Abigail remained behind the wheel and shut the car door. "I'd like to talk to you about a case on the Beara Peninsula." She hesitated a fraction of a second. "It involves an American named Keira Sullivan."

～ Chapter 20

Beara Peninsula, Southwest Ireland
8:00 p.m., IST
June 23

Eddie O'Shea hunched his shoulders against the fierce wind and lashing rain. A proper gale had kicked up since the guards and the Americans had left. How poetic, he thought, holding his cap on his head as he pushed on up the dirt track. He'd left his pub in his brother Patrick's hands, but there wouldn't be a crowd—surely he wouldn't manage to burn the place down before Eddie could get back.

Rain pelted his face with such force it might have been hundreds of tiny needles. The landscape was all gray and green. It seemed fine and normal to him, but he expected that Keira Sullivan would have found a way to capture it in a painting and make it feel special. Eddie had lived on this land his entire life. His ancestors went back a thousand years or more on the Beara, or so his mother had insisted— and who was he to argue?

A Yank with Irish blood coming to the village because of an old story about fairies and other such nonsense wasn't all that unusual. Eddie didn't pay attention to such things, typically.

But this story, and this Yank, were different.

He came to a dip in the upward sweep of the hills and crossed a wooden bridge over a winding stream, just as he had ever since he'd first sneaked off from his mother the first time at three years old.

He paused at the fence and caught his breath, shifting to keep the wind at his back. The grass and the rocks would be slick. The ground would be muddy. There'd be manure piles to navigate. Eddie had no illusions that he'd have ever made a good farmer.

I don't want to go into the pasture.

But he knew he had to, if any measure of peace of mind was to be his.

The guards, Keira and the big man—Simon Cahill—had crawled around in the old ruin without finding a thing except the bloody remains of a dead sheep. Eddie had pried at least some of the details from Seamus Harrigan, a regional detective with the Garda who'd stopped by the pub for a bowl of soup. Harrigan didn't know what to make of the American folklorist and her tale, but they hadn't found her backpack in the rubble—or, he'd said, any Irish artifacts. Nothing. Harrigan had said "artifacts" with a scowl. But he didn't disbelieve her. He'd told Eddie that Keira had been sincere—and quite beautiful. He just didn't know what was fact and what was imagination.

Harrigan had liked Cahill, too. Everyone did.

Eddie frowned at the fence. He'd stalled long enough. He'd have been over it by now as a boy. He stood on a rock to give him more height, and felt a pull in his thigh as he climbed over the fence, catching his trousers on a sharp barb. He could just hear his brother snorting with laughter—not Patrick, the brother minding the pub.

He was an aimless, jobless ne'er-do-well if there'd ever been one, but always cheerful, not a bad word to say about anyone. Eddie couldn't say that about Aidan, a farmer and the eldest of the O'Shea brothers.

Three of them—just as in the old story their grandmother had told their mother and she had told her sons.

The same story that had lured Keira Sullivan to Ireland, and her mother before her.

Has to be. It's all that makes sense.

Eddie's boot sank two inches into the muck and manure on the opposite side of the fence, but he managed not to fall. He preferred to stay in the pub on such days. Whip up a mutton stew, sweep the floors or just sit with a pint and contemplate his life.

More by instinct than memory, he found his old boyhood trail that ran across the open pasture above the stream. He and his brothers had taken it a thousand times. There were several more fences to cross and more wind and rain to brave. When Eddie started down into the trees, he felt a mix of trepidation and excitement. He was out of the worst of the gale now, and he could see matted grass where Keira, Simon and the guards had come through.

Eddie had known they wouldn't find anything.

Thirty years ago, Keira's mother had gone exploring out in this same spot. She took the bus from Dublin and camped in the hills by herself, and Eddie and his brothers, just teenagers themselves, hadn't bothered her. These were the days before Ireland's economic boom—long before the Beara Way, the nearly two-hundred-kilometer mix of marked trails, lanes and roads that snaked down one side of the peninsula and back up again. It was popular with walkers and bikers, and Eddie had seen a boost in business, thanks to its proximity to his pub. But the isolation and remoteness of the Beara hadn't seemed to bother Eileen O'Reilly.

She hadn't been pretty—certainly not the striking beauty her daughter was—but Eddie remembered she'd had a nice manner about her. She'd talked to his mother about the story of the three brothers and their dance with the fairies over the stone angel. Even then, his mother was apparently the only one left in the village who'd ever heard of the tale. She believed, as Eileen did, that the back-and-forth between the brothers and the fairies would resume if the angel were ever found. That it was meant to be.

Eddie had never spent so much as two seconds of his life looking for the thing.

He didn't believe the stone angel existed, and he didn't believe in fairies, either.

So why are you here instead of in your warm, dry pub?

Disgusted with himself, Eddie crept through the wet grass and undergrowth to the ruin, as gray as the sky above him. The place was no secret to him. No great discovery. He and his brothers had come out here many times. If there'd been an ancient angel to find, surely they'd have found it. But he hadn't been out to the ruin in years, and he knew his brothers hadn't.

In her last hours, his mother had begged Eddie to tell her the story she'd told him and her mother had told her. *"The one about the farmer, the hermit monk and the ne'er-do-well. Tell me that one, Eddie, my good boy."*

He'd sat on a wood stool by the fire and told it to her over and over as he watched her fade away.

"I'm going to the angels, Eddie...I can see Saint Ita now..."

His mother had been a faithful churchgoer and believed in angels, and in fairies, too. None of it mattered to Eddie.

She died two days after Eileen O'Reilly had gone home to Boston.

The rain eased, and Eddie walked closer to the ruin. A fallen tree lay half in the stream—Seamus Harrigan had described how he and

Simon had dragged it there from in front of the hut's open doorway. They'd discovered the remains of the ladder Keira had built for her escape, but nothing else.

Eddie felt terrible that she'd been up here, trapped and frightened, and he'd been none the wiser. He and his brothers would have gladly come to her rescue. But that was another part of her tale that Harrigan had found both amusing and curious—Keira's insistence that for most of the night and day she was stuck in the ruin, she was unafraid, confident of her ability to get out of there on her own.

Having known her just a short time, Eddie was nonetheless unsurprised by her strength and determination, never mind how those same qualities could also lead her astray.

He approached the entrance to the old hut and saw clearly how the hillside had eroded under the front corner on the chimney side. Keira had been lucky, indeed, not to be killed or seriously injured.

But what was this?

Eddie frowned, gingerly making his way to the spot where the uprooted tree had been. A holly tree grew up the hill close to the chimney—or what remained of it—and there, leaning into its waxy leaves and healthy branches was a shovel, as if a farmer had abandoned it moments ago.

Had the guards used it to dig in the ruin when they'd looked around here this morning?

But no, Eddie thought, rubbing his fingertips over the top of the shovel's sturdy wooden handle. It wasn't left here by a farmer or the guards. He couldn't say who'd left it, but he knew it had been left for him, put there against the holly tree as if whoever had done it had known he would come and figured he'd be fool enough to miss it if it wasn't right there under his nose.

Rain ran off the end of Eddie's cap as he squatted for a closer look.

Bits of gray mortar were stuck to the blade and there were fresh nicks, indicating the shovel had been used recently.

There you have it.

Eddie rose and pulled off his cap, smelling the wet wool as he ran his forearm across the top of his head. Someone had been digging here. And the digging had caused the old hut to cave in while Keira was inside, escaping her black dog.

Digging for what?

But Eddie knew the answer to that question.

Digging for the stone angel in his mother's story.

He remembered how Eileen O'Reilly had returned to the village that fall, and never mind the wool cape she wore, it was easy enough to see she was expecting a baby. She'd stayed for a week that time, roaming the hills in every manner of weather, speaking to no one. Eddie had wanted to help her, but what could he do? He and his brothers had just buried their mother.

"Ach," he said aloud, "that was a long time ago."

Eddie picked up the shovel and placed it on his shoulder. If it'd been left for him, then it was up to him to figure out what to do with it, wasn't it?

When Eddie was within a few yards of the dirt track, something by the rocks on a steep incline above him drew his eye. The rain was pounding again. The wind howled, and fog surged down from the hills like a live thing. He pictured himself back at the pub with a mug of coffee laced with whiskey and whatever Patrick had prepared for supper—it wouldn't be any good, whatever it was, but it'd be hot.

Wiping rain off his face with cold fingers, Eddie tried to make out what was up there on the hill. Whatever it was, it didn't belong there or he wouldn't have noticed it.

Dread tightened in his chest.

I don't want to go up there.

But even as he formed the thought, he was on his way. The hill grew steeper, and he lowered the shovel and used it as a walking stick, although he knew he'd be destroying any trace evidence on it. He watched the detective shows. He knew about such things.

He was panting now from the exertion, and the rain was coming down so hard, whenever he took a breath he'd get a mouthful. Rocks abounded, big enough to serve as places to sit and look out at the landscape, in fairer weather and if he ever had a mind for gazing at the scenery.

He didn't see anything but rock, grass, sheep and sheep dung. He leaned on the shovel, ready to give up—eager to believe whatever he'd seen had been a trick of his imagination.

As he stood up straight, he felt his heart skip and his chest tighten further, so that his breaths came only in shallow gasps, as if his body was responding already to what his mind couldn't grasp.

Slumped amid the rocks was a dead sheep—or what was left of her. Her woolly coat soaked up the rain. Even from where he stood, Eddie could see she'd been dead for at least a few days.

She hadn't died of natural causes.

He saw that, too. Saw that some evil bastard had brutalized the poor creature, tortured her without mercy until she breathed her last.

He'd never seen such a sight in all his life.

Eddie made a sign of the cross, grabbed the shovel and ran, slipping on wet rock and grass, stepping in dung and mud as he tried to keep his footing on the steep slope.

He had to get the guards, call Seamus Harrigan and tell him what he'd just seen.

And he had to get that image out of his mind, he thought desperately, although he knew he never would.

The image of that sorry, innocent beast would be with him until his dying day.

Eddie arrived at his pub soaked to the bone, with the shovel heavy on his shoulder and his heart still racing from fear and horror. The rain had stopped, and he decided he'd get warm and dry before he called the guards.

As he lowered the shovel from his shoulder, he automatically glanced at the picnic table next to the pub entrance to see if Patrick hadn't cleaned up out here. It would be just like him to forget. Even with the rain, people would come outside for a smoke.

Eddie noticed a backpack on the table's back bench. It wasn't the first time a hiker or cyclist had left one behind. He set the shovel down and had a look, unzipping the main compartment, welcoming the chance to do something ordinary—something to take his mind, even for a moment, off the shovel, the dead sheep...his deep uneasiness about what was to come.

He found a flashlight, a compact emergency blanket, a Boston Red Sox cap.

His heart thumping, Eddie dug deeper into the backpack and pulled out a sketchpad and a plastic bag of artist's pencils.

He stood up straight, shocked down to his toes and no longer cold or hungry.

It was Keira's missing backpack, sitting out here in front of his pub as big as life.

~Chapter 21

Boston, Massachusetts
4:00 p.m., EDT
June 23

A part of Keira knew she was dreaming again. Another part was convinced that Simon was making love to her. That the feel of his hands on her was real. His mouth, his tongue. They'd come together in the sunlight—somewhere. She didn't know where, but it didn't matter. He was unrelenting, caring, so incredibly sexy. He thrust deeply into her, and she gave herself up to a thousand different sensations, a want that was as emotional as it was physical.

A noise jolted her awake.

"We're landing," Simon said next to her.

Keira sat up straight, still aroused. He was working a Sudoku puzzle. He gave no indication she'd cried out in orgasmic ecstasy in her sleep—which meant she hadn't, because otherwise, he'd have said so.

"Dreaming?" he asked.

"Not about slugs and spiders." She noticed he'd nearly erased a hole in one of the squares on his puzzle. "You're not supposed to guess, you know. It just messes you up more."

"I didn't guess. I just was wrong."

"Well, it's a seven."

He glanced at her. "You can't know that in two seconds."

"No, I can. Look. There's a seven in the box above and a seven in the box below and—"

"Right. It's a seven." He smiled at her. "I hate this game."

In ten minutes, they were on the ground. Keira set her watch back on Eastern Daylight Time. She hadn't been in Ireland long enough for her body to adapt to Irish Summer Time, but it wasn't on Boston time, either. Two flights across the Atlantic in one week—never mind the rest of what she'd experienced—had taken a toll.

So had sitting thigh-to-thigh with Simon on a plane for seven hours. Every nerve ending in her body seemed electrified. He, on the other hand, struck her as completely unaffected by their proximity.

Suddenly hot, she slipped off her sweater. "I hope you and Owen have Fast Rescue business you can discuss. I wouldn't want you making this trip for nothing."

He shrugged. "I'm not that involved with Fast Rescue business."

"What about your job?"

"I'm between assignments."

"Do you have a family you could visit?" She grabbed her bag from under the seat, trying to stave off a sudden sense of panic at having Simon attach himself to her. "A father, mother, brothers, sisters, ex-wives, pets, estranged children—someone?"

He shut his Sudoku book. "None of the above."

"You're not all alone in the world, are you?"

"I didn't say that."

"What about girlfriends, a fiancée, an ex-fiancée you owe money?"

His vivid green eyes sparked with amusement. "Panicked at the idea of having me around, are you, Keira?"

"I don't need a bodyguard, and I'm sure you have better things to do—"

"Not today I don't." He got to his feet, easing into the center aisle. As big as he was, he moved gracefully. "Relax. It's not unusual for someone to bond with their rescuer."

"You didn't rescue me."

"Did I or did I not pull you out of that place?"

"You did, and I'm grateful, but I'm sticking to my story that I would have gotten out of there on my own."

"Tell it to your grandkids."

He didn't relent as they got off the plane. By the time they went through customs and met Owen, Keira had let go the last of her erotic dream. But she still made sure that Simon sat up front with Owen and not in the backseat with her.

"Your uncle's invited you to dinner," Owen said.

"Summoned or invited?" Keira asked.

"Is there a difference with him?" Owen merged into a line of traffic exiting the airport. "He won't say so, but he's glad you got out of Ireland in one piece."

"I was never in any real danger."

Neither man in the front seat responded, and Keira sat back, jet lag and erratic sleep gnawing at her. And nerves, she admitted. She was accustomed to being on her own, not having anyone fretting about her. She could be smart, stupid, reckless, cowardly—who would care? She had friends and colleagues, but no one who'd even think to sound the alarm when she didn't call from Ireland as promised. Having Bob O'Reilly as an uncle when she lived in San Diego was very different now that she was in the same city with him.

And men, she thought, noticing the black waves of Simon's hair in the late-afternoon east-coast light. She recalled the sensation of running her fingers through his hair as if it'd been real and not just an adrenaline-generated dream. She'd hardly dated since moving to Boston. Before that—the truth was, there'd never been anyone remotely like Simon in her life. Which threw her more than the idea that her intense reaction to him was natural, expected even, under the circumstances. Falling for him just wasn't going to get her anywhere.

Simon looked relaxed, not the least bit torn about having kissed her. "So, Owen," he said casually, "have you and Ab set a wedding date?"

Owen didn't answer right away, then said simply, "No."

"What's the delay?"

Keira raised her eyebrows at Simon's bluntness, but Owen kept his tone even. "There's no delay. Abigail's preoccupied with her work right now. She can have all the time she needs. I'm patient."

"Don't let her mistake patience for indifference."

"Words of wisdom from Simon Cahill?"

"Damn straight. Marriage will change your lives. You'll want kids, right? You've got places here, in Austin, in Maine. You come and go as you please right now. Ab dives into a case. She's a dog-with-a-bone sort of detective."

"Simon, you're giving me a headache."

"Ab's got all this on her mind, Owen. Mark my words."

"She hates being called Ab."

"What about Abby?"

"Hates that, too."

Simon grinned. "Good to know."

Abigail was pacing in her kitchen when Owen arrived with Keira and Simon. Despite Owen's warning, Keira was surprised at how preoccupied and agitated the BPD detective looked.

Simon, undeterred, walked up to Abigail and slung a big arm over her shoulder. "Hey, Ab, when's the wedding?"

She gave him a dark look and slid out from under his arm. "Don't think I can't take you on, Cahill, because I can."

"Did I just get deleted from the wedding guest list?"

"You were never on it." Her expression softened as she turned to Keira. "Bob's out back waiting for you. I'm waiting for a call."

They all took the hint and headed out to the small backyard.

Scoop Wisdom was on his knees in his tidy vegetable garden. "Hey, Keira," he said, rising with a metal colander of fresh-picked peas tucked under one well-muscled arm. He was a compact, bulldog of a man with a shaved head and a take-no-prisoners demeanor. "Welcome home. Good flight?"

"It was long."

He glanced at Simon and grinned. "I'll bet."

Bob O'Reilly thumped down the stairs from his third-floor apartment and sighed at Keira. "You look like you just got plucked from an Irish ruin in the nick of time. Scare the hell out of me, why don't you?"

"I'm sorry I worried you."

He grunted. "You've been going off like that since you were a little kid. You'd think I'd be used to it."

"I've also been very good at taking care of myself since I was a little kid."

"No choice, seeing how your mother was in another world half the time. A good thing you grew up in the country. When you were four years old, Eileen called me in a panic because she couldn't find you. One minute, you're drawing pictures on the back porch. Next minute, you're off in the woods. Packed yourself a couple of slices of bread and went in search of fairies or some damn thing."

"Frogs," Keira said. "I remember."

Simon, looking amused, sat at the round plastic table and stretched out his legs, his hands folded on his stomach as he watched her and her cop uncle. She was too restless to sit. "I'm not four anymore, Bob," she said.

"Twenty-nine doesn't seem so old to me, either." He nodded to Simon. "Thanks for rescuing her."

Simon leaned back deeper into his chair. "Not a problem."

"I know Keira insists she was three seconds from getting out of there on her own—"

"More like three minutes," she said.

Her uncle pointed a thick finger at her. "Don't think you're not like your mother, because you are. Instead of copying Bible verses on goatskin and living alone in the woods, you paint pictures of fairies and thistle and go off to the wilds of Ireland by yourself. No damn difference."

"She doesn't use goatskin—she uses a beautiful cotton paper. The true illuminated manuscripts were done on vellum made from the skins of cows, goats or sheep, but the real thing is hard to come by these days and very expensive."

"You're pushing my buttons, Keira."

Scoop stepped out of his tiny garden with his colander of peas. "What's this about your sister, Bob?"

"Nothing." He snatched up a can of charcoal lighter fluid, squirting it over the heap of charcoal. "Forget it."

Keira noticed Simon's eyes narrowed on her as if he'd just penetrated a secret corner of her life. She shifted her attention to Scoop. "My mother is a religious hermit. She lives alone in a cabin in southern New Hampshire."

"Since when?"

"Last summer. It's one reason I returned to Boston."

Scoop's shock was evident. Keira thought she understood. The younger detective had known her uncle for years. They'd worked cases together. But Bob had obviously never mentioned that his sister had become a religious hermit. "Is she—you know..."

"Mentally stable? Yes, she is," Keira said. "She's a kind, good person. I drove out to see her before I left for Ireland. She's doing well—she's working on an illuminated manuscript, a mix of calligraphy and illustrations of Bible passages. The true illuminated manuscripts are centuries-old—"

"Before printing presses," Scoop said, pragmatic.

Abigail emerged from her apartment, her expression tight as she pinned her gaze on Keira. "I just got off the phone with the Irish Garda detective you and Simon met this morning—"

"Seamus Harrigan." Keira sank onto a chair at the round table. "What's going on?"

"The village barman, Eddie O'Shea, came upon the carcass of the sheep that presumably was the source of the blood at the ruin where you were trapped."

"Had the dog—"

"No," Simon said, serious now, as he got up and stood behind Keira, putting a hand on her shoulder. "It wasn't the dog, was it?"

Abigail shook her head. "No. Someone deliberately brutalized the sheep. It was a female—she was carved up pretty bad." Abigail looked away a moment, staring at the ground as if she didn't want to make eye contact with anyone in the yard. "I guess it was a gruesome sight."

"The poor animal," Keira said, her stomach lurching as she thought of the blood, the entrails, the bits of wool at the ruin. She met her uncle's eyes, but he didn't say a word, and she shifted back to Abigail. "How's Eddie?"

Abigail gave a curt sigh. "Shaken up, according to Harrigan. O'Shea's been around sheep all his life, and he's never seen anything like this."

"Where was the sheep in relation to the ruin?" Simon asked.

"About three hundred yards above it. It was on a steep hill among a lot of rock, I gather. After you and Keira and the police all left, O'Shea went up to see the ruin for himself. He took a different route on the way back and spotted the sheep."

"So whoever it was—" Keira paused, picturing the beautiful, rugged landscape. "Whoever mutilated the sheep either gathered blood and entrails and took them down to the ruin or dragged the body up the hill."

"It's possible," Abigail said, "that this person was using the ruin as a hideout, or even a base for his games. Harrigan said they're looking for other mutilated animals and checking for any reports of similar acts elsewhere Ireland. But they're keeping an open mind. They have to."

"Did Eddie see anyone?" Keira asked.

"Not that he's told the police, no. If you mean fairies—"

"I don't mean anything or anyone."

But even as Keira resisted Abigail's sudden scrutiny, Bob picked up a bag of charcoal and dumped a heap into the grill. "So, Abigail," he said, his tone deceptively mild. "What were you doing talking to our friends in the Garda?"

"Harrigan called."

"How'd he get your number?"

"I called and left it. I didn't know Harrigan would be the one to call me back. At first I had trouble understanding his accent, but hearing it just makes me want to check out Ireland one of these days."

"Abigail."

"I wanted to know what was going on, and I called. Simple."

"There's no connection between your drowning in the Public Garden and a bloody sheep carcass in Ireland."

Abigail ignored him and turned to Keira. "Would you mind taking us through what happened in Ireland? I know you've already spoken to Seamus Harrigan—"

"I don't have a problem going through it again," Keira said.

She expected her uncle to comment, but he didn't. Simon dropped into a chair next to her. Abigail, still visibly tense, sat in an Adirondack chair next to Owen, whose focus was almost entirely on her. Keira couldn't help but notice just how much he was in love with Abigail—and she with him. She'd automatically gravitated toward him. But her difficult mood was impossible to miss. She was just a year or two older than Keira but had pursued a single-minded dedication to law enforcement since the murder of her husband on their honeymoon eight years ago. Keira had never experienced such tragedy and violence in her own life.

Scoop settled at the table with his colander and, using his fingers, snapped off the ends of the peas one by one. Bob lit the coals and stood back, watching his grill, listening. Keira was most aware of Simon, sitting as still as he had throughout their flight, watching her as she told the story of how she'd ended up trapped in a ruin on a stretch of windswept Irish coast.

She kept to the facts and didn't elaborate, left out her emotions and questions. If she'd learned nothing else during her brief stay at the police academy, she'd learned how to talk to cops.

When she finished, Scoop, halfway through his colander, shook his head. "I don't see how this ruin spontaneously collapsed. It must have had help."

"Maybe the fairies did it," Bob interjected.

Keira noticed a change in Abigail's expression. "There's more, isn't there?"

Abigail nodded. "I wanted to hear your story first. The barman says he found an old shovel at the ruin—before he ran across the sheep."

Simon sat forward. "Where?"

"Propped up against a tree where he couldn't miss it. Harrigan says it wasn't there this morning, or he'd have seen it."

"It wasn't there last night, either," Simon said.

Keira felt the late-day sun hot on the back of her neck. "I didn't see it. Do the police think someone went out to the ruin after we left this morning, before Eddie got there?"

"Possibly," Abigail said.

"I'm not going to get worked up over a shovel," Bob said, then glared at Abigail. "You're chewing on something else. What is it?"

She settled back in her Adirondack chair and addressed Keira. "Eddie O'Shea also discovered your backpack on a picnic table outside his pub."

This news got to Keira. "How did it end up at the pub? It was in the ruin—it got caught in the collapse. I don't know if it was buried in rubble or not. The police tried to look around inside this morning, but they didn't get far. Too risky."

"You'd just been through a difficult twenty-four hours," Abigail said, "and you were focused on the stone angel and then on the sheep's blood. Is it possible the backpack was within easy reach of the entrance, even with the collapse?"

"I don't know." Keira jumped to her feet, restless, more shaken than she wanted to admit. "The key to my rented cottage was in my backpack."

Abigail gave an almost imperceptible shake of her head. "It's not there now."

Scoop tossed the last of his snap peas in the colander. "That probably explains the unlocked door and missing note. Our guy lets himself in, finds the note, gets rid of it and forgets to lock up on his way out. He dumps the backpack, and some hiker finds it and leaves it at the pub."

"Maybe," Keira said. "But there was no way anyone could have known I wrote that note, and I didn't notice anything else missing."

"Harrigan plans to talk to Eddie O'Shea again tomorrow," Abigail said. "He'll go back up to the ruin and take another look."

Bob sighed at Keira. "I can't believe you went to Ireland chasing a fairy story."

"It's a great story, and I went to Ireland to do my work. You investigate homicides. I investigate old stories." Not investigate, precisely, but she'd made her point.

Her uncle stood back from the flames. "When I investigate a homicide, I'm never thinking fairies did it. You're not a detective, Keira. You don't think like one. You don't have the training."

"I didn't get trapped because I was trying to be something I'm not."

"No, I guess not." When he looked at her this time, his eyes were filled with pain and worry. "How bad was it in that place?"

Her throat caught. "Pretty bad." She attempted a smile. "There were slugs."

Scoop made a face. "I hate slugs." He nodded to his garden. "I had to go on the warpath against them during a rainy spell earlier this month. They were eating everything. What kind of slugs were in the ruin with you?"

"Black ones, about six inches—"

He shuddered. "Stop. I can't take it."

Even Abigail managed to grin at the prospect of Scoop Wisdom getting the creeps over slugs. "How did you learn about this story about the brothers and the fairies?"

Bob lifted a package of preformed hamburger patties out of a cooler. "What difference does it make?" He ripped open the package and started laying patties on the grill. "Scoop, you got enough peas for all of us?"

"More than enough," he said.

Abigail didn't relent. "The story, Keira?"

"Drop it," Bob said.

"I'm just asking a question, Bob. It's not an interrogation."

But it was, Keira thought with sudden clarity. Abigail was in detective mode, and it was irritating Bob. His reaction struck Keira as out of proportion to the offense, and she suspected it had something to do with her mother's trip to Ireland thirty years ago.

"Never mind," Abigail said quietly. "I'm sorry, Keira. You've had a long day—"

"A woman who lives on the street where my uncle and mother grew up told me the story. Supposedly my mother looked for the village when she was in Ireland before I was born."

Her uncle was seething. "She went to a lot of places when she was in Ireland, and it was thirty years ago. Leave her alone."

Keira turned to Simon and tried to lighten the mood. "Now I could use rescuing."

"Nah." He gave her a reassuring smile. "You're three minutes from crawling out of this one on your own, too."

"Can you sketch this angel for us?" Abigail asked. "The dog, the ruin?"

Keira didn't bother to hide her relief at the slight change in subject. "I can try."

"I'll see what I can scrounge up for drawing materials." Abigail re-treated into her apartment, returning in a few moments with a stack of printer paper and a mug of colored pencils, crayons and markers. "I know these aren't the kind of supplies you're used to—"

"They're fine. Thanks."

"It'll help us visualize your experience, and it could jog your memory, produce some detail you haven't thought of."

Keira picked through the mug, choosing a black fine-point felt-tip pen. "I don't know if I can capture the moody beauty of that evening. My ancestors are from Ireland," she said. "My great-great-grandfather O'Reilly came over during the famine years in the late 1840s. My grandmother was born in Ireland."

"But this wasn't your first trip?" Abigail asked.

"My fourth. Eddie O'Shea and his brothers have lived on the Beara Peninsula their entire lives. Their family goes back there hundreds of years. Being a basic tumbleweed myself, I'm drawn to that sense of place—that continuity of home."

Simon leaned forward over the table without crowding her. "Is Patsy McCarthy from the Beara Peninsula?"

"No—another village in West Cork. Her grandfather worked in the copper mines. The copper veins drew ancient settlers—the ruin is up in the hills above a megalithic stone circle. Some people believe that's fairy ground."

She stared at the blank page a moment, visualizing the Irish land-scape, the hidden ruin, the ivy, the snarling dog. *Had* the dog snarled? Had he meant to harm her? Or was he just reacting to the dead sheep?

"The sheep's blood wasn't there," she whispered. "Not when I arrived."

No one spoke, and she let her instincts lead her pen to the right spot on the paper. She drew quickly, but carefully, trying to get the details right without overfocusing on them.

She put the pen down. She was aware of the burgers sizzling on the grill. Scoop had gone upstairs with his colander. Abigail was leaned back in her chair, Owen next to her, Bob still at the grill. Simon hadn't moved.

"I can't believe I felt safe when someone was smearing the blood of a murdered sheep a few yards from me." Keira looked at the two detectives and the two search-and-rescue experts. "Someone was there. I didn't imagine the voice."

"But you still felt safe," her uncle said, all the ferocity gone out of his voice now.

"Afterward. Not at first. But afterward—in the dark." She appraised her sketch. The basics were there. Dog, stream, gray stone, debris. The dead tree. At least a sense of the moody light. "Yes. I felt safe."

"What about the angel?" Abigail asked. "Can you draw it?"

"Not as easily. I can draw what I saw—what I remember. It won't have the kind of detail you're probably looking for." It took several false starts, several different pencils and markers, before she managed to draw an angel that even came close to what she'd seen that night. "I can't..." She sighed. "It was more beautiful than this. Truly a work of art."

Bob leaned over her shoulder. "Patsy's always liked her angels," he said.

Something in his voice made Keira look up, but he quickly returned to the grill. Scoop came down the back stairs with a bowl of steamed peas, and Abigail and Owen went inside and brought out a platter of paper plates, condiments, buns and a bowl overflowing with a green salad—a well-practiced ritual, Keira realized.

"Jet-lagged?" Simon asked, close to her.

She remembered the feel of his thick thighs against her on the long flight across the Atlantic. "Very. The sheep is disturbing, Simon.

Eddie O'Shea didn't deserve to find such a horror. If I attracted whoever killed that poor animal to the village—"

"You're not responsible for what someone else does."

His clear, succinct words helped center her, but they didn't chase away all her sense of guilt at Eddie's grisly discovery. "It's not a co-incidence," she said. "The story, my presence, the dead sheep."

"I don't think so, either."

And the man who'd drowned, she thought. Was his death not a coincidence, either?

"I'm going to see Patsy in the morning," she said abruptly.

Her uncle's eyes were half-closed. "She's an old woman, Keira."

"I know. I'll be careful what I tell her. I don't want to upset her. I just want to know if there's some part of this story—some tidbit her grandfather told her that she hasn't thought about in years—that could help make sense of things. Then I'll talk to Colm Dermott."

"Are you planning to go back to Ireland?" Abigail asked.

"I certainly hope to, but I'm not wild about staying in my cottage alone until I have a better fix on what's going on. Maybe the Irish police will trace the dead sheep back to some hiker who has nothing to do with me."

Her comment was met with silence, which Keira took as skepti-cism—they all believed the poor mutilated sheep had everything to do with her own ordeal.

With a sudden burst of energy, she reached for a bright green marker and drew a cheeky leprechaun on one of her discarded sheets.

Scoop Wisdom gave a mock shudder. "I don't know, Keira. I think I'd rather run into a mean black dog coming out of the Irish mist than that little sucker."

Everyone laughed, but when dinner was served, Keira didn't eat a bite.

⌒Chapter 22

Beacon Hill
Boston, Massachusetts
9:00 p.m., EDT
June 23

As soon as Owen pulled in front of the Garrison house on Beacon Street, Keira grabbed her brocade bag from next to her on the backseat and leaped out, shutting the door behind her. Simon watched her charge for the front door. "She's got a lot of energy for someone who's been through what she has in the past few days."

"She could just be anxious to put some distance between you and her," Owen said.

"True enough."

"Simon—" Owen sighed, threw the car into Park. "What the hell's going on?"

"I wish I knew."

Simon kept his eyes on Keira as she set her bag on the step and dug out her keys. If she locked him out, he could always ask Owen to let him in. It had been a torturous flight. He'd done one damn

Sudoku puzzle after another to stay awake. Whenever he'd dozed off, he'd ended up dreaming about making love to the woman next to him.

He acknowledged he was restless. He was accustomed to search-and-rescue missions and changing time zones—to long flights, as well.

So it had to be Keira. The mess she was in.

Kissing her out in the windswept Irish countryside.

"What about John March?" Owen asked.

An image of the FBI director's face wasn't exactly how Simon wanted his memory of kissing Keira interrupted, but nothing he could do now. "What about him?"

"Does he know you're here?"

"I left a message for him before I left London. Said I was off to rescue a damsel in distress." Simon shrugged. "He hasn't called back. The less you know about my business with March, Owen, the better. It hasn't followed me back here, if that's what you're asking."

"I don't know if I should have called you in London after all."

Simon summoned his sense of humor from deep inside. "And spared me a night in an Irish cottage with our flaxen-haired fairy princess?"

"Simon...I swear..." Owen sighed again. "Do you know what you're doing?"

"I'm about to carry my bag upstairs. How many flights up to the attic apartment with no phone?"

"Three. The last one's steep and narrow." Owen added dryly, "Don't trip."

Simon grabbed his own bag from the backseat, thanked Owen for the ride and, with a fresh burst of energy, headed for the elegant brick house, running up the steps and catching the front door just before it could shut tight.

Keira had a decent jump on him. He started after her, taking the stairs two and three at a time, but dropped his pace down to one. Owen hadn't been kidding. The last flight of stairs in particular was steep and narrow, clearly not built for someone Simon's size.

When he reached the attic, he noted that Keira had left the front door slightly ajar. He took that as a positive sign.

"You can come in," she said, "but watch your head."

He had to duck to get through the door. The apartment had low, slanted ceilings, its open floor plan easing any sense of claustrophobia. A pine table doubled as a work space, an arrangement she'd duplicated at her Irish cottage. One edge of the table was lined with art supplies. Open shelves held books and additional supplies, and a desktop computer with a massive flat screen sat on a rickety-looking cart.

A couch, a chair and a coffee table formed a small seating area in front of three windows that looked out on Boston Common.

Simon plopped his bag onto the scuffed hardwood floor.

Keira's eyes were on him, serious. "I appreciate everything you've done for me, Simon. I know I've had a bad time of it, but I don't want to take advantage of your generosity."

"Tell me you want to stay here alone tonight in a way that I'll believe."

"I didn't—" She paused, obviously fighting to hang on to her self-control. "I didn't expect the sheep. I keep thinking about that blood. And the shovel—my backpack. I feel terrible for Eddie."

"He strikes me as a man who's seen a thing or two in his day."

"And he has his brothers and all those guys at the pub." The thought seemed to cheer her somewhat. "My backpack turning up is odd. Maybe Scoop's right and a hiker found it and just dropped it off at the pub and went on his way. But maybe it was someone who knew exactly what it was and left it for Eddie—someone who wanted to remain anonymous. Last night, Simon, you mentioned a man you saw—"

"You saw him, too, didn't you?"

She nodded. "I had a strange conversation with him the night before I was trapped. Nothing ominous—just unusual. Like he knew things about me."

"A fairy prince?" Simon's tone was only half lighthearted.

"A hard-bitten looking one, if he is," Keira said, almost managing a smile. "I'm not suggesting he's involved, certainly not that he'd brutalize a sheep."

"Seamus Harrigan seems competent. He'll investigate—"

"You're right."

"It's been a long day," Simon said simply.

She averted her eyes, and he could see that they'd filled with tears.

His heart nearly stopped. "Keira…"

"There's one more piece of this—I don't know where it fits, or even if it does fit. My mother came home from Ireland pregnant with me. She dropped out of college. She's never talked about what happened. When I ask her about my father, she just—" Keira sucked in a breath, turned to him. "She tells me that my father was John Michael Sullivan. And he was. I know that. He adopted me after he and my mother were married when I was a year old. He died in a car accident when I was three, and I barely remember him."

"I'm sorry, Keira."

"By all accounts, he was a wonderful man. My uncle thought the world of him. He was an electrician—salt of the earth. The rock my mother needed."

"You went to Ireland in search of your birth father?"

"Yes and no." All the tension and fear of the past few days seemed to have welled up inside her to the point of bursting. But she exhaled, blinking back any remaining tears. "I went because of Patsy's story—the book I'm doing. But also because I thought I might find some answers, or at least make my peace with not having them. I had a happy childhood, Simon. My mother's a loving, open woman, deeply committed to her faith. But over the past few years, she's pulled further and further away from everyone and everything she knows."

"And you blame yourself?"

"If this is what she wants, I can accept that. I just…" Keira raked her fingers through her hair, suddenly looking exhausted. "I keep thinking if I'd stayed closer to home, if I'd shown more interest in her life—"

"Keira, don't. You're not responsible for your mother's happiness."

"It's one thing to know that—it's another to feel it in your gut. The truth is, I'm not even sure she actually got pregnant when she was in Ireland."

"The monk in your story's a hermit. Do you think he inspired your mother in some way?"

She lifted her shoulders and let them fall in an exaggerated shrug. "Who knows?"

"So, I'm trying to picture your mother," Simon said. "Does she look more like her brother or more like you?"

Keira stared at him, and he thought he might have gone too far—but then he saw the spark in her eyes, the crack of a smile. "You're impossible, Simon. You know that, don't you?"

"Laugh hard, live long—or at least well."

He went over to her microscopic kitchenette and pulled two glasses and a bottle of Jameson's whiskey off an open shelf. Keira didn't need him there. She had all those cops she could call on in a pinch, and she was smart, capable and resourceful—not such a flake after all.

Maybe telling himself she was a flake was his own way of keeping his distance.

Not that he was doing a good job of it, he thought as he set the glasses on the foot of counter space and opened the whiskey, splashed some into the glasses.

He handed her a glass, watched her take a sip. "Keira, I want you to know that I don't make a habit of kissing someone I've just rescued. Never mind if that someone quibbles about who did the rescuing. This morning—"

"It seems like a million years ago, doesn't it?"

"Actually, no."

Color rose in her cheeks, but he decided it wasn't from embarrassment. She was remembering their kiss, too.

"Simon, I know you're doing a favor for Owen—"

"It's gone beyond that, Keira."

"I suppose it has. I don't even know that much about you, and—well, here we are." She spun over to the table with her glass of whiskey, but didn't sit down. "How did you get into search-and-rescue work?"

"I started picking up skills in high school and college." It was the truth as far as it went. "My father died when I was fourteen. Learning how to survive and to help other people in extreme conditions gave me something to do."

"What happened to your father?"

"He was killed in the line of duty. He was a DEA agent."

"How awful. Do you have any brothers and sisters?"

He shook his head. "Cousins, and my mother remarried not long after—a guy with three kids from a previous marriage." He walked over to the table and picked up a book with a beautifully illustrated cover of a girl running into a magical forest. He immediately recognized Keira's distinctive style. A collection of fairytales. Her photo with the flowers in her hair was on the back. "Is this a recent book?"

"Last year. Normally I don't keep my books out in the open—I prefer to focus on current projects. But I looked up a poem before

I left for Ireland—"The Fairies," by William Allingham. '*Up the airy mountain, Down the rushy glen...'*"

"'*We daren't go a-hunting for fear of little men.*'"

Keira smiled, obviously pleased. "You know it?"

"My father taught it to me."

"It's a fun one. Some believe Irish fairies are angels who aren't good enough to be saved nor bad enough to be damned. Others believe they're the remnants of the old Irish pagan gods and heroes who went underground to live. I'm not trying to prove or disprove Patsy's story on any level—I just want to record it accurately. That comes first. Then I want to come up with illustrations that will capture its essence."

"Your personal connection?"

"I don't know for sure I really have a personal connection. I went to see my mother the afternoon before the auction, and she wouldn't tell me a thing."

Simon could see his comment had triggered Keira's tension again and shifted the subject. "Do you need quiet and solitude to work?"

"It depends." She pulled off her sweater and tossed it onto the back of a chair, looking more relaxed. "Sometimes I lose myself in what I'm doing and nothing distracts me. I could be anywhere, and it wouldn't matter. Other times I need total peace and quiet. I know I have an attic apartment, but I'm not exactly the artist-in-the-garret type."

"What about the cottage you rented in Ireland?"

"I expected to get a mix of time to myself as well as time with other people."

"You were also on a mission," he said.

She nodded. "I had personal as well as professional reasons to go to Ireland. I should have told you about the personal reasons." She took two quick sips of her drink and set the glass down, then pointed to her couch. "It's a pullout."

"Unlike the couch at your Irish cottage," he said. "What'll you do if you have nightmares about slugs and spiders again tonight?"

"Trust me, I won't. I'll fetch some linens." She eyed him with a frankness he found both unsettling and sexy. "I can see you're not going to your boat."

She retreated into her bedroom. Simon sat on the sofa and put his feet up on the coffee table—it looked as if that was okay to do—and flipped through Keira's fairytale book. Her work, which clearly appealed to both adults and children, had heart, imagination and a style that was uniquely hers. Even the art snob at the auction had been captivated by the two paintings she'd donated, although he'd probably never admit it.

But she still didn't own a phone, Simon thought, getting to his feet when she returned with an armload of linens. He took them from her. "Go on to bed," he said. "I'll take it from here."

"I can help."

Watching Keira shake out sheets was more than he could take right now if what she wanted was sleep. "I can handle it."

"You've been at my side since you yanked me out of the ruin," she said, touching his arm. "Thank you."

"You're welcome. Now, that's it, right? No more gratitude." He set the bedding on a chair. "It gets in the way after a while."

But she didn't take her hand from his arm, and he knew it didn't have a damn thing to do with gratitude. He was tired, she was tired. Simon knew he should just send her to bed and tell her to put a chair in front of her side of the door and he'd do the same on his side. So they wouldn't be tempted.

He'd just never been one always to do what he thought made sense.

He whispered her name, and it was enough. They were kissing before he knew he'd even moved. The taste of her, the feel of her slim body against him, were just what he'd imagined during the long trip across the Atlantic.

Need ripped through him, immediate, hot. He wanted to be inside her, now.

She opened her mouth to their kiss and pressed herself hard against him, as if she'd been thinking about this moment, practicing it in her mind.

"I dreamed about this on the plane," she said between kisses. "For all those hours. It was worse than my nightmare, I swear."

She laughed, and it was sexy and a little wild and good to hear. Simon relished the spark in her eyes, the flush in her cheeks as the trauma of the past two days receded. He scooped her up and laid her on the couch. She was slim and lithe and had long, graceful limbs that tantalized his imagination. The rugby shirt and jeans had to go. He wanted to feel her smooth skin in his hands. He wanted to taste every inch of her and make her ache for him.

Something in his expression must have alerted her, because she draped her arms around his neck, skimmed her fingers up into his hair, then locked her eyes with his. "Make love to me, Simon. Let me make love to you. It's right. I know it is."

"You trust your instincts."

"It's not just instincts." She lifted herself to him, kissed him. "Remember, I brought water and food and a flashlight with me out to the ruin."

"No rope," he said.

"If I'd had a rope, I'd have climbed out of there in time to make that call to Bob, and you'd still be in London. And, anyway, who goes hiking with a rope?"

He kissed her again, and it was all he could do not to rip off all their clothes. She slipped her hands under his shirt, placing her palms on the small of his back, and he caught the hem of her shirt. He heard her breathe, give a small gasp of awareness of what came next. But he had her shirt off in seconds. He cast it aside.

She lay back on the couch, and now he saw a touch of self-consciousness in her. He didn't look away. He gazed at her, her skin creamy, almost translucent.

"You're beautiful," he said.

Her hands trembled, but not with nervousness, he decided, as she went to unfasten her bra. "I can't get it…damn…"

Simon tried the clasp, couldn't get it either, and just ripped it. "I'll buy you a new one," he said, tossing it onto the floor with her shirt. But she didn't say anything, and he wasn't sure she could. "I didn't do all those damn Sudoku puzzles on the plane for no reason."

He skimmed his hands over the swell of her breasts. She moaned softly, lying back onto a lacy pillow. He went with her, lost in the taste of her, the feel of her pulse quickening under his touch.

She started to wriggle out of her jeans, and he helped her, drawing them down her slender legs, adding them to the pile on the floor.

"I don't…" She fought for a breath. "I've never…"

"Never, what, Keira?"

"It's so fast. You, me."

"But it's right," he whispered, slipping his hand between her legs, felt her response, saw the same want and need in her eyes that were in him. "Tell me if you want me to stop."

"No. Oh, no." She smiled, moved against him as he eased his fingers into her. "Don't stop."

"Good," he said, and he circled, probed and thrust, until finally she grabbed at his shirt.

"Your turn," she said raggedly, clawing at him.

They dispensed with his clothes, and she drew him back to her, drifting her fingers over his flesh just as he'd dreamed last night and again on the plane, but reality was ever so much better.

"Now," she said, guiding him to her. "Simon...please..."

He didn't hold back, and they joined together in a frenzied haze of desire, heat and hunger. His body was ahead of his mind, responding, giving, taking, never doubting. He felt her body shudder and quake beneath him, her fingers digging into his upper arms as she came and came, then came again. Finally, he let go, thrusting fast and deep and hard, aware of her clutching his hips now, drawing him into her, taking him with her as they rose to the next peak together.

In the stillness that followed, he felt her heart racing and smiled. "It's a wonder we didn't fall off this little couch."

"We managed to fit."

"Oh, yes," he said. "We certainly did."

He saw the flush in her cheeks, and she slipped out from under him, gathered up her clothes, pulled on her rugby shirt and underwear. Her blond hair shone in the city lights pouring through the small windows. Her eyes gleamed with that gorgeous cornflower blue. If she couldn't believe what they'd just done, she didn't show it.

She waved a hand at the bedding. "If you need help with the sofa bed, just let me know. It's still early, I know—my body's not on Irish time or Boston time. I'm beat."

"Keira."

"Don't say anything. Please. This was perfect. No regrets. I just..." She adjusted her shirt, pushed back her hair. "We both need to get some sleep."

"Not going to trust your invisible electric fence tonight?"

She grinned at him. "Not a chance," she said, heading into her bedroom and shutting the door firmly behind her.

Simon noticed a light under her door. Well, he thought, she had to be tired. And he supposed part of her was thinking she needed to figure out what was going on before she got in over her head with him.

Part of him was thinking he should get a flight back to London in the morning.

But regrets?

No regrets, whatsoever, he thought, pulling open the sofa bed. The mattress was hellishly thin, but he'd endured worse conditions than an artist's garret on Beacon Hill. He shook out the sheets and a summer-weight blanket. A white lace sachet fell out, filled with some kind of scented herb. Lavender, he suspected.

And the lace would be Irish.

Of course.

⌐ Chapter 23

Jamaica Plain, Massachusetts
9:30 p.m., EDT
June 23

Abigail brought a glass of white wine outside, thinking she'd be alone, but Bob was at the table with a beer, and Scoop was weeding his garden in the semidarkness of the long June night. Owen was back from dropping Keira and Simon off, but he was inside on a call from a training team in Hawaii.

Scoop stood up from his tomato plants. "Oh, my aching back," he said with a grin.

Bob grunted. "Do you even feel pain?"

"Only when I have to. This thing with Keira—I don't know. I'll be around tomorrow if you need any help."

"Thanks," Bob said, unusually somber.

But Scoop didn't respond, and Abigail could see they were all troubled by the news from Ireland. The mutilated sheep raised the stakes. She'd heard the concern in Seamus Harrigan's voice when he'd relayed Eddie O'Shea's discoveries to her, a marked change from when they'd talked earlier in the day. Clearly, the Irish detective didn't know just what they were confronting.

"I should be the one talking to this Irish cop," Bob said.

Abigail shook her head. "No, you shouldn't be."

He started to say something, but Scoop nodded toward the back steps. "Hey—look who's here."

Fiona O'Reilly jumped off the steps into the yard. "Hi, guys. Owen says he'll be out in a sec." She cheerfully kissed her father on the cheek. "How're you doing, Dad? You look grumpy."

"Hi, kid," Bob said, obviously struggling to dismiss his somber mood. "What're you doing out running around in the middle of the night?"

"It's not even ten o'clock. I told Colm Dermott I was stopping by here, and he asked me to give this to Abigail." Fiona handed a file folder to Abigail. "I went to a lecture he gave at BU tonight on Irish folklore and the sea. It was amazing. I'm seriously considering switching my major to Irish studies."

"There are no more jobs for someone with a degree in Irish studies than a degree in harp," Bob said, teasing her, but he nodded to the folder. "What's that all about?"

Fiona shrugged. "I don't know. Colm didn't say."

"Shouldn't you be calling him Professor Dermott?"

"He said Colm is fine. He and Keira are friends— I love to talk about Irish music with him." She turned to Abigail and Scoop. "I'm majoring in classical harp, but I'm totally into Irish music right now. I still want to visit Keira in Ireland."

"Don't count on it," Bob said.

Fiona rolled her eyes. "I'm nineteen, Dad. I have a passport. I can buy my own ticket and go."

"You're a student. You don't have any money. Besides, Keira's back in Boston, at least for a couple days."

"She is? Why? What happened?"

"Nothing you need to worry about. You have a ride back to your apartment?"

"Yeah," Fiona said, clearly distracted by news of her cousin's sudden return. "I just wanted to drop off the folder. Dad..."

Bob looked up at her. "Is your ride a he?"

"It's a friend."

"The fiddle player in your band?"

Abigail recalled a very cute fiddler the other night at the auction and noticed Fiona blush as she answered her father. "As a matter of fact."

"Why didn't he come in? What's he doing, sitting out in his car waiting for you?"

"Yes—"

"I'll walk you out," Bob said, but he reached over and tapped the folder. "Well?"

Abigail sighed, annoyed. "It's the guest list for the auction at the Garrison house. I ran into Colm earlier today and asked him for it."

"You didn't run into him. You looked him up. Why?"

"You know why, Bob."

A muscle in his jaw worked. Scoop blew out a breath but said nothing.

Fiona frowned. "What's going on? Why's Keira back in Boston? What does this list—" She stopped, then winced. "Oh. I get it. You want to know if the man who died in the Public Garden was on his way to the auction. To see Keira? Is that what you think?"

"Abigail's speculating," Bob said, making it sound like an accusation.

Abigail tried not to let her irritation with him get to her. "It's an informal, incomplete list. Colm says they're not that sophisticated an operation."

Bob got to his feet. "You want to waste your time, fine." He turned to Fiona. "Let's go meet your fiddle player."

"Dad..."

"Did I ever tell you I took fiddle lessons as a kid?" he asked her.

That obviously piqued Fiona's interest, but as she headed out with her father, she glanced back at Abigail with a worried look.

With O'Reilly father and daughter gone, Scoop shook his head at Abigail. "You're playing with fire. We're talking about Bob's family."

"I'm just doing my job." She flopped back in her chair. "I didn't mean for Colm to give these names to Fiona."

"That's the risk you took. Turn the Sarakis case over to someone else, Abigail."

Since Scoop never interfered with her conduct on the job or off, clearly he thought she was seriously out of line. Abigail drank some of her wine. "I'm not on a fishing expedition, and I'm not trying to provoke Bob. You tell me what you'd do, Scoop, under the circumstances."

"I just told you. I'd turn the case over to someone else."

"No, you wouldn't." She paused, feeling a twinge of guilt. "I didn't have a clue about his sister. Makes you wonder what else he hasn't told us, doesn't it?"

"Don't go there."

Abigail didn't back off. "Come on, Scoop. You don't like this situation any more than I do. Bob's sister is a religious hermit, and his niece goes off to Ireland to investigate an old story about a stone angel and is damn near killed—and I've got a dead guy who was obsessed with the devil."

"Would he have been interested in this missing angel?"

"Possibly. His sister and brother-in-law are dealers in fine art and antiques. They have a particular interest in Classical and Medieval works. I don't know where this angel falls—"

"Keira said it could be from Wal-Mart for all she knows."

"Someone messing with her head?"

"Maybe it was part of an animal sacrifice. Grab an angel statue, torture a sheep."

"That's sick," Abigail said. "From what I can gather, Victor Sarakis's interest in evil and the devil was intellectual—I don't see him having anything to do with that sheep."

"Carving up a sheep like that is pretty damn evil, if you ask me," Scoop said. "But angels, devils. Not the same thing."

"Lucifer is a fallen angel. He was an archangel—the highest order of angels."

"Gabriel, Michael. Those guys are archangels, right?"

Abigail smiled. Scoop had a remarkable ability to change the mood of a conversation, depending on what he wanted to accomplish. "Right. Lucifer couldn't accept that he was a creation of God—he wanted to be an autonomous power. He rebelled against God, and God threw him out of heaven."

"Rough," Scoop said.

"In a nutshell, Lucifer becomes Satan. The devil. He's in a perpetual fight with God for supremacy. He recruits others to acts of rebellion against God's will. He demands loyalty above all else, but he doesn't care about being loved or feared—his overriding emotion is hatred, specifically, hatred of God."

Scoop, eminently practical, nodded. "So the rest of us have to choose between God and Satan."

"That's fundamental to the understanding of the devil and evil—we choose. Satan will do anything to get us to choose the path of evil, and therefore him." Abigail thought back to the book Charlotte Augustine had loaned her. "There's a lot more to this subject, but so much hangs on this basic concept."

"I can imagine," Scoop said, then gave Abigail an incisive look. "Do you think your guy's interest in Lucifer had a hand in his death?"

"I don't know."

"A lot of people believe in angels and the devil, Abigail."

"But not everyone has a room filled with flame-spewing, fork-tongued devils," Bob said as he rejoined them, picking up his empty beer bottle off the table with a calm that Abigail found unsettling. "That's what Abigail here is fixed on, Scoop."

She forced herself not to respond, and Scoop just shrugged.

Bob continued. "Keira paints pretty pictures of folktales and flowers. No devils. Her only interest in angels is the one in this crazy story."

"All right," Scoop said, starting for the back steps to his second-floor apartment. "I've had enough. I'm going on up. You two can fight it out."

Abigail didn't blame him. In his place, she'd have fled inside a long time ago.

She opened the folder Fiona had delivered and peeked at the printout of names. Victor Sarakis's name was no secret. Colm could easily have figured out what she was up to and checked the list, deleted names if he'd wanted to. Not that he had any reason, but she realized she hadn't been all that clever in asking him for the list.

"You weren't aware of Keira's reasons for going to Ireland, were you?"

Bob remained on his feet, but he seemed uncertain, which wasn't like him. Finally, he sighed, shaking his head. "Keira doesn't confide in me or anyone else. She's an O'Reilly, after all. She does what she needs to do." He returned to his chair at the table. "That was you last summer in Maine, Abigail. You had to check out that tip on your own. You shut out Scoop, me, your father, the Maine police. It's just that you're not used to shutting people out, and Keira is."

"Maybe she doesn't want to be used to it."

"I don't know about that. She wants to do things, see the world, draw, paint, talk to people. But deep down I think she's worried she's going to end up a recluse like her mother."

"Does she blame herself for her mother's decision to become a religious hermit?"

Bob didn't answer and seemed to stare out at nothing.

"Bob," Abigail said, "do you blame yourself?"

She half expected him to tell her to mind her own business, but he didn't. "Eileen came home from Ireland pregnant with Keira. She was nineteen—quit college. She's never talked about what went on in Ireland. Not to me, not to our folks. As far as I know, she never told a friend. I don't even think she told her husband. He was a great guy. He adopted Keira, loved both of them—" Bob paused, raked his forearm over the top of his head. "Hell of a thing, his death. Freak accident in the Callahan Tunnel. They happen, you know. Freak accidents."

Abigail ignored the jibe. "Do you think Keira latched on to this old story because her mother looked for the village when she was in Ireland and hoped it'd lead her to her father?"

"John Michael Sullivan was her father. Keira missed him like crazy when he died. She was just this little tyke, but you could see it. She kept wanting her mother to read her stories and poems. One after another. Eileen loved it. Helped her, too. They moved to southern New Hampshire, and she opened an art supply store. I got out there when I could." He looked up at the darkening sky. "I don't know what more I could have done."

"Bob, it's not your fault."

He shifted his gaze back to her. "What, that my sister's abandoned her family, her friends, the whole damn world to live by herself in a cabin with no running water, no electricity? Keira doesn't have a phone, but her nutty mother..." He stopped himself. "I respect

Eileen's religious convictions, but this life—it isn't her, Abigail. Her choice isn't easy on the rest of us, but we could live with it if we thought it was her. It's not. She's never married again, but she's always been social—lots of friends, all that. Now she sits in the woods and doesn't see anyone for days on end."

"What about Keira? It must feel as if her mother's rejected her, even if that wasn't her intention."

"We haven't talked that much about it. My opinion, she's not trying to talk Eileen out of the woods so much as trying to figure out what it means about who she is. Keira's pretty as hell, but she— well, you've seen her. She marches to the beat of her own drummer."

"Sounds like an O'Reilly to me," Abigail said with a smile. "Except the pretty part. You're not pretty, Bob."

He grinned at her. "I hope to hell not. You know why Keira went to the police academy? Because she figured that was what an O'Reilly would do."

"She thinks you're disappointed in her for not becoming a police officer?"

"Nah. That's not it. She's pissed she wasted her time at the academy when she could have been drawing pictures of fairies and research-ing crazy old stories."

"Not everyone figures out what they want to do in life at age five. You did. A lot of us take a winding road."

"You're a good detective, Abigail."

His praise caught her off guard. "Thanks."

"I'm sorry you came to the job the way you did, but you'd have found your way to it, eventually."

"I don't believe that. I'd have finished law school if Chris hadn't died. My life changed because of his death."

"What are you doing, Abigail?" he asked suddenly. "If you have a legitimate reason to think your drowning case ties back to Keira, you could turn it over to someone else. But you don't want to, do you? You latched on to it because you wanted to pick a fight with me. Why?"

"I didn't want to pick a fight with you, Bob. I'm just—"

"Just doing your job? That's crap. You've been prickly for a while now, looking for distractions. Something. What's going on?"

"Nothing."

It was true as far as it went. Abigail hadn't spent much time exploring her feelings, but she had to admit that she'd been out of sorts for several weeks.

"Everything okay with you and Owen?"

"Everything's fine. We have unusual lives, that's all."

"Afraid of losing him?"

She shook her head. That wasn't it, she thought. Not even close, but she couldn't put her finger on exactly what was troubling her, either. "I'm not afraid of anything, Bob. Really."

"We're all afraid of something," he said.

"I meant in terms of Owen and me. What are you afraid of?"

He gave her an irreverent grin. "Marriage. All right. I guess I shouldn't give you advice on your relationship with Owen seeing how I have two ex-wives."

But for once, Abigail didn't let him use humor to pull back from a conversation about his emotions. "You got married thinking it'd be forever, didn't you?"

He surprised her by answering. "The first time." He shrugged. "The second time I had a feeling I was biting off more than I could chew, but I did it, anyway."

Abigail knew Bob's first wife—the mother of his three daughters—better, but she'd met his second wife, and she could see his point. His two wives had been polar opposites of each other. He'd overcompensated with the second for what he regarded, as only Bob could, as mistakes with the first.

"You did too hot and too cold," Abigail said. "Now you need to find your Goldilocks woman. The one who's just right."

He snorted. "She's going to have to find me, because I'm not looking. I'm spending my money on a new sound system. Scoop and I are buying a boat." Bob exhaled at the now dark sky. "Abigail...I wish I knew what the hell went on with Keira in Ireland."

"I know, Bob. I do, too."

"This Simon character's a bruiser. Looks as if he's not going anywhere. He'll figure out what to do if Keira's stuck her hand in fire. And she's always been good at taking care of herself." He looked at Abigail, his eyes focused now, alert, sharp. "If you had information that Keira was in trouble, you'd tell me, wouldn't you?"

"Yes. If I had anything. I don't."

"You didn't bite my head off, Abigail. Why not?"

"Scoop reminded me we're talking about your family. Your niece, your sister. Even your daughter."

But Bob responded to her serious tone with a victorious snort. "That's it. I'll be damned. I've got it now." He slapped the table, obviously excited about whatever he'd just figured out. "You're not afraid you won't have kids. You're afraid of what happens if you *do* have kids."

Abigail jumped to her feet, grabbed Colm's folder and her wineglass. She wasn't having this conversation with Bob, not now—not even as a way for him to keep from thinking about his own problems.

He didn't take the hint and kept going. "You're afraid of what kids will mean to you and Owen, your lives. He's on the go all the time, you chew on a case night and day. Kids would change that. You're worried he won't—"

"Good night, Bob."

He waited until she was on the back steps before calling to her. "I'm right."

She ignored him and went inside. She set the wineglass in the sink and opened the folder on the counter, telling herself she was just doing her job and not looking for a distraction. She didn't want to think about Bob's comment. He was good at reading people. Had he just read her?

She scanned the printout of Colm's database, saw that the list was alphabetical by last names. She didn't see a Sarakis or an Augustine. There was one Butler, but not Liam.

Bob had regarded her asking for the names not as thoroughness on her part but as a deliberate thumb in his eye. He didn't want there to be a connection between the auction and Victor Sarakis's death, and Abigail couldn't blame him.

She headed for the bedroom, just wanted to forget about everything.

Owen had the paint can open at his feet. "What's up?" she asked, easing beside him in the doorway.

"I don't know about the color after all. This shade isn't my favorite." He slipped an arm around her waist. "If you love it, I can live with it. Blue's fine."

"Meaning you hate it," she said.

He kissed the top of her head. "That would be one way to put it."

She laughed. "Then let's pick out a color we both like, okay? Owen, honestly—I consider this place as much yours as mine. I want you to speak up and not just go along with me."

"Fair enough." He nodded toward the backyard. "How's Bob?"

"Worried. Hey, did you notice the way Simon and Keira looked at each other tonight?"

"No."

She elbowed him playfully. "You did, too. I don't know that much about Simon. He's okay, though?"

"If you'd seen him in Armenia—" Owen stopped, nodded. "I'd trust him with my life."

"You're careful about who becomes a Fast Rescue volunteer, right?"

"Absolutely. Simon's one of our best."

"I'm still wide awake." She slid out of Owen's embrace and set the top back on the paint can. "Since we're not going to be painting tonight, why don't you tell me what you know about our man to the rescue."

"I have a better idea," Owen said, grabbing her up into his arms and carrying her to the bed.

Abigail didn't object. Given what Owen clearly had in mind, she could definitely wait until morning to talk to him about Simon Cahill.

~Chapter 24

Beacon Hill
Boston, Massachusetts
7:00 a.m., EDT
June 24

Dying for coffee, Keira listened for sounds of life in the next room. She didn't know why she should be self-conscious now, but she was. She pressed her ear to her bedroom door. She couldn't hear breathing, a running faucet, the drip of a coffeepot—nothing. She cracked open the door. She didn't want to wake Simon, but, even more, she didn't want to catch him stretched out temptingly on her sofa bed.

"It's safe to come out," he said with a note of irony in his voice.

She threw open the door. "I'm trying to be polite."

He was dressed—lightweight pants and a dark polo shirt—and sitting at the table with a classic collection of Irish folktales, the sofa bed put away, the linens folded and stacked on a chair. He looked freshly showered and shaved, but she hadn't heard the shower.

"No nightmares?"

She shook her head. "How was your night?"

"I dreamed about fairy princesses."

Keira wasn't going near that one.

He set his book on the table. "These are addictive."

"Aren't they? Sean O'Sullivan put together that collection. He was the chief archivist of the Irish Folklore Commission during its entire existence in the mid-twentieth century. It was a nationwide effort to gather and preserve folktales. Its work is now part of the National Folklore Collection at University College Dublin—literally millions of pages of transcripts, tens of thousands of photographs and audio and video recordings. It's incredible, really."

"Quite an undertaking."

"Sean O'Sullivan was from the Beara Peninsula."

But Simon rose. "Let's go see your storyteller."

Keira grabbed her various sketches as she and Simon headed out, fetching her car and stopping for coffee and muffins on the way to South Boston. She called Patsy on his cell phone, but didn't get an answer. "She goes to church most mornings. My grandmother did, too, especially in the last few years before she died."

"Did your grandparents always live in South Boston?" Simon asked.

She shook her head. "No, they moved to Florida when my grandfather retired from the police department. He's still there." She smiled, thinking about him. "He keeps trying to get me to learn golf. He loves the weather in Florida—he can play year-round. I've told him I've seen golfers playing in gale-force winds in Ireland."

"If you wait for perfect weather, you wouldn't play much."

Keira enjoyed the normalcy of their conversation. She pointed out the simple duplex where her grandparents had raised her mother and uncle, imagined them on just such a warm early summer morning.

They parked in front of Patsy's house, one of only a handful of single-family houses in the neighborhood, and Keira rang the doorbell. During their first visit, Patsy had explained that she'd managed to keep her home after she was widowed at a young age because her husband had insisted on having good life insurance. She'd worked various office jobs over the years, but it was that insurance that had made the difference—she'd wanted Keira to know.

When there was no answer, she knocked. Again, no response from inside the house. "She should be home from church by now— it's just up the street."

"Maybe she's out back," Simon said.

They headed up the sidewalk and pulled open an unlocked, rickety white wooden gate between Patsy's house and the looming triple-decker next door, making their way back to a tiny, fenced-in yard crammed with bird feeders, birdhouses, leprechauns and gnomes. But Patsy wasn't there, either.

Keira climbed the steps onto the back porch, where a lone wind chime dinged once in the slight stir of a breeze. She raised her hand to knock on the back door, but saw that it wasn't latched all the way. "Simon…"

He touched her hand. "Let me go first." He opened the door. "Mrs. McCarthy? My name's Simon Cahill. I'm with Keira Sullivan."

"Hi, Mrs. McCarthy," Keira called, trying to sound cheerful.

She followed Simon into the kitchen, half expecting to find Patsy at the table with a cup of tea. Instead, her teapot, decorated with green shamrocks, sat on the counter. Magnets of American flags held an array of postcards of Irish scenes to her refrigerator. In their handful of meetings, Keira had enjoyed Patsy's sense of humor. Patsy was comfortable with her romanticized view of an Ireland she knew more now from memory and stories than from experience.

"Her bedroom's upstairs?" Simon asked.

"I think so." Keira nodded to the hall door. "That'll take us to the dining room and living room. There's a small study, too. The stairs are in the front entry."

Simon gave a curt nod. "Stay close, okay?"

Halfway down the hall, he stopped in the open doorway to the dining room, and when she stood next to him, Keira saw why. Scores of angels were set out on Patsy's lace-covered oval table, all facing the door as though to greet whoever walked in. They ranged in size from barely an inch to two feet tall and were constructed of a variety of materials—porcelain, pottery, silver, copper, gold, wood, glass, wax and origami paper.

Three silver-framed photographs of a pretty blond-haired girl stood among the angels. One appeared to be at her First Communion. In another, she was teetering on roller-skates at about age twelve.

In the third, she was standing next to a teenage Bob O'Reilly, both dressed to the nines for what had to be a high school prom.

Simon pointed to a prayer card propped up against a multicolored glass angel.

Deirdre Ita McCarthy.

"She must be Patsy's daughter. Oh, Simon. She was just nineteen when she died. I had no idea. Patsy never said a word."

"Were these angels and pictures here when you visited her?"

"No—none of them."

"We need to find her," Simon said.

Keira took shallow breaths, her tension mounting as they moved down the hall. When they reached the study, Simon swore and spun around quickly, grabbing her around the waist, stopping her. "Keira, don't look, sweetheart."

She clutched his arms. "Simon, what is it?"

"Your friend's dead."

"Oh, no…no…" Keira cried out, lunging toward the study, but Simon kept his arms tight around her. She saw blood spattered on the white woodwork. Her eyes filled with tears. "Are you sure—"

"I'm sure. There's nothing we can do for her, Keira. She's been dead at least a day." He kissed the top of her head. "I'm so sorry."

"Simon, the blood…" She forced herself not to hyperventilate. "It wasn't a heart attack, was it?"

"No."

"I have to see."

"Yeah. I know." He eased his hold on her. "Just stay out here in the hall. It's best we don't contaminate the scene, and it's a tough sight. A lot of blood. We need to call the police."

Her fingers digging into his arms, Keira peered past him into the study and saw Patsy sprawled on the floor in the middle of a hooked rug, her pastel pink sweater drenched in blood.

"Was it—can you tell—" She gulped in air, pulling herself together as she loosened her grip on Simon. "Can you tell if she suffered? If she was tortured, like the sheep…"

"She wasn't tortured."

"There was time for whoever killed the sheep to get back here and…" Keira broke off, unable to finish the thought. "There's a phone in the kitchen."

But he was already dialing 911 on his cell phone, his arm dropping to her waist as they returned to the kitchen. Keira was reeling, her head spinning as he provided a crisp, detailed report to the dispatcher. She remembered the dead man in the Public Garden just a few days ago, pictured the blood and entrails at the ruin and ran out to the back porch, half tripping down the steps to the yard.

The priest from the other night in Boston was there, white-faced and motionless. "Father Palermo," Keira whispered, choking back tears.

She could see he knew something horrible had happened. "Mrs. McCarthy didn't come to mass this morning. I walked over here to check on her. It's the second morning in a row she's missed mass. It's not—" His voice faltered. "It's not like her. Miss Sullivan…"

"I'm sorry, Father. I'm afraid Patsy's dead."

Keira realized how blunt her words sounded. She didn't know if she should have told him even that much. She realized the police would want to talk to him, and, in any case, she didn't want to be the one to describe the scene.

He gaped at her, obviously trying to absorb the news. "What—"

But Fiona appeared on the concrete alley-like walk to Patsy's backyard. Her blond hair was pulled back neatly, and she had her Irish harp with her, tucked under one arm as she stared, clearly in dread, at Father Palermo and then her older cousin.

"Fiona," Keira said, "what are you doing here?"

Her eyes—that O'Reilly cornflower blue—widened in obvious fear, and she about-faced and took off back out to the street.

Keira could hear police sirens in the distance as she turned to the priest. "I have to go."

He nodded, and she charged after her cousin.

∽ Chapter 25

South Boston, Massachusetts
9:30 a.m., EDT
June 24

Abigail jumped out of her car just down the street from Patsy McCarthy's house and raced up the sidewalk, intercepting Bob before he could get to the door. She leaped in front of him. "You can't, Bob," she said. "You know you can't go in there—"

His eyes were blue steel. "Get out of my way, Abigail."

She didn't budge. He was a senior BPD detective. If he wanted to see the scene, the BPD officers posted outside would let him in. But it wasn't a good idea. Abigail had been at her desk at BPD Headquarters, doing paperwork to mollify her partner and get her head screwed back on straight, when word spread that a seventy-nine-year-old woman had been knifed to death in South Boston. That kind of outrage always got to everyone. She'd known instantly, in her gut, that it was Keira Sullivan's storyteller.

Then came the news that Bob's niece was the one who'd found the body.

And his eldest daughter was there.

Even her partner was shaken. Tom Yarborough was an ambitious SOB. Twenty-nine, and he thought he should be running the department. But he'd understood when Abigail had abandoned her computer and charged out to the scene.

Police vehicles crowded the street. Some of Patsy McCarthy's neighbors had ventured out in front of their houses in shock.

"Bob," Abigail said, "you can't investigate this one. Stay out of it. You'd be telling me the same thing—"

"Where's my daughter?" His eyes didn't change, remained hard, flinty. "Where's Keira?"

"Let me find out, okay? I imagine they're with the responding officers."

He looked past her to the simple house. "What the hell was Fiona doing here?"

"I don't know, Bob," Abigail said, feeling his anguish despite his rigid self-control. "I just got here myself."

"I'm going in there, Abigail. Going to try and stop me?"

Abigail sighed, stepping away from him. "No."

In his position, she'd do the same. She'd done the same eight years ago when she'd flung herself at her dead husband's body.

She followed him past the patrol officers posted at the door who didn't, as she'd expected, question his presence. No one would.

They worked their way back to the study, where Patsy McCarthy's tiny body lay on a blood-soaked rug. "She hooked that rug herself thirty years ago," Bob said in a near whisper. "Look at it. It's like new. It's a scene from Ireland—a farm, a couple of sheep."

"Bob..." Abigail had to push back a rush of emotion. "I'm sorry."

"Not your fault. You didn't kill her."

The grim-faced lead detectives—experienced men Bob and Abigail both knew well—said it looked as if she'd been stabbed twice.

Once for the blood. Once for the kill.

"This was no way for an old woman to die," Bob said softly. "For anyone."

He continued down the hall, and Abigail was struck by his easy familiarity with the house. She pictured him running through there as a kid and couldn't imagine his pain now. But he stopped at the dining room, and Abigail grimaced. More detectives were in the room, carefully documenting the strange scene.

"Damn, Bob," Abigail whispered, her eyes fixed on one of a trio of pictures in the middle of dozens and dozens of angel figurines on the table. "That's you. The girl—"

"Patsy didn't set up this stuff. Her killer did."

He turned around and stalked back up the hall.

Abigail charged after him, her heart racing.

Out on the street, Bob stood under a scraggly maple tree and stuffed a stick of gum into his mouth. "Patsy believed in fairies." He didn't look at Abigail as she stood next to him in the thin shade. "She wouldn't admit it, but she did. Told me she'd hear the cry of a banshee just before someone close to her died. She said the first time she could remember hearing one was when as a little girl in Ireland when her kid sister died of some dread disease."

"I could do without hearing a banshee," Abigail said.

"Yeah. Patsy told me that quaint little story when I was nine or ten. Scared the living hell out of me." Bob chewed hard on his gum. "She was a simple woman, Abigail. She never asked for much out of life. She never got much, either."

"We'll find out what happened. Who did this to her."

"You know how many unsolved homicides are stacked up on my desk?

There are no guarantees. Save the platitudes for someone who doesn't know any better." He looked back toward the house, lace curtains in the front windows. "Sorry. I didn't mean to bite your head off."

"Forget it."

"I'm going to find Fiona and Keira."

"If there's anything I can do—"

"I'll let you know."

Abigail saw his daughter and his niece coming around from the backyard and left Bob to them. She returned to the house and made her way to the kitchen, where she found Simon Cahill chatting with a couple of patrol officers. He struck her as remarkably self-possessed for someone who'd just found an old woman murdered in her own home. Then again, she thought, she'd observed that same control in Owen. She didn't know if their search-and-rescue work developed such composure, or if they could do that work because they were naturally that way. A little of both, maybe.

"You must be wishing you'd stayed in London," she said.

"No sense wasting time wishing for something that can't happen. Bob O'Reilly's here?"

"Outside with Fiona and Keira."

Simon waited a half beat, then said, "You and O'Reilly are right up to the line separating personal and professional business."

"I'm up to it," she said. "Bob's crossed it."

His very green eyes leveled on her. Then he flipped a business-size card at her. "This was under Patsy's teapot." He nodded to the counter behind him. "There."

Abigail winced when she saw it was one of Bob's cards.

"I figured I'd give it to you," Simon said.

She regarded him with new insight. It wasn't everyone who'd notice a business card under a teapot with a dead woman in the next room, much less think to pocket it and give it to her. "Simon," she said, "do you mind telling me who the hell you are?"

"Stewing about me isn't going to help find whoever killed Patsy McCarthy."

He headed out through the back door. Abigail started to follow him and make him talk, but two more detectives came down the hall. She debated giving them Bob's card. Had he given it to Patsy? Did his daughter have one, and had she given it to her? Keira?

Abigail knew they weren't her questions to ask or answer.

If she'd been one of the detectives walking toward her right now, she'd want the card. Period. No games from a colleague.

But she tucked the card into her pocket. "You guys need to talk to Bob," she told the detectives. "Ask him when he last saw the victim."

"Abigail—"

"Just do it," she said and walked past them up the hall.

Fiona was still crying, her nose red, her cheeks raw, a tearstained tissue squished in her hand. She'd wiped her eyes, cried some more, wiped her eyes again. "Don't leave me, Keira," she said, sniffling as her father approached them. "Dad's going to—he's not going to understand."

"Give him a chance, but don't worry. I'm not going anywhere."

Her uncle was stoic, but Keira had learned to read the little signs and could see he was shaken—and furious, she thought. Apoplectic under his outward calm. A woman he'd known all his life murdered in her own home. His daughter and niece on the scene. He was a cop—an experienced detective—and he'd feel as if it was his fault, somehow, that he could have done something, stepped in before some maniac slipped into Patsy's house and killed her.

Keira could identify with such guilt. She couldn't shake the feeling that she'd set into motion the events that had led to the horror in the house behind her.

But her uncle held his emotions in check as he greeted his daughter. "Hey, kid." His tone was gentle, even kind. "How're you doing?"

"Oh, Dad. I feel so bad."

"I know. It's an awful thing."

Fiona nodded, tears welling in her eyes. "I liked her so much. She reminded me of Grandma with her Irish accent."

"They both were something. Should have seen them when we were kids, the two of them standing out here on the street laughing over little things. The weather, a new recipe. They'd argue, too. Remember how your grandma could argue?"

"She hated to lose," Fiona said, sniffling as she tried to smile.

"Patsy was the same way. We'll get you down to Florida, and your grandpa can tell you stories about the two of them. He thought Patsy was a loon, but he liked her."

Fiona continued to cry, and when Bob touched her shoulder, she fell into his arms and sobbed into his chest. He glared over the top of her head at Keira. "You want to tell me what the hell's going on? Did you introduce Patsy and Fiona—"

"No, Dad," Fiona said. "It wasn't Keira."

But her cousin sank against Keira's car, shaking with silent sobs. Keira stuffed her own grief down deep and explained what she knew, what she herself had just learned from Fiona. "Fiona's taking Irish music lessons a couple of blocks from here. She started after college let out for the summer. She walked over one day to see where you grew up and ran into Patsy at her church. Patsy reminded her of Gran—she wasn't hiding anything from you—"

"I didn't know about the lessons," Bob said, cutting her off. "I didn't know about Patsy. In my book, that's hiding something."

Fiona stood up straight, her face red from crying. "Dad—"

"You recognized Patsy when you saw her with Keira the other night in Boston."

"I never said I didn't."

He pointed a finger at her. "Don't bullshit me, Fi. Not now. I'm sorry she's dead. I'm sorry you're upset. But what you have to do right now is make sure you've told me every damn thing you know. Everything. Don't leave out anything, no matter how small or stupid or embarrassing you think it is. Understood?"

Fiona nodded, but instead of her father's stern words beating her down, they seemed to strengthen her. "I can't get my head around what was done to her, Dad. It's—it's beyond comprehension."

"Yeah. It is." He turned to Keira, his gaze unrelenting, like nothing she'd ever seen in him before. "What about you and Simon? When did you get here?"

"Around eight-thirty. I tried calling, I rang the doorbell. When I didn't get an answer, we went around back—"

"Hell, Keira. The body in the Public Garden, the mess in Ireland— and now this."

"I don't like it, either," Keira said.

Fiona sobbed, lifted her head. "Mrs. McCarthy was the sweetest woman, Dad. How could anyone hurt her?"

"I don't know, Fi, but it doesn't matter if she was sweet or a pain in the neck, she didn't deserve to die this way."

"I didn't see her, Dad. Mrs. McCarthy. Keira stopped me before I—"

"One good thing, anyway. Was it always just the two of you when you visited, Fi? No plumber, electrician, mailman, neighbor?"

"It was always just the two of us. I saw her maybe a half-dozen times, usually after my lesson, sometimes before—I'd catch her on her way home from church. That's what I was hoping to do this morning. She liked to talk, and if I had somewhere else I needed to be..." Fiona's eyes filled with fresh tears. "That's awful of me, isn't it, Dad?"

"No, it's not awful, Fi. Patsy would understand. She was nineteen once herself."

Fat tears spilled down Fiona's cheeks. "I walked over here one day after my lesson to see your old neighborhood. I went past Saint Ita's—your old church—and some of the church women were setting up for a bazaar in the parish hall. An angel bazaar. They had angel everything—food, decorations, knitted items, music." Fiona talked at a lightning speed, as if she needed to get everything out in one breath. "Patsy and some of the other women were displaying their collections of angel figurines. Patsy's was the best by far. Have you seen it, Dad? It's unbelievable."

"She collected angels for a long time."

"Father Palermo said some of them might be valuable. I hope... Dad, you don't think someone was trying to rob her, do you?"

"Too early to say. Did you go to this bazaar?"

Fiona nodded, perking up slightly. "I bought two handmade angel Christmas ornaments for presents, and I had a piece of angel food cake with green frosting."

Her father gave a halfhearted grin. "Gross."

"It wasn't that bad. Dad, Patsy had all of Keira's books—she loved them." Fiona went pale again. "I can't believe what's happened."

"I know, kid. It's a tough one." Bob turned to Keira, his expression showing more of his anguish now and less of his fury. "Were you already in touch with Patsy when Fiona got to know her?"

Keira nodded. "Patsy e-mailed me around the same time, but she never mentioned she knew Fiona." Keira hesitated, then added, "She never mentioned she had a daughter, either. Bob, the angels, your prom picture—"

"I need to get Fi out of here," he said.

Keira gave up on trying to pry information out of him. Now wasn't the time. Fiona pulled away from her father, some color returning to her cheeks. "I'm meeting my friends at the Garrison house for a practice session. Dad, I just want to play my music right now. Please..."

"No problem, kid. I'll drop you off. Keira?"

"I'll wait for Simon."

"Thought you might." But his attempt at humor—normalcy— faltered, and he said, "I know this is hard, Keira. I'm sorry you have to deal with it. We'll talk later, okay?"

"Sure."

"You know how to reach me if you need me."

"Yeah. Thanks."

Keira watched him walk up the street with Fiona. He was the one rock of her life—her tight-lipped, emotionally repressed uncle who'd never told her he'd taken his neighbor's long-dead daughter to their high school prom. What, Keira wondered, had happened to Deirdre McCarthy?

Her head ached, and she was wiped out and yet, at the same time, still keyed up, replaying in her mind walking through Patsy's house, finding her body, then going out into the yard and seeing Fiona and Father Palermo. Waiting for the police to arrive. Noticing how Simon, who'd dealt with countless disaster scenes in his search-and-rescue work, had met the responding officers with such calm and professionalism.

She looked around for him now, but saw only cops, crime scene technicians and a few reporters setting up, trying to figure out what was going on and whether it merited full coverage.

The detective who'd taken her statement earlier joined her in the shade. He was a tall, gray-haired, serious man she didn't recognize from any social gatherings at her uncle's place. "I just spoke to Detective Browning," he said, nodding back toward Patsy's house. "She told me you ran into trouble in Ireland. Mind telling me what happened?"

As if it mattered if she did mind. Nonetheless, she appreciated the gesture. "Not at all. Can I ask you a quick question first? I didn't realize Patsy McCarthy had a daughter until this morning. Do you know how she died?"

"You're an O'Reilly, all right. You like to ask the questions."

"Does that mean you're not going to give me an answer?"

He sighed. "I don't know how she died, Ms. Sullivan. It's one of the things we're looking into."

Because of the prom picture and the prayer card, she thought, but before she could ask a follow-up question, the detective—Boucher was his name, she remembered now—steered her back to the subject at hand. Ireland, and what had happened there.

⌒ Chapter 26

Simon found the priest walking from one colorful gnome and leprechaun to another in Patsy McCarthy's backyard, as if they had the
power to tell him who had killed their owner. "I encouraged her to
share her angels with the rest of the congregation," he said, more
to himself than to Simon. "We had a bazaar a few weeks ago—it
was my idea. I helped her get all her angels out, pack them up, haul
them to the church, unpack them, pack them up again..." He
sighed, looked up, his face shiny with tears and sweat. "It was a
chore, Mr. Cahill. I don't understand why she'd go to the trouble
of taking them out again. The police asked me—I didn't know
what to say."

"We don't know that it was her," Simon said.

"Ah. I see what you're suggesting." His skin turned even more
ashen. "You mean her killer could have done it."

"I mean her killer almost certainly did do it."

"That's..." Palermo swallowed visibly. "That's hard to accept, Mr. Cahill, isn't it?"

"When did Mrs. McCarthy start collecting angels?"

"Her daughter started the collection as a little girl. After Deirdre's death, Patsy kept adding to it as a way to stay close to her daughter. I wasn't here then, of course, but she told me. She loved all her angels, but the ones original to Deirdre's collection were her particular favorites." Palermo patted the head of a three-foot-tall gnome and tried to smile. "Did you ever wonder who actually buys these things and puts them in their gardens? Patsy had such a sense of mischief about her."

"That's what I understand," Simon said.

But the priest's eyes filled with tears, and he turned away. "We all enjoyed the bazaar. It was a fine day. Patsy made Irish bread and apple crumble. It was as if...I'm not sure I can explain. It was as if her daughter was there with her."

"Father—"

"Deirdre was murdered, Mr. Cahill."

Somehow, Simon wasn't surprised.

"It's a horrible story. Patsy never told me. I looked it up. Deirdre was kidnapped on her way home from work. She was missing for several weeks—her body washed ashore not far from here." Palermo moved on to a small figure of a lithe pink fairy. "She was tortured and sexually assaulted."

"Her killer?"

"A road worker named Stuart Fuller. He'd moved in a few blocks from here not long before he kidnapped Deirdre—he didn't grow up in the neighborhood."

"He was caught, then?"

Palermo shook his head. "No. As it turns out, he committed

suicide before the police could arrest him. Patsy didn't like to talk about what happened, except to say she believed with all her heart and soul that Deirdre is an angel."

"Did she tell you she was in touch with Keira Sullivan?"

"Patsy adored Keira's illustrations and couldn't wait to meet her." He smiled suddenly, some of his color returning. "She loved the idea of being part of one of Keira's books. I think she enjoyed the attention, to be honest."

"She never discussed her daughter's murder with Keira, either."

"That doesn't surprise me, frankly," Palermo said. "Patsy believed Deirdre had the gift of prophecy—that angels spoke to her and guided her throughout her short life. There's a famous story about Saint Ita—Deirdre's namesake—and Saint Brendan, another famous Irish saint. Do you know it, Mr. Cahill?"

Simon shook his head, and he noticed Keira on the concrete walk, motionless.

"Brendan was one of Saint Ita's students—he came to her convent in Ireland as a tiny boy. She was like a foster mother to him. Even after he left, he would come back to visit and ask her advice. He was an explorer. Some say he came to North America a thousand years before Columbus." Palermo choked up, then smiled through his tears. He seemed unaware of Keira's presence. "He's known as Brendan the Navigator. Doesn't that have a nice sound to it?"

"My father's name was Brendan," Simon said, just to break some of the priest's tension. "He was something of a wanderer himself."

"Was he?" Palermo took a breath, got hold of himself. "Brendan once asked Ita what were the three things that most pleased God, and she told him a pure heart, a simple life and generosity."

"Not a bad answer."

Palermo smiled suddenly. "Yes, indeed. Then Brendan asked what three things most displeased God, and Ita said a hateful tongue, a love of evil and greed."

"What do you think, Father?"

"I think that Saint Ita was a wise woman, but I hope she never knew the kind of person who could do what was done to Patsy, or to Patsy's daughter that terrible summer thirty years ago. How can we even comprehend such acts of depravity and evil?" But he didn't wait for a response. "I haven't been in this parish that long, but sometimes I feel as if I knew Deirdre myself. Her murder lingers in the lives of the people she knew, but so does her spirit."

Simon saw Keira turn pale and knew she'd put it all together—that Deirdre McCarthy was murdered the summer Eileen O'Reilly came home from Ireland pregnant.

He started to go her, but Keira bolted back toward the street.

Simon turned to Palermo. "Excuse me, Father——"

"Of course," Palermo said. "Please tell Keira how sorry I am."

"I will."

By the time Simon reached the street, Keira had jumped into her car and sped away. He dug out his cell phone. Abigail Browning and Bob O'Reilly had left, and no way was Simon asking one of the other cops for a lift.

He called Owen. "I could use a ride."

"I heard about Patsy McCarthy. Simon, Abigail called——"

"She's onto me, I know. She won't care that I'm in law enforcement or that I work for her father. She'll care that I've been like a son to him since I was a kid and he never told her, and she'll care that you've known for eighteen months and, likewise, haven't told her."

"She's not just suspicious, Simon," Owen said calmly. "She knows."

Simon tried to smile. "Not one to underestimate, that Abigail. All the more reason to set your wedding date. Get her thinking about picking out flowers instead of whether or not she should trust you."

"She can trust me. That's not an issue. None of this is anything you need to worry about right now. What about her father?"

"No worries. I'll deal with Director March. Just come pick me up."

"Where are you?"

Simon told him and disconnected, then dialed Will Davenport in London. "Up for a trip to Ireland?"

"I can leave in ten minutes."

"You didn't even ask what's going on."

"All right. What's going on?"

Simon gave him the short version. "When you get to Ireland, talk to a Garda detective named Seamus Harrigan. Find Eddie O'Shea. Do this, Will, and we're even. I mean it."

"This Keira Sullivan—"

"Don't go there."

"I looked up her Web site. Very pretty. You can always use my place in Scotland for the wedding."

Will's place in Scotland was a castle. "Keep me posted on what you find out in Ireland."

Simon tucked his cell phone back in his pocket. His calls were done.

Now it was time to learn more about the murder of Deirdre McCarthy thirty years ago.

～ Chapter 27

Back Bay
Boston, Massachusetts
11:00 a.m., EDT
June 24

Keira ran up the three flights of narrow stairs to Colm Dermott's office in an ivy-covered Back Bay building overlooking the Charles River. His door was open, and she burst in, set the Ireland sketches on the corner of his desk and forced back tears. "I'll explain everything," she said, "but first I need to borrow your phone."

"Keira, dear heaven—"

"Patsy McCarthy's been murdered. Colm…" She was breathing hard after running up the stairs. "It's bad."

"Here." He thrust his cell phone at her. "Call whoever you need to."

She went to the window, watching a lone sculler on the river as she dialed Simon's number. He'd insisted on giving it to her as they'd waited for the police to arrive at Patsy's house, never mind that she didn't own a phone herself.

He picked up on the first ring, but she spoke before he could. "I can come get you."

"Too late," he said. "Owen beat you to it. I dropped him off on Beacon Street and borrowed his car. I figure if you and I are going to be hanging out together, it's easier if I have my own car."

"I'm sorry I took off—"

"Don't," he said, surprising her with his intensity. "I just want to know you're okay."

"I am. I'm at Colm's office." She noticed the sculler lift his oars out of the water and sit back, coasting a moment, as if he just wanted to enjoy the perfect Boston June morning. "I didn't know about Patsy's daughter."

"So I gathered."

"She was killed the summer my mother went to Ireland. They were the same age. My uncle took Patsy's daughter to the prom. They all grew up together, Simon, and I never had a clue. I didn't know Deirdre McCarthy even existed."

"It sounds as if it was a particularly horrific murder," Simon said, as if that explained thirty years of silence.

Keira turned away from the window. Colm nervously held the sketch of the black dog in midair, but he was looking at her, as if she might suddenly crack into little pieces. She tried to relax some of the tension in her muscles as she continued speaking to Simon. "I keep thinking there's a subtext to everything Patsy told me over the past few weeks. Something I've missed. I videotaped her telling the story—Colm has a copy."

"The police will want it," Simon said.

"I brought the original with me to Ireland. I don't know if this is on the tape, but I remember Patsy saying she was worried she was talking too much, trusting too easily. I didn't think anything of it at the time. I assumed she meant me and just had the jitters over being taped. That's natural—it all seems so exciting until someone sticks a camera in your face." Keira looked down again at the river, but her sculler was out of sight. "Simon, what if Patsy was talking about someone else?"

"Keira, just tell the police everything, and let them do their job. You've done all you can at this point."

"I know, but what if Patsy told someone else that story—someone who decided to look for the ruin and the angel, and then turned around and killed her?"

Simon didn't answer.

"You've thought about this, too," Keira said. "If it's the same person who killed that sheep in Ireland, left me trapped in the ruin—maybe even tried to kill me—and took the stone angel, then Patsy would have known who it was. Murdering her kept her from telling anyone."

"Whoever was responsible obviously wanted a lot of blood," Simon said.

Keira felt her mouth go dry. "Just like with the sheep."

"I'll tell the police here and in Ireland about the tape—"

"Where are you right now? At the Garrison house?"

A half-beat's pause. "I'm at BPD Headquarters."

"You're looking into Deirdre McCarthy's murder. How—" But she stopped herself, then sighed. "I'll be damned. You're a cop, aren't you? What are you—a fed, right? ATF, FBI, the marshals?"

"It's complicated."

"Are you a spook? What would happen if I Googled you? Would my computer blow up? Would I end up on some watch list?" But Simon didn't answer, and she knew he wasn't going to. "You know the FBI director is Abigail's father, right?"

"Yes. I know."

His tone told her everything. "Oh. I get it now. You're an FBI agent. Do Owen and Abigail know?"

"Focus on your own situation. We'll talk later."

She pictured his vivid green eyes and could almost feel her fingers in his hair. She'd made love to him with such abandon last night. But as close as she'd felt to him then—even now—she realized she didn't know Simon at all. He was charming, good-looking and very sexy, but also controlled—and he was a federal agent.

"You have secrets, Simon."

"Everyone has secrets."

She thought of her mother, her uncle—Patsy. And a teenage girl murdered thirty years ago. "I'm driving out to see my mother after I talk to Colm. Simon, I'm sorry you had to be there this morning, but I can't imagine having had to find Patsy without you."

"Keira…" But he didn't go on.

"Good disaster planner that you are," she said, "I figure you'll want directions to my mother's cabin."

He sighed softly. "I could fall in love with you, you know."

Her heart jumped, and she smiled, even as she bit back more tears. "I'd like that," she said, and gave him directions to her mother's cabin.

When she hung up, Colm exhaled and rushed to her, hugged her fiercely, then stood back. "Keira," he said, his voice cracking. "Dear heaven, tell me everything."

He listened intently, without interruption, as she filled him in.

When she finished, he shook his head with obvious emotion. "I'm so sorry. What a grisly business. Of course I'll find the tape of Patsy telling the story. I haven't watched it yet myself, but I'll get it to the police straight away."

She jotted down her uncle's phone number, then added Simon's. "If you need anything, call my uncle or Simon, okay? I don't have Abigail Browning's number, but feel free to get in touch with her, too—"

"I will, indeed. And I'll take a closer look at your sketches," Colm said, then added briskly, "If I can be of any assistance at all in finding this bloody bastard—"

"I just don't want anyone else to get hurt. If I'm responsible in any way—"

"Don't do this to yourself, Keira," Colm said. "Let the police sort out what's going on. You've done all you can. Just be with your family and friends now and remember the good times you had with Patsy."

She smiled at him. "I like hearing you say her name with your Irish accent."

He kissed her on the cheek. "Happier times are ahead, Keira."

"It's hard to believe that right now. Well, I should go. I need to see my mother and tell her about Patsy."

Colm grabbed his cell phone and tucked it into her hand. "Take it." His eyes sparked, and he winked at her. "I remember this Simon Cahill from the auction, and I have a feeling you'd be wise to stay in touch with him."

Keira felt a rush of heat. "Probably so. Thank you for the phone."

Colm gave her a quick grin. "I'll be taking up a collection for you for a phone of your own."

"I don't blame you. You're a good friend, Colm."

She ran down the stairs and out to the street, jumping in her car and heading out to Storrow Drive and onto Route 2. In less than two hours, she'd be at her mother's cabin.

~ Chapter 28

Boston Police Department Headquarters
Roxbury, Massachusetts
11:25 a.m., EDT
June 24

Simon stood in a small, hot room in the sprawling headquarters of the Boston Police Department with the file of Deirdre McCarthy's murder in front of him and Norman Estabrook, soon to be in federal custody, on the phone.

"You're a dead man, Cahill," Estabrook said.

Simon didn't have time to listen to threats. "Yeah, whatever."

"I trusted you."

That was a lie. Estabrook didn't trust anyone. Simon didn't care.

Abigail Browning materialized in the doorway of the room where the BPD had led him, her arms crossed, her remarkable self-control firmly in place. He doubted now was the time to tell her how much she reminded him of her father.

Estabrook wasn't finished. "I have feds swarming over me right now because of you."

"Trust me now, Norm." Estabrook hated being called Norm. "Give yourself up peacefully, or they'll kill you."

"I didn't get to be a billionaire by giving up. You're dead, Cahill."

"How'd you find out about me?"

"Process of elimination. *You* trust *me* now. You're dead. Dead, dead, dead."

Estabrook could be remarkably petulant, but he typically wasn't one for empty threats. He was a portly, bland-looking, dangerous forty-year-old who thrived on risk and beating the odds. But Simon wasn't worried. After months of helping Estabrook plan, execute and survive his adventures—of insinuating himself into Estabrook's life—Simon was glad to be rid of him. Estabrook had decided to cross the line from ultrarich thrill seeker to international criminal. No one had done it to him.

"First I kill John March," Estabrook said. "Then I kill you."

"Send me a postcard from prison. It'll be your biggest adventure ever."

Estabrook sputtered, and Simon disconnected. He'd had enough.

John March's daughter walked into the room. "Well, Special Agent Cahill, should I ask what that was all about?" But she just nodded to the file. "I see you and I are here for the same reason. What do we have?"

"An ugly murder, Detective."

She picked up Deirdre McCarthy's high school graduation picture. "Sweet-looking kid, wasn't she? No wonder she ended up collecting angels."

Simon nodded. Deirdre was pretty, but it was her kindness that people who knew her had told police most defined her. If there were demon-fighting angels, Deirdre McCarthy wouldn't have been one.

Her mother, on the other hand...Patsy McCarthy had calmly predicted to more than one investigator that she would die fighting the devil with her bare hands. Simon thought of the tiny, crumpled body on the hooked rug and wondered if her premonition had come to fruition.

Abigail set the picture back down. "I see you're armed," she said.

"I had to look like a proper FBI agent before I came in here." But Simon couldn't pull off irreverence. He'd read the summary of the exhaustive investigation into Deirdre's kidnapping, torture, rape and murder. Now her mother was dead, slain in her own home. He looked again at Deirdre's picture, taken on a day when kids thought about their lives ahead of them. And a year later, she was dead. "Her killer stalked her for at least two weeks before he grabbed her. He took pictures of her—police found them in his apartment afterward."

"Deirdre didn't know she was being stalked?"

"She never filed a police report or said anything to her mother."

"Would she have?"

Simon didn't hesitate. "She'd have told her mother. It was just the two of them. She was a sweet kid who told her mother everything."

"Nobody tells anyone everything." Abigail swallowed visibly as she continued to flip through the file. "She was kidnapped on the summer solstice. No wonder Bob hates this time of year. I had no idea about this poor girl—not a damn inkling. He never said a word."

"He wouldn't. It's not how he's wired."

She sucked in a sharp breath but didn't argue. "How long did this monster have her?"

"Three weeks. You don't need to read the file to know what he did to her."

"No, I imagine I don't."

"Killing her was an afterthought. Either he just got tired of her, or he knew she couldn't live much longer. He slit her throat and dumped her body in Boston Harbor."

"Bob never even hinted..." Abigail's expression tightened as she came to the photographs taken after Deirdre's body had washed ashore. "Eight years I've worked here, and I've never heard of this case." She shut the file. "The killer—Stuart Fuller. Who was he?"

"A twenty-four-year-old road worker. He wasn't on the radar—no record. He grew up in a rough family. The father was in and out of prison and beat the hell out of his wife, and she beat the hell out of their kids. They lived all over the place. Stuart moved to South Boston to get away from his family two months before he kidnapped Deirdre."

Abigail had no visible reaction. "How did the police find him?"

"They didn't. He set himself on fire and jumped in Boston Harbor a week after Deirdre's body turned up."

"It was the right guy?"

"Police found overwhelming evidence—"

"That's not what I asked."

Simon had known it wasn't, but he didn't give her an answer.

She folded her arms on her chest again, pacing in the small room. "For seven years, I didn't know who killed my husband. Why, what happened. Any of it. I met Bob when I was still a recruit. He wasn't easy to win over."

"I can imagine," Simon said.

She didn't seem to hear him. "He's taught me so much."

"Abigail, that hasn't changed—"

"I believed I was teaching Bob what it's like to lose someone close to you to violence, when all the time, he knew and just never said anything."

"Some people bury something like that down deep and learn just not to go there."

"You had it right. Bob doesn't need a reason to be emotionally repressed. It's natural for him." She stalked to the door, but turned to Simon, her expression softening slightly. "Where's Owen?"

"I dropped him off on Beacon Hill. Fiona O'Reilly's at the Garrison house practicing with her friends." Simon tried to smile. "We could hear the Irish music all the way out on the street."

"I hope it's therapeutic for her."

"Yeah. Hope so. Today's been a tough one."

She gave a curt nod. "Bob?"

"He took off two seconds after Owen and I got there."

"Did he say where—"

"No. He didn't say a word to either of us."

"He's got the bit in his teeth, then."

Simon nodded. "I expect so."

"We don't need Bob O'Reilly going off half-cocked. One more question for you, Simon, before I leave." Her dark eyes leveled on him. "Just how well do you know my father?"

"As I said, some people learn to bury the bad and just don't go there."

John March had lost a friend and undoubtedly blamed himself for Brendan Cahill's execution, and to tell his daughter required confronting those feelings—that reality—in a way that keeping silent didn't.

Abigail took in Simon's nonanswer. "I have to be somewhere right now, but we're not finished."

"Hope not." He grinned at her. "I like weddings."

She scowled at him. "You're even less invited than you were last night."

But he saw some of the tension go out of her, if only for a moment, and she left, shutting the door behind her.

Simon opened Deirdre McCarthy's file again and turned to the last page Abigail had looked at.

It was a report on the Fuller family submitted by a BPD detective sergeant named John March.

Speaking of people who buried their emotions. Abigail had to have seen her father's name. She didn't miss anything.

According to everyone who knew him back in his BPD days, March had been hardworking, hard-driving and ambitious, putting himself through law school at night, figuring out how he could advance his career and still be a decent husband and father.

And friend, Simon thought, visualizing his own father's execution. What did John March owe the memory of the friend whose son he believed he'd helped orphan?

Simon knew the answer, because John March had lived it.

He set the file on the table and left. He wanted to be with Keira—now, not later. Deirdre McCarthy's murder had hung over Keira's life since the summer she was conceived, but no one—not her mother, her uncle, her grandparents or Patsy herself—had told her or her younger cousins about the girl next door, the friend who'd lost her life to violence.

And yet Simon understood why they hadn't.

Once he was on the road, navigating the busy urban streets, he called March's private number, barely letting the FBI director get out a greeting. "Do you care that Norman Estabrook just threatened to kill you?"

"No."

"I didn't think so. How long before you take him down?"

"Hours. He's still in Montana. We have him under surveillance. He's not going anywhere." March paused, then added, "We're monitoring his calls."

Simon had assumed as much.

"You're not calling to tell me Norman Estabrook hates me,"

March said. "You're in the middle of a mess that could explode in both our faces."

"You heard about Patsy McCarthy."

"Yes, I did," March said, a crack of emotion in his voice.

"You remember her, then."

"Her daughter's murder was one of the toughest cases I ever worked on, Simon. If I could forget it—well, I'm not sure I would. It's a reminder of what some people in this world are capable of doing."

"How'd you find out about the mother's murder? Who're you keeping tabs on, me or Abigail? Or have you been keeping tabs on Patsy McCarthy all these years?" March didn't give an answer, and Simon gritted his teeth. "All of the above, probably."

"Is Abigail—"

"She's in the thick of things, which is what you'd expect, isn't it?"

"Then she knows I worked on Deirdre McCarthy's murder investigation," March said. "That's not what's important now. Finding her mother's killer is. Simon, you need to walk away from this. It's not your fight. Go back to London, go fishing in Scotland with your friend Sir Will."

"Will's in Ireland."

"Of course. I should have known. The two of you are too independent for your own good. Dare I ask about Keira Sullivan?"

It was Simon's turn to avoid answering.

He heard March's soft sigh. "You do know how to complicate your life. There's no going back once we move forward with Estabrook, Simon. You have no illusions about that, I hope."

"My cover's pretty much blown as it is, and there's never any going back in life, anyway."

"I guess there isn't," March said with a note of melancholy that took Simon by surprise. "You've been clear-eyed and full-throttle since you were fourteen years old."

"Maybe so. Director March—John." Simon kept his eyes on the busy Boston street. "Did the right guy set himself on fire and jump into Boston Harbor thirty years ago?"

"Yes." There wasn't a hint of doubt. "Stay in touch," the FBI director said and hung up.

Simon tossed his phone onto the passenger seat. John March was as professional, honest and decent a man as there was, but he'd also kept his friendship with his dead friend's son secret from his daughter for twenty years. But Simon knew all about keeping secrets.

He hit the gas pedal, picking up speed.

"I was having the adventure of my life in Ireland while my best friend, the best person I've ever known, was in the hands of that monster."

Nineteen-year-old Eileen O'Reilly's words from Deirdre's case history had jumped off the page at Simon. Who could blame her for not telling her daughter about Deirdre's murder? And who could blame Keira, now, for wanting to understand her mother?

Simon gripped the wheel, half wishing Norman Estabrook would call and threaten to kill him again.

It would be a long drive out to the woods of southern New Hampshire.

He peeked at the speedometer.

Never mind, he thought—he'd get there in less than two hours. Way less.

~Chapter 29

The lunch crowd was descending on the busy, upscale health club under the Augustines' showroom on Clarendon Street. Abigail watched men and women with lives very different from her own burst into the locker rooms, jump onto treadmills, each with its own built-in little television, and climb onto weight machines. Several stretched on mats. One older guy crunched abs on an exercise ball. He looked as if he'd crunched about two million abs in his day.

All in all, Abigail would have preferred to strap on her iPod and go for a run along the Charles River, pump up her endorphins and just not think about an old woman killed in her home among the angel figurines her murdered daughter had collected—not think about the brilliant, honorable, frustratingly secretive man who was her father. She'd tried calling him on her way out to Clarendon

Street, but she only got his voice mail. She didn't leave a message. She figured he was avoiding her or talking to Simon—maybe both.

She didn't call Owen. He knew about Simon, she realized. Owen was thorough in everything he did, but especially in his work with Fast Rescue.

She expected lies and secrets in her work. They came with the territory—part of her job was to peel them back to get to the truth.

Secrets and lies weren't supposed to be part of her personal life.

But she was determined not to think about that for a while.

Instead, she was standing next to a stack of freshly folded white towels on the health club's front desk.

A lean, tanned man in a black tracksuit emerged from a back room. He was about Bob's age but in a lot better shape. "Thank you for waiting, Detective Browning," he said. "We spoke on the phone earlier. I've been expecting you. I'm Ron Zytka—I manage the health club. It's okay to talk here?"

"No problem."

"Charlotte and Jay Augustine stopped by just before you called. They're still very shaken up about Charlotte's brother." Zytka grabbed a perfectly folded towel from the top of the pile, shook it out and spread it out on the desktop, preparing to refold it. "Understandably."

"Did you know Victor?"

"Not really." He carefully folded the towel lengthwise into thirds. "I ran into him with Charlotte a few times, and she introduced us. I could pick him out of a crowd, but that's it. He wasn't a member here—not the type."

Zytka finished folding the towel and set it back on top of the pile. As far as Abigail could see, the towel looked exactly the same. She'd called him that morning before news of Patsy McCarthy's murder had reached her. Now she didn't know what difference the Augustines' exercise habits made. But she persisted. "I notice you check people in. You must keep a record—"

"We do, and I already checked to see if Charlotte and Jay were in the day Victor drowned, because I figured you'd ask. They weren't, but the kid who works for them was. I think he's actually the brother's employee. The poor man who drowned."

"Liam Butler was here?"

"That's right. He could use the club as a guest of the Augustines. We offer a limited number of day passes to people in the building. But he was here on his own—he has a six-month membership." Zytka pointed to a line of treadmills in front of a floor-to-ceiling window. "He always uses one of the treadmills over there."

Given the placement of those particular treadmills, Abigail noticed, Liam could watch people come and go into the building with little concern they would see him. "You're sure it was the same day—"

"Yes, Detective," Zytka said. "It was the day of the drowning. I can show you the log if you want."

"What time was he here?"

"Liam signed in just before six that evening." Zytka's hands shook as he lifted the refolded towel and took the one underneath it.

"Did Liam's behavior strike you as unusual?" Abigail asked.

Zytka licked his lips and averted his eyes, not because he was hiding something, she thought, but because he was uncomfortable, even afraid—but of what? He was an officious sort. He could simply be worried that one of the health club patrons would overhear him and question his discretion as a manager.

But Abigail suspected Zytka's nervousness had more to do with Victor Sarakis's death and Liam Butler's behavior that night. "We can talk in your office if you'd like—"

"I checked the log, Detective Browning," he said without looking at her as he unfolded the towel. "Liam Butler took out a membership two months ago. I can give you the exact date if you want. Since then, he comes several times a week, sometimes twice in the same day."

"If he was helping out upstairs—"

"He shows up here on days he doesn't work. I checked with my staff, and they've noticed. My opinion?" Zytka sucked in a breath and plunged ahead. "I think he's been spying on the Augustines."

"He couldn't just be training for a marathon?"

"No. I know the difference."

Abigail stood back a moment. "Mr. Zytka, did Liam Butler or the Augustines ever discuss angels or devils or evil with you?"

Zytka was so startled, his elbow jerked and struck the tower of towels, toppling several of them. He caught them as they fell and shook his head. "No—no, nothing like that. Detective, what—"

"Listen, thanks for your time," Abigail said, leaving her card for him on the counter. "If you think of anything else, call me, okay?"

"I will." He rubbed the back of his lean neck and suddenly seemed less sure of himself. "Listen, I don't want to get Liam into trouble if he just—you know. If he didn't do anything. I'm not accusing him…"

Abigail thanked him again for his time, and left.

When she got back out to her car, she called Tom Yarborough. She'd avoided him when she'd seen Simon. "Can you meet me at Victor Sarakis's house?"

"What's going on?"

"Sarakis's assistant was at a health club down the street from the Public Garden the night he drowned. Liam Butler. He hasn't told the truth."

"Give me the address," Yarborough said. "I'll get in touch with Cambridge PD and meet you there."

~Chapter 30

Near Mount Monadnock
Southern New Hampshire
12:30 p.m., EDT
June 24

Eileen Sullivan belted out the words to one Irish song after another as she stacked wood in front of her cabin. She could hear the Clancy Brothers in her mind, although she couldn't remember the last time she'd played a CD, listened to a radio. Her voice was terrible—Keira couldn't sing a note, either. They weren't the ones in the family with the musical talent.

A cool wind kicked up, and for a moment, Eileen let herself think it was a breeze off Kenmare Bay on her face. She shut her eyes and pictured herself dancing in an ancient stone circle above a quiet, gray harbor on the Beara Peninsula, and she hugged a log to her chest as if somehow it could bring her there—back to Ireland, back in time.

Before Deirdre's death.

That monster had Deirdre when I danced that night.

Eileen opened her eyes. She tried to sing again, but the words didn't come. She'd hoped singing and sweating and praying would finally chase away the demons that had been crawling over her since Keira's visit. Her distress wasn't Keira's fault—none of it was her fault. How could it be, when she didn't even know about Deirdre?

I should have told Keira about her.

About Deirdre's awful death, yes, but, even more so, about her life.

"You'll go to Ireland and have adventures. Oh, Eileen! I know you'll have the adventures of your life there. You'll have to tell me everything when you get home."

They'd laughed and planned some of the adventures Eileen would have—seeing the Cliffs of Mohr, kissing the Blarney Stone, finding long-lost cousins. Tracking down the village where Patsy McCarthy's story of the three brothers and the stone angel was to be Eileen's biggest adventure.

"You have to go alone. You know you do, Eileen. You'll never find the hermit monk's ruin if you don't. That'll be half the fun of it, going alone will. You can feel it's the thing to do, can't you?"

Deirdre had always had a gift of knowing. Not true prophecy in the way Eileen had been taught its meaning, but simply of knowing— of understanding people, opening herself to see into their hearts. Her intuition in those weeks before Eileen had left for Ireland had been keen, unrelenting.

"If something happens to me while you're in Ireland, promise me you won't regret a thing. Please, Eileen. Promise me."

Eileen blinked back tears, remembering how she'd refused that one request on the grounds that such a promise would somehow jinx Deirdre. In the years since her death, Eileen had come to see that Deirdre hadn't had a premonition about her imminent murder. She hadn't known she was being stalked. It was just Deirdre being Deirdre—she was a nurse's aide, and she'd lost her father as a teenager, knew her mother had lost a sister young. Every day was to be treasured.

She also had known Eileen, how hard she could be on herself—
how undeserving she often felt. That was *her* nature, and Deirdre,
with her uncanny ability to look into people's hearts, had only wanted
her friend to have a good time in Ireland. To trust herself to let go
and come home with no regrets.

What had Deirdre seen when she'd looked into her killer's heart?

"Stuart Fuller."

Eileen spoke his name aloud to remind herself of his humanity. A
supernatural creature hadn't murdered Deirdre. A man had made the
deliberate choice to stalk her, kidnap her, torture, rape and kill her.

Tears spilling down her cheeks, Eileen set the log on her woodpile.
She needed to get back to work on the illuminated manuscript. She'd
decided to shift to another, happier passage and leave aside serpents
for the moment. For most of the past week, she'd been preoccupied
with finding the perfect one to illustrate the Fall of Adam and Eve.

No wonder I keep thinking about demons. Eileen brushed her tears with
her sleeve. Seeing an ordinary snake curled up on a sunny rock that
morning had helped perk her up. It was a part of the natural order
of life out on her wooded hillside.

She looked at the beautiful landscape, focusing on a robin perched
on a hemlock branch. She found comfort in her solitude, in her
routines and rituals. They quieted her mind and eased her soul.

To a point, anyway.

*"You have to look for the village, Eileen. Imagine if you find the angel!
How happy Mum would be."*

Eileen smiled now, shaking off her melancholy as she thought of
her daughter in Ireland, having adventures of her own.

She stacked the last of the wood and propped her splitter against
the chopping block, then headed back into her cabin. She'd clean up,
and then she'd sketch angels. She didn't have Keira's artistic gifts—

her spark, her joy of drawing, painting, creating. It was all hard work for Eileen, but that wouldn't have bothered her if the results were what she wanted. But they never were. She would put her heart and soul into this one illuminated manuscript, and that would be it. No more.

She peeled off her zip-front sweatshirt and tossed it on the back of her work stool.

A sound distracted her.

She went still, listening.

Music…

The sound of a harp, playing a melody so sweet it seemed to pierce her straight to her soul, floated through her tiny cabin.

Eileen placed a hand on her worktable, steadying herself.

She heard a whisper now.

"Deirdre Ita…she died for your sins, Eileen…you know she did…"

And she turned, she gasped.

A stone statue stood on the hearth of her woodstove.

An angel.

~ Chapter 31

Kenmare, Southwest Ireland
5:35 p.m., IST
June 24

Eddie O'Shea waited impatiently for Mary Feeney, his cousin Joe's wife, to finish checking a middle-aged American couple into the mid-priced inn right in the heart of Kenmare. It wasn't as fancy as the busy town's five-star hotels, but, with its sleek modern furnishings, it was fancy enough. Eddie liked Kenmare all right but couldn't wait to finish his business there and get back home.

The couple went merrily off to their room, and he stepped forward to Mary's desk and gave her his friendliest smile. "Do you believe in fate, Mary?"

"No."

She was just twenty-nine and had the prettiest red hair Eddie had ever seen, but she'd always been a bit of a shrew as far as he was concerned. "Well, I do, and it's fate that brings me here. I've never asked anything of you, have I? And I wouldn't now, except I've no choice. The guards'll be coming for me before sundown if I don't figure something out."

She raised her pale blue eyes to him. "I hope they throw away the key."

He grinned in an attempt to soften her up a little. "Oh, come, Mary, what would you do without family?"

"Enjoy my life," she said, then sighed behind her elegant desk. "What can I do for you, Eddie?"

"Look up an American who was here on the summer solstice."

"Name?"

"I don't have a name."

"Then I can't help you."

"At least I think it's a man we're looking for—"

"*You're* looking for," Mary said.

True enough. "He wore a black sweater with a zipper, and he stayed here by himself. He ate dinner in your restaurant. I have the receipt—"

"You do? Well, then—"

"Part of the receipt, I should say. It's been torn." By a mysterious black dog…but Eddie wasn't going into that with someone as without imagination as Mary Feeney. "There's no credit-card number or room number."

Mary rolled her eyes in clear disgust. "Eddie, I'm not a miracle worker. I can't be expected to remember a man because of his sweater."

But Eddie was determined, and he smiled big for her. "What if I told you he lost his wallet and there'll be a reward?"

"It sounds as if he lost his sweater."

She could cover for her shrewish nature with wit and humor when it suited her. The sweater wasn't lost, Eddie thought. It'd been ripped off its wearer by Keira Sullivan's black dog, who'd bolted out of the roses in front of her cottage not three hours ago and dropped the sweater at Eddie's feet. It was torn and bloody, and Eddie wasn't taking any chances by giving it to the guards and getting himself locked up. He'd collected Patrick and Aidan, and they'd smuggled him off to Kenmare.

"If it was a wallet your man lost," Mary said, all superior and sarcastic, "you wouldn't need me to find out his name and address for you, now, would you?"

"I've never been a good liar."

"Your only charm, Eddie." She faced her computer monitor and clicked keys, her lips pursed in that sour way of hers. "In any event, this man's not the sort who'd offer a reward for anything."

"Ah. You do remember him."

"I do, indeed," she said softly, then eyed Eddie, a gray look to her fair skin now. "You'll stand here all night if I don't help you."

"You have a bad feeling about him, don't you, Mary?"

Before she could answer, a lean, fair-haired man walked up to Mary's desk. She blushed, and, married woman or not, Eddie couldn't blame her. The man was good-looking and obviously belonged in one of the five-star hotels, not Mary's little inn.

Instead of greeting Mary, he turned to Eddie. "My name's Will Davenport," he said, his accent identifying him as an upper-class Brit. "Simon Cahill sent me."

Eddie wasn't as shocked as he might have been at mention of the big, black-haired Yank who'd come to Keira's rescue.

"You're Eddie O'Shea, aren't you?" Davenport asked.

Eddie tried not to gape at the man. "How did you—"

"You and your brothers are too honest not to leave a trail."

Somewhere in Will Davenport's words was a compliment, Eddie thought, but no matter. At least he was getting no more argument from Mary.

"How do I know you're telling the truth?" Eddie asked.

Davenport didn't hesitate or look miffed. "Simon got into an argument about Irish weather when he was at your pub the other night. He says everyone liked him, regardless."

That sounded like Keira Sullivan's black-haired rescuer, but Eddie was still wary.

"All right, then," Davenport said. "Seamus Harrigan is the name of the Garda inspector looking into what happened in your village."

"That's not hard to find out."

The Brit's hazel eyes narrowed, and Eddie detected a seriousness about him—a competence that went beyond getting his brothers to rat him out. Davenport said quietly, "The woman who told Keira Sullivan the story that brought her to Ireland was found murdered this morning in Boston."

Mary gasped, and Eddie, an awful sickness in his stomach, stood up straight, and put out his hand. "It's good to meet you, Will Davenport. I could use any help you have to offer before this devil strikes again."

~Chapter 32

Cambridge, Massachusetts
12:40 p.m., EDT
June 24

As Abigail mounted the front steps to Victor Sarakis's Cambridge house, she was struck by how abandoned the place looked. The grass was taller. Dandelions blew in the afternoon breeze. He was just a week dead, and his home looked more than merely neglected. It looked as if he'd died without anyone in the world who'd cared about him.

Liam Butler's car was in the driveway, but obviously he hadn't worked up the energy or focus—or whatever it would take—to get out the lawn mower.

Or shut the door, Abigail thought, noticing that it was slightly ajar.

She rang the doorbell and waited a few seconds. When there was no answer, she knocked, the door swinging open about a foot.

But as she started to announce herself, she heard music coming from the direction of the devil room.

Irish music.

It was a kick-up-your-heels tune that sounded familiar but she couldn't name.

Why would Irish music be playing in Victor Sarakis's house?

The music paused, and Abigail could hear laughter and talking now—kids.

"It's just not there yet. Let's go through it one more time, okay, guys?"

Fiona.

Abigail stifled a gasp, recognizing the voices of Fiona O'Reilly and her musician friends.

A tape?

Drawing her weapon, Abigail stepped into the foyer. Yarborough and the Cambridge PD would be here any minute.

The music started again, and she noticed the pocket doors to the devil room were wide open. She couldn't see anyone...it had to be a recording.

But where? And why?

Pushing back an image of Bob if he'd been with her, she followed the music into the room with its disturbing collection of devil imagery. On the far wall, the door to the climate-controlled room stood partially open like an invitation—a temptation.

Fiona shrieked with laughter, she and her friends finding delight in having just messed up the piece they were practicing.

Abigail stepped into a small, dark, windowless room. With her free hand, she felt the side wall and switched on an overhead light. The room was obviously once a large closet that had been converted into this climate-controlled space. Floor-to-ceiling shelves were crammed with more items that reflected Victor Sarakis's interests.

The music and the voices of Fiona O'Reilly and her friends were coming from a tape recorder set up on an oak desk. It was a trick,

Abigail thought. A mind game by someone who'd expected her, who wanted to unnerve her.

Oh, God.

Photographs—a dozen of them, at least, tacked to a bulletin board propped against the leg of a desk.

Fiona...Madeleine O'Reilly, Jayne O'Reilly.

Bob's daughters.

There was blond-haired Fiona in front of the Garrison house on Beacon Street.

Red-headed Madeleine at soccer practice.

Little blond Jayne eating an ice cream cone in Lexington with her friends.

Abigail steadied herself. Where the hell was Liam Butler?

She headed back out into the main room and reached for her cell phone with her free hand, dialing Scoop. "I need to put you in charge of finding Bob's daughters. All three of them. Owen's with Fiona on Beacon Hill. I have no idea where Madeleine and Jayne are."

"What about Keira?"

"Find her, too." There were no pictures of Keira on the bulletin board, but Abigail wasn't taking any chances. As unemotionally as possible, she described the scene at Sarakis's house. "Yarborough's on the way with the Cambridge guys."

Scoop swore under his breath. "What else can I do?"

"I haven't told Bob yet." It'd be tough, telling Bob, and she needed to stay focused on what she was doing. "Find him, Scoop. Find him now. Tell him."

"It's done."

She stepped out into the main hall, her gun still drawn. "Scoop, I don't know what's real and what's a mind game. This creep—"

"Doesn't matter right now. We cover all the bases until we know what's going on. Be careful, Abigail. Wait for Yarborough."

But she saw blood smeared on the hardwood floor and heard a moan down the hall. Butler? One of the O'Reilly girls? "I can't wait."

⟜ Chapter 33

South Boston, Massachusetts
12:50 p.m., EDT
June 24

Bob O'Reilly walked from his old street to Saint Ita's, his boyhood church, just as he had so many times growing up. His colleagues were still processing the scene of Patsy's murder. They'd be at it a while. He couldn't stand the thought of her dying the way she had, but how many times had she told him she'd die fighting the devil with her bare hands? And it had been a quick, if bloody, death. Her killer hadn't toyed with her the way Deirdre's had.

The lead detective, a guy Bob had helped train, had pulled him aside and said they believed Patsy's killer had set up the angels and the pictures in the dining room after she was already dead.

That was something, anyway.

Saint Ita's was a white sided building that looked as if it belonged on a New England town green. He almost ran into a sobbing white-haired woman on the front walk. She identified herself as a friend of Patsy's and told him the priest was in the attached parish hall. Bob was relieved. He hadn't stepped foot in Saint Ita's since Deirdre's funeral all those years ago, and now, at least, he could avoid the sanctuary.

He found Father Palermo sitting on an old pew pushed up against the wall for extra seating. In his open palm was a delicate white porcelain angel, a small Irish harp in her arms that Bob recognized immediately.

"That was one of Deirdre McCarthy's favorites," Bob said. "It wasn't a gift. She picked it out herself."

Palermo nodded without looking up.

"Patsy gave it to you?"

"Yes. At our angel bazaar a few weeks ago."

"Interesting that of all her angels, she parted with that one."

Bob glanced at the empty room, imagined it filled with tables and displays of angels, imagined Patsy beaming proudly, because hers would have been the best collection there—and because it would reflect well on Deirdre's memory.

Palermo didn't respond, and Bob said, "So, Father, if I dug into your background, would I discover your real name isn't Michael Palermo?"

The priest raised his dark eyes to Bob, but he didn't try to read them. If he was right, Palermo had practiced for this moment.

When Palermo still didn't speak, Bob continued. "Stuart Fuller had a younger brother. Nice kid, apparently. I never met him. He was just fourteen when Deirdre was killed. Lousy family. Abusive parents, lots of sudden moves, lots of different schools. So you know what the kid did?"

Palermo lowered his eyes again to his angel. "He found an escape—a way out of the darkness."

"He created a fantasy world for himself. He filled one notebook after another with *National Geographic* articles on islands in the Mediterranean."

"How did you learn about these notebooks, Detective O'Reilly?"

There was no sharpness in Palermo's tone, no bitterness, just curiosity—as if he'd played out the different ways this all would end and hadn't come up with this one. "My father was a cop," Bob said.

Palermo shook his head. "Your father didn't tell you about the notebooks. He was a regular beat cop—the people here say he loved being on the street."

Bob shrugged. "He never wanted to be a detective. He knew I did—everyone did. People said things in front of me. I paid attention. It's not in the file on Deirdre's murder, about this kid and his notebooks. I doubt anyone's around anymore who'd remember."

Not true. John March remembered. He had worked the investigation as a young BPD detective, and Bob had talked to him just before heading over to Saint Ita's, asking the FBI director if there was anything he could think of about the people Stuart Fuller had left behind. Mother, father, brothers, sisters, friends.

March told him about the notebooks.

When Palermo didn't say anything, Bob resumed. "Palermo's the capital of Sicily, the largest island in the Mediterranean. I heard the brother turned to religion after Stuart's death. Funny how these things work out, isn't it?"

Palermo didn't answer right away. "Maybe so, Detective O'Reilly. Maybe so."

"Patsy figured out who you were, didn't she?"

"We never discussed it."

"She figured it out, Father. Trust me. I grew up a couple of doors down from her. I helped her bury her only daughter. Giving you that angel was Patsy's way of telling you she didn't blame you for what your brother did."

Palermo looked up, and this time his eyes brimmed with tears.

"She didn't deserve to lose Deirdre. She didn't deserve what my brother did."

"No, she didn't."

Palermo sank back against the pew, but he kept a tight grip on the angel figurine. "Patsy asked me to drive her to Beacon Hill to see Keira Sullivan before she left for Ireland—and I realized then that she knew I was Stuart's brother. It wasn't anything she said. But there's no doubt in my mind that she had me pegged."

"Did she kill your brother, Father?"

His expression softened, and Bob could see how the members of his church had come to love him as their priest. That was the word from the detectives back at Patsy's house—that she and everyone else adored Father Palermo. "You know in your heart she didn't kill Stuart," Palermo said. "After Deirdre's body turned up, Patsy figured out where Stuart had taken her. Where he killed her. Where he was hiding. She didn't tell the police."

"How did she figure it out?"

"She told me an angel came to her. I am a priest, Detective O'Reilly. That part's not a lie. But I don't believe she meant, literally, that an angel told her."

"Stuart called her," Bob said, seeing it now.

"He told her that he wanted to ask her forgiveness."

"Patsy didn't believe that line, did he?"

"No. She knew he was manipulating her. He wanted to relish her pain. My brother fed off other people's suffering, Detective O'Reilly. Patsy's grief and horror were as satisfying to him in their own way as what he did to her daughter." Palermo got heavily to his feet. "Stuart lured Patsy out to the boat where he was hiding. He set himself on fire in front of her. She blamed herself for not stopping him."

"Could she have?"

"Who's to say? I doubt it, personally. She was glad he couldn't hurt anyone else, and she was glad he'd suffered. She didn't regret that she didn't tell the police that Stuart had called her. She knew they'd stop her from going out to him—"

"Damn straight," Bob said.

Palermo hesitated before he continued. "I'm convinced Stuart planned that call to Patsy right from the beginning. He wanted to make them both suffer. Patsy and Deirdre. Mother and daughter."

Bob grimaced, but he said, "Unusual for someone like that to commit suicide."

Palermo didn't comment. He looked tired, ashen, but he attempted a smile. "Patsy was so happy when Keira came into her life." He gave a small laugh. "She was someone else Patsy could tell her stories to."

"She was quite a storyteller."

"The best. She loved Keira's work—a lot of the people in the church do. She has quite a following here."

"That's nice," Bob said tightly, uncomfortable with mention of his niece.

"Patsy believed good things would happen if the stone angel in the story of hers was ever found—she loved the idea of it as much as anything. Detective O'Reilly, I never meant..." Palermo shook his head, his eyes filling again with tears. "It doesn't matter what I meant. My brother played a terrible, twisted game with her, but what have I done?"

"Did you ever think she was in danger?"

"No. I saw no danger, Detective. I felt none."

"The only person responsible for the violence against Patsy is the one who committed it. Period. The same with Deirdre."

"Life isn't that black-and-white, is it?"

"Some things aren't. This is."

Bob thought of Abigail and her investigation into the drowning in the Public Garden. He'd been so impatient with her. He wasn't the only one, but how many times in the past years had he told her not to hold back just because she was taking heat? If she had a legitimate reason to pursue a line of questioning, a theory, then she should do it.

"Did you know Victor Sarakis, Father?"

"Just his name. He's the man who drowned the night I drove Patsy into Boston to see Keira."

"Liam Butler, Charlotte and Jay Augustine?"

He shook his head. "No." Palermo pulled open the outer door and bright sunshine streamed into the hall. "If you think of any other questions, Detective O'Reilly, I'll be here."

"I have to report what I know about you, Father."

"Yes. Of course you do. I'm sorry I lied about who I am. And I'm sorry about Patsy, Detective. I only knew her a relatively short time, but I was very fond of her."

"I didn't stay in touch with her the way I should have."

"From what I saw, she found a way to carry on with her life. We were all affected by what my brother did thirty years ago. Your sister's new life, I'm sure, is partly a result of—"

Bob stopped abruptly in the doorway. "What do you know about my sister?"

Palermo reddened. "Just what everyone else in the parish knows. She came to mass from time to time before she finished building her cabin. People here like her and appreciate her commitment to her faith, but they're surprised she chose this life. They're not being critical of her. They just didn't expect it because she's such a people person."

"Eileen's always been hard on herself."

"That's not the purpose of the life she's chosen."

"It's hers."

Palermo said nothing.

"Has Keira talked to anyone else in the church about their old family stories?" Bob asked.

"Not specifically, no, but word has gone out that she wants to talk to people who emigrated from Ireland in the last century."

"Anyone you know who's involved in this Boston-Cork conference?"

Palermo shook his head.

"What about people who collect Irish art and whatnot?"

"That's a broad group—"

"Someone who'd know Patsy, my sister, my niece," Bob said.

"Well, the Murphys, of course. They're avid collectors. I heard they bid on one of your niece's paintings at the auction, but I don't believe they were actually there."

Bob knew the Murphys. "Did you tell the detectives about them?"

"No—"

"Do. Go on up to Patsy's house and tell them. They'll want to know." Bob felt his cell phone vibrate. "I have to go. Be where we can find you."

Palermo nodded, clutching the angel and looking pale and shaken as Bob headed back outside. He glanced at the readout on his cell phone and sighed as he saw Scoop Wisdom's name and answered. "I hope to hell you're not calling to talk to me about compost piles."

"Everyone's okay, Bob," Scoop said. "I'm on my way to the Garrison house. Owen's there with Fiona. The Lexington police have Madeleine and Jayne. They're okay. They're all okay."

Bob had to lock his knees to keep them from going out from under him. "Bring me up-to-date. What the hell are you talking about?"

Bob stood in the summer sun on the sidewalk of his youth. Scoop described the pictures and tape Abigail had discovered at the Cambridge house of her drowning victim. Victor Sarakis. The man whose death Bob had insisted was an accident unrelated to the auction on Beacon Street that night. To Keira. To his family.

He pushed back the guilt. "What about Keira?" he asked when Scoop had finished.

"She's on her way to see her mother—"

Bob swore, cutting Scoop off, and looked back at the parish hall. Killing Patsy may have been expedient, but it also had been part of the plan. Setting up the angels, the pictures, the prayer card. Finishing Stuart Fuller's work. Mother and daughter were both dead now. Patsy, Deirdre.

Bob thought of the devils in Victor Sarakis's house.

They were chasing a devil. That was for damn sure.

Billie and Jeanette Murphy, longtime members of Saint Ita's, had let Eileen build her cabin on their land in southern New Hampshire. They'd bid on one of Keira's paintings. They collected Irish art.

Patsy had told Keira her Irish stories.

And someone had watched, plotted, manipulated and, finally, taken action.

"He wanted to make them both suffer. Patsy and Deirdre. Mother and daughter."

Bob felt the hairs on the back of his neck stand on end. "Scoop, it's Eileen and Keira. They're this bastard's target. They're the main event for this devil."

"How the hell—never mind. We'll get the state and local guys out to your sister's place. Can you can give them directions?"

"Follow the bread-crumb trail through the ferns—no, I can't give them directions. I've never been out there. We need to find the Murphys. They own the land. They'll know."

"I'm on it, Bob."

He gave Scoop their names, where to find them. "Cahill's on his way to New Hampshire," Scoop said. "He's FBI—Keira must have given him directions."

"FBI?" Bob tried to smile; gallows humor had always been his defense. "Can't wait to see Keira when she figures out she's fallen for a Fed."

"Think she's fallen for him?"

"Hard and fast. It's the only way she does things." Bob's chest felt tight. "Scoop…I can't lose them."

"You won't. I have to get moving, Bob."

"Yeah, go. I'm on my way to Cambridge. Scoop—" Bob choked up. "Thanks."

But Scoop had already hung up.

~ Chapter 34

Near Mount Monadnock
Southern New Hampshire
1:00 p.m., EDT
June 24

The city and suburbs of Boston gave way to rolling hills, woods and farmland as Keira drove west and then north into New Hampshire, but the picturesque scenery gave her no sense of relief as she pulled over to the side of the quiet secondary road just before the turn for her mother's cabin. Colm Dermott was on the phone, and she didn't want to risk losing service before he could finish what he'd called to tell her.

Jeanette and Billie Murphy—the couple who owned the land on which her mother had built her cabin—had purchased the second painting she had donated to the auction.

"I didn't see them, but I arrived late—"

"They weren't there." Normally so cheerful, Colm sounded tense, strained. "They bought the painting through a third party. Keira, this is troubling—Jay and Charlotte Augustine acted as intermediaries for the Murphys. They're fine art and antiques dealers in Boston. Charlotte Augustine is Victor Sarakis's sister."

"But Colm—he's the man who drowned."

"Yes," he said.

Keira tried to contain her shock. She rolled her window down, her heart racing as she listened to the stream that ran alongside the road. She was all alone out here. There were no other cars, no houses, no people in sight.

"The Augustines telephoned the bid on behalf of the Murphys," Colm said. "I'm trying to find the volunteer who took the call. I'm positive the Augustines didn't attend the auction. Their names aren't in the database of people we invited or on any of the sign-in sheets. Not everyone signed in, of course, but I don't remember meeting them. I would think I would have. I made a point of greeting everyone who attended, and I have a good head for names. Keira," he said, increasingly breathless, "the police will want this information, won't they?"

"Yes, absolutely they will, Colm. Have you heard of the Augustines? Do you know anything about them?"

"I looked them up on the Internet. They seem to be respected and knowledgeable dealers."

"Do they specialize in Irish works?"

"Not that I can see, no."

"I'm not thinking of my painting—I can't imagine it's what the Augustines are into." She felt a warm breeze, heard crows in the distance. "I'm thinking of Patsy McCarthy's stone angel. Would that interest them, assuming it's Celtic or even Celtic Revival?"

"It would interest a lot of people, Keira."

She sighed. "I can't imagine some high-class Boston dealers crawling around in an Irish ruin for a statute they'd have no reason to believe exists." Keira paused, suddenly feeling isolated on the quiet road. Her throat tightened with emotion. "But I can't imagine someone killing an old woman in her own home, either."

"That surely was a terrible thing," Colm said.

"Has anyone picked up the Murphys' painting?"

"Not yet."

"Colm—you've been incredible. I'll lose cell coverage any minute, so I can't call the police myself—"

"I have the numbers you left me right here. I'll try your uncle first. Keira…please, be careful. This is worrying."

"I don't have far to go. I'll be at my mother's cabin soon."

After they disconnected, Keira drove another mile before turning onto a narrow dirt road that took her deeper into the woods and finally dead-ended in a small circle. She got out and stood a moment, catching her breath amid the pine trees and sugar maples. Just a week ago, she'd come out here to talk to her mother about her trip to Ireland. Despite her ambivalence over her mother's new life, Keira had looked forward to seeing her. The prospect of finding out about her birth father had intrigued her, but it was the story of the three Irish brothers and their battle with the fairies over possession of a stone angel—the possibilities it presented to her as both an artist and a folklorist—that had fired her imagination.

She located the trail that led to her mother's cabin just as a stiff, sudden gust of wind blew strands of her hair in her face. She hadn't even thought to pin up her hair that morning. She'd been in a hurry to see Patsy and to get her black-haired search-and-rescue expert out of her apartment before anything else happened between them.

Except he was also an FBI agent.

Keira doubted that was Simon Cahill's only secret. He was a charmer if ever there was one, but he was also a man of many layers.

Another breeze stirred. She picked up her pace, navigating tree roots, rocks and low-hanging tree branches, pushing through the tall ferns that flanked the narrow trail. Ordinarily, she would have enjoyed the hike, especially on such a beautiful summer day, but today she felt only dread at the prospect of facing her mother, telling her about Patsy and pleading with her to talk—about Ireland and her long-dead friend.

And if she couldn't talk, at least engage with her daughter the way she used to, if only for a few minutes. Listen. Be there. Was that so selfish to want?

Keira forced herself to dismiss any need on her part. She'd only known Patsy for a matter of weeks. Her mother had known her all her life.

Why not turn around and go back to Boston? Why even tell her?

Keira tripped on an exposed rock, but regained her balance before she fell. The stumble brought her out of her thoughts, and she focused again on her surroundings. For the entire drive, she'd debated whether to leave her mother in blissful ignorance. Let her pray and work in her isolated world. Wasn't that what she wanted? But Keira had kept driving, and now she kept walking, because she didn't have a choice. She had only to envision Patsy's body, and the angels and pictures on the dining room table, and she knew she couldn't turn back.

As she came to the rustic cabin, Keira was struck by the similarities of the site she'd chosen to that of the ruin in Ireland. Although the landscape was more thickly wooded here than the open countryside on the Beara Peninsula, and there were no sheep or ancient stone circles in the area, the hill dipping down to a stream and the remoteness of the spot brought Keira back to her search for the ruin of Patsy's hermit monk hut on the evening of the summer solstice.

She gave an exaggerated shudder to rein in her active imagination and stepped up to the cabin's back door, calling through the screen. When there was no answer, she didn't hesitate, just pulled open the door and poked her head inside. "Hey, Mum—it's me, Keira."

But still there was no answer. She hadn't considered that her mother might be at the spring fetching water or checking on the Murphys' country house—or even just out in the woods listening to the birds.

She went inside, calling again as she headed through the rustic kitchen into the cabin's main room. Her mother had left a series of sketches of various serpents on her worktable.

She must have gone outside for a break, Keira thought, venturing out the front door.

She noticed the faint smell of sawdust and several freshly split logs awaiting their addition to the neatly stacked woodpile. With the woodstove her mother's only source of heat, the work to keep it stocked was never ending. Keira would have helped, but that wasn't an option in the new rules her mother adopted for her life.

The fenced-in garden was quiet in the afternoon sun. It included flowers as well as vegetables, which Keira had taken as a positive sign that this isolated existence really was what made her mother happy.

She heard a muffled sound down toward the stream.

A moan.

Her heart jumped, even as she saw a wet, dark smear on the tree stump her mother used as a chopping block, and it was as if she were back at the ruin in Ireland, standing up from the fallen tree covered in sheep's blood.

Except this wasn't sheep's blood.

Mum—where are you?

A splitter was propped against the chopping block. Keira took it in both hands, but there was no blood on the metal head.

The wind gusted through the trees, and she could hear the stream tumbling over rocks below her on the hillside.

She pictured him peering down at her in the rubble of the ruin, so calm, so competent. She didn't care that he'd obviously thought she'd been reckless, or that she'd worked for hours in grueling conditions to construct her makeshift ladder. That didn't matter—she couldn't think of anyone she'd rather have at her side right now.

She steadied herself. She'd chopped wood with her mother as a kid. She could wield a splitter if she had to.

She saw a shadow—a movement—among the hemlocks on the hillside.

It wasn't a squirrel or a wild turkey, or even the wind.

Someone was there.

~Chapter 35

Near Mount Monadnock
Southern New Hampshire
1:25 p.m., EDT
June 24

Simon's cell phone rang a few miles after he'd crossed into New Hampshire from Massachusetts. Before he could speak, Will Davenport said, "I have information, Simon."

"Are you having trouble getting to Ireland?"

"I'm here in Kenmare."

"Even our Moneypenny couldn't get you there this fast. Helicopter, Will, or were you already there when I called?"

"I anticipated you'd need my assistance."

Simon tensed, hearing the note of seriousness in his friend's voice. "Go ahead, Will. What's up?"

"An American named Jay Augustine arrived in Shannon on a flight from Boston on the morning of June twenty-first," Will said. "He rented a car at the airport and stayed in Kenmare that night. He returned to Boston the next day on a flight out of Shannon. He would have arrived midafternoon."

Given Will's extensive sources inside and outside government, Simon wasn't surprised at how much his friend had managed to discover in such a short time.

Will was also thorough, and he had a labyrinthine, suspicious mind.

"The timing fits," Simon said. "Who is he?"

"Jay Augustine is the brother-in-law of the man your Keira found dead in Boston before she left for Ireland herself."

Simon swore. He was keeping an eye out for the turn onto the dirt road that would take him to Eileen Sullivan's cabin. At the speed he'd been going, he figured he couldn't be too far behind Keira. "Go on," he said tightly. "There's more, isn't there?"

Will continued with his grim report. "Physical evidence—a blood-stained sweater—places Augustine at Keira's ruin on the Beara Peninsula. He and his wife are fine art and antique dealers in Boston, Simon. They would know the value of an ancient Irish artifact and have access to potential buyers."

"Money could explain wanting to beat Keira to the angel and make off with it. It also could explain leaving her in the rubble of that ruin. But the sheep, Will…" Simon broke off, controlling his anger. Keira had gone to Ireland to research an innocent story of mischief and magic, hoping to understand her mother and learn more about her birth father—perhaps, in a way, both her fathers. The one who'd given her life and the one who'd adopted her.

Simon saw his turn, took it and realized he was losing cell coverage.

"Simon?"

"I'm about to lose you, Will. I'm in the woods, on my way to Keira and her mother. Augustine didn't do much to cover his tracks."

"That means he has an escape plan," Will said. "What do you want me to do?"

"Inform the Irish police—"

"Are you kidding? They're on my elbow right now." But Will's touch of humor faded almost immediately. "This man's a cold, calculating predator, Simon."

"Yeah," Simon said, but he knew his phone had died.

The road was narrow and dotted with potholes, but he drove faster. Will and the Irish police would get word to Boston law enforcement about Jay Augustine. In the meantime, Simon would find Keira and her mother.

He rolled down his window, heard birds and felt the breeze. He could understand the appeal of building a cabin out in the woods. He lived on a boat himself, although for most of the past eighty-plus miles, he'd pictured Keira on his boat with him. If she didn't know about boats, he could teach her. If she did, he could just watch her paint Irish fairies and rainbows.

An image of Patsy McCarthy interrupted Simon's visions of sailing the seven seas—any sea—with his fairy princess.

He kept driving.

Chapter 36

Cambridge, Massachusetts
1:30 p.m., EDT
June 24

Charlotte Augustine shrieked on the front walk to her brother's house. "You can't stop me! I have a right to be here. I'm Victor's next of kin." She pushed at the Cambridge PD officer restraining her. "Let me go, damn you!"

Abigail stepped out of the house and ducked under the yellow tape two officers were still unfurling to mark off the crime scene. Two Cambridge detectives, who reminded her of Bob, glowered at her, but they didn't impede her.

Tom Yarborough fell in behind her. He was fair-haired, driven and absolutely the most cynical law enforcement officer Abigail had ever met, and she'd met plenty. He hadn't let her out of his sight since he'd arrived twenty minutes ago, finding her on her knees in a pool of blood as she tried to save Liam Butler's life. The Cambridge police and paramedics had since descended.

"Actually, they can stop you," Abigail told Charlotte.

"What's happened? My husband—Liam—"

"Liam's in tough shape. He's been stabbed repeatedly." But deliberately left alive, if barely so, Abigail thought. In order to suffer or to distract police, at least for a little while. Maybe both. "I found him in the sunroom. I did what I could. Paramedics are with him now."

"Will he..." Charlotte trembled, unsteady on her feet. "He'll live, won't he?"

"I don't know."

She put a hand to her mouth. "Oh, no...no."

"Where's your husband, Charlotte?" Abigail asked quietly.

"Did Liam—did he tell you who did attacked him?"

It was a question Abigail had no intention of answering. Liam had been at best semiconscious, unable to respond to any of her questions or instructions—finally, she'd just applied pressure to the worst of his wounds and waited for medical help to arrive.

"Mrs. Augustine—"

"I don't know where Jay is."

"Did you know that Liam was spying on you and your husband?"

Charlotte wobbled and took in shallow breaths. "I have no idea what you're talking about."

Abigail shook her head. "I think you do, Charlotte."

"Go to hell. You have no right to tell me what I know and what I don't know."

Yarborough moved slightly behind Abigail, but he said nothing. She noticed the dandelions going to seed in the unkempt yard and remembered the traditional, expensive clothes Victor Sarakis had been wearing the night he drowned. A man of contradictions, but wasn't everyone? Charlotte herself wore a female version of her brother's attire—light-colored khakis, a dark pink polo shirt, tennis shoes, simple gold jewelry. Nothing antique, nothing Celtic—nothing to indicate she had an interest in Irish artifacts.

"Mrs. Augustine," Abigail said, "when's the last time you were in your brother's climate-controlled room?"

Her hand dropped from her mouth. "What? Why?"

Abigail debated, then answered. "There's a bulletin board in there that's covered with photographs of the daughters of another detective—"

"They're not Victor's doing!"

"I believe we're dealing with a serial killer, Charlotte. You can help us stop him by telling us what you know."

She sagged, taking a step backward toward the street. She looked as if she might faint, but she rallied, even as tears streamed down her cheeks. "The spying—it was Victor's doing. He asked Liam to help him. He—they—" Charlotte faltered, wiped her tears with her fingertips. "They were trying to help me."

"How?" Abigail asked.

"Everything's happening so fast…"

"Just stick to the facts. You can sort out all the emotions later. Okay? How did your brother think he was helping you by spying on you and your husband?"

"I wanted a divorce," she blurted, then waved a hand dismissively. "Jay travels so much. That's where he is now. Traveling."

"Traveling where?"

"I don't know. He didn't tell me. He often doesn't. He's on the road a lot because of his work. Our work, I mean." She squinted at Yarborough, then at Abigail. Except for her red cheeks, there was no sign of tears now. "Jay is…remote."

"Have you told him you want a divorce?"

"No. No, I haven't." She wrapped her arms around herself,

hugging herself as if she was cold. "I'd hoped Victor's death was an accident. If he was murdered—can you imagine what that'll do to my life?"

Abigail stiffened and gave Yarborough a sideways glance, saw that Charlotte's comment had hit a wrong note with him, too. Never mind cooperating with the police and, if her brother had been murdered, finding his killer—making sure no one else got hurt.

But Charlotte Augustine didn't seem to think there was anything off-putting about her remark. "Detective Browning, I know you have to explore all the possibilities, but I don't see how these photographs of the detective's daughters or the attack on Liam have anything to do with me or my husband. What if Liam's the one responsible for the bulletin board, and this detective found out and attacked him?"

"That didn't happen," Yarborough said.

Charlotte went ashen. "I'm sorry, I..." Fresh tears welled. "I want to help if I can. Go ahead. Please. Ask me any questions you want to."

"Keira Sullivan," Abigail said. "Do you know her?"

A flicker of recognition.

Yarborough took a half step forward. "The truth, Mrs. Augustine."

She tightened her hug on herself and looked toward the house as the door opened and paramedics carried out Liam Butler on a stretcher. "Oh, Liam," she whispered.

"Charlotte," Abigail said, "how do you know Keira Sullivan?"

"I don't. We—we've never met. I just know her name. Her work. Victor showed me one of her illustrated books the day he drowned. That afternoon. I didn't tell you. He came out to the house..." She bit on her lower lip. "It was the last time I saw him."

Abigail could see that Charlotte wasn't finished and didn't interrupt her pause.

"I only remember because I liked the illustrations. They're so original—so cheerful. I was surprised Victor liked them, considering his obsession with the devil and evil."

"Why did your brother show you Keira's book?" Abigail asked.

"I don't know!"

But that wasn't the truth, and Yarborough, clearly losing patience, shook his head. Instead of pouncing on Charlotte for her obvious dissembling, he spoke quietly to her. "You have a lot bottled up inside you, Mrs. Augustine. You just lost your brother. It's tough. We know that." His tone was reassuring, friendly. "It'd do you good to finally let it all out. Tell us everything. Let us decide what helps and what doesn't. Don't censor yourself."

She dropped her arms to her sides. "It has been hard. So hard. I wish now I'd pushed Victor to give me more information, but I didn't. And now it's too late."

"There was an event on Beacon Hill the night he drowned," Abigail said. "A benefit for a folklore conference. Keira Sullivan was there. So was one of the girls whose pictures are on the bulletin board. Did Victor—"

"He wasn't invited. Jay and I weren't, either."

"Charlotte—"

"I don't know why Victor showed me that damn book! He was *spying* on me, Detective Browning. He was trying to help, but still." She suddenly kicked the top off a dandelion, sending little white seeds floating into the air. "He didn't like Jay."

Her tone had changed, and Abigail resisted the temptation to jump in with another question. Yarborough remained impassive at her side.

Charlotte squashed what was left of her dandelion with her toe. "I want this all to go away. But it won't, will it?" She raised her gaze to Abigail. "Liam didn't know why Victor was having him spy on Jay and me. Victor didn't tell him. There was no need to tell me—I saw for myself what was going on with Jay. I just didn't want to admit it."

"But Victor did tell you," Abigail said.

Charlotte nodded. She wasn't shaking now. "He said there were times when he'd look at Jay and think he was looking into the eyes of the devil. I wanted to believe it was an exaggeration. I didn't want to believe Jay was that bad."

"He is, though," Yarborough said. "Isn't he?"

"I think so," Charlotte said, hugging herself again.

Out on the street, Abigail saw Bob O'Reilly pull up to the curb, jump out of his car and show his badge to a Cambridge police officer, who didn't stop him.

Abigail didn't contain herself. "Bob—your daughters—"

"They're safe. They're with Scoop, Owen and the Lexington police." But he didn't look even marginally relieved as he narrowed his eyes on Charlotte Augustine. "Jeanette and Billie Murphy."

She gasped as if he'd stuck her with a needle and she lunged for the street, but Abigail and Yarborough both grabbed her before she could get a half step. Charlotte calmed down, and they let her wriggle free.

Bob hadn't moved. "You acted on behalf of the Murphys and bought one of my niece's paintings at the auction the night your brother drowned."

"I told Detective Browning already that my husband and I weren't there."

"You phoned in the bid. I just talked to the Irish professor who's heading up the conference—"

"He's wrong."

"The Murphys are your clients. They're into their Irish heritage." Bob was steady, focused. "They'd love to get their hands on an Irish Celtic stone angel like the one in Patsy McCarthy's story."

Charlotte turned to Yarborough, as if he could help her, but he just stepped back from her. She started shaking again. "Please—the Murphys aren't involved in any of this. I didn't tell you about the painting because I knew you'd jump to the wrong conclusion."

Bob remained icy. "You picked up the painting this morning."

"No—"

"Charlotte," Abigail said without sympathy, "no more lies and half truths."

She stared down at the ground. Some of the fight seemed to go out of her. "I delivered the painting to Billie Murphy's office in Boston. He wasn't there. I left it with his receptionist."

"Whose idea was it to bid on it?" Bob asked.

Charlotte clamped her mouth shut and refused to answer.

Even Yarborough gave a little hiss—no more playing the nice, patient police officer—but Bob remained calm to the point of scary. He rocked back on his heels. "Mrs. Augustine," he said, "you're going to tell us what you know."

Abigail glanced at the paramedics sliding the stretcher into the back of an ambulance. Liam Butler was fighting for his life, and this woman was playing games. "You need to stop thinking about how this situation is going to affect your business and your social life."

"The Murphys are new clients," Charlotte said weakly. "They're from working-class South Boston, but they have a spectacular home now on the waterfront. They're wonderful people. They have exquisite taste—"

Bob cut her off. "I grew up with them. I know who the hell they are. They looked after a woman who was just found knifed to death in her own house. The Murphys were good to her. They own the land in New Hampshire where my sister built a cabin. How did you meet them, Mrs. Augustine?"

"My husband. Jay—I don't know how he met them."

"He insinuated himself into the Murphys' lives, Patsy McCarthy's life—*my* life." Bob's tone hardened even more. "Where is Jay now?"

"I told Detective Browning—he's traveling."

"He's not traveling."

"No," Charlotte mumbled. "Please."

"My sister's name is Eileen Sullivan. She's a religious ascetic. She—"

Charlotte was sobbing quietly now. "I know. I don't know her, but we— Jay and I have been out to the Murphys' house in New Hampshire."

Bob didn't say a word, but Abigail could feel her own knees going unsteady under her. Jay Augustine knew how to get to Eileen Sullivan's cabin. She was there. Keira was on her way.

"Bob…"

He turned and walked back out to the street.

Yarborough nodded to Abigail. "Go. I'll see to Mrs. Augustine and fill in the Cambridge guys."

"Tom—"

"It's Bob's family, Abigail. Go."

She tried to smile. "I might have to revise my opinion of you."

He ignored her, and she ran to join Bob. She didn't know what she could do to help, but he didn't have to be alone.

Chapter 37

Near Mount Monadnock
Southern New Hampshire
1:45 p.m., EDT
June 24

Keira sank onto her knees on the bank of the stream in front of her mother, whose moan of pain had been the sound she'd heard. Her mother sat with her knees tucked under her chin in the shade of a white pine, her hands and feet bound tightly with blood-soaked rope.

She was bleeding from a dozen slashes on her arms and shoulders. Superficial wounds, Keira thought. Designed to elicit pain and a lot of blood, not to kill. Not yet, at least.

"I can feel the Irish wind on my face," her mother whispered, her lips cracked and bloodied from where she'd bit down during her torture. "Oh, I can see the green—such a green. Deirdre won't fly. She would love to see her mother's birth place and meet her Irish relatives, but she's too afraid to get on a plane."

"Mum…it's Keira." She had to fight to keep herself from sobbing. "You're in New England. Be with me now, okay?"

Her mother's eyes flickered, and she tried to sit up straighter. "Keira, please tell me you understand. I didn't tell you about Deirdre because I couldn't. She was—she was the best of us, and she was taken from us…"

"I know, Mum. I understand."

A few feet from them, the stone angel stood among the ferns at the edge of the stream, as beautiful as the night of the summer solstice when Keira had spotted it on the hearth of the collapsing ruin.

"Run, Keira." Her mother groaned in pain. "Leave me. *Please*."

"Don't talk. Save your strength."

"We can't let him kill again."

He was there, Keira realized. In the trees, just as he'd been in Ireland. Lurking, enjoying the fear and suffering he was causing.

Jay Augustine.

Using the edge of the splitter, she managed to whack through the rope on her mother's ankles. The rope on her wrists, yanked tight and soaked with blood, would be impossible to cut with any precision—she'd need a sharp knife.

"Can you walk?" she asked her mother.

"Yes…but, Keira, take the splitter. Run as fast as you can. Let him amuse himself with me—I'll buy you as much time as I can."

"I'm not leaving you."

Keira rose, slipping in the mud as she hung on to the splitter and, with her free hand, helped her mother up. *Distract and disrupt.* It was one commandment she remembered from her police academy days for just such a situation. She didn't have to take on Jay Augustine. She simply had to distract him and disrupt his plans, get her and her mother away from him if she could.

"He's evil, Keira," her mother said. "He's not insane. He's chosen this path."

"I know, Mum."

Her mother was reasonably steady on her feet despite the blood, her bound wrists. "He doesn't believe in angels or saints—or fairies and magic. Or the devil himself. He just wants to commit violence and play his games. Feel his own power."

"What does he have for weapons?"

"Knives. Two that I saw. And fear. He uses fear as a weapon."

At least if he didn't have a gun, Keira thought, he couldn't just shoot them from the bushes. She had no doubt he was watching, taking pleasure in her reaction to her mother's condition—plotting his next move. If the splitter deterred him, it wouldn't be for long. He'd think of some way around it.

Her mother faltered, shivering not with cold, Keira realized, but with the agony of her wounds—with her own fear. "He killed Patsy. He told me. She told him that story of hers. He manipulated her, too. It's not your fault. It's not her fault. Oh, Keira."

Keira focused on taking the next step, paying attention to any movement, any sound in the nearby trees and undergrowth. "Let's just keep moving."

Her mother sobbed, then nodded, as if summoning her resolve.

A crunching sound came from the hill above them. "Keira, Keira." A man's voice, chiding her as if she were a recalcitrant child. "Don't you see? Your mother wants to suffer for the sins of her past. She needs to suffer."

Keira maintained her hold on the splitter.

The man stepped out from the cover of several small hemlocks. He was middle-aged, trim, dressed neatly in slacks and a button-down shirt and lightweight jacket. But she saw spots of blood on his slacks, his knuckles, one cheek, and his eyes shone with an excitement that struck her as sexual, physical.

Keira pushed back her own fear. "Jay Augustine, right?"

He seemed momentarily surprised, then gave her a mock bow. "I did anticipate that my identity would be discovered. Part of the fun, in fact." But before Keira or her mother could speak, he continued. "While your saintly mother was cavorting in Ireland, indulging in fairies and magic and sins of the flesh, her best friend was being tortured and raped. She never told you, did she, Keira?"

"Why would she tell me? Any mother would want to protect her child—"

"I'm offering your mother redemption. I left her alive deliberately so she can watch me brutalize you, just as Deirdre's killer did her. You, the daughter conceived in sin—your mother can suffer the worst pain she's ever known, and thus be free."

Keep him talking, Keira thought. "You don't care about redemption—"

"I offered Patsy redemption. She set her daughter's killer on fire."

Keira's mother shook her head. "No. Not Patsy. She didn't kill Stuart. I'd have if I'd known where to find him, but Patsy didn't kill him."

"She wanted to—she let it happen. She always knew she'd have to pay for what she did. When I came for her, she knew her moment had come. I could see it in her eyes."

Keira scoffed at him. "You killed Patsy because she could identify you to the police. You wormed your way into her life, and she told you the story about the stone angel. With what happened in Ireland, you knew she'd figure out your role, and you killed her to protect yourself. Everything else is a narrative you've established for your own amusement."

He ignored her, his arrogance almost palpable. "Do you really think you can take me on with that ridiculous ax?"

Only if I have no choice, Keira thought. "Killing that poor sheep in Ireland wasn't about redemption."

"Practice, my dear Keira." He held up a double-edged assault knife covered in what Keira assumed was her mother's blood. Perhaps Patsy's, too. He smiled. "Practice."

She did her best to hide her revulsion. "You won't stop with me or my mother. You'll always want more, and you'll pay for it. Someone will make you pay."

"Not you, though, or your mother. And not today."

"Why didn't you kill me in Ireland?" Keira asked quickly, trying to distract him from his knife.

For the first time, he looked uncomfortable.

"You didn't expect me to find the ruin, did you?" She kept any fear out of her tone. "You thought you'd beat me to it. You're a planner— you're not spontaneous. You had to think on your feet when I showed up. Did you assume I'd die there?"

"I didn't want you to." He sounded sincere, as if the thought of her death had troubled him. "I wanted you here, now. I wasn't meant to kill you in Ireland. That way."

"The dog…he wasn't yours. He threw you off your game."

"Too late to help you. The ruin started to collapse and exposed the angel." He gestured with his knife at the simple, mesmerizing statue. "Look at her, Keira. Her beauty and grace. Have you seen Deidre's picture? They look so alike."

"How did you meet Patsy?" Keira asked, hoping his ego would lull him into lowering his guard, give her an opening, or just keep him talking until Simon could get there.

"We met the day she displayed her silly angels at the church. Most were junk, but a few were of value." He raised his knife to eye level. "I've enjoyed the chitchat, but don't think you're in control. You're not tough, Keira. Don't pretend you are. I can end your mother's suffering in an instant. I can kill you in an instant. It's my choice."

He was almost spitting his words now, but not because of exertion and fatigue, Keira realized. The thrill and anticipation of what he had planned were getting to him. Her pulse throbbed in her ears, and her hands felt clammy as she gripped the heavy splitter, edging closer to him. If he wanted to keep talking, she'd talk, but she knew she had to be prepared to defend herself and her mother.

"If I know about you," Keira said, "the police do, too."

That seemed to throw him off, but only for a moment. "Drop the ax," he said.

Keira knew she'd gone as far with him as she could. He was done talking. "Technically, it's not an ax," she said. "It's a splitter."

With an unexpected surge of energy, her mother stomped on his instep, and Keira whipped the splitter at him. He ducked away from the sharp edge, and she caught him in the midsection with the back of the metal head. He yelped in pain and stumbled, dropping his knife, charging into the woods.

"The police will catch up with him," Keira said, reaching an arm around her mother's waist and helping her to a boulder. She picked up Augustine's knife.

Her mother shook her head. "He'll come back. He's obsessed— he wants to do Deirdre's killer one better. Stuart Fuller enjoyed Patsy's suffering almost as much as he did Deirdre's. Mother and daughter…"

"Maybe, but Augustine's also an art dealer. He'll want to profit from the angel. Does he have a buyer? Did he tell you?"

"The Murphys. They think he's legitimate—"

"They won't for long."

Keira cut the ropes on her mother's wrists.

"It stops here, Keira," her mother said, wincing as she eased her bloody hands in front of her. "We can't let this man kill again."

"We won't, Mum. Simon's on his way. He'll be here soon. He'll help us find this bastard."

"Keira—Simon? Ah, the way you say his name. Did you meet him in Ireland?"

"Boston, actually." She managed a smile. "But I fell for him in Ireland."

Simon slowed his pace on the trail out to Eileen Sullivan's cabin in the woods, thinking he'd heard singing up ahead.

It *was* singing.

Really bad singing, he thought. He recognized "Irish Rover," a song his father used to belt out in the shower a long time ago, but this version had a desperate, half delirious sound to it. A warning? A distraction?

Simon stepped off the trail into knee-high ferns, ducking behind a thick oak tree for cover as a middle-aged man plunged down the trail, both arms out for balance as he negotiated a sharp turn.

He was panting, sweating.

He had to be Jay Augustine.

Simon jumped out onto the trail in front of him. "Stop—FBI. Keep your hands where I can see them—"

Augustine ignored him, turned and bolted into the woods on the opposite side of the trail. Simon raced after him, tackled him and dropped him facedown onto the ground. Hard, right into the middle of a low, thorny bush. Augustine moaned and tried to get up, but Simon held him down.

Moving fast, he got his knee into the middle of Augustine's back and, his eyes on Augustine's hands, cuffed him in about three seconds flat, then patted him down. He found an assault knife in a sheath on Augustine's belt. There was a second, empty sheath.

"Where's Keira?" Simon kept his knee in place. "Where's her mother?"

"Let me go, and I'll tell you."

"You look a little worse for the wear. Keira nail your ass?"

"She'll bleed to death," Augustine said, spitting his words. "So will her mother. Slowly, painfully. You know I can make it happen."

"That wasn't you singing, so I'm guessing they're okay."

Just then, Keira swooped down through the trees with a wood splitter held high.

"Whoa," Simon said. "Easy, there."

She lowered the splitter, breathing hard, hair flying in her face, eyes shining with fury as she focused on Augustine. "Your only way out now is to turn yourself into a bat or a snake, you bastard," she said, "and I'll bet you can't do that."

Augustine raised his chin and grinned at her, enjoying her anger—her hatred—as if he'd accomplished something. Simon didn't ease up on him at all.

A woman who had to be Keira's mother staggered down the nearby trail, bloody, holding an assault knife in one trembling hand. She stepped closer, and Simon couldn't tell if she planned on shoving the knife in Augustine's heart. If she tried, he'd have to stop her.

"That was you singing, Mrs. Sullivan?" he asked her.

She nodded, staring at Augustine. "I thought it would help cover Keira's running and perhaps throw him off, and keep me from having to..." She didn't finish her thought, instead lowering her knife. "I didn't want to scream. I didn't want to give him the satisfaction. I love that song, and I didn't know what else to do."

"We'll belt out some Irish songs together sometime," Simon said, then winked at her. "You, me and the Clancy Brothers."

Keira started toward her mother. "Mum..."

But Eileen Sullivan raised her bloodshot eyes to Simon. "Is your voice better than mine?"

He grinned at her. "A wee bit, ma'am," he said in his best Irish accent.

Sirens sounded in the distance. The local and state police would be arriving soon, and Simon wouldn't be surprised if a few Boston cops were thrown into the mix for good measure.

He saw a glimmer of a smile from Eileen Sullivan as she turned to Keira. "I like his wit," she said, then fainted in her daughter's arms.

— Chapter 38

Cambridge, Massachusetts
8:00 p.m., EDT
June 24

Abigail showed her badge to the police officer posted at Liam Butler's hospital room. Prosecutors were still debating whether to charge him with anything, but she doubted they would.

It was late in the evening, the end of a very long day.

Liam looked as if he was sleeping. The worst gash was in his abdomen, but no vital organs were seriously affected. The paramedics and doctors had intervened in time. They'd stopped the bleeding, given him blood and stitched him up. He was on pain medication, but what he needed most now, they said, was time to heal. He'd have scars from his ordeal, but otherwise he'd make a full recovery.

Emotionally, Abigail didn't know. He'd endured a horror few people had ever survived.

And he'd made a lot of mistakes.

Only he wasn't alone when it came to mistakes.

What promised to be a thorough, painstaking investigation had begun. Authorities in Boston, Cambridge and Ireland had already begun retracing Jay Augustine's steps over the past few weeks and months, when he'd gone from being a respected fine art and antiques dealer to a killer handcuffed in the New Hampshire woods.

Charlotte Augustine had already hired a lawyer and a spokesperson to manage media inquiries and to portray her as another of her husband's victims.

Maybe she was, but she hadn't told the truth to the police, either.

Abigail couldn't tell if Liam was aware of her presence. His parents and brother would be arriving soon from Chicago. "Hey, Liam," she said. "It's Abigail Browning. Are you awake?"

"I'm sorry," he mumbled without opening his eyes.

She hadn't expected any response. "Your folks will be here soon," she said.

This time he didn't respond.

Bob O'Reilly entered the room, jerking a thumb back toward the nurses' station. "The nurses are worse than the Cambridge cops. I thought they were going to frisk me before they let me in here."

Abigail was heartened by the return of his wry sense of humor.

He stood next to her at Liam's bed. "Cambridge PD's annoyed with you for not telling them about the devil room," he said.

"You didn't tell them, either."

Bob shrugged. "Hell, I thought your guy tripped on his shoelaces."

"We're still not sure he didn't, figuratively speaking—I realize he was wearing loafers. But it still could have been a freak accident."

"You don't believe that."

She shook her head. "No, I don't. Maybe we'll learn more when the rest of the autopsy results come in. The medical examiner's already taking a closer look at the preliminary results. You'd think there'd have been some obvious sign of a struggle."

"Maybe Victor thought he was up against a devil and didn't struggle."

"Not *a* devil, Bob. *The* devil or one of his minions. There's a distinction—"

"One you don't need to make." Bob grimaced at the sight of the thin, bandaged kid in the bed. "At least Augustine didn't slice and dice his brother-in-law the way he did that sheep in Ireland. What he had in mind for Keira and Eileen..."

"Bob—"

"It worked out," he said. "That's what counts."

"How's your sister?"

"She'll be okay. The bastard didn't lay a finger on Keira. She and that ax." He shook his head. "She's tougher than she looks, that one."

"And your daughters—"

"I think Fi's got a crush on Scoop. Something new to keep me awake nights."

Abigail smiled at Bob's bravado. As far as she could see, there wasn't an O'Reilly who wasn't tough.

"Augustine told people he was in New York the day Victor drowned."

"Yes, well, supposedly he was in New York when he was in Ireland, too."

"He wanted that angel—wanted to beat Keira to it. He knew he could get the Murphys to pay him a fortune for it. Figured he could always take the money and disappear. Start up again under a new name."

"He and Charlotte have only been married two years," Abigail said. "Who knows what we'll find when we dig deeper into his past?"

"Charlotte told Yarborough that she and Jay met after he found some of the pieces for her brother's devil collection. Didn't mention that tidbit to you, did she?"

Abigail shook her head. "Jay told us that day at Victor's that he and

Charlotte met over a Renaissance tapestry he'd helped Victor find. Did he hook up with Patsy through the Murphys, or vice versa?"

Bob rubbed the back of his thick neck, his fatigue evident. Today had shaken him, Abigail thought. But she knew he wouldn't stop until he had a solid sense of the time line of the past few weeks. What Jay Augustine had done. When. Why. How. All of it.

"He turned up for the angel bazaar at Saint Ita's," Bob said. "I just came from there. Showed Father Palermo a picture of this maniac. Several dealers stopped by the bazaar looking for bargains—some figurine some poor old lady had squirreled away for years and didn't realize was valuable. Palermo remembers Patsy and Augustine taking a shine to each other."

"He's a manipulative son of a bitch," Abigail said.

"He befriended the Murphys. He and Charlotte are legitimate dealers—Billie and Jeanette had no reason to suspect that anything was wrong. Patsy eventually figured out he was no good." Bob dropped his hand from his neck and looked at Abigail, his cornflower-blue eyes filled with pain. "In the end, she knew."

"He loved it all. Patsy's story and the possibility of finding a valuable Irish Celtic artifact. The tragedy of her daughter's death. Her killer's bizarre death." Abigail bit down on her lower lip to control a wave of emotion. "Keira. Her mother."

"Yeah," Bob said. "He loved it all."

"Keira knows she had nothing to do with bringing him into Patsy's life, doesn't she?"

"She knows. I'm just not sure how much that helps."

Liam's eyes, swollen from his ordeal, opened, focused on the two detectives. "I should have told you..."

Bob sighed at him. "Life's full of should haves, kid." He spoke as if he was just laying out an obvious truth. "Get used to it. You have a lot more mistakes ahead of you."

"Geez, Bob," Abigail said, "remind me not to have you come visit if I'm ever in the hospital."

He glanced at her, obviously mystified. "What?" But he turned back to Liam. "Detective Browning and I are experienced investigators, and we took a house tour with Augustine. I should have known something was wrong when that twisted son of a bitch didn't get the creeps in the devil room."

"Me, too," Liam mumbled. "But Victor..."

"Weird guy, but he was okay, huh?"

Liam stirred, more conscious now. "Victor figured it out. He knew what Jay was. I thought Jay was just hiding money and stealing from Charlotte. I got his log-in information for his accounts. Bank, credit card. Victor—he checked them out. He must have found something."

"Receipts for Jay's tickets to Ireland, maybe," Abigail said.

"He didn't tell me. That day..." Liam's eyes closed, and he was clearly fading again. "He said he had the devil on his heels. I didn't...I thought it was just...you know, Victor being Victor."

"Rest up, kid," Bob said. "You'll need your energy for when you look for a new job. Nothing involving devils this time, okay?"

Liam's mouth twitched with humor. "Thanks."

Bob didn't speak again until he and Abigail had exited the hospital and were outside in the warm, clear, beautiful June evening. "Yarborough's still annoyed with you for being right about your drowning. Me, I'm getting used to the idea."

"No, you aren't, and I don't care. I wish I'd been wrong."

"Better to die tripping on a crack in the sidewalk than believing you're being chased by the devil."

"We'll prove Augustine was in Boston that night," Abigail said.

"Yeah, but the bastard had me beat," Bob said, matter of fact. "Keira and Eileen are alive because of what they and Simon did, not because of what I did. I let my assumptions drive my conclusions."

"Augustine had us both beat," Abigail said.

"I don't know, though. Go back through the time line. We'd have had to be damn lucky to get ahead of Augustine any sooner than we did. Even if Butler had told us what he and Victor had been up to, he didn't know that Augustine was a killer. We're just a couple of detectives, Abigail. And we didn't kill anyone."

She walked out to her car. Bob had parked right behind her. She got out her keys but didn't step off the curb. "My father worked on the Deirdre McCarthy murder investigation."

"Yes, he did. Abigail—" He broke off, seemed to try to find the right words. "Deirdre's death is something I got used to not talking about."

It was as close to an apology as she'd ever get from Bob O'Reilly. "You I can understand. You were just a kid yourself thirty years ago. But my father…"

"He's not that much older than me. It was a tough investigation. I didn't know him that well, but you were a toddler when Deirdre was killed, Abigail." Bob took a pack of gum from his pants pocket, tapped out a piece and gave it to her, then tapped one out for himself. "Why would your father tell you about an unspeakable act of violence that happened when you were still in diapers?"

Abigail supposed he had a point, but she didn't want to get into it. He'd had a hard enough day without taking on defending her father. "Not me, Bob. I was out of diapers by then."

"No kidding? I thought my girls would be going to kindergarten in diapers." He headed for his car, but stopped after a few yards and called back to her. "You'll be a good mother, Abigail."

She pushed back a tug of emotion. "Yeah. I think so."

Two minutes later, she was in her car, tossing Bob's stick of gum into her little trash bag. She didn't chew gum that wasn't sugar free, and he didn't chew gum that was.

She stuck her key in the ignition, pushing back her fatigue. She was on her way to the triple-decker she shared with Bob and Scoop— and Owen, she thought.

Her eyes teared up, and suddenly she couldn't wait to be home.

~ Chapter 39

Jamaica Plain, Massachusetts
9:00 p.m., EDT
June 24

Keira laid a handful of loose-leaf lettuce in Scoop's dented colander. "I must really look like hell for you to let me in your garden."

He was picking lettuce a few feet down the row from her. The garden was his turf. He'd all but posted No Trespassing signs. He smiled at her. "Tough for you to look like hell, Keira."

"It's been a long day," she said without further explanation.

"Yeah. But working in the garden helps, doesn't it? Puts life into perspective. I'll wash the lettuce, toss it with this nice balsamic vinaigrette I whipped up." He rolled back onto his heels. "Feeling better already, aren't you?"

"I am," she said, standing up. "Thanks, Scoop. Thanks for everything."

"You're welcome, but I didn't do a damn thing except listen to Fiona O'Reilly play harp for a couple hours—"

"You got Madeleine and Jayne into protective custody, and you were the one who had to tell Bob about the pictures."

"Yeah. There was that."

The thought of the pictures—the thought of Jay Augustine stalking her cousins—made Keira sick to her stomach. She could only imagine how her uncle felt. But they were a ruse, a part of Augustine's game. Fiona, Madeleine and Jayne were never his targets.

"I didn't ask enough questions around here," Scoop said. "Bob and Abigail needed an objective voice, and I wasn't there. They weren't letting anyone in, given their crappy moods, but I should have forced myself in."

"We all did our best." Keira brushed dirt off her hands as she got to her feet. "I guess that's all we can ask of ourselves."

Scoop rose next to her with his colander. "Let this guy Cahill in, Keira. The two of you. It's new, but it's for real. That's not one of the things I missed the past week."

His words took her by surprise. "Scoop—"

But he'd already bolted for the stairs up to his apartment. Keira stepped out of the garden, carefully avoiding tramping on any of his tender plants. Scoop wasn't easy to figure out, but none of them was—him, her uncle, Abigail.

And Simon, she thought. He'd stayed at her side after he'd tackled Jay Augustine. The police had arrived within minutes. Augustine had gone silent by then, but Keira knew his cold stare would stay in her mind forever. But he was in police custody now. He couldn't hurt anyone else.

Simon was in Abigail's kitchen with her and Bob. Talking cop talk, probably. Keira wanted to stay close to her mother, who'd given in to her brother's wishes not to go back to her cabin. She'd had her wounds stitched up at a local hospital.

Augustine was, indeed, very good with knives.

She was half asleep in an Adirondack chair now. It was her first visit to the triple-decker Bob had bought with his two colleagues.

"Doing okay, Mum?" Keira asked her.

She managed a small, reassuring smile. "Never better."

Owen walked out into the tiny yard with two tall glasses of iced tea, handing one to Keira and the other to her mother.

Keira relished the normalcy of drinking iced tea on a warm summer night. "You knew Simon was FBI?"

Owen nodded without hesitation. "I did."

"For how long?"

"Eighteen months."

"And you didn't tell Abigail," Keira said, making it a statement.

"It turned into a bigger deal than it should have. Simon and I didn't really become friends until recently. The Armenian earthquake in particular—he's tireless. He's also one of the bravest men I've ever known."

Keira smiled. "Scary almost, isn't it?" But she couldn't sustain any real humor and instead dropped into a chair at the table, drinking some of her tea. "In other words, you never expected for you and Simon and Abigail to become friends."

"Fast Rescue has a lot of volunteers."

"Do you know what he does with the FBI?"

Owen looked uncomfortable. "Keira…"

"I'm guessing he's used his disaster-preparedness consulting as cover. I imagine he's had to tell the BPD and state detectives who he is by now, if not the details. Is that going to cause him problems?"

"Nothing he can't handle, or so he tells me." Owen pulled out a chair next to her and sat down. He could be exacting and intense, but he was also one of the kindest men Keira had ever met. "Simon's status was a confidence, not a secret."

"A distinction without a difference if you're the one in the dark. I'm not talking about myself. I'm just getting to know Simon." Never mind last night, she thought with a welcome surge of heat. "Abigail, though. Yikes. She must not be real pleased."

Owen shrugged, obviously not worried. "That's one way to put it. I've known Simon long enough to say this, Keira. He's the same man whether or not he's wearing his badge."

She knew what he was saying—that there'd been no pretending this week. The man she'd met—the man she'd made love to, had fallen for so hard and fast—wasn't part of an act.

But she'd known that. "Badge, hell, Owen. I'm just glad he showed up when he did this afternoon. Otherwise I'd have had to do serious bodily harm to that cretin."

"I heard about your ax," Owen said with a smile.

"Splitter. Now *that's* a distinction with a difference. An ax has a proper blade. If I'd had to tackle Augustine myself—" She stopped herself, not wanting to dive too deep into the bottomless ocean of might-have-beens. "It doesn't matter. I'm just relieved I didn't have to do more than I did."

"Which was enough."

"That whole deadly force thing is what bit me at the police academy. There's usually one thing in particular that gets people who don't make it through training, and that was mine."

"You dropped out. You didn't flunk out—"

"Another distinction without a difference."

"Maybe so. I'm not in law enforcement, but I know that the purpose of deadly force is to stop, not to kill."

She leveled her eyes on him. "There you go."

Simon had been gentle with her mother and professional with the police, but Keira knew he'd have used deadly force on Jay Augustine if he'd had to. He didn't just have handcuffs on him—he had a 9 mm Sig Sauer. Of course, he'd made wisecracks once the immediate danger had passed. He had an uncanny ability to sense when people were at their breaking point and knew how to ease their tension, to make them smile in spite of themselves, to remind them that life was too damn short to be serious all the time, even over serious matters.

And yet all the while, Keira knew he had other things on his mind—the life and work he'd dropped to check on her in Ireland.

The long June day was slowly giving way to darkness when Fiona arrived with her two younger sisters, and Bob emerged from Abigail's apartment, his emotion palpable as he took all three daughters into his arms. "Kiss your aunt," he said, nodding to his bandaged sister. "She's lucky to be alive with this crazy bastard come to cut her into ribbons."

Keira watched her cousins surround her mother, crying, hugging. Her mother's reserve, the inevitable result of living alone for so many months, lifted, and she let Jayne, the youngest, sit on the arm of her chair.

Without any warning, Bob broke into an Irish song as he lit the grill.

He had an amazing voice. Keira and her young cousins gaped at him, and he grinned. "What, haven't you ever heard me sing?"

"Not like *that,* Dad," Fiona said, obviously impressed.

Simon walked out into the yard, and Keira's heart jumped at the sight of him with his black curls, his green eyes, his confident manner. He winked at her, then joined in the singing, his voice just as amazing as her uncle's. The two of them adopted Irish accents, and Fiona got up, inserting herself between the two men and hooking one arm with each, the three of them step dancing merrily as they sang.

The tears came next as they belted out a sad song. Fiona, her sisters, Bob and his sister all cried openly. Keira couldn't stop herself from sobbing, but she noticed that Simon remained dry-eyed, just kept singing with that beautiful voice. When they switched to a jauntier tune, he scooped her up and spun her across the clipped grass. She didn't know any of the moves, but he showed her, holding her close, his eyes sparking with humor, and, she thought, desire as he sang and danced with her.

He tightened his arms around her. "Just don't you and your mother start singing," he said, and with one smooth move, swept Keira up and off her feet.

She shrieked in surprise and started to laugh, and she couldn't imagine anywhere else she'd rather be.

The dissecting of events began over dinner, just as Keira had known it would.

Colm Dermott joined the crowd as Abigail, tense and quiet, set the table, refusing help from anyone. He placed a computer disk in the middle. "The police have the original, but I'd copied it onto my computer and burned it onto a disk. I'm quite handy, I'll have you know." But he sighed, his humor not taking hold as he tapped the disk case with one finger. "Patsy doesn't say a word about this bloody bastard. It's just her telling her tale. What a tale it is, too! She was a fine storyteller, Keira."

"Here's my theory," Bob said, breaking the uncomfortable silence that had descended over the table. He glanced at his daughters, and Keira half-expected him to send them upstairs. But he didn't, and continued. "We're talking about Deirdre now. I don't doubt Michael Fuller—now known as Father Michael Palermo—was telling the truth when he said his brother called Patsy and got her out to his boat just as he jumped into the harbor in flames."

Eleven-year-old Jayne O'Reilly scrunched up her face. "That's gross, Dad."

"Yeah. It is." He winked at her. "Not everyone's as loving and wonderful as your dad, right, kid? Okay. Back to my theory. Let's say our fourteen-year-old Michael Fuller knows what his big brother has done and what a monster he's become."

Abigail sat across from Owen, not looking at him as she spoke. "Hadn't Stuart moved out by then?"

"Yeah, but he stayed in touch with Michael. Who knows, maybe he knew his little brother was on to him. Stuart didn't leave much of a trail. Nowadays, it's harder not to, but thirty years ago..." Bob shrugged. "So Michael's caught between a rock and a hard place. He doesn't have enough evidence—at least in his own mind—to take to the police. He's worried his brother's going to get wind of his suspicions and disappear, and who knows how many girls like Deirdre he'd kill before police caught up with him."

"This is an awful scenario, Bob," Abigail said. "This kid had no one he felt he could trust."

Bob didn't respond right away. He winked at Madeleine and Jayne, as if to remind them they were safe, and he stood behind Fiona, who sat between Owen and Scoop, and patted her on the shoulder, then gave his sister a nod. "Eileen, you okay? You hanging in there?"

"Keep going," she said in a tight whisper.

Keira watched her uncle move back over to the grill and pick up a barbecue fork. She had no idea if he was offering a theory that he'd just come up with, or if it was one he'd contemplated on and off over the past thirty years.

He stirred the coals and continued. "Michael figures his only way out is to take matters into his own hands. By now, Deirdre's body has washed up on shore. The police are searching for her killer. Michael knows who the killer is, where he is—but he makes up his mind not to tell the police. Instead, he waits until Stuart passes out from drinking, douses him with gasoline and sets him on fire."

Madeleine gasped, but Fiona and Jayne listened silently, wide-eyed. Keira pictured her uncle at twenty, learning the fate of the monster who'd so brutally and terribly slain his friend. The girl he'd taken to the prom. Patsy's daughter.

"There were less violent options," Abigail said.

Scoop shook his head. "Kid didn't want a less violent option."

"That's right," Bob said. "Michael wanted his big brother to burn for what he'd done. To suffer, here on earth. He wanted him to have a chance to ask forgiveness for his evil acts and save his eternal soul."

"Did it work out that way?" Fiona asked.

"Witnesses say Stuart was on fire when he leaped into the harbor."

"Did his younger brother watch?" Keira asked, then added, "At least according to your theory."

"There's no evidence putting Michael on the scene," her uncle said.

Abigail tilted her chair back. "Whatever he did or didn't do, I can't imagine knowing your brother's a killer and believing you're the only one who can stop him."

Simon stretched out his long legs. "Maybe your theory is off just a little, Bob. Maybe Stuart Fuller actually thought he was the devil, and he set himself on fire, thinking he'd survive."

Bob made a face. "That's creepy, Cahill. I've got freaking goose bumps now thinking about it."

Colm Dermott shuddered. "Aye," he said. "I do, too."

Keira shared their revulsion, but her mother leaned forward, wincing in pain. "It's also possible that Stuart Fuller really was Satan."

Her brother snorted. "Well, if he was Satan, he's a dead Satan, because I saw his body. In fact, Abigail, your father showed it to me. Hell. That was a long time ago."

Fiona got to her feet and hugged her father. "I'm sorry about your friend, Dad."

"Yeah, kid. Thanks."

But Owen rose and invited her and her sisters into Abigail's apartment for ice cream. Keira saw how good he was with the girls and wondered if Abigail noticed.

"Maybe I should have kept my mouth shut," Bob said, returning to the table.

"No," Abigail said, staring at the retreating O'Reilly girls. "They'll remember that you leveled with them and didn't shut them out. But it can be tough, seeing what we see in our work and then thinking about bringing kids into the world. If I could wave my magic wand and rid the world of violence, I'd do it. I'd put us right out of business."

"I know you would, kid, but if it's magic wands you need—talk to Keira."

Bob grinned, then laughed, and Abigail groaned and threw a plastic spoon at him.

Simon put a hand on Keira's thigh and leaned close to her. "Something's come up with my work," he said in a low voice. "I have to go."

"Your consulting work or your FBI work?"

"It could take some time."

"That's not an answer, Simon."

"You won't be able to reach me for a while, but don't worry." He squeezed her thigh and smiled. "I'll find you."

After Simon left, Abigail and Scoop retreated to their apartments, and Colm bid everyone good-night, whispering to Keira on his way out that Patsy's story was, indeed, perfect for her new book. "She wouldn't want that devil to ruin it," he said, "and she'd be so proud."

Her uncle closed up the grill. His daughters had come back out with their ice cream and watched as if they were seeing a side of him they'd never seen before. He pretended not to notice, but Keira thought he did.

"Looks as if it'll be me and the womenfolk tonight," he said. "I don't have enough beds, but I want you all to stay. Keira, Eileen—you, too. It'll be a crowd, but it's been a hell of a day. For a while there…" He shook off whatever he'd started to say. "Eileen, it'll be like the old days. Remember when we thought it was a big deal to sleep on blankets on the living room floor?"

She smiled. "We thought we were living large, didn't we?"

He pulled out his wallet and took out a cracked picture. "I've never shown you kids my prom picture." He held it in front of the citronella candle lit on the table as the girls gathered around him. "This is me. And this—" He paused to clear his throat and pointed gently to the pretty blond girl with him. "This is Deirdre Ita."

Fiona touched his arm. "Dad…"

"She was named for an Irish saint, and she loved angels and a good story."

"Oh, she did, Bob," his sister said.

As Keira listened to her mother and uncle talk and laugh, one story spinning into another about the friend they'd lost so long ago, she wondered if Simon had known this was coming, and that was at least part of the reason he'd chosen that particular moment to make his exit.

When they blew out the candles for the night, her uncle tucked an arm over her shoulder. "Well, kid, where's your fairy prince?"

"Simon, you mean? He had to leave. I think he might object to being called a fairy prince—"

"Do you, now? Interesting character. On my way back here from Cambridge, I got a call from a state detective I know. Your by-the-book type. Worse than Abigail's partner, that prig Yarborough. In a nutshell, this guy said they didn't find any damn stone angel by the stream, and we all should shut the hell up about one before we get carted to the loony bin."

"But, Bob," Keira said. "I saw it myself."

"You saw a rock. So did your mother. The woods out there are full of rocks. They don't call New Hampshire the Granite State for nothing." He yawned, dropping his arm back to his side. "Stress can do weird things to your mind."

"Then as far as the police are concerned, there's no stone angel?"

"No stone angel," her uncle said. "Of course, that's not what I told the State guy. I told him maybe the fairies took it. He threatened to come out here and shoot me himself. No sense of humor. But, who knows? I keep thinking about your backpack showing up at that Irish pub, and that scrap of sweater the barman in Ireland says he found."

Keira gave him a sharp look. "Bob, I didn't know you believed in fairies—"

"I don't. I just keep an open mind."

"Well," she said, "there was an old man in Ireland..."

"What old man, Keira?"

"I shouldn't say old. He was probably about your age—"

He grinned at her. "That's definitely not old."

As they all headed upstairs, Keira related her encounter with the man at the picnic table the night before the summer solstice, and her uncle listened, amused, curious. When she finished, he said, "I think you should go back to Ireland."

"I do, too."

Bob had a bedroom for his daughter, but they'd already made mats on the floor out of blankets, their aunt stretched out among them, saying she didn't want the couch. "Will you be staying?" she asked Keira.

"Yes, Mum. I'd love to stay."

She didn't want the couch, either, and settled on the floor with her mother and cousins. Bob put on the DVD Colm had brought.

Patsy was at her kitchen table with a pot of tea and a plate of brown bread, and she had on a pastel blue sweater, her eyes bright and filled with life. "Once upon a time," she said in her Irish lilt, "there were three brothers who lived on the southwest coast of Ireland..."

Keira bit back tears and felt her mother take her hand. "This is how Patsy would want to be remembered," she whispered. "For telling a good story."

It was true, Keira thought. And she knew what she had to do. She'd camp out here tonight with her family, and tomorrow she'd head back to Ireland. There was unfinished business there, although she couldn't put her finger on what it was.

And there was Simon.

She would trust him to find her.

~ Chapter 40

East Boston, Massachusetts
10:00 p.m., EDT
June 24

Simon had his feet up on the table on the top deck of his boat and didn't rise to greet John March, who seemed to have come out to the Boston Harbor pier alone—although that was unlikely if not impossible.

The FBI director's presence was not unexpected. He'd warned Simon he was on his way.

"My voice is hoarse," Simon said. "I've been singing Irish songs."

"You always could sing."

"Maybe that could be my new job."

"Hell of a day, Simon."

"Yeah."

March looked out at the harbor, the city lights glistening on the dark, still water. "I wonder what would have happened if I'd remained a Boston cop. Deirdre McCarthy's murder is one of those cases that stays with you, eats at you forever. I know that from a law enforcement point of view, it doesn't matter if the victim of a crime—a brutal murder—is a good person or a bad person. We have a job to do, regardless. But Deirdre…" The FBI director shook his head with emotion. "Deirdre was a good person."

"You wanted out of BPD before her murder. You were always ambitious."

"Her murder helped me to understand why. Abigail can do that work in a way I never could." He sighed at Simon. "You've complicated my life. You know that, don't you?"

Simon shrugged. "You can handle it."

"Reporters are already calling to ask me what I remember about Deirdre's murder. They know Abigail's my daughter." He gave a grim smile. "Wait until they find out about you, Simon."

"You're not just talking about my FBI status."

"That's right. There's also your father."

"Yes. There's my father."

"Someone will start digging and find out we were friends and that he died the way he did. Maybe it's time I talked about him. Brendan Cahill was a dedicated Federal agent. He deserves better than my silence."

"You have nothing to hide," Simon said.

"That's not the point, is it? Talking reminds me of my own failings, but that part doesn't get me so much. I wish I could have saved him, Simon. That's the truth of it." But March didn't linger on the thought and smiled suddenly. "Your father could sing, too. Do you remember?"

"He's the one who taught me my first Irish drinking song."

Simon thought of Keira and how much she still didn't know about him. Then again, she was nosy by nature—curious, she'd say. It was how she could sit in an old woman's kitchen and get her telling stories, and it was why she was interested in the first place. That curiosity—that sensibility—showed up in her artwork. She could go off to Ireland by herself for six weeks, but she wasn't a loner.

"Simon?"

He gave himself a mental shake. "What's going on with Estabrook?"

"We're making our move now. He's still in Montana—I'm expecting a call in few minutes. It'll be a big story. Simon, you need to drop out of sight for a few weeks."

He'd figured as much. "I'm on my way to Scotland. Will's castle. He wants me to play golf."

"And if Fast Rescue needs you?"

"Owen's up to speed on the situation. I'll be back in action as soon as possible."

"You're good, Simon. You don't crack under pressure."

"I don't know. I've fallen for a folklorist who paints pictures of Irish fairies."

March cracked a smile. "I hear she's also quite capable of defending herself. Sounds as if she's a woman right up your alley."

"It's going to take her a while to put this week behind her. She'll do it her own way, just as you did.... Stuart Fuller?"

"I was sitting in Patsy's kitchen eating brown bread and drinking tea when he called her. She knew what we were up against before we did. She believed he was the devil—not that he thought he was the devil. That he was, in fact, Satan."

"Did she tell you?"

March shook his head. "No. I figured it out later. She should have told me, but she didn't. Not for Fuller's sake, Simon. But she shouldn't have had to witness what he did to himself."

"So he did kill himself?"

"Yes, but that wasn't his intention. He believed he could survive the flames."

Simon took a moment to digest that one. A twenty-four-year-old killer luring the mother of a victim of his violence to watch him set himself on fire. "Figured he'd burn a while, prove how evil he was, then, what, set Patsy on fire?"

"Probably." March got heavily to his feet. "I promised your father I'd look after you if anything happened to him—"

"You have, John." Simon rose and put out his hand. "Thank you."

The two men shook, then March surprised Simon by embracing him. "Brendan would be proud of you."

"Tell Abigail about him." Simon stood back and smiled, remembering his father on a summer night just like this one. "He was named after an Irish saint. Brendan the Navigator."

"That tape of his execution…"

"Letting me see it was the right thing to do. Maybe not with another kid, but with me—it's when I knew you understood me. It's when I started listening to you. If you hadn't come along when you did, done what you did—" Simon gave the FBI director a broad grin. "I'd probably just be getting out of prison right about now."

And for the first time in many visits, and most likely many days, John March threw back his head and laughed.

~Chapter 41

Jamaica Plain, Massachusetts
11:30 p.m., EDT
June 24

Abigail couldn't contain her surprise and delight when she entered her living room and saw Keira Sullivan's painting of the Irish cottage that had caught her eye at the auction. She'd never been to Ireland and wasn't Irish, but it didn't matter. Something about the painting—about Keira's work—had captivated her.

"Owen," she said, turning to him, "where did this come from?"

"Simon left it for you. For us, really, but it's more for you. He says if you're happy, I'm happy, and this'll make you happy."

"It does. It's beautiful."

"He wants to know if he's back on the guest list for the wedding."

"Now we'll have to invite him, assuming…" She didn't go on.

"There'll be a wedding, Abigail," Owen said, slipping an arm around her. "Sooner rather than later, I hope."

"It's complicated."

"Only because we're making it complicated. We're lucky. We

have friends, family, resources, work we love—and we have each other. I love you, Abigail. I want to spend the rest of my life with you. I'm patient, but only to a point. Let's get married."

"We don't have everything figured out."

"We don't need to."

It sounded so simple when he said it. "I've been launching myself into the future. I haven't done that in a long time. Before Chris was killed, I had so many plans. Then I didn't. I focused on making detective and finding his killer. That was it. Nothing else. For seven years."

Owen kissed her softly. "We can plan together," he said. "You don't have to figure everything out by yourself."

"I keep thinking about Bob bottling up that poor girl's murder for all these years. Owen, I don't want us to shut each other out. Bob's one of the best men I know. I'd trust him with my life without hesitation. He's a great detective. But I'll bet you he never told either woman he married about Deirdre McCarthy."

"He's protective."

"Yes, but I think Simon got it right. He said Bob learned just not to go there—he put a wall up around that part of his past. I was never that way with Chris's death. I went there every day."

"Because his murder was unsolved," Owen said.

"I don't go there every day anymore. Owen—I love you so much. I love thinking about you, and I do. I think about you every day." She looked at the painting. "Our first wedding present. It's incredibly generous of Simon. Now we owe him—"

"He'd disagree. Hates having people owe him."

She just saw the card. "*Dear Ab*,'" she read aloud. "*Enjoy the painting. Let me know when you pick a wedding date. I think of you as a long-lost sister, even if you're not Irish.*'" She shook her head at Owen and smiled. "Simon does have a way about him. He's cheeky, though, isn't he?"

But there was a loud knock on the back door, and Abigail wasn't surprised when she found Bob and Scoop there with yellow pads and sharpened pencils. "The girls and my sister and niece are asleep," Bob said, "but I need to go through it all again."

"I'm not asleep," Keira said, appearing behind Bob and Scoop. "I'm not a cop, but can I join you?"

Abigail looked back at Owen, but he was already clearing off the kitchen table. It'd be a long night. Then a knock came at the front door, and as she headed down the hall, she couldn't even imagine who it'd be. Yarborough? The mayor? Reporters?

But it was her father, standing by himself on the welcome mat. "Hello, Abigail."

Her breath caught. "Dad. Tell me nothing's happened to Simon—"

"Nothing's happened to him," her father said. "He's fine."

"Cahill's a fun guy," Bob said from behind her in the hall, "but I have a feeling a lot of people want to kill him."

"One in particular at the moment."

"Norman Estabrook," Scoop said, then shrugged at the surprised looks. "I made a few calls."

Abigail noticed her father's slight smile. He was adept at keeping his emotions under tight wraps, but she could tell he had a genuine fondness for Simon. He stepped inside her small apartment, shrugged off his suit jacket. "I wouldn't worry," he said. "The people who want to kill Simon always end up dead or in prison."

Bob, Scoop and Owen obviously liked and understood that answer, but Abigail saw Keira's pale look. Keira knew little about Simon, but she was clearly in love with him. *We could be friends,* Abigail thought, and sat at the small kitchen table between her and Owen.

"May I join you?" her father asked.

Abigail nodded. "I'd love it," she said.

Before he sat down, he put an arm around Keira. "You can trust Simon," he said.

His tone gave Abigail a jolt, and she realized that Simon hadn't been kidding in his note. He *was* like a long-lost brother, because the way her father had just spoken about him…it was as if he were talking about a son.

~Chapter 42

Beara Peninsula, Southwest Ireland
7:00 p.m., IST
August 3

Keira walked down the lane from her cottage with her Irish sweater pulled tight against her in the chill of the wind and damp evening air. She'd begun to notice the days getting shorter, dawn coming a little later, night a little sooner, on the southwest Irish coast. She imagined life in the village before electricity, and it was easy to understand how telling stories by the fire had taken hold here.

As she turned the corner onto the main village street, she could hear an uproar at the pub. Laughter, arguing, hoots of protest. Her step faltered.

Simon.

She picked up her pace, breaking into a run. She hadn't pinned up her hair, and she could feel it tangling in the wind. A cold, damp mist swept up from the harbor. It was a good night for a warm pub, an even better night to be back with Simon.

When she pulled open the pub door, she forced herself to calm down, not look as if she'd just been chased by ghosts or wild dogs—although there'd been none of that in her weeks at her cottage. There'd been a lightness, tranquility, on her quiet lane. She liked to think Patsy's wish had been fulfilled and the stone angel was back where it belonged—somehow, some way.

Keira tucked back some wild strands of hair and caught her breath. She wasn't wrong. It was Simon who'd caused the uproar in the pub.

He stopped midargument and stood up from his stool at the bar. He had on an Irish sweater, and his black hair was a little longer, curling into the wool. His eyes, as green as the hills outside the pub door, sparked, and he smiled. "I had a feeling it'd be easier to find you this visit."

Eddie O'Shea polished a beer glass behind the bar. "Ah, Keira. You didn't have to get yourself into a pickle this time, now, did you?"

The local men gathered at the tables exchanged amused glances. None admitted to believing she'd seen the stone angel up at the ruin, or that the black dog had been anything but a stray, or that they knew anything about an old man in wellies or how her backpack and that shovel had ended up for Eddie to find.

They believed in the devil, though, who'd killed the sheep that awful night, who'd killed Patsy McCarthy in South Boston and had tried to kill Keira and her mother in the woods of southern New Hampshire.

But in the weeks since Keira had returned to the cottage, the horror of those days had receded. She'd worked tirelessly on her collection of tales from Irish-born American immigrants, taking time to roam the hills and play tourist, buying a pottery vase in Adrigole, riding Ireland's one cable car from the tip of the Beara Peninsula to Dursey Island, crawling through castle ruins. Colm Dermott had visited her with his wife and four children, and she'd hooked her laptop up to the Internet.

Seamus Harrigan had stopped by to tie up any loose ends of Jay Augustine's havoc in Ireland. The Irish detective had his own theories.

For starters, he believed that killing the sheep had been opportunistic—of the moment, when the poor beast wandered in front of Augustine on his search for the ruin. Harrigan's team had found a bucket Augustine had undoubtedly used to carry the blood and entrails off with him.

A grisly thought that disturbed even Harrigan, an experienced detective.

Once Augustine found the ruin and started digging, the dog attacked him, and he hid in the trees. Then Keira turned up and ducked into the ruin, thinking the dog was after her.

Augustine, still nervous about the dog, decided he had to take action. The ruin was already showing signs of collapsing. He whispered her name and triggered a bigger collapse, then grabbed Keira's backpack and ran.

But before leaving the ruin, he dumped his bucket of blood and entrails.

On his way out of town, he slipped into Keira's cottage and stole her copy of the tape of Patsy telling her story—and, when he saw the note on the counter detailing her whereabouts, he snatched that, too.

As for the angel—Harrigan had his doubts there'd ever been a stone angel in the ruin. "But if you want to believe there was, Keira," he'd said, with a flash of his very blue eyes, "you go right ahead."

And Keira had decided, who was she to argue with an Irish detective?

Harrigan, who had relatives in the village, said he had a story or two he'd like to tell her one of these days, and he spoke to her as if he knew she'd be back.

A few of the locals had pulled her aside to entertain her with tales of their own. None admitted to knowing the story about the three Irish brothers and the stone angel.

But throughout her weeks in the village, Keira had dreamed of this moment.

Simon set down his glass. "Sorry, fellas. Another time. We'll pick up where we left off."

He walked over to Keira and whisked her up into his arms, and the men all hooted and laughed as he carried her effortlessly out to the street. He didn't set her down until he reached the lane that led down to the harbor.

"A boat," she said. "I should have known."

"It's borrowed."

"Someone else who owes you his life?"

"The same person."

"Will Davenport," she said. "Eddie told me about him."

"Will's fishing in Scotland, but he wants to meet you. It's the flowers in your hair on your Web site."

"I suspect it's because he's your friend, and he knows I'm smitten."

"Smitten?" Simon grinned at her. "A word for a fairy princess, don't you think?"

She laughed, and he led her along the pier, fitting in with the Irish fishermen. But he was a man who could fit in anywhere. When they reached the boat, he scooped her up again, carrying her below, as if he'd been thinking about this moment for days.

He laid her on the bed, and she threw her arms over her head, sinking into the soft, warm sheets and taking in the welcome shock of being with him.

"Keira..." He stared into her eyes. "We're a couple of wanderers."

"At least for now." She threaded her fingers into his hair. "Let's wander together."

He quieted her up with a kiss. "Keira, Keira," he whispered, kissing her again and again. "I've missed you."

The next kiss lasted a long time, and all she wanted was it to go on forever. She smoothed her palms down his neck and over his shoulders, loving the feel of his warm sweater, his firm muscles. When he deepened their kiss, tasting her, she sank even deeper into the soft bed, feeling the want spread through her.

"I've dreamed about you," she said. "I knew you'd find me. I never doubted—"

He slipped his hands under her shirt, lifting his mouth from hers and smiling. "I thought that might get your attention."

"You were right." She relished the feel of him on her bare skin. "Simon...I'm not just falling in love with you any longer. I am in love."

"I've thought about you saying that for all these weeks. Keira," he whispered, skimming his hands up her sides, "I love you."

He curved his palms over her breasts, and she couldn't talk, just let herself take in that he was finally here, with her, making love to her. In seconds he had her clothes off, and his, and all she wanted was to give herself up to the feel of him. She couldn't get enough of him. Not now, not ever.

He pulled back the covers, holding her in his arms. "Are you cold?" he asked.

She smiled, running her hands up his strong back. "Not for long, I imagine."

His mouth found hers again, a deep, lingering, erotic kiss that fired her skin and her soul. She could feel his focus—his purpose. He could pluck survivors out of rubble because of his ability to zero in on a mission. She was more out of control.

A challenge, she thought. A distraction.

"We belong here," she said. "Right now, this moment..."

He kissed a trail lower and found her nipple, and she cried out in surprise and pleasure at the feel of his tongue. She heard the Irish wind howling outside. Appropriate, somehow. They'd met in Boston, Keira thought, but it was Ireland that had brought them together. She'd have fallen for him if they'd met over a pint at Eddie O'Shea's pub.

"Keira," he said, "stop thinking."

And he touched her, licked her, forcing all thought right out of her brain.

She drew her legs apart, and he raised up and drove into her, slowly, deeply, warmth as well as hunger in his green eyes. She responded, savoring every thrust, every inch of him, her pulse quickening, her skin tingling. Her release came suddenly, as the wind beat against the small boat and Simon cried out her name, and she knew they were where they were meant to be.

Afterward, they made their way back out to the pier, bundled in wool sweaters as the wind died down again. Keira looked up toward the barren hills, and against the stars and the moon, she saw the silhouette of a man in an Irish cap and wellies up among the rocks and sheep. He was trailed by a troop of dancing shadows—fairies, she thought, and whether they were real or imagined, she didn't care.

Simon slipped an arm around her, and she knew he'd seen them, too.

"My father's home village is up the coast," he said. "I've heard there are stories there of farmers, fishermen, fairies and magic."

Keira leaned against him, welcoming his warmth and strength. "I can't think of anything I'd rather do than sail the Irish coast with you."

"Up for an adventure, are you?"

She smiled. "Always."

~ Epilogue

Beara Peninsula, Southwest Ireland
7:00 p.m., IST
August 6

Bob O'Reilly entered the toasty pub and noticed that no one seemed to care that he was soaked to the bone and dripping on the floor. He'd walked down the lane from the cottage his crazy niece had rented for another month. She'd arranged for a cot in the living room and sent him and her mother tickets to Ireland.

What could he do? A free trip to Ireland. He had to go.

He peeled off his rain jacket and hung it on a coat tree with a lot of others just as faded and worn.

The barman, Eddie O'Shea, eyed him as he filled a beer glass from the tap. "Well, Detective, did you have a good walk?" He said "detective" as if he thought it was pretty funny Bob was a cop.

Bob shook some of the rainwater off his head. "The weather's lousy, and the air smells like wet sheep."

"Ah, but you love it, don't you?"

"I'm not saying."

He eased onto a high stool next to his sister. The scenery on the Beara Peninsula reminded him of some of the postcards Patsy McCarthy had tacked to the wall in her front hall.

And it reminded him of stories his mother used to tell.

He'd stay a week in Ireland. Then he had to get back to work.

He didn't know about Eileen. She might just stay forever. She'd finished her illuminated manuscript before heading to Ireland. Colm Dermott had hired her to help work on the Boston-Cork conference. Bob figured she'd have to find a place to live that at least had flush toilets. But she was already loving the idea of the job. Billie and Jeanette Murphy, horrified at how Jay Augustine had manipulated them, had set up a scholarship in Patsy's name and were sending the first recipient to the conference.

It'd be weeks yet before the Augustine investigation was wrapped up. Bob wasn't in charge of it—he wasn't even part of it, except as a witness. He didn't like that, but what could he do? The rest of the autopsy results were back on Victor Sarakis. Still no smoking gun on how he'd drowned in two feet of water, but the medical examiner had taken a closer look at Victor's body. He'd taken a solid hit on his left temple, undoubtedly when he struck the concrete edge of the pond. It wouldn't have killed him or probably even knocked him out, but it could have rung his bell enough to disorient him. And there was a bruise on Victor's back that could have been from his brother-in-law standing on him.

One or the other, or both, could have prevented Victor from fighting off that devil.

Jay Augustine's actions weren't arbitrary or nuts, Bob thought. Augustine'd had a mission. It just hadn't included grabbing a BPD detective's daughter off the street. He'd wanted a mother and daughter. A religious ascetic who lived in the woods and a pretty artist and folklorist.

Eileen and Keira...

Bob let the thought go. The bastard was behind bars where he belonged.

And I'm on vacation.

On his first day in Ireland, and Eileen's first day back in thirty years, they'd walked up to the ruin where Keira had nearly met her end on the summer solstice and all that bit about a dog and an angel and fairies had occurred. Maybe it was the old hut of the hermit monk from Patsy's story. Maybe it wasn't. It didn't matter—it was definitely the place where his sister had holed up for three days in a gale all those years ago.

But maybe, ultimately, that didn't matter, either.

"Keira called before you got to the pub," Eileen said. "She wants to arrange for us to spend Christmas in Ireland. You, me, the girls. We'll stay in fancy places in Dublin and Kenmare. Can you imagine, Bob?"

"I can imagine how much it'd cost."

"Her illustrations have caught on, and she's never been a big spender."

"What about Simon?"

"Oh, he'll be there, too," Eileen said. "I know he will, don't you?"

"At least I won't be the only male. That's what I know."

But he could imagine Fiona's excitement in particular at the prospect of spending Christmas in Ireland. She'd drag him to pubs to listen to music. Probably make him sing. She was getting her younger sisters into Irish music—Madeleine had taken right to the fiddle. Jayne was more like him and not that enthralled.

Eileen's cheeks were flushed with the anticipation of it all. "You can see it, can't you, Bob? All of us together for Christmas."

"Oh, yeah. I can see me in some damn five-star hotel with those girls of mine."

Eddie sighed with amusement. "You Yanks," he said, setting a pint of Guinness in front of Bob.

"American as apple pie," Bob said, raising his glass to Eddie with a wink.

"If you think the weather's bad now, wait until you're here at Christmas. The damp will sink into your bones."

"You keep the pub open?"

"All but Christmas Day."

"Good. I'll talk Keira out of putting us up in a five-star hotel."

Eddie laughed, but when he set a pot of tea and a small plate of steaming brown bread in front of Eileen, Bob saw her eyes film with tears. She was thinking of Patsy, he knew. And maybe Deirdre. He drank some of his Guinness and didn't speak.

"Ah, Eileen," Eddie said with a twinkle in his eyes, "sitting there you don't look a day over twenty."

She smiled through her tears. "Well, aren't you a big liar."

He laughed. "You've been missed all these years."

"I have a story to tell," she said with a catch in her voice. "A true story. Some of it's sad, and some of it's not. I can keep it to myself if you'd like."

Bob kept his mouth shut, but Eddie said, "No, tell it. It's a rainy, windy night, a good one for a story. Tell it start to finish, and don't leave out a word."

He closed the pub for the night. Several of the local men stayed, gathered at the small tables, nursing beers and coffee as the weather roared outside.

Eileen started tentatively, with her and Bob and Deirdre growing up together on the same street. She covered it all, from then until now, and Bob hadn't realized what a storyteller his sister was. All those months by herself in that cabin, chopping wood, hauling water, fending for herself—and praying, of course. She still prayed a lot. He didn't mind. He hoped now and then she put in a good word or two for him.

As she wrapped up, she said, "Deirdre always wanted to see Ireland. She truly was an angel."

"She still is, then," Eddie said, a little choked up himself.

"We used to talk about running off to Ireland and having adventures and romances."

"And here you are, back again."

"Because of Keira. Deirdre would be pleased at her happiness."

"And yours."

Eileen smiled. "Yes. Mine, too. I don't know who Keira's father was— I just know I was trapped in that ruin for three days in a proper Irish gale, and I loved hard and well for that time."

"But John Michael Sullivan," Eddie said with some emotion. "He was the love of your life, wasn't he, Eileen?"

She bit back tears. "Eddie…"

"If you hadn't come home from Ireland expecting, you'd never have let yourself look at him. You were the college girl. He was the boy from the neighborhood."

In the past thirty years, Bob had never thought of Eileen's relationship with her husband that way, but he saw her blush and had a sudden appreciation for the barman's wisdom.

"We loved each other," Eileen murmured.

Eddie O'Shea leaned over the bar, his eyes intense now, certain. "You didn't lose Deirdre or John Michael because of anything you did here. Your daughter's a blessing."

Bob couldn't take anymore. "I don't know about that. She's off sailing the Irish coast with some black-haired rake of an Irish fairy prince, drawing pictures of leprechauns and thistle and sticking me here in the back end of nowhere—"

He didn't get to finish—the locals were on him. He bought a round of drinks, and they laughed and argued and talked politics and sheep and fairies. Eileen didn't take part, but that was okay. Bob could tell she was listening, and she was happy, in the company of friends. He could feel all her anguish and guilt fall away. A mad affair that was meant to be was long over, and she knew what she knew about her daughter's father and that was all.

Not everything in life needed to be explained.

When they finally headed back to the cottage, the rain had stopped, and Eddie O'Shea joined them on the walk up the lane. His two brothers fell in beside him. It was a night for mischief, they said—and the three of them headed up the dirt track off into the dark Irish hills.

Bob stood with his sister in front of the pretty stone cottage with its pink roses, and they looked out at the starlit sky and the eerie mist above the harbor.

"We're in the company of angels, Bob," Eileen said softly.

"Yeah, sis." He slung an arm over her shoulders and thought of Deirdre and Patsy and John Michael, and he felt them all with him now in the Irish wind. "We surely are."

The New York Times

BOOK OF
WORLD
WAR · I

The New York Times

BOOK OF
WORLD
WAR · I

Edited by Christine Bent

Arno Press ● New York ● 1980

A Note to the Reader
In the interest of legibility, complete front pages of *The New York Times* could not be reproduced. The editor has included only the most important news articles from each issue of the newspaper. They appear in this book on redesigned pages under a copy of the original masthead.

The art of printing newspapers in the early 1900's obviously was not what it is today. In addition, original copies of *The New York Times* were not available to the publisher. This volume, therefore, was created from 35mm microfilm copies of *The Times*.

Copyright © 1914, 1915 1916, 1917, 1918, 1919, 1920 by The New York Times Company.

Copyright © 1980 by The New York Times Company.

Library of Congress Cataloging in Publication Data
Main entry under title:

The New York times book of World War I.

Compilation of articles that appeared in the New York times from 1914 through 1919.
1. European War, 1914–1918—Sources. I. Bent, Christine, 1949-
II. New York times
D505.N73   940.3   80-16366
ISBN 0-405-13465-7

Manufactured in the United States of America.

Book design by Moffit Cecil and Mary Smith.

Contents

Introduction vii

1914 1

1915 51

1916 103

1917 159

1918 221

1919 305

Introduction

The history of World War I, or "The Great War" as it was known to contemporaries, graphically unfolds with every headline, article and illustration in this unusual volume. It has also been the detailed subject of weighty books, perhaps hundreds in number, by learned and eminent historians. Some have covered the multitude of aspects—social, political, historical, diplomatic, economic, racial, religious, and even philosophical—that characterized that gigantic struggle. Others have analyzed these aspects as manifestations of a new and revolutionary era in human history—the age of technology, the age of the masses, a period which encompasses our own lifetimes.

An examination of several facets of the peace treaty which were designed to make this vast confrontation the "war to end all wars" leads one to believe that it may have constituted the *raison d'etre* for another, perhaps more terrifying world conflagration after a respite of only two decades.

In December 1918 President Woodrow Wilson set sail aboard the *George Washington*, for the war-ravaged "Old World" via the French harbor of Brest. When he arrived in Paris, it is reported, he was received in an atmosphere of unrestrained adulation and joy. His well-publicized goal was to be the architect of a just conclusion to the Great War that would, at the same time, purge Europe and the world of age-old injustices, intolerances and inequalities. He girded himself for a battle of persuasion with crafty leaders of both allied and enemy nations. He armed himself with broad ideals that reflected the optimism of his own "New World," the advice of learned, if sometimes not too professional, friends and consultants, and his scholarly research and considerable contemplation. This former Princeton professor, expert on the orderly workings of American constitutional government, was determined to play a decisive role in the construction of a lasting peace. There were some men in his entourage, less morally inspired than he, perhaps, and certainly less far-seeing, who brought with them more narrow considerations of national interest—considerations of economic gain, political power, even of imperial design. Wilson, however, stood squarely for ideals of international justice.

Nor was President Wilson modest or limited in his moral program for this new international order. On January 8, 1918, he had outlined his proposals to the American Congress and thus to the world. Fourteen in number, these principles he considered to be universally binding on all men, friend and foe alike.

> "We entered this war because violations of right had occurred which touched us to the quick and made the life of our own people impossible unless they were corrected and the world secured once and for all against their recurrence. What we demand in this war, therefore, is nothing peculiar to ourselves. It is that the world be made fit and safe to live in, and particularly that it be made safe for every peace-loving nation which, like our own, wishes to live its own life, determine its own institutions, be assured of justice and fair dealings by the other peoples of the world, as against force and selfish aggression. All of the peoples of the world are in effect partners in this interest and for our own part we see very clearly that unless justice be done to others it will not be done to us. The program of the world's peace, therefore, is our program, the only possible program, as we see it . . ."

Wilson's Fourteen Points called for freedom of the seas; free trade among nations; open covenants in international politics, the liberation of the oppressed nationalities of Austria-Hungary; the limitation of Turkish sovereignty over non-Turkish races, particularly in the Balkans; the immediate restitution and reconstruction of invaded and ravaged territories; objective and democratic solutions to colonial questions; and the two most important points of all were concerned with the right of self-determination as it related to nationality and statehood; and the establishment of an international body which would guarantee the objective application of all of these principles and, at the same time, would resolve all future difficulties between sovereign states and peoples—a League of Nations. The League of Nations was to take form out of the chaos of horrifying, brutal 20th-century warfare. It was to rejuvenate the earth with free, noble and altruistic ideals. It would prohibit war forever and ensure justice and security for sovereign states and for individuals. These benefits would accrue even to the weak, the poor, and the tiny nations which possessed no great armies, limited resources, and great geographic liabilities. Just before the *George Washington* docked in Brest on December 13, Wilson is reported to have made an eminently moral request of one of his trusted staff members. "Keep me informed as to what is right and I will fight for it. But see to it that I have a solid basis of information."

None of the great powers had entered the war of 1914 with clearly defined aims. Each had taken up arms for different reasons which often changed as drastically as the volatile military situation. The basic program of each was, therefore, limited to victory in the field and the fulfillment of secret obligations to companion states in payment for aid, alliance and military cooperation. These were the nefarious secret treaties that so astonished and repulsed Woodrow Wilson. Such secret treaty obligations were not, in the opinion of many diplomatic historians, wholly reflective of the Allied war aims. They were, however, formulated to help resolve the peace whenever it came about, to ease the pressure of conflicting issues between wartime partners and, in some instances, to give recognition to long-standing national interests and aspirations. In the case of Italy, they were employed to induce the Italian government to abrogate its alliance with the Central Powers and to enter the war on the side of France, Great Britain and Imperial Russia.

In addition, the age of popular democracy and intricate national industrial effort had brought with it the reality of a united war effort which demanded the *total* participation of an entire population in the pursuit of "national interests." As a consequence of "total war," entire nations were either "in the right" or "in the wrong," "brutal aggressors" or "innocent victims of warmongers" depending upon which side was making the moral evaluations and, in the case of World War I, upon which side was winning. In essence, World War I was really the first international struggle in which the concept of "national war guilt" played a crucial role. Although, in historical retrospect, many of the causes of World War I seemed to have been shared by national leaders on both sides of the trenches, it became critical for the Allies to affix to their prodigious war efforts lofty moral goals, thus to engender far greater sacrifice and blind patriotism in their citizenry, and to win over public opinion in the United States as well as the American government to their own "just" cause. "Open diplomacy," "self-determination," "free-trade," "world order through impartial world government"—were these not noble aims to which all popular governments could easily aspire? Was not justice in international relations a more compelling reason for military victory than territorial acquisition or economic advantage? Conversely, what was more "immoral" than the violation of Belgian neutrality or the shelling of French cathedrals, and what was less in keeping with the principles of a new world order than the autocratic government of the Kaiser or the Emperor?

Wilson was confident, and with reason, that his democratic allies (Imperial Russia, now defunct, had always presented a considerable embarassment in this respect) would welcome his principles and would concur unanimously that a peace treaty would have to include provisions for world government. Support for Wilson's point-of-view also came, as would be expected, from representatives of those peoples who aspired to national states of their own or to the restoration of territories that constituted their "historic homelands"—the Poles, the Czechs, the Slovaks, the Slavic minorities then under Austro-Hungarian or Turkish rule, the Jews, and many more obscure minorities whose nature, origins, and ethno-historical claims were all but unknown to either Wilson or his staff of experts. Nonetheless he was gratified by their faith in him, and he was almost overwhelmed with the realization that even the enemy, now close to defeat, also had accepted (indeed, had counted upon) the application of his proposals to the peace treaty.

Thus assured, and resplendent in his aura of self-righteousness, the American President took his evangelical program to Versailles and his place alongside other world leaders at the most ambitious peace conference in the history of mankind. On a scale far greater than that of the Congress of Vienna, twenty-seven nations, large and small, had sent modern versions of Talleyrand and Metternich to Paris. They all wanted to join in the negotiations and to share, publically at least, the responsibility for a new world. Privately, of course, they endeavored to make certain that their "just" national claims were recognized and satisfied in the treaty terms. Some great leaders, Clemenceau of France for one, were not totally convinced that small powers, especially from far-away continents, ought to debate issues of such vital and controversial a nature as the borders of the new Germany or the creation of a *cordon sanitaire* around the vanquished German people. Even Wilson's Secretary of State, Robert Lansing, had deep reservations about the entire conference and the need to give real power to an international government. These reservations stemmed from Lansing's quiet belief that the President's statesmanship was on a par with the "fantasy of an opium addict." To Lansing, the League of Nations was a utopian concept and foreign policy meant American policy serving the national interest. He wanted peace at top speed, and the return of the United States to its own affairs and its own boundaries as soon as possible. He envisioned a considerable risk—that America would be obliged, through the application of Wilson's principles and concepts, to come to the aid of Hottentots and Wallachians even when the national interest called for no such efforts. Superficially, however, and for a brief time at least, Wilson's moral standards and his priorities for discussion during the conference prevailed.

What went wrong? Why were the victors at Versailles unable or unwilling to establish the lasting peace which Wilson envisioned? The very nature of the Fourteen Points may have been, but only in part, to blame for their apparent failure. From the vantage point of the pulpit and from the viewpoint of the reformer, these were lofty, objective, passionately desirable principles. Did they, however, reflect the international situation or a profound understanding of the European scene? Did they truly consider the facts of history, no matter how distressing, or the background history of the war? What is more important, did they misconstrue the real nature of the 20th century? Frankly stated, were some aspects of Wilson's program for world order and peace more dangerous in what they implied or generated than the ills they were constructed to banish?

"Open covenants of peace, openly arrived at" and "diplomacy shall proceed always frankly and in the public view" were Wilsonian phrases that possessed a deeply moral and democratic cast. In the 19th century, diplomacy had, in most instances, been in the hands of a coterie of professional diplomats, representatives of the powerful classes of their respective states. An in-group, often above the passions of their own people and many times able to quell the more amateurish foreign policy programs of their less-informed colleagues in the national government, these diplomats settled disputes, declared war, gave away or exchanged territories (often not their own), and made plans for both colonial and territorial acquisition. Frequently they transferred or disenfranchised minorities, placing them into the hands of alien sovereigns. Just as often, they settled disputes adroitly in a sly game of reciprocity—all of this for the sake of the "balance of power" and "international stability." Negotiations and terms of agreement were, for the most part, secret, and what was offered for public edification was many times just the "tip of the iceberg." For most of the 19th century, however, despite wars, disputes and hostile alliances, a major conflagration had been avoided. Wilson, however, read diplomatic history differently, and from the point of view of a 20th century theoretician of democracy. Was not Bismarck a leading advocate of secret diplomacy, a weaver of tangled hostile alliances, a representative of an autocratic government, a persecutor of Poles and Czechs, an imperialist, and a natural enemy of the French and other democratic nations? Finally, was he not a German and had not the Germans (and their imperialist compatriots the Austro-Hungarians) started the war? In short, according to Wilson, it was secret diplomacy (more precisely, secret diplomacy in the hands of autocratic, elitist manipulators) that provided a contributing factor in international tension and strife. Get rid of secret diplomacy, take from the elitist diplomats their nefarious power, replace both with popularly approved treaties and agreements concluded by representatives of the democratic masses (who were always equitable and just if only told the "truth") and you take a giant step towards everlasting peace.

At the peace conference, when Clemanceau, Lloyd George and Orlando, rightly or wrongly, were most concerned with concretizing their war gains and fulfilling both their national aims and their obligations to allies, Wilson was more interested in settling the new frontiers of Europe according to "moral" standards, and establishing the League. When the provisions and promises of the secret agreements became widely known, Wilson chose to disregard them. They were immoral, not in the least democratic, and therefore irrelevant, both to an eventual peace treaty and to a possible world government.

And the national leaders who insisted on meeting their terms were crafty manipulators who, in no way, represented the real will of their co-citizens.

When the Prime Minister of Italy, Orlando, after having waited patiently for the conferees to honor Italy's war claims (based upon the secret London Agreement of 1915), saw all of the assurances and promises to his government ignored, he became "Orlando Furioso." He warned Wilson that Italy—and the Italians—would press for the Adriatic port of Fiume (Rijeka). The American President replied that the Italian people would never attempt to rob the young Slav state of its only real port. "I know the Italian people better than you do," he said to the astonished Orlando. Then the President released the details of his disagreement to the press, and the Italian people, not nearly as "fair and as equitable" as they ought to have been according to his theories, turned upon him in wrath. A few years later this wrath and frustration would turn into warm support for the revisionist and expansionist policies of Mussolini.

Wilson, deeply sincere in his convictions, was dedicated to a spirit of dilettantism, the reflection of an American suspicion of an elitist corps. Several of the fourteen points, especially "open diplomacy" reflected this unequivocally. He had failed to investigate other possibilities—or perhaps they just did not occur to him—that secret diplomacy may often be more effective; that complicated matters involving intricate details are often misunderstood and misinterpreted by the masses; that popularly held concepts about foreign nations might destroy chances for arbitration or compromise; and finally that modern governments, both democratic and dictatorial, often create popular opinion through massive programs of persuasion. When Wilson "went to the Italian people," it was a personal act of open diplomacy. The Italian people, far from being flattered because he had bypassed their governmental representatives, were furious. They were also furious because they felt that their wartime sacrifices had been in vain.

Self-determination was another principle that sounded better in theory than it was in terms of practicality. It was easy to talk of self-determination for Poles, Italians, diverse Slavic nations, Romanians and Hungarians. It was quite another task to fix the geographic limitations of their self-determination so that, even between the newly "liberated" peoples, there would be no lasting enmities or friction. Because Wilson had access to the "truth", he chose not to study the facts—and the facts about the national minorities constituted a maze of contradictions. The Austro-Hungarian Empire, one of the "guilty" parties in the Great War, was to be punished by dismemberment. This would serve to fulfill the national aspirations of the many peoples it had so "brutally" suppressed. Wilson never imagined that national minorities, like the Great Powers, would be interested not only in self-determination and regaining their "historic homelands," but in territorial expansion, access to mineral deposits and raw materials, shipping and docks, and manpower. Nor did he consider that many of these national minorities had conflicting claims, or that some of them would never be self-sufficient. To the contrary, they would always, even as sovereign states, be at the mercy of their larger, stronger neighbors.

The Treaties of Saint Germain, Neuilly and Trianon and their grave defects were certainly not engineered by Woodrow Wilson, but they unquestionably reflected the Pandora's box opened up by the destruction of the multi-national Austro-Hungarian Empire. This destruction was demanded by the victors in the name of national self-determination although it was also an instance of the victor punishing the vanquished. Was Europe more stable when Czechoslovakia became the beneficiary of three and one half million Sudeten Germans and masses of Hungarians and Poles? Was Hungary to accept with gratitude the fact that its territory had been reduced from 109,000 square miles to 36,000 square miles and almost two million Magyars given to Romania and one million more to Czechoslovakia? What about the German populations in the new Poland and the Poles in the reconstituted Germany; or the Austrians who now resided in Italy; or the thousands of Bulgarians who were incorporated, along with their farms and villages, into Romania? The cause of world stability may have suffered a stunning blow with the destruction of the dual Monarchy. There arose a power vacuum in Eastern Europe and the Balkans, a vacuum which both Hitler and Stalin attempted to fill within a few decades. Such was the result of diplomacy based on prayer house generalizations and moralisms.

Throughout the Fourteen Points there were other serious instances of this moralistic dilettantism. In reality, and even under international law, according to experts like Hans Kelsen, the establishment of a League of Nations did not properly fall into the legitimate scope of the peace negotiations. As Kelsen stated in 1938: "From the technical legal standpoint there was never any justification for the inclusion of the statute of the League of Nations in the text of the treaties. There were no practical reasons for making this wholly inorganic union of two kinds of provisions which were so much at variance in their purpose, and the resulting disadvantages are far from negligible." The disadvantage was the tying in of a world government to a treaty designed to punish. The Germans were at first excluded from the League and so were the "deserters," the Soviet Russians. Yet throughout the proceedings of the conference, Wilson insisted on the implementation of his fourteenth point.

As we now unfortunately know, the Great War was not "the war to end all wars." It was World War I. In 1939 another war, even more horrible, began. Some say it was just a continuation of the first world conflagration. Others maintain that we are still paying for the failure of the Paris peacemakers to rise above their passions and their fears and to establish a truly just and lasting peace. Wilson may have been a better, more principled man than his contemporaries; nonetheless, his lofty program to achieve world peace was no more realistic than their narrow nationalistic maneuvers and vendettas. Wilson had failed to come to grips with the realities of the world. The other Versailles statesmen failed to turn the peace conference into a vehicle to rise above these realities. The Germans were punished harshly and exiled, along with the Russians, to the fringe areas of the international community. They returned with a vengeance.

Sanford Louis Chernoff

1914

"All the News That's Fit to Print."

The New York Times.

THE WEATHER

Local showers today; Tuesday, fair; fresh, shifting winds, becoming northwest.

For full weather report see Page 17.

VOL. LXIII...NO. 20,610.   NEW YORK, MONDAY, JUNE 29, 1914.—EIGHTEEN PAGES.   ONE CENT In Greater New York, Jersey City and Newark. | Elsewhere TWO CENTS.

HEIR TO AUSTRIA'S THRONE IS SLAIN WITH HIS WIFE BY A BOSNIAN YOUTH TO AVENGE SEIZURE OF HIS COUNTRY

Francis Ferdinand Shot During State Visit to Sarajevo.

TWO ATTACKS IN A DAY

Archduke Saves His Life First Time by Knocking Aside a Bomb Hurled at Auto.

SLAIN IN SECOND ATTEMPT

LAID TO A SERVIAN PLOT

AGED EMPEROR IS STRICKEN

Special Cable to THE NEW YORK TIMES.

SARAJEVO, Bosnia, June 28, (By courtesy of the Vienna Neue Freie Presse.)—Archduke Francis Ferdinand, heir to the throne of Austria-Hungary, and his wife, the Duchess of Hohenberg, were shot and killed by a Bosnian student here today. The fatal shooting was the second attempt upon the lives of the couple during the day, and is believed to have been the result of a political conspiracy.

This morning, as Archduke Francis Ferdinand and the Duchess were driving to a reception at the Town Hall a bomb was thrown at their motor car. The Archduke pushed it off with his arm.

The bomb did not explode until after the Archduke's car had passed on, and the occupants of the next car, Count von Boos-Waldeck and Col. Morizzi, the Archduke's aide de camp, were slightly injured. Among the spectators, six persons were more or less seriously hurt.

The author of the attempt at assassination was a compositor named Gabrinovics, who comes from Trebinje.

After the attempt upon his life the Archduke ordered his car to halt, and after he found out what had happened he drove to the Town Hall, where the Town Councillors, with the Mayor at their head, awaited him. The Mayor was about to begin his address

Archduke Francis Ferdinand and his Consort the Duchess of Hohenberg

Slain by Assassin's Bullets.

of welcome, when the Archduke interrupted him angrily, saying:

"Herr Burgermeister, it is perfectly outrageous! We have come to Sarajevo on a visit and have had a bomb thrown at us."

The Archduke paused a moment, and then said: "Now you may go on."

Thereupon the Mayor delivered his address and the Archduke made a suitable reply.

The public by this time had heard of the bomb attempt, and burst into the hall with loud cries of "Zivio!" the Slav word for "hurrah."

After going around the Town Hall, which took half an hour, the Archduke started for the Garrison Hospital to visit Col. Morizzi, who had been taken there after the outrage.

As the Archduke reached the corner of Rudolf Street two pistol shots were fired in quick succession by an individual who called himself Gavrio Princip. The first shot struck the Duchess in the abdomen, while the second hit the Archduke in the neck and pierced the jugular vein. The Duchess became unconscious immediately and fell across the knees of her husband. The Archduke also lost consciousness in a few seconds.

The motor car in which they were seated drove straight to the Konak, where an army Surgeon rendered first aid, but in vain. Neither the Archduke nor the Duchess gave any sign of life, and the head of the hospital could only certify they were both dead.

The authors of both attacks upon the Archduke are born Bosnians. Gabrinovics is a compositor, and worked for a few weeks in the Government printing works at Belgrade. He returned to Sarajevo a Servian chauvinist, and made no concealment of his sympathies with the King of Servia. Both he and the actual murderer of the Archduke and the Duchess expressed themselves to the police in the most cynical fashion about their crimes.

PARIS PRESS FEARS WAR

But Thinks There Will Be an End of Ferdinand's Projects.

Special Cable to THE NEW YORK TIMES.

PARIS, Monday, June 29.—The French press devotes a great deal of space to Archduke Ferdinand's assassination. The general tone indicates a belief in the end of his projects and reputed intention to make Austria a greater Slav power. Combined with the admitted hostility of Servia and the opposition of Russia, French interests caused him to be regarded as the European stormy petrel.

A note of genuine regret is that, deprived of the Archduke's strong personality, Austria inevitably will be more subject to German influence. Several journals express the fear that the consequences will be sufficiently serious again to plunge the Balkans, if not Europe, into a conflict.

TRAGEDY MAY ALTER POLITICS OF EUROPE

Late Archduke's Ambitions Regarded with Distrust in Many of the Capitals.

WANTED A TRIPLE EMPIRE

And His Designs on Slavic Territory Had Long Threatened to Bring About Trouble.

Special Cable to THE NEW YORK TIMES.

LONDON, Monday, June 29.—A new situation has been created in Europe by the tragedy at Sarajevo. While the crime cannot but arouse universal horror and indignation for the as-

2

sassin and sympathy for the victims, there are political considerations which make it an event of as high importance from that point of view as in its personal dynastic aspects.

In Russia, England, and France the Archduke Francis Ferdinand was regarded as one of the most serious dangers to European peace. Even in Germany his accession to the throne was viewed with apprehension. A man of strong opinions and great will power, he already, as heir to the throne, exercised a potent influence upon Austrian policy. He was a strong supporter of Aerenthall, whose tenure of the Austrian Foreign Office saw Europe on the verge of war, and throughout the more recent developments in the Balkans some of the difficulties encountered by European statesmen in limiting hostilities to Southeastern Europe arose from the Archduke's insistence on what he regarded as the full measure of Austria's rights.

Russian diplomacy for some time past has been convinced that Francis Ferdinand's policy ultimately would bring about a crisis in Austro-Russian relations, and military movements in the great Slav empire which only a few months ago created a sensation in the Continental press were defended by Russian newspapers on the ground that they were necessary precautions against Austria.

Germany, which in 1909 threatened a mobilization of her army unless Russia agreed to Austria's annexation of Bosnia and Herzegovina, afterward used her influence in a contrary direction, and Kaiser Wilhelm's counsels of moderation to his Austrian ally undoubtedly were not without their effect upon the course of events immediately preceding and following the Balkan war.

The dead Archduke's dream was what is known in Austria-Hungary as trialism. His object was to prevent that disruption of the dual monarchy which it has so often been predicted would follow the death of Emperor Francis Joseph. Trialism is a device for consolidating the empire, which at present is a dual State, controlled in Austria by Germans and in Hungary by Magyars.

In this disposition of nationalities the Slav elements of the population do not play their proper rôle in the body politic of the empire. Trialism aims at reconstituting the State with three instead of two populations, one of them predominantly Slav, just as one is now predominantly German and the other predominantly Magyar. A necessary corollary of trialism is the increase of the Slav populations of the empire by the inclusion of the Slavonic races of the Balkans.

Whether such an ambition ever could be realized is open to doubt. The actually existing hatred of Austria by Servia and other Slav peoples of the Balkans would have to disappear first or be ground out under the heel of a military despotism.

The effort to develop these ambitions by the latter process naturally would be alarming to Russia, which dreams of a Slav empire extending over the Balkan States.

It is a curious instance of the irony of fate that the Archduke, whose ambition was the annexation of a Slav kingdom, was stricken by the hand of a youthful enthusiast, who dreamed of "a greater Servia" that would unite under one sceptre Servians of the present kingdom of that name and their Slavonic brethren of Bosnia, Herzegovina, Dalmatia, and Croatia. While the importance of the Archduke's assassination in the field of in-

ternational politics is thus seen to be great it may also have vast effects upon the internal fortunes of Austro-Hungary.

The new heir apparent, while popular in Vienna, is described as a young man of no remarkable ability, and the process of disintegration of the empire might very well be helped by a régime the head whereof was a weakling. The oft-repeated prediction respecting the breaking up of the empire on the death of Francis Joseph, however, is discredited by well-informed observers of Austrian affairs. In the conscriptional army the Government possesses not only a weapon to repress separatist movements, but an instrument whose power may weld together the various elements of which the dual kingdom is composed.

MAY MEAN INTERVENTION.

Grave Consequences of a Change of Ferdinand's Policy.

A couple of revolver shots probably never before formed a connection between such a line of complicated causes and such an infinite variety of possibly still more complicated effects as those which yesterday killed Archduke Ferdinand and his wife, the Duchess of Hohenberg.

Since the absorption of Herzegovina and Bosnia in 1908 by Austria, the ambition of Servia has been to keep that Empire in check, and to secure for herself a strip of coast line on the Adriatic. Keeping pace with that ambition has been that of Austria to extend her narrow coast line southward, and to absorb all the Slav territory possible. This last ambition has often found expression in the words of the ill-fated heir presumptive to the Austrian throne.

He realized that the days of the dual monarchy might end, through German or Russian intervention, with the death of the venerable Francis Joseph, and to preserve the entity of the empire he conceived the idea of a triune empire made up of Magyar, Slav, and German states.

It was in pursuance of this policy that Herzegovina and Bosnia were added to the Slav territory of the Empire and caused guns to be leveled across the Danube six years ago.

But these guns did not then explode. At the time it seemed as though Servia, backed up by Russia, might force Austria to withdraw, when Germany came to the rescue of her ally and caused Russia to dismiss her Foreign Minister and abolish her Pan-Slavonic policy. A state of armed neutrality then ensued until the Balkan war.

The maintenance of the Turk in Europe had long been acknowledged by the powers to be a vital necessity — not because of any particular desire to befriend the Turk, but solely because the downfall of the Turkish Empire would mean a disruption of the relative strength of the mutual bond on which reposed the peace of Europe.

Aside from the Pan-Slavonic force represented by Russia tending to destroy this equilibrium was the other force represented by Austria-Hungary and the Archduke Ferdinand's scheme for a triune empire.

But while Russia would have gained access to the Mediterranean by the destruction of European Turkey, Austria-Hungary would have left that territory as a rampart against Russia on the east and have forced her way through the heterogeneous mass of Macedonia to the Aegean or the Strait of Otranto. In other words, Austria would have liked the land north of Greece as a Slav appendage to her German and Magyar nationalities.

It is no wonder, therefore, that the Austro-Hungarian scheme found more sympathy in the chancelleries of Western Europe than the Russian, which the defeat of Turkey by the little Balkan nations in the late war has perceptibly strengthened.

One power, however, kept Austria in line, and has continued to keep her in line, even in the present Albanian imbroglio. That power is Italy, to whom Austrian control of the Adriatic would be fatal.

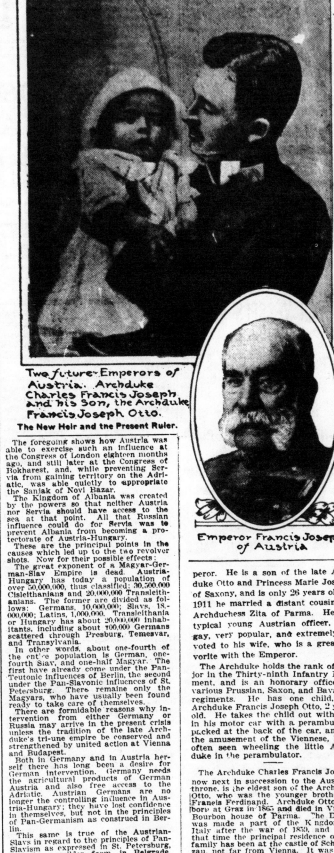

Two future Emperors of Austria. Archduke Charles Francis Joseph and his Son, the Archduke Francis Joseph Otto.

The New Heir and the Present Ruler.

Emperor Francis Joseph of Austria

The foregoing shows how Austria was able to exercise such an influence at the Congress of London eighteen months ago, and still later at the Congress of Bokharest, and, while preventing Servia from gaining territory on the Adriatic, was able quietly to appropriate the Sanjak of Novi Bazar.

The Kingdom of Albania was created by the powers so that neither Austria nor Servia should have access to the sea at that point. All that Russian influence could do for Servia was to prevent Albania from becoming a protectorate of Austria-Hungary.

These are the principal points in the causes which led up to the two revolver shots. Now for their possible effects:

The great exponent of a Magyar-German-Slav Empire is dead. Austria-Hungary has today a population of over 50,000,000, thus classified: 30,500,000 Cisleithanians and 20,000,000 Transleithanians. The former are divided as follows: Germans, 10,000,000; Slavs, 18,000,000; Latins, 1,000,000. Transleithania or Hungary has about 20,000,000 inhabitants, including about 700,000 Germans scattered through Presburg, Temesvar, and Transylvania.

In other words, about one-fourth of the entire population is German, one-fourth Slav, and one-half Magyar. The first have already come under the Pan-Teutonic influences of Berlin, the second under the Pan-Slavonic influences of St. Petersburg. There remain only the Magyars, who have usually been found ready to take care of themselves.

There are formidable reasons why intervention from either Germany or Russia may arrive in the present crisis unless the tradition of the late Archduke's tri-une empire be conserved and strengthened by united action at Vienna and Budapest.

Both in Germany and in Austria herself there has long been a desire for German intervention. Germany needs the agricultural products of German Austria, and also free access to the Adriatic. Austrian Germans are no longer the controlling influence in Austria-Hungary; they have lost confidence in themselves, but not in the principles of Pan-Germanism as construed in Berlin.

This same is true of the Austrian-Slavs in regard to the principles of Pan-Slavism as expressed in St. Petersburg, and, in a milder form, in Belgrade, Sofia, and Bukharest.

The situation caused by the revolver in the hands of the Servian student is one of infinite possibilities.

NEW HEIR IS POPULAR.

Charles Francis Joseph a Young Man of Good Impulses.

Special Cable to THE NEW YORK TIMES.

LONDON, June 28. — Archduke Charles Francis Joseph, the new heir to the throne of Austria-Hungary, is a nephew of Archduke Francis Ferdinand, and a great-nephew of the Em-

peror. He is a son of the late Archduke Otto and Princess Marie Josepha of Saxony, and is only 26 years old. In 1911 he married a distant cousin, the Archduchess Zita of Parma. He is a typical young Austrian officer, very gay, very popular, and extremely devoted to his wife, who is a great favorite with the Emperor.

The Archduke holds the rank of Major in the Thirty-ninth Infantry Regiment, and is an honorary officer in various Prussian, Saxon, and Bavarian regiments. He has one child, the Archduke Francis Joseph Otto, 2 years old. He takes the child out with him in his motor car with a perambulator packed at the back of the car, and, to the amusement of the Viennese, he is often seen wheeling the little Archduke in the perambulator.

The Archduke Charles Francis Joseph, now next in succession to the Austrian throne, is the eldest son of the Archduke Otto, who was the younger brother of Francis Ferdinand. Archduke Otto was born at Graz in 1865 and died in Vienna. Bourbon house of Parma. The Duchy was made a part of the Kingdom of Italy after the war of 1859, and since that time the principal residence of the family has been at the castle of Schwarzau, not far from Vienna. It was here that the Princess Zita was married on Oct. 21, 1911. Her half-brother Henry is now head of the house. Their father, Duke Robert, who died in 1907, was married first to Princess Maria Pia of the Two Sicilies, and second to Princess Maria Antonia of Parma, whi still lives at Schwarzau. Princess Zita is a child of the second union and was born at the Villa Pianore, near Viareggio, on May 9, 1892.

Of her nineteen brothers and sisters many are feeble-minded, but the Archduchess Zita herself has always been extremely healthy and of considerable mental brilliancy. She received an old-fashioned convent education, but is fond of tennis, hunting, and outdoor sports in general, and already has made a position for herself at the imperial court.

"All the News That's
Fit to Print."

The New York Times.

THE WEATHER
Fair today and Thursday; fresh
north and northeast winds.
For full weather report see Page 15.

VOL. LXIII...NO. 20,640. ...   NEW YORK, WEDNESDAY, JULY 29, 1914.—EIGHTEEN PAGES.   ONE CENT In Greater New York, Jersey City and Newark. | Elsewhere TWO CENTS.

AUSTRIA FORMALLY DECLARES WAR ON SERVIA; RUSSIA THREATENS, ALREADY MOVING TROOPS; PEACE OF EUROPE NOW IN KAISER'S HANDS

Notice Sent to the Powers of the Opening of Hostilities.

SERVIAN VESSELS SEIZED

Sharp Fighting Begins Along the River Drina on the Bosnian Frontier.

COUNTER INVASION PLAN

Montenegrin and Serb Armies to Invade Bosnia and Start a Rebellion There.

GREY'S PEACE PLAN FAILS

Kaiser Declines to Join in Conference to Exert Pressure on Austrian Ally.

BUT REPLY IS CONCILIATORY

And London Still Has Faith That His Influence Will Avert General Conflict.

Special Cable to THE NEW YORK TIMES.
LONDON, Wednesday, July 29.—Austria-Hungary declared war on Servia yesterday. The declaration was made at noon to the Servian Government by means of an open telegram. The Austro-Hungarian forces followed up the declaration by seizing two Servian vessels at Orsova, on the Danube, together with a number of boats.

The question whether the Austro-Servian war can be localized and a European Armageddon can be avoided now depends, so far as anything can depend on one man, upon Emperor William.

THE NEW YORK TIMES correspondent referred yesterday to the hopes of the British Foreign Office that the Kaiser's personal influence would be exercised for peace. Now that Germany has refused to accept Sir Edward Grey's suggestion of an ambassadorial conference and Austria

has declared war on Servia, the only hope of avoiding that greater conflict, which the whole world apprehends, lies in the conversations that are proceeding directly between Vienna and St. Petersburg, and particularly the turn which can be given them by the German monarch.

The Kaiser's Role.

THE TIMES correspondent is informed on the best authority that great hopes are based on Emperor William's influence in this direction. This information is reflected in The Times editorial this morning, which says:

"There is reason to believe that in the most exalted quarter of Germany the maintenance of European peace is warmly and honestly desired. The pressure from all manner of influential personages and groups is doubtless being exerted to overcome the pacific leanings of the Emperor. It may tax his powers of resistance severely, but in foreign affairs he is the undoubted master and he has often shown that he has a will and judgment of his own. We still hope with some confidence that they will be exerted on the side of that peace which it has often been his honorable boast he helped to keep for six and twenty years.

"Our Paris correspondent repeats that grounds exist for the belief that Germany has already given a better proof of her wish for peace than is known to France."

In London Germany's reply to Sir Edward Grey's proposal is not looked upon as a diplomatic rebuff. The tone of the reply was conciliatory, and Prince Lichnowsky, the German Ambassador here, explained that Germany, while most anxious to co-operate with Great Britain in the attempt to find a settlement, was unable to accept the rôle of a mediator so far as the Austro-Servian dispute was concerned, as she must eschew anything calculated to create the impression that she was not in entire harmony with her Austrian ally. The German Ambassador particularly insisted on the weight which Germany attaches to co-operation with Great Britain with a view to localizing the conflict.

The conversations at St. Petersburg between Count Szapary, the Austrian Ambassador, and Premier Sazonoff, are understood to be proceeding on a tone which gives good hope that it will be found possible to prevent the conflagration spreading beyond the present limits.

Up to a late hour this morning no definite confirmation had been received here of the various reports that Russia had begun a general mobilization.

Statements that the army corps in the west and southwest of Russia were being brought up to their war strength were accepted without hesitation as part of the precautionary

Text of Austria-Hungary's Declaration of War.

VIENNA, July 28.—Austria-Hungary's declaration of war against Servia was gazetted here late this afternoon. The text is as follows:

"The Royal Government of Servia not having replied in a satisfactory manner to the note remitted to it by the Austro-Hungarian Minister in Belgrade on July 23, 1914, the Imperial and Royal Government finds itself compelled to proceed itself to safeguard its rights and interests and to have recourse for this purpose to force of arms.

"Austria-Hungary considers itself, therefore, from this moment in a state of war with Servia.

(Signed) "COUNT BERCHTOLD,
"Minister of Foreign Affairs of Austria-Hungary."

Russia Announces Its Wish to Remain at Peace Yet Is Determined to Guard Its Interests.

ST. PETERSBURG, July 28.—The Russian Government tonight issued the following official communication:

"Numerous patriotic demonstrations of the last few days in St. Petersburg and other cities prove that the firm pacific policy of Russia finds a sympathetic echo among all classes of the population.

"The Government hopes, nevertheless, that the expression of feeling of the people will not be tinged with enmity against the powers with whom Russia is at peace, and with whom she wishes to remain at peace.

"While the Government gathers strength from this wave of popular feeling and expects its subjects to retain their reticence and tranquillity, it rests confidently on the guardianship of the dignity and the interests of Russia."

measures which every country in Europe, big or small, with the exception of Spain, Portugal, and Switzerland, considered necessary. The news of the issue of orders for a general mobilisation of Russian forces would mean that a great European conflict would be precipitated.

May Strike First at France.

Berlin dispatches state that Germany has made it quite clear in St. Petersburg that even "a partial mobilisation" will be answered immediately by the mobilisation of the German Army, which, according to one dispatch, "nothing could then hold back."

This is in accordance with what is known of the German war policy. The German General Staff does not contemplate simultaneous campaigns on a great scale against both France and Russia. France can mobilize nearly as quickly as herself. Russia takes some weeks to mobilize and more weeks to move her armies from mobilization centres to the frontier.

Germany's safety lies in taking advantage of the slowness of Russian mobilization. She will content herself with a comparatively slight screen of troops along her Eastern frontier to hold back the Russians

and will launch all her striking force against the French lines of defense, hoping to pierce them and break the back of the French armies before Russia is ready to act.

The next few hours is likely to show whether Germany thinks the extensive military movements which are taking place along the Russian side of the German-Austrian frontiers constitutes a partial mobilization.

In this connection extreme importance attaches to the statement made in a special dispatch to THE NEW YORK TIMES from St. Petersburg that Russia will declare a general mobilization if Austria occupies Belgrade.

A military expert who is acquainted with the European situation said, when shown the dispatch, that he hoped the correspondent's forecast was incorrect, for such a step would precipitate an Armageddon, as Germany could not afford to throw away the advantage which the slowness of Russian mobilization, the chief weakness of the Dual Alliance, gave her, and would immediately strike at France.

Probable Plans of Opposing Armies.

The Servians are reported to have formed a division in the Sanjak of Novi Bazar and to be concentrating strong forces on the River Lim, which

4

Map Showing Frontiers of Continental Nations Which May Be Involved in War.

runs through the Sanjak. Montenegrin troops are stated to be in close contact with the Servian forces.

The object of these movements, according to The London Times, is apparently to threaten Herzegovina and Bosnia, where the nature of the ground is favorable for guerrilla operations.

Rumors of fighting on the Drina River that forms the frontier between Bosnia and Servia, were circulated in Vienna and Berlin. Part of the Austro-Hungarian forces is expected to advance across the Drina in the direction of Kraguoyevatz. The Servian forces, on the other hand, are expected to cross into Bosnian territory with the object of raising an insurrection among the Bosnian Serbs.

It is stated on Austrian authority that the object of Austria-Hungary is to crush and disarm Servia and, in particular, capture the Servian artillery and compel Servia to reduce her army in future to inoffensive proportions.

Austria-Hungary also is determined to sieze Mount Lovtchen, a Montenegrin stronghold, which commands the important naval base of Bocche di Cattaro, despite the opposition which Italy is expected to offer to this proceeding.

Three Italian training ships now on a visit to the Clyde have been recalled.

Austrian naval concentration has been ordered at Fiume.

The Russian authorities have ordered all lights along the Russian Black Sea coast extinguished, with the exception of the Chersonesf Lighthouse near Sebastopol harbor. Sebastopol itself is open only to Russian warships.

Russia has ordered the mobilization of fourteen army corps in the neighborhood of the Austrian frontier, but these orders are understood to be merely preparatory, not final. In diplomatic circles it is stated that Germany will not reply to this partial mobilization unless a Russian army is mobilized also in the north.

Two French Cabinet councils were held yesterday. No mobilization order has been issued, but considerable military preparations are being made. All officers and men on leave have been recalled to the colors. The French Socialists have issued a manifesto calling upon the Government to use its influence in Russia in favor of peace.

Military preparations are proceeding in Holland and Belgium, with the view of maintaining the neutrality of those countries against an attack by the great powers.

Great enthusiasm prevailed in the Hungarian Chamber when Count Tiza, the Prime Minister, announced the outbreak of war and declared the situation demanded a deed of arms, not words. Count Apponyi, leader of the Opposition, supported the Premier. The Parliament was prorogued by royal decree.

Patriotic demonstrations took place in St. Petersburg, the crowds cheering the friendly embassies and legations, including those of Great Britain and Servia.

The Times St. Petersburg correspondent reports the growth of pessimism in official circles. News of the Austro-Hungarian occupation of Belgrade would inflame public feeling. Russian statesmen are convinced that England alone can save the situation, and that Sir Edward Grey's proposals by no means exhaust all his possibilities of persuasion.

BRITAIN PREPARES HER NAVY.

Crews of Second Fleet Filling Up—Navy Yards Are Active.

Special Cable to THE NEW YORK TIMES.

LONDON, July 28.—Precautionary measures are being taken by the British naval authorities. There was great activity at Portsmouth today,

chiefly in getting ships of the second fleet ready to answer a quick call. The crews are being filled and all leave is stopped. Strong infantry detachments are guarding all the magazines.

There is also considerable naval activity on the Humber. The eighth destroyer flotilla arrived and coaled. Submarines and a cruiser took up stations at the mouth of the Humber. The tanks of the Admiralty's oil fuel depot at Killingholme have been spotted with green, black, and red paint to render them unobservable from the sea.

A flotilla of submarines and three seaplanes have arrived in Dover naval harbor.

"All the News That's
Fit to Print."

The New York Times.

THE WEATHER
Partly cloudy today; Friday, fair;
moderate to fresh north winds.
☞For full weather report see Page 17.

VOL. LXIII...NO. 20,641.   NEW YORK, THURSDAY, JULY 30, 1914.—EIGHTEEN PAGES.   ONE CENT In Greater New York, Jersey City and Newark. | TWO CENTS

RUSSIA EXPECTS WAR, MOBILIZES 1,200,000 MEN;
CZAR ALSO SUMMONS RESERVISTS TO THE COLORS;
BELGRADE BOMBARDED AND OCCUPIED BY AUSTRIA;
KAISER IN COUNCIL ON NAVAL PREPARATIONS

St. Petersburg Convinced Political Miracle Only Can Avert War.

CZAR WOULD HEAD ARMY

Grand Duke Nicholas and War Minister Soukhomlinoff Seconds in Command.

PRAYERS FOR SERB VICTORY

Sacred Ikon Presented for King Peter's Forces—Great Patriotic Demonstrations.

BALTIC LIGHTS OUT NOW

Warsaw Arsenal Reported Blown Up — Bombs In Post Office — Revolution Rumor Denied.

New York Times-London Chronicle Special Cable Dispatch.
ST. PETERSBURG, July 29.—This evening Russia's intervention in the Austro-Servian conflict appears to be imminent. Certainly, after the receipt of the news of the bombardment of Belgrade I was so informed at the Foreign Office.

Russia even now will take steps to stay Austria's mobilization, being pushed forward actively, and an official announcement has been issued that a general mobilization will be Russia's reply to Austria's action.

The Vienna theory that the war is a mere punitive expedition is not admitted by Russia. The utmost admitted is that if Austria retires immediately there may still be room for diplomatic efforts.

Measures have been taken on the Baltic and at Sebastopol for the preparation of two fleets and there has been hurried promotion of officers.

Gradual transfer of the control of the railways to the War Office is proceeding.

These and other stirring events all indicate that the decisive moment is approaching.

Czar Summons Immense Number of Reservists; His Ukase Sweeps Empire for Additional Soldiers

ST. PETERSBURG, July 29.—An Imperial ukase, issued by the Emperor tonight, calls to the colors an immense number of reservists. The men called out are:

First—All the reservists of twenty-three whole governments and of seventy-one districts in fourteen other governments.

Second—Part of the reservists of nine districts of four governments.

Third—The naval reservists in sixty-four districts of twelve Russian governments and one Finnish government.

Fourth—The time-expired Cossacks of the territories of Don, Kuban, Terek, Astrakhan, Orenburg and Ural.

Fifth—A corresponding number of reservist officers of the medical and veterinary services, in addition to needful horses, wagons and transport services in the governments and districts thus mobilized.

A fateful manifesto expected tonight had not been forthcoming to the time of wiring.

Nothing could be more warlike than the official and popular attitude just now, and yet I found moderate people who still hold that the possibility of peace remains if Austria will but evacuate Belgrade immediately after its occupation.

Many people here eagerly grasp at the hope that the British fleet will intervene by a demonstration or otherwise to help Russia to bring pressure to bear on the Middle Empire.

Russia Believes the Die Is Cast.

By The Associated Press.
ST. PETERSBURG, July 29.—In Russian eyes the die is cast. Only a political miracle can avert war.

Russia does not swerve from her determination to support Servia, and partial mobilization has been ordered. There is every indication that the whole vast military machinery of Russia will soon be set in motion.

Should, as is understood, Emperor Nicholas become generalissimo of the forces an immense wave of enthusiasm will sweep over Russia.

The political parties have sunk their differences. The general attitude is not "jingoistic," but one of resolute confidence in the justice of the country's cause, and readiness to make all sacrifices.

The proposal attributed to Austria to discuss terms when Belgrade has been occupied is regarded as impossible. It is pointed out that before the opening of hostilities Russia proposed to Austria a direct exchange of views which Austria rejected.

[The foregoing paragraphs were passed by the censor without revision—a fact which is considered highly significant.]

Czar's Seconds in Command.

It is considered probable that Emperor Nicholas will become the Generalissimo of the Russian forces, his seconds in command being his second cousin, Grand Duke Nicholas Nicholaievitch, and Gen. Soukhomlinoff, the Minister of War.

The cadets of the naval school were promoted today to the rank of officers. In addressing them, the Emperor said:

"I have given orders that you should be incorporated in the navy in view of the serious events through which Russia is passing. During your service as officers, do not forget what I say to you—trust in God and have faith in the glory and greatness of our mighty country."

By orders of the Emperor, the enforcement of the legislative resolution restricting the acquisition of real estate by companies and also restricting the inclusion of Jews on Boards of Directors has been temporarily suspended.

The Maritime Bureau has announced the closing of additional lights, both in the Baltic and Black Seas.

In Yalta and the surrounding districts in the Crimea a state of reinforced protection or a modified form of martial law has been proclaimed.

Great Patriotic Demonstrations.

A great patriotic demonstration took

Czar Nicholas II of Russia

place on the Nevsky Prospect this afternoon. A procession was formed and with banners flying marched to the Servian Legation, where there were speeches, singing, and cheering. Thence the procession moved to the French and British Embassies, where similar scenes of enthusiasm were indulged in. The German and Austrian Embassies were guarded on all sides by strong detachments of police, and nobody was allowed to stop on the adjacent footpaths.

At the Kauzan Cathedral a special service was held and prayers were offered for victory to the Slav arms. The cathedral was thronged, and the officiating priest, after the ceremony, presented to the Servian Minister a fac simile of the ikon of the Holy Virgin of Kazan for the Servian Army. The Minister handed the ikon to officers who are starting for the front tonight.

A monster demonstration in favor of Servia was held at Moscow.

At Odessa processions marched through the streets bearing the portraits of Emperor Nicholas and the Kings of Servia and Montenegro, and cheering for Servia, France, and Great Britain.

A confident feeling prevails here of Great Britain's support. Germany's attitude is regarded as incomprehensible, except on the assumption that she is anxious for a trial of strength at the present moment.

Austria Occupies Belgrade

LONDON, Thursday, July 30.—A Vienna dispatch to the Exchange Telegraph Company says:

After a heavy bombardment by the Danube gunboats, Belgrade was occupied by the Austrian troops Wednesday.

"All the News That's Fit to Print."

The New York Times.

THE WEATHER
Partly cloudy today and tomorrow; moderate northeast winds.
For full weather report see Page 17.

VOL. LXIII...NO. 20,642. ...   NEW YORK, FRIDAY, JULY 31, 1914.—EIGHTEEN PAGES.   ONE CENT In Greater New York, Jersey City and Newark. | Elsewhere TWO CENTS.

KAISER CALLS ON RUSSIA TO HALT WITHIN 24 HOURS; IF SHE REFUSES GERMANY, TOO, WILL MOBILIZE; ENGLAND AND FRANCE READY, BUT HOPE FOR PEACE; AUSTRIANS DRIVE SERVIANS BACK FROM BELGRADE

Kaiser's Blunt Questions to the Czar Extreme Expedient to Avert War.

SENDS PEACEMAKER, TOO

Czarina's Brother, Grand Duke of Hesse, at St. Petersburg to Urge Peace.

CALL TO ARMS PREPARED

Would Add 2,000,000 Men to the Army and 80,000 to the Naval Forces.

AUSTRIA TO ATTACK RUSSIA?

Report That She Will Force the Issue by a Declaration of War Today.

Special Cable to THE NEW YORK TIMES.

BERLIN, July 30.—"Peace or mobilization within twenty-four hours," that, according to high authority, is the German Government's summary of the situation tonight.

The Kaiser's Government, as a last extreme move on behalf of peace, launched today a peremptory demand upon St. Petersburg for an unqualified explanation of Russia's "menacing mobilization" on the German and Austrian frontiers. Russia has been given to understand that unless these movements are abandoned forthwith Germany will respond in kind.

Little hope is cherished in Berlin that Germany's demand will be complied with. Indeed, a report which has just reached here that Russia's reserves in twenty-three districts have been called up seems like a defiant answer to Berlin's representations. In fact, hope that peace can be maintained has been all but abandoned.

Although Germany does not say she will declare war if Russia's military preparations are not canceled, and only threatens to retaliate with a counter demonstration, no secret is made of the fact that a counter-demonstration would be tantamount to war.

Mobilization a Mere Formality.

The fiction is still propagated by the Foreign Office, the War Office, and the Admiralty that no mobilization in any sense of the word has so far taken place, but when it does come it will turn out to be a mere formality. Germany at this hour is as ready to take the field as she will be when the ominous red placards formally gazetting the fact are posted on the public hoardings.

Late this afternoon the officials of the embassy of a certain great power applied to a wholesale provision firm for ten barrels of flour. They were informed that no such order could possibly be filled as everything already had been commandeered for the army and the navy.

Mobilization, it is understood, will call out all reserves for the years extending back to 1908, or the so-called "active reserve." This would mean in the case of the navy roundly 80,000 men and in the case of the army 2,000,000 men.

Decision at Wednesday's Council.

Germany's momentous decision to take a strong stand at St. Petersburg today was made at the New Palace, at Potsdam, last night at a council of war.

The council lasted far into the night. It was presided over by the Emperor in his capacity of Supreme War Lord, and included the Chancellor, the Foreign Secretary, the Minister of Marine, the Chief of the General Staff of the Army and the Chief of the Admiralty Staff, and a number of other distinguished military, naval, and civilian personages. Admiral Prince Henry of Prussia, fresh from England, also was present, as well as the Crown Prince, who, in accordance with Prussian traditions, will lead one of the German armies.

Gen. von Falkenhayn, the Minister of War, informed the conference that, while complete Russian mobilization, in a technical sense, had not taken place, the dispositions at the St. Petersburg War Office were of such an unmistakable character that Germany could only consider them as formal preliminaries to actual mobilization.

The conference came to the conclusion, after hearing satisfying reports from Gen. von Falkenhayn and Gen. von Moltke, Chief of the General Staff, as to the state of Germany's own preparedness, that the moment had arrived to launch a pointed question at St. Petersburg in regard to the significance of Russia's measures. It was decided that while Russia's reply to Germany's inquiry was pending Germany must not delay taking preliminary counter-precautions.

It was determined, according to the Government-controlled Lokal Anzeiger, that Russia must finally be given to understand that Berlin was no longer inclined to view with indifference the "continuous rattling of the Russian sabre in Germany's face." Germany has come to the conclusion that only the plainest speaking on her part can perhaps, at the eleventh hour, still preserve Europe from Armageddon.

"We believe," says The Lokal Anzeiger, "that the next twenty-four hours will bring forth decisions of enormous importance."

The Lokal Anzeiger this afternoon caused a sensation by publishing an extra announcing that the "entire German Army and Navy had been ordered to mobilize." People stood discussing the news excitedly on the streets. Twenty minutes later, however, another extra of the same paper appeared with the following strange announcement:

"Through a gross misdemeanor an extra edition of the Lokal Anzeiger was circulated this afternoon with the information that Germany had determined to mobilize. We herewith state that this news was incorrect."

One explanation of this incident is that the Lokal Anzeiger, wanting to be first in the field with the news, printed an "emergency" extra edition and that carriers and others who for several days had been drilled in "smartness" overreached themselves and obtained possession of the extra before being authorized to take it from the Lokal Anzeiger's premises.

Panic at Saarbrucken.

There was an extraordinary war panic today at Saarbrucken, Alsace. The populace indulged in mad competition to buy up the available supplies of provisions. Shops of all kinds were stormed and there was a run on the savings bank. Potatoes, flour, salt, sugar, and tinned vegetables soared to unprecedented prices, and paper money was frequently refused.

All bridges in that region are guarded by troops, and trains bound for France are carefully inspected.

The Town Council of Breslau held a secret session today to discuss ways and means of provisioning the city in case of war with Russia.

Two motor cars, said to belong to Grand Duke Orloff and Grand Duke Nicholas of Russia, were seized at Saarlouis. The cars contained a typewriter, a field writing desk, and several field chairs. Two chauffeurs and a servant were detained. They appear to have been bound for Paris.

King Peter of Servia (seated) looks back on his lost country as Austrians and Germans claim the land.

7

Where Austrian and Servian Forces Are Fighting.

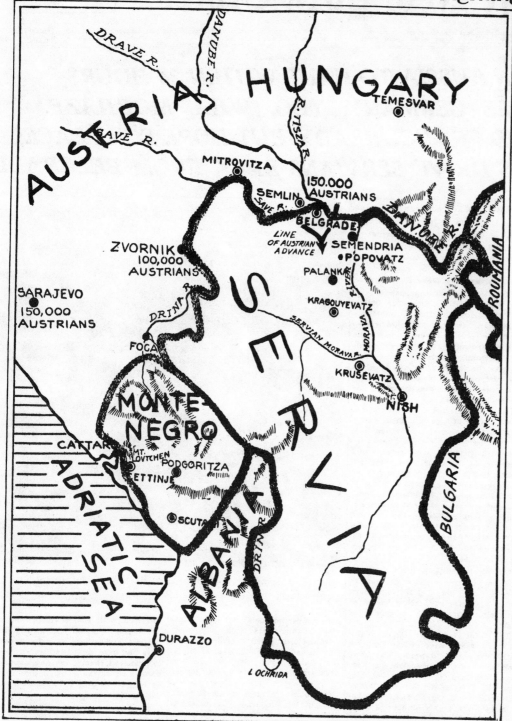

Belgrade was occupied yesterday by the Austrians. Another force which crossed into Servia at Senendria advanced along the road leading to Palanka and ultimately to Nish. An invading force at Losnitza, to the west of Belgrade, was repulsed. There were reports in Berlin of a fierce battle at Focha, in Bosnia, in which 1,000 men were said to have fallen. An attack by the Austrians on Mount Lovtchen, in Montenegro, also was reported, but a dispatch from Athens announced that the Montenegrins had occupied the Austrian port of Cattaro, which is dominated by the fort on Mount Lovtchen.

Of the 500,000 Austro-Hungarian soldiers in the field against Servia, 150,000 are operating from Semlin as a base, 100,000 from Zvornik on the River Drina, 150,000 from the Bosnian capital, Sarajevo, and 100,000 from Milanovatz, on the Danube.

CALLS OUT MEN OF 50.

Austria Using Very Last Line of Reserves—No Excuse Accepted.

Special Cable to THE NEW YORK TIMES.

LONDON, July 30.—How great are Austria's preparations for war, not merely on the Danube but for war with the great powers, is shown in a letter received today by a London commercial firm from a Bohemian firm with which it has intimate dealings.

The letter, which was seen by a NEW YORK TIMES correspondent, says:

"We are fully at war. For Austria it would be easy to blow Servia off the map, but Servia does not go to war without being encouraged by Russia. This means that we have to deal with a greater enemy than Servia. It means the whole Slav race, which wants to cross Europe from east to west through Austria-Hungary.

"All the fighting men in our country got orders on Sunday night to present themselves for service within twenty hours—not only the reservists, the Landwehr, and Landsturm men up to 42 years, but men up to 50 years of age have been called to the colors.

"On Monday morning we could do no business. We had only to say goodbye to all our workpeople. Hardly any one left except the girls of the button, crystal, and other departments."

The letter proceeds to give countermanding instructions consequent on this paralysis of business. The writer tells of one man who, though convalescing after a severe illness, had to equip himself and set out. No excuse is accepted. He goes on:

"One of our packers wished to take a train two hours later than the others. He was told that he would be severely punished if he did so."

An important fact is contained in the casual mention that all these troops are being sent, not to the lower Danube but to the Galician frontier—the border of Russia.

The tremendous force being called out may partly be measured by the fact that the Landsturm, and even older veterans, are being summoned. Even at the time of the Franco-German war the Landsturm was not called on. It is the arm reserved for the very last resort. There has been no call on the Landsturm, either in Austria or Prussia, since the war of 1866.

TO DECLARE WAR ON RUSSIA.

Austria Will Act Today, According to St. Petersburg.

LONDON, Friday, July 31.—A dispatch from St. Petersburg to Reuter's Telegram Company, says it is believed in St. Petersburg that Austria will declare war against Russia today.

The dispatch adds that if this should be the case it is understood that Emperor Nicholas will go to Moscow to deliver a pronunciamento in the Uspensky Cathedral.

BENEFITS TO US FROM WAR.

Statist Sees Great Economic Gains —May Make Us World's Banker.

Special Cable to THE NEW YORK TIMES.

LONDON, July 30.—The Statist will say tomorrow:

"A great war in Europe will probably bring economic advantages to the United States. It will enable it to sell its great crops in places which will give a much greater income than if there was no war.

"Almost every industry will derive more or less advantage. American investors and bankers should get in much profit from the ability to buy back from Europe great quantities of securities at attractive prices in payment for the foodstuffs and raw material exported from the United States.

"The United States can become, as it has this week, the world's greatest market for capital, and if the American people rise to their opportunity they can do a great deal to mitigate the disastrous economic consequences which would otherwise result in many countries from a great European war.

"It is obvious that for the time being the money markets of Europe will be closed to the demands for new capital of Canada, Brazil, Argentina, Mexico and other countries, and at such a time the prestige the United States would be immensely enhanced if it were to take the place of Europe and meet the pressing needs of these borrowing countries.

"It is possible that the United States may participate in the great loans that will have to be raised in Europe if almost the whole continent becomes engaged in war. Possibly the participation will be indirect rather than direct.

"For the United States to gain benefit from the position as the wealthiest nation in the world, it is essential that American investors should not only have confidence in the future of their own country, but also believe that, war or no war, the world will continue to progress.

"In brief, a great war in Europe will give the United States an opportunity of assuming the post of world banker, by supplying capital freely to countries and individuals in all parts of the globe who need it and can provide the required security. Should the American people take advantage of the golden opportunity afforded them by the outbreak of war, it will mean not diminished but increased prosperity for the United States."

"All the News That's Fit to Print."

The New York Times.

THE WEATHER
Generally fair today and Monday; gentle to moderate south winds.
For full weather report see
PAGE 3, SPORTS SECTION.

VOL. LXIII...NO. 20,644. ....   NEW YORK, SUNDAY, AUGUST 2, 1914.—88 PAGES, In Seven Parts, Including Picture and Rotogravure Section, Real Estate Directory, and Review of Books.   PRICE FIVE CENTS.

GERMANY DECLARES WAR ON RUSSIA, FIRST SHOTS ARE FIRED; FRANCE IS MOBILIZING AND MAY BE DRAWN IN TOMORROW; PLANS TO RESCUE THE 100,000 AMERICANS NOW IN EUROPE

Germany's War Challenge Delivered to Russia at 7:30 Last Evening

EMBASSY THEN DEPARTS

Enrollment of Reservists Begun Throughout the Czar's Vast Empire.

STIRRING SCENES ATTEND IT

Hardly a Family but Loses a Protector, Yet They Take the Call Submissively.

FRANCE HAS TILL MONDAY

Reply to Germany Due Then, but Issue May Be Forced Earlier.

ITALY REMAINS NEUTRAL

Triple Alliance Obligations Not Touched, She Says—Feared a Revolution.

LUXEMBURG INVADED.

Germans Seize a Neutral State Between Them and Paris.

LONDON, Aug. 2.—The Germans have invaded the Duchy of Luxemburg. They seized the Government offices and telephones. The news reached here in a Reuter telephone message from Brussels at 4 A. M. New York time.

Luxemburg is a neutral State southward of Brussels, with its borders on Germany and France. A straight line drawn between Berlin and Paris would pass through the heart of the Duchy of Luxemburg.

Special Cable to THE NEW YORK TIMES.

LONDON, Sunday, Aug. 2.—The news that Germany had declared war against Russia reached London from St. Petersburg late last evening, only

---

Chronology of Yesterday's Fateful Events

12 Midnight—Germany demands that Russia cease mobilization and gives a twelve-hour limit.

2 A. M.—King George of England, after an audience with Premier Asquith, telegraphs to the Czar, making a strong appeal for peace.

12 Noon—The time limit of Germany's ultimatum to Russia expires.

5:15 P. M.—Emperor William signs an order for the mobilization of the German Army.

7:30 P. M.—The German Ambassador at St. Petersburg delivers to the Russian Government a declaration of war in the name of Germany and leaves St. Petersburg.

First Shots Fired in the Russo-German War.

BERLIN, Aug. 1.—A German patrol near Prostken was fired on this afternoon by a Russian frontier patrol. The Germans returned the fire. There were no losses.

Prostken is a village of 2,300 inhabitants, in East Prussia. It is situated about two and one-half miles west of the international boundary line, on the Konigsberg & Lyck Railroad. The nearest Russian village is Grajevo, about three miles across the international boundary.

Kaiser Forgives Enemies, Prays for Victory.

BERLIN, Aug. 2.—The Emperor again spoke from a window of the Castle tonight to a crowd of 50,000 beneath, who cheered and sang patriotic songs until he appeared. He said:

"I thank you for the love and loyalty shown me. When I enter upon a fight let all party strife cease. We are German brothers and nothing else. All parties have attacked me in times of peace. I forgive them with all my heart. I hope and wish that the good German sword will emerge victorious in the right."

The speech was thrice interrupted by vociferous cheering. At its conclusion the Kaiser bowed in all directions, retiring amid a frenzied demonstration.

The Imperial Chancellor also addressed the assembly, saying:

"All stand as one man for our Emperor, whatever our opinions or our creeds. I am sure that all the young German men are ready to shed their blood for the fame and greatness of Germany. We can only trust in God, Who hitherto has always given us victory."

An imperial decree convokes the Reichstag on Aug. 4.

---

half an hour after a Central News dispatch from Paris had raised the hopes of all by the statement that Germany had extended for forty-eight hours, that is, until Monday noon, the period in which Russia and France could reply to the German ultimatums.

The first of these ultimatums was one demanding that Russia cease the mobilization of her army in twelve hours.

The second was a note presented by Baron von Schoen, the German Ambassador in Paris, to Foreign Minister Viviani calling upon France to inform

Germany whether in the event of the outbreak of war between Germany and Russia, France would remain neutral.

These notes were regarded as diplomatic skirmishing, designed to cover the hard fact that Germany was bending all her energies to the delivery of the first blow, which might affect the whole course of the war, now officially begun.

In the history of modern warfare an official declaration of war is either accompanied or preceded by an actual stroke of war.

In London this morning it is be-

lieved Germany would not officially declare war upon Russia unless her plans for a rapid attack had been entirely completed. Where or how the first blow will be struck is a matter of the widest speculation.

France Next to Be Involved.

France's reply to the German request as to the former's attitude in case Germany engaged in war with Russia is stated to have proved unsatisfactory to Berlin. It was bound to be. Germany could count confidently on it being so. Therefore, according to speculation in London this morning, the eventual news is likely to show that Germany has taken an unsatisfactory reply from France for granted, and while declaring war on Russia has struck or has made her chief preparations to strike at France. This, of course, is pure speculation, and THE NEW YORK TIMES correspondent mentions it for what it is worth.

The established facts, bearing on the crisis in yesterday's developments, are important to note. The first is that the effort made by King George to bring influence to bear on the Czar in favor of peace failed of effect.

The terms of the King's telegram are guarded as the strictest secret. All information THE TIMES correspondent could obtain was that the message was of a highly personal and confidential nature. It followed an interview with Premier Asquith at 2 o'clock yesterday morning.

Italy Feared a Revolution.

The second development was a confirmation of the report that Italy would remain neutral as long as she was assured that her interests were not menaced.

From an official source THE TIMES correspondent learns that the Italian Government was practically forced to this decision by the apprehension that the taking up of arms on behalf of Austria in a quarrel, precipitated by the hereditary enemy of Italy, would have caused an immediate revolution in Italy.

Italy's abstention is a serious blow to the Triple Alliance and may yet prove an important factor in determining, if not the issue of peace or war, at least the duration of the conflict.

One of the ways suggested to prevent the outbreak of war was that Italy and Great Britain should combine and declare themselves on the side of France and Russia. The suggestion utterly disregarded the treaty by which Italy was bound to the Triple Alliance, but it was given some color of vraisemblance by the fact that the

Four Nations of Europe Now at War.

The Boundaries of Germany, Russia, Austria-Hungary and Servia, and the Scene of the First Shots Between Germany and Russia.

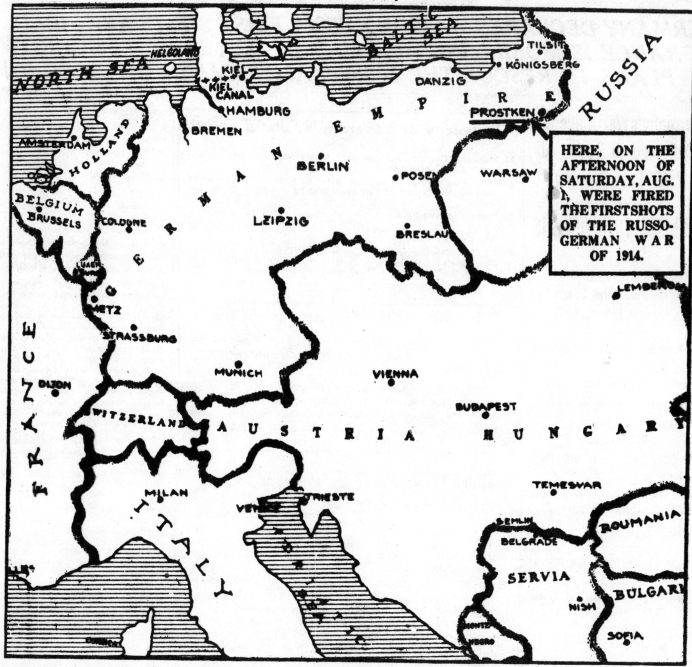

HERE, ON THE AFTERNOON OF SATURDAY, AUG. 1, WERE FIRED THE FIRST SHOTS OF THE RUSSO-GERMAN WAR OF 1914.

British and Italian Ambassadors in various capitals have been working together in a manner which indicated that the Italian Government preferred any peaceable solution of the war to the treaties which bound her to Germany and Austria.

The third important development of the night was the news that the French Government had issued orders for general mobilization.

This came a few hours after the severance of telephonic communications between London and Paris. The French Government informed the British authorities that the telephone was cut for ordinary communication in order to prevent any leakage of news.

Up to 2 o'clock this morning practically no news beyond the announcement of the mobilization had been received here from Paris.

The fullest confirmation of the general mobilization was obtained in London by the issue of a notice to the French Embassy here. This called upon all Frenchmen liable to military service to return to France within twenty-four hours. The news speedily became known in Soho, the French quarter of London, and this morning bands of enthusiastic Frenchmen paraded through Leicester Square.

The almost complete severance of telegraphic and telephone communication with Paris was shown by the fact that a London paper which had made most elaborate arrangements to obtain a special wire, under a guarantee that nothing in the nature of leakage of military secrets could possibly occur, had not received a word out of Paris up to 3 o'clock this morning.

Telephonic and telegraphic communications with the Continent were generally interrupted.

KAISER SIGNS ORDER MOBILIZING HIS ARMY

"Let Your Hearts Beat for God and Your Fists on the Enemy," Cries Chancellor.

BERLIN, Aug. 1.—Emperor William, at 5:15 o'clock this evening, signed an order mobilizing the German Army.

A semi-official statement says that the threatening danger of war necessitates that military measures be taken for the protection of the German frontier and railway lines. Restrictions, therefore, on the postal, telegraph, and railway services are inevitable, owing to the requirements of the military authorities.

It was officially announced that the time limit of the German ultimatum to Russia expired at noon.

An official communication published in the North German Gazette says the Russian Emperor on July 29 telegraphed to Emperor William urgently requesting him to help in averting the misfortune of a European war and to try to restrain his ally Austria-Hungary from going too far.

Emperor William replied that he would willingly take up the task of mediator, and accordingly diplomatic action was initiated in Vienna.

While this was in progress the news that Russia was mobilizing arrived in Berlin, and Emperor William telegraphed to the Emperor of Russia that his rôle as mediator was by this endangered, if not made impossible.

The communication adds that a decision was to have been taken in Vienna today in regard to the mediation proposals in which Great Britain had joined Germany, but that meanwhile Russia had ordered the full mobilization of her forces. Upon this Emperor William addressed a last telegram to Emperor Nicholas emphatically declaring that his own responsibility for the safety of the German Empire had forced him to take defensive measures.

The German Imperial Chancellor, Dr. von Bethmann-Hollweg, addressed a huge procession of demonstrators today from the window of his official residence, making a stirring speech, in which he said:

"At this serious hour in order to give expression to your feelings for your Fatherland you have come to the house of Bismarck, who with Emperor William the Great and Field Marshal von Moltke welded the German Empire for us.

"We wished to go on living in peace in the empire which we have developed in forty-four years of peaceful labor.

"The whole work of Emperor William has been devoted to the maintenance of peace. To the last hour he has worked for peace in Europe, and he is still working for it. Should all his efforts prove vain and should the sword be forced into our hands we will take the field with a clear conscience in the knowledge that we did not seek war. We shall then wage war for our existence and for the national honor to the last drop of our blood.

"In the gravity of this hour I remind you of the words of Prince Frederick Charles to the men of Brandenburg:

"'Let your hearts beat for God and your fists on the enemy.'"

Enthusiastic cheers and the singing of the national anthem greeted the close of the Imperial Chancellor's speech.

EXPECTS TURKEY TO FIGHT.

Her Ambassador Looks for Hostilities with Servia.

SWAMPSCOTT, Mass., Aug. 1.—A. Rustem Bey, the Turkish Ambassador, who is spending his vacation here, said

Latest Estimates of the Land Forces of the Four Powers Now Engaged in War

Russia.	
In European Russia.	
Infantry	838,000
Cavalry	304,000
Artillery	98,000
Total	1,240,000
In Asiatic Russia	300,000
On first reserve (estimated)	1,500,000
Grand total	3,040,000

(It is thought that Russia could mobilize for effective use in Europe about 1,240,000 men.)

Servia.	
Five brigades, consisting of	
Infantry	97,680
Artillery	8,880
Cavalry	3,390
Engineer Corps	4,685
Ambulance	4,855
Ammunition	5,750
Commissary, &c.	5,935
One cavalry brigade, including nine horse batteries, mountain artillery, &c.	22,764
Garrison troops	16,562
Total	168,501
First reserve troops, who have served in the army within the last 12 years	99,451
Second reserve troops, who are held subject to call for 6 years after passing from the first reserve	56,678
Grand total	324,630

Germany.	
Infantry	487,874
Rapid-fire gun corps	24,021
Cavalry	85,702
Field artillery	91,409
Heavy artillery	34,669
Scouts	24,045
Railroad and other corps	48,669
Total	795,930
First reserve (trained troops)	454,000
Landwehr	600,000
Grand Total	1,849,980

Austria.	
Infantry	196,957
Cavalry	47,151
Field artillery	37,099
Heavy artillery	9,934
Auxiliary corps	20,841
Total	312,552
Austrian Reserves—	
Infantry	41,157
Cavalry	4,400
Artillery	3,002
Hungarian Reserves—	
Infantry	27,430
Cavalry	5,623
Artillery	3,191
Grand Total	399,361

In time of war this strength can be doubled, but the above listed troops are immediately available.

tonight that in his opinion Turkey soon would become involved in war with Servia.

He expressed the opinion that a general European war was probable, and notwithstanding the fact that Turkey recently had signed a treaty with the Serbs, his country would again be arrayed in arms against them.

WILL RESPECT BELGIUM.

France Promises It Unless Other Power Violates Neutrality.

BRUSSELS, Aug. 1.—Antony Klobukowski, French Minister to Belgium, called today on M. Davignon, the Minister for Foreign Affairs, and informed him that the French Government would respect the neutrality of Belgium in the event of war, in conformity with its previous declarations.

Should Belgian neutrality be violated by another power, France, he said, would then take the necessary measures.

Norway Will Keep Out.

CHRISTIANIA, Aug. 1.—A Government decree, issued today, declares the complete neutrality of Norway.

SWISS TAKE PRECAUTIONS.

Parliament Summoned to Guard Republic's Independence.

BERNE, Aug. 1.—The Swiss Federal Parliament has been summoned to meet on Monday, to consider measures to safeguard the independence of Switzerland and to appoint a commander in chief of the army of 175,000 men called to the colors by a mobilization order.

The house will also deal with a measure for the issue of five-franc notes.

German Officials Hurry Home.

CAPE TOWN, Aug. 1.—The German Consul General, with his staff, left for England today on the steamer Saxon. The offices of the Consulate General have been closed.

Sweden Declares Its Neutrality.

STOCKHOLM, Aug. 1.—The Swedish Government today issued an official notification of its strict neutrality in the European conflict.

GREECE MOBILIZES; MAY FIGHT BULGARS

They Cannot Agree on Boundary Question, but Rumania Is Trying to Settle Squabble.

MONTENEGRIN-SERVIAN PACT

Prince Peter, King's Youngest Son, Announces They Will Fight Side by Side.

NEW YORK TIMES-London Chronicle Special Cable Dispatch.

MILAN, Aug. 1.—A special evening edition of the Secolo makes the announcement from Bucharest that Montenegro intends to fight side by side with Servia. Prince Peter of Montenegro, who arrived in Bucharest yesterday, said in an interview:

"Union between the two countries will now undoubtedly be realized. I may say before my departure to Cettinje that a project of military and financial union has already been agreed upon. Each country will retain its own King and its own sovereignty.

"The union already exists in fact. All that is now necessary is a formal announcement to the world at large."

The same journal's special correspondent at Salonika states that the Graeco-Bulgarian commission which is now sitting to settle the boundary dispute abruptly terminated its sittings through inability to reach an agreement, and another war looms up on the horizon. Negotiations, however, are still proceeding between Athens and the Rumanian capital to devise a means of preserving the treaty of Bucharest, but the Greek Government, hard pressed, has ordered a general mobilization as a precautionary measure.

All the State archives at the Franco-Servian Bank have been transported to Salonika under strong escorts of Servian officials and soldiery.

German infantrymen advancing in France.

Belgian peasants search through debris that was once their village after a battle between Belgian and German soldiers.

"All the News That's Fit to Print."

The New York Times.

THE WEATHER
Fair today and tomorrow; gentle northeast winds, becoming southeast tomorrow.
For full weather report see Page 18.

VOL. LXIII...NO. 20,646.   ....

NEW YORK, TUESDAY, AUGUST 4, 1914.—EIGHTEEN PAGES.

ONE CENT In Greater New York, | Elsewhere Jersey City and Newark. | TWO CENTS

ENGLAND WILL PROTECT FRENCH COAST AND DEFEND BELGIUM; GERMANY RECALLS ENVOY; HESITATES AT FRENCH FRONTIER; HER ARMY SEIZES RUSSIAN TOWNS, NAVY WINS A VICTORY

Britain Only Waits for German Ships to Fire on France.

PLEDGED TO GUARD COAST

Fleet Attack in Channel England's Signal to Strike, Grey Tells Commons.

WILD CHEERS GREET HIM

Reads Belgium's Appeal for Protection and Says England's Interests Are at Stake.

POINTS TO HOLLAND'S PERIL

Navy, Regulars, Reserves, and Territorials All Fully Prepared for Conflict.

CHANGES IN THE CABINET

John Burns, Opposed to War, Retires—Kitchener May Take War Portfolio.

Special Cable to THE NEW YORK TIMES.

LONDON, Tuesday, Aug. 4.—All England is in martial array, and she is ready to strike the moment the German fleet fires upon the Channel coast of France.

This policy of determination to defend the French coast was announced by Sir Edward Grey in a speech to the House of Commons yesterday, and was greeted with the wildest applause.

The Foreign Minister said the French fleet was in the Mediterranean and her northern coasts defenseless.

"If a foreign fleet engaged in war against France should come down and battle against those defenseless coasts we could not stand aside," he exclaimed.

Sir Edward read the appeal of the King of the Belgians for diplomatic intervention to safeguard the integrity of that country, and asserted that if the integrity of Belgium were destroyed that of Holland also would be lost.

As a result of the policy announced, John Burns, President of the Local Government Board, resigned from the

King Albert's Appeal to King George; Asks England to Protect Belgium

LONDON, Aug. 3.—King Albert of Belgium sent this telegram to King George today:

"Remembering the numerous proofs of your Majesty's friendship and that of your predecessor, of the friendly attitude of England in 1870, and the proof of the friendship which she has just given us again, I make a supreme appeal to the diplomatic intervention of your Majesty's Government to safeguard the integrity of Belgium."

Cabinet owing to his inability to agree. Mr. Burns was once a member of the council of the Workmen's Peace Society.

It is announced as practically certain this morning that Lord Kitchener will take charge of the War Office.

Commons in Memorable Session.

The sitting of the House of Commons will rank among the most memorable in history. Sir Edward Grey's speech was characterized by suppressed fire and unadorned simplicity. It rang with accents of sincerity and vibrated with high patriotic feeling. The House never listened to a speech more effective in its purpose. That purpose was to prove that British neutrality, in the face of the present conflict in Europe, was impossible unless Great Britain was prepared to forfeit her own self-respect and the world's confidence. Honor, duty, and interest required British intervention, the Minister said.

Sir Edward spoke without bitterness, but the impression he conveyed was that Germany was a wanton disturber of European peace. He made no allusion to Russia.

The most striking feature in the attitude of Sir Edward Grey's audience was the enthusiasm of the Irish Nationalists. The Liberal benches seemed sombrely acquiescent.

Irish Applaud Grey.

The most applause came from the Conservatives, while the Irishmen acclaimed Sir Edward Grey's determination to stand by France with resounding enthusiasm. William Redmond and Dr. Lynch, the latter of whom fought against Great Britain in the Boer war and was condemned for treason, waved their handkerchiefs vehemently while they applauded. The old links of historical association of Celtic feeling explained the warm sympathy of the Irishmen for France.

One of the most dramatic scenes of the day was the intervention of John Redmond. For the first time in many years the Irish leader associated himself heart and soul with the feelings of the average Englishmen in the face of the great national emergency. Mr. Redmond spoke briefly, but with an eloquence that thrilled the House. Now, in these times of trial and danger for Great Britain, he said, the Irish people turned to the British democracy with anxiety and sympathy. He recalled how in 1776, at the moment of dire peril for England, 100,000 Irish volunteers leaped to arms.

"Today," he said, "there are in Ireland two large bodies of volunteers.

I say to the Government they may tomorrow with safety withdraw every one of their troops from Ireland, and the coasts of Ireland will be defended from foreign invasion by her armed sons. In this matter the armed Catholics of the South will gladly join arms with the armed Protestants of the North."

Clinches Home Rule.

Cheers, wherein Liberals, Tories, and Nationalists participated with equal warmth, proclaimed their delight at this vibrant speech, so eloquent and timely. The battle for home rule is already won. Redmond's little gem of oratory made the assurance of its early triumph doubly sure. That England's danger is Ireland's opportunity is now true in quite a new sense.

It was noticeable that Mr. Asquith warmly cheered the Nationalist leader.

Sir Edward Grey, in his speech, made a pointed allusion to Ireland when he spoke of it as the one bright spot in the picture. He stressed this in order that it might be understood abroad that Ireland would not weaken England's arm in this momentous crisis.

Government Free to Decide.

Sir Edward Grey spoke seventy-five minutes, and the House of Commons listened with an absorption that was almost painful in its tension. After a recital of the course of European affairs since 1906, he said that in the present crisis "we have perfect freedom to decide." The Government was free, he said, consequently Parliament was free. The present crisis had not originated in any question affecting France, he asserted, but in a dispute between Austria and Servia.

"France is involved in this war simply because she has undertaken to fulfill an obligation of honor," said he. "Great Britain is under no such obligations of honor, but for years she has had a friendship with France. Whether that friendship involves obligations, let every man look into his own heart and feelings and construe the obligations for himself."

Sir Edward did not disguise his own feelings. He spoke of France with an emotion for which his audience was quite unprepared from a man of his apparently cold and passionless nature. He pointed out that the French fleet was in the Mediterranean. The northern and western coasts of France are absolutely unprotected by French ships, he said, because the

French Government confidently relied on the friendship of the British Government.

Then came a passage which stirred the House to its very depths and made every man who listened tingle with emotion. "If a foreign fleet came down the English Channel and bombarded and battered the unprotected coasts of France," he exclaimed, "we could not stand aside with our arms folded." Tremendous cheering and applause broke afresh when he added, "And I believe that to be the feeling of this country."

Italy as a Key.

He asked the House to consider the possible consequences of a European conflagration. Italy is neutral, he said.

Here there were Radical cheers. "Yes," said the speaker, turning to the benches whence the cheers had come, "Italy is neutral because she regards this as an aggressive war." Loud applause followed this.

"But suppose," he went on, "Italy departs from her attitude of neutrality. She might depart from it at a moment when the keeping open of the trade routes of the Mediterranean might be vital to us. A negative attitude by us at this moment would expose Great Britain to most appalling risks. France is entitled to know, and know at once, whether or not in event of an attack on her northern and western coasts she may depend on Great Britain for support.

"Therefore, Sir Edward said, on Sunday afternoon he gave written assurance to the French Ambassador that if the German fleet came into the Channel or through the North Sea to undertake operations against the French coast or French shipping the British fleet would give all the protection within its power.

Questions German Assurances.

This was not a declaration of war, Sir Edward carefully added.

He said that yesterday afternoon he received from the German Government assurance that if Great Britain would pledge itself to neutrality the German fleet would not attack the northern coasts of France.

"I only heard that shortly before I came into the House," said Sir Edward, "but it is far too narrow an engagement."

He next turned to the question of the neutrality of Belgium.

"If the independence of Belgium goes, the independence of Holland follows," he said. If France were beaten to her knees, which, assuredly he did not anticipate, and if Belgium, Holland, and Denmark fell under the same domination, then assuredly in Gladstone's words the world would see an unmeasured aggrandizement of a single power."

In conclusion Sir Edward said that, though no final decision to resort to force had been reached, Great Britain stood ready. The efficiency and readiness of the navy and army were never at a higher mark.

"Never have we been more justified in reposing confidence in the power of the navy to defend our commerce and shores. Suffering and misery will follow in the train of war, yes, but no neutrality will protect us from that. The situation has developed with such startling rapidity that the British people does not realize all that is involved, but when it does realize the issues at stake and the magnitude of the danger in Western Europe, then, I am confident, the Government will be supported by the determination, courage, resolution, and endurance of the whole country."

Sir Edward Grey's speech must be taken in conjunction with the orders for the mobilization of the British Army, which, it is officially announced, will be given by Royal proclamation today. The reserves will be called out, and the territorial forces be embodied.

No doubt exists that Sir Edward's exposition of the situation means that England will be involved. Sir Edward laid two contingencies necessitating British action—one a raid on the French coasts by German ships, the other the invasion of Belgium by German troops.

Germany's designs of a naval attack on the French North Coast is problematical, but her plans in regard to Belgium are clearly indicated by the ultimatum addressed to the Belgian Government on Sunday evening.

The ultimatum gave Belgium twelve hours to reply, and it required Belgium to facilitate the movements of German troops through her territory. This demand was a flagrant breach of the Treaty of London of 1839, whereby the powers guaranteed the neutrality of Belgium. The King of the Belgians appealed to King George for aid.

According to The Daily Mail, in its ultimatum to Belgium, Germany went further than was indicated in Sir Edward Grey's statement. The paper learns that Germany demanded from Belgium an attitude of friendly neutrality, which should extend to the passage of German troops through Belgian territory, promising in return to maintain, on the conclusion of peace, the independence of the Kingdom of Belgium and its possessions, and threatening, in the event of refusal, to treat Belgium as an enemy.

The Belgian Government replied that a violation of Belgian neutrality would be a flagrant violation of the rights of nations and that to accept such a demand as that presented by Germany would mean the sacrifice of the honor of the nation, which was conscious of its duty. The Government, it was added, was firmly resolved to repel aggression by all the means in its power.

Pay Homage to the King.

The King and Queen stood on a balcony at Buckingham Palace last night and received the homage of 10,000 subjects. The royal couple stood bareheaded while the multitude below, with waving hats and handkerchiefs, cheered and sang the national anthem.

The crowd went to the palace from Parliament Square as soon as the Government's policy was made known. For more than an hour the throng around the Victoria Memorial grew more and more dense until their Majesties appeared with the Prince of Wales and Princess Mary. Immediately there was such an outburst of cheering as rarely has been heard before in this country. When their Majesties retired a large number of people still remained, talking quietly, and looking up at the windows of the palace. Cries of "Down with Germany!" were heard as a large body of Frenchmen and Englishmen marched through Victoria Street with the tricolor and the union jack waving side by side.

Profoundly impressive scenes were witnessed at the railway stations all over the kingdom, when the regulars, territorials, and naval reserve men entrained for various ports. The self-restraint of the crowds was splendid, but everywhere there were evidences of the deep and anxious interest taken by the people in the tremendous events of the moment. Although it was a holiday, there had been demonstrations and excitement from early morning. The London terminals were thronged with men answering the call to arms. As more of the men arrived the holiday makers were leaving for the day, and the great stations echoed with cheers and patriotic songs. The sailors were the men of the hour, but were the calmest people in the stations.

There were exciting scenes around Whitehall throughout the day, crowds vainly besieging the War Office and the Admiralty, waiting for news. Along the pavement in front of the House of Commons the roadway was lined with spectators. An ovation was accorded to Premier Asquith when he left the Cabinet meeting at 7 o'clock.

Earlier an incident occurred that might have had serious results. A crowd of 2,000 persons surrounded a man distributing leaflets headed, "Should England Fight for Belgium's Neutrality? No!"

The pamphlet aroused the wrath of the crowd, and the man was violently hustled about, while policemen interfered and tried to get him away. He was finally put in a motor bus.

The Daily Telegraph says it is understood that the Cabinet has reserved the right for troops to be employed on the Continent if the circumstances render such a step desirable. The navy will, it is believed, take immediate and active steps to protect the French Channel ports from molestation.

By calling out all the reserves of the navy the Admiralty can obtain, allowing for those absent at sea and sick, an aggregate of 200,000 officers and men with which to place the ships of the Third fleet on a war footing. The First and Second fleets already are fully manned with their active service complements.

To Take Merchant Ships.

The Admiralty is now empowered to requisition merchant ships for the service. A royal proclamation in The London Gazette says a national emergency exists, and the defense of national interests makes it necessary immediately to employ ships to transport the auxiliary service. The Lord Commissioners of the Admiralty may take British vessels without requisition and arrange terms of compensation with the owners as soon as possible after taking them.

England Ready, but Waiting.

By The Associated Press.

LONDON, Aug. 3.—Great Britain has mobilized her forces and awaits. Today she is not a belligerent power, nor is she a neutral one. The Government has given France assurances that the English fleet will not permit the German fleet to attack the French coast. It has not as yet pledged itself to contribute an army to the continental war.

The British Government regards with the deepest distrust Germany's violation of Belgium's neutrality, but makes no declaration as to whether it considers that measure provocation for war.

The pronouncement of the Government policy—the result of two days of almost continuous deliberations—was made to the House of Commons this afternoon by Sir Edward Grey, Secretary of State for Foreign Affairs.

Belgian soldiers move into position for another attack on the German trenches.

Meanwhile the German Embassy in London is exerting every effort of diplomacy to induce Great Britain to hold aloof from the conflict and to bring public opinion to Germany's side. The counselor of the German Embassy issued a strong appeal for the neutrality of Great Britain, asserting that Germany would agree to keep her fleet from attacking the northern and western coasts of France if England would pledge neutrality, and argued that England would gain more in the end by standing outside the European war and using her influence as mediator when the moment was ripe.

Grey Dispels Doubt.

Sir Edward Grey dispelled the shadows of doubt which flickered over the Triple Entente in the minds of many Liberals by exposing some milestones in the history of the rapprochement, revealing it as essentially a national one with France, without definite obligations. Finally, on the one tremendously vital question—a question upon the answer of which the British Empire and the whole world are hanging—whether the Government considers that Germany's policy compels Great Britain to go to war, the Foreign Secretary left an impression of doubt. That doubt may reflect the mind of a Cabinet not wholly unanimous, and the interpretation drawn by many is that Sir Edward Grey's speech to Germany was a hint that if she would keep her soldiers off Belgian soil and her battleships away from the coast of France that will be the price of Great Britain's armed neutrality.

The Admiralty announced that the mobilization of the navy was completed in all respects at 4 o'clock this morning. This was due to the measures taken and the voluntary responses of the reserve men in advance of the general proclamation.

The Admiralty has issued an order prohibiting the use of wireless within the waters of the United Kingdom by merchantmen, which must dismantle their apparatus when ordered.

There is every probability of the formation of a coalition Government in the British Isles to tide over the present crisis. Andrew Bonar Law, the Marquis of Lansdowne, and Arthur J. Balfour, three Opposition leaders, were in consultation with Cabinet Ministers today.

John Burns, President of the local Government Board, has resigned. He is in disagreement with the war policy of the Government.

It is rumored that Viscount Morley of Blackburn, Lord President of the Council, contemplates resigning from the Cabinet. It is understood that the resignation of John Burns has not yet been accepted.

A strong belief was prevalent today that Field Marshal Earl Kitchener is about to be appointed British Minister of War. His return to his post in Egypt was canceled.

Sir Edward Grey's Speech.

Sir Edward Grey made two statements in the House of Commons today. In the first he said he had "given France assurance that if the German fleet came into the English Channel or through the North Sea to undertake hostile operations against the French coast or shipping the British fleet would give all the protection in its power."

The Foreign Secretary said the British fleet had been mobilized and the mobilization of the British Army was taking place, but that no engagement had yet been made by the British Government to send an expedition abroad. He continued:

"I understand that the German Government would be prepared if we would pledge ourselves to neutrality to agree that its fleet would not attack the northern coast of France. That is far too narrow an engagement."

The House broke out into cheers at this remark

Sir Edward then recited the history of Belgian neutrality, saying:

"Our interest is as strong today as it was in 1870. We cannot take a less serious view of our obligations now than did the late Mr. Gladstone in that year. When mobilization began I telegraphed to both the French and the German Governments asking whether they would respect Belgian neutrality. France replied that she was prepared to do so unless another power violated that neutrality. The German Foreign Secretary replied that he could not possibly give a response before consulting the Imperial Chancellor and the German Emperor. He intimated that he doubted whether it was possible to give an answer, because that answer would disclose the German plans.

"We were sounded last week as to whether if Belgian neutrality were restored after the war it would pacify us, and we replied that we could not barter our interests or our obligations."

Another burst of cheering greeted this declaration.

Appeal from Belgians.

Sir Edward then read a telegram from the King of the Belgians to King George making a supreme appeal for diplomatic intervention to safeguard the independence of Belgium. The telegram was as follows:

"Remembering the numerous proofs of your Majesty's friendship and that of your predecessor, of the friendly attitude of England in 1870 and the proof of the friendship which she has just given us again, I make a supreme appeal to the diplomatic intervention of your Majesty's Government to safeguard the integrity of Belgium."

In his second statement in the House of Commons, after the conference of Ministers in regard to the German ultimatum to Belgium, Sir Edward said:

"A message has been received from the Belgian Legation here stating that Germany sent to Belgium at 7 o'clock last evening a note proposing to Belgium friendly neutrality, coupled with the free passage through Belgian territory of German troops, promising the maintenance of Belgian independence at the conclusion of peace and threatening in case of refusal to treat Belgium as an enemy. The time limit of twelve hours was fixed for the reply."

This statement was received with murmurs from all parts of the House and then Sir Edward continued:

"Belgium answered that an attack on her neutrality would be a flagrant violation of the rights of nations, that to accept the German proposal would be to sacrifice her honor, and, being conscious of her duty, Belgium was firmly resolved to repel aggression by all possible means."

The Belgium reply was received with loud cheers by the members, and Sir Edward concluded with the declaration that the British Government had taken the information received into grave consideration and that he would make no further comment.

In other parts of his speech Sir Edward said:

"The intervention with Germany in regard to the independence of Belgium was carried out by England last night. If the independence of Belgium should be destroyed the independence of Holland also would be gone."

The Foreign Secretary then asked the House to consider what British interests were at stake.

"Do not imagine that if a great power stands aside in a war like this it is going to be in a position to exert its influence at the end," said he. "I am not quite sure whether the facts regarding Belgium are as they reached this Government, but there is an obligation on this country to do its utmost to prevent the consequences to which those facts would lead if they were not opposed. We have as yet made no engagement for sending an expeditionary force out of this country, but we have mobilized our fleet and the mobilization of our army is taking place. We must be prepared and we are prepared to face the consequences of using all our strength at any moment—we know not how soon—to defend ourselves.

"So far as the forces of the Crown are concerned, the Premier and the First Lord of the Admiralty have no doubt whatever of their readiness and their efficiency. They never were at a higher mark of readiness. There never was a time when confidence was more justified in their ability to protect our shores and our commerce. If the situation develops as it seems probable it will develop, we shall face it. I believe when the country realizes what is at stake it will support the Government with determination, with resolution, and with endurance."

From all parts of the House there came roars of cheering.

Obligations of Honor.

"It is said we might stand aside and husband our resources in order to intervene in the end and put things right," he went on. "If in a crisis of this kind we ran away from our obligations of honor and interest with regard to the Belgian treaty, I doubt whether whatever material force we might possess at the end would be of much value in face of the respect we should have lost."

Here he was interrupted by more loud cheering. He continued:

"If we engaged in war we should suffer but little more than if we stood aside. We are going to suffer terribly in this war whether this country is at peace or war, for foreign trade is going to stop."

Sir Edward gave an explanation of what occurred during the Moroccan crisis of 1911. He said he took precisely the same view in 1912. He continued:

"It was decided that we ought to have a definite understanding in writing, and that the conversations which had passed between military and naval officers of France and England were not binding on either side.

The Foreign Secretary then read a letter he wrote Dec. 22, 1912, to the effect that if either Government had grave reason to expect an unprovoked attack by a third power it should discuss whether both Governments should act together to prevent aggression. He then continued:

"That is our starting point, and that statement clears the ground as to the settlement of our obligations. The present crisis has not originated in a matter which principally concerns France. No Government and no country had less desire to be involved in the Austro-Servian dispute than France. France was involved because of its obligations of honor. We have a long-standing friendship with France. As to how far that friendship entails obligations, let every man look into his own heart and feelings and construe the extent of our obligations."

Pledges Ireland's Support.

Andrew Bonar Law, leader of the Opposition, said he was sure the country had taken the course it had because it had been forced upon the country, and in his opinion England had absolutely no alternative.

Wild cheering from all parts of the House greeted John E. Redmond, the Nationalist leader, when he assured the Government that every soldier in Ireland might be withdrawn tomorrow and the coasts of Ireland would be defended against invasion by her armed sons, the Catholics of the South and the Protestants of Ulster.

James Ramsay MacDonald, Socialist and Labor member, said he was not persuaded that Great Britain was in danger nor that her honor was involved. He was convinced, he said, that she should have remained neutral.

The House adjourned until 7 o'clock for a consultation between the leaders of all the parties.

Still Fight for Neutrality.

A small group of radicals during the period of adjournment of the House of Commons met and adopted a resolution that after hearing Sir Edward Grey's speech they were of the opinion that there was not sufficient reason for Great Britain to intervene in the war, and urging the Government to continue negotiations with Germany with a view to maintaining British neutrality.

When the house reassembled the Foreign Secretary made his statement with respect to Belgium. These members then protested that the Secretary had not made out a case for war.

Phillip E. Morrell, a Liberal, said the best that could be said for the entente after eight years was that it was going to land England in a war simply because a few German soldiers wanted to cross Belgium. The Laborites joined in the protest, asserting that it was a war made by the diplomats, not by the people. J. Keir Hardie asked what action was going to be taken the alleviate the sufferings of those who would be hard pressed by the war. He said he would do all he could to arouse the workingmen against the proposals of the Government.

The Chancellor of the Exchequer, David Lloyd George, announced that the Government had made arrangements for war risks for ships' cargoes, of which full details would be given later. Regarding the complaint of Hardie that the bill was for the protection of a small section of the community, the Chancellor said it was essentially a measure to protect the whole credit system, and unless steps of that kind were taken hundreds of thousands, perhaps millions, of workmen might be thrown out of work.

Arthur J. Balfour, one of the leaders of the Opposition, in winding up the debate said that the speeches of those persons who criticised Sir Edward Grey's speech did not represent even the views of the parties to which the speakers belonged.

The Cabinet held a session during the recess and was escorted to and from the House by cheering crowds.

"Good Old Winston."

The people of London generally were undemonstrative, apparently being more curious than excited. Occasionally there was cheering as some Cabinet Minister was seen leaving his office for the House of Commons or on his return from the House and when the guards at the palace gates were changed. But, on the whole, Londoners preferred to spend the holiday in their usual quiet manner. As evening drew on, however, and anxiety as to the attitude the Government intended to adopt increased, the people became more excited, and Winston Spencer Churchill as he walked from the Admiralty to the Commons was greeted with cries of "Good Old Winston."

Premier Asquith was greeted in a similar manner and escorted from his home to the precinct of the House by a cheering crowd, and other members of the Cabinet, as well as members of the House, received a cheer as they passed into the historic building to hear what England intended to do in the hour of her crisis.

John Redmond, the Irish Nationalist leader, came in for a splendid reception as he left the House, the news of his speech, in which he said every soldier would be withdrawn from Ireland, having preceded him.

Field Marshal Lord Roberts, the Marquis of Lansdowne, and Andrew Bonar Law, leader of the opposition, who visited the Prime Minister in Downing Street, were soon surrounded by a great crowd, which followed and cheered them, but the Ambassadors, including the German representative who went to the Foreign Office several times, and the Russian representatives, who sat in the House during Sir Edward Grey's speech, being little known to Londoners, passed unnoticed.

When Parliament adjourned a procession was formed, composed mostly of young men carrying Union Jacks and the tri-color, and marched through Whitehall, Trafalgar Square, Leicester Square, and Piccadilly Circus, singing all the way.

It is announced that the bank holiday has been extended to Thursday. This only applies to banks and will give the Government time to complete arrangements to meet the financial situation, so other business will continue as usual.

PRESIDENT ADVISES CALMNESS

No Cause for Alarm, He Says, in Conditions Here Due to the War in Europe.

CAN HELP REST OF WORLD

And "Reap a Great, Permanent Glory"—President Confers with Leading Senate Republicans.

Special to The New York Times.

WASHINGTON, Aug. 3. — To the Washington correspondents of newspapers, who called on him in a body today for their regular semi-weekly interview, President Wilson expressed confidence in the preparedness of the United States to meet the financial situation growing out of the European war, and "to straighten everything out without any material difficulty." The main thing for Americans to do, he said, was to keep their heads, so as to produce a state of mind that would enable this country to help the rest of the world. That America would arise to the occasion the President had no doubt, and he emphasized the assertion that this country could reap a great permanent glory out of the help she would be able to extend to other nations.

The President said that he knew from his conferences with the Secretary of the Treasury that there was no cause for alarm over the financial situation, and he asserted that the bankers and business men of the country were cooperating with the Government "with a zeal, intelligence, and spirit which make the outcome secure."

Here is what the President said to the newspaper correspondents:

No Cause for Excitement.

Gentlemen, before you question me I want to say this: I believe it is really unnecessary, but I want to tell you what is in my mind. It is extremely necessary, it is manifestly necessary, in the present state of affairs on the other side of the water that you should be extremely careful not to add in any way to the excitement. Of course, the European world is in a highly excited state of mind, but the excitement ought not to spread to the United States.

So far as we are concerned, there is no cause for excitement. There is great inconvenience, for the time being, in the money market and in our Exchanges, and, temporarily, in the handling of our crops, but America is absolutely prepared to meet the financial situation and to straighten everything out without any material difficulty. The only thing that can possibly prevent it is unreasonable apprehension and excitement.

If I might make a suggestion to you gentlemen, therefore, I would urge you not to give currency to any unverified rumor, to anything that would tend to create or add to excitement. I think that you will agree that we must all at the present moment act together as Americans in seeing that America does not suffer any unnecessary distress from what is going on in the world at large.

The situation in Europe is perhaps the gravest in its possibilities that has arisen in modern times, but it need not affect the United States unfavorably in the long run. Not that the United States has anything to take advantage of, but her own position is sound and she owes it to mankind to remain in such a condition and in such a state of mind that she can help the rest of the world.

I want to have the pride of feeling that America, if nobody else, has her self-possession and stands ready with calmness of thought and steadiness of purpose to help the rest of the world. And we can do it and reap a great permanent glory out of doing it, provided we all co-operate to see that nobody loses his head.

I know from my conference with the Secretary of the Treasury, who is in very close touch with the financial situation throughout the country, that there is no cause for alarm. There is cause for getting busy and doing the thing in the right way, but there is no element of unsoundness and there is no cause for alarm. The bankers and business men of the country are cooperating with the Government with a zeal, intelligence, and spirit which make the outcome secure.

Can't Use Government Ships.

What the President said to the newspaper men was repeated by him in other words to other callers. These callers learned from him tht the Administration was doing everything within its power to provide merchant vessels for carrying foodstuffs and other products from this country abroad and to bring back from Europe the tens of thousands of Americans who are practically stranded there. As to using Government ships for that purpose, the President remarked that this was easier said than done. He indicated that the Government did not have sufficient ships to be of any substantial benefit.

A proclamation of neutrality, Mr. Wilson said, would be issued as soon as it could be completed by the State Department. The President told his callers that the United States had not directly or indirectly made any offer to use its good offices to bring about peace in Europe. He said he had not heard of a suggestion by the Queen of Holland that the United States unite with her country to offer mediation.

The President indicated that he did not believe that there was any necessity for Congress to remain in session on account of affairs in Europe. What was in his mind in this connection was demonstrated this evening, when, at his request, Senators Gallinger, Smoot, and Brandegee, all Republicans of long service and prominence in the upper house of Congress, called at the White House to discuss arrangements by which the pending legislative programme could be put through in the shortest possible time. What the President most desired to accomplish through this conference with Republican leaders of the Senate was an understanding by which no obstruction would be placed in the way of action on legislative measures backed by the Administration.

President Wilson at this conference turned down a request from the Republican leaders that, in view of the business uncertainty growing out of the European war, the pending trust legislation programme be postponed until the next session of Congress. Senators Gallinger, Smoot, and Brandegee told Mr. Wilson that in their opinion the anti-trust bills would lead to further business troubles.

President Wilson assured his callers that in his opinion business would be hurt more if left uncertain as to what the anti-trust bills were to be. He declared that he was determined that final action on the bills should be taken at the present session of Congress and asked the Senators whether the Republicans would conduct a filibuster against them. Nothing of this kind was to be expected, he was told, though the Republicans reserved the right of voting against the bills.

After leaving the White House the Senators said they saw no reason why Congress should remain in session after Sept. 1.

French troops relax for a moment in a shell hole.

"All the News That's Fit to Print."

The New York Times.

THE WEATHER
Fair today; partly cloudy, warmer Thursday; moderate east to southeast winds.
[Full weather report see Page 12.]

VOL. LXIII...NO. 20,647.   ....   NEW YORK, WEDNESDAY, AUGUST 5, 1914.—TWENTY PAGES.   ONE CENT In Greater New York, Jersey City and Newark.

ENGLAND DECLARES WAR ON GERMANY; BRITISH SHIP SUNK; FRENCH SHIPS DEFEAT GERMAN, BELGIUM ATTACKED; 17,000,000 MEN ENGAGED IN GREAT WAR OF EIGHT NATIONS; GREAT ENGLISH AND GERMAN NAVIES ABOUT TO GRAPPLE; RIVAL WARSHIPS OFF THIS PORT AS LUSITANIA SAILS

State of War Exists, Says Britain, as Kaiser Rejects Ultimatum.

MUST DEFEND BELGIUM

King George Issues Call to Arms and Thanks the Colonies for Their Support.

ENVOY LEAVES BERLIN

British Foreign Office Makes Final Announcement One Hour Before Time Limit.

VOTE $525,000,000 FUND

England Takes All Foreign Warships Building in Her Ports —Two from Turkey.

JAPAN TO AID ENGLAND

To Smash the Kiel Canal Probably English Fleet's First Attempt Against Germany.

Special Cable to THE NEW YORK TIMES.

LONDON, Wednesday, Aug. 5.— War is on between England and Germany. An ultimatum to the German Government that the neutrality of Belgium must be respected was rejected by the Kaiser's Government and the British Foreign Office announced last night that a state of war existed.

The time limit for Germany's reply was set at midnight, but the Foreign Office announced that as Germany had given his passports to the British envoy at an earlier hour, the state of war existed from 11 o'clock.

King George has issued his proclamation mobilizing the army and has sent a message to the colonies thanking them for their hearty support in the hour of national emergency.

The Government has assumed control of all the railways and the Admiralty has taken over all the foreign

British Declaration of War With Germany, Following Rejection of Her Demand

LONDON, Aug. 4.—Great Britain declared war on Germany at 7 o'clock tonight.

An earlier announcement that Germany had declared war on Great Britain was due to an error in the Admiralty's statement.

The Foreign Office's Statement.

The British Foreign Office has issued the following statement:

"Owing to the summary rejection by the German Government of the request made by his Britannic Majesty's Government that the neutrality of Belgium should be respected, his Majesty's Ambassador at Berlin has received his passports and his Majesty's Government has declared to the German Government that a state of war exists between Great Britain and Germany from 11 o'clock P.M., Aug. 4."

Declaration Announced to Germany.

BERLIN, Aug. 4.—Shortly after 7 o'clock this evening William Edward Goschen, the British Ambassador, went to the Foreign Office and announced that Great Britain had declared war with Germany. He then demanded his passports.

England Calls All Unmarried Men From 18 to 30 To Serve King and Country in This Hour of Need

LONDON, Wednesday, Aug. 5.—A War Office advertisement appears in the morning papers headed: "Your King and Country Need You."

The advertisement says that the empire is on the brink of the greatest war in the history of the world, and appeals to all unmarried men between the ages of 18 and 30 years to join the army immediately.

warships now building in English ports.

The House of Commons has voted a fund of $525,000,000 for the emergency.

England Cool in Great Crisis.

England is facing this, the greatest crisis in her history, with calmness and courage. Sir Edward Grey's exposition has made it clear that the war is none of her seeking, and that she goes into it because her honor and her self-preservation alike compel her to do so. There is neither any sign of panic nor flame of war fever. All parties and all classes present a united front. The few exceptions are not worthy of mention. The protests that the Labor members of Parliament and a few Liberals have made in the House of Commons do not represent the prevalent feeling either in the ranks of labor or among the avowed pacifists. The peace-at-any-price advocates are submerged beneath the huge majority who would have welcomed peace with honor but prefer war to dishonor.

Liberal newspapers like The Westminster Gazette, The Daily Chronicle, and even The Daily News accept the situation as inevitable.

" 'Here we stand, and we can do

no other.' The Germans will recognize that famous phrase," says The Westminster Gazette, "and understand that it expresses the feelings of the vast majority of the British people."

The demeanor of the crowds last evening and this morning began to betray growing excitement. A procession of a thousand young men marched along by Whitehall and up the Strand, cheering. It was headed by a squad carrying the Union Jack of England and the tricolor of France. As it passed Trafalgar Square there was some booing, but the cheering outweighed it. Fleet Street last evening was jammed by crowds watching the bulletins. Occasionally they sang "The Marseillaise" and "God Save the King."

Soon after the announcement of Germany's declaration of war against Belgium was displayed on the bulletin boards the crowds, evidently believing no greater news was likely to come, quietly dispersed, and by 11 o'clock Fleet Street was as quiet as usual.

Would Smash Kiel Canal.

Premier Asquith's statement in the House of Commons yesterday that the German Government had been asked to give satisfactory assurances on the question of Belgium's neutrality by

midnight was generally regarded as meaning that England was prepared to strike at once if the reply was unfavorable.

The German fleet is concentrated for the defense of the Kiel Canal. Its destruction will be the first object of the British fleet.

Germany's compliance with the British ultimatum was not expected. Germany, according to a statement emanating from her London embassy, would have consented to refrain from using Belgian ports and would have confined her violation of neutrality to the inland districts if Great Britain would agree to hold aloof. It is obvious that a compact on such lines would have been useless to Great Britain. Belgian neutrality is strategically important in two ways—by sea to Great Britain and Germany and by land to Germany and France. If England abnadoned it in its land aspect, nobody, not even the Belgians, would have been willing to defend it when it was threatened in its sea aspect.

It seemed unlikely from the start that Germany would desist, because it was a matter affecting the military plans of ther General Staff. The whole German theory of war is to make plans years ahead and have everything, down to the last railway siding, ready for their execution and to carry them out without deviation. It is probable that the present plan was made as long ago as when Anglo-German hostility was an axiom, and there was no question in German minds of so shaping their strategy as to keep Great Britain neutral.

German Ships in Peril.

As was anticipated, Germany's first naval effort was to deal a heavy blow to the Russians in the Baltic, but as yet there is insufficient evidence that it succeeded or that the Russian fleet was rendered powerless. Germany's most urgent need, according to experts, is to assemble all her available naval forces on the west, principally in the North Sea, but, these experts say, the Germans are not likely to seek battle, hoping the strength of their adversaries may be reduced by the action of mines and torpedoes.

Two German cruisers seem to be in peril. The battle cruiser Goeben, on the way from the Mediterranean, is reported to have passed Gibraltar, steaming westward. She will not venture through the English Channel, and must travel homeward via the west coast of Ireland and north of Scotland. An attempt certainly will be made to intercept her, and the need of carrying assistance to her may bring about a fleet action. The German cruiser Breslau is reported to have shelled Bona before proceeding westward toward Gibraltar. Her position seems perilous in the extreme.

The government took over the railways to complete the co-ordination of the railway facilities, in view of the military and naval requirements and the needs of the civil communities. The staff of each railway remains as before. Supreme control is vested in a committee composed of the General Managers of the chief railways.

The Acting Chairman is H. A. Walker, manager of the London & Southwestern, who is well known among American railway men. The committee was formed some days ago. The Great Eastern is not represented, possibly because its General Manager, H. W. Thornton, is an American.

News Flashed to Navy.

When the announcement of the state of war was made by the Foreign Office, and the quietness of the Summer night was suddenly broken by the raucous cries of the news venders, the streets were practically empty. The ordinary troops of theatregoers were conspicuous for their absence.

Midnight was considered the fateful hour when orders would be flashed by wireless to the British Navy to begin operations.

Reports which had spread during the evening that German warships had sunk a British mine finder and chased the destroyer Pathfinder, were taken as another instance of Germany's method of taking an unfair advantage and acting before war actually was declared.

Sir John Jellicoe, who has been long regarded as predestined to head the fleet in case of war, has taken supreme command, with Rear Admiral Madden as Chief of Staff. Sir John Jellicoe, who is familiarly known as " J. J.," is a typical, keen-faced officer, distinguished for his personal courage as well as for scientific gunnery. He has the German decoration of the Red Eagle. Lord Kitchener is taking the Administrative part of the work of the War Office, where Lord Haldane is assisting Mr. Asquith.

The only panicky note which struck the English press hard came from The Evening News, which came out in a poster headed " Treachery " and stating that Lord Haldane's German sympathies made his apointment to the War Office a matter of suspicion to France. THE NEW YORK TIMES correspondent saw Lord Haldane at Whitehall yesterday afternoon walking toward Westminster. When accosted he said there was nothing he could say.

Lord Haldane did yeoman service when at the War Office, and a Liberal paper says the worst news Germany could receive is that he has returned to the department.

England's war with Germany is likely to be purely a naval conflict for the time being. Germany will keep her fleet sheltered at Wilhelmshaven and trust to her submarines and torpedo boats to reduce the strength of the British investing fleet. The reported sinking of a mine-layer probably is due to this. The feature of the Anglo-German war will be the strewing of the North Sea with floating mines.

Asquith's Impressive Speech.

The first chapter of the critical events of the day was unfolded when Premier Asquith read his statement in the House of Commons. The Premier read in a firm and measured voice, and his hand shook as he held the typewritten copy. His words were listened to in a silence that was almost uncanny, so tense and overwrought was the crowded House.

After he had read the telegrams exchanged between London and Berlin and London and Brussels, Mr. Asquith's announcement of the ultimatum to Germany demanding an answer by midnight was greeted with prolonged applause. There was a strange note of solemnity in the deep cheers that rolled up from all sides like thunder waves beating on a rockbound shore. Plainly enough the telegrams had eaten deep into the feelings of the audience, revealing Germany's disregard of the law of nations in browbeating Belgium.

Until yesterday afternoon a strong minority of the Liberal Party was in favor of British neutrality. Sir Edward Grey's speech reduced the minority to small proportions. Today's events almost extinguished it.

Even the Labor members, despite their sworn devotion to neutrality, were unfavorably impressed by this sample of German methods. A Scotch Radical member, who hates war, said: " Germany leaves us no alternative but to fight. We are standing for public law; she is trampling upon it.

"It is another struggle in the incessant conflict between right and force, wherein the rival champions in the last generation were Gladstone and Bismarck. Mr. Gladstone, who was a most peaceful statesman, said he would spend every shilling of the British exchequer and employ every soldier in the British Army in the defense of the independence of Belgium."

Goes to Belgium's Defense.
By The Associated Press.

LONDON, Aug. 4.—Great Britain and Germany went to war tonight. The momentous decision of the British Government, for which the whole world had been waiting, came before the expiration of the time limit set by Great Britain in her ultimatum to Germany demanding a satisfactory reply on the subject of Belgian neutrality.

Germany's reply was the summary rejection of the request that Belgian neutrality should be respected.

The British Ambassador at Berlin thereupon received his passports and the British Government notified Germany that a state of war existed between the two countries.

The British Foreign Office has issued the following statement:

Owing to the summary rejection by the German Government of the request made by His Britannic Majesty's Government that the neutrality of Belgium should be respected, His Majesty's Ambassador at Berlin has received his passports, and His Majesty's Government has declared to the German Government that a state of war exists between Great Britain and Germany from 11 o'clock P. M., Aug. 4.

A mob gathered outside the German Embassy in Carlton House Terrace tonight. The demonstrators groaned and hooted and finally stones were thrown, which broke windows. The German Ambassador, Prince Lichnowsky, and the members of his staff were in the garden, but quickly withdrew to the house. A force of mounted and foot police reinforced the regular guard and drove the crowd away.

A thousand persons assembled tonight before Buckingham Palace and cheered until the King and Queen, the Prince of Wales, and Princess Mary appeared on the balcony.

The statues of military heroes are being draped with flags.

All Europe Now in Arms.

All Europe is now in arms. On the one hand Austria-Hungary and Germany are opposed by Russia, France, and Great Britain, Servia and Montenegro.

Italy has declared her neutrality, but is mobilizing. Belgium, Holland, and Switzerland have mobilized.

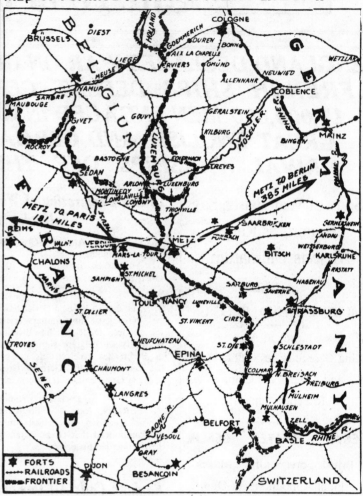

Map of Fortified Frontier of France and Belgium.

FORTS
RAILROADS
FRONTIER

Cunarder Slips Out; Will Pick Up British Cruisers as Escorts.

GERMAN SHIPS NEAR

Liner to Head for Newfoundland, Where Other English Ships Will Meet Her.

FRENCH CRUISERS OUTSIDE

Wireless Code Messages from Telefunken Station at Sayville Aid German Cruisers.

Cruisers Off the Coast
French.—Cruisers Conde and Descartes.
British.—Cruisers Berwick, Essex, and Lancaster.
German.—Cruisers Dresden, Strassburg, and Karlsruhe.

As the Cunard liner Lusitania left this port for Liverpool at 1 o'clock this morning, she was picked up outside Sandy Hook by the British cruiser Essex, which had just convoyed the White Star liner Olympic to the end of its transatlantic journey past three German cruisers off this coast and almost into New York Harbor.

The Lusitania was due to leave its pier at 12 o'clock. It was expected at that time that a wireless message would be received from either the Berwick, Lancaster, or Essex, the three British cruisers now off the Atlantic Coast, that one or all of them would escort the Lusitania on its trip across the Atlantic.

Word that the Lusitania could leave port safely had not come through the air at 12 o'clock. Capt. Dow had not yet received the word to cast off. It was believed by the crowd at the pier that at the last minute it had been decided that the danger was too great, and that the sailing was to be postponed.

A few minutes before 1 o'clock Chief Officer Johnson, who had been sent to the British Consulate, returned in an automobile to the pier and hurried on board the Lusitania.

Captain Orders Lights Out.

A few minutes later Capt. Dow gave the order, " All lights out." Those at the pier heard the order repeated again and again from one end of the boat to the other, and then, practically dark, the big ship glided out into the river.

It was not known to be a certainty that the Lusitania would have the convoy of the Essex until after the Olympic arrived.

The Lusitania has on board 100 passengers in the first cabin, 50 in the second, and 50 in the third, and carried 2,200 sacks of mail. All passengers were notified that lights in the staterooms must be blanketed when the vessel passed Ambrose Channel, and in the passageways of the ship oil lamps were to replace the customary electric lighting. The ship is to make the trip with no lights showing except the running lights at the masthead and on the sides. Passengers were allowed on deck, but warned that no lights must be shown.

H.G. WELLS' VISION OF ARMAGEDDON

Germany Prepares to Reap the Harvest That Bismarck Sowed.

RIGHTEOUS WAR BEGINS

Europe's Quarrel with the Kaiser and His System, Not with His People.

PEACE OF WORLD IN SIGHT

Novelist, Writing Just Before War Declaration Yesterday, Said England Had to Enter the Fight.

BY H. G. WELLS.
Author of "The World Set Free," "The War in the Air," &c.

Copyright, 1914, by the New York Times Co.
Special Cable to THE NEW YORK TIMES.

LONDON, AUG. 4.—At last the intolerable tension is over. Europe is at war. The monstrous vanity that was begotten by the easy victories of 1870-71 has challenged the world. Germany prepares to reap the harvest that Bismarck sowed. That trampling, drilling foolery in the heart of Europe that has arrested civilization and darkened the hopes of mankind for forty years—German imperialism and German militarism—has struck its inevitable blow.

The victory of Germany will mean the permanent enthronement of the war god over all human affairs. The defeat of Germany may open the way to disarmament and peace throughout the earth. To those who love peace there can be no other hope in the present conflict than her defeat, the utter discrediting of the German legend—ending it for good and all—of blood and iron, the superstition of Krupp, flag-wagging, Teutonic Kiplingism, and all that criminal sham efficiency that centres in Berlin.

Never was a war so righteous as is the war against Germany now; never any State in the world so clamored for punishment; but be it remembered that Europe's quarrel is with Germany as a State, not with the German people, with the system, not with the race.

The older tradition of Germany is a pacific, civilizing tradition. The temperament of the mass of the German people is kindly, sane, amiable. Disaster to the German Army, if it is unaccompanied by such a memorable wrong as dismemberment or intolerable indignity, will mean the restoration of the greatest people of Europe to the fellowship of the western nations.

The rôle of England in the huge struggle is as plain as daylight. We have to fight if only on account of the Luxemburg outrage. We have to fight. If we do not fight England will cease to be a country to be proud of and we shall have a dirt bath to escape from.

But it is inconceivable that we should not fight, and, having fought, then in the hour of victory it will be for us to save the liberated Germans from vindictive treatment, to secure for this great people their right to a place in the sun as one united German-speaking State.

First, we have to save ourselves and Europe, and then we have to stand between the Germans on the one hand, and Cossack revenge on the other.

Sure Germany Will Be Defeated.

For my part, I do not doubt that Germany and Austria are doomed to defeat in this war. It may not be a catastrophic defeat, though even that is possible, but it will be a defeat. There is no destiny in the stars and every sign is false if this is not so.

They have provoked an overwhelming combination of enemies. They have underrated France. They are hampered by bad social and military traditions. The German is not naturally a good soldier. He is orderly and obedient, but not nimble or quick-witted. Hence his sole considerable military achievement is his not very lengthy march to Paris in 1871.

The conditions of modern warfare have been almost completely revolutionized and in a direction that subordinates massed fighting and unintelligent men to the rapid initiative of individualized soldiers.

On the other hand, since those years of disaster, the Frenchman has learned the lesson of humility. He is prepared now sombrely for a similar struggle. His is the gravity that precedes astonishing victories. In the air, in the open field, with guns and machines, it is doubtful if any one fully realizes the superiority of his quality to the German.

This sudden attack may take him aback for a week or so, though I doubt even that; but in the end, I think, he will hold his own even without us, and with us I venture to prophesy within three months from now his tri-color will be over the Rhine, and, even suppose his line gets broken by the first rush, even then I do not see how the Germans are to get to Paris or anywhere near Paris.

I do not see how, against the strength of modern offensive and the stinging power of an intelligent enemy in retreat, of which we had a little foretaste in South Africa, the exploit of Sedan can be repeated.

A retiring German army, on the other hand, will be far less formidable than a retiring French army, because there is less devil in it, because it is made up of men taught to obey in masses, because its intelligence is concentrated in old, autocratic officers; because it is dismayed when it breaks ranks.

The German Army is everything the conscriptionists dreamt of making our people. It is, in fact, an army about twenty years behind the requirements of contemporary conditions.

Issue With Russia More Doubtful.

On the eastern frontier the issue is more doubtful because of the uncertainty of Russian things. The peculiar military strength of Russia, the strength she was never able to display in Manchuria, lies in her vast resources of mounted men.

A set invasion of Prussia may be a matter of many weeks, but the raiding possibilities in Eastern Germany are enormous.

It is difficult to guess how far a Russian attack will be directed by intelligence, how far Russia will have to blunder very disastrously, indeed, before she can be put upon the defensive.

A Russian raid is far more likely to threaten Berlin than a German to reach Paris.

Meanwhile there is a struggle on sea. In that I am prepared for some rude shocks. The Germans have devoted an amount of energy to the creation of an aggressive navy that would have been spent more wisely in consolidating their European position. It is probably a thoroughly good navy, and, ship for ship, the equal of our own, but the same lack of invention, the same relative uncreativeness that kept the German behind the Frenchman in things aerial made him follow our lead in naval matters, and if we erred, and I believe we have erred, in overrating the importance of big battleships the German has at least very obligingly fallen in with our error.

The safest and most effective place for the German fleet at the present time is the Baltic Canal. Unless I underrate the powers of the waterplane there is no safe harbor for it. If it goes into port anywhere that port can be mined and bottled up. Ships can be destroyed at leisure by aerial bombs, so that if they are on this side of the Kiel Canal, they must keep at sea and fight, if we let them, before their coal runs short, a battle in the open sea.

In that case their only chance will be to fight against odds, with every prospect of a smashing, albeit we shall certainly have to pay for victory in ships and men. In the Baltic we shall, notably, get at them without the participation of Denmark, and their ships may have considerable use against Russia, but in the end even there the mine, aeroplane, and destroyer should do this work.

So I reckon that Germany will be held in the east and that the west will get her fleet practically destroyed.

We ought also to be able to sweep her shipping off the seas and lower her flag forever in Africa, Asia, and the Pacific. All the probabilities seem to me to point to that.

There is no reason why Italy should not stick to her present neutrality. There is considerable inducement at hand for both Denmark and Japan to join in directly they are convinced of the failure of the first big rush on the part of Germany.

All those issues will be more or less definitely decided within the next two or three months. By that time, I believe, German imperialism will be shattered, and it may be possible to anticipate the end of the armaments phase of European history.

France, Italy, England and all the smaller Powers of Europe are now pacific countries. Russia, after a huge war, will be too exhausted for further adventure. Shattered Germany will be revolutionary. Germany will be as sick of the uniforms and imperialism idea as France was in 1871, as disillusioned about predominance as Bulgaria is today.

The way will be open at last for all these Western powers to organize a peace.

That is why I, with my declared horror of war, did not sign any of these "stop the war" appeals.

Declarations that have appeared in the last few days are that every sword is drawn against Germany. Now is the sword drawn for peace.

Over 17,000,000 Fighting Men of Eight Nations Now Engaged in the Colossal European War

DUAL ALLIANCE.

	Regular Army.	Reserves.	Total War Strength.
Germany	870,000	4,480,000	5,300,000
Austria-Hungary	390,000	1,610,000	2,000,000
Total	1,260,000	6,040,000	7,300,000

TRIPLE ENTENTE AND ITS ALLIES.

	Regular Army.	Reserves.	Total War Strength.
Russia	1,290,000	3,800,000	4,590,000
France	720,000	3,280,000	4,000,000
England	254,500	476,500	731,000
Belgium	42,000	180,000	222,000
Servia	32,000	208,000	240,000
Montenegro	50,000	......	50,000
Total	2,388,500	7,944,500	9,833,000
Grand Total			17,133,000

The above figures do not include the naval forces of the nations.

TWO GERMAN WARSHIPS TAKEN, ANOTHER SUNK

French Fleet in the Mediterranean Reported to Have Won a Victory.

PARIS, Aug. 4.—An unofficial report from Algiers says that a French fleet has captured two German cruisers, the Goeben and the Breslau.

A Havas dispatch from Algiers says that it is reported there that French warships have sunk the German cruiser Panther.

A previous report from the Governor of Algeria, in a telegram to the French Government, said that the German cruiser Breslau fired eight broadsides (about sixty shells) into the French fortified town of Bona this morning.

One man was killed and some buildings were damaged.

The German gunboat Panther, which is reported to have been sunk by French cruisers, was one of the smallest vessels in the Kaiser's navy, but also one of the most renowned, for it happened that four times she was the storm centre of various incidents of international politics. It was the Panther that blew the Haitian gunboat Cretè-à-Pierrot out of the water in Bnaives Bay in 1902.

In the fall of 1905, when she was still stationed in South American waters, her commander sent a detail of sailors ashore at Itajahy, Brazil, to seize a deserter. This action was disavowed by the German Government and the vessel's commander reprimanded.

"All the News That's Fit to Print."

The New York Times.

THE WEATHER
Fair today; unsettled, warmer Friday; gentle to moderate south winds.
For full weather report see Page 14.

VOL. LXIII...NO. 20,648.   ....   NEW YORK, THURSDAY, AUGUST 6, 1914.—EIGHTEEN PAGES.   ONE CENT In Greater New York, Jersey City and Newark.   Elsewhere TWO CENTS

BELGIANS DEFEAT GERMANS, KILL OR WOUND 3,500 MEN; BRITISH THIRD FLOTILLA HAS A BATTLE IN THE NORTH SEA; RUSSIANS DRIVE OUT THE GERMANS AND ENTER PRUSSIA; GERMANY SAID TO HAVE SENT AN ULTIMATUM TO ITALY

Severe Check to German Arms in the First Belgian Fight.

BATTLE LASTS FOR HOURS

Victors Afterward Fall Upon Detached German Forces and Annihilate Them.

Belgian Aviators Show Their Mettle—Forts Resist Heavy German Fire.

GERMAN PRINCE IS COMING

Reported Near Liege with 30,000 Fresh Troops, Ready to Attack Today.

FRENCH ARMY RUSHING UP

Force Has Already Effected Junction with Belgians—English Army Expected.

Crown Prince Bringing Aid; German Loss So Far, 3,500

Special Cable to THE NEW YORK TIMES.
AMSTERDAM, Thursday, Aug. 6, 3 A. M.—The German Crown Prince is hourly expected before Liege at the head of 30,000 fresh troops. The Germans now have crossed the river by means of pontoon bridges, developing the attack on Liege.

In yesterday's battle 3,500 Germans were killed or wounded.

The Postmaster of Vise met his death like a hero. The Germans ordered him to send telegrams to assist them. He refused and was shot.

BRUSSELS, (via Paris,) Aug. 6, 1:38 A. M.—Several thousand dead and wounded is the toll paid by the German Army of the Meuse for its attack on Liege in an attempt to force its way to the French frontier.

The Belgians made a heroic defense, repulsing the Germans after heavy and continuous firing. The assailants were unable to renew the assault.

The Belgians delivered a vigorous counter-attack on Germans who had passed the forts, killing all of them.

Eight hundred wounded Germans are being transferred to Liege, where they will be cared for.

The fortified position in and around Liege had to support yesterday the general shock of the German attack.

The forts afforded admirable resistance to the German shells. Evegnee Fort, which was in action all day, was absolutely unharmed.

The Belgian aviators proved themselves every whit as good as the Germans.

One Belgian squadron attacked and drove back six German squadrons.

The War Office announces that after fierce fighting in the environs of Liege the situation is excellent so far as the Belgians are concerned.

"The Germans," the announcement says, "were driven back by a heroic attack made by a Belgian mixed brigade, which had already earned for itself the highest honors. No German who passed the fort survived."

Another official bulletin says:
"The Belgian losses are trifling compared with those of the Germans."

MINE LAYER DESTROYED

Small German Coast Steamer Fitted as Auxiliary Sunk by the Amphion.

ALLIES SEIZE MANY PRIZES

Special Cable to THE NEW YORK TIMES.
HARWICH, Aug. 5.—The third flotilla left this port for the open sea at daybreak this morning and went into action almost immediately.

Heavy gun firing was heard at intervals throughout the day, and this evening the cruiser Vigo, anchored off Harwich pier, received a wireless message to be ready to receive 200 prisoners. The authorities were also requested to prepare to receive wounded who were being brought in by a torpedo boat.

Later the flotilla returned to port, little the worse for the encounter. The light cruiser Amphion, flagship of the flotilla, had her batteries slightly damaged.

Twenty-eight wounded were brought ashore and taken to the Shotley Naval establishment, opposite Harwich. Of the wounded twenty-two were Germans and six English.

As the flotilla steamed out of the harbor at daybreak the crews of the vessels still to go lined up and heartily cheered their comrades. Soon afterward a Hook of Holland boat, crammed with passengers, mostly Americans, and an Antwerp boat, equally crowded, passed the flotilla. The passengers realized the significance of the departure and cheered lustily. They received hearty response from the sailors.

During the day there were alarming rumors that the houses between Harwich and Walton would be blown down tonight as being in the line of fire from the shore batteries.

German Ultimatum to Italy Is Reported; Italy About to Declare War on Austria?

LONDON, Thursday, Aug. 6.—It is reported that Germany has sent an ultimatum to Italy. The report lacks official confirmation but is regarded here as not improbable.

There have been rumors that Italy, owing to the strong antagonism existing between Austrians and Italians, was likely to break away from the Triple Alliance and declare herself on the side of England.

LONDON, Thursday, Aug. 6.—The Telegraph in a late edition today says it is believed in diplomatic circles that Italy is on the eve of declaring war on Austria. Italy's alliance with Austria was never popular with Italians. The two peoples, in their aims and aspirations as regards Asiatic affairs and the Balkans, are notoriously irreconcilable, says The Telegraph.

Lusitania Fleeing Before German Cruisers, Says Wireless Message Picked Up at Portland

Special to The New York Times.
PORTLAND, Me., Aug. 5.—The Cunard liner Lusitania, according to an intercepted message picked up here by an amateur, is being pursued by two German cruisers and is heading back for Portland or Boston at full speed.

A later dispatch from a British cruiser said that she was on her way to render any possible assistance and advised the Lusitania to continue at top speed to the nearest port.

It is believed that the pursuing German cruisers are the same ones which have been reported to be cruising about off this coast for the last two days.

Tonight, far out to sea, searchlights are flashing beams of light across the heavens, but their source has not yet been determined.

Herman Winter, Assistant General Manager of the Cunard Line, said last night that he knew nothing of the pursuit of the Lusitania or of any orders for her to return.

"All the News That's Fit to Print."

The New York Times.

THE WEATHER
Local thunder showers, somewhat cooler, late today and probably Tuesday; moderate south winds today.
☞For full weather report see Page 10

VOL. LXIII...NO. 20,652. ....   NEW YORK, MONDAY, AUGUST 10, 1914.—TWELVE PAGES.   ONE CENT In Greater New York, | Elsewhere Jersey City and Newark. | TWO CENTS

FRENCH ARE DRIVING THE GERMANS BACK IN ALSACE; AUSTRIANS GO TO AID KAISER THERE; GERMANS IN LIEGE, BUT FORTS ARE UNTAKEN; FRENCH AND BRITISH NEAR; GERMANS IN A NAVAL FIGHT, LOSE A SUBMARINE

German Forces in Alsace Fall Back Upon Neu Breisach.

RETREAT CALLED A ROUT

Alsatian Populace Welcomes Gen. Joffre with Frenzied Joy-- French Losses 'Not Excessive.'

Special Cable to THE NEW YORK TIMES.

PARIS, Aug. 9.—The French arms have triumphed in the first fighting in Alsace, although the report that they have followed up their capture of Altkirch and Mülhausen by taking Colmar, lacks confirmation.

Altkirch was taken by a French brigade on Friday night. The German brigade which was intrenched there, after offering some resistance, took flight under cover of darkness, pursued by a regiment of French dragoons.

The French cavalry advanced on Saturday morning along the railway across the low country, and at 5 o'clock arrived at Mülhausen, a large industrial town, which was unfortified, and captured it in less than an hour.

The only important military fact developed by this engagement is that with equal numbers the Germans are unable to sustain a French bayonet charge; but the occupation of Alsace will have a great moral influence.

The Germans retired from Mülhausen upon Neu Breisach, fourteen miles to the north, first firing a great number of the Mülhausen buildings, notably provision shops and fodder stores. They also burned the forest of Hard, near Colmar.

The Alsatians, who have been terrorized by the German military authorities, welcomed the French with open arms.

Kaiser Off to the Front to Take Command; Paris Believes This Is Signal for Big Battle

LONDON, Aug. 9.—A dispatch from Rome to The Daily Mail says that a report is current that Emperor William has left Berlin in a motor car for the Alsatian frontier.

A dispatch to the Exchange Telegraph Company from Rome says that, on the contrary, Emperor William has arrived at Aix-la-Chapelle to join his army.

PARIS, Aug. 9.—The military critic of the Journal des Debats considers the report from Rome that Emperor William has left Berlin to join the general staff of the German Army on the Alsatian frontier shows that the Germans are ready to engage the French in great force, and that a general engagement is impending.

British Beat Off German Submarines, Sinking One

LONDON, Monday, Aug. 10, 1:30 A. M.—The Admiralty has announced that one of the cruiser squadrons of the main fleet was attacked yesterday by German submarines. None of the British ships was damaged. One German submarine boat was sunk.

No details are given as to the place at which the fight occurred. The submarine sunk by the British fleet was the U 15, which was built in 1912 and displaced 300 tons. She carried a crew of twelve men.

KAISER MADE A BOAST.

"Will Sweep Through Belgium," He Once Told a British Officer.

Special Cable to THE NEW YORK TIMES.

LONDON, Monday, Aug. 10.—According to the view of a very high military authority quoted by The Daily Telegraph, the severe check inflicted by the Belgian garrison at Liege on the Seventh German Corps is of cardinal importance.

The German General Staff made no secret of the fact that they expected an easy task in marching through Belgium.

An officer of the German War Office recently stated that they counted on the benevolent neutrality of Belgium at the worst, and more probably the King of the Belgians would range himself on the German side.

Some time ago a British military mission at the Kaiser's invitation attended manoeuvres of special importance near Berlin. In conversation with the senior British officer present the Kaiser said: "I shall sweep through Belgium thus," and he waved his arm in the air.

MILITARY VALUE OF LIEGE'S HEROISM

Joseph Reinach Says It Nullifies the Effects of the Germans' Deliberate Aggression.

CALLS THE WAR BRIGANDAGE

No People Can Put Itself Under Ban of Civilization with Impunity, French Statesman Declares.

By JOSEPH REINACH,
Member of the French Chamber of Deputies—Principal Secretary of Gambetta in 1881-1882.

Special Cable to THE NEW YORK TIMES.

PARIS, Aug. 9.—There is today no more glorious town in history than Liege. Its forts have already stopped the forward march of the invaders. The more than three days' advantage of their deliberate aggression given to the Germans in mobilizing is lost.

It is not only to the mass of the Belgian Army that the heroic defenders of Liege have given time to complete mobilization and concentration, but also to the French Army, to our northeastern troops, massed between Lille and Montmédy, and to the British expeditionary force.

The consequences of the resistance of Liege, which has caused the admiration of the civilized world and manifest surprise to the German Army, are not, even from a purely military point of view, facts of trivial importance. Even on the battlefield it is not only the big battalions that count.

Many fragments of information had already indicated that the German Army, strong in numbers and well prepared as it was, did not enter upon this war with the self-confidence it possessed in 1870.

Heavily charged with lies though the atmosphere be, a dim ray of light penetrates the darkness. Never had any war in such a degree the appearance, as it has the reality, of a piece of brigandage. It is impossible that Germany should not now have a vague consciousness of the horror with which the action of her Government struck the world.

Peoples do not put themselves under the ban of civilization with impunity. One cannot carry into a war against all that is implied in treaty rights, international law and justice when against it is put the pride of peoples who are struggling for the holiest causes.

It is hard to fight with the sun in one's eyes. It was not a sentimental philosopher, but the most hard-headed of soldiers, the very genius of war, Napoleon, who said: "In war morale and opinion are more than half of the business."

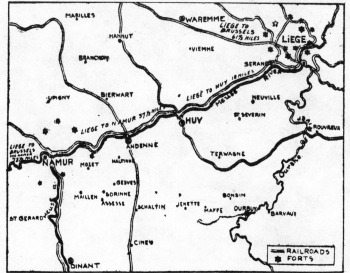

Area of French-Belgian-German Campaign

France's colonies contributed to her troop strength significantly throughout the war. In these photos, Algerian cavalry men and Turco foot soldeirs (also from Algeria) march through Belgium.

"All the News That's Fit to Print."

The New York Times.

THE WEATHER
Fair today and Friday; gentle to moderate shifting winds.
For full weather report see Page 18.

VOL. LXIII...NO. 20,655. .....   NEW YORK, THURSDAY, AUGUST 13, 1914.—SIXTEEN PAGES.   ONE CENT In Greater New York, Jersey City and Newark. | Elsewhere TWO CENTS.

BELGIAN LEFT WING WINS AS GREAT BATTLE BEGINS; ALLIED ARMIES DRAWN UP BEFORE KAISER'S MILLION MEN; GERMANS ADMIT HEAVY LOSSES ON RUSSIAN FRONTIER;

Huge Army of Germans Moves on Brussels and Battle Opens.

BIG CAVALRY FORCE LEADS

Belgians the Victors in First Encounter of the Greatest Conflict in History.

CLASHES ON 200-MILE LINE

Invaders Are Armed with 4,000 Field Guns and 1,200 Rapid-Fire Guns.

Belgians' Left Wing Drives Back Germans

Special Cable to THE NEW YORK TIMES.
LONDON, Thursday, Aug. 13—A Brussels dispatch received this morning says:

"The Belgians have routed the Germans in a fierce encounter between the Belgian left wing and massed German cavalry, infantry and artillery.

"The Belgians displayed wonderful control under the fierce fire, and their victory has aroused the liveliest enthusiasm along the whole line of the allied troops."

Special Cable to THE NEW YORK TIMES.
LONDON, Thursday, Aug. 13.—The first encounters in the greatest battle in history seem to be taking place along nearly the whole front of 200 miles.

The German concentration along the Liege-Luxemburg-Metz line now seems to be complete and fifteen army corps with two Austrian corps are in Belgium or within striking distance of the French frontier.

The total strength of this force is estimated at 1,000,000 men with 700,000 infantry, 50,000 cavalry, 4,000 field guns and howitzers, and 1,200 machine guns. This is about double the strength of the force which von Moltke had at his disposal in 1870.

Before a decisive success is obtained there will be a several days' battle, probably the bloodiest of all time.

Allies or French troops are in contact with the Germans on almost the whole line.

Such news as has been received here confirms the view that the main German advance will be through central and Southern Belgium and Luxemburg.

Private advices received in London last night from Belgium intimated that a German attack upon Brussels and the capture of the city were regarded there as imminent.

The residents of Brussels themselves have shown no signs of panic, having full confidence in the ability of their army to hold off the German attack, which is not expected by them to develop in great force, owing to the necessity of the Germans pushing forward every available man to the French frontier.

The private messages which reached London, however, spoke with expectation of a German occupation of Brussels.

An Englishwoman and well-known writer who arrived in Belgium yesterday with a mission to report events from a woman's point of view for a London paper was brusquely sent back to the seashore by the chief correspondent of the paper, who said it was the height of folly for any Englishwoman not forced to be in Belgium to venture there.

English correspondents are likely to be regarded as spies by Germans and summarily shot.

Special Cable to THE NEW YORK TIMES.
PARIS, Aug. 12.—It is thought here that the first big battle of the war has begun near Tirlemont, Belgium, and that it is the intention of the Germans to try a stroke at Louvain and Brussels.

To Strike England at Sea While Land Battle Is On, Germany's Plan, According to London Times Critic

Special Cable to THE NEW YORK TIMES.
LONDON, Thursday, Aug. 13.—Col. Repington, the London Times military expert, says:

"We are on the eve of a great struggle on the Meuse. Surrounded as she is by powerful enemies, a great victory is very necessary for Germany at this moment. Will she strike by sea when she strikes by land? This is the only blow open to Germany which can do us mortal hurt if it succeeds. The chances are against success, and with every day of the war the last chances become less, because our land forces are daily growing in numbers and solidity.

"We must regard the problem through German eyes, and however much we may disbelieve in the German solution, we must be prepared for a stroke which would accord with the German soldiers' theories of war."

Atlantic Safe, But No Reassurance as to North Sea, Where, Admiralty Says, Germans Have Spread Mines

LONDON, Aug. 12.—The British Admiralty has sent out cruisers which will ply the Atlantic to protect trade routes. The French Government also has sent out warships to search for German cruisers known to be in the Atlantic.

"The enemy's ships," says the official Admiralty report, "will be hunted continuously, and although some time may elapse before they are run down, they will be kept too busy to do much mischief.

"A number of fast merchant vessels, fitted and armed at British arsenals, also are patrolling the routes and keeping them clear of German commerce raiders. With every day that passes British control of trade routes, especially those of the Atlantic, becomes stronger.

"In the North Sea, where the Germans have scattered mines indiscriminately, and where the most formidable operations of the naval war are proceeding, the Admiralty can give no reassurance."

Even the dogs were put to good use in the defense of the country, as these Belgian soldiers move to the battle line at Termonde.

"All the News That's Fit to Print."

The New York Times.

THE WEATHER
Generally fair today and Tuesday; gentle to moderate shifting winds.
☞For full weather report see Page 5.

VOL. LXIII...NO. 20,659. ..... NEW YORK, MONDAY, AUGUST 17, 1914.—TWELVE PAGES. ONE CENT In Greater New York, Jersey City and Newark. | TWO CENTS Elsewhere

JAPAN GIVES GERMANY A WEEK TO QUIT THE FAR EAST; TWO AUSTRIAN WARSHIPS SUNK BY FRENCH FLEET; GERMANS SHIFT BELGIAN ATTACK TO THE SOUTH

Japan Notifies Germany She Must Give Up Kiau-chau at Once.

AND WITHDRAW SHIPS

ONE WEEK FOR A REPLY

Cites Alliance with England—Tells United States Neutral Interests Will Be Guarded.

TOKIO, Aug. 16.—Japan sent an ultimatum to Germany Saturday night at 8 o'clock, demanding the withdrawal of German warships from the Orient and the evacuation of Kiau-chau and giving Germany until Sunday, Aug. 23, to comply with the demand. Otherwise, the ultimatum asserts, Japan will take action.

The general expectation here is that the ultimatum will be followed by war.

Takaaki Kato, the Japanese Foreign Minister, simultaneously with the dispatch of the ultimatum, conferred with George W. Guthrie, the American Ambassador, and made to him a broad statement calculated to assure the United States that American interests in the Far East would be safeguarded and the integrity of China upheld.

Owing to doubts whether communications with Berlin were assured,

Japan in order to insure the arrival of the ultimatum forwarded it to Berlin by six channels, including Washington, London, and Stockholm. The Government also notified Count von Rex, German Ambassador to Japan, and likewise retarded the time limit for a reply until Aug. 23.

Germany Storing Provisions.

Inspired utterances express regret at the inability to maintain neutrality, but say that Great Britain, the ally of Japan, is compelled to defend herself against the aggressions of Germany. Moreover, it is pointed out that Germany is making preparations day and night at Kiau-chau, where it is storing provisions, while its warships are scouring the seas of Eastern Asia to the great detriment of commerce, and that its converted cruisers are seizing English merchant vessels. Such actions, it is argued, are directly calculated to disturb the peace of Eastern Asia, and, accordingly, after full and frank communication with Britain, Japan has found herself compelled to send an ultimatum to Germany.

Count Okuma, the Japanese Premier, today invited the peers, the newspaper men, and the leading business men of Tokio to come to his office at noon, at 4 o'clock, and at 6 o'clock in the afternoon, respectively, when he made known to them the terms of the ultimatum and announced that he would give out the negotiations in connection with the alliance. The Japanese War Office also summoned all newspaper men at 1 o'clock this afternoon, in order that they might receive instructions in regard to the publication of news in the event of a state of war coming into force.

Ministers Counsel Calmness.

The text of the ultimatum created a profound impression, although it had been predicted that Japan was making ready to precipitate war. Count Okuma and Takaaki Kato, in addressing the

Japan's Ultimatum Demanding That Germany Quit the Far East and Surrender Kiau-chau

TOKIO, Aug. 16.—This is the ultimatum sent to Germany by Japan:

"We consider it highly important and necessary in the present situation to take measures to remove the causes of all disturbances of the peace in the Far East, and to safeguard the general interests as contemplated by the agreement of alliance between Japan and Great Britain.

"In order to secure a firm and enduring peace in Eastern Asia, the establishment of which is the aim of the said agreement, the Imperial Japanese Government sincerely believes it to be its duty to give the advice to the Imperial German Government to carry out the following two propositions:

"First—To withdraw immediately from Japanese and Chinese waters German men-of-war and armed vessels of all kinds, and to disarm at once those which cannot be so withdrawn.

"Second—To deliver on a date not later than Sept. 15 to the Imperial Japanese authorities, without condition or compensation, the entire leased territory of Kiau-chau, with a view to the eventual restoration of the same to China.

"The Imperial Japanese Government announces at the same time that in the event of it not receiving by noon on Aug. 23, 1914, an answer from the Imperial German Government, signifying its unconditional acceptance of the above advice offered by the Imperial Japanese Government, Japan will be compelled to take such action as she may deem necessary to meet the situation."

merchants, members of Parliament and others, counseled a calm attitude. They insisted that Japan had no ambition for territorial aggrandizement.

JAPAN NOTIFIES BRYAN.

Mikado's Envoy Says Neutral Interests Will Be Guarded in Far East.

Special to The New York Times.

WASHINGTON, Aug. 16.—The Administration received its first official news of Japan's ultimatum to Germany tonight when the Japanese Ambassador, Viscount Chinda, delivered it to Secre-

tary Bryan in the form of a written announcement. At the same time the Ambassador communicated Japan's assurance to this Government that she would use the utmost effort to safeguard the interests of all nations not immediately concerned in the operations in the Far East.

After the Ambassador's call it became known that the United States Government had determined not to be drawn into the controversy between Japan and Germany in any way. It is said that this Government considers satisfactory the promise of Japan to restore the territory of Kiau-chau to China eventually.

Ambassador Chinda and Mr. Bryan conferred at the home of the Secretary of State. With the substance of the ultimatum to Germany the Japanese Ambassador presented the communication from the Foreign Office at Tokio, and added a strong statement concerning Japan's purposes of maintaining the territorial integrity of the Chinese Republic by restoring to her the territory of Kiau-chau.

While the statement made no direct reference to the United States, it gave assurance that the interests of all powers interested in maintaining the territorial status quo in the Far East would be protected to the utmost.

It developed as a result of the conference that Japan had no assurance up to the present time that its ultimatum had been delivered to Germany, owing to the cable difficulties with that country. In order to make certain of its delivery, a copy of the ultimatum will be communicated to Berlin through the channels of the American Government.

To many of the best-informed persons in Washington, Japan's warlike attitude toward Germany came as a surprise. There had been conflicting advices of an official character, and some officials chose to believe that Japan had no intention of becoming involved in the European struggle.

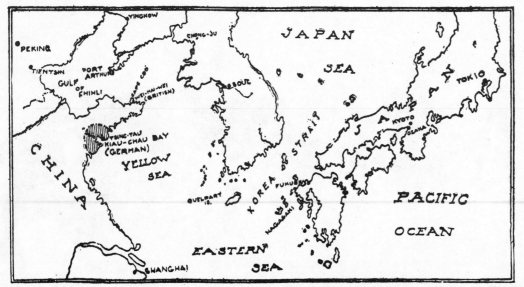

KIAU-CHAU, GERMANY'S FAR EASTERN COLONY NEAR JAPAN

"All the News That's Fit to Print."

The New York Times.

THE WEATHER

Unsettled, probably showers and cooler today; partly cloudy Friday; gentle to moderate winds.
☞For full weather report see Page 17.

VOL. LXIII...NO. 20,662. ....

NEW YORK, THURSDAY, AUGUST 20, 1914.—EIGHTEEN PAGES.

ONE CENT In Greater New York, Jersey City and Newark.

BIG ARMIES IN BATTLE NEAR WATERLOO; ALLIES FALL BACK, MAY QUIT BRUSSELS

Heavy German Pressure Forces the Allies to Withdraw.

READY FOR FINAL STRUGGLE

Hot Fighting on Tuesday Followed by Continued Advance by Germans Yesterday.

BRUSSELS AWAITS CAPTURE

Streets Barricaded, but It Cannot Resist Much—May Be Cut Off from Antwerp.

Special Cable to THE NEW YORK TIMES.

BRUSSELS, Aug. 19.—It was the turn of the Germans today to move forward. The enemy appeared in considerable force at several points on our front and pressed in overwhelming numbers.

The allies gave ground slowly, evacuating advanced positions, which were occupied as the result of yesterday's great cavalry drive.

The Germans fired several shells into Tirlemont without doing any damage, and the allies have now narrowed the front, occupied in a new defensive position, close to the capital.

The next move on the part of the invader is eagerly awaited.

Louvain is occupied.

We are now faced by a large army, and the next twenty-four hours should witness important developments.

BELGIAN LINES FORCED BACK.

Germans Compel Retirement of Advanced Troops of Enemy.

Special Cable to THE NEW YORK TIMES.

BRUSSELS, Aug. 19, (Dispatch to the London Daily News)—The Germans showed signs of pushing forward in force against the center of the Belgian position yesterday. The cavalry division and cyclist corps, which had been holding the advanced troops of the Kaiser in check, has fallen back on the main force.

The Brussels papers were invited to recall all their correspondents near the troops. One of the last to come was the representative of La Derniere Heure, from whose account of yesterday's operations the following is taken:

"At this moment the new advance of the Germans toward the interior of Belgium is preparing. Before the overwhelming weight of numbers the Belgian cavalry withdrew in good order.

"Our advanced troops were commissioned to hold the enemy as long as possible before falling back to our second line in intrenched position, made strong as it possibly can be to meet the German attack. A complete line exists, covering the approach to Louvain, Brussels and Antwerp.

"Yesterday's fighting started at 3.30 A. M. At dawn a German aeroplane flew low over our front. First one volley was fired at it, and then a second. The machine caught fire in the air and fell in the German lines.

"After several feints the attack developed about 6 o'clock. Strong forces of cavalry and infantry, supported by artillery and machine guns, poured down on the village. It was no mere skirmishing this time.

"A furious battle was soon raging along a seven-mile front, the points of attack being on the north of the line and on the south.

"The enemy tried to push through. They were opposed by a determined resistance. The cavalry dismounted and occupied trenches and bravely withstood the hail of fire for two hours. While the Belgian cavalry were acting as infantry behind earthworks, a party of German cavalry got in behind them and shot their horses.

"Inch by inch the ground was fought. Numbers of Germans were killed in their relentless move forward. The Belgian defenders suffered rather serious loss in their stubborn defense.

"At Berdingen the resistance was equally praiseworthy. In a trench where seven cavalrymen were making a great fight, Lieut. Count Wolfgang Dursel was struck by a bullet in the head and fell. His companions pressed around him.

"'I have got my account,' he said. 'You leave me. Do your duty.'

"He breathed his last a little later.

"When their retreat was ordered each Belgian cavalryman did his best to help the comrades whose horses had perished in the raid.

"At this point two Belgian squadrons, totaling about 240 men, showing great bravery, were holding 2,000 Germans. In spite of their superior numbers the Germans could claim no distinct advantage, but after two hours' resistance the Belgian retreat was sounded.

"When our cavalry retired the Germans advanced in great numbers and occupied Diest. They wrecked the railway station and bombarded the town. The terrifed inhabitants fled from it by the only route that remained open, and soon a struggling mass was rushing across the open country in search of a place of safety.

"The inhabitants of Tirlemont fared better. Seeing the inevitable approaching, three trainloads of refugees were hurriedly gotten away. As the last train left German shells were flying over the town, and several houses were in flames."

Following the announcement that the seat of Government and the royal family had moved to Antwerp, there was a large exodus of people from Brussels yesterday, particularly for the coast.

French Report Further Advance Into Lorraine; Admit Germans Have Recaptured One Village

PARIS, Aug. 19, 10:55 P. M.—The following official statement was given out tonight:

"Latest advices are to the effect that the French Army has reached Morhange (Morchingen) in Alsace-Lorraine, 19 miles southeast of Metz. Our advance was very rapid in the afternoon beyond the River Seille, especially the central part of our line. At the end of the day we reached Delme, on one side, and Morhange on the other.

"There is little change in the situation in Upper Alsace. We continue to advance in the Vosges. The Germans have retaken the village of Ville, where we had an outpost. Our troops on the Seille have occupied Chateau Salins and Dieuze, but face well fortified and strongly held positions. Our progress at first was necessarily slow.

"Our cavalry has had a successful encounter with the Germans at Florenville, Belgium. Very large German forces, it is announced, are crossing the Meuse between Liege and Namur.

"One of the French Brigadiers has asked the Commander-in-Chief to make public the following fact: A French Hussar, made prisoner, was dragged by German soldiers into an Alsatian village and his throat was cut before the villagers, who testify to the deed."

FRENCH TAKE THE OFFENSIVE

Battle Ground Picked on Which the Battle Will Take Place.

Special Cable to THE NEW YORK TIMES.

BRUSSELS, Aug. 19, (Dispatch to the London Daily News.)—The news reaches me by eye-witnesses from the front, Genappe, Wavre, and Gembloux, which for the present are forbidden ground to journalists, that the French are assuming the aggressive and hunting the Uhlans out of the woods back across the road between Namur and Brussels.

Further, from a good source, I have news that the French Generals have chosen their battle grounds and have the Germans now in such a position that they cannot avoid fighting a battle in which two-thirds of their northern force must be engaged if it is to face the body of the French, which has been rolled up into Belgium. This battle will decide the fate of Brussels, if that is not already decided, by giving it as a bait to Germany. It will also in large measure decide the fate of the war on this northern side, perhaps of the whole. The temptation to say more is considerable. What I have said is permissible, for the French have already shown their hand.

Things are being made very difficult for us now in the way of getting even stale news, but I managed a hurried run late in the afternoon today toward the eastern line to reassure myself that things were quite as I had expected.

It is a curiously subtle thing, this question of attack and defense. I could feel the difference in the atmosphere at the different points where they have touched the line, and there is not the slightest doubt from what I saw that the pressure is slowly turning against the invaders. There is real ground to hope that in a week or so they will be on the defensive and fighting for their lives.

The carnage will be awful. The German officers (such is the statement one of them made in a Belgian paper) have sworn not to return unless victorious, and to any one who knows the unbending stuff, heroic or brutal, just as you view it, of Prussian officers, it is quite certain that they will keep their oath.

Down at Dinant and Namur the battle is likely to be worse in the sense that it will be a rushing lance-to-lance and bayonet-to-bayonet affair up and down the steep hills by the Meuse, but at the battlefield which the French have chosen their artillery will get full play, and unless the Germans abandon their usual massed formation the slaughter will be terrible.

Wherever the English are, too, there will be a lot of cut and thrust work as well as good marksmanship.

Brussels is very nervous this evening, and there seems to be reason for it. All the official statements as to the situation are reassuring, but so they have been every day.

Brussels' nerves are taut. Notices posted in the streets tonight that any one with arms in his possession should deposit them with the police, as otherwise he was liable to be shot by any invaders, attracted the crowds all the evening.

25

Significant, too, are the barricades and intrenchments, now put all round the city, especially to the south and east.

Bruxelloise are sadly reconciled. If their beautiful city must be sacrificed in the great game the powers are playing, why, then, it is only on a level with the usual rôle of Belgium in which Fontenoy, Jemappes, Fleurus, Ligny, Neerwinden, Waterloo, and a score of other great battles have been fought.

BELGIANS ADMIT FALLING BACK

But Say German Delay Has Made for Defenders' Advantage.

LONDON, Thursday, Aug. 20.—A Havas dispatch from Brussels gives this official communication concerning the present state of the field operations in Belgium:

"After having lost much time and a great number of men, besides important war material, the Prussian right wing has succeeded in gaining on both banks of the Meuse the ground to bring them into contact with the allies' armies.

"The German troops on the north bank of the Meuse comprise sections of different army corps, whose efforts have been directed toward the capture of Liege and who are now disengaged. There are also bodies of cavalry, thanks to which the Germans have been able to make considerable disturbance and extend themselves north and south.

"On the south the allied Belgian and French armies have been able to repulse them but on the north on the contrary they have had a free field, and could penetrate in small bodies far into the country.

"In a word, the Germans have taken a number of our positions, but have wasted fifteen days in arriving at this result, which is greatly to the honor of our army. It is not a question of single battle evolutions or captures of certain parts of the country or of towns. These matters are secondary in regard to the object assigned our troops in the general dispositions. This aim cannot be resolved and the most penetrating minds will be unable to discover it owing to the necessarily vague particulars furnished concerning the operations."

"Fighting is proceeding on the whole front, extending from Basle, Switzerland, to Diest, Belgium, and in these numerous contacts the more the opposing armies approach each other and the nearer come the deciding battles, the more one must expect to hear of an advantage on this side and of yielding on that.

"In operations so vast and with those engaged using modern arms, too great attention must not be paid to the operations in our immediate vicinity. Au evolution, ordered in a particular previously determined aim is not necessarily a retreat. The engagements of the last few days have had the result of rendering our adversaries very circumspect. The delay of the enemy's advance had the greatest advantage for our general plan of operation.

"There is no need for us to play into the hands of the Germans. That is the motive of the movement now being carried out. Far from being beaten, we are making arrangements for beating the enemy under the best possible conditions.

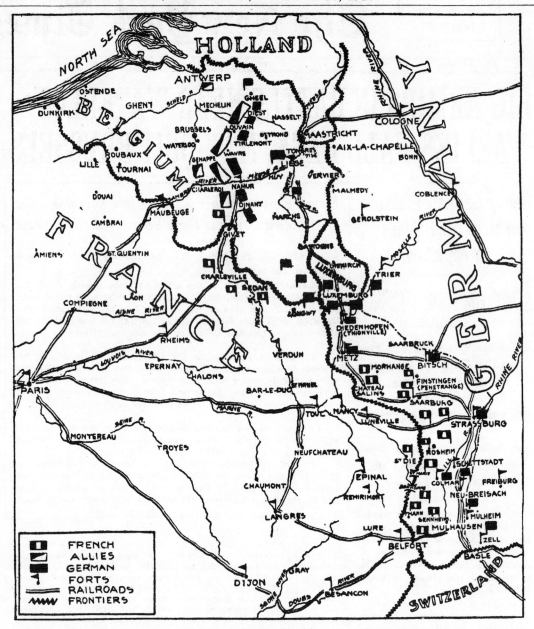

Where Germans and Allies Confront Each Other in Belgium and Alsace-Lorraine.

"The public should in this matter place full confidence in the commander of the army and remain calm and trustful of the outcome of the struggle, not doubtful. Meanwhile the newspapers should abstain from mentioning the movements of troops being published. Secrecy is essential to the success of our operations."

Another Havas dispatch from Brussels, sent in a very vague form, leads to the belief that the Germans made a surprise advance close to the Belgian positions defending Brussels. They encamped for the night, but a Belgian aviator discovered their position and revealed it to headquarters in time. Cavalry was hurried forward, and after some marching and countermarching the Germans retired.

PRESSURE OF BATTLE BEGINS.

Forces In Contact Along the Wide Front in Belgium.

LONDON, Thursday, Aug. 20.—A Reuter dispatch from Brussels says that the German advance posts, covering the region between Gembloux and Jodoigne, are being gradually pushed back before the advance of Belgian and French forces.

The Belgians and French are now in close junction and in contact with the advance lines of the German Army.

It was again reported yesterday that the German attack had been made on direct orders of Emperor William himself to his Generals in the field.

A previous Reuter dispatch, sent at 7 o'clock Tuesday night, said:

"A fierce battle is in progress between the Belgians and Germans along an extended front. Large numbers of refugees are arriving from Tirlemont."

This curt announcement was generally accepted in London as indicating the beginning of the first great battle in the war of eight nations.

The Brussels correspondent of the Exchange Telegraph Company says:

"It is becoming practically impossible to get news away from Brussels, as the censor forbids any information concerning the movements of troops being published. However, it is certain that a tremendous battle is in progress with the area stretching from Diest and Tirlemont as far as Givet.

"The general impression here is that no effort will be made to concentrate for the defense of Brussels, as the attacking German force would not be of sufficient strength to warrant such concentration."

PARIS, Aug. 19.—A dispatch to the Paris Midi from Brussels says cannonading was distinctly heard in Brussels at 6 o'clock this morning.

The correspondent adds that it is understood that a German Army is marching upon Brussels by way of Huy and Jodoigne.

An official announcement today said the retirement of Belgian troops toward Antwerp was rumored, but not confirmed.

It was officially explained that even were the reports of the retirement true, it would be neither a grave sign nor unexpected. The defensive organization of Belgium, as conceived by Gen. Brialmont and presented in technical works, provided that Antwerp be regarded as a last defense. It has been fortified with care, and is now a vast intrenched camp upon the flank of the enemy.

Details of the fighting at Dinant between the French and German troops show that the carnage was terrible. The first French force, although cut to pieces, held a position until another force came up with artillery, which destroyed a bridge.

A young Candian soldier, obviously less than happy about being in World War I.

"All the News That's Fit to Print."

The New York Times.

THE WEATHER

Thunder showers today; probably fair tomorrow; moderate shifting winds.

☞For full weather report see Page 15.

VOL. LXIII...NO. 20,665.   NEW YORK, FRIDAY, AUGUST 21, 1914.—SIXTEEN PAGES.   ONE CENT In Greater New York, Jersey City and Newark. | TWO CENTS Elsewhere

GERMAN CAVALRY FORCE CAPTURES BRUSSELS; BELGIAN ARMY RETIRES TO DEFEND ANTWERP; FRENCH WIN IN ALSACE, CHECKED IN LORRAINE

French Reoccupy Muelhausen, Driving Germans Out with the Bayonet.

OTHER GAINS IN ALSACE

Germans' Position Weakened by the Loss of Gebweiler and Morhange.

CHECK FRENCH IN LORRAINE

Advancing Prussians Intrench Themselves Before Briey, with Support from Metz.

PARIS, Aug. 20.—The reoccupation of Mülhausen, Alsace, by French troops is announced officially here today.

The recapture of the town was preceded today by a very severe battle, during which the French troops took one of the suburbs at the point of the bayonet. They also took as the result of their victory six German cannon and six ammunition wagons.

The official note says the situation in the Vosges Mountains is unchanged. In Upper Alsace the French have occupied Gebweiler, 14 miles southwest of Colmar.

The official announcement continues:

"Our troops have met with brilliant successes in Alsace, especially between Mülhausen and Altkirch.

"In Lorraine, the day was less fortunate for us. Our advanced troops found themselves faced by exceptionally strong positions. They were forced by a counter attack to fall back in a body, which is solidly established on the Seille, and along the canal from the Marne to the Rhine."

The situation in the Duchy of Luxemburg and in Belgium is unchanged.

German Losses Heavy.

LONDON, Friday, Aug. 21.—A dispatch to the Havas Agency from Belfort, by way of Paris, says:

"The battles around Mülhausen have been particularly bloody for the Germans who, knowing the French would spare as much as possible the Alsatians and their property, hid themselves in houses protected by the Red Cross, whence they fired upon the French.

"The French directed a violent rifle and artillery fire upon their assailants, causing veritable carnage. Every German leaving the houses was shot down.

"A battery of six guns, with their caissons filled with ammunition, was captured from the Germans. They were taken to Belfort, where crowds of curious people gathered to see them. Eighteen other guns captured today are expected to reach Belfort tomorrow, together with 600 prisoners."

VALUE OF FRENCH VICTORIES.

Paris Believes German Position in Alsace Now Dangerous.

By G. H. PERRIS,

NEW YORK TIMES-London Daily Chronicle War Service.

Special Cable to THE NEW YORK TIMES.

PARIS, Aug. 20.—Rumors that there has been prolonged and severe fighting in southern Alsace are to some extent confirmed this afternoon by an official dispatch saying that Mülhausen has been reoccupied by the French after a stiff action, in the course of which six cannon and six artillery wagons were captured. Again a French bayonet charge proved irresistible.

German Position Endangered.

Though the Germans have held out so long, and must therefore be in strong force, their position in southern Alsace is becoming somewhat dangerous. It is true that the French have lost the village of Ville, at the head of one of the branch lines of railway leading from the Vosges Mountains to Shlestadt, but by way of compensation they have taken Gebweiler, a textile manufacturing town of 14,000 inhabitants and the largest industrial centre in Alsace after Mülhausen.

With the French fixed at Gebweiler, Cerney, Thann, and Mülhausen, there would seem to be no safe German position west of the Rhine and south of Colmar. The old village of Morhange, which has just been occupied, has been made in recent years a considerable German garrison town, covering the important strategic railway centre of Benestroff, whence forces could be thrown by several lines upon the frontier. Large barracks and magazines overlook the dull country, much cut up by lakes and streams.

Château Salins and Delme, otherwise less important and detached places, have recently been connected by a strategic railway.

The most advanced of the positions that have been captured was just such a little inferno as that described by Lieut. Bilse in "Aus einer kleinen Garnison." Many of the old French population had emigrated, and the remainder were very restive under their German masters.

Looking still further north, a slow German advance is reported in the region of Longwy and Briey. The

Temps says that the Germans have intrenched themselves before Briey, with support from the garrison of Metz.

Positions Deemed Impregnable.

Special Cable to THE NEW YORK TIMES.

PARIS, Aug. 20 (Dispatch to The London Standard).—All French and German military writers have concurred hitherto in considering the country about Mülhausen as almost impregnable, and it will be interesting to learn how the French success was achieved. The public scarcely recognizes the importance of the feat, which reflects immense credit on the staff which conceived it and the gallantry of the troops in executing it.

Far from seeking to exaggerate victories, the Government notices are sober, almost to excess, in reporting doings at the front.

As for the army in Belgium, nobody has any idea, even approximately, of the disposition of the French, British and Belgian forces.

French Victory Near Luneville.

LONDON, Aug. 20.—A dispatch to The Times from Paris says that the first point at which the Germans crossed the French frontier was at Cirey-sur-Vesouse. Since then there has been continued fighting in that region until a day or two ago when it ended in the victorious advance of the French forces, who inflicted a decisive defeat on the enemy and drove them back across the frontier east of Lunéville.

The correspondent says that the laconic reports of the French Minister of War give little idea of the desperate struggle that occured around the handful of villages scattered along the French border. Point after point was taken and retaken by one side or the other.

He gives the following story of the fighting at the village of Badonviller, as told by the villagers:

"The village was occupied by a battalion of chasseurs as a covering force and was prepared for defense by numerous trenches. The battle began on Aug. 10. The Germans bombarded the village compelling the

chasseurs to evacuate it. The latter retired on Celles and afterward took up a position on Donan Ridge.

"After nightfall the Germans increased the bombardment and the inhabitants sought refuge in cellars as a continuous rain of shells kept wrecking the houses and setting them afire. It was a terrible sight. Women fell on their knees and prayed, while children cried piteously.'

"The chasseurs retired defending every house, foot by foot, and making the Germans feel their fire. The sun rose on a village in ruins. It had been under bombardment fifteen hours. When the Germans entered they fired first on all the windows and down loopholes into the cellars. No corner was spared."

Special Cable to THE NEW YORK TIMES.

ROTTERDAM, Aug. 20 (Dispatch to the London Daily News).—A private message from Berlin states that forty-eight trains were required to convey the Austrian troops for use against France to Leopoldshöhe, near Basle, and that eight Austrian regiments also proceeded to Baden, via Constance.

WATCH SKY FOR MESSAGES.

British Public Told to be on Lookout for Aeroplane Notes.

LONDON, Aug. 20.—Aeroplanes now are playing the part in war which formerly only carrier pigeons could perform, and seem to have greater possibilities than pigeons.

An official notification issued tonight to the people of England requests them to be watchful for messages dropped from aeroplanes, describes the peculiar wrappings which will inclose messages and instructs the finders to forward them immediately to the addresses they bear.

French aeroplanes scattered messages to the inhabitants of Alsace in the early days of the war, and the Russians adopted the same method for announcing the proclamation of Emperor Nicholas to the Poles.

French Airship Hit by Ninety-seven Bullets In Daring Flight to Drop Bombs in Germany

LONDON, Aug. 20.—Adolphe Pegoud, the noted French aviator, has returned to Paris from the war zone to get a new aeroplane. According to a Paris dispatch to the Exchange Telegraph Company, the wings of Pegoud's old machine were riddled by ninety-seven bullets and two shells when he made a flight of 186 miles into German territory with a military observer.

Pegoud could not say just where he had been except that he recrossed the Rhine and blew up by means of bombs two German convoys.

Capt. Finck, a military aviator, Pegoud said, had destroyed a hangar near Metz and wrecked a Zeppelin, and also destroyed three aeroplanes which were in the hangar.

Belgians Withdraw as the German Host Advances.

HEADQUARTERS GIVEN UP

Abandonment of Louvain Leaves the Capital an Easy Prey for the Invaders.

ENTER WITHOUT RESISTANCE

Belgians Hint Their Retirement Fits Into the Big Campaign Plan of the Allies.

PARIS, Aug. 20, 11 P. M.—The German cavalry have occupied Brussels. This official announcement was made tonight.

Strong columns are following up this movement.

The Belgian Army is retiring on Antwerp without having been engaged by the Germans.

The official statement says:

"In conformity with a prearranged plan, the Belgian field army retreated to the intrenched camp of Antwerp, after brilliantly fulfilling their duty.

"Antwerp has a double role. It is a formidable intrenched camp, fortified on most modern lines, and is the base from which the Belgian army can threaten the German flank and co-operate effectively with the allies.

"The Antwerp defenses consist of three fortifications, whose power of resistance can be heightened by flooding a large area around all the works. Antwerp is fully equipped with the most perfect appliances.

"To besiege the fortress the Germans would have to detach imposing forces and a large siege train. This they are not likely to do. If they do not, they will be obliged to cover themselves against the operations of the Belgian Army, which is intact, thanks to the skilful retreat and augmented by the Antwerp garrison.

Liege Forts Holding Out.

It is to e added that the Liege forts still hold out. Those at Namur have not yet been attacked. They are as strong as the forts at Liege and have been considerably strengthened in the last two weeks.

"From this it would seem that the advancing German armies are caught between the positions of Namur and Antwerp, a distance

This Belgian soldier, in a heavily fortified post, awaits the enemy in Antwerp.

from each other of thirty-five miles, as the crow flies.

"The German situation is, then, a difficult one, since they lack the chief postulates of a plan of march through Belgium. Namely, free passage of the Meuse, a route by Liege and Namur, and inaction on the part of the Belgian Army."

No Resistance Offered by City.

NEW YORK TIMES-London Daily Chronicle War Service.

Special Cable to THE NEW YORK TIMES.

GHENT, Aug. 20.—The Prussian cavalry this morning were very active along the whole front of the allies. Small bodies of Uhlans have been close around Brussels and also in the neighborhood of Malines, (thirteen miles northeast of Brussels.) My information does not enable me to say whether Malines is still occupied by the Belgians.

A German aeroplane flew over Brussels this morning and was seen at Ghent.

Just as I was leaving Brussels for the coast today [the censor has here evidently elided the words, "the German cavalry entered Brussels."] They met with no resistance, in accordance with instructions of the Belgian authorities. They were, however, coldly received. The streets were deserted and some brave persons manifested their grief by draping the national flag with black.

ANTWERP IS MAKING READY.

Houses Destroyed That Would Shelter Foe—Flood Gates Open.

NEW YORK TIMES-London Daily Chronicle War Service.

Special Cable to THE NEW YORK TIMES.

AMSTERDAM, Aug. 20.—A correspondent, who left Antwerp this afternoon and made his way over the Dutch frontier, telephones late tonight from Rosendaal that Antwerp is being put in a stage of defense. The woods are cut down over a wide area and the villas are being destroyed outside of the town so as to afford no shelter to the Germans. New earthworks are to be seen everywhere in the fields and part of the country of the fortification line has been flooded.

A party of French staff officers who arrived today were loudly cheered.

Two fast steamers from the Dover-Ostend route lie in the Scheldt to take away the Queen and royal family and Court if the Germans enter the town.

Great herds of cattle have been driven in from the country and are now in the parks, and everything is being done to provision the town.

The Chamber is to meet in the Flemish Opera House and the Senate in the Dutch Theatre.

LOUVAIN SLIMLY DEFENDED.

Only 3,000 Belgians Left There to Check the German Advance.

Special Cable to THE NEW YORK TIMES.

BRUSSELS, Aug. 20, (Dispatch to The London Daily News).—Today the Germans occupied Louvain, which was until this morning the headquarters of the Belgian army, and to-morrow they may be in Brussels.

The first hint I got of what was afoot was on returning from Antwerp early in the afternoon. At a crossroads below the railway line I met a whole company of Belgian infantry and artillery marching away from Louvain. They were moving in perfect order except for the dust. The men had not been in action.

Earlier in the day I had noticed an enormous number of loaded motor cars, and it had been whispered that the army headquarters would be transferred immediately.

On my return to Brussels I hurried out toward Louvain. Soon I met many indications of what had happened.

A force of about 3,000 men, or perhaps more, had been left in the trenches to meet the enemy and cover the retreat. With these the Germans, who had advanced by three roads from Diest, Tirlemont, and Hamme-Mille, on the Eghezee road, had a sharp encounter. The Belgians fought stubbornly, and by all accounts their losses were far smaller, as they have been in each encounter, than those of the assailants.

They beat the Germans back at all points in the first attack, and could have held the position, a wounded man told me, against an even greater number for much longer, but in the lull following the attack they drew back quietly. They were well upon their way when the Uhlans rode into the town.

There is a story among the refugees that Louvain has been fired, but that seems hardly likely. At all events, from a distance of about two miles I saw no trace of burning of any extent.

Pitiful Crowds of Refugees.

At this point I was stopped by an enormous crowd of refugees flocking along the Brussels road on foot and in vehicles and by Red Cross cars. The sight was pitiful—of all these people leaving their homes.

By far the greater number were women with young children, whose fathers were at the front. Some were old men and women, driven out by fear begotten by the stories, which have been circulated freely, of German atrocities. These, in fact, have of late been the only items of news that seemed to go uncensored, and it would have been far better if they had been blue-pencilled with the rest.

"All the News That's Fit to Print."

The New York Times.

THE WEATHER
Thunder showers, cooler today; probably fair Tuesday; moderate to fresh southwest to northwest winds.
☞ For full weather report see Page 11.

VOL. LXIII...NO. 20,666.   ....   NEW YORK, MONDAY, AUGUST 24, 1914.—FOURTEEN PAGES.   ONE CENT In Greater New York, Jersey City and Newark. | TWO CENTS

GREAT BATTLE ALONG 150-MILE BELGIAN LINE; GERMANS ENGAGED FROM MONS TO LUXEMBURG; RUSSIAN ARMY PUSHES FIFTY MILES INTO PRUSSIA

French and British Take Offensive Against Huge German Army.

INVADERS ARE HURRYING UP

French War Office Says It Will Take Several Days' Fighting to Decide.

BATTLE GROUND DIFFICULT

Combat Going On Amidst Dense Woods—London Sees Peril to Germans' Right Flank.

PARIS, Aug. 23, 11 P. M.—This announcement was issued tonight by the War Office:

"A great battle is now in progress along a vast line, extending from Mons to the frontier of Luxemburg. Our troops, in conjunction with the British, have assumed everywhere the offensive.

"We are faced by almost the whole German Army, both active and reserve.

"The ground, especially on our right, is thickly wooded and difficult. The battle is likely to last several days.

"The enormous extent of the front and the great number of forces involved make it impossible to follow step by step the movements of each of our armies.

"We must await the result of the first phase of the combat before we can form any conclusion as to the situation. Otherwise we should be giving to the press divergent and contradictory news, since such a battle is naturally made up of actions and reactions which follow and connect in a continuous manner.

"In the Vosges the general situation determined us to withdraw our troops from Donon and the Saales pass. Those points were no longer of any importance, since we occupied the fortified line beginning at Grande Couronne de Nancy.

"Luneville is occupied by the Germans, and at Namur the Germans are making great efforts against the forts, which resist energetically."

A dispatch to the Petit Parisien says that the French troops have thus far met with success in the battle along the line from Namur to Charleroi.

Germans Rushing Troops Up.

LONDON, Monday, Aug. 24.— Only fragmentary information is reaching here as to the battle between the allies and Germans in Belgium.

A Central News correspondent in Rosendaal, Holland, telegraphs:

"There is no doubt that a big battle is now in progress in the neighborhood of Charleroi. The Germans are rushing troops in that direction. Only 3,000 troops are left in Brussels, which is more isolated than Liege.

"The Germans have occupied all the villages between Louvain and Alost, in order that the passage of their main army across Belgium may not be interrupted. There are no Germans, except scouting patrols, around Ghent."

A dispatch to the Havas Agency from Ostend says bloody fighting is reported to have taken place at Luttre, ten miles north of Charleroi, and that an important battle is raging in the Province of Hainaut, (in which both cities are situated.)

According to the Ostend correspondent of The Daily Mail, two German columns are marching south toward Valenciennes, one by way of Ninove, Grammont, and Ath, the other by way of Hal, Braine-le-Comte, and Mons.

A dispatch to The Times from Ostend asserts that the German lines extend from Tamise, near Antwerp, southwest through Puers and Zele, and thence southeast to Gosselies and Charleroi.

It adds that most automobilists who have tried to get through the German lines from or toward Brussels have had their cars confiscated. In exchange for the cars the Germans have given papers, payable by the French Government, supposedly out of the indemnity which the Germans hope to collect.

In another dispatch The Times correspondent says:

"I am credibly informed that not fewer than 200,000 German troops are moving in the vicinity of

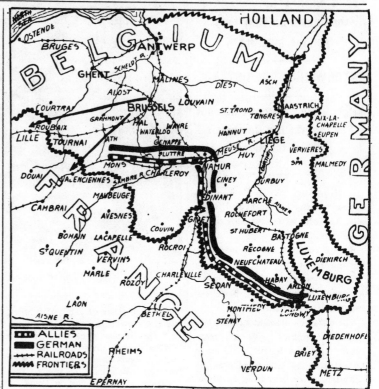

Brussels. A garrison of 10,000 is encamped at Kochelberg, and a very strong artillery force is proceeding in motor lorries to Grammont and Audenarde."

The Reuter correspondent at Antwerp sends two interesting pieces of information. Touching the general operations south of Brussels, he telegraphs:

"The French troops are engaged with the German forces, which were encamped near Marche, in the centre of Belgian Luxemburg, and have moved off southward."

He also records renewed activity by the main Belgian Army, now in Antwerp. He says:

"Belgian flying columns have cleared the environs of all Germans. Our troops have visited the Campine and Waes districts and also the environs of Malines, (halfway to Brussels,) but discovered no trace of the enemy anywhere."

GERMAN FORCE OF 200,000

Have Moved Past Brussels—Allies in Position to Meet Them.

Special Cable to THE NEW YORK TIMES.
OSTEND, Aug. 22, (Dispatch to The London Daily News.)—The position of the Germans in Belgium is as follows: They are in peaceful occupation of Brussels and have begun to push southwest unchecked toward Courtrai and the French frontier.

Their advance patrols and cavalry are well on their way.

On Friday morning the cavalry entered [censored] almost ten miles from Brusels, but up to Saturday midday no German troops, t my certain knowledge, had entered Ghent. The Germans have passed to the south of the city, and only a few, if any, are likely to enter the town.

No German troops are at Bruges or Ostend.

Of my own knowledge I may say that the position of the English, Belgian, and French is entirely satisfactory in regard to the present German rush.

I have the evidence of a French aviator that the movement of the allies to combine and intercept the opposing forces has already begun. It will, however, be some days before the issue is definitely forced.

Probably the Germans, of whom, according to a moderate estimate, 200,000 have passed through and around Brussels, will continue to march, even if their communications are cut here in the north, and will try to break through to join the second army, which, they are confident, will succeed in entering by the way of Luxemburg, and the third, which, they hope, may force the gap of Belfort.

From different sources I have information that many of the regiments in Brussels are from the eastern side of the empire, and probably the interchange of troops, to avoid the possibility of neighbors fighting half-heartedly, caused considerable delay in the German mobilization.

Czar's Troops Capture Johannisburg, Ortelsburg and Intersburg.

ALL EAST PRUSSIA IN PERIL

Invaders, Said to be in Virtual Control Beyond the Vistula, Rush On to Koenigsberg.

GERMANY DENIES DEFEATS

Special Cable to THE NEW YORK TIMES.

ST. PETERSBURG, Aug. 23, 8 P. M., (Dispatch to The London Times.)—I have just received news that the Russian left has completely enveloped the remnants of the Germans holding the lake region.

The Russians have occupied Johannisburg, in the southeast of East Prussia, and have pushed on fifty miles to Ortelsburg, twenty miles southeast of Allenstein, in the centre of East Prussia, on the line of the German retreat toward the River Augerab and the Mazur Lakes, is in Russian hands.

The Russians are even now sweeping the environs of Insterburg and have occupied Darkehmen, twenty miles south of Insterburg.

A glance at the map will show that the line from Thorn to Danzig is now within the sphere of Russian operations.

Unless the Germans are able to bring up strong reinforcements, which is doubtful, owing to the seizure of the railway and important roads by the Russians, the latter may now proceed to the investment of Koenigsberg.

The flight of the inhabitants from Willenburg is variously interpreted here. Some of the military men attribute it to the Russian advance on Mazur Lakes, others believe it directly due to another Russian movement from Poland toward Allenstein, sixty-five miles south of Koenigsberg, which, if substantiated, threatens serious consequences for the German forces in Northern Prussia.

The Novoe Vremya critic points out that the Russian Army advanced sixteen miles within two days on the march from Bilderweitchen to Gumbinnen, which might be regarded as a memorable achievement even in times of peace.

JAPAN DECLARES WAR; KIAO-CHAU READY TO FIGHT

Imperial Japanese Edict Directs Army and Navy to Begin Operations at Once.

TOKIO, Aug. 23.—The Emperor of Japan today declared war upon Germany. This action was taken at the expiration of the time limit of Japan's ultimatum to Germany demanding the surrender of Kiao-Chau. The Japanese Government has ordered the beginning of operations on land and sea.

The imperial rescript declaring war upon Germany was issued this evening, and officially inaugurates hostilities in the Far East. The proclamation of the Emperor sent a thrill through the country. Japan's entrance upon the fulfillment of her obligations to her ally, Great Britain, responds to the popular will from one end of the land to the other. Cheering crowds assembled today before the buildings occupied by the Department of Foreign Affairs and the administration of the navy. This evening there were lantern processions through the streets. The popular manifestations, however, do not approach the enthusism which preceded the war with Russia.

Passports to German Envoy.

Count von Rex, the German Ambassador in Tokio, has received his passports. He probably will leave here for America, either on the Minnesota, sailing on Aug. 27, or the Manchuria, which sails on Aug. 29. George W. Guthrie, the American Ambassador, will represent Germany. The Diet has been convoked in special session for Sept. 3.

The Austrian cruiser Kaiserin Elizabeth, which recently was at Tsing-Tau, the seaport of Kiao-Chau, is reported to have sailed. She perhaps will go to a neutral port and disarm. It is believed this action will keep Austria out of the war in the Orient, although unforeseen circumstances may force Japan to change her policy in this regard. No action has been taken relative to Austria, and the Foreign Office explains that Japan will remain friendly to Austria unless Austria adopts an attitude which it regards as offensive.

It is reported here that Germany has been trying to transfer the German railroad in Shantung, China, to America. Tokio believes, however, that the United States, pursuing the policy of neutrality outlined by President Wil-

Emperor of Japan Commands His Forces to Use All Their Strength in War on Germany

TOKIO, Aug. 23.—The text of the imperial rescript issued by the Emperor of Japan declaring war on Germany is as follows:

"Issued at Tokio, Aug. 23, 6 P. M.

"We, by the grace of Heaven, Emperor of Japan, seated on the throne occupied by the same dynasty from time immemorial, do hereby make the following proclamation to all our loyal and brave subjects:

"We hereby declare war against Germany, and we command our army and navy to carry on hostilities against that empire with their strength, and we also command our competent authorities to make every effort, in pursuance of their respective duties, to attain the national aim by all means within the limits of the law of nations.

"Since the outbreak of the present war in Europe, the calamitous effect of which we view with grave concern, we on our part have entertained hopes of preserving the peace of the Far East by the maintenance of strict neutrality, but the action of Germany has at length compelled Great Britain, our ally, to open hostilities against that country, and Germany is at Kiao-Chau, its leased territory in China, busy with warlike preparations, while its armed vessels cruising the seas of Eastern Asia are threatening our commerce and that of our ally. Peace of the Far East, is thus in jeopardy.

vessels cruising the seas of Eastern Asia are threatening our commerce and that of our ally. Peace of the Far East, is thus in jeopardy.

"Accordingly, our Government and that of His Britannic Majesty, after full and frank communication with each other, agreed to take such measures as may be necessary for the protection of the general interests contemplated in the Agreement of Alliance, and we on our part, being desirous to attain that object by peaceful means, commanded our Government to offer with sincerity an advice to the Imperial German Government. By the last day appointed for the purpose, however, our Government failed to receive an answer accepting their advice. It is with profound regret that we, in spite of our ardent devotion to the cause of peace, are thus compelled to declare war, especially at this early period of our reign and while we are still in mourning for our lamented mother.

"It is our earnest wish that by the loyalty and valor of our faithful subjects peace may soon be restored and the glory of the empire be enhanced."

son, will not accept the offer. President Wilson's announcement of American neutrality has greatly pleased the Japanese.

The newspapers express surprise at the extent of American suspicions regarding Japan's motives in issuing the ultimatum, but leading writers express a firm confidence that a better understanding will be had with the people of America.

Approved by England.

Premier Okuma says that documentary evidence will show that England not only requested Japan's assistance, but approved her entire programme. A dispatch from Peking says the German Minister and Chinese Foreign Office were about to sign an agreement regarding Tsing-Tau when Japan's decision was announced, whereupon the Chinese Foreign Office decided not to proceed. Other dispatches say that President Yuan Shih-kai is satisfied with Japan's attitude and pledges.

ZEPPELIN WRECKED BY SHELLS, SAYS PARIS

German Machine Brought Down Near Celle—Exploits of the Aviators.

PARIS, Aug. 23.—The Zeppelin airship No. 8, according to a War Office announcement made today, has been destroyed by French shells at a point between Celle and Badonviller. The airship was coming from the direction of Strassburg.

Badonviller is in the Department of Muerthe and Moselle, nineteen miles southeast of Lunéville.

Two Die in Burning Aeroplane.

LONDON, Aug 23.—According to information from Ostend a German aeroplane caught fire near Brussels, and two German officers on board were burned to death.

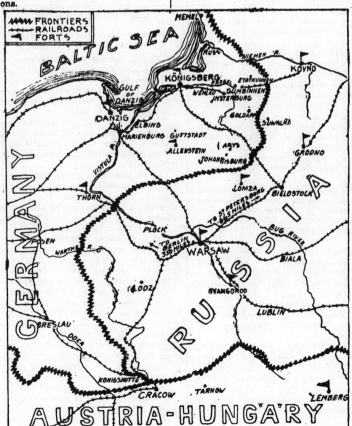

"All the News That's Fit to Print."

The New York Times.

THE WEATHER
Generally fair Sunday, preceded by showers; Monday, fair; moderate shifting winds, becoming west.
For full weather report see Page 15.

VOL. LXIII...NO. 20,672. ...   NEW YORK, SUNDAY, AUGUST 30, 1914.—88 PAGES, In Seven Parts, Including Picture and Rotogravure Sections, Real Estate Directory, and Review of Books.   PRICE FIVE CENTS.

FRENCH RIGHT WINS, BUT THEIR LEFT IS TURNED, AND PARIS ORDERS HOUSES DOWN FOR SIEGE

FRENCH VICTORY AT GUISE

Right Wing of Big Army Wins, But the Left Suffers Defeat.

GERMANS MOVE ON LA FERE

Their Cannonading Heard at Amiens—Stories of Their Great Losses Confirmed.

PARIS PREPARES FOR SIEGE

Paris, Sunday, Aug. 30, 12:59 A. M.—This announcement was made by the War Office this morning:

"In Lorraine our forces have advanced. We occupy a line along Mortagne (possibly Montagne) and our right wing is pushing forward.

"There is no news from the Meuse.

"A violent battle occurred yesterday (Saturday) in the region of Lannoy, near Lille, (and also near) Signy L'Abbaye, and Chateau Poicien, but the results have not been decisive, and the attack will be resumed tomorrow.

"Four French army corps engaged in a violent battle on the left wing.

"The right wing of these four corps, taking the offensive, drove back on Guise the Tenth German Corps and the Guard, both suffering considerable losses.

"Our left was less fortunate. The German forces are advancing in the direction of La Fere," (a town in Aisne, fourteen miles northwest of Laon, and a fortress of the second class.)

Official announcement is also made that the Military Governor of Paris has ordered all residents of the zone within action of the city's defending forts to evacuate and destroy their houses within four days from today, (Sunday.)

This brief dispatch chronicles three

These soldiers of the French infantry still carry the tension of battle in their faces after halting the Germans in a desperate battle outside Montagne.

Summary of War News

The left flank of the main French Army has been reinforced, and the War Office announces that four army corps met and defeated a German corps and the guard, driving them back on Guise, twenty-five miles northeast of St. Quentin. It is admitted, however, that the left flank of the force was repulsed, probably at St. Quentin, where the Germans report a British defeat. The Germans are marching on La Fere, one of the forts in the second line of French defenses. La Fere is eighty miles from Paris.

The Military Governor of Paris has ordered all residents of the zone within the line of fire of the city's defending forts to abandon their homes and destroy them before next Thursday.

The War Office announces that there was desperate fighting near Lille all day Saturday, without decisive result, and that the engagement will be resumed today.

German Army Headquarters in Berlin announces that Gen. von Hindenburg, after a three-day battle near Gilgenburg and Ortelsburg, defeated the Russian Army proceeding from the River Narew, which consisted of five army corps and three divisions.

It is also reported that five Russian army corps have been defeated by the Austrians and Germans south of Allenstein, where the Russians were reported on Friday.

Austria's War Office says that the Austrian troops are pursuing the Russians from Krosnik, and that another Austrian Army has invaded Russia and has occupied Zamose, in Russian Poland. The regions to the west, north, and southwest of Lemberg, Galicia, are being held, and the Austrian forces have advanced to the Dniester River against a strong invading force.

On the other hand, St. Petersburg says that the Russian Army is drawing a net around Lemberg and is making ready for a great battle with the Austrian forces, which have been reinforced by the Germans.

The French War Office says that the Russian Army has completely invested Koenigsberg and has occupied Allenstein.

England's Foreign Office announces that East Prussia is being rapidly overrun by the Russian Army, and that the German Army, consisting of three army corps and several divisions, have been repeatedly defeated, losing heavily in men and guns.

The first detachment of Canada's expeditionary force, consisting of 1,000 men of the Princess Patricia Light Infantry, has left for the front on board the White Star liner Megantic.

Field Marshal Lord Roberts says that Great Britain may require hundreds of thousands of men for the present conflict.

The Japanese have again drawn fire from the Kaio-Chau fortifications, when a shell was thrown at a small landing party at Cape Jaeschke. No damage was done.

different battles in the crucial war area of Northern France, aside from the fighting in Lorraine, in which the French troops seem to be winning some success.

One of these is proceeding near Lannoy a little northeast of Lillle and close to the Belgian frontier.

A second battle is in progress fifty miles south of Lille, close to La Fere, a fortified place in the second line of French defenses. A dispatch from Berlin tells of the defeat of a British force at St. Quentin in that region. Paris now recounts a success at Guise, twenty-five miles to the northeast of St. Quentin, but admits that the left wing of the same army (comprising four corps, or at least 160,000 men,) has been beaten back and that the Germans are marching on La Fere.

With its right wing at Guise and its left wing pushed back toward La Fere, this French army will be fronting to the northwest, and there is apparent danger that the Allies' line will be broken to the southward, if, indeed, the Germans with their strong turning movement have not already forced their way through there or to the westward.

The third battle, mentioned in the French War Office dispatch, is being fought forty miles to the east of Guise, at Signy l'Abbaye and Château Porcien. These are small places on the road from Rheims to Rocroi, Belgium, and are about ten miles apart.

ALLIES ARE REINFORCED.

Germans Attacking Vigorously and Paris Not Too Confident.

PARIS, Sunday, Aug. 30.—Yesterday was a long and anxious day in Paris. As the War Office had nothing to issue, the pessimists began to show themselves, and everybody asked what is going on in the north.

As far as could be learned, the French troops appeared to be intact, except for the losses inevitable in a week's heavy fighting over a vast front.

Every day had seen reinforcements moving up to aid the troops engaged on the Belgian frontier. The French, operating along the interior lines, were able to shift an army corps from one part of the front to another swiftly, and it is stated that the Allies are probably in a stronger position now than last Sunday.

Train service between Paris and Boulogne was suspended yesterday until further notice. When the announcement was made in the afternoon it was supposed here that the step was taken because the allied armies were about to engage the Germans on or near the railroad line running into Boulogne.

Apparently the Germans, owing to the increasing pressure of Russia, are throwing themselves against the intrenched positions of the Allies, and are suffering very severely. They are still hopeful of being able to break through the lines in Northern France.

The New York Times.

THE WEATHER
Fair Monday; Tuesday, fair, warmer; moderate shifting winds, becoming south.
For full weather report see Page 11.

VOL. LXIII...NO. 20,673. .... | NEW YORK, MONDAY, AUGUST 31, 1914.—TWELVE PAGES. | ONE CENT In Greater New York, Jersey City and Newark. | Elsewhere TWO CENTS.

BLOWING UP HOUSES OUTSIDE PARIS FORTS; FRENCH LEFT AGAIN DRIVEN BACK BY GERMANS; BRITISH LOSS, 6,000; LINES ARE REINFORCED

BOMBARDS PARIS FROM AIR

German Lieutenant Drops Five Bombs, Wounds Two Women.

"German Army at the Gates; You Can Do Nothing but Surrender," They Read.

CITY PREPARING FOR SIEGE

Cattle Gathered and Storehouses Filled—People Sobered by Crisis, but Not Downcast.

Blowing Up Houses So Forts Can Fire

Special Cable to THE NEW YORK TIMES.
PARIS, Aug. 30. [Dispatch to London Daily Mail.]—Thousands of houses, shops, and factories are being blown up to clear the field of fire for the Paris forts. The sound is faint, because it is sixty or eighty miles distant. I hear it coming from the Valley of the Oise.

LONDON, Aug. 30.—A Paris dispatch to the Exchange Telegraph Company says:

"A German aviator flew over Paris this afternoon and dropped five bombs, which fell in the most populous quarter of the city. In one case two women were wounded.

"One bomb fell in front of the shop of a baker and wine merchant at the corner of Rue Albouy and Rue des Vinaigriers; two fell on Quai de Valmy, one of which did not explode and the other struck the walls of the Night Refuge behind St. Martin's Hospital. Two others were dropped in the Rue des Caillettes and Rue Marcin, neither of which exploded."

"The aviator, who signed himself Lieut. von Heidsen, dropped manifestoes on which was written:

"'The German Army is at the gates of Paris; you can do nothing but surrender.'"

The territory over which a German aeroplane flew yesterday afternoon, dropping bombs, is in the northeastern part of Paris, and scarcely a mile from the heart of the city. In the district are the big military hospital, the Hospital St. Louis, St. Lazare Prison for women, the Church of St. Laurent, which dates from the sixteenth century; the North Railway station, the magnificent Church of St. Vincent de Paul, the Lariboisière Hospital, one of the largest in Paris; several colleges and several theatres.

Count Johann Heinrich von Bernstorff, the German Ambassador to the United States said yesterday afternoon that he had received no confirmation from his home Government that a German aviator had flown over Paris and dropped bombs. He reiterated in this connection what he had previously said with regard to the Zeppelin raid over Antwerp, namely, that if Paris had been attacked from the air he was certain that the assault was directed against the fortifications, and not against the city in general.

Count von Bernstorff said he really could not countenance the idea that his countrymen would drop bombs on places occupied by women and children. Such an action, he added, would be against all the traditions of the German Army.

KITCHENER TELLS OF BATTLE.

British Losses 6,000, but Troops Have Been Reinforced.

Special Cable to THE NEW YORK TIMES
LONDON, Aug. 30.—Lord Kitchener issued the following statement tonight through the official press bureau:

"Although official dispatches from Sir John French on recent battles have not yet been received, it is possible now to state in general outline what the British share in the recent operations has been.

"There has, in effect, been a four days' battle, on the 23d, 24th, 25th, and 26th of August. During the whole of this period the British troops in conformity with the general movement of the French armies, were occupied in resisting and attacking the German advance and in withdrawing to new lines of defense.

"The battle began at Mons on Sunday. During this day and part of the night the German attack, which was stubbornly pressed and repeated, was completely checked on the British front.

"On Monday, the 24th, the Germans made a vigorous effort in superior numbers to prevent the safe withdrawal of the British Army and to drive it into the fortress at Maubeuge. This effort was frustrated by the steadiness and skill with which the British retirement was conducted, and, as on the previous day, very heavy losses, far in excess of anything suffered by us, were inflicted upon the enemy, who in dense formation and enormous masses marched forward again and yet again to storm the British lines.

"The British retirement proceeded on the 25th, (Tuesday,) with continuous fighting, though not on the scale of the previous two days, and by the night of the 25th the British Army occupied the line of Cambrai-Landrecies-Le Cateau.

"It had been intended to resume the retirement at daybreak on the 26th, (Wednesday,) but the Germans' attack, in which no less than five corps were engaged, was so close and fierce that it was not possible to carry out this intention until afternoon.

"The battle on this day was of a most severe and desperate character. The troops offered a superb and most stubborn resistance to tremendous odds, and at length extricated themselves in good order, though with serious losses. No guns were taken by the enemy except those the horses of which were all killed or which were shattered by high explosive shells.

British Losses 5,000 to 6,000.

"Sir John French estimates that during the whole of these operations from the 23d to the 26th, inclusive, his losses amount to 5,000 or 6,000 men.

"The losses suffered by the Germans are out of all proportion to those which we suffered. In Landrecies alone on the 26th, as an instance, a German infantry brigade advanced in the closest order into a narrow street, which they completely filled. Our machine guns were brought to bear on this target from the end of the town.

"The head of the column was swept away. A frightful panic ensued, and it is estimated that no less than 800 to 900 dead and wounded Germans were lying in this street alone.

"Another incident, which may be chosen from many like it, was a charge of a German Guard cavalry division upon the British Twelfth Infantry Brigade, when the German cavalrymen were thrown back, with great loss and in absolute disorder.

"These are notable examples of what has taken place over practically the whole front during these engagements, and the Germans have been made to pay an extreme price for every forward march they have made.

"Since the 26th, apart from cavalry fighting, the British Army has not been molested. It has rested and refitted after its exertions and glorious achievements.

Fresh Guns and Men Received.

"Reinforcements amounting to double the loss sustained have already joined, every gun has been replaced, and the army is now ready to take part in the next great encounter with undiminished strength and undaunted spirit.

"Today the news is again favorable. The British have not been engaged, but the French armies, acting vigorously on their right and left, have for the time being brought the German attack to a standstill.

"Sir John French also reports that on the 28th the Fifth British Cavalry Brigade, under Gen. Chetwode, fought a brilliant action with the German cavalry, in the course of which the Twelfth Lancers and the Royal Scots Greys routed the enemy and speared large numbers in flight.

"It must be remembered throughout that these operations in France, vast though they are, are only one wing of the whole field of battle.

Summary of War News

Blowing up of the houses outside the Paris forts to permit a clear range for the defending forts has begun.

A German aeroplane flew over Paris yesterday and dropped several bombs, wounding two women.

The French War Office announces that the advance of the German right wing has caused the French left to yield ground again.

France has called out the 1914 reserves, the young men, and boys.

Lord Kitchener announces that the British losses were between 5,000 and 6,000 in four days of fighting, beginning a week ago yesterday, against superior numbers of Germans, on whom the British inflicted heavy losses. He adds that reinforcements amounting to double the losses sustained have already joined, every gun has been replaced, and the army is now ready to take part in the next great encounter with undiminished strength and undaunted spirit.

The Czar's forces have advanced in East Prussia to the German lines at the Vistula and are bombarding Thorn and Graudenz. As they advance the Russians are changing the railway lines to their gauge.

Russians and Austrians are in battle in Poland, where the Czar's troops are said to have won a big victory. Near Lemberg, in Austrian Galicia, they have also won, capturing many men and guns.

British losses in the naval battle in the North Sea, where the Germans were defeated, were 29 dead and 40 wounded.

Japanese troops have been landed at several points on the coast near Kiao-Chau.

Apia, Germany's capital city in the Samoan Islands, has surrendered to a British force from New Zealand.

Canada's expeditionary force has disembarked at Quebec, where it will await the arrival of a transport to convey it to the front.

German reports say that Turkey is preparing to enter the war against England and Russia.

ALLIES' FLANK PUSHED BACK

Paris Admits German Pressure Proved Too Severe.

ROAD TO PARIS STILL HELD

One German Corps Reported Wiped Out, Perhaps by Pau's Army Fresh from Alsace.

Republic's Forces on the Left Engaged--British After Heavy Losses Ready for Battle.

PARIS, Aug. 30, 11:30 P. M.—An official statement issued by the War Office tonight said:

"The passage of the German right wing has obliged us to yield ground on the left."

"The situation generally remains the same as this morning. After a lull, the battle has been resumed in the Vosges and Lorraine.

"On the Meuse at Sassaye, near Dun, a hostile regiment of infantry, endeavoring to cross the river, was almost annihilated."

Gen. Lacroix, former Commander in Chief of the army, takes a hopeful view of the situation, saying:

"The Germans continue their turning movement on the right. We have replied by assuming the offensive at Novion Porcien, and at Guise. The result is indecisive in the first direction, but our attack will be resumed.

According to La Liberté, the Germans have penetrated a short distance further on the River Somme.

The British, in conjunction with the French left, have resumed a vigorous offensive.

Further west the French troops are said to have checked the enemy's advance guard.

At the other extremity of the line on the Meuse the French are offering a strong and successful resistance, which extends along nearly the whole front.

La Liberté says:

"Our offensive succeeded on our right, but was checked on our left. The Germans gained ground toward La Fere, as announced. At any rate, we hold firm and even under attack—a sure sign of the confidence of our army."

Gen. Pau, recently commander of the Alsace invading force, but since recalled to aid the Allies in Northern France, was in Paris today for a brief visit to the Minister of War. He will return to the front very soon.

The Ministry of War announces that it has been decided to call out the class of 1914, which will give at least 200,000 additional troops, and also to call out the active reserve and the eldest classes of the territorial reserve.

THE WAR SITUATION.

Important Advance of German Right Wing—Allies Waiting for Russian Diversion—Austrian Army Concentrates Against the Russians.

Written for THE NEW YORK TIMES
BY AN ASSOCIATE EDITOR OF THE ARMY AND NAVY JOURNAL.

The German invasion of France has now reached a point where any delay is dangerous for them. They have successfully pushed the Allies back from one position to another, but have not gained the decisive victory that is so necessary for the success of their plan of operation.

The retreat of the left wing of the Allies to St. Quentin and Porcien is an important gain for the Germans. They now confront the strongly fortified defensive curtain running from La Fere to Reims, and have the choice of massing their troops to attempt to force an advance around either flank of this curtain. The uncertainty allows the Germans to concentrate all of their troops at the point selected, while the Allies must hold a force of defenders in both positions.

In spite of large losses the Allies still hold an unbroken line running from St. Quentin, twenty-five miles northwest of Laon, eastward through to Porcien to the Meuse River, near Sedan, and then southeast through Verdun and Nancy to the Vosges Mountains, near St. Die; here the line turns south along the line of the passes to Belfort and the Swiss border. At only one point along the line do the dispatches show signs of an aggressive movement, so necessary if the Allies wish to stop the further advance of the German invasion. This is in the district east of Nancy, where the French aggressive is being stubbornly opposed by the army of Prince Rupprecht of Bavaria.

The historical successes of French armies have come from their assumption of an active offensive plan of campaign, and the natural tendency of the people would lead to an energetic aggressive move. The most significant feature of the war to date has been not the overpowering advance of the Germans through Belgium, but the defeat of the first French aggressive move into Lorraine.

The dictates of careful strategy call for the French to avoid any disaster to their armies until the Russians have had time to push their campaign in force. The general plan of the French campaign calls for gradual withdrawals after causing as much delay as possible, when outnumbered by the German forces. However, this plan does not mean a quiet defensive all along the line, but an aggressive defensive, including advances against the enemy wherever possible.

The candid statement issued by the British Press Bureau yesterday stands the test of a critical comparison with news from other sources. It shows that the British Regular Army regiments are not yet all at the front. The British forces in the fight at Mons and in the series of rear guard actions during the fifty-mile retreat to St. Quentin can hardly have numbered more than 125,000. With reinforcements they may now number 150,000 men. Additional troops are coming both from the home battalions and from the colonies, but it is evident that the full British strength will not be placed in the firing line before October.

The line occupied by the Allies is naturally a stronger position than that of the Germans. The Allies are closer to their reinforcements and their bases of supply. They have convenient rail lines parallel to their front, available for transporting troops to any threatened part of their line. The Germans are getting further from their bases of supply, and

cannot so conveniently move reinforcing troops from flank to flank.

The German invasion has so far been successful at every point, though the advance has probably been slower than they had planned. No advance could have been faster than the one that they have made from Louvain to St. Quentin. They have stuck to the heels of the retreating Allies with a tenacity and with a strength that show a well-planned forward movement that can be stopped by the Allies only by an extreme effort.

In numbers the German and Austrian forces are by now probably inferior to the Allies, but the strength of an army does not depend on numbers alone. In the maxim of Napoleon, based on the experience of his successful campaigns, "the strength of an army, like the quantity of motion in mechanics, is estimated by the mass multiplied by the velocity. A swift march enhances the morale of the army and increases its power for victory."

The advantage in morale must certainly lie with the German armies at present. However, for their success they have to pay the penalty of longer lines of communication, more exposed to attack. Their safety lies in strenuously pushing the advantage gained and in keeping the Allies so busy that they will not have a chance to undertake any counter-attack. This will result in a steady aggressive, resulting in a continuous battle until the question is decided whether the Germans can break through the second French line of defense, or whether, thrown back from this, they will have to retreat out of France.

Steady Russian Advance.

The steady advance of the Russian Army into Germany continues, despite a stubborn German defense. The investment of Königsberg is confirmed, and the Russian occupation of Allenstein is reported. This places the Russian advance on a line running from Königsberg southwest through Osterode to the vicinity of Thorn. The reported attack on Graudenz indicates a salient at this point of the line.

The reported crossing of the Vistula River by Russian forces in Prussia will, if confirmed, show that the Russians have completed the first stage of their invasion, and that they are about to enter on the invasion of Germany proper, where they will have to face the immense armies of the German reserves. This will call for a large increase in the Russian forces at the front, and may cause some delay in their advance in force west of the Vistula.

The plans drawn up by the German General Staff for a defense against Russia are known to include a stubborn defense of the line of the Vistula River. Germany has strongly fortified the cities of Danzig, Thorn, Posen, and Breslau. She has also defended the river crossings at Marienburg and Graudenz by lines of detached forts. The German military writers have generally mentioned a temporary occupation of East Prussia by the Russians as an expected feature of the war. Germany's real defense against the Russian invasion is expected to come west of the Vistula River.

Delayed reports from the Austrian border show that the Austrian invasion of Poland is being made by a force of from four to seven corps. Yesterday's reports state that the success of the Russian advance on Lemberg is forcing this Austrian invading army to turn eastward to reinforce the Austrian forces that are charged with the defense of Galicia.

The Russian successes in Galicia so far more than balance the Austrian successes in Poland. Apparently Austria will soon need all her available forces to oppose the advance of this strong Southern Russian Army, estimated at 300,000 men.

These planes are part of the infamous squadron commanded by the German war hero, Baron von Richthofen.

"All the News That's
Fit to Print."

The New York Times.

THE WEATHER
Partly cloudy, warmer today; un-
settled Monday; gentle, variable
winds, becoming south.
For full weather report see
PAGE 6, SPORTS SECTION.

VOL. LXIII...NO. 20,679.   NEW YORK, SUNDAY, SEPTEMBER 6, 1914.—90 PAGES, In Seven Parts, Including Picture and Rotogravure Section, Real Estate Directory, and Review of Books.   PRICE FIVE CENTS.

GERMANS TAKE RHEIMS WITHOUT A BATTLE;
REPORT CAPTURE OF 410 GUNS AND 12,000 MEN;
ALLIES SIGN A PLEDGE TO STAND TOGETHER

NO PEACE TILL ALL AGREE

Britain, France and Russia Will Stand by Each Other Till the End.

BAR GERMAN OVERTURES

Special Cable to THE NEW YORK TIMES.

LONDON, Sept. 5.—The Foreign Office announces that England, France, and Russia by an agreement signed today have given mutual pledges to stand by one another until the finish of the war. Each Government declares that it will not conclude peace separately during the present war, and that when peace terms are discussed no one of the Allies will demand conditions of peace without previous agreement with the others.

This means that the Allies are determined to stand or fall together, burying any special interests and refusing, each for itself, any possible German overtures.

The Observer says there is reason to think that indirect approaches had already been made to France by Germany, ("which seems to imagine that every nation has its price.")

There is no actual evidence that Germany has endeavored to induce any of the powers concerned to forsake the Allies' cause, but such a thing is conceivable in the later stages of the war, and so the agreement has been reached. Its purpose is to show Germany and the rest of the world the firm unity of the Allies. At the Foreign Office an official said to THE NEW YORK TIMES correspondent:

"This agreement means that the Allies are absolutely determined to stand together in this war for freedom, fighting together for the right and to vanquish an enemy who threatens the whole world. Until thrown together by the outbreak of hostilities the Entente had been a rather loosely constructed organization, with no definite undertaking, as far as England was concerned, to join with the others in military operations against any enemy. The French and Russians were pledged to assist each other, but England was not. Now the more or less informal Entente of the three countries becomes an absolute alliance, with each pledged to co-operation in war as well as politics."

Text of Agreement to Make No Separate Peace; Allies Will Accept Only Such Terms as Suit All

LONDON, Sept. 5.—Following is the text of the protocol signed today by representatives of Russia, France and Great Britain:

London, Sept. 5, 1914.

The undersigned, duly authorized thereto by their respective governments, hereby declare as follows:

The British, French, and Russian Governments mutually engage not to conclude peace separately during the present war.

The three governments agree that, when the terms of peace come to be discussed, no one of the Allies will demand conditions of peace without the previous agreement of each of the other Allies.

In faith whereof the undersigned have signed this declaration and have affixed thereto their seals.

Done at London in triplicate this fifth day of September, nineteen hundred and fourteen.

(Signed)   E. GREY,
(British Secretary for Foreign Affairs.)

PAUL CAMBON,
(French Ambassador to Great Britain.)

BENCKENDORFF,
(Russian Ambassador to Great Britain.)

It is stated here that the agreement not only assures military unity of purpose, but equal voices in the final settlement after the war. It is hoped that when the peace negotiations begin one effect of this agreement will be the avoidance of any dispute over a division of spoils. This, of course, takes into consideration the feeling which generally prevails here that the Allies will be successful in the end.

Officials said today, when asked why Belgium had no part in this agreement, that it was an agreement only for the Triple Entente. Belgium was not being ignored, and, as a matter of fact, this new understanding made it more certain than ever that Belgium would obtain full reparation for the wrongs done her, as both England and France were fully pledged to make good Belgium's losses to the greatest possible extent.

May Have Effect on Italy.

It may prove that this agreement will have considerable effect in Italy. Advices indicate that Italy is wavering and is about to join the conflict on the side of the Allies. With the Allies' firm front demonstrated by this agreement, Italy may see the advantage of casting her lot with them.

Just what Italy intends to do is not known here, although there is hope that she will join the Allies. Her aid would be welcome, but, so far as can be learned, England is not trying to influence her. Germany is now openly endeavoring to keep her out of the struggle.

ALLIES GIVE UP FORTRESS

Berlin Tells of Taking of Rheims, the Last on Northern Line.

TURNING MOVEMENT GOES ON

French Authorities Say Germans Are Still Advancing Toward the Southeast.

MILLION MEN WAIT BATTLE

The capture by the Germans of Rheims, eighty-five miles northeast of Paris, the last fortress in the second line of defense north of the French capital, was announced by the Berlin War Office in the following dispatch, sent yesterday to Count von Bernstorff, the German Ambassador to the United States, and given out in this city last night:

BERLIN, Sept. 5. (By wireless via Sayville.)—Rheim has fallen into German hands without resistence.

Army of Gen. von Bülow captured until today 12,000 men, 260 heavy and 150 light guns, six colors.

Another dispatch from Berlin, forwarded to the German Ambassador by the same means, was mutilated in transmission. It referred to Great Britain's foreign policy, discussing particularly the question of violation of Belgian neutrality, and concluded:

"Weekly report Imperial Bank shows increase gold reserves 27,000,-000." (Does not say whether marks or dollars.)

The announcement from Berlin confirms the rather mystifying bulletin, issued by the French War Minister early yesterday morning, wherein it was stated that the enemy was "passing Rheims."

LONDON, Sept. 5.—An official statement issued in Berlin and received here by Marconi Wireless, says:

"Rheims has been taken without any fighting. Owing to the rapid advance of our army little attention can be paid to booty and guns and wagons have been left standing in the open fields quite abandoned. These will be collected by troops in due course."

The dispatch then takes up the situation in other fields, saying:

"Reports from the war correspondents of Viennese newspapers state that the whole situation in the northern theatre of war has been changed for the better by the victory of the armies commanded by Gen. Auffenburg and Gen. Dankl.

"As an example of the brilliant work of the armies in the field the correspondents relate that wounded Russian infantry who tried to beat a hasty retreat under cover were stopped by the renewed direct fire the moment they attempted to make any movement. Later the bodies of a large number of soldiers who had been killed by shrapnel were discovered near th is place.

"Officers of a Scutari detachment on their arrival in Vienna were received by Emperor Francis Joseph and afterward entertained at a banquet by the Minister of War, Gen. Ritter von Krobatin.

"It is reported that France through the intermediary of a group of banks has offered the Italian Government the loan of one milliard ($200,000,000) on favorable terms, but that the Italian Prime Minister refused the offer.

"Greece has called up ten classes of naval reserves for manoeuvres in order to give the national defense new stimulus."

"All the News That's Fit to Print."

The New York Times.

THE WEATHER
Partly cloudy, cooler today; fair, cooler Tuesday; fresh north to northwest winds.
For full weather report see Page 11.

VOL. LXIII...NO. 20,680.　　NEW YORK, MONDAY, SEPTEMBER 7, 1914.—TWELVE PAGES.　　ONE CENT In Greater New York, Jersey City and Newark. | Elsewhere TWO CENTS.

GERMANS MOVING FARTHER AWAY FROM PARIS; FRENCH REPORT CLAIMS GAINS FOR THE ALLIES; BRITISH SAY ENVELOPING MOVEMENT FAILED

FRENCH TELL OF SUCCESS

Part of German Right Wing Is Reported Driven Back.

ENGAGEMENT IS EXTENDING

British Forces, Aided by French, Said to Have Flanked Their Foes.

GERMANS' SHIFTS MYSTIFY

Paris Wonders if They Are Retreating—Kaiser Reported at Nancy—Attack On There.

PARIS, Sept. 6, 11:16 P. M.—This official communication was issued tonight:

"First—The allied armies have again come into contact on our left wing, under good conditions, with the right wing of the enemy on the banks of the Grand Morin.

"Second—Fighting continues on the centre and right in Lorraine and the Vosges. The situation remains unchanged.

"Third—Around Paris the engagement begun yesterday between the allied army and the flank of the advance guard of the German right has extended. We have advanced to the River Ourcq without great resistance.

"The situation of the allied armies appears good as a whole.

"Fourth—Maubeuge continues its heroic resistance."

A bulletin, issued in the afternoon, said:

"The advanced lines of the Allies for the defense of Paris came in contact yesterday with the right wing of the Germans, who appeared in a covering movement in strong force on our right and advancing toward the southeast. A short engagement resulted to the advantage of the Allies."

Reports Germans Are Flanked.

LONDON, Sept. 6.—A dispatch to The Times from Boulogne says that the Mayor of that city is reported to have received a telegram this morning stating that Gen. Joffre had succeeded in turning the German lines, and that Sir John French had gotten around on the left of the German Army.

The Boulogne Tellegramme says that the Germans, who had occupied Lille, Valenciennes, Armentieres, Douai, and Palleuil, departed quickly from those cities Saturday afternoon.

A Reuter dispatch from Berlin by way of Amsterdam says the Germans are attacking the forts at Nancy, and that Emperor William and the German General Staff are present there.

Information reached Dover tonight that train service between Paris and Dieppe had been stopped.

Movements of Four German Armies.

WASHINGTON, Sept. 6.—Dispatches to the French Embassy today from Bordeaux indicate that the German forces in four divisions are proceeding in a turning movement toward the south rather than pushing forward to Paris. They say:

"Their First Army on the 5th reached La Ferte and Montmiral; the second Chantilly, and continues southward. Rheims has been occupied by the Third, and the Fourth moves also southward.

"Fighting continues in Lorraine without decisive results.

"The situation as to material and morale in Paris satisfactory. Have the army needed for the defense of the capital."

GERMAN MOVE MYSTIFIES.

Paris Wonders if It Is a Retreat or Something Else.

By G. H. PERRIS.
NEW YORK TIMES-London Daily Chronicle War Service.
Special Cable to THE NEW YORK TIMES.

PARIS, Sept. 6.—It is still too early to say anything definite about the purpose of the extraordinary German movement to the southeast.

I learn, however, and this is the essential point, that the Allies are fully in touch with what now looks like an attack, converted into a retreat.

Thus the scene of the recent fighting has been practically evacuated by both sides and the centre of interest is transferred, for the moment at least, to the rear of the French Army of the Meuse.

Perhaps the desperate purpose of the German movement is to break through to the eastward and unite with the armies of Metz and Strassburg. This would involve an incredible sandwiching of forces, and we must await developments.

Meanwhile Paris is frankly disappointed.

A number of Sixth Dragoon Guardsmen are in Paris today obtaining remounts. They look very fit, but their khaki tunics badly need mending. They have fought all the way down from Belgium to Compiegne and Senlis, and told me Homeric tales of the last battle.

German and British batteries came into action against each other, they say, at a distance of no more than 500 yards. The British got the pitch first, wiped out the German gunners, and captured eleven guns.

There was a tremendous charge in which the dragoons were accompanied by their shoeing smith, armed only with a hammer, which he wielded with deadly effect.

A minor engagement took place yesterday afternoon between the advance guards of the army defending Paris and a German force, which appeared to be covering on the south the southeastward movement of the mass of the German right wing. The result was favorable to the French.

KAISER DIRECTS HIS WAR LEGIONS

Has Gone to Front for Conflict Which Berlin Regards as a Death Struggle.

Special Cable to THE NEW YORK TIMES.

BERLIN, Sept. 4 (Dispatch to The London Daily Telegraph).—A critical battle between France and Germany is on. The Emperor has joined the army of the Crown Prince. This is the first appearance of the Kaiser in the actual theatre of operations. It can have but one meaning—a death struggle.

The opposing forces are fighting on almost equal terms. Such advantage in numbers as may rest with the Germans is offset by the French position of defense.

So confident are the Germans of ultimate success that they are beginning a movement of troops from the western theatre of operations to the east. Two corps from Belgium have entrained for East Prussia, but the last German force has been called out.

The Landstrum, comprising men between the ages of 25 and 45, have been ordered to the colors. This must bring the number of troops actually under arms to 100 divisions. New units are being rushed to the front every day. They fill the gaps made by the constant fighting, and Germany has been prodigal with her sons.

On my way to Berlin I came through a train loaded with German wounded. They had been sent back from Namur. All were cases which were classified as slightly wounded, although it was plain that some of them had been previously hurt.

The plan of sending back the slightly wounded is new in the German Army. Badly hurt soldiers are held at the base hospitals, but it is planned to send all the lightly hit to spend their convalescence with their families and friends.

This relieves the Government of the expense of maintaining these men during the period of their inaction and it is also hoped that the soldiers will get well of their hurts more quickly in the circle of their friends.

BRITISH ARE CONFIDENT

Allies Have Frustrated German Attempt to Envelop Their Forces.

BUT MORE MEN ARE NEEDED

No Doubt, Says London, of the Individual English Fighter's Superiority Over the Foe.

BERLIN TELLS OF VICTORIES

Reports Allied Forces in Flight, Paris Deserted, and Austrians Driving the Russians Back.

LONDON, Sept. 6.—The operations of the British Army in France last week are reviewed in a statement issued by the Official War Information Bureau today. The statement reads:

"It is now possible to make another general survey, in continuation of that issued on Aug. 30, of the operations of the British Army during the past week.

"No new main trial of strength has taken place. There have, indeed, been battles in various parts of the immense front which in other wars would have been considered operations of the first magnitude. But in this war they are merely incidents of strategic withdrawal and contraction of the allied forces, caused by the initial shock on the frontier and in Belgium and by the enormous strength which the Germans have thrown into the west theatre, while suffering heavily through weakness in the eastern.

"The British expeditionary army has conformed with the general movement of the French forces and acted in harmony with the strategic conceptions of the French General Staff. Since the battle of Cambrai on Aug. 26, where the British troops successfully guarded the left flank of the whole line of French armies from a deadly turning attack, supported by an enormous force, the Seventh French army has come into operation on the British left.

Constant Rear-Guard Action.

"This, in conjunction with the Fifth

Army on our right, has greatly taken the strain and pressure off our left. The Fifth French Army, in particular, on Aug. 29 advanced from the line of the Oise River to meet and counter the German forward movement, and a considerable battle developed to the town of Guise.

"In this the Fifth French Army gained a marked and solid success, driving back with heavy loss and in disorder three German army corps—the Tenth, the Guard, and a reserve corps. It is stated that the commander of the Tenth German Corps was among those killed.

"In spite of this success, however, and all the benefits which followed from it, the general retirement to the south continued, and the German armies, seeking persistently after the British troops, remained in practically continuous contact with our rear guard.

"On Aug. 30 and 31 the British covering and delaying troops were frequently engaged. On Sept. 1 a very vigorous effort was made by the Germans, which brought about a sharp action in the neighborhood of Compiègne. This action was carried through by the First British Cavalry Brigade and the Fourth Guards Brigade, and was entirely satisfactory to the British.

"The German attack, which was most strongly pressed, was not brought to a standstill until much slaughter had been inflicted upon them and ten German guns had been captured. The brunt of this creditable affair fell upon our Guards Brigade, who lost in killed and wounded about 300 men. After this engagement our troops were no longer molested. Wednesday, Sept. 2, was the first quiet day they had since the battle at Mons on Aug. 23.

"During the whole of this period marching and fighting have been continuous, and in the whole period the British casualties, according to the latest estimates, have amounted to about 15,000 officers and men.

"The fighting having been in open order upon a wide front, with repeated retirements, has led to a large number of officers and men, and even small parties, losing their way and getting separated. It is known that a very considerable number of those now included in the total will rejoin the colors safely.

Foe's Losses Thrice as Great.

"These losses, if heavy in so small a force, have in no wise affected the spirit of the troops. They do not amount to one-third of the losses inflicted by the British force upon the enemy, and the sacrifice required of the army has not been out of proportion to its military achievements.

"Drafts of 19,000 have reached our army or are approaching the men on the line of communication, and advantage has been taken of the five quiet days that have passed since the action on Sept. 1 to fill up the gaps and refit and consolidate the units.

"The British Army is now south of the Marne and is in line with the French forces on the right and left.

"The latest information about the enemy is that they are neglecting Paris and are marching in a southeastern direction toward the Marne and toward the left and centre of the French lines.

"The First German Army is reported to be between La Ferte-sous-Jouarre and Effises Boffort.

"The Second German Army, after taking Rheims, is advancing on Château Thierry and to the east of that place.

"The Fourth German Army is reported to be marching south and on the west of the Argonne, between Suippes and Ville Jourbe. All these points were reached by the Germans on Sept. 3.

Enveloping Movement Thwarted.

"The Seventh German Army has been repulsed by a French corps near Dienville(?).

"It would therefore appear that the developing (enveloping?) movement on the Anglo-French left flank has been abandoned by the Germans because it was no longer practicable to continue such a great extension, or because the alternative, a direct attack upon the allied lines, is preferred.

"Whether this change of plan by the Germans is voluntary or whether it has been forced upon them by the strategic situation and the great strength of the allied armies in their front will be revealed by the course of events.

"There is no doubt whatever that our men have established a personal ascendency over the Germans, and that they are conscious of the fact that with anything like even numbers the result would not be doubtful. The shooting of the German infantry is poor, while the British rifle fire has devastated every column of attack that has presented itself.

"Their superior training and intelligence have enabled the British soldiers to use the open formation with effect, and thus cope with the vast numbers employed by the enemy.

"The cavalry, who have had even more opportunities for displaying personal prowess and address, have definitely established their superiority.

"Field Marshal Sir John French's report dwells on the marked superiority of the British troops of every arm of the service.

"'The cavalry,' he says, 'do as they like with the enemy until they are confronted with twice their numbers. The German patrols simply fly before our horsemen. The German troops will not face our infantry fire. As regards the artillery, they have never been opposed by less than three or four times their numbers.'

Brave Deeds Described.

"The following incidents have been mentioned: During the action at Le Château on Aug. 26, all the officers and men of one of the British batteries had been killed or wounded, with the exception of one subaltern and two gunners. These continued to serve one gun and kept up a sound raking fire and came out unhurt from the battlefield.

"On another occasion a portion of a supply column was cut off by a detachment of German cavalry. The officer in charge was summoned to surrender. He refused and, starting the motor off at full speed, dashed safely through, only losing two lorries.

"It is noted that during a rearguard action of the Guards brigade on Sept. 1 the Germans were seen giving assistance to our wounded.

"The weather has been very hot, with an almost tropical sun, which has made long marches trying to the soldiers. In spite of this they look well and hardy, and the horses, in consequence of the amount of hay and oats in the fields, are in excellent condition.

WHEN DIPLOMATS ABANDONED PARIS

Cosmopolitan Crowd Left for Bordeaux in the Dimness of a Darkened City.

SIEGE IS AWAITED CALMLY

Parisians Show Confidence in Gen. Gallieni's Ability to Defend the Capital.

Special Cable to THE NEW YORK TIMES.

LONDON, Sept. 6.—The scenes attending the departure for Bordeaux of the majority of the Paris Diplomatic Corps are thus described by G. H. Perris, the Paris correspondent of The Daily Chronicle:

"Their Excellencies left the Quai d'Orsay Station, and none who saw it is ever likely to forget the scene. I groped my way in the deep, narrow streets about the office on the south side of the river. In the last few nights I have conceived a perfectly practical affection for the much-slandered moon. You see, they are saving coal and electricity; moreover, it is advisable to give no guidance to hostile airships; so off the boulevards the streets are hardly lighted at all. Last night it was only two-thirds of a moon, and the dim, mysterious light on the riverside was altogether fitting for what was afoot.

A Sight to be Seen Only Once.

"You may see again such alarm as carried scores of thousands of Parisians southward in the last few days, but we are never likely again to see the abandonment of the first city of Europe at dead of night by a cosmopolitan crowd of diplomatists.

"There was Sir Francis Bertie [the British Ambassador] in a black suit and bowler hat, talking to the Marquis Visconti-Venosta, the Italian Ambassador himself, Signor Tittoni, being another distinguishable figure, in gray and soft felt hat. Ambassador Herrick had come down with his wife to say good-bye to his confrères, and M. Isvolsky, the Czar's envoy, was chatting with the Spanish Ambassador.

"The windows of each carriage of the special train were labeled with the names of the countries whose representatives it was carrying off. There was even an inscription for the more or less imaginary Republic of San Marino; but no one appeared to answer to this honorific name. There were the Persian Minister and M. Romanos, a black-bearded Greek, and the Russian Military Attaché in uniform, and les braves Belges, and all sorts of servants, including a Chinese nurse feeding a yellow baby with coal-black eyes. At last a soft-toned horn was blown, and the train rolled away. Say what you like about adventurous Herr Taube and the possibly approaching legions of his still more reckless Kaiser, it is no pleasant thing to see the world's delegates pack up their traps and leave the splendid City of Paris to its fate.

"President Poincaré, accompanied by all the members of the Ministry, left for Bordeaux at 5 A. M. Friday, and they were followed in two special trains by the Presidents and members of the Senate and Chamber of Deputies, with other official persons. The main body of the staff and the reserves of the Banque de France had already been removed. The higher legal functions of the republic will be represented in the provisional capital by fifteen Judges taken from three divisions of the Court of Cassation.

"Thus Paris is derobed of her accustomed majesty. Her great monuments remain only because they cannot be shifted. The perspective of the Champs Elysées is as glorious as ever.

DIPLOMATS' EFFORT TO PROTECT PARIS ART

Ask the United States Government to Join in Representations to Germany.

WASHINGTON, Sept. 6.—Neutral diplomats have asked Ambassador Herrick to sound the American Government on the question of making joint representations to Germany to protect certain buildings and works of art in the attack on Paris. This is the substance of official advices received today.

While there is no intimation that the French doubt their ability to protect their capital, a bombardment is regarded as probable, it is believed, and the establishment of neutral zones and avoidance of unnecessary destruction of world-famous buildings in Paris is being discussed there.

The United States is looked upon as the natural leader in such a movement, and Ambassador Herrick, it is understood, has asked for instructions.

At Brussels recently, Minister Whitlock and the Spanish Minister prevailed upon the Burgomaster to permit the peaceful entry of the Germans, as the town was unfortified, and an attack meant certain destruction and useless loss of life.

Ambassador Herrick, it is thought, will probably be informed that the United States will transmit communications from other countries and discuss the subject with Germany, but will do no more than act as a channel of communication.

Days Big With Destiny, Says President Wilson

America is greater than any party. America cannot properly be served by any man who for a moment measures his interest against her advantage. The time has come for great things. These are days big with destiny for the United States, as for the other nations of the world.

A little wisdom, a little courage, a little self-forgetful devotion may, under God, turn that destiny this way or that. Great hearts, great natures will respond. Even little men will rejoice to be stimulated and guided and set an heroic example.

Parties will fare well enough without nursing if the men who make them up and the men who lead them forget themselves to serve a cause and set a great people forward on the path of liberty and peace.

—From President Wilson's letter to Representative Doremus.

"All the News That's
Fit to Print."

The New York Times.

THE WEATHER
Fair Sunday; Monday cloudy, probably late showers; fresh east winds.
For full weather report see Page 5, Sports Section.

VOL. LXIII...NO. 20,686. ....

NEW YORK, SUNDAY, SEPTEMBER 13, 1914.—92 PAGES, In Seven Parts, Including Pictures and Rotogravure Section, Real Estate Directory, and Review of Books.

PRICE FIVE CENTS.

WHOLE GERMAN LINE RETIRES, HOTLY PURSUED; ALLIES WIN FIRST PHASE OF THE GREAT BATTLE; WILSON SOUNDS THE KAISER ON PEACE TERMS

GERMANS RETIRE IN HASTE

Collapse of Their Right Wing Affects Line to Verdun and Nancy.

LOSE MANY MEN AND GUNS

LUNEVILLE IS RECAPTURED

London Sees in Growing Success Proof of Fatal Error by Kaiser's Strategists.

PARIS, Sept. 12. 11:30 P. M.—An official statement issued tonight says:

"Notwithstanding the fatigues occasioned by five days of incessant fighting, our troops are vigorously pursuing our enemy, which is in general retreat.

"This retreat appears to have been more rapid than the advance. This has been so precipitate at certain points that our troops have gathered up at the general quarters, notably at Montmirail, charts, documents, and personal papers abandoned by the enemy, and also packages of letters which had been received or were ready to be forwarded.

"In the district of Fromentieres the enemy abandoned several batteries of mortars and a number of caissons of ammunition.

A later bulletin said:

"First—On our left wing the general retreat of the Germans continues before the French and British forces, who have reached the lower courses of the Aisne.

"Second—Likewise in the centre the German armies are retreating. We have crossed the Marne between Epernay and Vitry-le-François. On our right wing the enemy has in like manner begun today a retiring movement, abandoning the region around Nancy. We have reoccupied Lunéville."

An official bulletin, given out in the afternoon, said:

"On our left wing the Germans have begun a general retreating movement between the Oise and the Marne. Yesterday their front lay between Soissons, Braine, and Fismes and the mountain of Rheims.

"Their cavalry seems to be exhausted. The Anglo-French forces, which pursued them, encountered on Sept. 11 only feeble resistance.

"At the centre on our right wing the Germans have evacuated Vitry-le-François, where they had fortified

themselves, and also the valley of the Saulx River. Attacked at Sermaize and at Revigny, they abandoned a large quantity of war material.

"The German forces which have been occupying the Argonne region have begun to give way. They are retreating to the north through the Forest of Bellenon.

"In Lorraine we have made slight progress. We occupy the eastern boundary of the Forest of Champenoux, Rehainvillers, and Gerbenviller.

"The Germans have evacuated St. Die.

"In Belgium the Belgian Army is acting vigorously against the German troops, who are before the fortifications of Antwerp.

"In the Servian field of operations, the Servians have occupied Semlin, Austria."

LONDON, Sunday, Sept. 13.—A Reuter dispatch from Paris says that the French occupied Soisons, Department of Alsace, at 6 o'clock last evening.

ALLIES IN ACTIVE PURSUIT.

Four Days of Successful Advance Described by British War Office

LONDON, Sept. 12, 11:25 P. M.—The official Press Bureau gave out this statement today:

"A summary, necessarily incomplete, may be attempted of the operations of the British expeditionary force and the French Army during the last four days:

"On Sept. 6 the southward advance of the German right reached the extreme point at Coulommiers and Provins, cavalry patrols having penetrated even as far south as Nogent-sur-Seine.

"This movement was covered by a large flanking force, west of the line of the River Ourcq, watching the outer Paris defenses and any allied force that came from them.

"The southward movement of the enemy left his right wing in a dangerous position, as he had evacuated the Creil-Senlis-Compiègne region through which his advance had been pushed.

"The Allies attacked this exposed wing, both in front and on the flank. On Sept. 8 the covering force was assailed by a French Army, based upon the Paris defenses, and brought to action on the line between Nanteuil-le-Haudouin and Meaux.

"The main portion of the enemy's right wing was attacked frontally by the British Army, which had been transferred from the north to the east of Paris, and by a French corps, advancing alongside it on a line between Crécy, Coulommiers, and Sezanne.

"The combined operations have up to the present been completely successful. The German outer flank was forced back as far as the line of the Ourcq River. There it made a strong defense and executed several vigorous counter-attacks, but was unable to

beat off the pressure of the French advance.

"The main body of the enemy's right wing vainly endeavored to defend the line of the Grand Morin River, and then that of the Petit Morin. Pressed back over both of these rivers and threatened on its right, owing to the defeat of the covering force by the allied left, the German right wing retreated over the Marne on Sept. 10.

"The British Army, with a portion of the French forces on its left, crossed this river below Chateau Thierry—a movement which obliged the enemy's forces west of the Ourcq, already assailed by the French corps forming the extreme left of the Allies, to give way and retreat northeastward in the direction of Soissons.

"Since Sept. 10 the whole of the German right wing has fallen back in considerable disorder, closely followed by the French and British troops.

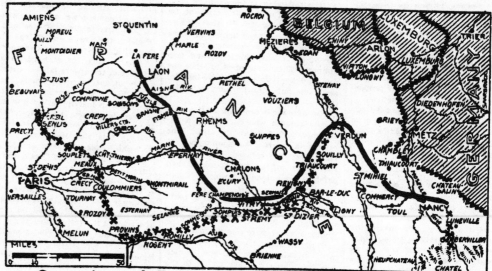

German Army at Its Furthest Advance—Approximate Position Today.

Since this map was prepared at 10 o'clock last night, on the basis of early evening advices, it has been announced that the advance of the Allies has been so rapid that they have now crossed the Marne between Epernay and Vitry.

"All the News That's Fit to Print."

The New York Times.

THE WEATHER

Showers this afternoon or tonight and probably tomorrow; gentle to moderate south winds.
For full weather report see Page 11.

VOL. LXIV...NO. 20,712   ...   NEW YORK, FRIDAY, OCTOBER 9, 1914.—SIXTEEN PAGES.   ONE CENT In Greater New York, Jersey City and Newark. TWO CENTS Elsewhere.

ANTWERP BOMBARDED FROM LAND AND SKY; KING AND PART OF THE ARMY MOVE OUT; CITY STILL HELD; ALLIES PRESSING NORTHWARD

TERRIFIC FIRE POURED IN

Germans Move Up to Second Line of Defense and Shell Antwerp.

ZEPPELINS SLAY AND BURN

Fleet Drops Bombs on Houses and Forts, Killing a Score and Setting Fires.

PLAN A VIGOROUS DEFENSE

LONDON, Oct. 8.—Having broken through the outer forts of Antwerp, the Germans are now bombarding the city and the second line of defenses. At the same time Zeppelins have appeared over the city dropping bombs, which are reported to have caused many deaths and added to the terror of the people, thousands of whom are fleeing from the city.

News has reached Bordeaux that King Albert, at the head of a part of the Belgian Army, marched out of Antwerp today. Such a move had been predicted to prevent the bottling up of the forces or capture if the city falls. A sufficient number of troops to man the fortifications has been left.

The bombardment of Antwerp has been so violent that the houses at Rosendaal, a Netherlands town more than twenty miles distant, have been visibly shaken, according to a telegram from that town to the Central News by way of Amsterdam.

Some wounded civilians have arrived at Rosendaal, and the Dutch Government has ordered all trains to proceed to that place to be held in readiness to transport the refugees and injured. Thousands of refugees have already arrived.

Throughout the entire night, the message adds, a red glare illuminated the sky.

Shells Near the Cathedral.

The correspondent of The Star at Ghent says:

"Antwerp was subjected to a furious bombardment throughout last night. Shells from the German sixteen-inch guns were falling early this morning in the Place Verte, close to the cathedral."

The attack on Antwerp began at midnight Wednesday, according to an official dispatch received in Amsterdam from Berlin, after Gen. Hans H. von Beseler, commander of the siege army at Antwerp, had notified the authorities of Antwerp, through the representatives of neutral States, that bombardment was about to open.

Zeppelins Kill a Score.

From Antwerp, under date of Wednesday, this report is received:

"The condition of panic among the people was increased today by the appearance at 11 o'clock this morning and at 3 o'clock this afternoon of German aircraft, which dropped bombs, destroying seven houses and killing a score of people.

"On account of the Zeppelins' successful attack, the large avenue leading to the railroad station quickly became black with a struggling mass of people eager to escape from the city. Seized with an unreasoning, terrible fear of a bombardment or of a charge of German cavalry, the people are transporting invalids, cripples, and even the occupants of lunatic asylums.

"The situation, however, quickly changed again. While at 2 o'clock even grown-up men were weeping with terror and were fighting for places around the railway station, at 6 o'clock everybody was again certain that the forces would be able to hold out against the Germans and even throw them back across the River Nèthe, while everybody was telling his neighbor how far superior the — guns were to the German heavy artillery.

"The people remaining in the 'y tonight are taking to the cellars, pared to hear the first German sh in the morning.

"The Belgian Ministers are trying to reach Ostend through Flanders and via Holland.

"The Belgian Army is marching into the city, tired out, leaving the guarding of the forts for the night to fresh —— troops."

[The blanks denote words cut out by the censor. They may relate to forces and guns sent to Antwerp by Great Britain.]

During Wednesday night no fewer than six Zeppelins flew over Antwerp, dropping bombs in all directions, the Central News correspondent at Amsterdam says. The extent of the damage done is not known, but one of the bombs damaged the Palace of Justice.

Reuter's Amsterdam correspondent says that Zeppelin airships cruising above the fortifications of Antwerp dropped bombs on some oil tanks at Hoboken, which caught fire. To prevent a general conflagraton, the other tanks were hastily drained.

Close to City, Says Berlin.

An official dispatch received here tonight from Berlin by the Marconi Wireless Telegraph Company says:

"It is reported from Dutch sources that fierce fighting occurred yesterday in the Nèthe district, (Province of Antwerp.)

"The Germans approached in a northerly direction from Forts de Wavre and de Waelhem and commenced a bombardment of Antwerp from these positions.

"Early in the morning the shrapnel shells already had caused great damage in many places, showing that the investing force is close to the city.

"The whole of the Belgian field army has been concentrated in the district between Antwerp, Lierre, (nine miles to the southeast of the city,) and the River Scheldt, in which area fighting is proceeding."

Both sides confirm the report that the Germans have succeeded in crossing the River Nèthe, but the trenches along the River Scheldt are still holding out against their determined attacks.

According to a message from Baarle-Nassau, the Netherlands, to the Nieuw Rotterdamsche Courant, the Germans occupied Turnhout, twenty-five miles east-northeast of Antwerp, this morning, presumably to join the attack on Antwerp from the east.

Thousands of fugitives have arrived at the Baarle-Nassau station. A train coming from the Dutch frontier was fired upon by the Germans, who destroyed the locomotive.

SOLDIERS' OWN DAILY.

It Is Handwritten and Is Passed Along from Trench to Trench.

Special Cable to THE NEW YORK TIMES.

PARIS, Oct. 29. — The Intransigeant gives details of the only newspaper in France which is untroubled by the censorship, though nearer the battle line than any other. It is called the Journal des Tranchées. It appears daily somewhere between Nieuport and Verdun. It is handwritten and passed along from trench to trench. There is only one copy per day. It is composed mostly of personalities with humorous references to the Germans. Under "Society Notes" it reported:

"A considerable party of our Teutonic visitors have just left the neighborhood of Rheims for a trip to the south. In order that nothing shall be lacking, the French Government is supplying special conductors for the tour, which is expected to be a long one."

The Intransigeant says that many of the best-known French journalists contribute to the new publication.

German hand grenade throwers clothed in steel armor look like a throwback from the Middle Ages rather than 20th-century soldiers.

"All the News That's Fit to Print."

The New York Times.

THE WEATHER
Local Showers today, unsettled Sunday.

VOL. LXIV...NO. 20,713. ... NEW YORK, SATURDAY, OCTOBER 10, 1914.—EIGHTEEN PAGES. ONE CENT In Greater New York, Jersey City and Newark. | TWO CENTS

LONDON HEARS THAT ANTWERP HAS FALLEN; CITY AFLAME UNDER RAIN OF GERMAN SHELLS; FRENCH CAPTURE 1,600 GERMANS NEAR ROYE

DESTRUCTION IN ANTWERP

Fire Spreads in Several Quarters and Many Non-Combatants Fall.

TERROR GRIPS THE PEOPLE

City Streets and Avenues of Escape Choked with Refugees —Rest Hide in Cellars.

Zeppelin Said to Have Been Brought Down—Some Public Buildings Struck by Shells.

Special Cable to THE NEW YORK TIMES.

LONDON, Saturday, Oct. 10.—The Morning Post says:

"We are informed on good authority that Antwerp has fallen.

"The news will be received with the profoundest regret by all who have watched the heroic defense that has been maintained by the Belgian Army.

"The foregoing has been submitted to the Press Bureau, which permits its publication but gives no confirmation."

"The regrettable news was conveyed last night by a representative of The Morning Post to Count de la Laing, the Belgian Minister, who was naturally much perturbed. He had not heard of the occurrence up to midnight and had no official confirmation of it."

The Daily Chronicle publishes the following:

"The Germans have entered Antwerp. The inhabitants are quite calm. Most of those who desired to leave the city did so before the bombardment commenced.

"This message has been submitted to the official censor, who has no objection to publication, but adds that 'the Press Bureau gives no confirmation of this news.'"

Desperate Fighting Reported.

Special Cable to THE NEW YORK TIMES.

ROTTERDAM, Oct. 9, (Dispatch to The London Daily News.)—The defenders of Antwerp are now fighting behind the second line of forts and are determined to resist to the last. The bombardment of the city goes on. Fire in the city is said to have reached tremendous proportions, and desperate fighting is proceeding.

It is confidently reported to me by a man who watched the bombardment of Antwerp from a distance that at 4:30 o'clock on Thursday afternoon he saw the guns of the forts concentrate their fire on one particular spot in the air: a number of shells burst together, and almost at the same moment he saw a large, cigarshaped body fall to earth. He has seen several Zeppelins in peace time, and is confident that the falling object was a Zeppelin. Bystanders, he says, were similarly confident.

Last night was a terrible one for the people of Antwerp, for the shells were literally rained on the town, and many civilians were killed and wounded before they could take shelter in cellars.

The special correspondent of the Nieuwe Rotterdamsche Courant, who left Antwerp this morning, relates that the first shrapnel fell on the town at 9 o'clock, and almost immediately fire broke out, especially in the neighborhood of the South Station. At Berchem, a southern suburb, grave damage was done.

During the whole night projectiles literally rained on the town, sometimes at the rate of more than twenty a minute. In the neighborhood of the station many houses were absolutely destroyed, while the Hippodrome has been burned to the ground. The Law Courts and Museum have been damaged.

Severe fighting is still proceeding outside the town, and many wounded were being brought from the fighting line. Belgian troops which had been fighting to the west of the Scheldt were repulsed by the Germans. They crossed the river and came into town.

Latest News Bulletins From Antwerp Showed City Aflame and Many Civilians Killed

Special Cable to THE NEW YORK TIMES.
Dispatch to The London Daily Chronicle.

ROSENDAAL, Oct. 9.—With the full force of their big guns, including 16½-inch howitzers, the Germans today are continuing the bombardment of Antwerp and the inner line of forts. Incendiary shells, which the Germans are pouring into the place, are having their effect, and the city is now burning at several points. Fire brigades are restricting the area of the outbreaks.

Many civilians have been killed by falling shells. Practically the town has now been deserted except for the Belgian troops.

Report That Bombardment Has Slackened.

LONDON, Saturday, Oct. 10.—The Daily Mail's Ostend correspondent, telegraphing late on Friday, says:

"Stubborn fighting is proceeding before the Antwerp fortifications. Four assaults have been repulsed at No. 4 Fort, at Vieux Dieu. The bombardment of the town appears to be somewhat diminishing in intensity."

200 GUNS SHELL CITY.

Two Forts Reported Silenced—Berlin Hears King Is Wounded.

LONDON, Oct. 9.—All reports received here show that Antwerp is being subjected to a heavy bombardment. The city has taken fire in several quarters, and public and private buildings have suffered severely. It is reported from The Hague that Forts 4 and 6 of the second line of defense have been silenced, but every account points to a determined, and, up to this time, a successful defense by the Belgians.

Reuter's Ostend correspondent says:

"In the operations against Antwerp the Germans are using no less than 200 guns of eleven, twelve, and sixteen inch calibre, some of them having a range of more than eight miles.

"The bombardment yesterday (Thursday) began at 9:30 o'clock at night and stopped at 10, only to be renewed with increasing violence at midnight.

"The British, French, and Russian Ministers were the last of the diplomatic body to quit Antwerp. They departed by boat at 11 o'clock last night after experiencing the first part of the bombardment."

The places in the city which thus far have suffered most severely are the Southern station, the Palace of Justice, the Avenue de l'Industrie and the quarters in these vicinities. The correspondent of The Evening Star adds that during the bombardment on Thursday night it was estimated that shells fell at the rate of twenty a minute. Many civilians were killed, he says. In addition to the Law Courts and the Museum, which, he says, were damaged by shells, fire broke out at many points in the city.

Another correspondent attributes the fires to incendiary bombs which, he says, the Germans threw. By noon on Thursday, it is reported, the city was burning in four places.

Saw Zeppelin Brought Down.

In a dispatch from Ghent, dated Thursday at midnight, the correspondent of The Star says:

"An officer whom I met states that the bombardment of the cathedral at Antwerp had begun at the hour he left that city, which was 10 o'clock Thursday morning. Fire had broken out in many places. The Germans were using their 16-inch howitzers with terrible effect on the inner ring of forts, but guns of smaller calibre were being employed for the destruction of the city itself.

"The airship which dropped a bomb on the Law Courts was subjected to a terrific fire, and must certainly have been hit. Other eye-witnesses of the Zeppelin flights over Antwerp insist that they saw one such craft hit by shells from the forts and fall to the earth.

"The Burgomaster of Antwerp has declared his intention of supporting the military in resisting to the last."

In a dispatch from Amsterdam, filed this afternoon, the correspondent of Reuter's Telegram Company says:

"The uninterrupted thundering of guns was heard at Rosendaal, Holland, from Antwerp throughout the night. The firing slackened a little in the early morning, but it has now resumed with full force.

"The sky last night was made red by the flames of burning Antwerp."

Borgerhaut, a suburb of Antwerp, was set on fire last night, according to an Amsterdam dispatch.

King Albert Reported Wounded.

Berlin transmits by wireless a report that has reached there that King Albert of the Belgians has been slightly wounded. An Amsterdam dispatch to Reuter's Telegram Company, dated to-

At the beginning of the war zeppelins were thought to be the ultimate offensive weapon.

A battalion of German infantrymen awaits the command to attack.

Along the Battle Front in France and Belgium.

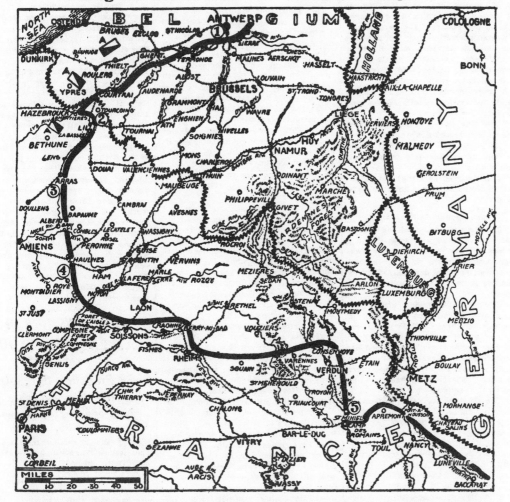

1. A vague report reaches London that Antwerp has fallen before the German attack, but this lacks official confirmation. Previous direct advices indicated that the city was under severe bombardment and that fires had spread to many quarters.

(2) Cavalry engagements of very extensive character and involving large forces, are still in progress north of Lille and La Bassée.

(3) Severe fighting continues along the hostile lines from Lens through Arras to Lassigny.

(4) The French official report records the capture of 1,600 Germans around Roye in the course of two days. There have been sharp encounters there.

(5) Neither side seems to be gaining much in the Woevre district, but the French are still endeavoring to expel the German force from St. Mihiel, on the banks of the Meuse.

(" A ") These represent detachments of Germans, probably cavalry in some force, which have been reported at points west and northwest of the main line of German defense.

day, however quotes the Nieuws Van der Dag of Ghent as saying that King Albert left Antwerp this morning and has arrived at Selzaete, a village near the Dutch frontier town of Sas van Ghent.

Railway and telegraphic communications between Berlin and Antwerp have been interrupted according to another wireless from the German capital. The message adds that the French Consul at Antwerp has transferred the archives of the Consulate to Rosendaal, Holland.

The Hague says the exodus of the panic-stricken people of Antwerp continues and it is reported there that the dikes have been opened.

The British Minister at The Hague has asked the Government to permit the free passage of a hospital ship to convey wounded from Antwerp to England. This, it is explained, is the only foundation for the report that Great Britain had asked the Dutch to allow British warships passage to Antwerp.

Leading Up to Antwerp.

The correspondent of The Morning Post at Antwerp, in describing the events leading up to the present situation at Antwerp, says:

"About a month ago the German commanders began to realize the danger of having the Belgian army occupying a fortified position which continually threatened the German lines of communication. The Germans threw out feelers to ascertain if Belgium would agree to keep her army in Antwerp in return for the German promise not to attack the town.

"The Belgians indignantly rejected all such proposals and replied by gallant sorties which, however, failed of complete success. The taking of Alost renewed the German conviction of the necessity for an aggressive campaign against the Belgians, which began after further German proposals for an agreement were rejected by the Belgians.

"Accordingly the Germans brought up some of their heaviest field pieces and opened with the bombardment of Malines. For a week afterward the Germans each day bombarded some open town outside of Antwerp with the idea that the fleeing civil population from these villages would wreck the morale of the Antwerp garrison.

"There is no question that this policy had its effect, and if the final event proves that Antwerp has decided not to endure the horrors of a bombardment no one can utter a word of censure. These streams of refugees are enough to break down the most heroic resolution, especially as the civic Government is kept completely engaged in finding food and shelter for the incoming horde.

"On Tuesday Fort Wavre-St. Catherines was put out of action. Later on the same day Fort Waelhem was damaged and became ineffective. Whatever the German shells struck they destroyed. On Thursday a Zeppelin attack on Antwerp failed, Fort Kessel succeeded in punishing the Germans severely, and the Germans shelled Boom and Lierre, sending the industrial population fleeing in a panic to Antwerp. By this time at least 50,000 refugees were in Antwerp.

"Thursday evening the German infantry attacked Lierre, Duffel, and Termonde, only the Duffel attack being successful. Up to this stage confidence had been general, but it now began to waver. Friday the bombardment of Lierre continued and the authorities began to consider the possibility of Antwerp's being occupied by the enemy.

"On Saturday the situation showed a slight advance by the Belgians, and on Sunday the German attack seemed to be slackening in its intensity. On Monday the German artillery made a furious attack on Lierre, and the City Counsel urged the Governor to continue the defense of the city without regard to property interests.

"On Tuesday there were further attacks on Lierre and at one point the Germans got a handful of men across the river by swimming, but they only came over to be killed. The German artillery attack was rather diffuse and the position was cheerful at nightfall, though savage fighting continued at Lierre."

Telegraphing from Ostend, the Daily Express's correspondent sends the following:

"The German plan for the reduction of Antwerp has carefully developed for many weeks past. The serious bombardment will only be begun when, in the opinion of the commandant, he is in a position to take the city with little delay. Emplacements for the big guns have been carefully constructed at most advantageous positions. These guns were brought from Namur and Maubeuge. The Germans have a large number of them at their disposal."

FAIL TO HEAD OFF ALLIES.

Germans Sought to Drive a Wedge to Isolate Antwerp.

LONDON, Oct. 9.—The Central News correspondent at Antwerp telegraphs under Thursday's date:

"The German effort toward north France, with a view of fixing a wedge between Antwerp and the Allies, has been nearly destroyed.

"Fierce fighting is occurring around Lille and south of there.

"Prisoners have been taken to Dunkirk and Ostend and a German aeroplane has been destroyed."

"All the News That's Fit to Print."

The New York Times.

THE WEATHER
Showers, cooler late today; fair, cooler Monday; fresh south winds, becoming westerly tonight.
☞ For full weather report see Page 11

VOL. LXIV...NO. 20,714.   NEW YORK, SUNDAY, OCTOBER 11, 1914.—96 PAGES, In Nine Parts.   PRICE FIVE CENTS.

ANTWERP FALLS, BUT BELGIAN ARMY GETS AWAY AFTER BLOWING UP FORTS; WIDE RUIN IN CITY; 2,000 BRITISH TROOPS DRIVEN INTO HOLLAND

GERMANS TAKE LAST FORT

Army and Thousands of Inhabitants Safely Out of Antwerp.

BOMBARDED FOR 40 HOURS

Damage to City and Loss of Life Believed to be Great, Though Reports Differ.

END CAME UNEXPECTEDLY

Armies Fought Desperately, Belgian Retreat Being Covered by a Heavy Fire.

Special Cable to THE NEW YORK TIMES.
ANTWERP, Oct. 9, via Flushing, Oct. 10, (Dispatch to The London Daily Chronicle.)—Antwerp was surrendered at 9 o'clock this (Friday) morning, after suffering a bombardment of forty hours. The damage wrought by shells has been terrible. The Hotel de Ville, the Palais de Justice, and the Art Gallery have suffered.

The terror of the last twenty-four hours before the surrender almost baffles description. Those of the inhabitants who had not fled took refuge in cellars. There has been a dreadful loss of life.

The end came sooner than was expected. The defense was spirited and gallant. I had a fortunate escape from the German fire, and got away by motor boat.

Berlin Reports the Capture.

LONDON, Oct. 10.—Antwerp surrendered to the besieging German force at 9 o'clock yesterday morning, and the Germans took possession of the city at 2:30 o'clock yesterday after the city had been under attack since Sept. 29. Official statements from the Press Bureau here and from Berlin make announcement of the surrender. The reports agree that the Belgian Army evacuated the city before its surrender.

The Press Bureau makes the bare statement that the city was evacuated. The first Berlin report received here by wireless says:

"This forenoon (Friday) several forts of the inner line of the fortifications of Antwerp have fallen. The town since midday has been in our possession.

"The commander and the garrison evacuated the fortifications. Only a few forts are still occupied by the enemy, and this is without influence on our position in Antwerp."

The capture of all the forts was announced later in a dispatch from Amsterdam. The correspondent of the Reuter Telegram Company wired that a message from Berlin conveyed a report issued from General Army Headquarters, dated Oct. 10, at 11 A. M., saying that the entire fortress of Antwerp, including all the forts, was in possession of the Germans.

Beaten back from their last defenses the Belgian garrison blew up their heavy batteries and withdrew to rejoin their comrades who previously had evacuated their positions.

A correspondent at The Hague sends interesting details of the surrender. He says:

"The war flag was removed from the Cathedral and a white flag raised in its place at 9 A. M. The actual surrender took place five and one-half hours later.

"It is declared here that the Cathedral of Notre Dame has not been damaged.

Last Desperate Fighting.

"The Germans delivered one of their last furious attacks between 6 and 7 o'clock Friday morning. The Belgians resisted them valiantly in their trenches, and the desperate fighting resulted in very heavy losses on both sides.

"During all Thursday night Zeppelin airships directed the firing of the German heavy artillery, the results of which were appalling.

"The German artillery forced its way across the River Nèthe, in which many of the artillerymen were drowned. The fighting has been indescribably sanguinary.

"The Belgians succeeded in blowing up two, and possible more, of their batteries and heavy artillery."

According to the Rosendaal correspondent of the Handelsblad of Amsterdam, the Germans entered Antwerp through the suburb of Berchem. The correspondent of the Amsterdam Telegraaf at Rosendaal learns from a Belgian medical officer that the Belgians blew up Fort de Meuxem, to the north of Antwerp.

The inner forts, like those further out, soon succumbed to the enormous shells, and on Friday morning several of these forts had fallen, opening the way for the Germans into the city. A few forts continued to hold out, and it was not until 11 o'clock this morning that the Germans, according to their own official report, were in complete possession of the city and fortresses. When they arrived yesterday they found that the Belgian field army and at least part of the garrison had anticipated them, and like the King and royal family had escaped.

Army's Safe Retreat.

A dispatch to The Nieuws van den Dag of Amsterdam says that when the capitulation of the city became inevitable the Belgian Army marched out methodically in order to occupy a long line of defense which would assure its retreat. For the purpose of gaining time a deadly fire was still directed at the enemy. When the troops were at a sufficient distance from the forts the latter were blown up.

The death roll resulting from the attack on and defense of Antwerp has not been compiled, and probably the full details will never be known, but all accounts describe it as being extremely large. The Germans, although their big guns cleared a path for them, had to sacrifice many lives in crossing the rivers and canals and in driving out the defenders, who held the intrenchments until the last.

The stubbornness of the Belgians and of those who went to their assistance cost them dearly, also, so that both sides will have long casualty lists. Of the loss of life in the city and the damage there are no reliable data available as yet.

The railway stations were made a mark for the shells from the big guns, but according to some of those who have reached here, the cathedral, which is on the other side of the city, nearer the Scheldt, while struck, was not badly damaged. The inmates of the hospitals and other institutions were removed on Thursday or earlier, so that they were well out of the way before the Germans arrived.

The Rotterdam Courant hears from a reliable source that the Belgians themselves destroyed the oil tanks in Antwerp, while another report indicates that Fort Waelhem was also destroyed by the Belgians.

From Rosendaal also comes the report that the Stuivenberg Hospital in Antwerp was hit by two bombs while the attack was in progress. Three hundred wounded soldiers in the hospital were removed to ships.

The correspondent of the Central News at Amsterdam, describing the wild flight of the people of Antwerp into Holland, says that one of the most distressing features was the large number of insane persons released from the asylum. Many of these are now roaming the country, creating fear and exciting disorders. The Dutch Government has issued an order warning the public not to act hastily in the cases of these unfortunates.

Many Dutch towns are filled with Belgian refugees. Flushing, Breda, Rotterdam, Rosendaal, The Hague, Amsterdam Terneuzen, Maastricht, and Dordrecht are so crowded with strangers that the streets are almost impassable. And still they come. The railway companies and many boat lines are transporting the refugees without charge. The Holland-Amerika steamship line is affording shelter to 1,000 persons here. The Dutch soldiers are feeding the refugees, distributing baskets of bread and meat as generously as is possible.

Refugees who arrived in London this afternoon from Antwerp brought the report from Ostend that a greater part of the Belgian Army had escaped from Antwerp.

While great crowds of refugees cross and recross the Dutch frontier in a frantic endeavor to get out of the danger zone, steamers coming to England from Ostend again are crowded with refugees of all classes. The rich and the poor are huddled together. Some remain at the ports of their debarkation, but many are proceeding to London, where relief committees provide lodgings and food. Several pathetic reunions among those who already have arrived here have occurred in the rooms of the committees. One woman who had become separated from her husband in the flight from Antwerp found him as he was making inquiries for her. Another fashionably dressed woman opened her purse to show that 5 francs was all she had left in the world. A middle-aged couple from the fashionable quarter of Antwerp were without means of any kind. The woman remarked: "Last week we were rich people. Now we are dependent on charity." A great many of the poorer refugees are being brought to England on Government transports.

LAYS ANTWERP'S RUIN AT ENGLAND'S DOOR

Berlin Prediction that Belgians Will One Day Denounce the "Seducer Across the Channel."

AMSTERDAM, (via London,) Oct. 10.—The Berliner Tageblatt makes the fall of Antwerp the text for a violent denunciation of England.

"Behind the Belgian defender," the newspaper says, "stood England, one may say, with whip in hand. When the thought rose in Belgian hearts to avoid useless destruction by capitulation, Britannia pronounced her veto. All were obliged to obey, even the King.

"This is the reason why the town, so full of life and industry, is severely damaged, and one day the maledictions of thousands will fall on the seducer across the Channel."

"All the News That's Fit to Print."

The New York Times.

THE WEATHER
Fair today and tomorrow, not much change in temperature; moderate west winds.
For full weather report see Page 11

VOL. LXIV...NO. 20,733. .....   NEW YORK, FRIDAY, OCTOBER 30, 1914.—SIXTEEN PAGES.   ONE CENT In Greater New York, Jersey City and Newark. | Elsewhere TWO CENTS.

TURKEY BEGINS WAR ON RUSSIA; WARSHIPS SHELL BLACK SEA PORTS; DEADLOCK ON LINES IN BELGIUM

CRIMEAN TOWN ATTACKED

The Breslau Bombards Theodosia—Goeben Sinks Two Ships.

NOVOROSSYSK SHELLED, TOO

Another Report Says the Hamidieh Only Demanded Caucasian Town's Surrender.

TOKIO, Friday, Oct. 30, 11:15 A. M.—The Russian Embassy here announces that Turkey has opened war on Russia.

Turkey is the tenth nation to enter the war. The other nine in the order of their beginning hostilities are: Austria, Servia, Germany, Russia, France, Montenegro, Belgium, Great Britain, and Japan.

Special Cable to THE NEW YORK TIMES.
PETROGRAD, Oct. 29. (Dispatch to The London Times.)—Turkey has begun hostilities by bombarding peaceful seacoast towns. Messages just received at Petrograd announce the simultaneous appearance this morning of the cruiser Breslau off Theodosia, Caucasia, and the cruiser Hamidieh off Novorossysk.

The German-Turkish warships shelled these unfortified places.

THEODOSIA, Crimea, via Petrograd, Oct. 29.—From 9:30 to 10:30 o'clock this morning a Turkish cruiser with three funnels bombarded the railway station and city, damaging the Cathedral, the Greek Church, a pier, and some sheds.

One soldier was wounded.

A branch of the Russian Bank of Foreign Commerce was set on fire.

At the conclusion of the bombardment the cruiser departed in a southerly direction.

NOVOROSSYSK, Caucasia, via Petrograd, Oct. 29.—The Turkish cruiser Hamidieh, which arrived here today, demanded the surrender of the city and the Government properties, threatening in case of refusal to bombard the town.

The Turkish Consul and other officials were arrested.

The cruiser withdrew.

The Turkish-German alliance is demonstrated in this photo of a Turkish artillery crew under the command of German officers.

Torpedoes the Yalta and Kazbek—Many Lost with Latter.

LONDON, Thursday, Oct. 30.—A Petrograd dispatch to Reuter's Telegram Company says:

"A dispatch from Kertch, a seaport in the Crimea, reports that near Takol Lighthouse the Russian steamer Yalta, from the Caucasus, was sunk by a torpedo launched by the Turkish cruiser Goeben. The crew and passengers were saved.

"The steamer Kazbek, which went to the rescue, was struck by two torpedoes and sank. Many persons aboard were drowned."

GIANT SUBMARINES TESTED BY GERMANS

Said to be Four Times the Size of Existing Craft—Can Cruise For Forty Days.

Special Cable to THE NEW YORK TIMES.
LONDON, Oct. 29.—The Daily Mail's Copenhangen correspondent says it is reported from Hamburg that two giant submarines are making trial trips at the mouth of the Elbe.

They are said to be four times the size of any existing submarines and to be able to keep at sea for forty days without having to replenish or even join mother ships.

At the outbreak of the war Germany was credited with having thirty submarines, of which twenty-four were kept in commission during 1913.

The latest known series, beginning with U 21, are 213 feet long, with a beam of 20 feet, and have three torpedo tubes and two guns mounted forward. Details of these vessels are not obtainable owing to the secrecy that shrouded their construction, but it is known that they have a surface speed of 17 knots and an under-water speed of about 12. Their average cruising speed will not exceed 10 knots, and this gives them a cruising range of about 1,000 miles under their own fuel. They can remain submerged about ten hours.

CANADIAN BORDER TALKING OF INVASION

Fear That Germans and Austrians Living in the United States May Attempt It.

Special to The New York Times.
OTTAWA, Ontario, Oct. 29.—Reports have reached here of a feeling of nervousness at certain places along the international border over the supposed danger of an invasion by Germans and Austrians living across the line.

Such fears are declared to be unnecessary because the Government is fully cognizant of conditions along the border, and in addition there will be from now until the end of the war a force of approximately 40,000 men mobilized and under arms in different parts of the country. These include about 10,000 on guard duty and home defense, and 30,000 in training for overseas service. This whole body would be an effective protection against any possible raid.

Summary of War News.

The Russian Embassy in Tokio announced this morning that Turkey had begun war on Russia. A Turkish cruiser yesterday bombarded Theodosia, in the Crimea, inflicting considerable damage. The Turkish cruiser Hamidieh appeared off Novorossysk, in the Caucasus, and demanded the surrender of the city, but departed without firing.

The French War Office announced the capture of German trenches in the region between the Aisne and the Argonne, and the repulse of all German attacks. A Bordeaux dispatch received in Washington told of the dislodging of some German outposts along the frontier between Moselle and the Vosges.

The German General Headquarters gave out a statement to the effect that the Germans were slowly gaining ground south of Nieuport and making good progress west of Lille. It also reported the repulse of French attacks southwest of Verdun and the occupation of the main French position.

Petrograd advices say that the main German armies in Poland have been widely separated and are in full retreat. On the East Prussian frontier both sides claim success.

The German cruiser Emden, flying the Japanese flag, entered the Harbor of Penang in the Straits Settlements and sank the Russian cruiser Jemtchug and a French destroyer.

The agent of the American Committee for Belgian Relief sends word to London that he fears the hungry Belgians, in desperation, may attack the authorities in some of the towns, which would be followed, he says, by great loss of life.

"All the News That's Fit to Print."

The New York Times.

THE WEATHER
Fair today and tomorrow; diminishing northwest winds.
☞For full weather report see Page 13.

VOL. LXIV...NO. 20,740. ...   NEW YORK, FRIDAY, NOVEMBER 6, 1914.—EIGHTEEN PAGES.   ONE CENT In Greater New York, Jersey City and Newark |

ALLIES LOSE AND RETAKE TRENCHES; KAISER WATCHES BATTLE IN FRANCE; RUSSIANS SEIZE TURKISH TOWNS

GERMANS ATTACK AT ARRAS

French Report the Result of a Day's Fierce Fighting a Draw.

KAISER DIRECTS A BATTLE

Sees the British Repulse Several Desperate Charges of His Men Near Armentieres.

GAIN FOR GERMANS AT YPRES

Berlin Also Announces Progress Near Lille, in the Argonne, and in the Vosges.

Kaiser Wilhelm and his staff touring one of the battlefields on the French front.

PARIS, Nov. 5.—Violent fighting today, particularly in the neighborhood of Arras, resulted in the repulse of the Germans, while the progress of the Allies in several directions is chronicled in the French official reports. Tonight's War Office communication says:

There is no new information on the operations at the north of the Lys.'

In a violent offensive movement by the Germans north of Arras we lost a few trenches, which later were retaken.

In the Argonne (region of St. Hubert) all the German attacks have been successfully repulsed.

Concerning the remainder of the battle front there is nothing of importance to report.

The official announcement given out this afternoon said:

On our left wing the allied forces have made slight progress to the east of Nieuport, on the right bank of the Yser. From Dixmude to the Lys the German attacks were renewed yesterday, but at a number of points with lessened energy, particularly with regard to the actions of their infantry.

The Franco-British lines have at no point drawn back, and our troops, undertaking the offensive, have made notable progress in several directions.

Between the region of La Bassée and the Somme the day was notable particularly for an artillery contest.

In the region of Roye we have maintained our occupation of Le Quesnoy-en-Santerre, and advanced perceptibly in the direction of Andrecy.

On the centre, between the Oise and the Moselle, there has been a recrudescence of the activity of the Germans, manifested particularly by their artillery fire.

Summing up, it may be said that the attacks of the enemy at various points on our front have been repulsed, in some instances after an engagement which lasted all day long.

On our right wing there is nothing new to report.

Belgians Repulsed, Berlin Reports.

BERLIN, (via London,) Nov. 5.—The German General Headquarters issued the following statement today:

Yesterday the Belgians, assisted by British and French troops, made a fierce attack by way of Nieuport between the sea and the inundated area, but they were easily repulsed.

Near Ypres, southwest of Lille and south of Berry au Bac, in the Argonne region, and in the Vosges our attacks are making progress.

BRITISH ROUT GERMANS AS KAISER WATCHES

Special Cable to THE NEW YORK TIMES.

IN NORTHERN FRANCE, Nov. 5, (Dispatch to The London Daily Chronicle.)—From the sea coast the tide of war in Belgium has flowed toward the south for two days. Now the Germans have been fiercely attacking the allied line. Heavy reinforcements of first line troops have been hurried up from Ghent and Bruges and thrown at once into the fighting zone.

The German attack was especially severe at two points in the Allies' long and thinly held line. An enormous mass of German infantry was hurled against Armentières. Around Arras the Germans launched two army corps against the Allies' defensive position. Both at Armentières and Arras the enemy was supported by a number of guns of heavy calibre.

At Armentières they brought to bear against our trenches a new type of mortar which throws a projectile weighing several hundred pounds. The ground around Armentières being too soft and yielding to sustain without artificial support the weight of this mortar, under cover of night the Germans dug a deep pit, filled it with concrete and mounted their pet gun on a wooden platform. At dawn they got to work and raked the Allies trenches with high-angle shell fire, the projectiles from

the mortar falling plump into the trenches. Despite their elaborate preparations the results of the shelling were disappointing. The shells buried themselves deep in the parapet of the trenches, making huge holes where they struck and giving the British a mud bath. On their impact these shells found no resistance from the soft clay-like soil, and their destructive force was therefore reduced to a minimum. An officer whose regiment was exposed to the full effects of the mortar fire, says that it did not put a single man out of action.

British Snug in Their Bomb-Proofs.

The advance trenches were subjected to severe shelling for three hours. The British dug themselves snugly into cover. Their trenches were furnished with bomb-proof shelters, where at the hottest moments of the bombardment the men took refuge. According to all the theories of all the German General Staff, three hours' bombardment by these heavy mortars should have reduced any army to pulp. The British gave no sign of life, and so, interpreting their silence significantly, the German commanders ordered their masses of infantry to carry the trenches which they concluded must be already filled with dead.

The assaulting columns came on in close formation. The word had been passed around and the British crept from their bombproof shelters and manned the trenches. So quietly was the manoeuvre executed that the attacking Germans had no suspicion of the deadly surprise in store for them. The British batteries had as yet not come into action. They were cleverly hidden in the fields behind and covered with brushwood. Then the guns spoke, and many German soldiers went down to rise no more. The British shells made great rents in the oncoming closely packed ranks of the Germans. Their advance stopped dead, and the survivors of the attacking columns went to earth, where they proceeded frantically to dig themselves into cover with their intrenching tools. The British infantry rifle fire found them by this time and punished them terribly.

Fought Under the Kaiser's Eye.

The attack was under imperial and royal auspices, for the Kaiser and the King of Saxony were present at the local German headquarters.

After another hour of shell fire directed upon our whole line, the mud-stained men who, molelike, had burrowed into the earth, crawled forth and, pulling themselves upright, faced the British bullets again. Shrapnel and rifle fire had no difficulty in finding these human targets. One could not help admiring the bravery of men who marched calmly and slowly toward certain death. That dull, gray-clad German line, urged forward by its officers, came on, leaving behind it at each step a trail of dead and dying.

The German artillery had ceased, for its infantry was creeping closer and closer to our trenches; but the fire from the trenches was telling, and under it the numbers of the assaulting columns were rapidly dwindling. No soldiers that ever faced an enemy could stand against this bullet storm. For the second time the German infantry wavered; then it went down as one man and sought cover. The attacking forces were an easy target for the British gunners and riflemen.

The minutes went by, and it became clear that if the Germans stayed where they were they must be annihilated. Their officers thought so, too, and ordered a fresh advance; but the men who had passed through such a hellish ordeal showed no inclination to rise up and close with the enemy.

Germans Break and Flee.

Here it was that the British chance came. The terrible punishment sustained in the advance had practically demoralized the Germans. Suddenly the British artillery and rifle fire ceased. A low word of command ran along the trenches. The mud-covered English appeared above ground; they clambered into the open; other lines followed the first; bayonets were fixed, and the khaki swarm swung forward. The coming of the British stimulated the hesitating German infantry into activity. They fired one volley, then sprang to their feet and went to the rightabout.

One line sought to cover the retreat. With fixed bayonets they faced the advancing British. A long, low murmur of satisfaction ran along the British front. The men broke into a cheer as they closed with the Germans, and bayonet met bayonet. There was thrust and parry, a swaying mass of struggling men in khaki and gray at death grips. Now it separated into two lines and broke clear. The men in gray were running and those in khaki were cheering—or attempting to cheer, for a stiff cross-country run with a bayonet fight at the end is trying to wind and limb. Back went the Germans and in pursuit went the British.

The Germans rallied around the mortar which earlier had been so active in shelling the British position. A desperate hand-to-hand struggle took place, the British devoting all their energies to capturing the gun. Its German defenders had fallen, and the prize was in English hands.

ARMENIAN CITIES TAKEN

Russians Report Victories Near Border—Turks Abandon Wounded.

BRITISH ANNEX CYPRUS

Turks Invade Persia—Accused of Trying to Force That Country to Help.

THE ALLIES DECLARE WAR

German Officer with a Plan to Blow Up the Suez Canal Sentenced to Prison for Life.

Special Cable to THE NEW YORK TIMES.

PETROGRAD, Nov. 5. (Dispatch to The London Daily Telegraph.)—News has reached Tiflis that the Turks suffered great losses in opposing the crossing of their frontier by the Russian Army. The entire battlefield was covered with their dead an dwounded. The feeling in the Ottoman Army is much depressed.

The Russian artillery was very skillfully handled nad struck panic into the ranks of the enemy.

On the eve of the outbreak of the war the Turkish Armenians were pitilessly plundered, and an army of them were arrested. The appearance of the Russian troops had a very tranquillizing effect, and the harvesting of the cotton crop has been resumed.

A large number of refugees from Turkish Armenia, who arrived at Odessa and expressed a wish to fight in the Russian Army are being sent round to Caucasia, where they will be embodied in a special corps.

PETROGRAD, Nov. 5.—A Turkish Army 90,000 strong, consisting of the Ninth, Tenth, and Eleventh Army Corps, is massed along the Caucasian frontier, according to the Novoe Vremya. Many villages have been occupied by Turkish outposts.

This Turkish Army the Novoe Vremya continues, would consist under normal conditions of 80 battalions of infantry, 60 batteries of artillery with 250 guns, and 40 squadrons of regular cavalry, but to it have been added 50 squadrons of Kurd cavalry, amounting to 20,000 men.

The following official communication has been received from the Russian General Staff:

In Caucasia one of our columns suddenly attacked the enemy near Ardost, (fifteen miles south of Kars, near the boundary of Turkish Armenia.) The Turks fled, abandoning their wounded.

Having dislodged the Turks from the village of Id, (about sixty miles west of Ardost, over the line into Turkish Armenia,) we took a great quantity of food. After a violent combat our troops seized Khorasan (in Turkish Armenia, thirty miles southeast of Id) and Col-Karaderbent. One hundred Cossacks attacked the trenches of the enemy and sabred the Turkish infantry.

One of our columns, having passed through difficult roads for a distance of fifty-three miles in thirty hours, encountered the Turks at Myssoune and Diyadin, (about thirty miles west of Bayazid, which is the capital of the Sanjak of Bayazid.) We dispersed a large body of Kurds and occupied Diyadin, where we took munitions of war and many prisoners. On Nov. 3 we occupied Bayazid, where we routed the Turkish troops, who resisted strongly.

AMERICAN MARINES LANDED AT BEIRUT?

Our Citizens in Constantinople Said to be in Danger and Preparing to Depart.

PARIS, Nov. 5.—The Temps has received a report stating that American marines have been landed at Beirut, Syria, for the protection of American interests.

GENEVA, Nov. 5.—A telegram has been received here from an American business man in Constantinople saying that Americans in the Turkish capital are in danger for the reason that the Turks cannot distinguish between Englishmen and Americans.

Continuing, this American declares that all business in Turkey is at a standstill, that the country is virtually in the hands of the Germans, and that all American business men are ready to depart.

According to advices reaching Geneva from Munich, fourteen German naval officers and fifty sailors, all in uniform, have left Munich for Turkey. They are traveling by way of Vienna.

LONDON, Nov. 5.—Telegraphing from Alexandria, Egypt, under date of Tuesday, the correspondent of Reuter's Telegram Company says:

"The Turkish authorities tried to prevent the departure of the British officials and other foreign subjects from Beirut, but the intervention of the American Consul in their behalf was successful. It was explained, however, that the idea of the detention was not to keep them as hostages, but to avoid the semblance of a final rupture, as the feeling there is resentful toward the Germans for plunging Turkey into war.

"The presence of the American cruiser North Carolina is expected to exercise a salutary influence on the popular feeling."

Special to The New York Times.

WASHINGTON, Nov. 5.—The Navy Department has not yet been advised that American marines have been landed at Beirut. The armored cruisers North Carolina and Tennessee are in Turkish waters, however, one of them being at Beirut, and officials of the Department said to-night that there would be nothing surprising if the marines were sent ashore.

While there have been no reports to the Navy Department indicating immediate danger of anti-Christian outbreaks in the neighborhood of Beirut, the commanding officers of the cruisers have full discretionary authority as to sending parties ashore.

British and French subjects in Turkey may elect to remain or depart, according to a statement made by the Turkish Minister of the Interior to American Ambassador Morgenthau.

The American Embassy is facilitating the departure of subjects of the allied powers in Turkey, as well as looking after American missionaries and interests.

PUTS GERMAN LOSSES AT 1,750,000 MEN

More Than One-Fourth of the First Line Gone, British Writer Estimates.

Special Cable to THE NEW YORK TIMES.

LONDON, Nov. 5.—Hilaire Belloc, writing to The London Daily Mail, estimates the German losses to date at 1,750,000 men.

"I know," he writes, "that this figure looks startlingly large, but the various steps by which it is arrived at are not, I think, open to criticism. It would be easy, by a little manipulation of the figures, to make out very much larger totals. I have attempted, on the contrary, to fix the lowest conceivable minimum."

The figure, 1,750,000, includes losses by sickness, fatigue, and accidents. The strict German losses in the field—men hit or caught—he puts at more than 1,250,000.

"These losses," he writes, "have, almost up to within the last two weeks or so, fallen in the main upon the trained troops of the enemy and with particular severity upon his body of officers. This loss of nearly 1,750,000 at very least, which has already fallen for the most part on the trained army, and equals the untrained mass behind it, has fallen most heavily on the first and best. It comes to more than a fifth of all the two possible categories combined; more than a fifth of those who can ever make real soldiers, and of these more than a quarter of the first line.

"There," he concludes, "is the chief military feature of the struggle at the present moment. Of all the available material for anything approaching a true army, a quarter has already gone."

WAR NOW NEAR ENGLAND.

Dispatch Bearer Under Shrapnel in the Morning Dines in London.

Special Cable to THE NEW YORK TIMES.

LONDON, Nov. 5.—As illustrating the nearness of London to the scene of the great battle in Belgium, a dispatch bearer who was seated at a table in one of the most fashionable restaurants tonight was dodging shrapnel this morning.

Moonlight, he told friends, had caused a heavy death rate among the Red Cross as they went about fields removing the wounded. Going about on dark nights with torches has been abandoned, and it is necessary for those on mercy bent to grope about to find wounded, who sometimes are Germans. The removal of the dead has cost additional lives among the British.

DOYLE TO WRITE WAR BOOK.

Material for It to be Gathered Direct from the Front.

Special Cable to THE NEW YORK TIMES.

LONDON, Friday, Nov. 6.—It is understood that Sir Arthur Conan Doyle means to write a book on the war, gathering material direct from the front and from those who have been there.

NEW AID TO SURGERY.

Dane Invents Apparatus to Photograph Interior of Stomach.

Special Cable to THE NEW YORK TIMES.

COPENHAGEN, Nov. 4, (Dispatch to The London Morning Post.)—An apparatus which should prove of considerable service to the surgical profession has been invented by M. Shirn Fredricksen. It photographs the interior of the stomach through the mouth, thus enabling doctors accurately to locate cancers, ulcers, and other abnormal affections.

The apparatus has been tested, and is said to have given successful results.

"All the News That's Fit to Print."

The New York Times.

THE WEATHER
Fair today and Sunday; warmer Sunday; light northwest winds.
☞For full weather report see Page 17.

VOL. LXIV...NO. 20,741. ...   NEW YORK, SATURDAY, NOVEMBER 7, 1914.—EIGHTEEN PAGES.   ONE CENT In Greater New York, Jersey City and Newark.

TSING-TAU SURRENDERS TO JAPANESE; GERMAN FORTS HELD OUT 2 MONTHS; BRITISH ADMIT LOSS OF GOOD HOPE

LAST ASSAULT WON A FORT

Then Germans Opened Negotiations Which Ended in Submission.

STOOD A SIEGE OF 65 DAYS

Garrison of 5,000 Pitted Against 25,000 Japanese Troops and Allied Warships.

HEAVY LOSS ON BOTH SIDES

Last Days of the Siege Marked by the Dropping of Bombs from Aeroplanes.

TOKIO, Saturday, Nov. 7, 11:25 A. M.—It is officially announced that the German fortress of Tsing-tau has surrendered to the Japanese and British forces.

It is officially announced that the first step in bringing about the surrender of the fortress occurred at midnight last night when the infantry charged and occupied the middle fort of the first line of defense. In this operation they took 200 prisoners.

The charge was led by Gen Yoshimi Yamada at the head of companies of infantry and engineers.

The Germans hoisted the white flag at 7 o'clock this morning at the Weather Observation Bureau of Tsingtau. The quick capitulation of the Germans was the cause of much surprise to the men of the army and navy operating against it and also to the people of Tokio.

In yesterday's official communication regarding the progress of operations it was announced that the bombardment continued, and that aeroplanes were dropping bombs and circulars into the besieged port. The circulars warned the civilian inhabitants not to take any part in military operations.

It had been suggested by the Japanese General Staff that the assault on the main positions around Tsingtau, the Iltis, Bismarck, and Moltke forts might be deferred until after the capture of the five forts south of the Haipo River, where behind strong defenses the German artillery and infantry were making a determined stand. These five forts are 2,400 feet from the Japanese trenches.

Complete casualty lists containing the names of the killed and wounded in the operations around Tsing-tau up to yesterday show that the British had two killed and eight wounded, their wounded including two Majors, and that the Japanese had 200 killed and 878 wounded. The total losses of the Japanese and Germans up to the time of the surrender were heavy.

SIEGE LASTED 65 DAYS.

Japan Engaged to Restore Kiao-Chau to China if Victorious.

The fall of Tsing-tau ends the most picturesque of the minor phases of the great world war now raging. On two continents and in many of the islands of the seas where colonies of the warring nations were planted combats of more or less interest have taken place, garrisons have been captured and towns occupied peacefully, but in the little German concession of the Shantung Peninsula of China there has been waged, on a reduced scale, a conflict which from all accounts has duplicated nearly all the features of the war in Europe, so far as the capture of fortified positions is concerned. The taking of Tsing-tau deprives Germany of her last foot of possessions on the Asiatic mainland, as well as her last strategic position outside of the German Empire in Europe.

For two months the little German garrison, nearly wholly composed of reservists who were living or doing business in China, held out against the land and sea attacks of the Japanese and of certain British detachments of both white and Indian troops that found themselves in China at the outbreak of the war. What the losses of the garrison have been are not known, but the official Japanese and British reports have indicated that Tsing-tau was taken at heavy cost of men on the part of the Allies.

WENT DOWN WITH 900 MEN

British Report Says Cradock's Flagship Caught Fire and Foundered.

LONDON, Nov. 6.—It is officially announced by the Admiralty that the British cruiser Good Hope caught fire during the engagement with the Germans off the coast of Chile last Sunday and foundered.

The Admiralty statement says it is believed that the British cruiser Monmouth, which the Germans reported as having been sunk, was run ashore. The cruiser Canopus, it adds, was not present at the time of the fight.

The Admiralty has not divulged the source of its news regarding the details of the battle, or whether it has heard from any of the crippled ships. The fact, however, that it says the Glasgow is not extensively damaged leads to the inference that she has reported from some port not far from the scene of the fight.

A dispatch to The Central News from Lima, Peru, says the Glasgow has arrived at Puerto Montt, Chile, and it may be from her that the news has come.

The statement says:

"The Admiralty now has received trustworthy information about the action on the Chilean coast.

"During Sunday, the 1st of November, the Good Hope, Monmouth and Glasgow came up with the Scharnhorst, Gneisenau, Leipzig, and Dresden. Both squadrons were steaming south in a strong wind and a considerable sea.

Germans Held Off.

"The German squadron declined action until sunset, when the light gave it an important advantage. The action lasted an hour.

"Early in the action both the Good Hope and Monmouth took fire, but fought until nearly dark, when a serious explosion occurred on the Good Hope and she foundered.

"The Monmouth hauled off at dark, making water badly, and appeared unable to steam away. She was accompanied by the Glasgow, which had meanwhile during the whole action fought the Leipzig and the Dresden. On the enemy again approaching the wounded Monmouth, the Glasgow, which also was under fire from one of the armored cruisers, drew off.

"The enemy then attacked the Monmouth again, but with what result is not known. The Glasgow is not extensively damaged and has very few casualties.

"Neither the Otranto nor the Canopus was engaged."

BATTLE RAGING AROUND YPRES

British and French Reports Tell of Advance—Berlin Also Claims Progress.

PARIS, Nov. 6, 10:40 P. M.—This official bulletin was issued by the War Office tonight:

To the north the fighting continues to be severe. According to the latest reports our offensive was proceeding in the region to the south and east of Ypres.

In the region of Arras and from Arras to the Oise several German attacks have been repulsed.

In the region of the Aisne we have retaken, to the east of Vailly, the village of Soupir, which was lost the other day.

In the Argonne the enemy keeps attacking violently, but without result.

On the heights of the Meuse and to the east of Verdun we have captured some trenches.

An afternoon bulletin said:

There was no perceptible modification, during the day or yesterday, anywhere on the front. The fighting continued between Dixmude and the Lys with the same characteristics as previously and without any marked advance or retirement at any point. There was violent cannonading to the north of Arras, and also directed upon Arras, without result for the enemy.

The German effort in Belgium and in the north of France continues. The Germans seem to have undertaken changes in the composition of their forces which are operating in this region, and are reinforcing their reserve corps, composed of new organizations, which have been very severely tested, with active troops with the idea of undertaking a new offensive movement, or at least to mitigate the bloody checks which have been inflicted upon them.

Between the Somme and the Oise and between the Oise and the Meuse there have been minor actions. We have consolidated our advance on the village of Andechy, to the west of Roye. A column of German wagons has been destroyed by the fire of our artillery, at long range, in the region of Nampcel, to the northeast of the forest of Aigue.

Near Berry-au-Bac we have retaken the village of Sapigneul, which had been captured by the Germans.

There has been a furious fight in the Argonne, where, as a result of fighting with the bayonet, our troops drove the Germans back.

In the Woevre district fresh attacks by the enemy have been repulsed.

To the southeast and to the east of the Grande Couronne of Nancy, in the region of the forest of Parroy and between Baccarat and Blamont, our advance posts have been attacked by mixed detachments of the enemy whose movements everywhere were checked.

"All the News That's Fit to Print."

The New York Times.

THE WEATHER

Fair, colder today; fair tomorrow; strong northwest winds on the coast diminishing.

VOL. LXIV...NO. 20,751. ....   NEW YORK, TUESDAY, NOVEMBER 17, 1914.—TWENTY PAGES.   ONE CENT In Greater New York, Jersey City and Newark. | TWO CENTS

GERMANS WIN BIG VICTORY IN POLAND; RUSSIAN ATTACK SETS CRACOW AFIRE; SNOW AND FLOOD HALT BELGIAN FIGHT

23,000 RUSSIANS TAKEN

Several Army Corps, Hurled Back, Forced to Abandon Some Guns.

KAISER REVEALS DANGER

German Public Informed at Last That the Czar's Hosts Are at the Frontiers.

RETREAT A GLORIOUS FEAT

Fatherland's Troops as Proud of It as the British Are of Their Withdrawal from Mons.

BERLIN, Nov. 16, (by Wireless Telegraph to London.)—This official communication was given out this afternoon:

The fighting in the east continues. Yesterday our troops operating in East Prussia repulsed the enemy in the region south of Stallupoenen. Troops from West Prussia successfully resisted the advance of Russian forces at Soldau and after a successful battle at Lipno drove them back in the direction of Plock.

Strong Russian forces are advancing along the right bank of the Vistula River. In this fighting we made 500 prisoners and captured ten machine guns up to yesterday.

A decision has been arrived at in the battle which has been going on for the last few days in continuation of our successes at Wloclawsk, in Russian Poland, on the Vistula, thirty miles northwest of Plock, where several Russian army corps in opposition to us were driven back beyond Kutno. According to the present reports we made 23,000 prisoners and captured over twenty machine guns, as well as some cannon, the number of which has not yet been ascertained.

Included in the information given to the press today in official quarters is the following:

Prince Dolgoroukoff, in an article appearing in the Russky Wufdomosty, published in Moscow, demands vainly the liberation of Russian Jews from special legislation.

People Told of Russian Danger.

BERLIN, (via London,) Nov. 16.—Germany again is under the sign of the Russian danger to quote the astrological metaphor frequently used by the Germans.

The combined German and Austrian armies, which by a well-timed and well-executed change in front and with timely reinforcements were able to sweep through Poland to the line of the Vistula and threaten Warsaw and Ivangorod, were in turn outflanked by the masses of Russians, and have fallen back to their own frontiers. The timid inhabitants of the border regions are leaving their homes for the interior.

The professional pessimists draw long faces and a certain amount of disquietude is being manifested in civilian circles in Berlin. There are many indications, however, that the retirement before Warsaw is not that of a beaten army, but of one which, realizing that it had failed in its object of a surprise campaign, promptly changed its strategic plan and retreated. Predictions are hazardous, but the great news of the next fortnight may come when the armies facing one another meet on Poland's wintery fields.

The common report is that Gen. von Hindenburg is ready to accept or give battle on the new ground he has chosen. The eighth army intrusted with the defense of East Pruseia again has a new commander. It originally was commanded by Gens. von Prittwitz and Gaffon and passed into the hands of Gen. von Hindenburg and Chief of Staff von Ludendorff. The new commander is Gen. von Bülow, one of a family of military brothers of high rank.

The retirement from Warsaw resembles in many respects that from the environs of Paris in September, the Germans in both cases assuming the great risk of running out of ammunition and supply trains, and exposing their flank and rear, hoping to smash a supposed demoralized army. They had hoped, in the Warsaw campaign, like Stonewall Jackson at Chancellorsville, to catch the enemy's right wing napping and roll up that portion of it west of the Vistula and press across the river and capture Warsaw. Holding strong the line from East Prussia on the north to Galicia on the south, they expected to be able to stand off Russia and devote their principal attention to the western campaign.

That is why, it is said, Gen. von Hindenburg in September transferred his headquarters from East Prussia to Breslau, in Silesia, acting in concert with the Austrian commanders' change of front against the Russians invading Western Galicia from the north.

The Russians were on the alert, however, and quickly retired to the safe side of the Vistula. The only important fighting was at Opatow, on the extreme southern flank. The Russians massed their troops in a generally north and south line behind the Vistula. They rushed their troops by railway, but were barely in time, for the Germans were actually entering one suburb of Warsaw at the same time the Siberian troops detrained in the town. The Germans had outrun their heavy artillery, which was delayed by bottomless roads. Plenty of Russian reinforcements came and the fighting became desperate and a retreat was finally ordered.

Proud of Their Retreat.

The Germans say they are as proud of this retreat as the English are of theirs after Mons. In another respect the retirement from Warsaw is like that before Paris. The German headquarters, it is said, forgot its geography.

In France a headquarters bulletin announced the beginning of the retreat promptly, but for a fortnight it gave virtually no news of the subsequent stages, mentioning in that period only three places. The German people were told promptly that the attempt against Warsaw was abandoned Oct. 28, but were not informed until Nov. 8 how far the retirement had progressed. Then the Germans had withdrawn 100 miles.

Although there are no official reports to this effect, advices have reached Berlin in soldiers' letters and missives from the wounded that pessimism in the ranks is limited and that confidence is maintained. One great change is noted in these letters since this campaign began. Early in the war the enemy's ability was decried. Now the officers admit that the Russians fight bravely; that the French artillery is remarkable, and that Tommy Atkins is a first-rate fighting man.

LONDON, Tuesday, Nov. 17.—A dispatch to Reuter's Telegram Company from Amsterdam says:

"The Sub-Prefect of Marienwerder, West Prussia, has issued a proclamation of warning to the effect that the Russian Army is advancing between Thorn and Soldau, (East Prussia,) but that it is expected that it will be met by strong forces which will shortly force it into a decisive battle."

CRACOW BESIEGED, SAID TO BE BURNING

Sortie from Przemysl Fortress Repulsed With Heavy Loss by Russian Artillery and Cavalry.

ROME, Nov. 16.—A special dispatch from Petrograd to the Giornale d'Italia says that the overwhelming advance of the Russians toward Cracow is overcoming all obstacles, both the difficulties of the passes and the desperate resistance of the Austrians. Cracow is entirely besieged on the northeast.

A sortie from Przemysl has been repulsed by Russian artillery and cavalry, which inflicted severe losses on the Austrians.

According to a dispatch from Venice to the same newspaper, Cracow is burning and its inhabitants are in flight.

Special Cable to THE NEW YORK TIMES.

LONDON, Tuesday, Nov. 17.—According to the Rome correspondent of The London Morning Post, news has reached Venice that part of Cracow is ablaze.

Cracow is invested on the north, and is expected to fall immediately. The inhabitants are in flight.

The Russian forces have made a very rapid advance and reached Cracow sooner than expected. For the Russians the fall of Cracow means the key to the industrial districts of Silesia, striking a vital economic blow at Germany.

Polish refugees and their families who have fled before the German invasion, encamped in the woods with what they managed to salvage of their belongings.

"All the News That's Fit to Print."

The New York Times.

THE WEATHER

Fair, warmer today; fair, colder Friday; south, shifting to west winds.

VOL. LXIV...NO. 20,753. ....   NEW YORK, THURSDAY, NOVEMBER 19, 1914.—EIGHTEEN PAGES.   ONE CENT In Greater New York Jersey City and Newark. | Elsewhere TWO CENTS

BIG GUNS IN DUEL ON FLANDERS FRONT; FRENCH IN A MINE TRAP NEAR ST. MIHIEL

Allowed to Win Village Which the Germans Then Blew Up.

DEADLOCK STILL IN BELGIUM

Both Sides Hold Their Ground in Muddy Trenches Around Ypres.

GERMANS GAIN NEAR CIREY

Berlin Reports the Taking by Storm of Chateau Chatillon and Neighboring Defenses.

PARIS, Nov. 18.—The following official bulletin was issued tonight:

The day has been marked by a very violent and almost uninterrupted connonade of our front in the north.

In the region of St. Mihiel the Germans have blown up the west part of Chauvoncourt, which they had mined.

There is nothing to report from other parts of the front.

The text of the afternoon communication was:

The day of yesterday, Nov. 17, passed much as did the day before. There were numerous artillery exchanges and some isolated attacks on the part of the enemy's infantry, all of which were repulsed.

From the North Sea to the Lys the front was subjected to a fairly active bombardment, particularly at Nieuport and to the east and to the south of Ypres.

Near Bixschoote the Zouaves, charging with the bayonet, brilliantly took possession of a forest which had been disputed between the enemy and ourselves for three days.

To the south of Ypres an offensive movement on the part of the enemy's infantry was repulsed by our troops. The English army also maintained its front.

From Arras to the Oise there is nothing new to report.

In the region of Craone our artillery on several occasions secured the advantage over the batteries of the enemy.

The bombardment of Rheims has continued. From Rheims to the Argonne there is nothing new to report.

In the region of St. Mihiel, in spite of counter-attacks by the Germans, we have retained in our possession the western part of the village of Chauvoncourt..

In Alsace the Landwehr battalions sent into the region of Ste. Marie-aux-Mines have had to be taken out for the reason that they lost one-half of their effective strength.

British Gain 500 Yards.

LONDON, Nov. 18.—The Official Information Bureau today gave out a statement as follows:

Our third division was subjected yesterday to a heavy attack, first from artillery and then from infantry, the brunt of both falling upon two battalions of the division. These were shelled out of their trenches, but they recovered after a brilliant counter-attack which drove the enemy back in disorder for some 500 yards.

During the day an attack was made also on a brigade of the second division. In this the enemy were repulsed with heavy loss.

Berlin Reports Argonne Successes.

BERLIN, (via London,) Nov. 18—An official communication issued today by the German General Headquarters says:

Fighting in West Flanders continues, and the situation on the whole remains unchanged.

In the forest of Argonne our attacks continue successfully. French sorties to the south of Verdun were repulsed.

An attack was made against our forces which had moved forward on the western bank of the River Meuse near St. Mihiel, and, although it was originally successful for the enemy, it broke down completely later on.

Our attack to the southeast of Cirey compelled the French to surrender some of their positions. The Château Châtillon was stormed and taken by our troops.

MAY BATTLE AGAIN ON WATERLOO FIELD

Germans Said to Have Constructed Concrete Trenches for a Winter Campaign.

Special Cable to THE NEW YORK TIMES
NORTHERN FRANCE, Nov. 18. (Dispatch to The London Daily Chronicle.) —A stinging hail storm swept the trenches in France and Belgium yesterday and covered them and the men imprisoned there with a white layer of icy-cold dampness.

At the time, which was toward midday, the heavy guns thundered from their concealed emplacements from Nieuport to La Bassée, and, since the German offensive was again due, the allied forces had to lie prone and wait. They waited patiently and bravely, although they were cold to the marrow and their clothes wet and sticking to their skins, their boots clogged with heavy mud, their feet soaked by the constant drip from their overcoats.

They await the next German offensive movement with confidence. Some are wondering whether another attack will be made before the end of the year, while others, apparently well informed, say that the Germans are on the point of retreating.

A Belgian who says he walked through the German lines from Brussels, informs me that German transport wagons have been choking the roads to Brussels for several days. He believes that these are being removed into a zone of safety before the fighting line has to be drawn back.

The Germans have a line of defense from Waterloo to Namur which they can utilize before defending the line of the Meuse. This line has been strongly intrenched. The field of Waterloo is said to be full of concrete trenches laid in such a way that they can be defended indefinitely and occupied in spite of the rigors of Winter and without causing discomfort to the troops. Here one of the great battles of the near future will be fought.

FIVE WARSHIPS JOIN FIRE.

Concentrate on Houses Where Germans Hid and Kill 1,700.

Special Cable to THE NEW YORK TIMES.

DUNKIRK, Nov. 18. (Dispatch to The London Daily News.)—A week ago the Germans near the coast noticed that the English warships' fire spared the houses on the sea front at Middelkerke. They accordingly took up their quarters in these houses.

Their plan became known to the British ships and the houses were suddenly bombarded fiercely by five vessels at once.

The German casualties were enormous. After the firing had ceased, stretcher parties went from house to house collecting the dead. A scouting officer watched the process and estimates the number of killed at 1,700.

PNEUMONIA IN THE TRENCHES.

Allies and Germans Have Many Cases—Some Remarkable Wounds.

Special Cable to THE NEW YORK TIMES.

BELGIAN COAST, Nov. 18. (Dispatch to The London Standard.)—There are many cases of pneumonia among the allied troops, and the disease is causing still more serious ravages among the troops of the Germans.

"It is marvelous," said a doctor to me today, "that there has been no epidemic during the Autumn. I attribute this largely to the fact that the bulk of the fighting for several weeks past has taken place within range of the purifying sea breezes. We have not had to deal with a single case of enteric or dysentery. Rheumatic fever and pneumonia are what we have most to fear now. After a man reaches the age of 45 prolonged exposure is almost sure to cause rheumatism, and, of course, no younger man is immune from it. Officers of 50 or 55 and upward are lucky if they escape it. They may continue to carry on till the heart begins to be affected, but then collapse is inevitable."

Some remarkable wounds have been noted by the surgeons here—notably that of a man shot through the head. He went on firing for half an hour, and stopped only because he was blinded by blood. He remembered then that he had felt "a slight blow" on the back of his head. The bullet had passed through and come out of his cheek.

LOST 2,700 AT DIXMUDE.

Dutch Report Heavy German Casualties—Nieuport Wrecked.

LONDON, Nov. 18.—The correspondent of Reuter's Telegram Company at Amsterdam sends the following:

"According to The Telegraaf's Sluis correspondent, the Germans occupying Dixmude have suffered heavy losses. In fresh fighting which has taken place there they lost 2,700 men.

"The town of Nieuport is badly damaged. Heavy cannonading was heard Tuesday in the direction of Ypres, indicating a renewal of heavy fighting there.

"Fugitives say that additional submarines are being constructed at Zeebrugge."

SHELL BELGIAN COAST TOWNS.

British Ships Destroy a German Military Base Near Zeebrugge.

LONDON, Nov. 18.—A Rotterdam dispatch to The Daily Mail says:

"The British fleet received information Monday which led them to carry out a vigorous bombardment at Knocke and Zeebrugge, on the Belgian coast. The Solvay Company's works on the Bruges Ship Canal, which are being used as a base for German military trains, were wrecked. A train of five cars filled with soldiers was struck by a shell, took fire, and was destroyed. Much damage was done to the German stores and supplies."

FLOOD MAROONS FIGHTERS.

Germans, Caught Amid Water, Have to Keep Low or Be Fired At.

Special Cable to THE NEW YORK TIMES.

LONDON, Nov. 18.—A correspondent of The Daily Mail, describing the fighting amid floods near the Yser River, says:

"The first snow fell on the eve of King Albert's birthday. It is believed that the Germans suffered terrible distress, as their trenches were already half under water. But, in any case, the spectacle before the trenches on both sides is a thing to shrivel imagination. It is a marvel that the Germans can endure it at all.

"In places the water is continuously deep and there is no possibility of burying the dead which float hither and thither.

"Out of the flood rise certain islands and island houses. In one such spot several hundred Germans were gathered and they were treated as a cat treats a mouse. The artillery did not shell them nor did the machine guns fire, but when any one of the group endeavored to wade, one of the few marksmen in the neighboring trenches picked him off. It was death to go and death to remain. Surrender on such occasions is the only alternative.

"A similar fate met a succession of Germans, each of whom showed the finest form of courage, between the trenches. Just outside of this fenland, for some unknown reason, the fallen bough of a tree, lying some 200 yards in front of the Belgians, was desired by the enemy. One man after another slipped from the German trench and ran for the log. A marksman fired, always with effect, and twenty-two German soldiers, one in succession to the other, were shot down. Then only was the attempt given up.

"The tragedy of the floods is not yet over. One group of German soldiers, who must be suffering terribly from hunger, are still enclosed in houses from which the waters allow no escape."

VON KLUCK KNEW HIS QUARRIES

Figaro Says He Picked Out His Soissons Position in 1913.

Special Cable to THE NEW YORK TIMES.

PARIS, Nov. 18.—According to the Figaro, Gen. von Kluck knew the quarries near Soissons, which have proved such an effective barrier to the French advance, long before his army was compelled to seek their shelter after the defeat on the Marne.

The Soissons correspondent of the paper says that in the Spring of 1913 an elderly German registered as M. Kluck at the principal hotel of the town, where his affability charmed every one. He showed great interest in the quarries, which, owing to the friable nature of the stone, have merely a historical value because 200 Russians took refuge there in 1814 and offered a prolonged resistance until they were finally smoked out by Napoleon's troops. "M. Kluck" spent a good deal of time exploring them and listened attentively to the stories about the Russians. Soon afterward a German company bought the quarries, ostensibly as a mushroom farm, retaining possession until the outbreak of hostilities.

The hotel keeper and others who met "M. Kluck" now assert that he is the original of the photographs of the German Generalissimo.

ASSAILS PARIS CENSORSHIP.

Clemenceau Says It Suppressed a Soldier's Widow's Appeal.

Special Cable to THE NEW YORK TIMES.

PARIS, Nov. 18.—Two days ago Georges Clemenceau wrote an editorial in L'Homme Enchaîné in which he called the attention of the authorities to a soldier's widow who was not rece:ving adequate assistance since her husband's death. At the point where he inserted the woman's letter with the words: "I have received the following moving letter," the censor obliterated her appeal.

Now Mr. Clemenceau attacks the treatment accorded him with the bitterest sarcasm. The woman, he says, "asks France: 'What will you do for me who have given my husband's life?' What do you reply, Socialist seigneurs, who contemplate from your gilded armchairs the results of your congress of international brotherhood; or you, smiling augurs of radicalism and moderation? You reply with Blucher's famous expression: 'Halt's Maul!' ('Shut your mouth!'). You impose upon the widows of the men who have died for France. It is too much. I conjure you in the public interest to stop. Who are you to bid all France be silent? I pray you, reflect! reflect!"

ANOTHER GERMAN GUN BURST?

Spanish Rumor of the Explosion of a 42-Centimeter Mortar.

MADRID, (via Paris,) Nov. 18.—The newspaper Pueblo Vasco of Bilboa says that another German 42-centimeter mortar has burst, killing a number of the gunners.

The Germans, according to the newspaper, are carefully concealing the new catastrophe.

BELGIAN VILLAGERS EVICTED.

Ordered from Their Homes During German Target Practice.

AMSTERDAM. (via London.) Nov. 18. —The German authorities in Belgium today issued a proclamation, according to the Handelsblad, ordering everybody in St. Nicolas and the surrounding villages to quit their homes until further notice, "as the Germans will be practicing firing in this district."

St. Nicholas is a town in East Flanders, twenty miles northeast of Ghent, on the railroad to Antwerp.

GERMANS ANTICIPATED ATROCITY CHARGES

Handbook Issued in 1906 Contains Form for Replying to French Accusations.

Special Cable to THE NEW YORK TIMES.
PARIS, Nov. 18 (Dispatch to The London Daily News.)—Among the many instances of German foresight in preparing for the present war not the least curious is a book called "The Military Interpreter," by Capt. von Scharfenort, Professor and Librarian of the Berlin Academy of War. This volume, published in 1908, says the Temps, is composed of reports, letters, circulars and notices for use in France during the German occupation.

On Page 22 is this model letter to the Commander-in-Chief of the French army in reply to a circular accusing the German troops of numerous violations of international law:

Letter to the Generalissimo of the Enemy:
In a circular of the Minister of Foreign Affairs you have reproached the German troops with numerous violations of international law. The German troops are alleged to have rendered themselves guilty of acts of hostility against ambulances; of having taken prisoner M. A. in the midst of the ambulance corps organised by him; of having made use of explosive bullets; of having forced the peasants of the environs of S— to work at digging trenches under the fire of the fortress; of having attempted to send food and munition trains, &c., under cover of the sign adopted by the Geneva Convention, and, lastly, a doctor, while tending a wounded Prussian soldier is alleged to have been killed by him.

I have made inquiry with the view of learning if anything had taken place which could have been transformed by informants unworthy of credence or of evil intention into the monstrosities you have denounced. An inquiry of this kind offered difficulties all the greater, inasmuch as the statements were drawn up in a form extraordinarily vague for official assertions of so grave a character. Every indication of the name of the place and the time is completely wanting in the two cases in which reference is made to witnesses and their statements. In the case of the explosive bullets and the peasants being forced to dig trenches, neither the tenor of the evidence nor the names of the witnesses or informers were indicated.

The inquiry conducted on our side has found a really but singularly distorted basis for one alone of the accusations brought against the German troops. It is correct that M. A. was arrested and that he was occupied in tending the wounded, but his arrest was not effected in midst of the ambulances. It was caused by the suspicion he was in communication with the garrison of S—. As to the duration of his detention the military authority alone could decide.

With reference to all other statements I must declare them entirely invented.

ROBERTS'S BODY AT ASCOT.

Taken to His Home There by Special Train—Service at the House.

ASCOT, Nov. 18.—Covered with the Union Jack, and with his khaki hat and sword upon it, the coffin containing the body of Field Marshal Earl Roberts now lies in the small room in his modest residence here, in which the great soldier conducted family prayers and in which there are a small altar and a crucifix.

The coffin arrived from Folkestone by special train this afternoon. The ceremony which followed was of a most simple description.

The coffin was borne by employes of the late Field Marshal's estate to his home, where a brief service, attended by Lady Roberts and her daughters, and a few privileged friends, was conducted by the rector of Ascot.

KIPLING'S TRIBUTE TO LORD ROBERTS

Reproaches England for Refusing to Hear His 'Pleading in the Market Place.'

LONDON, Thursday, Nov. 19.—The Daily Telegraph publishes the following poem, by Rudyard Kipling:

LORD ROBERTS.
[Copyright, 1914, by Rudyard Kipling.]

He passed in the very battle-smoke
Of the war he had desired.
Three hundred miles of cannon spoke
When the Master Gunner died.

He passed to the very sound of the guns,
But before his eye grew dim
He had seen the faces of the sons
Whose sires had served with him.

He had touched their sword-hilts and
greeted each
With the old, sure word of praise;
And there was virtue in touch and
speech,
As it had been in old days.

So he dismissed them and took his rest,
And the steadfast spirit went forth
Between the adoring East and West
And the tireless guns in the North.

Clean, simple, valiant, well-beloved,
Flawless in faith and fame;
Whom neither ease nor honors moved
A hairsbreadth from his aim.

Never again the war-wise face,
The weighed and urgent word
That pleaded in the market-place—
Pleaded and was not heard!

Yet from his life a new life springs
Through all the hosts to come;
And glory is the least of things
That follow this man home.

This Canadian howitzer, so large that it had to be loaded with a hoist, is an example of the "big guns" used in WWI.

"All the News That's
Fit to Print."

The New York Times.

THE WEATHER
Fair today and Friday, not much
change in temperature; moderate west winds.
For full weather report see Page 17.

VOL. LXIV...NO. 23,781. .....   NEW YORK, THURSDAY, DECEMBER 17, 1914.—TWENTY PAGES.   ONE CENT

GERMANS SHELL THREE ENGLISH TOWNS; SCORES ARE KILLED AND MORE HURT; RAIDING SHIPS ESCAPE BRITISH FLEET

ATTACK ANGERS ENGLAND

Shelling of Unfortified Towns Arouses the Entire Country.

BUT IT FAILS TO FRIGHTEN

Worth Two Corps to Army, Says Newspaper—German Policy Called "Senseless."

MAY APPEAL TO NEUTRALS

Officials Hold That The Hague Convention Has Been Flagrantly Violated.

Special Cable to THE NEW YORK TIMES
LONDON, Dec. 16.—From a myriad of special editions of the afternoon papers London learned of the action on the east coast. The news created excitement and tense interest, but not the slightest apprehension, nor was there any trace whatsoever of panic. On the contrary, London was well pleased with the event, and perfectly confident of the outcome.

There is intense indignation over the bombardment of unfortified places, which is generally looked upon as a bit characteristic of the Germans. If the German action was designed to frighten England, it completely failed. Judging by the attitude of the London public, England is really well pleased that the Germans have finally come out, and there was the utmost confidence today that the attacking ships never would get back.

During the day the news came in fragments, and even at a late hour this evening there was nothing to indicate how extensive the action had been, nor what was still ensuing. The Admiralty's statement, "the situation is developing," aroused the keenest interest, and the hope that it meant some general engagement between the great fleets, so confident is the public of the ability of England's naval forces to vanquish the Germans. Keen as its interest was, London found time to smile at this message a Scarborough railway engineer sent to his wife: "Shells are falling thickly around me, but I am all right."

There was an unprecedented demand for newspapers. The news tickers, which are much more extensively utilized here than in New York, were surrounded all day. In financial circles the news was received calmly. Throgmorton Street even showed jubilation. "It is the best bull point for some time," was the consensus of opinion, and so it was throughout the city. England has been determined in this war, but has outwardly shown little ferocity. This east coast event will arouse the whole nation to a pitch of anger hitherto unknown.

The Pall Mall Gazette says: "It is worth two army corps to the new army. 'Frightfulness' will produce no effect on the nerves of the country. This outrage on humanity will rouse a stern, cold anger in the hearts of the sturdy men of the north. Those who have hesitated will hesitate no longer."

"Is it the big thing?" is the headline over The Pall Mall Gazette's column of comment, which contains this answer to the inquiry: "Every one will hope it is."

The Evening News says: "Scarborough is unfortified, and its complete destruction would not have been of twopenny worth of good to the Germans. Was it a feint to draw off our forces or was it merely an attempt at that 'ruthless revenge' so violently demanded by the German press?"

The Evening Standard's naval expert calls the German action a senseless policy, and advocates harsh treatment of the prisoners, saying: "We shall probably manage to see to it that few German cruisers return to their harbor. If we are wise we shall hang any prisoners taken. Then and then only shall we render ourselves immune from similar raids in the future."

Commander Carlton Bellair, the well-known naval commentator, said: "The only conceivable object in undertaking such a perfectly useless act of war is to create a state of alarm and divert troops and guns to the east coast instead of the front. Obviously we have got statesmen who are not going to play that game."

The Westminster Gazette's expert says: "The only respectable thing about the raid is that it cannot be done without considerable risk. From a military standpoint there seems no explanation for an adventure of this kind, unless it is part of something far larger and more far-reaching. As an effort to divide our fleet to prepare for an action on a grand scale as a prelude to an invasion in force, it would have to be judged as one move necessary to a great campaign. Simply as an isolated event, undertaken for no other object than to do damage for the sake of doing it, it stands condemned and can hardly go unpunished."

The Pall Mall Gazette, reporting conversations heard in the streets, quotes one sailor who was on the cruiser Hogue as saying: "Maybe they are out for a big scrap. If they are they'll get all they want and a bit over."

"How many Germans will get back?" he was asked. He answered: "Tell me how many are out first."

"They got the Fisher touch in the Atlantic," said another. "They'll get the Fisher-Jellico touch this time, and it won't be nice."

The manager of a Strand toyshop said that during the noon hour he sold more flags today than he had during the last fortnight.

USED BRITISH SIGNALS.

Raiders Taken for Friendly Ships Till They Began to Fire.

Special Cable to THE NEW YORK TIMES.
SUNDERLAND, Dec. 16, (Dispatch to The London Morning Post.)—There is a suspicion that the enemy's warships must have had some useful information in the first place.

It is said that they displayed British signals and were taken for friendly ships until their guns began to fire.

Only one child in another family in the old town escaped, the father, mother, and two other children being killed. The shells went through the roof of the church. At the Vicarage, Canon Ormsby was in bed when the bombardment began. The household sought refuge in the cellar.

The house was unroofed, and most of the rooms damaged, but no one in the vicarage was injured. Among the victims were several children, who were on their way to school. A group of volunteers were watching the bombardment from the coast when a shell fell among them, killing seven men.

The Lighthouse a Target.

The ships appear to have made a target of the lighthouse, which, however, escaped severe damage. The town is almost entirely in darkness tonight as the result of the shelling of the gas works. The electric light station, however, has escaped.

The bombardment of West Hartlepool appears to have been heard at several places on the Durham coast. At Easington the firing was audible, and at Horden the reports were felt so violently that windows rattled. Many at Horden saw two German warships firing in the direction of West Hartlepool, the flashes being plainly visible, as were also the stabs of flame which denoted that the guns on shore were replying.

At Blackhall Rocks, five miles from West Hartlepool, spectators saw the German ships firing broadsides, then wheeling around and firing their opposite broadsides from about 8 o'clock until 8:45. Flames could also be seen on land, as though some structure had been set on fire, but these flames afterward died down.

After the guns on shore replied the Germans cleared off and were lost in the mist.

At Redcar terrific firing was also heard a few miles off the coast a little before 8 o'clock. The forms of three cruisers could then be discerned looming out of the haze, and the flashes from their guns were easily observed from the promenade.

Among the places attacked were Seaton Carew, practically a seaside suburb of Hartlepool, and Teesmouth. Three shells fell near the railway station at Seaton Carew, making deep holes.

NEUTRALS' LOSS BY MINES.

Twenty-two Vessels and at Least 77 Lives Toll for Four Nations.

Special Cable to THE NEW YORK TIMES.
STOCKHOLM, Dec. 16, (Dispatch to The London Morning Post.)—A survey of events snows that through submarine mine disasters Sweden has lost eight ships, and that from fifty to sixty lives have been sacrificed; Denmark, six vessels and six lives; Norway, five vessels and six lives, and Holland, three vessels and fifteen lives.

It is estimated that the loss to Sweden through the destruction of these vessels and their cargoes will amount to more than $2,500,000.

1915

"All the News That's Fit to Print."

The New York Times.

THE WEATHER
Local snow or rain today; partly cloudy Thursday; moderate west winds, becoming variable.
☞ For full weather report see Page 18.

VOL. LXIV...NO. 20,815.   NEW YORK, WEDNESDAY, JANUARY 20, 1915.—EIGHTEEN PAGES.   ONE CENT In Greater New York. | TWO CENTS Jersey City and Newark.

ZEPPELINS KILL 5 IN RAID ON ENGLAND;
ONE BROUGHT DOWN BY WARSHIP'S GUNS;
BOMBS FALL AT NIGHT ON SIX TOWNS;
KING'S SANDRINGHAM HOME A TARGET

Royal Family Left for London Before the Raiders Came.

YARMOUTH SUFFERS MOST

Buildings Torn Apart and Four Residents Killed as Aircraft Sweep Over City.

GERMANS USE SEARCHLIGHT

Flashes Seen and Whirr of the Motors Heard, but Darkness Hides Enemy from View.

TRAVELED OVER 400 MILES

Seen in Early Morning as They Left the German Base to Cross the North Sea.

LONDON, Wednesday, Jan. 20.— Under cover of darkness, several German aircraft, presumably all Zeppelins, raided the County of Norfolk, on the east coast of England, last night.

One of the Zeppelins was brought down near Hunstanton, a little watering place north of Sandringham, the seat of the royal palace, in the western part of the county. The Central News dispatch which reports this adds that the Zeppelin was brought down by the fire of a warship.

Besides dropping bombs close to Sandringham Palace, without doing any great damage, the German airmen attacked the seaport of Yarmouth, Cromer, a watering place forty miles northwest of Yarmouth, and Sheringham, in the same neighborhood; Beeston, and King's Lynn, ninety miles west of Yarmouth and near the Wash.

If the German raiders hoped to blow up the royal residence while the King and Queen were in it, they missed their mark, for King George and Queen Mary, with their family, who had been staying at Sandringham, returned to London yesterday morning to resume their residence in Buckingham Palace.

Five Known Dead

Only scattering reports have reached here from the towns that were bombarded, but it is known that at least five persons have been killed, four in Yarmouth and one in King's Lynn.

The damage done to property by the bombs was apparently small except at Yarmouth, but the noise of the terrific explosions caused a panic in several places. In Yarmouth the people in their fright, rushed pellmell out of the houses.

The raiding Zeppelins apparently flew across the North eSa during the day, timing their arrival so as to attack without any alarm being given.

A Copenhagen dispatch to a London morning paper reported increased activity among the German air fleet, and told of a huge Zeppelin being seen yesterday morning close to the southern border of Denmark.

Three German airships, according to a dispatch from Amsterdam, passed over the Island of Ameland, in the North eSa, at 2:30 o'clock yesterday afternoon. They were flying in a westerly direction, according to advices received from Nes, the principal town of the island.

The Attack on Yarmouth.

Six hours later, or about 8:30 o'clock in the evening, an aircraft appeared over Yarmouth, which is 100 miles across the sea from Ameland.

It was dark at the time of the attack, and it was impossible, therefore, to see the aircraft, which some believe was an aeroplane, and not a Zeppelin.

The whirring of the propellers and noise of the engine first attracted attention to the arrival of the Germans. It was evident that the machine carried a searchlight, as flashes of light could occasionally be seen coming from it.

Scarcely had the noise of the engine been heard in the city than there came the sound of explosions, as the raiders hurled their bombs. From five to seven of these were thrown, and considerable damage to property resulted.

One bomb fell in Norfolk Square, close to the sea front, and another on the south quay. A third struck the York Road Drill Hall, fragments of the casing of the shell crashing through the glass roof of the billiard room of the headquarters of the National Reserve. A fourth missile fell near the Trinity Station.

The concussion resulting from the exploding bombs broke the windows in a number of shops and houses.

Street Wrecked, Four Killed.

The greatest damage done by any bomb resulted from one that fell in St. Peter's Plain, near St. Peter's Church. This damaged a whole row of houses, breaking all the windows and littering the street with débris, consisting of slate from the roofs and brick.

One man was found outside his home on St. Peter's Plain. His head had been crushed. He was identified as Samuel Smith, a shoemaker.

A woman who has not yet been identified was also found dead, while a soldier was discovered in Norfolk Square with a wound in his chest. A dispatch from Yarmouth says there was a fourth victim.

Great excitement prevailed in the town, and special constables, the police, and the military were called out to calm the people, who rushed out of their homes when the explosions took place. The electric supply was immediately cut off and the town was plunged in darkness. Because of this shutting off of light, the full extent of the damage and loss of life is still unknown.

After the attack on Yarmouth, which lasted only about ten minutes, the German air craft sailed away in a southwesterly direction.

Other Towns Assailed

Cromer, on the coast to the northwest of Yarmouth, was also attacked by an aircraft, but the result is not known.

At Sheringham, five miles from Cromer, a bomb dropped in Wyndham Street went through a house, but did not explode, apparently because the fuse became detached in the descent.

Two bombs dropped at Beeston did no damage. These bombs measured nearly four inches in diameter.

King's Lynn was visited at about 10:45 o'clock and from five to seven bombs were dropped there. One report says it was an aeroplane that did the damage, but this seems to be disproved by other reports.

The police say that two houses in King's Lynn were demolished by the bombs and that one house was damaged in Bentinck Street. In one house a boy of 17 years was killed. His father was buried in the débris of their demolished home, but was taken out alive and later sent to a hospital. In another house a mother and her babay were slightly injured.

The same Zeppelin that attacked King's Lynn apparently sailed northward and attacked Sandringham.

Several bombs were dropped in that neighborhood, and one fell close to the royal palace. That building was not damaged, however, and so far as the reports go, little harm was done in the vicinity.

It is supposed that the Zeppelin that bombarded King's Lynn and Sandringham is the one which, according to report, was brought down at Hunstanton, a little to the north and on the coast.

From all the places that suffered from the raid word comes that the night was quite calm, but very dark and cloudy. This made it entirely impossible for the people in the towns over which they passed to distinguish even the outlines of the aircraft, though the droning of their motors could be distinctly heard.

FLASHLIGHT IN SKY FOLLOWED BY BOMBS

Five Rained Down on Great Yarmouth, Rocking the Town With Their Explosions.

Special Cable to THE NEW YORK TIMES.
GREAT YARMOUTH, Jan. 19, (Dispatch to The London Daily Chronicle.) —About 8:30 this evening German aircraft dropped five bombs into Great Yarmouth. The first warning the town received was a flashlight in the sky, and then came the bombs.

The airship arrived from the north and passed off due south, and some of the people on the Marine Parade say they saw its outlines. It was not more than five minutes passing over the town. Considerable excitement prevailed, and people rushed into the streets, the children screaming. The flashes from the bombs were seen by many hundreds of persons who ran to South Quay. The military authorities ordered all the lights out on the Marine Parade.

At 10 o'clock came news that another aircraft was expected, and this did not allay the public fears. Householders followed the advice given by the police and military, and for the most part kept indoors, those having basements immediately taking refuge there. Tramcars and motors were held up by sentries and ordered to put their lights out.

I learn that immediately the airship was overhead two lights were observed to be flashed from a house near the Aquarium Theatre, and people fancy there has been treachery.

I also learn that the Mayor, Alderman McCowan, had a narrow escape, for an Alderman of the Town Council saw a bomb fall in Norfolk Square practically against the Mayor's house. It dropped in a grass patch.

People in the places of amusement distinctly heard the reports of the bomb explosions, and foundations and roofs of buildings were shaken. Windows, too, were broken, and several persons were cut by falling glass.

So far as I could ascertain, two persons were killed in Lancaster Road.

One of the Raiders Wrecked
By Fire of Warship, London Hears

LONDON, Jan. 20, 2:15 A. M.—A Zeppelin has been brought down at Hunstanton, a few miles north of Sandringham, according to a dispatch from King's Lynn to the Central News.

The dispatch adds that the Zeppelin was brought down by the fire of a warship.

This was told me by Dr. Dix, who picked them up. Red Cross workers were sent out to attend to the injured.

RAID HAD BEEN EXPECTED.

Weather Conditions, It Had Been Pointed Out, Were Favorable.

Special Cable to THE NEW YORK TIMES.

LONDON, Wednesday, Jan. 20.—A projected German air raid on England was the subject of considerable discussion during the past week, and speculation was indulged in as to the date when it might be expected. It has been recognised by experts that Zeppelins under favorable weather conditions and with luck on their side might succeed in reaching the English shores, and in doing an appreciable amount of damage.

In case of aeroplane raids, experts say, daylight is essential to their success, whereas Zeppelins can travel during the night. The atmospheric conditions at present are entirely favorable to such a raid. After the recent stormy weather there is a period of comparative calm with right winds and absence of rain. The skies are cloudless, but not bright enough to make aircraft easily distinguishable by the naked eye from the earth.

A prominent aviation expert writing on Sunday on the prospect of a visit from hostile air craft said:

"The full moon is on Jan. 31, but given a spell of calm weather we may expect the Zeppelins regardless of the moon phase. By the law of averages, the time is at hand for a cessation of wind and rain. These and other indications point, in the writer's opinion, to an early visit, probably this week."

A message from Amsterdam last night reporting the passage westward of three German airships over the Dutch Frisian Islands awakened little concern, as similar reports hitherto had not been followed by any consequences. The last of these reports was on Jan. 6, when it was said three Zeppelins had been seen that morning off the French coast, between Calais and Gravelines, going in the direction of England.

The news of today's raid was not allowed to be circulated until nearly midnight, when it was too late to reach the general public, but among those who got to know of it, speculation at once became rife regarding the possibility of the visitors taking in London during the course of their trip. Up to 3 o'clock this morning, however, there was no sign of them, and reports from Kings Lynn that they were believed to have departed eastwards, seem to indicate that the capital is to be spared a visit this time.

The authorities had made all arrangements in expectation of a raid, for as soon as the news from Yarmouth came in members of anti-aircraft corps stationed at various points of the metropolis received immediate warning, and the full strength of the special constable force was called out to be ready in case of emergencies.

It was only yesterday that a special set of regulations were issued instructing the police, both ordinary and special, how to act in the event of a raid, so that if Zeppelins had come they would have found the capital fully prepared to receive them, so far as preparation can be said to be possible at all.

The fact that bombs were dropped near Sandringham, the King's Norfolk home, has not failed to arouse considerable comment.

DANES SAW A ZEPPELIN.

Big Craft Close to Border Yesterday Morning.

Special Cable to THE NEW YORK TIMES.

COPENHAGEN, Jan. 19, (Dispatch to The London Daily News.)—Increased activity is noticeable among the German air fleet in the North Sea.

A Zeppelin of the large type was observed today approaching North Slesvig, a few miles south of the Danish frontier. It flew at a great altitude parallel to the frontier and disappeared to the southeast.

An aeroplane, supposed to be German, passed over Jutland this morning, traveling westward to the sea.

ZEPPELIN EVERY 3 WEEKS.

Reported Output of Supertype at Germany's Friedrichshafen Plant.

Although, from time to time, some general information has come from the Swiss towns on Lake Constance near Friedrichshafen in regard to the activities at the Zeppelin plant there, this information has principally been limited to the results of distant observation.

It has been stated that the plant produced a super-Zeppelin every three weeks, which immediately vanished, being sent to the hangars at Düsseldorf, Hamburg, or elsewhere; that on Dec. 15 seven super-Zeppelins had thus been prepared, and that an eighth one was ready, but had been seriously damaged by the raid of Commander Briggs and his British naval hydro-aeroplane on Nov. 21.

The first authentic description to be found of these super-Zeppelins, of which Germany should now possess

ten or eleven, was given in The Messaggero of Rome by one of the Italian journalists, who toured Germany in early November at the expense of the Kaiser and was supposed, on his return to Italy, to write informing articles about the Fatherland so that Italians would be eager to join in the fray. The journalist spent thirty hours inspecting the plant at Friedrichshafen and here is what the correspondent of The Messaggero wrote:

"On the average a super-Zeppelin is turned out every three weeks, so that, barring accidents, there will be eighteen super-Zeppelins by next Spring. The new Zeppelins carry a crew of from twenty-five to thirty men and a cargo of from forty-five to fifty bombs.

"The underneath part only is protected by aluminium sheets, which are below the car, and cover the whole length of the envelope for mitrailleuses, which are reached by internal spiral shafts.

"The super-Zeppelin is about 140 meters long by 15 wide, and can rise at the rate of about 1,000 meters in three or four minutes.

"The bombs are to be dropped by a man in a basket let down to 150 meters below the car. There is a special winding apparatus to raise and lower the basket. By this means the bombs can be dropped accurately, without hindrance from the aluminium sheet, and if the basket is struck by a shot the rest of the airship is not affected."

In an introduction preceding the foregoing the writer stated that he had been told that the Germans had thirty Zeppelins of all types, but that the super-Zeppelins, while rigid and having compartments like the others, were raised by a patent gas, which, while nearly as light as hydrogen, was not explosive. Italian scientists seriously doubted the truth of this last observation.

FRENCHMAN UNAIDED, WINS GERMAN TRENCH

Drives Out Foe and Calls Up His Regiment to Occupy Captured Ground.

Special Cable to THE NEW YORK TIMES.

NORTHERN FRANCE, Jan. 19, (Dispatch to the London Daily Chronicle.)— The General commanding the district was waiting on the platform to greet Thorel, a young infantryman, on the hospital train from the trenches. He looked such a boy, this young wounded infantryman, as he was carried from

the train, but he smiled through his pain as the General congratulated him on his bravery and examined his medaille militaire, which Gen. Joffre himself pinned on his breast.

Thorel is one of the youngest heroes of the war. It was near Ypres that his regiment was ordered to retake the ground that the French had lost a little while before. The first attack failed, and the second was being attempted when it was decided, in view of the difficulties of the ground, to postpone it until night. Thorel was in the front rank and carried along by his enthusiasm, he did not hear the order to retire and continued to dash forward, believing he was being followed by his comrades.

At last he reached a deserted trench and sprang into it. Then when there was time to look around he found to his surprise he was alone.

Retreat was impossible, for as he peeped ahead he saw crowds of Germans coming and going in another trench only 25 metres away. The time had come to act, and his mind was soon made up. Making a rest for his rifle under the shelter he brought the sights on a German and pulled the trigger. The German fell, then a second fell and a third. A brisk volley came from the German trench, but Thorel was under good cover and was not hit.

He continued firing rapidly, and more than 150 of his 200 cartridges had been expended when the Germans, persuaded by his activity that the trench was strongly held, bolted to another position further to their rear. Some of them in their flight fell to the bullets of the still unconquered young infantryman.

At last, all his ammunition gone, Thorel retired and told his officer about the unoccupied trench in which he had made his lonely fight, and about the other trench that the Germans had deserted under his fire. The French at once advanced, and in the trench from which the Germans had been driven they found arms and ammunition as well as many evidences that the Germans suffered severely. The heroism and coolness of one young fellow had won this position for his regiment.

This wreck is all that was left of the zeppelin that was shot down during the attack on London.

"All the News That's Fit to Print."

The New York Times.

THE WEATHER
Cloudy, warmer; rain late today, warmer tomorrow; fresh southeast winds.

For full weather report see Page 22.

VOL. LXIV...NO. 20,831.   ...   NEW YORK, FRIDAY, FEBRUARY 5, 1915.—EIGHTEEN PAGES.   ONE CENT *In Greater New York.* | ...

GERMANY PROCLAIMS A WAR ZONE AROUND GREAT BRITAIN AFTER FEB. 18; SAYS NEUTRAL SHIPS WILL BE IN DANGER

Blunt Statement That No Vessel Will Be Safe After That Date.

DECREES VON TIRPITZ POLICY

Every British Merchant Vessel Found in Zone to be Destroyed.

MERELY A 'PAPER BLOCKADE'

But May Bring Protest from the United States and Other Neutral Nations.

CAUSES NO SURPRISE HERE

Shipping Men Not Alarmed, but Say It Is Violation of International Law.

BIG BLUNDER, SAYS LONDON

Certain to Arouse Other Nations, Is British View—'Inconceivable!' Cries F. R. Coudert.

Special Cable to THE NEW YORK TIMES.
LONDON, Friday, Feb. 5.—A German proclamation declaring " the waters around Great Britain and Ireland, including the whole English Channel, a war zone from and after Feb. 18," reached London after midnight.

The proclamation [printed in full elsewhere on this page of THE NEW YORK TIMES] says that " every enemy merchant ship, found in this zone, will be destroyed, even if it is impossible to avert dangers which threaten the crew and passengers."

England, however, sees the chief blunder in this part of the communication: " Also, neutral ships in the war zone are in danger, as in consequence of the misuse of neutral flags ordered by the British Government on Jan. 31 and in view of the hazards of naval warfare, it cannot always be avoided that attacks meant for enemy ships endanger neutral ships."

Scandinavia and the United States are particularly affected by this part of the proclamation. Neutral trade with Great Britain can only be carried on under risks which, even when they were largely supposititious, as was the case when the U-21 was lurking in the Irish Sea, aroused a storm of protest.

The proclamation was received here too late for general editorial comment in this morning's papers. The first impression created by the declaration, however, was that the German Government had committed the greatest of all blunders which could be laid at the door of German statecraft. It is regarded here as more materially affecting interests of neutral nations than endangering British supplies.

Conditions under which the North declared a blockade of the Southern coasts in the American civil war were different from this in essential features. The lives of the men engaged in blockade running were not endangered, save in exceptional circumstances, whereas the power of submarines to make a blockade effective by preventing transit of cargoes without causing loss of life is limited.

The Germans can only render effective such a " blockade " as they propose by the menace of submarine attacks as planned by Admiral von Tirpitz.

The Daily Chronicle's naval correspondent says:

" Germany can fulfil none of the conditions of the blockade, and any attempt, however wild, by the Germans to ignore, for example, the American flag on the strength of their paper blockade, would be a hostile act toward the United States. To sink an American liner with her passengers and crew would be an atrocity that would almost inevitably mean war."

CRIES "GOD PUNISH ENGLAND!"

Leipsic Paper Declares That "Wild Events" Are About to Occur.

Special Cable to THE NEW YORK TIMES.
ROTTERDAM, Feb. 4. — The Neuste Nachrichsten of Leipsic publishes an outburst against Great Britain in an article headed " God Punish England! " It says:

" The curtain rises upon the world's stage, and a new act is beginning. We are those who can decide the fate of England's trade if we will only advance to the attack.

" Though the stronger, England must bow to our will. The blockade of England is effective. Any one directing his ship's keel toward England does so at his own risk.

" Are our submarines the only weapon we can use to this end? Time will tell this. However, it is certain that we are prepared and ready. We shall stop this transport of men and war materials to France by every means in human power..

" You may roll your eyes round, oh, England! and cry aloud that we are doing deeds which fill the world with horror, but not the world. Oh, no! Only the world of English Pharisees one hears cry that England will win because she has the longer purse and the greatest credit. The longer purse can be emptied and the greater credit shattered.

" We are at work. Fight to the death against England! At the present moment transports of English troops are continuing to reach France, but the near future will be rich in wild events."

BERLIN, Feb. 4. (By Wireless to Sayville, L. I.)—German newspapers, including the Kreuz-Zeitung, Vossische Zeitung and Tageblatt, refer to an alleged order of the British Government that British ships employ the neutral flag. The Kreuz-Zeitung says:

" What is this command, but an admission by the English that ' we are unable longer to protect our flag? ' Furthermore, it is a gross violation of international law, and one of its consequences inevitably will be that neutral flags can no longer protect neutral shipping for the reason that it will be impossible for German naval officers to tell whether it is borne rightfully or not.

" Consequently, German submarines will have to direct their torpedoes also at neutral ships, if neutral powers do not see to it that this misuse of their flags, ordered by the British Admiralty, does not take place."

WASHINGTON VIEWS DECREE SERIOUSLY

Germany's Submarine War On Merchant Ships May Become a Grave Issue.

Special to The New York Times.
WASHINGTON, Feb. 4.—Germany's submarine war upon British merchant shipping is developing into one of the mammoth issues of the war—one which may be full of serious consequences for the United States and other neutral powers—because the incidental destruction of neutral vessels in these raids would develop vital diplomatic conditions.

These features of the new German policy fathered by Admiral von Tirpitz, Chief of the German Admiralty, were driven home when February was ushered in with the destruction of several British merchant ships that were torpedoed by the U-21 and other German submarines. Tonight further emphasis was given to the tremendous possibilities of the situation when it became unofficially known in Washington that the German Admiralty had today issued a communication declaring a " war zone " around the British Isles.

This Admiralty announcement serves notice on the world that it is the purpose of the German Navy, by submarine attacks, to destroy British, French or Russian merchant craft wherever found in British waters while leaving or entering the ports of that country. It warns every British and also every neutral shipmaster that he will enter British waters at his own risk after Feb. 18. Fifteen days grace are given to British ship owners in which to warn the Captains of their merchant craft not to approach British shores.

The German Admiralty announcement comes swiftly on the heels of the decision of the British Government in the Wilhelmina case, ordering the treatment of cargoes of grain and flour destined for Germany or Austria as conditional contraband, subject to seizure and confiscation. The British decision to seize the cargo of provisions now being carried across the Atlantic by the Wilhelmina grew out of the announcement that the German Government had decreed the confiscation of all grain and flour to conserve that nation's food supply.

It is believed in high circles here that the German decision to treat all waters around the British Isles as a war zone, in which every British merchant ship will be subject to submarine attack and destruction, is a response to the British decision to treat as conditional contraband all foodstuffs destined for Germany. It is regarded as a corollary of the issues between the British and Germans over the question of food supplies, the German purpose being to cut off the shipment of supplies to the British people if the British Government will not permit foodstuffs not destined for the use of the German Army to be shipped into Germany for use by German non-combatants.

Purposes of the Move.

The larger elements of the situation developed by Germany's war zone decree are believed to be these:

First—Germany hopes by her policy of submarine warfare to stifle British shipping and cripple the British merchant marine, at least to the extent of making it extremely dangerous, if not impossible, for ships flying the British flag to leave or enter the ports of England, Scotland, Ireland, or Wales.

Second—Germany hopes—if her submarine war is successful—to demoralize the shipping of food supplies into England from the United States and other countries and to make the submarine a serious peril to the food supply of the British nation, and thus dominate the British position of trade supremacy unless an effective means of defense can be devised.

Third—It is possible that the German submarine peril may force a change in the British policy with respect to the transfer of belligerent merchant ships to the American and other neutral flags on the theory that it may be found advantageous to the British Government to permit interned German ships to transfer their registry to the American flag in order that they may be utilized for carrying supplies to England.

Fourth—Neutral merchant ships, whatever the German notice may say, would not be subject to attack and destruction by the German submarines because this would involve serious breaches of international law, and if neutral ships were immune, the impossibility of using British ships might render it absolutely necessary to use American ships, interned German ships transferred to neutral flags, and other neutral vessels in order to maintain shipments into England.

Fifth—If neutral ships are destroyed in the war zone proposed to be established, new and critical issues involving the relations of Germany with neutral nations may be produced.

Von Tirpitz Policy.

These are some of the elements of the situation as seen by Washington officials. The announcement that " every enemy merchant ship found in this war zone will be destroyed even if it is impossible to avert dangers which threaten the crew and passengers," is taken to mean that Admiral von Tirpitz's declaration of some weeks ago that merchant ships of England, France, and Russia approaching British shores would be torpedoed is to be carried rigidly into effect.

The development of the seagoing, seakeeping submarine of nearly 1,000 tons displacement and about 3,000 miles radius, capable of making twenty-one knots' speed on the surface and fifteen while submerged, is the factor that makes possible the consummation of the policy announced in the German Admiralty statement. Smaller coast defense submarines would not be able to make the threat of such a policy effective, but the seakeeping submarine would enable Germany to attack British merchant ships, not only in the English Channel and the North Sea, but also in the Irish Sea and off the west coast of Ireland, as well as off the north coast of Scotland.

The German Admiralty announces that " neutral ships in the war zone are in danger, as, in consequence of the misuse of neutral flags ordered by the British Government on Jan. 31, and in view of the hazards of naval warfare, it cannot always be avoided that attacks meant for enemy's ships endanger neutral ships."

This is not interpreted in Washington as meaning that Germany would deliberately embark on submarine attacks on American or other neutral ships, but it is regarded as a warning to American and other neutral ships that they will be entering a war zone and dangerous water territory, should they approach the British or French coasts after Feb. 18. It means that neutral ships may be hit by mistake, or that they may run upon and be sunk by unspent torpedoes fired by German submarines that may have missed their mark. If British ships were to use neutral flags as a subterfuge they would not be immune from attack.

On Feb. 3 THE NEW YORK TIMES printed a Washington dispatch which set forth that Germany's war of submarines on English merchant ships might have an important bearing on British policy with respect to the transfer of German ships to neutral flags. The source of the information contained in that dispatch cannot be disclosed, but it was pointed out tonight that the statements therein contained were emphasized by the announcement today by the German Admiralty.

The only notification the State Department so far has received from Germany pertains to the north and west coasts of France. On that communication the State Department issued the following announcement this evening:

"The department has received a telegram from the American Ambassador at Berlin, dated Feb. 2, stating that the German Admiralty had issued a proclamation urgently warning all merchant vessels not to approach the north and west coasts of France, as it is the intention of the German Government to use all the means of war which it has at its disposal against British troopships and ammunition shipments to France. The German Government recommends that merchant vessels bound for the North Sea take the north of Scotland course."

Text of Germany's 'War Zone' Decree Threatening to Sink Merchant Ships

BERLIN, Feb. 4, (by Wireless to Sayville, L. I.)—The German Admiralty issued the following communication today:

The waters around Great Britain and Ireland, including the whole English Channel, are declared a war zone from and after Feb. 18, 1915.

Every enemy merchant ship found in this war zone will be destroyed, even if it is impossible to avert dangers which threaten the crew and passengers.

Also, neutral ships in the war zone are in danger, as in consequence of the misuse of neutral flags, ordered by the British Government on Jan. 31, and in view of the hazards of naval warfare, it cannot always be avoided that attacks meant for enemy ships endanger neutral ships.

Shipping northward, around the Shetland Islands in the eastern basin of the North Sea and in a strip of at least thirty nautical miles in breadth along the Dutch coast, is endangered in the same way.

There has been published in Germany recently what purports to be a secret order, issued by the British Admiralty to British merchant ships, instructing them to make use of neutral flags.

"Neutrals Must Take the Consequences"—Hollweg

LONDON, Friday, Feb. 5.—"England treats the United States as a besieged fortress," declared Dr. Theobald von Bethmann-Hollweg, the Imperial Chancellor of Germany, in discussing with a Danish correspondent Great Britain's attempts to prevent imports of food into Germany, according to a Copenhagen dispatch to the Exchange Telegraph Company tonight.

"Winston Churchill," continued the Chancellor, "wants to starve a people, numbering 70,000,000, in this barbarian fashion. Against this effort Germany will use every opportunity to take revenge.

"With regard to the complaint that we are injuring neutral interests, neutral powers have not protested against England's action and they must take the consequences. We certainly are not going to die of famine."

HOUSE UPHOLDS VETO OF THE ALIEN BILL

Friends of Measure Fail by Four Votes to Override President's Action.

ALL DAY GIVEN TO DEBATE

Changes of Front Shown by 13 Members in the Final Action on the Measure.

Special to The New York Times.

WASHINGTON, Feb. 4. — President Wilson's veto of the Burnett Immigration bill, sent to the House a week ago today, will stand. The House this afternoon, by a vote of 261 to 136, refused to pass the bill over the veto by the constitutional two-thirds vote. It was, however, a close call for Mr. Wilson. A change of four votes would have given the friends of the bill a victory over the President.

It was the third time the House had undertaken to pass an immigration bill containing the literacy test over a President's veto. Two years ago today an attempt to get the necessary two-thirds to override the veto of President Taft failed. President Cleveland also vetoed a like measure. Today was notable as the anniversary of the passage of the Burnett bill by the House. It was a foregone conclusion that if the bill passed the House it would pass the Senate, the last vote there being 50 to 7.

Of the 425 members of the House, 399 were present. The entire day was given over to debate under the five-minute rule. At times the discussion arose to unusual heights of oratory. On one side the appeal was made for the oppressed and downtrodden of other lands, and on the other the argument for fair play to the American workman was urged.

Mr. Moore of Pennsylvania, who closed the debate for the Republicans in opposition to the measure, began his remarks by reading from an ancient document adopted once upon a time in his district in the City of Philadelphia, which declared that all men were born free and equal, and among other things complained that the King of England in that day was preventing immigrants from coming to this country.

Mr. Moore appealed for the principles of the Declaration of Independence. To the argument that the Federation of Labor was asking for the passage of the Burnett bill, he said that there were only 2,700,000 members of the federation, while there were 30,000,000 laboring men outside that organization who made no complaint of competition from immigrant labor and were willing to keep the door open for those who wanted to come.

Mr. Burnett of Alabama, author of the bill and Chairman of the Immigration Committee, in closing the debate read from one of President Wilson's volumes of history an extract which set forth the argument against the admission of the southern European immigrant whose assimilation, it was asserted, was a task that was straining our institutions and putting undue burdens on our civilization. Mr. Burnett said that the pending bill with its literacy test had passed one house or the other seventeen times, and notwithstanding the President's demand in his veto message, that the question should be passed on by a party platform and a popular vote, it had been put in several platforms and public opinion was in favor of it.

As long ago as 1896, he said, the Democratic platform had asserted that there should be protection from excessive immigration, and the Republican platform had favored a literacy test.

It was several minutes before order could be restored when Mr. Burnett closed. The House broke out into cheers.

Mr. Sabath of Illinois led those Democrats who were opposed to the bill. Letters were read by him from the officers of the Garment Workers' Union, the Amalgamated Garment Makers, the Laundry Workers, the Bakers' Union, the United Neckwear Union, the United Trades of New York, the Cabinet Makers' Union, the Wood Turners' Union, the Shirtmakers' Union, and others in New York.

The whole number of members voting today was 397. When the bill passed a year ago the whole number voting was 378. The number voting on the conference report on Jan. 7 was 321. Of members who had gone on record heretofore on the measure, 13 changed their votes. Eight Democrats—Beakes of Michigan, Goeke of Ohio, Kindel of Colorado, Park of Georgia, Reed of New Hampshire, Taylor of Alabama, Whaley of South Carolina, and Williams of Illinois, who voted for the bill on its original passage and also for the conference report last month—voted today not to reverse the President.

Three Republicans, who previously voted against the bill, today voted to pass it over the veto. These were Cooper of Wisconsin and Drukker and Parker of New Jersey. Shreve, Republican, of Pennsylvania, changed from "Nay" to "Yea," and Steenerson of Minnesota, who had voted against the bill, answered "Present" when his name was called.

The 261 votes for passing the bill over the veto were cast as follows: Democrats, 166; Republicans, 78; Progressives and Progressive Republicans, 16; independent, 1.

Against the bill the vote was: Democrats, 101; "insurgent" Democrat, 1; Republicans, 32; Progressives and Progressive Republicans, 2.

'WAR ZONE' DECREE NO SURPRISE HERE

But New York Shipping Men Say Germany Will Be Unable to Carry It Out.

WILL CANCEL NO SAILINGS

Representatives of shipping companies operating between New York and British ports, when informed last night of the contents of the latest German proclamation, were inclined to treat the whole matter as a bluff. "They can't get away with it," "Business as usual," "No suspension of sailings," "No change in existing conditions"—these were some of the remarks made by the officials of transatlantic lines, who seemed to have little confidence in the ability of the Germans to carry out their threats to the Allies or that implied by the warning to neutral shipping.

Some of them, however, admitted that there was a possibility of serious risk and that later developments might bring on a difficult situation. No one was inclined to think that there was anything in the German notice which would call for diplomatic action by neutrals, although the suggestion was made that if the dangers hinted at by the Germans were actually realized some action might be expected from the Government of the United States and those of the neutral North Sea countries.

Cancel No Sailings.

Charles P. Sumner of the Cunard Line said: "This makes no difference at all to us. Our business will go on as usual, without any fear of such action as is threatened by the Germans. There is nothing at this time to call for the cancellation of any of our sailings. The postponement of the Transylvania's sailing from Liverpool from Feb. 6 to Feb. 13 was due purely and simply to the fact that she could not be got ready in time."

A representative of the French Line said: "Up to the present we have seen no reason to change our sailings, and there is no reason why we should make any alterations in our schedule in the immediate future. We have been well aware from the first that the Germans might try something of this sort, but we are fully satisfied that the British and French fleets can keep the narrow seas open for their own traffic, as well as for that of neutral countries."

"I should think that was more or less of a bluff," said T. Ashley Sparks of the Scandinavian-American Line. "British waters, as far as I can see, are no more in a state of war now than they have been since Aug. 4. The German Navy is bottled up with the exception of its submarines, and their activities have been only sporadic, and, in my opinion, have reached their maximum. I do not see any reason to believe that we shall suspend sailings, and I don't believe that this proclamation will affect shipping to any appreciable extent. It may put the war rate of insurance up a little, but that is all."

Liverpool to Remain Open.

"I am very much interested in this new move of Germany's," said Harold Sanderson, Chairman of the Board of Directors of the International Mercantile Marine Company, who landed yesterday from the Adriatic. "Such action was not altogether unexpected, but I do not think its effect will be important. There will no doubt be other submarine raids such as that off Liverpool last week, but it will make no difference. Liverpool will be kept an open port. I do not think that purchase of ships by the United States Government will have much effect on the situation one way or another. Freight rates are high at present, not because of the quantity of freight, but because of the congestion in loading. If you do buy ships under these conditions, what are you going to do with them?"

William Van Doorn of the Holland-America Line said: "The Germans haven't the ships to make such threats effective. Their submarines cannot do very much when their actions are compared with the magnitude of the field. Any action they might take to carry out this declaration will have to be in the main through mines, and a skillful pilot can dodge a mine field. I have had no instructions from the other side to postpone any of our sailings, and such orders would certainly have come if the situation were regarded as dangerous in Holland. If things keep on getting worse, there is a chance, I think, that the neutral States of Northern Europe might take some action through their diplomatic representatives at Washington; but there seems to be nothing in the present state of things to call for such steps."

"I can't say at this time," said Philip A. S. Franklin, President of the Atlantic Transport Line and a Director of the International Mercantile Marine, "what effect this is likely to have on the transatlantic lines, for the proclamation is unexpected and its full implication and actual force may not be seen at once. Such action as might be taken by the steamship lines in consequence is a matter for extended and careful consideration. We have a new problem every day in war times and the situation is constantly changing. So we have to think the whole situation over very carefully before we take any steps at all."

Sees No New Danger.

"I don't see that this new pronouncement means anything more than what we are already facing," said W. L. Walther of the Scandinavian-American Line, "for British waters and the neighboring seas have practically been in a state of war from the beginning. If the German warships had been able to leave their home ports British waters would have been dangerous from the very start for British merchant shipping. As to the reference to neutrals, there is no reason to believe that German ships are any more likely than British to attack neutral shipping. They look at the flag. Of course, if there is reason to believe that the cargo is destined for the enemy, that is a different matter; but I see nothing in this new angle of the situation which calls for any action or any attempt to secure diplomatic conferences on the part of neutral shipping companies."

Horace G. Philips, Secretary of the International Mercantile Marine, said: "I had heard nothing of this declaration before this, and can hardly say offhand what action would be likely to result on the part of the transatlantic navigation companies. It is quite a new move, and the whole question will have to be looked into before it would be possible to express an opinion as to what may be done by the steamship lines."

"All the News That's Fit to Print."

The New York Times.

THE WEATHER
Fair today and tomorrow; moderate northwest winds.

VOL. LXIV...NO. 20,806 ...   NEW YORK, TUESDAY, MARCH 2, 1915.—EIGHTEEN PAGES.   ONE CENT In Greater New York, Jersey City and Newark. |

ALLIES REPLY TO SUBMARINE WAR BY CUTTING OFF ALL GERMAN SUPPLIES; UNITED STATES LIKELY TO PROTEST

All Cargoes Going In or Out of Kaiser's Realm to be Stopped.

ASQUITH PROCLAIMS IT

British Premier Cheered by Vast Throng as He Exclaims "That Is Our Reply!"

AVOIDS WORD "BLOCKADE"

Asserts That Germany's Policy Has Stripped Her of Right to "Diplomatic Terms."

ASSURES NEUTRALS' SAFETY

Their Crews to be Protected and Their Ships and Cargoes Not to be Confiscated.

WAR COST $7,500,000 A DAY

But Prime Minister Says It Will Be Increased—Warns the World Peace Talk Is Idle Now.

Special Cable to THE NEW YORK TIMES.
LONDON, March 1.—Premier Asquith announced in the House of Commons today the purpose of England and France to cut Germany off from all trade with the rest of the world. If the fleets of the Allies can prevent it no commodities of any kind whatsoever, except those now on the seas, shall reach Germany until the war is ended. This, the Premier said, was England's reply to Germany's submarine blockade and that it was forthwith effective.

A crowded House listened to Mr. Asquith's speech, which members agree was a superb piece of oratory, marked by high eloquence and vibrant with patriotism. The passage which aroused the greatest applause was that "This, Sir, is our reply" to the German block-

ade. It was greeted with prolonged cheers by all the members without distinction of party.

Mr. Asquith said he must use "some very plain language about the so-called German blockade," an expression which, as applied to submarine warfare, he called grotesque. With Winston Spencer Churchill, first Lord of the Admiralty, sitting just behind him, he proceeded to describe "the German policy of piracy and pillage."

"It came as no surprise," he explained, "for here is a power which began the war with the cynical repudiation of a solemn treaty and has waged it not impulsively, but systematically. Confronted by this situation can we sit quiet?" There was silence at the question. Then he added, "We think we cannot."

The Premier said that for a blockade to be effective it must be made effective by ships of war. "Where," he inquired, "are the German ships of war? They have only twice been seen on the open sea, and in both cases their object was the same—the murder of civilians and the destruction of undefended seaside towns. Let them see British ships and they show a clean pair of heels."

"Not all!" called a member.

"Well, retorted the Prime Minister, "I admit that some suffered misadventure."

He took up a document and read it—the British reply. It amounted to this: That all goods going to Germany or coming from Germany would be held up.

"The words blockade and contraband," he said, "do not occur in this declaration. And why? Germany has forfeited all rights to diplomatic terms. Nor is the alliance to be strangled with a net work of juridical niceties."

All forms of economic pressure, he said, would be used, and if neutrals suffered inconvenience "we regret it." "But," he went on, "we did not initiate the new warfare and we promise the neutrals that we shall not assassinate their seamen or destroy their goods."

He added almost in an aside that there had been no rejection of the representations of the United States, which were under careful consideration. Germany, the Premier said, had no right to object if hardship came upon her civil population, for Bismarck had expressly authorized the methods which Great Britain had been forced to pursue.

Mr. Asquith's resolute language created an extremely favorable impression and aroused much enthusiasm when he said that "after seven months of war the country and the empire are every whit as determined—if need be at the cost of all they could command in men and money—to bring their righteous cause to a triumphant issue."

ASKS NEUTRALS TO BE PATIENT

Asquith Emphasizes That Seized Ships Are Not Necessarily To Be Confiscated.

By The Associated Press.
LONDON, March 1.—Premier Asquith in announcing today the intention of England and France to cut off all trade with Germany emphasized that vessels and cargoes that would be seized were not necessarily liable to confiscation and begged the patience of neutral countries in the face of a step through which they were likely to suffer. He added that in making such a step the Allies had done so in self-defense.

"We are quite prepared," he went on, "to submit to the arbitrament of neutral opinion, and still more to the verdict of impartial history, that in the circumstances in which we have been placed we have been moderate, we have been restrained, we have abstained from things that we were provoked and tempted to do, and we have adopted a policy which commends itself to reason, to common sense, and to justice."

Every member of the House not at the front in khaki, or unavoidably detained, was in his seat to hear the Prime Minister's speech, and there was frequent cheering. The galleries were packed. When the Premier concluded his set statement, and, turning to the Speaker, said:

"That, Sir, is our reply!" there was a tremendous outburst of applause.

Oddly enough, the German reply to the American note seeking to solve the situation growing out of Germany's declaration of a naval war zone was handed to Ambassador Gerard at Berlin today, and Premier Asquith, in his speech, said that Great Britain and her allies were still carefully considering the American note to them on the same subject. That the British Government had rejected the proposal, he stated, was "quite untrue."

Costs $7,500,000 a Day.

The tremendous cost of modern warfare, which the Premier estimated now at $7,500,000 daily to the Allies alone, and likely to grow to $8,500,000 or more daily in April, was one theme of the Premier's address. He gave these figures in asking for a supplementary vote of credit, making a total of £362,000,000 ($1,810,000,000,) to prosecute the war to March 31, 1915. This the House unanimously granted.

The entire struggle with Napoleon cost England only £1,831,000,000 ($9,155,000,-000) and the South African war only £211,000,000 ($1,055,000,000.) These were Mr. Asquith's figures.

Before the Premier had finished, the newspapers were on the streets proclaiming "Our Answer to Germany" in big letters, and it was apparent everywhere that the entire nation had been

chafing for reprisals against the sinking of merchant craft by submarines.

Dardanelles Operations.

Referring to the attack on the Dardanelles, the Premier said that there had been no impairment of strength of the Allies in France or in Flanders as a result of withdrawals of men for service in the campaign against Turkey.

"We shall continue to give the fullest and most effective support there," he added, referring to the western front. "Neither has there been, for the purposes of the Dardanelles operations, any weakening of the grand fleet. The enterprise was carefully conceived, with distinct political, strategical and economic objects."

The Premier said that the operations against Turkey again illustrated the close co-operation among the Allies. He referred to "the splendid contingent of the French navy, which shares the glory and hazards of the enterprise."

The Dardanelles operations also demonstrated, he said, the copiousness and variety of British naval resources. The Queen Elizabeth was Great Britain's newest superdreadnought, with a power of range never before known, while at her side was the Agamemnon, the predecessor of the dreadnought.

Referring to the new credit measure which the Government presented, Mr. Asquith said:

"The Government is making this large pecuniary demand with the full conviction that after seven months of war the country and the empire are every whit as determined as ever—if needs be at a cost of all we can command in men and money—to bring the righteous cause to a triumphant issue.

"There is much to encourage and stimulate us in what we see—in the heroism of Belgium and Servia and in the undaunted tenacity wherewith our allies hold their far-flung lines until the moment comes for an irresistible decisive advance. We have no reason to be otherwise than satisfied with the progress of recruiting. I can assure the House that, with all the knowledge and experience gained by the Government, we were never more confident than today of the power and will of the Allies to achieve an ultimate victory."

The Submarine Warfare.

Turning to the subject of Germany's submarine activities and the situation which they have brought about, Mr. Asquith said:

"I may say that the suggestion which has been put forth from German quarters, that we have rejected certain proposals or suggestions made to two powers by the United States, is untrue. All we have stated to the United States so far is that we have taken this matter into careful consideration in consultation with our allies.

"I shall have to use some very plain language. It did not come upon us as a surprise that war has been carried on by Germany with systematic violation of all the conventions and regulations under which, by international agreement, it was thought to mitigate warfare. She has now taken a further step by organizing an under-sea campaign of piracy and pillage. Can we—here I address myself to neutrals—sit quiet, as though we were still under the protection of the rules of civilized warfare? I think we cannot."

Mr. Asquith ridiculed what he called the German theory of blockade and asked: "Where is the German fleet?' It had been seen on the sea only twice since the war began, he said.

"The plain truth is that the German fleet is not blockading, cannot blockade, and never will blockade the English shore," the Premier continued. "The measures to be adopted by France and Great Britain, however, will not involve risks to neutral vessels or neutral lives. The Allies will hold themselves free to capture goods of presumed enemy origin or destination. There is no form of economic pressure whereto we do not consider ourselves entitled to resort.

"If neutrals suffer inconvenience the Allies will regret it, but neutrals should remember that this phase of the war was not initiated by us. We do not propose to assassinate their seamen or destroy their ships."

Peace Talk Untimely.

Referring to "whispers of peace," Premier Asquith remarked:

"It is not the time to talk peace. Those who do so, however excellent their intentions, are victims of grievous self-delusion. It will be time to talk peace when the great purposes of the Allies are in sight of accomplishment."

Referring to the two occasions on which German warships had been seen by the British at sea, Mr. Asquith said that the object of the Germans in both cases was "murder and wholesale destruction of property and undefended towns." He described the German campaign aginst British shipping as grotesque and puerile and said that it was a perversion of language to call it a blockade.

"The gravity of our immense task increases each month," he continued. "The call for men has been responded to nobly, both at home and throughout the empire. That call has never been more urgent than today."

Referring to recent labor troubles, the Premier said that the first duty of all concerned was to go on producing with might and main what the safety of the State required. If that were done the Government would insure prompt and equitable settlement of disputed points affecting the labor world. In cases of proved necessity, the Premier said, the Government would give, on behalf of the State, such help as lay in its power.

"Soldiers and sailors, employers and workmen in the industrial world, are partners and co-operators in one great enterprise, to achieve the purposes wherefor we and our allies embarked on this long and stormy voyage," he continued. "We must draw on all our resources, both material and spiritual. We have not relaxed, nor shall we relax until the pursuit of every one of our ends is accomplished."

The Premier made an appeal for a display of the inbred qualities of the race—self-sacrifice, patience, tenacity, unity and inflexible resolve.

Treat Raiders as Murderers.

Admiral Lord Charles Beresford invited the Premier to state whether Germans who engaged in submarine attacks or raids on unfortified towns and were captured would be tried for murder. Mr. Asquith declined to give any definite assurance, but he said:

"No doubt the Government will take into serious consideration what is the status under international law of persons engaged in this campaign."

GERMANY ACCEPTS, BUT ON CONDITIONS

Will Make Concessions on War Zone Food Embargo Matter Only If England Will.

AMSTERDAM, (via London,) March 2.—Germany's acceptance of the proposals made in the United States note regarding food supplies and the war zone, is based upon the condition that Great Britain shall make similar concessions, says a Berlin dispatch to The Telegraaf.

BERLIN, March 1, (via London.)—Germany's reply to the American note concerning the naval war zone was handed today to Ambassador Gerard. It corresponds in general with the forecast of some days ago.

The Foreign Office characterizes the German reply as "acceptance with few modifications" of the American proposals.

The reply suggests that, in accordance with the principles of international law, the importation should be permitted not only of foodstuffs, but also of such raw materials as are urgently necessary for the peaceful civilian population.

The American note and the German reply probably will be published here tomorrow afternoon.

REPRISALS LIKELY TO DRAW PROTEST

Washington Believes Wilson Will Not Accept the New Policy of the Allies.

AWAIT REPLY TO NOTE

Officials Think the Attitude of the Belligerents Disregards Our Rights.

WASHINGTON, March 1.—The impression was general in official quarters tonight that a strong protest would be made against the action of the Allies in announcing their determination to cut off all trade to and from Germany, which was regarded as an unprecedented and novel step.

Officials pointed out that in the reprisals which the belligerents were making toward each other there was a singular forgetfulness of the fact that whatever might be the violations of international custom between those countries at war, this could not affect the status of international rules as between the United States and countries with which she was at peace.

Assurances given by Great Britain that today's note was not a reply to the recent proposals of the United States for an adjustment of the entire situation which led to the retaliatory measures gave ground for some hope that the measures taken might be only of a temporary character. In this connection, the State Department issued the following statement:

The British Ambassador has presented the following instructions from his Government:

"When presenting joint Anglo-French communication you should inform United States Government that communication received from them through the United States Ambassador in London, respecting a possible limitation of use of submarines and mines and an arrangement for supplying food to Germany is being taken into careful consideration by his Majesty's Government in consultation with their allies."

The text of the British note, which was the same as the statement made in the House of Commons by Premier Asquith, was given out at the State Department, with the information that the French note was practically identical.

Creates Complex Problem.

Copies of the notes were immediately sent by Secretary Bryan to President Wilson. State Department officials admitted that one of the most complex problems of the war had arisen. Officials were unanimous in their opinion that the notification could not be called a "blockade," although it had virtually the effect of the same.

Secretary Bryan refused to discuss the note with correspondents further than to say that it was not in response to any communication sent by this Government, but came as an independent announcement from England and France.

"I have no comment whatever to make," said Mr. Bryan.

Similar reticence was shown by other Administration officials, but it is known that the action of the Governments of the Allies in laying this embargo on German trade is giving serious concern. What course the Government will take is not known, but profound consideration will be devoted to the very material problem that has been presented before any definite announcement of policy is made. It is the understanding here that the action of England and France is supported by all the Allies, and that it is their purpose to stand in solid array behind the decision to prevent all commodities from leaving or entering Germany.

The effect of this embargo on neutral trade will be far-reaching and staggering. Its strict enforcement will mean that shipments to Germany of American cotton, as well as foodstuffs and goods that are not even contraband, in neutral bottoms, must stop, if the Allies are able to maintain the embargo by naval force. It also means that Germany will not be able to ship dyestuffs, potash, and other products as return cargoes in American cotton ships going into Germany.

The ships, cargoes, and crews of neutrals are not to be injured, but the vital point with the neutrals will be the fact that the embargo proposes to cut off their trade in its entirety with Germany, regardless of what the cargoes may be.

Blockade Without the Name.

The move of the Allies is regarded here as virtually a blockade of the German coast without declaring a formal blockade. It marks a departure from the established rules of international law and is being justified by England and the Allies as a retaliatory measure based on the German substitution of indiscriminate destruction for regulated capture.

Under previously existing international law and practice it has been permissible for neutrals to send foodstuffs, not destined for the use of the enemy, and goods that are not contraband, like cotton, into a belligerent country. This will cause severe hardships to neutral nations. Southern members of Congress are greatly concerned over it. It is also known that the State Department is very much disappointed. Coming after American cotton had begun to move in a steady stream into Rotterdam, for shipment up the Rhine, and into Bremen, the embargo is expected to have a disastrous effect upon the cotton trade. The movement of American cotton in Germany had the effect of raising the price of the product. The cutting off of the German market is expected to depress the market again.

Sir Cecil Spring-Rice, the British Ambassador, and M. Jusserand the French Ambassador, delivered the joint note to Secretary Bryan this morning, and at the same time the British Ambassador presented his instructions with regard to his Government's further consideration of the American note.

It was noted generally that the communication from England and France did not use the word blockade, and at the French and British Embassies here there was an avoidance of the same word. The notes leave much, therefore, to be explained.

It was regarded as practically certain that the United States would reply promptly with an inquiry as to how the step was to be carried into practice, together with a protest against the announcement that commerce between the German and neutral countries hereafter would be interrupted by the Allies.

Just when the United States Government will act on the latest note is dependent to some extent on when the replies are received to the informal communication looking to an abolition of submarine warfare on merchant ships and the shipment of foodstuffs to the civilian population of belligerents. Germany's answer is said to be on its way, and officials expect that it will be practically an acquiescence to the principle of the American proposals. From Great Britain, not a word had come in several days until today's statement that the matter was under consideration.

Disregards Precedents.

Officials realized that, except for diplomatic correspondence, the points of which might be easily exhausted without remedy, there was no way for neutral Governments to enforce their protests and still maintain their neutrality. The general disregard of precedents, it was pointed out, has made the position of neutrals more delicate in the present circumstances than ever before, though to embargoes by the United States and the non-intercourse act arose in the early part of the nineteenth century, during the Napoleonic wars.

A blockade was declared by Great Britain against the German coast from the River Elbe to the port of Brest, (France, inclusive.) Napoleon, then in a somewhat similar situation which led camp at Berlin, proclaimed a counter-blockade against the entire British coast and prohibited commerce with England. Great Britain then retaliated by issuing an order in council prohibiting neutral vessels from trading with the ports of France and her allies, and with all ports of Europe from which the British flag was excluded.

"Against the several orders and decrees," writes John Bassett Moore, former Counselor of the State Department, "the United States protested and as measures of retaliation resorted to embargoes and non-intercourse, and in the case of Great Britain, which was aggravated by the question of impressment, eventually to war."

That these questions were never definitely settled is indicated in the correspondence between the United States and its commissioners who finally arranged the treaty of Ghent in 1814.

Cabinet to Take It Up.

The entire subject probably will be laid before the Cabinet tomorrow by President Wilson.

Senator Hitchcock of Nebraska, another Democratic member of the Committee on Foreign Relations, said:

"Heretofore the international law affecting warfare has been made by the belligerents alone. I think it is time that the neutrals co-operated to make rules that will protect their right to trade. Any such movement, of course, to be effective would have to be very vigorously undertaken, and the United States would have to be spokesman for the neutrals. I think the United States should exert herself to unite the neutrals for this purpose."

Senator Walsh of Montana, who had defended the right of the Dacia to carry goods across the ocean under the American flag, said that the action of the Allied Governments proposed a blockade similar to the Napoleonic blockade in the early part of the last century which was known as "the paper blockade."

Senator Stone of Missouri, Chairman of the Committee on Foreign Relations, said tonight:

"The effect of the Anglo-French proclamation is to close out our commerce from Germany. I regard it as a very unfortunate performance, to express it mildly."

Senator Stone declined to give his views as to the possible remedy the United States would take, for the reason that it would do no good to discuss that phase of the subject.

It was reported again tonight that the Administration had given consideration to declaring an embargo on foodstuffs intended for all belligerents in retaliation for the interference with American shipping, but officials close to the President previously had said they did not expect he would ask Congress to authorize such an embargo.

TURKS MASSING ON DARDANELLES

Essad Pasha Hurriedly Gathers Troops—Fort Dardanus Is Reported Silenced.

RUSSIA NOW CO-OPERATING

Has Expelled the Turks from the Trans-Caucasus and Dominates the Black Sea.

Special Cable to THE NEW YORK TIMES.

ATHENS, March 1, (Dispatch to The London Daily News.)—The Turkish forces are hurriedly concentrating on the Asiatic side of the Dardanelles under Essad Pasha, the defender of Janina.

LONDON, Tuesday, March 2.—According to The Daily Mail's Athens correspondent, Fort Dardanus, twelve miles up the Dardanelles, on the Asiatic side, has been silenced by the allied fleet.

The correspondent adds that diplomatic reports from Constantinople indicate that serious rioting there was suppressed after many arrests had been made.

The attack of the allied fleet on the Dardanelles has been considerably interrupted by bad weather. The Official Information Bureau issued this statement last night:

"The operations in the Dardanelles are again delayed by unfavorable weather. A strong northeasterly gale is blowing, with rain and mist, which would render long-range fire and aeroplane observation difficult."

Another official report says that one marine was killed and three were wounded on the British battleship Vengeance in the attack on the forts on Friday.

The operations of the allied fleet in the Dardanelles, as perhaps presaging quick developments in the Balkan situation, dominates the military situation on sea and land. The more optimistic minds expect Constantinople to fall; but there is a noticeable disposition to realize that the ships face no easy task, notwithstanding the twenty-mile range of the superdreadnought Queen Elizabeth. Whether any progress has been made since the outer forts were demolished has not been made known officially.

"All the News That's Fit to Print."

The New York Times.

THE WEATHER

Fair today and Sunday; moderate west to northwest winds.

Full weather report on Page 16.

VOL. LXIV...NO. 20,874. ....   NEW YORK, SATURDAY, MARCH 20, 1915.—TWENTY PAGES.   ONE CENT *In Greater New York, Jersey City and Newark.*

ALLIES LOSE THREE BIG BATTLESHIPS IN NEW ATTACK ON DARDANELLES; 600 FRENCH DROWN, BRITISH SAFE

Irresistible, Ocean and Bouvet Go Down, Hitting Mines in Strait.

OTHER VESSELS CRIPPLED

Gaulois and Inflexible Out of Action and Turks Say Others Suffered from Shell Fire.

FLOATING MINES DID HAVOC

But British, Undaunted, Are Sending Ships in Place of the Lost Craft.

ADMIRAL CARDEN DISPLACED

Announcement of De Robeck's Succession to Command Made in Admiralty's Report.

Allied Admirals Confer On the French Flagship

Special Cable to THE NEW YORK TIMES.

TENEDOS, March 19, (Dispatch to The London Daily Chronicle.)—A conference is being held on the French flagship Suffren. The English and French Admirals and Captains have assembled on the vessel. Important action is pending.

LONDON, March 19.—Three battleships of the allied fleet, the Irresistible and the Ocean, both British, and the Bouvet, French, were blown up and sunk by floating mines yesterday afternoon while engaged, with seven other warships, in attacking the forts in the Narrows of the Dardanelles.

The British battle-cruiser Inflexible and the French battleship Gaulois also were hit by shells from the Turkish forts and damaged.

Practically all the 630 men making up the complement of the Bouvet went down with the vessel, which sank within three minutes after she fouled

the mine, an internal explosion taking place aboard the ship.

Of the 1,500 men on board the two British battleships that were sunk few were lost, the crews being transferred to other warships under a hot fire. The British Admiralty remarks that the casualties " were not heavy, considering the scale of the operations."

The waters in which the ships were lost had been swept of mines, but, judging from the Admiralty report, other mines, set adrift by the Turks, floated down with the current and caused the disaster among the allied ships gathered inside the entrance to the Dardanelles.

In its official account of the operations, the effect of which upon the Turkish forts is not known, the Admiralty announces that the battleships Queen and Implacable are being sent to take the place of the lost vessels. It also chronicles the fact that Vice Admiral Carden was succeeded on Tuesday by Rear Admiral de Robeck in command of the fleet. The stated reason for Carden's retirement is illness.

Operations in the Dardanelles are being continued. It is understood that the engagement was resumed to-day.

Battle Scene from Tenedos Hill Thrills Beholders.

GUNS SHAKE LAND AND SEA

Forts Respond Fiercely to the Terrific Bombardment of Warships.

TWO MAGAZINES EXPLODE

Great Columns of Water Rise as a Warship, Probably the Bouvet, Is Blown Up.

Special Cable to THE NEW YORK TIMES.

TENEDOS, March 18, (Dispatch to The London Daily Chronicle.)—Standing on the summit of the hill of St. Elias and facing the mouth of the Dardanelles, one sees an unforgettable sight. On the left are the white cliffs of the European

shore. On the right, over the low coast of the Troad, is the lakelike expanse of strait, stretching up to the Narrows, and the Town of Chanak, where the Turks have the strongest of their forts.

As I watched (it was about 10:30 this morning) I saw four British battleships enter the strait, the Inflexible leading. Behind came the Queen Elizabeth, with a torpedo boat on either side of her. She opened fire. Two explosions rent the air, and the belching flame from the guns showed that one shell had been sent to the Asian and one to the European shore.

The effect was almost instantaneously seen. From Chanak a dense column of smoke rose. From Kilid Bahr fort on the other side there were flames as well as smoke.

Further firing was heard from the fleet. A little later a conflagration could be seen higher up the Narrows, responding to the flash and boom of the heavy guns.

At 11:30 o'clock four of the French battleships entered the strait, the Suffren, Gaulois, Bouvet, and Charlemagne, following five other British warships.. The French ships were soon in action and engaged the forts with a vigorous fire.

This tremendous bombardment, however, was still incomplete and at 12:15 o'clock other British warships, which had been at anchor below us, moved in stately procession to the strait in a single line.

By 12:45 the whole firmament seemed to be rocking under the tremendous roar and crash of the cannonade from warships and the answering fire from the forts, which were now all in full outburst.

Europe seemed to be belching flame across at Asia and Asia answering back again, and the usually placid waters of the Dardanelles were now pitted and churned with white splashes and erratic foam.

Two great columns of water followed explosions, probably from submerged mines. One warship near the Asiatic coast (the distance was too far to enable her identity to be distinguished) could be seen apparently on fire. A volume of black smoke followed and hid from view six of the British warships which a moment before could be seen heading up the strait with their funnels belching flame at a furious rate.

Fire from the ships and forts had now become deafening and a new dull, deep note was entering into the noise, as one judged from the howitzers of heavy type brought into play from the forts.

A change of operations took place at 1:30, four of the British battleships moving so as to allow six others to approach the narrows. But the incessant flashes and booming remained constant, and the very sky seemed overcast with the emanations of the guns.

There was a brief lull about 2 o'clock for an hour and then again at 3 the whole crescendo of thunderous sound broke out again.

The scene was awe-inspiring, the last touch being given by an aeroplane, which could be seen dimly through the smoke wreaths in the sky, flitting like some supernatural object over the combat. And as it moved, one could see below, as if there were some mysterious connection, vivid flames shooting up from west of Chanak.

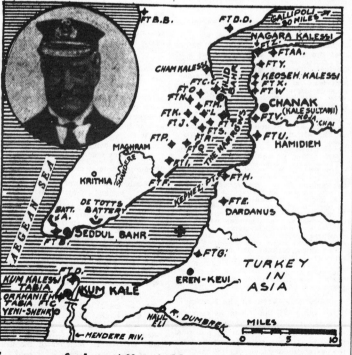

Scene of the Allies' Heavy Naval Losses

Star shows approximately the point where the Bouvet sank. Insert picture is that of Rear Admiral De Robeck, new commander of the British attacking forces.

MEMEL OCCUPIED BY RUSSIAN FORCE

Tilsit Also Menaced by Hosts Pouring Into East Prussia from the North.

GERMAN TRENCHES FLOODED

LONDON, Saturday, March 20.—Beyond the operations in the Dardanelles the most important news of the day concerns the reported occupation by the Russians of Memel, a German port on the Baltic, as announced in the German official communication. Memel is a town of considerable importance in Northeastern Prussia, and the presence there of Russian forces is taken by military observers here to indicate that the Russian Generals have decided to attempt a big sweep down through East Prussia, in an endeavor to compel the Germans to fall back from Northern Poland.

Again, North Poland has been transformed into an immense bog by the thaw, which has set in just as Field Marshal von Hindenburg has started his offensive against Przasnysz. It is declared that it is impossible, except at widely separated high places, to move, let alone fight.

The Germans, however, seemingly anxious always to be doing something, have started an offensive in Central Poland, where they have commenced an attack on the Russians in the region of the Pilica River. There is also heavy fighting in Galicia, the Carpathians, and Bukowina, despite the heavy snow. In Bukowina the Austrians, having received reinforcements, have resumed a strong offensive, says a Bucharest dispatch to The London Times.

PETROGRAD, March 19, (Dispatch to The London Morning Post.)—Russians are advancing steadily upon East Prussia. One column is now fighting in German territory, within a few miles of Memel, and a second is fighting in the neighborhood of Tauroggen, close to the German frontier, and one march from Tilsit. The Russian successes in this region are particularly gratifying to them, inasmuch as they are fighting in enemy country, even though within their own political frontiers.

Nearly 200 miles due south of Memel the Russian lines have advanced within half a march of the German frontier. Apparently the Germans here are quite broken beyond the power to organize an adequate defense. They have more difficulty in surrendering now than ever before, as the exasperation of the troops, especially those drawn from the nationalities over which the Baltic Germans tyrannized for centuries, are disinclined to give quarter. This fact also counts toward the explanation of the increasing cases of open desertion by German troops, which is quite a new phenomenon in this war.

South of the Lower Vistula the Germans are being incommoded by overflowing rivers, which in some cases have flooded them out of their trenches. A heavy cannonading is kept up in several sections on this front from the Bzura to Lopushno. In the neighborhood of the Pilica, where the Germans have made yet another series of violent attacks, their activity has been brought to a standstill by the steady resistance of the Russians.

The favorite tactics of the Germans, the so-called lightning attacks, have succeeded nowhere in this war, but continue to be attempted. The Russian artillery caught the last attempt with a withering fire which dispersed the usual dense formations.

The Carpathian front continues to occupy the least space in the bulletins, which, considering it is the main front, indicates that important movements are in progress which will be communicated when they have been completed. Meantime the following incident of the fighting in this region is interesting:

On Monday night three German companies under cover of fog reached a Russian trench held by only half a company, who were driven out. The Russians moved up two companies to retake it. They were met by heavy firing, but charged with bayonets, and practically destroyed the German superior force. Three officers and ninety-three men, all that were left alive after the bayonet charge, were taken prisoners.

It would appear that the German units have been seriously reduced in numbers, since the Russians reckoned two of their companies were sufficient to turn three German ones out of an intrenched position and annihilate the force besides.

MEN WORTH MORE THAN SHIPS

Naval Opinion Finds Comfort in Loss of Pre-Dreadnoughts.

Special Cable to THE NEW YORK TIMES.

LONDON, Saturday, March 20.—The Daily News naval expert says:

"The loss of the Irresistible and the Ocean is a serious blow from a material point of view, but let us remember in the first place that trained men are far more important than old pre-dreadnought battleships, and in the second place, that these vessels would not have been sent to the eastern Mediterranean if we could not well have afforded to spare them from the main theatre of naval operations, the North Sea. These were among our oldest ships, but the fact that we have there at least one of our very newest shows that the naval position in home waters is giving Lord Fisher no cause for anxiety.

"At the beginning of the war we had forty pre-dreadnought battleships to Germany's twenty, and after seven months of fighting we have now thirty-six to her twenty. On the other hand we have increased our strength in ships of the latest type at a far greater rate than Germany can possibly have done.

"The French battleship Bouvet is the first important unit which our Allies have lost so far, though they have had two destroyers, three torpedo boats, and two submarines sunk.

"The damage inflicted upon the other ships shows the fortifications are increasing in importance as the strait is penetrated."

The *Irresistible* was one of the ships sunk in the British effort to take the Dardanelles.

All of the three vessels sunk by mines in the Dardanelles on Thursday were representatives of a by-gone age of naval construction, being pre-dreadnought battleships of which class Great Britain had forty when the war began and France had twenty-one.

These ships were regarded as the most formidable craft of their sort afloat fifteen years ago. Sloping roofed turrets and double barbettes had just come into use, succeeding for a time the round turret and the single barbette.

The Irresistible was a sister ship of the Formidable, which was torpedoed in the English Channel, off Portsmouth, on Jan. 1. She had a displacement of 15,000 tons, a speed of 18 knots, and a complement of 780 men. Her main batteries consisted of four 12-inch guns and twelve 6-inch guns, and her secondary battery of sixteen 12-pounders, (heavy,) two 12-pounders, (light,) six 3-pounders, and two Maxims. She was laid down in 1898 and was completed in 1902. She had been refitted.

The Ocean was a sister ship of the Canopus, which was sent in October to join the British South Pacific squadron, but did not arrive until just after its destruction off Coronel, Chile, Nov. 1, 1914, by the German squadron under von Spee. The displacement of ships of this class is 12,950 tons. The Ocean's speed was 18¼ knots, and she carried a complement of 750 officers and men. She had the same main battery as the Irresistible, and her secondary battery was almost identical. She was laid down in 1898 and completed in 1900. She also had been refitted.

The Bouvet was an even older and lighter battleship than the British. She was laid down in 1896 and completed in 1898. Her displacement was 12,205 tons, and her speed 17 knots. Her regular complement was 630 officers and men. In her main battery were two 12-inch guns, two 10.8-inch, and 8 5.5-inch. Eight 4-inch guns, ten 3-pounders, and twenty 1-pounders completed her armament.

The Implacable, which has been ordered to the Dardanelles to take the place of the Irresistible, is the last ship of her class now afloat, while the Queen, sent to take the place of the Ocean, has the same displacement, armament, and speed as the Irresistible.

The Henri IV., ordered by France to the Dardanelles, is a comparatively small battleship, laid down in 1897 and completed in 1902. Her displacement is 8,950 tons and her main battery comprises two 10.8-inch and ten 5.5-inch guns.

"All the News That's Fit to Print."

The New York Times.

THE WEATHER

Fair today; increasing cloudiness tomorrow; moderate northwest winds.

For full weather report see Page 13.

VOL. LXIV...NO. 20,884. NEW YORK, TUESDAY, MARCH 30, 1915.—TWENTY PAGES. ONE CENT In Greater New York, Jersey City and Newark. | Elsewhere TWO CENTS.

140 LIVES LOST AS SUBMARINES SINK TWO SHIPS

Germans Blow Up Liner Falaba, Carrying 160 Passengers and Crew of Ninety.

MANY KILLED BY TORPEDO

Bolt Hurled at Steamer as Crowded Lifeboats Are Being Lowered Into Water.

ONLY 5 MINUTES' RESPITE

Survivors Assert that Germans Made No Effort to Save Drowning Victims.

STEAMER AGUILA ALSO SUNK

Shells Fall on Deck and Around Escaping Boats—One Capsized and a Woman Passenger Killed.

LONDON, March 29.—More than 140 lives were lost in the sinking by German submarines of the African liner Falaba and the British steamer Aguila, bound from Liverpool for Lisbon.

The Falaba, which was torpedoed in St. George's Channel on Sunday afternoon, carried a crew of 90 and about 160 passengers, and of this total only 140 were rescued. Of those rescued eight died from exposure.

The Aguila had a crew of 42 and 3 passengers, and of these 23 of the crew and all the passengers were lost.

In both cases, on sighting the submarine, the Captain tried to escape by putting on all speed possible, but the underwater craft overtook the steamers, showing that Germany now has some of her most modern submarines engaged in the blockade operations against England.

The Captain of the Falaba, who was one of those lost, was told that he had five minutes to get his passengers and crew into the boats, but, according to survivors, before this was possible, a torpedo was fired, striking the engine room, and causing a terrific explosion. Many persons were killed, and the steamer sank in ten minutes.

Trawlers which happened to be in the vicinity rescued most of those who were saved; others got away in the boats which were ready for launching and which were quickly lowered when the order came to abandon the ship. Those who were still aboard the steamer when the explosion occurred were thrown into the sea, and the fishermen worked for an hour or more picking up those who managed to keep themselves afloat.

The skipper of the fishing boat Eileen Emma, which participated in the rescue work, reported that no effort was made by the crew of the submarine to assist the persons who were struggling in the water.

The Eileen Emma sighted the submarine shortly after noon, her skipper said, and followed the craft for more than an hour.

Fired on Lifeboats.

The Aguila was attacked off the Pembrokeshire coast. The submarine, which in this case was the U-28, opened fire with her guns, shells from which killed a woman passenger, the chief engineer, and two of the crew. Even after the crew had begun to lower the boats, according to the story of the survivors, the Germans kept up their fire, and some of the boats were riddled with bullets.

The Captain of the trawler Ottilie, who was notified by the commander of the submarine that the Aguila had been sunk, went to the rescue and picked up three boats containing nineteen of the crew. The fourth boat, which contained the other members of the crew, could not be found, and it is presumed that she foundered. On their arrival at Fishguard several of the crew wore bandages, having been wounded by shells from the submarine.

Another Dutch steamer, the Amstel, of 853 tons, has been blown up by a mine off Flamborough Head.

With regard to the sinking of these vessels the British Admiralty tonight issued the following statement:

"Twenty-three members of the crew and three passengers are missing from the steamer Aguila.

"The steamer Falaba, which also sank, carried a crew of about 90 persons and about 160 passengers. About 140 survivors have been picked up, eight of whom, including the Captain, died afterward. It is feared that many persons on the steamer were killed by the explosion of the torpedo.

"The Dutch steamer Amstel, a vessel of 853 tons, belonging to P. A. Van Es & Co. of Rotterdam, when on a passage from Rotterdam to Goole, England, struck a mine at 4 A. M., March 29, in a German minefield off Flamborough (Yorkshire, England.) The crew has been landed in the Humber by the Grimsby trawler Pinewold."

There is a slight discrepancy between the admiralty's statement of casualties in the case of the steamer Falaba and the list supplied at the offices of the Elder, Dempster Steamship Company, owners of the vessel. The company's statement shows that so far as is known fifty-two first-class passengers, thirty-four second-class passengers and forty-nine of the crew of the Falaba were saved. Four of the passengers and four of the crew are reported killed, and sixty-one passengers and forty-three of the crew are missing.

Raider Outspeeds Ship.

FISHGUARD, Wales, March 29.—Capt. Bannerman of the Aguila said the submarine fired across the bows of the steamer, but he speeded up to fourteen knots to clear the undersea vessel. The submarine was making eighteen knots, however, and quickly overtook them.

The attempt of the Aguila to escape seemed to arouse the anger of the Germans, for they gave the crew and passengers only four minutes to leave the ship. But before the time was up the submarine opened fire which was kept up rapidly while the crew was launching the boats, killing the chief engineer and two of the crew and wounding several others.

One member of the crew said that a boat in which were ten sailors, a woman passenger, and a stewardess was fired on and the passenger was killed while the stewardess was thrown into the water and drowned. Finally the boat capsized and sank.

The Captain of the Ottilie, which picked up the remaining boat, said the submarine was the U-28, and apparently a new craft.

Jeered at Drowning Men.

Special Cable to THE NEW YORK TIMES.

CARDIFF, March 29, (Dispatch to The London Daily Chronicle.)—It was entirely due to the foresight of Capt. Wright of the steam drifter Eileen Emma that many more lives were not lost in the sinking of the liner Falaba, for he was able to save more than 140 of them. Many of these were transferred to other boats, and altogether 116 survivors, including the chief engineer, were landed at Milford Haven. It is believed that twenty others were saved.

Red Cross nurses were soon busy attending the injured. Many of the survivors were scantily clothed and shivering with cold. Very little property was saved. The Falaba was carrying a cargo and specie. On board were officers and men of the R. A. M. C.

The survivors expressed themselves very strongly with regard to the conduct of the crew of the submarine. They say that when the men were struggling in the water those on the deck of the submarine laughed and jeered. As some of the drowning men came to the surface they naturally held up their hands to try to grasp something to save themselves, and nothing seemed to give more amusement to the German crew than to watch the actions of these victims. After seeing that the vessel was doomed to sink, the survivors say, the submarine dived below. All speak highly of the perfect order on board the vessel before she sank. There was no panic, the Captain was on the bridge, and the wireless operator was at his post.

One man told me he was in the water for an hour before he was picked up. "Barely 10 minutes after we received the order to leave the ship, and before the last boat had been lowered," he said, "I heard a report and the vessel heeled over. The Germans had actually fired a torpedo at a range of about 100 yards when they could distinctly see a large number of passengers and the crew, including the Captain, the purser, and other officers were still on board. It was a dastardly thing to do. It was nothing but murder in cold blood. When we had been in the boats for two hours we were picked up by the Eileen Emma and two other trawlers.

"About 6 o'clock in the evening a destroyer came along, took us on board, and landed us at Milford Haven."

Another passenger gave a graphic description of what he termed "this murderous affair."

"The passengers," he said, "were largely composed of Government officials, traders, and merchants, about 150 in all. When we sighted the submarine coming up behind us we were going at full speed. But that was only from 12 to 13 knots, and the submarine quickly overtook us. She first came on our port side and signaled to us to stop and threatened to sink us if we did not obey. The Captain at once hove to.

Five Minutes to Get Away.

"The commander of the submarine then called out in excellent English that we should have five minutes in which to leave the vessel. He immediately turned his submarine around to our starboard side about 300 yards away and with its nose pointing direct to our midships. Meanwhile we lowered the boats as quickly as our crew could, but several of them did not get down properly and were upset. The people were soon struggling in the water.

"Another boat was actually half way down and full of passengers when the submarine fired a torpedo without the slightest warning. I was one of a small party of passengers and officers who had not got into the boats, and I distinctly saw the torpedo coming. It came straight toward where we were standing and we ran to the fore part of the ship to escape it. The torpedo struck the vessel amidships and she immediately gave a list to starboard and went down about ten minutes afterward. It was a slight explosion, more like the sound of a small gun. The party, of whom I was one, jumped overboard into the water about four minutes before the Falaba sank.

"The main deck was then awash. I was in the water for about an hour, swimming and floating. I had to swim among the wreckage and a number of dead bodies. At last I was picked up by one of our own boats, with four others, including the first officer. The Captain jumped into the water about the same time as I did. He was one of the last to leave the ship, and he swam in the sea for a long time and was finally picked up by one of the boats, but I was afterward told he died from exposure immediately after being rescued. I also heard that eight or nine of the crew died from injuries after being landed.

"The submarine was flying the German ensign, and I did not really believe she would fire a torpedo so soon. It was murderous. The people were swimming around the ship, and a boat but half way down the davits was sent flying into the water, for the shock of the torpedo snapped the davits.

"If the Germans had only given us ten minutes, I believe all our passengers and crew would have been saved."

Two officers who refused to give their names said: "It was murder, simply murder. We saw the submarine away in the distance on the starboard side. It seemed to say stop, but we made a bit of a run for it, hoping we should outdistance her. It was a murderous game. They fired a torpedo while the people were still on board and one of the boats actually was being lowered. They made no attempt to save anybody and there was only one trawler in sight."

Offered Life Belt to Woman.

There were seven women on board the Falaba, and of these all except one, a stewardess, were saved. She, too, might have been saved owing to the chivalry displayed by a young officer. This officer, observing that the stewardess was without a life belt, took off his own and insisted on putting it on her. She, however, refused to take it and the consequence was that both officer and stewardess were among the drowned. It is believed that of the officers only the Third and Fourth, the Chief Engineer, and the wireless operator were saved.

W. McCall of London, one of the survivors, gave me a thrilling description of the sinking of the ship. He said:

"Every one on board became excited at the news that a submarine was so near, and all the passengers crowded on deck to have a look at the craft. Our skipper put on full speed, but it was very soon seen that we stood no chance of getting away. The submarine came after us like a greyhound, and in three-quarters of an hour after we had sighted her she came within hailing distance. Judging from the photographs I have seen of submarines, this was one of the latest and biggest. She carried a good-sized gun, and this was trained on the Falaba as soon as the submarine got near us. The first thing the commander of the submarine did was to send up a rocket. Then, coming near, he hailed our skipper and ordered him to get his passengers into the boats at once, adding in good English: 'I'm going to sink your boat.' The boats were lowered immediately and the passengers were served with lifebelts, but no one was allowed to take any personal belongings."

W. A. Austin, one of the survivors, said that when the submarine was sighted she was flying a flag that looked remarkably like a white ensign. When the torpedo struck the vessel about fifty persons were standing on the poop. Austin said, and all must have been killed when the explosion occurred.

"We were among the last to leave the ship," he said. "We got into a lifeboat in which there were about forty people. We found the boat leaking badly, and within twenty minutes or so she became filled with water and capsized. After the Falaba sank the submarine made away toward Ireland. The crew standing on deck made no effort to rescue any one, but actually trained their guns on us."

Dr. Gros had a marvelous escape. He was floating about helpless when a Corporal of the R.A.M.C. went to his aid and swam with him toward the Eileen Emma. She took them aboard, but the Corporal died on deck.

Captain Gallant to the Last.

Special Cable to THE NEW YORK TIMES.

LIVERPOOL, March 29, (Dispatch to The London Daily News.)—Members of the Falaba's crew who arrived at Liverpool last night told of the brave manner in which Capt. Davis met his death. A deck steward named J. Turton said:

"From the boat I was in I saw the Falaba up to the time she sank. The Captain stuck to his post until the vessel was practically submerged. His last act was to hoist the Elder Dempster house flag on the sinking ship. While the boats were being lowered he blew the ship's whistle as a signal for assistance, and attracted the attention of the trawlers which saved us. Along with the Captain at the last were Chief Officer Baxter, the chef and three stewards named Noble, Ford, and Musker. They jumped to a trawler which had come alongside, and the Captain in doing so struck his head and fell into the sea. When pulled into the boat he died almost immediately."

The wireless operator in an interview said it was 12 o'clock at noon on Sunday when he was ordered by the chief officer to send out the S O S signal, as the ship was being chased by a submarine.

"I sent the signal," he said, "giving our position, and it was answered from Land's End. In order to emphasize the urgency of the call and anticipating what might happen I added that our ship had been torpedoed and was sinking. I remained in the cabin for about six or seven minutes, then the chief officer came to me and said nothing further could be done, as the submarine had overhauled us.

"I managed to get into one of the boats, but almost as soon as it touched the water it began to sink, part of the side having been burst through. A passenger with a piece of rope held the crack together as well as he could, but the water poured in and soon we were up to our waists in water. Only the buoyancy of the lifeboat kept us from going under.

"There were sixteen of us, and two, a passenger and a member of the crew, were washed away."

Another passenger, Mr. Taylor, said he distinctly saw the crew on the deck of the submarine laughing.

Torpedo Upset Boat.

CARDIFF, Wales, March 29.—One of the Falaba's passengers, in telling of their experiences, said that when the submarine ordered the passengers to take to the boats, the boats were lowered immediately and the passengers received life belts, but no one was allowed to take any personal effects.

"Then followed a horrible scene," said the passenger. "Some of the boats were swamped and the occupants were thrown into the sea. Several were drowned almost immediately.

"Barely ten minutes after we received the order to leave the ship I heard a report; and saw the vessel keel over. The Germans had actually fired a torpedo at her at a range of about 100 yards, when a large number of passengers, the Captain and other officers were still distinctly to be seen aboard."

All the passengers and officers say that the submarine fired a torpedo before all the boats were lowered, and while many persons were still aboard the steamer. One officer said:

"I was sitting in a boat which was suspended from the davits and was waiting for two women passengers, when another officer shouted, 'Look out,' and I then saw the bubbles marking the track of a torpedo.

"There was a tremendous crash, and the boat fell from the davits and turned over, throwing the passengers and crew into the icy water. The water was frightfully cold, and there were many who died from exposure."

The Quartermaster of the Falaba, describing the scene of the destruction of the steamer, said:

"All on bord helped splendidly in the rescue work. There were eight women on board. One of them, who hesitated about entering a lifeboat, I threw overboard. There was no time to argue the matter. Luckily she was picked up. Two other women who refused to leave the ship were drowned.

"The scene was awful with scores of people struggling in the water, owing to the overturning of the boats. The submarine was in the midst of them, and I saw at least twenty men on her. They stood and laughed.

"Captain Davis was on the liner when she sank. I pulled him into our boat with a boathook. Poor fellow, he was alive then, but he expired immediately afterward. Our small boat was within twenty yards of the submarine when she fired, and I saw the torpedo's propeller as it shaved us and went on its deadly journey."

CALLS IT SAVAGERY.

London Paper Says Germany Affixes Brand of Infamy to Her Name.

Special Cable to THE NEW YORK TIMES.

LONDON, Tuesday, March 30.—The Morning Post in an editorial on the sinking of the Falaba and Aguila says:

"Germany has boasted that the opinion of the civilized world does not interest her and certainly will not deflect her from her appointed course, and now we have evidence which not even our most incorrigible sentimentalists can ignore that she means what she says. To vent her hatred of this country there is no barbarity from which she will shrink, not even the shelling of women passengers as they seek refuge in the boats of a sinking ship. Very well, we must henceforth reckon with that fact.

"While Germany thus fixes the brand of infamy on her name it is our business first of all to take all measures for thwarting this reckless savagery, and next to make it plain that a dear account will be inexorably exacted for these crimes. It is true that the conscience of this country would never allow us to take reprisals in kind, whatever Germany does in the way of murder and outrage. We could not stoop to the lex talionis, but that does not mean that we are to suffer these things passively, that we are to let bygones be bygones when the time to exact the settlement shall arrive, and extend to the criminals an act of general oblivion and forgiveness. To consent to such counsel would be not only weak but treachery to civilization and humanity.

"It has become a vital world interest that the spirit which has made these deeds of horror possible shall not be only humiliated but utterly broken, and that the people who have fostered that spirit should be made to repent in bitterness and sorrow. It is our bounden duty to posterity not less than to the present generation to see to it that in its ending the way of the transgressor shall be hard."

Says Germans Are Desperate.

The Times says:

"We hope that the grief, caused by the loss of innocent life, and the indignation, excited by the manner of it will not find vent or be spent in violent language and vain abuse of the enemy. That will only enhance his satisfaction and increase the jubilation which will be felt in Germany at the successful murder of a number of British civilians.

"The lesson we must take to heart is that we are at war with a people who will stick at no means to accomplish their end. It is not a new lesson, but it has not hitherto been thoroughly learned. There are still considerable sections of people in this country who have regarded the war as a thing that does not intimately concern them and who hold their own petty affairs more urgent than the need of carrying it on with the utmost vigor of which we are capable.

"The wholesale murder of non-combatants on the high seas should open their eyes, and the exulting derision with which it has been accomplished should convince them of the kind of enemy with which we have to deal.

"The Germans are evidently desperate. The new turn given to their submarine campaign indicates the failure of its first objective, which was to put an end to our foreign trade. That has failed, and the present move is a result. Having declined to be frightened by a sham blockade, we are to taste the frightfulness inflicted on the helpless Belgians."

The Daily News says: "If these cases are not the ferocities of individual brutes, but the settled ruthlessness of a new phase in the campaign, the Germans cannot complain whatever differential treatment is hereafter meted out to their submarine crews. Men who deliberately kill unarmed merchant sailors and helpless women have clearly no place in the ranks of honorable combatants of any kind, and can shelter their conduct behind no orders whatever. The sinking of the Falaba has, it is believed, involved the loss of something like 150 lives. It is mere massacre, of no military significance whatever, for the presence of a few officers on board cannot be held to make the torpedoing of an unarmed liner with all on board a warlike operation.

"It weakens in no respect this country's power to conduct the war, but it does strengthen very materially the determination of Englishmen so to conduct it as to bring to strict account the men who can do such things as this and laugh at them, and the nation and Government which can condone and extol them."

The Daily Telegraph says:

"These terrible incidents are a sequel to all the conferences at The Hague. Conventions were drawn up to rob war of some of its terrors. The enemy has not only torn up these instruments, but, utilizing all the dearly won triumphs of mechanical science, has invented new forms of barbarious inhumanity.

"These outrages have occurred at the moment when it is being urged that it is our duty to forgive and forget and conciliate, when we are being exhorted to cultivate love for a country capable of the perpetration of such heartless crimes."

The Official Reports of War Operations.

RUSSIA.

PETROGRAD.—On the front west of the Niemen we have everywhere stopped the German counter-offensive. A battalion of the Twenty-first German Corps, which was advancing, Sunday, over the ice on Lake Dusia with the object of getting in our rear, was attacked with the bayonet near the village of Zebrziski and annihilated.

The enemy's siege batteries at Ossowetz have almost entirely ceased fire. Fighting continues between the Skwa and Orzyc Rivers. In an extremely desperate battle for the village of Vakhi we captured nine machine guns.

In the Carpathians, between Morlitze and Bartfeld, the Austrians on Saturday made persistent but fruitless attacks near the villages of Gladycheff and Reghetow. In the direction of Baligrod, on the left bank of the Upper San, in the sector of Radzielouw, Poliankа, Zavoy, and Javorjutz, we have made progress and have taken more than 600 prisoners and four machine guns. Near Kozlouwka, on Saturday, we repulsed new German attacks.

AUSTRIA.

VIENNA.—Fighting in the Carpathians continues. A Russian attack yesterday on the heights west of Benyavoelgy was repulsed, the enemy losing heavily. Regiments of the Fourth Cavalry Division and troops of the First Landsturm Infantry Brigade, fought magnificently, and repeatedly repulsed numerically stronger hostile attacks.

North of the Uzsok Pass Russian night attacks failed under heavy firing from our positions.

On the Southeast Galician front there were artillery duels. Russian forces, which advanced across the Dniester River, east of Zaleszezyki, were driven back after a vigorous fight.

At some points in Russian Poland and in West Galicia, artillery duels have taken place. A Russian night attack at Loscsina, in Poland, failed completely.

FRANCE.

PARIS.—(*Night Report*)—The enemy has bombarded Nieuporttown and Nieuport-Bains, (two miles to the northwest,) but the damage done to the bridge thrown across the Yser, was not of great importance.

In Champagne there has been artillery action in the neighborhood of Beausejour.

In the Argonne there has been cannonading and bombs have been thrown, principally in the region of Bagatelle, where both sides remain very active.

Everywhere else the day has been calm and no infantry action has taken place.

(*Day Report*)—In the region of Ypres a German observation post was blown up by the French with a mine.

At Les Eparges the Germans attempted to regain the trenches lost by them on March 27. After a violent struggle, the French gains were on the whole maintained in their entirety. The Germans obtained a footing in a few sections of their old trenches, but on the other hand the French made progress at other points.

GERMANY.

BERLIN.—On the west front the day of yesterday passed rather quietly. Only in the Argonne and in Lorraine were there minor engagements, and these were successful for the Germans. General von Kluck was slightly wounded by shrapnel while inspecting advanced positions of his army; his condition is satisfactory.

German troops have stormed Tauroggen, across the Russian frontier northeast of Tilsit, and taken 300 Russian prisoners.

A Russian attack on the railroad from Wirballen to Kovno, at a point near Pilwiszki, broke down.

The Russians suffered heavy losses in the Krasnopol district. More than 1,000 Russians were taken prisoners, among them being a squadron of lancers with their horses and five machine guns.

A Russian attack to the northwest of Olechanow was repulsed.

"All the News That's Fit to Print."

The New York Times.

THE WEATHER

Fair and cooler today; fair tomorrow; fresh northeast winds.
For full weather report see Page 13.

VOL. LXIV...NO. 20,906. ...   NEW YORK, WEDNESDAY, APRIL 21, 1915.—TWENTY-TWO PAGES.   ONE CENT In Greater New York, Jersey City and Newark.

'AMERICA FIRST,' WILSON'S SLOGAN

World Crisis Coming and We Are the Mediating Nation, He Tells Associated Press.

URGES STRICT NEUTRALITY

Not for Selfish Reasons, but to Qualify for Great Tasks Ahead.

NOYES ON UNBIASED NEWS

Explains Non-Partisan Standard of the Association—Publishers' Body Meets Today.

Strict neutrality, extreme caution in the publication of unconfirmed news, and "America first" were the keynotes of a speech by President Wilson that aroused great enthusiasm among newspaper editors and publishers from all parts of the country at the luncheon of The Associated Press at the Waldorf-Astoria yesterday.

Each telling point the President made in his speech, every word of which he seemed to weigh before uttering, was applauded by the audience of more than 300 at the tables and by a gallery of about 100 men and women.

The importance attached to his clear statement of the neutrality policy of his Administration was reflected in a request made by Melville E. Stone, Secretary and General Manager of The Associated Press, just before the Chief Magistrate was introduced, that all newspaper reports of the President's speech be based on the verbatim copy to be taken by a stenographer and supplied to all of the newspapers and news-gathering associations represented.

Frank B. Noyes of The Washington Star, President of The Associated Press, praised President Wilson's masterful maintaining of true neutrality, and said that the President had borne his great responsibility nobly. The applause that the laudatory remarks received would have done justice to a Democratic Nominating Convention. All arose and drank a toast to the President, and arose again when the orchestra struck up "The Star-Spangled Banner," and again when the President stood up to speak.

Function of The Associated Press.

In introducing President Wilson, the guest of honor, Mr. Noyes made brief reference to the scope of The Associated Press, saying he believed that it was "the greatest co-operative-non-profit making organization in the world." Its function, he said, was to furnish its members a service of world news untainted and without bias of any sort.

"To insure this," he said, "we have formed an organization that is owned and controlled by its members, and by

them alone; one that is our servant and not our master. So we are here today, Democrats and Republicans; Protestants, Catholics, and Jews; Conservatives and Radicals, Wets and Drys; differing on every subject on which men differ, but all at one in demanding that, so far as is humanly possible, no trace of partisanship and no hint of propaganda shall be found in our news reports.

"Because of its traditions and its code, and perhaps also because of the never-ceasing watchfulness of 900 members, it has come to pass that few people on earth are capable of giving the management of The Associated Press any points on maintaining a strict, though benevolent, neutrality on all questions on which we can be neutral and still be what we are—loyal Americans. We know, too—none better—that the genuine neutral, the honest neutral, is always the target of every partisan, and we find some solace that this fact is now being demonstrated to the world at large.

"Today, however, we willingly lower our crest to one who has demonstrated in these agonizing times his mastership of the principles of true neutrality, and who, fully realizing the dreadful consequences of any departure from these principles, has nobly borne his terrible burden of responsibility in guarding the peace, the welfare, and the dignity of our common country.

"Our distinguished guest, who so honors us today, may surely know that in the perplexities and trials of these days, so black for humanity, he has our thorough, loyal, and affectionate support.

"God grant him success in his high aims for the peaceful progress of the people of the United States."

BIGGER ZEPPELINS ORDERED BY KAISER

Raid Results Disappoint, So Huge Fliers Are Building to Carry Large Bombs.

GENEVA, (via Paris,) Wednesday, April 21.—German and Swiss newspapers published in towns around Lake Constance, where the Zeppelin works are situated, say that Emperor William seems displeased at the results obtained by the Zeppelin airships in recent raids, and has ordered much larger dirigibles constructed.

Two of the new aircraft, the newspapers assert, are to be finished each month. Formerly one airship was built every three weeks. The number of workmen at the Zeppelin plant have been nearly doubled and the machinery has been greatly augmented.

Count Zeppelin has arrived at Friedrichshafen to supervise the execution of the new order, the object of which, according to the newspapers, is organized raids against Paris and London.

BRITISH PRISONERS HUNGRY

LONDON, May 17.—A representative of The Daily Mail describes today a trip he made around Germany, in the course of which he visited several camps where war prisoners are interned. The writer, who is a citizen of a neutral nation, says:

"The principal complaint of the Britishers was the insufficiency of the food which is furnished according to the German standards of living, and these are admittedly lower than the British standards. All the men I interviewed said the food was insufficient. Some of them said they were starving."

The correspondent appeals to Britishers at home to send food and clothing to the war prisoners.

AUSTRIANS MASS ON ITALY'S BORDER

Yesterday Given as Latest Date Set for Consideration of Vienna's Proposals.

ISONZO RIVER FORTIFIED

German and Austrian Envoys Reported Ready to Leave Rome—Buelow Denies It.

PAPAL TROOPS ENLISTING

Accord Between Italy and Rumania Held to Presage Joint Intervention in the War.

Italy Requisitions Liners in New York Service.

GENOA, April 20, via Paris, April 21.—A number of Americans have been seriously inconvenienced because steamers, including the Italian liner America, on board which they had engaged passage, suddenly suspended their sailings for New York, owing to the fact that they had been taken over by the Italian Government.

The America was to have sailed today.

ROME, April 20.—Reports received here today from Austria say that the Dual Monarchy is hurriedly gathering troops on the Italian frontier to face a possible invasion by Italian soldiers.

A large contingent of Austrian troops, the reports say, have been quartered at Monfalcone, Ronchi, and Sagrado. The Austrians also are said to have fortified strongly the whole line of the Isonzo River with intrenchments, behind which batteries already are in position.

The Messaggero says that Michael de Giers, the new Russian Ambassador to Italy, is delaying his arrival in Rome because of his desire before leaving Petrograd to arrange with his own Government for the conclusion of a thorough agreement between Russia and Italy, not only concerning Italy's intervention in the war, but with regard to Italy's position when peace is reached.

The Messaggero adds that an almost perfect accord continues to exist between Italy and Rumania, and that therefore Italy's neutrality is approaching its end, although nobody can fix the day that Italy will enter upon hostilities.

"We would be blind still to hope for a good result from the 'Vienna conversations,'" the Messaggero continues. "This has been a dilatory game. It was proposed by Prince von Buelow, the German Ambassador, and accepted by Austria and Italy because for va-

rious reasons both countries considered it convenient to postpone the day of reckoning."

Special Cable to THE NEW YORK TIMES.
ROME, April 20, (Dispatch to The London Daily News.)—The German and Austrian Ambassadors accredited to the Quirinal and the Austrian Ambassador and Bavarian Prussian Minister accredited to the Vatican are secretly preparing for departure, evidently convinced that a rupture of diplomatic relations may occur at any moment.

The Austrian Ambassador at the Quirinal, Baron Macchio, has already sent his family to Innsbruck and granted leave of absence to the embassy staff. Prince Schonburg-Hartenstein, the Austrian Ambassador to the Holy See, will probably anticipate his Summer vacation and leave Rome at once.

The question of the custody of the archives of the several embassies has been already satisfactorily settled. The Pope yesterday received in audience Mgr. Csiszariz, the Austrian Embassy's ecclesiastical consultor, who on behalf of Emperor Francis Joseph, proposed that the custody of the Venetian Palace, which is the Ambassador's residence and Austrian Crown land, should be assumed by the Vatican. The German Embassy archives will probably be transferred to the Venetian Palace.

Prince von Buelow has transferred his villa to his brother-in-law, Prince Camporeale, with the idea doubtless of avoiding its sequestration in the event of war. The Prince's precaution is being copied by many German landowners in Italy, who are thus openly evading the law.

BRYAN SCORES PEARY FOR EXPANSION TALK

Calls It "Little Less Than a Crime" for a Prominent Man to Stir Up Neighboring Nations.

WASHINGTON, April 20.—Secretary Bryan said today that before criticising Rear Admiral Peary's recent speech on possible territorial expansion of the United States he had written the Admiral for verification of his remarks and received an authenticated copy. Mr. Bryan's comment on the speech, as given out today at the State Department, was in part as follows:

"Rear Admiral Peary, speaking at a Republican banquet in New York recently, said: 'We cannot stand still. A hundred years hence we shall either be obliterated as a nation or we shall occupy the entire North American world segment.'

"The advantages of free speech are so great that we are compelled to accept with these advantages the evils that follow from an occasional abuse of the privilege by persons sufficiently prominent to secure publicity for their views. It is to be regretted, however, that a man known to the public should so much enjoy indulging his imagination as to be indifferent to the effect which his utterances may have upon this country's relations with other nations.

"Admiral Peary does not, of course, claim to be inspired—he is simply expressing his private opinion; but his name, unfortunately, gives wings to his words. He fixes 100 years as the period during which it will be necessary for this Government to secure control of the continent or disappear. Such a prediction from an obscure man would be foolish; from one in his position it is little less than a crime. His prediction is based upon an assumption which has been demonstrated to be false—namely, that a nation must constantly expand or go into decay.

"It has been a century since the boundary line between the United States and Canada was established, and yet both countries are more prosperous to-day than they were a hundred years ago. This country shares the larger part of North America with several Spanish-speaking republics, and there is no reason why there should be any dispute between them in a century or in many centuries. The idea that a nation can grow only geographically is as un-American as it is untrue."

Admiral Peary on reading the above declined to comment upon or discuss it, but pointed out that he first presented the idea "that the entire North American world segment is the eventual destiny of the United States" in a public address in London in November, 1903, when he said:

"The attainment of the north pole is particularly an object for American pride and patriotism. The North American world segment is our home, our natural, ultimate destiny. Its bounds are the isthmus and the pole. We are negotiating for the isthmus, (the Hay-Varilla treaty was signed Nov. 18, 1903.) We must find and mark the pole."

REAL WORK OF WAR IS DONE AT NIGHT

Soldiers on the Advancing French Front Spend Most Days in Rest or Play.

AVIATOR'S QUEER GROUCH

Back, Angry from Flight Because Bombs Wouldn't Drop After He Picked a Fine Target.

From a Staff Correspondent.
Special Cable to THE NEW YORK TIMES.
PARIS, April 20.—To continue the story of my trip along the French battle front, the first installment of which was cabled yesterday:

Daytime in the trenches is usually quiet beyond an occasional artillery bombardment. The real work is at night. So men during the day sleep in dugouts or laze about, playing cards and writing letters, all except the sentinels on duty.

It is queer to see cigar boxes nailed up as letter boxes, with inscription giving the name of the division and sector.

It is strange, where the trenches pass through the woods, to see men perched aloft in the tops as in a ship's crow's nest, watching patiently, guns in hand, for the slightest movement in the enemy's line.

Back of the trenches we visited was a target where sharpshooters practice daily. The target is so arranged that if a man misses the bullets pass on to the Germans.

We got views of German "frightfulness" during the trip. We were in Amiens when the German aeroplanes made their demonstration against the cathedral. It was early morning, and we were just getting ready to go to the lines, thirty miles distant. Bombs fell only a few hundred yards from us and killed several woman and children. None touched the cathedral.

The Major of artillery I have referred to told us of a German attack on his position shortly before our arrival, which was communicated to the French outposts by the screams of women. A French company advanced, but a German officer cried out:

"Don't fire. We have women with us."

The Germans had taken all the women of the village and driven them ahead with a small detachment. The French charged suddenly on the flank, rescued the women, and killed the German drivers, who had got too far ahead of their column. The French artillery then smashed the advance.

At another point we visited was a Russian who had been a prisoner of the Germans, and escaped to the French lines. He said that over 300 Russians were in a little village near by, and that the Germans treated them like slaves, and made them do all the work, including looting everything from the houses, all of which was sent to Germany. He said that everything of the slightest value was taken, especially linen and copper.

A Toast in a Cave.

In this section we paid special attention to what went on behind the trenches. We viewed the field hospital stations, field kitchens, officers' quarters—all the dugouts. We even looked at a dugout cowbarn where the Colonel's cow peacefully chewed her cud and supplied fresh milk to the officers' mess. Every day she was taken through a trench to a pasture and brought back at night for milking.

At the end of this portion of the tour we were taken to the officers' dining room for a glass of wine.

We descended the narrow earth steps below ground into a cavern 4 feet by 12. A rough pine table ran lengthwise, with benches on either side. There was a small tunnel in the centre of the roof running to the outer world in which was fixed a pane of window glass.

I noticed that the usual bouquet of wild flowers in a pot made from a German shell occupied the centre of the table. At one end of the table was our escort's Colonel in corduroys and a dozen officers, several in the bright uniforms of the headquarters staff. The Colonel solemnly poured out the wine, and then stood as near straight as possible under the low earth roof.

I knew a toast was coming. I knew it would not be an idle one. This man had been talking of his son and relatives lost in this war, but he deplored all thought of a present peace. His tone was solemn, but with all the grace of the banquet hall he said:

"Gentlemen, to the victory of the forces of civilization I raise my glass."

We drained our cups to the bottom in silence.

An Aviator's Real Grouch.

I only saw one disgruntled man in the French Army. He was an aeroplanist with what I called an honest grouch. We had just arrived at the aero station when this flier appeared from the clouds. As his machine touched the ground he stood in his seat, took off his helmet, and banged it angrily on the ground. His leather coat followed. Then he flung himself over the side and stamped about the field.

He was very young. As we approached him he was investigating a hole in his shoe heel, from which he extracted a shrapnel ball. He then fingered several holes in the wings of the aeroplane, gently breathing curses.

He was asked to explain his trouble. It appeared that he had been over the German lines with bombs. Just when he had picked out for destruction a nice place of military value the lever controlling the bombs refused to work, so he was forced to return with the bombs still under the seat of the machine. He pointed at them with loathing.

While returning he was chased by a German aeroplane. When it got within fifty yards he emptied his revolver at it and saw it careening earthward. He pulled out the weapon and extracted the empty shells, but again pointed to the bombs and refused to be comforted.

While we were there, several machines received equipment of bombs. The engines were started, the pilots appeared, got into their leather clothes and climbed aboard.

They did not even bother to speak to those remaining behind. Perhaps this might be their turn never to return, but they simply gave the signal to let go and disappeared into the sky. It is all in the day's work.

I talked with several of these men. All say the French aero fleet is now showing superiority to the German in every way, and that only occasionally is battle offered, and then only when the Germans know the Frenchman has not a mitrailleuse aboard.

Like all others in the French Army, these aeronauts, who see more of what is happening than others, pay high tributes to the Germans as a brave, strong enemy, who must be beaten thoroughly in order to be beaten at all. One of them said:

"We fly over them and see almost nothing. There is scarcely a single motor on the roads back of their lines. All their transports move at night. If organization were everything, they would be invincible."

Last Glimpse of Spring's Glory.

On our last afternoon we were taken to another mountain top, crowned with a dense pine forest. Impenetrable thickets concealed the batteries, painted the same color as the foliage. Our Captain called attention to the barrels of the seventy-fives pointing skyward, cleverly concealed by trees. These guns are specially mounted to bring down aeroplanes. They can swing at any angle and in any direction and be fired as rapidly as revolvers.

We penetrated deeper into the forest to the searchlight station, so cleverly hidden under pine boughs as to be impossible to discover in the daytime. We climbed up to the platform.

Below we could see for miles down the valley. Near us was a little orchard planted with peach and plum trees in full blossom. At our feet a soldier was playing a violin made from a cigar box. The man played beautifully. Before the war he was first violinist at the opera in Bordeaux. He played "The Star-Spangled Banner," and then broke into an air from Massenet's "Therese."

Our Captain signaled that it was time to leave. We went through the pines toward the peach orchard, the stirring strains of the "Marseillaise" following us.

The odor of peach blossoms filled the air. All the earth was green and fresh.

I realized that Springtime had come to France, and with it a greater confidence in the future than ever before in her entire history.

DENOUNCES FOE'S POLICY.

England Assails Germany for Her Retaliatory Measures.

LONDON, April 20.—Through Walter Hines Page, the American Ambassador, the British Foreign Office today sent a protest to Washington to be forwarded to Berlin denouncing the retaliatory measures Germany has taken against thirty-nine British officers as a result of the special treatment accorded to thirty-nine submarine prisoners in England.

The note explains that the Germans are humanely treated and protests against the close confinement of the British officers. Virtually the only difference between the treatment of the German submarine prisoners and other German prisoners, the note says, is that the former are in the naval barracks instead of in the detention camps.

The Foreign Office is still without information as to the names of the British officers against whom retaliatory measures have been adopted in Germany, the United States not yet having obtained the names from Germany.

EXULT OVER AIR RAIDS.

German Papers Speculate on the Effects in England.

Special Cable to THE NEW YORK TIMES.
ROTTERDAM, April 20, (Dispatch to The London Daily News.)—After a long and weary wait for aerial success, Germany is delirious with joy over the visit of Zeppelins to England last week. The papers are still full of extraordinary praise. The Hamburger Fremdenblatt, writing apparently with a confused idea of English geography, says the aerial cruisers flew over the mouth of the Thames and passed by way of Kent across Sussex. It proceeds:

"With what feelings did London awake the morning after the German airships had been within a few miles of London and flown over Brighton, which on Saturday afternoons in Summer shows half London on its sands. It must be a painful experience for London's population of clerks to have our aerial cruisers so near their place of work in the city and right over the place of recreation and sport and to know their former proud and century-long inviolability has been broken.

"We are filled with expectations. What has been done can be done again. Spring is in the air, birds are on the wing, space is free, the nights are dark. What are distances! Unhindered our airships arrive, unhindered they go, having carried out the deed watched by proud and thankful Germany. Britons have learned that between heaven and earth there are things undreamed of in their philosophy, and they are German things."

ITALY'S NEW BIG GUN.

Special Cable to THE NEW YORK TIMES.
PARIS, April 20.—Italy has a forty centimetre cannon more powerful, but lighter and less cumberous than the Krupp monster, according to a prominent Italian politician's statement to the Excelsior. The King attended trials of the weapon three days ago at Genoa.

The explosions caused popular demonstration, everyone thinking they were the signal for mobilization, which the Excelsior's informant declares is practically complete, every able-bodied man born after 1876 having already joined the colors.

A British gun crew prepares to fire another round at the enemy on the western front.

"All the News That's Fit to Print."

The New York Times.

THE WEATHER
Generally fair today and Sunday; light to moderate variable winds.
For full weather report see Page [illegible].

VOL. LXIV...NO. 20,909. ... NEW YORK, SATURDAY, APRIL 24, 1915.—TWENTY PAGES. ONE CENT In Greater New York, Jersey City and Newark. | [illegible]

GERMANS GAIN; BIG NEW BATTLE ON NEAR YPRES

French Driven from Trenches Northeast of the City; British Hold Fast.

CHARGES OF POISON BOMBS

Gen. French Says Germans Won by Using Them; Denies German Counter Charges.

GERMANS CAPTURE 30 GUNS

And 1,600 French and English Prisoners Are in Their Hands, Berlin Reports.

BRITISH HOLD HILL NO. 60

Furious and Protracted Bombardment with Heavy Guns Fails to Dislodge Them.

LONDON, April 23.—That a severe engagement has taken place near Ypres is confirmed by the official reports, but these are so contradictory in their claims that the actual result of the preliminary fighting is not known.

To those outside the War Offices of the belligerent nations it would appear, however, that after their loss of Hill No. 60 and their failure, after repeated attempts, to recapture it, the Germans have begun an offensive from the northeast against the Anglo-French line in front of Ypres, which was the scene of such bloody battles last Autumn, and also against the Belgian line further west.

The Germans assert that, with a rush, they drove the Allies back to the Ypres Canal, taking 1,600 British and French prisoners, and a number of guns. The French account admits that the Allies had to fall back, but it is pleaded in extenuation that this was due to the use by the Germans of asphyxiating gas bombs.

Paris asserts that in counter-attacks the Allies took many German prisoners and that the Belgians repulsed attacks launched against them.

It is believed here that these operations are only the beginning of another battle of Ypres.

Sir John French Accuses Germans.

Field Marshal Sir John French, Commander in Chief of the British forces in France and Belgium, communicates the following under today's date:

Yesterday evening the enemy developed an attack on the French troops on our left in the neighborhood of Bixschoote and Langemarck, on the north of the Ypres salient.

This attack was preceded by a heavy bombardment, the enemy at the same time making use of a large number of appliances for the production of asphyxiating gas. The quantity produced indicates long and deliberate preparation for the employment of devices contrary to the terms of The Hague Convention, to which the enemy subscribed.

The false statement made by the Germans a week ago, to the effect that we were using such gases, is now explained. It obviously was an effort to diminish neutral criticism in advance.

During the night the French had to retire from the gas zone, overwhelmed by the fumes. They have fallen back to the canal in the neighborhood of Boesinghe. Our front remains intact, except on the extreme left, where the troops have had to readjust their line in order to conform with the new French line.

Two attacks delivered during the night on our trenches east of Ypres were repulsed. Fighting continues in the region north of Ypres.

This morning one of our aviators, during a reconnoissance which he completed successfully, damaged a German aeroplane and forced it to descend. Our flying corps has brought down another German machine near Messines.

Paris Confirms French's Charges.

PARIS, (via London,) April 23.—The following French official statement regarding the fighting in the western theatre of war was given out here tonight:

In Belgium the surprise due to the asphyxiating bombs used by the Germans to the north of Ypres has had no grave consequences.

Our counter attacks, vigorously supported by British troops on our right and also by Belgian troops on our left were developed with success. The Anglo-French troops gained ground toward the north, between Steenstraate and the Ypres-Poelcapelle road. Our allies took prisoners belonging to three different regiments.

Germans Tell of Success.

BERLIN, (via London,) April 23.—There was given out in Berlin today an official report on the progress of hostilities, reading as follows:

In the western arena of fighting, during the evening of yesterday, we advanced from our front at Steenstraate, east of Langemarck, against the positions of the enemy north and northeast of Ypres. With a rush our troops moved forward along a line extending as far as the hills south of Pilken and east of Douon. At the same time they forced their way, after a stubborn fight, across the Ypres Canal at Steenstraate and Het Sae, where they established themselves on the western bank of the canal.

The villages of Langemarck, Steenstraate, Het Sae and Pilken were taken. At least 1,600 French and British soldiers were taken prisoners, and thirty cannon, including four heavy British guns, fell into our hands.

GASES 'ONLY INCIDENTAL.'

Germans Deny Using Asphyxiating Shells, but Accuse Allies.

LONDON, April 23.—Replying to British complaints that the Germans are using shells the gases from which asphyxiate their antagonists, a wireless dispatch from Berlin says:

"The German troops do not fire any shells the sole purpose of which is to spread asphyxiating or poisonous gases. Such gases as develop incidentally upon the explosion of German shells are less dangerous than those emanating from ordinary British, French, and Russian shells.

"Smoke-developing contrivances used by the Germans in hand-to-hand combats are in no manner contrary to the laws of warfare. On the other hand, it appears from official communications that our opponents have been using illegal poisonous gas shells for several months."

WILSON STUDYING PEACE PROBLEM

Fitting Himself for Duties That May Fall to Him After the War.

SOME OBJECTION TO US NOW

But That Will Pass When Peace Prospect Opens, It Is Believed—President Seeing Few Visitors.

Special to The New York Times.

WASHINGTON, April 23.—President Wilson's exclusiveness these days is explained by the close study he is making of all phases of the international situation with a view to be thoroughly prepared to take an active part in an effort to bring peace to Europe should the opportunity be presented for the exercise of the good offices of the United States Government. For several weeks the President has seen few visitors, and it was made known the other day that he would not be able even to follow his custom of receiving the pupils of out-of-town schools who throng Washington in the early Spring.

He spends many hours each day in his study, it is said, with his desk piled with documents relating to the matters to which he is devoting attention, and he is credited with being engaged in a consistent attempt to fix in his mind the main points of the historical, geographical and legal problems that must be understood by any one who is to take a prominent part in negotiations having to do with the adjustment of the differences that have set most of the world on fire.

This course of the President and other related things indicate that by no means has he been impressed with the view that the Government of the United States has been disqualified as the peacemaker. Through private correspondence he is in touch with opinion in the chancelleries of Europe concerning the prospects of peace and the chance that this Government will be called on to lend a hand in the restoration of normal conditions.

It is supposed here that Col. E. M. House of New York and Texas, the President's close friend, who went to Europe ostensibly to co-ordinate the work of the various American relief organizations, is keeping the President fully informed as to sentiment among those who will have the ultimate say in the inception and conclusion of peace measures. Other friends and official advisers are understood to be keeping Mr. Wilson informed as to the situation, and he is giving marked attention to their letters.

Officials of the Administration and, of course, the President is included, are fully aware of the irritation felt in some of the warring countries against the Government, but in spite of this the opinion prevails that this feeling may not disqualify the United States from serving as the leader in a movement to restore amicable relations. A prevailing view said to be held by some of the men high in the Government is that when the time for making peace arrives the animosity toward America will have moderated and it will be realized that, as the nation least involved in the war, directly or indirectly, the United States must have a large share in the adjustment of the problems that will confront all those immediately concerned.

It is realized that in some of the belligerent countries there is a strong belief that the United States is not observing the neutral attitude that was proclaimed by President Wilson at the outbreak of hostilities. This belief appears to be most firmly fixed in Germany, whose Ambassador in Washington, Count von Bernstorff, has voiced the popular opinion of his Government and people in virtually accusing the United States Government of a breach of faith toward Germany in carrying out its obligations to the countries at war. But officials here are inclined to contend that when the passions now at fever heat have cooled under the prospect of peace, even the German Government will realize that the course of the United States has been correct, and that it has been and desires to continue a friend of all the powers that are engaged in the present world struggle.

In its desire to see peace in Europe, however, this Government's interest is not confined to keeping itself in a position which would lead to its possible selection as the chief peacemaker. It regards as of equal importance that it shall remain the firm friend of all the parties now at enmity, so that it will be able to take a foremost part in a movement for a post-bellum world congress that will revise and codify the principles of international law and perhaps provide means for the maintenance of permanent peace.

That is the greater mission of the United States, it is held, and the President's current study of war questions and their ramifications is said to be intended as a preparation for the leading rôle that he may be called upon to play in what is likely to be the greatest international gathering that the world has ever known.

RECENT NOTE FAILS TO CONVINCE GERMANS

Press Comments Bitterly on Our Neutrality and Sale of Arms to the Allies.

BERLIN, April 23, (via London, April 24.)—The American Government's answer to the recent memorandum of Count von Bernstorff, the German Ambassador to the United States, has not yet reached the Foreign Office in any official form. While the officials there are unwilling to comment on the newspaper versions of the reply, it is said that the answer, if it has been correctly transmitted, will scarcely cause surprise here, as little hope had been entertained that the United States would abandon her traditional policy.

The newspapers continue to assert that the American policy is so one-sided that it is impossible to term it neutrality. The Kreuz Zeitung today recalls President Wilson's declaration that the sale of submarines is inconsistent with the spirit of true neutrality, and asks where it is consistent to draw a distinction between submarines and cannon or shrapnel.

"Even if the American standpoint regarding the export of arms is accepted in principle," the Kreuz Zeitung says, "the American Government, by failing to take advantage of the opportunity to force Great Britain to permit foodstuffs to enter Germany by holding up shipments of arms until this is permitted, again demonstrates its non-neutrality."

The newspaper maintains that good will is lacking in the United States, adding: "It can be neutral, but it does not wish to be."

The Zeitung Am Mittag says:

"Secretary of State Bryan knows very well that the wholesale supply of arms and munitions is worth more to the Allies than ten army corps."

The Taglische Rundschau of Berlin says:

"America takes all possible trouble over the ammunition requirements of our enemies, ostensibly from a love of neutrality. She does not trouble about the possible food requirements of Germany; this also is done from a love of neutrality."

The Vossische Zeitung of Berlin says: "Washington should recognize that such an attitude on the part of America will not speedily be forgotten in Germany."

The Lokal Anzeiger of Berlin says: "The German standpoint on this question is founded on thoroughly established principles and practice of international law. The American standpoint can be explained only by the profits of the armament firms."

The Morgenpost of Berlin, under a headline reading "Remarkable Neutrality," says:

"This answer sounds like a mockery of the German standpoint as presented by Count von Bernstorff, although, of course, this is not Secretary Bryan's intention. Nobody outside the White House believes that the delivery of arms and other supplies is not a violation of neutrality and that its prohibition would be unneutral. But it remains for Mr. Bryan to proclaim with such cynical frankness that the weapon trade to one belligerent is real neutrality."

Die Post of Berlin makes no comment except for the headline, "America Further Shows Its Character."

EFFECTS OF POISON BOMBS.

Soldier Says They Stupefy the Subject Somewhat Like Chloroform.

Special Cable to THE NEW YORK TIMES.
LONDON, Saturday, April 24.—The Morning Post correspondent, in his description of the fighting near Ypres, says:

"In the course of this battle considerable use is being made by the enemy of their asphyxiating bombs—their newest example of 'frightfulness,' to which official reference has already been made.

"An informant who has come under the influence of one of them tells me that he was a good fifty yards from it when it exploded. He does not know if the fumes are actually poisonous, because he had time to get away from them before they overcame him; but he describes their first effects as stupefying—something similar to the beginning of unconsciousness under chloroform."

GERMANS ARE HURLING VAST MASSES ON YPRES

Fully 80,000 Fresh Troops Employed—Bloodiest Battle of the Campaign.

Special Cable to THE NEW YORK TIMES.
ROTTERDAM, April 22, (Dispatch to The London Daily Mail.)—The Germans have begun a vigorous attack on the Yser, which they have been preparing for more than a week, and would appear to have scored an initial success. The attack is still going on, and great masses of troops are being poured through Brussels for the front. All the troops that were on guard on the Dutch frontier have left there for the Yser, and reports to hand show that the enemy is making a great effort to break the allied line, and to this end he is throwing every available man against the positions to the north of Ypres, while the allies are attacking in strong force to the south of Ypres.

The German losses during the last few days have been tremendous. They have advanced against the allied trenches with desperate courage, new troops dashing forward over masses of dead and wounded. Bruges is filled with their wounded, and accommodation is wanting for the huge batches which continue to arrive. The bloodiest battle of the western campaign is now raging. It is reported that the German artillery has been extremely effective and the expenditure of shells tremendous. The movement of troops still continues. The Germans are throwing reinforcements forward in an effort to win this great battle for Ypres. Antwerp is isolated from the south. Carts filled with goods are being sent back to the

city, and the Belgian railways are entirely monopolized by troop trains.

Standing at the most southerly point of the Dutch frontier, one of my correspondents reports that during the last three days he has clearly seen German troops marching into Belgium as they marched at the beginning of the war, the only difference being that their guns were not so numerous as in August.

The troops came from the direction of Aix-la-Chapelle. Yesterday afternoon he made careful notes and calculations, and he estimates that he saw 80,000 men pass. "It was the greatest trek I have ever seen. The men were as closely packed as growing corn," he said.

Special Cable to THE NEW YORK TIMES.
LONDON, Saturday, April 24.—A Morning Post correspondent in the north of France, under date of April 22, writes:

"Still extending in area, the present battle in Flanders continues to rage with great severity. It has now become the biggest engagement that the British Army has entered upon on its own initiative since this war began. It has become obvious from the enormous concentration of artillery that the Germans had brought to bear not only upon our recently acquired position on Hill No. 60, but upon our rear lines and upon Ypres, that they were willing to accept a full-dress battle and were preparing the ground for a stupendous effort. Reinforcements, it is calculated, to the extent of a full army corps have been rushed forward to this point from Belgium.

"Yesterday they launched their first great attack upon Hill No. 60, exceeding in vigor by far any of the previous counter attacks they had delivered against that position. Apparently countless masses of men were hurled against us, debouching from the straggling wooded country. From their stronghold at Zandvoorde they are enabled to re-form and come at us in mass in the open country before the village of Zwartelen on the eastward side of the ridge. Their losses have been appalling, even in this war of colossal losses. Not only have we a great park of artillery cleverly placed and in possession of the range to a nicety, but our latest surprise for the Germans, namely, our formidable array of machine guns, has made their reception extraordinarily warm. Still, charging from the cover of the woods, these dense masses of men cannot but overwhelm the front lines

opposed to them. Our rifles grow too hot to hold after the unceasing fire, and one thin line of scooped-out trenches is not tough enough to resist a rush.

"It is a very different question with our defensive lines on the hill, and there is no danger of these being rushed. The enemy has not caught us napping by any means, for it was fully realized that our first success would evoke a strong effort on his part. Supports we have in plenty, and proof of our strength in our centre in this sector is that the Germans are trying to extend on the wings. Our losses continue surprisingly light, considering the importance of this battle.

"The devoted town of Ypres continues under constant bombardment. The German siege guns include some of their 17-inch howitzers.

"The Duke of Württemberg's army is leaving a hideous record of slain. I understood that the whole of the territory we have been acquiring recently is seamed with burial places of German dead to such an extent that the country is likely to become insanitary, if it is not already so."

GERMANS AIM AT CALAIS.

British Expert Says They Can Throw 500,000 Men on Ypres.

LONDON, Saturday, April 24.—Discussing the latest German effort to break through the British line at Ypres, the military correspondent of The Daily Mail says:

"The critical moment has arrived. The immediate object of the Germans is the capture of Ypres, which they regard as the key to Calais. For this movement picked troops have been transported to the Flanders front, as evidenced by repeated reports from Holland and the elaborate troop movements in Belgium. The British blow at Hill No. 60 was an effort to strike first.

"If the German report of the capture of four heavy guns is true the enemy must have made an advance of at least two or three miles, as heavy guns never are placed near the front, and often are four or five miles behind the advanced trenches.

"The Germans still are bringing up large reinforcements, throwing every available man into the gap. They have probably half a million men available without depleting the eastern front, and many men might be spared from Po-

land, where the roads render military operations impossible for the present."

TROOPS BLINDED BY BOMBS.

German Invention Said to Have Destroyed Sight of 500 in One Attack.

Mme. Henriette B. Maloubier of New York, who returned on the Touraine yesterday from a trip to Montbéliard, her native town in France, which is near Belfort, on the eastern frontier, said that an officer who came to the town from the firing line in Alsace told her that incidents occurred which did not appear in the bulletins issued by the War Office in Paris.

"For example," she said, "he told me that the Germans had attacked the trenches with hand grenades filled with a burning liquid that scattered over the faces and hands of the soldiers. The Germans did not advance, it is true, but over 500 of the French soldiers were blinded for life.

"A new kind of explosive is being made in the South of France at the Government factories for the use of aeroplanes, and portable bridges have been constructed to cross the river Rhine at three points.

"New regiments have been raised and trained in various districts in France and dispatched from Marseilles on the transports France, Provence, Lutetia, and other chartered vessels to take part in the siege of Constantinople and the Dardanelles."

Mme. Maloubier found conditions in France very much changed by the war. All the big cities she passed through from Havre to Montbéliard were dark at night, and the streets quite deserted. Scarcely any horses were to be seen, as all those fit to work had been requisitioned for military purposes.

At the railroad stations, Post Offices, restaurants, stores, offices, and cafés women were filling the places of the men, who had left everything to fight for France. Old men, who were too feeble to withstand the rigors of the trenches, she said, were doing duty as gendarmes and policemen.

Mme. Maloubier's husband is fighting at the front in the 405th Regiment of Infantry.

Commandants Fleury, Lacombe, and Thomassen, and Captain J. Hunebelle of the French Army, arrived on the Touraine to purchase horses, motor trucks, and munitions of war for their Government.

The only protection from the poisonous "mustard gas" was this strange looking headgear.

"All the News That's Fit to Print."

The New York Times.

THE WEATHER
Fair and continued warm today and Tuesday; light, variable winds.
For full weather report see Page 13.

VOL. LXIV...NO. 20,911.   NEW YORK, MONDAY, APRIL 26, 1915.—SIXTEEN PAGES.   ONE CENT In Greater New York, Jersey City and Newark. | TWO CENTS Elsewhere.

GERMANS GAIN MORE GROUND AT YPRES; BEGIN TERRIFIC DRIVE NEAR LA BASSEE

St. Julien and Kersselaere Taken Northeast of Flanders Centre.

1,000 BRITISH CAPTURED

Berlin Says Advance Continues, but Paris Asserts Allies' Lines Are Holding.

BIG FIGHT TO SOUTHWARD

Bavarian Prince Directs Onslaught on British Lines Southwest of Lille.

Germans Reported Driven Back Over Yser

Special Cable to THE NEW YORK TIMES.
NORTH OF FRANCE, April 25.— At the moment of writing (mid-day) I learn from quasi-official sources that the French have succeeded in retaking nearly all the lost ground during last night. The battle still continues.

The Germans have been driven back over the Yser.

Drei-Grachten is at this moment neutral ground. Neither the Belgians nor the Germans occupy it.

Our losses are considerable. The hospitals are full.

The German losses must also have been terrible on account of their massed formation of four abreast, for when one column fell another immediately took its place.

LONDON, April 25.—The fighting about Ypres has resulted in further marked advantages for the Germans, according to the Berlin official report, which covers the operations up to this morning, while the Paris communiqués deal with the fighting of Saturday and Sunday, too.

The Germans say that north of Ypres they retain the ground gained on Friday, while they assert that on Saturday they captured the villages of St. Julien and Kersselaere, (further to the east,) and "advanced victoriously toward Grafenstafel."

Following is the German official report:

We obtained further results at Ypres. The ground captured on April 23 north of Ypres was still retained yesterday in spite of the attacks of the enemy. Further east we continued our attacks

Cloud of Chlorine Borne by a Favoring Wind Germany's Novel Weapon That Swept Allies' Front; Was Released from Bottles of the Liquefied Gas

Special Cable to THE NEW YORK TIMES.
LONDON, Monday, April 26.—A correspondent of The Daily Chronicle, telegraphing from the North of France, in a message dated April 25, describes the use of chlorine gas by the Germans.

"On the evening of the 22d," he says, "the French soldiers who manned the first line trenches saw rising from the German trenches, a short distance away, a number of white fuses, evidently intended as signals. Almost at once all along the German trenches a thick curtain of yellow smoke arose and was blown gently toward the French trenches by a northeast wind. This curtain, which advanced like the 'yellow wind' of Northern China, offered this peculiarity, that it spread thickly on the ground, rising to a height of sixteen feet only.

"The French soldiers were naturally taken by surprise. Some got away in time; but many, alas, not understanding the new danger, were not so fortunate and were overcome by the fumes and died poisoned. Among those who escaped, nearly all cough and spit blood, the chlorine attacking the mucous membrane. The dead were turned black at once.

"The effect of this poisonous gas was felt over about six kilometers of ground in length by two kilometers deep. Farther than that the gas was too much diluted with air to kill, but suffocated many.

"About fifteen minutes after letting the gas escape the Germans got out of their trenches. Some of them were sent on in advance with masks over their heads to ascertain if the air had become breathable. Having discovered that they could advance, they arrived in large numbers on the area on which the gas had spread itself some minutes before and took possession of the arms of the dead men. They made no prisoners. Whenever they saw a soldier whom the fumes had not quite killed, they snatched away his rifle and threw it in the Yser and advised him ironically to lie down 'to die better.'

"I call your attention here to the fact that these were not asphyxiating bombs that the Germans used; they were big, reinforced bottles of gas, compressed at high pressure, which the Germans placed on top of their trenches, and of which they opened the taps when it seemed to them that the wind coming from behind them would carry on the poison to the enemy's trenches.

"It is possible that the use of chlorine gas may one day turn against the Germans themselves. Should the wind veer suddenly, they would be the first victims of their attempt."

and took by storm the Solaert farm, southwest of St. Julien, as well as the villages of St. Julien and Kersselaere, and advanced victoriously toward Grafenstafel. During these engagements about 1,000 Englishmen were taken prisoners and several machine guns were captured.

A British counter-attack against our position west of St. Julien was repulsed early this morning with very heavy losses to the enemy.

West of Wiel attempts of the British to make an attack were quenched at the very start by the fire of our artillery.

In the Argonne we repulsed an attack by two French battalions north Four de Paris.

In the Meuse hills, southwest of Combres, the French suffered a heavy defeat. We began an attack at this point, and in the rush broke through many French lines lying one behind the other. The French attempted at night to take away from us the captured territory, but again failed with heavy losses to them. Twenty-four French officers and 1,000 men, with seventeen cannon, remained in our hands after these engagements.

Between the Meuse and the Moselle fighting at close quarters occurred only at certain places. On our southern front, the fighting at Ailly has not yet come to a conclusion. A French night attack in the woods of Le Prêtre failed.

In the Vosges a dense mist prevented all military activities yesterday.

The French account, on the other hand, asserts that the Allies' counter-attacks continue with success, and that the British hold all their positions, and repeats the charge that the Germans are using bombs containing asphyxiating gases. The report reads:

To the north of Ypres the battle continues under conditions favorable for the troops of the Allies. The Germans have attacked at several points along the British front from various directions — north, northeast, and southwest, but they were not able to gain ground.

On our side we have made progress on the right bank of the canal through vigorous counter-attacks.

On the rest of the front there is nothing to report.

The German attack on Saturday in the Woevre, or in the Meuse Hills, was directed against the French positions to the southwest of Combres, and, according to the Berlin statement, the French suffered a severe defeat. Paris, however, says that in a counter-attack the Germans were completely driven out of the French first line, which they had pushed back.

These offensive movements by the Germans have been made possible by the state of the ground on the eastern front, where operations are virtually impossible until the Spring floods have subsided. Taking advantage of these conditions, the German General Staff transferred a large number of troops to the west to make another big effort, which shows that they are not content to pursue a passive policy.

It is believed that half a million new German troops have reached Flanders, and that more guns and material are to be used than were provided for the original attempts to destroy the allied armies in the west—attempts which met with failure both in August and in October.

NEW GERMAN ATTACK NEAR LA BASSEE

Bavarian Crown Prince Gains in Efforts to Pierce British Lines.

Special Cable to THE NEW YORK TIMES.
NORTH OF FRANCE, April 25. (Dispatch to The London Morning Post.)— Two of the most important events in the great battle which is in progress, occurred between Friday night and this morning at La Bassée and along the section of the Furnes-Ypres Canal, between the latter town and Bixschoote. It is as yet premature to speak in detail of the former until the official communiqués shall have been issued. Suffice it to say that the army of the Crown Prince of Bavaria has launched a great effort against Givenchy and Cambrin of such extreme violence that some temporary advantage has accrued to the Germans.

In dense masses they are beating against our positions, regardless of their losses, in an endeavor to drive a wedge through the British lines. These are unbroken, and the troops are holding out heroically against heavy odds.

It is another such wedge that has caused the battle north of Ypres, where several Hungarian regiments seem to have been introduced to fill the gaps in the Duke of Württemberg's army.

This battle is unique as being the first great event of the kind in the history of Canada; for the Canadian troops can claim it as their own, and the glory of it. They were holding the extreme left of the British line.

Preparing the ground by means of their poison bombs, the Germans, driving through Langemarck and Pilkem, forced a passage across the canal between Steenstraate and Het Sas, reaching the village of Lizerne.

The French zouaves and fusiliers marines and the Belgian riflemen, caught in the stupefying fumes of the gas bombs, were taken at a disadvantage, and, despite the valiant efforts of their supporting lines, were forced to give way. Pouring their masses across the canal, the Germans then swung to the left and attacked a considerable portion of the Canadian forces in the rear. The Canadians, facing both ways, fought like lions, for it was bayonet work now, and the hardy Colonials, practically back to back, were battling for their lives.

Meanwhile supports, of which the British have great bodies at all points of their line, hurried up and mingled with the Zouaves, who had by this time reformed. In one deadly rush upon the Germans they cut their way clean through to the surrounding Canadians, and the whole mass charged on to recapture the lost positions.

Not only were the Allies' trenches recovered, but, still sweeping onward, the Canadians gained a footing in the lines that the Germans had previously occupied.

In this onrush whole companies of the Germans were wiped out, great numbers of machine guns were captured, and the German field guns, which had closely followed the advancing infantry, were compelled to beat a hasty retreat to safer quarters.

The Canadians had saved the line, and, though they have lost heavily, they had given more than they received.

Among the equipment captured during the fighting has been a new device for throwing these asphyxiating bombs. It is in the shape of a steel fork, which is planted in the ground, and is simply a great catapult. Working with a screw to pull back the spring, it throws a bomb about the size of a football a distance of 300 yards, and in a wind the effect of the fumes can be felt almost a mile away.

The driving of British mines under Hill 60 must rank as one of the great feats of this war. The tunnel was pushed out for over half a mile from the British trenches before it got below the slopes of the hill, which is a round, smooth, knoll-like elevation. There it began to work round to the right below the line of the German trenches, which garnished the hill top. For another half mile it so circulated, apparently at a too great depth for the sound-detecting instruments to reveal the work.

At three points heavy charges, each of several tons of a new and exceedingly powerful explosive, were placed, which were fired at intervals of ten seconds. Practically the whole side of the hill was blown clear away.

So tremendous was the cataclysm that I do not think they even found many bodies, although the German trenches were full of men and the hill was defended like a fortress.

MARCONI SAYS ITALY SEEKS TO AVOID WAR

Invasion and Treatment of Belgium Turned His Countrymen Against Germany.

Have Come to Realize the Task Before Them—Inventor Perfecting Wireless Telephone.

That German sentiment in Italy may be described as negligible, and that a majority of the Italian people favor intervention in the present war on the side of the Allies, was the statement made yesterday by William Marconi, the inventor of wireless telegraphy. Mr. Marconi, who arrived here Saturday on the Lusitania, left Italy three weeks ago, and in the two weeks that intervened between his leaving Italy and his departure for New York, was in France and England, in both of which countries he observed what he termed a tenacious determination to fight this war through to the end desired by the Allies.

First, Mr. Marconi talked of his own country and her position in the European crisis.

"Italy's position," said Mr. Marconi, "has been a very delicate one. A false move on her part might have the most serious consequences for the nation, and she has had to be alert and on guard all the time. Italy's position, because of her being in alliance with Germany and Austria-Hungary, was rendered doubly difficult. We have had no quarrel with Germany, and the alliance may have been beneficial to Italy, until militarism gained the upper hand in Germany. The Italian nation did not approve of this war, and as a member of the Triple Alliance, Italy felt that she should have been consulted. Had she been this war, that staggers humanity, might possibly have been averted.

"Statements that Italy has been holding off in the effort to drive a hard bargain with Vienna are in my opinion unjust and untrue. I do not believe that my country has been trying to drive a hard bargain with Austria, but rather that Austria has been making advances in the effort to win the favor of Italy. Italians do not feel that their relations with Austria have been any too pleasant or that Italy has been treated any too fairly by Austria. Italy has been irritated by Austrian encroachments, and by harsh treatment of Italians within the borders of the Austro-Hungarian empire."

"Do you think that Italy will enter this war on the side of the Allies?" Mr. Marconi was asked.

Majority of Italians for Allies.

"That is a question that is very difficult to answer," he replied, "and I do not feel in a position to say at this time whether or not Italy will go in. The majority of Italians favor the Allies. There can be no doubt of that, and a great many of them favor going to war on their side. There is also a large peace party in Italy which, while not favoring war, is nevertheless ready to stand behind the Government in the event the step is taken. As for German sentiment in Italy, my own personal opinion is that it is negligible.

"For instance, as indicative of Italian sentiment, I only have to call your attention to the fact that there is in Italy a very strong democratic element which belongs to what is known as the Social Democratic Party. The majority of these Social Democrats are laboring men and from the first they have been horrified at the treatment accorded Belgium. The invasion of that little neutral State by the Germans is something they cannot stand for, and if for no other reason, they are against Germany because of this act against the Belgians. This is my own opinion, and in stating it I do so under the conviction that I know my own country pretty well.

"The Italians, I should mention, have always entertained an admiration for the great German military machine as a machine, but that is all. The methods of that machine have not the approval of the Italian people. They do not and could not approve of German methods of warfare, such as, for instance, the cruelty and the destruction that have marked their invasion of Belgium.

"But to revert to the question as to whether or not Italy will become a participant in this war. The military men say that Italy will go in, but some of the great politicians maintain that her entry is doubtful. However, it is a fact that all preparations have been made, and Italy is ready, should it be decided to take the step. Up to the present no definite opinion has been had as to Italy's procedure from any one in a high responsible position. But it is out of the question for Italy to go with Germany and Austria-Hungary. If she goes it will be with the Allies. Of that I am certain."

Mr. Marconi was asked concerning the readiness of the Italian Navy for active service.

"The Italian Navy," he answered, "is fit and its officers and men well trained. A number of new ships have been commissioned, among them several dreadnoughts. I have recently met many of the officers and have seen a number of the ships myself. I can say that everything that could be done has been done to bring the fleet up to a state of efficiency, and it is my personal opinion that the Italian fleet will give a fine account of itself if it is called into action. The commander of the fleet is the Duke of the Abruzzi, and Americans know what a fine and capable type of seaman he is. Under his direction the fleet has been undergoing a constant training in marksmanship and manoeuvring exercises, and never before in its history was the fleet so ready as now.

Economical Situation Excellent.

"Furthermore, the economical situation in Italy at the present time is excellent. Recently a very good loan was floated without outside assistance, and in the event the country becomes involved I am convinced that the Italian people are ready and willing to make great sacrifices should it become necessary to give further financial support to the Government.

"Since the beginning of the war I am of the opinion that Italy has sincerely and honestly made every effort to remain in an honorable neutral position, and at the same time to safeguard Italy's own vital interests. Personally, I hope that the situation will so adjust itself that Italy can keep out of the war. I hope peace will not be long delayed. But if Italy should be compelled to enter I can only repeat that she is ready.

"I doubt if the great body of Americans appreciate the full extent of the great tragedy of Europe. If you could see the maimed and ruined I am quite certain that all America would be still more ardently for peace than is now the case. My sincere hope is that the American Government and people will continue to exert every pressure to bring about a termination of the conflict."

Speaking of the impressions gained in his recent journey through France, Mr. Marconi said:

"In France at the start of the war the people seemed to lack the French spirit and appeared to be discouraged. But all that has disappeared, and today France and the French people are quite as determined as their British ally to see this war through to the end. The effort made in certain quarters to stir up feeling between the British and French and to create the impression that all was not harmony between them has completely failed. England and France are working hand in hand and are in perfect accord as to the course to be pursued. This is the impression I gained in my recent visits to those two countries.

"As for the British, they have at last awakened to a serious realization of the task that confronts them, and what is known as British bulldogishness—tenaciousness is probably a better word—is now asserting itself. For the first few months the English did not seem to grasp the full extent of the job they had in hand. In the last three months this has changed and now they have buckled down, and the tenacious spirit of the people is in the ascendant."

Mr. Marconi said that it was the Italian and not the British Navy, as reported in the interview he gave out on his arrival, which is using the Marconi wireless telephone system as a part of its system of intership and intersquadron communication. In some instances, he said, communication had been established between ships as far apart as 100 miles. At the present time, he added, his efforts were being directed toward the perfection of the invention for moderate and not long-distance communication. He confirmed the report, printed some days ago, that the wireless telephone would probably be on the market in the United States within the present year.

KURDS MASSACRE MORE ARMENIANS

All Inhabitants in Ten Villages Near Van Said to Have Been Killed.

APPEAL SENT TO WILSON

By Head of Church—Evidences of Fearful Outrages Seen in Deserted Settlements.

STORY OF GREAT EXODUS

TIFLIS, Transcaucasia, April 24, (via Petrograd and London, April 25.)—Refugees who have reached the Russian line report that the massacre of Armenians by Mohammedans is being continued on even a greater scale. They say that all the inhabitants of ten villages near Van, in Armenia, Asiatic Turkey, have been put to death.

On being advised of massacres at Eizerum, Berjan and Zeitun, and of the conditions at Van, the Katolikos, head of the Armenian church at Etchmiadzin, near Erivan, cabled to President Wilson an appeal to the people of the United States on behalf of the Armenians.

Robert M. Labaree, an American missiona y of Urumiah, Persia, who visited the Serbian villages and with whom the refugees were quarte/ed, 6ays he found the humanity of the poeple as broad as their means were limited. The village Governments or Relief Committ'es ha issued eight pounds of flour to each refugee in six weeks.

The Associated Press received reports of the massacre of 800 of the villagers in Urza and of 720 in Salmas. The painful uncertainty concerning the 15,000 survivors of Urza was confirmed by a journey through Salmas. Three weeks had failed to obliterate the signs of the slaughter. Pools of blood still marked the execution places in Haftevan. The caps of thirty-six victims lay where a mud wall had been toppled over on them. A young man named Hackatur related the story of his escape from a well in which the bodies of the dead had been crammed. He fell with others and was tossed into the well, but he managed to wriggle through the bodies lying on top of him and escaped at nightfall.

Not all the Christians lacked the courage or means for self-defense. At the desolated Catholic mission at Hosrova, where forty-eight victims of the massacre were buried, Elizabeth Marcara, an Armenian girl, told how she and young David Ishmu battled with the Kurds. Her story later was amply confirmed.

"When the Kurds burst the village gates," said Miss Marcara, "we took rifles and mounted to the roof. I fired eighty shots. The Kurds were forced to withdraw outside the village wall. There I killed two and David two. Later we killed four more, one of whom was the Chief. The Kurds abandoned their plunder, and carried off their dead.

"The battle lasted three hours. The death of their Chief caused the Kurds to flee. We came from the roof and recovered the things the Kurds had left behind them. Reinforced, I fled with my relatives. We saw the Kurds engaged in the pillage of Hafgvan and fired on them, but they escaped with their booty.

"Near Dilman we were attacked by fifteen Kurds, of whom I killed one. After the Russians defeated the Kurds and Turks near Khoi a soldier told the Persian Governor about me, and he sent for me and offered me the chieftainship of a regiment of Turks if I would fight the Russians."

GREAT EXODUS OF CHRISTIANS

Thousands Suffered Greatest Hardships to Escape Enemies.

DILMAN, Persia. April 24. (via Petrograd to London, April 26.—The exodus of from 20,000 to 30,000 Armenians and Nestorian Christians from Azerbaijan Province, the massacre of over 1,500 of those who were unable to flee, the death from disease of 2,000 in the compounds of the American mission in Urumiah, and possibly an equal number of refugees in the Caucasus have been confirmed.

When it became known on the night of Jan.1 and 2 that the Russian forces had left Urumiah about 10,000 Christians fled, most of them without money, bedding, or provisions. Vehicles and camels and donkeys were for hire only at prices at which they might previously have been bought.

A majority of the people started out afoot, through mud knee-deep, across the mountain passes in freezing weather. At Dilman they were joined by many more from Salmas plain. But for Father de Cross of the Roman Catholic Mission at Horova, near here, the disaster might have become historic. After assuring the safety of the sisters of the mission, Father de Cross joined the pilgrims and managed to secure bread and shelter for many of them.

The caravansaries were so crowded that few persons could lie down in them, and thousands slept in the mud and the snow. Children were born on the roadside or in the corner of a caravasary.

Arriving at Julfa, on the Russian border, passport difficulties added to the troubles of the fleeing people. Maddened women threw their children into the Araxes River or into pools in order to end their sufferings from cold and hunger.

Father de Cross had to put his back against a wall to fight off the famished mob when he began distributing bread. The mud and cold and the shelterless nights, during which the garments of the refugees were frozen knee high, continued for three weeks, until the people were slowly dispersed by rail. Meantime, hundreds of them had not slept under a roof or near a fire.

Isaac Yonan, a graduate of the Louisville (Ky.) Theological Seminary, was among the refugees. He kept a diary of the happenings during the exodus. This related that among the refugees from Urumiah were an old man and his two daughers-in-law, with their six children, three of them babes in arms. The oldest child was 9 years old. They were eight days on the way, averaging twenty miles daily through the mud. The old man became stuck fast in a pool and at his own request was left there to die. One woman gave birth to a child during the march and an hour afterward was again plodding along with the other refugees.

Two of the children were lost in a caravansary, but were taken up by Cossacks along with forty other persons. The soldeirs displayed great humanity, often giving up their horses to the women.

One young woman carried her father for five days, when he died. A woman was found dead by the roadside with her infant, still living, wrapped up in her clothing.

In a single day twenty persons died in the railway station at Kakhitchevan, across the border in Russia. The entire casualties aggregated hundreds. People died unheeded and unmourned; in fact, those who died seemed to be envied by the living.

GERMANS ADMIT USING POISONOUS GAS BOMBS

Say the Allies Made Them First, Germany's Are More Deadly.

LONDON, April 25.—Reuter's Amsterdam correspondent sends the following special article concerning the German successes near Ypres as printed by the Frankfurter Zeitung:

"It is, indeed, possible that our bombs and shells rendered it impossible for the enemy's troops to remain in their trenches or artillery positions, and it is even probable that, in point of fact, projectiles emitting poisonous gases were employed by us, for the Germany Army commander has permitted no doubt to exist that, as a reply to the treacherous projectiles of the English and French, which have been constantly observed for many weeks, we on our side also would employ gas bombs or whatever one may call them.

"The German Army commander, moreover, declared that from German chemistry considerably more effective substances might be expected, and our army commander was right."

PARIS, April 25.—Military writers are discussing the use of asphyxiating bombs, the Figaro quoting the German General Friedrich A. J. von Bernhardi as having advocated their use.

Since the contents of these bombs have become known it is urged that preventive measures be taken, as well as reprisals against the enemy.

"All the News That's Fit to Print."

The New York Times.

THE WEATHER

Local showers today and probably Thursday; cooler Thursday; moderate, variable winds.
For full weather report see Page 15.

VOL. LXIV...NO. 20,913. .....

NEW YORK, WEDNESDAY, APRIL 28, 1915.—TWENTY-TWO PAGES.

ONE CENT In Greater New York, Jersey City and Newark. | TWO CENTS Elsewhere

ALLIES BATTLE FOR A FOOTHOLD AT DARDANELLES

Report Troops Making Progress Ashore, but Turks Say Invaders Are Repulsed.

FRENCH HOLD KUM KALE

Seize Asiatic Side of Entrance to Strait While Other Forces Land on Gallipoli Peninsula.

TURKS RESIST STRONGLY

Announce That They Have Driven Many of the Troops Back to Their Ships.

FLEETS COVER THE LANDING

Constantinople Reports One British Torpedo Boat Sunk and Another Damaged—Heavy Losses Reported

LONDON, April 27.—On the narrow, rocky Gallipoli Peninsula in Turkey a picturesque assortment of allied troops landed Sunday, supported by the fire of the warships, and is trying to batter its way through thousands of Turkish troops, led by German officers, in an effort to force the Dardanelles—the main gateway of the Ottoman Empire—and reach Constantinople.

A report from Paris says that French troops have occupied Kum Kale, the Turkish fortress on the Asiatic side of the entrance to the Dardanelles, and the British report says the attack is progressing. But a Turkish communication received tonight declares that although the Allies landed forces at four points, these forces are being beaten back to the coast, while the Moslems in the French ranks are deserting the tricolor and casting their lot with the co-religionists.

A joint War Office and Admiralty statement issued tonight says:

"After days of hard fighting in a difficult country the troops landed on Gallipoli Peninsula are thoroughly making good their footing with the effective help of the navy. The French have taken 500 prisoners."

The statement appends the following, which, it says, is officially published at Cairo:

"The allied forces under General Sir Ian Hamilton have effected a landing on both sides of the Dardanelles under excellent conditions. Many prisoners have been taken and our forces are continuing their advance."

French Take 500 Prisoners.

PARIS, April 27.—An official communication on the operations at the Dardanelles, issued tonight, says:

During the disembarkation Sunday of the allied forces at the Dardanelles French troops, comprising infantry and artillery, had been designated particularly for operations at Kum Kale, on the Asiatic side. This mission was completely and successfully fulfilled.

Aided by the cannon of the French fleet and under the fire of the enemy our troops succeeded in occupying the village, and have continued its occupation despite seven counter attacks at night, supported by heavy artillery.

We took 500 prisoners, and the losses to the enemy appear to have been considerable.

The general disembarktion of the allied forces continues under good conditions.

Turks Tell of Repulsing Attack.

CONSTANTINOLE, April 27, (via Amsterdam and London.)—The Turkish War Department today gave out the following official statement:

Under the protection of warships the enemy attempted to land troops Sunday at four points on the west coast of Gallipoli, namely, at the south of Sighin Dere, on the coast in the district of Avi Burun, to the west of Gaba Tepeh, on the coast of Teke Burun and in the neighborhood of Kum Kale.

The troops of the enemy, which landed at Teke Burun, were forced to retreat at the point of the bayonet, and were pushed back to the coast. These forces on Monday night were obliged hastily to return to their ships. The Turkish attacks at all points are progressing successfully.

Simultaneously a fleet approached the Dardanelles in order to force the strait from the sea, but it was obliged to retreat before our fire.

The forces of the enemy which landed at Kum Kale advanced under the protection of warships, but, despite a heavy bombardment from all sides, our troops drove them back to the coast. Part of these forces on Monday night were obliged hastily to return to their ships.

400 Dead; 200 Prisoners.

The enemy lost 400 men killed and 200 taken prisones. Our losses were insignificant.

A party of Moslem soldiers who landed with the French troops on this point of the coast deserted the French and joined our forces.

Before Gaba Tepeh we captured a number of English and Australian soldiers, among them a Captain and a Lieutenant.

When the enemy's fleet approached the strait our fire sank one of their torpedo boats and damaged another so severely that it had to be towed to Tenedoc. The enemy did not undertake any operations from the sea against the Dardanelles the following day.

LONDON, Wednesday, April 28.—The Daily Mail's Athens correspondent says:

"The bombardment of the interior forts of the Dardanelles, which began Sunday, continued today (Monday) and resulted in heavy damage to the forts.

It is reported that the forts on the coast, near Smyrna, also were bombarded, but this report has not been confirmed.

A Petrograd dispatch to The Times says:

"According to the Odessa correspondent of the Russky Slovo the result of last week's operations by Russian torpedo boats off the Anatolia coast is four Turkish steamers and twenty-four sailing vessels destroyed—a serious matter for Turkey, considering the paucity of her transport resources."

SAVED BRITISH LINE BY NIGHT ASSAULT

Into a Dark Wood Held by Germans the Canadians Charged with Bayonets.

MOON ONCE SHONE FORTH

And Revealed the Terrible Struggle Over Dead and Dying—How Gas Routed French.

Special Cable to THE NEW YORK TIMES.
LONDON, Wednesday, April 28.—The Times publishes an account of the fighting near St. Julien from one who took part in it, clearly a Canadian Highlander. Describing the opening of the engagement, he says:

"It was 4:30 in the afternoon of Thursday that our pickets reported a sudden retiring movement on the part of our French allies on the left of the Canadian division on the Ypres-Langemarck Road.

"The strong northeast wind, which was blowing from the enemy's lines across the French trenches, became charged with a sickening, suffocating odor which was recognized as proceeding from some form of poisonous gas. The smoke moved like a vivid green wall some 4 feet in height for several hundred yards, extending to within 200 yards of the extreme left of our lines. Gradually it rose higher and obscured the view from the level.

"The rifle fire, which hitherto had been desultory, increased in volume, but tended to become more and more erratic, as is always the case when men fire at random or without any clear idea of their mark.

"Soon strange cries were heard and through the green mist, now growing thinner and patchy, there came a mass of dazed, reeling men who fell as they passed through our ranks. The greater number were unwounded, but they bore upon their faces the marks of agony.

"The retiring men were among the first soldiers of the world whose sang-froid and courage have been proverbial throughout the war. All were reeling through us and round us like drunken men."

After describing the earlier stages of the fight the writer goes on to tell how Canadians were sent to retake the wood near St. Julien, which the Germans had captured. It was a dark night before they came in front of the wood where the Germans had been entrenching themselves since 4 o'clock in the afternoon.

"Here a halt was made," says the soldier. "It was pointed out that the enemy were occupying a strong position in the rear of the British lines and that they must be driven out of it at all costs. It was whispered also that some British guns had been taken during the afternoon and that it would be our bit to retake them. It was well understood by all that we were in for bayonet work and that we should not be supported by artillery.

"We moved out in column of companies, forming by fours, to pass through a narrow gateway. This passed, we deployed in long lines of half companies, the second half of each company keeping about thirty yards in the rear of the first.

"All the battalions marched in this formation and each first half company knew that its pals in the second would not fail to support it when it came to

"The Tenth Battalion had the post of honor in the van. Its gallant Colonel, Russell Boyle, fell leading it.

"It wanted but a few minutes to midnight when we got to a hollow which was almost 300 yards from the wood. The moon now reappeared at intervals, and we could have done without her.

"Whispered orders were given to fix bayonets, which were obeyed in a flash. Overcoats, packs, and even officers' equipments were dropped, and we immediately advanced in light order.

"Scarcely had we reached a low ridge in full view of the wood when

APPEAL TO TURKEY TO STOP MASSACRES

Ambassador Morgenthau Instructed to Make Representations on Request of Russia.

WASHINGTON, April 27.—An appeal for relief of Armenian Christians in Turkey, following reported massacres and threatened further outrages, was made to the Turkish Government today by the United States.

Acting upon the request of the Russian Government, submitted through Ambassador Bakhmeteff, Secretary Bryan cabled to Ambassador Morgenthau at Constantinople to make representations to the Turkish authorities asking that steps be taken for the protection of imperiled Armenians and to prevent the recurrence of religious outbreaks.

Ambassador Bakhmeteff called at the State Department late today with a dispatch from his Government, which included an appeal to the President of the United States for aid, forwarded through the Russian Government from the Catholics of the Armenian Church at Etchmiadzin, in the Caucasus.

"The request from the head of the Armenian Church to this Government, forwarded through the Russian Ambassador," said Secretary Bryan, "is the first official notice the department has received of the reported Armenian massacres. Our action was taken as a matter of humanity."

The Russian Embassy today gave out a translation of a recent speech by the Minister of Foreign Affairs in the Duma, in which the presence of Russian troops in Persia was explained. The Foreign Minister said:

"The presence of our troops in Persian territory by no means involves a violation of Persian neutrality. Our detachments were sent to that country some years ago for the definite purpose of establishing and maintaining order in districts contiguous to our possessions, of high economic importance to us, also to prevent the seizure of some of these districts by the Turks, who openly strove to create for themselves there, especially in the district of Urumiah, a convenient base for military operations against the Caucasus. The Persian Government, not having the actual power to maintain its neutrality, met the Turkish violation of the latter with protests, which, however, had no results."

SAYS POISON GASES KILLED CANADIANS

British War Office Asserts That Medical Evidence Proves This.

LONDON, April 27, 11:40 P. M.—The British War Office, in a statement tonight supplementing its previous charges that the Germans are using noxious gases in their fighting, says:

"Medical evidence shows that Canadian soldiers have lost their lives in the recent fighting, not from wounds, but from poisoning by gases employed by the enemy."

Where Allied Troops Have Landed to Attack Dardanelles Forts.

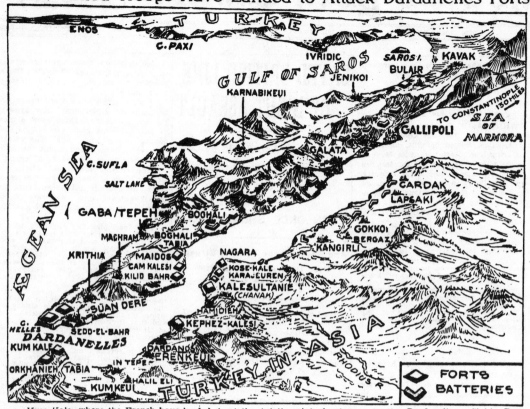

FORTS
BATTERIES

Kum Kale, where the French have landed, is at the Asiatic point of entrance to the Dardanelles. Sighin Dere, another point of landing, while not on the latest map of the region, is said to be just east of Sedd-El-Bahr, across the Strait from Kum Kale. Gaba Tepeh, a third landing point, is on the other coast of the Gallipoli Peninsula.

a perfect hell of fire was loosed on us from rifles and machine guns, which the Germans had placed in position behind the undergrowth skirting the wood.

"Instantly the word was given to charge, and on we rushed, cheering, yelling, shouting, swearing, straight for the foe.

"At first the Germans fired a little too high and our losses, until we came within fifty yards of them, were comparatively small. Then some of our chaps began to drop. Then the whole front of the line seemed to melt away, only to be instantly closed up again.

"Cheering and yelling all the time, we jumped over bodies of wounded and tore on.

"Of the Germans with the machine guns, not one escaped, but those inside the wood stood up to us in most dogged style. We were so quickly at work that those at the edge of the wood could not have got away in any case. Many threw up their hands and did not refuse quarter.

"Pressing on into the wood itself, the struggle became a dreadful hand-to-hand conflict. We fought in clumps and batches, and the living struggled over the bodies of dead and dying.

"At the height of the conflict, while we were steadily driving the Germans before us, the moon burst out. The clashing bayonets flashed like quicksilver and faces were lighted up as by limelight.

"Sweeping on, we came upon lines of trenches which had been hastily thrown up and could not be stubbornly defended. Here all who resisted were bayoneted. Those who yielded were sent to the rear.

"The trench fighting presented a spectacle which it is not pleasant to recall."

HOW GAS AFFECTED MEN.

Instinctively Fled from Trenches, if They Did Not Lose Consciousness.

PARIS, April 27.—Thirty-one French soldiers who were shot as they were leaving trenches near Ypres, when the Germans attacked them with asphyxiating gases, were brought today to the American Hospital. In addition to gunshot wounds, they are suffering from inflamed bronchial tubes and their eyes are swollen from the poisonous fumes.

These men say that as soon as they breathed the noxious gases released by the Germans they suffered acutely, their eyes stinging and their throats contracting. Some of the soldiers became unconscious almost immediately. Others, scarcely conscious, acted on instinct, and, crawling out of the trenches, staggered away from them. The connecting trenches were so choked with fugitives who had fallen unconscious that many soldiers were compelled to climb out and make their way toward the rear over the open ground.

As soon as the Germans perceived that the French were leaving their trenches overground they opened up an intense rifle and machine-gun fire along that portion of the front, which is about three miles in extent. It was this fire which caught the wounded brought to the American Hospital, they having been picked up by French troops held in reserve. These reserves, counter-attacking, carried the greater part of the trenches which had been evacuated.

The narratives of the wounded men differ in some respects. The physicians at the hospital attribute this to the psychological effects of a wholly new experience. Some patients say that the Germans threw bombs which on exploding distributed the gases. The majority, however, speak of having seen a thick, lemon-colored smoke arising in front of the German trenches and concealing them as if a heavy curtain had been let down. The gases hung close over the earth, and, propelled by a gentle breeze, crept toward the French earthworks, scarcely 100 yards away.

The physicians believe that no permanent harm is likely in the case of those who were not stifled to death. The survivors suffer poignantly from inflamed membranes, but will recover without treatment. In some cases pneumonia or bronchitis may follow.

It is the opinion of the physicians that the vapors must have been chlorine or gas of a sulphurous nature. It is hardly believed that carbon monoxyde was used, as this gas cannot be perceived with the eye.

It is evident from the stories of the soldiers that the wind must be just right to give full effect to the gases, for if released in a strong breeze the fumes would be dissipated and blown about before reaching the objective point. Meteorological charts of Northern France show that the prevailing breezes are from the south and southeast, which would favor the Allies rather than the Germans in the extensive use of gases.

Chemists generally think the gases can do little harm in the open air, and require so many favorable conditions as to make their successful use limited.

Some of the soldiers speak with scorn of the asphyxiating "bombs."

"Their famous bombs killed nobody," said one of the wounded Frenchmen. "They just put to sleep those who breathed the fumes. Then the Germans came up and killed the sleepers. Fortunately help came, and we finished by smashing them."

CALLS FOR RESPIRATORS.

British War Office Asks Women to Make Protectors Against Gas.

LONDON, Wednesday, April 28.—The War Office has issued an invitation to the heads of British households to make supplies of simple respirators, which are required by the troops at the front as a protection against asphyxiating gases.

The respirator is made of gauze or fine wire, and is worn over the nose and mouth. Such devices are frequently used by laborers who are compelled to work in smoke or dust.

PEACE DELEGATES REACH THE HAGUE

American Women Arrive in Time for Opening Session of the International Congress.

GERMAN DELEGATE SPEAKS

Says War Which Has Caused So Much Suffering Must End—Mrs. Andrews Gives American View.

THE HAGUE, (via London,) April 27.—The forty-two delegates from the United States to the International Women's Peace Congress, who were held up on the steamer Noordam because of Great Britain's order stopping traffic to Holland, arrived here today.

The delegates reached The Hague in time for the opening meting of the Congress tonight, at which an earnest desire to bring the world's war to a conclusion and insure a durable peace was strongly expressed by delegates belonging to both belligerent and neutral nations.

Besides the 886 Dutch delegates the gathering, which was presided over by Aletta Jacobs, comprised fifty-one women from America, three from Austria, nine from Denmark, five from Belgium, (who arrived by special permission of the German military authorities,) nine from Hungary, twelve from Sweden, fifteen from Norway, twelve from Germany, two from Great Britain, and one each from Chile, Armenia, Italy, and Canada.

Stirring addresses of greeting were delivered by Anita Augspurg of Munich, Mme. Tubjerg of Denmark, Katherine Courtney of London, Olga Misar of Vienna, Anna Kleman of Stockholm, M. S. Fanny Fern Andrews of Boston, Vilma Gluecklich of Dudapest, Rosa Genoli of Milan, Dr. Keilkau or Norway and Mia Boissevain of Amsterdam.

A thrill seemed to stir the audience as the women of the various nations uttered sympathetic references to the sorrows the hardships of their sisters. Dr. Anita Augspurg aroused the enthusiasm of the delegates when she declared that womanly feelings were above all race hatreds and that the German women stretched out their hands for friendship and international love.

Miss Courtney of England reciprocated with the assurance that English women recognized the women of other nations as sisters and were heartily thankful to the neutral nations for calling the gathering, declaring that all women in their hearts wished for peace.

Mrs. Andrews said that never before had she such faith in the power of women to effect a great purpose. Every woman in the United States, she declared, sympathized with the objects of the congress.

Vilma Gluecklich, one of the Hungarian delegates, argued that women would not be worthy of "their coming franchise" unless they proved that they were doing something to abolish the war.

An address which held her auditors spellbound was delivered by Signorina Genoli, the only Italian delegate. Speaking in French, and with great earnestness, she said she saw the horrors of war impending in Italy.

The men, who were starving because of the stoppage of trade, demanded to be sent to the front to fight, where they would be certain to obtain food, she said. Even the Italian Peace Society had declared in favor of war, but the women of Italy were praying against such a calamity befalling them.

Dozens of messages from every country except Belgium were read by Dr. Boissevain.

Dr. Jacobs, in her speech of welcome, said:

"We who convened this congress never called it a peace congress, but an international congress of women to protest against the war and to discuss ways and means by which war shall become an impossibility in the future."

Dr. Jacobs added that one of the most powerful means to attain this end would be the introduction of woman suffrage in all congress.

The congress was held in the Zoological Gardens.

Special Cable to THE NEW YORK TIMES.
ROTTERDAM, April 27, (Dispatch to The London Daily Mail.)—The American women delegates to the International Women's Peace Congress arrived here today on the liner Noordam. The delegates, who included Miss Jane Addams, appeared to be more interested in the big battle in Flanders than in the prospects of peace.

Special Cable to THE NEW YORK TIMES.
LONDON, April 27.—The steamer Noordam, with the American delegates to the Women's Hague Peace Congress aboard, sailed from Deal today for Holland after being held up for nearly three days by the Admiralty. Permission for the steamer to pass through the North Sea was given by the Admiralty after the American Embassy had interceded, responding to the importunities of the women.

The Admiralty consented to make an exception of the Noordam as a courtesy to the American women, although possibly the Admiralty is not in sympathy with the cause for which the women are assembling at The Hague.

The Noordam is the only steamer which has been allowed to leave England this week for Holland.

LONDON, April 27.—No fewer than 180 British women applied for permits to attend the peace congress at The Hague, but at the behest of the Foreign Office the list was weeded out to a maximum of twenty-four. Even these are still in England.

Reginald McKenna, the Home Secretary, questioned on this subject today in the House of Commons, said the Foreign Office considered it altogether undesirable that so many women as originally contemplated should attend a conference near the seat of war, where agents of Great Britain's enemies were active in endeavoring to procure fragments of intelligence concerning the movements of British troops and warships.

The Home Secretary repudiated the suggestion that the delegation of British women had in any sense an official character. He said the Government was not encouraging international congresses in the present circumstances.

"All the News That's Fit to Print."

The New York Times.

THE WEATHER

Increasing cloudiness, rain by to-night and tomorrow; moderate shifting winds, becoming southeast.
☞For full weather report see Page 19.

VOL. LXIV...NO. 20,922.　　　NEW YORK, FRIDAY, MAY 7, 1915.—TWENTY-TWO PAGES.　　　ONE CENT In Greater New York, Jersey City and Newark. | TWO CENTS Elsewhere.

RUSSIANS ARE BEATEN, LOSE TARNOW; RETREATING FROM MOUNTAIN PASSES; AUSTRO-GERMAN ARMY SWEEPING ON

Three Rivers Crossed and Gorlice, Jaslo and Dukla Also Taken.

MAY CAPTURE FLEEING ARMY

High Mountain That Protected Great Base at Tarnow Taken by Storm.

LINE SMASHED BY NEW GUNS

Czar's Legions Wither Under Terrific Fire of Austrian 42s and Smaller Howitzers.

TWO BALTIC PORTS MENACED

Russian Foreign Minister, Through Washington Embassy, Denies Foes Are Victorious in Carpathians.

VIENNA, May 6. (via London, May 7.)—The victorious advance of the Austro-German armies in West Galicia continues. The Northern wing has captured Tarnow. The southern wing has crossed the Wisloka River and the Russians are retreating eastward of the Lupkow Pass. An official communication issued late this evening by the War Office says:

At 4 o'clock this afternoon the last Russian positions on the heights east of the Dunajec and the Biala Rivers were gained by our troops.

Tarnow was captured by us at 10 o'clock this morning.

The strategic achievement of rolling up a hostile battle front by a flanking attack, of which Chancellorsville is one example in modern history, is now in full progress in West Galicia. Favored by continued good weather, mile after mile of the Russian Carpathian front has been rendered untenable by the steady, unchecked Austro-German advance.

The Austrian cavalry and infantry followed the Gorlice turnpike. The supporting artillery dropped shells on the road from Zmigrod to Jaslo, one of the principal lines of the retreat for the Russians in the Kukla region.

The Russian forces have been in full retreat since dawn on May 5, and are being closely followed by the Austrian Carpathian army, according to official

German Armies Operating on a Scale Unparalleled in the History of War

LONDON, May 6.—The Germans, in consort with their Austrian allies, are putting forth an effort, the extent of which has never been approached in the history of war. Throughout virtually the whole length of the eastern front they are engaged with the Russians, while in the west, in addition to their attacks around Ypres, they are on the offensive at many points. At other points they are being attacked by the French, British, and Belgians.

Far up in the Russian Baltic Provinces, heretofore untouched by the war, the Germans are attempting to advance toward Libau and Riga. On the East Prussian frontier they are engaged in a series of battles, and with a big gun are bombarding at long range, as they did Dunkirk, the Russian fortress of Grodno. In Central Poland they have had to defend themselves against a Russian attack. In Western Galicia they are attacking with all their strength the Russian flank and compelling the Russians to abandon the Carpathian passes which were gained at such cost during the Winter.

advices reaching here. More than 50,000 prisoners have already been captured by the Austrians in West Galicia.

Think Russians Can't Escape.

Field Marshal von Hoetzendorf's plan is working out with precise regularity with respect to this section of the front. Confidence is expressed by headquarters that the principal portion of the Russian army under General Radko Dimitrieff, which is attempting to defend positions in the Carpathians to the west of Lupkow Pass, cannot make good its retreat. Detachments of this army may work their way out, but it is declared that the bulk of the army, with the heavy artillery and baggage, can scarcely succeed in avoiding capture, in view of Field Marshal von Hoetzendorf's rapid advance through the Gorlice breach in the lines.

On the northern front the Russians held on desperately to Tarnow and Wal Mountain—a fortified crest 1,500 to 2,000 feet high between the Biala and Dunajec Rivers—to enable them to get great quantities of stores accumulated behind Tarnow away and cover the retirement of the armies to the southward. The Russians fortified this mountain until it was a veritable Gibraltar, but the Archduke's men attacked it with a desperate valor and were well served by their artillery. This struggle may go down in history with that for Putiloff Hill, to the south of Mukden, in the Russo-Japanese war.

The question as to whether the Russians can make a successful stand on the line of the Wisloka River is the important one from the Austro-German military viewpoint. If they cannot, the breach in the Russian line is considered complete, and the situation for the Russian Carpathian armies will undoubtedly be critical.

Great Mortar Fire Overpowering.

The heaviest artillery was employed in these operations. The 42-centimetre mortars in action were, however, not the noted German guns, but of Austrian make. They were designed originally for coast defense purposes, but have been found exceedingly valuable for land warfare. They fire projectiles 650 pounds heavier than the German mortar and are understood to be comparatively mobile and quickly set up. The

effect of these mortars during the artillery preparations for battle is described as overpowering. Shells from them have reached the supply depots behind Tarnow.

The Austrians are also equipped with highly effective smaller howitzers of a new type, which were put into the field during the later stage of the war.

The fighting is taking place in the difficult country of mountain spurs and foothills of the Northern Carpathians, and the successes of the Germanic forces are not being won without the hardest efforts. All hills and bridges in the rear of the original Russian lines had been fortified with triple rows of trenches, in preparation for such an emergency, and the Russians, with all the advantages of prepared trenches and gun positions, are putting up a stubborn resistence.

Many unverifiable rumors concerning the number of prisoners taken by the Austrians are in circulation. Some report, say that the total number of prisoners reached between 100,000 and 150,000 today and yesterday, but the authorities themselves warn against credence being placed in any particular set of figures. Probably they themselves do not know within thousands now many Russians have been taken prisoners.

The text of the War Office announcement of the operations issued today follows:

Forces of the Teuton allies are advancing successfully along the entire front in West Galicia. Troops of the enemy, still intact, are attempting, by taking up favorable defensive positions, to cover their hasty retreat.

The strong Russian forces in the Beskid region are being seriously menaced by the flank attack of our victorious armies. Already we have forced the fighting in the regions of Jaslo and Dukla, and the engagement now in progress will complete the annihilation of the Third Russian army.

The number of prisoners in our hands has been increased to more than 50,000.

On the remainder of the front the situation remains unchanged.

In the Orova Valley a strong Russian attack on the hill of Ostry has been repulsed with great slaughter of the enemy.

Berlin Cheered by Victories.

BERLIN, May 6, (via London.)—The military developments of the last week have had a visible effect on popular feeling in Berlin, which is decidedly more optimistic. Operations in the Russian province of Courland, on the Bal-

tic, in Galicia, and in Belgium indicate that German forces are taking the offensive on a large scale, and that greater events are to be expected.

Further developments in Galicia are awaited with breathless interest, as it is believed that the events on this section of the front may give a decisive turn to the entire Eastern campaign. The view held here is that the whole Russian position in the Carpathians has now become precarious.

The operations of the Austro-German force which is now threatening the Russian lines between the Dunajec and Biala Rivers is regarded as a first-class performance, from a German military standpoint, particularly as it is the result of a frontal attack against strongly fortified positions.

The Austrians crossed the Dunajec near its confluence with the Vistula, although the Russians were strongly protected behind a dike on the eastern bank.

The Austrians, behind a dike on the west shore, advanced pontoons by night, cutting through the dike and depositing the pontoons among high reeds along the shore. They refilled and resodded the cut each night. In this way a sufficient number of pontoons was concealed in three nights for effecting a crossing of the river. When these preparations had been completed a terrific artillery bombardment enabled the Austrians to bridge the stream with comparatively little loss.

The Austro-German attack near Gorlice is described as an unparalleled artillery performance. The Russians believed their position to be absolutely impregnable. The artillery of the allies, from 42 centimeters down, so completely overwhelmed the Russians, however, that the Austro-German infantry was able to take the opposing positions at the first rush.

Attack on the Nida a Blind.

These operations were veiled by a heavy bombardment of the Russian positions along the Nida River last week, the Germans and Austrians meanwhile bringing up a powerful force, including an enormous amount of artillery, to the Dunajec for the great push eastward toward Lemberg.

The Russians still hold one strong position on a range of hills, more than 1,000 feet high, near Tuchow, but this position is now threatened from both the north and south. Artillery is already preparing the ground for an attempt by infantry to dislodge the Russians.

In view of this situation it is generally believed in Berlin that the operations in Galicia during the next ten days will yield big results.

The War Office report of the latest operations there follows:

In the war area to the east of Tarnow and to the north of that place as far as the Vistula River, and on the right bank of the Dunajec River, fighting continued far into the night. The number of prisoners so far taken has reached to more than 40,000. It is worthy to note that this is on the Russian front.

In the Beskid Mountains, on the Lupkow Pass Road, an attack is being made by the forces under General of Cavalry Von der Marwitz simultaneously with an attack made by the Austro-Hungarian army which is co-operating with the Germans. These attacks are progressing favorably.

The bulletin concludes: " We not only forced a crossing of the Wisloka at several points, but firmly put our hands on the Dukla Pass, the road and the place.''

GERMAN GAINS NORTH AND SOUTH

Allies Lose Two Positions Near Ypres—Retake Hill 60 Trenches.

LONDON, May 6.—Several successes along the western front are recorded in today's official German statements. Berlin reports that the Kaiser's forces have made progress southeast of Ypres, but makes no mention of the recapture

Theatre of Austro-German Victory in West Galicia.

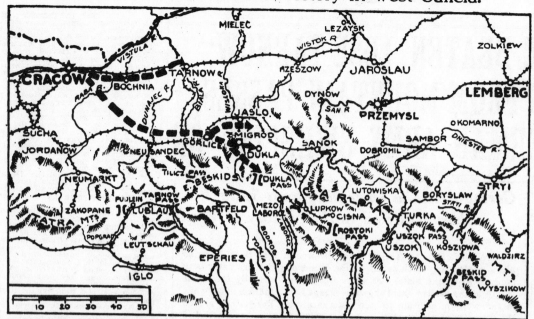

It is announced from Vienna that both the northern and southern wings of the great Austro-German Army, which was concentrated at Cracow, is succeeding in its task of rolling up the battle front of the Russians in Western Galicia. The heavy dotted lines on the map show the advance of the Austro-German Army.

The northern wing, after forcing the passage of the Dunajec River, and storming Wal Mountain, is reported to have captured Tarnow, the great Russian base in that region.

The southern wing, according to Vienna and Berlin reports, has crossed the Rivers Dunajec, Biala and Wisloka, captured the towns of Gorlice, Jaslo and Dukla, and the head of the Dukla Pass, and forced the Russians to retreat far eastward beyond the Lupkow Pass.

This means, in the opinion of military critics the collapse for the time being at least, of the entire Russian campaign in the Western Carpathians, and, in the view of military circles in Vienna, the probable capture of the bulk of the Czar's Army which has been operating in Western Galicia and through the Carpathians in the foothills on the Hungarian side of the range.

---

by the British of more of the trenches on Hill 60, (reported by Field Marshal Sir John French, who says that no German attacks occurred elsewhere on his front).

Other German claims relate to successes in the Woevre, where the Berlin War Office reports that in an attack along the northern side of the St. Mihiel wedge the Germans took upward of 2,000 prisoners, and that they repulsed French attacks on the southern section of the wedge near Flirey. This, as usual during the last few weeks, disagrees with the French account of the actions, although the Paris communiqué admits that the positions lost in the forest of Ailly, near St. Mihiel, have not all been retaken, and that in Alsace the Germans have recaptured a position at Mamelon.

Germans Take Two Farms.

Following is the Berlin official report:

Over the whole front artillery duels have taken place. We made further progress near Ypres (Belgium) and have taken the van Helpe farm and another farm near the Messines-Ypres Railway. We made 100 prisoners and took fifteen machine guns.

In the forest district to the west of Combres we made an advance and captured four French officers and 135 men. We also took four machine guns and a mine-thrower.

In our attack yesterday in the Ailly Wood we achieved our objective by forcing the enemy to evacuate his positions. More than 2,000 Frenchmen, among them 21 officers, were made prisoners. We also took two cannon and several machine guns and mine-throwers. The number of Frenchmen killed was extremely large.

The enemy attacked us in the region north of Flirey and near Croix des Carmes. North of the former place the enemy pushed forward as far as our trenches. At one point in this sector fighting continues. At all other points the French were beaten back. In the Vosges an advance against our position north of Steinbrück was repulsed.

Winning Back Hill 60 Trenches.

The British War Office tonight issued the following communication:

There is nothing to report on the British front except the recapture by us yesterday evening of more of our lost trenches on Hill 60, southeast of Ypres, and that fighting still continues in that locality.

Elsewhere the enemy has shown no disposition to attack.

The French War Office this afternoon gave out a report on the progress of hostilities, reading as follows:

To the north of Ypres we repulsed with facility a night attack made by the Germans from Steenstraete.

To the south of Ypres, the Germans yesterday, at a point near Zwartelan, attacked the trenches of Hill No. 60, occupied last month by British troops. Their very violent onslaught, during the course of which they again made use of asphyxiating gases, made them masters in the beginning of this position, but our allies subsequently delivered a counter-attack and recaptured a portion of the trenches previously lost.

In the Forest Ailly the counter-attack delivered by us toward the end of the day made slight progress, and we recaptured a portion of the position where the German had succeeded in gaining a footing in the morning. During the night the Germans delivered a counter-attack against our position at Mamelon, to the east of Sillakerwasen, the summit of which they reoccupied. All the remainder of our gain in the direction of the River Fecht has been consolidated and maintained.

"Today was calm. There is nothing to report," was the Paris night bulletin.

TALKS OF YIELDING YPRES.

London Daily News Says the Eastern Salient Is in Danger.

Special Cable to THE NEW YORK TIMES.

LONDON, Friday, May 7.—The Daily News, in an editorial, says that the position at Ypres is again critical. Owing to the success of the new method of "frightfulness" adopted by the Germans in poisoning the air, the salient has become perilously narrow, and it would cause little surprise, though much regret, if it were found necessary to sacrifice it and readjust the line west of the town.

URGE THAT BRITISH USE POISON GAS TOO

Special Cable to THE NEW YORK TIMES.

LONDON, Friday, May 7.—The Cabinet is now considering the question whether the Allies should employ poison gases against the Germans, according to The Daily Chronicle, which editorially argues that "it is clear from all the evidence that the German asphyxiating gases possess serious military importance, and the enemy will continue to use them, probably on a growing scale, whenever conditions are favorable. A new and formidable weapon has been introduced into warfare, and, much as we may regret its introduction and censure the gross breach of international faith by which it was introduced, neither regrets nor censure will win battles.

"Unless our troops are to feel that they fight an unfair battle, with one hand tied behind their backs—and that is a feeling which, if justified, might destroy all the morale of even the bravest soldiers—we must fight gases with gases, and do so with the least possible delay. We must arm our front with equipment at least as deadly as the German gas equipment, and, if possible, deadlier. This is not a matter to stand arguing about, posing pros and cons, whether in Parliament or elsewhere. In justice to our own soldiers we need to act, and act promptly; and at the same time there ought to be as rapid a development as possible of defensive measures, not merely for the wearing of respirators, but of the spraying of alcohol, ammonia, and other chemical agents.

"Every humane person must deplore that warfare has entered on this new phase, but we cannot prevent its being entered on; all we can do is to see that our men are not put at a relative disadvantage by it. If normal weather returns, with the normal preponderance of southwest winds the enemy may come to be sorry for their own barbarous innovation; but the fact that the Allies are compelled to copy it will not in any sense exonerate Germany for having introduced it, nor take the crime of having introduced it out of the category of those things for which an account must be duly exacted at the end of the war."

Slow Torture, Says An Officer.

The Chronicle prints a letter from a British officer who visited in hospital some of the men who were disabled by gas on Hill 60.

"The whole of England and the civilized world," he says, "ought to have the truth fully brought before them in vivid detail, and not wrapped up as at present. When we got to the hospital we had no difficulty in finding out in which ward the men were, as the noise of the poor devils trying to get breath was sufficient to direct us.

"There were about twenty of the worst cases in the ward, on mattresses, all more or less in a sitting posture, propped up against the walls. Their faces, arms and hands were of a shiny, gray-black color. With their mouths open and leaden-glazed eyes, all were swaying slightly backward and forward, trying to get breath. It was a most appalling sight—all these poor, black faces struggling for life—what with the groaning and the noise of the efforts for breath.

"There is practically nothing to be done for them except to give them salt and water to try to make them sick. The effect the gas has is to fill the lungs with watery, frothy matter, which gradually increases and rises till it fills up the whole lungs and comes up to the mouth; then they die. It is suffocation; slow drowning, taking in some cases one or two days. Eight died last night out of twenty I saw, and most of the others I saw will die, while those who get over the gas invariably develop acute pneumonia.

"It is without doubt the most awful form of scientific torture. Not one of the men I saw in the hospital had a scratch or wound. The Germans have given out that it is a rapid, painless death—the liars! No torture could be worse than to give them a dose of their own gas."

DARDANELLES GAINS PRAISED BY ASQUITH

Operations Being Pressed Forward Under Highly Satisfactory Conditions, He Tells House.

DESCRIBES THE LANDING

29,000 Men Put Ashore the First Day—Fierce Resistance of the Turks Causes Heavy Losses.

LONDON, May 6.—The operations in the Dardanelles are being pressed forward under highly satisfactory conditions, Premier Asquith told the House of Commons this afternoon in the course of a statement upon the combined naval and land attacks on the Gallipoli Peninsula.

The Premier spoke in part as follows:

"At daybreak of April 25 the landing occurred, the troops making use of six landing places. By nightfall 29,000 men had been disembarked in the face of fierce opposition by infantry and artillery intrenched behind successive lines of wire entanglements.

"The leading troops of the Twenty-ninth Division were held up all day to the west of Sedd-el Bahr, but at sunset they succeeded in a fine attack along the heights, which made possible the taking of a good position covering the disembarkation of the remainder of the division.

"The landing brigade of the Australian and New Zealand corps went ashore at Gaba Tepe at 4:30 o'clock in the morning in complete silence. The enemy opened a heavy fire at point-blank range, but the beach was rushed with good effect and the attack carried out with the utmost dash up the slope.

"French forces effected a landing at Kum Kale and advanced with great gallantry. Every report speaks of the magnificent co-operation of the naval forces. I regret the casualties were very heavy, including the death of Brig. Gen. Napier.

"During April 26 the disembarkation continued. The troops ashore were subjected to continuous and determined attacks from the enemy, but these in every case were repulsed with heavy losses. The Twenty-ninth Division, under command of General Hunter, with great valor carried the Turkish position at Sedd-el Bahr, which consisted of rocky ravines, ruined houses and wire entanglements.

"By evening of April 27 the 29th Division was firmly established across the Gallipoli Peninsula, having advanced two miles from the point of landing. They were joined by the French troops who, having fulfilled the task of silencing the hostile batteries on the Asiatic Coast which interfered with the landing on the Gallipoli Peninsula, had recrossed the strait. The Australian and New Zealand Corps defeated every counter-attack and steadily gained ground.

"The disembarkation continued on April 28 and 29. By May 2 a further advance had been made by the French and British troops on the southern end of the peninsula, and the Australian and New Zealand corps had been reinforced by the Royal Naval Division.

"All the News That's Fit to Print."

The New York Times.

THE WEATHER
Fair today and Sunday; fresh to strong southwest to west winds.
For full weather report see Page 21.

VOL. LXIV...NO. 20,923.   NEW YORK, SATURDAY, MAY 8, 1915.—TWENTY-FOUR PAGES.   ONE CENT In Greater New York, Jersey City and Newark. | TWO CENTS.

LUSITANIA SUNK BY A SUBMARINE, PROBABLY 1,000 DEAD; TWICE TORPEDOED OFF IRISH COAST; SINKS IN 15 MINUTES; AMERICANS ABOARD INCLUDED VANDERBILT AND FROHMAN; WASHINGTON BELIEVES THAT A GRAVE CRISIS IS AT HAND

SOME DEAD TAKEN ASHORE

Several Hundred Survivors at Queenstown and Kinsale.

STEWARD TELLS OF DISASTER

One Torpedo Crashes Into the Doomed Liner's Bow, Another Into the Engine Room.

BOATS PROMPTLY LOWERED

But Ship Goes Down So Quickly Many Must Have Gone with Her —No Officers Reported Saved.

Passengers at Luncheon—Warning Had Been Given by Germans Before the Ship Left New York.

LONDON, Saturday, May 8. —The Cunard liner Lusitania, which sailed out of New York last Saturday with 1,918 souls aboard, lies at the bottom of the ocean off the Irish coast.

She was sunk by a German submarine, which sent two torpedoes crashing into her side, while the passengers, seemingly confident that the great, swift vessel could elude the German underwater craft, were having luncheon.

How many of the Lusitania's passengers and crew were rescued cannot be told at present. Official statements from the British Admiralty up to midnight accounted for not more than 500 or 600, and unofficial reports tell of several hundreds landed at Queenstown, Kinsale and other points.

Up to midnight 520 passengers from the Lusitania had been landed at Queenstown from boats. Ten or eleven boatloads have come ashore and others are expected.

A press dispatch says seven torpedoes were discharged from the German craft and one of them struck the Lusitania amidships.

Probably at least 1,000 persons, including many Americans, have lost their lives.

Sank in Fifteen Minutes.

The stricken vessel went down in less than half an hour, according to all reports. The most definite statement puts fifteen minutes as the time that passed between the fatal blow and the disappearance of the Lusitania beneath the waves.

There were 1,253 passengers from New York on board the steamship, including 200 who were transferred to her from the steamer Cameronia. The crew numbered 665.

No names of the rescued are yet available.

Story of the Attack.

The tug, Stormcock, has returned to Queenstown, bringing about 150 survivors of the Lusitania, principally passengers, among whim were many women, several of the crew and one steward. Describing the experience of the Lusitania, the steward said:

"The passengers were at lunch when a submarine came up and fired two torpedoes, which struck the Lusitania on the starboard side, one forward and another in the engine room. They caused terrific explosions.

"Captain Turner immediately ordered the boats out. The ship began to list badly immediately.

"Ten boats were put into the water, and between 400 and 500 passengers entered them. The boat in which I was, approached the land with three other boats, and we were picked up shortly after 4 o'clock by the Storm Cock.

"I fear that few of the officers were saved. They acted bravely.

"There was only fifteen minutes from the time the ship

was struck until she foundered, going down bow foremost. It was a dreadful sight."

At the time this dispatch was sent from Queenstown two other vessels were approaching the port with survivors.

The Cunard Line received a message saying that a motor boat, towing two boats containing fifty passengers, and two tugs with passengers, was passing Kinsale. A majority of the rescue boats are proceeding to Queenstown.

An Admiralty report states that between 500 and 600 survivors from the Lusitania have now been landed, many of them being hospital cases. Several of them have died. Some also have been landed at Kinsale, but the number has not yet been received.

Hit 10 Miles Off Kinsale Head.

This greatest sea tragedy of the war because of the terrible loss of lives of non-combatants and citizens of neutral nations, took place about ten miles off the Old Head of Kinsale about 2 o'clock in the afternoon.

A dispatch to the Exchange Telegraph from Liverpool

quotes the Cunard Company as stating that "the Lusitania was sunk without warning."

According to a Queenstown dispatch the Lusitania was seen from the signal station at Kinsale to be in difficulties at 2:12 P.M. and at 2:33 she had completely disappeared.

This indicated, the dispatch added, that the liner was afloat twenty-one minutes after what evidently was the beginning of her trouble.

Official announcement was also made here last night by the Cunard Line that the Lusitania remained afloat at least twenty minutes after being torpedoed, and that "twenty boats were on the spot at the time." Sixteen more boats, officials of the line said, had been dispatched to the scene for rescue work.

As soon as the Lusitania's wireless call for assistance was received at Queenstown at 2:15 o'clock, Admiral Coke, in command of the naval station, dispatched to the scene all assistance available.

The tugs Warrior, Storm-

THE LOST CUNARD STEAMSHIP LUSITANIA

x Where the first torpedo struck. xx Where the second torpedo struck.

NO. 1—Navigating Bridge, Officers' Rooms, Roofs of Public Rooms, Marconi House and Docking Bridge.

A, OR BOAT DECK—Captain's Rooms, First Class Library, Grand Entrance, Passenger Elevators, First Class Lounge, Music Room, Smoking Room and Veranda Café, Second Cabin Promenade and Lounge.

B, OR PROMENADE DECK—Forecastle Head, Head Front of Promenade Deck, Observation Corridor, First Class Staterooms, Regal Suites, En Suite Rooms,

Grand Entrance and Passenger Elevators, First Class Staterooms, Dome of Dining Saloons, Second Cabin Promenade, Drawing Room, and Second Cabin Smoking Room.

C, OR UPPER DECK—Forward Capstan and Windlass Machinery, Third Class Smoking Room and Ladies' Room, Third Class Covered Promenade, Third Class Main Entrance, First Class Children's Dining Saloon and Nursery, Grand Entrance and Passenger Elevators, First Class Grand Dining Saloon, Engi-

neers' Quarters, Second Cabin Main Entrance, Second Cabin Staterooms and Promenade.

D, OR SALOON DECK—Stewards' Quarters, Third Class Main Dining Saloon, First Class Staterooms, Grand Entrance and Passenger Elevators, First Class Grand Dining Saloon, Galleys and Pantries, Second Cabin Dining Saloon, Second Cabin Staterooms, Stewards' and Cooks' Quarters.

E, OR MAIN DECK—Seamen's Quarters, Third Class Cabins, Grand Entrance and Passenger Elevators, First Class Staterooms, Firemen's Quarters, Second Cabin Staterooms, Stewards' Quarters.

F, OR LOWER DECK—First Class Baggage Rooms, Third Class Cabins, Coal, Stores, Wine Rooms, Firemen's Quarters, Mail Room, Mail Sorting Room, and Stewards' Quarters.

BELOW DECK F—Boilers, Engine Room, Pump Room, Tanks, and Shaft Tunnels.

cock, and Julia, together with five trawlers and the local life boat in tow of a tug, were hurried out to sea. It was thought it would take most of them about two hours to reach the spot where the Lusitania was reported to be sinking.

One dispatch received here said the liner was eight miles off the Irish coast when she finally went down.

London Torn With Anxiety.

All the afternoon, following the first startling message from Ireland and the fragmentary bulletins, indicating a possibility of heavy loss of life, London waited with intense anxiety for further news.

This anxiety grew steadily through the evening as hour after hour passed without any definite statement from an authoritative source as to the extent of the disaster.

The Cunard offices, which will remain open throughout the night, were besieged by a great crowd, largely composed of women, many of them weeping bitterly as the hours passed and no definite news came of those aboard the Lusitania.

Accommodation was provided inside the offices for those who had relatives or friends on the steamer, while hundreds waited outside, eagerly reading the scanty bulletins which told of rescue boats arriving at Kinsale and Queenstown, but gave no names of the saved, and consequently did not allay the anxiety.

There was a gleam of hope in the general gloom soon after

8 o'clock, when this announcement was made unofficially:

The Cunard Company has definitely ascertained that the lives of the passengers and the crew of the Lusitania have been saved.

This was speedily proved untrue, however, but the more optimistic still refused to credit the early reports of the swift sinking of the big liner. It was believed that her watertight bulkheads would tend to keep her afloat, and if she floated a reasonable length of time before going down, it was possible that rescuing ships got to her side in time to save all on board.

Owing to the fact that all the news of the Lusitania came through the Admiralty, and that only fragments filtered through at intervals, the crowds got increasingly more impatient, though the Cunard officials posted quickly all bulletins received.

Late in the evening the Admiralty felt compelled to give out notice that it was not holding back any known facts, but did not feel justified in giving out rumors.

Americans Besiege Embassy.

The American Embassy and Consulate and the American newspaper offices were flooded with telephonic inquiries from Americans as to the fate of the passengers on the Lusitania, but there was no definite news there until after midnight, and the only hope that could be held out was that some boats had landed survivors and others had been seen making for the

shore. The Embassy decided to remain open all night, so that any news that was received could be made public.

Up to 1 o'clock no news tending to allay the public anxiety had been received in the city. Then dispatches, issued by the Admiralty, indicated that among the survivors landed at Queenstown were some injured, presumably by the explosion.

A later dispatch from the same source increased the apprehensions in this direction. Those wounded are being sent to the naval and military hospitals.

A press dispatch from Queenstown reported that 400 passengers and crew had been landed at Kinsale. This stated that none of the first-class passengers had been saved, but this is proved not true by private dispatches.

Cross Section of the Lusitania.

An Admiralty statement states, however, that the survivors from the Lusitania landed at Kinsale numbered about eleven.

A private telegram from Clonakiety to Dublin says that several hundred passengers had landed that from the Lusitania.

DISASTER BEARS OUT EMBASSY'S WARNING

German Advertisement Practically Foretold Lusitania's Fate on Day She Sailed.

AND IS REPEATED TODAY

Passengers Also Said to Have Received Telegrams — Shipping Men Heard of Threats.

That the Germans intended to make an effort to sink the Lusitania had been the common impression in shipping circles for weeks. When the German Embassy advertisement, warning Americans not to go to Europe aboard vessels flying the British flag, was printed last Saturday many professed to see in that warning the promise of an early attempt on the part of German submarines to send the great Cunarder to the bottom.

The German Embassy advertisement appeared in the newspapers the day that the Lusitania left New York on her last voyage. Its appearance naturally attracted wide attention, and there was much apprehension felt among those shipping men who had maintained from the first that the Lusitania, despite her great speed, was not immune from submarine attack. A torpedo, they said, could travel faster than any ship, and should the Lusitania or any other liner pass within short range of a submarine all the speed in the world could not get those ships out of the way of a properly aimed Whitehead torpedo.

Advertisement Appears Again.

The German Embassy advertisement which it may be noted appears in THE NEW YORK TIMES for a second time this morning, and which caused so many persons to have what is sometimes termed "a hunch" that all would not go well with the great liner, reads:

NOTICE.

Travelers intending to embark on the Atlantic voyage are reminded that a state of war exists between Germany and her allies and Great Britain and her allies; that the zone of war includes the waters adjacent to the British Isles; that in accordance with formal notice given by the Imperial German Government, vessels flying the flag of Great Britain or of any of her allies are liable to destruction in those waters and that travelers sailing in the war zone on ships of Great Britain or of her allies do so at their own risk.

IMPERIAL GERMAN EMBASSY.
Washington, D. C., April 22, 1915.

The Lusitania sailed from New York at 12:20 P. M. a week ago today, and the insertion of the advertisement was the subject of most of the conversations of those aboard her, as well as their friends and others who had gone to the pier to wish them a safe voyage. The passengers for the most professed to have no fear that the Lusitania was running any danger, and not one, so far as is known, canceled his passage because of the German Embassy's warning.

Expected a Convoy.

Charles P. Sumner, the General Agent in New York of the Cunard Line, was on the pier when the Lusitania sailed, and when asked if he considered that the German warning placed the Lusitania in peril, he replied that he did not. As for submarines, he added that he had no fear of them whatever, pointing out at the same time "there is a general system of convoying British ships," and adding that the British Navy was responsible for all British ships and "especially for Cunarders."

"The Germans," said Mr. Sumner, "have been trying to spoil our trade for some time. I anticipate that from this time on every German method that can be devised will be used to keep people from traveling on our ships."

Just before the Lusitania sailed there was a report that some of the passengers had received warnings in the form of unsigned telegrams that it would be best for them to sail by some other vessel than the Lusitania, and that the Lusitania would be torpedoed when she neared or got into European waters.

Alfred Gwynne Vanderbilt was said to have received one of these warning telegrams. The anonymous sender of the Vanderbilt warning was said to have worded the warning in this way:

"Have it on definite authority that the Lusitania is to be torpedoed. You had better cancel passage immediately."

Several other passengers were reported to have received similarly worded warnings, but none of them took the matter seriously and all refused to become alarmed.

Denied by Line's Agents.

When officials of the Cunard Line were questioned concerning these reported anonymous telegrams they said that investigation of the rumor was made before the liner sailed and that it was ascertained that not one of the passengers named had received any of any kind from any source as to any danger traveling by the Lusitania might entail. This denial was repeated at the Cunard Line offices yesterday.

After the Lusitania sailed, and up to the moment it became known that she had been torpedoed, reports were current that the Germans were about to deliver their heaviest blow against British transatlantic shipping.

A few days ago it was stated by a man who had followed the submarine activities of the Germans closely that the Germans would get her before three weeks. He said he did not expect the attempt to be made until the German Embassy advertisement had appeared three times, as promised, in the American newspapers. Similar prophecies came to the ears of at least one leading shipping man in New York, and there is reason to believe that London was informed of these gloomy forecasts concerning the safety of the big liner.

Following the fire on the French liner Touraine, which it was asserted was started by a German agent on board the ship, all ships flying the flags of the Allied nations have been closely inspected before sailing from New York. All these lines are maintaining a secret service of their own and every passenger who is not known to the agents of the line, or their secret service men, is carefully scrutinized before and after boarding outbound vessels.

LINER UNPROTECTED, CAPTAIN COMPLAINED

"Admiralty Never Trouble to Send Out to Meet Lusitania," Turner Said.

WARNED OF MINES BEFORE

Officer Now Here Asserts the Only Vulnerable Spot Was Right Under Engine Room.

In spite of the warnings that had been received from time to time that the Germans would make an attempt to blow up the Lusitania, Captain William T. Turner expressed no fear for the safety of his ship when he sailed from New York last Saturday.

"I wonder what the Germans will do next?" was his only comment when he read the advertisement in THE NEW YORK TIMES sent out by the German Embassy warning Americans that they sailed at "their own risk" on British ships, which were liable to destruction in the war zone.

When Captain Turner was questioned by a TIMES reporter regarding the ship being met off the Irish coast by British torpedo destroyers, he replied:

"The Admiralty never trouble to send out to meet the Lusitania. They only look after the ships that are bringing the big guns over, like the Orduna and the Transylvania, last voyage. On the eastward trip I never saw a warship until we reached Liverpool. The ship is steaming under three sections of boilers, and will average about twenty-two knots if the weather is fine, which ought to bring her into Liverpool about Friday evening."

One of the Cunard officers now in port, who was on the Lusitania on her last voyage, yesterday confirmed Captain Turner's statement that the liner had not sighted a single warship before arriving at Liverpool.

Cautioned by Wireless.

"We received a warning by wireless from one of the warships stating that mines had been laid forty miles south of the Old Head of Kinsale and advising a strict lookout," he said. "Captain Turner is one of the best shipmasters I have ever known, courageous to the extreme, and always at his post, calm and confident in himself and his crew.

"We passed ten miles west of the Fastnet and about seven miles southwest of Kinsale, which lies about forty-seven miles east northeast of the Fastnet. Every precaution was taken by the Captain when we neared the danger zone. All boats were swung out ready to lower and life rafts and collapsible boats were uncovered and ready for launching. Two lookout men were posted on the foc'sle head, two more in the crow's nest, and two officers on the bridge. In addition either Captain Turner or J. C. Anderson, the staff Captain, were on the bridge when land was sighted until we reached Liverpool.

"You see that it is impossible for a master to take a ship into harbor like driving an automobile into a town. Coming in from the Atlantic he has to get his bearings either from the Fastnet or Kinsale, and that is where the German submarines evidently laid for him. In my opinion the Germans had two or three submarines between the Fastnet and Kinsale, so that they could signal his approach if he managed to run past the first one and the other would get the ship.

"The after section of boilers on the Lusitania have been shut down since the beginning of the war and her average speed was not more than twenty-two knots, but in time of danger the Chief Engineer might make a spurt up to twenty-three for a little while. To sink the ship, the torpedo must have struck her right under the engine room, because that was her only vulnerable spot."

The officer explained that the number of firemen and coal trimmers was smaller than normal on account of the boilers shut off, and there were fewer stewards, as the number of cabin passengers was fewer than usual at this season of the year.

Warning of Passengers Denied.

There were rumors before the Lusitania sailed that some of the passengers, including Charles Frohman, Alfred G. Vanderbilt, and Charles Klein, had received telegrams warning them not to sail on the ship. This was denied by the agents of the Cunard Line, who sent a wireless message to Captain Turner asking him to investigate the rumor. At 11 o'clock last Saturday night a reply was received which read:

"No one received telegrams of the kind indicated. Turner."

On the previous voyage there were rumors that the Lusitania was to be attacked and A. J. Drexel, Mrs. W. B. Leeds, and Mr. and Mrs. Harry Lehr canceled their passages at the last moment and sailed on the American liner New York. Mr. Drexel told a TIMES reporter that he had not been warned in any way but had changed his ship on account of Mr. Lehr, who had weak nerves and did not like submarines. On the Lusitania's last voyage no one cancelled, and the passenger list was the biggest eastward sailing this year.

The color of the Lusitania's funnels was changed from red with black top to black by Captain David Dow last November, and her superstructure forward by the bridge was changed from white to gray, but afterward was restored to its original color.

It was Captain Dow who raised the American flag on the Lusitania nearing Liverpool on Jan. 30, which provoked considerable comment at the time, as it was stated that he had been ordered to do so by the Admiralty.

Captain Turner said on the last previous voyage of the Lusitania that the instructions issued by the Admiralty to all shipmasters nearing the danger zone were: "Show neutral colors or none."

The Lusitania carried life boats and rafts sufficient to accommodate 2,605 persons. These included twenty-two life boats which carried sixty-eight persons each; twenty Chambers collapsible boats, carrying fifty-four each; twelve McLean-Chambers collapsible boats with a capacity of forty-nine each; two Henderson collapsible boats, carrying forty-three each, and fourteen life rafts, with capacities varying from twenty to forty each. There were also nearly 3,000 life preservers on board.

The life-saving apparatus is examined every voyage in Liverpool by the Board of Trade officials when the boats are lowered into the water and the life jackets placed on deck for inspection.

Roosevelt Calls It An Act of Piracy.

Special to The New York Times.

SYRACUSE, N. Y., May 7—Colonel Roosevelt tonight characterized the sinking of the Lusitania as "an act of piracy."

"I do not know enough of the facts," said the Colonel, "to make any further comment or to say what would be proper for this Government to do in the circumstances.

"I can only repeat what I said the other day when the Gulflight was attacked. I then called attention to the fact that months before the German war zone was established, and deeds such as the sinking of the Lusitania were threatened, that if such deeds were perpetrated they would represent nothing but mere piracy."

BULLETINS STIR UP WAR SYMPATHIZERS

Arguments and Fights Follow Sinking of the Lusitania —One Arrest.

The first reports of the sinking of the Lusitania by a German submarine posted on the bulletin boards around the city caused great crowds to gather and stirred heated arguments and a number of personal encounters. The police stationed at these places had their hands full keeping the peace.

When Paul Zeider of 416 West 126th Street passed Times Square at 6:30 o'clock last evening he saw on the bulletin board the news that the Germans had sunk the Lusitania. He shouted: "Hurragh for the Germans!" and threw his hat in the air. There was an angry outcry, and a dozen men rushed for him. When Traffic Policeman MacDonald, stationed at Broadway and Forty-third Street, had shoved his way into the centre of the small riot, he had to call Patrolman Foley to help rescue Zeider. The German sympathizer failed to appreciate this service, and began struggling with the policemen. He was then taken to the West Forty-seventh Street Police Station and locked up on a charge of disorderly conduct.

In front of THE TIMES bulletin board, in Herald Square, in Park Row, and, in fact, everywhere people congregated to talk about the sinking of the Lusitania, there were angry arguments.

171 ABOARD WERE AMERICANS.

Nationalities of First and Second Cabin Passengers Announced.

The first and second class passengers on the Lusitania, according to the Cunard office here, are divided into the following nationalities: British, 700; American, 171; Dutch, 5; Russian, 3; Greek, 3; Swedish 1; Mexican, 1; Swiss, 1; Italian, 1.

A table was prepared showing the nationality of the third-class passengers, but it was made on the assumption that the third-class passengers of the Cameronia had been tionalities who, it was learned later, had not gone aboard the Lusitania. All of those who left on the Lusitania were provided with passports from their Consular representatives, which had been approved by the British Consulate here.

"All the News That's Fit to Print."

The New York Times.

THE WEATHER

Fair today and tomorrow; continued cool; moderate north winds.
☞For full weather report see Page 21.

VOL. LXIV...NO. 20,929.　　　NEW YORK, FRIDAY, MAY 14, 1915.—TWENTY-TWO PAGES.　　　ONE CENT In Greater New York. | Elsewhere

PRESIDENT TELLS GERMANY WE WILL OMIT NO WORD OR ACT REQUIRED BY THE SACRED DUTY OF MAINTAINING OUR RIGHTS, VIOLATED BY SUBMARINE WAR ON MERCHANT SHIPPING; APPEALS TO GERMAN SENSE OF JUSTICE AND HUMANITY

CALLS SITUATION GRAVE

And Suggests Disavowal of the Acts of the German-Commanders.

REPARATION IS EXPECTED

"So Far as Reparation Is Possible for Injuries Which Are Without Measure."

LOOKS FOR PROMPT STEPS

"To Prevent Recurrence of Anything So Subversive of the Principles of War."

EMBASSY NOTICE IRREGULAR

"No Warning of an Unlawful or Inhumane Act Can Be Accepted as an Excuse."

Special to The New York Times.

WASHINGTON, May 13.—"The Imperial German Government will not expect the Government of the United States to omit any work or any act necessary to the performance of its sacred duty of maintaining the rights of the United States and its citizens and of safeguarding their free exercise and enjoyment."

This is the final paragraph of President Wilson's note to the German Government regarding the Lusitania disaster, which was made public tonight.

The note which was cabled by Secretary Bryan to the American Ambassador in Berlin today for delivery to the German Foreign Office tomorrow morning calls on Germany in vigorous but courteous language to abandon her submarine warfare against merchant vessels, and to disavow the acts of her submarine commanders in cases where American ships have been attacked or the lives of American citizens lost or endangered.

TURKS TORPEDO BRITISH WARSHIP

Predreadnought Goliath Sunk in Dardanelles, with Loss of 500 Men.

VICTIM OF DESTROYERS

They Attacked Her Just Within the Strait—Twenty Officers and 160 Men Saved.

LONDON, May 13.—The British battleship Goliath has been torpedoed in the Dardanelles. It is believed that 500 lives have been lost.

Announcement of the loss of the battleship was made in the House of Commons this afternoon by Winston Spencer Churchill, First Lord of the Admiralty, who said:

" The Goliath was torpedoed last night in a torpedo attack by destroyers while protecting the French flank just inside the strait.

" Twenty officers and 160 men were saved, which, I fear, means that over 500 were lost.

" The Admiral commanding at the Dardanelles also telegraphs that the submarine E-14, which, with so much daring, penetrated to the Sea of Marmora, has reported that she sank two Turkish gunboats and a large Turkish transport."

Reuter's Amsterdam correspondent says that Turkish Headquarters has made the following announcement, (probably referring to the Goliath:)

" A portion of the Turkish fleet in the forenoon attacked an English ironclad near Morto Harbor, at the entrance to the Dardanelles. She was struck by projectiles in three places, namely, the Commander's bridge, amidship, and astern, and sank immediately."

The Goliath is the fifth battleship unit to be lost during the investment of the Dardanelles. On Dec. 13, 1914, the Turkish battleship Messudiyeh was sunk by a British submarine, which dived under five lines of mines to reach her prey. On March 18 the Ocean, a sister ship of the Goliath; the Irresistible, a sister ship of the Formidable, which was lost in the English Channel by torpedo or mine on Jan. 1, and the French battleship Bouvet were sunk by mines while bombarding the forts on the Dardanelles.

All these battleships were of the predreadnought type. The Goliath, when she was completed in 1900, was noted for being one of the fastest ships of her class, making over her registered speed of 18¼ knots an hour. Her waterline length was 400 feet; her beam 74 feet, and her draught 26½ feet. Her displacement was 12,950 tons, and her officers and men numbered 750, or, as a flagship, 780.

The Goliath carried four 12-inch and twelve 6-inch guns, twelve 12-pounders, (ten heavy and two light;) six Maxims, and four 18-inch submerged torpedo tubes.

It has been reported, but the report lacks confirmation, that another British battleship, the Lord Nelson, stranded inside the strait and was destroyed by Turkish gun fire. The report emanated from Constantinople via Berlin on April 5. Since then, however, the name of the Lord Nelson has appeared in the British Admiralty reports of the action of the Franco-British fleets.

Government, will make reparation "so far as reparation is possible," for the injuries done by German agents.

3. The German Government, it is also confidently expected, "will take immediate steps to prevent the recurrence of anything so obviously subversive of the principles of warfare for which the Imperial German Government have in the past so wisely and so firmly contended."

Opinions Are Divided.

Such opinions as were expressed tonight in unofficial circles indicated that there was likely to be a divided view as to whether the President's message to the German Government meant war or a continuance of friendly diplomatic relations between the two nations. Germany has already refused to abandon her submarine warfare unless England for her part, would consent to relinquish her "starving-out" policy directed against Germany.

In calling on Germany to cease her submarine attacks on merchant vessels the United States does not offer any counter proposition. Having this in mind, one opinion prevailing in Washington tonight is that the course of the United States, outlined in the note, is likely to result in a severance of dealings between the two Governments and an ultimate resort to hostilities.

This, however, does not appear to be the prevailing interpretation in Administration circles. The feeling there is that the note opens the way for diplomatic exchanges. It is pointed out that if Germany construes the note in the spirit which pervades it, she will suffer no loss of dignity by responding in a way that will afford the United States Government no opportunity for offense, and will lead to mutual agreements which will produce the results that are insisted upon by President Wilson.

Opens Way for Exchanges.

At the same time some persons here find it difficult to escape the conviction that the German Government will not be willing to abandon its submarine warfare on the merchant ships of Germany's enemies. Judged by some of the views expressed at Tuesday's Cabinet meeting, it is believed that the response of the United States to this attitude would be the severance of diplomatic relations with Germany without resort to war and a synchronous declaration to the world that this nation could afford to have no further dealings with a Government which refused to comply with the rules of civilized warfare.

Submarine Reprisals.

In an examination of the note, attention is concentrated on the concluding paragraph and the paragraph which refers to the manner of conducting submarine war against unarmed merchantmen. The last mentioned reference holds that the submarine cannot undertake reprisals

The principle is laid down and emphatically maintained that American citizens engaged on peaceful missions are entitled to take passage on the merchant vessels of any nationality, even on the merchant vessels of Germany's enemies, and are immune from any attack on he high seas which places heir lives in jeopardy.

Appeal to Humanity.

Throughout the note there is an evident intention shown by the President to appeal to Germany's sense of right, justice, and humanity. But the concluding paragraph informs the German Government in unmistakable language that a failure to correct or abandon the abuses of which the United States complains, will cause this Government to take its own course in order to bring about what it insists the German Government should do of its own volition.

With te possible exception of the closing paragraph perhaps the most striking feature of the note is the virtual insistence that Germany abandon her submarine warfare on merchant shipping, not only with reference to the vessels of the United States and other neutral nations, but also the merchant vessels of Germany's enemies which fly the flags of Germany's enemies.

Abandon Submarine Attacks.

It is not stretching the purpose of President Wilson's words to say that he calls on Germany to abandon the terms of her war zone order, so far as it applies to submarine attacks on merchant ships of any nation, including a belligerent, or the destruction of any merchant ship, no matter what flag she carries, until after her passengers and crew have been allowed to leave her in safety.

The points made by the President in this communication may be summarized in the following groupings:

1. The German Government should disavow the acts which resulted not only in the sinking of the Lusitania, but those which disabled the American ship Gulflight and the American ship Cushing, as well as the destruction of the British steamer Falaba, with the consequent death of Leon C. Thrasher, an American citizen.

2. The German Government, in the "confident expectation" of this

against merchant vessels with any success, and the President's reasons for this view are given as follows:

"It is practically impossible for the officers of the submarine to visit a merchantman at sea and examine her papers and cargo. It is practically impossible for them to make a prize of her, and, if they cannot put a prize crew on board of her, they cannot sin her without leaving her crew and all on board of her to the mercy of the sea in her small boats. These facts, it is understood, the Imperial German Government frankly admit. We are informed that in the instance of which we have spoken time enough for that poor measure of safety was not given, and in at least two of the cases cited, not so much as a warning was received. Manifestly submarines cannot be used against merchantmen, as the last weeks have shown, without an inevitable violation of many sacred principles of justice and humanity."

Recalls Asquith's View.

The language quoted above practically advances the same ideas as those put forth by Mr. Asquith, the Prime Minister of Great Britain, in the House of Commons on March 1 as follows:

The responsibility of discriminating between neutral and enemy vessels and between neutral and enemy cargoes obviously rests with the attacking ship, whose duty it is to verify the status and character of the vessel and cargo, and to preserve all papers before sinking or capturing the ship. So, also, the humane duty to provide for the safety of crews of merchant vessels, whether neutral or enemy, is an obligation on every belligerent.

It is upon this basis that all previous discussions of law for regulating warfare have proceeded. The German submarine fulfills none of these obligations. She enjoys no local command of the waters wherein she operates. She does not take her captures within the jurisdiction of a prize court. She carries no prize crew which can be put aboard prizes which she seizes. She uses no effective means of discriminating between neutral and enemy vessels. She does not receive on board for safety the crew of the vessel she sinks. Her methods of warfare, therefore, are entirely outside the scope of any international instruments regulating operations against commerce in time of war.

The Gulflight Case.

A feature of the American note is that it charges that the American oil tank steamer Gulflight was disabled by a torpedo fired by a German submarine. It has never been publicly disclosed whether the German Government has admitted that the injury to this vessel was due to submarine activity. On Tuesday the State Department gave to the press a circular statement issued by the German Government saying that orders and instructions had been given repeatedly to German submarine commanders to avoid attacking neutral vesels not carrying contraband or engaged in hostile acts. A portion of this circular statement was omitted from the text as made public by the State Department, and it is suggested tonight that this deletion embraced an acknowledgment by Germany that the Gulflight had been attacked by a German submarine and had not been the victim of a British mine.

Embassy Advertisement.

Another feature of the note that attracts attention is the paragraph which refers to the action of the German Embassy in Washington in inserting an advertisement in American newspapers warning American citizens not to take passage on ships of Germany's enemies. President Wilson makes reference to the "surprising irregularity of a communication from the Imperial Government's Embassy at Washington addressed to the people of the United States through the newspapers," but he adds that he does so only to point out that no warning that an unlawful and inhumane act will be committed can be accepted by this Government in excuse or palliation for that act.

As has been said in Washington dispatches to THE TIMES, the note is an appeal to German conscience. It calls on Germany on grounds of humanity as well as of international law to abandon its submarine warfare, and gives the Imperial Government an opportunity to disavow the acts of its submarine commanders. The President states flatly that he is loath to believe that these acts had the sanction of the German Government. The plain intent of one portion of the communication is to show emphatically that this Government holds that American citizens on innocent missions have just as much right on a belligerent merchant vessel as they have on a vessel flying the American flag.

The declaration in the American note to Germany of Feb. 10 that this Government would hold the German Governmen to "strict accountability" for acts occasioning the loss of American vessels or the lives of American citizens on the high seas is emphasized in the note. The President repeats the term "strict accountability," but softens it by the statement that this Government does no understand that the Imperial Governmen questions the rights which the United States maintains belong to its ships and citizens.

Although the President praises Germany for high principles of equity which have actuated and guided her in the past, he refers to "acts of lawlessness," but again gives the German Government the opportunity to take no offense over this term, for he expresses the belief that the commanders of the German vessel which committed these acts did so "under misapprehension" of the orders of the German naval authorities. The President takes it for granted that the commanders of German submarines were expected to do nothing that would involve the lives of noncombatants.

"The Government and the people of the United States," says the President, "look to the Imperial German Government for just, prompt, and enlightened action in this vital matter with the greatest confidence, because the United States and Germany are bound together not only by special ties of friendship but also by the explicit stipulations of the treaty of 1828 between the United States and the Kingdom of Prussia."

Take Hopeful View.

It is evident from the note that the President, while feeling that the position of the United States demanded emphatic representations that would leave no doubt of the resentment felt by the American Government and people over the sinking of the Lusitania, intended that his language should convey an appeal to the German Government's heart and conscience rather than a demand for a new deal based on material grounds.

In the belief that the German Government will construe the note in this spirit, officials of the Government hold to the hope that what the President desires to see accomplished in the way of abandonment of the German submarine warfare on merchant vessels will be accomplished by peaceable means.

His Lucky Thirteen.

The note was written originally by the President in shorthand. This is a familiar method of Mr. Wilson in making memoranda, and the fact that he utilized it in writing the momentous communication sent today to Berlin indicates that he had his thoughts well in mind and understood in advance perfectly what he intended to say. The shorthand characters of the President filled six pages of ordinary note paper. After he had set down the communication in this way the President transcribed it on his own typewriter. As far as known, no official or clerk of the White House had any part in the transcription of the document until after it had been presented to the members of the Cabinet. Not even Secretary Bryan saw it in advance of that time.

The note is dated today, May 13. It was suggested tonight that the President purposely held it over from yesterday before transmitting it to Germany. He has always regarded 13 as his lucky number.

A copy of the note was delivered to Count von Bernstorff, the German Ambassador, tonight by the State Department as a courtesy, and copies were similarly cabled to the American Ambassadors at London, Paris, and Petrograd for their own information.

Publication of the text was arranged for by Secretary Bryan, who announced that the document was to be released for use in editions of morning newspapers reaching the American public near earlier than 5 A. M. Friday.

NAVAL LOSSES IN THE WAR TO DATE.

GREAT BRITAIN AND HER ALLIES.

Date of Loss.	Name.	Displacement. Tons.
	BATTLESHIPS, (SIX BRITISH.)	
Oct. 27, 1914	Audacious	23,000
Nov. 26, 1914	Bulwark	15,000
Jan. 1, 1915	Formidable	15,000
Mar. 8, 1915	Irresistible	15,000
Mar. 8, 1915	Ocean	12,950
May 13, 1915	Goliath	12,950
	(ONE FRENCH.)	
Mar. 19, 1915	Bouvet	12,205
	CRUISERS, (TEN BRITISH.)	
Aug. 6, 1914	Amphion	3,440
Sep. 5, 1914	Pathfinder	2,940
Sep. 20, 1914	Pegasus	2,185
Sep. 22, 1914	Aboukir	12,000
Sep. 22, 1914	Cressy	12,000
Sep. 22, 1914	Hogue	12,000
Oct. 15, 1914	Hawke	7,350
Oct. 31, 1914	Hermes	5,600
Nov. 1, 1914	Good Hope	14,100
Nov. 1, 1914	Monmouth	9,800
	(ONE FRENCH.)	
Apr 26, 1915	Leon. Gambetta	12,416
	(TWO RUSSIAN.)	
Oct. 11, 1914	Pallada	7,775
Oct. 28, 1914	Jemtchug	3,050
	(ONE JAPANESE.)	
Oct. 17, 1914	Takachiho	3,700
	GUNBOATS, (TWO BRITISH.)	
Sep. 3, 1914	Speedy	810
Nov. 11, 1914	Niger	810
	(TWO RUSSIAN.)	
Oct. 20, 1914	Kubanetz	1,200
Oct. 29, 1914	Donets	1,200
	(ONE FRENCH.)	
Oct. 28, 1914	Zelee	680
	DESTROYERS, (TWO BRITISH.)	
May 1, 1915	Recruit	880
May 8, 1915	Maori	1,035
	(ONE JAPANESE.)	
Sep. 4, 1914	Shirotaye	380
	(TWO FRENCH.)	
Oct. 28, 1914	Mousquet	303
Feb. 20, 1915	Dague	450
	SUBMARINES, (FOUR BRITISH.)	
Oct. 18, 1914	E-3	725
Nov. 3, 1914	D-5	550
Apr. 8, 1915	E-15	725
May 3, 1915	Unknown	550
	(THREE FRENCH.)	
Dec. 14, 1914	Curie	398
Jan. 17, 1915	Saphir	390
Mar. 18, 1915	Unknown	390
	TORPEDO BOATS, (THREE FRENCH.)	
Oct. 9, 1914	347	98
Oct. 9, 1914	338	97
Jan. 15, 1915	Unknown	..
	(ONE JAPANESE.)	
Nov. 11, 1914	30	110
	AUXILIARY CRUISERS, (FIVE BRITISH.)	
Sep. 8, 1914	Oceanic	7,333
Oct. 30, 1914	Rohilla	4,240
Jan. 14, 1915	Viknor	2,960
Feb. 15, 1915	Clan McNaughton	4,985
Mar. 11, 1915	Bayana	5,948
	(ONE RUSSIAN.)	
Oct. 29, 1914	Prut	5,500

Total, forty-eight vessels of about 253,978 tons.

GERMANY AND HER ALLIES.

Date of Loss.	Name.	Displacement. Tons.
	BATTLESHIPS, (ONE TURKISH.)	
Dec. 13, 1914	Messudiyeh	10,000
	CRUISERS, (EIGHTEEN GERMAN.)	
Aug. 27, 1914	Magdeburg	4,550
Aug. 28, 1914	Koeln	4,350
Aug. 28, 1914	Mainz	4,350
Aug. 28, 1914	Ariadne	2,660
Sep. 13, 1914	Hela	2,040
Nov. 3, 1914	Yorck	9,050
Nov. 6, 1914	Cormoran	1,604
Nov. 8, 1914	Geier	1,604
Nov. 9, 1914	Emden	3,600
Dec. —, 1914	Friedrich Karl	9,050
Dec. 8, 1914	Scharnhorst	11,600
Dec. 8, 1914	Gneisenau	11,600
Dec. 8, 1914	Nurnberg	3,450
Dec. 8, 1914	Leipzig	3,250
Dec. —, 1914	Koenigsberg	3,400
Jan. 24, 1915	Bluecher	15,500
Jan. 25, 1915	Gazelle	2,645
Mar. 14, 1915	Dresden	3,600
	(TWO AUSTRIAN.)	
Aug. 16, 1914	Zenta	2,300
Nov. 6, 1914	Kaiserin Elisabeth	4,000
	(ONE TURKISH.)	
Apr. 3, 1915	Medjibieh	3,432
	GUNBOATS, (NINE GERMAN.)	
Aug. 9, 1914	Moewe	650
Aug. 17, 1914	Tsingtau	168
Aug. —, 1914	Hedwig von Wissmann	199
Aug. —, 1914	Vaterland	168
Oct. 18, 1914	Komet	...
Nov. 6, 1914	Tiger	900
Nov. 6, 1914	Iltis	900
Nov. 6, 1914	Jaguar	900
Nov. 6, 1914	Luchs	900
	(ONE AUSTRIAN.)	
Oct. 23, 1914	Temes	440
	(ONE TURKISH.)	
Oct. 31, 1914	Burak Reis	500
	DESTROYERS, (NINE GERMAN.)	
Aug. 28, 1914	V-187	650
Oct. 6, 1914	S-126	487
Oct. 17, 1914	S-119	420
Oct. 17, 1914	S-118	420
Oct. 17, 1914	S-117	420
Oct. 17, 1914	S-115	420
Oct. 20, 1914	S-90	400
Nov. 6, 1914	Taku	280
Nov. 23, 1914	S-124	420
	SUBMARINES, (NINE GERMANS.)	
Aug. 9, 1914	U-15	250
Oct. 24, 1914	Unknown	250
Oct. 30, 1914	Unknown	250
Nov. 23, 1914	U-18	650
Feb. 28, 1915	Unknown	250
Mar. 4, 1915	U-8	250
Mar. 4, 1915	U-2 Type	250
Mar. 10, 1915	U-12	250
Mar. 28, 1915	U-29	800
	(ONE AUSTRIAN.)	
Oct. 17, 1914	Unknown	...
	TORPEDO BOATS, (TWO GERMAN.)	
May 1, 1915	Unknown	..
May 1, 1915	Unknown	..
	(TWO TURKISH.)	
Apr. 20, 1915	Unknown	..
Apr. 20, 1915	Unknown	..
	AUXILIARY CRUISERS, (NINETEEN GERMAN.)	
Aug. 5, 1914	Koenigin Luise	945
Aug. 27, 1914	K. Wilhelm der Grosse	5,521
Sep. 12, 1914	Spreewald	2,414
Sep. 14, 1914	Cap Trafalgar	9,854
Sep. —, 1914	Bethania	4,348
Oct. —, 1914	Itolo	105
Oct. —, 1914	Rhios	150
Oct. —, 1914	Soden	150
Oct. —, 1914	Markomannia	2,840
Oct. —, 1914	Graecia	1,697
Oct. 17, 1914	Ophelia	1,153
Nov. 6, 1914	Ruhin	....
Nov. 6, 1914	Berlin	9,834
Nov. —, 1914	Karnak	4,437
Nov. 8, 1914	Locksun	1,020
Feb. 20, 1915	Holger	5,300
Apr. 8, 1915	Prinz Eitel Friedrich	4,650
Apr. 26, 1915	Kronprinz Wilhelm	5,162
Apr. 30, 1915	Macedonia	2,779

Total, seventy-five vessels of about 192,899 tons.

"All the News That's Fit to Print."

The New York Times.

THE WEATHER
Partly cloudy today; showers at night or Tuesday; moderate shifting winds.
☞For full weather report see Page 17.

VOL. LXIV...NO. 20,909.　　　　　NEW YORK, MONDAY, MAY 24, 1915.—EIGHTEEN PAGES.　　　　　ONE CENT In Greater New York, Jersey City and Newark.

ITALY DECLARES WAR UPON AUSTRIA; GERMANY WITHDRAWS HER ENVOY; ITALIAN CHASSEURS EXPEL INVADERS

TEUTON ENVOYS TAKE LEAVE

Von Macchio Receives Passports; Von Buelow to Go With Him.

ENVOYS TO POPE GO ALSO

Italian Ambassador to Austria Gets Word to Withdraw from Vienna.

WHOLE NATION REJOICING

Rome Ablaze with Flags and Great Crowds Parade to National Airs of the Allies.

30,000 ITALIANS PRISONERS

Detained in Germany and Austria, Although Enemy Nationals Are Allowed to Leave Italy.

ROME, May 23.—Italy is at war with Austria-Hungary. Official announcement of the declaration of hostilities was made by the Government last night at 8:15 o'clock, simultaneously with the issuance of an order for general mobilization. The state of war begins tomorrow.

Passports were handed to Baron von Macchio, Austro-Hungarian Ambassador to Italy, at 3:30 o'clock this afternoon, and he will leave tonight or tomorrow morning.

Three special trains have been held in readiness, one for Baron von Macchio, one for Prince von Bülow, and the Prussian Envoy to the Holy See, and the third for the Bavarian Envoy to the Quirinal and the Vatican. The Italian Ambassador at Vienna, the Duke of Avarna, has been recalled.

Enthusiastic Throughout the Country.

Although drastic action has been loked for momentarily, Italians of all classes were electrified by the swiftly moving events. Reports from all towns in Italy say that the decree of mobilization was received everywhere with the greatest enthusiasm. Processions and demonstrations were held in all towns, the people acclaiming

Text of the Formal Declaration of War Presented by Italy to Austria-Hungary

VIENNA, May 23, (via Amsterdam and London, May 24.)—The Duke of Avarna, Italian Ambassador to Austria, presented this afternoon to Baron von Burian, the Austro-Hungarian Foreign Minister, the following declaration of war:

Vienna, May 23, 1915.

Conformably with the orders of His Majesty the King, His august Sovereign, the undersigned Ambassador of Italy has the honor to deliver to His Excellency, the Foreign Minister of Austria-Hungary, the following communication:

" Declaration has been made, as from the fourth of this month, to the Imperial and Royal Government of the grave motives for which Italy, confident in her good right, proclaimed annulled and henceforth without effect her treaty of alliance with Austria-Hungary, which was violated by the Imperial and Royal Government, and resumed her liberty of action in this respect.

" The Government of the King, firmly resolved to provide by all means at its disposal for safeguarding Italian rights and interests, cannot fail in its duty to take against every existing and future menace measures which events impose upon it for the fulfillment of national aspirations.

" His Majesty the King declares that he considers himself from tomorrow in a state of war with Austria-Hungary."

The undersigned has the honor to make known at the same time to His Excellency, the Foreign Minister, that passports will be placed this very day at the disposal of the Imperial and Royal Ambassador at Rome, and he will be obliged to His Excellency if he will kindly have his passports handed to him.

AVARNA.

the King and wishing victory for the country.

In some places portraits of the King and Queen were carried triumphantly through the streets by crowds singing the national airs and war songs popular with their grandfathers and fathers who fought in 1848, 1859, 1860 and 1866, or who climbed the scaffolds to meet the Austrian executioners.

In Rome early this morning great crowds gathered around the Quirinal to await the ministers who called on the King for the purpose of discussing the situation and signing decrees. When Premier Salandra and Signor Sonnino, the Foreign Minister, left the palace the people cheered them enthusiastically. The troops changing guards at the Royal Palace were the object of a stirring manifestation amid

" Vivas " for the army and for war.

General Zuppeli, Minister of War, and Vice Admiral Viale, Minister of Marine, remained with the King for a considerable time after the others left, and later they had a conference with Lieut. Gen. Cadorna, Chief of Staff, and Vice Admiral Phaon di Revel, Chief of the Naval Staff.

From Germany come reports that considerable resentment is felt in official circles there against what is alleged to be the obstinacy of the Austrian diplomacy responsible for the failure of the negotiations with Italy initiatew by Prince von Bülow, the German Ambassador. The suggestion had even been made that Austria should be left alone to fight Italy, but pledges taken by the German General Staff and by the German Em-

peror personally with Emperor Francis Joseph resulted in the triumph of those advocating Austro-German solidarity, even in a new war against Italy.

According tot the Giornale d'Italia,

the problem concerning the diplomats accredited to the Vatican has been solved satisfactorily. The Austrian and German diplomats, ignoring the situation in Italy, will depart, as though they were merelytaking their Summer vacations before the regular time. It had been urged by some that the Italian Government move energetically with respect to these diplomatic representatives, and by others that the Vatican resist any effort to force them to withdraw. But these extreme measures failed, and thus the Law of Guarantees remains untouched.

Alarming reports have been received from the Italian border towns that Italian residents in the Austrian Tyrol are experiencing great difficulty in returning to Italy, and in many cases have been placed under arrest.

Austria Gets War Declaration.

LONDON, Monday, May 24.—The Italian Ambassador at Vienna yesterday (Sunday) afternoon presented a formal declaration of war to Baron Burian von Rajece, the Austro-Hungarian Foreign Minister.

This announcement is made in a Vienna dispatch to Reuter's Telegram Company, sent by way of Amsterdam.

A Stefani dispatch from Rome says that the Italian Foreign Minister sent on Sunday a circular dispatch to the Italian representatives abroad, detailing the negotiations with Austria and declaring that the Royal Government, supported by the Parliament and the natiton, had decided to avoid all delay, and had therefore notified the Austrian Ambassador that he must consider a state of war as existing from tomorrow, (Monday.)

The Italian Navy, ranked sixth in the world, made history with its daring attacks on the harbors of Cattaro and Durazzo.

"All the News That's Fit to Print."

The New York Times.

THE WEATHER
Fair today, showers tomorrow; variable winds, becoming light southwest.

VOL. LXIV...NO. 20,957. ....   NEW YORK, FRIDAY, JUNE 11, 1915.—TWENTY-FOUR PAGES.   ONE CENT In Greater New York, Jersey City and Newark. | Elsewhere TWO CENTS

PRESIDENT WILSON TELLS GERMANY THAT SHE HAS NO RIGHT EVEN TO ENDANGER LIFE ON SHIPS UNARMED, UNWARNED; 'ON THIS PRINCIPLE THE UNITED STATES MUST STAND'; AGAIN ASKS ASSURANCES THAT SUCH ATTACKS SHALL CEASE

President Wilson's Answer to Germany's Note

The Secretary of State ad Interim to the American Ambassador at Berlin:

You are instructed to deliver textually the following note to the Minister of Foreign Affairs:

In compliance with your Excellency's request I did not fail to transmit to my Government, immediately upon their receipt, your note of May 28 in reply to my note of May 15, and your supplementary note of June 1, setting forth the conclusions, so far as reached, by the Imperial German Government concerning the attacks on the American steamers Cushing and Gulflight. I am now instructed by my Government to communicate the following in reply:

The Government of the United States notes with gratification the full recognition by the Imperial German Government, in discussing the cases of the Cushing and the Gulflight, of the principle of the freedom of all parts of the open sea to neutral ships, and the frank willingness of the Imperial German Government to acknowledge and meet its liability where the fact of attack upon neutral "ships which have not been guilty of any hostile act" by German air craft or vessels of war is satisfactorily established, and the Government of the United States will in due course lay before the Imperial German Government, as it requests, full information concerning the attack on the steamer Cushing.

With regard to the sinking of the steamer Falaba, by which an American citizen lost his life, the Government of the United States is surprised to find the Imperial German Government contending that an effort on the part of a merchantman to escape capture and secure assistance alters the obligation of the officer seeking to make the capture in respect of the safety of the lives of those on board the merchantman, although the vessel has ceased her attempt to escape when torpedoed. These are not new circumstances. They have been in the minds of statesmen and of international jurists throughout the development of naval warfare, and the Government of the United States does not understand that they have ever been held to alter the principles of humanity upon which it has insisted. Nothing but actual forcible resistance or continued efforts to escape by flight when ordered to stop for the purpose of visit, on the part of the merchantman, has ever been held to forfeit the lives of her passengers or crew. The Government of the United States, however, does not understand that the Imperial German Government is seeking in this case to relieve itself of liability, but only intends to set forth the circumstances which led the Commander of the submarine to allow himself to be hurried into the course which he took.

Your Excellency's note, in discussing the loss of American lives resulting from the sinking of the steamship Lusitania, adverts at some length to certain information which the Imperial German Government has received with regard to the character and outfit of that vessel, and your Excellency expresses the fear that this information may not have been brought to the attention of the United States. It is stated that the Lusitania was undoubtedly equipped with masked guns, supplied with trained gunners and special ammunition, transporting troops from Canada, carrying a cargo not permitted under the laws of the United States to a vessel also carrying passengers, and serving, in virtual effect, as an auxiliary to the naval forces of Great Britain.

Fortunately these are matters concerning which the Government of the United States is in a position to give the Imperial German Government official information. Of the facts alleged in your Excellency's note, if true, the Government of the United States would have been bound to take official cognizance in performing its recognized duty as a neutral Power and in enforcing its national laws. It was its duty to see to it that the Lusitania was not armed for offensive action, that she was not serving as a transport, that she did not carry a cargo prohibited by the statutes of the United States, and that, if in fact she was a naval vessel of Great Britain, she should not receive clearance as a merchantman; and it performed that duty and enforced its statutes with scrupulous vigilance through its regularly constituted officials. It is able, therefore, to assure the Imperial German Government that it has been misinformed. If the Imperial Government should deem itself to be in possession of convincing evidence that the officials of the Government of the United States did not perform these duties with thoroughness, the Government of the United States sincerely hopes that it will submit that evidence for consideration.

Whatever may be the contentions of the Imperial German Government regarding the carriage of contraband of war on board the Lusitania, or regarding the explosion of that material by the torpedo, it need only be said that in the view of this Government these contentions are irrelevant to the question of the legality of the methods used by the German naval authorities in sinking the vessel.

But the sinking of passenger ships involves principles of humanity which throw into the background any special circumstances of detail that may be thought to affect the cases; principles which lift it, as the Imperial German Government will no doubt be quick to recognize and acknowledge, out of the class of ordinary subjects of diplomatic discussion or of international controversy. Whatever be the other facts regarding the Lusitania, the principal fact is that a great steamer, primarily and chiefly a conveyance for passengers, and carrying more than a thousand souls who had no part or lot in the conduct of the war, was torpedoed and sunk without so much as a challenge or a warning, and that men, women, and children were sent to their death in circumstances unparalleled in modern warfare. The fact that more than 100 American citizens were among those who perished made it the duty of the Government of the United States to speak of these things, and once more, with solemn emphasis, to call the attention of the Imperial German Government to the grave responsibility which the Government of the United States conceives that it has incurred in this tragic occurrence, and to the indisputable principle upon which that responsibility rests.

The Government of the United States is contending for something much greater than mere rights of property or privileges of commerce. It is contending for nothing less high and sacred than the rights of humanity, which every Government honors itself in respecting, and which no Government is justified in resigning on behalf of those under its care and authority. Only her actual resistance to capture, or refusal to stop when ordered to do so for the purpose of visit, could have afforded the Commander of the submarine any justification for so much as putting the lives of those on board the ship in jeopardy. This principle the Government of the United States understands the explicit instructions issued on Aug. 3, 1914, by the Imperial German Admiralty to its Commanders at sea to have recognized and embodied, as do the naval codes of all other nations, and upon it every traveler and seaman had a right to depend. It is upon this principle of humanity, as well as upon the law founded upon this principle, that the United States must stand.

The Government of the United States is happy to observe that your Excellency's note closes with the intimation that the Imperial German Government is willing, now as before, to accept the good offices of the United States in an attempt to come to an understanding with the Government of Great Britain by which the character and conditions of war upon the sea may be changed. The Government of the United States would consider it a privilege thus to serve its friends and the world. It stands ready at any time to convey to either Government any intimation or suggestion the other may be willing to have it convey, and cordially invites the Imperial German Government to make use of its services in this way at its convenience. The whole world is concerned in anything that may bring about even a partial accommodation of interests or in any way mitigate the terrors of the present distressing conflict.

In the meantime, whatever arrangement may happily be made between the parties to the war, and whatever may, in the opinion of the Imperial German Government, have been the provocation or the circumstantial justification for the past acts of its Commanders at sea, the Government of the United States confidently looks to see the justice and humanity of the Government of Germany vindicated in all cases where Americans have been wronged or their rights as neutrals invaded.

The Government of the United States, therefore, very earnestly and very solemnly renews the representations of its note transmitted to the Imperial German Government on the 15th of May, and relies in these representations upon the principles of humanity, the universally recognized understandings of international law, and the ancient friendship of the German nation.

The Government of the United States cannot admit that the proclamation of a war zone from which neutral ships have been warned to keep away may be made to operate as in any degree an abbreviation of the rights either of American shipmasters or of American citizens bound on lawful errands as passengers on merchant ships of belligerent nationality. It does not understand the Imperial German Government to question those rights. It understands it also to accept as established beyond question the principle that the lives of noncombatants cannot lawfully or rightfully be put in jeopardy by the capture or destruction of an unresisting merchantman, and to recognize the obligation to take sufficient precaution to ascertain whether a suspected merchantman is in fact of belligerent nationality or is in fact carrying contraband of war under a neutral flag. The Government of the United States deems it reasonable to expect that the Imperial German Government will adopt the measures necessary to put these principles into practice in respect of the safeguarding of American lives and American ships, and asks for assurances that this will be done.

ROBERT LANSING,
Secretary of State ad Interim.

Bryan Explains His Idea of "The Real Issue"—For Persuasion, Not Firmness or Force

WASHINGTON, June 10.— William Jennings Bryan, in an appeal "to the American people," put on the wires tonight eleven minutes after President Wilson's note to Germany, asks them to hear him before they pass sentence upon his laying down the portfolio of Secretary of State n the midst of international stress.

Interpreting the new American note to Germany, which he refused to sign, as conforming to the "old system" of firmness based on potential force, and characterizing himself as a champion of the new system of persuasion instead of force, and as "an humble follower of the Prince of Peace," he pleads for the United States to lead the world "out of the black night of war."

Mr. Bryan tomorrow will issue another statement, an appeal, he says, to "German-Americans." With that he says he will rest his case.

Mr. Bryan's statement, headed "The Real Issue," follows:

An Appeal for Judgment.

To the American people:

You now have before you the text of the note to Germany—the note which it would have been my official duty to sign had I remained Secretary of State. I ask you to sit in judgment upon my decision to resign rather than to share responsibility for it.

I am sure you will credit me with honorable motives, but that is not enough. Good intentions could not atone for a mistake at such a time, on such a subject, and under such circumstances. If your verdict is against me, I ask no mercy; I desire none if I have acted unwisely.

A man in public life must act according to his conscience, but, however conscientiously he acts, he must be prepared to accept without complaint any condemnation which his own errors may bring upon him; he must be willing to bear any deserved punishment, from ostracism to execution. But hear me before you pass sentence.

The President and I agree in purpose; we desire a peaceful solution of the dispute which has arisen between the United States and Germany. We not only desire it, but, with equal fervor, we pray for it; but we differ irreconcilably as to the means of securing it.

If it were merely a personal difference, it would be a matter of little moment, for all the presumptions are on his side—the presumptions that go with power and authority. He is your President, I am a private citizen without office or title—but one of the one hundred million of inhabitants.

But the real issue is not between persons, it is between systems, and I rely for vindication wholly upon the strength of the position taken.

Force Versus Persuasion.

Among the influences which Governments employ in dealing with each other there are two which are preeminent and antagonistic—force and persuasion. Force speaks with firmness and acts through the ultimatum; persuasion employs argument, courts investigation, and depends upon negotiation. Force represents the old system—the system that must pass away; persuasion represents the new system—the system that has been growing, all too slowly, it is true, but growing for 1,900 years. In the old system war is the chief cornerstone—war, which at its best is little better than war at its worst; the new system contemplates an universal brotherhood established through the uplifting power of example.

If I correctly interpret the note to Germany, it conforms to the standards of the old system rather than to the rules of the new, and I cheerfully admit that it is abundantly supported by precedents—precedents written in characters of blood upon almost every page of human history. Austria furnishes the most recent precedent; it was Austria's firmness that dictated the ultimatum against Serbia, which set the world at war.

Every ruler now participating in this unparalleled conflict has proclaimed his desire for peace and denied responsibility for the war, and it is only charitable that we should credit all of them with good faith. They desired peace, but they sought it according to the rules of the old system. They believed that firmness would give the best assurance of the maintenance of peace, and, faithfully following precedent, they went so near the fire that they were, one after another, sucked into the contest.

Never So Frightful as Now.

Never before have the frightful follies of this fatal system been so clearly revealed as now. The most civilized and enlightened—aye, the most Christian—of the nations of Europe are grappling with each other as if in a death struggle. They are sacrificing the best and bravest of their sons on the battlefield; they are converting their gardens into cemeteries and their homes into houses of mourning; they are taxing the wealth of today and laying a burden of debt on the toil of the future; they have filled the air with thunderbolts more deadly than those of Jove, and they have multiplied the perils of the deep.

Adding fresh fuel to the flame of hate, they have daily devised new horrors, until one side is endeavoring to drown noncombatant men, women, and children at sea, while the other side seeks to starve noncombatant men, women, and children on land. And they are so absorbed in alternate retaliations and in competitive cruelties that they seem, for the time being, blind to the rights of neutrals and deaf to the appeals of humanity. A tree is known by its fruit. The war in Europe is the ripened fruit of the old system.

This is what firmness, supported by force, has done in the Old World, shall we invite it to cross the Atlantic? Already the jingoes of our own country have caught the rabies from the dogs of war; shall the opponents of organized slaughter be silent while the disease spreads?

As an humble follower of the Prince of Peace, as a devoted believer in the prophecy that "they that take the sword shall perish with the sword," I beg to be counted among those who earnestly urge the adoption of a course in this matter which will leave no doubt of our Government's willingness to continue negotiations with Germany until an amicable understanding is reached, or at least until, the stress of war over, we can appeal from Philip drunk with carnage to Philip sobered by the memories of an historic friendship and by a recollection of the innumerable ties of kinship that bind the Fatherland to the United States.

Some nation must lead the world out of the black night of war into the light of that day when "swords shall be beaten into plowshares." Why not make this honor ours? Some day —why not now?—the nations will learn that enduring peace cannot be built upon fear—that good-will does not grow upon the stalk of violence. Some day the nations will place their trust in love, the weapon for which there is no shield; in love, that suffereth long and is kind; in love, that is not easily provoked, that beareth all things, believeth all things, hopeth all things, endureth all things; in love, which, though despised as weakness by the worshippers of Mars, abideth when all else fails.

W. J. BRYAN.

The New York Times.

THE WEATHER
Showers late today; Sunday, probably fair; moderate south winds, becoming west.
For full weather report on Page 17.

VOL. LXIV...NO. 20,965. ...   NEW YORK, SATURDAY, JUNE 19, 1915.—EIGHTEEN PAGES.   ONE CENT In Greater New York, Jersey City and Newark. | TWO CENTS

BERLIN FACTIONS IN A STRUGGLE OVER OUR NOTE

Von Tirpitz Fighting Hard to Save Submarine System Which He Built Up.

GRIM DRAMA BEHIND SCENES

Military and Political Leaders Sharply Divided Concerning American Demands.

STIRRED BY FATE OF U-14

Germany Hears British Fishermen Sank Her After Getting a Humane Warning.

LAY BLAME TO KING GEORGE

Assail Monarch for Rewarding Merchant Captain Who Rammed Under-Sea Raider.

MEYER-GERHARD REPORTS

Emissary's Story Impresses the Foreign Minister—Reply Probable in Ten Days.

By a Staff Correspondent.
Special Cable to THE NEW YORK TIMES.
BERLIN, (via The Hague,) June 18.—A fascinating and perhaps historic drama is transpiring behind the scenes as a result of the American note, those in high places holding widely diverging views on the stand that Germany ought to take according as they attach supreme importance to Germany's political or military interests.

While powerful influences are working for a modus vivendi, even at the cost of a modification of the submarine warfare provided certain objects can be gained, it is known that Grand Admiral von Tirpitz, who conceived and made possible the submarine warfare, sees in President Wilson's demand the ruin of his whole life work, and a surrender probably would be followed by one of the biggest sensations of the world war.

An important new emotional factor has been injected into the question by reports printed here that the destruction of the submarine U-14 was directly due to the humane conduct of her commander. She was fired upon and sunk by an English "fishing steamer" after her commander had signaled to the fishermen that they had five minutes in which to leave their vessel.

Recalls Thordis Incident.

In this connection the Local Anzeiger prints a column communication from "A Highly Placed Personage," bitterly recalling that King George had given the Distinguished Service Order to the merchant Captain of the steamer Thordis for ramming and sinking a German submarine, while the Admiralty made him a Lieutenant in the Naval Reserve, "thus rewarding, justifying, and encouraging ramming and other hostile acts by merchantmen." The communication adds:

"There is not the slightest doubt that England, by this official act of the King, forfeited all further claims upon our submarines to live up to the usual rules of naval warfare in the future. It would not be a practice of humanity, but of criminal weakness, justly challenging the scorn of England, to suggest to our brave submarine sailors, who hourly risk their lives for the Fatherland, that in future they should first call upon and halt English merchantmen. From this viewpoint the procedure against the Lusitania, whether she was armed or not, was, in all circumstances, fully justified, and similar procedure on the part of our submarines toward every other British merchantman will be justified as a necessary measure and self-defense against the tricky attacks of English merchantmen upon German men-of-war in violation of international law, and which are openly praised and rewarded by King George. To Mr. Wilson's demand that in this case justice and humanity demanded the hailing and peaceable stopping of the Lusitania by the submarine King George has already given his answer that such considerations of humanity and international law would have been answered by the sinking of our submarine and that the Captain of the Lusitania would have been assured of the King's high reward."

Army Bitter Toward Us.

Another equally important emotional factor is the unanimous and bitter resentment of the army over American ammunition. Some interesting light was thrown upon this in the course of a conversation yesterday with a division chief of the Grand General Staff who had just returned from the front. He said: "After the Lusitania affair Americans perhaps are able to understand how we feel. They have only to think of their own indignation over the loss of a hundred and odd Americans to consider how we at the front feel over more than 50,000 German soldiers being killed and twice as many maimed for life by American ammunition. So far this is a conservative estimate. It is cruel hypocrisy to tell us we must not sink ships bringing ammunition to kill our soldiers because there happen to be Americans on board."

This general feeling in the army is most significant.

WHY LUSITANIA PLANS SHOW GUN OUTLINES

Made Before Ship Was Built— Merely Indicate Where Rifles Could Be Mounted.

Special Cable to THE NEW YORK TIMES.
LONDON, June 18.—Perverse ingenuity, according to general opinion here, is the only way to characterize the publication in New York of a picture of the Lusitania in an attempt to show that the Cunarder was armed with twelve six-inch guns on her trip that ended in her being sunk by a German torpedo.

According to word reaching here today, this picture was reproduced from the May 14 issue of Engineering, a London publication. Investigation by THE NEW YORK TIMES correspondent today reveals that if any such picture was printed as being reproduced from Engineering to show that the Lusitania was armed on her fateful voyage it is a pure fake.

In its issue of May 14 Engineering republished a group of ten old sketches of the Lusitania, all of which were published eight years ago, when the Lusitania was built. These sketches, all made by the ship's engineers, show sectional views of the Cunarder and the plans of her decks. They were all made, as Engineering clearly explains, by the engineers before the Lusitania was constructed.

At the time the Lusitania was built provision was made, as these sketches show, for emplacements for twelve guns so that the guns could be mounted if the Lusitania ever was impressed into service as a Government auxiliary. But no occasion ever arose for the Lusitania to be used as an auxiliary and no guns ever were mounted on the emplacements.

To use the words of Engineering, which printed a 1,000-word article on the Lusitania in the issue of May 14: "To facilitate a correct understanding of the designs of the vessel we reproduce two of the cross sections of the ship which originally appeared in Engineering eight years ago, when the vessel was built. That issue is now out of print."

No other sketch of the Lusitania appears anywhere in Engineering. On the reproduction of the sketch of the promenade deck emplacements for two six-inch guns on the starboard and two on the port side are indicated, while on the shelter deck, immediately below, emplacements for four six-inch guns are indicated on both sides of the ship. At each spot indicated is the tiny outline of a gun, and running across the rounded line which is meant to show where the emplacement was to be built is the inscription "6-inch gun." The sketches of the promenade deck and the shelter deck are entirely separate, while above appears a sectional outline of the Lusitania showing the whole interior and the noses of guns sticking out.

This sectional view carries out faithfully, so far as the cramped space in which it is reproduced will allow, the outlines of the promenade and shelter decks. The six-inch guns popping out through tiny holes are so small as hardly to be observed without a microscope. Viewed in the light of the explanatory article running with the sketches any one would know immediately that the designs were those of the Lusitania before she was built and not the Lusitania as completed.

It is a familiar fact to every one who ever traveled on the Lusitania that the emplacements for the guns were shown as a feature of the ship's many attractions, the ship's crew always explaining that the Lusitania was originally built to serve as an auxiliary, if needed, and that the guns then would be mounted.

At the Admiralty it was pointed out today that the Lusitania never was impressed into the Government service after the day she was launched, and that no guns ever were mounted on the emplacements. Not at any time has it been asserted that the Lusitania did not have gun emplacements, but it has been insistently asserted by the Admiralty and again by every witness this week at the Lusitania inquiry here that she never was armed with any guns.

STAHL INDICTED ON PERJURY CHARGE

German Who Swore He Saw Guns on the Lusitania Must Face the Federal Court.

INQUIRY NOT YET ENDED

Three Government Officials Testify and Other Indictments May Be Returned.

Gustav Stahl, the alleged German reservist, who made an affidavit that he had seen guns on board the Lusitania on the day before she sailed on her last voyage, was indicted on a charge of perjury by the Federal Grand Jury yesterday. The perjury charge is based on his testimony before the Grand Jury, during which examination he repeated that he had seen the guns on the Lusitania as set forth in his affidavit filed by the German Embassy in Washington and now in the hands of the State Department.

The name of Paul Koenig, who, it is said, was known to Stahl as Stemler, and who is the chief of the secret service of the Hamburg-American Line, is mentioned by name in the indictment. The indictment sets forth that on June 10 there was pending before the Grand Jury an investigation concerning Koenig and others and that Stahl was among the witnesses called in the course of that investigation. It then goes on to say that Stahl testified in substance and to the effect that on April 30 he went aboard the Lusitania, then with one Leach, and that while on the vessel he saw four guns on one of the decks of the steamship, two forward and two aft, and all mounted on wooden blocks and covered with leather. The indictment further charges that at the time of so swearing Stahl did not believe it to be true that he had been on board the Lusitania and had seen the four guns.

The indictment, in conclusion, charges that there were no guns upon the decks of the Lusitania on April 30. "Therefore," the Grand Jury charges, "that Stahl, after taking an oath before a competent officer to truly depose and testify, did wilfully, knowingly and feloniously and contrary to his said oath, depose and state material matters which were not true and which he did not then believe to be true, and thereby did commit wilful and corrupt perjury against the peace of the United States and their dignity and contrary to the form of the statute of the United States in such case made and provided."

Stahl will be araigned before Judge Russell in the criminal branch of the United States District Court on Monday. He is now in the Tombs in default of $10,000 bail. Should he be convicted of perjury he may be sentenced to prison for five years or fined $10,000, or both.

The indictment of Stahl does not mean that the Government's investigation of the Lusitania affidavits, and the way in which they were procured, is at an end. On the other hand it is proceeding vigorously. Three witnesses, all Government officials, were before the Grand Jury yesterday in connection with the case. Heinz Hardenberg, who was found in Cincinnati a week ago today and brought here to be examined by the Grand Jury has not yet appeared before that body, although the Government agents insist they can produce him when his testimony is desired.

"All the News That's Fit to Print."

The New York Times.

THE WEATHER
Partly cloudy today and Friday; warmer Friday; moderate west winds.

VOL. LXIV...NO. 20,970. NEW YORK, THURSDAY, JUNE 24, 1915.—TWENTY PAGES. ONE CENT In Greater New York, Jersey City and Newark. | Elsewhere TWO CENTS.

LEMBERG TAKEN BY AUSTRO-GERMANS; LLOYD GEORGE GIVES BRITISH LABOR SEVEN DAYS TO MAN WAR FACTORIES

WARNING IN THE COMMONS

Strikes and Lockouts Barred by Munitions Bill, Which Passes First Reading in Commons.

LONDON, June 23.—David Lloyd George, the Minister of Munitions, has given British labor seven days in which to make good the promise of its leaders that men will rally to the factories in sufficient numbers to produce a maximum supply of munitions of war.

This was the most striking statement in the new Minister's speech in the House of Commons today in the course of outlying the munitions measure, which is designed to control not only the output, but the men responsible for it.

The first of the seven allotted days will begin tomorrow, and with its dawning will be launched a great campaign to recruit the workers.

"I had a fresh discussion with the trade-union leaders," said Mr. Lloyd George in his speech, "and told them if an adequate supply of labor could not be secured compulsion was inevitable. The union representatives answered: 'Give us a chance to supply the men needed in seven days. If we cannot get them we will admit that our case is considerably weakened.'

"The seven days will begin tomorrow," continued Lloyd George, "and advertisements will appear in all the papers. The Union representatives have engaged 150 town halls as recruiting offices, and the assistance of every one has been invited."

There will be no age limit for the men enrolled. They will not wear uniforms, but will have to give their full time to the work, and they will receive a certificate attesting that they are working for King and country.

The Munitions bill makes strikes and lockouts illegal, provides for compulsory arbitration, limits the profits of employers, creates a voluntary army of workmen pledged to go wherever they are wanted, and contains other provisions which will give the Minister full powers to carry out the plans he has devised to develop the production of munitions.

After emphasizing the absolute necessity of vast supplies of guns and ammunition, which he described as the great essential of victory, the Minister announced that he had sent David Thomas, managing director of great colliery companies in South Wales, and known as the "British Coal King," to represent the munitions department in the United States and Canada. Respecting this appointment the Minister said:

"In consequence of the great importance of the American and Canadian markets and the numerous offers to provide munitions, it is very desirable that we have some one over there. Accordingly, we have sent a very able business man, Mr. D. A. Thomas, who will be given the * * * fullest responsibilities for the discharge of his important duties There is not the slightest idea of superseding our existing agencies. They have worked admirably, and have saved us many millions. Mr. Thomas will co-operate with the Messrs. Morgan with a view to expediting supplies."

The Minister, in winding up the debate on the bill, said he would hold himself responsible for the supply of ammunition at the front and would make himself thoroughly acquainted with what was going on there.

This was in answer to Sir Arthur Markham, Liberal, who said that if Mr. Lloyd George was not going to be independent of the War Office, by which he meant Lord Kitchener, his scheme was foredoomed to failure.

Mr. Lloyd George, continuing, said he was sure that Lord Kitchener would agree that the Minister of Munitions should have a free hand. He hoped that the bill would be printed by Friday, when the members could read it, and they would see that it satisfactorily disposed of most of the criticisms.

The bill passed its first reading. It will receive its second reading Monday.

Speaking of German preparation, the Minister said:—

"Germany has been piling up material. Until she was ready she was friendly with everybody. During the Balkan crisis none could have been more modest or unpretentious. She had a **benevolent smile for France. She walked arm in arm with Great Britain through the chancelleries of Europe. We really thought an era of peace and good-will had come. At that moment she was forging and hiding away enormous war stores to attack her neighbors unawares and murder them in their sleep.**

"If that trickery is to succeed, all the bases of international good will will crumble to dust. It is essential for the peace of the world that it shouuld fail, and it is up to us to see that it does so. It depends more upon Great Britain than on any one else to see that it fails.

"One of the pillars of good government is that evil-doing shall be punished; that is equally true in the sphere of international government. Valor alone will not achieve success, or the valor of our brave men at the front would have achieved it long ago. We must strain every resource of the machinery of organization at our disposal so as to drive conviction into the heart of every nation over the whole world that those Governments who deceive their neighbors to their ruin do so at their peril."

The Minister's peroration was greeted with loud and prolonged cheers.

Mr. Llyod George admitted that the shortage of munitions was serious, in view of the standard set up by this war. This fact, he continued, was doubtless as well known in Germany as it was in England.

"The duration of the war, the toll of life and the amount of exhaustion created by the war, ultimate victory or defeat depend upon the supply of munitions," the Minister declared. "That is cardinal. Where the Allies are making progress on any part of the line it is due to their superiority in munitions. The Allies have superiority in men, both in numbers and in quality. I have been told that the Central European powers are turning out 250,000 shells a day. We can not merely equal, but if we are in earnest we can surpass that output."

Sir Richard Ashmole Cooper, a member of a large chemical manufacturing concern, who previously had frequently complained that the British War Office, by refusing to deal with responsible agents, had neglected to obtain large available supplies of munitions, made the specific declaration in the House of Commons today that he was in a position to offer the Government 3,000,000 shells made in England, 8,000,000 shells made in Canada, and 10,000,000 shells made in the United States. Sir Richard also said he could deliver 1,000,000,000 rifle cartridges and 2,000,000 rifles, beginning in October, and added:

"If this offer is not accepted I want to know the reason why."

Mr. Lloyd George, replying to Sir Richard, said the War Office had asked Sir Richard to give it the names of the firms which were prepared to supply such large quantities of munitions. The result of this, the Minister added, was the receipt of the name of one firm, which, on inquiry, was found to be engaged in lithographing.

The Munitions Minister deprecated what he termed all the wild and irresponsible talk of there being plenty of shells available. He said he was scouring the country for them and was prepared to take every shell that could be produced.

Continuing, Mr. Lloyd George referred to his recent interview with Albert Thomas, who holds the post similar to his own in France, and said he had been very much reassured as to what France had done and could do in this regard. "If we can within the next few months," Mr. Lloyd George went on, "produce as much ammunition as can the French establishments, the Allies will have an overwhelming superiority in the first great essential of victory.

"The Germans undoubtedly—we may as well recognize it—anticipated the duration of this war as no one else has done. They realized it would be a great trench war, and they had organized an immense supply of machinery applicable to these conditions. We assumed that victory was due us as a tribute from Fate. Our problem is to organize, not to take it for granted. To do this the whole engineering and chemical resources of this country and of the Empire must be organized. When this has been done France and ourselves alone will overlap the entire Teutonic output.

"With regard to the supply of material," Mr. Lloyd George said, "it may be necessary to take complete control of the metal market in order to be sure that valuable material is not wasted in non-essentials. In the meanwhile the department is procuring full information regarding stocks of raw and semi-manufactured metal.

"I am sorry to say," the Minister continued, "that there are indications of the holding up of supplies of material in certain quarters for higher prices. This is the cause of serious delay, and this practice must be brought to an end."

"We must appeal to the men at a time of dire peril to put forward their whole strength in behalf of their fellows now in the field and to rely upon the nation to see that they have fair play at the end of the war.

"I have a guarantee from the employers that no advantage will be taken of any relaxation in the regulations. As many skilled men as possible will be brought back from the ranks in the army; but the task will be difficult, as the men prefer fighting to working in the shops.

"The trade unionists have promised to get all the munition workers the Government requires in seven days to go anywhere needed to turn out munitions. If the scheme succeeds there will be no need for compulsion, which will be so much the better."

Mr. Lloyd George pointed out that he would have the power to enforce contracts entered into by the voluntary army of workers and to maintain discipline in the yards. A munitions court will be established to decide disputes, and there will be a limitation in the profits of the establishments working for the State.

"It will take months before we can obtain the maximum output," Mr. Lloyd George went on. "Existing firms are unable to deliver goods in accordance with agreement because they cannot man the machines. It is entirely a question of labor. If I could lay my hands on an adequate supply of skilled labor I could double in a few weeks our supply of machine guns.

"I cannot forecast Germany's next move. If she skings her forces from the east to the west it is vital for the lives of our troops, and, in order to enable them to maintain their positions, that every available machine should be produced. It is essential that trade union restrictions which interfere with a great output of munitions shall temporarily be suspended at once. There must be a stoppage in slackness, and an end must be put to the practice of employers pilfering each other's men. There must be no strikes or lock-outs during the war."

Dealing with the difficulties which he had to overcome, the Minister of Munitions said he early recognized that existing armament firms were inadequate to supply the new or old armies. A vast improvement already had been made by inviting business men to organize in their own localities. For instance, through local organization in one town alone 150,000 shells monthly already were being turned out there, and these figures were expected to rise to 250,000.

Great Britain, Mr. Lloyd George said, would be organized into ten munition areas. In London, he said, there would shortly be another Woolwich arsenal able to turn out prodigious quantities of war material.

Mr. Lloyd George emphasized the fact that he intended to rely largely upon decentralization, and real progress, he said, had already been made since the establishments of the Munitions Department.

GERMAN WEDGE DRIVEN FAR

Berlin Believes That the Russian Forces Are Split in Twain.

LONDON, Thursday, June 24 — The Russians have lost Lemberg. They occupied the Galician capital on Sept. 3 last and had held it continuously until Tuesday, when the combined Austro-German forces compelled them to retreat from the city, which is only sixty-odd miles due west from the nearest point of the Russian frontier.

Whether the fall of Lemberg means that the Russian army operating south of it in Southeast Galicia is effectively cut off from the army to the north, stretching across Poland to the Baltic, cannot yet be said. The newspapers of both Vienna and Berlin say this is the case and that the Russian arms have received a blow from which they cannot recover.

If the stroke proves as crushing as the Teutons predict, its effect, military observers here say, soon should be felt in the transfer of vast German forces to the West, where for days they have been hard pressed by the French.

Up to midnight last night Petrograd had not conceded the fall of Lemberg. Previous dispatches from the Russian capital, however, related details of what purported to be the systematic withdrawal of the Russians from the town, and if these details prove correct it is believed in military circles here that when the count is taken of the Austro-German booty it will be not large, for, as was the case at Przemysl, the Russians are said to have worked hard to move everything of military value.

"All the News That's Fit to Print."

The New York Times.

THE WEATHER
Partly cloudy, probably local showers today; Monday probably fair, with lower temperature; light to moderate variable winds.
For full weather report see Page 6.

VOL. LXIV...NO. 21,008. NEW YORK, SUNDAY, AUGUST 1, 1915.—90 PAGES, In Seven Parts, Including Picture and Rotogravure Sections and Review of Books. PRICE FIVE CENTS.

YEAR OF WAR SEES FOES DETERMINED; NO WHISPER OF PEACE BY EITHER SIDE; SITUATION FROM NATIONAL VIEWPOINTS

BRITISH REVIEW BY CARSON

Attorney General Says England Is Aroused as Never Before.

FRANCE DOGGED AND GRIM

And Russia, Despite Reverses, Will Do Her Part—Czar's 1914 Defiance Reissued.

GERMANY CONFIDENT, TOO

Advantages Are With Her to Date, Berlin Experts Declare—Make Much of Submarines.

The end of the first year of the war in Europe finds both sides apparently confident, certainly determined to fight on indefinitely, with no whisper of peace audible. Reviews of the year's operations are presented below from different national viewpoints — British, French, Russian, German. All seem marked by the same characteristic—a dogged determination to carry the conflict to the bitter end and to win.

BRITAIN MUST WIN, AND WILL, SAYS CARSON

Attorney General Sums Up Twelve Months of Conflict, and Sees Only Encouragement Ahead.

LONDON, July 31.—Sir Edward Carson, the Attorney General, has prepared for The Associated Press a signed statement giving a broad outline of the first year of the war from the British standpoint, together with an expression of what he declares to be the unalterable purpose of the British Government and people to carry on the war to a successful conclusion. The statement follows:

How long will the war last, and what will be the result? To such questions as these any British subject can give but one answer, and that is that the war will last until the cause of the Allies has been brought to a successful issue and Europe and the world have been relieved from the ideals involved in the aggression of Prussian domination. The word peace does not enter into our vocabulary at the present time. It is banished from our conversation as something immoral and impossible under existing circumstances. And yet we are the most peace-loving people in the world; a nation which throughout the globe, within its many dominions, his inculcated good government and social and industrial progress and the free exercise, in its widest sense, of civil and religious liberty.

Rightly or wrongly, we have in the past devoted our energies and our intelligence not to preparations for war, but to that social progress which makes for the happiness and the contentment of the mass of our people. And this, no doubt, is the reason why other nations imagine that we, as a nation of shopkeepers, are too indolent and apathetic to fight for and maintain these priceless liberties won by the men who laid the foundation of our vast empire.

The Nation Determined.

But they are entirely mistaken in forming any such estimate of the temperament or determination of our people. Great Britain hates war, and no nation enters more reluctantly upon its horrible and devastating operation; but at the same time, no nation, when it is driven to war by the machinations of its foes, who desire to filch from it or from its co-champions of liberty any portion of their inherited freedom, is more resolved to see the matter through, at whatever cost, to a successful issue.

A year of war has transformed Great Britain. Of our navy I need hardly speak. It has upheld to the fullest extent the great traditions which fill the pages of history; in the past it has driven its enemies off the seas; it holds vast oceans free for almost the uninterrupted commerce of neutral powers and it has preserved these highways for its own supplies of material and food almost without interruption. I do not minimize the peril of the submarines, which is in process of being dealt with through the careful and zealous watchfulness of our Admiralty, but, while the submarine has enabled the Germans to commit savage and inhuman atrocities contrary to the laws of civilization and against the settled rules of international law, it has done nothing to affect the vast commerce of our empire.

Ther German submarine attack has signally failed to hamper our military operations. Under the protection of our navy hundreds of thousands of men have been brought to the fighting area from the most distant parts of the empire. Troop ships are crossing daily to France, and not a single ship of a single soldier has been lost in the passage. The manner in which our troops have received their supplies is a source of satisfaction to us and admiration to our enemies.

Volunteer Army Matchless.

At the commencement of the war we were not, and never did pretend to be, a military nation. An expeditionary force of 170,000 men and a small territorial army of 260,000 men for defense against invasion was all we could boast of, but today Great Britain teems with military camps in which millions of men of the finest material are being trained and equipped to cope with every emergency.

No other nation in the world ever produced or hoped to produce, a volunteer army of such proporitons. Each day brings to the colors thousands of men who had never thought of military service before, and each day, as our enemy grows weaker, the infancy of our strength is growing into manhood, and with increasing virility and prowess. No doubt some people are foolish enough to be influenced by the misrepresentations which are a part of the equipment of our German enemies, who represent us a decadent race. But they know little of the spirit of our people.

As the problem unfolds from day to day and the task before us expands in its herculean form, our spirit becomes more determined and our efforts and organization quietly shape themselves to meet the emrgencies that are before us. That all this is being accomplished without dramatic demonstration and foolish boasting is not a sign of weakness, but of strength.

Tribute to Britain's Allies.

The splendid heroism of our Russian and French allies is not only an example which stimulates us, but it is an additional incentive to our national honor to carry on to an end the obligations we have undertaken. And if for the moment we are confronted with the impossibility of offensive action by our brave Russian allies, and are compelled to wage a costly and diffiuclt war against the Turks in the Dardanelles, as well as against our enemies in Flanders, we cheerfully resolve to fit ourselves for the situation which confronts us.

It is, of course, true that our country has not been accustomed to organization and discipline, which leads unthinking men from time to time to imagine that there could be a different discipline in the coal fields or the workshops from that which prevails in the trenches; but all that is a mere temporary difficulty and it cannot impede the country, which has made up its mind to win if it has to spend the last man and its last dollar in the process.

The success of the recent war loan shows how anxious our people are to invest their money in the prosecution of the war. Not only is it the largest loan that ever has been floated, but it represents not merely the accumulation of capital of a few large banks but the hard-earned savings of small investors in every part of the country. Although our shores are not invaded and we have not experienced the impelling necessities of a war waged in our own country, yet there is hardly a family in any village in the land that has not willingly sent its sons to fight our battles in foreign lands. While I see day by day more and more anxiety from every man to do his share, I can see no sign nor trace of wavering in any section of the community.

Admonition to Neutrals.

We have the right to say to neutrals that our cause is just; that the war has been forced upon us, and that we are making and are going to make every sacrifice that makes a nation great to bring our cause to a successful conclusion. We have a right, I think, to ask neutrals to examine their own consciences as to whether they have done everything that neutrals ought to do or can do in insisting that the laws of humanity and the doctrines of international law, which have been so carefully fostered in times of peace, are carried out.

But, however that may be, our courage is undaunted. It grows into exaltation by reason of the difficulties that surround us, and we will go on to the end without fear or trembling and in the certain inspiration of a victory which will restore to the world that peace which can alone bring happiness and contentment to the mass of its citizens.

EDWARD CARSON.

RUSSIA REPEATS RESOLVE TO TRIUMPH

Czar's Solemn Declaration of Aug. 1, 1914, Reprinted—Year's Operations Reviewed.

PETROGRAD, July 31.—"I hereby solemnly declare that we will not conclude peace until the last enemy soldier has left our land."

These words of Emperor Nicholas of Russia, uttered at the Winter Palace on Aug. 1, 1914, are reproduced in the press of Petrograd on the anniversary of the war. A message in The Bourse Gazette today, printed in all the languaages of Russia's Allies, says:

"For a year past the enemy has been threatening the freedom of the world. We deeply appreciate the self-sacrificing aid of the Allies in exerting a combined pressure on him on all sides.

"A firm confidence in victory in a community of world-wide interests and in the final triumph of right fires the spirit of the nation. It has been our guiding star throughout this year of bloodshed. It will serve us in the coming months, maybe years, of this terrible struggle.

"Russia greets her Allies—France, Great Britain, Belgium, Serbia, Montenegro, Japan, and Italy. All hail to their heroic loyalty and firm determination to stand by her to the end; till light dispels the gloom."

From a person who, although not connected officially with the War Department, is in close touch with the Government officials and is well acquainted with the military situation and the Russian state of feeling, The Associated Press has obtained the following review of the first year of the war:

"The end of the first year of the war finds Russia's potential fighting ability undiminished. Her armies are intact, her resources virtually untouched; and the dettermination of her people, the morale of her troops have only been deepened with the growing realization of the enemy's strength.

"The campaign on the eastern front must be viewed in relation to the enormous extent of territory over which battles have been waged, from the Baltic to Bukowina. The far-flung advances and retreats here have had no more significance relatively than gains and losses of a thousand yards on the western front. To interpret Russia's temporary loss of territory as German success is to ignore Russia's rôle to engage as great a part of the enemy's forces as possible, to relieve pressure on her allies. Russia's refusal to accept battle in disadvantageous conditions, even though she must temporarily abandon territory, has kept her armies and defensive lines unbroken.

"It is the assertion of Russian authorities that every German advance has cost Germany more men, both relatively and actually, than it cost Russia. They regard Germany as now committed definitely to a campaign which is carrying the German armies further and further from their bases; and to abandon this campaign would be disastrous defeat for her. Moreover, it is maintained that not even the territorial ambitions of Germany have been realized, since the German objectives on this front have not been fully attained.

"The advance of the Austrians into Southern Russia in the early stage of the war met with full defeat. It was followed by Austria's loss of Galicia. General Ivanoff, at the head of the southern Russian armies, carried on one of the most brilliant offensive campaigns of the war. The present stage may possible be regarded as an uncompleted repetition of this earlier movement.

"Furthermore, the repeated German drives at Warsaw from the west have cost the enemy tremendous losses. It was only after six weeks of the most intense fighting in the Bura region due west of Warsaw last Winter that the Germans recognized the futility of attempting to break the Russian front by direct frontal movements. On the other hand, by exacting a heavy toll of lives in rear-guard actions during the carefully ordered retreats and by keeping her own army intact, Russia successfully performed her appointed task.

"The East Prussian aggressive, which manifested itself periodically, and latterly the Baltic campaign, never have been regarded otherwise than as diversions. A parallel to these movements is found in the Bukowina operations, in their relation to the general Galician campaign. Their chief importance has been to draw men from other fronts, where more serious fighting has been in progress.

"While it is understood the fate of the Turkish provinces on the Caucasian front will be determined by the general course of the war, this should not minimize the genuine military successes Russia has achieved in the distant field. Russia did not desire to expend her strength in Asiatic Turkey, but when opposed by the threatening Turkish advance in December, she exerted her power, flung back the Turkish army at Sari Kamysh, and began a series of movements which carried the Russian arms to Van and the approaches to Bitlis and Mush, in Turkish Armenia."

NEVER WAS SO FIT

Count de Montebello Reviews Successes of Last Year and Looks Confidently to the Future.

PARIS, July 31.—A year of war finds "France fit to continue the struggle to the end and confident of the outcome," says Count Adrien Lannes de Montebello in a review of the first twelve months of hostilities given to The Associated Press. Count de Montebello, a recognized authority on military affairs, was one of the strongest advocates of the three-year military service law and its co-author with the ex-Premier, Louis Barthou. He was formerly Deputy from Rheims and Vice President of the Committee on Military Affairs of the Chamber of Deputies. His grandfather was Marshal Lannes, at whose death on the battlefield of Essling Napoleon is said to have wept.

Count de Montebello's review follows:

"France was not expecting war, and her preparations therefore were less complete than those of her adversaries, who, knowing their intentions, had accumulated an immense supply of fighting material and disposed of their troops in such a manner as to strike the most powerful blow of which they were capable.

"Germany threw against Belgium and France fifty-two army corps, or almost her entire military force as mobilized in August. Under the impact of the German advance the French armies, with their British allies, suffered initial reverses and great losses, especially in the battle of Charleroi. While the French armies were in retreat a national Ministry was formed and the civil population of France organized for war. The French and British armies stood on the line of the Marne from a point near Paris to the Eastern frontier of France. They received the shock of more than 1,200,000 German troops, and defeated them with somewhat inferior forces. The Germans were outlied and outfought in a vast general action over a line of more than 120 miles.

"The French troops were too exhausted by their fifteen days of marching and fighting to make their victory decisive. The Germans checked their retreat upon the line of the Aisne, and had sufficient time to dig in. The battle of the Aisne developed by the Germans endeavoring to turn our left and by the simultaneous French effort to turn the German right. This contest resulted in a race for the sea in the obstinate two months' battle along the Yser in October and November. The Germans again failed and finally gave up that part of their offensive on account of their terrific losses.

"Simultaneous with the battle of the Marne, though forming no part of the battle front of what has been called the battle of the Marne, were the operations in the Argonne, the Woevre, and the Grand Couronne de Nancy. The army of the German Crown Prince, marching on Verdun, and the army of Crown Prince Rupprecht of Bavaria, marching on Nancy, both were defeated in some of the bloodiest engagements of the entire war.

"The ultimate result of these defeats was the liberation of that part of the ancient province of Lorraine left to France after 1870 from the occupation of the German Army. The German forces had penetrated fifteen or eighteen miles. They were not only driven out before the 1st of November, but since then the French have invaded Upper Alsace, of which they now hold a considerable part. This country, taken from France in the war of 1870-71, has been reorganized and is under control of a civil Government, which restored the school and judicial system of France.

"From the battle of Charleroi to the end of the first year of the war the Germans achieved no successes on the western battle front save the slight advance at Soissons during the floods of the River Aisne and the advance at Ypres, partially lost afterward, at the time of the first attack with the assistance of asphyxiating gas.

"The successes of the Allies since the battle of the Marne are in the recapture of Thann, Steinbach, Hartsmans-Weller-kopf, Metzeral, La Fontenelle, together with considerable territory in the Alsatian Vosges; the capture of an entire German position in the Forest of Le Prêtre, along the wedge the Germans are still holding in the French lines at St. Mihiel; an advance of a mile along a front of ten miles at Beausejour, in the Champagne country; the capture of Neuve Chapelle by the British, the capture of Notre Dame de Lorette, Carency, and Neuville St. Vaast, and an advance of two or three miles along a front about seven miles north from Arras by the French, and the clearing of the left bank of the Yser of the enemy by the Belgian Army.

"Never since the war began has the French Army been so fit to continue it to a triumphant conclusion as today. We have not only carried on the war with success during the year, but we have accumulated immense reserves of every necessity for continuing the war until it has been won. Our reserve troops in depots and under training are relatively greater than those of the Germans. The army is absolutely confident. The people behind the army, to a man, are equally so.

"The French people, through no fault of theirs, have suffered and are suffering today, but they are equal to every hardship, every effort necessary to drive the war to a final victorious conclusion."

GERMAN WAR WRITERS BREATHE CONFIDENCE

Major Moraht Reviews Army Operations of First Year of War and Captain Persius the Naval.

BERLIN, July 31.—Major Ernest Moraht, the military correspondent of the Berliner Tageblatt, reviewing the twelve months of the war for The Associated Press, says:

"A year ago a coalition with a powerful numercal superiority, declared war on Austria-Hungary and Germany. The hostile countries have a far larger population than have the two Central Powers, and their combined armies originally outnumbered those of the latter. The Central States, however, have known how to improve this difficult situaton by alternately taking the offensive and defensive on the western and eastern fronts.

"In the west the German armies, in a rapid, triumphant advance, carried their standards to within fifty miles of Paris and have kept them flying there since mid-September. Even though the right and left wings of our wide-flung battle front in France and Belgium have been bent back since then (because there was no other method for the time being of counteracting the numerical superiority of the British, French and Belgians), still we held the positions fortified during the nine mnoths, firmly in our hands, so that almost all of Belguim and the northeastern departments of France have been occupied by the troops of Germany.

"In the east the Austro-German armies first held up the Russian millions on the Galician frontiers and then were forced to retire before a manifold numerical superiority, to intrench themselves on the rest of the Carpathians and to beat back until May 1 the Russian assaults with heavy losses. Meanwhile Field Marshal von Hindenburg, in East Prussia, was able to destroy several large Russian armies and free East Prussia; to occupy conjointly with Austrian troops, Poland almost to the Vistula River, and in the northeast to carry the war into the Russian provinces.

Offensive in Galicia.

"While the positions in the war in the west continue to surge to and fro, and three great attempts made to break through our lines, in the Winter, Spring and Summer, were repulsed with awful losses to our enemies, the German and Austro-Hungarian armies on May 1 launched a great offensive against the Russian main armies in Galicia.

"In the series of battles and under constant pursuit, the Russians were hunted out of 48,470 square miles of Galicia, their principal force was severed at several places, and they were driven eastward and northward.

"The west bank of the Vistula in Poland has been cleared of Russian armies. The siege of Warsaw is about to begin and Field Marshal von Hindenburg, in the northward, has pressed forward against Riga and now has reached the vicinity of the city after numerous victories. The successes of the Germans have cost the Russian army millions in dead, wounded and prionsers. The Russian Empire possesses only fragments of its mighty armies and no longer can supply these adequately with arms and munitions. Their fate will be decided very shortly. The Russian forces will be destroyed or forced to flee deep into the interior to the eastward.

"The battles in the West have cut so deeply into the French strength that now 18-yar-old lads must bear arms. Great Britain's original army has been destroyed and only enough substitutes can be raised to hold a forty-four mile front in Belgium. The British losses, particularly those of officers, have been very heavy. The army of 3,000,000 men which Lord Kitchener promised six months ago has not yet appeared, and our opponents in the West never again will be able to raise superior forces to expel the Germans from the country.

"The action in the Dardanelles, which has been in progress for months against the Turks, shows results for the British and French only in great losses of men, ships and war supplies of all kinds. The Turkish army steadily is improving in numbers and quality. The Turkish fortifications are quite as strong as they were at the outset. The prospects of the attackers reaching Constantinople, therefore, have vanished and since none of the Balkan States are willing to enter the Anglo-French service, and since the Russian army, which should have participated from Odessa, has been destroyed in Galicia, it is difficult to see any chances for France and Great Britain.

Should Italy send an army to the Dardanelles, it will find a superior Turkish Army ready to receive her. Italy, after conducting mobilization secretly for nine months, entered the field against Austria-Hungary at the end of May. An Italian Army 1,000,000 men strong, has been attempting for two months to sweep over the fortified Austrian passes and to cross the Isonzo River, behind which the Austro-Hungarian defensive army occupies strong positions. All the attempts of the Italians up to the present have been unsuccessful. The cost to the attackers has been hundreds of thousands in dead and wounded. Austria-Hungary grows stronger day by day and, although its valiant struggle is a difficult one against Italian superiority in numbers, it will be able to bar the way to the coastland and to Trieste and Tyrol. Meanwhile Italy has lost her entire colony at Tripoli to the Arabs and apparently is about to declare war on Turkey.

"The Serbian Army, after great losses in the Winter, has undertaken no military operations, being content to guard the frontiers of its country on which there no longer is an Austro-Hungarian Army.

"The other Balkan States are about to decide which side they shall take in the war. Since Russia's forces have been driven back and badly beaten and a German and Austro-Hungarian Army has been arrayed near the frontier of Rumania, Bulgaria has come to an understanding with Turkey, and Greece remains the opponent of Italy, and an increase in the number of our enemies under control of the Entente Allies no longer is to be anticipated by Austria-Hungary.

"The Germans have every reason, therefore, at the end of the first year of the war to consider their sacrifices in blood and treasure have been rewarded. We are well prepared for a continuance of the war. Onr nation still possesses determination to conquer and to make the necessary sacrifices. Our supplies of war material are assured by efficient organization. Our finances are far from exhausted, and there is no lack of provisions. Our fleet, despite a few losses among the cruisers, is ready to be thrown into the struggle at the proper moment and in full strength, and our submarines in all the seas are the dread of our enemies. Thus their offensive has changed to a defensive, and the prospects of eventual victory for the Central Powers is materially increased."

GERMAN NAVY IN THE WAR.

Although the main German and British fleets have not been matched in battle, the ending of the first year of the war finds that Germany has distinguished herself at sea, says Captain I. Persius in a review prepared for The Associated Press. Captain Persius, formerly an officer of the German Navy, is a recognized authority on German naval affairs, and is naval expert of the Berliner Tageblatt. He says Germany's policy has been to attempt to weaken her chief opponent at sea by using submarines and mines to a point where there will be some prospect of success of an attack on the main British fleet. His review follows:

"The German fleet may boast that the offensive spirit it has displayed has constituted the most prominent and decisive feature of all the naval war theatres. War was declared against Russia on Aug. 1, and on Aug. 2 the cruiser Augsburg bombarded the Russian war port of Libau. The declaration of war against France was issued Aug. 3, and on the following day the cruisers Goeben and Breslau shelled the troop embarkation points of Phillipeville and Bona, on the North African coast. Finally England declared war on Aug. 4, and on the 8th the minelayer Koenigin Luise planted mines at the mouth of the Thames one of which destroyed the cruiser Amphion.

"We thus see that from the very beginning German warships displayed a spirit of daring offensive. Not only in European waters but in distant seas we heard of victorious combats wherein our cruisers were engaged. In a majority of cases the foreign cruisers, like the home units, fought against much superior forces.

"In Germany the gigantic task of our sea forces is in no wise underestimated. We know that the British fleet alone, so far as material strength is concerned, is considerably more than twice our superior, but we are certain that the same heroic spirit of determination to win exists in the fleet as in the army, and that we can depend upon the efficiency of our material which, even though inferior in quantity, can brave comparison with that of any other power for excellence in construction of artillery and machinery.

Opponent Worthy of Respect.

"We do not forget that the British fleet, first in the world and of glorious history, is an opponent worthy of all respect. nevertheless, at the close of the first year of the war, it may be said without exaggeration that its achievements do not measure up to our expectations. It has lacked, it seems, the iron determination and ability to conquer.

"The British Admiralty has held strictly to 'the strategy of caution.' The German submarine danger is, we realize, partly responsible, but it cannot be questioned that, as a consequence of undeniably evident lack of initiative, the prestige of the British sea power no longer stands so unshaken throughout the world as formerly. British forces have been victorious only in engagements where they were overwhelmingly superior, as at the Falkland Islands, and even this is not claimed by the British press to be an unconditional success because the battle was too costly in time and sacrifice.

"Our naval authoritites followed generally the principle of keeping battleships in harbor while attempting to weaken the enemy through minor warfare, particularly with submarine and mines, to a point where the attack on the main fleet will offer some prospect of success. How correct this strategy was is proved by the past twelve months. Thanks to the effectiveness of our submarines, which excited the justified admiration of the whole world, it has been possible sorely to wound the British fleet.

"In addition, our submarine arm has busied itself since the beginning of the year in an entirely unexpected way, as a destroyer of commerce. Views may differ as to the final outcome in this field, but it is undeniable that a nation like Germany, whose commerce has been driven from the seas, but which can subsist without imports, has an extraordinary advantage over a country dependent almost entirely, like Britian, upon importations of food and raw materials across the water. The submarine danger unquestionably weighs like a nightmare upon the inhabitants of the sea-washed land. The future results of the wide extension, as we hope, of the fruitful activity of our sumarines cannot be predicted, but the expectation is generally cherished in Germany that the submarine campaign will help to accelerate the demand for peace in England.

"Every type of warship has fallen victim to German submarines—the battleships Formidable, Triumph, and Majestic, the armored cruisers Hogue, Cressy, and Aboukir, the Russian armored cruiser Pallaba, the cruisers Hawke and Pathfinder, and the British destroyer Recruit, for example—and neither the express steamer nor the slow fishing boat is safe from our deadly torpedoes.

Aerial Offensive a Success.

"In addition, the aerial arm of the service has won many laurels. Zeppelins crossed the North Sea safely, even to London and back and German aeroplanes participated in the destruction of the enemies' war and merchant ships. The question whether airships and aeroplanes could be used offensively at sea must, in the light of the achievements of our aircraft, be answered affirmatively.

"German aircraft have even fought successfully against the dreaded submarines. A Russian submarine was destroyed in the Baltic by bombs from an aeroplane, and at least one British submarine met the same fate in the North Sea.

"The general fear of submarines is responsible for the remarkable spectacle of the heavily armed and strongly armored battleships rarely venturing to leave sheltering harbors—ships which before the war were counted as decisive factors in sea power, but find themselves condemned to inactive rôles. Clashes of heavy battleships, like those in distant waters, have borne out the old rule that superiority in numbers, artillery, and speed make up the decisive factor for victory.

These Polish infantrymen use shell holes as rifle pits on the East Prussian front.

"All the News That's Fit to Print."

The New York Times.

THE WEATHER
Fair today, partly cloudy tomorrow; moderate west to northwest winds, becoming variable.
☞For full weather report see Page 17.

VOL. LXIV...NO. 21,037. ....   NEW YORK, FRIDAY, AUGUST 20, 1915.—TWENTY PAGES.   ONE CENT In Greater New York, Jersey City and Newark. | Elsewhere TWO CENTS.

WHITE STAR LINER ARABIC, TORPEDOED WITHOUT WARNING WITH 26 AMERICANS ABOARD, SINKS IN ELEVEN MINUTES; 391 SAVED, SOME INJURED; TWO AMERICANS AMONG 32 MISSING

WOMAN NEW YORKER LOST?

U-Boat Emerged and Fired Torpedo Without Slightest Warning.

PASSENGERS SAW PERIL

Watching Attack on Another Vessel When Fatal Bolt Struck the Arabic.

BOATS QUICKLY LAUNCHED

But Many Persons, Including a Woman, Were Hurled Into Sea —Maimed Reach Queenstown.

LONDON, Friday, Aug. 20.—The big White Star Line steamer Arabic, formerly a favorite ship of the Liverpool-Boston service, but which on her present trip was on the way to New York, was torpedoed and sunk by a German submarine at 9:15 o'clock yesterday morning southeast of Fastnet.

The steamer, according to a statement of the White Star Line, was attacked without warning and went down in ten minutes. Of the 423 persons on board—181 passengers and 242 members of the crew—32 are missing and are believed to have perished.

Most of those who have not been accounted for belong to the crew. Only six of the passengers are reported missing.

Whether any of those not accounted for are Americans has not yet been determined, but there were only twenty-six citizens of the United States on board, twenty-two being in the second cabin and four in the steerage. The Arabic carried no first-class passengers, having lately been turned into a two-class liner.

Survivors at Queenstown.

The survivors, who left the steamer in the ship's boats and were picked up later by passing vessels, arrived in Queenstown tonight. They are being accommodated by the White Star Line in hotels and boarding houses in the little town which so short a time ago cared for the survivors and the dead of the Lusitania.

Details of the sinking of the Arabic

President Wilson's Warning to Germany

" The very value which this Government sets upon the long and unbroken friendship between the people and Government of the United States and the people and Government of the German nation impels it to press very solemnly upon the Imperial German Government the necessity for a scrupulous observance of neutral rights in this critical matter. Friendship itself prompts it to say to the Imperial Government that repetition by the commanders of German naval vessels of acts in contravention of those rights must be regarded by the Government of the United States, when they affect American citizens, as deliberately unfriendly."—From the American note to Germany, sent on July 21.

are lacking, but that the loss of life was not greater was doubtless due to the fact that the weather was fine and that steamers plying the German submarine zone now keep their boats swung out and are otherwise prepared for emergencies.

The torpedo that sunk the Arabic struck her on the starboard side 100 feet from her stern. The vessel had left Liverpool Wednesday afternoon and taken a southerly course, well off the Irish coast, doubtless with a view of avoiding the submarines which frequent the waters nearer the shore.

When some fifty miles west of where the Lusitania was sunk in May the

Ship's Whole Side Blown Out; Many Survivors Injured

Special Cable to THE NEW YORK TIMES.

QUEENSTOWN, Aug. 19, (Dispatch to The London Daily News.)—Three hundred and seventy persons who were rescued from the Arabic were landed at Queenstown at 6 o'clock this evening. A large number of them were badly injured. The ship sank in six minutes, according to some survivors, almost the whole of one side being torn out of her.

Several of those who were injured were engaged in watching another ship which was being torpedoed when their own vessel was struck.

The survivors were four hours in the ship's boats before they were rescued.

German submarine came to the surface and launched a torpedo.

The marksmanship of the Germans, as in the case of the Lusitania, was deadly accurate, and like the Lusitania, the big liner quickly settled and soon disappeared from view.

Some of the survivors, according to reports received here, say that they had just witnessed the torpedoing of a British steamer, presumably the Dunsley, and that this had caused great alarm on board the Arabic.

In their fright the passengers had rushed for life preservers, and had barely adjusted them when the German submarine turned its torpedo against the Arabic's side.

Ten life boats and a number of life rafts were quickly got over the side of the steamer, and into these a large number of the passengers and members of the crew scrambled.

Many of the passengers, however, fell into the water, but they got hold of the rafts and clung to them and later were rescued. One woman who fell into the sea screamed pitifully for help. The weather and tidal conditions being favorable, two sailors swam to her assistance and succeeded in lifting her upon a raft.

Among those who were rescued were Captain William Finch, commander of the Arabic, all the deck officers, the chief engineer, the surgeon, the purser, the assistant purser, the chief steward, and the third-class steward.

Submarines Have Sunk 67 Ships Since Our Last Lusitania Note

Between Feb. 18, when the German " war zone " decree went into effect, and July 21, the date of the last American note to Germany, 218 vessels were destroyed by German submarines, with a loss of 1,652 lives.

Since then the losses have been as follows:

Date.	Name.	Class.	Nationality.	Loss.
July 26	Rubona	Ship	Russian	0
" 24	Star of Peace	Trawler	British	0
" 22-25	Danae	Steamer	French	0
" 22-25	Henry Charles	Trawler	British	0
" 22-25	Kathleen	Trawler	British	0
" 22-25	Activity	Trawler	British	0
" 22-25	Prosper	Trawler	British	0
" 22-25	Frith	Steamer	British	4
" 22-25	Perseus	Trawler	British	10
" 22-25	Briton	Trawler	British	6
" 25	Leelanaw	Steamer	American	0
" 26	Fimreite	Steamer	Norwegian	0
" 26	Grangewood	Steamer	British	0
" 25-27	Emma	Steamer	Swedish	0
" 25-27	Maria	Schooner	Danish	0
" 25-27	Neptunis	Schooner	Danish	0
" 25-27	Lena	Schooner	Danish	0
" 25-27	Mangara	Steamer	British	0
" 28	Iconic	Trawler	British	0
" 28	Salacia	Trawler	British	0
" 28	Tagnadelen	Bark	Swedish	0
" 28	Westward Ho	Trawler	British	0
" 29	Princess Marie Jose	Steamer	Belgian	0
" 29	Fortuna	Brig	Swedish	0
" 31	Iberian	Steamer	British	8
" 27-31	Quest	Trawler	British	0
" 27-31	Strive	Trawler	British	0
" 27-31	Achieve	Trawler	British	3
" 27-31	Athena	Trawler	British	0
" 27-31	Coriander	Trawler	British	0
" 27-31	Fitz Gerald	Trawler	British	0
" 27-31	Two unnamed	Trawler	British	0
Aug. 3	Ranza	Steamer	British	3
" 5	Grimbariat	Trawler	British	6
" 5	Portia	Trawler	British	0
" 5- 9	Mai	Steamer	Swedish	10
" 5- 9	Geiranger	Steamer	Norwegian	0
" 5- 9	Westminster	Trawler	British	0
" 5- 9	Harbor Wiper	Trawler	British	0
" 5- 9	Benardna	Trawler	British	2
" 5- 9	Jason	Schooner	Danish	0
" 10-11	Oakwood	Steamer	British	0
" 10-11	Morna	Bark	Norwegian	0
" 10-11	Francois	Bark	French	0
" 10-11	Baltzer	Bark	Russian	0
" 10-11	Young Admiral	Trawler	British	0
" 10-11	George Crabbe	Trawler	British	0
" 10-11	Illustrious	Trawler	British	0
" 10-11	Calm	Trawler	British	0
" 10-11	Trevire	Trawler	British	0
" 10-11	Welcome	Trawler	British	0
" 10-11	Utopia	Trawler	British	0
" 11-13	Osprey	Steamer	British	0
" 11-13	Summerfield	Steamer	British	0
" 11-13	Jacona	Steamer	British	0
" 11-13	Aura	Steamer	Norwegian	3
" 11-13	Bonny	Trawler	British	0
" 14-18	Maggie	Trawler	British	0
" 14-18	Thornfield	Steamer	British	0
" 14-18	Isidoro	Steamer	Spanish	?
" 14-18	Rumulus	Steamer	Norwegian	0
" 14-18	Mineral	Steamer	Norwegian	0
" 18-19	Grodno	Steamer	British	0
" 18-19	Serbio	Steamer	British	0
" 18-19	Dunsley	Steamer	British	0
" 19	Arabic	Steamer	British	32

The total since July 21 is 67 ships and 84 lives lost, and since Feb. 18,285 ships and 1,736 lives lost.

"All the News That's Fit to Print."

The New York Times.

THE WEATHER

Sunday rain; Monday fair; moderate to fresh south to southwest winds.

VOL. LXIV...NO. 21,029.   NEW YORK, SUNDAY, AUGUST 22, 1915.—90 PAGES, In Seven Parts.   PRICE FIVE CENTS.

ITALY, FLEET AND ARMY WAITING, DECLARES WAR ON TURKEY; FRENCH ARMY IS NOW READY TO BEGIN A GREAT OFFENSIVE; ARABIC NOT CONVOYED AND GOT NO WARNING, PAGE CABLES; PRESIDENT GIVES BERLIN CHANCE TO EXPLAIN BEFORE ACTING

PAGE SENDS ARABIC REPORT

Cables Affidavits of Americans That Liner Was Not Warned.

VESSEL HAD NO ESCORT

Admiralty Statement and Captain's Story Bear Out Tales of the Survivors.

WILSON MOVES CAUTIOUSLY

Will Give Germany a Chance to Explain—Open Talk of Diplomatic Break.

Berlin Silent on the Arabic, Press Under Tight Curb

BERLIN, Aug. 21, (via London, Aug. 22, 1:35 A. M.)—No statement is obtainable in official quarters regarding the sinking of the steamer Arabic. The tendency, however, seems to be to consider the question without excitement.

The press thus far has avoided comment of any nature.

This dispatch contains the only reference to the Arabic obtainable from Berlin Saturday.

Special Cable to THE NEW YORK TIMES

LONDON, Aug. 21.—Ambassador Page cabled a report to Washington today giving the details of the sinking of the Arabic, and making the point that from statements communicated to him the submarine fired its torpedo without giving the slightest warning. That is the Ambassador's official report, based upon all the information available.

The Ambassador talked with James Colman, an American citizen, who had been living in London for some years and had sold his property here in the last few months, so as to return to America. He was aboard the Arabic. Mr. Colman called at the Embassy to assure Mr. Page that the

torpedo was fired without the slightest chance being given to the passengers to save their lives.

"The first any one knew of the torpedo," he said, "was while some were looking at the steamer Dunsley foundering a little distance away. Suddenly the cry went up that a torpedo was coming toward us. Captain Finch was zigzagging his vessel, for evidently he had already spotted the submarine, and was trying to avoid it. Before any one of us fully realized it, crash came the torpedo into the ship, almost knocking the ship over, it seemed. The Germans did not fire any shot across the bow of the Arabic to stop her, and did not make any effort to ascertain if there were Americans aboard. It was simply a cold-blooded attack with utter disregard of the consequences.

"Every American on the ship to whom I have since talked agrees that the Germans apparently were determined to kill every one."

NEW FOE FOR THE MOSLEMS

LONDON, Sunday, Aug. 22.—Italy has declared war against Turkey, according to a Steffani News Agency dispatch from Rome.

This announcement receives confirmation in an official telegram from Constantinople received in Amsterdam and transmitted to The Central News with the added information that the Marquis di Garroni, the Italian Ambassador at Constantinople, presented the declaration yesterday and demanded his passports.

The reasons given in the note for Italy's declaration of war were the support of Turkey of the revolt in Libya and the prevention of the departure of Italian residents from Syria.

A Reuter dispatch from Constantinople, via Berlin and Amsterdam, says that the Ambassador has left the Turkish capital.

The Italian Government, says another dispatch from Rome, has telegraphed to all its representatives abroad a circular setting forth the questions at issue between Italy and Turkey. The circular closes with these words:

"In view of these obvious infractions of categorical promises made by the Ottoman Government, and following upon our ultimatum of Aug. 3, provoked by evasions of the Ottoman Government, particularly with regard to the free departure of Italian subjects from Asia Minor, the Italian Government has sent instructions to its Ambassador at Constantinople to declare war upon Turkey."

"Time for Words Has Passed," Says Roosevelt; He Declares It Not Enough to Dismiss Bernstorff

OYSTER BAY, N. Y., Aug. 21.—Ex-President Theodore Roosevelt issued this statement tonight:

I see it is suggested in the papers that the German answer to our last note—that is, the sinking of the Arabic by a German submarine and the consequent murder of certain American citizens—will be adequately met by the Administration dismissing Bernstorff and severing diplomatic relations with Germany. I earnestly hope the Administration will not take this view, for to do so would be a fresh sacrifice of American honor and interest.

The President's note to Germany in February last was an excellent note, if only it had been lived up to. But every subsequent note has represented nothing but weakness and timidity on our side, and the sinking of the Lusitania and of the Arabic, the attacks on the Gulflight and the Falaba, and all the similar incidents that have occurred, represent the arrogant answers which this weakness has inspired. Germany will care nothing for the mere severance of diplomatic relations.

The time for words on the part of this nation has long passed, and it is inconceivable to American citizens, who claim to be inheritors of the traditions of Washington and Lincoln, that our governmental representatives shall not see that the time for deeds has come.

What has just occurred is a fresh and lamentable proof of the unwisdom of our people in not having insisted upon the beginning of active military preparedness thirteen months ago.

FRENCH EAGER TO BEGIN

Times Correspondent Hints at Advance 'Before Leaves Are Red.'

From a Staff Correspondent.
Special Cable to THE NEW YORK TIMES.

PARIS, Aug. 21.—With an officer of the General Staff—the same who accompanied me on previous trips to the front—I have just visited three points on the French battle line, heretofore barred to correspondents.

I waited for this trip in preference to the privilege of describing rides in aeroplanes or visits to famous generals or similar "stunts," in order that I might obtain the closest view of the French army accorded to anybody.

For weeks there have been "reliable" rumors concerning the "German plan when the Russian campaign is over." We have been regaled with details of just how and where Germany intended to hurl new millions of men and shells. There have been disturbing whispers. In fact, Paris has been so crazy with misinformation that the idea has scarcely occurred to any one that perhaps the army's higher command might

have an entirely commendable plan of its own for the ultimate victory of the French arms.

This is not to be an account of fighting, such as the spectacle of the Battle of the Labyrinth permitted me to describe. Of all the war I have seen, this trip seemed the least like war.

When I rode through the majestic pine forests between the mountain peaks of the Vosges there was not a sound to disturb tranquility of thought, although armies were secreted there, watching. When I walked through the meadows of Lorraine I could scarcely believe there was anything but peace in all the world, although several times observers informed the party that we were unnecessarily exposing ourselves to German artillery.

But artillery did not breathe a sound those beautiful afternoons. When, from observatory posts on the lofty ranges in the north I looked down upon the dense and tranquil woods, I knew them full of hidden troops and cannon. Afterward I saw them close, but it was like the quaint forest life of old story books—these Summer encampments.

Men Playing and Bathing.

Everybody was happy. Men played quoits and ninepins or fished and bathed in the streams, and slept at night on pine boughs in funny little houses of rough bark or mud. Perhaps it was the pines and balsam that proved so delusive, but one could not realize that only a few yards further on were the trenches where sentries never slept. On this peaceful excursion I did not get shot at once,

"All the News That's Fit to Print."

The New York Times.

THE WEATHER
Cloudy today and Friday; not much change in temperature; strong northeast winds.
☞For full weather report see Page 15.

VOL. LXIV...NO. 21,040.　　　　NEW YORK, THURSDAY, SEPTEMBER 2, 1915.—TWENTY PAGES.　　　　ONE CENT In Greater New York, Jersey City and Newark. | TWO CENTS

GERMANY GIVES A WRITTEN PROMISE TO SINK NO LINERS WITHOUT WARNING; POPE BEGINS NEW MOVE FOR PEACE

BERLIN YIELDS TO PRESIDENT

Bernstorff Brings Pledge for Safety of Non-Combatants at Sea.

DISAVOWALS TO COME NEXT

Oral Assurances Quickly Followed by a Formal Letter from the Ambassador.

VICTORY, SAYS WASHINGTON

Recognition of Fundamental Principle of Our Demands, Lansing Asserts.

GERMANY'S NOTE TO FOLLOW

Way Now Clear for Settlement of Lusitania Case and Whole Submarine Question.

Special to The New York Times.

WASHINGTON, Sept. 1.—Any doubt that may have remained of Germany's intention to acknowledge the justice of this Government's contentions respecting the illegality of the German submarine warfare and to furnish guarantees of a new line of policy was removed today when Count von Bernstorff, the German Ambassador, gave to Secretary Lansing, both orally and in writing, assurances that liners would not be sunk by German submarines without warning and that provision would be made for the safety of noncombatants. This expressly concedes the major contention of the American Government as set forth in the three notes on the sinking of the Lusitania.

The only qualification of the German pledge was that this practice would be adhered to, provided the liners did not try to escape or offer resistance. But that is hardly a qualification, for the United States has acknowledged that resistance or effort to escape on the part of a merchant vessel would give the submarine the right of attack.

The importance of Count von Bernstorff's assurances, which were given in the form of a quotation from Germany's forthcoming note in answer to the American representations concerning the Lusitania, is indicated by a brief statement, made by Secretary Lansing, in giving out the text of an informal communication from the German Ambassador. Mr. Lansing said that the only comment needed was that the Ambassador's communication appeared to be " a recognition of the fundamental principle for which we have contended."

This conservative description of the German assurances, however, hardly represents the gratification with which Count von Bernstorff's statement has been received. It is not beyond the mark to say that officials are elated and feel that not only have President Wilson and Secretary Lansing won a notable diplomatic victory, but that the danger of war with Germany is definitely removed.

No Quibble Intended.

Count von Bernstorff's note to Mr. Lansing seems to leave uncertain the question whether the duty of visit and search, now pledged by the German Government regarding ''liners,'' will apply equally to freighters and passenger ships. But it is clearly understood that no such quibble is intended, and it was officially explained at the State Department that the death of an American sailor on a belligerent merchantman, whether a passenger or freighter, would be regarded as probably even more serious than the death of an American passenger. This view was explained on the ground that the sailor would be carrying out simply his normal calling, while the passenger might be regarded as voluntarily putting his life in jeopardy.

The full text of the German note, replying to the last American communication on the sinking of the Lusitania, of which Count von Bernstorff quoted one sentence, has not been received in Washington, and it may be delayed until the Arabic case is definitely disposed of. But when it comes it is hoped that it will in set terms clear up all uncertainties regarding the scope of the pledge to exercise visit and search hereafter before sinking merchantmen. The German word translated as " liners " might in itself clear the whole subject.

One strong reason for believing that the German Government does not intend now to quibble over the difference between passenger and freight vessels lies in the known motive prompting of the publication of the promise at this time. Some weeks ago German officials let the American Government understand that the reply to the last Lusitania note would not be delivered before the United States sent forward its protest against the British blockade. The change of mind in this respect resulted from a desire on Germany's part to show her willingness to meet the wishes of the United States without regard to Great Britain's course. A desire to show this friendliness before Great Britain had a chance to make any further concessions to American demands might also explain the haste with which an isolated sentence from the coming formal note was cabled to the German Ambassador for transmission to the State Department.

Bernstorff's Success.

It is not difficult in all this to see the initiative of Count von Bernstorff. The circumstances under which he wrote his note this morning made it certain that he did so without consultation with his Government, although, of course, that did not rob the quoted sentence of its formal character. It has been known for a long time that Count von Bernstorff was bending all his efforts to prevent a break between Germany and the United States. And to avoid that contingency he has pressed upon the German Chancellor the seriousness with which the marine incidents were viewed in the United States and the necessity of meeting that view by official concessions rather than by argumentative notes in justification of the submarine war, or by unofficial propaganda in this country. Today's events show he has succeeded.

As expressed at the State Department this afternoon, the next move is Germany's. This probably means that until the full text of the note is received the United States will not formally accept the assurances as satisfactory. Or it might mean simply that the policy upon which those assurances were based, which, as Count von Vernstorff pointed out, was agreed to in Berlin before the sinking of the Arabic, must be formally applied to the Arabic in order to close that incident.

The German Ambassador's statement that the policy was agreed to before the Arabic incident confirmed the report, first printed in THE NEW YORK TIMES, that there had been some embarrassing delay in the German Admiralty in giving effect to the policy of the German Chancellor. While a disavowal of the sinking of the Arabic is certain to follow, the assurance that attacks without warning would not be made in the future, it is believed that the reported loss of the offending German submarine will obviate the necessity of Germany accompanying that disavowal by the punishment of any German officer or official.

What remains now to meet the American demands is a disavowal in the Lusitania, reparation for lives lost on belligerent and American ships, and for damage done in mistaken attacks on American vessels. But it is quite probable that the German Ambassador in his conversations with Mr. Lansing has already indicated fully that American suggestions as to how reparation can be made will be satisfactory to Germany. A formal disavowal of intention to injure Americans will probably be accepted in view of Germany's present conciliatory stand as sufficient response to the American demand for a disavowal of the act of the submarine commander immediately responsible for sinking the Lusitania.

How Delay Was Gained.

It is believed that the German Ambassador conveyed informally to Mr. Lansing news of the German order ameliorating conditions of submarine warfare when he called at the State Department following his telegram ten days ago in which he asked that no action be taken until the German position could be sent out. His telegram made it certain that there had been a change of front on Germany's part. It is hardly likely that he would not have fully explained that inference to Mr. Lansing, who waited, however, till the statement could be made on official direction from Berlin with a textual citation of the assurance.

For some time back, dating probably from the Ambassador's New York telegram, if not before, the German plan as to the final disposition of the whole controversy has been clearly outlined. The ameliorating order was to be communicated officially to the United States as an assurance for the future. A disavowal of the sinking of the Arabic would clear up that incident. Then would come an invitation to the United States to suggest a way in which reparation for loss of American lives and property could be adopted. No difficulty is expected on that score.

While the State Department was reluctant this afternoon to add anything to Mr. Lansing's statement appended to the press copy of the Ambassador's note it was said that the general principle, such as the German assurances conceded, would ordinarily cover all incidents to which it was applicable, even if the incident arose subsequent to the events about which the first dispute arose. That makes it certain that no developments of fact regarding the loss of the Arabic will be allowed to impair the complete understanding toward which the United States and Germany seem to be rapidly coming.

It is not believed here that the new German policy will have any marked physical effect upon the results of her submarine warfare.

"All the News That's Fit to Print."

The New York Times.

THE WEATHER
Fair and colder Monday; probably fair Tuesday; northwest gales diminishing.

VOL. LXV...NO. 21,065. ...　　　NEW YORK, MONDAY, SEPTEMBER 27, 1915.—EIGHTEEN PAGES.　　　ONE CENT In Greater New York, Jersey City and Newark. | Elsewhere TWO CENTS

ALLIES ATTACK FROM SEA TO VERDUN; SMASH 20 MILES OF GERMAN FRONT; 20,000 PRISONERS, MANY GUNS TAKEN

Greatest Advances Made in Champagne and North of Arras.

SOUCHEZ AND LOOS TAKEN

British Capture of the Latter Threatens the Germans' Possession of Lens.

A 70-HOUR BOMBARDMENT

It Preceded French Assaults Which Won 15 Miles of Trenches Near Perthes.

LONDON, Sept. 26.—The great allied offensive in the west began yesterday was successfully continued today. Tonight the net result is the taking of more than 20,000 unwounded German prisoners, the occupation of twenty miles of German trenches, (the German lines having been penetrated at some points to a depth of two and one-half miles,) and the capture of upward of thirty field guns, besides other war material.

The attack which resulted in the French and British victories began Saturday morning. For several weeks there has been an almost incessant bombardment with big guns, which late last week increased in intensity, particularly in the sectors where the infantry attacks took place.

The French, who have the most important gain to their credit, directed their chief onset against the German lines around Perthes, Beauséjour, and Souppes, in Champagne, where in December they made a considerable gain of ground. Saturday's attack, however, backed by a tremendous artillery fire, gave them possession of more territory than they had retaken from the Germans since the latter dug themselves in after the battle of the Marne.

According to the French account the Germans in Champagne were driven out of their trenches over a front of fifteen miles, varying in depth from two-thirds of a mile to two and a half miles. The French in this engagement captured more than 12,000 prisoners, and apparently the advantage is being pressed still further.

Weakens German Argonne Positions.

The importance of this gain lies in the fact that every yard of ground taken in this region weakens the German position around Verdun, from which the Germans might be compelled to retire should the French succeed in making any further advance.

The French also have regained, first the cemetery and then the whole town of Souchez and trenches east of the Labyrinth in the Arras district, which was the scene of much heavy fighting earlier in the year. This battle was fought in co-operation with the British, who attacked on either side of La Bassée Canal. The attack to the south of the canal, Field Marshal Sir John French reports, was a complete success. Trenches on a five-mile front were taken at this point, the victors penetrating the German lines 4,000 yards.

This push forward gives the British possession of the road from Lens to La Bassée, which was used by the Germans for moving troops and supplies north and south, and threatens to outflank the German troops holding the town of Lens.

British Only Twelve Miles from Lille.

Hill No. 70, one of the positions taken on the road, is less than a mile directly north of Lens, with Hulluch, which also fell into the hands of the British, is at the end of the road near La Bassée. It is only twelve miles from Hulluch to Lille, the chief city of Northern France.

North of the canal the British, although they fought all day yesterday, were unable to hold the ground gained and had to fall back to the trenches which they had left in the morning. The attack, however, accomplished one purpose, as, according to Sir John French, German reserves were sent to check this move, this giving the British south of the canal an opportunity to consolidate their new positions unmolested.

A somewhat similar manoeuvre took place to the north and south of the Menin Road, east of Ypres, and the results were the same. North of the road the British were unable to hold the ground taken, while to the south they gained about 600 yards of the German trenches and consolidated the ground won. So far as is reported, the British took 2,600 prisoners, with nine field guns and several machine guns.

The repulse of a German division near Loos, northwest of Lens, with considerable casualties and the loss of materials, is admitted in the German official communication made public in Berlin today. The War Office also announces the evacuation of Souchez and of an advanced German position north of Perthes, between Rheims and the Argonne forest; but it insists that "all attempts to break through failed."

French Bulletins of Victory.

The text of the Paris night statement follows:

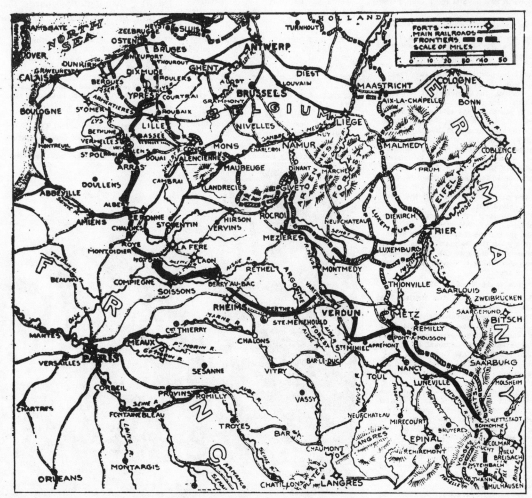

Western Battle Front, Scene of Allies' Great Drive

1. Hooge, the northern limit of the British attack.
2. Here the British captured five miles of trenches.
3. The British capture of Hill 70, a mile from Lens, threatens the German occupation of that town.
4. Loos, captured by the British, is about twelve miles from Lille, the most important city of Northern France held by the Germans.
5. Souchez, after months of fighting, now entirely in French hands.
6. Perthes, middle of the Champagne line, along which the French captured fifteen miles of trenches.

Our attack to the north of Arras has realized fresh progress. We have occupied by sheer force all the village of Souchez, and have advanced toward the east in the direction of Givenchy.

More to the south we reached La Folie and pushed to the north of Thelus, as far as the destroyed telegraph lines. We made in the course of this action about a thousand prisoners.

In Champagne our troops continue to gain ground. After having crossed on nearly the whole front extending between Auberive and Ville-sur-Tourbe, the powerful network of trenches, passages, small forts, and shelters perfected by the enemy during long months, our troops advanced toward the north, compelling the German troops to fall back on their trenches of the second position, from three to four kilometers (one and seven-eighths to two and a half miles) to the rear. The struggle continues on the whole front.

We have reached l'Epine de Vedegrange and passed the cabin on the road from Souain to Somme-py, and the hut on the road from Souain to Tahure. More to the east we are holding the farm of Maisons de Champagne.

The enemy has suffered by our fire and in hand-to-hand struggles very important losses. He left in the works which he abandoned considerable material, which has not yet been inventoried. Already the capture of twenty-four field guns is recorded.

The number of prisoners is increasing steadily, and is actually more than 16,000 men, not wounded, of whom at least 200 are officers.

The total number of prisoners captured on the whole front by the allied troops in two days is more than 20,000 men not wounded.

Won on 15-Mile Champagne Front.

The successes of yesterday are recorded in the French afternoon report as follows:

In Artois we maintained during the night the positions which we yesterday won. These include the Château de Carleul, the cemetery of Souchez, and the last trench which the enemy continued to occupy to the east of the fortified position called the Labyrinth.

In the Champagne stubborn fighting continues on the whole front. Our troops have penetrated the German lines along a front of 25 kilometers (about 15 miles) for a depth varying from one to four kilometers, (.62 miles to 2.48 miles.) Our troops in the course of the night maintained all the positions conquered.

The number of prisoners actually enumerated exceeds 12,000 men.

Except for one surprise action of our artillery on the German works in the region of Launois, in the Ban-de-Sapt, there is nothing to report on the rest of the front.

British Hold List of Their Gains.

The night report of the British field headquarters says:

There has been severe fighting today on the ground won by us yesterday, the enemy making determined counterattacks east and northeast of Loos.

The result of this fighting is that, except just north of Loos, we hold all the ground gained yesterday, including the whole of Loos itself.

This evening we retook the quarries northwest of Hulluch which we rewon and lost yesterday. We have in this fighting drawn in the enemy's reserves, enabling the French on our right to make further progress.

The number of prisoners collected after yesterday's fighting amounted to 2,600. Nine guns have been taken and a considerable number of machine guns.

Our aeroplanes today bombed and derailed a train near Loffres, east of Douai, and another, which was full of troops, at Tohult, near St. Amand. The Valenciennes station was also bombarded.

The text of the afternoon report of the British Commander in Chief in France follows:

Saturday morning we attacked the enemy south of La Bassée Canal to the east of Grenay and Vermelles. We captured his trenches on a front of over five miles, penetrating his lines in some places for a distance of 4,000 yards.

We captured the western outskirts of Hulluch, the village of Loos, and the mining works around it, and Hill 70.

Other attacks were made to the north of La Bassée Canal, which drew a strong reserve of the enemy toward the point of the line, where hard fighting occurred throughout the day with varying success. At nightfall our troops north of the canal occupied their positions of the morning.

We made another attack near Hooge on either side of the Menin road. An attack north of the road succeeded in occupying Bellewaarde farm and ridge, but this subsequently was retaken by the enemy.

In the attacks to the south of the road we gained 600 yards of the enemy's trench, and we consolidated the ground won.

The reports of captures up to the present include about 1,700 prisoners and eight guns, besides several machine guns, the number of which is not yet known.

The report in Friday's German communiqué that we attempted to make an attack on the previous day south of La Bassée Canal, which broke down under hostile artillery fire, is false. No attack was attempted.

German Report Admits Reverses.

The War Office in Berlin has issued this communiqué:

The battles in the continuation of the British and French offensive, which had been prepared for months, have progressed without bringing our assailants considerably nearer to their aim.

In the sector of Ypres the enemy suffered heavy losses and had no success.

Southwest of Lille the enemy succeeded in repulsing one of our divisions near Loos from its advance line of defense to its second line. Naturally we had considerable losses, including material of all kinds inclosed between the two positions. A counterattack is progressing favorably.

"Voluntarily" Left Souchez.

We voluntarily evacuated the ruins

Escorted by a detail of guards, German prisoners of war captured at Verdun, are marched off to prison camps.

of the village of Souchez. Other attacks on this front were easily repulsed, at several points with the heaviest of losses for the enemy. The Thirty-ninth Regiment of Landwehr especially distinguished itself. This is the same regiment which sustained the principal attack north of Neuville in May.

Belgians Successful, Too.

The Belgian official communication issued today, says:

The enemy artillery has not been very active. There have been several actions with heavy guns at various points along the front.

In the evening of Sept. 25 our troops captured a German observation post on the right bank of the Yser. The garrison of the post (fifteen men and one commissioned officer) and a grenade-thrower were taken. The occupation of the post obliged the Germans to evacuate trenches extending 200 meters (about 650 feet) along the Yser.

Soldiers such as these were responsible for the French victory.

"All the News That's Fit to Print."

The New York Times.

THE WEATHER
Showers today or at night; partly cloudy Friday; moderate south to southwest winds.

For full weather report see Page 12.

VOL. LXV...NO. 21,022. ....   NEW YORK, THURSDAY, OCTOBER 14, 1915.—TWENTY-TWO PAGES.   ONE CENT In Greater New York, Jersey City and Newark. | TWO CENTS Elsewhere.

EIGHT KILLED IN AIR RAID ON LONDON; SERBS DEFEAT BULGARS; RUSSIANS GAIN; GERMANS RETAKE TRENCHES AT SOUCHEZ

BULGAR DIVISION ROUTED

SAVOFF REFUSES TO FIGHT

TEUTON HOST PRESSES ON

But Serbs in Retiring Make Fierce Resistance—Greece Repudiates Treaty.

PARIS, Thursday, Oct. 14.—Private advices reaching Bucharest say that a Bulgarian division was almost annihilated in a fierce battle near Kraguyevatz, (Kniashevatz?) Serbia. These advices reach here in a dispatch to the Havas Agency, dated Tuesday.

A Havas dispatch from Turnu-Severin, on the Danube, in Western Rumania dated Tuesday, says:

"The Bulgarians yesterday bombarded a Serbian train laden with munitions between the stations of Badjtuitza and Zaiecar. They destroyed the station at Tabacovatz and a number of wagons. Another Bulgarian attack in the Vraio region is reported."

Bulgars Driven Over Nischava River.

Special Cable to THE NEW YORK TIMES.

GENEVA, Oct. 13. (Dispatch to The London Daily Express.)—Telegrams from Innsbruck state that the Bulgarians have concentrated a large cavalry force at Vidin (on the Serbian frontier) where they are awaiting the Austro-Germans.

The Bulgarians have forced the Serbian frontier on the River Nischava, but were driven back. Sanguinary fighting here continues.

On the Belgrade-Semendria front the Serbians are resisting strongly, but in Bosnia and Herzegovina they are greatly outnumbered and have been forced back.

Coincident with the attack on Serbia the enemy have entered Montenegro at Mokrino and Perasto. The Montenegrins are fighting like lions.

Serbia's only hope now rests in quick aid from the Franco-British forces.

TEUTON ADVANCE AGAINST SERBS SLOW

Invaders Meet Strong Resistance as They Move South From the Danube.

LONDON, Thursday, Oct. 14.—The Serbians, although greatly outnumbered by armies with superior equipment, are making a stubborn defense of their country against the Teutonic host, and while the Austro-German progress is steady, it is very slow, and probably will become slower when the mountains where the Serbians are strongly intrenched are reached.

Zeppelins Raid London, Killing 8 Persons And Wounding 34; Property Damage Slight

LONDON, Thursday, Oct. 14, 12:30 A. M.—Zeppelin airships have made another raid over London, dropping bombs. Eight persons are reported to have been killed and about thirty-four injured. The material damage done is said to have been small.

The Home Office soon after midnight made the following report on the raid:

A Zeppelin raid was made yesterday evening over a portion of the London area, when a certain number of incendiary and explosive bombs were dropped. The material damage done was small. A few fires resulted, but they were quickly put out by the fire brigade. The Admiralty will issue a statement today when particulars are available.

At present it is only possible to say that no public buildings were injured and that the casualties so far reported number two women and six men killed and about thirty-four injured. With the exception of a soldier killed all these were civilians.

These figures include all the casualties reported at 11:45 oclock Wednesday evening.

Zeppelin Appears Along the Marne and Drops Bombs

PARIS, Thursday, Oct. 14.—A Zeppelin flew over Chateau Thierry (on the right bank of the Marne) last night and dropped five bombs, all of which fell outside the town. No one was injured and there was no property damage. The airship then turned back to its own lines.

The latest German War Office report of the operations says:

The resistance of the Serbians was sufficient to hold up only slightly our forward movement. South of Belgrade the village of Zaleznik and the heights east of the village, on both sides of Topeiderska, were stormed. Attacks upon Pozarevac are continuing most favorable. The Pozarevac-Gradiste road has been crossed in a southerly direction.

Pozarevac is on the Morava River a few miles southeast of Semendria.

The official report from Vienna says:

Our attacks are proceeding everywhere in spite of most severe resistance on the part of the enemy. On the Lower Drina our troops ejected the enemy from several trenches. South of Belgrade we captured stubbornly contested vantage points. Serbian counterattacks always failed with heavy enemy losses.

The Serbian official version of the situation covering Oct. 11 and the night of Oct. 11-12 has been received in a delayed dispatch from Nish, which says:

curred south of Gradiste and southwest of Semendria. Semendria was evacuated in the direction of the village of Lipa. Near Semendria a fierce engagement was fought. The enemy succeeded in occupying Lipa, but at heavy cost.

On the Danube front fighting occurred. There has been no action since, as the enemy had such heavy losses. The battlefield is covered with bodies.

The enemy also attacked near Belgrade, at Velika, Mokri, Loug, and Tourlak.

On the Save and Drina fronts there is nothing of importance to report.

Referring to previous actions the statement says:

On the 9th in the fighting north of Pokarechez (Pozarevac) one of our battalions reached an enemy battery, but was unable to bring the captured battery back to our lines. Our troops dismounted the guns, and brought back all the machine guns except two. The men carrying the latter were killed on the way.

On the 10th the enemy opened a violent bombardment on our positions at Zabrezge. He used asphyxiating shells, which, however, caused no disorder in our ranks. Our soldiers immediately donned masks, and a detachment charged the enemy through the cloud of gas. Taken by surprise, the enemy retreated, some of the troops even recrossing the Save.

Three hours later the enemy renewed the attack, preceding it by a further bombardment of gas shells, but when the enemy troops charged our men not only repulsed them, but captured an officer and thirty soldiers.

Discord Among Bulgarians.

The Allies are closely watching developments in the internal situation in Bulgaria, where many of the people are averse to fighting against the Allies, particularly Russia. It is reported from Paris that General Savoff, former Bulgarian Minister of War and former Commander in Chief of the Bulgarian Army, has resigned his command rather than fight against Russia. It is thought that the advent of Russians in Bulgaria might result in a change in the policy of that country even thus late in the day.

In the meantime the Russians have no easy task before them if they intend to land in that country. Varna and the other Bulgarian ports on the Black Sea, where a landing might be made, have been strongly fortified under the direction of German officers and are protected by mine fields. The Russians could sail up the Danube, as that is an international waterway, but it is doubtful if they have the necessary transports, while to cross Rumania would require the consent of the Government of that country, which, although considered friendly to the Entente powers, might not wish to lend the displeasure of Germany.

Some disappointment is expressed here at the decision of Italy not to participate. Italy has laid claim to great influence in the Balkans and is known to have aspirations in Asia Minor, which the junction of Germans and Turks, it is pointed out, would virtually bring to an end. With superfluous forces and excellent transport facilities, the view is held in London that Italy is in a better position than any of the Allies to lend a hand, and the hope is expressed that she will yet do so.

TERRIFIC ATTACKS FORCE FRENCH BACK

Violent Bombardment, Followed by Desperate German Assaults, Win Ground Near Souchez.

DRIVE PARTLY CHECKED

French Also Fall Back Before Attacks of Germans in Vosges.

LONDON, Oct. 13.—In a series of desperate assaults, preceded by a destructive bombardment with heavy guns, the Germans today succeeded in penetrating the French trenches in a wood near Souchez.

This information is contained in both German and French official reports, the latter while describing the fighting in more detail than the former, insisting that the assaults were repulsed with heavy loss except in the limited area specified. Intense artillery actions are reported at points south of the Somme and thence along the front to the Moselle.

Paris Admits Loss Near Souchez.

Following is the text of the Paris official report issued tonight:

The enemy renewed today with strong forces his attacks to the northeast of Souchez, against the wood "le Bois en Hache," to the east of the road from Souchez to Angres; against our positions on the approaches to the five highways on the crest of Vimy; against the small fort, previously taken by us in the Givenchy Wood, and the neighboring trenches.

Despite the extreme violence of the bombardment which preceded these attacks, despite the desperate nature of the renewed assaults, the enemy was able to penetrate only some parts of the trenches in the Givenchy Wood which had been completely shattered by shells of heavy calibre. Everywhere else we conserved all our positions and repulsed the assault of the Germans, who suffered very heavy losses.

Artillery actions of particular intensity are reported to the south of the Somme, in the sector of Lihons. In Champagne, to the north of Souain and Massiges, in Argonne, to the north of La Harazee, and between the Meuse and the Moselle, to the north of Flirey.

In the Vosges we dispersed by our fire an enemy attack against our positions in the valley of La Laucne.

French Afternoon Report.

The text of the French afternoon communication follows:

At the conclusion of the bombardment reported yesterday, the enemy last evening delivered an infantry attack against our positions to the northeast of Souchez. These attacks, like the preceding ones, were everywhere completely repulsed.

Last night saw artillery actions of great intensity, in which both sides took part, between the Somme and the Oise; in the region of Andechy, and to the east of Rheims, in the direction of Moronvillers. Batteries of the enemy have delivered a violent cannonade in the region to the south of Tahure and to the east of Butte de Mesnil. Our artillery held this fire back effectively, and in the meantime we were making further progress from trench to trench at a point to the east of the earthwork known as "the Trapeze."

"All the News That's Fit to Print."

The New York Times.

THE WEATHER
Fair Monday; local rains Tuesday; shifting winds, becoming south-east and south.
For full weather report see Page II.

VOL. LXV...NO. 21,066. ....   NEW YORK, MONDAY, OCTOBER 18, 1915.—EIGHTEEN PAGES.   ONE CENT In Greater New York, Jersey City and Newark. | Elsewhere TWO CENTS

ALLIED FORCES INVADE BULGARIA, DEFEAT ARMY AND CAPTURE STRUMNITZA; MACKENSEN ASKS FOR MORE TROOPS

ALLIES WIN SWIFT VICTORY

Defeat Bulgars on Serbian Soil and Pursue Foe Over the Border.

NEW ALLIED ARMY ON WAY

Part May Land at Saloniki and Part May Descend on Bulgarian Coast.

GERMANS REPORT ADVANCES

Heights South of Belgrade Are Stormed While Gallwitz Pushes Along the Morava.

Strumnitza Taken by the Allies

Special Cable to THE NEW YORK TIMES.

LONDON, Monday, Oct. 18, 4:20 A. M.—A dispatch from Rome, just received by The Daily Chronicle, reports that the allied British, French, and Serbian forces have occupied Strumnitza, in Bulgaria, after having been attacked by 40,000 Bulgarians at Vilandovo, in Serbia, whom they defeated and pursued into Bulgaria.

Capture Officially Confirmed

LONDON, Monday, Oct. 18, 5:10 A. M.—Strumnitza, in Bulgaria, has been occupied by the allied armies of Great Britain, France, and Serbia, according to official advices telegraphed by the Reuter correspondent at Athens.

Various points, dominating the railway from Saloniki to the interior, have been occupied by allied troops, the correspondent adds, and the protection of the line is regarded as assured.

LONDON, Monday, Oct. 18.—The allied forces from Saloniki have begun operations against the Bulgarians with unex-pected zeal, and already the Serbo-Anglo-French forces have penetrated into Bulgarian territory, just north of the Greek boundary, and are attacking the Bulgarian stronghold of Strumnitza, which is about five miles from the Serbian frontier.

Advices to this effect come from Saloniki by a Reuter message by way of Athens.

It is declared that "the fall of Strumnitza is imminent," and the dispatch continues:

"The Serbs, aided by the Allies, repulsed the Bulgarians, who retreated on Strumnitza.

"It is learned from diplomatic sources that Field Marshal von Mackensen, the German Commander, has demanded reinforcements."

A Rome dispatch quotes this message from Athens, published in the Idea Nazionale, dealing with the operations:

"Serbo-French troops initiated after their success at Vilandovo, a rapid counter-offensive action and penetrated into the enemy's territory and are marching victoriously on Strumnitza, the occupation of which is probable, owing to the feeble resistance of the enemy.

"One-third of the Serbian army has been sent against Field Marshal von Mackensen on the Drina, Save and Danube Rivers, while the other two-thirds have been placed along the eastern front against the Bulgarian forces. The latter at many points have taken the offensive."

This Rome dispatch gives the only inkling of the result of the battle which early Athens messages said was proceeding between French troops and the army of 40,000 Bulgarians, who were reported in Saturday's dispatches as attempting to cut the railroad near the bridges between Hudovo and Vilandovo, about twenty miles from the Greek frontier.

One dispatch from Athens said the Bulgarian artillery was bombarding the Vilandovo garrison, which was offering a stout resistance. Allies were also reported in contact with the invaders near Gievgeli, about nine miles from the frontier. These movements of the Allied forces probably marked the beginning of the drive into Bulgaria, Vilandovo being about twelve miles southwest of Strumnitza.

The allied troops are going to the aid of the Serbians as fast as the railroad facilities from the base will permit. A Malta dispatch of Reuter's says that "signs are not wanting that the Allies in the course of the next few days will be landing strong new forces at Saloniki." Meanwhile France has formally declared war on Bulgaria as from Oct. 16, at 6 A. M.

In addition to pushing the expedition landing at Saloniki, the British, according to a dispatch from Athens to the Paris Journal, will operate along the Bulgarian-Turkish coast at Dedeaghatch and Enos, from which points quick access may be had to the route the Teutonic forces must take to reach Constantinople.

Coasts Mined by Bulgaria.

The Bulgarian Government has announced officially that mines have been laid along the coasts of the Black and Aegean Seas. Lights have been extinguished and the Port of Dedeaghatch has been closed, except to neutral merchantmen.

In their resistance to the Teutonic-Bulgarian invaders the Serbians are being helped by the weather, which is cold and Winter-like. The rains have set in and are impeding the movements of troops and guns, which, at the best, must be slow over what answer for roads in the Balkan States.. The Germans, however, say they have taken the heights south of Belgrade, while along the Danube the army of General von Gallwitz is pushing the Serbians back.

The official report of the operations issued by the Berlin War Office yesterday reads:

The German, Austro-Hungarian and Bulgarian troops continue victorious in Serbia.

All the heights south of Belgrade are in German hands. General von Gallwitz's army has thrown the enemy behind Ralja, southwest of Semendria.

General Boyadjieff's Bulgarian army has forced a passage of the lower Timok and stormed Glopovica mountain, 1,198 metres high, and made prisoners of 200 Serbians. He also took eight cannon. The Bulgarians also have advanced toward Pirot.

General von Mackensen's army up to the present has taken sixty-eight Serbian cannon.

Sofia Reports Many Successes.

The latest Bulgarian official bulletin, received from Sofia yesterday, is dated Friday and is as follows:

Yesterday, despite the bad weather in the theatre of operations—rain and fog and snow on the mountain tops—our armies pursued the offensive slowly, with great exertions, all along the whole front.

On the western slopes of the great Balkan range our troops reached the line of Novokorito, Aldinatz, Repuchnitza, Ravnoboutche, and Tzrnivrh. In the Valley of Nichava our forces occupied the important strategical point of Vraja.

In Macedonia our advance proceeded rapidly. In the region of the Upper Bregalnitza Valley our troops have attained the line of Dratcha, Tchoukagolak, Tchjavka Peak, and Colak Planina, and occupied Tzarevoselo, Pehtchevo, and Beroyo.

A heavy Winter rain fell yesterday in the Austro-German theatre. Nevertheless, the German advance continued, the Serbians being repulsed on the whole front south of Belgrade.

The armies of our allies have reached the line of Rouschani, Pinossava, Lechtani, and Pitopek, and in the Moravo Valley have reached the line of Oudovitche, Salakovatz, Smolianaz, and Gradevo. The Serbians have evacuated the bank of the Danube as far as Golubatz.

The Vienna War Office bulletin has this to say of operations:

Austro-Hungarian and German battalions stormed yesterday in an encircling attack from the north and west the Serbian positions on the Avala Mountains. Austrian troops, advancing on both sides of the road from Belgrade to Grocka, captured the heights of Velky, Malmein, and Pasuli-isse.

Southwest of Semendria and southeast of Pozarevac the enemy was again repulsed by the Germans.

The Bulgarians crossed the Timok below Zaievar and stormed the height of Glogovica, east of Knazevac, capturing 200 prisoners and eight guns. Their attack is everywhere progressing.

Additional reports, says another dispatch from Sofia of the same date, show that the Bulgarian losses in the fighting at Trin and Bosgilegrad were 70 killed and 500 wounded, instead of 18 killed and 190 wounded, according to the figures first available. It is added that the second day's operations by the Bulgarians were notably successful, especially in the direction of Sultan-Tepe, which is con-sidered one of Serbia's strongest positions.

Teuton Force Estimated at 280,000.

The Austro-German troops on the Save-Danube front are estimated at fourteen divisions, (280,000 men,) according to a dispatch to the Paris Temps from Nish under Saturday's date. The Teutonic pressure continues in the region of Pozarevac.

"The Bulgarians," the dispatch continues, "are attacking with large forces along the line between Zaiecar and Kotchane, in the vicinity of Timok and Breganitza. They have succeeded in passing Raikov, Savat, and Stoikovo Brdo.

"To the south the Bulgarians have forced back the Serbians in the region of Kniazevac.

"In the region of Kriva and Palanka, situated on the Kumanovo-Kustendil road, the Bulgarians made an attack with several regiments and succeeded in reaching Tchoupiro Brdo, whence they can menace the cities of Kumanovo and Vranie, and the Nish-Saloniki railroad. At Kotchane, on the Breganitza River, the Serbians are successfully resisting an attack by two Bulgarian divisions.

"The situation is becoming serious, especially in the region of Kumanovo, as it appears that the Bulgarians plan to seize the railroad on this side and separate the Serbian army from the allied troops coming up from Saloniki, and then turn toward the north through the Morava Valley in order to reach Nish.

"The prompt arrival of the Allies at Kumanovo and Vranie is necessary, and the Government and army, as well as all Serbians, are awaiting them with growing impatience."

In its efforts to repress the dissatisfaction that has manifested itself among the people and in the army at its course in turning against Russia, the Bulgarian Government has dismissed summarily from the diplomatic service M. Majoroff, its Minister to Petrograd, who when relations were broken off was quoted in a Russian newspaper as criticising Premier Radoslavoff's policy. He is also to be prosecuted. General Radko Dimitrieff, who has been leading a Russian army against the Austro-Germans, and all other reserve officers who have not returned to Bulgaria are to be considered deserters and treated as such.

OFFICIAL REPORT ON ZEPPELIN RAID

Extensive Damage Inflicted in Five Distinct Areas of London.

ONE SMALL HOTEL WRECKED

Described as a Haphazard Attack, Airships Flying Too High to See Definite Targets.

LONDON, Oct. 17.—The following account of the Zeppelin air raid on Wednesday night was prepared by a writer appointed by the Home Office:

"On the evening of Oct. 13 another aerial attack was directed against London, which differed in no material respect from those made on previous occasions. The enemy's vessel or vessels flew high, at an altitude chosen, no doubt, in order to prevent as far as possible the danger of damage or destruction from anti-aircraft guns.

"The darkening of the metropolitan area, together with the height at which the aircraft traveled, certainly prevented the enemy from discovering the exact position of places of importance.

"As on the last occasion, the official report issued in Berlin proves the raiders to have been grossly in error in most cases as to where they were dropping their bombs, and if we can suppose that they had really some definite objective, other than mere haphazard destruction of the lives and property of noncombatants, then, owing to the height at which they flew, they entirely failed to attain that objective.

"Except for one chance shot, the damage was exclusively on property not connected with the conduct of the war. Of the 127 persons killed or injured, none, save one or two soldiers, who were in the street at the time, were combatants.

Failed to Cause a Panic.

"As for the moral effect for which presumably the enemy was seeking—that was all to his disadvantage. The raid occurred at an hour when practically no one except children was in bed, and, though the shops in the principal shopping areas were closed, places of entertainment were full, and the masses of the population were about their ordinary evening's pleasure or at business.

"A very much larger number of people, therefore, were aware of the enemy's presence than on previous occasions, but the population of London, though hundreds of thousands heard the sound of bursting bombs and the guns, remained cool and free from panic. There were, if possible, even less signs of excitement than on the previous occasions. The official warnings to take shelter were better observed, and when the aircraft passed and the guns ceased firing, most of the people who had been watching the bombardment went quietly to bed, and were undisturbed by the second raid, which took place about midnight in another part of the London area.

"In the theatres, from which the sounds of the firing and explosions could plainly be heard, there was a commendable absence of panic. Altogether the imperturbability of the people of London would appear to offer a striking contrast to the behavior of the population on the occasion of rehearsals of aircraft attacks recently said to have been made on certain German towns.

Bomb Misses Big Crowd.

"When the results of the raid were examined next morning five distinct areas could be distinguished in which damage was done. The first of these is an area in which there is little or no residential property, some large buildings devoted to various kinds of business, and comparatively wide streets. In this area bombs were dropped containing high explosives, which in four cases fell upon the streets, and in the fifth upon the back premises of one large building thronged with people.

"One of the bombs, which apparently was of large size, penetrated the street into the subways containing gas and water mains, and, in exploding, melted the gas pipes, setting alight a fire which, though slight in extent, lasted for several hours. The explosion of this bomb damaged the buildings round about considerably, and destroyed almost all the glass in the neighborhood. It also was responsible for a number of casualties, which will all be the subject of an inquest. Those killed were either sitting in the front rooms of the buildings or were working or walking in the streets.

"The second area contains a large block of residential flats, some of which are occupied as offices. Like many other blocks of flats in London, this one has a stretch of garden behind the buildings, and one of the enemy's high explosive bombs fell in this garden, close to the flats themselves. One or two rooms on the ground floor were totally wrecked, and on the first floor considerable damage was done. Another bomb fell on the top of one of the buildings, demolishing the top story. In this area there were no casualties, though several narrow escapes.

Concrete Resists Bomb.

"The third area contains two damaged business premises. The first of them is a large modern building constructed of reinforced concrete and with steel and concrete roof and flooring. Two bombs were dropped on this building, one of them actually on the roof and one on the pavement immediately beneath the doorway. The bomb on the pavement appears to have exploded sideways. At any rate, the damage done, which consisted chiefly of broken glass and plaster, occurred mainly in the houses on the other side of the street. The bomb which dropped on the roof of the building itself did little damage.

"In the same area a bomb was dropped on the roof of a small hotel, the ground floor of which was occupied as an office. In this case the strength of the building, which was an old one, was not sufficient to withstand the force of the explosion, and the whole of the hotel, which consisted of three floors of the building, was entirely blown up. Fortunately in this area those indoors had been warned by the sound of previous explosions, and by taking refuge in the lower floor they escaped injury altogether. In this area, as by a curious coincidence in one other, the effect of the bombs was severely felt in a small restaurant opened in the interests of Belgian refugees.

"The fourth district in which damage was done is one consisting entirely of what may be called working-class property, with small, low buildings, some of them used to house small shops of various businesses, but in most cases occupied, and in many cases overcrowded, by private residents of the poorer classes.

"In this area more bombs were dropped than in those previously described, and the damage done was exclusively suffered by private traders or householders, who behaved with the utmost heroism and coolness and who suffered damage and, in some cases, loss of life with no compensating military value for the enemy. One group of small houses in this area was entirely destroyed by a single explosive bomb, and in the ruins, above which floats an evil smell of gas and drains, are to be found, torn and covered with dust, account books and documents of some small business which up to 9:30 on Wednesday night no doubt kept alive the owner and his family.

"In another spot in this district a bomb fell on top of a building used for keeping dairy cattle. None of the cattle was killed, though one was injured. The dairyman, with presence of mind and coolness, made his way to the top story of his house near by, in which all the windows were broken and most of the ceilings destroyed by the force of the explosion, and brought down his children to safety below. On his way down stairs on the last journey a further explosion blew him backward on to the floor of one of the rooms, but he succeeded in bringing all his family out unharmed. After the aircraft passed they returned to their rooms until they were wakened again by the sound of guns about midnight.

"In the last area covered by the raid—this time in a suburb—there is not a single factory or business house and hardly any shops. There are no military encampments, no store sheds, no aerial defenses, and not even searchlights. All the property consists of detached or semi-detached houses surrounded by small gardens. It was in this district that, for some obscure reason, the largest number of bombs were dropped, and they must have been launched by what the commander of a Zeppelin in his interview on the last raid described as 'rapid fire.'

"The actual period of bombardment did not last a minute, and the distance from the spot where the first bomb dropped to the last could not have been more than 600 yards. Within sixty yards no less than five fell together, while, near by, three fell in a single garden, which did not measure more than thirty yards square.

"The striking and fortunate feature of the bombardment in this district, and, indeed, of the whole attack on this occasion, is the number of cases in which the bombs dropped, not on the buildings, but on the ground. In only three cases in this suburban area were houses actually struck; though, of course, the force of the explosion was sufficient to destroy whole houses, even at a considerable distance.

Sleeping Women Hurled Into Street.

"Here there were many astonishing escapes. In one instance a bomb fell on a narrow passage, separating two houses, the entire fronts of which were blown out, causing the upper bedroom floors to collapse. In one of the upper bed rooms a mother and daughter were sleeping. They were thrown out onto the street through the place where the ground floor window should have been, both escaping with their lives.

"In the next house a little boy lying in his cot was buried under the débris of the wrecked roof of the house, and in order to release him the whole roof had to be lifted up, so securely was the cot pinned down. There was not a stick of furniture nor a piece of china left whole in either of these two houses; only two small pictures remained with the glass unbroken.

"A large house a few yards away suffered very badly. A bomb fell right on the centre of it, killing instantly two children and severely injuring a third child and the father and mother.

"In the road in which this occurred there are twenty houses without doors or windows, and every house is heavily pitted with shot marks. In one of the houses, where a woman was sitting on a sofa, the door of the room was forced open with such violence that the lock was wrenched from its fastenings and struck the wall within a few inches of the woman's head.

"At another point where a bomb fell in the street, a young man was saying good-night to a woman at the front door of the house. He was killed by a fragment of the bomb and the woman was severely injured. At this point also an old man, who was walking on the pavement, had his arm blown off and died in the hospital shortly afterward."

SAY ALLIES' DRIVE USED 1,620,000 MEN

Germans Publish Another 'Secret Order' Found on a Dead French Officer.

BERLIN, Oct. 17, (By Wireless to Sayville, L. I.)—The following official communication was issued today:

"The hopes put by our enemy in their last offensive and the forces they employed in it are illustrated, aside from General Joffre's order of Sept. 14, which has already been published, by the following order found on a dead French staff officer:

East Army Headquarters, Third Bureau. No. 12,975. General Headquarters, Sept. 21.

Secret order for northern and middle army groups.

To all regiments must be explained, possibly in the following way, the enormous force of the blow which will be executed by the French and British armies:

In the operations will take part thirty-five divisions under General Castelnau, eighteen divisions under General Foch, thirteen English divisions, and fifteen cavalry divisions, among which are five English. Further prepared to enter the battle are thirteen infantry divisions and the Belgian Army. Three-quarters of the French forces will participate in the central battle, helped by 2,000 heavy and 3,000 field guns. The provisions of munitions are now larger than at the beginning of the war.

All the preliminary conditions for certain success have now been removed. It will be remembered that only fifteen divisions and 350 heavy cannon entered into the last offensive near Arras. JOFFRE.

As a division consists of 20,000 men, it will be seen that the alleged order of Joffre indicates that the Allies employed 1,620,000 troops in the recent drive.

PARIS, Oct. 17.—A Paris paper today gives an account of how General Joffre directed the operations during the battle in the Champagne region. Taking a post close to the front, in an innkeeper's kitchen where a telephone had been installed, General Joffre, bending over a large scale map, listened to officers at the telephone, at intervals giving his orders in an absolutely calm voice.

In this position, the newspaper account says, General Joffre remained longer than twenty-two hours—from 9 o'clock in the morning until 7:30 the next morning—neither eating nor drinking during the whole time. At the end of that period, after marking certain places on the map, he put down his pencil and said: "It is over. Let us go take a bite."

'LEAGUE FOR MARRYING OF BROKEN HEROES'

Started by a Clergyman, Who Wants Englishwomen Thus to Sacrifice Themselves.

LONDON, Oct. 13.—The Rev. Ernest Houghton, a Bristol rector, has issued an appeal to patriotic women of the nation to give their lives to ameliorate the condition of maimed heroes of the war by marrying them. He has launched a "League for the Marrying of Broken Heroes."

Mr. Houghton contends that the example of France shows that unions thus arranged promise a greater percentage of happiness than is customary from the methods in England, because they are based upon a high degree of unselfishness.

Strict secrecy is promised as to the identity of women prepared to immolate themselves after the plan of the league until the arrangements for their marriage are complete.

RUSSIAN ARMY TOLD NOT TO SPARE SHELLS

Order Issued to Forces in the South—Output Increased Many Fold.

Special Cable to THE NEW YORK TIMES.

LONDON, Monday, Oct. 18.—A dispatch to The Daily Mail from Odessa dated Thursday, says:

"A new order has been issued to our southern armies not to spare ammunition. Ammunition supplies are now fully organized and the output at present is several times what it was four months ago."

MISS CAVELL SHOT BY GERMAN OFFICER

Englishwoman, Condemned to Death, Said to Have Fainted Before Firing Party.

Special Cable to THE NEW YORK TIMES.

AMSTERDAM, Oct. 17, (Dispatch to The London Daily Mail.)—Such details as it is possible to collect here concerning the execution of Miss Edith Cavell, at Brussels, are as follows:

The charge against her was of aiding Belgians to escape to England. It is stated that she hid them in her house and provided them with money and addresses in England, and helped to smuggle them across the frontier. A German military court found her guilty and sentenced her to death by shooting.

The execution ground was a garden, or yard, in Brussels, surrounded by a wall. The German firing party of six men and an officer were drawn up in the garden and awaited their victim. She was led in by soldiers from the house near by, blindfolded with a black scarf. Up to this minute the woman, though deadly white, had stepped out bravely to meet her fate, but before the rifle party her strength at last gave out and she tottered and fell to the ground, thirty yards or more from the spot where she was to have been shot.

The officer in charge of the execution walked to her as she lay prone on the ground motionless. The officer then drew a large service revolver from his belt, took steady aim from his knee and shot the woman through the head. The firing party looked on as the officer quietly returned his revolver to its case and ordered the soldiers to carry the body to the house where charge was taken of it by a Belgian woman, acting under instruction of the Spanish Minister, who had undertaken the responsibility for the body, pending arrangements for burial.

The execution has shocked the whole Belgian community, who speak of it as the bloodiest act of the whole war.

"All the News That's
Fit to Print."

The New York Times.

THE WEATHER
Fair, much colder Friday; fair
Saturday; moderate northwest
winds, becoming variable.
☞For full weather report see Page 12.

VOL. LXV...NO. 21,090. ....   NEW YORK, FRIDAY, OCTOBER 22, 1915.—TWENTY PAGES.   ONE CENT In Greater New York, Jersey City and Newark. | Elsewhere TWO CENTS.

HURRIED EDITH CAVELL TO DEATH AT NIGHT, IGNORING THE PROTESTS OF DIPLOMATS AND TRYING TO HIDE HER FATE FROM THEM

WHITLOCK MAKES REPORT

News of Sentence Was Kept From Him for Several Hours.

HIS FINAL APPEAL WAS VAIN

Nor Had He Been Able to Gain for Miss Cavell a Chance to Consult Her Counsel.

NO CHARGE OF ESPIONAGE

But Prisoner Admitted Having Aided Allied Soldiers to Escape to England.

LONDON, Oct. 21.—The full report of the circumstances of the condemnation and execution of Miss Edith Cavell, an Englishwoman and head of a training school in Brussels, for helping English, French, and Belgian soldiers to escape from Belgium, made by Brand Whitlock, the American Minister at Brussels, to Walter H. Page, the American Ambassador at London, was issued by the British Government this evening.

How the Secretary of the American Legation, Hugh S. Gibson, sought out the German Governor, Baron von der Lancken, late at night before the execution, and, with the Spanish Minister, pleaded with him and the other German officers for the Englishwoman's life, is graphically related in a memorandum from Mr. Gibson. This document makes reference to an apparent lack of good faith on the part of the German authorities in failing to keep their promises to inform the American Minister fully of the trial and sentence.

Minister Whitlock telegraphed to Ambassador Page on Oct. 12: "Miss Cavell sentenced yesterday and executed at 2 o'clock this morning, despite our best efforts, continued until the last moment."

Final Appeal Just Before Execution.

Mr. Whitlock's final appeal was in the form of a note sent by a messenger late on the night of the 11th to Governor von der Lancken, reading as follows:

"Mon cher Baron: Je suis trop malade pour vous présenter ma requête moi-même, mais je fais appel à votre générosité de coeur pour l'appuyer et sauver de la mort cette malheureuse. Ayez pitié d'elle.

"Votre bien dévoué.
"BRAND WHITLOCK."

[Translation.]

"My dear Baron: I am too sick to present my request myself, but I appeal to your generosity of heart to support it and save from death this unhappy woman. Have pity on her.

"Yours truly.
"BRAND WHITLOCK."

Mr. Whitlock also called the attention of the Governor to the fact that Miss Cavell had nursed German soldiers:

Mr. Deleval, Counselor of the American Legation, reported to Minister Whitlock:

"This morning Mr. Gahan, an English clergyman, told me that he had seen Miss Cavell in her cell yesterday night at 10 o'clock and that he had given her Holy Communion and had found her admirably strong and calm.

Happy to Die for England.

"I asked Mr. Gahan whether she had made any remarks about anything concerning the legal side of her case, and whether the confession which she made before trial and in court was in his opinion perfectly free and sincere. Mr. Gahan said she told him she was perfectly well and knew what she had done; that, according to the law, of course she was guilty, and admitted her guilt, but that she was happy to die for her country."

London Contrasts the Execution of Edith Cavell With Mild Treatment of Woman Spy in England

LONDON, Oct. 21.—English newspapers draw a parallel between the summary execution of Miss Cavell in Belgium and the course taken in England concerning Mrs. Louise Herbert, who was sentenced to six months' imprisonment as a spy.

Mrs. Herbert's appeal was heard at Durham yesterday. She is a German, and the wife of an English curate at Darlington. She admitted that she had sought information regarding munitions and intended to send this information to Germany. The Judge asked her yesterday:

"Did you intend to send the information to Germany if you got the chance?"

"Yes, I did," she replied.

Mrs. Herbert also admitted that she had corresponded with Germany through friends in Switzerland.

The Judge, astonished by her frank answer, remarked: "This woman has a conscience—she wishes to answer truthfully and deserves credit for that. At the same time, she is dangerous."

He affirmed the sentence of six months' imprisonment.

Secretary Gibson's report says that Conrad, an official of the German civil branch, gave positive assurances on the 11th that the American Legation would be fully informed of the developments in the case, and continues:

"Despite these assurances, we made repeated inquiries in the course of the day, the last one being at 6:20 P. M. Mr. Conrad then stated that sentence had not been pronounced, and specifically renewed his previous assurances that he would not fail to inform us as soon as there was any news.

"At 8:30 it was learned from an outside source that sentence had been passed in the course of the afternoon, before the last conversation with Mr. Conrad, and that execution would take place during the night."

Secretary Gibson thereupon sought the Spanish Minister, with the American Minister's note for clemency, and, with Mr. Deleval, they went to von der Lancken's quarters. Finding the Governor and his staff absent, they telephoned to them, asking them to return on a matter of the utmost urgency. The Governor with his staff returned shortly after 10 o'clock.

Governor Denied the Sentence.

Secretary Gibson's report to Minister Whitlock continues:

"The circumstances of the case were explained to him, and your note was presented. He read it aloud in our presence. He expressed disbelief in the report that sentence had actually been passed, and manifested some surprise that we should give credence to any report not emanating from official sources. He was quite insistent on knowing the exact source of our information, but this I did not feel at liberty to communicate to him.

"Baron von der Lancken stated that it was quite improbable that sentence had been pronounced, and even if so it would not be executed in so short a time, and that, in any event, it would be quite impossible to take any action before morning.

"It was, of course, pointed out to him that even if the facts were as we believed them to be, action would be useless unless taken at once. We urged him to ascertain the facts immediately. This, after some hesitancy, he agreed to do. He telephoned to the Presiding Judge of the court-martial, and returned to say that the facts were as we had presented them, and that it was intended to carry out the sentence before morning.

"We then presented as earnestly as possible your plea for delay. So far as I am able to judge we neglected to present no phase of the matter which might have had any effect, emphasizing the horror of executing a woman, no matter what her offense, and pointing out that the death sentence had heretofore been imposed only for actual cases of espionage, and that Miss Cavell was not even accused by the German authorities of anything so serious.

Gibson Warned of Reprisals.

"I further called attention to the failure to comply with Mr. Conrad's promise to inform the legation of sentence. I urged that, inasmuch as the offenses charged against Miss Cavell were long since accomplished, and as she had been for some weeks in a prison, delay in carrying out the sentence could entail no danger to the German cause. I even went so far as to point out the fearful effect of a summary execution of this sort upon public opinion, both here and abroad; and, although I had no authority for doing so, called attention to the possibility that it might bring about reprisals."

Spanish Minister's Urgent Appeal.

Mr. Gibson's report continues:

"The Spanish Minister forcibly supported all our representations and made an earnest plea for clemency. Baron von der Lancken stated that the Military Governor was the supreme authority in matters of his sort, and that an appeal from his decision could be carried only to the Emperor, the Governor General having no authority to intervene in such cases.

"After some discussion he agreed to call the Military Governor on the telephone and learn whether he had already ratified the sentence, and whether there was any chance for clemency.

"He returned in about half an hour and stated that he had been to confer personally with the Military Governor, who said he had acted in the case of Miss Cavell only after mature deliberation; that the circumstances in her case were of such a character that he considered the infliction of the death penalty imperative, and that he must decline to accept your plea for clemency or any representation in regard to the matter.

"Baron von der Lancken then asked me to take back the note which I had presented to him. To this I demurred, pointing out that it was not a requête en grâce, but merely a note to him transmitting a request to the Governor, which was itself to be considered as the requête en grâce.

"I pointed out that this was expressly stated in your note to him and tried to prevail upon him to keep it. He was very insistent, however, and I finally reached the conclusion that, inasmuch as he had read it aloud to us, and we knew he was aware of its contents, there was nothing to be gained by refusing to accept the note, and accordingly I took it back.

"Even after Baron von der Lancken's very positive and definite statement that there was no hope, and that under the circumstances 'even the Emperor himself could not intervene,' we continued to appeal to every sentiment to secure delay.

"The Spanish Minister even led Baron von der Lancken aside in order to say very forcibly a number of things which he would have felt a hesitancy in saying in the presence of the younger officers and of Mr. Deleval, a Belgian subject.

Our Services to Germans Recalled.

"His Excellency talked very earnestly with Baron von der Lancken for about a quarter of an hour. During this time Mr. Deleval and I presented to the younger officers every argument we could think of. I reminded them of our untiring efforts on behalf of German subjects at the outbreak of the war and during the siege of Antwerp. I pointed out that, while our services had been gladly rendered, and without any thought of future favors, they should certainly entitle you to some consideration for the only request of this sort you had made since the beginning of the war.

"Unfortunately our efforts were unavailing. We persevered until it was only too clear that there was no hope of securing any consideration for the case. We left shortly after midnight, and I immediately returned to the legation to report to you.

"HUGH GIBSON."

Counselor of Legation Deleval reported to Mr. Whitlock that on the failure of the German authorities to reply to Mr. Whitlock's request of Aug. 31 that Mr. Deleval be permitted to see Miss Cavell in order to have all necessary steps taken for her defense, another letter was dispatched on Sept. 10, to which a German reply on Sept. 12 refused the request, but referred him to Attorney Kirschen, who had been assigned for the defense.

Documents Kept from the Defense.

Attorney Kirschen, Mr. Deleval reported, stated that Miss Cavell was being prosecuted for helping soldiers cross the frontier, and that lawyers defending prisoners before a German military court were not allowed to see their clients before trial, and were not permitted to see any document of the prosecution, but that trial was developed so carefully and slowly that it was possible to have a fair knowledge of all the facts and present a good defense for the prisoner.

"I informed Mr. Kirschen," Mr. Deleval's report continues, "of my intention to be present at the trial so as to watch. He dissuaded me from taking such an attitude, which, he said, would cause great prejudice to the prisoner, because the German judges would resent it and feel that it was almost an affront if I was appearing to exercise a kind of supervision on the trial."

Mr. Deleval's report says that Attorney Kirschen assured him repeatedly that the Military Court of Brussels was always perfectly fair, and that Herr Kirschen would keep him informed of all developments in the case, but that Herr Kirschen failed to give him any information, and that after the trial Mr. Deleval learned from other sources the following:

Miss Cavell Admitted the Charges.

"Miss Cavell was prosecuted for having helped English and French soldiers, as well as Belgian young men, to cross the frontier and go to England. She admitted by signing a statement before the day of the trial and by public acknowledgment in court that she was guilty of the charges, not only that she had helped these soldiers to cross the frontier, but also that some of them had thanked her in writing when arriving in England.

"This last admission made her case more serious, because if it had only been proved she had helped soldiers to traverse the Dutch frontier, and no proof was produced that those soldiers had reached a country at war with Germany, she could have only been sentenced for an attempt to commit the crime, and not for the crime being duly accomplished.

"As the case stood, the sentence fixed by the German military law was the sentence of death."

The report of Mr. Deleval says that Miss Cavell, in her oral statement before the court, disclosed almost all the facts of the prosecution. She spoke without trembling and showed a clear mind, and often added some statement of greater precision to her previous depositions.

"When she was asked why she helped these soldiers to go to England," the report of Mr. Deleval continues, "she replied that she thought if she had not done so they would have shot by the Germans. Therefore she thought she only did her duty to her country in saving their lives.

"The military prosecutor said the argument might be good for English soldiers, but that it did not apply to Belgian young men, who would have been perfectly free to remain in the country without danger to their lives."

Herr Kirschen made a good plea for Miss Cavell, says the report, but the military prosecutor asked the court for a death sentence for her and for eight others of the thirty-five persons on trial. The court seemed not to agree, and judgment was postponed. The trial lasted two days, ending Oct. 8.

Not Allowed to See a British Clergyman.

Mr. Deleval's request on the 10th for permission for an English clergyman to see Miss Cavell was denied, the report says. He was told she could see the three Protestant clergymen attached to the prison.

On the evening of the 11th Mr. Deleval learned from unofficial sources that the sentence of death had been passed at 5 o'clock in the afternoon, and that Miss Cavell would be shot at 2 o'clock in the morning.

On Oct. 9 Mr. Whitlock notified Ambassador Page that a sentence of death had been asked for, but that he had hopes the Court might decline to grant it. Mr. Whitlock added that he felt it would be useless to take any action until the sentence was pronounced.

Whitlock's Appeal to Germans.

The letter sent by Mr. Whitlock to Baron von der Lancken at the hands of Mr. Gibson on the night of the 11th, follows:

"Your Excellency:

"I have just learned that Miss Cavell, who is a British subject and consequently under the protection of my Embassy, was this morning condemned to death by sentence of court martial. Without going into the causes which led to such a severe sentence, and one which, if all the reports which have reached me are correct, is more severe in this case than in all others which have been tried by the same tribunal, I hope to be able to appeal to the sentiments of humanity and generosity of His Excellency, the Governor General, on behalf of Miss Cavell, in order that the sentence of death which has been passed against her may be commuted, and that this unhappy lady be not executed.

"Miss Cavell is the head nurse of a surgical institute of Brussels. She has spent her life in alleviating the sufferings of others, and at her school have been trained numerous nurses who, throughout the world, in Germany as in Belgium, have kept watch at the bedsides of patients. At the beginning of the war Miss Cavell gave her services to German soldiers as well as to others.

"Failing other reasons, her humanitarian career is of a nature to inspire pity for her, and, in advance, to secure her pardon.

"If the information given me is correct, Miss Cavell, far from hiding herself, with laudable frankness admitted all the facts laid to her charge, and the information she supplied was the cause of aggravating the sentence passed upon her.

"It is with confidence and hope of its being favorably received that I pray your Excellency to present to the Governor-General my request for grace in favor of Miss Cavell.

"I take this occasion to renew to your Excellency assurances of my high consideration.

"BRAND WHITLOCK."

Every Possible Effort Made.

In a report to Mr. Page Mr. Whitlock wrote:

"I know that you will understand without my telling you that we exhausted every possible effort to prevent the infliction of the death penalty, and that our failure has been felt by us a very severe blow. I am convinced, however, that no step was neglected which could have had any effect.

"From the date we first learned of Miss Cavell's imprisonment we made frequent inquiries of the German authorities and reminded them of their promise that we should be fully informed as to developments. They were under no misapprehension as to our interest in the matter."

The British Foreign Office, in a note to Ambassador Page, asking him to express to Mr. Whitlock and his staff the British Government's grateful thanks for their efforts in behalf of Miss Cavell, says:

"Sir Edward Grey is confident that the news of the execution of this noble Englishwoman will be received with horror and disgust, not only in the allied States, but throughout the civilized world.

Not Even Charged with Espionage.

"Miss Cavell was not even charged with espionage, and the fact that she had nursed numbers of wounded German soldiers might have been regarded as a complete reason in itself for treating her with leniency.

"The attitude of the German authorities is, if possible, rendered worse by the discreditable efforts successfully made by officials of the German civil administration at Brussels to conceal the fact that the sentence had been passed and would be carried out immediately.

"These efforts were, no doubt, prompted by a determination to carry out the sentence before an appeal from the finding of the court-martial could be made to a higher authority, and show in the clearest manner that the German authorities were well aware that the carrying out of the sentence was not warranted by any consideration. Further comment on these proceedings would be superfluous."

Sir Edward Grey adds that he is fully satisfied that the American Legation left no stone unturned to secure a fair trial for Miss Cavell and a mitigation of her sentence.

Stayed in Brussels to Give Help.

LONDON, Oct. 21.—The Morning Post publishes a letter from a cousin of Miss Cavell concerning her devotion to her work as a nurse:

"My cousin's intense devotion to the alleviation of suffering caused her to devote her life to nursing in Brussels," the letter says. "She voluntarily remained there to continue her work when the city was taken by the Germans. She would have nursed a German with as much tender care as an Englishman.

"In a letter to me she said: 'We have no wounded here now. The Allies do not come here, and the Germans are sent back to their own country. The few that remain are nursed by their own countrywomen, so we are denied the great consolation of being of use in our own special way.'

"She allowed the womanly quality of compassion to get the better of prudence and self-interest. For this she has suffered untold miseries and died a martyr's death."

MISS CAVELL'S DEATH INFLAMES ENGLAND

Her Execution is Denounced as 'the Most Damnable Crime of the War.'

LONDON, Friday, Oct. 22.—The story of the execution of Edith Cavell, as told in the correspondence sent by the American Minister at Brussels to the American Ambassador at London, is printed in full in the morning papers, which predicted that it will send a wave of indignation throughout the country.

In Trafalgar Square yesterday all heads were bared to the memory of Miss Cavell. One speaker, holding in his hand a wreath to her memory, to be placed on the plinth of the Nelson Column, exclaimed:

"Who will avenge the murder of this splendid Englishwoman?" In response to this appeal many new recruits came forward.

The London papers, in their editorials, while paying tribute to the fine efforts of the American diplomatic representatives in her behalf, characterize her execution as "the most damnable crime of the war."

The Daily Graphic says:

"The documents issued are a record of such foul and damnable infamy as all Germany's bloody crimes in this war cannot equal; for this was cold, calculated, and deliberate murder. Not heaven itself, nor all the mercy of all the angels, could find a mediatory expiation."

The Daily Mail in an editorial says:

"It is a deed which in horror and wicked purposelessness stuns the world and cries to Heaven for vengeance."

The Daily Telegraph says:

"We cannot be too grateful to those American and Spanish officials who worked with such passionate zeal in behalf of our unhappy countrywoman."

Special Cable to THE NEW YORK TIMES.

LONDON, Friday, Oct. 22.—The Daily Chronicle says of the Cavell case this morning:

"The papers communicated by the American legation at Brussels regarding the trial and execution of Miss Cavell record surely one of the most appalling wickednesses yet perpetrated in this war. We pity the man, born of woman, who can read them unmoved. One may safely affirm that, having regard to her transparently humanitarian motives and all the circumstances of the case, no Government in the world but the German would have inflicted the death penalty on such a culprit. They not merely inflicted it, but compassed its infliction with a mixture of duplicity and brutality that must make every decent human being's gorge rise.

"Only less amazing than the futile cruelty of the thing is the series of lies and subterfuges whereby it sought to trick the American Legation and to secure that Miss Cavell should be dead before they could finally protest. The sense of the whole civilized world can be left to judge between this helpless woman and her murderers."

"All the News That's Fit to Print."

The New York Times.

THE WEATHER
Fair Monday and Tuesday; warmer; moderate north winds.
For full weather report see Page 13.

VOL. LXV...NO. 21,603. .... NEW YORK, MONDAY, OCTOBER 25, 1915.—EIGHTEEN PAGES. ONE CENT In Greater New York, Jersey City and Newark. | Elsewhere TWO CENTS

ARREST GERMAN FOREIGN OFFICE MAN HERE AS A SPY WITH EXPLOSIVES TO BLOW UP SHIPS LEAVING NEW YORK

BOMB FACTORY IN HIS ROOM

Prisoner, an Officer in the Kaiser's Army, Carried Map of Harbor.

MECHANIC AID ALSO TAKEN

Telescope Device Found in Lodgings, with Supply of Most Powerful Explosive.

The attempt by two Germans to buy ten pounds of picric acid, the chemical which enters into the composition of most high explosives, from a New York firm a few weeks ago resulted yesterday afternoon in the arrest in a wood near Grantwood, N. J., of Robert Fay and Walter Scholz, who are locked up in the Weehawken police station on the charge of conspiracy.

Fay, according to papers found in the apartments which the two men shared at 27 Fifth Street, Weehawken, is a Lieutenant in the German Army. It is said that he took part in the battle of the Marne, and came to the United States last April.

Other documents found in his rooms indicate a connection, according to the Federal Secret Service men and the New York and New Jersey detectives who made the arrest, with the German Foreign Office. What this connection was no one would say last night, but it is intimated that there can be no doubt that he had close relations with Wilhelmstrasse.

Fay is 34 years old and a man of culture and refinement. He speaks English fluently and possesses a striking personality. Scholz is 27 and a mechanic, who has been in this country two years. It is said that he represented himself as Fay's brother-in-law.

Held for Conspiracy.

The two men are held on the charge of conspiracy, and will be arraigned this morning before Recorder Rander in Weehawken. But it is understood that they are believed to have been connected with a recent explosion in a West Shore Railroad elevator in Weehawken, and it is intimated by the detectives that there is reason for connecting them with the series of explosions in ammunition factories, of bomb explosions on board steamers carrying supplies to the anti-German coalition in Europe, which has been a feature of the American export trade in munitions for the last few months.

Explosions Said to Have Been Set by Spies on Ships and in Powder Plants Making Munitions

ON STEAMSHIPS.

Sailed	Sailed
March 6—Touraine.	May 8—Bankdale.
April 27—The Devon City.	July 9—Minnehaha.
April 29—The Lord Erne.	July 24—Craigside.
April 29—Cressington Court.	Sept. 8—Athinai.
May 1—Sandland.	Sept. 13—Sant' Anna.
May 1—Lord Downshire.	Dynamite found on Arabic on
May 2—Kirkoswold.	Aug. 4.
May 8—Strathtay.	

IN THE MUNITION PLANTS.

April 1—Equitable powder plant, Alton, Ill.
March 5—Du Pont plant, Haskell, N. J.
April 4—Caps for shells exploded in Pompton Lakes, N. J., freight depot.
May 10—Du Pont plant, Carney's Point, N. J.
May 15—Two explosions same place.
May 25—Explosion same place.
July 15—Central Railroad grain elevator, Weehawken.
Aug. 11—Westinghouse Electric plant, Turtle Creek, Penn.
Aug. 29—Dupont plant, Wilmington, Del.

In the men's rooms, and in a compartment in a West Hoboken storage warehouse which it is said they rented, were found explosives of the highest power, together, according to the police story, with mines fitted out with apparatus for attaching them to the sterns of ships.

The apprehension of the two men began with the activity of Acting Detective Captain Thomas Tunney, in charge of the dynamite squad at New York Police Headquarters, who was ordered by Commissioner Woods some time ago to devote his energies to hunting down the men who have been concerned in the placing of bombs on merchant ships. Tunney and his men thereupon started a careful scrutiny of every place in Manhattan where high explosives are manufactured, stored, or sold, and every man who came or went, who bought or sold anything, was carefully looked over and investigated. It was some time ago that the two Germans who tried to make the purchase of picric acid came under Tunney's observation. His men followed them when they left the place where they had tried to buy the explosives, followed them across the river into New Jersey, and up to the apartment house in Fifth Street, Weehawken.

Secret Service Joins Work.

For some time after that New York and New Jersey detectives kept a watch on the two. It was discovered, according to the police, that they were in the habit of taking a trolley car to a lonely spot near Grantwood, there to make experiments with explosives, small quantities of which they took with them. After the police had found this out Chief William J. Flynn of the Federal Secret Service was notified, and he sent up two of his men, James Bush and James E. Savage, to take part in the investigation.

Yesterday afternoon Captain Tunney, Detective Lieutenant Barnetz, and several of his men, accompanied by Fifth Deputy Police Commissioner Guy H. Scull and Inspector of Combustibles Healy, crossed over to Jersey and were joined by Bush and Savage, Detective Lyons of Weehawken, and Detective Lieutenant Charles Gillman of Union Hill.

The two men who had been under surveillance left the apartment in Fifth Street about the middle of the afternoon, carrying something with them in a suitcase. They got on a car to Grantwood and one of the detectives took the same car and went along with them.

The others followed in an automobile, keeping as near to the street car as they could, until the two suspects got off, near Grantwood. Then the officers came up rapidly, followed the two into the wood, and made the arrest.

The article which the two had in the suitcase, according to the police, was something believed to be a bomb, made on the model of a telescope. The outer casing was an iron pipe four inches in diameter. Within it was another pipe, and still another, and it is believed that the space between was to have been filled with explosives.

The two men were taken back to the Weehawken Station, where they were still being questioned by the Secret Service men at midnight. Meanwhile others of the party of Federal and local detectives went back to the apartment on Fifth Street and searched it. There, they say, they found the documents proving the connection of Fay with the German Army and the German Foreign Office. They found also 200 letters in German, mostly addressed to Fay, which are now in the possession of the Secret Service officers and are being translated. And they found a United States Coast Survey map showing New York Harbor with all its docks and piers in great detail.

There was a raised platform in one of the rooms on which were a considerable number of mechanisms of various kinds which the police believe to be intended for the manufacture of bombs. There were also four suitcases containing twenty-five sticks of dynamite and twenty-five pounds of trinitrotoluol, which is one of the highest of known explosives, and is the one used in most

high explosive shells. This is more powerful than anything in the outfit of Erich Muenter, alias Frank Holt, the German-American who last July set off a bomb in the Capitol at Washington and later committed suicide in the jail at Mineola, L. I., where he had been confined after an attempt to murder J. P. Morgan.

From information obtained in the observation of previous days and confirmed by papers found in the apartment occupied by the two men the police thereupon went to the Victor Storage Warehouse at 245 Clinton Avenue, West Hoboken, where they found five packing cases which it is said Fay and Scholz had put away there.

Mines to Blow Up Ships.

In these cases, according to the police, were five explosive mines, contained in steel boxes, with attachments which are believed to be designed for fastening the mines to the rudders of steamers. It is the theory of the Secret Service mechanics, who have inspected the mechanism, that the rush of water from the propeller would start a clockwork device which would bring about the explosion of the mine at a certain time.

There were also, according to the police, other bombs which might have been intended for placing inside ships among the cargo to start fires, as has been done several times during the past few months.

Then, after the apartment had been ransacked, the detectives went to Herzog's garage on Main Street, Union Hill, where they found a high-power automobile in Fay's name. It is said to be capable of ninety miles an hour.

In Degan's boathouse, on the Hudson, they found a high-power motor boat, which would have been able to run all over the waters about New York at a speed such as could have been approximated by very few other craft of any description in the harbor.

It is believed that the factory where the men made their explosives was somewhere near Grantwood, and the police are now searching all that neighborhood in the hope of finding some clue which may lead them to the plant.

J. C. Harperson, proprietor of the rooming house at 27 Fifth Street, Weehawken, where Fay and Scholz made their home, said that he knew nothing of the men prior to their appearance at his house about a week ago, when they engaged their rooms. He said he had had no difficulty with them and that they had been quiet and unobtrusive.

Fay Cool Under Grilling.

The two made not the slightest resistance when arrested; Fay, indeed, gave himself up with a quiet smile to the detectives, and remained unruffled after hours of grilling by Secret Service men and the New York and New Jersey police. Deputy Police Commissioner Scull, who himself was formerly in the Secret Service, took charge of the quizzing of Fay and was still at it at midnight.

Despite the statement that Scholz was Fay's brother-in-law, the police are inclined to believe that he was only a subordinate, and that Fay is the principal and the brainy man of the two. Neither of the men would say anything last night, and no clue to their connections in Germany could be obtained, aside from those which the police found in their correspondence.

When it was suggested that a man named Scholz had once had an intimate connection with the personal entourage of Emperor William II. the Secret Service men said that there was no reason to believe that this was the man.

The bombs which have been exploded from time to time this Summer in the cargoes of outward-bound liners carrying munitions of war have been all set off by clockwork, so far as is known, although as a rule no fragments of the infernal machine have been found. But clockwork bombs under water, such as those found in the Clinton Avenue storage warehouse, are believed to be, have been used very rarely.

It was some such idea that was conceived by Bushnell, the inventor of the first submarine, who planned to attach mines to be exploded by clockwork to the British ships off the New England coast in the Revolutionary War; and a similar plan was entertained by Robert Fulton when he experimented with submarines in the war of 1812.

But with the development of electrical appliances engineering ingenuity ran more to contact mines or those exploded from the shore by an electric spark, and the clockwork mine as an implement of warfare against warships has practically disappeared.

For the purpose of being fastened under the stern of a merchant ship, however, it seems to be well adapted; the clockwork not starting so long as the vessel is lying at dock, but only being set off by the rush of water from the propeller when the ship steams out to sea.

The New York Times.

THE WEATHER
Fair Sunday and Monday; moderate northwest to north winds.
For full weather report see Page 21

VOL. LXV...NO. 21,106. ...   NEW YORK, SUNDAY, NOVEMBER 7, 1915.—104 PAGES, In Seven Parts, Including Picture and Rotogravure Sections and Review of Books.   PRICE FIVE CENTS.

KITCHENER OFF TO AID IN BALKANS; RETAINS POST AS WAR SECRETARY; NISH CAPTURED BY THE BULGARS

KITCHENER RUMORS SPREAD

Government Strongly Denies That He Is Out of the Cabinet.

FITTED FOR THIS TASK

Has Knowledge of the East— May Go On to Egypt to Study Its Defenses.

LONDON PAPER SUPPRESSED

The Globe Seized for Insisting That War Secretary Had Offered His Resignation.

LONDON, Nov. 6.—Earl Kitchener, the British War Secretary, has gone to the eastern theatre of war at the request of his colleagues, apparently to study the situation in that now critical field of conflict.

Disturbing rumors concerning the departure of Kitchner from the country and stories that he had resigned from the Cabinet, or was about to do so, filled London all day. To settle these reports two official statements were issued during the day and another tonight, the latter stating in behalf of the Cabinet that the War Secretary's journey was being made at the express wish of his colleagues.

This official statement was issued earlier in the day.

"Earl Kitchener, at he request of his colleagues, has left England for a short visit to the eastern theatre of war."

At night this additional bulletin was issued:

"The statement that Earl Kitchener has resigned his post as Secretary of State for War has already been authoritatively denied. It is equally untrue to suggest that Earl Kitchener has tendered his resignation or that his visit to the King had any relation to any such subject, or that his visit to the Eastern theare of war in any way betokens that such resignation is contemplated.

"On the contrary, this visit is undertaken by him in discharge of his duty as Secreatary of State for War, which duty he has no intention of abandoning."

May Visit Egypt and Gallipoli.

The announcement that Lord Kitchener was to visit the East did not come as a surprise in well-informed circles. It was generally believed when it became known he was about to undertake a mission that the Balkans would be his destination, for there is no man in the British Empire better equipped with a knowledge of near Eastern affairs, military and political, than he.

It is thought that his activities will not be confined to this theatre of the war, however, but that he will visit Egypt to inspect the defenses of the Suez Canal against a possible German or Turkish attack; Mesopotamia, where the British expedition is doing bigger things than was expected of it, and is now nearing Bagdad; and the Dardanelles, where steps are being taken to push the operations to a conclusion.

Besides this, it is understood that his duties will include efforts to co-ordinate the work of the general staffs of the Allied Armies.

It is thought impossible for Premier Asquith to hold both offices of Prime Minister and Minister of War for any length of time. The Earl of Derby, Director of Recruiting, has been mentioned as a possible incumbent during Earl Kitchener's absence.

When the vote of credit is introduced by the Premier in the House of Commons on Wednesday there will be full opportunity for debate and for the extraction of such information as the Government is then in a position to furnish.

The Globe Seized; Resignation Denied.

The London Globe, which has been bitter in its attacks on the conduct of the war and which announced yesterday that Kitchener had resigned, was seized and suppressed by the police today. In today's issue it stuck to its guns and again asserted that Kitchener has resigned because of "manoeuvres and machinations" of politicians. It added that King George had refused to accept his resignation.

This reiteration brought forth another authorized categoricol statement to the contrary, as follows:

"Not only is it untrue that Earl Kitchener has resigned, but it is equally untrue that his Lordship ever tendered his resignation to the King."

This action against The Globe is the first action of the kind taken by the authorities since the outbreak of the war against a daily paper in the United Kingdom. Some weekly papers, both in England and in Ireland, including The Labor Leader, were similarly treated some time ago, but The Labor Leader, after a secret trial of the case, was allowed to resume publication.

Linked with Joffre's Visit.

Comment in the morning newspapers indicated a belief in some quarters that the sudden development regarding Earl Kitchener related to the visit of General Joffre, the French Commander in Chief, to London recently. In this connection The Weekly Nation made an interesting revelation,

"General Joffre's visit," it says, "has been one of the personal sensations of the war. Our politicians expected to find a strategist; they saw, rather, the orator and enthusiast. It would not be right to say they were carried off their feet, but the air has been magnetic, and resulting decisions have been rapid. Who, on such authority, can dispute them?"

The Daily Chronicle editorially points out the various possibilities of the situation. First, the probability of a marked addition to the importance of the General Staff in London, the tendency of which would be to separate clearly the administrative responsibilities of the War Minister from the strategic responsibilities of the Chief of Staff, and make the War Minister's rôle different from that which Earl Kitchener hitherto has filled. Secondly, it added, there was a remote possibility of some kind of joint staff being constituted by the Allies at Paris for the purpose of pooling military councils.

"If this were done," says The Chronicle, "the head of the British section would manifestly occupy a very important position.

"Thirdly, it is possible that in view of the importance of our Near Eastern armies, some higher eastern command might be constituted to co-ordinate their action. For such a post Lord Kitchener's peculiar authority in Oriental matters might be thought to mark him out. Fourthly, there are a number of problems centring more closely on India."

The Daily Mail also points out that General Joffre's visit was concerned with the decision to secure closer co-operation of the Allies. "It was recognized," says The Mail, "that time was being lost and decisions delayed by references from London to Paris and vice versa, and that Germany had a great advantage in centralized staff control of military operations. What is wanted is a General Staff with the ablest available soldier to co-ordinate British operations and provide equipment equal or superior to the German."

Praise for Kitchener.

Nearly all the morning papers pay high tribute to Earl Kitchener, acknowledging the debt which the nation owes him. Even The Mail, which formerly had attacked the War Minister, says that he "is entitled to claim all the credit of the considerable achievements accomplished under his unfettered direction, and he must also bear all the blame for shortcomings.

"Whatever regrets the public may feel at the temporary absence of an old and trusted servant may be assuaged by the prosecution of the war with greater vigor. * * * For the conception of new armies running into the millions, Lord Kitchener deserves the greatest credit."

The Times, remarking that circumstances lately have freed the Field Marshal from the whole business of recruiting, which had been his great preoccupation during the first year of the war, says:

"Lord Derby's scheme now is in full progress and Lord Kitchener's presence at the War Office cannot materially assist it. He is therefore at liberty to divert his attention to other matters. Of these, by far the most urgent is the new development of the war in the Near East, a theatre of which Lord Kitchener possesses long standing and first hand knowledge. It would not be unnatural, therefore, if for the time being he were to devote himself entirely to consultation with the Allies for a settlement of that tangled problem."

"It is generally believed," says The Post, "that Earl Kitchener's business will necessitate a stay so prolonged that it will be necessary to fill his place at the War Office before long. It is true that he has not resigned, but the importance of his present errand makes it certain that his resignation is only delayed.

"The suggestion has been made that Lord Haldane be brought back to the War Office, but this is probably unfounded."

The Graphic, urging the Government not to delay disclosure of the actual facts, suggests that Lord Derby, who is now in charge of British recruiting, would make an excellent War Minister. The Graphic says it is conceivable that Earl Kitchener has arrived at the conclusion that he can serve his country better in the field than in Whitehall.

"A new and important campaign," the newspaper continued, "is opening in the Balkans, and the country would gain renewed confidence if it knew that Earl Kitchener would assume the chief command. His administrative work at the War Office is practically ended. The new armies he has raised are trained and in the field. The work of collecting still further armies can safely be entrusted to other hands. Lord Derby has done splendid work in this respect, and it may be that Lord Kitchener feels that now the soldier's task is more pressing than that of the administrator."

SERBS' WAR CAPITAL FALLS

Bulgarian Army Marches Into Nish But Gets Little Booty.

TEUTONS ALSO SWEEP ON

Form Junction with Main Bulgar Force and Quick Advance Is Looked For.

ALLIES RUSHING UP TROOPS

Those Already in the Field Defeat the Bulgars in the South.

LONDON, Sunday, Nov. 7.—Bulgarian troops have occupied Nish, the Serbian war capital, which gives them complete control of the railway from Prahovo, on the Danube, and thus opens a through route for the central powers to Sofia and Constantinople.

In addition to this Teutonic success, which caused the more gloom in London yesterday because of the coincidence with the disturbing rumors about Lord Kitchener, the main Bulgarian and German armies have effected a junction at Krivivir, northwest of Nish.

As a result of the union of forces the campaign against Serbia, which has been somewhat slower than expected, will probably move at a faster pace. In fact, the invasion of King Peter's domain is already gathering more headway. Official reports from Berlin and Vienna indicate that all the invading forces are making progress against Serbia's resistance, except in the south, near the Greek frontier.

In that region, however, according to reports coming from the German Legation at Athens and also from Serbian sources, the British, French, and Serbians, who are evidently in superior force, have inflicted a severe defeat on the Bulgarians at Izvor, ten miles west of the Vardar River, and at the entrance to Babuna pass, where the French left wing joins the right of the Serbian southern army. The Bulgars are reported to be retreating toward Veles. British cavalry and French infantry are said to be engaged in this battle.

Allies Rushing Up Troops.

More allied troops are being sent from Saloniki to the scene of the fighting, in the hope that they will be able, by the capture of Veles, to compel the Bulgarians, who advanced west of Uskub and Veles, to retire and clear the Saloniki-Mitrovitza railway so that assistance can be sent to the Serbs' northern army.

All assistance that reaches the Serbians must apparently be sent by the British and French, for, despite the defeat of the Zaimis Government and the triumph of Venizelos in the Greek Chamber, there is no evidence yet that Greece intends to change her policy of " benevolent neutrality " and join the war on the side of the Allies.

Meanwhile Rumania, like Greece, is remaining neutral in the face of agitation in favor of intervention to aid the Allies.

No news is forthcoming concerning the Russian expedition, which was reported early in the week to have been massed on the Rumanian frontier. Russian attacks are, however, preventing the Austro-Germans from dispatching any additional troops from her front to the Balkans.

There is evidence of renewed allied activity on the Gallipoli Peninsula, and the impression prevails here that another big attempt will be made to open the straits before the German ammunition reaches the Turks.

The Petit Parisian's correspondent at Saloniki takes a cheerful view of the situation in the south. He cables under date of Friday:

" The Serbian situation has improved in the view of the British and French staffs at Saloniki. British troops, in splendid form, now have taken their place in the first line.

" The Serbians are still holding on at Prilip, according to a wireless message. The Bulgarians subjected the French at Krivolak to an intense bombardment for forty-eight hours. The net result was one man wounded.

" Fresh troops left today for the Serbian front as well as convoys of arms, munitions, and provisions."

Teuton Report of Successes.

The official bulletin issued in Berlin says:

In the valley of the Western Morava fighting goes on. To the southeast of Cacak the town of Kraljevo has been taken. The enemy is being pursued to the east of Kraljevo, and Etubal has been reached.

The Zupanyevac sector has been crossed. In the valley of the Morava our troops pressed on after the enemy as far as Obrez-Sikirica.

By means of a clever stroke our troops took possession of Varvarin during the night. More than 3,000 Serbians were taken prisoners.

At Krivivir a connection between the fighting German and Bulgarian main forces has been established.

The army of General Boyadjieff (Bulgarian) has defeated its opponents near Lukovo and near Sokobanya. More than 500 prisoners were taken and six cannon were captured.

After battles which lasted three days the fortified capital of Nish was captured yesterday afternoon, notwithstanding the stubborn resistance of the Serbians. During battles in the headlands 350 prisoners and two cannon fell into the hands of the Bulgarians.

The Austrian official report on operations in the Balkans says:

Austro-Hungarian forces operating on the Montenegrin border stormed on Thursday Ilinobordo Mountain, east of Trebinje, thus breaking through the Montenegrin main position. Yesterday the enemy was thrown back near the Klobuk Runs.

The Austro-Hungarians of General von Koevess's Army gained the defile of Kisura, south of Arilje. Another column drove the enemy across the Jelica and southeast of Cacak.

German troops occupied Kraljevo further southeastward German and Austro-Hungarian detachments crossed the Western Morava.

General von Gallwitz's Army is approaching Ravini, north of Krusevac. Nish is in Bulgarian hands. They also took Banja and the heights west of Lukovo.

This bulletin of the Bulgarian War Office, which reached London last night, apparently refers to Thursday's fighting:

On Thursday in the direction of Aleksinac (about twenty-three miles northwest of Nish) our troops reached Soko-Banja. After heavy fighting we captured the advance positions of Nish on the northern and eastern front of the fortress, taking 2 guns, 8 ammunition cars, and 400 prisoners.

On the railway between Kulajevats and Sorlijig we captured 1 engine and 103 wagons with a great quantity of material for troops.

South of Strumitza our troops were attacked by numerically superior Anglo-French forces. We repulsed them by heavy counterattacks at the point of the bayonet, inflicting severe losses. The fighting against the French is developing favorably for us on the front of Krivolak-Sonitchi-Glava.

An official bulletin issued by the Montenegrin Consul at Paris says:

Since Nov. 1 the activity of the enemy has been most pronounced on the entire Herzegovinian frontier. Furious infantry attacks against our positions have been supported by intense fire from heavy artillery. Fighting has been going on day and night all week.

Our troops are vigorously repulsing every assault of the Austrians, who have succeeded in occupying only one unimportant point on the frontier. Their losses are enormous. Ours are light.

SERB CAMPAIGN WON IN BERLIN OPINION

Newspaper Think the Fall of Nish Has Settled Conflict In Teutons' Favor.

From a Staff Correspondent.
Special Cable to THE NEW YORK TIMES.
BERLIN, Nov. 6.—The occupation of Nish again gives the German press occasion to hymn praise of the Bulgar ally, the principal cause of rejoicing being the fact that this capture gives the Teutonic forces possession of all the important railroad junctions.

All the papers prophesy that the last link of the railway from Belgrade to Constantinople will soon be in the hands of the central powers. The Berlin Gazette says:

" The opening of the Danube resulted in direct connection between the central powers and Turkey, and now the fall of Nish will soon give us a direct rail line, since only a few isolated stretches north of Nish are still held by the Serbs. It will not be much longer before the Orient express again runs from Berlin and Vienna to Sofia and Constantinople. With the loss of Nish, the Serbs are forced to give up not only an important base of operations, but also numerous magazines and immense war supplies, thus greatly lowering the Serb armies' power of resistance."

The military expert of the Vossische Zeitung estimates the length of railway from Belgrade to the Bulgar border as 214 miles. He says that the Bulgarians have occupied 61 miles and the Austro-Germans 98 miles between Nish and Papatchin. He goes on:

" We may soon expect the junction of the Austro-German with the Bulgarian main forces, when the way from Belgrade to Constantinople will become free, a complete victory over the Serbs.

" For the present we do not hold the theory that the decision of this world war will be in the Balkan theatre, as our opinion is that the decision has practically been reached on the battlefields of Central Europe. But one can state with all certainty that the Oriental campaign as such has been won for us by the fall of Nish. There are only fifty-five miles to go and we are as good as finished with our task."

Major Moraht in the Tageblatt writes:

" Now that Nish has fallen, this part of the Bulgarian line will likewise press forward toward the Morava Valley in faster marches. Apart from the effectiveness of the Bulgarian artillery, the principal factor, hastening Nish's end was probably the demoralization of the Serb Army.

" There is nothing more in the way to prevent the complete union of the entire Bulgar east army with Mackensen's left wing. Undoubtedly the Bulgars will know, as we have done in Belgium and are still doing in West Russia, how to convert a Serbian fortress to our own use, thereby materially strengthening the Bulgarian fronts on this side.

" The immediate result is ever-lessening prospect of the Anglo-French expedition being able to defer the fast approaching finish of Serbia."

Count Reventlow, in the Tageszeitung, looks beyond Nish to Egypt, and says:

" The way to Constantinople through Serbia will soon be open. Thereby one object of the Balkan campaign is achieved, which, to be sure, is only preparatory to a greater object and goal."

A well-informed Sofia correspondent wires:

" Regarding reports that Bulgaria is undertaking new steps at Athens, protesting against the landing of the Entente troops, I was informed in the highest source that the reports are without foundation. The Bulgarian Government does not need to undertake such steps, as the troops already landed by the Entente Powers already are beaten, and a further landing is highly improbable. One cannot ask the impossible of Greece.

" If Greece tried forcibly to prevent the Entente Powers' action she would be drawn into the war, which, as a result of her geographical position, would be a catastrophe, but the Entente, on its part, will take care not to irritate Greece further so as not to lose it entirely. On the other hand the Greek Government spontaneously declared to the Bulgarian Government that it was in no way assisting the already landed troops and that shortly it would send a new note to the Entente, protesting sharply against the violation of its neutrality."

RUSSIANS CAPTURE 8,500 IN GALICIA

Surprise Attack Demoralizes Gen. von Linsingen's Austrian Forces on the Stripa.

But Berlin Reports 6,000 Prisoners Taken and Attacks in North Repulsed.

PETROGRAD, Nov. 6, via London, Sunday, Nov. 7.—The official communication issued tonight reports the capture by the Russians of 8,500 prisoners as the result of a surprise attack near the village of Semikovitze [Sienikowce] on the Stripa River.

The text of the statement follows:

West of Riga, near the village of Uchine, we repulsed several attacks. German counterattacks continue south of Lake Sventon. Further south, as far as the Pripet region, there is no change.

According to supplementary reports we took twenty-two officers and 712 men prisoners and captured seven machine guns and two guns in the fight near the village of Kostioukhova, west of Rafalovka. We repulsed enemy attacks in the direction of the village of Budki, driving him back in disorder to his trenches.

The period of extremely desperate fighting in the region of the village of Semikovitze and on the western shore of Lake Ischkuve has now ended. Swift frontal surprise attacks undertaken some days ago, including the crossing of the River Stripa near the village of Semikovitze, justified all our expectations. We took over 8,500 men prisoners, besides capturing a number, not yet determined, of officers and machine guns. Our valiant troops had to overcome the greatest difficulties while sending the enormous number of Austrian and German prisoners to the rear and across the River Stripa and Lake Ischkuve.

Bulgarian infantry advances against heavy Serbian artillery fire.

The New York Times.

THE WEATHER
Fair today and Thursday; moderate northwest winds.
☞ For full weather report see Page 15

VOL. LXV...NO. 21,109. ...   NEW YORK, WEDNESDAY, NOVEMBER 10, 1915.—TWENTY-TWO PAGES.   ONE CENT In Greater New York, Jersey City and Newark. | Elsewhere TWO CENTS.

AUSTRIAN SUBMARINE SINKS ANCONA; 270 SAVED, 312 MISSING FROM LINER BOUND FOR NEW YORK FROM NAPLES

LOST IN MEDITERRANEAN

She Is Believed to Have Left Italian Port Only Yesterday

SURVIVORS AT BIZERTA

They Report That the Undersea Craft That Sunk Steamer Was a Large One.

SOME VICTIMS WOUNDED

Agent of the Line Thinks It Likely Some Americans Were Aboard the Vessel.

ROME, Nov. 9, (via Paris.)—The Italian liner Ancona, bound from Naples to New York, has been sunk by a large submarine, flying the Austrian colors.

She carried 422 passengers and 160 men were in the crew.

Two hundred and seventy survivors, some of them wounded, have been landed at Bizerta.

The Ancona sailed from New York for Naples on Oct. 17. She had on board 1,245 Italian reservists and a general cargo. She arrived at Naples on Oct. 29, and was due to sail from Naples for New York yesterday.

William Hartfield of the firm of Hartfield, Solari & Co., 1 State Street, agents for the Italia Societa Navigazione a Vapore of Naples, which owned the Ancona, said last night:

"The Ancona has accommodation for forty-eight first-class passengers, and usually has a few Americans on the westward voyage to New York and Philadelphia. She is commanded by Captain Massardo, who is a very skillful navigator and a careful man.

"I understood she was to have left Naples today, but had not received any cablegram from the head office. I will send a dispatch at once and ask if there were any Americans on the passenger list."

Mr. Hartfield characterized the sinking of the Ancona as "an unnecessary crime" and "absolute murder."

Most of the Ancona's passenger list, Mr. Hartfield went on, had been made up hitherto of women and children. He believed she carried a large number of women and children on her present voyage.

The Ancona, he added, carried a crew of 160 men, all of them being Italians.

At no time, he said, did the Ancona carry guns or munitions of war, because it was against the rules of the company to carry war munitions on the same vessels with passengers.

One Explanation of Austrian Flag.

Shipping men recalled last night that Italy and Germany had not declared war on each other, and it was suggested that if a German submarine was responsible for sinking the Ancona the raising of the Austrian flag was very easily explained.

The Ancona was built in Belfast in 1908. She was a twin-screw steamer of 8,210 gross tonnage, 482 feet long, and with a beam of 58 feet.

The Ancona has been in the Italian Line service six years, and without her cargo was valued at more than $1,000,000. She played a prominent part in the rescue of passengers from the burning Fabre liner Sant' Anna in mid-Atlantic in September last, coming to the Sant' Anna's aid and taking off more than 600 passengers. The Sant' Anna succeeded in checking the fire and proceeded to the Azores without further assistance.

For several months before Italy's entrance into the war the Ancona was engaged in carrying home Italian reservists from this country and supplies for the Italian Government. On one of her trips from New York to Naples late in August last year the Ancona was stopped by the British at Gibraltar and twenty-four Germans and one Austrian were taken off the ship.

Bizerta, where her survivors were landed, is a French naval station on the north coast of Africa, about thirty-five miles northwest of Tunis.

Since the beginning of October Captains and officers of incoming steamers have reported sighting submarines in the Mediterranean and usually off the African coast.

The Lamport & Holt steamer Voltaire sighted a big submarine off Tunis on her way to New York from Genoa, according to her officers, just after daybreak. Apparently the commander must have mistaken the steamer for a cruiser on account of her gray-painted funnel and hull and dived under the surface about two miles off on the port bow. When the Voltaire reached Gibraltar the officers heard that a French and a British steamer had been torpedoed on the same day, that they sighted the submarine off Tunis.

They said that the German and Austrian submarines kept over to the African Coast, to be out of the way of the British and French torpedo boat destroyers and cruisers patrolling from Gibraltar to the Dardanelles to guard the transports.

SUBMARINES ACTIVE IN MEDITERRANEAN

Eight Other Vessels Had Been Reported Sunk There Within a Week.

On Oct. 18 Count von Bernstorff, the German Ambassador, announced that he had received an official communication from Berlin to the effect that German submarines had recently sunk twenty-three vessels, including four transports, belonging to the Allies in Mediterranean waters.

This was the first intelligence which conveyed an idea of the extensive operations of the German boats in the waters in question. Since then the losses reported have been:

Date.	Name.	Nationality.
Oct.—		
18—Amiral Hamelin..	French transport	
23—Unknown	....	Italian
20—Marquette	......	British transport
27—H. C. Henry....	British	
Nov.—		
4—Friargate	....	British
4—Dabra	....	French
4—Calvador	....	French
4—Ionio	....	French
5—Sidi Ferruch	....	French
7—Yasakuni	....	Japanese
8—Yser	....	French
9—Ancona	....	Italian

Austrian submarines have not hitherto been active beyond the Adriatic. But the Italian battleships Amalfi and Giuseppe Garibaldi were sunk by them on July 6 and July 19 respectively; and the submarines Medusa and Nereide also met the same fate—June 17 and Aug. 7. The French armored cruiser, Léon Gambetta, was sunk off Otranto, Italy, April 26, by the Austrian submarine U-5.

GERMANY REDOUBLES FIGHT ON DEAR FOOD

Issuance of Meat Cards to Civilians Imminent—State Confiscates All Oils and Fats.

From a Staff Correspondent.
Special Cable to THE NEW YORK TIMES.
BERLIN, Nov. 9.—At a caucus today of the National Liberal members of the Reichstag it was resolved that the fight against the high cost of living due to the war was at present the most important question growing out of the conflict and that further measures should be taken along the lines of the food ordinances already put into effect. The resolutions demand the introduction of meat cards; also the establishment of a far-reaching system of leaves of absence for soldiers at the front in order to maintain the efficiency of the industrial trades and of agriculture. In addition, the sharpest punitive measures against food speculators were advocated, including the loss of civic honors, and the immediate introduction of graduated taxes on war profits was demanded.

New milk cards will be issued in many Berlin boroughs on Nov. 15, and there is official intimation that preparations are being made for introducing meat cards in the near future. The Bundesrath also has passed an almost revolutionary measure for the confiscation by the State of all stocks of animal and vegetable oils and fats having food value, which will be distributed and apportioned to the various industries by the newly organized State War Corporation, modeled on the breadstuffs monopoly which has functioned so successfully.

Among the many interesting means employed to wean the public away from eating meat and to restrict its consumption is an exposition of meatless dishes which an association of Berlin housewives has just opened.

LARGE BRITISH FORCES ARE LANDED IN SERBIA

And Decisive Move Is Near— Berlin Reports 300,000 Allies Are There.

Special Cable to THE NEW YORK TIMES.
SALONIKI, Nov. 9. (Dispatch to The London Daily Telegraph.)—There are good grounds for hoping that the misfortunes of the Serbians have ended and that the tide which has been running against them has reached its high-water mark and that what is left of their sorely tried country will be saved from invasion.

Large British forces have arrived and more are expected.

The Allies will soon be in a position to take a decisive offensive.

LONDON, Wednesday, Nov. 10.—Newspapers of Berlin, as quoted by the correspondent at Copenhagen of the Exchange Telegraph Company, say that the Allies already have landed 300,000 men at Saloniki.

In spite of this, however, every hour adds to the peril of the Serbian armies, which are fighting desperately to hold back the Austro-Germans pressing them from the north and the Bulgarians, invading their country from the east, until the asistance their allies are sending can reach them.

The Bulgarians have extended their grip on the Belgrade-Saloniki railway north and south of Nish, and have occupied Leskovac, south of the captured capital, and Aleksinac, to the north. At the latter point they are in close touch with the German Army, which, after occupying Krusevac, extended its left wing as far as Gyunis, on the left bank of the Bulgar Morava.

The Austro-Germans, advancing southward, are making progress except in the west, where they are being held by the Montenegrins. The invading forces are now reaching the most difficult part of Serbia, the mountainous region, where the natives, knowing every hill and gully, can offer the strongest resistance. The Austrians and Germans, however, are plentifully supplied with mountain guns, with which they expect to drive the defenders from their fastnesses.

Allies Clear Railroad to Velon.

In the south the ever-growing strength of the French and British forces is beginning to tell. They are carrying on an energetic offensive against the Bulgars, have managed to keep the railway clear as far as Veles, and are barring the Bulgars' route to Monastir.

A Paris Havas dispatch from Athens filed on Monday says the French have reached Gradsko on the railroad from Krivolak to Veles. A Bulgarian attack against Krivolak, with heavy forces of infantry and artillery, is reported to have been repulsed, after which the French occupied the village of Komental.

On the Anglo-French front, northwest of Guevgeli, the advance of the Allies continues, and the Bulgarians now occupy only the village of Ourmandi in Serbian territory.

A dispatch from Rome tends to confirm the recent reports that Italy will send troops to Albania to aid the Serbs.

It states that a semi-official note has been issued which says that while Italy did not participate in the recent expedition of the Allies to assist Serbia she has found a better way to oppose the Austro-German-Bulgarian attack upon Serbia.

This way, the note says, was opened by the Bulgarians themselves, when they threatened to invade Albania to reach the Adriatic, a design so dangerous to Italy's interest that, the mere threat must oblige Italy to take appropriate measures to frustrate it immediately."

A Bucharest dispatch by way of Geneva says that 60,000 Albanians are preparing to attack the Serbians in the rear at Monastir and Prizrend.

Official Reports of Operations.

The text of yesterday's German official statement concerning the operations follows:

South of Kraljevo and southwest of Krusevac the enemy has been driven out of his rear-guard positions. Our troops are continuing the advance. The heights near Gyunis, on the left bank of the Morava, were stormed.

The booty taken at Krusevac was increased to about 50 cannon, including 10 heavy pieces. The number of prisoners was increased to 7,000.

The army (Bulgarian) of General Boyadjieff on the evening of Nov. 7 had reached the Morava at a point northwest of Aleksinac, which is to the northwest of Nish. Southwest of Nish, in conjunction with other Bulgarian troops advancing from the south, this army has taken Leskovac. The Austrian War Office version of the advance says:

On the Montenegrin frontier the situation is unchanged.

One group of Austro-Hungarian troops fighting in Serbia has occupied Ivanjica, and another group has ejected the enemy from height positions on the road from Ivanjica to Kraljevo. The German forces have dislodged the enemy from an intrenched position south of Kraljevo. South of Trstnick our battalions are engaged in battle. On the sector of

Kraljevo a German division is advancing southward. The Bulgarians have captured Leskovac.

Repulse of Austrian attacks was reported in the official statement issued by the Montenegrin War Office at Cettinje yesterday as follows:

Important artillery engagements occurred along the entire front on Nov. 7. The enemy threw forward his infantry in attacks at various points without attaining successes.

A delayed dispatch from Sofia, dated Sunday, says,

"The booty captured at Nish, consisted of forty-two guns, thousands of rifles, much ammunition, 700 railway cars, and many automobiles. The retreating Serbians abandoned numerous guns, machine guns, and rifles which have not been counted. Thus far 5,000 prisoners taken at Nish have been counted."

Members of the Rumanian Parliament who are being interviewed by Premier Bratiano to obtain their views upon the international situation have been told that the hypothesis of action against Russia need not be considered, says the Bucharest correspondent of the Petit Parisien of Paris.

"The prohibition of the transit of ammunition to Bulgaria," the Prime Minister is quoted as having said, "proves our sympathy for the Entente. I repudiate any policy which expects profits without corresponding sacrifices, but neither will I make sacrifices without the probability of success."

There is no change in the attitude of Greece, although it is considered significant that at the moment that Bulgaria has again protested against the hospitality accorded the allied troops at Saloniki the Greek Government has applied to the Allies for financial assistance—an application which is receiving favorable consideration. The Greek Government has also renewed to the Allies an expression of its firm determination to maintain neutrality and of its sincere goodwill toward the Entente powers.

Austrian War Office Reports Successes on the Frontier.

VIENNA, Nov. 9, (via London.)—The following report of the operations on the Italian frontier was issued today by the Austrian War Office:

"The situation is unchanged. Several Italian attacks on the Isonzo front against Zagora, and in the Dolomites against the lower ridge of the Col di Lana were repulsed."

TALE OF KITCHENER GOING TO INDIA

Washington Heard Rumors That Serious Unrest Among Natives Was Calling Him There.

'Kitchener Gone to the Near East I Hope, for a Short Time'—Asquith

LONDON, Nov. 9.—In his speech at the Lord Mayor's banquet tonight, Prime Minister Asquith said that Lord Kitchener, Secretary for War, had gone to Paris at the request of his colleagues, and had had fruitful conversations with the Premier and War Minister there.

"He has gone thence, I hope, for a short time only," continued the Premier, "to survey at close quarters the situation in the Near East. He takes with him the complete confidence of his colleagues and countrymen. He takes with him the authority of a great soldier and administrator, with an unrivaled knowledge of the Near East. I have every reason to know that his mission is regarded with unqualified approval and warm sympathy by our allies."

Special to The New York Times.

WASHINGTON, Nov. 9.—Reports were current here today that, according to confidential information that had reached the capital, Earl Kitchener, the British War Secretary, who recently left London so suddenly, was bound, not for the Balkans but for India, where, according to the story, serious unrest

confronted the British authorities and the Nizam of Hyderabad, an influential native Prince and staunch supporter of British rule, had been deposed by his people.

No confirmation of any such serious condition in India could be obtained at the State Department or the British Embassy, and persons who would be in a position to hear such important news expressed doubts as to the truth of the report. It was surmised that it was merely a phase of persistent rumors that things in India were in a bad way politically.

The statement of Premier Asquith at the Lord Mayor's banquet in London tonight that Lord Kitchener had gone to survey the Near East situation at close range, and that he hoped the War Secretary would be gone for only a short time, was thought to dispose of the story that Kitchener was going to India on a serious errand.

Information that has reached Washington indicates that efforts have been made by German agents ever since the outbreak of the great war to cause disaffection among the natives of India. Evidence has been gathered to show that a large amount of money has been used in propagating hostility to the British authority. According to one report reaching here forty German agents were recently captured in Persia by Russian troops, while they were attempting to make their way into India. Later there was an uprising in Singapore, and it was plain that a concerted movement was on foot to make trouble in the Indian Empire.

The United States Government received a complaint that German agents were at work in the Philippines, presumably to organize an expedition that would proceed against British colonies. Investigation brought no confirmation of this story, but officials had reason to believe that efforts were being made by German agents near the Philippines to bring about an uprising in India.

That the British Government has been uneasy over the attempts to cause trouble in India has been known here. Information has been received that newly recruited troops were being sent from England to India to take the places of the regulars withdrawn to take part in the Dardanelles campaign and the fighting in France and Belgium. None of the reports that have come here have indicated that the British Government regarded the Indian situation as serious. On the contrary, it was felt that if there were any outbreaks they could be handled without great difficulty by the forces in that country.

These Serbian gunners are ready for the Austrian troops advancing on Nish, Serbia.

"All the News That's Fit to Print."

The New York Times.

THE WEATHER
Snow or rain today; partly cloudy tomorrow; fresh southeast winds, shifting to northwest.
For full weather report see Page 21.

VOL. LXV...NO. 21,142.   ...   NEW YORK, MONDAY, DECEMBER 13, 1915.—TWENTY-TWO PAGES.   ONE CENT In Greater New York, Jersey City and Newark. | Elsewhere TWO CENTS

PRESIDENT DEMANDS ANCONA DISAVOWAL AND REPARATION, ALSO PUNISHMENT OF THE GUILTY SUBMARINE COMMANDER, IN NOTE REQUIRING THAT AUSTRIA'S COMPLIANCE BE PROMPT

THREATENS GOOD RELATIONS

Government Said to Be Prepared for a Diplomatic Break.

NO LOOPHOLE FOR PARLEYS

Vienna's Contention That Ancona Was Trying to Escape Is Brushed Aside.

ACT 'A WANTON SLAUGHTER'

"Illegal and Indefensible," "Condemned by World as Inhumane and Barbarous."

Special to The New York Times.

WASHINGTON, Dec. 12.—Apparently leaving no loophole for compromise or discussion, the United States Government has called upon the Government of Austria-Hungary for prompt compliance with a demand for disavowal and reparation on account of the sinking of the Italian-American liner Ancona by an Austro-Hungarian submarine, and the punishment of the submarine's commander. The text of the formal diplomatic communication containing the demand was made public by the State Department today.

The demand follows a statement informing Austria-Hungary that "the good relations of the two countries must rest upon a common regard for law and humanity." The note arraigns the shelling and torpedoing of the liner as "inhumane," "barbarous," and a "wanton slaughter" of "helpless men, women, and children."

Not in any of the diplomatic notes of this Government to Germany concerning the Lusitania was such direct and menacing language used. As a consequence of this communication, which bears all the marks of being an ultimatum, the gravest danger threatens the continuance of relations between the Governments of Austria-Hungary and the United States.

"Ultimatum" is the term used by some officials in describing the substance of the American position. Generally in Administration circles the view appears to prevail that President Wilson and Secretary Lansing have burned all bridges behind them, and are prepared to take extreme measures to showing their resentment if the Vienna Government declines to comply with the demands made. In diplomacy "demand" is about the strongest word that can be used, and it is used twice in the Ancona note.

Must Accede Within a Week.

The course the United States will pursue is understood to have been determined upon. A reasonable time will be given Austria-Hungary in which to reply to the communication before further action is taken. The word "prompt" as used in the note is understood to mean that Austria-Hungary must accede to the demand of the United States within a week, at the most. If the demand is not complied with, immediate severance of diplomatic relations is regarded as certain.

The Administration has been sensitive over the criticism, heard most frequently during the critical period of the Lusitania negotiations, that all the action of the Government in dealing with Germany's destruction of merchant vessels, with the loss of innocent lives, was confined to writing diplomatic notes. With particular reference to this criticism, it is declared by officials that the note on the Ancona case means exactly what it says, and that the country should be prepared for a break in the relations between Washington and Vienna if the Austro-Hungarian Government does not promptly accede to the demand to "denounce the sinking of the Ancona as an illegal and indefensible act, that the officer who perpetrated the deed be punished, and that reparation be the payment of an indemnity be made for the citizens of the United States who were killed or injured by the attack on the vessel."

The manner in which the American note dismisses the Austrian contention that the Ancona sought to escape removes that phase of the incident from the field of discussion. A point-blank refusal to accept the Austrian view seems to be a correct construction of the American position. Judged by what is being said in a guarded way by officials here, the Austro-Hungarian Government must either accept or reject what is demanded by the United States. There is no half-way point in the negotiations, according to the official view.

Although the character of the action that would be taken by this Government should Austria-Hungary decline to comply promptly with the demands made is not clearly set forth in the comments of officials, it is evident that the Government has in mind a severance of diplomatic relations. Such a course would dispose also of the incident involved in the admission yesterday to Secretary Lansing by Baron Zwiedinek, Chargé d'Affaires of Austria-Hungary, of the genuineness of a letter signed with his name suggesting that the Austro-Hungarian Consulate General in New York might be able to procure "at slight expense" passports of neutral countries to enable Austrian reservists to proceed in safety from the United States to their own country. Should diplomatic relations between the two Governments be severed, Baron Zwiedinek and all the other members of the embassy staff would be dismissed from the United States. The Administration is deferring decision in the matter of the Zwiedinek letter until the Ancona case has been disposed of.

Baron Zwiedinek was furnished with a copy of the Ancona note when he called at the State Department yesterday.

After listening to the views of officials high in the Administration's councils, cautiously expressed though they are, it is impossible to escape the conviction that from now on the United States Government will not follow any velvet-glove procedure in dealing with such incidents as that of the Ancona. The vigorous language of the note to Austria-Hungary is declared to be in keeping with a new policy that found its first public expression in that portion of President Wilson's address to Congress last Tuesday in which reference was made to what the President termed the disloyal attitude of some American citizens of foreign birth whom he accused of being engaged in bomb plots and other conspiracies in the interest of European belligerents. The Administration is said to have determined to go ahead in protecting American interests at home and abroad and on the high seas without regard to the possible cost.

The note to Austria-Hungary suggests that the President and the Cabinet have fully determined to go to the limit in all cases involving disregard by European belligerents for the lives of American noncombatants on merchant vessels on the high seas. It is the opinion here that the Administration is hopeful that its attitude toward Austria in the Ancona case will make Germany realize that the desire for satisfaction indicated by the United States in connection with the sinking of the Lusitania was emphatic and that the relations between Berlin and Washington will be unsatisfactory so long as the Lusitania controversy remains unsettled.

GERMAN PRESS VIEWS ON NOTE TO AUSTRIA

Ridder Hopes for Arbitration, Saying President Wilson's Demands Are Unjust.

Comments on the Ancona note by German newspapers in the United States follow. Bernard Ridder, in the New Yorker Staats-Zeitung, expresses the hope that Austria-Hungary will ask for arbitration, and says:

"President Wilson's Ancona note is his first concise and statesmanlike document, and, if his premises were unassailable, he would find the whole nation solidly behind him.

"Unfortunately President Wilson rests his demands on an erroneous assumption. Brushing aside the Declaration of London of 1907 and that of Paris of 1856, both of which were concluded to guide nations over disputed ground, he bases his demands on the law of nations as it existed before the Declaration of Paris. Of this law, however, the nations of Europe—and inferentially also the United States, for Lincoln wished to sign it—spoke as is stated in the preamble of the Declaration.

"If the Austro-Hungarian submarine commander had spared the Ancona, Austria-Hungary claims, the steamer would have carried on her return trip death for the Austrian soldiers. American lives must be held sacred everywhere, but not at the cost of making unjust demands on other nations, and so long as the President's interpretation of the law of nations is not proved to be correct, however pleasant it may be to all of us, his peremptory demands on Austria-Hungary cannot be called just. American honor, like Caesar's wife, should be above suspicion. This is, however, not inevitably the case in this instance."

From the Cincinnati Volksblatt.

The President can effectually protect American citizens from submarine danger by issuing to them the order promulgated in England in the Russo-Japanese war, to the effect that British subjects must stay away from belligerent ships. There is no reason apparent why the President should not proceed in this manner and thereby avoid unnecessary friction with foreign countries. If the President has set his heart upon involving our country in the European war he will not accomplish his design. Congress is everything but pleased with the President's conduct of foreign affairs.

ELEVEN AMERICANS KILLED.

Total Loss of Life from Torpedoing of the Ancona Was 205.

The steamship Ancona was torpedoed and sunk on Monday, Nov. 7, off the north coast of Africa, near the naval station Bizerta, with the loss of 205 lives. Eleven American citizens were among the victims. They were Alexander Patativo, his wife, and four children; Mrs. Francesco Mascolo Lamura, Pasquale Laurino, Mrs. Giuseppe Torrisi, Mrs. Louis Cupo, and her three-year-old son. Mrs. Cupo was the wife of a druggist at 94 St. Mary's Avenue, Rosebank, Staten Island; she went to Italy in July for her health.

Two other Americans were cabin passengers on the Ancona; they were saved. These were Dr. Cecile L. Greil of Washington Square, this city, and Giuseppe Torrisi.

The Ancona, according to the officers and the survivors among the passengers, was attacked without warning about 1:15 P. M. by a big submarine flying the Austrian colors. The first shells were fired from a distance of five miles. The commander of the Ancona stopped his ship immediately, because most of the 428 passengers on board were women and children. The submarine then approached the steamer at full speed, firing from a gun in her bows. One of the shells carried away the chart room on the bridge. In the meantime the passengers were ordered to take to the boats. Panic ensued.

Dr. Greil said that one shell entered the port hole of her cabin, killing the maid as she was getting her papers together to leave the ship.

While the boats were being lowered from the deck, filled with women and children, Dr. Greil said, the submarine continued to fire all around the ship, which threw the passengers into greater terror. Many of the shots pierced the hull of the Ancona above the water line. The vessel did not commence to sink until after a torpedo had been fired at her from a distance of 300 yards.

"All the News That's Fit to Print."

The New York Times.

THE WEATHER
Fair today, partly cloudy tomorrow; not much change in temperature; light variable winds.
For full weather report see Page 17.

VOL. LXV...NO. 21,160. ...   NEW YORK, FRIDAY, DECEMBER 31, 1915.—EIGHTEEN PAGES.   ONE CENT In Greater New York, Jersey City and Newark. | Elsewhere TWO CENTS

AUSTRIA REPLIES THAT SHE HAS PUNISHED U-BOAT CAPTAIN FOR NOT TAKING ACCOUNT OF THE PANIC ON THE ANCONA; SHE OFFERS US REPARATION FOR THE AMERICAN LIVES LOST

REPLY SURPRISES CAPITAL

Official Circles Had Believed Vienna Would Propose Arbitration.

DISPUTE CLEARED AWAY

View Held in Washington That Other Issues Involved Are Now Settled.

NOTE 3,000 WORDS LONG

Ambassador Notifies State Department That Text Is Being Forwarded.

Special to The New York Times.

WASHINGTON, Dec. 30.—News that the Austrian note informs the American Government not only that Austria intends to uphold the principles of humanity, but already has punished the commander of the submarine that sunk the Ancona will come as a complete surprise to the State Department and the Austrian and German Embassies. Government officials here, guided by rather gloomy dispatches from Vienna, had thought that the best that could be hoped for with regard to the punishment of the officer would be the suggestion that the point be arbitrated.

It is considered here that the Austrian reply, which also offers reparation, clears up the entire dispute.

In the first American note on the Ancona. sinking Secretary Lansing summarized the demands of the United States in these words:

"As the good relations of the two countries must rest upon a common regard for law and humanity, the Government of the United States cannot be expected to do otherwise than to demand that the Imperial and Royal Government denounce the sinking of the Ancona as an illegal and indefensible act; that the officer who perpetrated the deed be punished, and that reparation by the payment of an indemnity be made for the citizens of the United States who were killed or injured by the attack on the vessel."

The reply of the Austro-Hungarian Government to the second American note on the Ancona case is en route to Washington. A cablegram from Frederic C. Penfield, the American Ambassador at Vienna, was received at the State Department this afternoon informing Secretary of State Lansing that the American answer was delivered to Ambassador Penfield at Vienna yesterday.

In making this announcement Secretary Lansing said that the message from the Ambassador gave no forecast of the note, but merely said that the reply had been delivered, that it was about 3,000 words long, and that it would be forwarded to Washington as soon as it could be translated and enciphered.

The message from Ambassador Penfield reached the State Department at 2:45 o'clock, and bore evidence of having been relayed from Vienna via Berne, Switzerland, in twenty-four hours. Up to midnight tonight the text of the note had not begun to come into the State Department telegraph offices. Experience has demonstrated that long cipher messages require not less than two days for transmission to Washington from Vienna. The text of the note is not expected to reach the State Department before tomorrow, and possibly not until Saturday.

Secretary Lansing maintained his custom today of not commenting on the Austrian situation. Not until he has had opportunity to consider carefully the Austrian response and confer with the President will the Secretary of State authorize any announcement indicating the effect the communication from Austria may have.

It had been expected that in the Ancona case Austria, while asserting her diplomatic independence of Germany, would follow Germany's Lusitania course point by point. But she has come to the point of important concessions much more quickly than her ally. The German Government was not asked to punish the commander of any of the offending submarines. In quarters here sympathetic with Austria, it had been held that the Austrian Government could not well punish an officer for obeying orders, especially in view of the statement justifying the officer issued by the Austrian Admiralty.

GERMAN ORDER HOLDS AMERICANS IN AUSTRIA

Consul at Vienna Refuses to Vise Passports Without Birth Certificates.

Special to The New York Times.

WASHINGTON, Dec. 30.—The following dispatch from Ambassador Penfield was received today:

Vienna, Dec. 28, 1915.

Secretary of State, Washington:

German Consulate at Vienna refuses to vise American passports for travel in the German Empire unless bearers present certificates of birth or naturalization. Americans here not possessing these documents are consequently being detained. Have presented matter to German Embassy, with request for modification of present regulations to enable American citizens to return to their homes, and informed the embassy at Berlin, requesting their good offices in presenting the matter to the German authorities. The above regulations practically exclude from Germany bona fide American-born and naturalized citizens, bearers of American passports but not the required additional documents, and will tend to work hardships and delay, making it practically impossible for such persons to embark from Holland. PENFIELD.

Ambassador Gerard on Dec. 22 notified Secretary Lansing that new regulations for viséing passports for use in Germany had been adopted, the pertinent parts applicable to American citizens being that a new visé of a passport by a German diplomatic or Consular officer would be required for each separate entry into Germany, that to obtain the visé the bearer of the passport must apply in person to the German diplomatic or Consular officer.

In order to compensate for an inferior fleet of surface vessels, Germany resorted to all-out submarine warfare, striking merchant vessels without warning.

1916

"All the News That's Fit to Print."

The New York Times.

THE WEATHER
Rain Sunday; Monday colder, probably fair; fresh south winds, becoming northwest and strong by Monday.
For full weather report see Page 22

VOL. LXV...NO. 21,162. ...   NEW YORK, SUNDAY, JANUARY 2, 1916.—124 PAGES, In Eight Parts,   PRICE FIVE CENTS.

LINER PERSIA TORPEDOED; HUNDREDS PERISH; THREE AMERICANS, ONE A CONSUL, ON BOARD; WASHINGTON SEES A NEW CRISIS THREATENED

SHIP IS SUNK OFF CRETE

British P. & O. Steamer Was on Her Way from London to Bombay.

ONLY FOUR BOATS GOT AWAY

160 Passengers and Crew of 250 to 300 Aboard, Most of Whom Perished.

DOUBT AS TO WARNING

Consul Skinner Strives to Get Facts and Names of Americans Who May Be Lost.

LONDON, Jan. 1.—The British passenger steamer Persia, bound from London for Bombay, was torpedoed and sunk off the Island of Crete in the Mediterranean, on Thursday, and it is believed that several hundred persons, some of whom were Americans, perished.

It is known that the majority of the passengers and crew were lost. Only four boats got clear of the liner before she sank. These boats were picked up by a steamer bound for Alexandria, and the survivors were expected there this morning.

Robert McNeely, American Consul at Aden, was a passenger on the Persia. Members of the Consul's family say that his brother was with him.

Two other American passengers are known to have been on the vessel when she left London. Charles H. Grant of 49 Federal Street, Boston, was on his way to Bombay. Edward Rose, a schoolboy, was on the way from Denver to Gibraltar. Rose probably landed at Gibraltar and was not on board the boat at the time she was sunk.

160 Passengers Aboard.

Sixty-one first-class passengers and eighty-three second-cabin passengers, including eight children, boarded the steamship at London, according to information obtained at the Peninsular & Oriental Line, owners of the liner. At Marseilles thirty-five of the first class and thirty-two of the second cabin boarded the vessel. The company estimates that after deducting the number of passengers leaving the ship at her various ports of call about 160 passengers were aboard when the vessel was sunk.

A Lloyd's dispatch says that most of the passengers and men of the Persia were lost.

A message from the Admiralty to the Peninsular & Oriental Company makes the definite announcement that the Persia was torpedoed. The disaster occurred at 1 o'clock on Thursday afternoon. The company does not know whether the vessel received a warning or not.

Cable communication with the East is so slow that details on the disaster are not expected to arrive for a day or two. A majority of the Persia's passengers were British, bound for India, including many women.

Lord Montagu was on the passenger list. He was proceeding to India to assume the post of Inspector of Mechanical Transport Vehicles. He appeared in the list of New Year honors, receiving the order of the Star of India for services in connection with the war. He was well known in America. He was prominent in athletics and has traveled extensively, visiting the United States, Japan, China, India and Egypt. He was a war correspondent in Rhodesia during the Matabele war. He was interested in railway and transport problems.

Crew of More Than 250.

The crew of the Persia numbered between 250 and 300 men. They were nearly all Lascars. There was not much cargo aboard the Persia, but she was carrying very heavy mail. The vessel carried no war materials.

The four boats which got away from the sinking vessel were capable of carrying 60 persons each, but it is not known if the boats were full.

Every effort is being made by Consul General Skinner to get some information about Robert McNeely, the American Consul at Aden, and the two other Americans known to be on the passenger list. The British Admiralty informed Mr. Skinner it had no information with regard to the fate of individual passengers. Mr. Skinner sent a cablegram to the American Consulate at Alexandria requesting the Consul to ascertain the fate of Consul McNeely and the other Americans.

The officers on board the Persia, it is learned, were ordinary booked passengers and were not on active service in the British Army.

Next to Lusitania Disaster.

Next to the Lusitania disaster the sinking of the Persia probably means a considerably heavier casualty list than that of any of the passenger-carrying ships that heretofore have fallen victims to the torpedoes of German or Austrian submarines. This deduction is based on the reports that the vessel carried several hundred passengers and crew, and that only four lifeboats got away from the vessel as she went down.

The Peninsular & Oriental steamship office will issue a list of the actual passengers as soon as possible.

At present only partial bookings are available.

The scene of the catastrophe, the seas between the Island of Crete and Alexandria, recently has been the graveyard of a number of fine ships, and only a few weeks ago the American tank steamer Petrolite narrowly escaped the guns of a submarine there.

The Persia, a vessel of 7,974 tons, was the first passenger ship lost by the Peninsular & Oriental Line during the war. Just prior to the departure of the vessel from London the company held its annual meeting. Chairman Inchcape remarked of the growing anxiety caused by the enlargement of the submarine danger zone and of the indebtedness of this company to the British Navy for complete immunity from casualty for their ships, and added prophetically: "Of course we cannot tell when a disaster may overtake us."

ATTACK SHOCKS CAPITAL

Strikingly Similar to That on Arabic After Lusitania Disaster.

U-BOAT PROBABLY AUSTRIAN

Situation Is Complicated by Vienna's Compliance with Our Ancona Demands.

OFFICIAL REPORT AWAITED

Comment Withheld Pending Details as to Whether Liner Was Fleeing or Resisting.

President Silent on Persia Till Facts Are Learned

HOT SPRINGS, Jan. 1.—Information regarding the situation with Austria was forwarded to the President by Secretary Lansing today, but its nature was not disclosed. Mr. Wilson would not comment on the possible effect of the sinking of the liner Persia, saying he could not form any opinion until he had more complete information.

Special to The New York Times.

WASHINGTON, Jan. 1.—Washington was shocked by the news that the P. and O. liner Persia had been torpedoed in the Mediterranean with a large loss of life. The attack was made just when hopes were highest here that the second note from the Austro-Hungarian Government not only would avoid a diplomatic rupture over the sinking of the Ancona but also would pave the way for a settlement of the submarine warfare controversy with Germany. This attack overlaps the Ancona issue with startling similarity to the manner in which the attack on the Arabic was thrust into the controversy over the Lusitania.

Washington officials are reserving judgment on the sinking of the Persia in view of the fact that when the details are known they may involve no new complications. Until detailed facts are obtained it will be impossible to gauge the diplomatic significance of the attack.

If the Persia was attacked without warning the fact undoubtedly would precipitate a real crisis; if torpedoed while attempting to escape the gravity of the situation would be reduced from a diplomatic standpoint, for it has not been the contention of this Government that liners are entitled to any immunity while attempting to escape or if they offer resistance. It is possible that the attack on the Persia was made by a submarine that had been out of touch with the Austrian Admiralty and which might not have been advised of the manner in which the Austrian Government had dealt with the submarine commander who attacked the Ancona, or had not received any new Admiralty instructions growing out of that case.

Lack of Harmony Suggested.

Still another suggestion heard here today was that perhaps the Austro-Hungarian Admiralty had not issued any new instructions on the basis of the Ancona settlement and that lack of harmony of opinion might exist between the Austro-Hungarian Admiralty and the Foreign Office, just as there was a clash of views in Germany between the Foreign Office and Grand Admiral von Tirpitz, head of the Admiralty, over the concessions made by Germany to the United States in the dispute over submarine warfare.

In this connection, it was pointed out tonight, no new instructions seemed to be called for under the position taken by Austria, the submarine commander who sank the Ancona being punished for infraction of existing instructions.

If the Persia was not trying to escape, and if she was not resisting the submarine, it is the expectation of the Washington Government that the Vienna Government or the Berlin Government, as the case may be, will immediately and in very convincing manner repudiate the attack and explain the circumstances.

Cabled press accounts of the attack on the Persia were widely circulated in Washington today and cast depression over the New Year's Day celebrations in official circles. The fact of the attack was confirmed in cablegrams from Robert G. Skinner, the American Consul General at London, to Secretary Lansing. These messages merely repeated the information given in the press dispatches. No direct information was received from any of the American diplomatic or Consular officers in regions bordering the Mediterranean. The American Consul at Alexandria, Egypt, is Arthur Garrels. Authentic official information is momentarily expected from him.

Consul General Skinner confirmed the report that three Americans were passengers on the Persia when she sailed from England—Robert Ney McNeely, bound for his post as Consul at Aden, Arabia, and Charles H. Grant, and another, Edward Ross, a boy, bound for Bombay, India. The fact that Americans may have lost their lives opened a possibility upon which officials did not like to comment.

If Consul McNeely is among those saved it is expected that he will send an early report to the Government.

Consul Skinner's Messages.

The first of the dispatches received from Consul General Skinner read:

From London, Jan. 1, 1916.
P. and O. liner Persia reported sunk, submarined, while approaching Alexandria. Robert N. McNeely, American Consul at Aden, going to post, left London as passenger. Nearly all on board perished. SKINNER.

A subsequent message from Mr. Skinner stated that 211 passengers boarded the Persia at London and that the ship picked up sixty-seven passengers at Marseilles. He said that at the time the ship was torpedoed 161 passengers were on board, and that four boat loads left the Persia in safety. The message was by no means clear. It was not given out textually. A paraphrase was issued stating that Mr. Skinner reported that sixty-one first-class passengers and eighty-three second-class passengers boarded the Persia at London, and that at Marseilles the ship picked up thirty-five first-class passengers.

All the agencies of the American Government have been set in motion to gather facts on the disaster. The general view in official quarters was that the position of the United States was sufficiently well known to Austria, and the Ancona negotiations have been under way a sufficient length of time to permit instructions to reach the submarine fleet. On every hand the news was received with astonishment.

The information forwarded by Consul General Skinner — information available at the British Admiralty—with other unofficial reports of the disaster, was sent to President Wilson at Hot Springs. The President will have Austria's satisfactory reply in the Ancona case and the news of the latest submarine disaster before him at the same time.

There is little room to doubt that the incident will mean new diplomatic action in which the United States will present to Austria again its unalterable policy that the laws of nations and humanity must be regarded by the belligerents in their warfare at sea. Severance of diplomatic relations, with all its possibilities, looms up as one of the eventualities, the same as it did in the case of the Lusitania, the Arabic, and the Ancona.

Although the nationality of the submarine which sank the Persia remains unestablished definitely, as was the case with the Yasaka Maru and the Ville de la Ciotat, the assumption generally is that it was an Austrian boat, because Count von Bernstorff, the German Ambassador, recently declared that no German or Turkish submersibles were operating in the Mediterranean.

ALLIES EXPECT TO WIN THE WAR BEFORE '16 ENDS

POINCARE IS SANGUINE

PARIS, Dec. 31, (Delayed.)—"Nineteen hundred and sixteen will be our year of victory," says President Poincaré in a message to "the officers and soldiers of France," which was distributed along the whole front tonight. The message, which is one of great simplicity, expresses the confidence of the entire nation in its defenders. The letter follows:

"Like you, my noble friends, I have read with emotion in the Army Bulletin, messages addressed to you on the eve of the New Year by the Mayors of our large cities. The same language is used by all these French cities, and it is easy today to draw from these numerous expressions the unanimous sentiment of the country.

"Everywhere you have seen maintained without effort this sacred union spontaneously established seventeen months ago under the menace of the enemy. Why would not the civil population follow the example of agreement and harmony which you give it? In the trenches and on the battlefields you hardly think of considering your personal opinions.

"Civil discord does not disturb the fraternity of arms, which, with its common perils and identical duties, binds one and all. You have your eyes fixed on an ideal which constantly diverts your attention from secondary objects, and you know that your patriotic mission cannot be performed by others.

"While you are thus sacrificing everything to the salvation of the nation, is it not natural that those Frenchmen whose age, health, or duties prevent them from meeting at your side the fatigue and perils of war work should at least repel harmful suggestions of hatred and conserve jealously the public peace?

"The Mayors of France have spoken of some of the charitable works resulting from the successful joining of hearts. Most of these institutions are destined to aid you, your aged parents, your children, your wounded or imprisoned brothers. In cities furthest from the front your condition thus remains constantly present in all minds and concentrates, as is well in view of the tragic realities of the time, the thoughts of those who might be inclined to forget.

"The mourning which has darkened the home of so many families, moreover, imposes on those who have been less severely afflicted the pious obligation of meditation and gravity. All the French people feel the same affliction, and there is not one who does not listen with respect to the stern lesson of the day—a lesson of courage, of patience, of will, of calm, of confidence, and of serenity.

The Problem Before France.

"Everywhere it is the same—a determined resolution to hold fast, to endure, and to vanquish. Every one knows the stakes of the war are great and that the outcome concerns not only our dignity, but our life. Shall we tomorrow be the vassals of a foreign empire? Shall our industries, our commerce, our agriculture, be placed forever under the influence of a power which openly flatters itself on aspiring to universal domination, or shall we safeguard our economic independence and national autonomy? This is a terrible problem, which admits of no half-way solution. Any peace which came to us with suspicious form and equivocal purpose would bring us only dishonor, ruin, and servitude. The free and pure genius of our race, our most venerated traditions, the ideas which are dearest to us, the interests of our citizens, the fortunes of our country, the soul of the nation, everything which has been left by our ancestors and all that we ourselves own, would be the prey of Germanic brutality.

"Who then would, by impatience or lassitude, thus sell to Germany the past and future of France? Yes, certainly, the war is long. It is rigorous and it is bloody, but how much future suffering are we spared by our present suffering? No French person desired this war. All the governments since 1871 have endeavored to avoid such a war. Now that it has been declared against us in spite of ourselves, we must carry it on with our faithful allies until we have gained victory, the annihilation of German militarism, and the entire reconstitution of France. To permit ourselves to falter even momentarily, would be to be ungrateful to our dead and to betray posterity.

"We must persevere obstinately in the will to win. Is it not the surest means of bringing about victory?

We Shall Not Become Wearied.

"In the war which we are carrying on so valiantly in France, Belgium, and the East, the part played by implements of destruction has become of essential importance, and it is the imperious duty of the Government to furnish you constantly with the most powerful weapons and an abundance of munitions. But moral power is the foremost consideration for final success. The beaten side will not necessarily be that which has had the heaviest losses or has endured the most misery. It will be the side which becomes wearied first. We shall not become wearied.

(A) STARB. BOW TORPEDO TUBE.
(B) ACCOMODATION FOR CREW OF 30, SUITABLE FOR LONG VOYAGE.
(C) TWO 900 H.P. DIESEL MOTORS, FOR SURFACE RUNNING.
(D) TWO 500 H.P. ELECTRIC MOTORS, FOR SUBMERGED RUNNING.
(E) TWIN SCREWS.
(F) STERN DIVING RUDDERS, DIVES ON AN EVEN KEEL, ALLOWING TORPEDOES TO BE FIRED DURING SUBMERGENCE.
(G) STERN TUBES.   (H) 3" GUNS IN RECESS.
(I) BROADSIDE TUBES, 8 TUBES IN ALL, 16 TORPEDOS ARE CARRIED.
(J) 3" GUNS IN RECESS.   (K) STARB. DIVING RUDDERS.
(L) GUN LYING IN RECESS IN DECK.
(M) GUN RAISED AND RECESS CLOSED, THE FIRST SHOT CAN BE FIRED IN 20 SECONDS.
(N) TWO PERISCOPES.

This illustration provides a detailed depiction of a German submarine used in WWI.

"All the News That's Fit to Print."

The New York Times.

THE WEATHER
Fair today, fresh northwest winds on the Coast; Sunday fair, slightly warmer.
For full weather report see Page 17.

VOL. LXV...NO. 21,168. ...   NEW YORK, SATURDAY, JANUARY 8, 1916.—EIGHTEEN PAGES.   ONE CENT In Greater New York, Jersey City and Newark. | TWO CENTS

GERMANY PLEDGES HUMANITY AT SEA; WILL ALSO PAY LUSITANIA INDEMNITY; AUSTRIA AND TURKEY TO JOIN IN PLEDGE

INCLUDES THE PERSIA CASE

If German U-Boat Sank Liner Commander Will Be Punished.

LUSITANIA DISAVOWAL NEXT

Only the Wording of the Agreement in That Case Now Believed to be at Issue.

FRYE SETTLEMENT AT HAND

Washington Regards the Whole U-Boat Problem Near End—Safety for All Noncombatants.

Special to The New York Times.

WASHINGTON, Jan. 7.—The whole aspect of the complicated and grave situation caused by Teutonic submarine attacks on merchant ships in the Mediterranean changed late this afternoon when Secretary Lansing announced that new written assurances had been received from the German Government regarding its attitude.

Equally important is the information, unofficially made known, that similar assurances will be furnished by the Governments of Austria-Hungary and Turkey. Incidentally, the German guarantees apply to the Persia case in such a way as to dissipate the international crisis over the sinking of that vessel.

These assurances were contained in a note which Count von Bernstorff, the German Ambassador, received from the Berlin Foreign Office this morning, and which he delivered in person to Secretary Lansing during a conference later in the day.

According to these assurances no German submarine will be allowed to sink an enemy merchant vessel in the Mediterranean until after safety has been accorded to passengers and crew—unless the vessel offers resistance or attempts to escape. This new pledge, broader than any previously given by the German Government to the United States, applies to freight as well as passenger vessels.

Additional assurances are given that any German submarine commander who

Germany's Pledge of Safety in Mediterranean and Promise to Punish Those Violating It

Special Dispatch to The New York Times.

WASHINGTON, Jan. 7.—After a visit of Count Bernstorff to the State Department today Secretary Lansing issued the following statement, comprising the text of the new written guarantees from the German Government:

The German Ambassador today left at the Department of State, under instructions from his Government, the following communication:

"(1) German submarines in the Mediterranean had, from the beginning, orders to conduct cruiser warfare against enemy merchant vessels only in accordance with general principles of international law, and in particular measures of reprisal, as applied in the war zone around the British Isles, were to be excluded.

"(2) German submarines are therefore permitted to destroy enemy merchant vessels in the Mediterranean—i. e., passenger as well as freight ships as far as they do not try to escape or offer resistance—only after passengers and crews have been accorded safety.

"(3) All cases of destruction of enemy merchant ships in the Mediterranean in which German submarines are concerned are made the subject of official investigation and, besides, subject to regular prize court proceedings. In so far as American interests are concerned, the German Government will communicate the result to the American Government. Thus, also, in the Persia case, if the circumstances should call for it.

"(4) If commanders of German submarines should not have obeyed the orders given to them they will be punished; furthermore, the German Government will make reparation for damage caused by death of or injuries to American citizens."

sinks a vessel in violation of the pledge thus furnished will be punished, and the German Government will make reparation for damage caused by the death of or injuries to any American citizen.

Pledges Germany's Allies.

Germany's guarantees are to be observed likewise by the Austrian and Turkish Governments. While this is not set forth in the communication delivered by the German Ambassador, it is understood that the German, Austrian, and Turkish Governments have confidentially come to an understanding among themselves agreeing to the rules under which submarines flying their respective flags are to conduct their warfare against merchant craft in the Mediterranean, and that the Berlin Foreign Office has taken the initiative in bringing about a common line of conduct between the central powers and their allies for observance in submarine warfare.

The pledge of the German Government is regarded as all the more important because it was given voluntarily by the Berlin Foreign Office without waiting for a request from the United States Government for information as to the manner in which German submarine warfare would be conducted in the Mediterranean. And particular significance is attached to the fact that the assurances thus given by the Berlin Government are a direct outcome of the Ancona and Persia cases.

SERBIAN RETREAT A HEROIC TRAGEDY

Flight to Sixth Capital in Two Months Through Albanian Mountains Described.

GUNS AND CONVOYS LEFT

Officers and Soldiers Wept as They Destroyed Them—Army Harassed by Guerrillas.

PARIS, Jan. 7.—Hardships encountered by the Serbian Army in its flight through the mountains of Albania are described in a letter to the Temps sent from Scutari on Dec. 11.

"This is the sixth capital Serbia has had during two months," says the writer. "After Nish it was Kraljevo, then Ras-

ka, Mitrovitza, Prisrend, and finally Scutari.

"As a tourist I am acquainted with the Alps, the Carpathians, and the Pyrenees, but I have never seen such goat paths for roads running along the edges of terrible precipices and the sides of peaks in the clouds. The officials of the Serbian Government rode little mountain ponies, but often they had to abandon their mounts and go on foot. I have seen their horses slip and fall into abysses. Sometimes one had to go on all fours. Some, to avoid vertigo, had to be guided with closed eyes.

"Then there was snow, which caused fresh suffering. Roads were worn through the snow a yard deep. Albanian guerrillas were taking pot shots at us from behind rocks high up or from opposite sides of the canyons.

"The army could not bring its guns and convoys through such country. When we began to enter it we had to destroy automobiles, wagons, vehicles, and every sort of gun. Officers and soldiers wept as they demolished their guns, those pieces of steel which they called their 'French friends,' the ordnance having been made at Creusot. The men had become attached to them and many artillerists served the same gun four years. Some officers refused to destroy their pieces, saying they preferred to use their last bit of strength in trying to save them; and some of them have succeeded and actually have brought their guns across.

"After all these sufferings from cold, hunger, and fatigue, many soldiers being barefoot, we are here.

"Altogether there have arrived by various routes 6,000 women and children. The tragedy of the situation is that the army has almost nothing to eat. The soldiers had no bread for four days, but small quantities of flour were kept for the women and children."

Germans May Have Sunk Persia.

During his visit to the State Department Count von Bernstorff also informed Secretary Lansing that an official dispatch from Berlin brought the information that the German Government only knew of the Persia disaster through the newspaper reports and was not aware that any German submarine sank the liner. That a German submarine may have sunk the Persia is inferred from the statement that "thus also in the Persia case if the circumstances should call for it." The American Government also is to be notified of such facts as are obtained. From this allusion to the Persia it is now believed here that should a German commander report that he attacked the Persia, and if it should be shown that the Persia neither tried to flee nor offered resistance, Germany would punish that commander and make reparation to the United States.

Similarly, the dispatch from Ambassador Penfield at Vienna stated that the Austrian Government had not been notified that any of its submarines sank the Persia, but that any information that the Vienna Government obtained from its commanders would be communicated to the United States. It was pointed out at the State Department today that neither from Vienna, Berlin, London, Malta, Cairo, Alexandria, nor Marseilles had the United States Government been able to obtain any facts regarding the sinking of the Persia that could be regarded as evidence that the steamer was torpedoed, or upon which this Government could act.

During his conference with Secretary Lansing, Count von Bernstorff again discussed the Lusitania case. While neither would disclose the result of the conference, there is authority for the statement that these discussions have made such progress that the Lusitania question soon will be settled to the satisfaction of both Governments. Germany will pay an indemnity for the loss of American lives in the destruction of the Lusitania. There will be some form of disavowal, but the wording of this has not been finally determined, and this is understood to be the only cause of the delay in the settlement. That there will be a prompt settlement is conceded.

Secretary Lansing would not today state the character of the note from Germany on the Frye case. He said this note would be made public tomorrow. It is understood that in this communication Germany grants what the United States asked. The note is declared to be satisfactory.

"All the News That's Fit to Print."

The New York Times.

THE WEATHER
Cloudy, warmer Monday, rain by night; Tuesday rain or snow, colder; south month in northwest gales, becoming northwest.
For full weather report see page 16

VOL. LXV...NO. 21,170.   NEW YORK, MONDAY, JANUARY 10, 1916.—TWENTY PAGES.   ONE CENT In Greater New York, Jersey City and Newark | TWO CENTS Elsewhere

ALLIES ABANDON ALL OF GALLIPOLI, ESCAPING FROM TURKS WITHOUT LOSS; MINE SINKS BATTLESHIP EDWARD VII.

WARSHIP'S CREW ALL SAVED

Only Two Men Wounded as Giant British Craft Is Abandoned.

SCENE OF DISASTER SECRET

Admiralty Gives Out Mere Bulletin of Accident, Withholding the Details.

LONDON, Monday, Jan. 10.—The British public received another severe shock from the announcement last night of the loss of the battleship King Edward VII., which has been blown up by a mine.

The brief official statement on this subject does not reveal the scene of the disaster. It reads:

"H. M. S. King Edward VII. has struck a mine. Owing to the heavy sea she had to be abandoned and sank shortly afterwards. The ship's company was taken off without any loss of life. Only two men were injured."

The King Edward VII. represented an investment of nearly £1,600,000 ($8,000,000), and was one of the finest of the last class of predreadnoughts, corresponding in general to the American ships of the New Jersey and Nebraska type. She was only slightly older than the Natal, which was sunk by an internal explosion about a week ago.

Special Cable to THE NEW YORK TIMES.
LONDON, Monday, Jan. 10.—Naval critics speak of the sinking of the King Edward VII. as a serious loss because, although she was nearly eleven years old, she was a valuable unit. She and her seven sister ships constituted a swift, powerful and homogeneous squadron."

She is the eighth battleship lost in the war, not one of which was destroyed in action. She also was the heaviest vessel lost, her displacement being 16,350 tons, against the Blücher's 15,500 tons.

There is much satisfaction over the fact that the officers and crew, numbering more than 800, were saved, in spite of the rough weather and heavy seas, attesting the discipline and resource of those aboard. The naval critics point out that, notwithstanding the British naval losses to date, the grand fleet is actually and relatively stronger than it was when hostilities opened.

A dispatch to The Daily Mail from Chatham says that a trainload of men from the sunken battleship King Edward VII. arrived there Sunday afternoon, and were taken direct to the naval barracks.

The King Edward VII. was a barbette

battleship of 16,350 tons displacement laid down on March 8, 1902, at Portsmouth Dockyard, when King Edward laid the first plate. She was launched on July 23 of the following year, the Princess of Wales, now Queen Mary, acting as sponsor.

The King Edward VII. was one of a class which included the New Zealand, Commonwealth, Dominion and Hindustan which were designed by the late Sir William H. White, formerly director of Naval Construction and later with the firm of Armstrong, Whitworth & Co., Ltd.

The day the building of the King Edward VII. was started was notable in the annals of British shipbuilding. Five minutes before the first plate was laid Queen Alexandra had named the battleship Queen before that vessel was launched from the same slip and blocks.

The King Edward VII. was 425 feet long, with a 78-foot beam. She was equipped with two triple-expansion vertical engines of 18,000 horse power, and made nineteen knots on her trial trip. She was armed with four 12-inch, four 9.2-inch and ten 6-inch guns in her main battery. She had a number of quick-firing guns of various calibres and Maxim guns and four torpedo tubes submerged. She carried 800 officers and men. The King Edward VII. was built under the direction of Rear Admiral W. H. Henderson and J. Black, Chief Constructor for the Admiralty. About 6,100 tons of material was used in her construction, including 675 tons of armor.

ONLY ONE HURT IN RETREAT

All Artillery Saved Except 17 Old Guns—These Reported Destroyed.

CAMPAIGN COSTLY FAILURE

Casualties and Sick Estimated at 200,000, While Five Battleships Were Sunk.

LONDON, Monday, Jan. 10.—The remaining positions held by the Allies on Gallipoli Peninsula have now been abandoned, with the wounding of only one man among the British and French, according to a British official statement issued last night.

A semi-official report from Constantinople, according to an Amsterdam dispatch to Reuter's Telegram Company,

claims "the capture by the Turks of a great enemy camp and nine guns, and the sinking of an enemy vessel with troops near Sedd-el-Bahr."

The British official communication follows:

General Sir Charles Monro reports the complete evacuation of Gallipoli has been successfully carried out.

All the guns and howitzers were got away, with the exception of seventeen wornout guns, which were blown up by us before leaving.

Our casualties amounted to one member of the British rank and file wounded.

There were no casualties among the French.

General Monro states that the accomplishment of this difficult task was due to Generals Birdwood and Davies, and invaluable assistance rendered in an operation of the highest difficulty by Admiral de Robeck of the Royal Navy.

News of the final evacuation of the peninsula has been expected for several days by the keener observers of the Near Eastern campaign, for the retirement of the troops from Anzac and Suvla Bay three weeks ago left no strategic advantage to the retention of the tip of the peninsula. Nevertheless, the news will be received with a pang of regret by the people of the British Isles, as well as the colonies.

However, the London morning papers comment with satisfaction and relief on the success of the operation of withdrawal. They consider, despite General Monro's generous tribute to Generals Birdwood and Davies, that credit for the remarkable double retirement should be attributed to General Monro himself. The Times says editorially:

"Twice within a few weeks General Monro has managed to remove his men and guns under the eyes of the Turks and their German officers. We doubt if a precedent for such an achievement can be found in the annals of war.

"The extraordinary freedom from casualties at Helles is explainable to some extent by the fact that, unlike Anzac and Suvla, it gave us one beach sheltered from the enemy's fire. But neither operation would have been possible with any but the boldest and steadiest troops. The Government may be congratulated on their prompt decision on the complete evacuation of the peninsula."

As regards the wisdom of the movement, The Daily Chronicle says:

"The evacuation of Suvla meant the renunciation of any offensive on the peninsula. That being so, the abandonment of Cape Helles is no longer a loss. It is a difficult and costly area to hold, for every spot in it is within range of the enemy's artillery, and could be shelled not only from the front, but across the strait from the forts on the Asiatic shore. Its occupation conferred on us no power of blocking the strait which we cannot still exercise through our occupation of Imbros and Tenedos, and it is not too much to say that the only motive left for holding it was the difficulty of getting the men off. Now this has been overcome there is ground for heartfelt satisfaction."

The King Edward VII. Sunk By a Mine

"All the News That's Fit to Print."

The New York Times.

THE WEATHER
Probably rain or snow today; Friday unsettled, probably rain, fresh east winds.
For full weather report see Page 21.

VOL. LXV...NO. 21,215. .....   NEW YORK, THURSDAY, FEBRUARY 24, 1916.—TWENTY-TWO PAGES.   ONE CENT In Greater New York, Jersey City and Newark.   TWO CENTS Elsewhere.

GERMANS HURL 280,000 MEN AT VERDUN; BATTLE NOW RAGING ON 25-MILE FRONT; BERLIN REPORTS PIERCING LINE 2 MILES

3,000 FRENCH CAPTURED

A Continuous Bombardment With Heavy Guns Preceded the Attack.

FRENCH FIRE EFFECTIVE

Stops the Germans at Herbebois, but They Carry Several Positions on the Meuse.

GERMAN GAINS IN ALSACE

700-Yard Front Penetrated 400 Yards, Though the French Retake a Part of It.

LONDON, Feb. 23.—The most ambitious offensive since the French advance in Champagne is now in progress to the north and northeast of Verdun, and has so far resulted in German gains of nearly two miles at various points along a twenty-five-mile front. Seven army corps (280,000 men) are assailing the French positions, the attack having been preceded by a bombardment of guns of heavy calibre. The French admit the loss of several positions, but assert that their counterattacks have checked the enemy's advance at other points, and that they have inflicted heavy losses upon their assailants.

Reports from Berlin say that 3,000 French prisoners were taken.

The French have also suffered the loss of trenches southwest of Altkirch, in Alsace, but there, too, report that they have recovered a part of the positions at first abandoned.

Germans Tell of Gains Near Verdun.

The official report from Berlin says:

In the neighborhood of the trenches captured by our troops Feb. 21 to the east of Souchez the positions of the enemy were considerably damaged by mining operations. The number of prisoners taken here was increased to 11 officers and 348 men. The booty consisted of three machine guns.

In the Meuse hills artillery duels continued with undiminished violence.

East of the Meuse River we attacked a position which the enemy has been fortifying for one and a half years with all means of fortress construction, in the neighborhood of the village of Consenvoye, in order to maintain an embarrassing effect on our defense in the northern sector of the Woevre.

The attack was delivered on a front extending well over ten kilometres (six miles) and we penetrated as far as three kilometres into the enemy lines.

Apart from considerable sanguinary losses, the enemy lost more than 8,000 men in prisoners and great quantities of material, the extent of which cannot yet be estimated.

In Upper Alsace our attack to the east of Heidwiler resulted in capturing an enemy position extending over a width of 700 meters and for a depth of 400 meters. About eighty prisoners were taken.

In numerous aerial engagements behind the enemy lines our aviators maintained the upper hand.

The official communication issued by the French War Office tonight says:

In Belgium the destructive fire of our artillery opened several breaches in the German trenches in front of Steenstraete.

To the north of the Aisne our batteries shattered enemy organizations on the Plateau of Vauclerg.

In the region to the north of Verdun the German attack, as was foreseen, developed into a very important action, for which powerful preparations were made.

Heavy Losses for the Germans.

The battle continued today with increasing intensity, and was energetically withstood by our troops, who inflicted extremely heavy losses on the enemy. The bombardment with shells of heavy calibre was uninterrupted, and our artillery responded with equal violence. It covered a front of nearly forty kilometres (twenty-five miles) from Malancourt as far as the region opposite Etain.

The actions of the German infantry were carried out by very heavy effectives, comprising troops of seven different army corps, who followed one another in the course of the day between Brabant-sur-Meuse and Ornes.

At the approach to the village of Haumont the enemy was not able, notwithstanding his efforts, to force us from our positions. In the Bois des Caures, of which we hold the greater part, our counterattacks stopped the enemy's offensive.

To the east of the Bois des Caures the Germans were able to penetrate the Wavrille Wood after a series of bloody encounters.

To the north of Ornes the enemy's attacks against our line at Herbebois were arrested by our counterattacks. There was no infantry action on the left bank of the Meuse, nor between Ornes and Fromézey.

French Alsace Trenches Taken.

In Alsace yesterday at the end of the day the enemy attacked our positions to the southeast of the Carspach Wood, southwest of Altkirch. An immediate counter attack drove him out from the greater part of the advanced sections where he had gained a footing.

The text of the French afternoon statement follows:

We have retaken some sections of the trenches in the woods of Givenchy.

In the regions to the north of Verdun the bombardment by the enemy, which has been energetically answered by us, continued throughout the night. Infantry actions have developed on a front of fifteen kilometers (more than nine miles.) The struggle is continued with violence along the right banks of the Meuse toward the southeast. East of this point a counter-attack enabled us to retake the greater part of the forest of Causres, situated in the salient occupied yesterday by the enemy to the north of Beaumont.

A strong German attack on Herbebois was stopped by our curtain of fire. According to statements of prisoners certain German units were completely destroyed in the course of these actions.

A desultory artillery duel continues in the region of Haute Charrière and of Fromézey in Lorraine. In the region of Nomeny our artillery has been very active. An enemy reconnoissance to the north of Létricourt failed to reach our lines.

In Herbebois we have evacuated the village of Haumont. We still hold the environs after a bitter fight, in which our troops inflicted very heavy losses on the enemy.

The British official report on the campaign in the west, issued tonight, reads as follows:

There was some artillery activity in the neighborhood of La Bassée Canal. North and east of Ypres our guns did considerable damage to the enemy's positions.

On our extreme left we shelled working parties last night, and in grenade fighting in a mine crater dispersed a party of enemy grenadiers.

AUTOMOBILE BATTERY DESTROYED ZEPPELIN

PARIS, Feb. 23.—An eyewitness of the destruction of Zeppelin L-Z 77 by French gunners on Monday, near Revigny, a town which lies nine miles northwest of Bar-le-Duc, thus describes the exploit:

"Two Zeppelins were signaled at 10:25 o'clock at night by an artillery officer in a listening post in the first-line trenches of the Argonne. The night was clear and the wind moderate. The officer could not see the airships, but he heard the noise of their engines and telephoned to the battery base, whence the news was forwarded to the army corps headquarters. All the batteries of the district were at once on the alert, and within five minutes searchlights were sweeping the heavens in all directions.

"The Zeppelins were first sighted by an officer commanding a battery of 75-millimeter guns. The nearest was then about two miles off, flying at an attitude of about 5,000 feet and rising rapidly. The second Zeppelin was some three miles behind the first. The officer was unable to get the elevation necessary to hit the airship, but he managed to give the exact position to the searchlight operators. From that moment until it was destroyed the first dirigible was never lost to view, and the searchlights never left it. As it was moving against the wind its progress was relatively slow.

"As soon as the warning reached Revigny, five automobiles, with searchlights and with special anti-aircraft guns, manned by naval gunners, started in pursuit. These guns throw a shell which is expressly designed to explode on contact with the aluminium-painted covering of the Zeppelins and to burst into flames once it is inside. As the car rushes along the road, the officer standing in the back of the car gives the range and directs the fire of the gun by the crew which work the gun lying on the flat of their backs.

"The guns on the moving automobiles opened fire as soon as they came within range. A shell burst just behind the Zeppelin, throwing it into strong relief, and immediately the gunners seized their opportunity. Another shell passed over the target, but the next, of the inflammable type, hit the mark squarely about seventy-five feet from the stern.

"There was a shout of triumph from the Frenchmen as the shell appeared to go through the body of the airship and to adhere to the right side of the framework, which it set afire. A few seconds later two other shells went through the rear of the car, badly damaging the steering and elevating mechanism.

"For an instant nothing seemed to happen, and then a thin red line crept along the side of the airship, which shone with a bright ruddy glow as the flames spread and moved upward. No explosion was heard as the Zeppelin began to fall. The great mass, now blazing more and more fiercely, descended slowly, while burning fragments of the cover fluttered away in the wind, and all the onlookers expressed surprise that the airship took so long to come down.

"The cargo of bombs, which there is reason to believe were to have been dropped on the inhabitants of Paris, exploded with a terrific roar as the Zeppelin struck the ground. Fragments of its car were hurled over 2,000 feet away, and the remainder of the huge framework collapsed in a heap, the fire continuing to burn for several hours."

Scene of Great German Drive at Verdun.

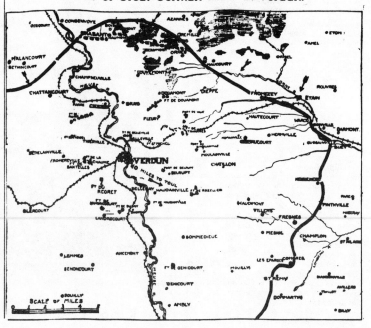

HOUSE IN REVOLT OVER ARMED LINERS; DEMOCRATS DEMAND THAT PRESIDENT CHANGE POLICY AND WARN AMERICANS

CONGRESSMEN NEAR PANIC

Fear Nation Will Be Drawn Into Conflict Unless President Yields.

Special to The New York Times.

WASHINGTON, Feb. 23.—A revolt in Congress against President Wilson's policy of dealing firmly with Germany's revival of submarine warfare—a revolt of dramatic surprise that came today, unexpectedly, suddenly—has produced a crisis in domestic politics and increased the gravity of a delicate international situation.

Leaders of the House of Representatives virtually served notice on President Wilson this afternoon that unless within forty-eight hours he agreed to warn American citizens that they must not take passage on armed belligerent merchant ships, which the Germans and Austrians threaten to sink on sight, the House by an overwhelming majority would issue the warning in the form of a resolution.

House leaders are to tell the President that persistence in his present policy will lead inevitably to war. They and their followers appear to be panic-stricken over the idea that hostilities with the Teutonic Empires are certain if the President does not yield to the clamor on Capitol Hill. The President's answer, already forecast, is that if American lives are sacrificed through the sinking of a merchant ship, armed or unarmed, by a Teutonic submarine, he will dismiss Count von Bernstorff, the German Ambassador, and Baron Zwiedinek, the Austro-Hungarian Chargé d'Affaires, recall Ambassador Gerard from Berlin and Ambassador Penfield from Vienna, and sever diplomatic relations with the German and Austrian Governments.

Crisis Comes Suddenly.

Veteran legislators said tonight that not for many years had they seen a situation so dramatic and sensational. None could recall any that had developed with such startling suddenness. All day there had been quiet conferences between House leaders among themselves and with Democratic leaders of the Senate. Then, unexpectedly, the storm burst. It was apparent that a majority of the House was ready to act. This majority—militant in knowledge of its strength and urged to action by what was described as a panic—demanded immediate action on a resolution of Representative McLemore of Texas, previously offered, directing that a warning be issued to American citizens not to take passage on armed belligerent merchant ships. A meeting of the Democratic members of the House Committee on Foreign Affairs was called at once to consider the affair. Afterward members who attended the meeting declared that sentiment was unanimous among them in favor of the McLemore resolution or a measure of similar purpose.

Speaker Clark and Representative Kitchin, the Democratic floor leader, while admitting to their party friends that they were in favor of having Americans warned to keep off armed merchantmen, labored with their associates not to attempt to force the President's hand today. In consequence of their efforts, the Foreign Affairs Committee decided to take no action until the President had been consulted. But this was agreed to with the significant understanding that the President would be told tomorrow that unless he modified his attitude toward Germany's armed merchantmen order within forty-eight hours, the House would adopt a resolution warning Americans not to take passage on vessels carrrying arms.

ASQUITH RESTATES BRITISH WAR AIMS

Will Not Sheathe the Sword Till Belgium and Serbia Are Avenged.

LONDON, Feb. 23.—Premier Asquith found himself unexpectedly face to face in the House of Commons today with a new demand for the Government's views on peace. He took up the gauntlet almost eagerly, and in a bristling fifteen-minute speech made it clear that the British Government's determination to wage war to the end without compromise had not abated a jot or tittle since the early days of the struggle.

The climax of Mr. Asquith's speech was reached in these words:

"I have stated in clear, direct, explicit and emphatic language what are the terms upon which we in this country are prepared to make peace. I will repeat them. They are familiar to our allies and well known to the German Chancellor.

"What I said Nov. 9, 1914, I repeat now: 'We shall never sheathe the sword which we have not lightly drawn until Belgium—and, I will add, Serbia—recover in full measure all and more than they have sacrificed; until France is adequately secured against aggression; until the rights of the small nations of Europe are based upon an unassailable foundation, and until the military domination of Prussia is wholly and finally destroyed.'

"What is there wanting in clearness and directness in that? I ask Mr. Trevelyan and the German Chancellor how I can make it fuller and more intelligible? Ho can I do more to convince him and all our enemies that not until a peace based upon these foundations is within sight of attainment, and not until then, shall we or any of our allies abate by one jot our prosecution of this war?"

The Prime Minister's stern declaration created a deep impression on all parts of the House, and this found deep reflection subsequently in the lobbies.

The occasion for his pronouncement was a speech which Philip Snowden of the Independent Labor Party, injected into the debate on the Consolidated Fund bill, a routine measure providing appropriations mainly for interest on the national debt.

Mr. Snowden urged that the time was ripe for peace negotiations, maintaining that there was little or no hope of a crushing victory on either side, and that if the war went on all the participants would be bankrupt in men and money.

He agreed that the present military situation was not necessarily evidence that a decisive military victory might not yet come to the Allies, though he said few men who took an intelligent and dispassionate view of the situation and the lessons it had taught would say that there was any reasonable ground for hope of a decisive and crushing military victory for either contending party.

If Great Britain was determined to continue in the expectation of crushing Germany, he said, her people ought to be convinced that it was the best method for establishing the international relations of the European powers. He, however, believed that a continued attempt to crush Germany would be the worst basis for the establishment of a just and lasting settlement.

The speaker asserted that all the nations, and especially Germany, were being driven to accept the evidence of this war of the futility of militarism, and the time was therefore ripe for making a movement in the direction of peace. In particular, Mr. Snowden maintained that the German Socialists were solidly in favor of peace, now that it had been proved that Germany was invulnerable from external attack.

The Premier said he welcomed Mr. Snowden's admission that the country was at one and would remain of one mind in demanding that the conditions of peace should be such as to secure the permanent attainment of the national aim.

"There is absolute unity in the country," he continued.

Mr. Asquith remarked that Mr. Snowden's statement on the military situation was a matter of opinion. "It is not mine," was his comment.

The real gist of Mr. Snowden's speech, added the Premier, was the contention that a genuine desire for peace existed in Germany. As evidence of this there was the report of the debate in the Reichstag and the Chancellor's speech in which he said he would welcome approaches from any quarter, but did not say he was prepared to make approaches himself.

The Premier referred in biting terms to the Chancellor's statement that Germany was not the enemy of small nations, and characterized the statement as "colossal and shameless audacity" after her treatment of Belgium and Serbia.

Mr. Asquith was followed by a score of speakers, for the most part applauding the Premier's position. Two or three so-called peace advocates, including Charles P. Trevelyan, Liberal member for the Elland Division of Yorkshire supported Mr. Snowden, but found themselves scarcely tolerated by their audience. The only applause in the course of any of the pro-peace speeches came from a spectator in the Strangers' Gallery, who was promptly ejected.

Stephen Walsh, for the Labor Party, denied that Mr. Snowden expressed the opinion of organized labor.

"The Allies cannot make peace overtures," he said, "while the tiger has its fangs in the vitals of Belgium, Serbia and Poland."

The House of Lords continued today the debate on the blockade. Lord Sydenham finally withdrew his motion for a stricter blockade after the Earl of Crewe, Lord President of the Council, had further clarified the Government's position.

Asquith Stirred His Audience.

Special Cable to THE NEW YORK TIMES.

LONDON, Thursday, Feb. 24.—The Chronicle this morning says:

"Never has Premier Asquith spoken with more passion and determination than he did this evening when, replying to the peace speeches made by Snowdon and Trevelyan, who pressed him to state clearly the conditions on which the British Government is willing to make peace, he reiterated his declaration of 1914, asserting that Great Britain will never sheathe the sword until Belgium recovers in full measure all and more than she sacrificed; until France is adequately secured against the menace of aggression; until the rights of the smaller nationalities of Europe are placed upon an unassailable foundation, and until the military domination of Prussia is wholly and finally destroyed. To the name of Belgium he now added the name of Serbia.

"'What,' he asked, 'is there wanting in the clearness or directness in that language? How can I make it more full or more intelligible? Not until peace based on those foundations is within sight and obtainable shall we or any of our gallant allies abate by one jot the prosecution of this war.'

"Into these concluding sentences Premier Asquith put all his heart and soul and strength. As he declaimed them in tones of thunder and with accents of intense conviction the glow of his oratory set the hearts of his audience on fire, and its feelings presently found expression in a great outburst of applause, which was renewed again and again."

BATTLE CRUISERS ENGLAND'S PRIDE

An Unknown Quantity at the Beginning of the War, They Now Lead the Line.

LONDON, Feb. 11, (Correspondence of The Associated Press.)—Speed, with sufficient gun power to cause the necessary destruction, is now the cardinal principle of the British naval strategy, and battle cruisers, an unknown quantity at the beginning of the war, have proved this principle to the satisfaction of every man aboard the battle cruiser fleet, which was visited this week in the North Sea by a correspondent of The Associated Press.

New battle cruisers before the war were not exactly objects of pride to their officers and crews. On account of the voracity with which they consumed coal, service on them was not popular and a Government harassed with demands for a reduction in naval expenditure had no reason to favor these refinements of the superdreadnought school.

To prove that the battle cruiser has redeemed its unfortunate early reputation, it is only necessary to point to the activities of this type of fighting craft since the war began. Battle cruisers brought von Spee's career to an end, and they were the only big ships which succeeded in getting into the North Sea engagements. So it is not surprising that these monsters, the biggest fighting machines afloat, are idolized by their officers and men.

A squadron at the opening of the war, the battle cruisers now form the nucleus of Great Britain's first-line fleet of naval offense. There are many new ships among the light cruisers attached to this squadron, but virtually every battle cruiser in it has been "blooded," to use the navy's equivalent for the army's baptism of fire, and the sailors manning them show the pride and poise of veterans.

When the mist lifted for a few minutes as the correspondent stood on the control bridge of one of the battle cruisers, the fastest fleet capable of actual offensive operations ever gathered under one flag appeared in view. There were more than 100 war vessels in the fleet, arranged in squadrons, with battle cruisers surrounded by their screen of faithful destroyers occupying the place of honor, but with every section, down to the humble, rusty but virtually necessary colliers, on the mark for a flying start if the eagerly-awaited coming-out of the German fleet is signalled.

One lone dreadnought, powerful enough to meet almost any foe, but painfully slow in comparison with the other units of the fleet, swung at anchor. The officers on the bridge jokingly explained that she formed the third line to come on and pick up the pieces, or, if necessary, to be sent out as bait for the wary German fleet.

The mobility of this fleet has thrown on it much of the patrol work in the North Sea, and it is accepted as a matter of course that should the German warships come out it will be the first unit of the British Navy to feel the shock of battle, as, on account of its speed, it will be able to get into action before the superdreadnought battleships reach the scene. Hence its claim to being the first line of offense, with the superdreadnoughts second, and the old battleships of the predreadnought period forming a powerful third line reserve. No land force ever has been so well protected against unforeseen disaster as the British Navy.

Increase in the size of the big guns does not worry the officers of the battle cruisers, who say that since their 13.5-inch guns can sink a battleship as far as the range can be found, any bigger guns would add to the weight of the ship and reduce the available space for turrets, without sufficient corresponding advantage. These officers talked about the much-heralded German 17-inch gun in a speculative way, but, even admitting the possibility of mounting it on a warship, they did not show any great concern.

This feeling of confidence in their ships is not a matter of theory, for the battle cruisers are the veterans of this war. In destructive power they have done only what was expected of them, but in their powers of resistance they have more than surprised their officers.

This wasteland is what was left after one of the most intensive artillery battles in World War I—the battle of Verdun.

"All the News That's Fit to Print."

The New York Times.

THE WEATHER
Fair Monday and probably Tuesday; rising temperature Tuesday; strong west winds, diminishing.
For full weather report see Page 17.

VOL. LXV...NO. 21,219. ...   NEW YORK, MONDAY, FEBRUARY 28, 1916.—EIGHTEEN PAGES.   ONE CENT In Greater New York, Jersey City and Newark. | TWO CENTS

GERMAN GUNS BLOW UP VERDUN FORTS; FOUR SHOTS DESTROYED DOUAUMONT; SINGLE SHOT LEVELS A SECOND FORT

FIERCE FIGHTING ON SLOPES

Those of Douaumont Strewn With Dead Bodies of Germans.

CHAMPNEUVILLE IS TAKEN

Village West of the Fort Falls— Talou Ridge Untenable for Either Side.

15,000 FRENCH PRISONERS

LONDON, Feb. 27.—Today's fighting in the Verdun region has been most intense around the armored fort of Douaumont, for the possession of which French and Germans are desperately contending. Apparently the Germans yesterday succeeded in throwing a force into this position and have maintained themselves there despite repeated counterattacks, of which the Berlin report mentions five. The capture of Champneuville and the Côte de Talou (both to the west of Fort Douaumont) and of the fortified wood of Hardaumont, to the east, is reported from Berlin. Paris asserts that the French still hold Hardaumont and that the Talou ridge is so swept by artillery fire as to be untenable for neither side.

The official statement from Berlin says:

On the heights to the right of the Meuse the French attempted by attacks, repeated five times with fresh troops, to reconquer the armored fortress of Douaumont. They were repulsed with sanguinary losses.

To the west of the fort our troops have taken Champneuville, the Côte de Talou, and have advanced as far as Nave on the southern border of the wood northeast of Bras.

To the east of the fort we took by storm the extended fortified works of Hardaumont.

In the Woevre plain vigorous fighting is taking place on the German frontier, the battles extending as far as the Côte Lorraine.

According to information at present in hand the number of unwounded prisoners amounts to nearly 15,000.

In Flanders our aeroplane squadrons repeated their attacks on the camp of the enemy troops.

A bomb attack on Metz by enemy aviators resulted in the injury or death of eight civilians and several soldiers. Several houses were damaged.

In the neighborhood of the fortress a French aeroplane was brought down in an aerial battle and by the bombardment of the anti-aircraft guns. The occupants of the machine included two Captains, who were captured.

On various portions of the front there were intense artillery and mine battles.

South of Ypres a British attack was repulsed.

The official communication issued in Paris tonight reads as follows:

In the region to the north of Verdun, following the violent actions of the preceding days, there has been some abatement in the efforts of the enemy in the course of the day, except between the height of Douaumont and the plateau to the north of the village of Vaux, where a strong attack carried out against our positions was repulsed.

To the east and west of the position of Douaumont, the slopes of which are covered with German bodies, our troops are pressing closely the enemy detachments which were able to gain a foothold there, and which are maintaining themselves with difficulty.

According to the latest reports, the Côte de Talou, rendered untenable as well for us as for the enemy by the bombardment of the artillery of both sides, is not occupied by any of the adversary forces.

In the Woevre, the enemy has come in contact with our advance posts in the direction of Blanzée and Moranville, where their efforts to debouch toward Hill 255 failed.

Between Soissons and Rheims destructive firing has been carried out on the enemy works in front of Venizel and to the east of Troyon.

In the Vosges there was an artillery duel at Hartmanns-Weilerkopf. We took under our fire and dispersed an enemy detachment in the region of Senones.

The text of the French afternoon statement follows:

In the region to the north of Verdun our troops during the night continued to reinforce their positions. There was no change on the front of attack.

To the east of the Meuse, where the snow fell in abundance, no new attack by the enemy was reported up to the close of yesterday, nor upon the Côte du Talou, nor upon the Côte du Poivre.

A strong German attack, launched in the region of the Haudromont farm, east of the Côte du Poivre, was broken down by our artillery and machine gun fire and by our counterattacks.

Another attack no less violent in the region of the woods of Hardaumont, east of Douaumont, had no more success.

In the Woevre the orderly retirement of our advanced posts was effected without the least interference from the enemy. To the west of the Meuse no infantry action took place.

In the Vosges, after artillery preparation, the enemy at nightfall yesterday attempted a strong attack on a front of two kilometers to the southeast of Celles in the Valley of the Plaine. The attack was completely checked.

This morning action by our batteries against the revictualing depots of the enemy at Vosewhir, north of Münster, gave good results.

The British official report reads as follows:

Last night we repulsed a small attack on our trenches north of the Ypres-Comines Canal.

Second Fort Blown Up.

The Berlin Tageblatt Dispatches.

Special Cable to THE NEW YORK TIMES.

GERMAN GREAT HEADQUARTERS, BEFORE VERDUN, Feb. 26.—The giant block of cement and steel armorplate that was Douaumont lies in ruins. A second fort not far off blew up, just as did Fort Loncin at Liége, as the result of a single large calibred shell crashing through to the ammunition magazine.

The organization of the attack on the north front of Verdun was a masterpiece in itself. Preparations of vast extent had first to be carried out in complete concealment from the enemy if the fight against the invincible fortress was to succeed.

To the great distance over which heavy artillery had to be brought without using railways were superadded the great difficulties resulting from continuous bad weather and the consequent condition of roads. Hundreds of men had first to build good roads.

Another of the difficulties was the proper laying of the beds on which the great guns rest, and on whose firmness depends in the first line the accuracy of our heavy gun fire. How unbelievably accurate was their fire is now known.

Yesterday there was hardly any firing of importance to be heard from the forts. On the other hand, prisoners said that the effect of our artillery was indescribably frightful; nobody could hold out long against it.

Verdun Victory Hinges Now on Ammunition; French Rush Men and Guns to Threatened Front

Special Cable to THE NEW YORK TIMES.

PARIS, Feb. 27, (Dispatch to The London Daily Mail.)—Wounded soldiers who have reached Paris say that the carnage among the Germans has been simply terrible. At many places the German dead formed huge dams across the ravines, impeding the water on its downward course to the Meuse. Every now and then one of these dams gives way, and the reddened stream swirls on again, carrying with it hundreds of corpses.

During the week of battle the French have not been idle, and along the eastern railway line have been rushing troops and munition trains night and day. The French Generals realize that victory in the present battle will go to the army which makes the best use of its artillery, and so battery after battery of light and heavy guns since Monday has been sent up to the Argonne and Meuse Heights.

The French hitherto have regarded their artillery offensive of last September in the Champagne as the greatest effort of the war, but the present battle upset all the calculations of the staffs and the consumption of shells of every calibre has greatly exceeded all estimates. The French have plentiful supplies, however, and if the battle ends for lack of munitions that lack will be on the German and not on the French side.

French Rushing Reinforcements to Verdun

OTTAWA, Feb. 27.—British lines in Belgium and France are being extended to replace French troops who are being rushed to the Verdun region to take part in the fighting "which has settled down to a terrific slaughter," according to advices received here from the battle front.

Approximately twenty army divisions (400,000 men) have been thrown into the battle by the Germans, while the French troops number fifteen divisions, cable messages say.

"All the News That's Fit to Print."

The New York Times.

THE WEATHER
Increasing cloudiness, probably snow today; snow tomorrow; not much change in temperature; moderate variable winds.
☞For full weather report see Page 19.

VOL. LXV ... NO. 21,220   NEW YORK, TUESDAY, FEBRUARY 29, 1916—TWENTY PAGES   ONE CENT   In Greater New York, Jersey City and Newark   Elsewhere TWO CENTS

GERMAN DRIVE AT VERDUN CHECKED; BATTLE STILL RAGES AT DOUAUMONT WHERE KAISER'S FORCE IS HEMMED IN

FIGHTING HAND TO HAND

Crucial Struggle Going On in the Centre of Battle Front.

FRENCH WIN BACK REDOUBT

And Still Hold Village Before Fort in Spite of Terrific German Attacks.

GERMAN RIGHT PRESSES ON

Teuton Forces in the Champagne, by a Sudden Stroke, Win a Mile of Trenches.

PARIS, Feb. 28.—Strong attacks are being pressed by the Germans to the north of Verdun today, but according to the official communications issued by the War Office the French lines are holding firm.

Counterattacks are being made by the French in the region around Fort Douaumont, and the Germans are said to have been driven out of a redoubt, west of the main works, in a hand-to-hand encounter.

The fortress itself apparently is still held by the Germans, but is "closely encircled" according to the War Office. In the village of Douaumont, a few hundred yards from the fort, there was a furious struggle last night, but the War Office announces that German attempts to capture the village resulted in failure.

Artillery fire continues with great intensity here, but on the west of the Meuse there has been a slackening of the bombardment.

An extension of the German offensive along the front to the east and southeast is indicated by the official bulletins. The afternoon statement reports a futile German attack against Manheulles, ten miles southeast of Verdun, which apparently indicates a German advance in that quarter. The night report chronicles two attacks on Fresnes in the same region. Both are said to have been failures.

Outside of the vitally important struggle at Verdun the most noteworthy feature of the official reports is the admission of loss of ground in Champagne. Here the Germans were able to occupy outer French trenches and also a supporting trench.

Fighting Hand to Hand.

The night bulletin of the War Office is as follows:

In the Argonne our heavy batteries and field guns shelled the roads of access of the enemy, particularly in the region of the Cheppy wood. This morning at Hill 285 we exploded a mine, the crater of which we occupied.

In the region to the north of Verdun artillery activity on both sides is still very spirited, except in the sector to the west of the Meuse, where an abatement of the enemy bombardment is reported.

The Germans during the course of the day attempted several partial attacks, which were driven back by our fire and our counterattack.

To the west of Fort Douaumont particularly our troops have engaged in hand-to-hand encounters with the adversary, who was ejected from a small redoubt, where he had succeeded in installing himself.

In the Woevre two attacks against Fresnes completely failed.

In Lorraine our artillery has displayed marked activity in the sectors of Reillon, Domebre, and Badonviller.

The afternoon bulletin of the French War Office reads:

In Belgium our batteries have bombarded German organizations located opposite Steeenstrate.

In Champagne, in the region of the Navarin Farm, to the north of Souain, the enemy was successful by a surprise attack in occupying certain trenches of our advance line; they also took a supporting trench.

In the region to the north of Verdun the bombardment has continued with intensity, particularly in the central sectors and on our right. There has been no further attack on the Côte du Poivre.

Furious Assaults on Douaumont.

Yesterday evening German forces made several attempts to occupy the village of Douaumont. Their efforts were broken by the resistance of our troops, who withstood the most furious assaults.

There is no change in the situation at the Fort of Douaumont, which still remains closely encircled.

The fighting is less spirited on the plateaus to the north of the village of Vaux.

In the Woevre district the enemy yesterday evening and last night assumed an attitude of greater activity. The railroad station at Eix, captured and recaptured several times by the attacks and counterattacks of the two opposing forces, now remains in our possession.

Twice in History Have Taken Verdun—Prussia's Finest Regiments.

One hundred and twenty-four years ago Verdun was captured from the Republican Army of France by a brigade from Brandenburg. Troops from this province also helped take it in 1870. Brandenburgers now make up the Sixth Division of the German Army which forms the Second Division of the Third Army Corps. This corps with the Ninth, Eleventh, and Eighth is famous for the charges it made on the forts of Liége, from Aug. 6 to 10, 1914. It was then incorporated in the Fifth Army under the command of the Prussian Crown Prince, whose plan of campaign, after the fall of the Belgian forts, was to attack immediately north of the barrier chain—Verdun-Toul and Epinal-Belfort—which runs southeast along the main roads from Luxemburg by Stenay, where the bridges cross the Meuse.

INFANTRY AGAIN A FACTOR

Paris Sees Vital War Lessons in the Verdun Combat.

TRENCHES ARE "SCRAPPED"

And the Old-Fashioned Pitched Battle Takes the Place of Deadlock.

Greatest Battle of War Now Concentrated Within Two Narrow Fronts.

Special Cable to THE NEW YORK TIMES.
PARIS, Feb. 28.—The French counterstroke at Verdun may mark the battle raging there as the beginning of the end of the war on the western front, according to military authorities here, reading between the lines of tonight's official bulletin.

That trenches have literally been scrapped and the long-drawn field fortress deadlock displaced by an old-fashioned pitched battle is the great lesson of the German attempt to take Verdun. But in teaching it there are good reasons to believe, according to the view here, that Germany may have signed her own death warrant.

What has been already indicated in the Champagne battle is now clearly proved by the German cannonade at Verdun: That under the concentrated fire of hundreds of great howitzers hurling shells weighing from one-half to three-quarters of a ton, even the strongest trenches are smashed into a defenseless chaos, and the mitrailleuse emplacements, which have previously rendered the heroism of infantry fruitless, are blasted into nothingness.

Foot soldiers have become once more, as throughout history, the decisive factor of warfare. Torn to pieces by shells, their front ranks melting under the cannonade, the waves of German soldiers nevertheless flowed incessantly over their comrades' bodies until at last General Joffre unleashed his waiting legions and man fought man as of old.

Two facts stand out clearly from the week's orgy of slaughter. The first is that German artillery cannot silence French, and the second is that if sacrifices are ignored and reserves are sufficient, infantry can advance despite the artillery and because of the practical obliteration of the mitrailleuses, may only be checked by infantry.

A Lesson for Allies.

Should Germany win five Verduns she cannot, it is held here, escape defeat, now that the Allies have learned that bloody lesson. Sooner or later the allied workshops will deliver the needed quantity of guns and munitions and the allied army will attain sufficient numerical superiority. Then will come a series of these blasting attacks, terribly expensive, but culminating inevitably, according to opinion here, in Germany's downfall. In the last resort only her infantry can save her, but her infantry has been wasted like sand from the banks of the Marne to the Riga swamps.

While the previous great battles of the war have been fought on fronts of thirty, fifty, or a hundred miles, what makes the Verdun struggle so appalling is its final concentration from a twenty-five-mile front into two short sections, each barely a mile across. The first is on the French left, and stretches from Champneuville to Côte du Poivre. The second is one the right and comprises the Douaumont spur, which is being attacked from the north and east simultaneously.

In the first section the German efforts were vain. The Kaiser's troops, directly they debouched from the ravine toward the crest, were swept away by a terrific fire from the French batteries across the Meuse, aided by mitrailleuses, which were comparatively sheltered from the German artillery.

Against Fort de Douaumont they succeeded on Saturday morning, but what they conquered and announced to the world was not a fort like the forts of Liége or Brest-Litovsk. It was armored and cemented, perhaps, as are the shelters in the Labyrinth or on Tahure Hill, but the frowning battlements and huge fixed cannon gave place six months ago to modern style rabbit-warren defenses.

The German capture, announced seven hours earlier than the usual bulletin for the Swiss afternoon papers, was just a strong position, not, as they indicated, the cornerstone of the Verdun defenses. And as a strong position it was recaptured in the afternoon by the French infantry.

Even had the counterattack failed, the German gain was far from all-important. Behind Douaumont spur are Forts Thiaumont, Damloup, Belleville, Souville, and St. Michel, the guns of which sweep the centre plateau, here bare of the woods that afforded some shelter in the attack on Fort de Douaumont.

TIDE HAS TURNED, PARIS BELIEVES

Kaiser's Troops Which Won Fort Are Now Surrounded.

PARIS, Feb. 27, (delayed.)—"A frightful massacre" is how German soldiers, taken prisoners in the battle of Verdun, describe the effect of the French artillery, machine gun, and rifle fire. But the impetus of the assaulting forces was not diminished thereby during the first four days because fresh troops were thrown unceasingly into the battle.

"Advance, no matter what the losses may be," was the order given to the German troops before the attack. This is verified by documents found on one of the captured officers.

The most critical moment in the six days' action was when the Germans gained a footing in the intrenched camp by the capture of Fort Douaumont. The least hesitation on the part of the defenders would have been disastrous. The Germans redoubled their efforts to take advantage of any confusion, but the French immediately began a counter-offensive.

French infantry advanced at double quick to the sound of the trumpet, and leaped at the first ranks of the Germans with fury. The clash was murderous to both sides. The thinned French ranks were not to be denied, but went on to the second German wing, while reinforcements were hurried to their support. The German lines wavered first west of Douaumont, then were driven out of the ruins of the fort.

A cry of triumph went up all along the French line, and the ardor of the counterattack was redoubled. In the meantime an artillery duel, surpassing in intensity any previous action of the war, added to the carnage.

The battle seems now to have reached a critical point. The assaulting forces have recoiled slightly in the region of Douaumont, leaving the regiments which occupied the fort cut off and surrounded by French troops.

The attacks upon the French left at Pepper Hill (Côte du Poivre) seemed to have failed completely. But the attacks, made repeatedly with such heavy masses as the Germans are constantly bringing up, it is admitted by military authorities, are always likely to make further gains, provided the officers are willing to pay the price in human life.

There is no exaggerated optimism to be found in military circles here, but the check of the Germans, attacking in such formidable numbers, is regarded by them as one of the great achievements of the war, and it is generally held that events have taken a turn quite favorable to the French arms in the last twenty four hours.

Premier Briand told representatives of the press today how the tide was turned.

"Caught between two warring fires," said Mr. Briand, "covered with shrapnel from all sides, attacked by our fresh divisions, surging upon the field of battle at an unexpected moment, the Germans saw their efforts stopped short. The struggle was a titanic one. Our heroic troops went into the melee frantically. Our light and heavy artillery dug sanguinary furrows in the compact ranks of the Germans.

"Finally exhausted, their ranks decimated, the German armies recoiled under our furious counterattacks.

"We have regained the advantage. Installed upon formidable positions, our heroic soldiers remained masters of the field of battle."

French Soldier Pictures the Fight for Douaumont; German Charge at One Point Blocked by Own Dead

Special Cable to THE NEW YORK TIMES.

PARIS, Feb. 28.—A wounded Colonial infantryman who reached Paris this morning gives THE NEW YORK TIMES correspondent a picture of the taking and retaking of Fort de Douaumont at Verdun.

"The German cannonade had leveled the parapets and trenches until the position looked like a newly plowed field," he said. "It seemed as if every gun in the world was concentrated upon that one point. The noise was far greater than in the battle of Champagne.

"Some Boche infantry were creeping up a narrow ravine on the right front, others were crawling through the wood directly before the position. Suddenly they surged forward in a gray mass from both quarters at once. There must have been 5,000 in the ravine and perhaps 20,000 from the wood. As the former reached the plateau a single shell burst right among them, flinging pieces in all directions. The front was enveloped in a storm of shells, fragments of men, and lumps of earth.

"Through the smoke one could see them advancing, heads down, as if sheltering themselves from rain. Soon the ravine head was choked with bodies. Others tried to clamber over and kept rolling down the hillside. The heaps of dead gave us a more effective barricade than our own intrenchments. They simply could not pass.

"But in front, where the slaughter was even greater, they came on incessantly.

"Truly, they are brave, those Boches. I would never have believed that human beings could face such a terrific fire. Yet they knew it was certain death, for the wounded were stifled under corpses or torn in pieces by fresh shells.

"Wave after wave advanced. At last they reached the spot where our fortifications had been on the spur of the hill, and began piling up bodies to protect them from our fire. Douaumont was theirs, but at ghastly cost.

"Further back our hearts were burning. Were the Germans to be allowed to consolidate their victory? For three days they had kept us idle while the gunners did all the work. Since we retook Caures wood they held us, saying it was a useless sacrifice.

"We watched our shells concentrate upon Douaumont, tearing the German defenses into fragments. Our hearts beat fast. Surely we should attack soon.

"At last our turn came. I took part in the Champagne charge, but it was nothing like this. We were mad. Nothing could have stopped us. Despite the German fire, which perhaps was hampered by the fear of hitting their own men on the spur, we hurled ourselves at them with the bayonet among the shell holes and ruined emplacements.

"This was real war as I had never seen it. For a moment it was furious and equal. Then came another blue-clad wave and another. We hurled them back, screaming, over the hillside. It was a battle without quarter. We only captured corpses.

"They had had enough. Fort de Douaumont was French once more.

"As we lay there, panting and too exhausted to cheer, I suddenly found that my thigh was bleeding from a deep stab. My boot was already full of blood, but I had not noticed it."

Although the French were victorious at Verdun, both armies suffered such staggering losses that it is said neither fully recovered. This pile of dead German soldiers is atop a hill renamed "Le Mort Homme" — The Dead Man.

The New York Times.

THE WEATHER

Increasing cloudiness, warmer Monday; probably rain Tuesday and warmer; moderate variable winds, increasing.

For the full weather report see Page 19.

VOL. LXV...NO. 21,226. ....   NEW YORK, MONDAY, MARCH 6, 1916.—TWENTY PAGES   ONE CENT In Greater New York, Jersey City and Newark. | Elsewhere TWO CENTS.

9-INCH SHELLS NOW FALLING IN VERDUN BUT GERMANS ADVANCE NO FURTHER; NORTHCLIFFE AT FRONT, SEES VICTORY

VERDUN NOT YET MUCH HURT

117 Shells Fell Saturday Night—Cathedral and Seminary Damaged.

DOUAUMONT FIGHT GOES ON

German Efforts to Take French Advanced Positions Near Vacherauville Result in Failure.

FRESNES UNDER HEAVY FIRE

Powerful Bombardments Sweep This and Other Towns of the Woevre, East of Verdun.

Berlin Sure Verdun Victory Will Be Worth the Cost

From a Staff Correspondent.
Special Cable to THE NEW YORK TIMES.

BERLIN, March 4 (Delayed). — In well-informed military circles here quiet confidence is expressed in the outcome of the titanic struggle around Verdun. While there is full realization of and grief over the heavy losses incurred by the Germans, there is also a firm belief that Verdun will fall on schedule time, and that the victory will be well worth its cost.

VERDUN, (via Paris.) March 5.—Nine-inch shells are falling around the gates, bridges, and railway stations of Verdun today. They come from long-range guns, seven miles away, and drop methodically.

The gendarmes on duty near one gate told The Associated Press correspondent he had kept a tally of those that fell last night, and that there were 117 of them. The correspondent, sheltered by a massive earth and stone work at one of the gates, counted projectiles exploding about three minutes apart in that neighborhood.

The German gunners are trying to break the communications through Verdun. Strangely enough, not a bridge nor an entrance to the abandoned fortifications has been struck directly. Splinters from shells have chipped some of the structures, but none of them has been destroyed.

The city is nearly empty. It is more like the ghost of a city than a modern, well-built town. There are no civilians and no soldiers here. Firemen have remained, however, and are busy stopping the work of the incendiary bombs. A detachment of gendarmes is on duty as a precaution against any stray plundering.

Twenty-two thousand persons locked their doors, and with a small allowance of personal baggage left the town by order. Transportation was provided for them without deranging the enormous military requirements of the moment. One can walk through miles of streets with shuttered windows without seeing a person.

The city is little damaged. The Associated Press correspondent did not see a building that had been hit in the Rue Mazel, the principal business street of Verdun. Only one place was open; it was the Café de la Paix, and its doors were wide for the convenience of the firemen and gendarmes. In front of it stood the aproned proprietor, the single civilian remaining in the city.

But off the Rue Mazel, in various quarters, houses had been struck by shells. One shell had hit the annex to the hotel Le Coq Hardi, well known to tourists. It was one of the first of the 13-inch shells that reached the city. The four-storied corner building had collapsed into second-hand building material.

Part of the Cathedral Wrecked.

Numerous other shells had fallen on the eminence where the cathedral of Notre Dame and the church buildings stand. One gable of the cathedral had been knocked off, and the handsome stained glass windows shattered by concussions. Otherwise the cathedral had not been injured. A girls' seminary, adjoining it, however, was a mass of ruins.

In one large house a life-size statue of Joan of Arc holding the flag of France stood upright among a wilderness of stone and woodwork. A child's doll, beheaded, lay nearby.

A cat, imprisoned in a second story of a residence, cried pitiously. The window was open, but the wooden lattice was closed. The cat was a huge black and white creature. The exploring party made efforts, mounting Zouave-fashion, to break the lattice, but were unable to do so, and finally notified the firemen, who promised to rescue the cat.

The Associated Press correspondent, with the officers of the General Staff, went to one of the forts defending Verdun. It was on the heights of the Meuse. On a clear day the whole field of the fighting which began thirteen days ago would have been easily visible, but in the sombre weather, with occasional flurries of snow, Douaumont, which has been taken and retaken several times, was barely discernible.

A tremendous cannonade was going on. Many hundreds of guns on both sides were in action, mostly of the heavier calibres. The detonations were not counted; they were great and small and near and remote. Two or three houses were burning in the valley. Occasionally a flash of fire was perceived on the edge of the horizon.

80,000 Shells Fell in One Sector.

An artillery officer in the party, in describing the bombardment on the first day of the action, said:

"Eighty thousand shells fell in one sector only a thousand yards long and 80,000 shells fell in seven hours and were so disposed that the crater of one cut into the craters of others, pulverizing and resisting substance.

"As a matter of fact, many shells did not explode because they struck the soft earth, which is saturated by the Spring rain, and—"

There was a ripping sound in the air at this moment, like the tearing of parchment, and something fell about 200 yards away.

"There," continued the officer, "is an example. The shell did not burst."

Say Germans Fired 6,000,000 Shells.

There was talk among the officers present as to the number of shells which had been used. The civilian remarked that he had heard that the Germans had thrown two million, but this was regarded by the technical observers in the party as a low estimate. The number was thought to be somewhere between four and six million.

"The difference between the French attack in Champagne last September and the German attack here," explained a General Staff officer, "is that our adversaries made no reply virtually to our three days' preparatory bombardment, while we have replied continuously with ever-increasing power, so that now our artillery dominates."

The Germans appear to have planned their attack on the same general lines as that of the French in Champagne, except that within an hour after the bombardment opened at 7 A. M., Feb. 21, an infantry attack in force was made on Haumont, which was taken on the twenty-second. The next day the French retired from Brabant. They recaptured it the same evening, but gave up Samogneux, Beaumont and Ornes and evacuated the marsh of Poivre.

Since then there has been little change in the situation. Bits of the line, like the village of Douaumont, a mere group of cottages, have been taken and retaken. The French artillery in the meantime having come up in great force.

The ground taken by the Germans is almost the same as that won by the French between January and April of last year. The commander at Verdun thought, as he put it, that the place did not have enough lungs, and that it was difficult to enlarge the line, and did so in a series of local actions lasting three months, taking a piece here and a piece there.

The Germans have now won back this terrain, and the lines on both sides rest where they did at the end of 1914. Those in the group went over the regional maps with markings of the positions then and those of this morning. They are almost identical.

Went Thirsty to Water Their Guns.

Some mention was made of the Aures Wood, and the artillery officer told of how a battery was in continuous action there for forty-eight hours, and how the men cooled the guns by slowly dropping their drinking water on them, enduring intense thirst rather than drink the water. They retired slowly, saving their pieces.

Confidence at headquarters is absolute. The small progress achieved by the Germans in the first three days' attack enabled the defenders to make every disposition to meet it, and if occasion arises, to counter-attack. Nothing, of course, may be said concerning what these preparations and dispositions are, except that they are on an enormous scale and, as the commanders see, certainly more than adequate.

The Crown Prince's Proclamation.

The Associated Press correspondent saw many German prisoners. They appeared to be in good physical condition and occasionally were talkative. They told of an order or proclamation by the Crown Prince, issued to the troops and read to them by their officers just before the attack began, saying in substance:

"We are about to pulverize the enemy's trenches with our artillery. They will be so torn up and disorganized that when you rush forward to occupy them you will find that you can do so at the parade march. You will find little or no resistance."

"Eighty thousand German dead is what the living find," said a general officer.

The correspondent has been to the front many times, but has never seen yet such activity behind the lines. The train service between Paris and the Verdun region for civilian passengers has been suspended, and it was necessary to come here by automobile. All the roads behind that part of the front are crowded with transports. There are three to four times more of these than one sees at the usual encampments. Near one station were shells piled up like cordwood in regular tiers about four feet high. They were mostly of large calibre, and in what to the inexpert eye looked like limitless thousands. "The food of our big pets," was what a gunner called them.

There were to be seen detachments of German prisoners and an infinite variety of material, including poles for the making of corduroy roads across the soft fields for the moving of the artillery, which the French manage to shift about with amazing facility.

GERMAN LOSSES 100,000

Northcliffe Says Whole Army Corps Were Wiped Out by French Fire.

By LORD NORTHCLIFFE.

Lord Northcliffe, owner of The London Times and The London Daily Mail, is the first person permitted by the French Government to go to the front at Verdun as a correspondent. He arrived there on Friday morning, and his first dispatch to The London Times of this morning appears below.

Special Cable to THE NEW YORK TIMES.

BEFORE VERDUN, March 4, via Paris, Sunday, March 5.—It is known that the Germans intended to attack later, but the premature Spring seemed to dry the ground sufficiently and accelerated their plans by six weeks.

Lord Northcliffe.

Deserters give more than usually valuable information. The French were fully prepared. So far the Germans have been effectively checked, with losses hard to exaggerate, while the French losses are really trifling. I know the official figures.

I have interrogated scores of prisoners, belonging to every corps engaged.

Their accounts agree—everywhere the losses are beyond anything known before. Thus, the German Third and Eighteenth Corps were 'entirely used up,' the Seventh Reserve lost half, and the Fifteenth three-quarters of their strength. The 113th Division and Fifth Reserve Corps and the Bavarian Erste Division were all 'used up,' while later came reinforcements, which suffered equally. The most conservative total estimate surpasses one-third of the forces engaged, or over 100,000 of Germany's picked troops.

A sudden change in the weather damaged the German plans. Never did wounded suffer so terribly. Imagine the horror of the French when their lookouts, trying to save the living among the German masses covering the plateau and slopes, found all had been frozen stiff by the icy wind.

Stupendous Quantities of Supplies.

As I approached the battle two things struck me: First, the huge quantity of all kinds of supply wagons; second, the terrific thunder of the cannonade, far surpassing anything I have heard in other battles. I looked across the city of which the enemy is making a second Ypres toward Douaumont, that gunless fort so magnified by the Germans, whose capture French Headquarters regard as "a simple episode of give and take in war." The Brandenburgers who now occupy the fort are suppiied precariously with food by their comrades at night, and are practically surrounded by the French.

The day was fine, and despite the horrible carnage the character of the ground forces me to describe this as a beautiful battle. Despite the cannonade birds were singing and Red Cross ambulances and motor convoys wound through picturesque roads. We counted twenty convoys of a hundred wagons each on one road alone. It is not only the Germans who know how to utilize auto transport.

Arrived at the battlefield there were a dozen vantage points from which with glasses, or indeed with the naked eyes, one can take in much that happened. Verdun lies in a great basin with the silvery Meuse twining in the valley. As it stands out in the sunlight it is difficult to realize that it is a place whose people have all gone save for a few of the faithful who live below ground. Ypres looked like that the first time I saw it soon after the war began.

The tall towers of Verdun still stand. Close by us is a hidden French battery and it is pretty to see the promptitude with which it sends its screaming shells back to the Germans within a few seconds of the dispatch of a missive from the Huns.

The storming of Fort Douaumont, as related by the German dispatches, is on a par with the sinking of the Tiger and the recent air bombardment of Liverpool. All the world knows that the Tiger is as she was before the Germans sank her in their newspapers, one of the finest ships in the world, and that the air bombardment of Liverpool was imagined in Berlin. The storming of Fort Dauaumont, unless and unarmed, is about as important—a military operation of little value. The announcement of the fall of Fort Dauoumont to the world evinces the great anxiety of the Germans to magnify anything concerning Verdun into a great event. It should also cause people to apply a grain of salt to German official communiqués before swallowing them.

I lunched at the simple headquarters of General Pétain, who drank tea with his brief meal. He discussed the battle as though only an interested spectator. He looks like Lord Roberts, though larger built. He spoke with great interest of the Australians and Canadians and the growth of the British Army. Both he and his staff are remarkable by a complete lack of excitement.

At another gathering of officers the talk touched on the question whether the British should attack now to relieve the Verdun pressure. Opinion was mostly adverse, but the French evidently feel that our army has reached the point of being able to bear England's full share in future operations. The French officers agree that Verdun's value is chiefly moral. They are confident the line would hold if the fortress fell. But if neutrals could see the poor quality of the Teuton soldiers they would be more impressed than by the fall of Verdun.

"What a pity your Highlanders can't meet them in fair fight. It would end the war in a month," said a French Captain as we passed a group of wretched, puny prisoners.

Germany must be near the end of her tether when 5 foot 4, narrow-chested youths are members of élite corps like the Third or Fifth Berlin Army Corps. The young prisoners had only ten weeks' training before going to the front. Some who came from Flanders after a short rest were told: 'We send you against the kindly French instead of the frightful English.' All were dazed and just able to rejoice that they had escaped alive. All agreed that there is no enthusiasm left in the German Army, and that home letters are invariably gloomy. Their boots were the only good thing about them, and show the need of our further tightening the blockade.

From tho reports which these men have received from their families during the last two months it appears that in the words of one of them "there reigns in Germany considerable misery." All agreed that butter is unobtainable and meat scarce, exctpt in Alsace and parts of Pomerania. Fat is almost unknown, even in the army. In other respects the food of the army is tolerable enough, though not good or abundant.

The real lessons of the Verdun battle is that the French, with comparatively small losses of men and ground, have repulsed forces originally three to one stronger.

Line-up of German Army.

Here is the disposition of the German armies on Feb. 21, when the battle began, running east from a point north of Varennes. On their extreme right were the 7th Reserve Corps, consisting of the 2d Landwehr and 11th and 12th Reserve Divisions in the order named. During the battle the 11th was relieved by the 22d Reserve. Next facing the French northeast of Verdun came the 14th Reserve Division, with the 7th Reserve Corps and 11th Bavarian Reserve Division as supports. These troops formed the right of the enemy's central force. Next came the 18th Corps and 3d and 15th Corps and Bavarian Ersatz Division in the order named. South of Etain, in the Woevre, were the 5th Landwehr Division and 5th Army Corps and lastly the 3d Bavarian Corps opposite Fresnes. By March 3 the Germans had brought the 113th Reserve Division to replace the used up 3d Army Corps and other corps were relieved by units not yet known.

The French are now confident that they have made concentrations of men and material sufficient to repel the strongest attacks. Bombardment by unlimited heavy guns may lead them to abandon outlying thinly held positions, but the defense of the central plateau will be unflinching.

Though the French withdrawal may have induced the Germans to think they were demoralized, they have now realized their mistake. Verdun is not likely to fall, and nothing leads one to suppose that the spirit and stamina of the enemy are equal to dislodging the French from their present formidable positions.

What Are the Motives of Attack?

What are the secret motives underlying the German attempt to break the French line at Verdun, in which the Crown Prince's army is incurring such appalling losses? Is it financial, in view of the coming war loan? Is it dynastic or is it intended to influence doubting neutrals?

The Germans made a good many of the faults the British made at Gallipoli. They announced that something large was pending by closing the Swiss frontier. The French were fully warned by their own astute intelligence department. Their aeroplanes were not idle, and if confirmation were needed it was given by deserters who, surmising the horrors to come, crept out of the trenches at night and lay down by the edge of the Meuse until morning and then gave themselves up, together with information that has since proved accurate.

Things went wrong with the Germans in other ways. A Zeppelin that was to have blown up important railway junctions on the French line of communication was brought down at Revigny. Then the gigantic effort of Feb. 21 was frustrated by the coolness and tenacity of the French soldiers and the deadly curtain of fire of their gunners.

The present attack is by far the most violent incident of the whole western war. The bombardment is continuing and the massed guns of the Germans are of greater calibre than ever have been used in such numbers. Yet the superb calm of the French people, the efficiency of their organization, and the equipment of every soldier convince one that the men in the German machine would never be able to compare with them, even if France had not the help of her allies.

Unique Episode of the War.

It cannot be pretended that the German attack has in it anything of a military necessity. It was urged forward at a time of the year when weather conditions might prove a serious handicap in moving big guns and in the observation by aeroplane. Changes in temperature are somewhat more frequent here than elsewhere, and so sudden are these changs that not long ago there occurred the following incident—one of nature's romantic reminders of her power:

The opposing French and German trenches, their parapets hard frozen, were so close that they were actually within hearing of each other. Toward dawn a rapid thaw set in and the parapets melted and subsided and two long lines of men stood up, naked, as it were, before each other, face to face, with only two possibilities—wholesale murder or a temporary unofficial peace for the making of fresh parapets. The situation was astounding—unique in the history of trench warfare.

The French and German officers, without conferring, turned their backs so that they might not see officially so unwarlike a scene, and the men on each side rebuilt the parapets without the firing of a single shot. This serves to illustrate the precarious weather in which the Germans have undertaken an adventure in which the elements play such a part.

HEARD VERDUN CANNON AT 125 MILES' DISTANCE

German Traveler Saw Ammunition Rushed Up and Prisoners Sent Back.

From a Staff Correspondent.

Special Cable to THE NEW YORK TIMES.

BERLIN, March 5.—Interesting details of the German preparations for the Verdun offensive are given by a traveler who has just returned from the Rhenish Palatinate, which borders upon Alsace-Lorraine:

"I spent the night of Feb. 20 in the well-known wine district, and heard a continuous, dull, droning from afar. My host next morning laughed when I asked the cause of the strange noise, and said it was the thunder of cannon. 'It's more than 125 miles to the front, but we've heard the firing for months. Since yesterday it has been particularly strong; something must be brewing behind Metz.'

"He was right. Next morning the further west I walked the louder grew the noise of battle. As I reached a railway near a small village I saw an incredibly long freight train drawn by two locomotives. The cars were marked 'provisions'; but most frequent were the long freight trains, with their well-known red labels marked 'ammunition.' Trains puffed past [number deleted by censor] me in the course of the afternoon.

"The great drive at Verdun did not come unexpectedly for the natives of the Palatinate and the adjoining border regions of Lorraine. The people have learned to draw shrewd inferences from the little they see. Since Christmas they have been convinced that something was brewing around Metz and would break after Feb. 15. From the beginning in January one ammunition train after the other rolled through toward the west front; the few soldiers on furlough were more reticent than ever; the hospitals were cleared as far as possible, and all transportable wounded were sent to the interior.

"Feb. 22 the first wounded began to arrive at the hospitals in the Palatinate—Brandenburgers and Silesians, cheerful, lively youngsters with their hearts in the right spot. One of them was asked where he came from. He assumed a mysterious look and answered: 'From Mesopotamia, direct from the Irak front.' Afterward some of the brave Brandenburgers became more confidential, and one of them said:

"'No matter where we were under fire, it was frightful. Our own losses kept within moderate limits, particularly after we Brandenburgers had taken a French position from which we were exposed to a flanking fire. But the French! They suffered terribly. Their first trenches into which we broke offered a horrible picture—shot to pieces, half caved in and torn to shreds, a mixup of burning and charred posts, shredded barbed wire, and crushed and smeared bodies. Those who followed us simply had to shovel the dirt into their trench graves.'

"As the first official reports of the new offensive appeared I went to a small town near Metz. Although it was still thirty-five miles to the firing line, the earth quaked, windows shook, pictures on the walls were constantly a-quiver; at night there were continuous flashes on the horizon, like heat lightning—the reflection from the fire of the German mortars. Next morning not less than four trains of French prisoners passed through the town; one stopped opposite my hotel. It was an endless chain of at least fifty covered freight cars, each containing fifty prisoners. They lay on the straw covered car floor, and seemed visibly relieved to have escaped the hell around Verdun. Their appearance was good and their equipment excellent.

"For the inmates of the next prisoner transport drinking water was placed in readiness on the platform of the railway station. It proved a picturesquely checkered gathering of Zouaves, Turcos and Sengral negroes; very few belonged to a French regiment of the line. Many wore the old blue coat with their field gray breches, and even the old red trousers and gold-braided Zouave jackets were numerously represented and made a comical effect in contrast with the field gray parts of the uniforms.

"A young corporal—in civil life a teacher at a girls' school—gave me the explanation: 'The field gray uniform is supplied only to those who have been a long time in the field, and then only piecemeal, to supply the wornout parts of the uniform; hence the mixture of fashions.' He concluded with a sigh: And now we are going to Berlin—or rather Doeberitz—rather differently, though, than we had dreamed it.'"

50,000 UNBURIED DEAD.

Said to be Bodies of Germans Lying Before Verdun Defenses.

PARIS, March 5.—It is stated semi-officially that the battle at Verdun continued yesterday throughout the day with the same intensity and without causing any change in the respective positions of the opposing armies. Fighting is still going on for definite possession of the village of Douaumont.

The situation as a result of this second phase of the German offensive is regarded as altogether different from that of the first days of the battle. The only progress made by the Germans was during the first two days of the second attack. For the last forty-eight hours they have not advanced.

The comparison is also in favor of the French by reason of the fact that the Germans have now lost the advantage of surprise, and also because the ground has been torn up to such an extent that it cannot be organized properly.

This information from semi-official sources points out that it must be demoralizing to the Germans to see some 40,000 to 50,000 corpses of their comrades lying before the French lines.

Sharper Watch by England Placed on Alien Sojourners

LONDON, Monday, March 6.—The Home Office has issued new and more rigid regulations for the control of Americans and other friendly aliens residing in or visiting the so-called prohibited areas, which include most of the towns or districts regarded as of military importance.

After March 18 aliens will not be permitted to enter any of these prohibited areas unless they possess either special police permission or an "identity book," which will be issued by the police authorities to approved persons after due investigation, and which must be constantly carried and shown on demand to any police or other official. Aliens who wish to visit any prohibited area, even for a single day, must apply several days in advance, to give time for investigation.

"All the News That's Fit to Print."

The New York Times.

THE WEATHER
Partly cloudy Thursday and Friday; rising temperature; moderate variable winds.
For full weather report see Page 22.

VOL. LXV...NO. 21,271. ... NEW YORK, THURSDAY, APRIL 20, 1916.—TWENTY-FOUR PAGES. ONE CENT In Greater New York, Jersey City and Newark. | Elsewhere, TWO CENTS.

PRESIDENT ADDRESSES CONGRESS AND NOTIFIES GERMANY THAT SUBMARINE WARFARE ON MERCHANTMEN MUST STOP OR WE SHALL BE COMPELLED TO SEVER RELATIONS WITH HER

VIEWED AS AN ULTIMATUM

Wilson Says He Is at Last Forced to Conclusion There Is But One Course.

SPEAKS FOR ALL NEUTRALS

Declares We Are the Responsible Spokesmen of the Rights of Humanity.

Special to The New York Times.

WASHINGTON, April 19.—Before a joint session of the Senate and House, President Wilson this afternoon, speaking in behalf of the rights of the United States and its citizens and the rights of humanity in general, announced that he had notified Germany that "unless the Imperial Government should now immediately declare and effect an abandonment of its present methods of submarine warfare against passenger and freight-carrying vessels, the Government of the United States can have no choice but to sever diplomatic relations with the German Empire altogether.

It was explained later at the State Department that immediately did not mean as late as two weeks hence, and that an answer to the American note, which was forwarded yesterday, was expected before Sunday.

The President's address to Congress and his note to Germany are paraphrases of each other, whole passages being identical. The President's quiet manner before Congress was made ominous by the known fact that his indictment of Germany had been communicated to the German Government. For in spite of the forced reserve of the President's manner and his expressions in both documents, they constitute the severest arraignment of a great power disclosed by the history of recent years.

The feeling of both the executive and legislative branches of the Government is that the severance of relations with Germany is now inevitable, although the hope and apparently the belief, at both ends of the avenue is that war will not follow. The note to Germany demands the immediate abandonment of the "present methods of conducting submarine warfare." But throughout the note and the President's address runs the inference, bluntly stated at the close of the note, that the use of submarines for destroying commerce is "of necessity utterly incompatible with the principles of humanity, the long-established and incontrovertible rights of neutrals, and the sacred immunities of noncombatants."

Must Stop Submarines Altogether.

This general statement and the demand upon the German Government must be construed together. It was explained by the State Department this afternoon that Germany must abandon not only her present methods of submarine warfare, but that warfare itself, as now directed against commerce, before any discussion of the possible use of submarines against commerce would be permitted. There are cases in which a submarine may properly and effectively be used against merchantmen, as where a merchantman is overhauled in fair weather near shore, but after a year of German failure to conduct submarine warfare within these limitations, the United States is determined that the whole submarine warfare against commerce be stopped in sign of good faith, before discussions are resumed.

It is over this point that the break with Germany is expected to come. Germany is expected to repeat what she said many times, that this warfare will be continued according to international law, but that she cannot surrender the arm altogether. This ordinarily, if believed, would be satisfactory to the United States. But, after a year of violations of such assurances, the American Government is determined that the warfare shall end altogether before it enters into a discussion of the terms under which it may be permitted. Germany is not expected to agree to this, and the sinking of a single merchantman by a German submarine in the meantime would, in all probability, be taken as the final signal for a rupture.

Guilty of Bad Faith

Through both note and speech runs the plain implication, and in one place is the plain statement, that Germany has been guilty not only of atrocities but of bad faith toward the United States. In the speech the German allegations regarding the Sussex are utterly ignored with the directed statement that the ship, unarmed and unwarned, was torpedoed by a German submarine. In the note the American Government says that the German allegations merely confirm other unquestionable evidence that the ship was torpedoed, adding the evidence in a detailed appendix.

In most of the references to the German violations of international law, both the speech and the note lay the blame on German submarine commanders, as if they, and not the German Government, had been guilty of dishonor in breaking a solemn pledge. But both documents add that these incidents have been too often repeated for any such explanation. In the note, for instance, the attack on the Sussex is described as "one of the most extreme and most distressing instances of the deliberate method and spirit of indiscriminate destruction of merchant vessels of all sorts, nationalities, and destinnations."

If the Sussex case stood alone, say the two documents, the United States might be satisfied with proper reparation and the due punishment of the offending submarine commander. But the commander is not believed to have acted on his own initiative. The note sums up this charge of deliberate bad faith: "Again and again the Imperial Government has given its solmen assurances to the Government of the United States that at least passenger ships would not be thus dealt with, and yet it has repeatedly permitted its undersea commanders to disregard those assurances with entire impunity."

Ruthlessness Increased.

The President, in beginning his address, reminded Congress that upon the first announcement of Germany's undersea warfare over a year ago the United States had protested because of the "practical certainty of gross and palpable violations of the law of nations." In spite of German protestations of care, he said, this warfare had grown "more and more ruthless, more and more indiscriminate as the months have gone by, less and less observant of restraints of any kind," till it had become "grossly evident that warfare of such a sort, if warfare it be, cannot be carried on without the most palpable violation of the dictates alike of right and of humanity."

The President referred in the bitterest terms to German attacks without warning on great liners like the Lusitania and the Arabic. Recent events, he added, showed the "Spirit and method of warfare which the Imperial German Government has mistakenly adopted, and which from the first exposed that Government to the reproach of thrusting all neutral rights aside in pursuit of its immediate objects."

In both papers the President refers to the "very genuine friendship for the people and Government of Germany" of the United States as explaining the only significant passage in the one paper that is not contained in the other, is the statement in the note to Germany that the German note of April 10, regarding the Sussex, gave the impression that Germany had "failed to appreciate the gravity of the situation." This is the note that has been generally condemned for its thinly veiled frivolity.

Cheers Greet the President.

The President, escorted by his Secretary, Mr. Tumulty; two Secret Service men, and committees of the House and Senate, entered the hall of the House by a door immediately behind the Speaker's desk one minute before 1 o'clock. With his customary lack of ceremony he advanced to the stand before the desk, while the House and galleries, standing, welcomed him with prolonged applause, and shook hands with Speaker Clark and Vice President Marshall, who sat together under the United States flag. Then taking from his breast pocket the copy of the speech which he had typed on his own machine, and generally holding by both hands to the reading desk, he slowly and solemnly began his message.

A large and notable company was gathered to hear the President. He stood in the middle of the concentric desks of white marble about the Speaker's desk, which shone brilliantly under the skylight, contrasting strangely with the sombre furnishings of the rest of the hall.

Immediatley over his head was the press gallery, with correspondents from all parts of the world. Around him were the employees and guards of the House. Seated on the steps at his feet were sprawling groups of pages, silent and awed for once. In the chairs placed near by in the well before the tables were members of the Cabinet and other high officers of the Government—Secretary of State Lansing, Secetary of War Baker, Secretary of Agriculture Houston, Secretary of Labor Wilson, Postmaster General Burleson. Attorney General Gregory, Solicitor General Davis, and Counselor Polk of the State Department.

Every seat on the floor was occupied, Senators in the first tiers near the President, representatives carrying the mass back to the rail at the rear. And behind the rail stood more representatives and attendants. The glass roofing of the hall cast a strange gray twilight over everything.

The only real color came from the galleries, filled with brightly dressed women. But even the bright Spring dresses were dulled and rich in the dusk under the heavy cornice running round the chamber directly over the upper seats of the galleries. And the silence tha oppressed the hall whenever the Presdient's reading paused, seemed to subtract from what light there was.

Mrs. Wilson Present.

Mrs. Wilson, the President's wife, sat with her mother, Mrs. Bolling, and friends and relatives in the Executive gallery, otherwise filled by the families of Cabinent officers and other high officials. Next to this gallery sat the diplomats, and their compartment, too, was crowded to the doors. Ambassadors, Ministers, and Secretaries sitting indiscriminately on the floors of the aisle and in the few seats. Teutonic representatives and representatives from the missions of their allies were notably absent. But the other side in the European struggle was there in force, with many from neutral legations—Colville Barclay, Counselor of the British Embassy; Mr. Brambella, Chargé d'Affaires of the Italian Embassy; Ambassador da Gama of Brazil, Minister Ritter of Switzerland, and many attachés and secretaries.

The President's slow delivery of his address took just sixteen minutes. His face was grave, but the deep tan of health added to the firmness of his expression. His voice was low, but it carried throughout the large hall. Sometimes he hesitated in his reading, or skipped a word, and had to go back for it, but these faults of the orator seemed to emphasize his unstudied delivery. He made no attempt at rhetorical flourishes, and his almost monotonous reading gave to the occasion the complexion he desired, the simple laying before Congress of a memorable State paper.

The restrained manner of the President's reading explained the complete absence of demonstration while he spoke. There could be no mistaking the solemn effect on his hearers. At the beginning, where the address was mostly a narrative of known events, there were restless coughs in the rear of the hall. But these disappeared as the address advanced and members looked to each other questioningly at some signfiicant passage.

When the President concluded there was a moment's silence. Then a burst of applause and one lone yell came from the Democratic side. The handclapping, as the members rose for the President's departure, quickly spread to the Republican side, though on that side not more than half the members applauded.

BREAK PREDICTED BY BRITISH PRESS

London Chronicle Says Germany Will Not Yield After Recent Submarine Successes.

Special Cable to THE NEW YORK TIMES.

LONDON, Thursday, April 20.—President Wilson's speech before the joint session of Congress is featured by the newspapers, which recognize that the controversy between America and Germany has reached a crisis which is likely to completely change the whole aspect of the war. Even the British Cabinet situation takes a secondary place in the public interest.

Indications from Germany as to the attitude the Berlin Government is likely to take in reply to the President's "last word" are awaited with the keenest anxiety.

"It is difficult to suppose," says The Chronicle editorially, "that the German Government, elated by its submarine successes of the past six weeks, will accept President Wilson's terms. Diplomatic relations between Berlin and Washington will be broken off. The resulting situation, of course, will not be a state of war, but it may easily develop into war if Germany perpetrates fresh atrocities of which American citizens are victims.

"This must be obvious to both parties. President Wilson has counted the cost, and presumably the Kaiser is counting it, too. If he decides that the continuance of submarining is worth a diplomatic breach with America, he will probably decide it is worth war, too. If, on the other hand, he desires to avoid war he would most naturally make his concession at a stage when it would also avert the breaking off of relations."

"All the News That's Fit to Print."

The New York Times.

THE WEATHER
Fair Sunday; Monday partly cloudy; light, variable winds.
For full weather report see Page 23.

VOL. LXV...NO. 21,281.   NEW YORK, SUNDAY, APRIL 30, 1916.—96 PAGES, In Seven Parts.   PRICE FIVE CENTS.

8,970 BRITISH AT KUT SURRENDER TO TURKISH FOES

Tigris Force Which Gen. Townshend Led Almost to Bagdad Is Starved Out.

RELIEF FORCE 20 MILES OFF

Hordes of Turks, Strongly Intrenched, Twice Defeated Efforts to Reach Town.

FLOODS ALSO HALT ADVANCE

England Laments Surrender, but Praises Commander for His Brilliant Defense.

LONDON, Sunday, April 30.—The British Tigris army under the command of Major Gen. Charles Townshend, which has been besieged at Kut-el-Amara, has surrendered to the Turkish foes. Exhaustion of supplies compelled the force to yield.

This official announcement was made here yesterday:

After a resistance protracted for 148 days and conducted with a gallantry and fortitude that will be forever memorable, General Townshend has been compelled by the final exhaustion of his supplies to surrender.

Before doing so he destroyed his guns and munitions.

The force under him consists of 2,970 British troops of all ranks and services, and some 6,000 Indian troops and their followers.

The eventual surrender of General Townshend had been expected since the recent failure of the forces under Lieut. Gen. Gorringe and General Keary to break through the Turkish position at Sannayyat, about twenty miles below Kut-el-Amara on the Tigris River, and an unsuccessful attempt to send to the blockaded army provisions by steamers. It had been touch and go with the small British force for many days.

The location of Kut-el-Amara, on a peninsula extending into the Tigris River, made it impossible to send supplies by air as there was no landing place for aeroplanes.

While a supply vessel a few days ago got beyond the main Turkish lines at Es-Sinn, it was a forlorn hope, as the Turks investing the city, advised of her coming, could have easily sunk her from shore, even if she had escaped the artificial barriers in the river.

As for the forces which attempted to relieve General Townshend, they met with almost continual misfortunes. Several times when it was believed they were on the point of success, rising waters made further progress impossible. After penetrating Turkish positions they were compelled to fall back or remain stationary, owing to the impossibility of attacking the position at Sannayyat, which was surrounded by

Scene of the Tigris Campaign Which Has Ended in Surrender

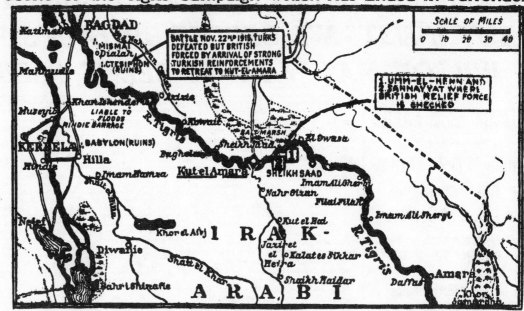

water. The British troops did actually attack the prepared position there, after wading through mud and water waist deep, but while meeting with some success, failure at other points made their sacrifices futile.

The British public never lost faith in General Townshend, and even now that he has been forced to capitulate after destroying everything at Kut-el-Amara that might be valuable to the Turks, they look back upon his campaign as a brilliant one.

END OF 10 MONTHS' CAMPAIGN.

Surrender Is a Climax of Disasters to British Forces.

The surrender of General Townshend's army to the Turks is one of the few instances of the war in which an entire fighting unit of important numbers has laid down its arms. It is one of the largest body of troops of the Entente Allies which has surrendered at one time and larger than any other captured French or British force.

Signs have not been wanting for a month that the Anglo-Indian force at Kut-el-Amara was in sore straits. Communication had been kept up by aeroplanes, but the official British statement of Friday that a vessel loaded with food had grounded four miles below the city was a strong indication that the force had lacked supplies to a dangerous degree.

A recent Turkish official bulletin said the position of the British at Kut-el-Amara was critical and that they were expecting to receive small supplies of food by aeroplane.

Up to a late day General Townshend had kept alive the hope that he would be relieved. King George sent a message of encouragement to him several weeks ago, and in a message sent out as late as April 7 the General said he expected to be relieved soon.

Less than a score of miles away down the Tigris is a relief army which for months had been attempting to reach the besieged forces. A few weeks ago several successes over the Turks were announced and hope then ran high in England that the mission would succeed.

The Kut-el-Amara disaster is an unfortunate ending of a campaign which for a short time promised to be crowned with remarkable success by the capture of Bagdad.

It was early in June, 1915, that General Townshend, moving northward on his way to Bagdad, captured Kut-el-

Amara with the Turkish force of 730 men and the Governor.

Led 40,000 Men Northward.

Townshend had with him two divisions of Anglo-Indian troops, or a few over 40,000 men. There are no towns deserving the name between Kut-el-Amara and Bagdad, and, receiving fresh supplies the following week, Townshend pushed on northward, part of his force following the old caravan trail and part the river, where his troops were transported by boats, most of which had been brought from India and were as primitive as those which the Turks and Arabs brought to oppose them.

The British van on Nov. 22 reached Ctesiphon, eighteen miles from Bagdad. There it was attacked by an overwhelming force, and, although on the following day it recovered the ground lost, Townshend saw nothing but a siege before him and no prospect of being reinforced for several weeks.

His water supply also gave out and the order was given to retreat southward. This retirement, accomplished under extraordinary disadvantages, was hailed in England as a remarkable achievement. Not only did General Townshend ward off the pursuing Turks with comparatively small losses, but he succeeded in taking with him all his wounded.

The main body pushed ahead, but on Dec. 5 Townshend determined to make a stand with the rear guards, at the scene of his previous victory, Kut-el-Amara. This guard, consisting of something over 10,000 men, made an intrenched camp around the place, while the remainder of his force passed on down the Tigris.

Kut-el-Amara is nothing but a mud collection of ramshackle houses on somewhat raised ground. Behind the river front are a mosque and a collection of one or two storied Arab houses.

Three days after he began to intrench, (that is, on Dec. 8,) Townshend's communications with the main body of troops were cut off, and ever since then he has been besieged, although few actual assaults have been made against his defenses since the middle of January.

Before that time almost daily attacks were made by the Turks. Townshend is said to have captured over 8,000 Turks and Arabs by sorties.

When it became evident that Townshend was so beset that he could not fight his way out, steps were taken to send a relief expedition. Thirty thousand Indian troops were dispatched and

two Anglo-Indian divisions, which had been fighting in France were transported to the head of the Persian Gulf, making, with the remnants of Townshend's main expedition, a relief force of 90,000 men. General Sir Percy Lake was placed in command of the entire forces, in succession to Sir John Nixon, and command of the relief expedition itself was given to Major Gen. Aylmer.

This expedition was poorly supplied in regard to transport and river gunboat service and Aylmer's march up the river again turned to a retreat after the first dash. The march began on Jan. 6, when the advanced guard left Gherbi, about eighty miles by river southeast of Kut-el-Amara. By Jan. 8 he had reached Sheikh Saad, forty miles to the north, where he defeated the Turks in two pitched battles. Between Jan. 15 and 19 he reached Orah, and on Jan. 21 he was at El Gussa, only eight miles from Kut-el-Amara. On the following day he attacked the Es Sinn intrenchments, which the Turks had built across the river, but failed to take them. Floods came to add to the trouble, due to lack of equipment, so that his position became almost as precarious as was Townshend's at Ctesiphon. Like him, Aylmer retreated.

Colonials Sent to Help.

Up to this time the campaign had been under the direction of the India Office, but the War Office in London now took a hand and a large body of Colonials, including the Thirteenth Division of Gallipoli fame, with full equipment and supplies was sent from Egypt, together with a flotilla of gunboats. In February Aylmer again started from his base at Gherbi and General Lake himself joined the expedition.

By the middle of March the expedition was near El Owasa and defeated the Turks there, after having met with a reverse at Felahie.

On April 5 the British force carried by assault the Turkish intrenched position at Umm-el-Henna, twenty-two miles from Kut-el-Amara. The next day the capture of Felahie was officially announced. Even then the relief expedition was about fifteen miles further away from Townshend's beleaguered force than it was on Jan. 21. Formidable masses of Turks were gathered on both sides of the Tigris below the invested town, holding intrenched and strongly fortified posts to contest the further advance.

The fighting in this region has been severe ever since, but the relief force, although gaining some ground, was never able to win a decisive victory.

The losses on both sides recently have been heavy. On April 14 it was admitted that the Tigris army had lost 8,100 men up to that time. Since then there have been several battles between the Turks and the relief expedition.

"All the News That's Fit to Print"

The New York Times.

THE WEATHER
Fair Saturday, warmer; Sunday fair; moderate south winds.
For full weather report see Page 19.

VOL. LXV...NO. 21,297.

NEW YORK, SATURDAY, MAY 6, 1916.—TWENTY PAGES.

ONE CENT In Greater New York, Jersey City and Newark.

GERMANY AGREES TO MODIFY SUBMARINE WAR, BUT INSISTS WE OPPOSE BRITAIN'S BLOCKADE; WILSON MAY WAIT TO SEE IF PLEDGE IS KEPT

DIPLOMATIC BREAK AVERTED

Germany's Note "Irritating but Acceptable," First View at Capital.

NEW ORDER TO U-BOATS

Must Apply General Rules of Visit and Search with Safety of Lives.

CABINET VERDICT WITHHELD

President to Give No Decision Until He Has Studied the Official Text of the Reply.

Special to The New York Times

WASHINGTON, May 5.—"Irritating but acceptable." That is the Administration's first view of the German response to the demand of the United States that the Imperial Government immediately declare and effect an abandonment of present methods of submarine warfare.

The Admintration is willing to construe the new instructions to German submarine commanders, which are disclosed in the response of the Imperial Goverment, as compliance with the American demand for a declaration that the objectionable methods of submarine warfare be abandoned. If the declaration is made effective by a cessation of illegal submarine practices the two Governments will continue on good relations.

The foregoing furnishes the gist of a tentative conclusion reached by President Wilson and his Cabinet during a session that lasted for more than two hours today. The unofficial press translation of the German note was laid before the President and his advisers a few minutes after they assembled in the Cabinet room of the White House at 11 o'clock and was read at the meeting. Technically, no decision as to a course of action by the United States Government was reached, but practically, judged by the agreement of opinion among the President and the members of his Cabinet, the position of the United States will be to regard the German answer as a Compliance with the demand of this Government. When the Cabinet adjourned it was with the understanding that each member should read and study the text of the German communication with a view to forming a matured opinion by the time of the next Cabinet session. The next regular meeting day of the Cabinet is Tuesday, May 9.

As the situation is understood upon the basis of information gathered after the Cabinet meeting, there will be no break in diplomatic relations between the two powers so long as Germany refrains from resuming illegal attacks upon merchant vessels, belligerent as well as neutral, armed as well as un-armed. Whether a formal response will be made to the German Government's note has not been determined. It was indicated at the Cabinet meeting today that a response might not be necessary, and that the only course essential for the United States to take would be negative—that is, to wait and see if the German Government was living up in good faith to the instructions issued to submarine commanders as the United States chose to construe those instructions.

The State Department announced tonight that it had received the official text of the German note which has been before the Cabinet in unofficial form as transmitted in press dispatches from Berlin. Copies of the official text will be laid before the President and his Cabinet for reading and study and a formal determination as to the attitude of this Governrent probably will be made known by Sunday, the first anniversary of the sinking of the Lusitania.

The President and his Cabinet advisers were irritated, and acknowledge it to themselves, over the language employed by the German Government in answering the American communication of April 18, demanding an abandonment of present methods of German submarine warfare. But they were willing to adopt the charitable view that this irritating language was used by Germany mainly for German consumption. That this view was correct was practically evident from information recieved by the State Department from James W. Gerard, the Ambassador to Germany concerning his conferences with Emperor William.

Kaiser Explains Note.

Mr. Gerard sent a long report in regard to his conversations with the Kaiser. Emperor William had expressed great friendship for the United States and a desire that the two Governments continue on amicable terms, but he told the American Ambassador that German public opinion must be considered in making any concessions to this Government concerning the conduct of German submarine warfare. It was apparent from what the Kaiser said that the Imperial Government believed it must so word its answer to the United States that the German people would not feel that their Government had been forced to modify the rules under which submarines had been operating. Submarine warfare against merchant vessels as conducted in accordance with the practices to which this Government has taken serious exception is very popular with the German people, and it is understood that the Kaiser emphasized this point in what he said to Mr. Gerard.

To a great extent the statement of the Kaiser tended to soften the irritating language employed by the German Minister for Foreign Affairs in his response to the American demand. The Kaiser gave Mr. Gerard the impression that Germany would go to great lengths to avoid a break with the United States, and that the German note must be construed in the light of this feeling. It is gathered that the attitude of friendliness and desire to avoid a break shown by the Kaiser had its effect upon the conclusion of the President and the Cabinet at their meeting today that the German note should be accepted as a

compliance with the demand of this Government.

No comment was obtainable from responsible officials as to whether this Government would respond to the expression of confidence contained in the German note that the United States would "now demand and insist that the British Government shall forthwith observe the rules of international law universally recognized before the war as are laid down in the notes presented by the Government of the United States to the British Government Dec. 26, 1914, and Nov. 5, 1915." It was recalled, however, that the United States had heretofore refused to recognize the right of Germany to make any promise contingent on certain action by one of Germany's enemies and had shown resentment of an attempt on Germany's part to point out the duty of the United States to another nation.

The conclusions reached by the President and the Cabinet in their interpretation of Germany's answer may be stated as follows:

1. Germany is very anxious to avoid a break with the United States.

2. Germany is equally anxious to mollify her own people with respect to dealing with the United States on the submarine issue.

3. Germany wishes the Unitet States to construe the new instructions to submarine commanders as a full compliance in good faith with all that the United States demands.

4. The only question that remains is whether Germany will live up to the letter and spirit of the instructions to submarine comamnders, and this can be determined only by waiting for developments.

5. For the time being, at least, the illegal warfare against merchant vessels on the high seas will be discontinued, and as long as this condition exists, the United States Government will have no quarrel with Germany.

REPLY NOT OUT IN BERLIN

But the Lokal-Anzeiger, Apparently Inspired, Praises Its Tone.

AND HOPES FOR ACCEPTANCE

Thinks the Concessions to Us Are Such as the Dignity of the Empire Demands.

BRITISH COMMENT SEVERE

Document Is Denounced as a Humbug and Solely Designed to Gain Time.

BERLIN, May 5, (via London.)—The German answer to the American Government's note with regard to Germany's submarine warfare has not yet been published here, and the newspapers generally refrain from any attempt to anticipate its contents or to forecast the consequences which may follow. The Lokal-Anzeiger, however, prints the following significant comment:

"Judging by what we have been able to learn concerning the spirit of the German answer to America, we cherish the expectation that the sense of justice of the American people which was emphasized in the American note will come into its own.

"The concession made by Germany in this connection is naturally as the dignity of the empire demands, solely born out of the consciousness of German strength, German successes, and the justice of our cause. The German standpoint can less be subjected to just criticism because of the fact that to the best of our knowledge it rests upon the basis of written international law and humanity repeatedly emphasized by America."

The Vossische Zeitung says: "Our investigations, made after the note was delivered, show that political circles cherish the hope that a conflict with America will be avoided."

LONDON PAPERS SCOFF AT VON JAGOW NOTE

LONDON, Saturday, May 6.—The interest with which Germany's reply to the United States was awaited here could hardly have been exceeded in America.

All the evening newspapers yesterday printed the note prominently by sections in successive editions. The greatest curiosity was expressed as to the reception of the note by the United States.

The morning newspapers, almost without exception, print editorials on the note and express more or less decided opinions on it.

The Daily Chronicle says:

"The purpose of the long rigmarole is simply to gain time. It adduces no new argument, it cites no unfamiliar fact or fable, it makes no offer to the United States, except on terms which render it valueless.

"We are told that the German Chancellor met the Budget Committee of the Reichstag in secret session and explained his policy, and the German stage manager does his best to create the impression that Berlin is offering wonderful sacrifices in its profound desire to conciliate Washington. In their sleeves, no doubt, the performers of this cynical play acting are laughing at the idiotic Yankees and speculating whether the Wilson Administration will be put off once more by shadows and words."

"It can only mean a break between America and Germany," says The Daily News. "The phraseology of the German reply, which manifestly was designed to impress the German people with the justice of their cause and to throw the onus of hostile action on America, is in itself sufficient in its oblique but calculated effrontery to impel the Government of a powerful and independent people to action.

"The essential fact is that America's specific demands are at every point either completely evaded or yet by a concession so emasculated by the condition on which it hangs as to be approximately a' flat refusal. On a plain reading the German note is a on possumus, nad on plain reading the American note foretold a break in diplomatic relations as a result of a non possumus."

Text of Germany's Reply to Our Note.

BERLIN, May 5, (by Wireless to Sayville.)—Following is the text of the note of the German Government in reply to the American note respecting submarine warfare, delivered yesterday by Gottlieb von Jagow, the Foreign Secretary, to Ambassador Gerard:

The undersigned, on behalf of the Imperial German Government, has the honor to present to his Excellency the Ambassador of the United States, Mr. James W. Gerard, the following reply to the note of April 20 regarding the conduct of German submarine warfare.

The German Government handed over to the proper naval authorities for early investigation the evidence concerning the Sussex, as communicated by the Government of the United States. Judging by the results that the investigation has hitherto yielded, the German Government is alive to the possibility that the ship mentioned in the note of April 10 as having been torpedoed by a German submarine is actually identical with the Sussex.

The German Government begs to reserve further communication on the matter until certain points are ascertained, which are of decisive importance for establishing the facts of the case. Should it turn out that the commander was wrong in assuming the vessel to be a man-of-war, the German Government will not fail to draw the consequence resulting therefrom.

In connection with the case of the Sussex the Government of the United States made a series of statements, the gist of which is the assertion that the incident is to be considered but one instance of a deliberate method of indiscriminate destruction of vessels of all sorts, nationalities, and destinations by German submarine commanders.

The German Government must emphatically repudiate the assertion. The German Government, however, thinks it of little avail to enter into details in the present stage of affairs, more particularly as the Government of the United States omitted to substantiate the assertion by reference to concrete

The German Government will only state that it has imposed far-reaching restraints upon the use of the submarine weapon, solely in consideration of neutrals' interests, in spite of the fact that these restrictions are necessarily of advantage to Germany's enemies. No such consideration has ever been shown neutrals by Great Britain and her allies.

The German submarine forces have had, in fact, orders to conduct the submarine warfare in accordance with the general principles of visit and search and the destruction of merchant vessels recognized by international law, the sole exception being the conduct of warfare against enemy trade carried on enemy freight ships encountered in the war zone surrounding Great Britain. With regard to these, no assurances have ever been given to the Government of the United States. No such assurances are contained in the declaration of Feb. 8, 1916.

The German Government cannot admit any doubt that these orders were given or are executed in good faith. Errors actually occurred. They can in no kind of warfare be avoided altogether. Allowances must be made in the conduct of naval warfare against an enemy resorting to all kinds of ruses, whether permissible or illicit.

But apart from the possibility of errors, naval warfare, just like warfare on land, implies unavoidable dangers for neutral persons and goods entering the fighting zone. Even in cases where the naval action is confined to ordinary forms of cruiser warfare, neutral persons and goods repeatedly come to grief.

The German Government has repeatedly and explicitly pointed out the dangers from mines that have led to the loss of numerous ships.

The German Government has made several proposals to the Government of the United States in order to reduce to a minimum for American travelers and goods the inherent dangers of naval warfare. Unfortunately the Government of the United States decided not to accept the proposals. Had it accepted, the Government of the United States would have been instrumental in preventing the greater part of the accidents that American citizens have met with in the meantime.

The German Government still stands by its offer to come to an agreement along these lines.

As the German Government repeatedly declared, it cannot dispense with the use of the submarine weapon in the conduct of warfare against enemy trade. The German Government, however, has now decided to make a further concession, adapting methods of submarine war to the interests of neutrals. In reaching its decision the German Government is actuated by considerations which are above the level of the disputed question.

The German Government attaches no less importance to the sacred principles of humanity than the Government of the United States. It again fully takes into account that both Governments for many years co-operated in developing international law in conformity with these principles, the ultimate object of which has always been to confine warfare on sea and land to armed forces of belligerents and safeguard as far as possible noncombatants against the horrors of war.

But although these considerations are of great weight, they alone would not under present circumstances have determined the attitude of the German Government. For in answer to the appeal by the Government of the United States on behalf of the sacred principles of humanity and international law, the German Government must repeat once more, with all emphasis, that it was not the German, but the British, Government which ignored all accepted rules of international law and extended this terrible war to the lives and property of noncombatants, having no regard whatever for the interests and rights of neutrals and noncombatants that through this method of warfare have been severely injured.

In self-defense against the illegal conduct of British warfare, while fighting a bitter sturggle for national existence, Germany had to resort to the hard but effective weapon of submarine warfare.

As matters stand, the German Government cannot but reiterate regret that the sentiments of humanity, which the Government of the United States extends with such fervor to the unhappy victims of submarine warfare, are not extended with the same warmth of feeling to many millions of women and children who, according to the avowed intention of the British Government, shall be starved, and who by sufferings shall force the victorious armies of the Central Powers into ignominious capitulation.

The German Government, in agreement with the German people, fails to understand this discrimination, all the more as it has repeatedly and explicitly declared itself ready to use the submarine weapon in strict conformity with the rules of international law as recognized before the outbreak of the war, if Great Britain likewise was ready to adapt the conduct of warfare to these rules.

Several attempts made by the Government of the United States to prevail upon the British Government to act accordingly failed because of flat refusal on the part of the British Government. Moreover, Great Britain again and again has violated international law, surpassing all bounds in outraging neutral rights. The latest measure adopted by Great Britain, declaring German bunker coal contraband and establishing conditions under which English bunker coal alone is supplied to neutrals, is nothing but an unheard-of attempt by way of exaction to force neutral tonnage into the service of British trade war.

The German people know that the Government of the United States has the power to confine the war to armed forces of the belligerent countries, in the interest of humanity and maintenance of international law. The Government of the United States would have been certain of attaining this end had it been determined to insist, against Great Britain, on the incontrovertible rights to freedom of the seas. But, as matters stand, the German people are under the impression that the Government of the United States, while demanding that Germany, struggling for existence, shall restrain the use of an effective weapon and while making compliance with these demands a condition for maintenance of relations with Germany, confines itself to protests against illegal methods adopted by Germany's enemies. Moreover, the German people knows to what considerable extent its enemies are supplied with all kinds of war material from the United States.

It will, therefore, be understood that the appeal made by the Government of the United States to sentiments of humanity and principles of international law cannot, under the circumstances, meet the same hearty response from the German people which such an appeal otherwise always is certain to find here. If the German Government, nevertheless, is resolved to go to the utmost limit of concessions, it has been guided not alone by the friendship connecting the two great nations for over one hundred years, but also by the thought of the great doom which threatens the entire civilized world should the cruel and sanguinary war be extended and prolonged.

The German Government, conscious of Germany's strength, twice within the last few months announced before the world its readiness to make peace on a basis safeguarding Germany's vital interests, thus indicating that it is not Germany's fault if peace is still withheld from the nations of Europe. The German Government feels all the more justified in declaring that responsibility could not be borne before the forum of mankind and in history if after twenty-one months of the war's duration the submarine question, under discussion between the German Government and the Government of the United States, were to take a turn seriously threatening maintenance of peace between the two nations.

As far as lies with the German Government, it wishes to prevent things from taking such a course. The German Government, moreover, is prepared to do its utmost to confine operations of the war for the rest of its duration to the fighting forces of the belligerents, thereby also insuring the freedom of the seas, a principle upon which the German Government believes, now as before, that it is in agreement with the Government of the United States.

The German Government, guided by this idea, notifies the Government of the United States that German naval forces have received the following order:

> In accordance with the general principles of visit and search and the destruction of merchant vessels, recognized by international law, such vessels, both within and without the area declared a naval war zone, shall not be sunk without warning and without saving human lives unless the ship attempt to escape or offer resistance.

But neutrals cannot expect that Germany, forced to fight for existence, shall, for the sake of neutral interests, restrict the use of an effective weapon, if the enemy is permitted to continue to apply at will methods of warfare violating rules of international law. Such a demand would be incompatible with the character of neutrality, and the German Government is convinced that the Government of the United States does not think of making such a demand, knowing that the Government of the United States repeatedly declares that it is determined to restore the principle of freedom of the seas, from whatever quarter it has been violated.

Accordingly, the German Government is confident that in consequence of the new orders issued to the naval forces the Government of the United States will also now consider all impediments removed which may have been in the way of a mutual co-operation toward restoration of the freedom of the seas during the war, as suggested in the note of July 23, 1915, and it does not doubt that the Government of the United States will now demand and insist that the British Government shall forthwith observe the rules of international law universally recognized before the war, as are laid down in the notes presented by the Government of the United States to the British Government Dec. 28, 1914, and Nov. 5, 1915.

Should steps taken by the Government of the United States not attain the object it desires, to have the laws of humanity followed by all belligerent nations, the German Government would then be facing a new situation in which it must reserve to itself complete liberty of decision.

The undersigned avails himself of this opportunity to renew to the American Ambassador assurances of highest consideration. VON JAGOW.

"All the News That's Fit to Print."

The New York Times.

THE WEATHER
Fair today, preceded by showers, cooler; strong northwesterly winds; tomorrow fair.
For full weather report see Page 21.

VOL. LXV...NO. 21,290. NEW YORK, TUESDAY, MAY 9, 1916.—TWENTY-TWO PAGES. ONE CENT In Greater New York, Jersey City and Newark. | Elsewhere, TWO CENTS.

PRESIDENT WILSON IN FINAL NOTE TO GERMANY ACCEPTS PROMISE OF NEW SUBMARINE POLICY, BUT REJECTS ANY CONDITION AS TO BLOCKADE

PRESIDENT ON DEFENSES

In Speech to Anti-Militarists He Says Force Must Back Up Opinion.

OUR 'SHALL' MUST BITE

Asserts That We Must Play Our Part in the Family of Nations.

EXPLAINS NAVY INCREASE

Due Simply, the President Says, to Growth of the Nation's Police Work.

Special to The New York Times.

WASHINGTON, May 8.—In a running conversation with a delegation from the American Union Against Militarism, such as he once gave to a group of woman suffragists, President Wilson this afternoon expressed his fundamental disagreement with the anti-preparedness advocates. He drew a sharp distinction between universal military training, which would enable the independent people of the country to bear arms effectively for their rights, and universal military service, which might put the force of the country under the control of a few. But even in regard to universal service he said his mind was still " to let."

The President intimated that he advocated stronger national defenses so as to strengthen the hands of the United States should the time come for its good offices in restoring the peace of the world. A country regarded as helpless, he said, " is apt in general counsel to be regarded as negligible; and when you go into a conference to establish foundations for the peace of the world, you must go in on a basis intelligible to the people you are conferring with."

Later he added that should a joint effort be made to keep the peace after the war, the United States would be expected to contribute her share to the force behind that movement.

Miss Lillian D. Wald of New York introduced the speakers, who included Rabbi Stephen S. Wise of the Free Synagogue; Max Eastman, editor of The Masses and former Professor of Philosophy at Columbia University, and Amos Pinchot. Others in the delegation were Dr. J. L. Elliott, Miss Alice Lewisohn, Dr. Frederick Lynch, and Miss Crystal Eastman of New York City.

The delegation as a whole presented a memorial asserting that after taking the President's advice to " hire large halls " they had found sentiment in the Middle West strongly against preparedness and had come to ask him where he would draw the line in further defenses.

" This is a year of madness," said the President in explaining his belief that adequate defenses were necessary to the maintenance of peace.

" In the circumstances," said the President a little later, " it is America's duty to keep her head, and yet have a very hard head."

He added that it was a " physical fact " that the United States did not have troops enough to patrol the Mexican border. When Miss Wald suggested that there was an effort to stampede the country into militarism, the President's answer was, " But it is not working."

Favors Reasonable Preparation.

In the course of his more formal remarks, the President said:

" I have never dreamed for a moment that America as a whole, its rank and file, had got any military enthusiasm or militaristic spirit, and I think that it is very necessary, in order that we should work this thing out wisely, that we should carefully discriminate between reasonable preparation and militarism, because, if you use the two words interchangeably, then, of course, the reasonable things that we ought to do take on a wrong and sinister appearance, and we seem to be working for the wrong things when we are in reality working only for the right—that is, the necessary things that are unavoidable in the circumstances.

" I think it would be a disservice not to recognize that there is a point of reasonable preparation, and that you can go to that point without changing the spirit of the country or violating its traditions, for the traditions of the country have not been those of a military helplessness, though they have been those of anti-militarism.

" The currents of opinion or, rather, the bodies of opinion, in this country are very hard to assess. For example, Mayor Mitchel of New York City and a group of gentlemen associated with him made a tour not unlike that which you made and had meetings, and they came back and reported in the most enthusiastic terms a unanimous opinion, not for universal military service, but very distinctly for universal military training, which, of course, is a very different thing.

" Now I quite see the danger that Mr. Pinchot perceives in the laws that he referred to, because they seem to associate military training with public authority and to draw that training into some sort of connection with military organization. It is not inconsistent with American tradition that everybody should know how to shoot and take care of himself. On the contrary, that is distinctly implied in our bills of rights, where the right to carry arms is reserved to all of us. There is no use carrying arms if you do not know what to do with them.

" I should say it was not inconsistent with the traditions of the country that the people should know now to take care of themselves; but it is inconsistent with the traditions of the country that their knowledge of arms should be used by a Governmental organization which would make and organize a great army subject to orders, to do what a particular group of men might at the time think it was best to have it do. That is the militarism of Europe, where a few persons can determine what an armed nation is to do. That is what I understand militarism to be.

" But a nation acquainted with arms is not a militaristic nation, unless there is somebody who can by an order determine what they shall all do with that force. I think we ought to be very careful not to let these different things seem as if they were the same.

Regular Army Inadequate.

" When you come to ask how much preparation you can make, that surely is a matter of judgment, and I do not see how you can find any absolute standard upon which to determine that question. Take Mr. Eastman's suggestion that we might have some arrangement by which the border of Mexico can be patrolled. There are not men enough in the existing American Army to patrol that border. That is the mere physical fact. When things are at sixes and sevens in a neighboring country, as in Mexico, and everybody apparently a law unto himself, there are not men enough to safeguard that border. And yet it is obviously the right thing to do to keep the disorders of one country from flowing over to disturb the peace of another country. That is not militarism, that is necessity.

" I do not need to tell you that I am just as much opposed to militarism as any man living. I think it is a deadly thing to get into the spirit of a nation, and I do not think there is the slightest danger of its getting into the spirit of this nation—only I have to determine a very practical problem.

" I have to determine how large an army is not unreasonable for the United States. The largest army proposed, that of the Chamberlain bill, is 250,000 men, and as compared with any European standard that is extremely small in a nation of 100,000,000.

" So that unless you regard it as a prophecy there is nothing extravagant in an army of 250,000 men. The traditions of the American people have always been for a very powerful navy. We have never been jealous of the navy even in our most sensitive moments."

One of the members of the committee asked if the navy had not been increased tremendously.

" Not tremendously," Mr. Wilson replied. " You see our tasks have increased tremendously. The amount of sea that we have found it necessary to police to take care of our distant possessions and be ready for exigencies of the most ordinary kind, quite independently of war, has increased tremendously, so that I earnestly hope that we may not antagonize reasonable protection in our effort to avoid militarism. I do not think it is going to need any very great effort to avoid militarism, because I quite agree with you that there we have got the sentiment of a great body of people behind us, and that, after all, is all that we care about.

Anxious for Peace.

" As to the general thing we are all most profoundly interested in, and that is peace, we want the peace of the world. Now, I do not know, I cannot speak about what I am going to speak about with any degree of confidence, I do not suppose any man can—but a nation which by the standards of other nations, however mistaken those standards may be, is regarded as helpless, is apt in general counsel to be regarded as negligible. And when you go into a conference to establish foundations for the peace of the world you must go in on a basis intelligible to the people you are conferring with."

A committeeman interposed to say that he was in London in 1895 at the time of the Venezuela complications and heard it said that if America had a great navy President Cleveland's message would have been regarded as an attempt at bullying, and unquestionably would have led to war.

" But this is not the year 1895," replied the President. " This is a year of madness. It is a year of excitement, more profound than the world has ever known before. All the world is seeing red. No standard we have ever had obtains any longer. In the circumstances it is America's duty to keep her head and yet have a very hard head; to know the facts of the world and to act on those facts with restraint, with reasonableness, without any kind of misleading excitement, and yet with energy, and all that I am maintaining is this: that we must take such steps as are necessary for our own safety as against the imposition of the standards of the rest of the world upon ourselves.

Must Play Our Part.

" We have undertaken very much more than the safety of the United States; we have undertaken to keep what we regard as demoralizing and hurtful European influences out of this hemisphere, and that means that if the world undertakes, as we all hope it will undertake, a joint effort to keep the peace, it will expect us to play our proportional part in manifesting the force which is going to rest back of that. In the last analysis the peace of society is obtained by force, and when action comes it comes by opinion, but back of the opinion is the ultimate application of force. The greater body of opinion says to the lesser body of opinion, ' We may be wrong but you have to live under our direction for the time being until you are more numerous than we are.' That is what I understand it amounts to.

" Now, let us suppose that we have formed a family of nations and that family of nations says the world is not going to have any more wars of this sort without at least first going through certain processes to show whether there is anything in its case or not.' If you say, ' We shall not have any war,' you have got to have the force to make that ' shall ' bite. And the rest of the world, if America takes part in this thing, will have the right to expect from her that she contributes her element of force to the general understanding. Surely that is not a militaristic idea. That is a very practical idea."

Miss Wald asked if this logically would not lead to a limitless expansion of America's contribution. The President replied:

" Well, logically, Miss Wald, but I have not the least regard for logic. What I mean to say is, I think in such affairs as we are now discussing, the circumstances are the logic. * * * Now, quite opposite to anything you fear, I believe that if the world ever comes to combine its force for the purpose of maintaining peace, the individual contributions of each nation will be much less, necessarily, than they would be in other circumstances; and that all they will have to do will be to contribute moderately and not indefinitely."

Explains Navy Increases.

Miss Wald remarked that the navy seemed committed to a policy of huge increase.

" Just let me say that there really has not been any material change," the President said. " The only difference is this: We have been going on from year to year making certain additions determined upon that year, all along looking forward to a series of years. Now, all that we have done is to evolve the rest of the program. It is not altered to any extent."

It was as the interview neared a close that one of the members of the committee asked whether the President believed in compulsory military service.

" I did not say I believed in it. To use the phrase of a friend of mine, my mind is to let on the subject. I would say merely that that was not contrary to American tradition."

" Mr. President," continued the questioner, " we are potentially more aggressive, because our economic organi-

President Wilson's Answer to Germany

SPECIAL TO THE NEW YORK TIMES.

WASHINGTON, May 8.—The American Ambassador in Berlin was instructed today by cable to deliver the following note to the German Minister of Foreign Affairs:

The note of the Imperial German Government under date of May 4, 1916, has received careful consideration by the Government of the United States. It is especially noted, as indicating the purpose of the Imperial Government as to the future, that it " is prepared to do its utmost to confine the operations of the war for the rest of its duration to the fighting forces of the belligerents " and that it is determined to impose upon all its commanders at sea the limitations of the recognized rules of international law upon which the Government of the United States has insisted.

Throughout the months which have elapsed since the Imperial Government announced, on Feb. 4, 1915, its submarine policy, now happily abandoned, the Government of the United States has been constantly guided and restrained by motives of friendship in its patient efforts to bring to an amicable settlement the critical questions arising from that policy. Accepting the Imperial Government's declaration of its abandonment of the policy which has so seriously menaced the good relations between the two countries, the Government of the United States will rely upon a scrupulous execution henceforth of the now altered policy of the Imperial Government, such as will remove the principal danger to an interruption of the good relations existing between the United States and Germany.

The Government of the United States feels it necessary to state that it takes it for granted that the Imperial German Government does not intend to imply that the maintenance of its newly announced policy is in any way contingent upon the course or result of diplomatic negotiations between the Government of the United States and any other belligerent Government, notwithstanding the fact that certain passages in the Imperial Government's note of the fourth instant might appear to be susceptible of that construction. In order, however, to avoid any possible misunderstanding, the Government of the United States notifies the Imperial Government that it cannot for a moment entertain, much less discuss, a suggestion that respect by German naval authorities for the rights of citizens of the United States upon the high seas should in any way or in the slightest degree be made contingent upon the conduct of any other Government affecting the rights of neutrals and noncombatants. Responsibility in such matters is single, not joint; absolute, not relative. LANSING.

Statement by Mr. Lansing

The following statement by Secretary Lansing was made public after the note was on its way to Berlin;

The greater part of the German answer is devoted to matters which this Government cannot discuss with the German Government. The only questions of right which can be discussed with that Government are those arising out of its action or out of our own and in no event those questions which are the subject of diplomatic exchanges between the United States and any other country.

The essence of the answer is that Germany yields to our representations with regard to the rights of merchant ships and noncombatants on the high seas and engages to observe the recognized rules of international law governing naval warfare in using her submarines against merchant ships. So long as she lives up to this altered policy we can have no reason to quarrel with her on that score, though the losses resulting from the violation of American rights by German submarine commanders operating under the former policy will have to be settled.

While our differences with Great Britain cannot form a subject of discussion with Germany, it should be stated that in our dealings with the British Government we are acting as we are unquestionably bound to act, in view of the explicit treaty engagements with that Government. We have treaty obligations as to the manner in which matters in dispute between the two Governments are to be handled. We offered to assume mutually similar obligations with Germany, but the offer was declined. When, however, the subject in dispute is a continuing menace to American lives it is doubtful whether such obligations apply unless the menace is removed during the pendency of the proceedings.

The treaty with the British Government referred to is the convention negotiated by ex-Secretary Bryan under which the two nations agree that any dispute arising shall be submitted to an investigating commission for one year before entering into hostilities. An offer to enter into such a treaty with Germany brought a request for information, but formal negotiations never were instituted.

---

zations are more active, more powerful, in reaching out and grasping for the world trade. The organization of the international corporation is one of the great trade factors of modern history, and it seems to me that if you hitch up this tremendous aggressive grabbing for the trade of the world with a tendency to back up that trade, there is going to be produced an aggressive nationalism in trade."

"It might very easily, unless some check was placed upon it by some international arrangement which we hope for," replied the President.

GERMAN PAPER FINDS U-BOAT POLICY BAD

Yielding Made Harder Because of Inflamed Public Opinion, Says Lokal Anzeiger.

BERLIN, May 8, (via London, May 9.)—A striking article on German relations, which is construed here as a criticism of Admiral von Tirpitz, appears in today's issue of the Lokal Anzeiger. After expressing approval of the German Government's reply to the American note the article says:

" The decision would have been easier if public opinion had not been influenced and inflamed in other directions by certain irresponsibles. It is just the same proposition as was the great mistake made in announcing the submarine war on commerce at the beginning of 1915 with great words and prescribing for the untried weapon successes which it could not obtain. It was wrong to preach that the submarine commercial war was the only effective weapon against England, although this may have been done with the best intentions.

" Neutrals were led to prick up their ears by the pompous announcement of the new war method, and difficult problems in international law were needlessly injected into the debate. A person can be a good organizer and still be a poor politician."

ENGLAND BUILDING ZEPPELIN TYPE CRAFT

Admiralty Official Refuses to Say How Many of the Airships Great Britain Has.

LONDON, May 8.—That England is building airships of the Zeppelin type was disclosed in the House of Commons today by Thomas James Macnamara, Financial Secretary of the Admiralty, in reply to the question of a member.

Mr. Macnamara said that it was not in the public interest to say how many such aircraft Great Britain possessed.

DELBRUECK TAKES REST AS FOOD RIOTS GROW

Berlin Sees Connection Between Minister's Absence and the Shortage of Eatables.

LONDON, Tuesday, May 9.—A Berlin official statement says that Clemens Delbrück, Minister of the Interior, and Vice Chancellor, who recently resumed work after three weeks' leave of absence on account of a furuncle, has not yet completely recovered, and has, therefore, been obliged to discontinue work for the present.

A Reuter dispatch from Amsterdam, commenting on this statement, says:

" The prolongation of the Minister's rest cure is believed to be closely connected with the recent food troubles in Germany and the inability of the Department of the Interior to force dealers in foodstuffs to sell their stocks instead of withholding them for higher prices."

All the Berlin papers give prominent place to accounts of the disturbances over the shortage of food, and especially to riots before butcher shops, where the police were frequently forced to interfere to protect the lives of the owners.

An ugly necessity of war—dealing with the wounded and dying. Here an American Red Cross first aid station is set up in a French town, and German prisoners are utilized by British soldiers as stretcher bearers.

"All the News That's Fit to Print."

The New York Times.

THE WEATHER
Fair Sunday; Monday rain; moderate, variable winds, becoming north and northeast.
For full weather report see page 18.

VOL. LXV...NO. 21,295.   NEW YORK, SUNDAY, MAY 14, 1916.—100 PAGES, In Eight Parts.   PRICE FIVE CENTS

135,683 SERIOUS, EARNEST AMERICANS EMPHASIZE DEMAND FOR PREPAREDNESS IN PARADE THAT MARCHES FOR 12 HOURS

EVERY CALLING IN THE LINE

Clergy, Doctors, Lawyers Join With Men of the Many Varied Trades.

CITY'S PLEA TO CONGRESS

Thousands of Women Tramp Fifth Avenue to Show Eagerness for Country's Defense.

GOOD SOLDIER MATERIAL

Hosts of Men Without Training March with Precision That Pleases Military Reviewers.

More Americans than have marched behind one leader since the Grand Review in Washington at the close of the civil war, paraded in New York yesterday to vitalize their belief in national preparedness. The Citizens' Preparedness Parade exceeded the most romantic expectations. The number of marchers, the manner of their marching, and their appearance as a multitude of individuals united in one mighty body to emphasize a single thought, made the parade perhaps the greatest procession of civilians that the world has ever seen.

The total number of marchers, according to a count made by THE NEW YORK TIMES, was 135,683. Of these 105,674 were male civilians, who marched i nthe industries and business branches represented. There 3,287 women by the same count, and the National Guard turned out with 2,994 men. Tt the end of the parade were 728 Spanish War veterans.

The only other estimate of the numbers marching was made by Colonel Charles H. Sherrill, the Grand Marshal, who figured the total as 144,000. Grand Marshal Sherrill estimated the number of marchers at 127,000 exclusive of the National Guard and women in the parade. He said that between four and five thousand women took part though this figure was doubted by Inspector Schmitberger, who believed that less than three thousand were in line. Colonel Sherrill stated that ten thousand members of the National Guard and three thousand Spanish War veterans marched in the demonstration.

The parade passed the reviewing stand for eleven hours. The Mayor's carriage, heading the parade, moved from the City Hall at 9:35 in the morning, and a few minutes later the Grand Marshal and his staff swung into line. At 10:30 Colonel Sherrill rode his prancing horse past the reviewing stand at Fifth Avenue and Twenty-fourth Street, and at 11:15 he reached the disbanding point, Fifth Avenue and Fifty-seventh Street, with the first marchers behind him.

Until after nightfall, then, the lines formed downtown, moved away, passed the reviewing stand, and disbanded at Fifty-seventh or Fortieth Street in practically an unbroken stream. They went by the reviewing stand at rates varying from 13,000 to 24,000 men an hour, a speed beyond the highest calculation made before the parade.

At 9:40 in the evening the last line went by the reviewing stand, and a three-inch field gun trailing behind was wheeled and fired.

In the Reviewing Stand.

The reviewing officers were Mayor John Purroy Mitchel for the city, Major Gen. Leonard Wood for the United States Army, and Rear Admiral Nathaniel R. Usher, Commandant of the Brooklyn Navy Yard, for the navy. For the entire duration of the parade General Wood stood in the reviewing stand, saluting the flag as many times as it passed and sitting only for the short and not frequent intervals when there were gaps in the column. Mayor Mitchel and Admiral Usher stood beside him throughout the whole time, except for about two hours, when they were the guests at luncheon of the Aldine Club in the Fifth Avenue Building.

The compelling, dominating fact of the parade was its unity. No dress, no banner, no individual for a moment detracted from the one big motive of the marching — civilian patriotic national preparedness. And yet the parade was such a representation of diversified citizenry as has never before been seen. The Presidents of banks and bank workers; manufacturers employing and employed; Supreme Court Justices, Judges of lesser courts and the lawyers who practice before them; brokers and brokers' clerks; insurance men from Presidents to office partners; the big men and the little men of almost every business and industry in the city; doctors, nurses, clergymen, and missionaries; civilians and soldiers; men and women, boys and girls; rich persons and poor; the leaders and the led in every walk of life were the units.

Flags by Thousands.

And though no uniforms were worn, except by members of the National Guard, there were distinctions of dress that made variety without clashing with the dominant note. The dress of all emphasized the Americanism of the marchers without giving distinctly military color to their display. There were thousands and thousands of American flags, hundreds of American Union packs, and other hundreds of red, white, and blue pennants—every marcher carrying a flag of some kind. There were uniform hats and hat bands in some sections; red, white, and blue neckties in others.

Every one who watched the parade or any part of it, those in the reviewing stand and those who craned their necks from rear rank positions on the

sidewalk, was impressed—they said so, and showed it—with the character of the men who marched. There were gray-haired men and small boys among the marchers, but for the most part the paraders were young men—between 20 and 35 years of age—who showed in face and figure that they were intelligent, sturdy Americans of the kind who might do much more than march. The storied anemic youth of the sweatshop, the sallow young man of the banking house, the pallid clerk of the business office was missing from the parade. If he exists he was strangely unseen yesterday.

And the way the men marched amazed those who only stood and waited while they passed. They were civilians without training, except for rare exceptions; they had not practiced for the parade; and yet they held lines twenty men in length, kept step with bands sometimes blocks away, saluted with their flags, fell into line and disbanded, without confusion, with a sureness and precision scarcely believable of civilians.

General Wood was impressed with this feature of the parade.

"It is a splendid showing," he exclaimed, when asked to express his feelings. "I congratulate the Grand Marshal with all of my heart. I am especially impressed with the fact that as many as 20,000 men have marched past the stand in an hour and not fewer than 13,000 in any hour and in such order. It is all the best example of citizen-marching I have ever seen."

Mayor Mitchel was thrilled. "It is a wonderful demonstration of the overwhelming sentiment of this city for adequate national preparedness," he said. "I have known all along that at St. Louis and elsewhere in advocating complete national preparedness I have been expressing the wishes of the vast majority of citizens of New York.

"This parade should demonstrate that sentiment to Congress in an unmistakable way. It should help in bringing that body to a more complete and satisfactory plan than it has yet evolved. The manifest enthusiasm and zeal of the thousands on thousands of citizens in this line today is merely symptomatic of the earnest and nobleminded demand of the American people for the upbuilding of the nation's defenses by land and sea. I congratulate with all my heart Colonel Sherrill, the other organizers of this splendid demonstration, and all the marchers in line for the patriotic services they have rendered. The showing made by the representatives of the City Government was a source of special gratification to me. I am informed that four times as many as could find places in line volunteered to march."

Joseph H. Choate, who was in the reviewing stand for several hours, said:

"The parade has exceeded the expectations of myself and of the National Security League. I am deeply impressed with the physical appearance and apparent intelligence of the men. They would make good soldiers. They have an earnest and brave bearing and show that they do not take their marching as play. They are in deadly earnest. The parade is bound to have a great influence on the country."

War seems a cause for celebration as these enthusiastic volunteers prepare to trade their civilian clothes for uniforms and learn the basics of soldiering.

"All the News That's Fit to Print."

The New York Times.

THE WEATHER
Partly cloudy Monday; showers Tuesday; moderate southeast to south winds.
☞For full weather report see Page 20.

VOL. LXV...NO. 21,303. ••••   NEW YORK, MONDAY, MAY 22, 1916.—TWENTY PAGES.   ONE CENT In Greater New York, Jersey City and Newark. | TWO CENTS

COSSACKS JOIN BRITISH ON TIGRIS; ROME EXPECTS GREAT ALLIED DRIVE; FURIOUS BATTLE RAGES AT VERDUN

SURPRISING RUSSIAN MOVE

Cavalry Reaches Gen. Gorringe "After a Bold and Adventurous Ride."

NEW ADVANCE ON KUT BEGUN

British Move North, Capturing a Redoubt West of the Tigris —Held on East Bank.

RUSSIANS MASS IN PERSIA

Austrians Reported in Bagdad and Germans Coming—Turks Guard Alexandretta.

LONDON, May 21.—The first news of the operations on the Tigris since the fall of Kut-el-Amara, sent today by Lieut. Gen. Sir Percy Lake, commander of the British forces in Mesopotamia, although it shows that the Turks are still holding the Sannayyat position on the left bank of the Tigris, where the British check made it impossible to carry out the relief of General Townshend, brings the astonishing intelligence that a body of Russian cavalry, after an adventurous ride, has succeeded in joining General Gorringe's forces on the south bank of the Tigris.

An official communication issued tonight concerning the situation along the Tigris says:

General Lake reports that on the 19th the enemy vacated the Bethalessa advanced position on the right bank of the Tigris. General Gorringe, following up the enemy, attacked and carried the Dujailah Redoubt. The enemy is still holding the Sannayyat position on the left bank of the river.

A force of Russian cavalry has joined General Gorringe after a bold and adventurous ride.

How this important junction was effected is still unknown, and the story will be awaited with intense interest. The supposition is that this detachment came from the Russian Army which is threatening Khanikin, but it still remains a puzzle where and how the Russians succeeded in crossing the river.

Their sudden appearance with General Gorringe has also raised the question whether the Russians have already cut the Bagdad Railway at Mosul. In any case the unexpected appearance of this body of cavalry is as great a surprise as was the first landing of the Russian troops at Marseilles, and is another instance of the swift and stealthy movement of the Russian forces in Asia Minor.

Junction Stirs British Speculation.

Special Cable to THE NEW YORK TIMES.

LONDON, Monday, May 22.—The dramatic appearance of Russian cavalry with General Gorringe's force means the British and Russians are now fighting side by side on land for the first time in the war.

Much speculation is heard as to which way the Russian troops came in their "bold and adventurous ride." It seems probable they came from Kermanshah, in which case the feat would be a brilliant one, since the route of some 150 miles would be through swamps, over mountains void of tracks, or with roads of the most primitive character.

The Daily News military correspondent warns his readers not to build too much on the news that a junction between British and Russian forces in Mesopotamia is imminent. He says:

"From all accounts the little known cross-country track from Kermanshah is quite impracticable for the movement of large bodies of troops and guns, and it is unlikely, though of course not impossible, that there is backing behind the Russian cavalry."

The same correspondent, dealing with the Turkish position at Kut-el-Amara, says:

"What seems probable is that General Baratoff, who reached Kasrishirin on May 10, is threatening Khanikin with a large force, and this has determined Khalil Pasha to contract his front and draw in his troops for a nearer defense of Bagdad. Kut-el-Amara lost its significance for the Turkish commander as soon as General Townshend surrendered. What he has now to do is to make the best arrangement he can for the defense of Bagdad against a converging movement which is threatening the town, keeping his eye on his communications with Mosul, which also is being threatened by the Russian force that seized Rowandiz a few days ago.

"The capture of Bagdad is of initial military importance, not only on account of its special strategical significance as the place where the high roads into Persia and down to the Persian Gulf meet, but also because it is a stepping stone on the way into Anatolia.

"As soon as General Baratoff or General Lake (it matters not which General is first there) reaches Bagdad the long-drawn-out front over which the Grand Duke's armies are operating will be contracted, and the Russian columns can be drawn in toward the centre in order to force the Turks to fight a pitched battle on the upper Tigris or upper Euphrates, as circumstances may dictate."

OFFICER'S STORY OF TRENCH FIGHT

French Lieutenant Describes Intense Struggle Involved in Small Local Gains.

NEW MACHINE GUN DEADLY

By GEORGES LE HIR,
Special Correspondent of The New York Times.

A VILLAGE NORTHWEST OF VERDUN, Thursday, May 18, (via Paris, May 21.)- The German drive for Verdun has degenerated into a regular ebb and flow of position warfare, in which local advances are the reward of individual dash and initiative.

This is especially the case on the west of the Meuse, where the French are steadily "nibbling" back the outlying positions around Hill 304, won by prodigious sacrifices.

In this fighting the French make unexampled use of the mitrailleuse, which is by general consent the deadliest of weapons in all this war of slaughter, and originally of French contrivance. The French have far surpassed the Germans, at first superior in the use of the mitrailleuse. The gun is particularly employed in local attacks, and the account that follows may be taken as typical of the present French methods of procedure before Verdun.

The point attacked was a section of a German trench, forming a salient on the northern slopes of the western spur of Hill 304 and commanding the ravine between the hill and Le Mort Homme, along which the Germans vainly tried to force home a massed assault during the early part of last week. This description is given me by the Lieutenant commanding the attacking company, to whom a bullet through the left forearm seemed an infinitesimal price to pay for the first occasion that he had led French soldiers to victory:

"About 1 o'clock this morning the fire of a battery of 75's was directed against converging German trenches, which formed a V-point forty yards in front of the French position. For two hours the hundred-yard sides of the salient were enveloped in an eruption of flame and smoke until the first light of dawn showed the German wire entanglements torn to ribbons. At half-past 3 o'clock four mitrailleuse sections began creeping forward in groups of five, dragging the new light mitrailleuses, which are especially suitable for such work. Each group aimed at reaching the V-point angle, from which they could enfilade both sections of the German trench.

"Sheltered by the smoke of bombardment and taking advantage of the shell holes and undulation» of the ground they made fair progress, when suddenly one of the heavy German shells landed full on a hole where the foremost group were crouching. The result was that horrible fragments of torn flesh and splintered steel were scattered over their comrades waiting in the French trench.

"The second group were little luckier for a German sentry in an armored turret shot three dead and wounded the fourth before a well-aimed shell reduced him to silence.

"The third section had better fortune, and as the cannonade died away into sudden silence, like a shock there began a rat-a-tat like the explosion of engines of distant motor cycles from a crest of earth, thrown up by a bursting shell, a scant five yards in front of the V-point, which showed that they had placed their weapon in position.

"The remaining group managed to reach a vantage point whence they could paritally sweep the other trench, but only after a furious hand-to-hand fight with an alert German patrol. This diversion prevented their getting sufficiently near, and they were soon forced to cease firing by the advance of our charging soldiers.

"The latter sprang forward in two lines, one against each side of the salient. On the left, where the mitrailleuse at the V-point enfiladed the trench, the task was easy. They paused a while on the brink of the trench, flinging grenades.

"The Germans had the choice of dying like rats in their shelters or coming out to meet a storm of bullets. They were frantic with fright. Some wallowed in the mud at the bottom of the trench to let the death stream pass over them and escaped for a moment, only to die later by the bayonets of our infantry. Others tried vainly to climb the steep trench walls. Of the 150 defenders only

Allies' Operations in Asia Minor

The armies of the Russian Grand Duke now have for their objectives Baiburt (1,) Erzingan (2,) and Diarbekr (3.) From Persia Russian forces are operating toward Mosul (4) on the Constantinople-Bagdad route, from Ban (5,) and against Khanikin Pass (6.) The British expedition reports the taking of a redoubt fronting them south of Kut-el-Amara (7.) It is here that Russian cavalry has joined the British expeditionary force.

two or three wounded survived to become prisoners when we finally occupied the position.

"Then the mitrailleuses, now reduced to three, were turned against the right side of the salient, where a desperate battle with grenades was progressing. The enemy fell dying under the leaden hail.

"Suddenly the rat-a-tat ceased, as the officers of the mitrailleuse groups perceived a French soldier, bolder than his fellows, who had hurled himself with his bayonet into the trench. Instantly he grasped the situation and shouted. 'Continue firing. Never mind me.'

"The rat-a-tat began again and he fell dead amid a heap of the enemy. Then the mitrailleuses became silent and our infantry leaped into the trench, bayonetting the remaining survivors or hurling grenades into a few deep shelters where a few might be lurking. That's how the French 'clean up' the enemy trenches northwest of Verdun."

MEUSE STRUGGLE GROWING

Germany's Loss Put at 300,000 as Battle Enters Fourth Month.

TRENCHES CHANGE HANDS

Paris Reports Winning Two on West Bank of the River, Berlin One.

GERMANS TAKE 1,300 MEN

Great Activity on East Bank Also, as Well as on Belgian Front—Many Air Battles.

Special Cable to THE NEW YORK TIMES.

PARIS, May 21, (Dispatch to The London Daily Chronicle.)—The battle of Verdun began on Feb. 21 amid wet and snow; it continues on May 21 in a blaze of hot sunshine. We know in these three months the German losses exceed 300,000. Fresh regiments are still being brought up to replenish the enemy's exhausted lines. An experienced officer reckons half a million tons of metal have been sprinkled over the Meuse hillsides, 3,000 German cannon having fired 15,000,000 shells during the battle.

It is only by the constant reminder of the dimensions and intensity of the effort that we can measure its failure and appreciate the valor of the French resistance.

The struggle recommenced yesterday afternoon along the northern face of Dead Man crest, Hill 295, which, the German dispatches to the contrary notwithstanding, has never ceased to be completely in the possession of the French. Something like 30,000 men are believed to have been engaged yesterday in repeated assaults on this two-mile front. On the east and steeper side of the position, the Crown Prince's troops concentrated in Crows' Wood and got into advanced trenches which had been badly shattered, but they were quickly thrown back to their own lines.

The fighting was more desperate on the north and west slopes, where the French recently progressed to the foot of Hill 295. After repeated assaults over ground torn up and parapets destroyed by preliminary bombardment some detachments got as far as French second positions, where they were broken and dispersed with heavy loss. Reinforcements were constantly brought up and new assaults were launched throughout last night, but without any change in the situation except an advanced trench on the west side of the hill was captured.

For a new hecatomb, the Crown Prince has gained a few yards of broken and exposed ground of no tactical value.

Both Sides Claim Gains.

LONDON, May 21.—The battle before Verdun continued last night and today with great violence on both banks of the Meuse. Paris and Berlin report local gains for their respective armies.

The lastest word from the French War Office tonight claims the capture of two German trenches near the west end of the front, along the road from Esnes to Haucourt. East of the Meuse French troops captured the Haudromont quarries.

The Berlin report of this afternoon says the German succeeded in advancing at Dead Man Hill, capturing 1,315 men and 31 officers from the French ranks. The Paris afternoon statements admits the loss of a first line trench on the Dead Man Hill front.

Arillery activity of great intensity occurred today on the Belgian Sector in Flanders.

There have been a number of air battles and raids, the results of which are given in the official reports.

French Gain Two Trenches.

The official communication issued by the French War Office tonight reads:

On the left bank of the Meuse the battle continued fiercely all day on the front between the Avocourt Wood and the Meuse. In the neighborhood of the road from Esnes to Haucourt an attack launched by our troops permitted us to occupy two German trenches. A small work which the enemy occupied on May 18 south of Hill 287 was entirely shattered by our artillery.

Immediately east of Hill 304 the enemy delivered against our positions an attack which after momentarily penetrating our first line trench, was completely driven back.

On the slopes west of Dead Man Hill a violent offensive action carried out by an enemy brigade was stopped by the fire of our machine guns and by our counterattacks. Enemy grenade columns which followed the assaulting waves were taken under the fire of our batteries and were obliged to fall back.

On the right bank of the Meuse the artillery struggle was very violent. In the sector of Douaumont our troops in a spirited attack captured the Haudromont quarries, which had been strongly organized by the enemy. We took eighty prisoners and four machine guns.

There were intermittent artillery actions on the rest of the front.

German aeroplanes carried out since yesterday two bombardments in the region of Dunkirk. About twenty shells were dropped last evening, killing four persons and wounding fifteen. Today another enemy squadron dropped about 100 bombs in the outskirts of Dunkirk. Two soldiers and a child were killed, and twenty persons were wounded.

Allied aeroplanes pursued the enemy machines and succeeded in bringing down two at the moment they were about to enter their own lines.

Immediately after the first bombardment fifty-three French, British, and Belgian aeroplanes flew over the German cantonments at Wywege and Chistelles, on which 250 shells were dropped.

German aeroplanes today dropped fifteen bombs on Belfort, but the material damage was insignificant.

Germans Capture 1,300 Prisoners.

The official communication issued today in Berlin is as follows:

On the south and southwest slopes of Dead Man Hill our lines were advanced after effective artillery preparation. Thirty-one officers and 1,315 men were taken prisoner and, in addition to other war material, sixteen machine guns and eight cannon were captured. Minor counterattacks by the enemy were abortive.

East of the Meuse it has been ascertained that the French attack with hand grenades in Caillette Wood on the night of May 20 was repulsed. There was no infantry action at this point yesterday. The firing on both sides at times was very violent. Minor expeditions west of Beaumont and south of Gondrexon were successful.

Near Ostend, (Belgium)—A hostile aeroplane was brought down by the fire of our anti-aircraft guns and fell into the sea. Four other machines were shot down in aerial encounters. Two of them fell within our lines, one near Lorgies, north of La Bassée, and the other near Chateau Salins. The remaining two fell within the enemy's lines, one in Borrus Wood, west of the Meuse, and the other beyond a hill east of Verdun.

Our aeroplane squadron again dropped bombs freely on Dunkirk during the night.

The official French statement of this afternoon says:

West of the Meuse the Germans continued during the night their attacks on our positions on Dead Man Hill. They were again repulsed by our curtain of fire, which shattered their attacks. The enemy succeeded, however, in occupying one of our first line trenches and also slopes west of Dead Man Hill.

East of the Meuse there was very heavy artillery firing in the vicinity of Fort Vaux, without any infantry actions.

In Lorraine an attack following a violent bombardment enabled the Germans to penetrate one of our trenches west of Chazelles. The first of our artillery and machine guns compelled the Germans a little later to return to their lines, leaving their dead and wounded in the evacuated positions.

Over the remainder of the front there was the usual cannonading.

A raid was made by enemy aviators in the region of Baccarat, Epinal, and Vesoul. The material damage was insignificant. Four persons were wounded slightly.

Our aviators last night threw numerous bombs on military establishments at Thionville, Etain, and Spincourt and on the camps in the vicinity of Azannes and Damvillers. The railway station at Lunes was bombarded, causing the rapid flight of trains and a large fire in the railway buildings.

In an aerial engagement between four of our aeroplanes and three Fokkers over Bezange Forest one of the enemy machines was brought down and another Fokker, being attacked, was compelled to descend to earth behind the German lines, while under the fire of our batteries, which destroyed it.

Airmen Active on British Front.

The British official statement on the western campaign reads:

Yesterday (Saturday) our aeroplanes had several successful encounters. An aviatik fell on fire into some trees near Abimfor Wood in the enemy's lines. one of its occupants being seen to fall out. Another hostile machine fell, in flames, near Contalmaison, also in the enemy's lines, after an encounter with one of our scouts. A third crashed to earth in our lines near Maricourt. One of our aeroplanes fell in the enemy's lines.

Much successful artillery work was accomplished. Early this morning a hostile machine landed undamaged in our lines. The pilot and observer were made prisoner.

Last night the enemy made three small attacks southwest of Wieltje. All were repulsed.

South of Souchez from 2 P. M. onward a heavy hostile fire was directed against our front trenches. Our artillery replied, shelling the hostile batteries and trenches.

Manzangarbe and Noeux-les-Mines and our trenches about Aultmille, Oviliers, Hulluch, and Sanctuary Wood have also been shelled. Our artillery silenced a hostile battery north of Namety Wood.

There has been some mining activity at the Hohenzollern Redoubt and north of La Bassée Canal.

The Belgian communication says:

Last night and today the artillery duels in the sector of Dixmude reached great intensity. In the direction of Steenstraete the action extended to an engagement with bombs. Yesterday in an aerial fight off Nieuport a Belgian aeroplane brought down a German machine, which fell into the sea.

WAR COSTS BRITAIN $150 EVERY SECOND

This Makes an Expenditure of $12,960,000 for Every Twenty-four Hours.

Special Cable to THE NEW YORK TIMES.

LONDON, May 17.—F. D. Acland, the Financial Secretary to the Treasury, speaking at a meeting here today, estimated the cost of the war to England at $150 a second.

This means an expenditure of $12,960,000 a day. Lloyd George's recent estimate was $10,500,000.

These cavalry men are just one of the Cossack troops that fought on the side of the Allies in WWI.

"All the News That's
Fit to Print."

The New York Times.

THE WEATHER
Local showers today; Sunday fair;
strong south, shifting to
west, winds.
For full weather report see Page 53.

VOL. LXV...NO. 21,315. ...   NEW YORK, SATURDAY, JUNE 3, 1916.—TWENTY-TWO PAGES.   ONE CENT In Greater New York, Jersey City and Newark. | TWO CENTS Elsewhere.

25 WARSHIPS WITH 7500 MEN LOST IN BATTLE OFF DENMARK; BRITISH FLEET HAS 14 VESSELS SUNK AND THE GERMANS 11; GERMANY ACCLAIMS IT A VICTORY, BUT ENGLAND IS CALM

FIRST NEWS SHOCKED BRITISH

But Later Bulletin Telling Foe's Loss Was More Assuring.

MOURN SIX BIG SHIPS GONE

Loss of Life Believed to be Heavy, but the Censor Withholds Unofficial Accounts.

FEW FACTS OF FIGHT KNOWN

Combat Began Wednesday Afternoon and Lasted Into Night —Six Zeppelins Took Part.

Loss Admitted by British

Battle Cruisers.
Queen Mary.
Indefatigable.
Invincible

Cruisers.
Defence.
Black Prince.
Warrior.

Destroyers
Tipperary.
Turbulent.
Fortune.
Sparrowhawk.
Ardent.
Three others.

London Statement of Foe's Loss

Battleships.
One battleship of Kaiser class
blown up.
Another of same class sunk.

Battle Cruisers.
Derfflinger or Lützow, blown up.
Another "disabled."
Another "seriously damaged."

Cruisers.
One "light" cruiser sunk.
Two others disabled.

Destroyers.
Six sunk.

Submarine.
One rammed and sunk.

LONDON, June 2.—Picking its way from its base in the Kiel Canal the German high sea fleet on Wednesday afternoon emerged into the North Sea and off the coast of Jutland, engaged a British fleet throughout the afternoon and night in what probably was the greatest naval battle in the world's history so far as tonnage engaged and tonnage destroyed was concerned.

When the battle ended Great Britain had lost the battle cruisers Queen Mary, Indefatigable, and Invincible, the cruisers Defense, Black Prince, and Warrior, and eight torpedo-boat destroyers, while the German battleship Pommern had been sent to the bottom by a torpedo and the cruiser Wiesbaden sunk by the British gunfire. In addition several German torpedo craft were missing and the small cruiser Frauenlob had last been seen badly listed and was believed to have gone to the bottom. These losses have all been admitted by Great Britain and Germany.

Aside from Great Britain's conceded losses, Germany claims that the British battleship Warspite, sister ship of the Queen Elizabeth, and one of the largest and most powerful ships afloat, had been sunk; that the battleship Marlborough, a vessel of 25,000 tons, had been hit by a torpedo, and a submarine had been destroyed. Great Britain also added to Germany's acknowledged losses with the claim that one dreadnought of the German Kaiser class—vessels of 24,700 tons, and carrying a complement of 1,088 men—had been attacked and destroyed by British torpedo craft; that another battleship of the same class was believed to have been sunk by gunfire; that one battle cruiser had been blown up, and two others damaged, and that a submarine also had been sent to the bottom.

Great Britain's admitted loss in tonnage was 114,810 for the six battle cruisers and cruisers. That of Germany, including the tonnage of the Wiesbaden, supposed to be of the Breslau class, (4,550 tons,) was 20,262. Adding the tonnage of the six destroyers and one submarine which the British say they sank, the figures would approximate 27,000. If, as the British allege, they also sank a dreadnought of the Kaiser class, the total German tonnage destroyed was 51,000.

The tonnage of the capital ships sunk by the Japanese in their fight with the Russians in the battle of Tshushima in May, 1905, aggregated 93,000. Twenty-one Russian craft were destroyed in this fight, including six battleships and four cruisers. The remainder of the sunken craft comprised coast defense and special service vessels and torpedo boats.

That the casualties in the fighting off Jutland were heavy is indicated by the fact that of the crew of some 900 on board the Indefatigable only two men are known to have been saved. Full details of the fight, in which Zeppelins are declared to have taken part, are being gathered by the British Admiralty, and pending their receipt the censor is withholding permission to correspondents to send out stories from London.

With their full complements the crews of the British ships lost would number over 5,000 men.

Rumors had been flying about London all day that a naval battle had taken place in the North Sea, but it was not until evening that the Admiralty gave out its official statement.

The news was flashed out in special editions of the evening newspapers, and caused greater consternation in the West End of London than had been witnessed on any previous occasion since the declaration of war.

The frankness of the Admiralty announcement concerning the serious nature of the British losses and the apparently small losses of the Germans in comparison led to the assumption in most minds that the British vessels must have been led into a mine field.

Following quickly upon the Admiralty announcement came the German official version of the fight, which, in general, confirmed the British account, but carried the assertion that the battleship Warspite also was sunk and other British battleships damaged.

Official Accounts of Battle.

The British Admiralty announcement reads as follows:

On the afternoon of Wednesday, the 31st of May, a naval engagement took place off the coast of Jutland. The British ships on which the brunt of the fighting fell were the battle cruiser fleet and several cruisers and light cruisers, supported by four fast battleships. Among these the losses were heavy.

The German fleet, aided by low visibility, avoided a prolonged action with our main forces. As soon as these appeared on the scene the enemy returned to port, though not before receiving severe damage from our battleships.

The battle cruisers Queen Mary, Indefatigable, and Invincible, and the cruisers Defence and Black Prince were sunk. The Warrior was disabled and, after being towed for some time, had to be abandoned by her crew. It is also known that the destroyers Tipperary, Turbulent, Fortune, Sparrowhawk, and Ardent were lost, and six others are yet to be accounted for. No British battleship or light cruiser was sunk.

The enemy's losses were serious. At least one battle cruiser was destroyed,

Scene of the Great North Sea Battle
[Shown by the Numerals 1 and 2.]

British Ships Lost in the North Sea Battle.

Queen Mary (sunk)

Indefatigable (sunk)

and one was severely damaged. One battleship is reported to have been sunk by our destroyers. During the night attack two light cruisers were disabled and probably sunk. The exact number of enemy destroyers disposed of during the action cannot be ascertained with any certainty, but must have been large.

Later in the evening this additional communication was issued:

Since the foregoing communication was issued a further report has been received from the Commander in Chief of the Grand Fleet, stating that it has now been ascertained that our total losses in destroyers amount to eight boats in all.

The Commander in Chief also reports that it is now possible to form a closer estimate of the losses and the damage sustained by the enemy fleet.

One dreadnought battleship of the Kaiser class was blown up in an attack by British destroyers and another dreadnought battleship of the Kaiser class is believed to have been sunk by gun fire.

Of three German battle cruisers, two of which it is believed were the Derfflinger and the Lutzow, one was blown up, another was heavily engaged by our battle fleet and was seen to be disabled and stopping, and the third was observed to be seriously damaged.

One German light cruiser and six German destroyers were sunk, and at least two more German light cruisers were seen to be disabled. Further repeated hits were observed on three other German battleships that were engaged.

Finally, a German submarine was rammed and sunk.

The official Press Bureau shut down late at night on unofficial accounts of the battle, issuing this bulletin at 11 o'clock:

Owing to lack of information we are unable to pass various accounts of the sea battle that are being submitted.

By tomorrow the Admiralty, no doubt, will possess fuller details, and then, if the articles are submitted, they can be properly dealt with.

How the Fight Started.

A few early evening dispatches from the Continent, largely from points in Denmark and Holland, give fragmentary but interesting details of the fight.

Says Germans Dropped Mines Behind.

A dispatch to the Exchange Telegraphy from Copenhagen says:

"During the retreat of the German fleet large numbers of mines were thrown out. Today several German floating mines were seen in the North Sea.

"Fishermen say that a cruiser struck a mine fifty miles northwest of the Wyl Lightship, outside Blaavandshuk. Only a few men of the crew were saved."

A dispatch of Thursday comes from Ringköbing, on the Danish coast, about thirty-two miles north of Horn Riff. It says:

"From 4 o'clock yesterday (Wednesday) and during the greater part of the night a heavy cannonade was heard from several points on the west coast of Jutland. Many windows were broken here, and people left their beds to ascertain the meaning of the firing.

"At midnight a Zeppelin passed off the coast.

"At 11 o'clock this morning (Thursday) a German destroyer appeared off Noerre Lyngvig Lightship with engine trouble and unable to proceed. At 3 o'clock in the afternoon another German destroyer arrived and left an hour later with the disabled destroyer in tow."

From Copenhagen comes this dispatch under today's date:

"The National Tidende says that last night ten German torpedo boat destroyers passed through the Little Belt from the north going very slowly.

"The newspaper adds that a torpedo boat, badly damaged, is lying off Lynvig, near Ringköbing.

"The Politken says that sentries fired numerous shots at a Zeppelin airship passing over France Island and that the airship withdrew over the international boundary. This, the newspaper adds, was the first time the Danish had fired against a belligerent airship."

Wounded Reaching Dutch Ports.

Advices from Dutch sources are largely concerned with reports of rescues of survivors of the combat. A dispatch from The Hague reads:

"A Dutch trawler has arrived at the Hook of Holland with one dead and seven live Germans who were saved from the naval battle.

A Reuter dispatch from Rotterdam reports the tugboat Scheldt entering the new waterway with dead and wounded men from the naval battle.

Lost Battle Cruisers Veterans.

Among the British vessels lost in the Jutland fight there were no more noted veterans of the navy than the battle cruisers Queen Mary, Indefatigable, and Invincible. The Queen Mary played a prominent part in the Heligoland Bight engagement under the command of Captain William Hall, who has since been prominent as chief of the intelligence division of the Admiralty. The Queen Mary missed the Dogger Bank action by being in drydock for minor repairs. A few weeks ago a large part of her crew came to London on shore leave, and upon their departure Captain Hall, their old commander, came to say farewell to them.

The Indefatigable and Invincible bore scars from the Falkland Islands encounter, where they had a prominent share in sinking Admiral von Spee's squadron, and from the Dardanelles, where they played a leading part in the bombardment of the strait. They had participated in previous North Sea actions.

When a correspondent visited the battle-cruiser fleet in the North Sea last Winter these three vessels were exhibited as the pride of the fleet, which had just come in from a scouting cruise that took them to the German coast. The Queen Mary was pointed out as the finest type of speed and gun power in the British Navy.

"All the News That's Fit to Print."

The New York Times.

THE WEATHER
Fair Sunday and Monday; moderate west winds.
☞For full weather report see Page 20.

VOL. LXV...NO. 21,316.

NEW YORK, SUNDAY, JUNE 4, 1916.—102 PAGES, In Seven Parts,

PRICE FIVE CENTS.

BRITISH NOW CLAIM SUCCESS IN GREAT SEA FIGHT; BEATTY HELD AND JELLICOE ROUTED FOE, SAYS LONDON; BERLIN DENIES DEFEAT; WESTFALEN REPORTED LOST

ELBING LOST, SAYS BERLIN

Admiralty Admits Cruiser Was Blown Up After a Collision.

WHOLE FLEET ENGAGED

Germans Insist the British Sea Force Was Twice as Large as Their Own.

SAY THEY HELD THE FIELD

And Declare the Result of the Battle to be Highly Satisfactory.

German Chancellor Thanks Navy in Name of the Empire

AMSTERDAM, via London, Sunday, June 4.—The Imperial German Chancellor has sent a congratulatory telegram to the commander of the High Seas Fleet, according to a Berlin dispatch.

The Chancellor's Message.

I beg your Excellency to accept my heartiest congratulations upon the grand success of the High Seas Fleet. Pride and enthusiasm prevail throughout the whole of Germany that the fleet has now also had an opportunity of showing a superior enemy, who considered himself invincible, with mighty blows what Germany's sea power is and can do. The Fatherland rejoices and is thankful.

The Fleet Commander's Reply.

I ask your Excellency to accept the heartiest gratitude of the High Seas Fleet for your stimulating and congratulatory message. The pride of the Fatherland, expressed in your Excellency's words, gives us hope that we will be able to contribute in part to Germany's value in the world. This hope is of importance to our fleet and an encouragement for the future.

BERLIN, June 3, (via London.)—A secondary official statement issued today by the Chief of the Admiralty Staff regarding the great naval battle in the North Sea says:

"In order to prevent fabulous reports, it is again stated that in the battle off Skagerak on May 31 the German high sea forces were in battle with the entire modern English fleet.

"To the already published statements it must be added that, according to the official British report, the battle cruiser Invincible and the armored cruiser Warrior were also destroyed.

"We were obliged to blow up the small cruiser Elbing, which, on the night of May 31-June 1, owing to a collision with other German war vessels, was heavily damaged, and it was impossible to take her to port. The crew was rescued by torpedo boats, with the exception of the commander, two other officers, and eighteen men, who remained aboard in order to blow up the vessel. According to Dutch reports they were later brought to Ymuiden on a tug and landed there."

Held the Field, Say Germans.

BERLIN, June 3, (by Wireless from a Staff Correspondent of The Associated Press.)—The first naval battle on a grand scale during the present war has been attended by results which, according to the information received here, are highly satisfactory to the Germans, not only in respect of the comparative losses of the two fleets, but in the fact that the Germans maintained the field after the battle. This is shown, German commentators assert, by the rescue of British survivors.

The full German high sea fleet was engaged, under personal command of Vice Admiral Scheer, the energetic German commander who succeeded Admiral von Pohl. The British fleet is now said to have been approximately twice as strong in guns and ships as that under Admiral Scheer.

Detailed reports have not yet been received, but the main engagement apparently occurred about 125 miles south-southwest of the southern extremity of Norway and 150 miles off the Danish coast. The battle was divided into two sections. The day engagement began at about 4 o'clock in the afternoon and continued until dark, or about 9 o'clock. This was followed by a series of separate engagements through the night.

The exact ranges and courses of the day fight have not been ascertained. It is assumed the ranges of the day engagement were not extreme, possibly at a distance of about eight miles, as the weather was hazy.

The German torpedo boats and destroyers were more effective than the British, accounting to a considerable extent for the successes of the Germans against an overwhelmingly superior force. It is understood the Queen Mary and the Indefatigable were both sunk in the day battle. It has not been learned when the Warspite and the other British warships went down. (The loss of the Warspite is denied officially by the British.)

All the German warships except those mentioned in the official report reached Wilhelmshaven safely. Thus far nothing has been reported regarding the extent to which any of these vessels were damaged. It is stated at the Admiralty that at least thirty-four British capital ships were engaged, and that the British torpedo flotillas were severely handled. The battleship Westfalen alone sank six torpedo boats during night encounters.

German personnel and material alike stood the test brilliantly, and the damage sustained by the German fleet is small in comparison with the British losses. The battleship Pommern, which was sunk, was commanded by Captain Boelken.

Entire Fleets in Action.

"Supplementing the official report of the Admiralty," says the Overseas News Agency, "it is stated by a competent authority that in the North Sea battle the Germans had in action the High Seas Fleet, with dreadnoughts and older battleships, battle cruisers, and also light sea forces, including torpedo boat and submarine flotillas. The Germans faced the greater part of the modern British navy.

"The German reconnoitering forces were commanded by Rear Admiral Hipper. These forces first entered into combat with the enemy's battle cruisers and light cruisers at about 5 P.M. Later the main forces on both sides took part in the fight. During the day battle German torpedo boats several times entered into action successfully, one of them three times. The fight kept on until 9 o'clock in the evening.

"During the night both sides made violent attacks with torpedo boats and cruisers, in which there were further British losses. The leading German ship annihilated six modern British destroyers."

HOSTS IN CHICAGO ON DEFENSE PARADE

CHICAGO, June 3.—The greatest parade ever held in Chicago, finished tonight after 130,214 persons, one-sixth of them women, had filed through the streets in the preparedness demonstration. The parade was eleven and a half hours in passing. The night division was made up largely of military organizations.

The parade was said by Major General Thomas H. Barry, Commander of the Central Department of the United States Army, who sat in the reviewing stand, to be the greatest and most inspiring spectacle he had ever seen.

The great parade, in close order, massed from curb to curb, rolled like a tide through the streets all day. It was as if the great skyscrapers were the banks of a river, and the marching thousands, each with an American flag, the current moving between them.

It impressed by its bulk, and by the absence to a large extent of the hilarity accompanying most parades. There were no floats, no comic costumes, and little of the holiday spirit apparent. The airs played by the bands either were patriotic or military. Patriotic songs were sung, or hummed, or whistled, for few knew the words. They did better, occasionally, with hymns.

The precision with which the parade moved was itself said to be a lesson in preparedness, for it was handled by Captain Raymond Sheldon of the regular army, by a system of telephones. The demonstration started promptly at 9 A. M., upon a salute of twenty-one guns.

130 TO 150 SHIPS IN FIGHT

Total Number of German Vessels Lost Nearly Equals the British.

Rear Admiral Hood and Host of Officers Among the British Who Went Down with Ships.

INQUIRERS BESET ADMIRALTY

All England Saddened by the Great Losses — Portsmouth Had Six Vessels Sunk.

King George Praises Fleet; Regrets That Germans Fled

LONDON, June 3.—Admiral Jellicoe and King George exchanged the following messages today on the occasion of the King's birthday:

The Admiral's Message:

On the occasion of Your Majesty's birthday the officers and men of the Grand Fleet in humble duty send their respectful, heartfelt wishes, with the loyal hope and determination that through victory for Your Majesty's arms and those of our gallant allies the blessings of peace may be restored.

The King's Reply.

I am deeply touched by the message you have sent in behalf of the Grand Fleet. It reaches me on the morrow of a battle which once more displayed the splendid gallantry of the officers and men under your command.

I mourn the loss of the brave men, many of them personal friends of my own, who have fallen in their country's cause. Yet even more do I regret that the German High Seas Fleet, in spite of its heavy losses, was enabled by misty weather to evade the full consequences of the encounter.

They always professed a desire for which when the opportunity arrived they showed no inclination. Though the retirement of the enemy immediately after the opening of a general engagement robbed us of the opportunity of gaining a decisive victory, the events of last Wednesday amply justify my confidence in the valor and efficiency of the fleet under your command.

GEORGE R. I.

LONDON, Sunday, June 4.—Latest reports from the British fleet, from neutral vessels which witnessed parts of the naval battle in the North Sea and from survivors, have caused the British public to believe that the engagement was not so near a defeat as it appeared at first, and in no wise a disaster.

128

The British losses, with all the craft engaged accounted for, are three battle cruisers, three armored cruisers, and eight destroyers. It is officially announced that the three destroyers previously unidentified are the Nomad, Nestor, and Shark.

The German losses are believed to have been about the same number of ships, although a much less aggregate of tonnage. The dreadnought Westfalen, of 18,600 tons, has been added to the German list. a wireless dispatch from Berlin stating that the German Admiralty admits the loss of this vessel. Another addition to the original German list is the new cruiser Elbing, displacing 4,000 to 5,000 tons.

British naval experts maintain that Great Britain continues to hold the supremacy of the sea by a safe margin and that her huge navy could better afford the losses it suffered than could the smaller German establishment.

The first reports of the heavy loss of life are confirmed. Great Britain mourns for more than 5,000 of her best seamen and the whole nation is oppressed with sadness.

There were about 6,000 men on the ships which sank and only a few hundred have been saved. The horrors of modern naval warfare, far exceeding those when wooden ships fought and continued to float, even when they ceased to be fighting units, were realized to their utmost. From five of the largest ships, which went under with a complement of more than 4,000 men, only seven junior officers and a few seamen were rescued.

Entire Crews Lost.

There were no surrenders and the ships which went down carried with them virtually their whole crews. Only the Warrior, which was towed part way from the scene of battle to a British port, was an exception.

Of some thousand men on the Queen Mary only a Corporal's guard is accounted for. The same is true of the Invincible, while there are no survivors reported from the Indefatigable, the Defence, or the Black Prince.

The manner in which the Queen Mary came to her end is described by an east coast town correspondent of The Weekly Dispatch.

The ship, according to this correspondent, was sunk by the concentrated gunfire of the German capital ships, causing her magazine to explode with terrific force. The forward part of the ship was blown away almost bodily, and the Queen Mary went down in less than two minutes.

Rear Admiral the Honorable Horace Lambert Hood, second in command to Vice Admiral Sir David Beatty, and Captains Sowerby, Cay, and Prowse of the Indefatigable, Invincible, and Queen Mary, were lost with many others, whose names are not yet known because the Government has not so far issued any casualty list.

Two well-known London clergymen, who volunteered to serve as Chaplains at the beginning of the war, Mr. Lyndell and Mr. Lepatourel, are among the missing. Mr. Lyndell is a nephew of Field Marshal Viscount French. He was to have been married at London Monday.

The only formal statement issued by the Admiralty yesterday referred to a eGrman wireless message to Washington, containing a report of the speech of the President of the Reichstag, in which the loss of the British battleship Warspite was again asserted.

Latest Figures on Losses in North Sea Battle

BRITISH.

Name.	Tonnage.	Personnel. [Few Survivors]
Queen Mary (battle cruiser)	27,000	1,000
Indefatigable (battle cruiser)	18,750	800
Invincible (battle cruiser)	17,250	750
Defense (armored cruiser)	14,600	755
Warrior (armored cruiser)	13,550	704
Black Prince (armored cruiser)	13,550	704
Tipperary (destroyer)	1,850	150
Turbulent (destroyer)	1,850	150
Shark (destroyer)	950	100
Sparrowhawk (destroyer)	950	100
Ardent (destroyer)	950	100
Fortune (destroyer)	950	100
Nomad (destroyer)	*950	100
Nestor (destroyer)	*950	100

*Not listed in last British register.

Totals.

Battle cruisers	63,000	2,550
Armored cruisers	41,700	2,163
Destroyers	9,400	900
Fourteen ships	114,100	5,613

GERMAN.

Name.	Tonnage.	Personnel. [Of whom many were saved.]
Pommern (battleship)	13,200	729
Wiesbaden (cruiser)	5,600	(estimated) 450
Frauenlob (cruiser)	2,715	264
Elbing (cruiser)	5,000	(estimated) 450
Six destroyers (reported)	6,000	(estimated) 600

[REPORTED BY BRITISH, BUT NOT ADMITTED BY GERMANS.]

Westfalen (dreadnought)	18,900	963
Derfflinger (battle cruiser)	26,600	(estimated) 1,200
One submarine	1,000	(estimated) 40

Totals.

[ADMITTED.]

Battleship	13,200	729
Cruisers	13,315	1,164
Destroyers	6,000	600
Ten ships	32,515	2,493

[INCLUDING GERMAN LOSSES REPORTED BY THE BRITISH.]

Two battleships	32,100	1,692
Four cruisers	39,915	2,364
Six destroyers	6,000	600
One submarine	1,000	40
Thirteen ships	79,015	4,696

"This is untrue," the statement declares, "that ship having returned to harbor."

"The loss of the destroyer Alcaster," the statement continues, "is also announced. This is untrue, that vessel also having returned to her base."

"The names of three British destroyers not hitherto identified, making a total of eight lost, reported in an official statement issued early in the day, are the Nomad, Nestor, and Shark.

"Statements in the same German wireless message as to three German merchant vessels being torpedoed without warning by a British submarine are without foundation."

William Hall, Chief of the Intelligence Division of the Admiralty, also denied during the day the loss of the Marlborough, as reported in Berlin, saying that she was hit by a torpedo but was safe in port.

It is impossible to visualize any coherent story of the great battle, which lasted many hours, with the different units at times fighting scattered engagements.

The British and German reports contradict each other flatly on the main facts. The British assert that the German fleet retired when the British battleships appeared, while the German official statement maintains that the German forces were in battle with the entire British fleet. The British assert that they had only two divisions engaged and that all the units of these were not able to participate in the fighting and, furthermore, that Admiral Sir John Jellicoe, commander of the grand fleet, remained in the area of the battle after the Germans had retreated, and swept it thoroughly in search of enemy ships and survivors.

The King's message to Admiral Jellicoe states that the Germans robbed the British of the opportunity of gaining a decisive victory by retiring immediately after the opening of the general engagement.

Battle Fought on Tested Lines.

Vice Admiral Beatty, commanding the battle cruiser squadron, presumably on his old flagship the Lion, was again in the thick of the action.

Every arm of the most modern naval warfare was employed—battleships, cruisers, torpedo boats, destroyers, submarines, and even Zeppelins. Apparently most of the destruction was accomplished by gunfire. British officers say that the battle was fought by the methods known and practiced by all navies, and that there were no surprises and no new devices of weapons or strategy.

How far the Zeppelins contributed to the German successes is a matter of dispute. Only one airship came within sight, according to British accounts, and she was soon damaged and withdrew. But the Germans lay stress on the assistance rendered by their air service, and neutrals report the presence of six Zeppelins in the

North Sea. The belief among the British public is that scouting Zeppelins kept the German fleet informed by wireless of the approach of the British numbers and formation.

Fishermen arriving at Dutch ports assert that 150 vessels of all classes took part in the battle.

Before the hostile fleets came into touch with each other Admiral Beatty with his battle cruiser squadron got between the German fleet and its base. He was compelled to withdraw, however, following the discovery of the presence of battleships with the German fleet.

The Central News reports that after the action the German fleet broke into two forces and made for their home ports after sowing a large number of mines. The British squadron, it is stated, succeeded in getting between the German battle fleet and the smaller German vessels, and after a brief engagement forced them into their own mine field, with disastrous results for the Germans.

A report from The Hague, as forwarded to the Central News, says that six German destroyers were sunk by the British and that a large cruiser, severely damaged, was towed into the harbor at Kiel.

From survivors come thrilling stories of the horrors and humanities of the battle. The British destroyer Shark acted as a decoy to lead the German ships into the engagement. She was battered to pieces by gunfire, and half a dozen sailors, picked up clinging to a buoy by a Danish ship, tell of her commander and two seamen serving her only remaining gun to the last minute, when the commander's leg was blown off.

Sang Anthem as Ship Sank.

There are stories of ships sinking with great explosions, of crews going down singing the national anthem, of merchant ships passing through a sea thick with floating bodies.

An Exchange Telegraph dispatch from Copenhagen says the German torpedo boat V-28 was sunk during the engagement. Three survivors, who were rescued from a raft by a Swedish steamship, reported that all the rest of the crew of 102 were lost.

According to this dispatch the survivors of the V-28 said they believed that twenty German torpedo boats were destroyed, and that the German losses as a whole were "colossal."

A lifeboat with German survivors from the German cruiser Elbing rescued Surgeon Burton of the British destroyer Tipperary. He had sustained four wounds.

The Admiralty was crowded all day with anxious men and women of all classes trying to learn the fate of relatives. Only the names of surviving officers were published today.

Many who have relatives and friends in the navy are ignorant of what vessels they are serving on. Accurate casualty lists cannot be issued until the identity of the survivors who have been taken to Holland and Scandinavian ports is known.

Portsmouth is a town of mourning. Three thousand of the men who went into the battle came from Portsmouth, and most of them leave families.

Wounded men from the battle have begun to arrive in London, cheered by the crowds assembled to meet them.

The Admiralty has no information concerning a report that the German dreadnought Hindenburg was sunk.

These gas masks are, from left to right, American, British, French and German. The design may have been different but the function was the same—to save the soldier from a slow and painful death from "mustard gas."

Peach pits were one of the main ingredients in the substance that lined the all-important gas mask so governments encouraged their patriotic citizens to eat plenty of peaches and deposit the valuable pits in barrels like this one.

"All the News That's Fit to Print."

The New York Times.

THE WEATHER
Fair today and probably Sunday; moderate west winds.
For full weather report see Page 18.

VOL. LXV...NO. 21,343. ... NEW YORK, SATURDAY, JULY 1, 1916.—TWENTY PAGES. ONE CENT In Greater New York, Jersey City and Newark. | Elsewhere TWO CENTS.

BRITISH SHELL STORM SHAKES FOE; RUSSIAN HOSTS TAKE KOLOMEA; FRENCH SEIZE THIAUMONT WORK

GERMAN LINES POUNDED

Million Shells Are Hurled Daily by British Guns

FROM YPRES TO SOMME

Defenses Smashed and Communication Trenches Wrecked, Stopping the Food Supply.

GERMAN RESPONSE FEEBLE

Night Raids by British Patrols Are Constant and Effective, Taking Many Prisoners.

BRITISH HEADQUARTERS IN FRANCE, June 30.—The fourth day of the British bombardment of the German positions sees no diminution of the volume of fire, which continues along the whole line without cessation day and night, cutting barbed wire entanglements, demolishing first and second lines of German trenches, and placing curtains of fire on the roads and communicating trenches.

All this week the British front has been alive with the most furious gunfire, in vivid contrast with the quiet Spring months when the world was asking why the British were inactive. Battery by battery guns have been arriving from England and have been tried out, and this week the curtain was lifted on an exhibition of their power. The proportion of large calibre guns, which are so useful, is large.

Considerably over 1,000,000 shells a day are being expended, and there seems to be no limit to the supply of them. The German artillery fire is heavy at some points, but in most cases seems half-hearted.

Wherever the correspondent has gone along the line the British have appeared to be firing two shells to the Germans' one. At some points in the face of the British concentration the German guns have seemed strangely silent, as if awaiting events.

British infantry actions have been limited thus far to raids under cover of artillery and trench mortar fire, which ascertain the state of the German wire entanglements and trenches. The new type of British mortar is capable of such rapid fire that six shots in the air at once proved highly serviceable, both in cutting of wire and the smashing of trenches.

Patrols report that German trenches at several places have been deserted and that the defense works and wire entanglements have been damaged badly.

At other parts the German line is strongly held, great alertness and spasmodic bursts of machine-gun fire and rifle volleys indicating a condition of apprehension.

British infantry last night carried on raiding as usual, and brought back prisoners from several places.

These captures have enabled the British to identify every German battalion opposite their lines. Some of the prisoners say that the British fire has been so heavy that it has destroyed the communication trenches and that the Germans have been unable to bring up food to their front line for three days.

During the night the sky from twenty to thirty miles in the rear toward the east was brilliant from dusk to dawn, as if with the glare of the aurora borealis. This was the only illumination along the roads for the movement of trucks and automobiles, none of which carried lights.

From a point near a group of batteries a correspondent witnessed a scene of grandeur under the canopy of a cloudless and moonless night, with broad sheets of flame and ugly flashes and darts of fire over the entire area of action.

The correspondent traveled from the northern to the southern end of the line with the roar always in his ears. He left the automobile at intervals to climb hills or go forward to artillery observation posts to see the results of the fire.

In the region from the Vimy Ridge to the Somme, vantage points of the rolling country permit the spectator, as in a gallery, to look out over the area behind the German lines and witness the panorama of bursting shells.

Just back of a German first line trench the village of Beaucourt-sur-Ancre, which when last seen was unharmed, with its green shade trees, had become in a day's time a wreck of fallen walls, with only a few stumps of trees standing, while shells still belabored the ruins.

When the correspondent returned from one of his trips forward, passing between batteries, he observed that, despite the torrent of shells, many batteries were not firing and that their gunners were resting in dugouts or washing or preparing their meals in their recesses from labor. Batteries placed well in the rear seemed to be waiting their turns.

Gangs were busy repairing the network of roads, some new, built to carry the heavy traffic of catterpillar tractors, steam and gasoline tractors, and columns of motor trucks which were bringing up shells.

"It took time to prepare all this, and all of it had to be brought from overseas," said an officer.

British Guns Hold the Mastery.

Special Cable to THE NEW YORK TIMES.

WITH THE BRITISH ARMY IN THE FIELD, June 29. (Dispatch to The London Daily Chronicle.)—For more than eighty miles, from the Yser to the Somme, the British guns are still shelling the German lines. They are shelling certain points along the German front opposite La Bassée, Vimy and further south, where the flat plains give way to long ridges of wooded hills, and with a deadly weight of metal.

I can speak as a man who has seen this thing on only a few miles of the line, but in that part it is certain the British artillery is stronger than the German. There comes back so far only a spasmodic reply, and I am told on all sections of the front British guns have the mastery in numbers.

All the horizon beyond the ground where I stood today was darkened by the fumes of shells. Not a minute passed without the crash of high explosives.

Raids that followed this shell fire at many points of the line killed many of the enemy and brought forth sufficient prisoners for the identification of the regiments and divisions confronting the British. For the first time there is absolute knowledge of every German unit in their order of battle, and it is a tribute to the work of the intelligence service that this certainty owing to the capture of prisoners confirms in every detail the reports already sent in from other sources of information.

The effect of the British military work on the German troops appears to have been deadly. Some prisoners say they had no food for three days, owing to the barrage fire, which prevented supplies reaching them by their communication trenches.

The weather has not been good for the gunners, and observations may have been a little hindered by the rain clouds which obscured the view, but today it seemed to me the British had the better means of observation. Immediately in front of where I stood I counted twelve British kite balloons poised above the lines so that observers could see far across the German trenches to their battery positions. Time was when I used to see "German sausages," as we used to call those balloons, staring down. Today there was not a single hostile balloon opposite those twelve of the British. Rapid destruction of six of them has, I fancy, caused the hauling down of the others. If they cannot put them up again, the Germans have lost the eyes of their artillery in places where they are not on high ground from which observation may be made more safely.

Germans Moving Troops.

It is too soon yet to say whether this gunfire, destructive over a wide area, will have any immediate effect in relieving the pressure upon Verdun. The Russian advance on the Eastern front already has caused the withdrawal of at least eight divisions. These include the Twenty-seventh Reserve Corps, the Eleventh Bavarian division, both from the Verdun area, and the Tenth Corps from the Champaigne.

About a Bavarian division a curious story is told on good evidence. It seems they revolted against the continual slaughter of German troops in the attempt to capture Verdun and refused to advance to the attack. It is said for this mutiny one man out of ten men throughout the division was sentenced to be shot, but they were reprieved when the King of Bavaria protested against this severity. They were then sent in disgrace to Russia. It is possible other German troops may have been taken from the Verdun area.

The combined activities of the Allies and France will prove that her calm confidence and heroic sacrifices were justified by this supreme rebuff to the German plans. The enemy is losing men, losing guns, losing heart. The work of the British guns is a terrible proof to me that the time was after all on the side of the Allies and was used to build up artillery which is now as strong as the foe's.

But though we are strong, the enemy also is strong, and the people in England will be wise if they do not place their hopes too high because our shellfire is spreading up and down the line.

As I said yesterday, the object of these bombardments is to kill Germans. That is being done and the number of their dead is rising. But behind the dead is a great living army, strongly intrenched and able to strike back heavy blows. There must be bloody fighting this year or next before the end comes, but the spirit of our troops is high, because after much waiting our guns are speaking loudly and in great numbers.

Some indication of the violence of the present artillery fire along the British front is afforded by the fact that in two days of the bombardment of Neuve Chapelle in March, 1915, 5,000 massed French and British field pieces and howitzers were unofficially reported to have fired 3,000,000 shells. There were intimations at the time that one reason for the halt of the attack was the exhaustion of the shell supply.

FIERCE STRUGGLE NORTH OF VERDUN

French Seize Redoubt at 10 A. M., Lose Part at 3 P. M., and Recover All at 4:30.

HARD FIGHTING AT HILL 304

Germans Capture French Position, Only to Lose It by a Counterattack.

PARIS, June 30.—French troops today recaptured from the Germans the Thiaumont work, northeast of Verdun, according to the War Office communication issued tonight.

A terrific struggle took place in that area. The Germans were driven out of the redoubt at 10 o'clock in the morning, after having held it for seven days. By a violent assault they entered the work at 3 o'clock in the afternoon, but the French counterattacked, and at 4:30, says the offficial bulletin, they had again gained full possession.

There was heavy fighting last night near Hill 304 west of the Meuse. In a terrific attack upon the French positions the Germans captured a fortified work in the first line of the French trenches, after the garrison had been buried under a storm of shells. The position was recaptured by a brilliant French counterattack, according to the afternoon bulletin of the French War Office.

The Germans also delivered a powerful attack on French positions in Avocourt Wood and west of Hill 304, but these efforts are said to have been checked, with heavy losses to the attackers.

The night bulletin of the French War Office reads:

> On the left bank of the Meuse the bombardment continued in the region of Hill 304, but no infantry action took place.
>
> On the right bank of the Meuse stubborn fighting was in progress all day. In the region of Thiaumont this morning about 10 o'clock our troops in the course of a very brilliant attack carried the Thiaumont work, notwithstanding the extremely violent curtain of fire brought to bear by the enemy.
>
> This afternoon the Germans multiplied their efforts to expel us. In the course of this offensive they sustained considerable losses. Toward 3 o'clock the enemy succeeded in re-entering the fort, but a vigorous counterattack enabled us at 4:30 o'clock to regain complete possession of it.
>
> A particularly violent bombardment occurred today in the Fumin and Chenois woods.

The afternoon communication of the French War Office reads:

> In Belgium last night at about 11 o'clock, following a preparatory artillery fire, German forces attacked a salient of our line not far from the road between Nieuport and Lombaertzyde. A counterattack was at once delivered which drove the enemy out of one section of trench where they had gained a footing.
>
> Between Chaulnes and Roye a

strong German reconnoitering party, caught under our fire, was dispersed before it could reach our trenches.

Between the Oise and the Aisne two other German patrols also were dispersed in like manner, one in front of Quennevières and the other at a point to the northeast of Vingre.

In the Champagne district a minor attack of the enemy with hand grenades upon our advanced posts to the west of Butte de Mesnil was easily repulsed.

On the left bank of the River Meuse the Germans last night increased their offensive activity against our positions stretching from Avocourt Wood to a point to the east of Hill No. 304. They directed upon the principal salients of our line a series of very violent attacks. These were preceded by intense bombardments and accompanied by the throwing of flaming liquids.

Between Avocourt Wood and Hill 304 all their endeavors were broken by our fire, which inflicted heavy losses upon them. To the east of Hill 304, after several fruitless assaults, the enemy succeeded in taking possession of a fortified work in our first line, the garrison of which had been literally buried by the German bombardment. At about 4 o'clock in the morning a brilliant counterattack on the part of our troops resulted in our again becoming masters of this work.

On the right bank of the river the bombardment has been very spirited in the sectors to the north of Souville and Tavannes, particularly in the region of Chenois. There was no infantry fighting at these points.

Berlin Reports Heavy Firing.

Berlin asserts that attacks by the French at various places yesterday and last night were repulsed. The official statement has this to say of the fighting on the French front:

Southeast of Tahure and near Maisons de Champagne advancing French detachments were sanguinely repulsed.

On the left bank of the Meuse (Verdun front) we made progress on Hill 304. On the right bank of the river there was no infantry activity.

The total number of prisoners taken by us since June 23 and during the repulse of the great French counter-attack was 70 officers and 3,200 men.

On the evening of June 27 Lieutenant Boelke shot down his nineteenth enemy aeroplane near the Thiamont Farm and yesterday Lieutenant Parachau brought down his fifth enemy aeroplane near Peronne.

RUSSIANS WIN GREAT BATTLE

Austrian Line in Southeast Galicia Smashed and Army in Full Retreat.

KOLOMEA AND OBERTYN FALL

Invaders Pass Mouth of Stripa in Sweep Westward—Germans in North Cross the Niemen.

LONDON, Saturday, July 1.—The announcement that the Russians had captured Kolomea, Galicia, reached London early today in a laconic special communication from Petrograd. This communication merely said:

"We have taken Kolomea, the most important railway centre in the Bukowina region."

The importance of Kolomea is obvious. The army which holds the town not only has cleared Bukowina of the Austrians, but is planted on the flank of the Austro-German central force in a position which may make a complete rearrangement of their line inevitable, according to military observers.

General Count von Bothmer had been maintaining his position ever since the Russian offensive began, and had been heavily reinforced by the Austro-German high command in the belief that if his position on the centre held firm the Austrian defeats in the north and south might be retrieved. Now suddenly his right flank has been defeated, and, in the belief of the British military experts, it will be virtually impossible for General von Bothmer to remain where he is any longer, for the Russians command, or at all events threaten, his communications and his whole right flank is at their mercy.

If General von Bothmer falls back toward Lemberg, the military observers say, his whole line must be rearranged further west. Then, they say, the question arises, will the Russians allow this serious operation without inflicting further grave losses? They add that it is becoming increasingly evident that the great captures of men, munitions, and stores by the Russians are a greater loss to the Austrians and Germans than even the extensive progress the Russians have made in Austrian territory, because the lack of immediately available men, munitions, and stores is likely to prove a tremendous handicap to any rearrangement of the Austro-German lines.

Russian Official Report.

PETROGRAD, June 30.—The War Office tonight announced the capture of Kolomea by the Russians in the following communication:

The troops on the Russian left wing today took the city of Kolomea, the most important railway centre in Bukowina (sic.) The enemy continues to fall back westward occupying positions previously prepared.

Northwest of Kimpolung, (southern Bukowina,) the enemy attempted an offensive with large forces. General Letchitzky's forces are carrying out the offensive under extremely difficult conditions, for torrential rains have played havoc with the roads, already bad.

Northwest of the confluence of the Lipa and Styr and along the line of Lutsk-Brody, the enemy bombarded our positions with heavy and light artillery and then undertook an offensive near the village of Garienki and Nataline. Our troops coolly allowed them to approach their barbed wire and then shot them down. In the region of the Lipa the enemy, having once been repulsed, is preparing a new attack.

The total prisoners from June 6 to June 28 is 212,000, including officers. Prisoners are still flowing in.

An earlier bulletin read as follows:

In the region south of the Dniester we are pursuing the enemy. The Austrians, panic-stricken in their flight, are leaving behind a large number of convoys. Military material and more prisoners have been brought in.

According to telegrams received here, the town of Obertyn was taken after a fight, as well as villages in the neighborhood north and south.

Northwest of the confluence of the Rivers Lipa and Styr our detachments under command of Colonel Grembezky, approached unperceived the settlement of Covbane and a village of the same name and took possession. After having put the garrison of Covbane to the bayonet we took possession of the village to which the enemy had fled in panic. Some prisoners were taken by us.

An action is in progress near the village of Pistyne, northwest of Kuty, (Galicia.) In the course of one of the combats here General Count Keller was wounded.

Near the village of Solovine, between the Rivers Stokhod and Styr, to the west of Sokul, the Germans attempted to take the offensive, after emitting clouds of gas, which failed to reach our lines, and which were partly blown back in the direction of the enemy. The German attack was repulsed, but an artillery duel continues.

Yesterday morning enemy aviators dropped thirty bombs on Lutsk.

On the Dvina front the enemy artillery has bombarded our positions southeast of Riga and the bridgehead above Ikskul. North of Illoukst the Germans last evening attempted to move forward, but were thrown back by our gunfire.

On the evening of Wednesday light and heavy German artillery opened a violent fire on our trenches in the Niemer sector northeast of Novo Grodek. Under cover of this fire the enemy crossed the Niemen and occupied the woods east of the village of Ghnessitche.

BRITAIN'S ARMY 4,000,000.

Best Cared For in History, Says Doctor—Crippled American Returns

Among the passengers arriving yesterday on the French liner Chicago from Bordeaux was Dr. Francis R. Holbrook of New York, who had been serving for the last thirteen months with the British Red Cross in Belgium and France.

"The British Army has attained to a high state of efficiency which I do not think is equaled by the Germans today. The soldiers fight bravely and with a steady determination to beat the enemy, and they are better taken care of than any army has been before in history."

The doctor said the health of the men in the trenches was much better than it was a year ago, and there were a great many less gangrene cases, as the treatment of wounds had been very much improved.

These French machine gunners were a small part of the troop force that fought to defend Verdun.

The New York Times.

"All the News That's Fit to Print."

THE WEATHER
Fair Sunday and Monday; moderate westerly and southwesterly winds.
For full weather report see Page 8.

VOL. LXV...NO. 21,344. ...   NEW YORK, SUNDAY, JULY 2, 1916.—90 PAGES, In Eight Parts, Including Pictures and Rotogravure Section and Review of Books.   PRICE FIVE CENTS.

BRITISH SMASH 7 MILES OF FOE'S LINE, TAKE 2 TOWNS AND 2,000 PRISONERS; FRENCH JOIN ATTACK, TAKE 3 TOWNS

ATTACK ON 25-MILE FRONT

British Right Pushes in 1,000 Yards and Takes Fortified Positions.

LEFT UNABLE TO HOLD ALL

Loses Some Trenches Taken from the Germans in the First Rush, Retains Others.

CONFLICT IS STILL RAGING

Great Offensive Begun After Seven Days of the Fiercest of Bombardments.

LONDON, July 1.—By a concerted attack today in great force on German trenches extending twenty-five miles north and south of the Somme River, the British and French troops made large and important gains, capturing at least five towns, and inflicting heavy losses on the foe.

Haig's soldiers bore the burden of the assault, moving against the foe on a twenty-mile front from near the Somme northward, beyond the Ancre River. Tonight they hold seven miles of German trenches, and the fortified towns of Montauban and Mametz, east of Albert, and have also captured some positions northeast of Albert, while others in that region are still in German possession.

North of the Ancre the advancing British met the fiercest resistance, and positions which were captured by the first rush of the offensive were afterward lost again.

On the British right the French struck simultaneously, and tonight the War Office at Paris announced the taking of Dompierre, Becquincourt and Fay, south of that river.

Announcement of the beginning of this great offensive was made soon after noon today in this bulletin of the British War Office:

An attack was launched north of the River Somme this morning at 7:30 in conjunction with the French. British troops have broken into the German forward system of defenses on a front of sixteen miles. The fighting is continuing.

The French attack on our immediate right is proceeding equally satisfactorily.

On the remainder of the British front raiding parties again succeeded in penetrating the enemy's defenses at many points, inflicting loss on the enemy and taking some prisoners.

British Achievements of the Day.

The night bulletin of the British War Office summed up the results of the day's great offensive as follows:

Heavy fighting continued all day between the Rivers Somme and Ancre and north of Ancre to Gommecourt, inclusive. The fight on the whole of this front still continues with intensity.

On the right of our attack we have captured a German labyrinth of trenches on a front of seven miles to a depth of 1,000 yards, and have stormed and occupied the strongly fortified villages of Montauban and Mametz.

In the centre of our attack on a front of four miles we have gained many strong points, while at others the enemy is still holding out and the struggle on this front is still severe.

North of the Ancre Valley to Gommecourt inclusive the battle is equally violent, and in this area we have been unable to retain portions of the ground, gained in our first attacks, while other portions remain in our possession.

Up to the present over 2,000 German prisoners have passed through our collecting stations, including two regimental commanders and the whole of one regimental staff.

The large number of enemy dead on the battlefield indicates that the German casualties have been very severe, especially in the vicinity of Fricourt.

Last night parties of our troops penetrated the German trenches at various points on the front between Souchez and Ypres, in each case inflicting casualties on the garrisons before withdrawing. One raiding party captured sixteen prisoners.

The French War Office bulletin tonight has this to say of the operations in this sector:

North and south of the Somme, following artillery preparation and reconnoissances carried out in the preceding days, Franco-British troops launched this morning an offensive on a front of about 40 kilometers, (25 miles.)

In the morning and during the course of the afternoon along the entire front attacked the allied troops gained possession of the German first position.

North of the Somme the French troops established themselves in the approaches to the village of Hardecourt and in the outskirts of the village of Curly, where the battle continues.

South of the Somme the villages of Dompierre, Becquincourt, Bussu, (?) and Fay have fallen into our hands.

The number of unwounded German prisoners captured by the French troops alone during the course of the day surpassed 3,500.

The official communication of the German Headquarter's Staff, issued today, had only a brief reference to the allied attacks. It read:

Repeated French and British reconnoitering attacks during the night were everywhere repulsed. A number of prisoners and some material remaind in our hands.

The attacks were preceded by intense fire, gas attacks, and mine explosions.

Early this morning, fighting activity appreciably increased on both sides of the Somme.

EXPECT TERRIFIC STRUGGLE

But Experts Doubt Present Drive Will End the War This Year.

ALLIES FACING STERN TASK

Special Cable to THE NEW YORK TIMES.

LONDON, July 1.—News of the launching of the British offensive on the western front keyed popular interest here today to the highest pitch. The public's impression is that the ceaseless effort of many months now is about to be put to the sternest test. Many experts believe that the military initiative has now definitely passed from the Central Powers to the Allies, and, while a majority incline to the view that a terrific struggle will be necessary before the maps to which Chancellor von Bethmann Hollweg pointed can be radically altered, some observers predict relatively quick decisions, chiefly on the ground that the training and temperament of the German masses are unlikely to stand the strain of continued assaults of an enemy superior in numbers and at least equal in its artillery.

The average man in the street is generally confident that "We'll soon have 'em on the run." Professor Albert Frederick Pollard of London University, whose lectures on the war have attracted much attention here, takes a different view. He sees no definite result this year. In an interview with THE NEW YORK TIMES correspondent today Professor Pollard said:

"Broadly speaking, it looks as though a real, but possibly a limited, offensive has been begun by the British and French on the western front, but it is impossible to tell now how far it will go for the moment.

"It hardly seems probable that the war can be ended this year, but that the final campaign against Germany will probably be left to next year, but, of course, everything depends on the degree of success attained in the various spheres of operations this Summer and Autumn, upon the impression produced by those operations on German public opinion, and upon the effect such a likely change of opinion might have upon the capacity of the German Government to carry on the war. So far as the British offensive goes, it may be taken for granted that preparations have been going on for the greater part of two years for a desperate campaign, so that at the present moment Great Britain probably is better equipped in guns and munitions than any other fighting force.

"Although it is undoubtedly true that German production of arms and ammunition has been enormously increased right along, she is not in as strong a position as she would like to be. Germany is producing more ore than at any previous time during the war, but the fact is outstanding that the quality of this ore is by no means up to the best standard. While Germany is taking large quantities of ore from the conquered territories in France and Belgium, the quality of it is not equal to that required to make the highest type of ammunition and other war material. This must be regarded as an appreciable drawback to Germany's producing strength for the purpose of carrying on the war.

"When one considers Germany's food supply, the effect of the Russian advance has to be regarded, for the Russian offensive must play an important part in that problem of the Central Empires. Russia now occupies many square miles of corn-growing country, on which Germany largely depended, and even if the Czar's forces are driven back, they will destroy the crops during their retreat."

Professor Pollard then referred to the British offensive in connection with the Verdun struggle.

"I have reason to know," he said, "that in February Germany, while not expecting to win the war in the sense which she hoped for in 1914, still counted upon the offensive at Verdun to knock France out, or, at least, to paralyze it for the purpose of a general offensive this year. Germany banked on Verdun to impress France with Prussian superiority, then hoped while France was staggering to deal a fatal blow to the British. France's magnificent resistance at Verdun upset Germany's calculations.

"When the Germans began to move against Verdun it is said General Joffre was delighted, because he expected they would involve themselves in operations from which they could not extricate themselves without discredit and disadvantage. Whether Joffre has got the Germans into that position remains to be seen. In any event he has drawn out a powerful force that has all it can do to make headway, and which would have been more usefully employed elsewhere.

"From all we know it would seem the British forces on the western front are superior to the German forces. Whether that superiority is sufficient to overcome the advantage possessed by the defensive remains to be seen, but certainly grounds exist for confidence."

British Say Baltic Ports Are Now Tightly Closed

LONDON, July 1.—British naval men home on leave after a period of participation in submarine operations in the Baltic, speak enthusiastically of the success attending their work, says The Star's Edinburgh correspondent.

"While nothing has been reported in the English or Russian papers," said one petty officer, "we imposed an iron rule in the Baltic, and the Germans are now beginning to feel the full effects of it in a terrible draught upon their larder. The blockade in the Baltic is now about as thorough as that which the Grand Fleet has established in the North Sea. Submarines of the Allies are a constant menace to Memel, the German timber port; Koenigsberg, and the ports in the Gulf of Danzig, as well as the Pomeranian ports, and the whole sea traffic of the German Baltic provinces is in a state of disorganization through the effectiveness of the submarine patrol."

"All the News That's Fit to Print."

The New York Times.

THE WEATHER
Local thundershowers Monday; fair Tuesday; moderate winds, except fresh on the coast.
For full weather report see Page 17.

VOL. LXV...NO. 21,345. NEW YORK, MONDAY, JULY 3, 1916.—EIGHTEEN PAGES. ONE CENT In Greater New York, Jersey City and Newark. | Elsewhere, TWO CENTS.

ALLIES FORGE AHEAD ON THE SOMME; TAKE FRICOURT, FRISE AND CURLU; 9,500 GERMANS CAPTURED IN 2 DAYS

STORY OF GREAT BATTLE

Night of Intense Shelling Before the Assault by Allied Troops.

FLAMES SWEPT THE HILLS

Darkness Pierced by Flashes of the Cannon and Signals of Colored Rockets.

TENSE HOURS FOR BRITISH

But the Men Went to the Front Singing—Prisoners Show Signs of Frightful Ordeal.

By PHILIP GIBBS.

London Daily Chronicle Dispatches.

Special Cable to THE NEW YORK TIMES.

WITH THE BRITISH ARMIES IN THE FIELD, July 1.—The great attack which was launched today against the German lines on a twenty-mile front has begun satisfactorily. It is not yet a victory, for victory comes at the end of battle, and this is only the beginning, but the British troops, fighting with splendid valor, have swept across the German front trenches along the great part of the line of attack, and have captured villages and strongholds which the Germans have long held. They are fighting their way forward, not easily but doggedly.

After the first day of battle we may say "All goes well." It is a good day for England and for France. It is a day of promise in this war in which the blood of brave men is poured out upon the sodden fields of Europe.

For nearly a week now the British have been bombarding the enemy's line from the Yser to the Somme. Those who watched this bombardment knew the meaning of it. They knew it was in preparation for this attack. They had to keep it secret, to close their lips tight, to write vague words lest the Germans should get a hint too soon, and the strain was great upon them and the suspense and the ordeal to the nerves became more trying because, as the hours went by, they drew nearer to the time when great waves of men, those splendid young men who had gone marching along the roads of France, would be sent into the open, out of the ditches where they had got cover from the German fire.

This secret was foreshadowed by many signs. Traveling along the roads one saw new guns arriving, heavy guns and field guns. Week after week the British were massing a great weight of metal. Passing them, men raised their eyebrows and smiled grimly. The tide of men flowed in from the ports of France, new men of new divisions. They passed to some part of the front, disappeared for a while, were met again in the fields and billets, looking harder and having stories to tell of trench life and raids.

First Hint of the Attack.

A week or two ago the whisper passed that we were going to attack, but no more than that, except behind closed doors. Somehow, by the look on men's faces, by their silence and thoughtfulness, one could guess something was to happen. There was a thrill in the air, a thrill from the pulse of men who know the meaning of attack. Would it be in June or July?

The guns spoke one morning last week with louder voice than yet had been heard upon the front, and as they crashed out all knew it was the signal for the new attack. Their fire increased in intensity, covering raids at many points of the line, until at last all things were ready for the biggest raid.

The scene of the battlefields at night was of terrible beauty. I motored out from a town behind the lines where through their darkened windows the French citizens watched the illumination of the sky, throbbing and flashing to distant shellfire. Behind the lines the villages were asleep without a twinkle of a lamp in any window. Here and there on the roads a lantern waved to and fro, and its rays gleamed upon the long bayonet and steel casque of a French territorial and upon the bronzed face of an English soldier who came forward to stare closely at the piece of paper which allowed a man to go into the fires of hell up there.

It was an English voice that gave the first challenge and then called out "good night" with a strange and unofficial friendliness as a greeting to men who were going toward the guns.

A mile or two more, a challenge or two more, and then a halt by the roadside. It was a road which led straight into the central fires of one of the great battlefields in a battle line of eighty miles or more, a small corner of the front yet in itself a broad and far-stretching panorama of the British gunfire. On this night of bombardment I stood with a few officers in the centre of a crescent sweeping round from Auchonvilliers, Thiepval, La Boisselle, and Fricourt to Bray on the Somme at the southern end of the curve. Here in two beetroot fields on high ground we stood watching one of the greatest artillery battles in which British gunners had been engaged.

Night View of the Battlefield.

The night sky was very calm and moist with low-lying clouds not stirred by the wind. It was rent with incessant flashes of light as shells of every calibre burst and scattered. Out of the black ridges and woods in front of us came the explosions of white flare as if the earth has opened and let loose its inner heat. They came up with the burst of an intense brilliance which spread along 100 yards of ground and then vanished abruptly behind the black curtain of night. It was the work of the high explosives and heavy trench mortars falling in the German lines over Thiepval and La Boisselle. There were rapid flashes of bursting shrapnel shells, and these points of flame stabbed the sky along the whole battlefront.

From the German lines rockets were rising continually. They rose high and their start-shell remained suspended for half a minute with intense brightness. While the light lasted it cut out the black outline of trees and broken roofs and revealed heavy white smokeclouds rolling over the German positions.

The were mostly white lights, but in one place red rockets went up. They were signals of distress, perhaps from the German infantry calling to their guns. It was in the zone of these red signals over toward Ovillers that the British fire for a time was the most fierce, so that sheets of flame waved to and fro as if fanned by a furious wind.

All the time along the German line red lights ran up and down like red dancing devils. I cannot tell what they were unless they were some other kind of signaling or bursting of rifle grenades. Sometimes for thirty seconds or so the firing ceased and the darkness, very black and velvety, blotted out everything, and restored the world to peace. Then suddenly at one point or another the earth seemed to open to the furnace of fires.

Down by Bray, southwards, there was one of these violent shocks of light, and then a moment later another by Auchonvilliers, to the north, and once again infernal fires began flashing, flickering, and running along the ridge with a swift tongue of flame, tossing burning feathers above the rosy smoke clouds, concentrating into one bonfire of bursting shells.

Over Fricourt and Thiepval, upon which the British batteries always concentrated, there was one curious phenomenon. It was the silence of all artillery by some atmosphere condition of moisture or wind, though the night was calm, or by the configuration of the ground, which made pockets into which the sound fell. There was no great uproar such as I have heard scores of times in smaller bombardments than this. It was all muffled. Even the British batteries did not crash out with any startling thunder, though I could hear the rush of big shells like great birds in flight.

Now and then there was a series of loud strokes, like urgent knocking at the doors of night, and now and again there was a dull, heavy tunderclap, followed by a long rumble, which made me think mines were being blown further up the line. But for the most part it was curiously quiet and low toned, and somehow this muffled artillery gave one a greater sense of awfulness and of deadly work. Along all this stretch of battle front there was no sign of men. It was all inhuman work, of impersonal powers, and man himself was in hiding from these great forces of destruction.

British Troops Going Up.

So I thought, peering through the darkness over the beetrooots and wheat, but a little later I heard the steady tramp of many feet and the thud of horses' hoofs, walking slwoly, and the grinding of wheels in ruts. Shadow forms came up out of the dark tunnel below the trees, black figures of mounted officers, followed by a battalion marching with its transport. I could not see the faces of the men, but by the shape of their forms I could see they wore their steel helmets and their fighting kit. They were heavily laden with their packs, but they were marching at a smart swinging pace, and as they came along they were singing cheerily. They were singing some music hall tune with a lilt in it as they marched toward the light of all the shells up there in the places of death. Some of them were blowing mouthorgans and others were whistling.

I watched them pass—all these tall boys of the north country regiment, and something of their spirit seemed to come out of the dark mass of their moving bodies. They were going up to those places without faltering, without a backward look, and singing.

I saw other men on the march, and some of them were whistling "The Marseillaise," though they were English soldiers. Others were gossiping quietly as they walked, and once light of bursting shells played all down the line of their faces, hard, clean shaven, bronzed, English faces with eyes of youth staring up at battle fire and unafraid. A young officer, walking at the head of his platoon, called out a cheery "good night" to me. It was a greeting in the darkness from one of these gallant boys who lead their men out of the trenches without much thought of self in that moment of sacrifice.

In the camps lights were out and the tents were dark. The soldiers who had been writing leters home had sent their love and gone to sleep, but the shellfire never ceased all night. A staff officer had whispered the secret to us at midnight in a little room when the door was shut and window closed. Even then they were words which could be only whispered and to men of trust: "the attack will be made this morning at 7:30."

The dawn came with great beauty. There was a pale blue sky flecked with white wisps of cloud, but it was cold, and over all the fields there was floating a mist which rose up from the moist earth and lay heavily upon the ridge so that the horizon was obscured. As soon as the light came there was activity in the place where I was behind the lines. A body of French engineers, all blue from casque to puttee and laden with their field packs, marched along with steady tramp, their grave, grim faces turned toward the front. British staff officers came motoring swiftly by, and dispatch riders mounted their motor cycles and scurried away through the market carts of the French peasants to the open roads.

We went further forward to the guns and stood on the same high fields where we had watched the night bombardment. The panorama of battle was spread around us, and the noise of battle swept about us in great tornadoes. I have said that in the night one was startled by the curious quietude of the guns, by that queer, muffled effect of so great an artillery, but now, on the morning of the battle, this phenomenon, which I do not understand, no longer existed. There was one continual roar of the guns, which beat the air with great waves and shocks of sound, prodigous and overwhelming.

The Greatest Bombardment.

The full power of the British artillery was let loose at about 6 o'clock this morning. Nothing like it has ever been seen or heard upon the front before, and all preliminary bombardment, great as it was, seemed insignificant to this. I do not know how many batteries are along this battle line or upon the section of the line which I could see, but the guns seemed crowded in vast numbers of every calibre, and the concentration of their fire was terrific in its intensity.

For a time I could see nothing through the low-lying mist and the heavy smoke clouds which mingled with the mist, and I stood like a blind man, only listening. It was a wonderful thing which came to my ears. Shells were rushing through the air as though all the trains in the world were driving at express speed through endless tunnels, in which they met each other with frightful collisions.

Some of these shells, fired from batteries not far from where I stood, ripped the sky with a high tearing note. Other shells whistled with that strange, sobbing, sibilant cry which makes one turn cold. Through the mist and smoke there came sharp, loud insistent knocks as the separate batteries fired salvos and great, clangorous strokes as of iron doors banged.

The mist was shifting and disssolving. The tall tower of Albert Cathedral appeared suddenly through the veil, and the sun shone a full few seconds on the golden Virgin and Babe which she held, head downward, above all this tumult as a peace offering to men. The broken roofs of the town gleamed white, and two tall chimneys to the left stood black and sharp against the pale blue of the sky into which a dirty smoke drifted above the whiter clouds.

I could see now as well as hear. I could see British shells falling upon the German lines by Thiepval and La Boisselie, and further, by Mametz and southward over Fricourt, high explosives were tossing up great vomits of black smoke and the earth all along the ridges. Shrapnel was pouring upon these places and leaving curly, white clouds, which clung to the ground. Below there was the flash of many batteries, like the Morse code signals by stabs of flame. The Germans were being blasted by a hurricane of fire.

Airmen Join in the Attack.

Over my head came a flight of six aeroplanes led by a single monoplane, which steered steadily toward the Germans. The sky was deeply blue above them, and when the sun caught their wings they were as beautiful and delicate as butterflies, but they were carrying death with them and were out to bomb batteries and to drop their explosives into masses of men behind the German lines. Futher away a German plane was up and the anti-aircraft guns were searching for him with their shells, which dotted the sky with snowballs.

Every five minutes or so a single gun fired a round. It spoke with a voice I knew, the deep, gruff voice of "Old Grandmother," one of the British 15-inches, which carries a shell large enough to smash a cathedral with one enormous burst. I could follow the journey of the shell by listening to its rush through space; seconds later there was the distant thud of its explosion.

Troopers were moving forward to the attack from behind the lines. It was nearly 7:30. All the officers about me kept glancing at their wrist watches. We did not speak much, but stared silently at the smoke and mist which floated and banked along the lines. There hidden were the men. They, too, would be looking at their wrist watches.

The minutes were passing very quickly, as men's live pass when they look back upon the years. An officer near me turned away and there was a look of sharp pain in his eyes. We were only lookers on. The strong men, the splendid youth that we had passed on the roads of France, were about to do this job. "Good luck go with them." Men were muttering such wishes in their hearts.

It was 7:30 o'clock. Our watches told us this but nothing else. The guns had lifted and were firing behind the first lines, but there was no sudden hush for the moment of the attack. The barrage by the British guns seemed as great as the first bombardment for ten minutes or so. Before this time a new sound had come into the general thunder of the artillery. It was like the rafale of French soixante-quinze, very rapid with distinct and separate strokes, but louder than the noise of the field guns. They were the trench mortars at work along the whole length of the line before me.

The moment for the attack had come. Clouds of smoke had been liberated to form a screen for the infantry and hid the whole line. The only men I could see were those in reserve winding along the road by some trees which led up to the attacking points. They had their backs turned as they marched very slowly and steadily forward.

The Charge of the Infantry.

At a minute after 7:30 o'clock there came through the rolling smoke clouds a rushing sound. It was the noise of rifle fire and machine guns. The men were out of their trenches and the attack had begun. The Germans were barraging the lines. The country chosen for the main attack today stretches from the Somme for some twenty miles northward. The French were to operate on the immediate right. It is a very different country from Flanders with its swamps and flats, and from the Loos battlefields with their dreary plain pimpled by slag heaps. It is a sweet and pleasant country with wooded hills and little valeys along the river beds of the Ancre and Somme and fertile meadowlands, and stretches of woodland where the soldiers and guns may get good cover.

It was different ground in front of us. The Germans were strong in their defenses. In the clumps of woodland beside the ruined villages they hid many machine guns and trench mortars, and each ruined house in each village was part of a fortified stronghold, difficult to capture by direct assault. It was here, however, and with good hopes of success, that the Allies attacked today, working westward across the Ancre and northward up from the Somme.

At the end of this day's fighting it is still too soon to give a clear narrative of the battle behind the veil of smoke which hides the men. There were many different actions taking place, and messages that come back at the peril of men's lives and by great gallantry of the signallers and runners give but a glimpse of the progress and the hard fighting. I have seen wounded who have come out of battle and prisoners brought down in batches, but eve□ they cax give only confused accounts of the fighting. At first it is certain there was not much difficulty in taking the first nine trenches along the greater part of the country attacked. The bombardment had done great damage, and had smashed down wire and flattened German parapets.

When the British left their assembly trenches and swept forward, cheering, they encountered no great resistance from the German soldiers who had been in hiding in their dugouts under the storm of shells. Many of these dugouts were blown in and filled with dead, but out of others, which had not been flung to pieces by high explosives, crept dazed and deafened men, who held their hands up and bowed their heads. Some of them in one part of the line came out of their shelters as soon as the guns lifted and met the British soldeirs half way with signs of surrender. They were collected and sent back under guard, while the attacking columns passed on to the second and third lines in the network of trenches.

Varying Success of the Attack.

But the fortunes of war vary in different places, as I know from the advance of troops, including the South Staffords, Manchesters, and Gordons. In crossing the first line of trench the South Staffordshire men had comparatively an easy time, with hardly any casualties, gathering up the Germans, who surrendered easily. The German artillery fire did not touch them seriously, and both they and the Manchesters had very great luck. But the Gordons fared differently. These keen-fighting men rushed forward with great enthusiasm until they reached one end of the village of Mametz, and then quite suddenly they were faced by a rapid machine gun fire and a storm of bombs. The Germans held the trench called Danzig Avenue on the ridge where Mametz stands and defended it with desperate courage. The Gordons flung themselves upon this position and had some difficulty in clearing it. At the end of the day Mametz remained in British hands.

It was those fortified villages which gave the men the greatest trouble, for the German troops defended them with real courage and worked their machine guns from hidden emplacements with skill and determination.

Montauban, to the northeast of Mametz, was captured early in the day, and the British also gained a strong point at Serre until the Germans made a somewhat heavy counterattack and succeeded in driving out some of the British troops.

Beaumont Hamel was not definitely in the hands of the attackers at the end of the day, but here again the British are fighting on both sides of it.

The woods and village of Thiepval, which I had watched under terrific shell fire in the preliminary bombardments, was one point of the first attack and the troops swept from one end of the village to the other and out beyond to a new objective.

They were too quick to get on, it seems, for a considerable number of the Germans remained in the dugouts, and when the British soldiers went past them they came out of their hiding places and became fighting forces again.

Further north the infantry attacked both sides of the Commecourt Salient with the greatest possible valor.

That is my latest knowledge, writing at midnight on the first day of July, which leaves the British beyond the German front lines in many places and penetrating the country behind like arrowheads between German strongholds.

The First Prisoners Brought In.

In the afternoon I saw the first batch of prisoners brought in in parties of 50 to 100. They came down, guarded by men of the border regiments, through little French hamlets close behind the fighting lines, where peasants stood in their doorways, watching these first fruits of victory. Some were wounded and nerve-shaken in the great bombardment. Most of them belonged to the 109th and 110th Reiments of the Fourteenth Reserve corps, and they seemed to be Prussians and Bavarians. On the whole, they were tall, strong fellows, and there were striking faces among them of men higher than peasant type and thoughtful, but they were very haggard and worn and dirty.

Over the barbed wire which had been stretched across a farmyard in the shadow of the old French church, I spoke to some of them, on one man especially, who considered all my questions with a kind of patient sadness. He told me most of his comrades and himself had been without food and water for several days, as our intense fires made it impossible to get supplies up the communication trenches. About the bombardment, he raised his hands and eyes a moment full of the remembered horror and said:

"It was horrible." Most of the officers had remained in the second line, but others had been killed.

OFFENSIVE GAINS GROUND

Two-Mile Advance Made by British at Some Points of Attack.

FRENCH NOW EAST OF FRISE

They Have Cut the Second Lines of the Foe South of the Somme.

KAISER'S LOSSES GROWING

London Says First Estimates Were Too Low—Desperate Resistance to Allies' Advance.

LONDON, Monday, July 3.—The official British dispatches issued yesterday report the continued success of the combined Anglo-French offensive. The Germans put into operation strong counterattacks during the night, and are apparently making desperate resistance, but the British troops have occupied Fricourt, three miles east of Albert, and the French have captured Curlu and Frise, and have seemingly nowhere had to yield the ground already gained.

The German lines in some places have been penetrated to a depth of two miles, and the prisoners taken by the French and British in the two days number nearly 10,000, according to the latest estimates that have been given out.

North of the Somme, where the French and British Armies make contact, various points of tactical value have been taken. The allied struggle is to extend the hold over the rolling plateau, from 300 to 500 feet high, which stretches around Albert.

At Fricourt, Contalmaison, and Gommecourt the Germans made a most desperate resistance, with a view to defending the high road which extends from Arras to Bapaume and Peronne, and which is one of the main arteries of the western operations.

British General Headquarters gave out the following report late last (Sunday) night:

Heavy fighting has taken place today in the area between the Ancre and the Somme, especially about Fricourt and La Boiselle.

Fricourt was captured by our troops about 2 P. M. and remains in our hands, and some progress has been made east of the village.

In the neighborhood of La Boiselle the enemy is offering stubborn resistance, but our troops are making satisfactory progress. A considerable quantity of war material has fallen into our hands, but details are not available.

On either side of the valley of the Ancre the situation is unchanged.

The general situation may be regarded as favorable. Later information of the enemy's losses shows that our first estimates were too low.

Yesterday our aeroplanes were very active in co-operatin with our attack north of the Somme and afforded valuable assistance to our operations. Numerous enemy headquarters and railway centres were attacked with bombs.

In one of these raids our escorting aeroplanes were attacked by twenty Fokkers, which were driven off. Two enemy machines were seen to crash to earth and were destroyed.

Some long distance reconnoissances were carried out in spite of numerous attempts by enemy machines to frustrate the enterprises. Three of our aeroplanes are missing. Our kite balloons were in the air the whole day.

The text of an official British announcement given out early in the evening said:

Substantial progress has been made in the vicinity of Fricourt which was captured by us at 2 P. M. today.

Up to noon today some 800 more prisoners had been taken in the operations between the Ancre and the Somme, bringing the total up to 3,500, including those captured on other parts of the front last night.

French Extend Their Gains.

The statement of the French War Office given out last night says:

North of the Somme the battle continued all day in our advantage in the region of Hardecourt and Curlu. East of this latter village we have carried a quarry which had been powerfully organized by the enemy.

South of the Somme we have obtained a footing in the second line of the German trenches at numerous places. Between the river and Assevillers the village of Frise has fallen into our hands, and also the Mereaucourt wood, further east.

The number of unwounded prisoners captured by the French soldiers during the two days' fighting, and who have been counted, is more than 6,000, of which at least 150 are officers. Some cannon and much other material has also fallen into our hands. Thanks to the very complete and very efficacious artillery preparation, and thanks also to the elan of our infantry, our losses have been very small.

AMERICAN POISON GAS SHELL

Advertisement Offering It for Sale Discussed by the Cabinet.

Special to The New York Times.

WASHINGTON, June 18.—Secretary Redfield laid before President Wilson and the Cabinet at their regular meeting today an advertisement in an American trade paper of a projectile for use in war which it is claimed contains and generates poisonous gases guaranteed to kill in four hours. The advertisement gave the name of a firm in Cleveland, Ohio, as the manufacturer of the shell.

According to information obtained after the meeting, the members of the Cabinet expressed horror that such a device should be manufactured in this country and that it should be advertised publicly for sale. The advertisement, it was understood, had been inserted in two foreign publications.

At first the members of the Cabinet were inclined to regard it as a grim joke designed to bring other products of the Cleveland firm into prominence or as being inspired from sources anxious to produce further ill-feeling in the United States over the European war, but they were assured that the advertisement was of a real device, and that the shell and the poison gases were for sale to Governments that were willing to use such means of warfare.

What was described as "the horribleness" of the advertisements occupied a considerable part of the discussion. Just what the Government can do if any action is determined upon, remains a moot question pending an investigation to be conducted through the Department of Commerce.

In a broad way, it was stated that the attitude of this Government in such cases is that where contributory violations of The Hague Convention occur within the United States, the Government will endeavor to stop them. It was agreed that the Government would have the right to prohibit the exportation of such a device on passenger steamers.

OUTCLASS GERMAN BIG GUNS.

British Weapons Said to be Better

Special Cable to THE NEW YORK TIMES.

PARIS, July 2, (Dispatch to The London Daily Telegraph.)—I am credibly informed that the British heavy guns now absolutely outclass the German or Austrian famous 42-centimeter guns which the German command sprang as a surprise at the outbreak of the war.

British supplies of munitions are so great that in the present offensive the question of economy of shells does not enter into account.

The French people have heard with pardonable satisfaction that the British asphyxiating gas has proved deadlier than any the Germans have invented.

"All the News That's Fit to Print."

The New York Times.

THE WEATHER
Fair today and Sunday, warmer Sunday; moderate east to southeast winds.
For full weather report see Page 13.

VOL. LXV...NO. 21,371. ...   NEW YORK, SATURDAY, JULY 29, 1916.—SIXTEEN PAGES.   ONE CENT In Greater New York, Jersey City and Newark. | Elsewhere, TWO CENTS

RUSSIANS TAKE BRODY, MENACE LEMBERG; BREAK THE GERMAN LINE IN VOLHYNIA; BRITISH WIN LONG-CONTESTED GROUND

ALL OF LONGUEVAL TAKEN

Last of Brandenburgers Expelled from Delville Wood Near Village.

PROGRESS MADE EASIER

London Expects Forward Movement of Offensive Will Be Greatly Facilitated.

GERMANS ATTACK IN VOSGES

Penetrate Advanced Trenches, but Are Driven Out by Bayonet Charges.

LONDON, July 28.—Tonight's official report of the British War Office shows that the British are continuing their successful progress. The whole of Longueval is now in their hands as well as Delville Wood, from which they drove the Fifth Brandenburg Division.

The final capture of Delville Wood is very gratifying to the British people. It was first taken on July 17, but was afterward abandoned. For many days the wood and the village of Longueval have been the scene of some of the heaviest fighting of the whole campaign.

The possession of this wood and of Longueval is expected to facilitate greatly the further progress of the Franco-British forces.

An attack by the Germans against French positions south of Sainte Marie Pass, in the Vosges, resulted in their gaining a lodgment in the advanced French trenches, according to the official statement given out in Paris tonight. The statement adds, however, that later the Germans were driven out with the bayonet.

Progress for the French on the right bank of the Meuse is reported.

Russians reconnoitring at Auberive, in the Champagne, the French official statement issued this afternoon says, penetrated the German trenches and cleared them with hand grenades. The Russians took some prisoners.

A German attempt to attack near Lihons, north of Chaulnes, was arrested by French infantry fire.

The Berlin report says strong British attacks against the German positions in Foureaux, or High Wood, in the Somme region, broke down yesterday under the German fire.

The official statement given out tonight by the British War Office says:

Continuing their success of yesterday our troops have captured the last enemy strongholds in Longueval, together with a number of prisoners.

In the vicinity of Pozières hand-to-hand fighting has continued throughout the day. Elsewhere on the battle front there was considerable artillery activity by both sides.

Two hostile aeroplanes were destroyed by one of our aerial patrols in the neighborhood of Bapaume yesterday.

70,000 Turks in Hungary; Aged Emperor at Budapest

LONDON, Saturday, July 29.—A Turkish army, estimated at 70,000 strong, is now concentrated on the Hungarian plains for the defense of Hungary, says a dispatch to the Exchange Telegraph Company from Lausanne, Switzerland.

The dispatch adds that the Austrian Emperor has gone to Budapest, where intense excitement prevails.

RUSSIANS PURSUING FOES

Take 9,000 Germans With 2 Generals and 46 Guns West of Lutsk.

DRIVE AUSTRIANS SOUTH

Communications of Whole Teuton Front Imperiled by Swift Advance.

BIG BATTLE IN LITHUANIA

Berlin Reports Leopold Attacked in Baranovitchi Region and Issue in Doubt.

Where Russians Broke the Teuton Lines.

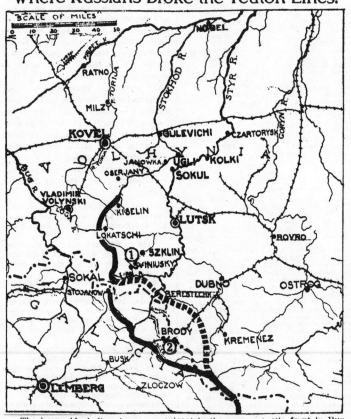

The heavy black line shows approximately the present battle front in Russia, from the Stockhod River through Northeast Galicia, the dotted line showing where the drive for Brody (2), captured yesterday, began a few days ago. North of Sviniusky (1) the Russians smashed the German line, capturing more than 9,000 prisoners, including 2 Generals, and 46 guns.

PETROGRAD, July 28.—The Russians, having driven the Austro-German forces from the line of the Rivers Slonevka and Boldurovka, have occupied Brody, the important Teuton base in Northeast Galicia, on the railroad from Dubno to Lemberg, and only fifty-eight miles from the Galician capital. In Volhynia the Czar's army has broken through the entire first line of the Teuton allies west of Lutsk, where they captured more than 9,000 prisoners, including 2 Generals, and 46 guns, and are following up their success.

Following is the text of the official report issued tonight by the War Office announcing these victories:

West of Lutsk, (Volhynia,) we took the offensive, and broke through the whole first line of the enemy, inflicting severe losses. Our troops are now advancing and the cavalry is pursuing the fleeing enemy.

In this district we captured 46 guns, including 6 mortars and 6 machine guns, and 50 officers, including 2 Generals and 2 commanders of regiments, and over 9,000 men.

In the valley of the Rivers Slonevka and Boldurovka, (Northeast Galicia,) the enemy has been defeated along the whole line, and is now being pursued in the direction of Brody. Explosions were heard in Brody, and fires were observed. Dense columns of goods trains were seen moving from there.

Later—At 6:30 o'clock Friday morning Brody was captured by our troops. The number of prisoners and the amount of booty captured are not yet known.

Another official statement issued earlier in the day follows:

In the district of Krevo an enemy aeroplane was hit by our artillery fire. It fell within the enemy lines.

In the districts northeast and southeast of Baranovitchi there were artillery duels and encounters between advance guards. We made small advances at some points.

In the region of the River Slonevka and the River Boldurovka our advance continues successfully.

VIENNA, July 28, (via London.)—An official statement given out by the Austro-Hungarian War Office today says:

Russian War Theatre.—On the upper part of Czarny Czereomsz River several Russian attacks failed.

In the region north of Brody the enemy continued yesterday during the whole day till late in the afternoon his assaults, but he was again repulsed and gained no ground. A fresh attack was undertaken in masses during the evening, and the Russians succeeded in penetrating our positions along the Brody-Leszniow road. Our troops continue the battle on the southern border of Brody.

Near Pustomyty, in Volhynia, Austro-Hungarians chase back the enemy who advanced to their intrenchment. Northeast of Sviniusky the local invasion of the Russians was replied to by counterattack.

In the middle of July the enemy resumed the offensive in Volhynia after a pause of four weeks. The total result has been that our front on a length of eighty kilometers (fifty miles) was pushed in to a depth of not over fifteen kilometers, (9 1/2 miles.) The enemy paid for this small gain of ground, owing to uninterrupted strong attacks, with enormous sacrifices.

"All the News That's Fit to Print."

The New York Times.

THE WEATHER
Fair today and probably Thursday; not much change in temperature; light north winds.
For full weather report see Page 19.

VOL. LXV...NO. 21,375. NEW YORK, WEDNESDAY, AUGUST 2, 1916.—TWENTY PAGES. ONE CENT In Greater New York, Jersey City and Newark. | Elsewhere TWO CENTS.

GERMANY DEFIES FOES' HUNGER WAR AS SECOND YEAR OF CONFLICT ENDS; ALLIES SEE TEUTON STRENGTH WANING

German Military Power on Point of Crumbling, Joffre Tells His Soldiers on War Anniversary

PARIS, Aug. 1.—The Bulletin des Armées will publish tomorrow an order of the day issued by General Joffre to the French Army on the occasion of the second anniversary of the outbreak of the war. The order of General Joffre follows:

Soldiers of the Republic:

Your third year of fighting has begun. For two years past you have been supporting with unfailing strength the weight of an implacable conflict. You have caused all the plans of our enemies to fail. You vanquished them on the Marne; you checked them on the Yser, and you beat them in the Artois and in the Champagne at a time when they were vainly seeking victory on the plains of Russia. Then your victorious resistance during a battle of five months' duration broke the German effort in front of Verdun.

Thanks to your stubborn courage, the armies of our allies have been enabled to manufacture arms, the weight of which our enemies today are experiencing over their entire front.

The moment is approaching when, under the strength of our mutual advance, the military power of Germany will crumble.

Soldiers of France, you may be proud of the work you already have accomplished! You have determined to see it through to the end! Victory is certain!

JOFFRE.

GERMANS TO FEED POLAND

Batocki Plans to Cut Rations of Belgians and French to Do It.

SAYS BLAME IS ON BRITISH

Food Dictator Declares Lord Grey Would Extend Hunger War to Conquered Territory.

KAISER PREDICTS VICTORY

Congratulates Army and Navy and Proclaims the Empire's Forces Invincible.

By CYRIL BROWN,
Staff Correspondent of The New York Times.
Special Cable to THE NEW YORK TIMES.

BERLIN, Aug. 1.—"If America's humanitarian desire to aid in feeding Poland is balked and frustrated by the opposition of England not one person will die of hunger, although the food rations will be short."

This is the personal answer of Germany's food dictator, von Batocki, to Viscount Grey.

The food Field Marshal, whose tremendous vitality and aggressive personality are as confidence-inspiring in his herculean job as those of Hindenburg and Linsingen, made it clear to THE NEW YORK TIMES correspondent that he considered Lord Grey's "arrogant and absurdly impossible terms dictated to Germany on which England would permit America to send foodstuffs into Poland not only a transparent and hypocritical play to the neutral gallery, but a subtle, cunning, and diabolical plot to draw Poland, Belgium, and Northern France into the theatre of the hunger war waged against humanity."

Accepts Responsibility.

"I am personally intensely interested in Lord Grey's reported reply to America's appeal," said von Batocki, "and particularly in his threat that England would exact retribution and inflict punishment for every civilian life lost as a result of insufficient food in the territories occupied by the armies of the Central Powers. I am indirectly responsible for the feeding of Poland, because when foodstuffs are sent to the point of famine there I must give of our stocks in Germany both for the army and for the civilian population. Thus there is no sugar in Courland, no sugar in Poland, or occupied Russia, for the retreating Russians destroyed all the beet sugar factories, and so, although sugar is short in Germany, I must apportion small quantities to these occupied territories.

"I am also intensely interested in the possibility of the neutral commission's ceasing its humanitarian work in France and Belgium, because in that case I would become responsible for feeding them. I must know what is needed in all the occupied territories outside of Germany, too. I am also indirectly in touch with Austria as well as directly with Serbia and Turkey.

"Herr Grey's threat of retribution and punishment frightens me, but fortunately there is an army between him and me. But firstly nobody will starve and secondly Grey will not catch me," and Herr Batocki smiled at the prospect of a personal encounter with Lord Grey.

The Food Dictator weighs nearly 200 pounds, has the muscular physique of a trained athlete, and the heavy hand of a professional prize-fighter, while certain scars on his cheek indicate that he was graduated from a fighting student corps.

"Although he threatens me with death if a single individual starves to death in the occupied territories," Herr von Batocki went on. "I nevertheless would be very happy to invite Lord Grey to visit Germany, Poland, Belgium, and Northern France and personally convince himself of the conditions and the work we are doing at home and in the occupied territories, and I should also be pleased to show him what the Russians did to Poland. I would be happy to have him bring along some of his poor relations among the allied statesmen, and would gladly explain to him my whole economic system, and would even promise to go to considerable trouble to get him safe conduct. Then Lord Grey could personally convince himself that England cannot starve Germany, nor Poland, nor Belgium, nor Northern France either. It might be a great step toward peace if the legend about starving out Germany were thus blasted.

"I personally feel that it is unjust to treat Belgium better than Poland. Either give something to both or give nothing, is my attitude.

Will Treat All Alike.

"I am no professional politician, and I speak this purely as my personal opinion from my economic viewpoint. What our statesmen will do in the matter of Grey's food ultimatum and how they will do it, is none of my business. But if our statesmen say 'break with England on this impossible proposal,' then it at once becomes very much my business. The whole responsibility will fall on me. I am not afraid of this responsibility. I shall have to care for everything in the food line in the occupied territories, and I will make it go, too. We shall still come out, and nobody will die of hunger, but food will be short. I shall treat Poland, Belgium, Northern France, and Germany as one economic and organic whole for the distribution of the necessaries of life. It will be hard on the Belgians, but better for the Poles and the Jews.

"Belgium will get a little less and Poland a little more, but, all the same, nobody will hunger. There will be an equal distribution of the absolute necessaries. Both in Poland and Belgium all will receive enough bread, potatoes, and salt, also some sugar, very little meat, also very little fat, and fish not at all. Naturally, they will get no coffee, tea, or spices."

To the question as to what Poland needed most, Herr von Batocki enumerated coffee, tea, fish, fat, and spices, among other things. He said that by measures in flagrant violation of neutral rights and international law England had prevented Holland's herring and Scandinavia's fish from reaching Germany and Poland, and had already caused intense hardship to the Poles, who were devout Catholics and, therefore, consistent fisheaters on Fridays. He said the Polish Jews, too, who largely subsisted on fish, were suffering intensely as a result of England's economic pressure on neutrals, particularly in the matter of fish exports to and through Germany.

"Lord Grey is too late with his generous proposals," continued the food dictator. "He should have spoken sooner. The harvest has already begun in Poland. Normally it should have begun a week ago, but it was delayed owing to the cold weather. I have been through Poland and know the country and the food conditions. Generally, this year's harvest is no worse than in peace times."

Must Control Railroads.

Herr von Batocki analyzed the features of Lord Grey's terms, which, he said, made them impossible of acceptance by Germany. In his personal opinion, particularly the neutral control of food distribution in Poland without the co-operation of the German Government, which would mean having independent strangers clothed with autocratic power in and behind the fighting and operating zones.

"We must have complete control of the railways at all times," he said. "Where there are so few of them we cannot have outsiders meddling with the military railways. Under Grey's terms no control over the railroads would be possible. It would simply lead to continuous friction with the neutral commissions in the matter of food transfers. Food shipments and distribution as between the army and the native population cannot be kept separate. As a practical example Warsaw may have to give potatoes to the army and we in turn may send potatoes to Warsaw. Furthermore in the agricultural districts of Poland the Russians in retreating took away many of the inhabitants as well as their horses. They destroyed the agricultural implements and machinery and burned down the barns and other farm buildings. As a result the German Army had to pitch in and help till the fields.

"The German Army plowed and planted several millions of acres in Poland. It will now help in the harvest and must further help in the farming in the future. The inhabitants alone cannot do it because the larger part of their horses, tools, and buildings are gone and the greatest part of the seed had to be sent from Germany. There also are whole regions where there are practically no farming inhabitants left, notably in the Baltic provinces. In Poland there are none at all immediately behind the front, so that the German Army has had and will continue to have to cultivate the land right up to the front."

Comforts for Belgians.

Herr von Batocki summed up his answer to Lord Grey as follows:

"Belgium and occupied France have until now been excluded from England's hunger war. The English have permitted foodstuffs to be brought into these territories under control of a neutral commission, and these were distributed as extra rations in addition to the foods produced in the country. As a result, food conditions in those occupied territories became in many respects, better than in Germany. Although from the German viewpoint this form of regulation gives rise to complaint, we nevertheless permitted it in order to make the lot of the native Belgian and Northern French populations as pleasant as possible. In addition our authorities, through the careful and thorough stimulation of agriculture in the territories occupied in the west, have assured to these territories the greatest possible food supply out of the present harvest now beginning. And while Germany's stocks of cattle became depleted as a result of the shortage of fodder, necessitating a limit to the consumption of meat on the part of the German population, cattle stocks in the occupied territories in the west have developed favorably, even better than in peace times, and the Belgian meadows today are richer in cattle than ever before.

"Much more hateful and ruthless has been Russia's attitude toward the Poles, Lithuanians, Jews, and other inhabitants of the vast Russian territory occupied by the German troops. This territory is so great and fruitful that the 1915 harvest would have sufficed adequately to feed the native population if the Russians before their flight had not destroyed as much as possible of the live stock and supplies, and even the standing harvest. Through their gruesome and senseless devastation of countless farmhouses and other buildings they condemned the unfortunate inhabitants to spend the Winter huddled together in the poorest shelters, to build which our troops aided the population as much as possible. After the occupation of this territory everything was done on our part to save that part of the harvest that had not been destroyed, and so to divide the food supplies that even in the large cities a famine was avoided.

Suffering in Larger Cities.

"The armies in the East were fed as far as possible from Germany in order to leave as much foodstuff as possible to the natives. Despite all this the situation was extremely hard for the poor population in many parts of the occupied territory, particularly in Warsaw, Lodz, and similar cities until the present harvest began. Naturally our authorities could not do England the favor of letting the inhabitants of Germany starve in order to send foodstuffs from Germany to the population of occupied territory to replace what the Russians had purposely destroyed.

A year ago the cries of the West Russian population were directed toward America and all neutral States whose desire to create in Poland as in Belgium an international relief work, has been shattered against the opposition of England. England would rather see Polish women and children starve than run the risk of having anything whatever reach the German population from Poland. England, therefore, procrastinated, delayed negotiations, and set up conditions which for military reasons were impossible of acceptance by Germany. The consequences, despite all the care of the German authorities, have had to be borne by the women and children of West Russia. But there was one thing that our authorities could at least take care of; namely, that this year's harvest in West Russia was prepared for in the best possible way. This could not be achieved entirely without sacrifices on the part of the German people, for large quantities of seed had to be exported from Germany into the districts devastated by the Russians. This sacrifice has had its result. As in Germany and the territories in the west a very good harvest stands on the fields of this vast region of Poland, Livland, and Courland. In many cases the crop is better than ever was the case under Russian government.

Calls It Hypocritical.

"This fact has afflicted the English hunger politicians with a nervous fear. They are seeking for a new way to continue their starvation plan in the new harvest year. They hypocritically offer to make easier the feeding of the native population, not only in Belgium, but in Poland, by permitting importation, but they fasten upon this offer conditions which they know in advance to be wholly impossible of acceptance, and Herr Grey has the hardihood to hold Germany responsible for the control system behind our fighting troops. The demand that nothing produced in the occupied territory be used for our army is, as is natural with English offers, utterly contrary to international law.

"This plan of the English to extend the hunger-war to Belgium, Northern France, and Poland, will come to naught. Our painstaking preparations for the new harvest in occupied territories and the rich stocks of cattle will not only feed the native populations, but will still yield a considerable surplus for our troops. There will of course be a lack of import articles such as fat, groceries, fish &c., which, to be sure, contribute to the agreeableness of life, but which are not absolute necessities. In this respect, therefore, the Belgians and the inhabitants of Northern France will, thanks to England's hunger-war policy, be not so well off as heretofore. They will have to be satisfied with what the German population also has to be satisfied with, and their stocks of cattle will have to be drawn upon more extensively. No military advantage whatever, but merely the harming of millions of innocent women, children, and aged persons will be the consequence of this new English procedure."

GERMANY REJECTS RELIEF.

Attacks Conditions Imposed by England for Admitting Food to Poland.

Special to The New York Times.

WASHINGTON, Aug. 1.—The German Government has informed the United States Government that, owing to "the unfounded and impracticable conditions" imposed by Great Britain on the shipment of food from America to Poland, further negotiations for co-operation in Polish relief work are fruitless.

Germany explains that through intensified cultivation of land in Poland and the prospect of good crops "relief action after Oct. 1 can apparently be dispensed with." It is admitted by Germany that "the population of Poland and Lithuania will to some extent suffer until the new crop is lodged," but the necessity for this is placed at the door of Great Britain.

The German statement is contained in a communication which was forwarded by cable by Ambassador Gerard at Berlin. It reads:

"From the very beginning the Imperial Government declared its readiness to offer its assistance in order that the distress apparent in those parts of Russia which are occupied by German troops and systematically wasted and deprived of all victuals for the use of the remaining inhabitants by the retreating Russian hosts be eased by the relief work of the United States of America, which is organized on such a great scale. The Imperial Government has particularly offered all guarantees consistent with the requirements of war that the imported foodstuffs will only serve the needs of the population of the territory occupied. Accordingly, the American relief might have been realized several months ago with the same provisions as in Northern France, had not the Government of Great Britain prevented its accomplishment by clinging to its unfounded and impracticable conditions. In this way it has become practically impossible to convey a considerable amount of foodstuffs from America to Poland by the expiration of the term set as the end of the relief work is Oct. 1. Accordingly, further negotiations are devoid of purpose. But on the other hand, thanks to the intense culture of the land affected by the Imperial Government by using all the means available and every effort possible in the occupied territory, and, owing to the favorable harvest prospects a relief action after Oct. 1, 1916, can apparently be dispensed with. The fact that the population of Poland and Lithuania will to some extent suffer until the new crop is lodged, and later on will sometimes have to put up with straitened circumstances, can, therefore, not be laid to the blame of the Imperial Government, but to that of Great Britain."

GERMAN INVINCIBLE, THE KAISER ASSERTS

Congratulates His Army and Navy on Another "Year of Glory on All Fronts."

AMSTERDAM, Aug. 1.—Emperor William, according to a telegram received here today from Berlin, has issued the following proclamation to the German forces on land and sea:

Comrades: The second year of the world war has elapsed. Like the first year, it was for Germany's arms a year of glory. On all fronts you inflicted new and heavy blows on the enemy.

Whether the enemy retreated, borne down by the force of your attacks, or whether, reinforced by foreign assistance collected and pressed into service from all parts of the world, he tried to rob you of the fruits of former victories, you always proved yourselves superior to him. Even when England's tyranny was uncontested, namely, on the free waves of the sea, you victoriously fought against gigantic superiority. Your Kaiser's appreciation and your grateful country's proud admiration are assured to you for these deeds, for your unshaken loyalty, for your bold daring and for your tenacious bravery.

Like the memory of our dead heroes, your fame also will endure through all time. The laurels which our ever-confident forces have won against the enemy, in spite of trials and dangers, are inseparably linked with the devoted and untiring labor at home.

This strength at home has sent an ever-fresh inspiration to the armies in the field. It has continually quickened our swords, has kindled Germany's enthusiasm, and has terrified the enemy. My gratitude and that of the Fatherland are due the nation at home.

But the strength and will of the enemy are not yet broken. We must continue the severe struggle in order to secure the safety of our beloved home land, to preserve the honor of the Fatherland and the greatness of the empire.

Whether the enemy wages war with the force of arms or with cold, calculating malice, we shall continue as before into the third year of the war. The spirit of duty to the Fatherland and an unbending will to victory permeate our homes and our fighting forces today as in the first days of the war. With God's gracious help I am convinced that your future deeds will equal those of the past and present.

Main Headquarters. WILHELM.

Another Berlin dispatch says the Emperor has sent a telegram to the Minister of War thanking "all who at home are ceaselessly laboring in loyal fulfillment of their duty to produce war material of the highest perfection to enable the army and navy to fulfill their gigantic daily task; all who either by intellectual or manual work give their best to maintain the nation's armor hard as steel and impenetrable, also all women who have undertaken the hard work of men apart from their normal duties."

SEE TEUTON FORCES NEAR EXHAUSTION

British Experts Think Kaiser's Boast Will Be Disproved Before Another Year.

AUSTRIA'S LOSSES 3,500,000

Only Half a Million Left to Fight, London Figures — German Reserves Gone.

Special Cable to THE NEW YORK TIMES.

LONDON, Aug. 1.—As military experts here view the situation on this second anniversary of Germany's declaration of war against Russia, they point to the great change in conditions since Aug. 1, 1915, and assert with confidence that the Kaiser's statement in his letter today to Chancellor von Bethmann Hollweg that the Fatherland is invincible will be disproved before the third year of the conflict is over.

Incidentally British observers are insisting that both Austria and Germany are nearing the point of exhaustion of available troops needed for a prolonged defense against the Allies on all fronts.

The early reports that a Turkish army corps had been moved to the support of the Austrian line on the eastern front were received with skepticism here, where it was thought that the Turks needed all their available men to meet the Russian onslaught in Armenia. Now that the report has received confirmation by eyewitnesses, among them the correspondent of THE NEW YORK TIMES on the eastern front, this use of the Ottoman forces is regarded by experts as giving a measure of Austria's dire distress. One military writer says:

"What have been the Teutons' losses in the two years of the war? The Germans admit the loss of about 4,000,000 men, and a most cautious estimate by allied statisticians adds about 900,000 to this total. If we add the losses of July and a portion of June, which have not yet been particularized in the German official reports, we have a total well over 5,000,000 men.

"Austria in the first fourteen months of the war had casualties of 2,5000,000. After that the Austrian Army enjoyed a certain immunity from wastage. General Ivanoff accounted for about 45,000 between September and the end of November, and probably put another 50,000 out of action in his December offensive. In the present operations General Brusiloff has taken over 300,000 Austrian prisoners and put another 300,000 hors de combat.

A conservtive estimate of the Austrian losses since September last must put them at no fewer than 680,000, so that the end of the second year of the war, which began with Austria's offensive against Serbia, brings the Austrian losses approximately to 3,500,000.

"The losses of the Austrians and Germans, therefore, cannot be less than 8,000,000, and probably 8,500,000. These figures do not, of course, represent the total losses, except in the case of Austria, of whose 3,500,000 the greater proportion are definitely out of action.

"Austria, like every other country engaged in the war, made extraordinary calls upon her population. She has about 6,000,000 men, that is to say about 12 per cent. of her population, available for service, if their mobilization were possible. The Russian occupation of Galicia interfered, to a great extent, with that mobilization, and it is doubtful whether Austria ever mobilized more than 4,500,000, or at the most 5,000,000 men. Of these a very large number have been absorbed in noncombatant service such as munition making, working on the railways, &c., and allowing for the young and old men, at present doing garrison duty or training in depots, Austria's military strength is now under 500,000.

"The loss of guns and material makes it impossible for Austria to release the men employed in the munition works, while for the very salvation of the two empires it has been necessary to retain a very large number of men in agricultural empoyment. The Russian experts say their recent offensive resulted in the enemy losing 66 per cent. of his effectives, but this may be a too hopeful view.

"At any rate it is evident that the Austrian Army has been terribly reduced in size and in fighting power, and that no effort the Germans can make can replace the battalions which have been obliterated in the recent fighting."

Colonel Feyler, the Swiss strategist, puts the German strength in the west at 1,476 battalions; that is to say, 1,622,000 men. In the east he puts about half that number, so that on all fronts he calculates the German Army as numbering about 2,500,000 bayonets. At the outset of the Verdun offensive the Germans asserted that they had a sufficient number of men to hold all the fronts, and, in addition, had or would have in the next six months a striking force of 1,500,000 men available for service on any front.

Estimating the German-Austrian losses as follows—before Verdun 300,000, in Trentino 50,000, in Volhynia 700,000, between Riga and the Pripet 50,000, in the allied offensive on the western front 100,000, and taking the normal losses on the other parts of the line at the rate of two men a mile of each front a day, on the thousand-mile front since the end of February at 300,000, a total of 1,500,000 is reached.

The Teutonic powers have about 1,250 miles of front to defend in the main theatres of the war. With the growing pressure of the Allies everywhere, apart from the special offensives, the Teutonic wastage is probably reaching the figure of ten men a mile a day, or 8,500 a day, or 250,000 a month.

POINCARE EXHORTS FRANCE TO VICTORY

President Tells the Troops That They Undertake a Crusade for Law and Liberty.

VERDUN'S FAME IMMORTAL

Struggle Not Yet Ended, but Fate's Scales Are Swinging in the Allies' Favor.

PARIS, Aug. 1.—The Bulletin des Armées, the official journal of the soldiers of the French Army, will publish tomorrow copies of letters exchanged between President Poincaré, David Lloyd George, British Secretary for War, and General Sir Douglas Haig, commander of the British troops in France.

President Poincaré's letter begins by saying:

"For the second time, my friends, we have to commemorate together a soul-stirring anniversary. Two years ago we lived hours that are not to be forgotten. Since then two sections of mankind have been grappling with one another and are fighting amid streams of blood. The nations who have let loose that stupendous catastrophe have not yet completely expiated their act. But justice is on its way."

The President recalls the events which preceded the declaration of war. He relates how the German troops entered French territory, and continues:

"Two years have passed, but amid the fatigues and perils these recollections, my friends, have remained vivid in your souls. Do not let them become obliterated, because it is they which give to this war its clear significance and bring to light the beauty of your task.

Attempt to Falsify History.

"Instinctively, mutilated France, which during forty-four years had imposed silence on her sorrow, understood in 1914 that the foe who was attacking her, blinded by pride and fanaticized by hatred, had no grievance to plead, no right to defend, no menace to ward off. It is in vain that today the aggressors are attempting to falsify history.

"They were at first less knavish and more cynical, when they flattered themselves in seeing in the treaties granted by them nothing but common scraps of paper. With insolent frankness they accepted the responsibility of their crime. The French people was not decided. The nation was conscious that theirs was a case of legitimate defense. It realized spontaneously that sacred union which is the main condition of victory and which found in the memorable sitting of the Parliament on the 4th of August, 1914, an imposing consecration.

"The war became immediately, in the whole force of the term, a national war. There is not a Frenchman who remained deaf to the call of his country. When you were called upon to protect our frontiers and save our natal soil you were not only conscious that your material interests were at stake: You knew also that you were going to defend your hearths, that you were going to defend all which constitutes France —traditions, ideas, moral forces, preserved and developed by a nation which will not die.

Undertake New Crusade.

"Among these French ideas one of the oldest and most deep-rooted is the horror of injustice. The violence meted out to Serbia and the invasion of Belgium still further enhanced the outburst of your patriotism and fortified your resolution to be victorious. You perceived that the cause of which you had become the champions outmeasured your lives, that it was greater than France herself, that it embraced in reality civilization and humanity.

"It is a new crusade that you have undertaken, a crusade for the the law of nations and for the liberty of peoples. The grandeur of your mission has exalted your courage, and you have revealed to the world the true France.

"All the News That's Fit to Print."

The New York Times.

THE WEATHER
Scattered thunderstorms today; Thursday probably fair; slight temperature changes; light north to variable winds.

VOL. LXV...NO. 21,382.   NEW YORK, WEDNESDAY, AUGUST 9, 1916.—TWENTY PAGES.   ONE CENT In Greater New York, Jersey City and Newark. TWO CENTS Elsewhere

ALLIES WIN 4-MILE FRONT ON SOMME; ITALIANS TAKE GORIZIA BRIDGEHEAD; RUSSIANS CLOSE IN ON STANISLAU

WIDE ADVANCE BY FRENCH

GERMANS ATTACK POZIERES

LONDON, Aug. 8.—British and French troops in a combined offensive north of the Somme have made substantial gains near Guillemont, west of Combles.

The French at the same time increased their gains north of Hemwood, some distance south of Guillemont, so that their advance in the last two days comprises the capture of the whole of a line of German trenches on a front of nearly four miles, penetrating to a depth of 300 to 500 yards.

According to the official statement this evening from British Headquarters, General Haig's troops have advanced 400 yards southwest of the village of Guillemont. The heaviest fighting developed at the railway station, which lies just north of the village. Here the battle continues with little change in the situation.

The French War Office reports an advance east of Hill 139, north of Hardecourt, and just south of the British line of advance.

The Germans made four attacks today on the trenches held by the Australians northwest of Pozières, following a very heavy bombardment. One attack, accompanied by the throwing of liquid fire, enabled them to occupy about fifty yards of a British trench. All other attacks, the official report tonight says, were repulsed. The text of tonight's official British report follows:

Southwest of Guillemont we advanced our line about four hundred yards. Fighting continues near Guillemont station.

Northwest of Pozières the enemy made four attacks on our trenches, again using flammenwerfer. Three attacks failed completely, but in one he managed to occupy about fifty yards of our trench.

The enemy shelled Longueval, High Wood and Pozières heavily and also the vicinity of Mametz.

Elsewhere along the front it was a quiet day except for some artillery activity in the Loos Salient and near Givenchy.

Take Front of Nearly Four Miles.

The night report issued by the French War office, recounting the French success north of Hem Wood, follows:

North of the Somme we increased our gains of yesterday, capturing a small wood and a trench strongly organized by the enemy north of Hem Wood, which we held in its entirety.

In fine, in these two days we have conquered north of the Somme the whole of a line of German trenches on a front of six kilometres (3.75 miles) to a depth of from three hundred to five hundred metres (325 to 542 yards.)

The French afternoon report telling of the repulse of German attacks east of Monacu Farm, follows:

North of the Somme our infantry operating on the right of the British, in the course of an attack by our allies on Guillemont, made an advance east of Hill 139, north of Hardecourt, and took forty prisoners.

East of Monacu Farm the Germans made two attempts this morning to recapture trenches which we took yesterday. Both attempts were repulsed

Triple Offensive of the Allies Delights London, Which Sees Auspicious Opening of Third Year of War

LONDON, Aug. 8.—Before the echoes have died of the mutual congratulations of the allied sovereigns, statesmen, and Generals on the auspicious opening of the third year of the war comes news of further Russian successes and of a victory for the Italian arms on the Isonzo front.

The surprising success of the Italians, who in two days have captured 10,000 prisoners, suggests that in addition to transferring General Koebess, an able Austrian General, from the Trentino front to Galicia, the Austrians also ventured to transfer troops from the Isonzo to the Russian front, in an endeavor to stem the Russian advance.

General Cadorna's victory has caused great rejoicing in London as one of the most promising successes in the new allied operations and a demonstration of the constantly growing power of the allied offensive on all fronts. Russia's new victories south of the Dniester and southwest of the Stanislau-Kolomea Railway afford equal satisfaction, and the prompt admission in the Berlin official statement of the retirement of the Austro-Germans south of the Dniester is taken here to indicate that the Russian victory in this quarter is weightier than yet announced by the Russian official dispatches. According to an unofficial report, the evacuation of Lemberg, the Galician capital, has already been ordered.

In the meantime, a new combined offensive by the Allies has begun on the western front, which is expected to lead to the severest fighting. Guillemont, around which heavy fighting is now in progress, is one of the strong positions in the German second system. It is expected that it will be defended, as was Pozières, with the utmost stubbornness.

by our infantry fire. The enemy was compelled to fall back, leaving a number of dead before our lines. The number of unwounded prisoners, taken yesterday in this region is 230, of whom two are officers.

The British afternoon statement follows:

The enemy, after his five fruitless attempts yesterday north and east of Pozières has not made any fresh infantry attacks, but is maintaining a heavy artillery bombardment on this front and on other portions of the battle area.

Last night our troops pushed forward in places east of Trones Wood, and fighting on the outskirts of Guille-

ment, near the station, is proceeding.

In the eastern portion of the Leipsic salient the enemy attempted a bomb attack on our lines, but was driven back without difficulty.

North of Roclincourt two of our raiding parties successfully entered the German lines and blew up some dugouts.

An enemy squadron of ten aeroplanes endeavored to cross our lines yesterday on a bombing expedition. They were cut off by one of our offensive patrols of four machines. The enemy's machines scattered, returning precipitately, pursued by our patrols. Two of the hostile aeroplanes had to make forced descents behind their own lines.

Scene of Allies' Gain North of Somme.

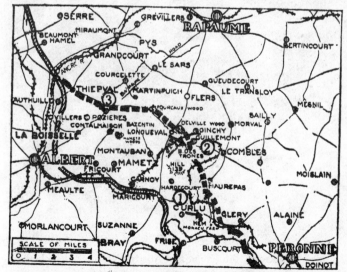

The greatest gain on the allied front north of the Somme has been made by the French, who have captured German trenches north of Hem Wood (1) on a front of nearly four miles. At the northern wing of this front British and French, in a combined attack, gained about 400 yards southwest of Guillemont, (2.) Northwest of Pozières (3) the Germans again made a series of determined counterattacks, the net result being the capture of a small portion of a British

ITALIANS PIERCE ISONZO FRONT

Rush to Victory Flower-Decked and Shouting, "Great Italy Forever!"

10,000 AUSTRIANS TAKEN

Thousands of Others Buried in Caverns Blocked with Debris from Mighty Bombardment.

Special Cable to THE NEW YORK TIMES.
MILAN, Aug. 8 (Dispatch to the London Daily Chronicle).—The long-awaited hour of Italy's grand assault on the Isonzo has sounded the first day's offensive on a thirty-mile front resulted in a haul of nearly 4,000 prisoners with an immense quantity of guns and war material, in fact, the largest prize taken since Italy went to war.

First particulars from private sources supplementing the official communiqué are now permitted publication by the censorship. This morning's late edition of the Secolo contains the following from its war correspondents, Signori Pino Alessi and Raffaele Garinei.

"At 7 o'clock Sunday morning, under an unclouded Summer sky, the huge orchestra of Italian guns began rending the air with a terrifying chorus all the way from Plava heights right down to Monfalcone, supported thence by a naval demonstration in the higher Adriatic against the enemy's coast between Duino and Miramare.

"The whole territory which had been plowed up by bombardments since July 14 was again subjected to a ceaseless hail of shells of every calibre for the space of nine hours. No such awe-inspiring cascade of fire ever before has been witnessed on the Italian front. So terrific were the incessant earthquake-like phenomena thereby produced that houses in the Gorizia plain were shattered or collapsed by the force of the seismic waves, while the mouths of vast caverns on the Carso, in which thousands of Austrian troops had hurried and crouched for refuge, were dammed and choked by tons of débris so as to become converted into living tombs.

"Only at 4 o'clock in the afternoon was the order given for the infantry to quit the trenches where they had passed so many months in pent-up impatience. The spectacle of these hardy warriors as they bounded forth to the fray recalled the heroes of legendary lore. Thousands of their front ranks wore round their helmets a floral garland specially woven and forwarded for the historic occasion by women of Thiene and Schio of Vorastica and Vicenza.

"To the stirring cry of 'Great Italy forever!' they bounded across the dales at bridgehead of Gorizia and lower down scaled the lines of Carso plateau, everywhere to engage in a hand-to-hand struggle with the foe. Ahead of the main masses went men bearing aloft big white discs mounted on slender gray-green painted poles so as to guide the gunners in lengthening the range as the great advance proceeded.

"All the News That's Fit to Print."

The New York Times.

THE WEATHER
Generally fair Monday and Tuesday; moderate temperature; light northwest winds.
For full weather report see Page 17.

VOL. LXV...NO. 21,401. .... NEW YORK, MONDAY, AUGUST 28, 1916.—EIGHTEEN PAGES. ONE CENT In Greater New York, Jersey City and Newark. | Elsewhere TWO CENTS

ITALY DECLARES WAR ON GERMANY; ROME EXPECTS RUMANIA TO FOLLOW; BULGARS IN KAVALA SHELLED FROM SEA

BUCHAREST NEAR TO ACTION

Crown Council Today May Put Rumania On Side of the Allies.

NEW COMMANDER FOR ARMY

Gen. Averescu, Who Favors Entente, Chosen — Bratiano Bent on Ending Neutrality.

OUTLOOK WORRIES AUSTRIA

Hungary's Plea for Coalition Cabinet Is Rejected and a Serious Political Crisis Impends.

Special Cable to THE NEW YORK TIMES.

ROME, Aug. 27.—Italy issued today a declaration of war on Germany. This move caused general satisfaction here, as it at last put an end to an intolerable situation.

In political circles this formal action by Italy is declared to be in strict conjunction with the entrance of Rumania into the war.

She promised to join the war over a year ago when Italy entered, but found it impossible, under the circumstances at that time.

Political leaders now confidently expect a declaration of war by the Bucharest Government.

It is felt here that Germany in the past has not been without pretext for breaking definitely with Italy, as, for instance, when Italy signed the pact of London. It is believed that Germany's patience with Italy was not only to protect her great interests in this country, but to deceive the German people still further. Germany on her side has continually protested that she has never done anything incompatible with her situation as an enemy of Italy, yet not declaring war on her.

Germany has denied that any of her soldiers were sent to fight Italy on her northern or northeastern frontiers. Unofficial reports have told of the presence of German troops there, but these reports have never been confirmed. It is said, however, that the Italian Government now has possession of proof of these and other acts by the Germans,

Allies Tell Greece They Won't Defend Thessaly and Ask What the Athens Government Intends

LONDON, Monday, Aug. 28.—A delayed dispatch from Athens says that the French and British Ministers on Thursday evening asked Premier Zaimis how far the Greek Government proposed to countenance the Bulgarian advance without resistance, pointing out that it would be of no military interest to the Entente Powers to defend Central Thessaly from invasion, as Saloniki was supplied from the sea and could not be cut off by land.

"The embarrassment of the Greek Government," continues the dispatch, "grows hourly in the face of popular resentment against the Bulgarian invasion. The Venizelist organs criticise the inaction of the Government, the Cretan declaring that the hour has come for action similar to that taken in 1909.

"M. Pachitch, former Serbian Premier, has arrived here on his way to Saloniki."

Greek People Stirred by Bulgar Invasion.

Special Cable to THE NEW YORK TIMES.

LONDON, Monday, Aug. 28.—The Daily Chronicle prints the following dispatch from Athens, dated there Aug. 24:

"Popular interest regarding the situation arising out of the Bulgar invasion of Greece increases with the approach of Sunday, the day on which a great demonstration of protest will be held here. The papers devote long articles to the situation. The Patris, a journal always well informed, makes the following interesting statement, which may be regarded as diplomatically inspired:

"'Recent events in Greece have given rise to a new exchange of views between the Entente Powers. As to the decisions that may be reached as a result we are not yet in a position to know, but what we can affirm is that the diplomacy of the Entente is recasting its views on Greece and examining whether the conditions imposed by the note of June 21 are sufficient to meet the altered conditions created by the Bulgar invasion. A decision will shortly be reached.'

As this photo shows, the Italian and Austrian troops had to be daring and adept to wage war against one another. Here Italian infantry move up a cliff that looks prohibitive. The troops used a similar method to move heavy artillery to mountain tops and passes throughout the war.

including the torpedoing of Italian steamers on the high seas.

BERLIN, Aug. 27, (by Wireless to Sayville.)—The following official announcement was made here today:

The Italian Government has declared through the Swiss Government that it considers itself, from Aug. 28, at war with Germany.

Crown Council Called in Rumania.

LONDON, Aug. 27.—The Rumanian Crown Council, which had been convened for 10 o'clock Monday morning, has been postponed until 5 o'clock in the afternoon, a Bucharest dispatch received in Amsterdam says.

According to another Bucharest dispatch, the King of Rumania has convened a conference of representatives of all the political parties, former Premiers, former Presidents of the Legislative Chambers, Ministers, and Government representatives, with the idea of ascertaining the views of all sections of public opinion on the present situation.

Special Cable to THE NEW YORK TIMES.

LONDON, Monday, Aug. 28.—The Bucharest correspondent of The London Times sends the following, dated Aug. 21:

"General Averescu (former Minister of War and in the councils of the Headquarters Staff one of the chief advocates of intervention) is stated in military circles to have been selected for chief command of the army.

"The German Minister, who on Wednesday had another audience of the King, is reported to have delivered to his Majesty an autograph letter from the Kaiser."

A Budapest dispatch to The Morning Post, dated Aug. 20, quotes the Bucharest correspondent of Népzava as saying, under date of the previous day:

"The general opinion expressed by the Bucharest press of all political shades is that a decision of the Cabinet is at hand. The Bina, a pro-German organ, says that, in spite of the fact that nothing of the nature expected by Premier Bratiano has happened on the European fronts and that the Entente Powers have achieved no prominent successes, the Rumanian Premier finds it fit and timely to abandon neutrality. Neither the Allies in the west nor Russia or Italy, it goes on, can boast of any great measure of success, 'yet the Rumanian Cabinet is feverishly preparing for war.'

"According to another Rumanian paper, the Steagul, 'the Bratiano Government has decided to enter the war on the side of the Entente,' and it warns the Government not to sacrifice the welfare of the country for reasons of sentiment.

"The Bucharest journal Dreptatea says that M. Filipesco declared to one of its representatives that Russian forces would proceed across the Polrudsha against Bulgaria within ten days and that the consent of the Rumanian Government had already been secured to this move, though the Government would enter a formal protest.

"All the News That's Fit to Print."

The New York Times.

THE WEATHER
Fair, continued cool today; tomorrow, fair; light west to southwest winds.

VOL. LXV...NO. 21,402.   NEW YORK, TUESDAY, AUGUST 29, 1916.—TWENTY PAGES.   ONE CENT In Greater New York. | Elsewhere Jersey City and Newark. | TWO CENTS

RUMANIA IN WAR, ATTACKS AUSTRIA; GERMANY DECLARES WAR IN ANSWER; EUROPE EXPECTS GREECE TO FIGHT

Rumania's King, Some of His Trained Soldiers, and a Group of Recruits.

RUMANIANS ENTER PASSES

Army Begins the Invasion of Transylvania in Two Directions.

HOPES TO SHORTEN WAR

Also to Realize National Ideal, Vienna Is Told in Declaration of Hostilities.

TWO CITIES ARE MENACED

LONDON, Tuesday, Aug. 29.—Rumania has declared war against Austria-Hungary, Germany has retaliated by declaring war against Rumania ,and fighting has already begun on the frontier of Transylvania.

The note declaring that Rumania, from 9 o'clock Sunday evening, considered herself in a state of war with Austria-Hungary was presented to the Austro-Hungarian Foreign Minister last night by the Rumanian Minister at Vienna, who personally visited the Ministry of Foreign Affairs.

The note was a lengthy document, in which Rumania set forth her grievances. The Paris newspaper La Liberté has received a summary as telegraphed from Geneva. According to this the

persecution of Rumanians by Austro-Hungarian officials is alleged, and it is charged that agreements which existed between Rumania and the former members of the Triple Alliance have been broken in letter and spirit from the time Germany and Austria entered the war. Italy, the declaration says, was obliged to detach herself from Austria and Germany.

Motives for Declaring War.

In conclusion, the communication sets forth as follows the motives in compelling Rumania to enter the war:

First—The Rumanian population in Austrian territories is exposed to the hazards of war and of invasion.

Second—Rumania believes that by intervening she can shorten the world war.

Third—Rumania places herself on the side of those Powers which she believes can assist her most efficaciously in realizing her national ideal.

An official statement issued in Berlin and forwarded by Reuter's correspondent at Amsterdam says:

After Rumania, as already reported, disgracefully broke treaties concluded with Austria-Hungary and Germany she declared war yesterday against our ally.

The Imperial German Minister to Rumania has received instructions to request his passports and to declare to the Rumanian Government that Germany now likewise considers herself at war with Rumania.

Rumania's decision to enter the war was reached at a meeting of the Crown Council held Sunday morning at the Controceni Palace, Bucharest. King Ferdinand presided, and the session was prolonged over a period of several hours. The Council consists of nineteen members, of which number it is believed that four to six opposed intervention.

Besides conferring with the council with whom the final decision rested, King Ferdinand had conferences with the leaders of all Rumanian political parties, including those favorable to intervention in the great war and those who had been the strongest supporters of Rumania continuing her neutrality.

The Rumanian military officials had discussed for some days what probably

would be the first step taken when war was declared and had dismissed all alien employes many of whom were Germans. An especially large number of Germans were employed in the technical services. General Averescu, former Minister of War, will have, it is said, chief command of the Rumanian Army.

The Bucharest newspaper, Adeverul, commenting on the council meeting, said:

"At last the decisive hour has struck. Events have dictated to the Government intervention and the realization of Rumanian's national claims. The King, in view of the recent events, like the late King Carlos, convoked the Crown Council. The politicians when they leave it will have to bow to its decision. The union of all parties must be effected before the greatness of the cause."

FIFTEEN NATIONS ARE NOW AT WAR

1914.

July 28—Austria declares war on Serbia.
Aug. 1—Germany declares war on Russia.
Aug. 2—Germany at war with Belgium.
Aug. 3—France announces a state of war with Germany.
Aug. 4—Great Britain declares war on Germany, and the latter declares war on Belgium and France.
Aug. 6—Austria declares war on Russia.
Aug. 8—Montenegro declares war on Austria.
Aug. 10—France announces a state of war with Austria.
Aug. 12—Great Britain announces a state of war with Austria. Montenegro declares war on Germany.
Aug. 23—Japan declares war on Germany.
Aug. 25—Austria declares war on Japan.
Aug. 28—Austria declares war on Belgium.
Nov. 5—Great Britain declares war on Turkey.

1915.

May 23—Italy declares war on Austria.
June 3—San Marino declares war on Austria.
Aug. 20—Italy declares war on Turkey.
Oct. 7—Announcement of a state of war between Russia and the Bulgarian Government.
Oct. 14—Bulgaria declares war on Serbia.
Oct. 15—Great Britain declares war on Bulgaria.
Oct. 16—Bulgaria announces a state of war with Russia.
Oct. 19—Italy declares war on Bulgaria.

1916.

March 9—Germany declares war on Portugal.
Aug. 27—Italy declares war on Germany, and Rumania on Austria.

The New York Times.

THE WEATHER
Fair, somewhat warmer Monday; overcast, warmer Tuesday; moderate south winds.
For full weather report see Page 13.

VOL. LXV...NO. 21,408. ...   NEW YORK, MONDAY, SEPTEMBER 4, 1916.—FOURTEEN PAGES.   ONE CENT In Greater New York, Jersey City and Newark. | TWO CENTS Elsewhere

ALLIES SMASH GERMAN SOMME FRONT, TAKE 3 TOWNS, OVER 2000 MEN, 62 GUNS; GREEK KING SWITCHES TO ENTENTE

ALL GREEK PARTIES UNITED

Allies Demand Control of Posts and Telegraphs and Expulsion of Teutons.

GERMAN MINISTER FLEES

Baron Sohenok and 30 Men with Grenades Barrioade Themselves in His House.

FLEET BLOWS UP U-BOAT

Traps Undersea Craft at Phaleron — May Establish Army-Navy Base at Piraeus.

Special Cable to THE NEW YORK TIMES.

ATHENS, Sept. 3, (Dispatch to The London Times.)—I learn from a reliable source that King Constantine has declared to the Entente Ministers that after Rumania's participation in the war he is disposed to reconsider Greek policy.

Special Cable to THE NEW YORK TIMES.

ATHENS, Sept. 3, (Dispatch to The London Daily Chronicle.) — After an eventful day the political situation is moving toward a satisfactory solution. Both sides may be said to have come to a tacit agreement to give their support to the Zaimis Cabinet, which will therefore cease to be an interregnum Cabinet and become a political Cabinet, enjoying the full confidence of the Crown and complete support of the Venizelist party.

I understand the King has expressed his belief in the expediency of Greece now leaving her neutrality. Venizelos, on the other hand, equally approves this solution, and, desiring the welfare of his country before place and power, will efface himself when he sees the realization of the policy for which he has fought so long.

Anglo-French Note to Greece.

A joint note was handed to the Government last evening by the British and French Ministers. It says that the enemies of the Entente are informed in divers ways, and especially by the Greek telegraph, of the Allies' movements. The Allies demand control of the posts and telegraphs, including the wireless; that the enemy agents of corruption and espionage leave Greece immediately and not return there until the close of hostilities, and that necessary measures be taken against such Greek subjects as have rendered themselves culpable as accomplices of this corruption and espionage.

It may be taken that the note will be accepted in its entirety and that we may look for the entry before long of Greece into the war on the side of the Allies.

Diplomats and politicians had a very busy day on Friday. Premier Zaimis at first received the Minister for War, General Calaris, and later M. Streit, former Minister of Foreign Affairs. About 11 A. M. Sir Francis Elliott motored to Dekelia and had a long audience with the King. Premier Zaimis in the afternoon received the French Minister, M. Guilleman, who called a second time toward 6 o'clock, accompanied by the English Minister. The diplomatic representatives informed the Premier of the coming presentation of the note from the Entente Powers, the contents of which were outlined subsequently in extra editions of the Greek papers, and caused a panic among the Teutons and their henchmen here.

German Minister Flees.

Count Mirbach, the German Minister, left in a motor car at 9 o'clock last night, taking with him six cold meals, which he ordered got ready for him at one of the hotels in Athens. It was reported that Baron Schenck, head of the German propagandists, also had fled. He has not left Athens, however, but barricaded himself in his house with the evident intention of making it a Fort Chabrol. He has with him a score of men, who are well supplied with hand grenades. Up to the moment of telegraphing he has been left unmolested.

During Friday night reports of Allied naval movements reached the local authorities, and yesterday was ushered in by an extraordinary event. About 6:30 in the morning a loud explosion aroused the people of Phaleron, and was also heard at Piraeus. The allied ships had the evening before sighted a submarine near the shore in Phaleron waters. It sank at once, but was prevented from getting away, and at the hour mentioned the craft was blown up.

Piraeus Probable Base of Allies.

LONDON, Monday, Sept. 4.—Events are moving very rapidly toward an early announcement of a most important change in the attitude of Greece, dispatches from Athens say. Already Venizelos and anti-Venizelos newspapers that for a year have been accusing each other of treason are beginning to preach unity in the face of the national crisis. Former Premier Venizelos has announced his unqualified support of the Cabinet of Premier Zaimis.

Reuter's Athens correspondent says the reconstruction of the Greek Cabinet with two adherents of Venizelos, General Danglis and M. Repoulis, is probable, while an official announcement of the postponement of the elections is a foregone conclusion.

In a note presented to the Greek Government diplomats of the Entente Allies demand that Baron von Schenck and sixty co-workers in behalf of the Central Empires be expelled from Greece. Several arrests already have been made, those taken into custody including the officers of the Austrian and German ships seized on Saturday.

BIG STROKE NORTH OF CLERY

Germans Are Swept Out of Positions On a 6½-Mile Front.

COMBLES IS NOW MENACED

French Reach Outskirts of Town Besides Taking Village of Forest — British in Ginchy.

GUILLEMONT ALSO IS WON

LONDON, Sept. 3.—In a severe stroke delivered by British and French troops on the Somme today, the German front for a distance of six and one-half miles, from Ginchy to Cléry, was smashed. Three towns were occupied by the Allies, Guillemont by the British, who also won a hold on Ginchy, and Forest and Cléry by the French. Two thousand prisoners were captured by Joffre's troops and "several hundred" by Haig's forces. The French night report chronicles the seizure of twelve cannon and fifty machine guns in the sector of Forest alone.

The wide assault on the German positions was made at midday and was carried out with great dash. At some points the Allies swept over trenches and strong positions to a depth of over three-fourths of a mile. The French troops in their advance reached the outskirts of Combles, which is also menaced by the British drive from the north.

The night bulletin of the French War Office, telling of the success, reads:

North of the Somme, after artillery preparation, French infantry, in conjunction with the British Army, attacked shortly before midday the German positions on a front of about six kilometers, (three and three-quarters miles,) reaching from the region north of Maurepas to the river, with remarkable dash, against which the resistance of the enemy was useless for the moment.

Our troops swept away large enemy forces and carried all their objectives. The villages of Forest, east of Maurepas, and Cléry-sur-Somme are entirely in our possession.

North of Forest we have taken all the German trenches along the road from Forest to Combles, as far as the outskirts of Combles. Between Forest and Cléry-sur-Somme we also carried all the enemy positions, and crossed at numerous points the road connecting these two places.

German counterattacks with heavy forces, launched against our conquered positions south of Forest, broke down under the fire of our batteries, and the enemy retired in disorder, leaving numerous dead.

Up to the present the number of unwounded prisoners in our hands exceeds 2,000, while the captured war material includes twelve cannon, taken in the single sector of Forrest, and fifty machine guns.

On the right bank of the Meuse, (Verdun sector,) the Germans made since this morning a series of violent attacks on our positions at Vaux and Chapitre. Repulsed several times along the whole front with heavy losses, the enemy had succeeded at the end of the afternoon in setting foot in one salient of our line, where the combat is continuing bitterly.

Shortly after beginning this action we attacked the German positions east of the village of Fleury. Our troops carried several trenches and powerfully organised works. Another attack was made by us northwest of the village of Fleury and enabled us to occupy a part of the crest from the village to Thiaumont work. In the course of these attacks we made 300 prisoners.

British Take Part of Ginchy.

The British War Office statement reads:

In co-operation with the French on our immediate right we attacked the enemy Sunday at several points. We captured part of Ginchy and the whole of Guillemont. Our front now runs some 500 yards east of Guillemont from Ginchy to near Falfemont Farm.

On the east side of Ququet Farm we also gained ground. We captured several hundred prisoners.

Between our right and the Somme the French made substantial progress, capturing a considerable number of prisoners. The fighting continues.

Aircraft did useful work, co-operating with the artillery and infantry. The enemy's aeroplanes, which made desperate attempts to interfere, were unsuccessfully engaged in many aerial fights and driven off with the loss of three machines destroyed and at least four others damaged, while we lost three.

The day bulletin of the British War Office Reads:

Last night generally was quiet. Fighting was in progress this morning near Mouquet Farm, south of Thiepval, and on the banks of the Ancre, and also on our right about Falfemont Farm. We gained ground.

Last night we carried out a successful raid on the enemy trenches north of Monchy, capturing prisoners.

The day report of the French War Office says:

On the Somme front our artillery activity continued during the night. There was no infantry engagement except four coups de main carried out by us on a German trench near Armancourt, which enable us to bring back some prisoners.

On the right bank of the Meuse the enemy violently bombarded our positions between Thiaumont, Fleury, and the Vaux-Chapitre Wood.

The night was calm on the rest of the front.

London Millions Saw Zeppelin Fall; Second Is Reported Hit by Shell

Night Crowds Rushed Into Streets, Cheered and Sang National Anthem, as Raider Burst, Riddled by Shells from Enfield Gun Factory—Thirteen Craft in Raid—Two Persons Killed.

Special Cable to THE NEW YORK TIMES.

LONLON, Sept. 8.—Thirteen Zeppelins constituted the raiding squadron that visited England last night, but only three of them got near the outskirts of London, and one of these was shot down about fifteen miles north of the city.

There are reports, however, that another one was hit and, disabled, drifted out to sea. A correspondent on the east coast says that when the searchlights found their objective, the anti-aircraft guns got to work and soon succeeded in driving one Zeppelin seawards. Three hours later this Zeppelin made a futile attempt to get inland. In the full glare of a powerful searchlight the raider was distinctly seen.

"It was kept in full view, and the guns made a grand practice," says this observer, "their shells bursting all about the Zeppelin. The raider was evidently hit, for after some minutes it became perfectly perpendicular, and in that apparently crippled and helpless plight it drifted away slowly over the North Sea and was lost to sight."

The casualties officially reported are two dead and eleven persons injured by the many bombs dropped by the raiders.

The following account by an eyewitness of the bringing down of the Zeppelin was given to THE NEW YORK TIMES correspondent by Sir Charles Inigo Thomas, former Secretary to the Admiralty:

"I was awakened about 2:30 o'clock by the information that gunfiring was going on. Looking from my windows, I saw the flashes of the guns in all directions. In a certain direction particularly there was a great display of searchlights, but the weather was foggy and nothing was very distinct. Suddenly about 2:45 o'clock there appeared a glow in the sky which gradually increased in intensity until it became something like a great star. This rapidly increased in size until it clearly assumed the shape of a Zeppelin. The whole looked like a mass of molten metal such as one sees falling out of a furnace pipe. The outline which at first was horizontal, gradually turned and became almost perpendicular, at the same time falling earthward. As it fell it seemed to shrink in size, until the last I saw of it was a sort of stream of deep-red fire. The first appearance of flame was noticeably of a yellow tint. I have said gradually, but of course the whole descent from the time the starlike centre appeared took no more than a minute, or perhaps a minute and a half."

Another eyewitness of the destruction of the Zeppelin writes: "When the guns opened fire, the Zeppelin already had been centred in a ball of light created by the myriad arms of pale light which shot up suddenly from the darkness. The Zeppelin was at a great height, so great, indeed, that it seemed just like a bar of polished steel about the thickness of an engine piston rod. There it remained apparently motionless and undecided which way to go while the guns peppered it without cessation.

"Shells burst around it, in front and behind, above and below, and it made a turn as if to go in the direction of the coast, but a shell burst ominously near its nose and caused it to swing around in the opposite direction. Its tail dipped and it made a move to ascend still higher, when a shell burst directly over it. Another descent was necessary, and three shells burst simultaneously below, behind, and in front of it. It seemed impossible for it to go north, south, east, or west, and there it remained for a second or two helpless, with shells bursting all around it.

"Then away up there in the centre of the ball of light something happened. It seemed as if a black shadow passed between our vision and the brilliant light. In the sky when we looked again the airship had gone. Firing ceased and the searchlights, splitting their focussed rays, shot backward and forward across the firmament, but the Zeppelin was gone. Under cover of a cloud of smoke she had made a wild dash upward beyond the ray of light and through the ring of bursting shells.

"Suddenly, away further to the north, a ball of fire in the sky riveted our attention. The ball spread in size, and there was a great explosion. The whole of London, north, south, east, and west, was illuminated by the one flash. The dome of St. Paul's and the towers at Westminster, hitherto obscured, stood out with remarkable clearness, and for a brief second it looked as if a panorama of the whole of London had been thrown upon a screen in a darkened hall.

"There was no need now to speculate as to the fate of the invader. Persons who came out into the streets raised cheer after cheer and sang the national anthem. The burning Zeppelin could now be seen falling nose downward to the earth like a huge blazing cauldron from which poured a spray of sparks."

Wreck Almost Fell on Them.

A Daily Chronicle dispatch from Cuffley says the Zeppelin brought down here this morning fell headlong, a blazing mass, with a tearing sound in a meadow midway on the road from Potters Bar to Enfield. This is the story of her bringing down told by reliable witnesses who were almost underneath the falling airship, who indeed most narrowly escaped destruction with her:

"We first heard the Zeppelin over us about 1 o'clock this morning," said Mr. Grey of Cuffley Hill Farm. "She remained overhead for about twenty minutes, then went away southward over Enfield. It was very foggy, and, as the ship was not illumined by searchlights, we couldn't see her, but we heard the sound of the engines die away in that direction. Ten minutes or a quarter of an hour later we heard gunfire and the sound of bombs dropping. Then we again heard the Zeppelin overhead. All that we could see at the time was a deep and general glow in the air. We thought the Zeppelin had dropped star shells. Then we looked up and saw the ship above us like a huge incandescent mantle with an orange centre of flame.

"Almost immediately one end of her dipped and the orange centre extended till she seemed all on fire. Then the Zeppelin, now in a vertical position, fell headlong. She dropped with a terrible tearing sound and struck the ground with a crash that could be heard for miles around. The wreckage burned for hours, lighting up the whole countryside. Every few minutes came a popping from her machine-gun ammunition.

"A policeman was the first on the scene. Then came a few villagers and myself and soon afterward a corps of special constables from Goff's Oak. We did our best with buckets of water from the pond near by and an old hose to put out the flames and rescue some of the bodies we saw entangled in that blazing wreck. Curiously enough at first we did not know whether she was one of our own airships or a Zeppelin, she made such a comparatively small patch on the ground for the reason, of course, that she struck nose on. Then we came across half of a propeller with a charred body mixed up with the wheel and immediately behind that two other bodies. On one of them we found a piece of cloth with some German buttons on it and nearby some German cartridges and a German cap. Then, for the first time, we knew it was a Zeppelin.

"About 4 A. M. parties of military arrived and took charge. From that time to 7 A. M. altogether eighteen bodies were taken out of the debris, together with some more or less damaged machine guns."

Sang "God Save the King."

Describing the scene which followed the destruction of the raider a suburban correspondent says: "As soon as it was realized that it was a Zeppelin in flames there was pandemonium. Everyone was shouting, hands were being clapped, steamers were using their sirens incessantly, and a few railway engines that were about were cock-a-doodling with steam whistles until the uproar resembled nothing so much as the advent of a new year in the shipping area.

"Gradually the glowing mass was lost behind the outlines of houses, but the sky for some time was lit up brilliantly. Then we talked excitedly. we wrung each other's hands and acted like children, till suddenly, in sweet contralto tones, were heard the opening bars of the national anthem, and there we stood, men, women, and children, singing 'God Save the King,' while the gathering light was heralding the approach of another Sabbath day."

Correspondents at points forty miles away from the scene of the Zeppelin's destruction report seeing a glow in the sky. For a radius of twelve miles around the spot great cheers went up from the watching crowds when it was realized that the raider was brought down. People asleep miles away were awakened by the shouts and rushed into the streets or appeared at windows in time to see the glow in the distance.

Revealed by Rift in Cloud.

Another eyewitness says:

"Above the clouds the enemy could easily have lurked. Unfortunately for the enemy the clouds drifted in the wrong direction for him, and this gave the searchlight men an opportunity of which they were not slow to avail themselves. Steadily round the edges of one large cloud bank the searchlights rested. If there was any Zeppelin behind it its only hope of remaining undetected was to stay and drift with it.

"Suddenly the cloud parted and through the gap and at a great height the gleaming outline of the Zeppelin was discerned. The cry of 'There she is!' was followed by the boom of a gun and an instant later a shell burst in what appeared to be close proximity to the raider."

New Drive of the Allies on the Somme.

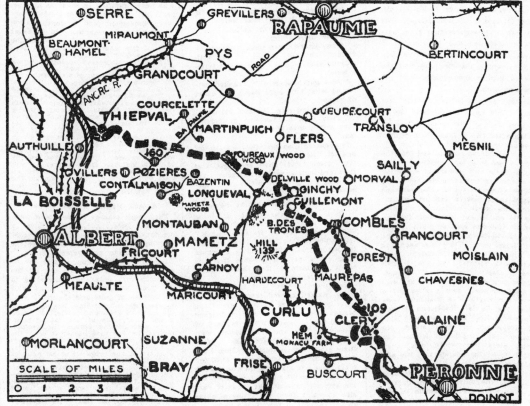

The broken line indicates the approximate position of the battle front before the Allies' drive of yesterday. The dotted line shows where the French and British troops pushed forward.

"All the News That's Fit to Print."

The New York Times.

THE WEATHER
Fair today and Tuesday; continued cool; gentle west winds.
For full weather report see Page 21.

VOL. LXVI...NO. 21,422. .... NEW YORK, MONDAY, SEPTEMBER 18, 1916.—TWENTY-TWO PAGES. ONE CENT In Greater New York, Jersey City and Newark.

Amazing Deeds of British 'Willies'; One Climbs Redoubt, Kills Men In It

New Armored Motor Monsters in Their First Test Also Knock Down Houses, Snap Off Trees and Leap Trenches Like Kangaroos.

BY PHILIP GIBBS.

Special Cable to THE NEW YORK TIMES.

The London Daily Chronicle Dispatches.

WITH THE BRITISH ARMIES IN THE FIELD, Saturday, Sept. 16.—Another day of great remembrance has been given to England's history by British troops, Sept. 15, that will not quickly pass out of the memory of the people, for on that day the British soldiers broke through the German third line of defense and went out into the open country and gave staggering blows to that German war machine which for two years, all but two months, seemed unthinkably strong.

It was a day of good success. Yesterday the British had the taste of victory and it was like a strong drug to their hearts, so that they laughed, even while blood was streaming down their faces, and they said: "By God, it's wonderful," when they came limping off the battlefields with wounds on fire and said: "We made 'em run like rabbits," when they lay on stretchers and could not move without a groan. And it was wonderful, indeed, for the day of victory came after two and a half months of continued and most bloody fighting. This new British army has not had an easy walk through after its time of preparation and training in the dirty ditches of the old trench warfare. Every yard of ground they had made since the dawn of July 1 was made by sheer, stubborn resolution to get forward, reckless of all cost in life or suffering. The first smash through of that great network of defenses had been made by masses of men flinging themselves upon positions which the Germans had the right to believe impregnable, and the price was high.

The task set the British soldiers yesterday would have been formidable on the first day of the great offensive. Coming after two and one-half months of the continuous fighting, it was startling in its boldness and showed that the Generals had supreme confidence in the men, in their own powers of organization and in the luck of battle that comes to those who work for it. The Germans believed the offensive had petered out. There was much evidence for that. They did not believe it possible that an army of the size and strength of the British could carry on an attack at the same fierce pace. They cherished the hope that the British divisions were broken and spent, that the British stores of ammunition were giving out, that the men were overtired. They still had faith in their own gun power, a defensive strength of a thousand guns against the British front and it was reasonable faith. They had been digging furiously on dark nights to strengthen the third line of defense, the famous Flers line which was, they thought, to be the boundary of the advancing British tide.

Yesterday I saw their prisoners coming off the battlefields in droves, and today hundreds of them in barbed wire cages behind the lines. They were dazed men, filled with gloom, tortured by a great bewilderment.

"It is your victory," said one of their officers, speaking to me in French. "It is our defeat; I cannot understand."

"Germany is kaput," said one of their noncommissioned officers. He meant that Germany is down, "in the soup," as the British soldiers would say. It was an exaggeration, for Germany still has a lot of fight left in her, but it was the belief of her captured soldiers yesterday.

Go Into Battle Cheering.

The British were exalted, excited by the smell of victory, exaggerating their gains in the belief that the last great smash had been made, and that the end of this war was at hand. They went out at dawn yesterday filled with the spirit of victory. Many of them went over, too, in the greatest good humor, laughing as they ran, like children whose fancy had been inflamed by some new toy. They were cheered by a new weapon which was to be tried with them for the first time, the "heavily armored motor machine guns of a new style" mentioned already in the official bulletin.

That description is a dull one compared with all the rich and rare qualities which belong to these extraordinary vehicles. The secret of them had been kept jealously for months. Only a few days ago it was whispered to me. "Like prehistoric monsters, you know, the ichthyosaurus," said the officer. I told him he was pulling my leg.

"But it's a fact, man." He breathed hard and laughed in a queer way at some enormous comicality. "They cut up houses and put the refuse under their bellies and walk right over 'em."

I knew this man was truthful, yet I could not believe him.

"They knock down trees like matchsticks," he said, staring at me with shining eyes. "They go clean through a wood."

"And anything else?" I asked, enjoying what I thought was a new sense of humor.

"Everything else," he said earnestly. "They take ditches like kangaroos; they simply love shell craters, laugh at 'em."

It appeared also that they were proof against rifle bullets, machine gun bullets, bomb and shell splinters, just shrugged their shoulders and passed on. Nothing but a direct hit from a fair-sized shell could do them any harm.

Called "Hush, Hush" by Some.

"But what's the name of these mythical monsters?" I asked, not believing a word of it. He said "hush." Other people said "hush, hush" when the subject was alluded to in a remote way, and since then I heard that one name for them is the "hush, hush," but their great name is tanks.

For they are real and I have seen them, walked around them, got inside their bodies, looked at their mysterious organs and watched their monstrous movements. I came across a herd of them in a field, and like a countryman who first saw a giraffe said: "Hell, there ain't no such animal." Then I sat down on the grass and laughed until the tears came into my eyes, (in war one has a funny sense of humor,) for they are monstrously comical, like toads of vast size emerging from the primeval slime in the twilight of the world's dawn.

The skipper of them introduced me to them.

"I felt awfully bucked," said the young officer, who was about five feet high, "when my beauty ate up her first house, but I was sorry for the house, which was quite a good one.

"And how about the trees?" I asked.

"They simply love trees," he answered.

When the British soldiers first saw these strange creatures lolloping along the roads and over the old battlefields, taking trenches on the way, they shouted, cheered wildly, and laughed for a day afterwards. Yesterday the troops got out of their trenches, laughing, shouting, cheering again, because the tanks had gone on ahead and were scaring the Germans dreadfully while they moved over their trenches and poured out fire on the German side. These motor monsters had strange adventures and did very good work, justifying their amazing existence.

Great Preparations for Attack.

For several days before the great blow was to be made and while there was heavy fighting in progress at most parts of the line, there was a steady forward movement and a concentration of all men and machinery to strike at the Flers line. The villages beyond the zone of fire where battalions had been resting suddenly became emptied.

The men had passed on higher up on the roads where there was a struggling tide of all the traffic of war, with supply columns, mule trains, guns, limbers ambulances, and troops from all parts of the empire surging, swirling, struggling slowly forward through the narrow village streets, up long winding roads, across trampled and barren fields, through the ruins of villages destroyed a year or more ago, and out into the country of evil menace, which is criss-crossed by old trenches and pitted with shell craters and strewn with the refuse of the battle two months back in history. Here a great army, with all its material of war, incredibly vast and crowded, lay waiting for the hour when it should be hurled to the great hammer stroke.

Attack Begins at Daybreak.

They were masses of men who were the night before the battle hidden in the darkness of the earth, not revealed even by the white moonlight except in huddled crowds and camps.

Before 6 o'clock, Summer time, all the guns were firing steadily and all the sky was very pale and shimmering in the first twilight of day, filled with the flashes of guns and shells. I went to the right of the line, hoping to see the infantry attack to the left of Leuze wood. Here one of the motor monsters was coming across the ground, but as the sun rose higher it drew the moisture out of all these shell craters and trenches and a dense white mist blotted out the ridge. For an hour or more the French troops who join the British line here, came across country. The British soldiers were moving forward on the left silently, with the mist about them. Overhead shells went rushing by. It was the usual bombardment, not so heavy as others I watched.

It was not until two hours after the first attack, by which time the British troops were in Flers, that the artillery Generals unmasked a number of new batteries, and there was an infernal pandemonium of noise, with every kind of gun and trench mortar flinging explosives over the lines which were now the German first line of defense.

Airmen Have a Great Day.

The machine gunfire rapped out in fierce spasms and the German archies were throwing up shells which burst all about the planes of the British airmen, who came like a flock of birds over the battlefields, flying low above the mists. They did wonderful things yesterday, those British air pilots, risking their lives audaciously in single combats with hostile airmen in encounters against great odds, in bombing enemy headquarters, railway stations, kite balloons, and troops, and registering or observing all day long for the artillery.

They were out to destroy the Germans' last means of observations, and they began the success of the battle by gaining absolute mastery of the air. Thirteen German aeroplanes, since reported by General Haig to be fifteen, were brought down and their flying men dared not come across the British lines to risk more losses.

It is impossible at this stage to give a detailed narrative of the great battle along the whole front of attack. It is still in progress and there are many troops engaged. It is only possible to give a general outline of the action and a few glimpses of separate advventures.

On the British side there was nothing of the killing character within their reach and knowledge which they did not use, and they turned the Germans' worst weapons against themselves.

Every material of war made by the home workers in British factories by months of toil was called in. Men went in with a resolve to break through the German third line without counting the cost, to smash down any opposition they might meet, and to go forward and far until they could get the Germans on the run.

A body of Scots went out to the battle lines to the tune of "Stop Your Tickling, Jock," but there was grim meaning in the music. It is no love song. The English soldiers had been practicing bayonet exercise harder than usual, and, with a personal interest beyond the discipline the men fought yesterday fiercely and ruthlessly. They want to get onto the heels of the Germans, and there were moments yesterday when they saw many pairs of heels.

The area of the British attack yesterday extended on the left from the ground north of Pozières to the line recently won to the north of Ginchy on the right, and its purpose was to break through the third German line below Courcelette, Martinpuich, and Les Boeufs, a distance of about six miles.

On the left, in front of Courcelette, there was hard and unexpected fighting. As it is now known, the Germans had prepared for an attack, and had massed troops in considerable force in the front and reserve lines. They sent out advanced patrols and bombing parties while the British [illegible] go over, and immediately there was a

Monster Armored Cars, Used by British in Charge, Defy Trenches, Barbed Wire, or Craters to Stop Them

LONDON, Saturday, Sept. 16.—Reference today in the official communication to a new type of armored car is the first official mention of a development which has been much whispered about recently in army circles. Those who have seen the new vehicles refer to them as "tanks," while the soldiers who have been handling them have given them the nickname of "Willis."

The object sought by the designers was to render a heavily armored motor car capable of being operated in the shell-torn and roadless wilderness of trenches, where a vehicle mounted on ordinary wheels could not be used.

Although no details of the car's construction have been published, The Times says: "Our inventors have not hesitated boldly to tread unbeaten paths. We may imagine the feelings of German infantry in shell-battered trenches when, in the uncertain light of dawn, they saw advancing upon them an array of unearthly monsters, cased in steel, spitting fire and crawling laboriously but ceaselessly over trenches, barbed wire, and shell craters."

BRITISH FRONT IN FRANCE, Sept. 15.—When the British brought into action today for the first time the new type of armored motor car capable, because of its powerful traction, of crossing trenches and shell craters, the soldiers cheered it even in the midst of shell fire as it moved along beside them in the charge. There has been nothing mor wonderful in this war than th spectacle of its advance toward the German line.

fierce encounter. The Germans came over in a rush. Many fell before the British rifle fire, but others managed to jump into portions of a trench and bombed their way up. Several of the machine guns were turned on them, and there were not many left alive.

But before the fight ended a new one began, for the British jumping-off time had come, and the assaulting troops rose as one man, taking no notice of what had happened, and swept across their own trenches, and the Germans, who were in them, and went straight across country toward Courcelette.

They came up immediately against difficult ground and fierce machine gun fire. Southeast of Courcelette, beyond the shell craters and bits of a broken trench, which the men had carried easily enough, sweeping the Germans down before them, stood the ruins of a sugar factory which the Germans had made into a redoubt with machine gun emplacements. It was one of those deadly places which had cost so many lives among the British in other parts of the battle ground, but they had a new engine of war to destroy the place.

Over the British trenches in the twilight of dawn one of those motor monsters lurched up and now came crawling forward to the rescue, cheered by the assaulting troops, who called out words of encouragement to it and laughed so that some men were laughing even when the bullets caught them in their throat. "Crême de Menthe" was the name of this particular creature, and it waddled forward right over the old German trenches, went forward very steadily towards the sugar factory. There was a silence from the Germans there, then suddenly their machine gun fire burst out in nervous spasms and splashed against the side of "Crême de Menthe," but the tank did not mind. The bullets fell from its sides harmlessly.

Walked Through Sugar Factory.

It advanced upon a broken wall, leaned up against it heavily until it fell with a crash of bricks, and then rose on to the bricks and passed over them and walked straight into the midst of the factory ruins. From its sides came flashes of fire and a host of bullets, and then it trampled around over the machine gun emplacement, "having a grand time," as one of the men said with enthusiasm. It crushed the machine guns under its heavy ribs and killed the machine gun teams with its deadly fire. The infantry followed in and took the place after this good help, and then advanced again around the flanks of the monster.

In spite of the tank, which did such grand work, the assault on Courcelette was hard and costly. Again and again the men came under machine gun fire and rifle fire, for the Germans had dug new trenches called "fabeckgraben" and "zollerngraben," which had not been wiped out by the artillery. They fought with great courage and desperation. Seventy men who advanced the first on part of these lines were swept down, seventy others who went forward to fill their places fell also, but their comrades were not disheartened, and at last carried the position in a great wave of assault.

Then they went on to the village. It was like all these villages in German hands, tunneled with a nest of dugouts and strongholds hard to take. The British troops entered it from the eastern side, fought yard by yard, stubbornly resolved to have it. A tank came along and plowed about, searching for German machine guns, thrusting over bits of wall, nosing here and there and sitting on heaps of ruin while it fired down the streets. By 6:30 last evening the village was taken. The British took 400 prisoners, and when they were brought down to Pozières last night they passed old "Creme de Menthe," who was going home. They held up their hands, crying "Gott in Himmel," and asked how they could fight against such monstrous things. The taking of Courcelette was a great achievement, skillfully planned and carried out by splendid men and one monster.

Attack Upon Martinpuich.

On the right of these troops there was a great assault upon Martinpuich and High Wood. Here also in High Wood the Germans had been ready for attack, and, being forestalled in that, they made a strong counterattack, which for a time had some success, driving the British back to the southern edge of the wood. The British troops had been heavily shelled beforehand, and they found the Germans in much stronger force than they had expected in that wood of bitter memory, but the British fought very gamely, some among them utterly without experience of the Somme kind of fighting, and they wilted a little before its ferocity of fire.

But the older men, veterans of a year's service or more, cheered them up, kept them steady, and led them. They counterattacked and regained their old line, and then, to their great joy, saw the tanks advancing through High Wood and on each side of it.

"It was like a fairy tale," said a Cockney boy. "I can't help laughing every time I think of it." He laughed then, although he had a broken arm and was covered in blood.

"They broke down trees as if they were matchsticks and went over the barricades like elephants. The Boches were thoroughly scared.

"They came running out of their shell-holes and trenches shouting like mad. Some of them attacked the tanks and tried to bomb them, but it wasn't a bit of good. Oh, crikey! it was a rare treat to see the biggest joke that ever was. They just stamped down the German dugouts as one might a wasps' nest."

Little Shelter for Attackers.

On the left of High Wood was a very fine body of troops who had no trenches to lie in, but they just lay out in shell craters under the constant fire of the whizz bangs, that is to say the field guns, firing at short range, which was extremely hard to endure.

"It was cruel," said one of these men, "but we went forward all right when the time came over the bodies of our comrades, who were lying in pools of blood, and afterward the Germans had to pay."

They were co-operating with some troops on their left who went straight for Martinpuich. These men went across No Man's Land for nearly 1,000 yards in six minutes' racing. They made short work of the Germans, who tried to snipe them from shell craters, and they only came to a check on the outskirts of Martinpuich, where they were received with a blast of machine gun fire.

"Hungry" Monsters Brought Up.

It was then the turn of the tanks. Before dawn two of them had come up out of the darkness and lumbered over the British front line trenches, looking toward the Germans as though hungry for breakfast. Afterward they came across No Man's Land like enormous toads with pains in their stomachs and nosed at Martinpuich before testing the strength of its broken barns and bricks. The men cheered them wildly, waving their helmets and dancing around them. One company needed cheering up for they had lost two of their officers the night before in a patrol adventure, and it was the Sergeants who led them over, but now, when they saw the ichthyosauri, they shouted with the others and laughed loudly.

Twenty minutes afterward the first waves were inside the first trenches at Martinpuich and in advance of them waddled a monster. The men were held up for some time by the machine guns but the monsters went on alone and had astounding adventures. They went straight through the shells of broken barns and houses, straddled on top of German dugouts and fired enfilading shots down the German trenches. From one dugout came a German Colonel with a white, frightened face, who held his hands very high in front of the tank shouting "Kamerad, Kamerad."

"Well, come inside then, said a voice in the body of the beast and a human hand came forth from a hole opening suddenly, and grabbing the German officer.

For the rest of the day the tank led that unfortunate man about on the strangest journey the world has ever seen.

Another tank was confronted with 100 Germans, who shouted "Mercy! Mercy!" and at the head of this procession led them back as prisoners to the British lines. Yet another tank went off to the right of Martinpuich and was so fresh and high-spirited that it went far into German lines as if on the way to Berlin.

Martinpuich in British Hands.

The men were not so fortunate as the monsters, not being proof against machine gun bullets and shell fire. The Germans concentrated a very heavy fire upon them and many fell. It was late in the evening before the whole of Martinpuich was taken after fierce fighting, and it was the crowning triumph of a successful day.

The troops on the left side of the line did well. They took forty German officers and 1,430 of other ranks. Against them was the Second Bavarian Corps, whom many of the British met before at Kemmel and the Hohenzollern redoubt, and Ypres, and were glad to pay off the old scores against them.

On the right of the troops at Martinpuich the attack was swinging up to Flers, across a wide stretch of difficult and perilous ground, strongly defended. The Germans were flinging over storms of shrapnel and high explosives, and many British fell, but the wounded shouted on the others if they were not too badly hit, and the others went forward grimly and steadily. These soldiers were superb in courage and stoic endurance, and pressed forward steadily in the broken waves.

The first news of success came through from an airman's wireless, which said:

"A tank is walking up the High street of Flers with the British Army cheering behind."

It was an actual fact. One of the motor monsters was there enjoying itself thoroughly and keeping down the heads of the Germans. It hung out a big piece of paper, on which were the words, "Great Hun Defeat, Special." An aeroplane flew low over the monster-machine, gunning the scared Germans, who fled before this monstrous apparition.

Later in the day it seemed to have been in need of rest before coming home, and two humans got out of its inside and walked back to the British lines, but by that time Flers and many prisoners were in the hands of the British, and the troops had gone beyond to further fields.

On the extreme right of the line of attack the fighting was hardest and fiercest of all, and is still very confused and uncertain to the north of Ginchy and in the direction of Gueudecourt. In this direction the Germans fought from the direction of Morval and Combles, and the shell fire was frightful in its violence. Nevertheless, the first rush forward was magnificent on the part of the troops. The Germans resisted stoutly along their first line. They kept up a severe rifle fire and machine-gun fire until the British were right on them, and then they fought bayonet to bayonet. Large numbers of them were killed, and the British swept through to the second line of trenches and took that.

Troops Go as Far as Gueudecourt.

A third wave passed through them to the third German trench, but before they reached this goal the German soldiers came out with their hands up and surrendered. The British went on and on. They went too far, these soldiers in their eagerness. One of the Colonels stood up on a hillock, blowing a hunting horn to fetch them back, but they did not hear and went on still further, unprotected by the troops on their right. The officers waved on their men with revolvers and many fell leading their companies. It was one of the greatest charges in history, but it drove out too far into the "blue" without sufficient co-operation with the troops, held up lower down by strong points and machine guns. What the situation is there tonight I do not yet know except that these men are fighting on the outskirts of Gueudecourt.

It was the hardest blow today that had been struck at Germany's heart and pride by British troops.

INVENTORS OF THE "TANKS."

Col. Swinton, Former "Eyewitness," and Major Stern Get Credit.

LONDON, Monday, Sept. 18.—Credit for the new traveling land forts, which have been used during the last few days on the British front, belongs to two men, Lieut. Col. E. D. Swinton of the Intelligence Department of the General Staff, and Major Stern. Lieut. Col. Swinton will be remembered as one of the officer "eyewitnesses" who wrote accounts of the early days around Ypres for British newspapers. Major Stern is a business man who has been for some time in the employ of the Government. The Daily Mail describes the new monsters as follows:

"These long, low, dust-colored tortoises have no resemblance to motor cars. They are, in fact steel land ships of immense power and wonderful capacity. In practice they can climb walls, push through dense woods, cross trenches and manoeuvre in and out of craters. One of the most remarkable facts about them is the secrecy with which the making of their thousands of parts was veiled in the midland town of their birth. The army likes them, but it is not placing too much reliance on what is for the present only an experiment."

BURY GERMANS ALIVE AT MOUQUET FARM

Men Refused to Come Up from Underground Shelters When Ordered to Surrender.

WITH THE BRITISH ARMY IN FRANCE, Sept. 17.—The British today took the Mouquet Farm. On two former occasions they had been on the premises, but were unable to remain there. It was a strong point on the right of the British battle line, where a garrison of Germans and their machine guns seemed proof against shell fire.

They had the usual deep cellars and runways underground, and, driven from one exit by shellfire, they would emerge from another. The British got entirely around their burrows and called down the cellar stairs for them to surrender. The Germans thought a counterattack would come to their assistance, as before. The British, however, assured them that none would come, as they had the trench all the way round the farm to prevent their exit or aid from coming to them. Still the Germans refused to yield, and the final result of this grim colloquy was that the British blew in all the cellar doors. But such persistent diggers were the Germans that the British are not certain but they had some under ground passage for escape.

The British also cleaned up the Danube trench in the old German first line near Thiepval, which is the hinge of the Somme battle line. As happened before and after the fierce general attack along the whole front, the succeeding days are spent in rectifying the line and cleaning up any strong points that still hold out.

Small bodies of British infantry have been in both the villages of Les Boeufs and Geudecourt, beyond Flers, which was taken Friday, and the British line is now close to these villages.

Talking with officers of corps engaged in the fighting of the last three days, they estimate the losses at from two to one to five to one for the Germans as against those of the British. In one sector the ratio was estimated at as high as eight to one. The superior volume of the British shellfire, now that the Germans are forced into the open, has a telling effect.

This strange looking machine is the first tank ever used. It was introduced by the British in the battle for the Somme.

"All the News That's Fit to Print."

The New York Times.

THE WEATHER

Partly cloudy Monday; not quite so warm; fair Tuesday, cooler; moderate west and northwest winds.
For full weather report see Page 21.

VOL. LXVI...NO. 21,443. ....　　　NEW YORK, MONDAY, OCTOBER 9, 1916.—TWENTY-TWO PAGES.　　　ONE CENT In Greater New York, Jersey City and Newark. | TWO CENTS Elsewhere.

GERMAN SUBMARINES SINK 6 TO 9 SHIPS OFF NANTUCKET;
ONE A LINER WITH MANY AMERICANS, BUT ALL ARE SAVED;
WASHINGTON SEES GRAVE PERIL IN RAIDS OFF OUR COAST

POSSIBLY THREE U-BOATS

Swift Harvest of Victims Follows the Visit of U-53 to Newport.

4 BRITISH, 2 NEUTRAL SHIPS

Red Cross Liner Stephano Is Torpedoed After the Passengers Take to Boats.

U.S. WARSHIPS GO TO RESCUE

Seventeen Destroyers Rushed from Newport—Crew of One British Ship Missing.

Nine Vessels Reported Sunk By Three German Submarines

NEWPORT, R. I., Monday, Oct. 9.—3 A. M.—It was reported without confirmation early this morning that three submarines were operating off the coast and that a total of nine vessels had been sunk by them.

The executive officer of the destroyer Drayton, which has just returned to port, says the Captain of the Nantucket Lightship wirelessed that the total number of vessels destroyed was nine.

The Captain of the lightship also said that three submarines were at work.

BOSTON, Oct. 8.—The submarine arm of the Imperial German Navy ravaged shipping off the eastern coast of the United States today.

Four British, one Dutch, and one Norwegian steamer were sent to the bottom or left crippled derelicts off Nantucket Shoals.

Tonight under the light of the hunters' moon the destroyer flotilla of the United States Atlantic Fleet was picking up passengers and crews of the destroyed vessels and bringing them into Newport, R. I. So far as known, there was no loss of life, although at a late hour the crew of the British steamer Kingston had not been accounted for.

According to a very definite report tonight two submarines were concerned in the work this afternoon. The Newport Naval Station has re-

ceived a wireless from the Captain of the lightship, stating that he recognized two submarines at work.

A submarine held up the American steamer Kansan, bound from New York for Genoa with steel for the Italian Government, but later, on establishing her identity, allowed the American to proceed. The Kansan came into Boston Harbor late tonight for her usual call here.

This submarine is believed to be the U-53, which paid a call to Newport yesterday and disappeared at sunset.

Day's Work of Havoc.

The record of submarine warring, as brought to land by wireless dispatches, follows:

THE STRATHDENE, British freighter, torpedoed and sunk off Nantucket. Crew taken aboard Nantucket Shoals Lightship and later removed to Newport by torpedo boat destroyers. The vessel left New York yesterday for Bordeaux, and was attacked at 6 A. M.

THE WEST POINT, British freighter, torpedoed and sunk off Nantucket. Crew abandoned the ship in small boats after a warning shot from the submarine's gun. Officers and men were taken aboard a destroyer. The vessel was attacked at 10:45 A. M. She was bound from London for Newport News.

THE STEPHANO, British passenger liner, plying regularly between New York, Halifax and St. John's, Newfoundland, sunk by opening valves when southeast of Nantucket, while bound for New York. Passengers and crew, numbering about 140, were picked up by the destroyer Balch and transferred to the destroyer Jenkins. The attack was at 4:30 P. M.

THE KINGSTON, British freighter, torpedoed and sunk southeast of Nantucket. Crew missing and destroyer searching for them. This vessel is not accounted for in maritime registers, and may be the Kingstonian. The attack was at 6 P. M.

THE BLOOMERSDIJK, Dutch freighter, torpedoed and sunk south of Nantucket. Crew taken aboard a destroyer. The steamer was bound from New York for Rotterdam, having sailed last night.

THE CHRISTIAN KNUDSEN, Norwegian freighter, torpedoed and sunk near where the Bloomersdijk went down. Crew picked up by destroyers. The vessel sailed from New York Saturday for London.

Whole Coast in Alarm.

The sensation created yesterday when the U-53 quietly slipped into Newport Harbor and as quietly slipped away, three hours later, was less than the shock in shipping circles when wireless reports of submarine attacks began to come into the naval radio stations just before noon today. Within a few minutes the air was literally charged with electricity as wireless messages of warning shot up and down the coast.

The submarine or submarines had taken a position directly in the steamer lanes, where they could hardly miss

anything bound for New York or bound east from that port.

Vessels of the allied nations and neutral ships carrying contraband of war scurried to get within the three-mile limit of the American shore. Several that were following the outside course shifted and made for the inside lane. The Stephano of the Red Cross Line, however, was caught outside the neutral zone. The destruction of this vessel was perhaps the biggest prize of the day. The craft had been sold to the Russian Government, and would have been used as an ice breaker after her present trip.

Holds Up the Kansan.

At daylight today the submarine was southeast of Nantucket and got in the way of the Kansan. The steamer was flying the American flag. She was stopped by the submarine at 5:30 o'clock. Assured that the Kansan was an American-owned vessel, the submarine later allowed her to proceed.

Captain Smith of the Kansan reported that he had been stopped in a wireless message to the Captain of the Nantucket Shoals Lightship. He said the submarine showed no colors, but from his meagre description of the warship naval men were satisfied that it was the U-53.

A half hour later the submarine encountered the Strathdene, commanded by Captain Wilson and under charter by the French Line. A subsequent message from the Nantucket Lightship stated that the Strathdene had been sunk at 6 o'clock this morning and that the crew of "twenty men" were on the lightship. The steamer carried a crew of thirty-four, so there was some doubt as to whether the lightship had picked them all up or had correctly reported.

Pursuing her hostile course, the submarine next came up with the West Point. The fate of the British freighter was told in the following wireless dispatch from her commander, Captain Harden, to the Naval Radio Station:

"British steamer West Point stopped by submarine and fired upon; getting boat ready. Position 30.25 north, 69 west. Get cutter."

Shelled by the U-Boat.

Later messages gave further details. One stated that the steamer was being shelled by the submarine when the message was sent at 11:15 A. M. A third message said that the vessel was attacked at 10:45 ten miles south of Nantucket. This message caused confusion regarding the exact position of the freighter. The steamer Kansan picked up the distress signals of the West Point and proceeded to her assistance. The Boston Navy Yard at 1:30 o'clock received a message from the Kansan stating that the West Point was sinking and that the Kansan was going to her aid. The disabled vessel was then fifty-five miles distant and the Kansan was making twelve knots.

Later a private dispatch added the information that the submarine, after stopping the West Point, ordered the crew into their small boats. The crew abandoned the ship, which was then torpedoed. It was in a sinking condition when last reported.

The distress signals of the West Point were picked up by the Government Radio Station at Newport, and immediately Rear Admiral Albert Gleaves, commander of the destroyer flotilla of the Atlantic Fleet, ordered virtually all his ships to the rescue.

Map showing location of Nantucket Lightship near which the U53 attacked British shipping yesterday

Our Last Warning to Germany On Her Submarine Warfare

From President Wilson's notice to Germany that submarine warfare on merchantmen must be kept within the law, April 18, 1916:

Vessels of neutral ownership, even vessels of neutral ownership bound from neutral port to neutral port, have been destroyed, along with vessels of belligerent ownership, in constantly increasing numbers. Sometimes the merchantmen attacked have been warned and summoned to surrender before being fired on or torpedoed; sometimes their passengers and crews have been vouchsafed the poor security of being allowed to take to the ship's boats before the ship was sent to the bottom. But again and again no warning has been given * * * and the lives of noncombatants, passengers and crew, have been destroyed wholesale and in a manner which the Government of the United States cannot but regard as wanton and without the slightest color of justification.

The Government of the United States has been very patient. * * * It has become painfully evident to it that the position which it took at the very outset is inevitable, namely, the use of submarines for the destruction of an enemy's commerce, is, of necessity, because of the very character of the vessels employed and the very methods of attack which their employment of course involves, utterly incompatible with the principles of humanity, the long-established and incontrovertible rights of neutrals, and the sacred immunities of noncombatants.

If it is still the purpose of the Imperial Government to prosecute relentless and indiscriminate warfare against vessels of commerce by the use of submarines, without regard to what the Government of the United States must consider the sacred and indisputable rules of international law and the universally recognized dictates of humanity, the Government of the United States is at last forced to the conclusion that there is but one course it can pursue.

"All the News That's Fit to Print."

The New York Times.

THE WEATHER
Fair and Continued cool Sunday; fair, slightly warmer Monday; moderate northwest winds, becoming variable.
For full weather report see Page 19

VOL. LXV...NO. 21,078. ...   NEW YORK, SUNDAY, OCTOBER 10, 1915.—114 PAGES, In Seven Parts, *including Picture and Rotogravure Section, Special Rotogravure Portrait of President Wilson's Fiancee, and Articles Sent Weather.*   PRICE FIVE CENTS

TEUTONIC FORCES CAPTURE BELGRADE AND DRIVE SERBS BACK ALONG DANUBE; BULGARS ARE ADVANCING TOWARD NISH

CONCERTED DRIVE NOW ON

Serb Capital Easily Taken by Main Army Under Von Mackensen.

DEFENDING FORCE RETIRES

And Will Await the Invaders in Prepared Positions in the Mountains.

ALLIES RUSHING UP TROOPS

LONDON, Sunday, Oct. 10.—Belgrade, the old capital of Serbia, or the greater part of it, has been occupied by the advancing host of Austro-German troops. Other bodies of Teutonic forces have crossed the Danube at four points below Semendria, and are reported to be driving the Serbians southward.

Announcement of these successes in the Balkan War area was contained in the German Army Headquarters bulletin, which said concerning these operations:

The main sections of two armies of the newly formed army group under Field Marshal von Mackensen have crossed the Save and Danube Rivers.

After the German troops of the army of the Royal and Imperial Infantry, under General von Koevess, had captured Ziguner Island and the hills southwest of Belgrade, the army succeeded in bringing the greater part of the city of Belgrade into the hands of the allies.

Austrian troops stormed the citadel and the northern section of the town of Belgrade. German troops stormed the New Konak, (the Royal Palace.) The troops are penetrating further through the southern part of the town.

The army of Artillery General von Gallwitz has forced crossings over the Danube at four points on the section below Samandria, and is driving the enemy in front of it toward the south.

The Austrian official statement concerning the operations says:

The Austro-Hungarian troops of the army of General von Koevess yesterday penetrated the northern part of Belgrade and stormed the citadel. Early this morning German troops from the west cut a path to the Konak (the royal palace.) Austro-Hungarian and German flags are flying from the castle of the Serbian kings. Both above and below Belgrade the

enemy watching the banks could nowhere resist the allies.

The capture of Belgrade had been expected, as it was not thought that the Serbians would make any serious attempt to defend the city, which lies on a point of land at the junction of the Save and Danube, jutting toward Austria, and could be attacked from three sides.

The real test of strength will come when the invaders reach the main Serbian positions in the mountains, where the Austrians were so severely defeated in December. The present, however, is a more formidable attack, a new army group having been organized under command of Field Marshal von Mackensen for that purpose. Its strength is not exactly known, but it is supposed that it is composed chiefly of Austro-Hungarians, with a stiffening of Germans, and is largely commanded by German officers.

Bulgar Army is Moving.

The Bulgarians, acting in concert with their new allies, are advancing from Sofia toward Pirot, on the Serbian frontier, the fortress which covers the road to Nish, the Serbian war capital.

No definite information is available yet as to the campaign plans of the Serbian commanders, but a Rome dispatch quotes the Military Attaché of the Serbian Legation there as saying that the Serbians would take the offensive against the Austro-German forces as soon as the Entente Allies' reinforcements came up. Even without the allied reinforcements, he asserted, the Serbians were quite able to meet the Austro-German invasion.

The French and British are now landing troops at the rate of 14,000 daily at Saloniki to send by railway to the assistance of Serbia.

With the Balkans thus taking their place with the Russian and western fronts as a centre of war interest, the Black and Aegean Seas will also be the scenes of activity, for as soon as Bulgaria strikes at Serbia the allied fleets will give the Bulgarian ports their attention.

Although the Bulgarian Minister at London, who has not received or asked for his passports, stated yesterday that Bulgaria had no quarrel with England, an attack on Serbia would be regarded by England as sufficient reason for a quarrel.

Turkey, according to a dispatch from Saloniki, is sending 50,000 men to Varna and Dedeaghatch to help in the defense of those Bulgarian ports.

Greece Assailed by Both Sides.

Greece's attitude is still somewhat obscure. The Greek Minister at Paris yesterday reiterated that Greece's neutrality would continue to be one of benevolence toward the Entente Powers. But more than that was expected, and the allied capitals are awaiting a definite statement from the new Greek Cabinet.

Meanwhile, Bulgaria, through her Premier, is reported to have warned Greece that she cannot continue to be regarded as neutral if she permits the landing of allied troops at Saloniki. On the other hand, the allied envoys at Athens are said to have told the Greek King that the landing of troops would go on.

GREECE WARNED BY BOTH SIDES

Bulgar Premier Objects to the Continued Landing of Allied Troops.

HINTS IT MUST NOT GO ON

But Allied Envoys, Talking Plainly to King, Say the Expedition Will Be Pushed.

LONDON, Oct. 9.—Strong representations are said by the Central News to have been made by Bulgaria to Greece against the landing of French and British troops at Saloniki.

The dispatch to the Central News which comes from Sofia, says that Premier Radoslavoff informed the Greek Minister that the landing of allied troops at Saloniki was not in harmony with the attitude of the Greek Government toward Bulgaria, as recently expressed. The Premier added that if the attitude of Greece was not altered, the Bulgarian cabinet could not be responsible for a change in the feelings of the Bulgarian people.

The Bulgarian Minister at Athens is said to have been instructed to make similar representations to the Greek Government.

ROME, Oct. 8, (via Paris, Oct. 9.)—King Constantine of Greece was told plainly by the British Minister, Elliot, during the audience granted him on Thursday, that Great Britain and France were determined to push through the military expedition, now being landed at Saloniki.

The Athens correspondent of the Giornale d'Italia says that the views of the Quadruple Entente governments were explained to the Greek ruler in very energetic terms by the British diplomat.

GREEKS CAN'T STOP ALLIES.

London Chronicle Declares Any Attack Means a Change of Rulers.

Special Cable to THE NEW YORK TIMES.
LONDON, Oct. 9.—The Chronicle says editorially this morning:

"Greece's default throws the whole burden on the allied expedition. It is at once a dishonorable and impolitic default, but it is not that of the Greek Nation nor of its Constitutional leader. It is the unconstitutional act of the German Emperor's brother-in-law, who occupies the Greek throne.

"The new Cabinet, we are told, does not propose to interfere with the Allies continuing to land troops at Saloniki. Let us add quite frankly that after what has passed it is not in a position to do so, and that to attempt interference would be practically a hostile act.

GUARDING GEORGE V. IN A ZEPPELIN RAID

"Sit on His Head if Necessary," Said Kitchener, and They Almost Had to Do It.

IGNORED GUARD'S "HALT!"

"Pass, King; Why in 'Ell Didn't You Sing Out?"—Village Rector and Neighbors Gather with Guns.

Cosmo Hamilton, the English dramatist, who for the last year has been an officer in the Royal Naval Aviation Corps and was held personally responsible for the safety of King George V. at Sandringham Palace during the Zeppelin raids, gave to a reporter from THE TIMES yesterday many intimate details of the life of England's ruler under war conditions. He also said that the rumors of the Prince of Wales having been shot in France were untrue.

"When I left Liverpool on Sept. 29 by the American liner New York," said Mr. Hamilton, "the Prince of Wales had just returned to his regiment in France, having been on a furlough and a visit to the King and Queen at Windsor Castle. On the day he is supposed to have been shot by the jealous husband of a French waitress near Ypres the Prince was visiting the New Zealanders in the hospital outside of Windsor. He is a very keen soldier, and is not the type of young man who would spend his time flirting with a waitress. His training and home bringing-up were against that sort of thing, and, moreover, such conduct would displease his parents very much."

With regard to the report that King George had told Premier Asquith that he would abdicate the throne immediately if the war terminated in an inconclusive peace, Mr. Hamilton said he thought it was quite likely to have happened.

"The driveling 'wait and see' policy of the political hucksters in power under Asquith," he continued, "has been so stultifying that it may have given rise to the impression that the Government would agree to a peace of that kind. But the country would never consent to such a course, and it would cause a revolution.

"The people have paid 33 per cent. of their earnings for income tax, and every man is willing to do his duty and die in defense of the country. The only clog on the nation is the party in power at Westminster, which has not improved much since the coalition. King George is a great little man, a sailor and a soldier every inch of him. There is not much connected with the Navy and the Army that he does not know about.

Soldiers Fond of the King.

"When the war first started it was the magic name of Kitchener that caused the thousands in England to enlist, but today the men in the trenches speak with affection of 'G. V.' which is their pet name for the King.

"The Tommy Atkins of today differs from his predecessors. He is sober, intelligent, and attentive to his duties. His one object is to defeat the enemy at all cost. The new army has leveled all class distinctions, and you will find the son of the Baron sitting side by side in the trenches on equal footing with the son of a baker. Six years' training were considered necessary by the War Office to make a good artillery officer, but the present war has shown us that more efficient officers can be turned out in six months. In the old days the cadets spent about three hours a day in studying and the rest of the time on pleasure jaunts.

"All the News That's Fit to Print."

The New York Times.

THE WEATHER
Fair, rain to tonight or Thursday; moderate northeast winds.

VOL. LXVI...NO. 21,459. ...   NEW YORK, WEDNESDAY, OCTOBER 25, 1916.—TWENTY-TWO PAGES.   ONE CENT

FRENCH BREAK GERMAN VERDUN LINE ON 4-MILE FRONT, ADVANCING 2 MILES; RUMANIANS LOSE THREE MORE TOWNS

FRENCH REWIN DOUAUMONT

They Also Take Thiaumont, Haudromont Quarries and Caillette Wood.

3,500 PRISONERS COUNTED

Great Activity of Air Scouts, Shelling Depots and Railway Lines, Presaged Drive.

BRITISH HOLD ON SOMME

Consolidate Newly Won Ground Near Gueudecourt While Artillery Chorus Continues.

PARIS, Oct. 24.—By a powerful stroke the French forces under General Nivelle opened an entirely new phase of the Verdun campaign today by piercing the

Defenders of Verdun Recapture in a Single Day Area Which It Took the Germans Two Months to Win

LONDON, Wednesday, Oct. 25.—Military experts here point out that the French coup at Verdun has regained virtually all the ground lost in the second battle of Verdun. This was accomplished with lightning suddenness in a single day, whereas the Germans occupied nearly two months in wresting this ground from the French.

The fort of Douaumont is the highest elevation on the right bank of the Meuse in the neighborhood of Verdun.

The Germans captured part of the fort on Feb. 25, four days after the battle of Verdun began. On March 31 they occupied the village of Vaux and announced that they had captured Fort de Vaux, which did not fall until June 1, according to the French reports.

Meanwhile, the Germans who had occupied part of the Douaumont Fort—a Brandenburg regiment belonging to the Fifty-eighth Infantry Division—found themselves in a precarious position. On May 22 the French made an assault upon their position and drove them into the inner works. Then two days later the Germans relieved them and occupied the entire fortifications.

Since May 24 Fort de Douaumont has been in German hands. Thiaumont Farm and the Haudromont Quarries, after changing hands several times, have been held by the Germans since July 1-2.

The German offensive at Verdun practically came to an end in the third week in July, when between the 15th and 20th 300,000 Germans were removed and sent to the Somme, where the Franco-British offensive had begun on July 1.

German lines on a front of more than four miles on the east bank of the Meuse. In the centre the advance reached a depth of nearly two miles. So far 3,500 prisoners and large quantities of war material have been captured.

The famous fort of Douaumont, which had already changed hands many times,

was captured, as well as the village of Douaumont, lying to the northeast. The French also took La Caillette Wood in its entirety, advancing to the western outskirts of the village of Vaux.

On the left wing Thiaumont Redoubt and the fortified farm of the same name fell into the hands of the victors, who, continuing their dash forward, stormed the quarries of Haudromont, establishing a new line along the road running from Bras through Haudromont Wood to Douaumont.

The fact that the Germans were withdrawing men and guns from Verdun to reinforce their hard-pressed lines on the Somme has been mentioned several times in the French official reports. This is emphasized again today in a dispatch from the correspondent of La Liberté on the Somme, who says that the growing intensity of the bombardment between the Ancre and the Somme indicates that the Germans are preparing for another attempt to remedy a situation which is becoming more critical for them each day.

Emperor William, adds the correspondent, has even been reported to be at Bapaume personally overseeing the preliminaries for the formidable counter-offensive in view, for which the German army on the Somme front is said to have received strong reinforcements in infantry, and more especially in artillery.

The French night report dealing with the Verdun operations says:

On the Verdun front after intense artillery preparation, an attack on the right bank of the Meuse was launched at 11:40 o'clock in the morning. The enemy line, attacked on a front of seven kilometers (four and one-third miles), was broken through everywhere to a depth which at the centre attained a distance of three kilometers (nearly two miles.)

The village and fort of Douaumont are in our hands.

To the left, our troops advancing beyond the Thiaumont work and farm, rushed the Haudromont quarries and established themselves along the road from Bras to Douaumont.

On the right of the fort our line runs to the north of La Caillette Wood along the western outskirts of the village of Vaux and the eastern border of Fumin Wood and continues to the north of Chenois Wood and the Damloup Battery.

Prisoners are pouring in. So far, 3,500, including about 100 officers, have been counted. The quantity of material captured cannot yet be estimated. Our losses were small.

The French official statement regarding aerial operations issued this afternoon says:

Aviation—On the Somme front one of our aeroplanes attacked with a machine gun enemy trenches in St. Pierre Vaast Wood.

On the Verdun front yesterday, despite a thick mist, our aircraft displayed activity and fought some twenty engagements.

Three enemy machines were brought down. One fell to the north of Azannes, another dropped near Ornes, and a third was seen to fall with a broken wing north of Romagne.

Following an engagement fought by one of our air squadrons with an enemy group in the vicinity of Verdun, one of our pilots descended within 100 meters of the ground in order to set on fire a shed and to open with his machine gun on a motor car.

In Lorraine two German machines were forced down in a damaged condition.

In Alsace one of our pilots felled an Aviatik, which landed near Cerney.

Yesterday our bombarding aeroplanes dropped three heavy calibre bombs on the railway station at Spincourt, and about twenty on enemy bivouacks at Azannes.

10 MORE SHIPS SUNK BY GERMAN U-BOATS

Five Norwegian, One Danish, and Four British Vessels Sent to the Bottom in the War Zone.

LONDON, Oct. 24.—The German campaign against merchant vessels continues unabated. According to announcements made today, ten more vessels have been sunk, five of them Norwegian, four British and one Danish. The crews of the lost vessels have been saved. The ships destroyed were:

	Tons.
The Secundo, Norwegian	
The Gronhaug, Norwegian	
The Gunn, Norwegian	483
The St. Estad, Norwegian	2,349
The Rensfien, Norwegian	
The Gulfborg, Danish	
The Midland, British	4,200
The Cluden, British	3,166
The W. Harkees, British	1,186
The Barbara, British	3,740

In addition to these the Danish schooner Libra has been set afire by a German submarine. The crew escaped.

The Midland, 380 feet long and built in 1913, was owned in London. She was last reported on a voyage from Melbourne to Las Palmas, during which she sailed from Cape Town on Sept. 17. The steamer Cluden was last reported at Karichi, British India, on Sept. 22. The British steamer Barbara was last reported as having sailed from Philadelphia, Sept. 28, for Queenstown. There are two Danish steamers named Gulfborg, one of 1,569 tons, the other of 138 tons.

Reuter's Stavanger correspondent says that the Norwegian bark Athenian, which has arrived at Egersund, reports that on Sunday she saw four Norwegian steamers set on fire by a German submarine. The Athenian escaped to Egersund and does not dare to put to sea again, says the correspondent.

Scene of Big French Stroke at Verdun.

The shaded portion of the above map indicates the extent of the ground gained yesterday by the French, on a front of over four miles and to an extreme depth of nearly two miles. The upper solid line shows where the French stood when the battle of Verdun began on Feb. 21 last, while the lower line indicates the extreme advance of the Germans.

"All the News That's Fit to Print."

The New York Times.

THE WEATHER
Overcast today; Sunday fair; slight temperature changes; west winds.
For full weather report see Page 19.

VOL. LXVI...NO. 21,483. NEW YORK, SATURDAY, NOVEMBER 18, 1916.—TWENTY PAGES. ONE CENT In Greater New York, Jersey City and Newark. | Elsewhere, TWO CENTS.

GERMANY TO DEPORT 300,000 BELGIANS; NATION IS WILD WITH GRIEF AND TERROR; ALLIES PLAN STRONG COUNTERSTROKE

BELGIAN VICTIMS DEFIANT

Sing Patriotic Songs As Packed in Cattle Trucks They Go To Exile.

30,000 ALREADY TAKEN

Despairing Women Throw Themselves Before Trains and Are Removed by Force.

TOURNAI OBJECTS, IS FINED

Representatives of Neutrals Are Appealed To for Aid to End the Deportations.

LONDON, Nov. 17.—Thirty thousand Belgians already have been deported to Germany, according to information received here through official channels.

Reports from the same sources say that the Germans plan to take some 300,000, judging from the order issued in a number of cities for all males over seventeen to report for inspection.

The Municipal Council of Tournai has formally declined to accede to the German demand, the reports say, protesting that hitherto it had acquiesced in all the German orders. General Hopffer thereupon imposed a fine of 200,000 marks, it is added, for the refusal of the Council to furnish a list of male inhabitants, with a further fine of 20,000 marks daily as long as the Council refused to give the list.

A circumstantial report from the Mons district says that the entire male population over seventeen years was summoned to report at German Headquarters at 8 o'clock on the morning of Oct. 26.

The priests, professors, teachers, local officials, members of the Food Committee, and the physically defective were dismissed, but, it is added, 1,200 men, composing 20 per cent. of the eligible males, both employed and unemployed, were selected and immediately placed on cattle trucks and started for Germany. Being ignorant of the purpose of the summons the men had assembled without clothing for traveling and without food. Relatives, who hurried to the station with food and clothing, were not permitted access to the men, the reports add.

The resolution of the Municipal Council at Tournai concerning the request by the German authorities for a list of workmen, says the Council decides to preserve its negative attitude, and adds the following:

"The City of Tournai is prepared to submit without resistance to all the exigencies authorized by the laws and customs of war. Its sincerity cannot be doubted, as it has shown perfect composure and has avoided any active hostility during the period of over two years that it has had to endure the present occupation, to billet the troops and feed them. The city has thus clearly shown that it is not animated by an undue spirit of bravado.

"But at the same time the Municipal Council could not furnish weapons against their own children, fully conscious that natural law and international law, which is derived from it, forbids them to do so.

"In his proclamation of Sept. 2, 1914, the Governor General of Belgium made this statement: 'I am not asking any one to renounce his patriotic feeling.' The city of Tournai remains confident in this statement, which must be considered as expressing the feeling of his Imperial Majesty, the German Emperor, in whose name the Governor General was speaking. Consequently, in following the call of honor and patriotism, the city remains faithful to a primary duty of which a higher German officer cannot fail to realize the nobleness.

"The members of the Municipal Council are confident that the loyalty and frankness of this attitude will help to avoid all misunderstandings between themselves and the German Army."

Reply of Military Chiefs.

The above resolution was dated Oct. 20. Under date of Oct. 23, Major Gen. Hopffer replied as follows:

"The fact that the municipality allows itself by the decision of the Town Council to oppose the orders of the military authorities in occupied territory constitutes an act of arrogance without precedence and is an absolute misunderstanding of the situation arising from the state of war.

"The state of affairs is clearly and simply this: The military authority commands and the municipality has to obey. If it fails to do this, it will have to support the heavy consequences which I have already pointed out in my previous explantion.

"The commander of the army has imposed on the town for its refusal to supply the required lists a fine of 200,000 marks, which has to be paid within the next six days, and he further adds that until the required lists have been put at his disposal the sum of 20,000 marks will have to be paid for every day of delay. This will hold good until Dec. 31."

Entire Population in Terror.

THE HAGUE, Nov. 17.—The number of Belgians deported by the Germans up to date, according to information given to The Associated Press today from a reliable source, apparently is between 80,000 and 40,000, and they are being deported at the rate of about 2,000 daily.

Antwerp, it was said, has been commanded to furnish 27,000 men, which is probably not more than 10 per cent of its able-bodied population, but the commune of Lessines has lost more than 2,000 from a total population, including women and children, of 7,000, repesenting virtually every able-bodied man, excepting officials.

The entire Belgian population, the narrator said, is terrorized because the people realize they are entirely helpless. Crowds of hysterical women and children gather at the railway and recruiting stations, and many women at Jamapes threw themselves on the rails to prevent the departure of a train of emigrants and had to be forcibly removed by German soldiers.

The men are frequently loaded into cattle cars and spend one or two days on the journey. They are strongly determined to refuse to work, believing that if they are not employed in military works they will be compelled to replace Germans and be forced to work directly or indirectly against the Belgian Army and its allies. The deported men in trains passing through Liège are declared to have been heard singing the Marseillaise and other patriotic airs.

The newspapers report a case near Valenciennes of sixty Frenchmen who, when impressed by the Germans, refused to work. They are declared to have been tied to posts for forty-eight hours, until half of them fainted from hardships and hunger.

Prominent Men Make Protests.

Many prominent Belgians are reported not to have hesitated to risk their liberty, by the strongest of protests to the German authorities against the deportations. Various official bodies have drafted resolutions of protest, and the Senators and Deputies of Antwerp and Hainault Provinces have taken especially strong action in the premises and are said to be daily expecting deportation.

Neutrals in Belgium, especially the Ministers, are receiving many appeals to try and induce their Governments to intervene. The newspaper La Libre Belgique, which has maintained a wide circulation throughout Belgium for more than a year, despite the alleged efforts of the Germans to discover its authors and suppress the sheet, has published a special number containing an appeal to the neutral nations.

The Antwerp order notifies students to bring their books and musicians their instruments. The authorities promise the men good wages and liberty to remit money from Germany to their families in Belgium. To all of them is offered an opportunity to sign a voluntary agreement to work. They are informed, it is stated, that if they refuse to sign they will be treated worse, but virtually all decline to do so.

Whenever the males assemble for deportations doctors examine them and the physically unfit are eliminated, together with municipal and relief organization officials. Those without regular employment are the first selected for deportation.

Skilled Workers Sought.

The principle object of the deportations, it was said, appears to be to secure silled workers. Men regularly employed have been enrolled from several communes. A large number was taken at Jamapes from factories which were running and were self-supporting, and bank employes were impressed at Mons. The relief organization in Luxembourg Province was carrying on public works and giving employment to many men, but the works stopped a month ago and the laborers thus rendered unemployed are being deported.

Despite the statements credited to German officers that the deported men will not be employed in military work, the Belgians are declared to fear the contrary, as it has been reported that large bodies of men have been taken to Northern France and employed in cutting timbers for trenches, and that others in Northern Belgium have been forced to dig trenches.

URGES AMERICANS TO SAVE BELGIANS

Lord Robert Cecil Says Nation Is Being Wiped Out by German Deportation Measure

LONDON, Nov. 17.—In a statement today, Lord Robert Cecil, Minister of War Trade, uttered a vigorous protest against Germany's deportation of Belgians, and declared that the people of France and England, no less than the people of Belgium, "hope that American public opinion will show itself, not only in a few short days or weeks of protests and criticisms, but in steady pressure upon the invaders of Belgium to conduct the war against the soldiers of the Allies in the trenches and not against the helpless civilians whom they have in their power."

Lord Robert reviewed the measures taken by the Entente Allies to provide relief for the Belgians, and characterized as "a lie" what he termed Germany's attempt to justify her action by saying that England was responsible for unemployment in Belgium.

"Three times during the last year," Lord Robert continued, "we have proposed to the Germans a definite scheme whereby the exports of Belgian manufactures and even imports of raw material might be made free under the control of the Belgian Relief Commission, and that the commission might control all the funds arising out of the trade. To none of these proposals have we had a reply. The Germans have consistently refused to do anything to assist the relief commission and Belgian industry. Instead they have exacted forty million francs a month from Belgium, requisitioned every kind of machinery and raw material, seized the funds of the national bank, and restricted exports.

"They have drained Belgium dry and stripped her bare, and we know all this policy was deliberately calculated to create a maximum amount of unemployment in order that when the proper moment arrived their slave raids might begin.

"Further, the Germans justify their action on the ground that the unemployment they themselves created had become so bad as to overstrain the resources of the poor relief. This is the most impudent thing even Germany has said since the war began. You might think the poor relief referred to came from Germany or from Belgium. As a matter of fact it comes from the Allies through the relief commission. This country alone in the last eighteen months has advanced some $50,000,000 for food and poor relief. This money goes from us freely, and without conditions, except that it shall be under neutral control.

"It is kind of the Germans to be so anxious not to overstrain our resources, but it is fair to ask what right the Germans have to make the charity of the world an excuse for enslaving those who receive it. The Belgians are going to Germany on no ordinary work. They are to be caught up and crushed in the machine, they will never return to Belgium. It is this grinding up of a nation piecemeal which is the most horrible feature of the sitution.

"Lastly, it must be remembered that the Allies can and will liberate Belgian territory. meanwhile they can and will bear the burden of keeping the Belgians from starvation. But they cannot protect the Belgians from slavery. They cannot insure that when Belgium is liberated it will be a nation and not a desert. It is only the neutrals who can do this by the exercise of their public opinion."

Lord Robert concluded with an expression of hope that the pressure of American public opinion would bring about this result.

WOOLWICH WONDERS SEEN BY HALL CAINE

Writer Says 17,000 Women and 50,000 Men Are Now Employed There.

HOW BIG GUNS ARE MADE

Female Hands Particularly Adept in Making Fuses and Filling Shells.

By HALL CAINE.

LONDON, Oct. 22.—When the Imperial Chancellor opened the Reichstag the other day he tried to account for the reverses of the German Army by saying it had had to face the whole world's output of ammunition. Nothing of the kind. We are not insensible of the importance of the contribution to our equipment which has come to us from foreign countries, especially one foreign country. Nor are we ungrateful for it. But if Germany must needs ignore or minimize the gallantry of our soldiers in the field and account for its losses in terms of shells, let it know that it has not been the men of the neutral nations but the women of our own empire who have been the determining force in battering its trenches and breaking its legions.

We have always been proudly conscious of what the sons of Britain have been doing at the front. But is it not time we realized, not merely in abstract phrases or yet definite figures, but vividly, tangibly, and as by the evidence of our own eyes, what the daughters of Britain are doing at home?

To do this we must get close to the mighty army of women in our munition factories and we cannot do better than take a first sight of them at their work at Woolwich. The enemy knows Woolwich, where and what it is, therefore there can be no danger of revealing secrets. But though the vast arsenal is at our doors few of us who sleep in London under the broad shadow of its wings have any real sense of its colossal presence, its immense significance, the tremendous force it stands for. Its origin dates back to the days of other wars, but when the present war began its workers were only 14,000 in all, without a woman of their number. Now there are 17,000 women within its high walls and 50,000 men besides.

Surely this and such as this is a scene proper for man's work only—for man's muscle, man's naked and blackened body, man's brain and man's nerve alone. Every instinct of our nature revolts against the thought that woman, with the infinitely delicate organization which provides for her maternal functions, should under any circumstances whatever take part in the operations such scenes require, and just as we feel that our men only may do work like this so we must see at the swiftest glance that to any question of which of our men should do it there can be one answer only—the skilled and brawny men who can do it best. Once across the threshold of the places I have attempted to describe, and there can be no test for the workers but one test—capacity. Capacity to fight this mighty battle with natural forces and compel them to obey man's will, capacity to turn out the largest number and most perfect specimens of guns and shells. Man-power for the field, yes, but man-power for the forgers also. To forget that in this hour would be fatal.

Part the Women Play.

But Woolwich has a world of operations that are entirely suitable for women, and in a few minutes more we are in the midst of them. There is a new shop entirely operated by women, having been built for them since the beginning of the war. The vast place covers an area which is apparently as great as that of Trafalgar Square. Two thousand women are here, and there is

room for 3,000 in all. Innumerable lathes, generally of small size, cover the cemented floor, with pulleys and wheels spinning in the air above them. It is a dense forest of machinery, pulsing and throbbing and whirring and tossing as from some unseen storm.

There is at first something so incongruous in the spectacle of women operating masses of powerful machinery (or indeed any machinery more formidable than a sewing machine) that for a moment, as you stand at the entrance, the sight is scarcely believable. But you go in and move around, and after a while the astonishing fact seems perfectly natural. Although most of the machines in this shop are small, some are large, and a few alarming. Here is a slip of a girl working one of the latter kind, a huge thing that has two large wheels like mill-wheels revolving at either side of her, and though she looks like a child in the jaws of some great, black monster, she does not seem to be the least afraid. Here is another young girl who is feeding a round disk with bits of metal that look like discolored farthings, and as her own particular Caliban eats them up it utters from its interior a hoarse grunt that hits you like a blow on the brain, yet she does not seem to hear.

All this sounds portentous in description, but at close quarters it looks astonishingly simple. The machines themselves seem almost human in their automatic intelligence, and, if you show a proper respect for their impetuous organism, they are not generally cruel. So the women get along very well with them, learning all their ways, their whims, their needs, and their limitations. It is surprising how speedily the women have wooed and won this new kind of male monster.

The vast workshop we are walking in is laid out on a simple methodical plan. The lathes are ranged in regular lines along the length of the place, with alleyways, called streets, between them. A few of the lathes seem to work almost automatically and to require little or no attention, but before each of the other machines a woman stands to start, stop, feed, and control it. Sometimes the machine goes wrong, a strap breaks or a tool wears out, and then a male mechanic, known as a setter, steps up to set it right. Sometimes it requires more than a woman's muscle to master it, and then a male laborer has to be called to pull the crank or turn the lever. In cross-streets forewomen sit at desks, or walk to and fro at the heads of their sections, and up and down the alleyways the under-forewomen, with their account books, pass from operator to operator to take tally of the work that has been done.

All Women in Overalls.

All the women wear the same uniform, a khaki-colored overall, girdled at the waist, and a cap of the shape of a bathing cap. This is in the interests of safety, lest the dress or the hair of the operator should be caught in the pulleys and belts of the machinery; but it has the further and not altogether negligible advantage, in the eyes of the male creature, of being extremely becoming. If there is any man in London who can pass through the workshops of Woolwich without thinking he has been looking at some thousands of the best-looking young women in the world, it is certainly not the present writer. Their hard work does not seem

to be doing much harm to their health, for their eyes are bright, their cheeks are fresh, and there is hardly any evidence of fatigue among them.

The clamorous and deafening noise of the machinery, its jar and whirr and clank, which make your temples throb, sings (after their first days in the factory) like music in their ears, and they would miss it if it stopped. They work day and night, in two shifts of twelve hours each, with a break of an hour for dinner and half an hour for tea. Their pay, which is usually by the piece, is generally large, the minimum being, I think, £1 a week, and the maximum £5 or £7.

But you realize that the lure of money is not the sole or yet the chief magnet that draws women to work for the war when you leave this immense workshop for the sinister-looking sheds in which the finished shells are filled. Everybody knows that a shell is not merely a lump of dead steel, but a living reservoir of compounds which have been brought up from the bowels of the earth and transformed into terrible explosives. Everybody knows, too, that somewhere the womb of the shell has to be loaded with its deadly charge. Therefore, there ought not to be any question of exciting public alarm (there is no reasonable cause for it) or any fear of betraying a secret to the enemy (it is no secret) if, as evidence of the moral and physical courage of the daughters of Britain, and as an example of the bravest single thing woman does for the war, risking her life at home even as man risks his life in the field, I describe the scene of what is known as the danger zone at Woolwich.

The Weighers of Powder.

A Zeppelin might drop a bomb on this noiseless place without doing much mischief. But what of the peril within itself, and the courage required to work in it? We walk along our causeway until we come to one of the detached wooden huts. The door is open (for fresh air is wanted) and electric light is streaming out of it. A dozen women are sitting within at two oblong tables, weighing and measuring out in little brass scales, like a chemist's, with all the care of apothecaries

small quantities of black, green, yellow, and blueish powder (which recall in their volcanic coloring the lakes of Kruisivik and the pits of Caltanasetta) and then pouring them into the open mouths of half empty shells that stand upright by their sides.

They talk very little—indeed, hardly at all. Perhaps their work requires all their attention; perhaps their spirits are under the spell of the deadly things they are dealing with. Some of them are wearing over their mouths and nostrils light green veils that are like the veils of Arab women inverted; others, in their indifference to danger, have tucked their respirators into their waistbands, and are working with nostrils and mouths exposed.

It is not for long we can bear to look on a scene like this, so fearfully charged with spiritual as well as physical tragedy, and when we step back to the causeway outside we breathe more freely. It is still very quiet. The moonlight is now shining clear on the wraithlike figures, which are moving silently to and fro in their rubber slippers. The river must be somewhere near, for we hear the sirens of the steamers that are sailing by, and sometimes the lap of the running waters. We have a sense, too, of the imminent presence of the great city that is unseen and unheard from here, though not far away. Its tumultuous life must now be at the high tide of early evening, with its darkened but crowded thoroughfares, its hurrying taxis, its glimmering theatres, its surging railway stations, and its faces, faces, faces everywhere. And is it only an effect of the strained and perhaps disordered condition of one's nerves, at sight of these brave and fearless women filling with deadly explosives the shells that are soon to batter down the trenches of the enemy who lies in wait behind them to kill their husbands and lovers on the battlefield, that, as one stands in the breathless silence of this sombre spot, one thinks one hears the low, deep, far-off booming of the great guns across the sea?

For centuries the spirit of mankind has knelt at the feet of its great creators, its Miltons and its Dantes, in awe of their awful imaginings. But what are the highest reaches of the imaginative mind compared with the realities of that mightiest of all tragic poets—war!

The war brought women out of their homes and into the factories to do the work that used to be done by men. These two photos show women working in munitions factories in Woolwich, England.

"All the News That's Fit to Print."

The New York Times.

THE WEATHER
Fair today; Thursday increasingly cloudy, warmer; east winds.

VOL. LXVI...NO. 21,487. ... NEW YORK, WEDNESDAY, NOVEMBER 22, 1916.—TWENTY-FOUR PAGES. ONE CENT

EMPEROR FRANCIS JOSEPH DEAD AFTER 68 YEARS ON AUSTRIA'S THRONE; CARL FRANCIS JOSEPH NOW EMPEROR

AGED RULER STRONG TO END

Refused to Obey Orders of Physicians and Gave Audiences Daily.

WAS UP ALL DAY MONDAY

But Is Reported to Have Received the Last Sacraments on Saturday.

REIGN FULL OF TROUBLE

His Death Amid War He Precipitated One of Many Hapsburg Tragedies.

LONDON, Wednesday, Nov. 22.—Emperor Francis Joseph died last night at 9 o'clock at Schönbrunn Castle, according to a Reuter dispatch from Vienna, by way of Amsterdam.

He had been suffering for some time from lung trouble, which a few days ago became acute.

A Geneva dispatch forwarded to Reuter's by way of Amsterdam yesterday quoted the Katolische Zeitung as saying the sacrament was administered on Saturday.

The Emperor retained his extraordinary vigor to the end, and his disinclination to obey the orders of his physician caused them the greatest anxiety. He insisted on giving audiences daily, and on Sunday conferred with Premier von Koerber for an hour, according to Vienna advices. He was out of bed all day Monday, it is stated, and in the evening received several visitors

The first intimation received here that his health was again the subject of solicitation was contained in a dispatch dated Nov. 12, emanating from a Vienna news agency, which reported that the Emperor had been suffering for some days from a slight catarrhal affection.

Subsequent reports from various sources, more or less conflicting, represented that his condition was becoming worse, but none indicated that his illness threatened to reach a critical state until the following bulletin was issued in Vienna early last evening:

"The seat of the inflammation in the right lung, established yesterday, has increased. The patient's temperature early this morning was 38.1 reaumur, at 2 o'clock 39.5, and this evening 39.6.

Breathing had accelerated to 30 respirations a minute. Appetite small and vitality visibly lowered."

What gave credence to the suspicion that his condition was much graver than the official bulletins indicated was the report, which still lacks official confirmation, that it had been decided to associate the heir to the throne Archduke Carl Francis, in the government of the country and that he was to assume the position on Dec. 2, on the sixty-eighth anniversary of the Emperor's ascension to the throne.

Telegraphing from Amsterdam the Central News correspondent says:

"Vienna reports that although the death of the Emperor had been expected, the news, which was printed in special editions of th enewspapers, made a deep impression on the public. A special Cabinet meeting was held. The heir to the throne, Archduke Charles Francis, has been for some time in Vienna.

"A meeting of the Hungarian Cabinet has been called at Budapest. Premier Tisza will afterward come to Vienna."

CAREER OF FRANCIS JOSEPH.

A Military Despot at First, He Afterward Became Just and Popular.

The Emperor Francis Joseph ascended the throne of Austria-Hungary in 1848. The sixty-eight years of his reign have seen the remaking of Europe, while at the present time almost the entire continent is at war.

Other nations have seen greater and more far-reaching changes than Austria in the two-thirds of a century covered by Francis Joseph's reign, but in no other of the greater powers have there been so many vicissitudes as those through which the aged ruler lived. He was born on Aug. 18 in the revolutionary year of 1830, and ascended the throne in the other revolutionary year 1848. Liberalism and Nationalism were beginning to show their full force when the boy of eighteen came to the throne from which his uncle had withdrawn in dismay at the problems confronting him. Francis Joseph began as the despot of a heterogeneous collection of races, held together by military power and the aristocracy of a favored nation. He was obliged to quell formidable attempts at secession, and was for some years apparently as powerful as any of his predecessors. Then came two disastrous wars, which cost Austria nearly all her Italian possessions, much of her prestige and her hegemony of the German States. A direct consequence of the second war was the "Ausgleich" of 1867, whereby the Hungarians, who had struck vainly for their liberty eighteen years previously, received nearly everything they had wanted.

At that point the fortunes of Austria were at their lowest ebb. But then came the close and very profitable alliance with Germany, which restored Austria to a strong position among the Powers. There was a Balkan policy which, if failing to reach Salonika, at least won Bosnia and Herzegovina; and Italy, though still at heart an enemy, became, in name at least, a friend. So, two years ago, it seemed as if the long career of Francis Joseph would end with his Empire once more on the upgrade.

The sudden rise of the Balkan League upset Austria's "Drang nach Osten." The Dual Monarchy seemed shut off from her chosen and ancient goal, the Aegean, and threatened on the south

by a power hostile to herself and friendly to Russia. But clever diplomacy neutralized much of the harm to Austrian interests resulting from the Balkan War, and only the strength of Serbian agitation, brought to a head by the murder of the heir to the Hapsburg throne, led to the final catastrophe.

Through all these vicissitudes the Emperor, whose task it was during most of his reign to keep together an Empire that, most observers predicted, must sooner or later break up, managed to grow out of the inexperience which weighed upon him when he first took up the sceptre, to throw off many of the traditions of absolutism which were incompatible with the duties of a constitutional monarch of the nineteenth century, and to make himself much loved in his own dominions and universally respected abroad. And he did this in spite of perhaps the most appalling series of domestic calamities that has ever befallen a king.

Succeeded in a Year of Revolutions

Francis Joseph succeeded to the throne of Austria in the year of revolutions, 1848. His uncle, the Emperor Ferdinand, was entirely unfit to meet the storm and stress of the rising tide of liberalism. His father, the Archduke Francis Charles, had abdicated his rights of succession in favor of his four His mother, the Princess Sophie, was an ambitious woman and persuaded

the Emperor to resign in favor of his eighteen-year-old nephew.

Francis Joseph at that time was far from being the wise statesman his later years proved him. He was a scholar, deeply read in jurisprudence, philosophy, and diplomacy. He was a famous linguist, and was fairly well acquainted with chemistry and natural science, but he could not realize the task before him. Austria has been cursed for centuries with the war of nationalities. Seventeen separate peoples, each with its own language and customs, each with its pride of race and love of freedom, are intermingled in the territories he ruled.

To satisfy them would have been difficult enough if each nationality had had a local habitation and could be allowed some form of autonomy within its own district. But there was none of this, and German and Magyar, Czech and Ruthonian rubbed shoulders on the streets and struggled for their own supremacy in every province and town of the empire.

The Europe the young Emperor had to face was far different from what it is now. Germany was still a congeries of States. Prussia had not yet risen to greatness by the genius of Bismarck and the Emperor William. It was still doubtful whether the Austrian Emperor, the claimant of the historic title of the Emperor, the direct successor of the Caesars, might not become the leader of the German world. Moreover, the

The Late Emperor Francis Joseph.

Austrian dominions extended beyond the Alps. In the north of Italy Venetia and Lombardy were under the imperial sway, and, with Italy still divided, constituted a constant temptation to interfere in the politics of that peninsula.

The immediate dangers which confronted Francis Joseph in his accession were revolts in these Italian provinces and in Hungary. The former were put down first. The King of Sardinia met with a heavy check in his attempt to wrest Italian soil from the alien power, and after the defeat of Novara, three months after the Emperor's reign had begun, was forced to pay a heavy indemnity.

In Hungary Austria met with a greater difficulty. Kossuth had kindled a fire of liberty which was beyond all the power of the empire to check, and only by calling upon Russia to aid with 100,000 troops were the brave patriots suppressed and their great leader forced to fly.

Dissolved the Reichsrath.

The young man of 20 who thus saw himself victorious after the severest trials was not likely to deny himself the fruits of his victory. Brought up in an absolute régime, surrounded by advisers of the old school, encouraged by his mother to preserve every particle of his prerogative, he proved himself for a time a thoroughgoing reactionary. In spite of his promise at his accession to resuscitate Austria upon the basis of "liberty and equality before the law," within three months he dissolved the Reichsrath, and two years later, on Dec. 31, 1851, he formally abolished the Constitution which had lingered only in name.

Henceforth for some years absolutism and military despotism were the rule in his dominions, and he gave himself up to the sordid amusements which have been the curse of so many monarchs. It is said that his awakening came in a dramatic fashion. On Feb. 15, 1853, as he was reviewing his army on the Schmeis, a young Hungarian, Joseph Libenyi, sprang from the crowd and aimed a blow at his throat with a long, sharp butcher's knife. Only the large buckle worn by Austrian officers saved Francis Joseph's life, and before the assassin could strike again he was seized by Count O'Donnel, an Irishman in the imperial service.

Francis Joseph, it is said, took the attack deeply to heart, and realized that there was something wrong with a régime which could lead to such an attack. He became more liberal in his views, and his marriage to the Princess Elizabeth of Bavaria in 1854 confirmed him in his altered policy. She was a liberal in every way, and his meeting with her was a happy day for Austria. As a matter of fact, there was something of chance about it. The Emperor's mother desired him to marry Elizabeth's elder sister, the Princess Helena, but Francis Joseph met the younger sister of the woman he had agreed to marry, and at once transferred his proposals to her.

Crushed in Two Battles.

At this period Austria was at the height of its power, but was soon to see it begin to decline. The struggle for a "United Italy" was entering upon its final stage, and in 1859 Napoleon III., in the pursuit of his tortuous diplomacy, joined hands with the King of Sardinia. They declared war upon Francis Joseph and crushed him at the battles of Magenta and Solferino. As a consequence he was forced to grant freedom to the rich Province of Lombardy.

Eight years later came another crushing blow. Prussia was strong enough to dispute the supremacy it had allowed to Austria in 1850. The complicated Schleswig-Holstein question gave the excuse, and in the Summer of 1867 Bismarck brought on war. With astonishing celerity, within seven weeks the battle of Königgrätz had been lost and won. Austria was prostrate before the genius of Moltke, and King William could dictate what terms he liked. Austria lost Venetia and was forced back upon itself. Its aspiration to control the destinies of the German-speaking peoples was crushed for ever, and Francis Joseph was left to face the difficult problem of governing his heterogeneous subjects undistracted by the claims of world politics.

His defeat in Italy in 1859 had already made him far more liberal in his policy. In 1860 he had undone the mistake of the first years of his reign and given to Austria a Parliament. In 1867 he opened at Pesth the first Diet of the Kingdom of Hungary. From this has been developed the dual Constitution which allows Austria and Hungary perfect autonomy in all internal affairs, but a common Ministry as far as foreign relations, war, and finance are concerned.

Moreover, in 1867, still further to win the allegiance of his Hungarian subjects, he was crowned their king. To this proud people this was no empty ceremony. Their King must come to Pesth and assume the historic crown of St. Stephen. Then he must ascend on horseback a mound of earth brought from every part of the monarchy and lunge with his sword north, south, east, and west, in token of his determination to defend every portion of his dominions. Then and then only would he be recognized as the true "Apostolic King."

Popular with Hungarians.

From this dates the surprising popularity of Francis Joseph with the Hungarians. Since that day again and again have Austrian and Hungarian stood at daggers drawn. Again and again has it seemed certain that the Dual Monarchy would be rent in twain, but at every crisis the personal popularity of the aged Emperor somehow prevented an open split. A few years ago, when the Hungarian Parliament denied the right of the crown to call out the reservists when necessary, the old Emperor's threat to abdicate as King of Hungary carried his point. Part of this feeling toward him he had engendered by his great linguistic gifts. German though he always professed himself in his early life to be, he could speak the tongue of every one of his subjects, and was able to discuss with them their grievances and aspirations.

The war with Prussia and the establishment of the Triple Alliance with the German Empire and Italy seemed to fix the position of Austria-Hungary in Europe. For years it was at peace, content to play a somewhat secondary, but none the less important, part in European affairs, till in 1908 it took a step which startled the world. In 1878, at the Congress of Berlin, Austria had received the right to administer the Provinces of Bosnia and Herzegovina. They still remained nominally subject to the suzerainty of the Sultan of Turkey, but they were governed entirely from Vienna.

Under the new régime they prospered exceedingly, and the complex nationalities and religions of what had been one of the danger spots of Europe dwelt in harmony side by side. Then came the fall of Abdul Hamid, and the rise of the Young Turk Party. Constitutionality was to be the order of the day in the Turkish Empire, and Austria feared that she might be asked to restore the two provinces. Moreover, she dreaded the rise of the Slavic idea and a movement on the part of Montenegro and Serbia to revive the old Serb Empire. So the aged Emperor, on Oct. 6, 1908, issued a decree formally annexing the two provinces to his empire, and promising them a liberal Constitution. Russia, France, and Great Britain protested, the Kaiser stood grimly behind his old ally, and, in spite of the heartburnings of the Triple Entente, the annexation became at once an accomplished fact.

Austria and the Dreibund.

To Germany's firm support of her ally on this occasion, when William II., in his own phrase, "Stood forth in shining armor," may be traced the series of international difficulties which have culminated in the present great war. The attitude of Germany aroused undying resentment in Russia as well as in Serbia, and caused considerable ill-feeling in Italy. Yet it was perhaps the most remarkable triumph of the Triple Alliance, and the most prominent instance in which German support proved invaluable to Austria.

Italy, Austria's deadly enemy for many years, became, on the establishment of the Triple Alliance, her reluctant friend through the very necessity of the Adriatic situation, which required that the two powers must either be allies or constantly on the verge of war. For thirty years peace has been kept between the two nations, and it is only now, when Italian interests and sympathy are both on the side of the allies against the German powers, that the Government of Italy has shown its hand.

Bismarck, to be sure, foresaw something of the sort from the first. "If a single Italian soldier faces west when the war comes," he is reported to have said, "I shall be satisfied." But the fact that the alliance held as long and successfully as it did has brought considerable advantage to both powers and, backed by Italy and Germany, Francis Joseph's empire seemed from 1883 to 1912 on the road to renewed prosperity and power.

The culmination of this era was the annexation of Bosnia and Herzegovina. Three years afterward the formation of the Balkan League and its victories over Turkey brought about a great change in the position of the Dual Monarchy. The road to Salonika was suddenly blocked by a young and vigorous confederation, and a tremendous impetus had been given to centrifugal and nationalistic movements among the Slavs f Austria-Hungary. The second Balkan war, which broke up the formidable league that threatened Austria on her southern frontier, has usually been attributed to the "Machiavellian wiles" of Austria. But, though Bulgaria was humbled, there remained a strengthened Rumania, an overgrown Greece, and, most serious of all for the Dual Monarchy, a Serbia which was greatly expanded, flushed with victory, and enthusiastic for union with the Serb peoples of the Hapsburg Empire. And it was the rise of Serbia, which, directly or indirectly, after the murder of the heir to the throne, led the statesmen of the Dual Monarchy to resolve at last to risk the very existence of their empire on an appeal to the sword.

Little that can be considered authentic has been known in this country of the part the aged Emperor played in the war. It was generally believed that it was at a hint from him that the Kaiser determined not to attend the funeral of the Archduke Franz Ferdinand, but if Francis Joseph had decided to maintain independence of action for his empire, he found it impossible to carry out this policy.

Berlin knew exactly what diplomatic steps Vienna was taking in the last frenzied hours before strife broke out, and, month by month, as the Austrian Army showed itself unable to hold off the Russians, the German influence grew. The Kaiser paid Francis Joseph a visit a few months after the war had begun, and it was followed immediately by rumors that a Zollverein after peace had been concluded had been already decided upon by the two empires. So in his last days the aged Emperor, weighed down with domestic sorrows and oppressed by the sufferings of his people from the war, saw his authority as a monarch steadily diminished and the prestige of his throne stolen by his ally.

Many Domestic Misfortunes.

Emperor Francis Joseph met with a series of domestic misfortunes which befall few men. The superstitious among his subjects, as again and again they have seen the imperial house plunged into mourning, have called to mind the curse of the Countess Karolyi. Her son was put to death in 1848 for participation in the Kossuth rising, and she called on heaven to blast the happiness of the Emperor, to exterminate his family, to strike him through those he loved, and to wreck his life and ruin his children.

The first in the long roll of Hapsburgs who met a sad fate was the Emperor's brother Maximilian, whom Napoleon III. sent on his mad expedition to Mexico and there deserted. Then came the mysterious death of his son, the Crown Prince Rudolph, in 1887.

He had been married for six years to the Princess Stéphanie, daughter of the King of Belgium. The marriage had been a loveless one, and the disappointment when, two and a half years after their union, a daughter and not an heir was born to them, was great.

In the Autumn of 1887 the Crown Prince met the Baroness Marie Vetsera. She was a beautiful woman and Rudolph conceived a violent passion for her at first sight. It was whispered that he even intended to resign his rights to the throne in order that he might put away the Princess Stéphanie. The Emperor heard the rumors and sent for his son. A stormy interview followed, but it was announced that the Crown Prince had determined to part from the Baroness.

A last meeting, according to the most reliable of the stories available, was arranged at Rudolph's hunting lodge near Mayerling. Bratfisch, a singer of note, drove them out, and an enjoyable evening was passed with Prince Philip of Coburg, Count Hoyos, and Bratfisch. It was noticed that Rudolph, contrary to his usual custom, drank heavily, and it was 2 o'clock before he left his companions.

Next morning at 7 o'clock Bratfisch went to awake him to go hunting. He found, lying upon a couch and completely covered with wild flowers, the Baroness dead, and on the floor near her side the Crown Prince, a heavy cavalry pistol in his hand and the back of his head blown off.

The Crown Princess Stéphanie herself a few years later contracted a marriage outside the circle of royalty with Count Elmer Lonyay de Nagy Lonya.

A nephew of the Emperor, the Archduke Johann, has disappeared, and whether he lives or is dead is unknown to this day. As John Orth, skipper of the vessel Santa Margaretha, he is believed to have been wrecked on the voyage to Chile, but many stories have been printed from time to time of his reappearance.

At the terrible fire in Paris which consumed a charity bazaar and burned to death numbers of the most prominent persons of the French capital, the Duchess d'Alençon, the sister-in-law of the Emperor, was one of the victims.

The Empress Elizabeth herself was foully murdered by an Anarchist. She was staying at Geneva in September, 1898, and was taking a walk from her hotel. She was without guards, for it has never been the habit of the Austrian royal family to hide themselves behind the police. A man named Luccheni sprang out upon her and killed her before any one could come to her assistance. When the aged monarch heard the news he exclaimed: "It seems that no sorrow is to be spared me."

Eight years ago his favorite grandchild, the pretty little Princess Elisabeth, who had married, against Francis Joseph's wishes, Prince Otto of Windisch-Grätz, shot her husband's mistress, with whom she surprised him at Prague.

The latest tragedy which afflicted the old Emperor, and the one which directly occasioned the great war in which his reign ended, was the murder on June 28, 1914, at Sarajevo, Bosnia, of his nephew and heir, the Archduke Francis Ferdinand, and the Duchess of Hohenberg, the Archduke's consort. This murder, by a band of Serbs who thought they were striking for Bosnian independence, brought on the war between Austria and Serbia, and then the great European war. It left the young Archduke Charles Francis Joseph, grandnephew of the late Emperor, as the heir to the throne.

Chief Servant of His People.

But with all his private griefs Francis Joseph ever bore himself as the chief servant of his people. He mixed freely among them, he received them in public audience, and worked harder at the business of governing than any of his Ministers.

Twice a week, when he was in Vienna, he received in audience any one who had a petition to lay before him. Standing at a table, he would greet the petitioner without formality, and, referring to a paper on which was a list of those who were to be admitted, he would inquire closely into the complaint in whatever one of the seventeen languages of his dominions the petitioner might happen to speak. On his hunting trips in the mountains he wandered about without ceremony, and many a mountaineer has had the Emperor stop at his cottage for a friendly chat or a few minutes' rest.

"All the News That's Fit to Print."

The New York Times.

THE WEATHER
Fair today; Friday rain, warmer; west winds, diminishing.
For full weather report see [illegible]

VOL. LXVI...NO. 21,502. .... NEW YORK, THURSDAY, DECEMBER 7, 1916.—TWENTY-FOUR PAGES. ONE CENT in Greater New York, Jersey City and Newark. | Elsewhere, TWO CENTS.

LLOYD GEORGE TO BE BRITISH PREMIER; TEUTON HOSTS OCCUPY BUCHAREST; JOFFRE'S RETIREMENT CONSIDERED

ALL PARTIES IN CABINET

Bonar Law and Derby Likely to Play Big Role in the New Ministry.

KING STRIVES FOR HARMONY

Confers with Leaders at Palace, but Bonar Law Refuses to Take the Helm.

LABORITES HOLD ALOOF

Look on the New Premier as an Enemy—Nationalists Also Withhold Support.

LONDON, Thursday, Dec. 7.—David Lloyd George, having overthrown the Asquith Cabinet, will become Prime Minister himself.

The new Government will be coalition, similar to the old one, but probably without the same measure of harmonious support which attended the formation of the first coalition Government, because its birth has created additional factional differences.

The official announcement, as made in the Court circular last night, read:

> The King gave a further audience this evening to Mr. Bonar Law, who intimated that he was unable to form an administration. Thereupon the King summoned Mr. Lloyd George, who, at his Majesty's request, undertook to endeavor to form an administration.

This result emerged from another day of active and hurried party conferences, and a day of intense suspense and interest throughout the country.

There was a prospect yesterday afternoon that the personal offices of the King might solve the situation, and many thought that the Asquith régime might be continued. The King called the party leaders to Buckingham Palace and conferred with them for more than an hour.

Mr. Asquith and Mr. Lloyd George of the Liberals, Mr. Bonar Law and Mr. Balfour of the Unionists, and Mr. Henderson of the Labor Party, were with the sovereign. It is many years since a British ruler assembled the representatives of the different factions face to face when they had shown themselves unable to settle their differences. But no such serious crisis had arisen before to require such action by the King.

Whatever passed in the conference is held secret, but the inference that the King tried to arrange a reconciliation appears a most natural one. The five statesmen departed separately, at 4:30 o'clock, four in their motor cars, and the workingmen's spokesman afoot.

According to persons who saw Mr. Asquith, he presented a worn and grave appearance. The war has left unmistakable marks upon his vigorous frame and features, but yesterday there was something more—a tinge of weariness, physical, as well as mental. Usually reserved and singularly unemotional, he betrayed signs of the strain in the very gesture with which he flung himself well back out of public sight in the corner of his motor car.

After Mr. Asquith returned to his official residence, he was visited by several of his colleagues in the late Government. Mr. Lloyd George was also in consultation with some of his supporters.

Afterward the King gave an audience to Mr. Bonar Law, who declined to undertake the formation of a new Ministry, and then to Mr. Lloyd George, who accepted the responsibility, as every one expected he would if the opportunity came to him.

The official announcement at night that Mr. Lloyd George had undertaken the task, with the co-operation of Mr. Bonar Law, was a notification that the new Government would be coalition. Any party Government would be impossible because neither the Unionists nor the Liberals have a majority in the House of Commons; either one must obtain the support of the Irish Nationalists or the Laborites to command a majority.

The Nationalists have refused to participate in the Government until home rule becomes established. The Laborites are sworn enemies to Mr. Lloyd George because they resent his accusations that the workingmen have put their personal interests above the national interests at times during the war.

That the Laborites are not likely to support a Lloyd George administration was further indicated at a meeting yesterday of the Parliamentary Committee of the trades unions, which adopted a resolution unanimously expressing profound regret "that certain statesmen, influenced by the press campaign, have, in the hour of the nation's crisis, entirely failed to observe loyalty and self-sacrifice, which they repeatedly urged upon the workmen during the war."

The resolution continues:

"Further, we earnestly hope that the present unseemly quarrel among those intrusted with great responsibilities shall immediately cease, and so set a better example to the workers."

Bonar Law, Sir Edward Carson, and the Earl of Derby probably will act under Mr. Lloyd George, as they supported his ultimatum to Premier Asquith regarding the formation of a smaller war council.

What New Government Means.

The country awaits the rising of the curtain on the next act of this historical and remarkable crisis with an expectancy which never surrounded the beginning of any previous Government. The Lloyd George Ministry means the direction of the war by a Dictatorship in the form of an Inner Council of the Cabinet and means the scrapping of those elder statesmen, whose supremacy in the councils of the nation, until they chose to withdraw from the scene voluntarily, has always heretofore been regarded by the British people as a matter of course.

Mr. Asquith, Mr. Balfour, Viscount Grey, and Lord Lansdowne "must go," the Lloyd George press has been crying. But their going will be attended by widespread misgivings among the people, who have thought their knowledge and experience as necessary to the Government as the push and driving power of the group which will succeed them.

Mr. Lloyd George is committed to the formation of a War Council, and the membership of that dictatorship will be the most important and crucial work he will have to deal with. Andrew Bonar Law, the Earl of Derby, and Sir Edward Carson, all of them Conservatives, are most talked of. Mr. Bonar Law and Lord Derby would be generally approved, but Sir Edward Carson has many critics, who concede his talents as a brillinat lawyer, but question whether he has also the stability, sound judgment and business experience for directing war measures.

The new Premier is confronted with the problem whether or not he will become a member of his own War Council. His scheme for the council, which he presented to Premier Asquith as the price of his continuance in the Asquith Cabinet, excluded the Premier on the ground that the general duties of the office did not leave time for daily sessions, to which the council must devote itself. The question whether or not Lord Northcliffe, to whom more than to any one, unless himself, Mr. Lloyd George owes his advancement, will enter the Cabinet is much discussed. If he does, the presence there of Mr. Asquith, Viscount Grey, and Mr. Balfour, whom Lord Norhtcliffe's newspapers call "the Haldane gang," apparently becomes entirely improbable.

Who will be Minister for Foreign Affairs and Chancellor of the Exchequer—two of the most important offices outside of the military and naval spheres—is a matter of speculation, on which predictions are all guesswork. The House of Commons will meet today, (Thursday,) but no notice regarding the new Government is expected. An official note last night says the proceedings will be formal and that no questions will be answered.

FRENCH ARMY CHIEF MAY GO

Nivelle, Now Commander at Verdun, Suggested to Succeed Him.

PETAIN FIRST PROPOSED

But He Is Said to Have Demanded Larger Control Than France Alone Could Grant.

Special to The New York Times.

WASHINGTON, D. C., Dec. 6.—That part of official Washington, inclusive of the foreign diplomatic body which follows with close attention the trend of events in Europe, is on the tiptoe of expectation over the prospect of momentous changes in the administration of the great war by the Entente Allies. The feeling of expectancy has been emphasized by bits of information that have drifted into Washington from European capitals indicating substantial basis for the guarded press comment from London and Paris concerning dissatisfaction over the conduct of the struggle with the Central Powers.

Beyond what is printed in the newspapers, little is known here as to the ins and outs of the reported Cabinet crisis in Great Britain. For many reasons, however, there is a disposition to credit suggestions that a new deal is impending in the Government of hostile operations by both England and France. What is known most definitely applies particularly to French conduct of the war.

The secret sessions of the French Chamber of Deputies now being held are expected to develop important changes, of which a hint has already been heard on this side of the Atlantic. It is known here that one of the chief questions the Chamber has been considering is the reorganization of the French high command and that this may include the retirement of General Joffre.

Dispatches from Paris, published in the newspapers, are already speaking of "considerable alterations at the front," of "steps taken and to be taken in reorganizing the high command," and of the "organization of an inter-allied command," all implying that General Joffre is to quit his present post.

That the great French commander is about to retire from active service in the field will come as a surprise to most people. But the considerations that have led to the understood decision to relieve him are regarded as paramount in the present circumstances. It is felt that General Joffre has done his work. He has organized a superb defense and made the French Army an instrument that is capable of bringing victory to the Allied arms under a younger and more active man. Joffre is 64.

When the decision was reached that General Joffre should relinquish his command General Petain, Commander of the French forces in the notable successful resistance of the German attempt to take Verdun, was picked as Joffre's successor. Difficulties arose, however, over accomplishing the contemplated change. It is understood that the proposal to Petrain was that he should command, personally and directly, all the allied forces in France—French, British, and Belgian.

Petain's rise in rank and fame has been remarkable. At the beginning of the war he was only a Colonel of infantry. When things were going badly at Verdun, Joffre took Petain out of the reserve army and appointed him commander of the forces defending that sector. He is a modest man, with marked objection to being advertised, and little has been heard of him in this country. But in the French Army he is looked upon as a wonderful soldier and some of those who know him have predicted that he would prove to be the superman who would eventually lead the French forces to victory.

After some discussion, however, General Petain, it is understood, has declined the flattering proposal of those who determine matters of policy in France. The whole story affecting his attitude has not reached this country, but enough is known to indicate that Petain's declination was due to a belief on his part that, in order to achieve victory, he must be invested with greater authority than it was proposed to give him.

How much power he demanded is not made clear. It may have been the supreme command of all the allied armies in their several fields of activity. Or it may have been that Petain felt that to gain the end he sought—victory for the allied cause—he should have not only command of the armies in France, but control over the resources of the nation. Perhaps, it is suggested, Petain may have insisted that all armies and all resources should be placed in his charge by the allied Governments. At any rate, the negotiations ended in his elimination, for the present, from the choice for supreme command.

"All the News That's Fit to Print."

The New York Times.

THE WEATHER
Fair, colder, diminishing west winds today; Thursday fair, cold.
For full weather report see 23.

VOL. LXVI...NO. 21,508. ....   NEW YORK, WEDNESDAY, DECEMBER 13, 1916.—TWENTY-FOUR PAGES.   ONE CENT In Greater New York, Jersey City and Newark. | Elsewhere TWO CENTS

GERMANY AND HER ALLIES OFFER TO NEGOTIATE FOR PEACE; NO TERMS NAMED IN NOTES TO NEUTRALS AND THE POPE; LONDON SKEPTICAL, BUT WILL CONSIDER THE PROPOSALS

THE CHANCELLOR'S SPEECH

Tells Reichstag Germany and Her Allies Are Unconquerable.

Disclaims Any Aim to Shatter or Annihilate Their Adversaries.

THRONG CHEERS HIS WORDS

Floor and Galleries Packed, While Huge Crowds Surround Building.

BERLIN, Dec. 12, (by Wireless to Sayville.)—Proposals by Germany and her allies to the Entente Powers to enter into peace negotiations were announced in the Reichstag today by Chancellor von Bethmann Hollweg in the course of a speech, during which he read an identical note submitted through the United States, Spain, and Switzerland.

Earlier in the day the Chancellor had received the representatives of these countries, which are protecting German interests in hostile countries, and had handed the note to them with the request that they bring it to the knowledge of the hostile countries.

In the note the four Central powers propose to enter forthwith on peace negotiations. The propositions, which they bring forth for such negotiations, are, according to their firm belief, appropriate for the establishment of a lasting peace.

The Governments at Vienna, Constantinople, and Sofia transmitted identical notes and also communicated with the Holy See and all other neutral powers."

Practically all the Members of Parliament answered the unexpected summons. The crowded House and thronged galleries listened in attentive silence when the Chancellor rose for his speech. The Chancellor first outlined the extraordinary political situation and then, insisting upon the achievements of the Central Powers, made the announcement which possibly may be the turning point in the war which for more than two years held the world under its spell.

Diplomats Hear Speech.

The galleries and the royal box were crowded when the Chancellor began speaking. All the Ambassadors and Ministers of foreign Governments were in the diplomatic box. The American Chargé d'Affaires, Joseph C. Grew, and Mrs. Grew were among those present, as were the Ministers of Argentina, Brazil, Chile, and the other States of Central and South America.

The Reichstag building was surrounded by a great crowd, and the adjoining streets were thronged. The people were intensely interested, and the Imperial Chancellor, on his arrival, was cordially greeted in the usual fashion.

The Chancellor began his speech in a clear, loud, ringing voice. His first utterances were greeted with applause on all sides, and at frequent points in his speech the assembly assented in demonstrative fashion. Later, however, when he touched upon the question of policy, differences of opinion made themselves felt, the applause coming mainly from the Catholic Centre and the Left. At the conclusion of his address a majority of the House applauded and the galleries joined in the handclapping.

The Chancellor said:

"The Reichstag had been adjourned for a long period, but fortunately it was left to the discretion of the President as to the day of the next meeting. This discretion was caused by the hope that soon happy events in the field would be recorded, a hope fulfilled quicker, almost, than expected. I shall be brief, for actions speak for themselves."

The Chancellor said Rumania had entered the war in order to roll up the German positions in the east and those of Germany's allies. At the same time the grand offensive on the Somme had as its object to pierce the German western front, and the renewed Italian attacks were intended to paralyze Austria-Hungary.

"The situation was serious," said the Chancellor. "But with God's help our troops shaped conditions so as to give us security which not only is complete, but still more so than ever before. The western front stands. Not only does it stand, but in spite of the Rumanian campaign it is fitted out with larger reserves of men and material than it had been formerly. The most effective precautions have been taken against all Italian diversions. And while on the Somme and on the Carso the drum-fire resounded while the Russians launched troops against the eastern frontier of Transylvania, Field Marshall von Hindenburg captured the whole of western Wallachia and the hostile capital of Bucharest, leading with unparalleled genius the troops that in competition with all the allies made possible what hitherto was considered impossible.

Vast Supplies Seized.

"And Hindenburg does not rest, military operations progress. By strokes of the sword at the same time firm foundations for our economic needs have been laid. Great stocks of grain, victuals, oil, and other goods fell into our hands in Rumania. Their transport has begun. In spite of scarcity, we could have lived on our own supplies, but now our safety is beyond question.

"To these great events on land, heroic deeds of equal importance are added by our submarines. The spectre of famine, which our enemies intended to appear before us, now pursues them without mercy. When after the termination of the first year of the war the Emperor addressed the nation in a public appeal, he said: 'Having witnessed such great events, my heart was filled with awe and determination.' Neither our Emperor nor our nation ever changed their minds in this respect. Neither have they now. The genius and heroic acts of our leaders have fashioned these facts as firm as iron. If the enemy counted upon the weariness of his enemy, then he was deceived.

"The Reichstag, by means of the national auxiliary war service law, helped to build a new offensive and defensive bulwark in the midst of the great struggle. Behind the fighting army stands the nation at work—the gigantic force of the nation, working for the common aim.

"The empire is not a besieged fortress, as our adversaries imagined, but one gigantic and firmly disciplined camp with inexhaustible resources. That is the German Empire, which is firmly and faithfully united with its brothers in arms, who have been tested in battle under the Austro-Hungarian, Turkish, and Bulgarian flags.

"Our enemies now ascribed to us a plan to conquer the whole world, and then desperate cries of anguish for peace. But not confused by these asseverations, we progressed with firm decision, and we thus continue our progress, always ready to defend ourselves and fight for our nation's existence, for its free future, and always ready for this price to stretch out our hand for peace.

Not Deaf to Peace.

"Our strength has not made our ears deaf to our responsibility before God, before our own nation and before humanity. The declarations formerly made by us concerning our readiness for peace were evaded by our adversaries. Now we have advanced one step further in this direction. On Aug. 1, 1914, the Emperor had personally to take the gravest decision which ever fell to the lot of a German—the order for mobilization—which he was compelled to give as a result of the Russian mobilization. During these long and earnest years of the war the Emperor has been moved by a single thought: How peace could be restored to safeguard Germany after the struggle in which she has fought victoriously.

"Nobody can testify better to this than I who bear the responsibility for all actions of the Government. In a deep moral and religious sense of duty toward his nation and, beyond it, toward humanity, the Emperor now considers that the moment has come for official action toward peace. His Majesty therefore, in complete harmony and in common with our allies, decided to propose to the hostile powers to enter peace negotiations. This morning I transmitted a note to this effect to all the hostile powers, through the representatives of those powers which are watching over our interests and rights in the hostile States. I asked the representatives of Spain, the United States and Switzerland to forward that note.

"The same procedure has been adopted today in Vienna, Constantinople and Sofia. Other neutral States and His Holiness the Pope have been similarly informed."

The Reichstag adjourned, to be reconvened at the call of the President. Prior to adjournment, the President of the Chamber declared that the nation and its representatives would always support the Chancellor in a policy which was farsighted and intelligent.

Await Answer Serenely.

The Chancellor then read the note, and, continuing, said:

"Gentlemen, in August, 1914, our enemies challenged the superiority of power in the world war. Today we raise the question of peace, which is a question of humanity. We await the answer of our enemies with that sereneness of mind which is guaranteed to us by our exterior and interior strength, and by our clear conscience. If our enemies decline to end the war, if they wish to take upon themselves the world's heavy burden of all these terrors which hereafter will follow, then even in the least and smallest homes every German heart will burn in sacred wrath against our enemies, who are unwilling to stop human slaughter in order that their plans of conquest and annihilation may continue."

German Chancellor Von Bethmann Hollweg.

Text of the Teutonic Notes to the Neutral Powers and the Pope

To the Neutral Powers.

BERLIN, Dec. 12.—Following is the text of the note addressed by Germany and her allies to the neutral powers for transmission to the Entente Allies:

"The most terrific war experienced in history has been raging for the last two years and a half over a large part of the world—a catastrophe which thousands of years of common civilization was unable to prevent and which injures the most precious achievements of humanity.

"Our aims are not to shatter nor annihilate our adversaries. In spite of our consciousness of our military and economic strength and our readiness to continue the war (which has been forced upon us) to the bitter end, if necessary; at the same time, prompted by the desire to avoid further bloodshed and make an end to the atrocities of war, the four allied powers propose to enter forthwith into peace negotiations.

"The propositions which they bring forward for such negotiations, and which have for their object a guarantee of the existence, of the honor and liberty of evolution for their nations, are, according to their firm belief, an appropriate basis for the establishment of a lasting peace.

"The four allied powers have been obliged to take up arms to defend justice and the liberty of national evolution. The glorious deeds of our armies have in no way altered their purpose. We always maintained the firm belief that our own rights and justified claims in no way control the rights of these nations.

"The spiritual and material progress which were the pride of Europe at the beginning of the twentieth century are threatened with ruin. Germany and her allies, Austria-Hungary, Bulgaria, and Turkey, gave proof of their unconquerable strength in this struggle. They gained gigantic advantages over adversaries superior in number and war material. Our lines stand unshaken against ever-repeated attempts made by armies.

"The last attack in the Balkans has been rapidly and victoriously overcome. The most recent events have demonstrated that further continuance of the war will not result in breaking the resistance of our forces, and the whole situation with regard to our troops justifies our expectation of further successes.

"If, in spite of this offer of peace and reconciliation, the struggle should go on, the four allied powers are resolved to continue to a victorious end, but they disclaim responsibility for this before humanity and history. The Imperial Government, through the good offices of your Excellency, asks the Government of [here is inserted the name of the neutral power addressed in each instance] to bring this communication to the knowledge of the Government of [here are inserted the names of the belligerents.] "

To the Vatican.

BERLIN, Dec. 12.—The note of the German Government, as presented by Dr. von Muhlberg, German Minister to the Vatican, to Cardinal Gasparri, Papal Secretary of State, reads as follows:

"According to instructions received, I have the honor to send to your Eminence a copy of the declaration of the Imperial Government today, which by the good offices of the powers instrusted with the protection of German interests in the countries with which the German Empire is in a state of war, transmits to these States, and in which the Imperial Government declares itself ready to enter into peace negotiations. The Austro-Hungarian, Turkish, and Bulgarian Governments also have sent similar notes.

"The reasons which prompted Germany and her allies to take this step are manifest. For two years and a half a terrible war has been devastating the European Continent. Unlimited treasures of civilization have been destroyed. Extensive areas have been soaked with blood. Millions of brave soldiers have fallen in battle and millions have returned home as invalids. Grief and sorrow fill almost every house.

"Not only upon the belligerent nations, but also upon neutrals, the destructive consequences of the gigantic struggle weigh heavily. Trade and commerce, carefully built up in years of peace, have been depressed. The best forces of the nation have been withdrawn from the production of useful objects. Europe, which formerly was devoted to the propagation of religion and civilization, which was trying to find solutions for social problems, and was the home of science and art and all peaceful labor, now resembles an immense war camp, in which the achievements and works of many decades are doomed to annihilation.

"Germany is carrying on a war of defense against her enemies, which aim at her destruction. She fights to assure the integrity of her frontiers and the liberty of the German nation, for the right which she claims to develop freely her intellectual and economic energies in peaceful competition and on an equal footing with other nations. All the efforts of their enemies are unable to shatter the heroic armies of the (Teutonic) allies, which protect the frontiers of their countries, strengthened by the certainty that the enemy shall never pierce the iron wall.

"Those fighting on the front know that they are supported by the whole nation, which is inspired by love for its country and is ready for the greatest sacrifices and determined to defend to the last extremity the inherited treasure of intellectual and economic work and the social organization and sacred soil of the country.

"Certain of our own strength, but realizing Europe's sad future if the war continues; seized with pity in the face of the unspeakable misery of humanity, the German Empire, in accord with her allies, solemnly repeats what the Chancellor already has declared, a year ago, that Germany is ready to give peace to the world by setting before the whole world the question whether or not it is possible to find a basis for an understanding.

"Since the first day of the Pontifical reign his Holiness the Pope has unswervingly demonstrated, in the most generous fashion, his solicitude for the innumerable victims of this war. He has alleviated the sufferings and ameliorated the fate of thousands of men injured by this catastrophe. Inspired by the exalted ideas of his ministry, his Holiness has seized every opportunity in the interests of humanity to end so sanguinary a war.

"The Imperial Government is firmly confident that the initiative of the four powers will find friendly welcome on the part of his Holiness, and that the work of peace can count upon the precious support of the Holy See."

Austria's Separate Statement.

LONDON, Dec. 12.—An official Austrian statement, referring to the peace offer, says:

"When in the Summer of 1914 the patience of Austria-Hungary was exhausted by a series of systematically continued and ever increasing provocations and menaces, and the monarchy, after almost fifty years of unbroken peace, found itself compelled to draw the sword, this weighty decision was animated neither by aggressive purposes nor by designs of conquest, but solely by the bitter necessity of self-defense, to defend its existence and safeguard itself for the future against similar treacherous plots of hostile neighbors.

"That was the task and aim of the monarchy in the present war. In combination with its allies, well tried in loyal comradeship in arms, the Austro-Hungarian Army and Fleet, fighting, bleeding, but also assailing and conquering, gained such successes that they frustrated the intentions of the enemy. The quadruple alliance not only has won an immense series of victories, but also holds in its power extensive hostile territories. Unbroken is its strength, as our latest treacherous enemy has just experienced.

"Can our enemies hope to conquer or shatter this alliance of powers? They will never succeed in breaking it by blockade and starvation measures. Their war aims, to the attainment of which they have come no nearer in the third year of the war, will in the future be proved to have been completely unattainable. Useless and unavailing, therefore, is the prosecution of the fighting on the part of the enemy.

"The powers of the Quadruple Alliance, on the other hand, have effectively pursued their aims, namely, defence against attacks on their existence and integrity, which were planned in concert long since, and the achievement of real guarantees, and they will never allow themselves to be deprived of the basis of their existence, which they have secured by advantages won.

"The continuation of the murderous war, in which the enemy can destroy much, but cannot—as the Quadruple Alliance is firmly confident—alter fate, is ever more seen to be an aimless destruction of human lives and property, an act of inhumanity justified by no necessity and a crime against civilization.

"This conviction, and the hope that similar views may also be begun to be entertained in the enemy camp, has caused the idea to ripen in the Vienna Cabinet—in full agreement with the Governments of the allied [Teutonic] powers—of making a candid and loyal endeavor to come to a discussion with their enemies for the purpose of paving a way for peace.

"The Governments of Austria-Hungary, Germany, Turkey, and Bulgaria have addressed today identical notes to the diplomatic representatives in the capitals concerned who are intrusted with the promotion of enemy nationals, expressing an inclination to enter into peace negotiations and requesting them to transmit this overture to enemy States. This step was simultaneously brought to the knowledge of the representatives of the Holy See in a special note, and the active interest of the Pope for this offer of peace was solicited. Likewise the accredited representatives of the remaining neutral States in the four capitals were acquainted with this proceeding for the purpose of informing their Governments.

"Austria and her allies by this step have given new and decisive proof of their love of peace. It is now for their enemies to make known their views before the world.

"Whatever the result of its proposal may be, no responsibility can fall on the Quadruple Alliance, even before the judgment seat of its own peoples, if it is eventually obliged to continue the war."

"All the News That's Fit to Print."

The New York Times.

THE WEATHER
Snow or rain today; Friday colder, probably fair; shifting winds.
For full weather report see Page 19.

VOL. LXVI...NO. 21,516. NEW YORK, THURSDAY, DECEMBER 21, 1916.—TWENTY PAGES. ONE CENT In Greater New York, Jersey City and Newark. | Elsewhere, TWO CENTS

PRESIDENT WILSON CALLS UPON ALL THE WARRING NATIONS TO STATE THE TERMS UPON WHICH THE WAR MAY BE ENDED; OUR INTERESTS, SERIOUSLY AFFECTED, MUST BE SAFEGUARDED

NOTES PREPARED ON MONDAY

And Forwarded to Belligerents and Neutrals Tuesday Morning.

IF THE WAR GOES ON

"It May Presently Be Too Late to Accomplish the Greater Things Which Lie Beyond."

FOR A PERMANENT CONCORD

In Which the United States Would Co-operate—Bernstorff Prohpesies a Conference.

Special to The New York Times.

WASHINGTON, Dec. 20.—President Wilson has called on all the belligerent nations to state the terms which might serve as a basis for the restoration of peace.

The texts of the communications sent by the President's direction to each group of combatants were made public tonight, and created a sensation throughout official Washington, particularly in the European diplomatic body.

"Now I am perfectly convinced there will be a conference," said Count von Bernstorff, the German Ambassador, when he learned the details of President Wilson's undertaking.

While the notes say that the President "would be happy himself to serve or even to take the initiative" to bring a statement of terms from the belligerents, they also assert that "the President is not proposing peace; he is not even offering mediation."

"He is merely proposing," asserts Secretary Lansing, whose name is signed to the notes, "that soundings be taken in order that we may learn, the neutral nations with the belligerent, how near the haven of peace may be for which all mankind longs with an intense and increasing longing."

There are two notes, one addressed to the Entente Governments and their smaller allies and the other to the Central Power group, led by Germany. Identical language is used in the communications except in one paragraph, where the changes are not material, except to the extent that the note to the Teutonic allies gives assurance to them that the President's course is not "prompted by a desire to play a part in connection with the recent overtures of the Central Powers."

Antedate Lloyd George's Speech.

Each note bears date of Monday, indicating that the communications were prepared before Mr. Lloyd George, the British Prime Minister, delivered his response in the House of Commons to the German peace offer. All were cabled on Tuesday morning.

The sensation created by the announcement of the President's action was accentuated by the general understanding that it had been determined by the President to take no hand in the present movement to end the war. Late Friday afternoon, following a meeting of the Cabinet, THE NEW YORK TIMES correspondent was told by one of the highest officials that it had been decided that the German peace offer would be forwarded to the Entente Governments without comment from this Government. It was explained that this action was definite, but it was desirable that the press should not say that the Government had determined to take no part in the peace movement because the President was anxious that the impression should not be created that the United States had closed the door to participation in any effort to end the war. Circumstances might arise in the future, it was explained, that would make it desirable for this Government to further a peace movement.

The announcement this evening that President Wilson had addressed communications to all the belligerents calling upon them for "such an avowal of their respective views as to the terms upon which the war might be concluded" caused astonishment among those who had gained the impression that the United States would make no move toward peace at this time.

Action Long Contemplated.

What produced the apparent change of purpose on the part of the Government? According to an explanation obtained tonight from a thoroughly informed official, there was no change. The President, it was said, had had in mind for weeks the idea of taking the action embodied in the notes sent on Monday and made public tonight. His hesitation in the matter, it was explained, was due to uncertainty as to when would be a propitious time to transmit the communications.

The decision to forward the German peace offer without comment had no application, it was stated, to the move of the United States made known today. That, it was said, was an independent move on the initiative of this Government. It had been determined upon before the German peace tender was announced, and, it was stated, would have been sent to the belligerents when the proper time appeared to have arrived if there had been no action by the Central Powers. Furthermore, it was pointed out that the President's notes did not contain an offer to act as mediator or urge the acceptance by the Entente Allies of the proposal of their enemies.

If the German Ambassador is elated, diplomats connected with the embassies of Entente nations are in a state of uncertainty over the effect of the President's course. They are cautious and courteous in expressing views concerning the President's action, and it may be said that one of the impressions they convey is that the notes of the United States may be construed merely as supporting the request of the British Prime Minister for a definite statement of peace terms from Germany. There is a definite opinion in the Entente embassies that Germany cannot now afford to conceal from her enemies the terms upon which she would go about seeking to make peace. The Entente nations, it is pointed out, are in accord with the declaration of the British Prime Minister that a peace conference cannot be obtained unless the Central Powers first make a definite statement of willingness to provide restitution and reparation for past offenses and guarantees for future peace.

Entente May Resent It.

This seemingly kindly reception of President Wilson's course will change materially, however, it is gathered, if it is concluded to be engaged in a move to force peace upon Europe. The Entente Governments, it was indicated, would not tolerate American interference to that extent. It was said in one quarter, informed as to the views of the Entente Allies, that if the people of the allied nations interpreted the President's note to their Governments as a suggestion that Great Britain and her partners did not know for what they were fighting, the action of the President would be resented.

Germany, however, is not disposed to make known in advance of any conference the terms upon which she will be willing to negotiate a treaty of peace. Her position, it is learned here, is that the best assurance of peace lies in having envoys of the groups of belligerent nations get together around a table and talk things over. If one side becomes dissatisfied it can withdraw; it does not commit itself to any guarantees or assurances in advance by entering the council chamber. Germany, it is said, is willing to furnish guarantees called for by Great Britain—that is, she is willing to give guarantees of an arrangement for a reduction of armaments and the formation of a league to enforce peace in the future. But it is strenuously insisted by those informed as to Germany's position that she is opposed to making any advance disclosure of her terms or to consent that these terms, even when laid before the Entente peace commissioners, should receive publicity pending an agreement.

What caused the President to make this unexpected move is a source of speculation in Washington tonight. From an excellent source it was learned that the President had the idea in mind of taking this action several weeks ago, and the impression was gained that at the time of its inception he feared another outbreak of reckless German submarine warfare which might compel the United States to become a party to the European conflict. It was for this reason, it is believed in some quarters, that he began to think seriously of making a move for peace. The belief is strongly borne out by the President's statement that if the war is not concluded soon it may reach a condition where "the situation of neutral nations, now exceedingly, hard to endure, may be rendered altogether intolerable." With that idea in mind the recent effort of Germany to bring the war to an end probably influenced him to some extent in making known to the belligerents his own views of what should be done to produce peace. But the determining thing that brought the President suddenly to the conclusion that he must move without delay, even at the risk of placing himself in the attitude of being offensive to the Entente Allies, remains a mystery outside of the inner official circle.

All Neutrals Threatened.

One of the best informed men in Washington, to whom THE TIMES correspondent went for guidance as to the meaning of the President's course, made the significant statement that if the war continued for any great length of time there would be nothing to prevent all the neutral nations from being drawn into the conflict. The time had come, it was said, when the United States was entitled to say to the belligerents, "We would like to know what are the objects for which you are fighting."

Those objects have been stated in general terms by the leaders of the belligerents themselves, the President contends in his communications, and he holds that their statements are in substantial agreement. All agree, he points out, that it is essential to secure weak nations against aggression, to provide security against future great wars and the abandonment of alliances by groups in favor of the formation of a league of nations to insure peace and justice throughout the world. His notes call upon the belligerents on both sides to state these terms definitely in order that a foundation for a move toward peace can be obtained.

That is the essential proposition he makes to the Entente Allies and the Central Powers. He wants an immediate opportunity, "for a comparison of views as to the terms which must precede these ultimate arrangements for the peace of the world."

Count von Bernstorff declined to comment on the President's note other than in the few words quoted in the beginning of this dispatch. It may be said, however, that a definite acceptance of the President's proposal will be sent by the German Government.

Surprised Official Washington.

By The Associated Press.

WASHINGTON, Dec. 20.—President Wilson's notes to the belligerent powers appealing to them to discuss peace terms proved a distinct surprise to official Washington. All had been led to believe that with the formal transmittal of the proposals of the Central Powers the United States would await further moves between the belligerents themselves, and that in view of the speech of Lloyd George and the announcements in Russia, France, and Italy, further action by neutrals would depend upon the next careful moves of the belligerents.

The tenor of official opinion throughout Washington, when the President's action became known, was that it immeasurably improved the prospects for some sort of exchanges looking toward an approach to peace discussions between the belligerents without impairing the position of the United States, should they finally be unable to find a ground on which to approach one another.

At the White House no statement whatever could be obtained as to whether any power had intimated how it would receive the note, and there was every indication that the same secrecy which prevented anything whatever becoming known about the President's action until it had been taken would surround any of the succeeding moves.

Nowhere on the surface appears any indication of the history-making events which diplomats generally are convinced must have happened since the German allies brought forth their proposals to dispel the general belief that such action on the part of President Wilson would be unacceptable to the Entente Powers.

British Embassy officials said they were utterly taken by surprise, were unable to explain it, and were emphatic in their statement that no exchanges had passed through the embassy here as a preliminary.

The wish and hope of the German powers that President Wilson would intercede in some way has long been well known and has been conveyed in different ways to the White House.

Recalls Roosevelt's Course.

The nearest parallel in world history for President Wilson's action was President's Roosevelt's move in 1905 to end the war between Russia and Japan. But in that case the President had been assured his proposal would not be disagreeable to either of the belligerents, and, curiously enough, it was through Emperor William of Germany that the preliminary soundings crystallized into the suggestion that President Roosevelt take the steps. Before that time President Roosevelt had conferred with Count Cassini, the Russian Ambassador here, and with Mr. Takahira, the Japanese Minister. In the Russian capital the American Ambassador, George Von L. Meyer, had conversations with Count Lamsdorff, the Russian Minister for Foreign Affairs. In Tokio American Minister Griscom had conversations with Count Komura, the Japanese Minister for Foreign Affairs. The outcome of all these preliminaries was that President Roosevelt was assured that he would not be humiliated by a rejection of his action.

There are indications that President Wilson began preparation of his note some time ago, probably even before the German proposals came out, and that the offer of the Central Powers and the succeeding developments made a more favorable opportunity for its presentation.

The fact that the President asks first only a clarification of terms is taken as indicating that he is not expecting an immediate conclusion. In a war involving so many conflicting interests not only between the two belligerent groups, but even between nations of the same group, it is realized that much time may be needed even to bring about the mere preliminaries of a conference. It is desired, therefore, to clear away as many of those preliminaries as possible, so that when a solution is near, either by victory or exhaustion, not a day of needless slughter may be necessary.

Officials expect the note to be received with general favor in Germany, but many believe the real test will come with its arrival in the Entente countries; where many influential persons have feared and sought to prevent any American intervention until the military situation changed. From the fact, however, that Lloyd George's reply to the Central Powers was milder than generally had been expected and still left the way open for further negotiations, it is believed that the Allies will meet the present note in at least a friendly spirit.

German Plan of Conference.

While German officials thoroughly understood that President Wilson made it clear that he was not in any sense offering mediation to the warring Governments, it was declared that should the negotiations reach that stage, Germany, being anxious to have the peace of Europe restored, willingly would agree to such procedure. Neither does it make any difference to Germany, it is said, whether the conference is composed of representatives of all the belligerents or just the coalitions.

So far as Germany is concerned, the view held here is that she would be perfectly willing that a committee of three, formed of a representative of the Central Powers, a representative of the Entente, and a representative of the United States, should hold preliminary discussions. The main idea of Germany and her allies is to get each set of belligerents into direct personal communication with the other. The method is considered of secondary importance.

ROOSEVELT WON'T COMMENT.

Silent on President's Note to the Belligerent Powers.

Theodore Roosevelt declined last night to comment on President Wilson's note to the belligerent Governments suggesting that they state peace terms. Extracts were shown to him at the Hotel Langdon. He insisted that he did not care to make a statement. He declined to avail himself of an opportunity to read the note in full.

The Colonel said he had heard nothing of the published statement that Congress intended to return to him the $40,000 Nobel Peace Prize awarded to him in 1907 and which he employed as a Foundation for the Promotion of Industrial Peace. Congress planned this action, it was said, because the fund never had been added to or employed as the Colonel had planned and because Mr. Roosevelt could be counted on to devote the money to some other public purpose. Mr. Roosevelt said he would have nothing to say concerning the matter until the money was delivered to him.

Comment of This Morning's Papers on the Note.

NEW YORK CITY.

Purveyors of German Peace.

From The New York Tribune.

The Tribune profoundly regrets that **President Wilson** should at this time **have** been moved to make any gesture **which**, however honestly intended to **promote** the cause of peace, will **inevitably tend** to complicate and not to **clarify** the **situation.**

In the eyes of Europe today the United **States is no longer** a nation dedicated to **the championship of noble principles** and **committed** to the support of a just **peace. Today and** henceforth we have **become the agents and** purveyors of a **German peace.** The nation that did not **protest when Belgium was invaded** could **not wait** until the liberation and restoration **of Belgium** were assured before **raising its** voice on behalf of what?—of whatever German purpose lies undisclosed behind the German peace proposal.

Request Cannot Be Ignored.

From The New York World.

What may come of the President's request can only be conjectured; but, for one thing, it cannot be ignored, and the answers must go further than any European statesman has yet gone in defining the objects of the war and the terms of peace.

The worst that can happen is that the war will continue without conclusive results. But in the meantime the United States and all other neutrals will have obtained a clearer notion of the measures which they must take, if the war is to continue, to protect their rights and safeguard their welfare. To that much consideration, at least, they are entitled from belligerents which have hitherto shown little respect for any neutral right from the violation of which they could profit.

Of one thing there can be no question. In trying to find a common ground upon which the warring nations can meet, President Wilson represents the sentiment of a vast majority of the American people, and that sentiment is without ulterior or selfish motive. The American people want nothing for themselves. They ask nothing out of this conflict except peace with justice and the common good of all mankind.

A Task of Definition.

From The New York Sun.

What President Wilson suggests to the statesmen of the belligerent powers is a task of definition. He categorically denies that he proposes peace. He does not offer mediation. He asks for formal disclosures of national aspirations and racial ambitions. The limitations he imposes on his present project he makes clear beyond the possibility of misconstruction. It is not how peace may be attained, but why war is maintained, that engages his immediate interest.

Serious as is the President's aim with respect of the conflict now devastating the world, it is to America less momentous than the change in our historical attitude toward foreign affairs which may eventually flow from its development.

Sees Striking Coincidence.

From The New York Herald.

Despite his disclaimer, the President's action in proposing, at this time, that the belligerent nations exchange views on possible terms of peace is bound to be construed by the peoples of those nations and by many Americans as having direct relation to the Berlin cry for peace. If the suspicion is not warranted the responsibility, if Mr. Wilson's alone, for the coincidence is striking. It will be surprising if the mere suspicion raised in nations that are fighting for their existence does not militate greatly against the end to which the President is aiming.

GERMAN PAPERS PLEASED.

Has Won Enduring Fame.

From the New-Yorker Staats-Zeitung.

The note which President Wilson yesterday addressed to the Governments of all the warring nations to move them to come to an exchange of views on the question of peace may prove to be a step of quite incalculable extent in the interest of all the peoples involved in the fearful war.

The dispatch of this note is an act of world-historic importance. Correctly estimating the situation, President Wilson has chosen the psychological moment for it. After the expressions of leading allied statesmen yesterday the conclusion that the Governments of England, France, and Russia were preparing to refuse the German offer was justified. The warning of the President, which in its impressive phraseology will have a tremendous influence, cannot be without effect upon even the most reluctant European statesman, for it is the power of truth which turns itself upon the spirits of these rulers, hardened by the tumult of the bloody struggles. The thankful relief of the hard-tried peoples of Europe will be a monument to the President which insures to his name a place of honor in history more enduring than images of marble or bronze.

May Signal End of War.

From the New Yorker Herold.

President Wilson's note calling for peace terms may be the signal for the end of hostilities. We are certain that this note is but the result of negotiations behind the scenes and that the speech of the German Chancellor and that of Lloyd George were merely preliminary acts in the drama, which is now unfolding itself before our eyes.

The President's note is drawn up in such a manner that the impression is conveyed that he is merely sounding the belligerents as to the prospects of peace, but in reality he would not have dared to come out openly in this manner if secret negotiations, whether he should do so, had not been answered by the belligerents in the affirmative.

All belligerents and all neutrals desire peace. But what kind of peace will it be? England knows already and so do the other belligerents. They have a general idea what the peace terms will be. They will be determined by the war map—or, rather, mainly determined. The Central Powers will yield some of the territory they have conquered. They will forego some advantages they might hold if they elected to continue fighting. But, on the whole, they will have their way in their main contentions. They have won the war.

WASHINGTON.

"An Independent Proposal."

From The Washington Post.

It is somewhat unfortunate that the President's proposal should come at a moment when it may be associated with the peace overtures of Germany and the reply of the Allies. It is clearly an independent proposal, decided upon before the German overtures were made. If the German Government should not regard it as an effort to swing neutral sentiment behind the Allies' demand for an explicit statement of Germany's position, the President's communication cannot fail to do good. It will induce the peoples of all warring nations to ask themselves why they are fighting.

BOSTON.

"President Wisely Leads."

From The Boston Herald.

If the President can have any influence in bringing the embattled nations to a common understanding of what this struggle is about, he should exert it. What they need is an internationalmindedness, a detachment from the prejudice and misinformation with which their minds have been instilled. From the effects of this we exempt neither side of the controversy. We think opinions freer and the people better informed in the great democracies of Great Britain and France than in the autocracies of Central Europe. But both sides can learn something of the others' points of view to advantage, and in this direction our President wisely leads.

NEW ORLEANS.

"Clear, Direct, and Fair."

From The Times-Picayune.

President Wilson's peace note to the warring nations takes the country by surprise, and apparently is as profound a surprise to the Governments addressed. The proposition is clear, direct, and fair to all. Its proponent places his finger upon the fatal defect of all the peace talk gone before—the fact that the 'authoritative spokesmen' of either side have 'never yet avowed the precise objects which would, if attained, satisfy them or their people.'"

Special to The New York Times.

MONTREAL, Dec. 20.—The Montreal Gazette will say tomorrow in a "box" conspicuously printed on its first page:

"The complete text of Premier Lloyd George's speech, as printed in yesterday's issue of The Montreal Gazette, contained more than 8,000 words. The Gazette was the only Canadian newspaper to carry the full text of this speech, and it was enabled to render this service to the reading public through its connection with THE NEW YORK TIMES, unquestionably the greatest of American newspapers.

"In addition to the report of the speech, THE TIMES also had cabled to New York a four-thousand-word picture of the scene at Westminster and a review of the Premier's declarations, written by Hall Caine. This cable The Gazette also received through THE TIMES service, making 12,000 words of cable dealing with the events of a notable day in the British House of Commons."

HAMPERED CABLING PREMIER'S SPEECH

Censorship Went Through Its Delaying Process in This as in Everything Else.

TIMES GAVE CANADA TEXT

All That Lloyd George Said, with Hall Caine's Description of Scene, Sent to Montreal from New York.

Special Cable to THE NEW YORK TIMES.

LONDON, Thursday, Dec. 21.—The Daily Chronicle prints the following under the heading, "Censoring Lloyd George's Speech:"

"Long reports of Lloyd George's great speech in the House of Commons on Tuesday were cabled to America. THE NEW YORK TIMES printed the speech in full, accompanied by a descriptive article by Hall Caine.

"The speech had to be censored at the press bureau before it could be sent to the cable office. This is obviously unnecessary and vexatious, and it casts suspicion on accredited correspondents, besides a great deal of delay. The censors think it is part of their duty to waste time censoring speeches of this kind. The work should be done at the cable office, and no time wasted over it.

"Such speeches are the best propaganda work we can issue to neutrals, and no difficulties of delays should be put in the way of their publication."

LONDON FINANCIERS PLEASED.

Approve Heartily Sentiments of Premier, Asquith, and Curzon.

Special Cable to THE NEW YORK TIMES.

LONDON, Thursday, Dec. 21.—The Morning Post's financial correspondent says:

"There was only one topic of conversation in the city yesterday, and it would be difficult to say which of the three speeches in the Houses of Parliament, the Premier's, Asquith's, or Curzon's, was more closely studied. All three, however, commanded approval, and some of the criticisms which had been offered on the previous night on Lloyd George's speech, based on brief extracts in the evening papers, were modified on perusal of the speech in its entirety. And although the point may be regarded by some as a small one, the city was very favorably impressed with the close similarity between the more important passages both in Curzon's and the Premier's remarks, as well as by the restraint in both.

"The situation is one in which if the war is long continued there must inevitably be calls for self-sacrifice throughout the community, and it is essential not only that patriotism should be stirred, but that confidence should be engendered. Therefore was this note of restraint particularly liked by businessmen."

LLOYD GEORGE'S STAND SHAKES VIENNA'S HOPE

AMSTERDAM, Dec. 20.—Some of the Vienna newspapers, commenting on the speech of David Lloyd George, the British Premier, express the opinion that rejection of the peace offer of the Teutonic allies by the Entente Allies is virtually certain. The Fremdenblatt says:

"After Mr. Lloyd George's speech the continuation of the world war is inevitable. Great Britain does not want to end the war until her aim has been attained. This aim Mr. Lloyd George designated by the dark word 'reparation.' He obviously demands reparation for the fact that the Central Powers dared defend themselves against world enemies standing under England's command. Fate will be allowed to take its course, and the day will come when Mr. Lloyd George, shudderingly, will recognize that England, by rejecting the peace offer, has really stuck its head into a noose with the rope in our hands."

President Wilson's Note to the Belligerent Nations

DEPARTMENT OF STATE,
WASHINGTON, D. C., Dec. 18, 1916.

The President directs me to send you the following communication to be presented immediately to the Minister of Foreign Affairs of the Government to which you are accredited:

The President of the United States has instructed me to suggest to the [here is inserted a designation of the Government addressed] a course of action with regard to the present war, which he hopes that the Government will take under consideration as suggested in the most friendly spirit, and as coming not only from a friend but also as coming from the representative of a neutral nation whose interests have been most seriously affected by the war and whose concern for its early conclusion arises out of a manifest necessity to determine how best to safeguard those interests if the war is to continue.

[*The third paragraph of the note as sent to the four Central Powers—Germany, Austria-Hungary, Turkey, and Bulgaria—is as follows:*]

The suggestion which I am instructed to make the President has long had it in mind to offer. He is somewhat embarrassed to offer it at this particular time, because it may now seem to have been prompted by a desire to play a part in connection with the recent overtures of the Central Powers. It has, in fact, been in no way suggested by them in its origin, and the President would have delayed offering it until those overtures had been independently answered but for the fact that it also concerns the question of peace and may best be considered in connection with other proposals which have the same end in view. The President can only beg that his suggestion be considered entirely on its own merits and as if it had been made in other circumstances.

[*The third paragraph of the note as sent to the ten Entente Allies—Great Britain, France, Italy, Japan, Russia, Belgium, Montenegro, Portugal, Rumania, and Serbia—is as follows:*]

The suggestion which I am instructed to make the President has long had it in mind to offer. He is somewhat embarrassed to offer it at this particular time, because it may now seem to have been prompted by the recent overtures of the Central Powers. It is, in fact, in no way associated with them in its origin, and the President would have delayed offering it until those overtures had been answered but for the fact that it also concerns the question of peace and may best be considered in connection with other proposals which have the same end in view. The President can only beg that his suggestion be considered entirely on its own merits and as if it had been made in other circumstances.

[*Thenceforward the note proceeds identically to all the powers, as follows:*]

The President suggests that an early occasion be sought to call out from all the nations now at war such an avowal of their respective views as to the terms upon which the war might be concluded and the arrangements which would be deemed satisfactory as a guaranty against its renewal or the kindling of any similar conflict in the future as would make it possible frankly to compare them. He is indifferent as to the means taken to accomplish this. He would be happy himself to serve, or even to take the initiative in its accomplishment, in any way that might prove acceptable, but he has no desire to determine the method or the instrumentality. One way will be as acceptable to him as another, if only the great object he has in mind be attained.

He takes the liberty of calling attention to the fact that the objects, which the statesmen of the belligerents on both sides have in mind in this war, are virtually the same, as stated in general terms to their own people and to the world. Each side desires to make the rights and privileges of weak peoples and small States as secure against aggression or denial in the future as the rights and privileges of the great and powerful States now at war. Each wishes itself to be made secure in the future, along with all other nations and peoples, against the recurrence of wars like this and against aggression or selfish interference of any kind. Each would be jealous of the formation of any more rival leagues to preserve an uncertain balance of power amid multiplying suspicions; but each is ready to consider the formation of a league of nations to insure peace and justice throughout the world. Before that final step can be taken, however, each deems it necessary first to settle the issues of the present war upon terms which will certainly safeguard the independence, the territorial integrity, and the political and commercial freedom of the nations involved.

In the measures to be taken to secure the future peace of the world the people and Government of the United States are as vitally and as directly interested as the Governments now at war. Their interest, moreover, in the means to be adopted to relieve the smaller and weaker peoples of the world of the peril of wrong and violence is as quick and ardent as that of any other people or Government. They stand ready, and even eager, to co-operate in the accomplishment of these ends, when the war is over, with every influence and resource at their command. But the war must first be concluded. The terms upon which it is to be concluded they are not at liberty to suggest; but the President does feel that it is his right and his duty to point out their intimate interest in its conclusion, lest it should presently be too late to accomplish the greater things which lie beyond its conclusion, lest the situation of neutral nations, now exceedingly hard to endure, be rendered altogether intolerable, and lest, more than all, an injury be done civilization itself which can never be atoned for or repaired.

The President therefore feels altogether justified in suggesting an immediate opportunity for a comparison of views as to the terms which must precede those ultimate arrangements for the peace of the world, which all desire and in which the neutral nations as well as those at war are ready to play their full responsible part. If the contest must continue to proceed toward undefined ends by slow attrition until the one group of belligerents or the other is exhausted; if million after million of human lives must continue to be offered up until on the one side or the other there are no more to offer; if resentments must be kindled that can never cool and despairs engendered from which there can be no recovery, hopes of peace and of the willing concert of free peoples will be rendered vain and idle.

The life of the entire world has been profoundly affected. Every part of the great family of mankind has felt the burden and terror of this unprecedented contest of arms. No nation in the civilized world can be said in truth to stand outside its influence or to be safe against its disturbing effects. And yet the concrete objects for which it is being waged have never been definitively stated.

The leaders of the several belligerents have, as has been said, stated those objects in general terms. But, stated in general terms, they seem the same on both sides. Never yet have the authoritative spokesmen of either side avowed the precise objects which would, if attained, satisfy them and their people that the war had been fought out. The world has been left to conjecture what definitive results, what actual exchange of guaranties, what political or territorial changes or readjustments, what stage of military success, even, would bring the war to an end.

It may be that peace is nearer than we know; that the terms which the belligerents on the one side and on the other would deem it necessary to insist upon are not so irreconcilable as some have feared; that an interchange of views would clear the way at least for conference and make the permanent concord of the nations a hope of the immediate future, a concert of nations immediately practicable.

The President is not proposing peace; he is not even offering mediation. He is merely proposing that soundings be taken in order that we may learn, the neutral nations with the belligerent, how near the haven of peace may be for which all mankind longs with an intense and increasing longing. He believes that the spirit in which he speaks and the objects which he seeks will be understood by all concerned, and he confidently hopes for a response which will bring a new light into the affairs of the world.   LANSING.

[*Copies of the above will be delivered to all neutral Governments for their information.*]

1917

"All the News That's Fit to Print."

The New York Times.

THE WEATHER
Fair, cold today; Saturday probably snow, warmer; northwest winds.
☞For full weather report see Page 21

VOL. LXVI...NO. 21,538. ...   NEW YORK, FRIDAY, JANUARY 12, 1917.—TWENTY-TWO PAGES.   ONE CENT In Greater New York. | Elsewhere Jersey City and Newark. | TWO CENTS

TERRITORIES OVERRUN, EVEN IN THE PAST, TO BE RESTORED; EXPULSION OF THE TURK AND REORGANIZATION OF EUROPE; THESE, WITH INDEMNITIES, ARE THE ALLIES' TERMS OF PEACE

NO AIM TO CRUSH GERMANY

Frank and Friendly Tone of Reply to President Pleases Capital.

WILSON'S COURSE IN DOUBT

But Unofficial Washington Thinks the Document Closes Door to Peace at Present.

BERLIN LIKELY TO ANSWER

One Forecast Says Teutons' Terms Will Be Made Known, Insuring Continuance of War.

Special to The New York Times.

WASHINGTON, Jan. 11.—The State Department this evening gave out for publication the reply of the Entente Governments to President Wilson's note of Dec. 18, addressed to the belligerent nations, in which he suggested that they state the objects for which they were fighting and indicate the terms upon which they would be willing to undertake an adjustment of the war.

Unlike the Central Powers group, the Entente Allies do not stand on the technicality that the President merely suggested that a modus be provided for ascertaining what the President desires. Instead they outline their terms and show in general a disposition to respond frankly and specifically to the request of the President. The reply expressly states that the Allies will not make known their war objects in detail until "the hour of negotiation," but it adds that these objects "imply in all necessity in the first instance" certain terms. These may be summarized as follows:

Restoration of Belgium, Serbia, Montenegro, with indemnities.

Evacuation of invaded territories of France, Russia, and Rumania, with reparation.

Reorganization of Europe under guarantees to insure to all nations respect and liberty of development.

Restitution of territories wrested in the past from the Allies by force or against people's will.

Liberation of Italians, Slavs, Rumanians, and Tcheco-Slovaks from foreign domination.

Enfranchisement of populations subject to the Turks.

Expulsion from Europe of the Ottoman Empire.

To these terms the Allies add that Russia has already clearly indicated her intentions toward Poland, and that if the Allies wish to free Europe from Prussian militarism, it has never been their design to "encompass the extermination of the German people and their political disappearance."

Frankness Pleases Officials.

On account of the frankness of the Entente reply it has created an excellent impression in high official quarters, where the Allies' attitude is construed as a hopeful sign for further exchanges between the belligerents and the United States. It should be understood, however, that this sentiment is not to be taken as an expression of the Administration view. There is no Administration view so far. That depends on the interpretation placed by President Wilson on the Entente reply. It should be understood also that opinion in official circles is not unanimous as to the meaning and effect of the Entente note. While officials were cautious in expressing themselves, no doubt is felt that some of them agree with a rather general unofficial view that the Allies have closed the door to peace at this time.

This unofficial view is shared at the German Embassy, where the answer of the Entente is, if expressions heard there this evening represent the real feeling, a real disappointment. But the Embassy finds a grain of comfort in the thought that the Entente's attitude will arouse the allies of Germany and make them more than ever determined to fight to a finish. The German idea is that while the people of Germany may take note of the assurance of the Entente that "it has never been their design to encompass the extermination of the German peoples and their political disappearance," the nations allied with Germany will find in the note the expression of a purpose to cause their territorial and political disintegration, and this will impel them to fight harder.

As to whether the Entente rejection of the peace offer of the Central Powers will cause Germany to undertake reprisals with her submarine craft, the flat statement was made in German circles that Germany would live up to her pledges given to the United States in the Sussex case. At the same time it was pointed out that Germany has reason to believe that Great Britain was arming merchant vessels for offensive action, and this might cause the Berlin Government to take its own measures to meet such a situation. The German Government, it was said, had never denied the principle asserted by the United States that merchant vessels had the right to arm for defensive purposes and, in fact, had no longer any differences with the United States over the principles of submarine warfare. But if British merchantmen carried guns forward, as well as aft, cases were likely to arise from the sinking of merchant vessels by German submarines that would have to be determined on the merits of each case.

The suggestion gained from this was that as the Allies had decreed that the war must go on, they could not expect Germany to permit departures from the rule that armed merchant vessels were immune from attack without warning by enemy craft, only when armed defensively, that is, with a gun carried aft. This suggestion is looked upon as emphasizing the statement of President Wilson in his note to the belligerents that if the war was prolonged the situation of neutral nations, "now exceedingly hard to endure," might "be rendered altogether intolerable."

The feeling that the Entente reply is favorable to the undertaking of President Wilson, outlined in his note of Dec. 18, is based in part on its friendly tone. In one high quarter it was said that the reply exceeded the expectations of officials of the Government because it stated the terms upon which the Entente would be willing to conclude a peace. This optimistic opinion was based on the view that the President's communication of Dec. 18 was not a peace note but merely an effort to induce the belligerents to state their terms for ending the war. In another official quarter it was held that the Allies had made a mistake in not placing greater stress on their willingness to enter into a league to insure peace. These views indicate the divergence of opinion in the Administration, and show that no definite conclusion as to the meaning of the Entente reply has been formed.

Only once in the reply does the Entente show any feeling over the initiative taken by President Wilson, and this is coupled with assurances intended to take away any sting. The communication, which came from Ambassador Sharp in Paris, and was introduced by the phrase, "the following is the translation of the French note," expresses objection to the "assimilation established in the American note between the two groups of belligerents." In other words, they object to an intimation that the objects for which the two groups are fighting are the same. But, after pointing out that "this assimilation, based on public declarations of the Central Powers, is in direct opposition to the evidence," the Entente acquit the President of meaning more than that it was claimed that the objects for which each group was fighting were similar.

It is clear from the statement of allied terms that the Allies are not willing to make peace until they have accomplished the objects they have pledged themselves to bring about. So satisfied are they that Germany will not agree to enter into peace negotiations on these basic conditions that they state frankly that they "believe it is impossible at the present moment to attain a peace which will insure them reparation, restitution, and such guarantees to which they are entitled by the aggression for which the responsibility rests with the Central Powers and of which the principle itself tended to ruin the security of Europe." It is this statement, taken in connection with the outline of terms, that convinces most observers here that the answer of the Entente makes peace impossible at this time.

What President Wilson will do now is problematical. It was said in an official statement from the State Department last week, authorized by the President, that there was no truth in reports that the President had determined to send a second note to the belligerent Governments, and to this was added that he did not even have in contemplation the sending of a second note. It was explained unofficially that the President could not determine whether a second note should be transmitted to the belligerents until he had read the answer of the Entente to his note.

That the President desires to take counsel before determining his course was indicated by the presence in Washington tonight of Colonel E. M. House, a close unofficial adviser, who came here to attend a dinner given this evening by Secretary and Mrs. Lansing to the President and Mrs. Wilson. It is the belief here that Colonel House was asked to come here mainly to express his views with respect to the Entente reply.

London Estimates Casualties of Germans at 4,010,160

LONDON, Jan. 11.—The total German casualties since the beginning of the war were placed at 4,010,160 in an official summary issued by the British Government today, which reads:

"A summary of the German casualties reported in official German casualty lists published during December gives a total of 88,291, which, added to those previously reported, brings the total German casualties to 4,010,160. The naval and colonial casualties are excluded."

WAR AIMS WON, GERMANY ASSERTS

Tells Neutrals She Fought for Liberty and Existence, and These Are Obtained.

ISSUES INDEPENDENT NOTE

BERLIN, Jan. 11, (by Wireless to Sayville.)—Germany today handed to the neutral Governments a note concerning the reply of the Entente to the German peace proposals, the Overseas News Agency announces.

"Our adversaries declined this proposition, giving as the reason that it is a proposition without sincerity and without importance. The form in which they clothe their communication excludes an answer to them, but the Imperial Government considers it important to point out to the Governments of neutral powers its opinion regarding the situation.

"The Central Powers have no reason to enter into any discussion regarding the origin of the world war. History will judge upon whom the immense guilt of the war shall fall. History's verdict will as little pass over the encircling policy of England, the revengeful policy of France, and the endeavor of Russia to gain Constantinople as over the instigation of the Serbian assassination in Sarayevo and the complete mobilization of Russia, which meant war against Germany.

"Germany and her allies, who had to take up arms for defense of their liberty and their existence, consider this, their aim of war, as obtained.

"On the other hand, the hostile powers always went further away from the realization of their plans, which, according to the declarations of their responsible statesmen, were, among others, directed toward the conquest of Alsace-Lorraine and several Prussian provinces, the humiliation and diminution of the Austro-Hungarian monarchy, the partition of Turkey, and the mutilation of Bulgaria. In the face of such war aims, the demand for restitution, reparation, and guarantee in the mouth of our adversaries produces a surprising effect.

Resents Insincerity Charge.

"Our adversaries call the proposal of the four allied (Teutonic) powers a war manoeuvre. Germany and her allies must protest in the most energetic fashion against such a characterization of their motives, which were frankly explained. They were persuaded that a peace which was just and acceptable to all the belligerents was possible; that it could be brought about by an immediate spoken exchange of views, and that therefore the responsibility for further bloodshed could not be taken. Their readiness was affirmed without reservation to make known their peace conditions when negotiations were entered into, which refutes every doubt as to their sincerity.

"Our adversaries, who had it in their hands to examine the proposition as to its contents, neither attempted an examination nor made counter-proposals. Instead, they declared that peace was impossible so long as the re-establishment of violated rights and liberties, the recognition of the principle of nationalities, and the free existence of small States were not guaranteed.

Text of Allies' Reply to Wilson

Ambassador Sharp to the Secretary of State:
(*Telegram No. 1,806.*)

AMERICAN EMBASSY,
Paris, Jan. 10, 1917.

The following is the translation of the French note:

The allied Governments have received the note which was delivered to them in the name of the Government of the United States on the 19th of December, 1916. They have studied it with the care imposed upon them both by the exact realization which they have of the gravity of the hour and by the sincere friendship which attaches them to the American people.

In a general way they wish to declare that they pay tribute to the elevation of the sentiment with which the American note is inspired and that they associate themselves, with all their hopes, with the project for the creation of a league of nations to insure peace and justice throughout the world. They recognize all the advantages for the cause of humanity and civilization which the institution of international agreements, destined to avoid violent conflicts between nations would prevent—agreements which must imply the sanctions necessary to insure their execution, and thus to prevent an apparent security from only facilitating new aggressions.

But a discussion of future arrangements destined to insure an enduring peace presupposes a satisfactory settlement of the actual conflict. The Allies have as profound a desire as the Government of the United States to terminate as soon as possible a war for which the Central Empires are responsible and which inflicts such cruel sufferings upon humanity. But they believe that it is impossible at the present moment to attain a peace which will assure them reparation, restitution, and such guarantees to which they are entitled by the aggression for which the responsibility rests with the Central Powers, and of which the principle itself tended to ruin the security of Europe—a peace which would, on the other hand, permit the establishment of the future of European nations on a solid basis. The allied nations are conscious they are not fighting for selfish interests, but, above all, to safeguard the independence of peoples, of right, and of humanity.

The Allies are fully aware of the losses and suffering which the war causes to neutrals as well as to belligerents, and they deplore them, but they do not hold themselves responsible for them, having in no way either willed or provoked this war; and they strive to reduce these damages in the measure compatible with the inexorable exigencies of their defense against the violence and the wiles of the enemy.

It is with satisfaction, therefore, that they take note of the declaration that the American communication is in nowise associated in its origin with that of the Central Powers transmitted on the 18th of December by the Government of the United States. They did not doubt, moreover, the resolution of that Government to avoid even the appearance of a support, even moral, of the authors responsible for the war.

The allied Governments believe that they must protest in the most friendly but in the most specific manner against the assimilation, established in the American note, between the two groups of belligerents; this assimilation, based upon public declarations by the Central Powers, is in direct opposition to the evidence, both as regards responsibility for the past and as concerns guarantees for the future; President Wilson, in mentioning it, certainly had no intention of associating himself with it.

If there is a historical fact established at the present date, it is the willful aggression of Germany and Austria-Hungary to insure their hegemony over Europe and their economic domination over the world. Germany proved by her declaration of war, by the immediate violation of Belgium and Luxemburg, and by her manner of conducting the war her simulating contempt for all principles of humanity and all respect for small States. As the conflict developed, the attitude of the Central Powers and their allies has been a continual defiance of humanity and civilization.

Is it necessary to recall the horrors which accompanied the invasion of Belgium and of Serbia, the atrocious régime imposed upon the invaded countries, the massacre of hundreds of thousands of inoffensive Armenians, the barbarities perpetrated against the populations of Syria, the raids of Zeppelins on open towns, the destruction by submarines of passenger steamers and of merchantmen even under neutral flags, the cruel treatment inflicted upon prisoners of war, the juridical murders of Miss Cavell, of Captain Fryatt, the deportation and the reduction to slavery of civil populations, et cetera? The execution of such a series of crimes, perpetrated without any regard for universal reprobation, fully explains to President Wilson the protest of the Allies.

They consider that the note which they sent to the United States in reply to the German note will be a response to the questions put by the American Government, and, according to the exact words of the latter, " constitute a public declaration as to the conditions upon which the war could be terminated."

President Wilson desires more: he desires that the belligerent powers openly affirm the objects which they seek by continuing the war; the Allies experience no difficulty in replying to this request. Their objects in the war are well known; they have been formulated on many occasions by the chiefs of their divers Governments. Their objects will not be made known in detail with all the equitable compensation and indemnities for damages suffered until the hour of negotiations. But the civilized world knows that they imply, in all necessity and in the first instance, the restoration of Belgium, of Serbia, and of Montenegro, and the indemnities which are due them; the evacuation of the invaded territories of France, of Russia, and of Rumania, with just reparation; the reorganization of Europe, guaranteed by a stable régime and founded as much upon respect of nationalities and full security and liberty of economic development, which all nations, great or small, possess, as upon territorial conventions and international agreements, suitable to guarantee territorial and maritime frontiers against unjustified attacks; the restitution of provinces or territories wrested in the past from the Allies by force or against the will of their populations; the liberation of Italians, of Slavs, of Rumanians, and of Tcheco-Slovaques from foreign domination; the enfranchisement of populations subject to the bloody tyranny of the Turks; the expulsion from Europe of the Ottoman Empire, decidedly alien to Western civilization. The intentions of his Majesty, the Emperor of Russia, regarding Poland have been clearly indicated in the proclamation which he has just addressed to his armies.

It goes without saying that if the Allies wish to liberate Europe from the brutal covetousness of Prussian militarism it never has been their design, as has been alleged, to encompass the extermination of the German peoples and their political disappearance. That which they desire above all is to insure a peace upon the principles of liberty and justice, upon the inviolable fidelity to international obligations with which the Government of the United States has never ceased to be inspired.

United in the pursuit of this supreme object, the Allies are determined, individually and collectively, to act with all their power and to consent to all sacrifices to bring to a victorious close a conflict upon which, they are convinced, not only their own safety and prosperity depend, but also the future of civilization itself.   SHARP.

Belgium's Separate Reply to the President.

Ambassador Sharp to the Secretary of State:
(*Telegram.*)

AMERICAN EMBASSY,
Paris, Jan. 10, 1917.

Copy of Belgian note as follows:

The Government of the King, which has associated itself with the answer handed by the President of the French Council to the American Ambassador on behalf of all, is particularly desirous of paying tribute to the sentiment of humanity which prompted the President of the United States to send his note to the belligerent powers, and it highly esteems the friendship expressed for Belgium through his kindly intermediation. It desires as much as Mr. Woodrow Wilson to see the present war ended as early as possible.

But the President seems to believe that the statesmen of the two opposing camps pursue the same object of war. The example of Belgium unfortunately demonstrates that this is in no wise the fact. Belgium has never, like the Central Powers, aimed at conquest. The barbarous fashion in which the German Government has treated, and is still treating, the Belgian ration does not permit the supposition that Germany will preoccupy herself with guaranteeing in the future the rights of the weak nations, which she has not ceased to trample under foot since the war, let loose by her, began to desolate Europe.

On the other hand, the Government of the King has noted with pleasure and with confidence the assurances that the United States is impatient to co-operate in the measures which will be taken after the conclusion of peace to protect and guarantee the small nations against violence and oppression.

Previous to the German ultimatum, Belgium only aspired to live upon good terms with all her neighbors. She practiced with scrupulous loyalty toward each one of them the duties imposed by her neutrality. In the same manner she has been rewarded by Germany for the confidence she placed in her, through which, from one day to the other, without any plausible reason, her neutrality was violated, and the Chancellor of the Empire, when announcing to the Reichstag this violation of right and of treaties, was obliged to recognize the iniquity of such an act and predetermine that it would be repaired.

But the Germans, after the occupation of Belgian territory, have displayed no better observance of the rules of international law or the stipulations of The Hague Convention. They have, by taxation as heavy as it is arbitrary, drained the resources of the country; they have intentionally ruined its industries, destroyed whole cities, put to death and imprisoned a considerable number of inhabitants. Even now, while they are loudly proclaiming their desire to put an end to the horrors of war, they increase the rigors of the occupation by deporting into servitude Belgian workers by the thousands.

If there is a country which has the right to say that it has taken up arms to defend its existence, it is assuredly Belgium. Compelled to fight or to submit to shame, she passionately desires that an end be brought to the unprecedented sufferings of her population. But she could only accept a peace which would assure her, as well as equitable reparation, security and guarantees for the future.

The American people, since the beginning of the war, has manifested for the oppressed Belgian nation most ardent sympathy. It is an American committee, the Commission for Relief in Belgium, which, in close union with the Government of the King and the National Committee, displays an untiring devotion and marvelous activity in revictualing Belgium. The Government of the King is happy to avail itself of this opportunity to express its profound gratitude to the Commission for Relief as well as to the generous Americans eager to relieve the misery of the Belgian population. Finally, nowhere more than in the United States have the abductions and deportations of Belgian civilians provoked such a spontaneous movement of protestation and indignant reproof.

These facts, entirely to the honor of the American Nation, allow the Government of the King to entertain the legitimate hope that at the time of the definitive settlement of this long war the voice of the Entente Powers will find in the United States a unanimous echo to claim in favor of the Belgian nation, innocent victim of German ambition and covetousness, the rank and the place which its irreproachable past, the valor of its soldiers, its fidelity to honor, and its remarkable faculties for work assign to it among the civilized nations.

                SHARP.

"All the News That's Fit to Print."

The New York Times.

THE WEATHER
Rain Thursday; fair, cold wave by night Friday.
For full weather report see Page 21.

VOL. LXVI...NO. 21,558. ... NEW YORK, THURSDAY, FEBRUARY 1, 1917.—TWENTY-TWO PAGES. ONE CENT In Greater New York, Jersey City and Newark. | Elsewhere, TWO CENTS.

GERMANY BEGINS RUTHLESS SEA WARFARE; DRAWS 'BARRED ZONES' AROUND THE ALLIES; CRISIS CONFRONTS THE UNITED STATES

A SHIP A WEEK FOR US

To and From Falmouth on a Prescribed Route.

BECOMES EFFECTIVE TODAY

Bernstorff Delivers a Note Which Ends Germany's Pledges to Us.

BECAUSE OF PEACE FAILURE

The Kaiser Now Proposes to Employ All Means of Sea Warfare at His Command.

CAPITAL TAKES GRAVE VIEW

President Studies Note Alone—Break Predicted in Some Quarters

President Amazed by News; Spends Evening Studying Note

WASHINGTON, Jan. 31.—When The Associated Press dispatches telling of the German note began arriving at the White House today President Wilson was in his office talking with a friend. Secretary Tumulty hurried to him with the news. The President could not believe it until he was assured that the information was contained in a formal note already before the State Department.

The President went to bed at 11 o'clock after spending the evening alone in his study with a copy of the German note. This apparently disposed of suggestions that some action might be taken before morning.

The President saw no callers, but is understood to have used the telephone freely.

As far as could be learned, no plans have been laid for him to go before Congerss, as he did to announce the sending of the Sussex note threatening to break off diplomatic relations.

WASHINGTON, Jan. 31.—The United States Government tonight faces its greatest international crisis since the Lusitania was sunk. With full knowledge that her action almost certainly means a break with America, Germany announced to this Government today that she intended to abandon the pledges she gave last year to observe the rules of international law in the conduct of her submarine warfare against merchant shipping. How a break can be avoided, observers here are unable to see. The gravity of the situation cannot be exaggerated.

Beginning at midnight tonight the German U-boats will sink without warning any merchant vessel, neutral as well as enemy, entering a prescribed zone that extends from north of the British Isles around into the Mediterranean to include even the waters of Greece.

That is the sum and substance of Germany's communication to this Government today, delivered to Secretary Lansing in Washington by Count von Bernstorff, the Kaiser's Ambassador, and to Ambassador Gerard, in Berlin, by the Imperial Foreign Office.

The United States Government is on record as determined to break diplomatic relations with Germany if pledges concerning submarine warfare are not observed in letter and in spirit. Today's notification of the Imperial Government brings the United States to the point where it must decide whether it intends to make good the following warning to Germany, contained in a note of April 18, 1916:

"Unless the Imperial Government should now immediately declare and effect an abandonment of its present methods of submarine warfare against passenger and freight-carrying vessels the Government of the United States can have no choice but to sever diplomatic relations with the German Empire altogether. This action the Government of the United States contemplates with the greatest reluctance, but feels constrained to take in behalf of humanity and the rights of neutral nations."

As a result of this warning, the German Government modified its instructions to submarine commanders so as to provide that merchant ships should not be sunk without warning unless they resisted or attempted to escape. But Germany qualified her promises with the statement that she would reserve to herself complete liberty of decision should the United States Government fail to require Great Britain to abandon her alleged illegal blockade, instituted for the purpose of starving out Germany. The German Government now takes the ground that as Great Britain and other members of the Entente have given notice of intention to crush the Central Powers, it is necessary for Germany to abandon her present methods of submarine warfare and use every means at her disposal to resist the Allies.

President Wilson Silent.

The course to be adopted by President Wilson on the basis of the German notification that unrestricted methods of submarine warfare are to be resumed cannot be ascertained tonight. The White House is absolutely silent. Efforts to obtain some word from President Wilson were futile. As far as known, the President had no conferences this evening with any of his advisers. Secretary Lansing remained at home. He declined to comment on the situation produced by Germany's action. From what was said in official circles the idea was obtained that the Administration would wait until tomorrow before undertaking to determine its exact course. All sorts of reports were in circulation, among them that Count von Bernstorff had already received his passports.

In some quarters it is believed that the President is tonight at work on a diplomatic communication to Germany warning that Government that a break in relations is inevitable if ruthless submarine warfare is resumed.

Crisis Not Unexpected.

President Wilson and his confidants have suspected for some time that Germany contemplated resuming ruthless submarine warfare. There is reason to believe that Ambassador Gerard's trip to this country last Autumn was for the especial purpose of telling the President that the German Government might not be able to hold out much longer against the popular sentiment behind the insistence of the von Tirpitz party that unrestricted submarine warfare should be undertaken without regard to the consequences. Knowing that a violation of the pledge Germany gave in the Sussex case would oblige this Government to break relations with Berlin, the Administration for months has been confronted by the apprehension that the von Tirpitz party would obtain the ascendency.

It may now be stated definitely that Secretary Lansing spoke the truth in his statement of Dec. 21, 1916, in which he explained President Wilson's reasons for sending his peace note of Dec. 18 to the belligerent Governments. Mr. Lansing's statement was regarded as alarming, and it caused a near-panic in the stock market. In it he said "we are drawing nearer the verge of war ourselves." So much excitement was caused by this remark that after a consultation with President Wilson he modified it so as to indicate that there was no intention on the part of this Government to change its policy of neutrality. But the first statement was much nearer the truth than the second.

In sounding the belligerent Governments as to the conditions upon which they might be willing to consider arrangements for ending the war, President Wilson had in mind that the danger was ever present that the German Government might abandon the pledge it gave in the Sussex case and resume ruthless methods of submarine warfare. Such a contingency, it was realized, would bring a break in diplomatic relations between Germany and the United States. There has been a general agreement among those best qualified to give an opinion that a break would in all likelihood lead to hostilities.

How long the Government has known in any definite way that Germany contemplated abandoning the pledge she gave in the Sussex case is something that cannot be ascertained from officials. All that was said by them today and prior to today indicated that they had no positive information that unrestricted submarine warfare was to be resumed, and the views they expressed on the subject were based merely on information as to the situation in Germany.

Sea Decree Forecast.

As late as this morning officials of the State Department declared that they had no knowledge indicating that there had been any change in Germnay's attitude on the submarine situation. It was known at that time that the German Government was to send some responses to President Wilson's address to the Senate, but the State Department disclaimed all knowledge of the character or substance of the communication. But if the United States Government was in ignorance of what Germany intended to do, that ignorance was not shared in the capitals of other nations.

It was public knowledge in England and France more than two weeks ago that the German Government intended to extend the limits of her original war zone with the idea of starving out the British Isles. On Jan. 2 THE NEW YORK TIMES printed a story to the effect that passengers arriving in New York the day before on the American liner Philadelphia and the White Star liner Baltic said it was generally believed in England and France that Germany would soon send out a warning to neutral nations of her intention to establish a deep-sea blockade of the British Isles.

Today's notification, confirming the information possessed in England on the subject more than a fortnight ago, furnishes what probably is the main reason for the action of the British Government this week in extending the "danger" area of the English Channel and the North Sea so as to include waters near to the coast of Holland and Denmark. The British Government, it is now believed, made this extension with a view to counteracting the starvation policy of the German Government, announced in the note delivered to the United States today.

It is apparent, therefore, that the German Government cannot with justice contend that its decision to abandon humane methods of submarine warfare was based on the British extension of the danger area. The action of Great Britain seems to have been inspired by advance knowledge of Germany's intention, and not to have furnished reason for the reprisal policy made known in the German note of today.

Bernstorff Delivers Note.

Count von Bernstorff went to the State Department shortly before 4 o'clock this afternoon and delivered to Secretary Lansing personally the German communication with the accompanying notification of the extension of the war zone area. When the Ambassador left the office of the Secretary of State neither he nor Mr. Lansing would furnish any information as to the purpose of the Ambassador's visit other than that he had delivered a communication from his Government.

When it became known that his communication contained notice of Germany's abandonment of her present methods of submarine warfare efforts were made by newspaper men to see Secretary Lansing, but without success. When Mr. Lansing left the State Department for his home later in the afternoon he was asked by newspaper men who encountered him in the corridor whether he would make a statement concerning the German communication.

"I have nothing to say at all," he answered.

It was expected that Mr. Lansing would go to the White House tonight, but he did not do so.

Apparently there was an agreement between the German Ambassador and the Secretary of State by which neither was to make any statement to the press interpretative of the German note. Count von Bernstorff declined to talk for publication, and it was evident that he realized the gravity of the situation and the danger that might come from any public comment on the new policy of his Government. The German attitude, however, appeared to be well understood in quarters where the views of the Central Powers are usually reflected accurately, and it was gathered from what was said in these quarters that Germany was well aware of the seriousness of her abandonment of her pledges to the United States, and had not decided to enter upon the new policy without careful consideration.

The German Government, according to information that has reached Washington, has more than 300 submarines, perhaps as many as 500, which will undertake the work of destroying shipping engaged in carrying cargoes to and from the territory of Germany's enemies. These submarines, it is understood, will be divided into flotillas or sections, each of which will perform blockade duty for a certain period and will be relieved in terms by submarines of another flotilla or section. A confident feeling exists in Teutonic circles here that not one ship will be able to escape the watchful U boats. There is reason to believe that this feeling represents the scope and character of Germany's intention in promulgating the new war zone order.

The German Government has undertaken this new policy with the intention of shutting off all supplies from the British Isles. In undertaking this course Germany holds that it is a step in the direction of forcing her enemies to accept peace, and can be defended on the ground that it will relieve the world from the most awful tragedy that it has ever experienced. Germany's purpose is "to play the game the other way around"; in other words, to force peace by means of ruthless warfare.

Under the terms of the notification delivered to this Government today, no merchant ships will be permitted to go in or out of the blockaded area without danger of being sunk without warning. The only reservation is that passenger vessels will not be interfered with if they are already at sea, but this immunity will extend only for the period of the current voyage.

Only One Vessel a Week.

Steamships of the American Line will not be molested if guarantees are given by the officers of the line that they do not carry contraband. But only one vessel of this line will be permitted to depart each week and the voyage must be between New York and Falmouth.

The privilege will be extended to vessels of the American Line to proceed from Falmouth to ports of Holland, but the voyage must be taken through a prescribed area thirty miles wide. It is not known in Washington whether such special provision will apply to merchant vessels of other neutral nations.

Germany defends this course on the ground that when the pledge was given in the Sussex case she reserved the right of resuming unrestricted submarine warfare if the United States failed to induce Great Britain to abandon her blockade of German ports and ports of neutral nations of Northern Europe.

The United States not having succeeded in bringing about a modification of the British blockade, the German Government, it is understood here, felt it could not hold out longer against German public opinion, and, to satisfy the pressure of its own people, was obliged to agree to resume the policy advocated by Grand Admiral von Tirpitz and a very strong following among influential men in the Empire. Great Britain, it is contended, has been trying to starve Germany for two years and Germany now feels that she has the right to undertake a starvation policy against England.

Those who sympathize with the German policy and have some knowledge of feeling in Germany on the subject predict that England can be brought to the verge of starvation in thirty days. It is contended in Germany that the British Isles have food supplies only sufficient to feed their people for that period.

The war, according to the German view, has now reached the basis of economic warfare, with each side trying to win by starving the other. The Central Powers, it is understood, regard it as more important at this stage of hostilities to keep food out of England than to keep out munitions.

Answers Wilson's Address.

Germany interpreted President Wilson's peace address to the Senate as inviting an answer from the belligerent powers. In this interpretation the German Government was influenced by the fact that a copy of the President's address, which had been cabled by the State Department to the American Embassy in Berlin, was furnished to the Berlin Foreign Office by Ambassador Gerard.

Germany was glad of the opportunity to make a response to the President's address, because it gave her the chance to explain that she was in accord with the sentiments expressed by the President as to the future relationship of nations.

She was also glad of the chance to say that the declared intention of the Entente Governments with respect to Turkey in Europe and certain other territory now held by the Central Powers was interpreted by Germany as a declaration of intention on the part of the Entente to crush Germany and her allies. After the Entente had gone on record to that effect, peace was out of the question, according to the German view, and it was impossible for the Central Powers to make further overtures with a view to ending the war. This was not merely the view of Germany and her allies, it was contended, but was the view of all Europe.

It was pointed out in the circles mentioned that the German position was if the British blockade had been modified so as to permit foodstuffs to pass to neutral ports of Northern Europe, legitimate trade would not have been interfered with by the Central Powers and there would have been no submarine issue.

At the same time the naïve admission was made that if legitimate trade had been carried on with neutral countries, these countries would have sold foodstuffs to Germany which, it was asserted, they had a perfect right to do.

It was learned tonight that the de-cision of the German Government to resume unrestricted submarine warfare was probably reached before President Wilson delivered his speech to the Senate on Jan. 22. It was not asserted that absolute advices to that effect had been received in Washington, but it was contended that the German decision must have been reached some time ago, because it would require considerable preparation to make the arrangements announced today for carrying the new war zone order into effect. This statement, which comes from a source friendly to the Central Powers, fits in with the information brought to the United States on Jan. 21 by passengers on the steamships Philadelphia and Baltic of Germany's intention to establish an extensive blockade to cut off supplies from the British Isles.

A decided reticence to discuss the situation created by the new German policy was manifested among Senators and Representatives this evening. It was apparent from the attitude of most of them that they appreciated the seriousness of the matter and felt that it would be unwise for them to talk.

A Senator said tonight that he believed that sentiment in the Senate and House was favorable to the adoption of a resolution warning Americans not to take passage on vessels which would be placed in jeopardy through the operation of Germany's new submarine methods. This Senator was not in sympathy with any such resolution, but he said he believed those who sided with him would be unable to prevent a warning resolution from being adopted if it were brought up for action in Congress.

Thinks Americans Oppose War.

For weeks inspired, authoritative, and almost semi-official statements have been coming from Berlin indicating an absolute decision not to resume unrestricted submarine warfare. The complete agreement of the Emperor, Chancellor von Bethmann Hollweg, General von Hindenburg, and General von Ludendorff, the four men in whose hands Germany's destiny lies, has been mentioned frequently in dispatches passing the censor. Information received only today, however, shows that a very careful campaign for the full use of sea forces has been under way recently. It has been urged as essential to Germany's existence, and it was represent-ed that it would be impossible now for President Wilson to get the American people behind him in a declaration of war. Congress was represented as opposed to war.

Germany, according to information received here, realizes that her action may result in a break of relations, but Berlin officials are prepared for the rupture. Tonight they were represented as feeling that the only other steps open to the United States was to call a conference of neutral nations to end the blockade or some other step which speedily would result in peace. Information received from the same source is that Admiral von Tirpitz, or his followers, had absolutely nothing to do with the new policy. On the contrary, it was said tonight that von Tirpitz was not, as has heretofore been supposed, removed from power because he advocated ruthless submarine warfare. The fact, according to this information, was that he was deposed because he did not effectively carry out the campaign he inaugurated. From German quarters tonight came the information that Germany now has from 800 to 500 submarines ready for the campaign.

The German view is that the new policy will improve general prospects of an early peace. Germany is represented as still being ready to discuss peace at any time. However, it is declared that German officials, both in this country and in Berlin, feel that the declaration of changed policy should make it clear that Germany and her allies are in the war to the last drop of blood.

Policy Laid to Hindenburg.

Unrestricted submarine warfare, it was declared, was determined upon as soon as the nature of the Entente reply to President Wilson's note became known and before the President's address to the Senate. The President's address, it was said authoritatively, come in the midst of the situation, and because of its nature it appeared for a time as if the new campaign might be postponed. However, it was explained, much preparation was necessary for the opening of such a campaign and nothing was to be gained by waiting. It is believed here that the policy was decided upon at a recent conference at the headquarters of the German General Staff, and that Field Marshal von Hindenburg played a most important part in its formulation.

It is expected that Austria-Hungary will take action similar to that of Germany with regard to the operations of its submarines in the Mediterranean.

Every public intimation from Germany in the last few months has been that an unrestricted submarine warfare, almost certain to bring in the United States, would be adopted only as a last act of desperation. German papers have said Germany would not dare oppose neutral opinion unless she were willing to have the rest of the neutral world added to her enemies.

Two opposing views of American hostility have been allowed to pass the German censor. The first was that the harm the United States could do to Germany as an active enemy was no greater than as a neutral supplying munitions and loans to the Allies, and that the crippling of allied shipping would be the turning point of the war. This apparently is the view now adopted. The other view, known to have been held by some high officials here, was that Germany might in desperation seek to involve the United States as an actual enemy on the ground that her influence at the peace conference would be a generous one.

Washington Officials Stunned.

Officials here, stunned at the suddenness of the German action, do not conceal their disquietude over the mental unpreparedness of the American public for what may be coming. The recent flood of peace discussion, started by the German offer, increased by the President's note, and again by the Entente reply, are thought to have turned public opinion in this country entirely away from the possibility of war, and to have focussed attention on the terms of a possible peace.

A revulsion is expected to take place in the Entente countries, with the result that the world war will enter a period of frightfulness unimagined heretofore. With the massing for huge offensives by land and the announcement of ruthlessness by sea, officials look forward to at least a Spring and Summer of unprecedented slaughter.

"Barred Zones" and "Safety Lanes" Outlined in Germany's Note.

"All the News That's Fit to Print."

The New York Times.

THE WEATHER
Fair, warmer today; fair, colder Monday.
For full weather report see Page 16.

VOL. LXVI...NO. 21,561. ..   NEW YORK, SUNDAY, FEBRUARY 4, 1917.—96 PAGES, In Eight Parts.   PRICE FIVE CENTS.

RELATIONS WITH GERMANY ARE BROKEN OFF; AMERICAN SHIP HOUSATONIC SUNK, CREW SAFE; MILITIA CALLED OUT; GERMAN SHIPS SEIZED

BREAK WITH AUSTRIA, TOO

Notice of Her Blockade Arrives as President Is Speaking.

EXPECTS NEUTRAL SUPPORT

President Expresses Belief That They Will Follow America's Course.

STILL HOPES AGAINST WAR

Mr. Wilson Unable to Believe That Germany Means to Carry Out Threat.

Special to The New York Times.

WASHINGTON, Feb. 3.—Diplomatic relations between Germany and the United States were severed today. It was President Wilson's answer to the German notice that any merchant vessel which entered prescribed areas would be sunk without warning. Count von Bernstorff, the Kaiser's Ambassador, has received his passports; in other words, he has been dismissed by this Government. James W. Gerard, the American Ambassador at Berlin, has been ordered to return home with his staff.

President Wilson made the sensational answer in a momentous address delivered before the two houses of Congress assembled in joint session this afternoon. Congress appears to be unanimous in a determination to stand by the President in whatever measures he takes. Party lines have been obliterated in the general desire to support the Administration in dealing with a critical situation that most observers expect to result in the entrance of the United States into the European conflict.

War has not been declared. The President in his address said: "We do not desire any hostile conflict with the German Government." But preparations for war are being made. Navy yards have been closed to the public. For the present private shipbuilding concerns and other plants engaged in Government work will take their own precautionary measures. Private shipbuilders have offered, to place their establishments under the control of the Government, and a provision authorizing the Secretary of the Navy to do this will be offered by the Naval Committee in the House on Monday.

German merchant ships at American ports are being closely guarded, and some have been seized. Our war vessels are said to have received precautionary orders. Army arsenals have been told to guard against danger. Public buildings here and elsewhere are being guarded also.

Break with Austria, Too.

Diplomatic relations with Austria-Hungary are to be severed also. This was made certain by the receipt by the State Department today of a note from the Vienna Government containing notice of adherence to the German submarine blockade policy. President Wilson did not know this when he went to the Capitol. Count Tarnowski von Tarnow, the newly accredited Ambassador of Austria-Hungary, who had reached the United States on Thursday, went to the State Department today to arrange for his formal presentation to President Wilson. Word was brought to him that Secretary Lansing would be unable to receive him. Hardly had the Ambassador gone when the department received a cable message from Frederic C. Penfield, the American Ambassador at Vienna, giving the text of the Austro-Hungarian adherence to the German war zone order. As Count Tarnowski has not been formally received by this Government he may not be dismissed in the same way as Count von Bernstorff was, but he will be invited to leave the country, with the members of his suite and embassy staff. Ambassador Penfield and his embassy staff will be ordered home. If war results it will be war not only with Germany but with Austria-Hungary and Turkey as well, and possibly with Bulgaria.

Demands Release of Americans.

Taking it for granted that war is inevitable, speculation is being indulged in here as to how soon the clash will come. That it will come soon is a general opinion tonight. A German submarine is reported to have sunk the American freight steamer Houstatonic. Word came officially today that Germany was holding as prisoners of war sixty-odd American citizens taken from merchant ships by a German raider. This Government has demanded their release immediately. If Germany refuses—and this is expected—the President may ask Congress to authorize him to take measures of reprisal. He will certainly do so if Germany does not spare American merchantmen entering the forbidden areas.

An important aspect of the situation to which little attention has been attracted is that President Wilson hopes that other neutral nations will join the United States in blacklisting Germany in proclaiming that Government as a pariah unworthy of association with other nations in the great world family. The President as his intention is understood, wants Germany "sent to Coventry," not to be spoken to until she has shown herself worthy of recognition again.

The United States stands ready to champion the integrity of neutral rights. Whether this will be done single-handed or with the co-operation of other neutral nations is not known. An exchange of views between the United States and the Foreign Offices of South America and Europe is expected to be in progress by Monday. In Spain's recent reply to President Wilson's note to the belligerent nations that country's willingness to participate in any concert of neutrals for the safeguarding and protection of the common rights of neutrals was indicated.

COUNT JOHANN VON BERNSTORFF

BERNSTORFF WAS NOT SURPRISED

But on Receiving Passports Did Not Hide His Concern Over Failure of His Efforts.

HAS NO SAFE CONDUCT YET

Details of Arrangements for His Departure Not Settled—His Wife an American.

Special to The New York Times.

WASHINGTON, Feb. 3.—Count von Bernstorff, who had been Ambassador from Germany to the United States since Dec. 30, 1908, received his passports promptly on the stroke of 2 o'clock this afternoon. These were broad enough to cover the German Ambassador, his family and all the members of the embassy suite, but no communication was delivered to the Ambassador to the effect that he would receive safe conduct from this country to Germany. This is a detail that will have to be arranged later.

The passports were delivered by Lester H. Woolsey, an Assistant Solicitor for the State Department, who is attached in a confidential capacity to the office of Secretary Lansing. Mr. Woolsey also delivered to the Ambassador the

Col. Roosevelt Squarely With the President

Special to The New York Times.

OYSTER BAY, N. Y., Feb. 3.— Colonel Theodore Roosevelt pledged himself tonight in support of President Wilson in upholding the honor of the United States, and offered his own and the services of his four sons to the country in case hostilities are not averted.

Plans for a volunteer army division, to be commanded by the Colonel, which his friends have worked on since the sinking of the Lusitania, again have jumped to the fore, and the Colonel tonight said he had asked the War Department for permission to raise such a body of troops.

"Of course, I shall in every way support the President in all that he does to uphold the honor of the United States and to safeguard the lives of American citizens," he said. "Yesterday I wrote to the War Department asking permission to raise a division if war is declared and there is a call for volunteers. In such event I and my four sons will go."

text of a note from Secretary Lansing, which was worded so as to embrace the main portions of the text of the President's address to the Senate. The note handed to Count von Bernstorff did not, however, embrace that part of the President's speech which declared that this Government did not desire any "hostile conflict" with Germany, and that only actual overt acts on the latter's part could make the President believe that Germany intended to disregard its long friendship with this country.

that he might find it necessary later on that "authority be given to me to use any means that may be necessary for the protection of our seamen and our people in the prosecution of their peaceful and legitimate errands on the high seas," the President said: "I take it for granted that all neutral nations will take the same course."

Bernstorff Promptly Notified.

The note of dismissal handed to Count von Bernstorff was practically a paraphrase of the President's address to Congress. It was signed by Robert Lansing, Secretary of State, and was given to the German Ambassador personally by Lester H. Woolsey, an assistant solicitor of the State Department who does most of the confidential legal work for Secretary Lansing. Mr. Woolsey went to the German Embassy on Massachusetts Avenue at exactly 2 o'clock and was received immediately by Count von Bernstorff. Mr. Woolsey's arrival at the embassy was timed to correspond to the moment when President Wilson appeared in the hall of the House of Representatives to inform Congress that diplomatic relations with Germany had been severed. With the note handed to the German Ambassador by Mr. Woolsey were the passports guaranteeing Count von Bernstorff safe conduct out of the United States. When and how he will depart and where he will go are questions to be determined. Count von Bernstorff is still at the embassy.

The concluding paragraph of the note of dismissal to Count von Bernstorff gives in brief form the action taken by this Government today, which breaks officially for the first time in history the friendly relations existing between Germany or any German State and the United States. That paragraph reads:

"The President has, therefore, directed me to announce to your Excellency that all diplomatic relations between the United States and the German Empire are severed, and that the American Ambassador at Berlin will be immediately withdrawn, and in accordance with such announcement to deliver to your Excellency your passports." And the Secretary of State, whose language was scrupulously courteous throughout his communication, had "the honor to be, your Excellency's obedient servant, Robert Lansing."

Precautions at Capital.

Washington is calm outwardly, but under the surface the excitement is intense. Having recovered from its first shock of realization that the break with Germany which might mean war had come at last, Washington began to discuss the situation and arrived at the conclusion that a break was the only possible outcome of the German notice that ruthless methods of submarine warfare were to be resumed. This, of course, applies to Washington generally. Official Washington showed a bit of excitement as the day wore along.It was impossible not to come under the spell of the air of activity in the Government Departments where the wheels were humming in a way suggestive of the period of the war with Spain.

Persons who have been in the habit of passing regularly in and out of Government buildings were stopped at the entrances and told that they could not enter unless they furnished evidence that they were Government employes or had engagements with officials. The great host of clerks who make their homeward way nightly through the White House grounds were politely told by policemen that the gorunds were closed to the public for an indefinite period. The gates leading to the footways were closed, and while the gates of the entrances to the driveways were open, they were guarded by policemen.

Suffragists bearing banners inquiring of President Wilson how long women must wait for liberty and what the President would do for suffrage kept up their vigil at the White House gates. It was bitterly cold, but the women stood their watches cheerfully. The part of the White House grounds closed today had never been closed except for the brief periods of ceremonial occasions.

Joseph P. Tumulty, Secretary to the President, said the grounds had been closed merely out of excess of caution. He thought it well to take that action in a time likley to lead to great popular excitement.

Decision Reached at Night.

President Wilson's decision to break with Germany at once was apparently reached in the still watches of the night. When he left the Capitol yesterday evening after consulting with sixteen Senators he did not indicate what course he intended to follow in dealing with the German Government. All that was known was thathe new submarine policy of Germany made a break inevitable. But when it was to come was problematical. The President had been advised by some of his conferees to break at once. Others had thought he should wait for an actual sinking of a merchantman without warning by a German submarine. Some—but they were few—suggested that another diplomatic note should be sent to Germany before a severance of relations. Which of these courses the President would be inclined to follow he did not indicate when he left the Capitol.

It was abut 10:30 o'clock this morning that the President sent for Secretary Lansing and told him that the had determined that diplomatic relations with Germany should be broken at once. He then arranged for addressing Congress at 2 o'clock. Secretary Lansing went back tothe State Department to make the necessary arrangements for dismissing Ambassador von Bernstorff and recalling Ambassador Gerard.

The scene when President Wilson appeared at the House at 2 o'clock was dramatic. Reports had been in circulation that the President had ordered a break with Germany, but comparatively few persons in that large audience were certain as to what attitude the President had decided to adopt. Floor and galleries were packed and jammed when the President entered the chamber. He got a cordial reception. In the thirty minutes that he stood at the rostrum facing that breathless, eager gathering of men and women, only twice did his hearers become really demonstrative. He had received a round of handclapping and a cheer or two when he appeared. Then the audience listened attentively to the President's words as he read from little printed pages.

Draws Volleys of Cheers.

The President had sketched the steps the Government had taken to bring Germany to a realization of her responsiblility to other nations in the conduct of submarine warfare. It was near the close of the address when the crowd broke into applause over his declaration that he had directed that all diplomatic realtions between Germany and the United States should be severed. A moment later there was another outbreak of approval when he said that he refused to believe that the German Government intended to do in fact what it had given warning of intention to do, but this applause was not very marked. When, near the very end of the address, the President said he would come before Congress again to ask authority to protect Americans on the seas if Germany carried out her threats, the audience burst into spontaneous cheering.

On the whole the businesslike and direct character of the address brought general commendation from those who heard it, and a careful canvass of opinion among Senators and Representatives showed that party lines were obliterated in the patriotic desire to prove to the President that the nation's legislators stood behind him in the most important and far-reaching action he has undertaken in his Presidential term.

CONGRESS THRILLED BY HISTORIC SPEECH

Tense Interest Is Followed by Cheers as Throng Filling the House Stands.

WILSON CALM, CONFIDENT

Unusual Precautions to Guard Him —Supreme Court Bench Attends in a Body.

Special to The New York Times.

WASHINGTON, Feb. 3.—When President Wilson stepped out on the Speaker's paltform at 2 o'clock sharp this afternoon to deliver the message which startled and thrilled the country, he faced probably the most impressive alliance that has gathered in the chamber of the House of Representatives in many years.

The news of the President's step, announced in a hurried extra issued by afternoon papers, had spread through Washington, and long before the time set for the speech the Capitol was crowded with people importuning members of Congress and officials for admission to the galleries. Hundreds of citizens standing about the corridors outside the chamber and thousands within and without the Capitol Building were unable to gain admittance to the House itself.

On the floor every member of the House was in his seat many minutes before the time set, thoroughly stirred by the impending announcement. For the first time in the history of joint sessions, so far as could be remembered tonight by officials in the Capitol. The Chief Justice and Associate Justices of the Supreme Court were present, sitting in a body in the front row of seats at the left of the Speaker's desk, while the members of the Cabinet were scattered about through the chamber. The rear of the House was filled with clerks of committees and others who have floor privileges.

Senators Solemnly File In.

The centre door of the chamber was thrown open at five minutes of 2 o'clock and the members of the Senate, preceded by the Vice President, filed in by twos with unusual solemnity, and ranged themselves in the seats reserved for them in the front of the chamber.

For the first time there were so few absentees among the members of both houses that the ushers were compelled to place chairs in the aisles to seat several of the visiting Senators.

In the diplomatic gallery on the north side of the chamber sat two members of the allied diplomatic corps, Minister Havenith of Belgium, and Jules Jusserand, the French Ambassador, both of whom watched the President intently all through the reading of his message. Dr. Paul Ritter, the Swiss Minister; Constantin Brun, the Danish Minister; Ambassador Naon of Argentina, Frank Polk, Counsellor of the State Department, and Breckinridge Long Third Assistant Secretary of State, were also in the diplomatic gallery.

Secretary Lansing alone of the members of the Cabinet was not in the chamber. Mrs. Wilson, an opera glass in her hand, sat in the executive gallery.

As the President appeared, those on the floor and in the galleries rose. There was an outburst of applause from the Democratic side emphasized with some cheering. A few Republicans joined in the hand clapping. A feeling of suspense and uncertainty kept it from lasting more than a few moments.

Speaker Champ Clark, in the chair, said formally: "Gentlemen of the Sixty-fourth Congress: I present the President of the United States." and the audience sank back in the seats.

President Calm and Confident.

The President was dressed almost youthfully in a smart cutaway instead of the frock coat in which he has appeared in public of late, and while his manner was wholly serious it was untinged with any unusual appearance of being oppressed with overwhelming burdens. His voice was calm and his attitude wholly self-possessed and confident.

As Mr. Wilson began reading, the atmosphere was tense, seeming to relax slightly as he proceeded with the recital of the history of the diplomatic correspondence over the submarine issue. His voice, although entirely audible from the first, grew clearer as he went on. As he concluded the reading of the last German note, with the words "All ships met within the zone will be sunk," the tension seemed to grow, and the suspense increased further as he announced that this Government had no alternative but to take the course it had mapped out for itself.

As he began the sentence, "I have, therefore, directed the Secretary of State to announce to his Excellency the German Ambassador," many members of Congress leaned forward to make sure of every word, and as he reached "that all diplomatic relations between the United States and the German Empire are severed," both sides of the chamber, without permitting him to finish the sentence, burst into a long round of applause, with cheers from the Southern Democrats.

The first man to applaud was Benjamin R. ("Pitchfork") Tillman of South Carolina, Chairman of the Senate Naval Affairs Committee; the second, sitting beside him, was Henry Cabot Lodge of Massachusetts, ranking Republican member of the Senate Foreign Relations Committee, and the President's bitterest critic in the Senate.

At two other points there was generous applause from both parties—when the President declared that "only overt acts" could convince him that Germany intended to carry out her threats, and when he declared that if she did so he would take the liberty of coming again before Congress to ask authority "to use any means that may be necessary for the protection of our seamen and our people in the prosecution of their peaceful and legitimate errands on the high seas." The last outburst was the loudest.

Audience Stands and Cheers.

Genuine emotion stirred Mr. Wilson as he reached the words, "God grant we may not be challenged to defend them [American rights] from acts of willful injustice on the part of the Government of Germany." The audience stood up and again applauded as he concluded.

As soon as the President left the chamber the joint session broke up, the Senate returning to its own hall, and the House reverting to the consideration of the Naval Appropriation bill.

All through his address the President found Congress in thorough sympathy with his position. The episode was completely lacking, however, in the wild scenes that would be expected in the event of a declaration of war. The applause and cheering was generous from Republicans and Democrats alike, but the predominant mood seemed one of regretful determination. The general feeling was that the parting of the ways had been reached, and that the President must be supported, but that extreme measures were justified only as an inevitable and deplorable necessity, because there was no alternative.

There was a feeling on the part of some members, however, that the excitement was no less tense because subdued. Not until after 11 o'clock this morning, when extras appeared on the street, did members of Congress realize that the break had come. Most of them had expected it soon, but the President's conference with Senators last night had given many of them the impression it might be delayed for days or even weeks.

One Senator said this afternoon that if, after today's warning, Germany should commit the "overt act" which she has threatened, and the President should go again before Congress with an actual war message the suppressed feelings of the country would be expressed in a wild wave of enthusiasm. All day today the two chambers were outwardly calm.

Downstairs in the corridors of the Capitol before the President arrived there was general confusion. Literally thousands of persons were gathered both inside and outside the House wing of the building watching for any chance to get to a place where they might see the President. Special officers were appointed to assist the Capitol police in their attempts to hold the people in check.

Arrival of the President.

Outside the Capitol several thousand persons stood and applauded the President as he reached the House wing. Motion picture cameras clicked, and there was a surge around the President's automobile as he left it.

Unusual precautions were taken to safeguard the President as he entered the elevator which carried him to the Speaker's room, where a committee of the Senate and House awaited. A large throng had congregated near the entrance to the Speaker's lobby, in this room being members of Congress, newspaper correspondents, Capitol attachés, and a few onlookers who had somehow gained admission to the middle floor before the doors were shut.

When the President stepped out of the elevator, four secret service men and two Capitol policemen ranged themselves between the Chief Executive and the crowd. Mr. Wilson took three steps and the door of the Speaker's office closed behind him.

Prior to the arrival of Mr. Wilson the most animated scenes were in the lobbies and smoking rooms back of the House chamber. Members of Congress by the score surged about two tables at one of which stood employees of the bookkeeper's office distributing gallery tickets. To each member of the Senate and House was alloted one ticket to the gallery, the shortness of the notice precluding distribution in the ordinary way.

Because of this an unusual and spectacular method of distribution was followed. Assistant doorkeepers called out the names of members of the House as one might at an auction sale and the legislators crowded and pushed one another in their hurry to get next to the ticket distributor. The tickets were not ready for distribution until about 1 o'clock and excited members grabbed their cards and rushed to a telephone to advise wives or others to hurry to the Capitol.

The galleries filled to the doors in less than an hour. Persons to whom tickets of admission were denied—that is, the general public—offered fancy prices for the pasteboards and pleaded with members of Congress to get them into the gallery somehow. In ninety cases out of a hundred these pleas were unavailing.

Only fifteen minutes was consumed in the reading of the address. The President left the Capitol as hurriedly as he came, and as he departed from the building he found outside a cheering throng who watched his automobile dash back to the Executive Mansion.

Cabinet Members Cheered.

Members of the Cabinet entered the Capitol a few minutes in advance of the President. As each entered a wave of applause swept through the congested corridors.

Hardly thirty men were in their seats in the House at 11 o'clock this morning when Claude Kitchin, the Democratic floor leader, whom Secretary Tumulty had asked to arrange for the joint session, introduced his resolution. the galleries, which had just begn to fill, were immediately emptied.

James R. Mann, the Republican floor leader, asked if any action would be required of the House at the joint session, to which Mr. Kitchin replied that he understood not. The word was quickly passed around, and members began to hurry to the chamber to find out what was to be expected.

"All the News That's
Fit to Print."

The New York Times.

THE WEATHER
Probably snow, colder by tonight;
Friday fair, much colder.
For full weather report see Page 21.

VOL. LXVI...NO. 21,565.   ...   NEW YORK, THURSDAY, FEBRUARY 8, 1917.—TWENTY-TWO PAGES.   ONE CENT In Greater New York | TWO CENTS
Jersey City and Newark.

LINER CALIFORNIA SUNK WITHOUT WARNING, MANY MISSING; GERARD AND ALL AMERICANS IN GERMANY HELD AS HOSTAGES; NO CONVOYS GRANTED, AMERICAN LINE CANCELS SAILINGS

AMERICAN, IN CREW, SAVED

Two Women and Several Children Among Missing; One Known Death.

TWO TORPEDOES HIT SHIP

Fired Without Warning from a Distance of 300 Yards, the Captain Asserts.

MAY BE THE 'OVERT ACT'

News Creates Great Excitement in Washington — Wilson Will Move Cautiously.

Special to The New York Times.

WASHINGTON, Feb. 7.—The State Department was officially notified tonight by Wesley Frost, American Consul at Queenstown, that the British steamer California of the Anchor Line had been sunk without warning off the coast of Ireland with 200 persons on board. Some of the passengers and crew, he reported, were still missing, including two women and several children.

There was at least one American survivor—John A. Lee of Montgomery, Ala., thought to have been a member of the crew, and who is reported by Consul Frost as having been saved.

Consul Frost's first message regarding the loss of the California reached the State Department late this afternoon, and was given out in paraphrase as follows:

"Anchor Line California has been sunk, bound for Glasgow, presumably from New York. Two hundred persons on board. One death, thirty hospital cases. Survivors reached here late tonight."

The State Department made public tonight additional information received from Consul Frost. This information is understood to have been received in a second message from the Consul, and declared that the California went down immediately, after having been fired at with two torpedoes, and that it was torpedoed without warning.

The text of Consul Frost's message containing this information was not given out by the State Department, but this paraphrase of the Frost message was issued:

"Consul Wesley G. Frost, at Queenstown, cabled the State Department to-

night that the British liner California had been torpedoed without warning off the Irish coast, and that one American, known to have been on board, was saved. Some of the passengers and crew still were missing, including two women and several children.

"The Captain of the ship was quoted as saying the submarine did not hail or give any warning before firing two torpedoes from a distance of 300 yards. The American survivor was John A. Lee of Montgomery, Ala., who was supposed to have been a member of the crew."

The statement in Consul Front's message that the California was sunk without warning at a distance of 300 yards, that women and children are missing, and that at least one American was on board, gives the California case a most grave aspect in the present crisis, and if this information is fully confirmed the cast may be regarded by the President as the overt act which he told Congress he was unready to believe Germany intended to commit.

Whether any Americans were or were not killed, complete proof that the vessel was attacked without warning without regard for the lives of men, women, and children on board, will present the gravest possible situation in the present crisis, as the mere presence of a single American on board means that an American life was jeopardized by an attack that is officially reported to have been without warning.

Consul Frost says that the Captain of the California is quoted as saying the submarine did not hail or give warning, but fired two torpedoes. Whether or not the Consul has been able to confirm the Captian's statement from other sources is not disclosed, but it is a fact that the announcement authorized by the State Department tonight, based on Consul Frost's dispatch, says without qualification or reservation the Consul reported that the vessel had been torpedoed without warning.

The mere fact that one American survivor was saved does not alter the issue as laid down in the various notes to Germany during the past two years, in which it has been steadily insisted upon, that the lives of Americans on any peaceful merchant steamers should not be "jeopardized" by unwarranted attacks.

If the steamer was attacked without warning and without affording safety for human lives, and lost no immunity through attempting to escape or through resistance, while Americans were on board, the issue is as serious as if those Americans had been killed.

That an American citizen on board was saved is to be attributed, it is said, to luck or good fortune and not to the observance of humane and international law codes by the German submarine commander. This Government has always insisted that warning must be given and that no merchant vessel should be sunk without first having afforded the passenger and crews on board an opportunity to escape.

Manifestly, it has been the contention of President Wilson and Secretary Lansing that this opportunity is not given if vessels that neither seek to escape nor try to resist are sunk without warning. In Secretary Lansing's note of June 9, 1915, to the German Government, the note that brought about Secretary Bryan's resignation, this Government's position was outlined in this phrase:

"Only her (the Lusitania's) actual resistance to capture or refusal to stop when ordered to do so for the purpose of visit could have afforded the commander of the submarine any justification for so much as putting the lives of those on board the ship in jeopardy."

It was then contended and has since been the position of this Governement that the lives of Americans must not ever be put in jeopardy by unjustifiable attacks by German submarines, and that it is just as serious to jeopardize those lives in this manner as to bring about the actual loss of American lives, so far as concerns the principle for which the United States Government has contended.

The case of the California as thus far reported is clearly regarded as ruthless submarine warfare by Government officials, and only awaits complete and undoubted confirmation to be regarded as a deliberate disregard of the pledges which Germany gave to the United States Government in formal writing.

The following extract from the note which Secretary Lansing, by direction of President Wilson, sent to Germany April 18, 1916, in the Sussex case, is considered the keynote of this Government's attitude toward the joepardizing of American lives of peaceful merchant steamers by submarine attacks without warning.

"Again and again, no warning has been given, no escape even to the ship's boats allowed to those on board. Great liners like the Lusitania and Arabic and mere passenger boats like the Susex have been attacked without a moment's warning, often before they have even become aware that they were in the presence of an armed ship of the enemy, and the lives of noncombatant passengers and crew have been destroyed wholesale and in a manner which the Government of the United States cannot but regard as wanton and without the slightest color of justification."

GERARD SENDS WORD TO EGAN

Minister to Denmark Told That Americans Cannot Leave.

ENVOY CANNOT USE CODE

Berlin Wants Assurance of Safety of Bernstorff and the German Crews Here.

WASHINGTON IS STIRRED

Inclined to Question Report of Such Radical Action by Berlin Government.

Special Cable to The New York Times.

COPENHAGEN, Feb. 7.—I am authorized by the American Legation to say that Minister Egan today received several sensational dispatches from Ambassador Gerard.

The latter telegraphs that the German authorities will not permit Americans to leave Germany at present. He says that he, his staff, and all American Consular officials will be detained until the fate of Count

LONDON, Feb. 7.—Addressing a meeting in London tonight, John Hodge, Minister of Labor, said he thought he was giving away no secret in saying that at the recent conference between representatives of the Entente Allies the determination had been arrived at to terminate the war by the end of Summer.

von Bernstorff and the German crews from the captured German ships in America has been decided.

The German authorities are denying Mr. Gerard the right to telegraph in code. All correspondence with the Copenhagen Legation is now in plain English.

Ambassador Gerard advised Minister Egan that the sailors captured on the Yarrowdale will be detained on the same grounds as the other Americans.

Confirmation from Berlin.

Special Cable to The New York Times.

BERLIN, Feb. 7, (via London, Feb. 8, 5:40 A. M.)—Ambassador Gerard is still without instructions from the Foreign Office as to his departure. These seem to be withheld until arrangements regarding Count von Bernstorff's repatriation are concluded.

BERLIN, Feb. 6, (via London, Feb. 7.) —The Foreign Office thus far has received no definite information in regard to the former German Ambassador at Washington, Count von Bernstorff, which probably must arrive before the details of Ambassador Gerard's departure can be decided.

Mr. Gerard has not yet received his passports, and does not know definitely when he will depart, although he has decided upon the route via Switzerland.

The rush of Americans seeking passports and information at the American Embassy lessened considerably today, and at the closing hour most of the work had been completed by the officials and employes.

AMSTERDAM, Feb. 7, (via London.)—According to Les Nouvelles of Maestricht, Holland, a dynamite factory at Schlebusch, near Cologne, was blown up on Jan. 27, causing the death of 200 persons, mostly women.

An explosion last Thursday on the railway between Aix-la-Chapelle and Louvain, this newspaper reports, caused the death or injury of 26 Belgian workmen.

"All the News That's Fit to Print."

The New York Times.

THE WEATHER
Fair, colder today and tomorrow; strong northwest winds, diminishing.
For full weather report see Page 10.

VOL. LXVI...NO. 21,584. ....   NEW YORK, TUESDAY, FEBRUARY 27, 1917.—TWENTY PAGES.   ONE CENT in Greater New York, Jersey City and Newark. TWO CENTS Elsewhere.

PRESIDENT ASKS BROAD POWERS TO MEET U-BOAT WARFARE; BILL INTRODUCED; REPUBLICANS OPPOSE UNLIMITED GRANT; LINER LACONIA SUNK; TWO AMERICANS, PROBABLY MORE, LOST

RIGHT TO ARM SHIPS ASKED

Special to The New York Times

WASHINGTON, Feb. 26.—President Wilson today asked Congress to provide means to enable the Government to maintain an "armed neutrality" in dealing with the unrestricted submarine warfare of Germany, which, besides checking the operations of American shipping, had brought about a situation "fraught with the gravest possibilities and dangers."

Appearing in person before the Senate and House, assembled in joint session, he read a brief address, the substance of which was that he should be authorized to supply armament and ammunition to American merchant vessels and "to employ any other instrumentalities or methods that may be necessary and adequate to protect our ships and our people in their legitimate pursuits on the seas." He asked also that "a sufficient credit" be voted to enable him "to provide adequate means of protection where they are lacking, including adequate insurance against the present war risks."

The President's address embodied the conclusions reached by himself and his Cabinet after it had become apparent that the German blockade was having the effect of paralyzing American trade with Europe. He was careful to indicate that he was not proposing a war measure, but he felt that the sanction of Congress was desirable, even though perhaps not essential, to enable him to provide means for arming ocean-going vessels of American register so as to permit them to defend themselves from U-boats in passing through the barred areas named in the German blockade proclamation of Jan. 31.

Although President Wilson told Congress that he was not acting because of the long-feared "overt act," news of the destruction of the Cunard liner Laconia, with Americans aboard, was received here as he was entering the doors of the Capitol, and was passed from mouth to mouth through Congress while he was speaking.

Text of President Wilson's Address to Congress

Gentlemen of the Congress:

I have again asked the privilege of addressing you because we are moving through critical times during which it seems to me to be my duty to keep in close touch with the houses of Congress, so that neither counsel nor action shall run at cross-purposes between us.

On the 3d of February I officially informed you of the sudden and unexpected action of the Imperial German Government in declaring its intention to disregard the promises it had made to this Government in April last and undertake immediate submarine operations against all commerce, whether of belligerents or of neutrals, that should seek to approach Great Britain and Ireland, the Atlantic coasts of Europe or the harbors of the eastern Mediterranean and to conduct those operations without regard to the established restrictions of international practice, without regard to any considerations of humanity even which might interfere with their object.

That policy was forthwith put into practice. It has now been in active exhibition for nearly four weeks. Its practical results are not fully disclosed. The commerce of other neutral nations is suffering severely, but not, perhaps, very much more severely than it was already suffering before the 1st of February, when the new policy of the Imperial Government was put into operation.

We have asked the co-operation of the other neutral Governments to prevent these depredations, but I fear none of them has thought it wise to join us in any common course of action. Our own commerce has suffered, is suffering, rather in apprehension than in fact, rather because so many of our ships are timidly keeping to their home ports than because American ships have been sunk.

Two American vessels have been sunk, the Housatonic and the Lyman M. Law. The case of the Housatonic, which was carrying foodstuffs consigned to a London firm, was essentially like the case of the Frye, in which, it will be recalled, the German Government admitted its liability for damages, and the lives of the crew, as in the case of the Frye, were safeguarded with reasonable care.

The case of the Law, which was carrying lemon-box staves to Palermo, disclosed a ruthlessness of method which deserves grave condemnation, but was accompanied by no circumstances which might not have been expected at any time in connection with the use of the submarine against merchantmen as the German Government has used it.

In sum, therefore, the situation we find ourselves in with regard to the actual conduct of the German submarine warfare against commerce and its effects upon our own ships and people is substantially the same that it was when I addressed you on the 3d of February, except for the tying up of our shipping in our own ports because of the unwillingness of our ship owners to risk their vessels at sea without insurance or adequate protection, and the very serious congestion of our commerce which has resulted—a congestion which is growing rapidly more and more serious every day.

This, in itself, might presently accomplish, in effect, what the new German submarine orders were meant to accomplish, so far as we are concerned. We can only say, therefore, that the overt act which I have ventured to hope the German commanders would in fact avoid has not occurred.

But while this is happily true, it must be admitted that there have been certain additional indications and expressions of purpose on the part of the German press and the German authorities, which have increased rather than lessened the impression that, if our ships and our people are spared, it will be because of fortunate circumstances or because the commanders of the German submarines which they may happen to encounter exercise an unexpected discretion and restraint, rather than because of the instructions under which those commanders are acting.

It would be foolish to deny that the situation is fraught with the gravest possibilities and dangers. No thoughtful man can fail to see that the necessity for definite action may come at any time, if we are, in fact and not in word merely, to defend our elementary rights as a neutral nation. It would be most imprudent to be unprepared.

I cannot in such circumstances be unmindful of the fact that the expiration of the term of the present Congress is immediately at hand by constitutional limitation and that it would in all likelihood require an unusual length of time to assemble and organize the Congress which is to succeed it.

I feel that I ought, in view of that fact, to obtain from you full and immediate assurance of the authority which I may need at any moment to exercise. No doubt I already possess that authority without special warrant of law, by the plain implication of my constitutional duties and powers; but I prefer in the present circumstances not to act upon general implication. I wish to feel that the authority and the power of the Congress are behind me in whatever it may become necessary for me to do. We are jointly the servants of the people and must act together and in their spirit, so far as we can divine and interpret it.

No one doubts what it is our duty to do. We must defend our commerce and the lives of our people in the midst of the present trying circumstances with discretion but with clear and steadfast purpose. Only the method and the extent remain to be chosen, upon the occasion, if occasion should indeed arise.

Since it has unhappily proved impossible to safeguard our neutral rights by diplomatic means against the unwarranted infringements they are suffering at the hands of Germany, there may be no recourse but to armed neutrality, which we shall know how to maintain and for which there is abundant American precedent.

It is devoutly to be hoped that it will not be necessary to put armed forces anywhere into action. The American people do not desire it, and our desire is not different from theirs. I am sure that they will understand the spirit in which I am now acting, the purpose I hold nearest my heart and would wish to exhibit in everything I do.

I am anxious that the people of the nations at war also should understand and not mistrust us. I hope that I need give no further proofs and assurances than I have already given throughout nearly three years of anxious patience that I am the friend of peace and mean to preserve it for America so long as I am able. I am not now proposing or contemplating war or any steps that need lead to it. I merely request that you will accord me by your own vote and definite bestowal the means and the authority to safeguard in practice the right of a great people, who are at peace and who are desirous of exercising none but the rights of peace, to follow the pursuit of peace in quietness and good-will—rights recognized time out of mind by all the civilized nations of the world.

No course of my choosing or of theirs will lead to war. War can come only by the willful acts and aggressions of others.

You will understand why I can make no definite proposals or forecasts of action now and must ask for your supporting authority in the most general terms. The form in which action may become necessary cannot yet be foreseen.

I believe that the people will be willing to trust me to act with restraint, with prudence, and in the true spirit of amity and good faith that they have themselves displayed throughout these trying months; and it is in that belief that I request that you will authorize me to supply our merchant ships with defensive arms should that become necessary, and with the means of using them, and to employ any other instrumentalities or methods that may be necessary and adequate to protect our ships and our people in their legitimate and peaceful pursuits on the seas. I request also that you will grant me at the same time, along with the powers I ask, a sufficient credit to enable me to provide adequate means of protection where they are lacking, including adequate insurance against the present war risks.

I have spoken of our commerce and of the legitimate errands of our people on the seas, but you will not be misled as to my main thought—the thought that lies beneath these phrases and gives them dignity and weight. It is not of material interest merely that we are thinking. It is, rather, of fundamental human rights, chief of all the right of life itself.

I am thinking not only of the rights of Americans to go and come about their proper business by way of the sea, but also of something much deeper, much more fundamental than that. I am thinking of those rights of humanity without which there is no civilization. My theme is of those great principles of compassion and of protection which mankind has sought to throw about human lives, the lives of noncombatants, the lives of men who are peacefully at work keeping the industrial processes of the world quick and vital, the lives of women and children and of those who supply the labor which ministers to their sustenance. We are speaking of no selfish material rights, but of rights which our hearts support and whose foundation is that righteous passion for justice upon which all law, all structures alike of family, of State, and of mankind must rest, as upon the ultimate base of our existence and our liberty.

I cannot imagine any man with American principles at his heart hesitating to defend these things.

"All the News That's Fit to Print."

The New York Times.

THE WEATHER
Cloudy, colder today; Thursday snow or rain; wind northeast.
For full weather report see Page 19.

VOL. LXVI...NO. 21,585. ... NEW YORK, WEDNESDAY, FEBRUARY 28, 1917.—TWENTY PAGES. ONE CENT In Greater New York, Jersey City and Newark.

PRESIDENT FINDS THE LACONIA'S SINKING AN 'OVERT ACT'; AWAITS FULL POWER FROM CONGRESS BEFORE TAKING ACTION; BILL REFRAMED AND STRENGTHENED FOR THE SENATE

LACONIA CASE "CLEAR CUT"

President and Advisers View It as Violation of Sussex Pledge.

FURTHER INQUIRY NEEDLESS

Next Step in Meeting the Situation Rests with Congress, Officials Hold.

WILSON READY FOR ACTION

May Arm Ships Anyway, Even if Congress Does Not at Once Grant Express Authority.

Special to The New York Times.

WASHINGTON, Feb. 27.—The sinking of the Cunarder Laconia by a German submarine 150 miles off the Irish coast, without warning, at night in rough seas, and with the loss of American lives, is regarded by President Wilson and his advisers as a clear-cut case of violation of the pledge which the German Government gave to the United States after the Lusitania and Sussex cases. From very high authority the statement was obtained tonight that the Laconia case is clear-cut."

The Laconia case constitutes the overt act which the President has indicated would be a first step toward compelling a more vigorous policy in dealing with Germany. No further facts are needed by this Government, and no inquiry is necessary to establish the facts of the case. That was acknowledged officially today, but for the present the situation rests with Congress, whose attitude is to determine the measure of resentment to be shown by the Government over Germany's paralysis of American trade and the killing of two American citizens.

Until Congress acts on President Wilson's recommendations that he be vested with broad powers to protect American ships and lives from German aggression the President will take no action in regard to the sinking of the Laconia.

Congress Prepares to Act.

The chances are excellent that Congress will pass a bill carrying out in practically complete form the recommendation for protection made by the President in his address before the two houses of Congress yesterday. The Senate Committee on Foreign Relations this afternoon finished its consideration of the bill proposed by the Administration and made few important changes in it. The House Committee on Foreign Affairs found plenty of opposition in its membership to the President's proposals, and was obliged to postpone further consideration of the measure until tomorrow. From present appearances an effort will be made to pass the bill in the House before adjournment tomorrow night and the Senate will begin its consideration on Thursday.

After a conference had taken place early this morning between President Wilson and Secretary Lansing, it was acknowledged in authoritative quarters that the sinking of the Laconia presented a clear-cut case of violation of international law and constituted an overt act. Later in the day a regular meeting of the Cabinet was held, but nothing that occurred there seems to have changed the international situation. The President is understood to be of the opinion that instead of again going to Congress, this time to ask that the sinking of the Laconia be construed as an act of war, the better plan is to wait until Congress has granted the authority to him to protect American ships and American lives on the seas, and use that power in a way that will make Germany realize that the United States means business. It is contended that this course is in strict accordance with the program outlined by the President in his address to Congress on Feb. 3 when he announced that he had directed that diplomatic relations with Germany be severed.

SURVIVORS LANDED SINGING

Chant "Rule, Britannia," and Cheer on Reaching Queenstown.

MRS. HARRIS AIDED CAPTAIN

Wife of American Army Officer Was Last Woman to Leave Sinking Cunarder.

MANY TALKED WITH U-BOAT

Special Cable to The New York Times.
LONDON, Wednesday, Feb. 28.—A Queenstown dispatch to The Evening News says that just before 11 o'clock Monday evening the rescue ship, with the survivors of the torpedoed Cunarder Laconia on board, came into port jubilant with melody led by the women, of whom there were a hundred forward, with their hair hanging loose over their shoulders and with inflated lifebelts fixed around them.

The whole crowd sang "Rule, Britannia," and then cheered and cheered again for the Captain and officers of the sloop which had picked them up.

The first to step ashore was an American, Mrs. Harris, wife on an American Army officer, and the last woman to leave the liner as it was sinking. She stuck bravely by Captain Irvine until he had to force her into a boat which had been intended for himself.

The last dinner of the voyage was over and some of the women had already turned in and were actually in bed. In the smokeroom men were playing auction bridge. Half a dozen children were romping in the saloon. The Laconia was showing no lights and keeping a sharp lookout.

No Sign of Submarine.

Immediately following a glimpse of uninterrupted moonlight at about 9:15 o'clock the first torpedo crashed into the liner, hitting her well aft. There was no sign of the attacker and nobody even saw the sharkfin wake of the torpedo on its journey. The ship shivered under the blow. Everybody felt it and knew what had happened, but there was not the slightest panic on board.

Captain Irvine instantly ordered the turning on of every light in the ship, and in half a dozen seconds the vessel was ablaze with electricity. The familiar boat drill, practiced zealously every day by all on board, was repeated all over again as if it were a drill and no more. All the boats, fully equipped and provisioned, were swung out. As the ship began to settle down, the women and children were taken off first, and the rest of the passengers followed.

A quarter of an hour after the ship had been struck she had listed heavily to starboard. Then, as the watertight bulkheads on the port side began to fill, she slowly righted herself and lay on an even keel once more.

The Laconia was sinking, but so slowly that the murderous U-boat, watching near by, bobbed up again close alongside and let fly another torpedo. Far amidships it crashed into the engine room, and that was the end of the Laconia. Within an hour of the first shot she sank, and Captain Irvine, the wireless operator, and several officers were swimming about in the moonlight.

Liner Sank by Moonlight.

All the boats were well out of range of the maelstrom as she went down. Round about in the flickering moonlight the little fleet of lifeboats lay rocking on the swell, their passengers watching her last struggles, every soul silent and tense with emotion.

Boat 15 was standing by with women passengers of the second class on board and a full complement of sixty persons all told. Suddenly, right under her bows, rose the submarine once more, as a long cloak of cloud trailed across the moon and darkened the sea.

"We could only see the beast dimly," said one of the women, "but it was a huge black shape, dwarfing us and drenching us as it rose. We could make out two guns on board, and big guns they were, too.

"Standing by, on the platform by the periscope, were two or three men, and one of them, who said he was commander, spoke to us in a very soft voice. His English was quite good, but guttural.

"'What is the name of your ship, her tonnage and her cargo?' he said.

"Somebody near me said: 'Don't tell the murderer anything; let's just sing "Rule, Britannia," at him and defy him to do his worst.' But the steward in charge of the boat wisely said, 'No, we had better not do that. We are entirely in his hands, and the best thing to do is to answer his questions. Then he sang out:

"'I want to tell you, first, that we have got women and children on board, in case you're thinking of sending us down as well as our ship.'

"The commander of the submarine then said: 'What's become of your Captain and where is he? I want him. Is he on board that boat?'

"Somebody replied that the Captain of the British ship was doing his duty in the place where a British Captain would always be found. To this the submarine commander could find no suitable reply, and after other questions he had asked had been answered he said no more beyond informing the crew of one boat that a vessel would be on the scene to pick them up.

"'Good night,' said he, and then he and his ship vanished, and nothing more was seen of them.

"For hours and hours the lifeboats cruised around in the empty sea, and it was after midnight when the flashlight of the first rescue ship picked them out and gathered derelicts one by one to its fold."

The American Embassy received word from Consul Frost at Queenstown late yesterday that a special train with the Laconia's survivors had left there at 8:25 o'clock in the afternoon for Dublin, and would reach Liverpool at 3:15 this morning. At Liverpool they are to take a special train to London, reaching here before 9 o'clock this morning.

Crowds Greet Survivors.

QUEENSTOWN, Feb. 27.—There was an unusual scene at the docks when the Laconia survivors landed at 11 o'clock in the evening. As the rescue ship was made fast a huge crowd of civilians, soldiers, sailors, and nurses began cheering and singing under the leadership of a shrill-voiced cheer-leader in the uniform of the Women's National Service Organization.

The first passenger to land was an American woman, Mrs. F. E. Harris, to whom this honor was accorded by the Captain's order because of her heroism in supervising the departure of the women and children from the sinking ship. She was the last passenger to leave the Laconia, standing by the side of the Captain and going the rounds with him, carefully checking off the women and children passengers to see that they were all in their places and provided with clothing, blankets, and tarpaulins.

After Mrs. Harris on the landing stage came other women and children from the Laconia, all clinging still to their lifebelts, and then the men passengers, some with lifebelts and some wearing lifesaving waistcoats of various types.

A string of automobiles was waiting for the party and its members were conveyed quickly to the Queen's Hotel, where nurses provided dry clothing and warm baths. In half an hour the men, women and children who had come off the rescue sloop in a varied state of disarray were ready for a really sumptuous meal of broth, salmon, turkey, and champagne which had been prepared for them.

In addition to the survivors brought to Queenstown, fifteen were landed at Bantry. Some of the passengers arriving here had failed to supply themselves with warm clothing when they left the ship, so that during their long hours in the open boats they suffered from cold. The Captain, Chief Engineer, Purser, and wireless operator were the last to leave the ship. They jumped from the deck to a lifeboat, but missed it and fell into the sea. They were picked up.

Everything possible was done to relieve the suffering of the American women, but the shock and the hardships of exposure to the cold proved fatal to Mrs. Hoy and her daughter.

The greatest attention is being paid here to the surviving passengers. Numerous residents have taken many of them into their homes. Mrs. Harris was entertained by the Commanding Admiral at the Admiralty House. Captain Irvine and the ship's officers and passengers proceeded tonight for Liverpool. The crew, except five men detained in the hospital, also have departed.

The New York Times.

THE WEATHER
Probably snow or rain today and Friday; wind northeast.
For full weather report see Page 21.

VOL. LXVI...NO. 21,586.   NEW YORK, THURSDAY, MARCH 1, 1917.—TWENTY-TWO PAGES.   ONE CENT In Greater New York. | TWO CENTS New England and Middle States. | THREE CENTS Elsewhere.

GERMANY SEEKS AN ALLIANCE AGAINST US; ASKS JAPAN AND MEXICO TO JOIN HER; FULL TEXT OF HER PROPOSAL MADE PUBLIC

WASHINGTON EXPOSES PLOT

Our Government Has Zimmermann's Note of Jan. 19.

BIG PROMISES TO MEXICO

Conquest of Texas, New Mexico, and Arizona Held Out as a Lure to Her.

BERNSTORFF CHIEF AGENT

German Embassy in Washington Head Centre of All Intrigues in This Hemisphere.

[The following dispatch was sent out by The Associated Press last night with the statement that its contents had been fully authenticated.]

WASHINGTON, Feb. 28.—The Associated Press is enabled to reveal that Germany, in planning unrestricted submarine warfare and courting its consequences, proposed an alliance with Mexico and Japan to make war on the United States if this country should not remain neutral.

Japan, through Mexican mediation, was to be urged to abandon her allies and join in the attack on the United States.

Mexico, for her reward, was to receive general financial support from Germany, reconquer Texas, New Mexico, and Arizona—lost provinces —and share in the victorious peace terms Germany contemplated.

Details were left to German Minister von Eckhardt in Mexico City, who by instructions signed by German Foreign Minister Zimmermann at Berlin, Jan. 19, 1917, was directed to propose the alliance with Mexico to General Carranza and suggest that Mexico seek to bring Japan into the plot.

These instructions were transmitted to von Eckhardt through Count von Bernstorff, former German Ambassador here, now on his way home to Germany under a safe conduct obtained from his enemies by the country against which he was plotting war.

Germany pictured to Mexico, by

Zimmermann Says Again Neutral Ships Will Be Sunk; Escape of the Orleans Only an Instance of Luck

Special Cable to THE NEW YORK TIMES.

BERLIN, Feb. 28. (via London.)—The report of the safe arrival of the freighter Orleans at Bordeaux did not cause much surprise here, as it was known that there were heavy fogs along the course most likely to be selected by the American vessel, which would naturally render the operations of the U-boats extremely difficult.

The fact that the Orleans, despite her speed, took nearly three weeks for the passage is regarded here as sufficient evidence that her course must have been roundabout and zigzaggy, it being assumed that she was not any too anxious to meet a U-boat.

"One swallow does not make a Summer," is the comment of the newspapers, who say it would be a mistake if the Americans supposed the U-boats had received orders to let American ships pass unmolested. No such orders have been given, according to the Berlin papers, who leave no doubt about it by quoting Foreign Secretary Zimmermann, who in an interview with a Spanish newspaper man recently took occasion to make the following unmistakable statement:

"We make absolutely no distinction in sinking neutrals' ships within the war zone. Our determination is unshakable, since that is the only way to finish the war the coming Summer, in which desire we all share."

This, it is held, can be interpreted in no other way than that American ships, like those of all other neutrals, must comply with the U-boat rulings or take the consequences.

The sinking of the Laconia, a much larger ship than the Orleans, which crossed the danger zone at about the same time, is regarded as proof that even in propitious circumstances, such as foggy weather, it is difficult to escape the U-boats.

"As a casus belli, the Orleans was a failure," says the Zeitung am Mittag, and it would seem as if the people here were rather glad it was.

Says It's Only Luck That No American Ship Has Been Sunk

AMSTERDAM, Feb. 28. (via London.)—Referring to President Wilson's statement to Congress in asking for power to arm American ships that the overt act had not yet occurred, the Cologne Volks-Zeitung says:

"It is only due to a lucky accident that American ships have not been sent to the bottom, and unless American ships avoid the danger zone the overt act is bound to come. There is no doubt that the arming of American merchantmen will mean a fight between submarines and American vessels, which necessarily will produce a state of war."

broad intimation, England and the Entente Allies defeated, Germany and her allies trumphant and in world domination by the instrument of unrestricted submarine warfare.

A copy of Foreign Secretary Zimmermann's instructions to von Eckhardt, sent through von Bernstorff, [printed in adjoining columns on this page of THE TIMES] is in the possession of the United States Government.

Document in President's Hands.

This document has been in the hands of the Government since President Wilson broke off diplomatic relations with Germany. It has been kept secret while the President has been asking Congress for full authority to deal with Germany, and while Congress has been hesitating. It was in the President's hands while Chancellor von Bethmann Hollweg was declaring that the United States had placed an interpretation on the submarine declaration "never intended by Germany" and that Germany had promoted and honored friendly relations with the United States "as an heirloom from Frederick the Great."

Of itself, if there were no other, it is

considered a sufficient answer to the German Chancellor's plaint that the United States "brusquely" broke off relations without giving "authentic" reasons for its action.

The document supplies the missing link to many separate chains of circumstances which, until now, have seemed to lead to no definite point. It sheds new light upon the frequently reported but indefinable movements of the Mexican Government to couple its situation with the friction between the United States and Japan.

It adds another chapter to the celebrated report of Jules Cambon, French Ambassador in Berlin before the war, of Germany's worldwide plans for stirring strife on every continent where they might aid her in the struggle for world domination which she dreamed was close at hand.

It adds a climax to the operations of Count von Bernstorff and the German Embassy in this country, which have been colored with passport frauds, charges of dynamite plots, and intrigue, the full extent of which never has been published.

It gives new credence to persistent reports of submarine bases in Mexican territory in the Gulf of Mexico. It takes cognizance of a fact long

recognized by American Army chiefs, that if Japan ever undertook to invade the United States it probably would be through Mexico, over the border and into the Mississippi Valley to split the country in two.

It recalls that Count von Bernstorff, when his passports were handed to him, was very reluctant to return to Germany, but expressed a preference for asylum in Cuba. It gives a new explanation to the repeated arrests on the border of men charged by American military authorities with being German intelligence agents.

Last of all, it seems to show a connection with General Carranza's recent proposal to neutrals that exports of food and munitions to the Entente Allies be cut off, and an intimation that he might stop the supply of oil, so vital to the British Navy, which is exported from the Tampico fields.

What Congress will do, and how members of Congress, who openly have sympathized with Germany in their opposition to clothing the President with full authority to protect American rights, will regard the revelation of Germany's machinations to attack the United States, is the subject tonight of the keenest interest.

Such a proposal as Germany instructed her Minister to make to Mexico borders on an act of war if, actually, it is not one.

No doubt exists here now that the persistent reports during the last two years of the operations of German agents not alone in Mexico, but all through Central America and the West Indies are based on fact. There is now no doubt whatever that the proposed alliance with Mexico was known to high Mexican officials who are distinguished for their anti-Americanism. Among them are Rafael Zubaran, Carranza's Minister to Germany, and Luis Cabrera, Carranza's Minister of Finance.

It is apparent that the proposal had taken definite form when Zubaran returned to Mexico City from Berlin recently. His return from his foreign post was covered by the fact that Carranza had called in many of his diplomats for "conferences."

Some time before that, Cabrera, while still at Atlantic City in the conferences of the American-Mexican Joint Commission, had suggested in a guarded way to a member of the American section, that he regretted that the commission had not succeeded fully in settling the difficulties between Mexico and the United States. For, he said, he had hoped it might continue its work and make peace for the world.

When pressed for some details of how the commission could restore world peace, Cabrera suggested that the American republics controlled the destiny of the war by controlling a large part of its supplies. Mexico, he intimated, might do her part by cutting off exports of oil. The American Commissioners dismissed his ideas as visionary.

Text of Germany's Proposal to Form an Alliance With Mexico and Japan Against the United States

[Supplied by the Associated Press as an authentic copy of the German Foreign Minister's note to the German Minister in Mexico.]

BERLIN, Jan. 19, 1917.

On the 1st of February we intend to begin submarine warfare unrestricted. In spite of this, it is our intention to endeavor to keep neutral the United States of America.

If this attempt is not successful, we propose an alliance on the following basis with Mexico: That we shall make war together and together make peace. We shall give general financial support, and it is understood that Mexico is to reconquer the lost territory in New Mexico, Texas, and Arizona. The details are left to you for settlement.

You are instructed to inform the President of Mexico of the above in the greatest confidence as soon as it is certain that there will be an outbreak of war with the United States, and suggest that the President of Mexico, on his own initiative, should communicate with Japan suggesting adherence at once to this plan. At the same time, offer to mediate between Germany and Japan.

Please call to the attention of the President of Mexico that the employment of ruthless submarine warfare now promises to compel England to make peace in a few months.

ZIMMERMANN.

President Insists on Passage of Senate Armed Ship Bill

Special to The New York Times.

WASHINGTON, Feb. 28.—The statement was authorized by the White House tonight that President Wilson would insist on the passage of the Senate bill giving him power to arm and protect mechant shipping.

Almost coincident with Zubaran's return from Germany, Cabrera returned to Mexico City, open in his expressions of anti-Americanism. Zubaran, before being sent abroad, had represented General Carranza here while the Niagara mediation conferences were proceeding and was no less avowedly anti-American than Cabrera.

Baron von Schoen Transferred.

Meanwhile, Baron von Schoen, Secretary of the German Embassy here, was transferred to the Legation in Mexico City. No explanation could be obtained of the reason for his transfer, and such investigation as was possible failed to develop why a Secretary from the United States should be sent to the German Legation in Mexico.

Baron von Schoen's association with the moves, if any at all, does not appear. The only outward indication that he might have been connected with them is found in the fact that he recently had been detached from the German Embassy in Tokio and was well acquainted with the Japanese Minister in Mexico City.

Carranza's peace proposal was openly pronounced by officials here as evidence of German influence in Mexico, who declared it was intended only to embarrass the United States. Then apparently, some influences showed their effect on the course of the Mexican Government, and on Feb. 25 Cabrera, the Minister of Finance, issued a statement describing the "amazement" of the Mexican Government that the American newspapers should have interpreted General Carranza's proposal to cut off exports of munitions as a suggestion that he might cut off shipments of British oil. They were, Cabrera declared, "entirely groundless," and that feature of the situation ended. There was an intimation that Germany's astounding proposal that Japan turn traitor to her allies had been answered by Tokio.

Count von Bernstorff's connection with the plot, further than serving as the channel of communication, is intensified by the fact that the German Embassy here was not merely the medium of delivering a message in this instance, but was really a sort of headquarters for all the German missions in Central and South America.

The German Naval Attaché, Captain Boy-Ed, and the Military Attaché, Captain von Papen, whose recall was forced by the State Department because of their military activities in this country, also were accredited to Mexico, and between the outbreak of the war and their departure from this country made at least one visit there.

Mexico Base for Raiders.

For months many naval officers here have believed that the mysterious German sea raiders of the South Atlantic must have found a base somewhere on the Mexican coast, and that such a base could not be maintained without the knowledge and consent of Mexican officials. Last November the British Chargé at Mexico City presented to the Carranza Foreign Office a notification that if it was discovered that Mexican neutrality thus had been violated the Allies would take "drastic measures" to prevent a continuance of that situation.

In a note almost insolent in tone, Foreign Minister Aguilar replied to the charge that, in effect, it was the business of the Allies to keep German submarines out of western waters, and that if they were not kept out, Mexico would adopt whatever course the circumstances might commend.

To German influences also have been attributed in some quarters the vigorous steps taken by the de facto Finance Minister to force loans from the Banco Nacional and the Bank of London and Mexico, owned by French and British capital. The institutions were closed by the Mexican officials and some of their officers imprisoned and held for weeks despite repeated protests by France, Great Britain and the United States.

Reports of German machine guns and German gunners in the Carranza army also have been persistent, although the relative importance of that to the proposed alliance is not fully established. It is recalled tonight, too, that last November, when the Mexican-American Joint Commission was making its futile effort to adjust the difficulties between the two countries, the Austro-Hungarian Ambassador at Mexico City, Count Kalman Kama Votkanya, made a trip to the United States on what he described as a "secret mission."

A suggestion interpreted by some officials as an indication that Germany might have made approaches to Mexico at that time was made by Cabrera in an address at Philadelphia on Nov. 10.

"The foes of the United States will certainly assume to be friends of Mexico," said Mr. Cabrera, "and will try to take advantage of any sort of resentment Mexico may have against the United States. Mexico, nevertheless, understands that in case of a conflict between the United States and any other nation outside America, her attitude must be one of continental solidarity."

Trails of German Secret Service.

It has been an open secret that Department of Justice Agents in their investigations of plots to violate American neutrality by setting on foot armed expeditions in Mexico more than once have uncovered what appeared to be trails of the German secret service. A few days ago Fred Kaiser, suspected of being a German agent, was arrested at Nogales on charges brought under the neutrality statutes, Department of Justice Agents declaring he had attempted to obtain military information on the American side of the border and had cultivated the society of American Army officers with an apparent intention of promoting those efforts.

Last July, when W. H. Schweibz, who claimed to be a former German army officer, escaped into Mexico at Nogales after arrest on similar charges, the Deputy Marshal who tried to follow him was stopped by Mexican authorities.

The full extent of the evidence of Germany's plotting against the United States, gathered by the American Secret Service, may become known only according to the course of the future relations between the two countries. It is known that much evidence of the operations of the German Embassy and persons who were responsible to it never has been permitted to come out because officials preferred to guard against inflaming the public mind in the tense situation with Germany.

The public amazement which a full exposition of the evidence in the hands of the Government would cause cannot be overestimated. Only today the Council of National Defense, created by act of Congress, issued an appeal to all Americans to show every consideration for aliens in this country.

"We call upon all citizens," said the appeal, "if untoward events should come upon us, to present to these aliens, many of whom tomorrow will be Americans, an attitude of neither suspicion nor aggressiveness. We urge upon all Americans to meet these millions of foreign-born with unchanged manner and with unprejudiced mind."

PACIFISTS PRESS VIEWS ON WILSON

Bryan, Jane Addams, and Others in Two Groups Confer with the President.

FEAR DECLARATION OF WAR

Approve Executive's Grasp of the Siuation—Bryan Wants Sea Restrictions.

Special to The New York Times.

WASHINGTON, Feb. 28.—William J. Bryan with other pacifists invaded Washington today to bring their influence to bear on the President and Congress to avert war with Germany. Mr. Bryan hurried here from Miami, Fla., last night.

Two groups, the first including Jane Addams, Professor Emily Balch, Joseph Cannon, and William I. Hull, and the second Amos Pinchot, Max Eastman, Paul Kellogg, and Lillian Wald, had conferences with the President this afternoon, both lasting more than an hour. Although none of the eight would discuss their conversations with the President in detail, they said they were impressed with the grasp of the situation the President showed, and that he had assured them he would use his best efforts, as he had in the past, to keep this country out of war if possible.

Mr. Bryan, after conferring in the morning with the leaders of the Emergency Peace Federation, went to the Capitol, where he talked with the members of Congress who are particularly friendly to his peace policies. Although he insisted that he believed the bills now pending before Congress to give the President power to deal with the German crisis should be phrased so as to leave no doubt that Congress was not in any sense declaring war, he would not say that he disapproved of the proposal to give the President added powers in the present emergency.

Asked to commit himself definitely on this point, he said he preferred not to give any one advice on the subject, as his attitude would depend altogether on the phraseology with which the bill was worded when finally approved by Congress.

Mr. Bryan insisted that particular emphasis should be laid on the part of the President's address to Congress in which he said he was not proposing war or measures which must lead to war.

"I am sure that in that the President correctly interpreted the hope of the people," Mr. Bryan said. "The people desire peace, but we have a war element in the country who are doing all in their power to manufacture war sentiment."

He contended that Americans should be prevented from traveling on armed ships, and also that passengers should not be allowed to travel on ships carrying munitions. He called attention in this connection to a dispatch in a New York paper of Feb. 24 saying that the British authorities at Halifax had taken off a number of women and children from a transatlantic steamer under a regulation forbidding them to travel on the ocean during the continuance of the present unrestricted submarine blockade while three American women who were on the same ship were allowed to remain.

"Is it possible," Mr. Bryan said, "that any one will say that our Government is less careful about its people than is the British Government? I believe that American citizens should be restrained from travelling on belligerent ships at a time like this. The Captain of a belligerent ship forfeits every life aboard if he tries to escape when warned to stop.

"Life is more important than merchandise and the first duty of those in charge of a passenger ship is to guard the lives of the passengers. A ship Captain cannot give to his passengers the care and protection to which they are entitled if his thoughts are on a contraband cargo.

"The President in his message said: 'I am not now proposing or contemplating war or any steps that might lead to it.' This statement is so plain that no one ought to suppose for an instant that the President desires Congress to surrender its exclusive right to decide whether the country should go to war and when it should go to war."

"All the News That's Fit to Print."

The New York Times.

THE WEATHER
Fair today; tomorrow rain or snow; moderate northwesterly winds.

VOL. LXVI...NO. 21,601. ...   NEW YORK, FRIDAY, MARCH 16, 1917.—TWENTY PAGES.   ONE CENT In Greater New York, New England and Middle States. / TWO CENTS / THREE CENTS Elsewhere.

REVOLUTION IN RUSSIA; CZAR ABDICATES; MICHAEL MADE REGENT, EMPRESS IN HIDING; PRO-GERMAN MINISTERS REPORTED SLAIN

ARMY JOINS WITH THE DUMA

Three Days of Conflict Follow Food Riots in Capital.

POPULACE TAKE UP ARMS

But End Comes Suddenly When Troops Guarding Old Ministers Surrender.

CZAR FINDS CAPITAL GONE

Returns from Front After Receiving Warning from Duma and Gives Up His Throne.

Empress Reported Under Guard or Hiding From Angry People

Special Cable to THE NEW YORK TIMES.
PETROGRAD, March 14. (Dispatch to The London Daily Chronicle.)—The Empress of Russia has been placed under guard.

LONDON, March 15.—According to information received here the Russian people have been most distrustful during recent events of the personal influence of Empress Alexandra. She was supposed to exercise the greatest influence over Emperor Nicholas.

It is stated that her whereabouts is not known, but it is believed she is in seclusion, fearing the populace.

The Empress Alexandra before her marriage to the Emperor of Russia in 1894 was the German Princess Alix of Hesse-Darmstadt.

PETROGRAD, March 15.—Emperor Nicholas of Russia has abdicated, and Grand Duke Michael Alexandrovitch, his younger brother, has been named as Regent.

The Russian Ministry, charged with corruption and incompetence, has been swept out of office. One Minister, Alexander Protopopoff, the head of the Interior Department, is reported to have been killed, and the other Ministers, as well as the President of the Imperial Council, are under arrest.

A new national Cabinet is announced, with Prince Lvoff as President of the Council and Premier, and the other offices held by the men who are close to the Russian people.

Petrograd has been the scene of one of the most remarkable risings in history, beginning with minor food riots and labor strikes last week Thursday. The people's cry for food reached the hearts of the soldiers, and one by one the regiments rebelled, until finally those troops which had for a time stood loyal to the Government gathered up their arms and marched into the ranks of the revolutionists.

Duma President Leading Figure.

Michael V. Rodzianko, President of the Duma, was the leading figure among the Deputies, who unanimously decided to oppose the imperial order, issued last week, for a dissolution of the House. They continued their sessions, and M. Rodzianko informed the Emperor, then at the front, that the hour had struck when the will of the people must prevail.

Even the Imperial Council realized the gravity of the situation, and added its appeal to that of the Duma that the Emperor should take steps to give the people a policy and government in accordance with their desires and in order that there should be no interference with carrying on the war to a victorious ending.

The Emperor hastened back to the capital, only to find that the revolution had been successful and that a new Government was in control.

The Empress, who, it is alleged, has been influential in the councils opposed to the wishes of the people, is reported to have fled or to be in hiding.

Although considerable fighting took place, it is not believed that the casualties are large. One report says that they do not exceed 500.

A few defenders of the old régime put up a last feeble defense last night from the roofs of the wrecked Astoria Military Hotel and St. Isaac's Cathedral, facing on two sides of the same square.

The city is now quiet and perfect order prevails. So far as is known, no foreigners were injured.

The Imperial Palace at Tsarskoe-Selo is said to have been in a state of siege, but thus far no firing has been reported between the guards defending the palace and the revolutionists and troops.

According to one report the Emperor expected trouble to follow from his decree dissolving the Duma, and so warned the residents of Tsarskoe-Selo to arrange to remain in the suburb for an indefinite period.

Czar Nicholas under guard at the palace at Tsarskoe-Selo (now called Pushkin) where he was held prisoner following his abdication.

Began From Strikes a Week Ago.

The most phenomenal feature of the revolution was the swift and orderly transition whereby the control of the city passed from the régime of the old Government into the hands of its opponents.

The visible signs of revolution began on Thursday, March 8. Strikes were declared in several big munitions factories as a protest against the shortage of bread. Men and women gathered and marched through the streets, most of them in an orderly fashion. A few bread shops were broken into in that section of the city beyond the Neva, and several minor clashes between strikers and police occurred.

Squads of mounted troops appeared, but during Thursday and Friday the utmost friendliness seemed to exist between the troops and the people.

This early period of the uprising bore the character of a mock revolution, staged for an immense audience. Cossacks, charging down the street, did so in a half-hearted fashion, plainly without malice or intent to harm the crowds, which they playfully dispersed. The troops exchanged good-natured raillery with the working men and women, and as they rode were cheered by the populace.

Long lines of soldiers stationed in dramatic attitudes across Nevsky Prospect, with their guns pointed at an imaginary foe, appeared to be taking part in a realistic tableau. Machine guns, firing rounds of blank cartridges, seemed only to add another realistic touch to a tremendous theatric production which was using the whole city as a stage.

On Saturday, however, apparently without provocation, the troops were ordered to fire on people marching in Nevsky Prospect. The troops refused to fire, and the police, replacing them, fired rifles and machine guns.

Then came a clash between troops and police, which continued in desultory fashion throughout Saturday night and Sunday. The Nevsky Prospect was cleared of traffic by the police and notices were posted by the commander of the Petrograd military district warning the people that any attempt to congregate would be met by force.

Until Sunday evening, however, there was not intimation that the affair would grow to the proportions of a revolution. The first serious outbreak came at 6 o'clock, when the men of the Volynsky Regiment shot their officers and revolted when they received an order to fire upon striking workingmen in one of the factory districts.

Another regiment detailed against the mutineers also joined the revolt. The news spread rapidly to the other barracks and four more regiments went over. Some of the revolting troops marched to the St. Peter and St. Paul Fortress on the left bank of the Neva, and after a brief skirmish with the garrison took possession of it.

Dissension spread among the troops, who did not understand why they should be compelled to take violent measures against fellow-citizens whose chief offense was that they were hungry and were asking the Government to supply bread. Several regiments deserted. A pitched battle began between the troops who stood with the Government and those who, refusing to obey orders, had mutinied, and even slain their officers.

A long night fight took place between the mutinous regiments and the police at the end of St. Catharine Canal, immediately in front of the historic church built over the spot where Alexander II. was killed by a bomb. The police finally fled to the rooftops all over the city and were seen no more in the streets during the entire term of the fighting.

Turning Point in Revolution.

Still, on Monday morning the Government troops appeared to control all the principal squares of the city. Then came a period when it was impossible to distinguish one side from the other. There was no definite line between the factions. The turning point appeared to come about 3 o'clock in the afternoon. For two hours the opposing regiments passively confronted each other along the wide Liteiny Prospect in almost complete silence.

From time to time emissaries from the revolutionary side rode to the opposing ranks and exhorted them to join the side of the people. For a while the result seemed to hang in the balance. The troops appeared irresolute, awaiting the commands of their officers, who themselves were in doubt as to what they should do.

Desultory firing continued along the side streets, between groups of Government troops and revolutionists. But the regiments upon whose decision the outcome rested still confronted each other, with machine guns and rifles in readiness.

Suddenly a few volleys were exchanged: there was another period of silent suspense, and the Government regiments finally marched over to join the revolutionists. A few hours after the first clash, this section of Petrograd, in which were located the Duma building, artillery headquarters, and the chief military barracks, passed into the hands of the revolutionary forces, and the warfare swept like a tornado to other parts of the city, where the scene was duplicated.

At first it seemed a miracle that the revolutionists, without prearranged plan, without leadership or organization, could in such a short time, with comparative ease, achieve a complete victory over the Government. But the explanation lay in the reluctance of the troops to take sides against the people and their prompt desertion to the ranks of those who opposed the Government.

Workingmen and Clerks Fight.

The scenes in the streets were by this time remarkable. The wide streets, where the troops were stationed, were completely deserted by civilians, except for a few daring individuals, who, creeping along walls and ducking into courtyards, sped from one side to the other. But the side streets were choked with people.

Groups of students, easily distinguished by their blue caps and dark uniforms, fell into step with rough units of rebel soldiers, and were joined by other heterogeneous elements, united for the time being by a cause greater than partisan differences.

Unkempt workingmen, with ragged sheepskin coats covering the conventional peasants' costume of dark blouse and top boots, strode side by side with well groomed city clerks and shopkeepers.

This strange army of people, mustered on the street corners, shouldered their newly acquired rifles and marched out to join the ranks of the deserting regiments.

The economic and industrial life of the city came to a complete standstill. Street car service was suspended from the beginning of the disorders and stores were closed. The two leading hotels which housed officers were wrecked. Others restricted their service to regular patrons. In response to an appeal by the revolutionist committees, citizens distributed food to the soldiers.

Duma Declares Government Ended.

On Monday the Duma members, except the Rightists, met in executive session, notwithstanding the order of the Czar dissolving their body. The result was a virtually unanimous vote to place the Duma squarely on the side of the revolution and to authorize the Executive Council of that body to declare the present Government overthrown, and organize a provisional Government.

President Rodzianko, who presided, sent a telegram to the Emperor, informing him of the developments and calling on him to listen to the voice of the people.

"'The hour has struck,'" he said, "'when the will of the people must prevail.'"

It was further stated in the telegram to the Emperor that a special committee, composed of the leaders of the various parties in the Duma, would submit a list of names for the new Cabinet.

Members of the Imperial Council also sent a message to Emperor Nicholas, outlining conditions and recommending a change in the internal policy in accordance with the decision of the Duma, dismissal of the present Cabinet and its reorganization in accordance with the desires of the people and their representatives. The message bore twelve signatures.

Simultaneously it was reported that all the Ministers except M. Protopopoff had resigned.

The following were named as the "staff of the temporary Government": Michael V. Dodzianko, H. V. Nekrasoff, A. I. Konovaloff, L. I. Dmitrukoff, A. F. Kerenski, M. S. Pshkeidze, V. V. Shulgin, S. I. Shidlovsky, Paul N. Milukoff, M. A. Makarauloff, V. N. Lvoff, V. A. Rjevsky, and Colonel Englehard.

Remarkable Scene at the Duma.

The scene at the Duma before the revolution was in full flame was extraordinary. The members stood about the broad corridors talking calmly, the serious priest members in long black gowns, with flowing hair, and members from the provinces in top boots and blouses mingling with well-groomed and frock-coated representatives.

At the front gates the troops began to assemble. They were without arms. They were the revolting regiments. One body in marching order entered the side gate and halted before the entrance. A Duma member spoke from the steps, explaining the attitude of that body and assuring the regiments that the Duma was with them.

Auto trucks packed with men, soldiers, and civilians, with and without arms, rolled up the circular drive and stopped before the door, while some occupant delivered a lurid oration, and then went on cheered by the crowds.

Then came a small army of citizen soldiers, factory workers, clerks, students armed with rifles taken from the captured arsenals, their pale faces and black Winter clothing forming a strange picture against the snow piled high in the Duma garden.

For an hour they stood in more or less military formation before the building, and at dusk marched away toward the centre of the city, followed by the revolting soldiers. The crowd was extremely orderly. A group of a dozen soldiers pushed into the corridor of the building and demanded to be allowed to address the members. A mild-mannered young civilian of the student type took them in hand with a little difficulty and led them into the open. A delegation asked for food. Immediately waiters from the Duma restaurant were sent out with trays of tea and food until the place was cleaned out.

At nightfall on Monday only one small district of the city, containing the War Office, the Admiralty Building, St. Isaac's Cathedral, and the Military Hotel, still resisted the onslaught of the revolutionary forces, and the battle for the possession of Petrograd came to a dramatic conclusion. In the Admiralty Building the Council of Ministers secretly gathered for a conference, and the last regiments loyal to old Government were drawn up as a guard.

While the Council sat in the last meeting which they were destined to hold, the building was surrounded and the besiegers poured rifle and machine gun fire upon the defenders.

For a few hours the fiercest battle of the day continued: the streets were swept by a steady fusillade and the crowds scattered for the nearest shelter, some of the people being compelled to spend the night in courtyards or corridors of office buildings or wherever they first found refuge.

Soldiers and workers banded together and took over the Duma immediately following the Czar's abdication.

Toward morning (Tuesday) there was a sudden lull, broken by exultant shouts, which deepened into a roar, and were succeeded by the Russian revolutionary "Marseillaise." The regiments defending the Admiralty had surrendered and gone over to the side of the revolutionists.

The Ministers in the Admiralty Building were then arrested and the Russian national colors were replaced by the red flag of the revolutionists.

During the day revolutionary publications appeared in the streets, with the simple caption "News." These contained a résumé of developments, and they were eagerly read by all classes. Rodzianko's telegrams to the Emperor and others to the commanders of the troops at the front were reproduced. The first message to the Emperor read:

> The situation is grave. Anarchy reigns in the capital. The Government is paralyzed. The transport of provisions and fuel is completely disorganized. General dissatisfaction is growing. Irregular rifle firing is occurring in the streets. It is necessary to charge immediately some person trusted by the people to form a new Government. It is impossible to linger, since delay means death. Praying God that the responsibility in this hour will not fall upon a crowned head.

Later President Rodzianko sent the following to the Emperor:

> The position is becoming more serious. It is imperative that immediate measures be taken, because tomorrow will be too late. The last hour has come when the fate of the fatherland and the dynasty are being decided.

Similar telegrams were sent to all the commanders at the front with an appeal for their support before the Emperor of the Duma's action. General Alexis Brusiloff, Commander in Chief of the armies of the southwestern front, and General Nicholas Ruzsky, Commander of the northern armies, replied promptly. General Brusiloff sent this message:

"Have fulfilled duty before fatherland and Emperor."

General Russky's reply read:

"Commission accomplished."

Petrograd Resuming Wonted Calm.

Today the city emerged from the week's nightmare of revolution and figuratively smiled under a brilliant flood of sunshine, following a series of gray days, ending with a snowstorm last evening.

Planks were pulled down from windows long closed. Stores, banks, and business establishments of every description reopened their doors for the resumption of ordinary activities as confidence in the new Government gained in force.

With the reopening of bread, sugar, tea, and meat shops queues of women with shopping bags and baskets lined up often to the length of a block to replenish stores exhausted by the long siege.

Truck sledges and little sleighs for hire, the most widely appreciated conveniences of Russian cities, began to appear again in the streets, which for six days had been absolutely void of any means of private transportation.

No newspapers, with the exception of the revolutionary publications, which sprang into life with the success of the revolt, have yet appeared.

The only visible signs of the clash of authority which turned the city into a battleground were the charred ruins of the jail, which are still pouring a cloud of smoke skyward, and here and there the remains of other police institutions and the homes of the few individuals who were regarded as offenders against the rights of the people.

In front of other Government institutions, which apparently it was not seen fit to destroy, were piles of charred embers, showing where wreckage and documents had been dumped and consumed.

It is evident that the strike of workingmen Thursday of last week provided the spark which set aflame the growing unrest and angry discontent with the Government that, pervading the entire population of Russia, had reached the ignition point.

Thus the small manifestations of hungry factory workers, crying for bread, changed in a single day into a revolution which swept the whole city, spread to the Government troops who had been called to hold the crowds in check, and, supported by the Duma, ended in the downfall of the Government.

The revelations in the Duma of Government stupidity and corruption, and the allegations of treason against the chief members of the Cabinet, sent a wave of protest through the country, and all political factions, except a small reactionary group, still cherishing traditional ideas of the old regime which existed before Russia received a constitution, declared themselves firmly against the sinister influences which had been undermining the best efforts of the country successfully to carry on the war.

Even the Imperial Council, which never before in the history of the country had allied itself with the popular will, held special meetings, in which attention was called to the "serious conditions to which the country had been brought by the unscrupulous designs of governmental heads."

People Against Government.

With unanimity unprecedented the entire population presented a solid front against the Government. The belief prevailed everywhere and was expressed that pro-German Court circles and the Government were doing everything in their power to interfere with the proper conduct of the war and to bring about a separate peace.

Stürmer, Rasputin, and Protopopoff formed a picturesque trio, known as "the dark forces" against which the chief animosity of the country was directed, but powerful as they were, these figures were declared to be only symbols of German influence which was "militating against the patriotic desire of the mass of the Russian people for war until victory."

After the assassination of Rasputin and the removal of Stürmer from the Premiership, the same Ministerial influence, wearing a new mask in the form of a changed Cabinet, Duma officials declared, still flourished with undiminished strength. Direct appeals were made to the Emperor by all sorts of representative bodies and influential officials to save the country from the disaster which threatened it and to appoint a new Cabinet which would have the confidence of the people.

But the Government, except for empty concessions and compromises, remained obdurate to all appeals and showed not the slightest inclination to change the direction of its policy or accede to the demands more and more loudly expressed.

It was the opinion of the majority of the Deputies in the Duma that, despite this state of affairs, an open revolution was impossible, as the country realized that a revolution would seriously interrupt the work of the war and would be playing into the hands of those who had this very end in view.

Open letters were printed in the Petrograd newspapers from popular Duma leaders, and proclamations were posted in the streets, urgently begging the population not to create demonstrations or cause disorders which might lead to interruption of the manufacture of munitions or paralyze the industrial activity of the city.

Manifestations already arranged for March 6, including a general strike and the marching to the Duma of a deputation of workingmen, were in this way averted. But the moment was only postponed. The people, who had been long vaguely disturbed by the political unrest and were convinced that they were being exploited by the hostile Government, received what they regarded as the last proof of the inefficiency and corruption of their own Government when they were apprised that the already insufficient supply of food had become still more meagre and that for some days it would be necessary to go without bread altogether.

Patient and long suffering by nature, this was too much for the population of Petrograd, who knew that the interior of Russia was stored with immense quantities of grain and all kinds of provisions, and, without other motive at first than to voice a demand for bread, the people paraded the streets and the demonstrations began which soon kindled into a revolution.

LONDON HAILS REVOLUTION

Expected Czar's Overthrow and Sees Brighter Prospects for the Allies.

THINK THE COUP DECISIVE

Well-Informed Observers Believe the Patriotic War Party Has Made Its Control Secure.

FEAR NO SEPARATE PEACE

With Weak Ruler Deposed and Pro-German Advisers Ousted, They Predict New Victories.

Special Cable to THE NEW YORK TIMES.

LONDON, Friday, March 16.—It is the belief in well-informed circles here that the Provisional Government which has been set up in Russia by the military party will be able to keep the upper hand in maintaining a policy that means the uninterruptedly vigorous prosecution of the war to a victorious end.

The overthrow of the Czar was expected, and observers here are confident that the Grand Duke as regent will have the solid support of the war party, while they are equally sure of the elimination of any element with a pro-German taint.

An Anti-German Uprising.

As the situation is explained to THE NEW YORK TIMES correspondent, the revolution simply means that German sympathizers within the Russian Government have been overthrown, and that no chance remains for a separate peace

being secretly arranged with Germany. This, it is felt, is the real basis of the revolution that has worked such a sudden change in Russian politics.

This revolution, which has been on the verge of boiling over for months, reached its crisis three days ago, when the military leaders, with the Duma behind them, started outbreaks in Petrograd and Moscow. It is evident from the way in which the uprising was conducted, says THE NEW YORK TIMES correspondent's informant, that it had been carefully planned and skillfully executed.

"After it got under way," he says, "there was no hesitation of movement until the members of the military party were masters of the situation. The details of what occurred in Petrograd and Moscow are lacking, but enough is known to show that they have been in a fever of sanguinary revolution for the last three days.

"Dashes of troops against the headquarters of the pro-German leaders, with the capture of Protopopoff and Stürmer as prisoners of war, were conspicuous features of the revolution. The houses of German sympathizers were burned in both cities, and the occupants either taken captive or forced to flee.

"Now that the military party is in control the situation is said to be settling down, with every prospect that the aim of the Revolutionists will be accomplished."

In fact, the situation was described last night as being "entirely satisfactory."

For months, said the informant of THE NEW YORK TIMES correspondent, Great Britain had been expecting an outcome of the Russian political crisis that would mean the solid intrenchment of the war party and the downfall of those seeking a separate peace with Germany. Now it may be confidently expected that Russia will play her part in the war with even greater vigor than before.

German-Born Czarina Blamed.

The Daily Chronicle in its leading article says:

"From a very early period the German-born Czarina and the clique of pro-German reactionaries whom her influence made powerful with the Czar were bent on ending the war prematurely in the interests of reaction. The Ministers set up under these auspices

have for over two years acted in defiance of public opinion. Their policy was not obscure; they hampered the army in respect of munitions, disorganized the country in respect of its distributive services, brought about artificial famine in a land which is one of the world's chief food producers, and themselves, through police agents, tried to stir up abortive revolts in order that they might plead military failure and internal revolution as a reason for withdrawing from the war.

"The people foiled them for long by magnificent and much enduring patriotism. When the Government left the army without munitions the local authorities—the zemstvos and unions of towns—stepped in and organised their supply. When police agents tried to bring about riots and strikes, the workmen's own leaders prevented their breaking out. When secret negotiations were opened up with Germany, the Duma blasted them by public exposure on the popular side.

"The Duma's demand for sympathetic and really national Government was enforced, first, by the Council of the Empire, normally the stronghold of high officialdom, and then by the Congress of Nobles, which represents the landed aristocracy.

"With the nobility, much of the bureaucracy, the army, the navy, the Duma, the professional classes, and the working classes all ranged against them, the 'dark forces' held obstinately on their way. The murder of the Czarina's favorite, the infamous Rasputin, only intensified the reaction, though its story and sequel showed significantly how far many members of the Imperial family were from supporting the reigning head and his consort in the policy which was jeopardizing the dynasty. But the Czar's blindness was incurable. In a kind of panic he got rid of every remaining progressive Minister; a nonentity of no importance from the Czar's personal circle was made Prime Minister, and the real power fell to Protopopoff, the strong man of the camarilla, who was to see their design through."

London Overjoyed at the News.

LONDON, Friday, March 16.—The news that "Great Russia" had joined the democracies of the world, and that one of the three great absolutist rulers of the world had resigned his throne in accordance with the demands of his people was received here with unmixed joy. There has been no illusion about Russia here. Particularly in the last year it had been well understood that the situation there has been the people against the throne.

"The people and the army are all for the war and against Germany," has been the word which came from Russia through all channels repeatedly. That the Court has been enshrouded in a pro-German atmosphere, and that the Emperor was a weak man, under the thumb of his wife and also under the domination of several members of the bureaucracy, some of whom were influenced only by the tradition of the old régime and others of whom were in the pay of German diplomats, had also been reported.

The men now in control of the destinies of the great empire of Eastern Europe are Russians who are anti-German and pro-Russian to the core, as the Russian developments are regarded here as wholly to the benefit of the Entente Powers in the war.

The revolution is commented upon editorially here with enthusiasm, mainly as a great triumph for the Entente and a great disaster for the Central Powers. The press describes it as the death of German hopes and a more crushing and more far-reaching blow than Germany has yet received. The Liberal papers also welcome it as a triumph of democracy, presaging great influence on the cause of liberty throughout the world.

There is a note of anxiety in some of the comments that troublesome developments may occur, but this note is not emphasized. Pity and sympathy are expressed for the Emperor, of whom the worst said is that he lacks intellectual and moral strength. Tributes are paid to his generous and lovable disposition and his ardent desire to serve his people, while his abdication is described as an act of unselfish patriotism, which it is hoped has saved his country from civil war and Petrograd from anarchy.

The provisional government holds a session in the Duma. Behind the speaker is the place where the Czar's portrait hung before his abdication.

"All the News That's Fit to Print."

The New York Times.

THE WEATHER
Rain by tonight; wind south; Sunday rain, strong northwesterly winds. For full weather report see Page 19.

VOL. LXVI...NO. 21,602. .....   NEW YORK, SATURDAY, MARCH 17, 1917.—TWENTY PAGES.   ONE CENT In Greater New York. | TWO CENTS New England and Middle States. | THREE CENTS Elsewhere.

THE ROMANOFF DYNASTY ENDED IN RUSSIA; CZAR'S ABDICATION FOLLOWED BY MICHAEL'S; CONSTITUTIONAL ASSEMBLY TO BE CONVOKED

WIDE REFORMS PLANNED

Universal Suffrage and Full Political Amnesty Are the Bases.

CROWDS CHEER PROMISE

Duma Committee and Workingmen Busy Planning for a Constituent Assembly.

FOOD PRICES FALL RAPIDLY

Calm Restored in Petrograd, but Partisans of Old Regime Are Still Being Arrested.

LONDON, Saturday, March 17.—Universal suffrage in elections to be held for members of a new constituent Assembly and full political amnesty will be features of the new régime in Russia, according to dispatches from Petrograd. In fact, Deputy Kerenski, the new Minister of Justice, who is a Socialist, accepted the portfolio on the stipulations that there should be absolute freedom of speech and of the press, and full political amnesty, and that the Assembly should be convoked.

Addressing an assemblage of thousands of soldiers and civilians from the gallery of the lobby of the Duma, M. Kerenski, says a Reuter dispatch from Petrograd, dated yesterday, announced that the Provisional Government took office by virtue of an agreement with workingmen's and soldiers' delegates. The council of these delegates approved the agreement by several hundred votes to 15. The first act of the new Government, M. Kerenski stated, was the immediate publication of a decree of full amnesty. Continuing, the Minister said:

"Our comrades of the second and fourth Dumas, who were banished illegally to the tundras of Siberia, will be released forthwith. In my jurisdiction are all the Premiers and Ministers of the old régime. They will answer before the law for all crimes against the people."

"Show them no mercy," many voices in the crowd exclaimed.

"Comrades," M. Kerenski replied, "regenerated Russia will not have recourse to the shameful methods utilized by the old régime. Without trial none will be condemned. All prisoners will be tried in open court."

"Comrades, soldiers, citizens, all measures taken by the new Government will be published. Soldiers, I ask you to co-operate. Free Russia is now born, and none will succeed in wresting liberty from the hands of the people. Do not listen to the promptings of the agents of the old régime. Listen to your officers. Long live free Russia!"

The speech was greeted by a storm of cheering.

The labor leader, Chkueidse, addressing the officers and soldiers, paid a glowing tribute to the soldiers and workingmen who had participated in accomplishing the revolution. He recounted the recent provocative efforts by the secret police in publishing proclamations regarding the murders of officers by soldiers. He exhorted the soldiers to regard their officers as citizens who had helped raise the revolutionary flag and as brothers in the great cause of Russian liberty.

Subsequently officers, soldiers, and workingmen carried M. Chkueidse on their shoulders through a cheering throng of soldiers and civilians.

Apparently the new Provisional Government is proceeding promptly to organize itself on a stable basis, to reconstitute the Governmental departments, and prepare steps for the vigorous carrying on of the war. There is no sign of serious hindrance to the completion of the work of this extraordinarily swift and successful revolution.

Former Premiers Golitzine and Goremykin have been placed in the Fortress of St. Peter and St. Paul, as have Generals Soukhomlinoff and Beliaeff, former Ministers of War; A. B. Protopopoff, former Minister of the Interior; J. G. Chtchegiovitoff and M. Makaroff, former Ministers of Justice, and M. Malakoff and General Kurloff, former Chiefs of Police. Other prominent persons under arrest are being detained temporarily in the Duma Building.

It is announced that there will be no further trials for political offenses, and that the Government has opened the bar to Jewish lawyers, who have been excluded heretofore.

At a conference of the members of the Duma Executive Committee and delegates representing the workmen, which lasted until 5 o'clock this morning, says a dispatch from Petrograd, an agreement was reached concerning the transitional period before the election of a constituent assembly. The executives insisted in the interests of the war on the necessity of order being re-established before holding the elections.

Search Houses for Sharpshooters.

Calm has been quickly restored in Petrograd, although numerous partisans of the old régime have been firing from roofs and garrets upon the troops and inhabitants. By order of the Executive Committee soldiers have entered the houses where firing is taking place and removed suspected persons.

Thousands of the police have been imprisoned. All the police stations have been destroyed or sacked, and all suspected houses are being searched for ammunition and arms.

According to a dispatch sent from Petrograd yesterday afternoon, the State Bank and all the private banks reopened during the day.

Stringent orders have been issued for the rearrest of a number of criminals who escaped during the liberation of political prisoners. Some of them, disguised as soldiers, have been pillaging private houses and threatening their occupants. Official orders have been issued that the criminals are to be shot at sight if they offer resistance to arrest. Genuine patrols and search parties are wearing distinguishing signs and also carry written authorizations.

Among the latest persons arrested is the Countess Klein-Michael, who is well known in Court circles and for a long time has been conspicuous as an intriguer and a tool for the dissemination of pro-German propaganda. Hitherto she had enjoyed immunity because of influential connections. The Countess was taken under guard to the Duma Building.

The factories have formed a police service for patrolling the factory districts, enrolling one out of every ten of their workmen.

The question of naming officers to replace those who were disarmed by their own troops is one which will be decided promptly.

In the present spirit of the officers and the men in the ranks there is no reason to apprehend disciplinary troubles, as the officers rejoice equally with the men in the overthrow of the autocracy. The officers have issued a proclamation to their men, in which they refer to the "accursed old régime."

There will be a great parade of troops in Petrograd today before the new Ministers.

In the meantime the Provisional Government is doing its utmost to straighten out the numerous tangles. The Duma and the Zemstvo Council are working hand in hand, although issuing separate proclamations.

Despite the non-appearance of newspapers the public is better informed of what is going on than ever before. A special squadron of motor cars have been commandeered by the Executive Committee, and these cars go about the city distributing printed bulletins free to everybody. Thus the most authentic news gains speedy circulation.

Through this motor service President Rodzianko has appealed earnestly to the people not to injure Government buildings, telegraphs, the water supply equipment, factories, &c., and also to continue the public services and avoid bloodshed.

In the meanwhile he is energetically tackling the food problem, and the public is confident that the combined efforts of the Duma and the Zemstvo will soon assure an adequate supply. Large stores of flour have been uncovered in various parts of the city. The prices of food are falling rapidly in the city.

A minor instance of the popular feeling was shown when the appearance of a few intoxicated persons on the streets caused such indignation that the culprits were promptly imprisoned.

GAVE UP SON'S RIGHTS, TOO

Czar Yielded at Midnight Thursday; Grand Duke Michael Yesterday.

DUMA IS NOW IN CONTROL

Executive Committee Acting with Cabinet It Chose After the Revolution.

NATION BACK OF CHANGE

New Ministers Assume Their Duties and Are Starting Preparations to Push the War.

PETROGRAD, Friday, March 16, 5 P. M., (via London, Saturday, March 17.)—Emperor Nicholas abdicated at midnight last night on behalf of himself and the heir apparent, Grand Duke Alexis, in favor of Grand Duke Michael Alexanderovitch.

Trains Are Rushing Food to Hungry Russian Cities

LONDON, March 16.—"Train service has continued throughout the revolution," says Reuter's Petrograd correspondent in a dispatch dated this afternoon. "Hundreds of previously idle cars are now rushing supplies to the populous centres, which actually faced starvation. Grain stores everywhere may be requisitioned at fair prices, and estates of over 125 acres may be taken over temporarily by the Local Committee.

"The Government has appealed to the conscience and sense of duty to humanity of the peasants to bring forward all the grain possible, saying that the nation is placed on its honor to do everything to relieve the food situation."

At 2:30 o'clock this afternoon Grand Duke Michael himself abdicated, thus bringing the Romanoff dynasty to an end.

The Government, pending a meeting of the Constitutional Assembly, is vested in the Executive Committee of the Duma and the newly-chosen Council of Ministers.

A manifesto to this effect was issued by the Duma Committee today and it will be telegraphed to the General Army Headquarters this evening.

Unless improbable events occur, Russia has today become a republic.

The outcome depends on how the manifesto of the new Government is received by the 6,000,000 soldiers at the front.

Except for the unqualified rejection of the throne by the Czar Nicholas II.'s only brother, the Grand Duke Michael, the Romanoff-Holstein dynasty might be preserved by any number of Czar Nicholas's kinsmen. But the title of Autocrat, since the days of the first Michael Romanoff, in 1613, may only be conferred by a Romanoff. As the Czar chooses no successor after the Grand Duke Michael, and the Grand Duke names no successor at all, the dynasty ends as a reigning house unless a new Government places it upon the throne. Even so, the Romanoffs might decline to recognize the authority of such a Government, as they assert that their right to reign and rule is entirely independent of the will of the people.

The house of Romanoff is descended from Andrei Romanoff, who is said to have gone to Moscow from Prussia in the fourteenth century. Michael Feodorovitch Romanoff was the first of the family to ascend the throne. This was in 1613, when he was 17 years old. He died in 1645. The direct male line of the Romanoffs terminated in 1730 and the female line in 1762, when the Holstein-Gottorp branch came into power and has since ruled.

lines where they are far beyond the old system of trenches and in real open warfare of the old style, which I, for one, never believed would come again. The enemy's lines were protected with a new belt of barbed wire, without which he can never stay on any kind of ground. But it was this which proved his undoing.

His massed attack against the Australian troops had a brief success, but the battalions of Prussian Guards, charging in waves, broke through the forward posts and drove a deep wedge into the British positions. Here they stayed for a time, doing what damage they could, searching around for prisoners and waiting perhaps for reserves to renew and strengthen the impetus of their attack. But the Australian staff officers were swift in preparing and delivering a counterblow which fell upon the enemy at 7:30. Companies of Australians swept forward, and with irresistible spirit flung themselves upon the Prussians, forcing them to retreat.

They fell back in an oblique line from their way of advance, forced deliberately that way by the pressure and direction of the Australian attack. At the same time the British batteries opened fire upon them with shrapnel. As they ran, more and more panic-stricken, toward their old lines, the greatest disaster befell them for they found themselves cut off by their own wire, those great broad belts of sharp-spiked strands which they had planted to bar the British off.

Rifles are Again Used.

What happened then was just an appalling slaughter. The Australian infantry used their rifles as never rifles had been used since the first weeks of the war when the old British regulars of the First Expeditionary Force lay down at Le Cateau on the way of their retreat and fired into the advancing tide of Germans so that they fell in lines. Yesterday in that early hour of the morning the Australian riflemen fired into the same kind of target of massed men not far away, so each shot found its mark.

The Prussians struggled frantically to tear their way through the wire to climb over it, crawl under it. They cursed and screamed, ran up and down each line, each in turn until they fell dead. They fell so that the dead bodies were piled upon dead bodies in long lines of mortality before and in the midst of that spiked wire. They fell and hung across its strands. The cries of the wounded, long, tragic wails, rose high above the roar of rifle fire and bursting shrapnel, and the Australian soldiers, quiet and grim, shot on and on till each man fired a hundred rounds, till more than 1,500 German corpses lay on the field at Lagnicourt. Large numbers of prisoners were taken, wounded and unwounded, and five Prussian regiments have been identified.

The Prussian Guard has always suffered from the British troops as by some dire fatality. At Ypres, at Contalmaison, in several of the Somme battles, they were cut to pieces, but this massacre at Lagnicourt is the worst episode in their history, and it will be remembered by the German people as a black and fearful thing.

PRESIDENT WARNS AGAINST TREASON

Proclamation Points Out Resident Aliens Owe Allegiance to United States.

SAME STATUS AS CITIZENS

Obliged, Like Them, to Report Treasonable Acts—Constitution and Law on Subject.

Special to The New York Times.

WASHINGTON, April 16.— President Wilson today issued a proclamation calling the attention of aliens and citizens to the acts which this country holds to be treasonable, and warning them that the laws for the punishment of treason will be vigorously prosecuted by the Federal Government. The proclamation quotes what the American Constitution says regarding treason, what the Criminal Code of the United States contains by way of Federal law against treason, and summarizes the

acts which the Federal courts have held to be treasonable.

Far-reaching importance attaches to the direction of the warning to aliens, and the declaration that "resident aliens, as well as all citizens, owe allegiance to the United States," and therefore are equally subject to the laws against treason and like crimes. At war the United States is in a very different position from a neutral. Bomb plotters now may be gripped with an iron hand. Not only are conspirators themselves subject to heavy penalties, but any one, even a German resident, who has knowledge of treasonable acts and fails to make known the facts to the authorities may be sent to prison for seven years and fined $1,000 for misprision of treason.

The President's proclamation follows:

Text of the Proclamation.

Whereas, All persons in the United States, citizens as well as aliens, should be informed of the penalties which they will incur for any failure to bear true allegiance to the United States;

Now, therefore, I, Woodrow Wilson, President of the United States, hereby issue this proclamation to call especial attention to the following provisions of the Constitution and the laws of the United States:

Section 3 of Article III. of the Constitution provides, in part:

Treason against the United States shall consist only in levying war against them, or in adhering to their enemies, giving them aid and comfort.

The Criminal Code of the United States provides:

Section 1—Whoever, owing allegiance to the United States, levies war against them or adheres to their enemies, giving them aid and comfort within the United States or elsewhere, is guilty of treason.

Sec. 2—Whoever is convicted of treason shall suffer death; or, at the discretion of the court, shall be imprisoned not less than five years and fined not less than $10,000, to be levied on and collected out of any or all of his property, real and personal, of which he was the owner at the time of committing such treason, any sale or conveyance to the contrary notwithstanding; and every person so convicted of treason shall, however, be incapable of holding any office under the United States.

Sec. 3—Whoever, owing allegiance to the United States and having knowledge of the commission of any treason against them, conceals and does not, as soon as may be, disclose and make known the same to the President or to some Judge or Justice of a particular State, is guilty of misprision of treason and shall be imprisoned not more than seven years and fined not more than $1,000.

Sec. 6—If two or more persons in any State or territory or in any place subject to the jurisdiction of the United States, conspire to overthrow, put down, or to destroy by force the Government of the United States, or to levy war against them, or to oppose by force the authority thereof, or by force to prevent, hinder, or delay the execution of any law of the United States, or by force to seize, take, or possess any property of the United States, contrary to the authority thereof, they shall each be fined not more than $5,000 or imprisoned not more than six years, or both.

The courts of the United States have stated the following acts to be treasonable:

The use or attempted use of any force or violence against the Government of the United States, or its military or naval forces.

The acquisition, use, or disposal of any property with knowledge that it is to be, or with intent that it shall be, of assistance to the enemy in their hostilities against the United States.

The performance of any act or the publication of statements or information which will give or supply in any way aid and comfort to the enemies of the United States.

The direction, aiding, counseling, or countenancing of any of the foregoing acts.

Such acts are held to be treasonable, whether committed within the United States or elsewhere; whether committed by a citizen of the United States or by an alien domiciled, or residing, in the United States, inasmuch as resident aliens, as well as citizens, owe allegiance to the United States and its laws.

Any such citizen or alien who has knowledge of the commission of such acts and conceals and does not make known the facts to the officials named in Section 3 of the Penal Code is guilty of misprision of treason.

And I hereby proclaim and warn all citizens of the United States and all aliens, owing allegiance to the Government of the United States, to abstain from committing any and all acts which would constitute a violation of

any of the laws herein set forth; and I further proclaim and warn all persons who may commit such acts that they will be vigorously prosecuted therefor.

SAYS AUSTRIA WON'T DECLARE WAR ON US

Willing to Leave Developments in Hands of Washington, According to High Authority.

BERNE, April 16, (From a Staff Correspondent of The Associated Press, formerly stationed in Vienna.)—The announcement is made on high authority that Austria-Hungary does not contemplate declaring war on the United States, that she is willing to leave further developments in the hands of the American Government.

The Government up to the last minute regretted what it considered to be the necessity of severing diplomatic relations with the United States.

When Ambassador Penfield informed Count Czernin, the Foreign Minister, of his intention of departing from Vienna, an intimation was given to him for the first time that the Austro-Hungarian Government intended to break off diplomatic relations with Washington in case the United States entered into a state of war with Germany. Mr. Penfield had planned to leave Vienna on April 4 or 5, but was informed that he would be received by the Emperor on April 5, the Emperor and Count Czernin having spent the first three days of that week at German General Headquarters.

On the day appointed the Ambassador was received by the Emperor, but the same evening the report was current that Mr. Penfield himself would receive

his passports. The news appeared authentic to the Ambassador, who, himself unwilling to investigate, asked the correspondent of The Associated Press to ascertain if the report was true. The correspondent learned from the highest source that the Austro-Hungarian Government did not intend to hand the Ambassador his passports, even though Congress declared a state of war and President Wilson signed the resolution. Thus The Associated Press became virtually the intermediary between the American Embassy and the Austro-Hungarian Government.

The Government made all needed arrangements for the Ambassador's departure, and to the last moment treated him as a diplomat going on leave of absence. Two representatives of the Foreign Office were at the station to bid farewell to the Ambassador and Mrs. Penfield, and, in the name of the Austro-Hungarian Government, presented Mrs. Penfield with flowers and other gifts.

The semi-official Fremdenblatt on April 10 pointed out in a leader that with diplomatic relations between Washington and Vienna intact and intercourse between the embassy and the State Department unchecked, certain military information likely to hurt Germany would reach the American Government, and this is considered one reason why the severance of relations became necessary.

In Austro-Hungarian Government circles the rupture itself was not popular, according to the general belief. In the Hungarian Diet the Government was attacked by the opposition for having severed relations, but a statement from the Government quickly quieted Premier Tisza's opponents. Nowhere in the monarchy could antagonism toward the United States be found, which was true also in the highest military circles and the various ministries. That diplomatic relations between the two countries had been severed appeared to cause, in fact, universal regret.

Nothing was said in the way of the departure of Chargé Grew and his staff, for the Government expressed itself as believing that no guarantees regarding the Austro-Hungarian diplomatic representatives in the United States would be needed.

"All the News That's
Fit to Print."

The New York Times.

THE WEATHER
Fair today and Tuesday; northwest
winds, becoming variable.
☞For full weather report see Page 17

VOL. LXVI...NO. 21,604. ••••   NEW YORK, MONDAY, MARCH 19, 1917.—EIGHTEEN PAGES.   ONE CENT In Greater New York | TWO CENTS New England and Middle States. | THREE CENTS Elsewhere.

THREE AMERICAN SHIPS SUNK, ONE UNWARNED, 22 MEN MISSING; U-BOATS REFUSE AID; MILITIA DEMOBILIZATION IS STOPPED

PATROL PICKS UP SURVIVORS

City of Memphis Crew Is Abandoned at Sea In Five Open Boats

VIGILANCIA SAW NO U-BOAT

29 of Her 43 Men Landed at Scilly Islands After She Is Torpedoed Unawares.

TANKER ILLINOIS ALSO LOST

Oil Ship and City of Memphis Were Returning to United States in Ballast.

LONDON, March 18.—The sinking of the American steamships City of Memphis, Illinois, and Vigilancia by German submarines was announced today. Fourteen men from the Vigilancia are missing, as are twenty-four men from the City of Memphis. The crew of the Illinois was landed safely.

[Later advices which were received by the State Department at Washington said that of the fifty-seven men on the City of Memphis fifteen had landed at Schull and thirty-four were on an Admiralty vessel, which was searching for the eight others.]

The City of Memphis, which left Cardiff Friday in ballast for New York, was sunk Saturday. When she left port the steamship had the Stars and Stripes painted on both sides. She encountered a submarine about 5 o'clock Saturday evening. The German commander ordered the Captain of the steamer to leave his ship within fifteen minutes.

The entire crew entered five boats, and the submarine then fired a torpedo which struck the vessel on the starboard side, tearing a great hole through which the sea poured. The steamer settled down quickly and foundered within a few minutes.

Three Boat Crews Picked Up.

In the night the boats became separated, and at 4 o'clock Sunday morning three boat crews were picked up by a patrol vessel and landed. These boats contained thirty-three men, mostly Americans. All of the officers were Americans. The officers believe that the other boats will be rescued.

Third Engineer Thompson of the City of Memphis, in an interview with the Central News, said that the submarine fired a warning shot for the steamer to slow down, and subsequently signaled for her to stop and for the crew to abandon the ship. Ten or eleven shells were fired at the vessel, which began to sink. Then followed a terrific explosion which caused the vessel to tremble all over, and within twenty minutes she sank, stern first. The

The proud captain and crew of the German submarine, U-53.

crew suffered a great deal from exposure during the night.

Thompson said the ship was on charter to discharge her cargo at Havre. From Havre she went to Cardiff, and the skipper, knowing he was in the danger zone, kept the flag, which was yards in length, flying at the masthead. Nobody seems to have expected an attack.

Captain Borum briefly consulted with the officers after the Germans ordered him by megaphone to leave the ship because it was intended to sink her, said Thompson. All agreed that there was no alternative. After describing the sinking of the steamer, Thompson continued:

"When the ship had been destroyed the German commander steamed to our boat and asked for the Captain, but none of our lads answered him. He then went from boat to boat until he found Captain Borum, who briefly conversed with him. I do not know what was said."

Flarelights Bring Rescuers.

"The weather was not too bad, but there were heavy swells. We kept the boats together, and during the evening we rowed together toward the coast. The night closed with a biting wind, and some of our young chaps were very sick. Our flarelights were seen between 3 and 4 o'clock in the morning by the patrol vessels, which rescued two boats crews. The other two had become separated. We lost everything we possessed."

The following American officers are known to have been landed: Chief Officer C. G. Laird, Chief Engineer W. I. Percy, Assistant Engineer F. Bevill, Third Engineer W. M. Thompson, Third Officer M. Dierland, Wireless Operators J. Welch and P. J. Donahue, and Electrician Phillips.

[The statements that the steamer, City of Memphis was sunk by gunfire, also that she was torpedoed, apparently are cleared up by the statements

of Third Engineer Thompson that she was first shelled and was sinking when "a terrific explosion, which caused the vessel to tremble all over," occurred. This seemingly would indicate that the steamer was torpedoed after she had been shelled.]

The Vigilancia was torpedoed without warning. The submarine did not appear. The Captain, First and Second Mates, First, Second, and Third Engineers, and twenty-three men of the crew have been landed at the Scilly Islands.

Exclusive of the final trip, she had traveled 79,801 miles in taking abroad horses for the Italian Government, cotton, and general merchandise, worth more than $900,000, this figure including the value of the last cargo delivered.

Built in Chester, Penn., in 1902, the City of Memphis, while in the coastwise trade in May, 1914, was chartered by the Government, in a crisis in the relations between the United States and Mexico, to transport supplies by way of Galveston to American troops occupying Vera Cruz. As she left Boston harbor a German freighter fired a salute from a brass gun mounted on deck.

Discharged from Government service in December, 1914, the City of Memphis loaded with cotton and started for Germany, the second American vessel to take a cargo of that character to that country. She steamed up the Weser River to deliver the merchandise and her commander was rebuked by the authorities for entering a river which was mined. Captain Borum replied he did not know the Weser had mines, and sailed for America.

"Skipper Without Fear."

Subsequent voyages took her to Italy five times, Rotterdam once, and France three times. Captain Borum was described yesterday by Mr. Pleasants as "an American skipper without nerves and without fear." When at Spezia, Italy, in December, 1915, the ship was chartered to McAndrew & Forbes, Philadelphia licorice dealers, to go to Turkey and bring a cargo of licorice to Philadelphia. Off Scalanova, Turkey, the American met British and French warships, which escorted her into the har-

bor, but before she could load they ordered her out on the ground that they were about to shell the town. The American withdrew, Scalanova was bombarded, and the freighter again entered.

While in the Turkish port Captain Borum entertained the authorities aboard his ship and his vessel was known as "the dove," being the only neutral craft in the harbor. After she sailed the Turks signaled him to return, but Captain Borum suspected they intended to place his vessel between the warships and the town in the event of bombardment and continued on his way. A second shelling did take place before the City of Memphis was entirely out of the harbor and the American ship, Mr. Pleasants said yesterday, was struck by Entente shells and slightly damaged.

On her voyage into the war zone the City of Memphis each night carried a reflector above an American flag painted on either side and the ship's name appeared in six-foot letters in several places.

The Vigilancia was of 4,115 tons gross, 45 feet beam and 330 feet long. She had a speed of thirteen knots, and her Captain was instructed to proceed to Havre via the Azores, where he was to call at St. Michaels for coal if necessary. The steamer was built for the Ward Line in 1890, and was engaged in passenger and freight service between New York and Cuban ports until 1914, when she was sold to engage in the cotton carrying trade from the United States to German ports. In 1915, when on her way to Bremen, she was stopped by a British cruiser and taken into Kirkwall.

The Globe Company of 140 Broadway bought the Vigilancia, which sailed on Feb. 28 for Havre under charter to Harber & Co., Inc., of 17 Battery Place for the outward voyage with a general cargo said to consist chiefly of provisions. She was delayed three days in sailing owing to a strike of the crew, who demanded a bonus of 75 per cent. of their wages as war risk. They finally sailed with a bonus of 50 per cent.

The Vigilancia was marked on her sides with the American flag and her name in letters that could be read three miles away. The hailing port, "New York," was painted on the port and starboard bows in letters five feet high.

Americans on Vigilancia.

The steamship was commanded by Captain F. A. Middleton and had a crew of forty-five, of whom twenty, including the Captain, were American citizens, including five Porto Ricans and one Filipino. Americans in the crew are:

B. D. O'Connell, mate, 35 Charles Street, New York; J. H. Smith, second mate, 42 Adams Street, Malden, Mass.; N. P. North, born in Denmark, naturalized, third mate; F. Brown, carpenter, Newport News; A. Gillard, Quartermaster, 141 Cleveland Street, Brooklyn; J. N. Loera, Quartermaster, San Juan, P. R.; S. Stamot, seaman; Fred Schwia, born in Norway, naturalized, chief engineer; E. A. Denton, first assistant engineer, 448 East 147th Street, New York; Walter Scott, Jr., second assistant engineer, Fitchburg, Mass.; Alexander Rodriquez, born in Porto Rico, oiler; M. Ruiz, fireman, Noyaquez, P. R.; C. W. Dawson, steward, 350 Washington Street, Newark, N. J.; J. A. Macdonald, born in Canada, had taken out first papers, baker; Walter Pitts, third cook, 191 London Street, Boston; J. Connors, waiter, Seattle, Wash.; E. Lopes, born in Porto Rico, messboy, no address; Paul T. Platt, wireless, 142 Sycamore Street, Winter Hill, Mass. The third assistant engineer, an American, had not been signed on when the list was compiled.

First Assistant Engineer Denton of the Vigilancia signed up on the vessel against the wishes of his wife, according to her story told last night. Mrs. Denton broke down when told at her home, 448 East 147th Street, the Bronx, of the sinking of the vessel.

"I have not heard from my husband since Feb. 28, when he signed on against my wishes," she said. "I had a horror of the sea, feeling that something would happen to him now that the German submarines are sinking vessels. He was out of work, and that is why he sailed." Mrs. Denton has two children, a boy 5 years old and a girl 9. She said her husband was 27 years old, and had crossed the Atlantic on the steamer Chemung the trip before she was sunk by a submarine.

Amos J. Mace, General Manager of the Globe Steamship Company, which is owned by Gaston, Williams & Wigmore, Ltd., of 140 Broadway, said last night that he had not received any message regarding the loss of the Vigilancia. He knew that the Vigilancia had been purchased by the firm, but could not tell the price.

The tank steamship Illinois was built in 1913 at Newport News for the Texas Oil Company of 17 Battery Place, New York, and sailed from Port Arthur, Texas, on Feb. 1; for London, under the command of Captain Iverson. There are no marine records to show her arrival or departure from London. She was a single screw vessel of 5,220 gross tons and was 390 feet long and 52 feet beam.

Arthur Barber, of the firm of Barber & Co., who dealt with the loading of the Vigilancia, said yesterday that she had about 3,000 tons of general cargo, including machinery, provisions, steel rails and other railroad material. He could not place any definite value on the merchandise, but believed it would be between $800,000 and $1,000,000.

The Illinois, from London for Port Arthur, Texas, in ballast, was sunk at 8 o'clock this morning.

Memphis Sunk by Gunfire.

Special Cable to THE NEW YORK TIMES.

LONDON, March 18.—A dispatch from a British port tonight reports that the City of Memphis, an American cargo steamer of Savannah, Ga., outward bound in ballast, had fallen a victim to submarine ruthlessness.

So far her commander, Captain Borum, with nine others in the same boat, are missing. Two boats were picked up at sea after their thirty-three occupants had been afloat eleven hours. Sixteen of those brought ashore are Americans.

The steamer received two gunfire warnings first and then a signal to abandon ship. The order was carried out in about fifteen minutes, four boats being lowering to hold the crew of fifty-seven. Three of the boats' crews are accounted for so far. Norwegians, Russians and Danes are among the men saved.

The submarine had got in close proximity to the City of Memphis before starting to shell her. Most of the ten or twelve shots fired had deadly effect, one knocking the smoke funnels out of her. The steamer disappeared stern first after twenty-five minutes, the Stars and Stripes flying at her peak as she took the final plunge.

The submersible did not fly the German flag as she appproached the four boats. On getting close, her commander put some questions to the occupants, one inquiring for the captain. He then went to the boat in which the Captain was. There is reason for thinking that this boat's crew has been picked up.

All the steamers' officers are Americans. They are: Chief Engineer Laird, First Engineer Percy, First Assistant Engineer Bevill, Third Assistant Engineer Thompson, Third Officer Dierlem, Electrician Phillips, and Wireless Operators Welch and Donoghue. The Americans are being looked after by a Consul.

Think Missing Men Were Picked Up.

QUEENSTOWN, March 19.—Officers of the City of Memphis who have been landed here say that the boat in which Captian Borum and eight men took refuge was pickeup by by a rescue steamer on Sunday morning empty. The officers think the boat met with some other steamer during the night and that the occupants were landed elsewhere.

Thirty-three refugees in all were landed in this neighborhood, sixteen of whom are American and seventeen of other nationalities. Nobody was injured. United States Consul Frost is caring for the survivors.

Consul Frost Reports Sinking.

WASHINGTON, March 18.—Consul Frost, at Queenstown, reported to the State Department tonight the sinking by a German submarine of the American steamer City of Memphis, saying forty-nine survivors had been picked up and that an Amirality vessel was searching for eight missing. The dispatch follows:

American steamer City of Memphis, Cardiff to New York, reported sunk by German submarine 4 P.M. March 17, thirty-five miles south of Fastnet. Fifteen survivors landed Schull 7 P.M today. Thirty-four survivors on Admiralty vessel, which continues search for eight missing. Will land Baltimore on Irish coast probably today.

Baltimore is a point on the coast a considerable distance west of Queenstown and Cork.

A second dispatch from Consul Frost stated that thirty-three survivors of the City of Memphis landed at Queenstown, and that seven Americans were among the fifteen landed at Schull. The message follows:

City of Memphis, thirty-three survivors now landed here, vessel sunk by gunfire, submarine large type, remained on the scene after crew left ship. Refused request tow boats to land. Weather not severe, but threatening. Survivors at Schull included Allen Carroll, second officer; — McPherson, second engineer; Robert Shea, surgeon; John Watkin, Henry Campany, Gus Campany, A.D. Henton, all Americans, and five Spanish, one Portuguese, one Swede, and one Russian.

The department announced that a dispatch form Consul General Skinner at London said it was reported the City of Memphis, the Illinois, and the Vigilance, (probably Vigilancia), all American steamers, had been sunk, the latter without warning. The message added that some of the crew of the City of Memphis has been landed and that a patrol boat had gone to pick up the crew of the Illinois.

A later dispatch from Consul General Skinner read:

American steamer City of Memphis, Cardiff to New York, reported sunk. Some of crew landed. Patrol boat gone to pick up rest. American steamer Illinois, London to Port Arthur, reported sunk. American steamer Vigilance alleged torpedoed without warning.

The Vigilancia

One of the Three American Steamships Sunk Within Twenty-four Hours by German Submarines.

MANY AMERICANS ON BOARD.

City of Memphis Had War Record—Two Others Lost.

Forty-eight men who were Americans by birth or by naturalization and nine others, several of whom were believed to be naturalized Americans, composed the crew of the American freight steamship City of Memphis, reported from London yesterday as having been sunk by shellfire. The vessel itself, valued at $600,000, had weathered safely many adventures in European waters on previous voyages since the war began. She was of 5,252 gross tonnage and 49 feet beam, 377 feet long and had a speed of fourteen knots.

Owned by the Ocean Steamship Company, known as the Savannah Line, the City of Memphis sailed from New York on Jan. 23 carrying 9,653 bales of cotton, valued at $600,000. This she delivered at Havre, France. She was on her way home in ballast when sunk.

Her Captain was L. P. Borum of Norfolk, Va., where he was born of American parents. Her other officers, all American-born except one, were: First officer, C.B. Laird, Savannah; second officer, A. Carroll, born in Nova Scotia, naturalized American; third officer, M. Dierland, address unknown here; W.I. Percy, chief engineer, Savannah; F. Bevill, first assistant engineer, Savannah; F. McPherson, second assistant engineer, New York, and W.M. Thompson, third assistant engineer, address unknown here.

Of the others on board the ship's surgeon, Dr. F. Shea, lived at 7 Van Ness Place, New York, and the wireless operators, J. Welch and P. J. Donohue, lived in New York. All of these were American born or naturalized Americans.

There were nine firemen, born in Portugal or Spain, some of whom were thought to be Americans by naturalization.

Every officer aboard had his American license, and every naturalized American his naturalization papers, in compliance with a rule laid down by the ship's owners.

While on her last voyage from New York the City of Memphis was halted off the Scilly Islands on Jan. 30 by a German submarine, whose captain demanded to see the papers she carried.

A mate went aboard the U-boat, and was informed that, inasmuch as the American carried a contraband cargo, she ought to be sunk, but because America and Germany were on friendly relations she might proceed. The U-boat commander said that if he caught the steamship again he would sink her without warning.

Leaving Havre after discharging her cotton, the City of Memphis put in at Cardiff, Wales, for enough bunker coal to enable her to steam to New York.

A message received here Saturday by W.H. Pleasants, President of the Ocean Steamship Company, from Captain Borum announced the ship's departure from Cardiff on Friday, so that she was less than forty-eight hours out when sunk.

The City of Memphis's last voyage to Europe was her tenth in the war zone.

Germans Retire on 85-Mile Line: Abandon Peronne and Noyon

British and French Cavalry Pursuing Teuton Rearguards—Allied Advance Extends from Arras to Soissons, to Depth of Twelve Miles, Recapturing Over Sixty Villages.

LONDON, March 18.—The German retirement in France, which continued yesterday at three separate points, spread today over a front of approximately eighty-five miles, from south of Arras on the north to Soissons on the Aisne. The important towns of Péronne, Chaulnes, Nesle, and Noyon were evacuated, together with scores of villages, some of them only slightly damaged as the result of military operations.

The advancing British and French troops, keeping in close touch with the German rearguard, have pushed forward to a depth of from ten to twelve miles. Allied cavalry rode into Nesle, northeast of Roge, at almost the same time.

The occupation of Noyon, one the Oise River, and the nearest point to Paris held by the Germans, removes the famous Noyon elbow or salient, from which some military men here expected the Germans to launch another drive on Paris.

The text of the British statement reads as follows:

We have occupied Nesle, Chaulnes, and Péronne.

Pressing back the enemy's rearguard, we advanced several miles during the past twenty-four hours to a depth up to ten miles in places on a front of approximately forty-five miles, from south of Chaulnes to the neighborhood of Arras.

During this period, in addition to the towns above mentioned, we gained possession of over sixty villages.

Two enemy raiding parties reached our trenches in the night northeast of the Vermelles area.

The text of the French night statement follows:

From the Avre to the Aisne on a front of more than sixty kilometers the advance of our troops continued during the course of the day. North of the Avre our cavalry this morning entered Nesle, and we immediately sent out patrols in the direction of the Somme. There were several engagements with enemy rearguard detachments, who resisted feebly. The inhabitants of Nesle acclaimed our troops.

Northeast of Lassigny we have up to the present advanced more than twenty kilometers in the direction of Ham.

Further to the south our light cavalry detachments, moving along the Valley of the Oise, occupied Noyon about 10 o'clock this morning.

Between the Oise and Soissons (Aisne sector) the entire German first line, as well as the villages of Carlepont, Morsain, Nouvron, and Vingre, fell into our hands. We have gained a foothold on the northern plateau of Soissons and occupied Crouy.

The French afternoon statement follows:

Between the Avre and the Oise our troops made important progress during the night. All the ground between our old lines and the Rove-Noyon road, from Damery as far as the Lagny height, is now in our hands.

There were rather spirited engagements with portions of the enemy rearguard, which terminated to our advantage, and did not impede our progress. The pursuit continues north of the Noyon road.

A dispatch from British Headquarters tonight in France says:

"So rapid became the pursuit of the Germans retreating in the Ancre and Somme sectors today that the British cavalry came into play after restless months of waiting. It has been a wonderful sight to see the cavalry squadrons moving toward the front for several days past. They have included some of the crack English regiments looking very grim and businesslike in steel shrapnel helmets and equipped with gas masks.

"The fine drying weather of the last three days has helped the pursuit, which in some places has reached solid ground that has been little damanged by shellfire.

According to French military cirtics, it is difficult to say where the Germans propose to establish a stable defense. The retreat of modern armies, encumbered with great supplies of material, can be effected only with extreme slowness, which permits an active and resolute adversary to maintain contact unceasingly.

The victorious entry of the French into Roye on the heels of the retiring Germans was marked by stirring incidents, in which 800 liberated citizens participated, regardless of danger. The inhabitants threw themselves in front of the arriving French soldiers, all shouting as they did so, "Vive la France!" Women hugged them, while old people grasped their hands. Tears were in the eyes of all, when suddenly a twelve-year-old boy began singing the "Marseillaise,' which was taken up instantly by the population. Onrushing waves of soldiers joined in, and it was to the strains of the national anthem that the French outposts left roye, pressing the retreating Germans.

"All the News That's Fit to Print."

The New York Times.

THE WEATHER
Fair, colder today; tomorrow warmer, probably rain; wind northwest.
For full weather report see Page 23.

VOL. LXVI...NO. 21,619.   NEW YORK, TUESDAY, APRIL 3, 1917.—TWENTY-FOUR PAGES.   ONE CENT In New York City. | TWO CENTS New England and Middle States. | THREE CENTS Elsewhere.

PRESIDENT CALLS FOR WAR DECLARATION, STRONGER NAVY, NEW ARMY OF 500,000 MEN, FULL CO-OPERATION WITH GERMANY'S FOES

Text of the President's Address

Gentlemen of the Congress:

I have called the Congress into extraordinary session because there are serious, very serious, choices of policy to be made, and made immediately, which it was neither right nor constitutionally permissible that I should assume the responsibility of making.

On the 3d of February last I officially laid before you the extraordinary announcement of the Imperial German Government that on and after the first day of February it was its purpose to put aside all restraints of law or of humanity and use its submarines to sink every vessel that sought to approach either the ports of Great Britain and Ireland or the western coasts of Europe or any of the ports controlled by the enemies of Germany within the Mediterranean. That had seemed to be the object of the German submarine warfare earlier in the war, but since April of last year the Imperial Government had somewhat restrained the commanders of its undersea craft, in conformity with its promise, then given to us, that passenger boats should not be sunk and that due warning would be given to all other vessels which its submarines might seek to destroy, when no resistance was offered or escape attempted, and care taken that their crews were given at least a fair chance to save their lives in their open boats. The precautions taken were meagre and haphazard enough, as was proved in distressing instance after instance in the progress of the cruel and unmanly business, but a certain degree of restraint was observed.

The new policy has swept every restriction aside. Vessels of every kind, whatever their flag, their character, their cargo, their destination, their errand, have been ruthlessly sent to the bottom without warning and without thought of help or mercy for those on board, the vessels of friendly neutrals along with those of belligerents. Even hospital ships and ships carrying relief to the sorely bereaved and stricken people of Belgium, though the latter were provided with safe conduct through the proscribed areas by the German Government itself and were distinguished by unmistakable marks of identity, have been sunk with the same reckless lack of compassion or of principle.

I was for a little while unable to believe that such things would in fact be done by any Government that had hitherto subscribed to humane practices of civilized nations. International law had its origin in the attempt to set up some law which would be respected and observed upon the seas, where no nation has right of dominion and where lay the free highways of the world. By painful stage after stage has that law been built up, with meagre enough results, indeed, after all was accomplished that could be accomplished, but always with a clear view, at least, of what the heart and conscience of mankind demanded.

This minimum of right the German Government has swept aside, under the plea of retaliation and necessity and because it had no weapons which it could use at sea except these, which it is impossible to employ, as it is employing them, without throwing to the wind all scruples of humanity or of respect for the understandings that were supposed to underlie the intercourse of the world.

I am not now thinking of the loss of property involved, immense and serious as that is, but only of the wanton and wholesale destruction of the lives of noncombatants, men, women, and children, engaged in pursuits which have always, even in the darkest periods of modern history, been deemed innocent and legitimate. Property can be paid for; the lives of peaceful and innocent people cannot be. The present German submarine warfare against commerce is a warfare against mankind.

It is a war against all nations. American ships have been sunk, American lives taken, in ways which it has stirred us very deeply to learn of, but the ships and people of other neutral and friendly nations have been sunk and overwhelmed in the waters in the same way. There has been no discrimination. The challenge is to all mankind. Each nation must decide for itself how it will meet it. The choice we make for ourselves must be made with a moderation of counsel and a temperateness of judgment befitting our character and our motives as a nation. We must put excited feeling away. Our motive will not be revenge or the victorious assertion of the physical might of the nation, but only the vindication of right, of human right, of which we are only a single champion.

When I addressed the Congress on the 26th of February last I thought that it would suffice to assert our neutral rights with arms, our right to use the seas against unlawful interference, our right to keep our people safe against unlawful violence. But armed neutrality, it now appears, is impracticable. Because submarines are in effect outlaws when used as the German submarines have been used against merchant shipping, it is impossible to defend ships against their attacks as the law of nations has assumed that merchantmen would defend themselves against privateers or cruisers, visible craft giving chase upon the open sea. It is common prudence in such circumstances, grim necessity indeed, to endeavor to destroy them before they have shown their own intention. They must be dealt with upon sight, if dealt with at all.

The German Government denies the right of neutrals to use arms at all within the areas of the sea which it has proscribed, even in the defense of rights which no modern publicist has ever before questioned their right to defend. The intimation is conveyed that the armed guards which we have placed on our merchant ships will be treated as beyond the pale of law and subject to be dealt with as pirates would be. Armed neutrality is ineffectual enough at best; in such circumstances and in the face of such pretensions it is worse than ineffectual; it is likely only to produce what it was meant to prevent; it is practically certain to draw us into the war without either the rights or the effectiveness of belligerents. There is one choice we cannot make, we are incapable of making; we will not choose the path of submission and suffer the most sacred rights of our nation and our people to be ignored or violated. The wrongs against which we now array ourselves are no common wrongs; they cut to the very roots of human life.

With a profound sense of the solemn and even tragical character of the step I am taking and of the grave responsibilities which it involves, but in unhesitating obedience to what I deem my constitutional duty, I advise that the Congress declare the recent course of the Imperial German Government to be in fact nothing less than war against the Government and people of the United States; that it formally accept the status of belligerent which has thus been thrust upon it; and that it take immediate steps not only to put the country in a more thorough state of defense, but also to exert all its power and employ all its resources to bring the Government of the German Empire to terms and end the war.

What this will involve is clear. It will involve the utmost practicable co-operation in counsel and action with the Governments now at war with Germany, and, as incident to that, the extension to those Governments of the most liberal financial credits, in order that our resources may so far as possible be added to theirs.

It will involve the organization and mobilization of all the material resources of the country to supply the materials of war and serve the incidental needs of the nation in the most abundant and yet the most economical and efficient way possible.

It will involve the immediate full equipment of the navy in all respects, but particularly in supplying it with the best means of dealing with the enemy's submarines.

It will involve the immediate addition to the armed forces of the United States, already provided for by law in case of war, of at least 500,000 men, who should, in my opinion, be chosen upon the principle of universal liability to service, and also the authorization of subsequent additional increments of equal force so soon as they may be needed and can be handled in training.

It will involve also, of course, the granting of adequate credits to the Government, sustained, I hope, so far as they can equitably be sustained by the present generation, by well conceived taxation.

I say sustained so far as may be equitable by taxation, because it seems to me that it would be most unwise to base the credits, which will now be necessary, entirely on money borrowed. It is our duty, I most respectfully urge, to protect our people, so far as we may, against the very serious hardships and evils which would be likely to arise out of the inflation which would be produced by vast loans.

In carrying out the measures by which these things are to be accomplished we should keep constantly in mind the wisdom of interfering as little as possible in our own preparation and in the equipment of our own military forces with the duty—for it will be a very practical duty—of supplying the nations already at war with Germany with the materials which they can obtain only from us or by our assistance. They are in the field and we should help them in every way to be effective there.

I shall take the liberty of suggesting, through the several executive departments of the Government, for the consideration of your committees, measures for the accomplishment of the several objects I have mentioned. I hope that it will be your pleasure to deal with them as having been framed after very careful thought by the branch of the Government upon whom the responsibility of conducting the war and safeguarding the nation will most directly fall.

While we do these things, these deeply momentous things, let us be very clear, and make very clear to all the world, what our motives and our objects are. My own thought has not been driven from its habitual and normal course by the unhappy events of the last two months, and I do not believe that the thought of the nation had been altered or clouded by them. I have exactly the same things in mind now that I had in mind when I addressed the Senate on the 22d of January last; the same that I had in mind when I addressed the Congress on the 3d of February and on the 26th of February. Our object now, as then, is to vindicate the principles of peace and justice in the life of the world as against selfish and autocratic power, and to set up among the really free and self-governed peoples of the world such a concert of purpose and of action as will henceforth insure the observance of those principles.

Neutrality is no longer feasible or desirable where the peace of the world is involved and the freedom of its peoples, and the menace to that peace and freedom lies in the existence of autocratic Governments, backed by organized force which is controlled wholly by their will, not by the will of their people. We have seen the last of neutrality in such circumstances. We are at the beginning of an age in which it will be insisted that the same standards of conduct and of responsibility for wrong done shall be observed among nations and their Governments that are observed among the individual citizens of civilized States.

We have no quarrel with the German people. We have no feeling toward them but one of sympathy and friendship. It was not upon their impulse that their Government acted in entering this war. It was not with their previous knowledge or approval. It was a war determined upon as wars used to be determined upon, in the old, unhappy days, when peoples were nowhere consulted by their rulers and wars were provoked and waged in the interest of dynasties or of little groups of ambitious men who were accustomed to use their fellow men as pawns and tools.

Self-governed nations do not fill their neighbor States with spies or set the course of intrigue to bring about some critical posture of affairs which will give them an opportunity to strike and make conquest. Such designs can be successfully worked out only under cover and where no one has the right to ask questions. Cunningly contrived plans of deception or aggression, carried, it may be, from generation to generation, can be worked out and kept from the light only within the privacy of courts or behind the carefully guarded confidences of a narrow and privileged class. They are happily impossible where public opinion commands and insists upon full information concerning all the nation's affairs.

A steadfast concert for peace can never be maintained except by a partnership of democratic nations. No autocratic Government could be trusted to keep faith within it or observe its covenants. It must be a league of honor, a partnership of opinion. Intrigue would eat its vitals away; the plottings of inner circles who could plan what they would and render account to no one would be a corruption seated at its very heart. Only free peoples can hold their purpose and their honor steady to a common end and prefer the interests of mankind to any narrow interest of their own.

Does not every American feel that assurance has been added to our hope for the future peace of the world by the wonderful and heartening things that have been happening within the last few weeks in Russia? Russia was known by those who knew her best to have been always in fact democratic at heart in all the vital habits of her thought, in all the intimate relationships of her people that spoke their natural instinct, their habitual attitude toward life. The autocracy that crowned the summit of her political structure, long as it had stood and terrible as

was the reality of its power, was not in fact Russian in origin, character, or purpose; and now it has been shaken off and the great, generous Russian people have been added, in all their naïve majesty and might, to the forces that are fighting for freedom in the world, for justice, and for peace. Here is a fit partner for a League of Honor.

One of the things that has served to convince us that the Prussian autocracy was not and could never be our friend is that from the very outset of the present war it has filled our unsuspecting communities, and even our offices of government, with spies and set criminal intrigues everywhere afoot against our national unity of counsel, our peace within and without, our industries and our commerce. Indeed, it is now evident that its spies were here even before the war began; and it is unhappily not a matter of conjecture, but a fact proved in our courts of justice, that the intrigues which have more than once come perilously near to disturbing the peace and dislocating the industries of the country, have been carried on at the instigation, with the support, and even under the personal direction of official agents of the Imperial Government, accredited to the Government of the United States.

Even in checking these things and trying to extirpate them we have sought to put the most generous interpretation possible upon them because we knew that their source lay, not in any hostile feeling or purpose of the German people toward us, (who were, no doubt, as ignorant of them as we ourselves were,) but only in the selfish designs of a Government that did what it pleased and told its people nothing. But they have played their part in serving to convince us at last that that Government entertains no real friendship for us, and means to act against our peace and security at its convenience. That it means to stir up enemies against us at our very doors the intercepted note to the German Minister at Mexico City is eloquent evidence.

We are accepting this challenge of hostile purpose because we know that in such a Government, following such methods, we can never have a friend; and that in the presence of its organized power, always lying in wait to accomplish we know not what purpose, can be no assured security for the democratic Governments of the world. We are now about to accept the gauge of battle with this natural foe to liberty and shall, if necessary, spend the whole force of the nation to check and nullify its pretensions and its power. We are glad, now that we see the facts with no veil of false pretense about them, to fight thus for the ultimate peace of the world and for the liberation of its peoples, the German peoples included; for the rights of nations, great and small, and the privilege of men everywhere to choose their way of life and of obedience.

The world must be made safe for democracy. Its peace must be planted upon the tested foundations of political liberty. We have no selfish ends to serve. We desire no conquest, no dominion. We seek no indemnities for ourselves, no material compensation for the sacrifices we shall freely make. We are but one of the champions of the rights of mankind. We shall be satisfied when those rights have been made as secure as the faith and the freedom of nations can make them.

Just because we fight without rancor and without selfish object, seeking nothing for ourselves but what we shall wish to share with all free peoples, we shall, I feel confident, conduct our operations as belligerents without passion and ourselves observe with proud punctilio the principles of right and of fair play we profess to be fighting for.

I have said nothing of the Governments allied

with the Imperial Government of Germany because they have not made war upon us or challenged us to defend our right and our honor. The Austro-Hungarian Government has, indeed, avowed its unqualified indorsement and acceptance of the reckless and lawless submarine warfare, adopted now without disguise by the Imperial German Government, and it has therefore not been possible for this Government to receive Count Tarnowski, the Ambassador recently accredited to this Government by the Imperial and Royal Government of Austria-Hungary; but that Government has not actually engaged in warfare against citizens of the United States on the seas, and I take the liberty, for the present at least, of postponing a discussion of our relations with the authorities at Vienna. We enter this war only where we are clearly forced into it because there are no other means of defending our right.

It will be all the easier for us to conduct ourselves as belligerents in a high spirit of right and fairness because we act without animus, not with enmity toward a people or with the desire to bring any injury or disadvantage upon them, but only in armed opposition to an irresponsible Government which has thrown aside all considerations of humanity and of right and is running amuck.

We are, let me say again, the sincere friends of the German people, and shall desire nothing so much as the early re-establishment of intimate relations of mutual advantage between us, however hard it may be for them for the time being to believe that this is spoken from our hearts. We have borne with their present Government through all these bitter months because of that friendship, exercising a patience and forbearance which would otherwise have been impossible

We shall happily still have an opportunity to prove that friendship in our daily attitude and actions toward the millions of men and women of German birth and native sympathy who live among us and share our life, and we shall be proud to prove it toward all who are in fact loyal to their neighbors and to the Government in the hour of test. They are most of them as true and loyal Americans as if they had never known any other fealty or allegiance. They will be prompt to stand with us in rebuking and restraining the few who may be of a different mind and purpose. If there should be disloyalty, it will be dealt with with a firm hand of stern repression; but, if it lifts its head at all, it will lift it only here and there and without countenance except from a lawless and malignant few.

It is a distressing and oppressive duty, gentlemen of the Congress, which I have performed in thus addressing you. There are, it may be, many months of fiery trial and sacrifice ahead of us. It is a fearful thing to lead this great, peaceful people into war, into the most terrible and disastrous of all wars, civilization itself seeming to be in the balance.

But the right is more precious than peace, and we shall fight for the things which we have always carried nearest our hearts—for democracy, for the right of those who submit to authority to have a voice in their own Governments, for the rights and liberties of small nations, for a universal dominion of right by such a concert of free peoples as shall bring peace and safety to all nations and make the world itself at last free.

To such a task we can dedicate our lives and our fortunes, everything that we are and everything that we have, with the pride of those who know that the day has come when America is privileged to spend her blood and her might for the principles that gave her birth and happiness and the peace which she has treasured.

God helping her, she can do no other.

The War Resolution Now Before Congress

This resolution was introduced in the House of Representatives last night by Representative Flood, Chairman of the Foreign Affairs Committee, immediately after the President's address:

JOINT RESOLUTION, Declaring that a State of War Exists Between the Imperial German Government and the Government and People of the United States and Making Provision to Prosecute the Same.

Whereas, The recent acts of the Imperial German Government are acts of war against the Government and people of the United States:

Resolved, By the Senate and House of Representatives of the United States of America in Congress assembled, that the state of war between the United States and the Imperial German Government which has thus been thrust upon the United States is hereby formally declared; and

That the President be, and he is hereby, authorized and directed to take immediate steps not only to put the country in a thorough state of defense but also to exert all of its power and employ all of its resources to carry on war against the Imperial German Government and to bring the conflict to a successful termination.

MUST EXERT ALL OUR POWER

To Bring a "Government That Is Running Amuck to Terms."

WANTS LIBERAL CREDITS

And Universal Service, for "the World Must Be Made Safe for Democracy."

A TUMULTUOUS GREETING

Congress Adjourns After "State of War" Resolution Is Introduced—Acts Today.

WASHINGTON, April 2.—At 8:35 o'clock tonight the United States virtually made its entrance into the war. At that hour President Wilson appeared before a joint session of the Senate and House and invited it to consider the fact that Germany had been making war upon us and to take action in recogniton of that fact in accordance with his recommendations, which included universal military service, the raising of an army of 500,000 men, and co-operation with the Allies in all ways that will help most effectively to defeat Germany.

Resolutions recognizing and declaring the state of war were immediately introduced in the House and Senate by Representative Flood and Senator Martin, both of the President's birth-State, Virginia, and they are the strongest declarations of war that the United States has ever made in any war in which it has been engaged since it became a nation. They are the Administration resolutions drawn up after conference with the President, and in language approved and probably dictated by him, and they will come before the two Foreign Affairs Committees at meetings which will be held tomorrow morning and will be reported at the earliest practical moment.

Unreservedly With the Allies.

Before an audience that cheered him as he has never been cheered in the Capitol in his life the President cast in the lot of America unreservedly with the Allies and declared for a war that must not end until the issue between autocracy and democracy has been fought out. He recited our injuries at Germany's hands, but he did not rest our cause on those; he went on from that point to range us with the Allies as a factor in an irrepressible conflict between the autocrat and the people. He showed that peace was impossible for the democracies of the world while this power remained on earth. "The world," he said, "must be made safe for democracy."

We had learned that the German autocracy could never be a friend of this country; she had been our enemy while nominally our friend, and even before the war of 1914 broke out. He called on us to take our stand with the democracies in this irrepressible conflict, with before our eyes "the wonderful and heartening events that have been happening in the last few weeks in Russia."

This artist's rendering depicts Woodrow Wilson delivering his war address to Congress.

He reaffirmed his hope for peace and for freedom, and looked to the war now forced upon us to bring these about; for, he said, a world compact for peace "can never be maintained except by a concert of the democracies of the world." The objects for which we fight, he said, are democracy, the right of those who submit to authority to have a voice in their own government, the right and liberties of small nations, the universal dominion of right, the concert of free peoples to bring peace and safety to all nations, and to make the world free. These have always been our ideals; and to accomplish them, we accept the war Germany has made upon us. In fighting it we must not only raise an army and increase the navy, but must aid the Allies in all ways, financial and other, and so order our own preparations as not to interfere with the supply of munitions they are getting from us.

I WANT YOU
FOR U.S. ARMY
NEAREST RECRUITING STATION

FILL THE BREECH

THE NAVY NEEDS YOU! DON'T READ AMERICAN HISTORY— MAKE IT !

U·S·NAVY RECRUITING STATION

FOLLOW THE FLAG

ENLIST IN THE NAVY
U.S.NAVY RECRUITING STATION
HALL BUILDING, 161 GRISWOLD ST. DETROIT

Part of the campaign to get men to enlist in the service of their country was very successfully accomplished with posters like the ones here.

"All the News That's
Fit to Print."

The New York Times.

THE WEATHER
Rain tonight and Friday; moderate
temperature; southeasterly winds.
For full weather report see Page 23.

VOL. LXVI...NO. 21,621. ... NEW YORK, THURSDAY, APRIL 5, 1917.—TWENTY-FOUR PAGES. ONE CENT In New York City. | TWO CENTS New England and Middle States. | THREE CENTS Elsewhere.

SENATE, 82 TO 6, ADOPTS WAR DECLARATION; ITS OPPONENTS SCORED; HOUSE ACTS TODAY; BERLIN FEARS OUR INFLUENCE ON RUSSIA

MAY BLOCK SEPARATE PEACE

America's Stand a Menace to German Negotiations with Duma Government.

COMMENT OF GERMAN PRESS

Can't Understand Reason for War; but Will Face Eleventh Enemy Bravely.

WISH FOR A BRYAN TREATY

Plan 'Foolishly Rejected' Would Have Held Us Off for a Year, Tageblatt Says.

Special Cable to THE NEW YORK TIMES.

BERLIN, April 4, (via The Hague.)—Reports of yesterday's proceedings in the American Congress, scant as they are, leave no doubt in the minds of the German people and Government that President Wilson will have his way in everything, and that their eleventh enemy is about to make his appearance in the theatre of war.

Nobody is excited here, but nobody is underestimating the effect of America's entrance into the war against Germany. In military circles it is considered that the immediate effect on the various fighting fronts will not be considerable. In political circles what is most feared is that America's action may influence the present rulers of Russia to a degree that they will resist the temptation to accept the peace offered by Germany. The masses of the German people are utterly at a loss to understand this war with a nation 4,000 miles away, with whom they have had no quarrel whatever. The news from America arrived so late thtat most of the afternoon papers abstained from lengthy comment, contenting themselves with explaining to their readers the workings of the Washington Government machinery. But the Tageblatt states the German position very lucidly as follows:

Sees the Hand of England.

" In his last speech the Chancellor prepared us for the fact that there was no chance of continuing on peaceful terms with the United States. If the English press pretended that it was just this speech that had knocked the bottom out of the barrel, this is only another of those tricks which have had such fatal success with American public opinion. The English press also hoped to minimize thereby the Chancellor's declaration that the German people would go into this war without

hatred or enmity, but would be sure to bear patiently this new burden.

" Are the American people in a like condition of mind? It is difficult to answer this question.

" It is a foregone conclusion that Congress will grant all of President Wilson's demands made in his message. He had little trouble to overcome the opposition which was raised against him in the last Congressional session. Of the few Senators who resolutely carried out the operations of obstruction against his policy very few are left, if English sources have informed us correctly. They gave way under the pressure of public opinion even in some of the Western States, where that Zimmermann letter seems to have had some effect after all.

" Since then there has been a feverish war propaganda. Meanwhile the Bryan pacifists did their best to avoid the worst. But it was quite clear that when once the war fever caught Madison Square there would be no stopping this hysterical wave.

" Hatred? Enmity? We know nothing about it. The emotions dictating to

Congress its action and which were nourished by President Wilson and his partisans were of another kind. They were nothing but anger over supposed violations of American rights. Despite all efforts to enlighten him President Wilson clung tenaciously to his original view, and he still upholds it with surprising acuteness.

" In order not to disavow his pretended pacifism, Mr. Wilson now seeks to avoid an American declaration of war against Germany. That is why he insists on a fiction, as though Germany by her U-boat war had been guilty of a warlike action, necessary now, for America has recognized the existence of a state of war.

Wish for a Bryan Treaty.

" We realize now what a big mistake it was that German policy saw fit to refuse to conclude the Bryan peace treaty such as England and other powers entered into with the United States. If such a contract existed today the United States would be compelled to submit even the gravest differences to a court or arbitration before breaking relations.

Text of War Resolution Adopted by Senate and the Detailed Vote Upon Its Passage

WASHINGTON, April 4.—Following is the text of the resolution declaring war upon the Imperial German Government, which was adopted by the Senate tonight:

Whereas, The Imperial German Government has committed repeated acts of war against the Government and the people of the United States of America; therefore, be it

Resolved, by the Senate and House of Representatives of the United States of America in Congress assembled, That the state of war between the United States and the Imperial German Government, which has thus been thrust upon the United States, is hereby formally declared; and

'That the President be, and he is hereby, authorized and directed to employ the entire naval and military forces of the United States and the resources of the Government to carry on war against the Imperial German Government; and to bring the conflict to a successful termination all the resources of the country are hereby pledged by the Congress of the United States.

The detailed vote of the Senate on the declaration of war was as follows:

FOR THE RESOLUTION—82

Democrats—43.

ASHURST,	JAMES,	OWEN,	SIMMONS
BECKHAM,	JOHNSON, (S. D.)	PHELAN,	SMITH, (Ariz.)
BROUSSARD,	JONES, (N. M.)	PITTMAN,	SMITH, (Ga.)
CHAMBERLAIN,	KENDRICK,	POMERENE,	SMITH, (S. C.)
CULBERSON,	KING,	RANSDELL,	SWANSON,
FLETCHER,	KIRBY,	REED,	THOMPSON,
GERRY,	LEWIS,	ROBINSON,	TRAMMELL,
HARDWICK,	McKELLAR,	SAULSBURY,	UNDERWOOD,
HITCHCOCK,	MARTIN,	SHAFROTH,	WALSH,
HUGHES,	MEYERS,	SHEPPARD,	WILLIAMS.
HUSTING,	OVERMAN,	SHIELDS,	

Republicans—39.

BORAH,	FRANCE,	LODGE,	SMOOT,
BRADY,	FRELINGHUYSEN,	McCUMBER,	STERLING,
BRANDEGEE,	GALLINGER,	McLEAN,	SUTHERLAND,
CALDER,	HALE,	NELSON,	TOWNSEND,
COLT,	HARDING,	NEW,	WADSWORTH,
CUMMINS,	JOHNSON, (Cal.)	PAGE,	WARREN,
CURTIS,	JONES, (Wash.)	PENROSE,	WATSON,
DILLINGHAM,	KELLOGG,	POINDEXTER,	WEEKS,
FALL,	KENYON,	SHERMAN,	WOLCOTT.
FERNALD,	KNOX,	SMITH, (Mich.)	

AGAINST THE RESOLUTION—6.

Democrats—3.

LANE,	STONE,	VARDAMAN.

Republicans—3.

GRONNA,	LA FOLLETTE,	NORRIS.

Eight Senators were absent, but all would have voted for the resolution. They were: Bankhead, Gore, Hollis, Newlands, Smith, (Maryland;) Thomas and Tillman, Democrats; Goff, Republican.

KEEN DEBATE FOR 13 HOURS

La Follette Scourged by Williams as Pro-German and Anti-American.

'TREASON' CRY AT NORRIS

Nebraska Senator Denounced for Hinting That Commercialism Prompted Nation's Course.

OPPONENTS 'WILLFUL MEN'

Three from Each Party—La Follette, in 4-Hour Speech, Assailed Great Britain.

President at Theatre Is Cheered by Audience

WASHINGTON, April 4.—President Wilson, attending a theatre tonight after working most of the day on war plans, was greeted with enthusiastic cheers. The orchestra played " The Star-Spangled Banner," and as the President was recognized the audience rose for a tumultuous demonstration.

Special to The New York Times.

WASHINGTON, April 4.—At 11 minutes past 11 o'clock tonight, the Senate, in the presence of a great throng on the floor and in the galleries, passed the resolution declaring a state of war between the United States and the German Government; and pledging all the resources of the United States for the successful prosecution of the war.

While the recorded vote was 82 to 6, the Senate's true alignment on the question of war is 90 to 6, as the absent Senators all favored the resolution. The House is expected to pass an identical resolution tomorrow by a still more overwhelming vote.

The six Senators opposing the declaration were equally divided between the two parties. They were La Follette of Wisconsin, Gronna of North Dakota, and Norris of Nebraska, Republicans; and Stone of Missouri, Lane of Oregon, and Vardaman of Mississippi, Democrats. All were members of the group of " willful men " whom President Wilson denounced.

Of the other six opponents of armed neutrality at the last session, Senators Cummins, Kenyon, and Kirby voted for the resolution tonight. Senators O'Gorman, Clapp, and Works have retired to private life.

182

Austria to Break with Us If We Join War on Kaiser

Vienna, April 3, (via London, Thursday, April 5.)—It appears certain that Austria-Hungary will sever diplomatic relations with the United States if Congress declares that a state of war exists between America and Germany.

The Government has placed a special car at the disposal of Ambassador Penfield, who will probably leave Vienna on Thursday. Before leaving Ambassador Penfield will be received by Emperor Charles. The Ambassador will travel by way of Switzerland.

The vote came after thirteen hours of debate, that had lasted continuously since 10 o'clock in the morning.

The passage of the resolution was marked by no outburst from the galleries. On the floor the Senators themselves were unusually grave and quiet. Many of them answered to their names in voices that quivered with emotion.

As the last name was called, and the Clerk announced the vote, there was hardly a murmur of applause. The great crowd was awed by the solemnity of the occasion and sobered by the speeches they had heard.

The resolution was adopted in the form approved by the Committee on Foreign Relations. Only one effort was made to change the committee's draft. That was in a substitute offered by Senator McCumber of North Dakota, in which the United States would simply proclaim certain principles of international law, with the warning that war would be made on any country violating them. Mr. McCumber cast the only vote for the substitute.

Throughout the long hours of discussion ony five speeches were made against the resolution, and all efforts in opposition to it ceased with the conclusion of Mr. La Follette's four-hour attack on the President and defense of Germany's course. The remaining hours of the session were consumed by brief statements from Senators, one after the other, telling why they regarded war as necessary, how they had gradually come to change from advocates of peace to believers that war was essential to the safety and honor of the nation.

Last Stand of Germany's Apologists.

Today's debate, slow-moving as much of it was, postponing for weary hour after weary hour the declaration for which the country waited, was in itself the culmination of almost three years of intermittent discussion.

That long discussion had the same subject on the part of most Senators as today's debate, resentment of German outrages of every sort, murders on the high seas, affronts to Americans in Germany, and gross violation of American hospitality by the Imperial representatives in the United States. During these three years, as was again the case today, there was a bi-partisan minority defending the acts of Germany, extenuating her offenses, and doing everything to hold the United States back from vigorous assertion of her rights.

Both these aspects were summed up in the speeches today, and both aspects seemed to lead to the end of today's debate—a solemn declaration of war against the house of Hohenzollern. For the subject matter of discussion has been increased from month to month by new German outrages, while the defenders of Germany in the Senate have presented a constantly dwindling front. The vote tonight, which every recent event insured would be overwhelming, might be regarded as the point of intersection of these two converging lines of change.

The loss of American sympathy for Germany was never more evident than it was in today's proceedings in the Senate. Senator Stone of Missouri, Chairman of the Committee on Foreign Relations, still held out for submission to German dictation, as did Senator Vardaman of Mississippi. And three Republican Senators spoke against war—La Follette of Wisconsin, Gronna of North Dakota, and Norris of Nebraska.

But Senator Hitchcock of Nebraska, next to Mr. Stone, the Democratic leader of the Foreign Relations Committee, who has been regarded by some as a pacifist, today took the last step in the march he began, when he accepted responsibility for the Armed Neutrality bill, by supporting vigorously the President's demand for war and handling the resolution embodying that demand. Senator Kirby of Arkansas, a Democratic member of the "little group of willful men," announced that as war was inevitable he would not weaken the country's stand before the world by voting against the resolution. Senator Kenyon of Iowa, who refused to sign the manifesto of Senators supporting the Armed Neutrality bill, announced his support of the war resolution in a ringing plea for the destruction of the "bloody dynasty of Hohenzollern," and his colleague, Senator Cummins, who fought the Armed Neutrality bill with all his might, was among the supporters of the war resolution.

As this gradual drift manifested itself more and more in the direction demanded by the country, old observers, inured to the deliberate processes of the Senate, got, perhaps, an added sense of climax from the debate. To them the apparently endless addresses were the breathless hush before the breaking of a tornado. They knew what the end would be; everybody knew it; and they could read its terrible significance in the most casual utterances of the day.

Plain Talk of "Treason."

The delay increased the tension that has followed the President's last call for an extraordinary session of Congress to the breaking point, and the break came at last with almost unprecedented violence. It came when Mr. Reed of Missouri, in restrained voice and deliberate manner, accused Senator Norris of treason, and Senator Williams of Mississippi, Pomerene of Ohio, and James of Kentucky, supported the charge, inferentially, by the severe questioning to which they subjected the Nebraskan.

The rules of the Senate expressly forbid accusing a Senator of motives unworthy of a Senator, but Mr. Norris admitted the extraordinary situation by not invoking the rule in his defense, and not resenting the charge. He denied the truth of the charge, but contented himself with saying that his accusers would in calmer moments regret what they had said.

The clash came over a sentence in Mr. Norris's speech for peace, in which he said that Congress, by declaring war, would "put the dollar mark on the American flag." As he explained his remark, he meant simply that the war in which the United States was about to engage had a commercial origin, that most of the persons slain by German forces had taken their dangerous voyages for the sake of profit, and that American exports to the Allies had caused the German blockade to be turned against Americans.

But his interlocutors were in no mood for explanations. Senator Reed sent for the notes of Senator Norris's speech, reread them to the Senate and declared them to be an insult to the President. Then, using the language of the Constitution's definition of high treason, he went on:

"If that be not giving aid and comfort to the enemies of the United States on the very eve of hostilities, I, at least, do not know what would give more comfort to a Hapsburg or a Hohenzollern. If that be not treason, it would at least give more comfort to the enemy, coming from a Senator of the United States, than if 1,000 or 10,000 private citizens rose in open revolt. If that be not treason, as the Senator from Mississippi [Mr. Williams] suggests to me, it grazes the edge of treason. We are going into this war, not to save money, but to pour out our blood that liberty might live. The President calls for war, not to save a few paltry dollars, but to vindicate the sovereign rights of the United States."

Senator Norris then made his explanation, denying any reflection on the President. The country, he said, was war-crazy; he admitted that war would certainly be declared, but under the influence of passion Senators, he said, had somewhat lost their reason.

"All except him," commented Mr. Williams, while his colleagues laughed.

Although the day's debate was slow, there was no filibustering. Even La Follette, though he began to talk in the middle of the afternoon and ended only after the lights were turned on, did not try to delay matters. He is naturally a long talker, and his criticism of President Wilson, his denunciation of Great Britain, and his defense of Germany were taken by his hearers, not as tactics of delay, but as a defense of himself in voting against war.

Some Stirring Moments.

At times the debate, under impulse of the mighty events it foretold, rose to the ancient heights of Senatorial traditions. Senator Hitchcock's speech, in which he frankly related his own change of opinion in the face of increasing evidences of Germany's determination to follow her ruthless course without regard to warnings or to rights, and his final plea for a united country for the war, made a profound impression.

Senator Lodge of Massachusetts, the scholar of the Senate, and a recognized authority on international law, made the speech that was expected of him.

And when Senator La Follette took his seat, Senator Williams in a vigorous reply rose to a flight of patriotic eloquence that gave the galleries the throb and thrill that they had been waiting for.

For these orations the stage of the Senate was grandly set. Every Senator was in his place and remained there. The rail of the Senate was lined by members of the House, who remained standing all day long and through the night till the end came. The galleries were crowded to the doors, and around the elevated rear of the galleries a packed line of tireless watchers, standing, carried the bowl of faces up to the lofty ceiling. If a few spectators withdrew, their places were instantly taken by others, waiting their chance in long lines at every door.

The crowd retained its density through the night, but as the evening wore on its character changed. Brilliantly dressed women, with escorts in evening clothes, came from dinner parties or theatres, seeking a more vital drama. Secretary Lansing, Counselor Polk, and Assistant Secretaries Phillips and Long of the State Department, Solicitor General Davis, and Secretary Tumulty were among the prominent officials in the evening audience.

Popular Celebration in France to Mark Our Entry Into War

PARIS, April 4.—A great national demonstration to mark the entry of the United States into the European war was proposed today to the French Government.

It was suggested that the demonstration should be of a popular character, in order to enable the French people to participate in it.

ARMY CALL READY FOR 500,000 MEN

War Department Has Universal Service Plan Worked Out and Waits on Congress.

BACKED BY GENERAL STAFF

Selective Conscription Scheme to be Submitted When War Resolution Passes.

Special to The New York Times.

WASHINGTON, April 4.—The plan of selective conscription, under which the first increment of 500,000 men is to be obtained under the universal military service plan of raising an army for the war with Germany, will be presented to Congress by the War Department as soon as that body adopts the war resolution.

In his address to Congress the President said that the entrance of the United States into the war would "involve the immediate addition to the armed forces of the United States already provided for by law in case of war at elast 500,000 men, who should, in my opinion, be chosen on the principle of universal liability to service, and also the authorization of subsequent additional increments of equal force as soon as they may be needed and can be handled in training."

The War Department has a well-worked-out plan, representing the views of the General Staff and Army War College, as to how this army may be raised and the machinery for registering and enrolling the various increments of 500,000 men.

But the plan has been carefully guarded, and Secretary Baker said today that the War Department's recommendations would not be made public until after they had been sent to Congress. While the department has a plan, Secretary Baker asserted today that the initiative with respect to the raising of an army rested with Congress, and that the Administration would carry out the will of that body as embraced in the legislation to be enacted.

In view of the President's recommendation in favor of universal liability to service, and the sentiment throughout the country in favor of universal military service, it is now assumed in Administration circles that the legislation soon to be enacted by Congress will be based on that principle.

In raising the first increment of 500,000 only young men of certain designated ages are to be called to the colors. These will include mainly unmarried men 18 to 19 years of age, but may include men up to 23. The age limits to be recommended by the War Department to Congress were not disclosed at the department today.

The unmarried males from 18 to 24 years of age in the United States at the beginning of the present year are estimated to have been as follows:

Between 18 and 19 years....	1,981,298
Between 20 and 24 years....	3,775,376
Total, 18 to 24 years......	5,756,674

These figures are based on the 1910 census plus a 10 per cent. increase suggested by the Census Bureau as approximately correct for the period 1910-1916. It is not to be assumed that all these unmarried men would be called to the colors or that they are all without dependents. In addition to exemptions in favor of married men, and others with dependents, there will also be exemptions in favor of men needed in war industries and men who fail to meet the proper military requirements.

After deducting from the 5,756,674 unmarried men between 18 and 24 years a percentage representing the physically incapable, as estimated from the results of examinations of applicants at army recruiting stations over a period of nine years, there would yet remain ten times as many men as would be required to fill the first increment of 500,000 men.

In the light of developments of the last two years in the European war the War College recently favored a first-line army of 1,500,000 and an army of 1,500,000 that could be in readiness in ninety days as the best military policy for the United States. Census figures indicate that the whole of such first-line army could be made up of men from 19 to 20, and that the other unmarried men from 21 to 24 years would supply a force twice as large as the proposed second-line army.

Careful Selection at First.

In picking the 500,000 men for the first call, as well as of the other increments, careful selection will be applied to bring into the service those with the fewest responsibilities. There will be a registration of all available men in the country, and from these lists the men will be chosen for the first call. It is expected that it will require about four months to complete these registration lists.

Want 20,000 Skilled Men.

It was announced at the War Department today that 20,000 mechanics and artisans were wanted at once to join the Quartermaster Enlisted Reserve Corps. Men of many trades, from blacksmiths and butchers to motorcyclists and tentmakers are wanted, and rapid promotion is promised to those who prove themselves fit. The call for these men was issued in the following form:

"Twenty thousand men, of all trades, wanted for the Quartermaster Enlisted Reserve Corps.

"Desirable persons qualified to fill the following named positions will be enlisted in the Quartermaster Enlisted Reserve Corps for a period of four years, unless sooner discharged by proper authority, and promoted to the higher grades as vacancies occur and the reservists' qualifications, education, and service justified. Promotions will be rapid in the case of men of high character who show most proficiency in their particular lines. The positions are as follows:

"Bakers, blacksmiths, butchers, cargaders, (pack trains,) carpenters, carpenters, (foreman,) chauffeurs, checkers, clerks, cooks, electricians and helpers, engineers, (steam,) farriers, forage masters, horseshoers, horse trainers, laborers, machinists and helpers, masons, (brick and stone,) mechanics and helpers, (automobiles,) motor-car masters and assistants, motor-truck masters and assistants, motor cyclists, overseers of labor, painters, painters, (foreman,) packers, (with pack trains,) pack masters, (foreman,) pack masters, plumbers, (foreman,) saddlers, (foreman,) saddlers, stablemen, stenographers, storekeepers, teamsters, tentmakers, train masters, typewriters, wagon masters, wagon masters, (assistant,) watchmen, wheelwrights.

"Recognizing that from patriotic motives many are willing to do their share to further the preparedness of their country to meet aggressions from foreign nations, Congress, on June 3, 1916, authorized the formation of the enlisted reserve corps as an auxiliary of the regular army, such reserves to be made up of men from all walks of life and skilled in various trades and businesses as indicated above."

"All the News That's Fit to Print."

The New York Times.

THE WEATHER
Clearing today; tomorrow probably fair; southwest gales.
For full weather report see Page 21.

VOL. LXVI...NO. 21,622. NEW YORK, FRIDAY, APRIL 6, 1917.—TWENTY-TWO PAGES. ONE CENT In New York City. | TWO CENTS New England and Middle States. | THREE CENTS Elsewhere.

HOUSE, AT 3:12 A.M., VOTES FOR WAR, 373 TO 50; $3,000,000,000 ASKED FOR ARMY OF 1,000,000; NATION'S GIGANTIC RESOURCES MOBILIZED

DEBATE LASTED 16½ HOURS

One Hundred Speeches Were Made—Miss Rankin, Sobbing, Votes No.

ALL AMENDMENTS BEATEN

Resolution Will Take Effect This Afternoon with the President's Signature.

KITCHIN WITH PACIFISTS

Accession of the Floor Leader Added Others to the Anti-War Faction.

Special to The New York Times.

WASHINGTON, Friday, April 6.—At 3:12 o'clock this morning the House of Representatives by the overwhelming vote of 373 to 50 adopted the resolution that meant war between the Government and the people of the United States and the Imperial German Government.

War will formally begin this afternoon when President Wilson will approve the resolution which was passed by the Senate Wednesday night and was approved by the House this morning without the crossing of a "t" or the dotting of an "i."

The House presented an impressive spectacle as the roll call proceeded on the adoption of the war resolution. Nearly every member was in his seat.

The galleries were crowded for the most part by men and women who had sat there all the evening, some of them since 10 o'clock yesterday morning when the House met. Some of the men and women were in evening dress. Men and women who were in the diplomatic box had come directly from dinner parties.

There were crowds also in the corridors outside the galleries, seeking a chance for a peep at the events inside.

Usually when the roll of the House is called there is much confusion, and it is often difficult to hear the responses of the Representatives as their names are droned by the reading clerk.

But there was a marked difference this morning. The House, which had been full of levity at times during the long debate, felt the solemnity of the moment. No sound disturbed the proceedings. Every member's answer came distinctly and was heard by the throng that listened almost breathlessly to the "Ayes" and "Noes" that followed the calling of the roll.

Miss Rankin Votes "No."

Miss Jeanette Rankin, the woman Representative from Montana, had been absent from the House most of the evening, but took her accustomed place while the roll call was in progress. When her name was called she sat silent. "Miss Rankin," repeated the clerk. Still no answer. The clerk went on with his droning, and floor and galleries buzzed.

On the second roll call Miss Rankin's name was again called. She sat silent as before. The eyes of the galleries were turned on her. For a moment there was breathless silence. Then Miss Rankin rose. In a voice that broke a bit but could be heard all over the still chamber she said:

"I want to stand by my country, but I cannot vote for war. I vote no." The "No" was scarcely audible.

And the maiden speech of the first woman Congressman ended in a sob. She was deeply moved and big tears were in her eyes.

It was a sympathetic House, however, and although most of the persons there were plainly in favor of the war resolution, a wave of applause swept through floor and gallery.

When the roll call had been completed and a slip containing the count handed to Speaker Clark the latter's gavel came down with a bang. The House became quiet instantly.

"On this motion," said the Speaker "the Ayes are 373 and the Noes are 50."

The cheers that followed drowned the Speaker's announcement that the resolution had been adopted. Then the floors and galleries cleared, Representatives and spectators knowing that war had again come to the United States.

The Senate adjourned Wednesday night, to meet again at noon today. As the resolution must be returned to the Senate, while that body is in session President Wilson will not receive the historical document for signature until this afternoon. From the moment of his approval war will be on.

The Early Morning Scenes.

At 1:20 o'clock this morning, when Representative Kelly of Pennsylvania began to express his views, the tally list showed that he was the eightieth member to address the House on the war resolution.

At that hour the galleries were crowded, women forming a majority of the spectators. All through the evening there were but few vacant seats in the executive gallery and the diplomatic box, while the other gallery space was filled. Members of the Diplomatic Corps and women in evening dress showed keen interest in the debate.

At 2:35 o'clock, when Representative Ray of New Jersey had delivered the 100th speech, the House by viva voce vote rejected amendments that had been offered to the war resolution.

These were the proposals of Representative McCullough of Ohio that "none of the military forces of the United States may be transported for service in any European country except on express approval of Congress," and of Representative Britten of Illinois to prohibit the use of troops in Europe, Asia or Africa, without the approval of Congress, except troops volunteering for such service.

At 2:40 o'clock Chairman Flood moved that the committee of the whole rise and report the resolution to the House. This was adopted, and Representative Fitzgerald, who had presided over the proceedings, made the report, after Speaker Clark had resumed the chair.

Then Chairman Flood moved the previous question and the motion was adopted by a viva voce vote without dissent. The third reading of the resolution was ordered in the same rapid fashion.

Representative Britten moved to recommit the resolution to the Foreign Affairs Committee with his amendment that no part of the military forces of the United States should be sent to Europe, Asia, or Africa without the consent of Congress, unless such as volunteered. Mr. Britten demanded a roll call, but not a sufficient number of members backed him.

The roll call on the resolution then began at 2:45 o'clock.

A Feast of Speeches.

While a heavy northeaster raged outside the Capitol the House went through last night and this morning the throes of the most important debate that had fallen to its portion in many years. Yet "debate" is hardly the word to apply to the long discussion of the business before the popular branch of Congress. It was a speechmaking festival, member after member having his say, with few making the effort to answer any of the arguments that had been advanced for or against war with the German Government.

Before the House met yesterday morning it was freely predicted that a mere handful of Representatives would vote against the war resolution. But after a speech by Representative Claude Kitchin of North Carolina, the Democratic floor leader, in which he argued against war and declared his intention of voting against the pending measure, there was seemingly a marked change among the contingent which had been wabbling between the two sides of the war controversy. Undoubtedly Mr. Kitchin swung a considerable number of weak-kneed ones to his side.

The speech of Mr. Kitchin and those of Mr. Mann, (Illinois,) the Republican floor leader; Chairman Flood of the Foreign Affairs Committee, and Mr. Cooper of Wisconsin, the ranking Republican member of that committee, were the most important contributions of the day's debate. Mann and Flood were for war; Kitchen and Cooper for peace. But the stirring episodes of the discussion—and there were several—were furnished by other Representatives.

Levity Amid the Solemnity.

Mr. Heflin, Democrat, of Alabama, called on Kitchin to resign his leadership. Party friends of Kitchin resented this and showed their resentment in hisses. Later on Mr. Burnett of Alabama, another Democrat, declared that Kitchin had converted him to the pacifist view and took occasion to make remarks about Mr. Heflin which angered the latter. The two Alabama members shouted at each other while Representative Fitzgerald, who was in the chair, pounded with his gavel. Grasping the mace, the Sergeant at Arms sought to quiet the disturbance and succeeded.

This incident was greatly relished by a large part of the members, who found keen enjoyment in egging on Burnett and Heflin. It was evident that the House was willing to inject a note of levity into a solemn occasion. This was particularly emphasized when Representative Talbott of Maryland, "the Father of the House," made an old-fashioned Star-Spangled banner speech that brought gales of laughter from the tired Congressmen, but at the same time aroused patriotic fervor on the floor and in the galleries.

No closure rule was adopted to limit debate which, unusual in the House, proceeded under a gentleman's agreement that no member should speak more than twenty minutes without unanimous consent. Later it was agreed to limit speeches to five minutes.

Flood Opens the Discussion.

"The crushing of Prussian militarism and the liberation of the world from the menace of Hohenzollern dynasty," was demanded by Chairman Flood of the Foreign Affairs Committee in opening the debate. He recited, one by one, the German offenses against the United States.

"Didn't Great Britain's mines sink the Evelyn?" asked Representative Cooper of Wisconsin.

"Great Britain has not taken an American life during the war," retorted Mr. Flood. "The Evelyn was sunk by a German mine in a German field near the German coast."

Mr. Cooper insisted that Great Britain's violations of international law had been flagrant, yet no war was declared against her.

"They talk about human rights," he shouted, "and yet men are assailed because they object to rushing this country into war for the right of free speech. A mob breaks up a meeting in Baltimore. I wonder if this mob comprised descendants of those who stoned Massachusetts troops who passed through that city during the civil war."

Mr. Cooper added that he was willing to fight for defense.

"There is a difference," he said, "in an American defending his home from invasion and going away hundreds of miles to engage in a brawl."

Mr. Britten of Illinois, Republican member of the Naval Committee and an advocate of preparedness, announced his purpose to oppose the resolution unless it included a proviso that only Congress should direct the sending of troops to Europe. His assertion that 90 per cent. of the American people were opposed to war was challenged by Mr. Glass of Virginia.

"How do you know the people oppose war?" Mr. Glass asked.

"Because I have been back home," said Mr. Britten, who added that there had been no public enthusiasm for a war parade in Chicago.

Kitchin's Stand Surprises Leaders.

The defection of Representative Kitchin, the Democratic floor leader, to the anti-war faction was the outstanding event in the debate. His opposition was known only to a few intimate friends. When other leaders heard of Mr. Kitchin's intention to speak against the resolution they urged him at least to remain silent and merely vote against the resolution. Representative Harrison, one of the Democrats of the Foreign Affairs Committee, appealed to him not to speak.

Mr. Kitchin's stand heartened the wavering pacifists, and after his speech Administration supporters increased their efforts to muster an overwhelming vote. Postmaster General Burleson was soon seen about the corridors.

Mr. Kitchin spoke with deliberation, reading his speech from manuscript—something he very seldom does. His enunciation was slow, and he spoke with almost a tremor in his voice. He was plainly overwrought, and when he left the chamber after speaking he was on the verge of tears.

At Mr. Kitchin's first announcement that he would vote against the resolution there was applause from perhaps a score of pacifists. When he concluded both sides of the House applauded him; but the applause was for Kitchin, the man, and his conscientious exposition of the reasons for opposing the war resolution, rather than for the sentiments he expressed. Administration leaders said that his speech had cost the resolution a number of votes.

Alabamians in a Rumpus.

At times during the afternoon the debate dragged, but under the influence of crowds that filled the galleries, bright lights, and increased attendance upon the floor the discussion became more lively in the night hours. It was during the late afternoon that Representative Burnett, an Alabama Democrat, who is only 5 feet in height, belligerently assailed Representative Heflin, also of Alabama, because the latter had virtually demanded the resignation of Mr. Kitchin as majority leader because of his speech.

"Start a petition and see how many men will sign it to have Mr. Kitchin resign!" shouted Mr. Burnett, addressing Mr. Heflin. "Are you going to enlist? Are you going to resign? Would you vote for conscription in this country?"

The confusion in the House was great, but above the uproar Mr. Heflin was heard shouting that he "would resign if necessary."

"A son of my sister has been on the border, and my son will go as soon as he is old enough!" he yelled. "I will go if it becomes necessary."

Mr. Burnett made an impassioned speech against the war resolution. He walked up and down the aisles in an excited manner, waving his arms and decrying the fact that the nation was being rushed into war. Mr. Burnett said that he had had doubts as to how he should vote, but finally made up his mind that he should oppose the resolution.

The pacifist trend was checked momentarily in the afternoon by Representative Clarence B. Miller of Minnesota, a Republican member of the Foreign Affairs Committee, who startled his colleagues by asserting that part of the Zimmermann note, which had been suppressed, proposed the establishment of a submarine base in Mexican ports and "an attack all along the border."

Mr. Miller asserted further that Carranza and Villa were dominated by Germany, that German reservists were now making munitions in Mexico and that a flood of German money was being poured into Mexico.

Secretary Lansing subsequently stated that the Zimmermann instructions contained "nothing of the sort" such as Mr. Miller asserted.

Why Wilson Must Sign Resolution.

The signature of the President to the war resolution is required because the legislation is in the form of a joint resolution, which must have Executive approval to become law.

As Congress has the exclusive right by the Constitution to declare war, action could have been taken without the President's assent.

A "concurrent" resolution, which becomes effective when adopted by the Senate and the House and does not require the President's signature, would have produced a state of war between the United States and the German Government from the moment the legislative formalities were concluded.

It was deemed more effective, however, to put the war declaration in the form of a "joint" resolution, requiring the President's approval, so that President Wilson could sign, and thus become a party to the warmaking transaction.

EBB AND FLOW OF DEBATE.

Pacifists' Pleas, with Interruptions, Provide Chief Interest.

WASHINGTON, Friday April 6.—Debate on the war resolution began in the House promptly at 10 A. M. yesterday, with Chairman Flood of the Foreign Affairs Committee making the opening statement. Galleries were then only half filled and fewer than half the members were present.

Under the unanimous consent rule, by which the resolution was considered, Representative Flood could move the previous question at any time after an hour and, if sustained, bring the measure to a vote. The debate began without any limitation.

"War is being made upon our country and its people," said Representative Flood in opening. "Our ships are being sunk. Our noncombatant citizens, including men, women and children, are being murdered, our merchantmen are denied the freedom of the seas. There is no choice as to our course. We are compelled by the acts of the German Government to enter into this most colossal war.

"The time for argument has passed; the time for heroic action is here, and our people will rally to the support of their Government in this high and patriotic hour and meet war's sacrifices and war's perils as a brave and patriotic people should.

"We should take our stand by the side of the allied nations which have been fighting humanity's battles for two and one-half years, determined that our power shall be so employed that complete victory shall crown their efforts and that Prussian militarism shall be crushed and the world shall be delivered from the threat and danger of the Hohenzollern dynasty."

Denounces Talk of Expediency.

Representative Siegel, Republican, of New York, favoring the resolution, said he could not disregard the fact that "though we cry peace, Germany answers by warring against us.

"During this week," he said, "intimations have come to me that political expediency required me to cast my vote against this resolution, and that contrary action on my part would mean a general effort from now on to end my Congressional career. I would be unworthy of American citizenship were I to be deterred from acting by such warnings. I say to my colleagues who are now hesitating that the people will know whether they are for this great land of freedom and religious liberty or whether they are going to be guided simply by the selfish question whether they will obtain more votes in 1918 by standing on the side of our foe. Let us give evidence to the world that we are united."

Representative Harrison, Democrat, of Mississippi, assailed pro-German sympathizers and pacifists.

"I would suggest to them," said he, "that they now employ their talents and eloquence, not in attempting to cause dissension among the American people, but in addressing Kaiser Wilhelm, Bethmann Hollweg, the Reichstag, and the author of that remarkable sample of diplomatic 'kultur,' the Zimmermann note."

Cooper First to Oppose.

The first expressions of opposition to the resolution came from Representative Cooper of Wisconsin, who launched into a defense of pacifists generally and himself particularly.

"I have been called a pacifist," he said. "I voted for all of these preparedness bills. This campaign of slander has no regard for the truth."

Mr. Cooper also defended his vote for the McLemore resolution.

"I was right then," he said, "and so were the 144 other members who voted for it. It should have passed. Canada does not permit its women to travel on armed ships, and neither should we. Every pacifist in the country knows I am not a pacifist in the sense in which that word is used. Does it mean because I do not want to go to war with a nation 4,000 miles away, because England and Germany have violated our rights, that I am not an American?"

Mr. Cooper broke his eyeglasses and found trouble reading certain documents. A dozen members rushed forward and laid spectacles on the table in front of him.

Mr. Cooper, turning to the Chair, said: "Mr. Chairman, I cannot surrender all of my time to trying on specs."

A roar of laughter swept the House.

Mr. Cooper asserted that the German Government had never promised unqualifiedly to abandon its submarine warfare. Representative Flood made loud demands to be heard, but Mr. Cooper would not yield.

Mr. Cooper stated in conclusion that while all would stand united when war came, he would not be one to vote to plunge the country into war.

Representative Foss, Republican, of Illinois, held that the issue was the defense of American rights on the high seas and of the America flag. He said that when war came the German-born American would be as loyal and patriotic as the American-born.

Representative Britten, Republican, of Illinois, said he was not a pacifist in any sense, but was opposed to the resolution. Some Democrats, he said, had told him they were opposed to the resolution, but would vote for it.

Representative Harrison of Mississippi and Heflin of Alabama, Democrats, called for names of such Democrats, and Mr. Britten replied by asserting that 75 per cent of the Democratic members were really personally not in favor of it, and that 90 per cent of the people of the country were against going into war.

Mr. Britten had read an amendment which he said he would later offer, providing that no part of the military forces of the United States should be ordered to do land duty in Europe until so directed by Congress. This aroused applause from a small number of members on both the Republican and Democratic sides.

Interest in the debate waned, and by 1:30 o'clock fewer than seventy-five members were on the floor. The diplomatic and executive galleries were empty and there were many unoccupied seats in the public gallery.

Representative Igoe, Democrat, of Missouri, stated that he would vote against declaring war because he thought his people desired that he should.

"With the passage of the resolution, however," he said, "my opposition will cease. I will vote for every measure to help carry on the war."

Sensation Over Zimmermann Note.

Representative Miller of Minnesota, Republican member of the Foreign Affairs Committee, sprung a sensation by asserting that an unpublished paragraph in the "Zimmermann note" offered to establish a submarine base in a Mexican port, supply Mexico with unlimited quantities of arms and ammunition, and send German reservists in the United States to Mexico.

This unpublished portion of the Zimmermann note, as read by Mr. Miller, was as follows:

"Agreeably to the Mexican Government, submarine bases will be established at Mexican ports from which will be supplied arms, ammunition, and supplies. All reservists are ordered into Mexico. Arrange to attack all along the border."

Representative Miller further stated that he understood that three German schooners had reached the western coast of Mexico, and that Villa was surrounded by German officers who had taken charge of the drilling of his men. Reliable information, he said, also was that the Carranza army was "not much better."

Rush to Hear Kitchin Talk.

Word that the Democratic floor leader, Kitchin, would speak and vote against the resolution quickly filled the chamber. He began his unexpected onslaught on the war resolution soon after 3 o'clock. After saying that he would not criticise those who would vote for it, he stated that he thought he should vote his convictions regardless of consequences.

Mr. Kitchin reached a height of earnestness when, after a pause, he said:

"My friends, I cannot leave my children lands and riches. I cannot leave them fame But I can leave them the name of an ancestor who, mattering not the consequences to himself, never hesitated to do his duty as God gave him to see it.

"Half the civilized world is now a slaughterhouse for human beings. This nation is the last hope of peace on earth, good will toward men. I am unwilling for my country by statutory command to pull up the last anchor of peace in the world and extinguish during the long night of a world-wide war the only remaining star of hope for Christendom.

"I am unwilling by my vote today for this nation to throw away the only remaining compass to which the world can look for guidance in the paths of right and truth and justice and humanity, and leave only force and blood to chart hereafter the path of mankind.

"By the passage of this resolution we enter the war, and the universe will become one vast drama of horrors and blood, one boundless stage upon which will play all the evil spirits of earth and hell. All the demons of inhumanity will be let loose for a rampage throughout the world. Whatever be the future, whatever be the rewards or penalties of this nation's step, I shall always believe that we could and ought to have kept out of this war."

Mr. Kitchin said he had reached a decision to vote against the war resolution after prayer for guidance and with a full realization of the possible consequences to himself.

"Profoundly impressed with the gravity of the situation," he went on, "appreciating to the fullest the penalties which war will impose, my conscience and judgment, after mature thought and fervent prayer for rightful guidance, have pointed out clearly the path of my duty, and I have made up my mind to walk in it, if I go barefooted and alone. I have come to the undoubting conclusion that I should vote against this resolution.

"If I had a single doubt, I would dissolve it in favor of the view of the Administration and of a large majority of my colleagues, who have so recently honored me with their confidence. I know that I shall never criticise any member for advocating this resolution. I concede, I know, that he casts his vote in accordance with sincere conviction. I know, too, that for my vote I shall not only be criticised but denounced from one end of the country to the other. The whole yelping pack of the defamers and revilers in the nation will, at once, be sicked upon my heels."

Cites Course Toward Britain.

Mr. Kitchin said that the United States did well to keep from war with Great Britain, although the latter nation had repeatedly violated American rights by closing to us the ports of neutrals, by unlawfully seizing ships and cargoes, by rifling mails, and making the North Sea a military area. The United States had protested, he said, and no American lives were lost because American ships remained away from the mine-strewn regions included in the British blockade area.

"We knew that these acts of Great Britain, although in plain violation of international law, were not aimed at us, but were inspired by military necessity," said Mr. Kitchin. "Rather than plunge this nation into war we were willing to forego our rights. I approved that course then and I approve it now.

"Germany declared a war zone sufficiently large to cover the ports of her enemy. She infested it with submarines and warned the neutral world to stay out. Though in plain violation of our rights and international law, we know that these acts are not aimed directly at us, but are intended to injure and cripple enemies with which she is engaged in a death struggle.

"We refuse to yield. We refuse to forego our rights for the time. We insist on going in. In my judgment we should keep out of the war with Germany as we kept out of the war with Great Britain by keeping our ships and our citizens out of the war zone of Germany as we did out of the war zone of Great Britain, and we would sacrifice no more honor and no more rights in the one case than the other.

"In this case no invasion is threatened. No foot of our territory is in danger. No vital right is contested. The acts of Germany are not directed directly at us. We are asked to make common cause with Great Britain and France, to support a cause, right or wrong. Every feeling of humanity combines to keep us out of war.

"When Congress has passed such a resolution as is now pending then and then only will it be the duty of the nation to make the voice of the Government its voice. Until then each person should have the inherent right to voice and vote his conviction."

Mr. Kitchin referred to the invasion of American rights in Mexico. The United States, he said, had not gone to war with Mexico, although the American flag was insulted, American lives were lost, and American property was ruthlessly destroyed.

Why Not Forego Violation of Rights?

"Why can we not, why should we not," he asked, "forego the violation of our rights by Germany and do as we did with Mexico and Great Britain and thus save the universe from being wrapped in the flames of war? I have hoped and prayed that God would forbid our country going into war with another for doing that which, perhaps, under the same circumstances, we ourselves would do."

Mr. Kitchin pictured a situation where the United States might be at war with Germany and Japan with the ports of this country closed and its vessels swept from the sea and the nation facing starvation. Would it be unreasonable to assume, he asked, that this nation would use desperate measures, probably in violation of international law?

Mr. Kitchin concluded with a pledge to merge his personal judgment into the will of the majority once Congress had declared war. It would be the duty then of all Americans, he said, to accept the mandate of the country when written into law.

"The voice of law will command a patriotic duty, will demand loyal and earnest and active submission and obedience," he concluded. "Until then each should have and does have the inherent right, and it is his bounden duty to himself and to the truth, to vote his convictions."

Following Mr. Kitchin, Representative Rogers of Massachusetts recited a long list of cases in which Germany had invaded the rights of the United States. The list compiled by the State Department showed that in two years and two months 226 American lives had been lost as a result of illegal attacks on vessels by German submarines.

While Representative Borland of Missouri was speaking Representative Flood interrupted to announce to the House the sinking of the unarmed American steamship Missourian without warning, and probably with the loss of American lives.

Representative London, Socialist, of New York, vigorously opposed the resolution. He said that in contrast with the fact that President McKinley in the war with Spain called only for volunteers, President Wilson's plan for conscription showed that the President realized the people were against the war. He said that war was indefensible.

Representative Sherwood of Ohio said that he was opposed to the resolution in a form which permitted sending troops abroad.

Non-Partisan Plea by Cannon.

Former Speaker Cannon, supporting the resolution, said that this was no time for partisan discussion; that the United States was not ready for war now, but must prepare at once.

Remarking that he had heard it suggested that the President should be impeached for arming American ships, Mr. Cannon said: "We would not make much headway there." He defended the loyalty of American citizens of German birth, and, amid enthusiastic applause, announced his intention of voting for war.

Representative Dill of Washington said that he had spent sleepless nights considering the war question, and stated that finally he had decided to vote against the resolution because he believed it the highest duty of the United States to keep out of the European conflict. Once in, he added, the Government would receive his entire support.

Intimates Kitchin Should Resign.

Representative Heflin, Democrat, of Alabama, told the House that he had been humiliated by the stand taken by Mr. Kitchin.

"If I had made it," he said, "I would have first resigned as majority leader, and after making it I would resign my seat in the House."

This statement was hissed from the floor, most of the hisses apparently coming from the Republican side.

"You may hiss, you who represent the Kaiser and not the President of the United States!" shouted Mr. Heflin.

The galleries and a few members applauded this statement. Mr. Fitzgerald, who was presiding, gave warning that the galleries would be cleared if there was a recurrence of the demonstration.

Mr. Heflin's arraignment of the pacifist group brought approving handclaps.

"You who have large populations of German constituents," he said, "think you are playing to them by opposing this resolution. As a matter of fact you reflect on their honesty and patriotism. I know of Germans who have offered to serve the American flag. I wish they had been here to hear Mr. Kitchin and Mr. Britten.

"The Kaiser today with the greatest war equipment in the world is stalking around with the though. He is to rule the world. He has fallen upon us and destroyed our commerce. He waves us from the sea and murders our citizens.

"God of our Fathers, how long will there be divided loyalty in this country, how long? We paid a fearful price to remain at peace with Germany. There is no peace when war is made upon us. We must fight, gentlemen, or surrender as a nation—surrender our honor, our independence, and tear down our flag."

Representative Sloan, Republican, of Nebraska, asserted that the sober second thought of the American people, including Congress, was being felt, and that ten days' delay of the vote would defeat the resolution in its present shape.

Representative Lenroot, Republican, of Wisconsin, said that he would support the resolution because not to do so would mean "that we will submit to Germany warring on us without using force to prevent it." He denied that England, in planting mines in the North Sea and creating a military zone there, had violated international law.

Toward 7 o'clock Chairman Flood, who was in charge of the resolution, sought an agreement to have the Committee of the Whole rise at 8 o'clock and report the resolution in the House, with a view to early action.

There was immediate opposition. Speaker Clark said that everybody ought to have a right to speak, and the House should stay in session until early in the morning or all night if necessary. Mr. Flood then withdrew his request and speechmaking was resumed.

Representative Burnett of Alabama, in the course of a speech against the resolution, challenged Representative Heflin to circulate a petition in the House to secure support for his declaration that the majority leader (Kitchin) should resign. He also asked his colleague to prove himself consistent by enlisting as a private in the army.

Interchanges between the two Alabamans were made to the accompaniment of shouts of applause from both sides of the chamber and the galleries.

Mr. Heflin, unable to obtain recognition, insisted on replying, shouting that he would resign and fight for his country.

Mr. Burnett continued his heckling, despite the roars of the members and the pounding of the gavel by Representative Fitzgerald, until the Sergeant at Arms produced the mace, symbol of the authority of the House, and compelled him to take his seat.

Only One Course, Says Mann.

Just before 9 o'clock Representative Mann, the Republican leader, took the floor to support the resolution.

"I wish," he said, "to pay a tribute to the courage of those members of the House who, in the exercise of the responsibility cast upon them, have expressed their opposition to this resolution. I want particularly to pay my tribute to the rare courage of the gentleman from North Carolina, (Kitchin.)

"I do not agree with them, but this is a time when members of this body, aye all citizens of the country, have the right to express their opposition to the war, for tomorrow, when the war is declared, it will become the duty of all citizens to hold up the honor and policy of the Republic.

"For two and one-half years I have done all in my power by voice and vote to keep this country out of the European war. I have believed that it was to the advantage not only of our people and our country, but to the advantage of civilization and humanity that we should keep out of the war at this time. But after all it was not because I was afraid of war. The American people may prefer peace, but they are not guilty of cowardice; it is not because we are afraid to fight.

"Now the situation is changed. The President of the United States, who has the responsibility of dealing with foreign countries and who is the spokesman of the people with the nations of the world, has asked us to declare war, and we have a resolution to that effect before us on which we must vote. We must vote to decide on war or vote down the resolution. What position would we be in if we should vote down the recommendation of the President? And what would be the effect on the rest of the world and on our own self-respect?

"The only thing left for us to do is to stand by the President, elected by the people. We cannot say to the world that our only goal is gold, that our only desire is wealth. We must, when the question is presented to us, declare that we will maintain the rights of Americans abroad as well as at home.

"There is a difference between a deliberate affront and an incidental injury. We have had incidental injuries from both England and Germany. A deliberate affront long ago would have brought a declaration of war. Now we are required to say that a deliberate affront has been made by Germany and there is nothing left for us to do but follow the recommendation of our Chief Executive and engage in war and maintain our rights and our civilization."

At 9 o'clock general debate and discussion under the five-minute rule began.

Chairman Flood's suggestion that all debate close at 11:45 o'clock brought a storm of "noes." Some members expressed a desire to reach a vote before midnight because of Good Friday.

War for Human Rights, Gardner Says.

Representative Gardner, Republican, of Massachusetts, said that the United States was not going to war for 200 murdered Americans, but for the rights of man.

"The South and North," said he, "did not settle their differences like money changers on the corner of the street. They settled it as men always settle their differences. Now the democracies of the world are struggling to their feet, and the knell of autocracy has been sounded. Too long have we suffered other nations to bear our burden in this war for liberty. Now we must descend from the seat of ease into the blood and dust."

Representative Decker of Missouri said that he believed in national honor, but did not think "we would sacrifice it if we did not go to war."

Pointing to the large oil paintings of Washington and Lafayette that were hanging near the Speaker's rostrum, Representative Fitzgerald, of the Appropriations Committee, invoked the spirit of those heroes in announcing his support of the war resolution and pledging every resource at the hands of Congress to prosecute the conflict to a successful termination.

"Practically all of the belligerent nations have violated American rights," said Mr. Fitzgerald. "But the one nation that has been contemptuous of us above all others, the one nation that has shown no regard for American rights is that nation which is tonight brought before the bar of our public opinion and upon which we pass judgment.

"No one can charge that Woodrow Wilson has hurried us into this war. I regret that war must come. But if we are to retain our self-respect, if we are to encourage those patriotic virtues without which we cannot exist, if we are not to be the laughing stock of the world, if we are not to be regarded as a nation of degenerates and cowards, there is nothing else to do but acknowledge that Germany has made war upon us and accept it.

"Although it will not be particularly pleasing to me, I believe it is the duty of the United States to co-operate with every other nation now engaged in making warfare against this enemy, to this end, that we may make common warfare against the common enemy of civilization."

HUGE BUDGET FOR WAR

$3,401,000,000 Needed for the Army and Navy at Once.

Special to The New York Times.

WASHINGTON, April 5.—Three billion four hundred and one million dollars is needed immediately to place the United States on a proper war footing and to meet the first expenses of actual operations in the war with the German Government. This fact was disclosed when William G. McAdoo, as Secretary of the Treasury, today sent to the Capitol the first of the estimates from the various executive departments of the Government based on "military necessity." These estimates call for the appropriation of $3,401,865,684.87, of which the sum of $3,400,932,484.87 is for the army and navy alone, while the rest is for use by other departments as collateral war expenditures.

This total of $3,400,932,484 will enable the Government to raise, organize, equip and officer an army of 1,000,000 men during the next year, but will not pay for the employment of that force beyond June 30, 1918; it will enable the navy to raise its enlisted strength of 150,000 men and the Marine Corps to increase its enlisted personnel to 30,000 men, in addition to certain active operations in the war.

The total of $3,400,932,484 is also in addition to the sum of $517,273,802 already provided for the navy's use during the next fiscal year by the Naval act of March 4, 1917, and the sum of $240,000,000 carried by the Army Appropriation bill which passed the House yesterday under a suspension of the rules.

"All the News That's Fit to Print."

The New York Times.

THE WEATHER
Fair today and tomorrow, rising temperature; wind northwest.

VOL. LXVI...NO. 21,626.
NEW YORK, TUESDAY, APRIL 10, 1917.—TWENTY-TWO PAGES.
ONE CENT In New York City. | TWO CENTS New England and Middle States | THREE CENTS Elsewhere

BRITISH BEGIN THE GREAT DRIVE, TAKE 6,000 PRISONERS; PLANS TO DISCUSS WITH ALLIES OUR SHARE IN THE CONFLICT; CONSCRIPTION FEATURE OF ARMY BILL MEETS OPPOSITION

HAIG STRIKES NEAR ARRAS

English and Canadians Break Through Lines on 12-Mile Front.

SEIZE FAMOUS VIMY RIDGE

Villages and Fortified Points Captured to Depth of Two to Three Miles.

"TANKS" LEAD THE ADVANCE

British Also Push Forward Toward Cambrai and North of St. Quentin.

LONDON, April 9.—The British troops launched a terrific offensive today on a twelve-mile front north and south of Arras, penetrating the German positions to a depth of from two to three miles. Many important fortified points were captured, including the famous Vimy Ridge.

Nearly 6,000 prisoners, mostly Bavarians, Württembergers, and Hamburgers, have been taken so far, and they continue to pour into the receiving stations. Large numbers of guns, trench mortars, and other war material have been captured. The advance continues, the British having blasted their way clear through the German front and rearward positions.

The line of advance extends from Givenchy en Gohelle, southwest of Lens, to the village of Henin, on the Cojeul River, southeast of Arras. The attack began at 5:30 this morning, after a terrible night of artillery fire. For the last week the British guns have been bombarding the German lines in this sector without cessation, but last night's bombardment outdid even the terrible bombardments that preceded the Somme offensive last year.

The honor of capturing Vimy Ridge, where the French lost thousands of men last year in an attempt to hold this dominating height, fell to the Canadians. This ridge protects the French coal fields lying to the eastward. Once before the British gained the crest of this ridge, but, under a tremendous concentration of German guns, they were compelled to give it up. All Winter long Canadians have held a footing on the ridge, with the German lines looking down on them. All the fighting today was against dominating positions on high ground, some of which had been held by the Germans for two years and were lavishly hemmed with wide belts of some of the toughest and longest-pronged barbed wire that has been seen in the war.

Along the greater part of the front, says Reuter's correspondent at the front, the advance of the infantry was strenuously opposed. Near Arras the Germans offered determined resistance and a large pocket of the Germans was reported to be still holding out at midday, although entirely surrounded. The famous redoubt named "The Harp," only a little less formidable than the noted "Labyrinth," was captured with virtually the whole battalion defending it. Several "tanks" were seen climbing Telegraph Hill, which commands "The Harp," and probably had much to do with the surrender of this position. Here three German battalion commanders were captured.

Along the railway running through to the valley of the Scarpe the British made good progress, while upon the Lens branch of the line they captured Maison Blanche Wood.

Battle Begins at Daybreak.

The early British report, which is timed 11:25 A. M., is as follows:

We attacked at 5:30 o'clock this morning on a wide front from south of Arras to south of Lens. Our troops have everywhere penetrated the enemy's lines and are making satisfactory progress at all points.

In the direction of Cambrai we stormed the villages of Hermies and Boursies and have penetrated into Havrincourt Wood.

"In the direction of St. Quentin we captured Fresnoy le Petit and advanced our line southeast of Le Verguier.

No estimate of the prisoners taken can yet be given, but considerable numbers are reported captured.

The text of the statement issued this evening reads:

The operations continue to be carried on successfully in accordance with the plan. Our troops have everywhere stormed the enemy defenses from Henin-sur-Cojeul to the southern outskirts of Givenchy-en-Gohelle to a depth of from two to three miles, and our advance continues.

The enemy's forward defenses on this front, including Vimy Ridge, which was carried by the Canadian troops, were captured early in the morning. These defenses comprise a network of trenches and fortified localities—Neuville, Vitasse, Telegraph Hill, Tilloy Lez Mofflaines, Observation Ridge, St. Laurent-Blangy, Les Tilleuls, and La Folie Farm.

Subsequently our troops moved forward and captured the enemy's rearward defenses, including, in addition to other powerful trench systems, the fortified localities of Feuchy, Chapelle de Feuchy, Hyserbad Redoubt, Athies, and Thelus.

Up to 2 P. M. 5,816 prisoners, including 119 officers, passed through the stations, and many more remain to be counted. Of these a large number belong to the Bavarian divisions, who have suffered heavy casualties in today's fighting. The captured war material includes guns and a number of trench mortars and machine guns, which have not yet been counted.

In the direction of Cambrai further progress has been made in the neighborhood of Havrincourt Wood. We have captured the village of Demicourt. In the direction of St. Quentin we captured the villages of Pontru and Le Verguier.

The aerial activity of the past few days has continued with great energy. Several successful bombing raids were carried out by us, our machines co-operating with our artillery with excellent results. Two hostile machines were destroyed and fifteen others were driven down and probably crashed. Two German kite balloons were brought down in flames. Ten of our airplanes are missing.

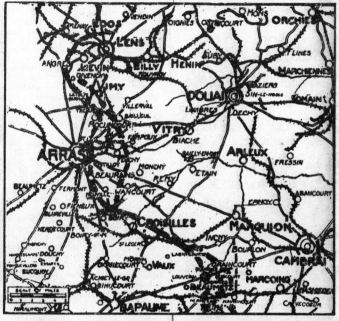

Scene of the New British Offensive.

The British, opening a tremendous offensive against the strong positions protecting the northern point of the Hindenburg line, broke through on a front of twelve miles, from Givenchy to Henin, advancing to a depth of from two to three miles. The extent of the advance is shown above.

British Destroying U-Boats at Rate of One a Day

The British have been destroying U-boats at the average rate of one a day since Feb. 1, and latterly at an even higher rate, according to information brought to New York yesterday by persons returning from Europe, who said they had the authority of naval officers and officials high in the Admiralty for the figures. In the month following the declaration of unrestricted submarine warfare British ships sank thirty-two submarines. Since then, it is said, the average number destroyed a week has been between seven and fifteen, with the number running as high as twenty-three in the week.

British naval officers assert their methods in fighting the submarine are being improved constantly. The small motor boat, known as the "submarine chaser," following in the wake of destroyers dragging cables or chains between them, has sunk most of the U-boats with a new explosive bomb, effective within a circumference of 200 yards. Airplanes are used also, while the practice of equipping merchant ships with guns forward, as well as aft, has caused the destruction of several U-boats.

British officers say the Germans profess to be turning out a submarine a day, but they do not see how submarines, manned by competent crews, can be sent to sea at this rate.

An Associated Press correspondent at the front says:

"After a beautiful and warm Easter Sunday the weather changed last night, and today's attack was carried out in a pelting rain driven before a gale in which was the sting of January cold. The airplanes, which have accomplished wonderful work since Thursday's "clearing the air" of German machines, were robbed of the opportunity to participate in the beginning of the offensive. Several intrepid British airmen ascended, but on account of the rain and low-lying clouds they could do little or nothing, and after being tossed about severely they descended.

"Today's attack also hit the northern hinge of the recent German retreat from Arras to the Aisne. The Germans evidently had expected a renewal of the offensive in the valley of the Somme, for in making the retreat in that sector they announced that they had completely disarranged the British offensive plans. Today's blow was Britain's answer."

The British also gained considerable ground at other points on the line. On the road to Cambrai they captured by storm the Boursies, Demicourt, and Hermies. Boursies is seven and a half miles southwest of Cambrai. The British also made progress in the Havrincourt Wood, south of the Bapaume-Cambrai Railway.

Farther to the south, in the neighborhood of St. Quentin, General Haig's troops captured the villages of Fresnoy, Pontru, and Le Vergnier, thus pushing forward their lines to within two miles of the St. Quentin Canal.

BERLIN FEARS RUPTURE WITH SOUTH AMERICA

Zimmermann Has Long Conference with Envoys from Brazil, Argentina and Chile.

LONDON, April 9.—A dispatch to the Exchange Telegraph Company from The Hague says that Dr. Zimmermann, the German Foreign Secretary, conferred for an hour on Sunday with the Ministers of Brazil, Argentina, and Chile. The dispatch says that it is thought in Berlin that the conference was connected with a possible rupture of relations between Germany and the three South American republics.

CARACAS, Venezuela, April 9.—The President-elect of the republic, Juan Vicente Gomez, has addressed a circular to the Governors of the States urging that steps be taken to assure maximum crops in order to avoid a scarcity of food supplies, "because," the circular points out, "we do not know the extent to which foreign disturbances will affect this country."

SANTIAGO, Chile, April 9. — Chile will maintain an attitude of neutrality in the war so long as she is not made the object of a direct attack, according to assurance given by Government officials.

CONGRESS AGAIN SHOWS A LEANING TO VOLUNTEERS

Anxious to Give Wilson the Forces He Asks, but Many Are Against Any Draft.

HOUSE COMMITTEE HOSTILE

Chairman Dent, Summoned to Conference by the President, Departs Unconvinced.

COMPROMISE TALKED OF

Some Favor Limited Test of a Volunteer Call — Senator Nelson Speaks Against Conscription.

WASHINGTON, April 9.—The Administration learned today that strong opposition existed in the House of Representatives to the conscription feature of the Army bill. President Wilson called to the White House Representative Dent, Chairman of the Committee on Military Affairs, and an hour's conference developed a sharp difference in views.

The President made it clear to Chairman Dent that he believe the safety of the nation rested on the action of Congress in this regard. He will make a similar exposition of the military situation tomorrow to Representative Anthony of Kansas, who has led the opposition to the draft plan among Republican members of the committee.

Secretary Baker found today among the members of the Military Committee decided opposition to the proposed Army bill. Not only is Chairman Dent opposed to the selective draft, as provided in the bill, but most of the committee are said to be against it.

That only about half a dozen of the twenty-one members of the committee were in favor of conscription was asserted today. Representative Kahn, Crago, and Tilson, Republicans, and Olney and Caldwell, Democrats, are regarded as steadfast advocates of the conscription plan. All other members may not be against the bill, but apparently they will support consription only as a last resort.

Chairman Dent is said to have told President Wilson that anti-conscription sentiment in the committee was strong, and that even if a Conscription bill was brought into the House there was doubt of its approval. He said that he and many other members of the House believed the volunteer system would suffice to raise an army. President Wilson did not share in this optimism.

Mr. Dent intimated that some form of compromise legislation might come out of the committee. He suggested that the legislation reported be for a temporary period, that is for the duration of the war, if anything approaching conscription was to be in the bill. He said today that he did not expect to report any measure for a week.

Mr. Dent added:

"There is no question on the part of any one as to giving the President all the men and money needed to carry on the war. The only controversy is as to the means of doing so."

There is some talk that because of Chairman Dent's attitude some other member of the House Committee may present the Administration bill if it is reported, as officials hope it will be, substantially in the form in which it was drawn.

Secretary Baker told the committee again today that the volunteer system would not meet the present emergency. He made little headway toward obtaining the acceptance of his views, it is said.

Secretary Baker is said to have urged the committee to reprot the bill as drawn because, for one thing, it would show Germany the earnestness of this country in entering the war. The psychological effect of a conscription measure, the Secretary feels, would be very great.

The Secretary has endeavored to impress the committee with the Government's desire not to raise a heterogenous army. It is seeking by selective draft to raise an army of active equally-aged men, who can take an aggressive part in warfare after training. The volunteer system, under which there would be a less systematic mobilization, is regarded as unfit for the present emergency.

Promotion for Guard Officers.

Mr. Baker approved a suggestion that instead of authorizing two increments of selective draft forces, 500,000 to an increment, the bill should authorize the President to call as many such increments from time to time as he deemed necessary to prosecute the war.

Mr. Baker said the only provision of the bill, which would militate against the continuance of National Guard units as such after they were drafted in the Federal service, was that the way was to be opened for National Guard officers to promotion to any part of the new armies. This provision was inserted in justice to officers of the guard and to provide an elastic and homogeneous military structure.

Mr. Baker explained also that the department had been unable to permit National Guard recruiting to proceed beyond the peace strength of the commands because of shortage of equipment, which would be supplied soon.

Chairman Dent and other members of the committee, however, think that the volunteer system is entitled to fair trial before conscription is attempted. It has been suggested that a compromise be accepted by the department—that the volunteer system be tried sixty to 120 days with the understanding that conscription be then taken up if the other plan failed. The disposition of the committee seems to be to separate the conscription issue from the broader question of universal military training and service and approach the army bill as an emergency measure.

Members of Congress are receiving letters both for and against the conscription program. Governor Ferguson telegraphed Representative Garner today that Texas opposed conscription.

Senator Nelson Wants Volunteers.

Debate on conscription occupied some time in the Senate during the discussion of the Army Appropriation bill, left over from last session. Senator Kirby, over from last session. Senator Kirby offered an amendment to authorize the President to call volunteers in lots of half a million each. The amendment is subject to a point of order, and probably will be disposed of that way without debate.

When a section authorizing advertising agencies to obtain recruits for the army whs reached, Chairman Chamberlain said that it was held necessary to get men, and instanced the fact that recruiting for the National Guard had not been successful.

Senator Nelson, a veteran of the civil war, declared in favor of a call for volunteers.

"I venture to say," said he, "that if the President calls for a volunteer army of 500,000 men, and says it is going to Europe and fight, there would be no trouble at all. What the boys dread above all is to be stationed in camp with nothing but drills and guard duty. What they want is to march and fight, and to meet the enemy."

The Senator added, however, that he did not think it was necessary to send an army to Europe at present.

Senator Stone urged an increase in the pay of privates to four or five times the present amount. He said that this might increase the Army bill, but it was worth it because the men who went to war would leave behind dependents.

During the discussion some Senators expressed wonder as to the War Department's course toward the National Guard. Senator Fall of New Mexico said that New Mexican units had been ordered mustered out on April 7, five days after the President asked Congress to declare war on the German Government.

Senators Wadsworth of New York and Smith of Georgia said they had received protests against a recent order forbidding the enlistment of additional volunteers in the National Guard. Mr. Wadsworth said that he had been informed that lack of equipment was the reason for the order, but that one New York regiment had marched out to service 1,350 men strong, leaving 300 complete equipments behind in their armory. Mr. Smith said his inquiries at the War Department had been met by the answer that the prohibition against enlistments was a temporary measure.

The rank of Brigadier General in the regular army is abolished by a provision of the bill. All general officers after its enactment would have no less rank than that of Major General. About thirty Brigadier Generals, now in active service, would become Major Generals. Committee members said the change was made in conformity with modern military practice abroad.

The new section also provides that the Chief of Staff shall have the rank of General, senior to all other army officers while in that position. This again parallels changes in navy practice, where the Chief of Operations has been made ranking Admiral of the navy. Similarly, departmental commanders would become Generals, and provision is made for the recreation of the grade of Lieutenant General, which vanished from army lists with the retirement of General Miles. With armies of the size now in contemplation this procedure becomes necessary in order that high command can be properly assigned.

MORGAN PREDICTS SUCCESS OF BONDS

Banker Tells Secretary McAdoo That Country Is Ready for the Great Investment.

Special to The New York Times.

WASHINGTON, April 9.—J. P. Morgan had a conference today with Secretary McAdoo in regard to war finance. Mr. Morgan expressed his satisfaction with the plan to issue immediately $5,000,000,000 in bonds with the understanding that $3,000,000,000 of the amount thus raised should be employed to buy the war bonds of the ally countries. He predicted that the bond issue would find the country ready for the investment and thought that the plan came at a very favorable time so far as the ability of the investment market to absorb the issue promptly was concerned.

To questions following the brief conference between the banker and the Secretary, Mr. McAdoo said that no details in regard to any feature of the plan had been discussed, and the chief matter talked of was the readiness of the money market to take up the bonds when issued, and this Mr. Morgan said was well assured.

The draft of the bill to authorize the bond issue was prepared in the Treasury Department today, and will be before the Ways and Means Committee of the House tomorrow. The committee will make it the special order of business and consider it until a vote is reached for a report.

The office of the Secretary of the Treasury is receiving an avalanche of approval and advice in regard to the loan. It is not improbable that the bonds will be issued in series and will be convertible in character. The terms mentioned today at the department were ten-twenties and twenty-forties. The interest rate for the amount first issued will be 3½ per cent.

In discussing the general features of the loan, Mr. McAdoo said tonight:

"The Administration will ask Congress for authority to issue $5,000,000,000 of Government bonds to meet the situation created by the war with Germany. The proposed bonds will be exempt from taxation and bear interest probably at 3½ per centum per annum. Two billion dollars of these bonds will be required to finance, in part, the expenditures involved in the proper organization and operation of the army and navy and the conduct of the war generally.

"Of course, a large amount of additional revenue will have to be raised by taxation, but this part of the problem is under consideration by the Ways and Means Committee of the House of Representatives. It will naturally take a reasonable time to discuss and agree upon the new items for taxation, which should not and, I am confident, will not become the subject of partisan treatment.

Three billion dollars of the proposed issue of bonds should be used to supply credit to the Governments making common cause with us against Germany to enable them to secure essential supplies in the United States and carry on the war with increased effect.

"The most serviceable thing we can do immediately for the common cause is to furnish credit to these foreign Governments who, in conjunction with us, are fighting Germany. This financial aid ought to be extended at the earliest possible moment. It will be trebly valuable and effective if extended now.

"The purpose is to purchase the obligations of the foreign Governments to which credit is given, such obligations to bear the same rate of interest and in other essentials to contain the same terms and conditions as the bonds of the United States.

"The bonds of the United States will be offered as a great popular loan, and the widest opportunity will be given to the public to subscribe, and by subscribing, to perform one of the most patriotic services that can be rendered to the country at this time.

"In view of the fact that the laws of the United States forbid the payment of commissions on sales of Government bonds, it is extremely gratifying to have received so many offers from bankers and others throughout the country of the free use of their services and facilities in making the proposed bond issue a success.

It is the purpose of the department to make use of these offers, and to seek the assistance of the Federal Reserve Banks, the national banks, the State banks and trust companies, the savings banks, insurance companies, private bankers, and investment bankers throughout the country in the public offering that will be made of the Government's bonds. Every Governmental agency, such as the Internal Revenue offices and Post Offices, will be asked to assist in this patriotic work.

"When the Congress shall have granted the necessary authority to make public offer of the bonds, I shall take the benefit of the counsel of the most experienced bankers and investors in the country as to the best means of making the offering a pronounced success.

"The wealth of the United States is so great, the investment resources of the country are so large, the strength of our banking situation is so phenomenal, and the patriotism of our people is so aroused, that I am confident that when the Government offers its bonds for public subscription the amount will be overwhelmingly subscribed.

"So many offers have been received from bankers, organizations and individuals tendering their services and facilities to the Government, free of expense, in placing the bonds at the disposal of the public, that it has been absolutely impossible for me to make personal acknowledgment and express my deep appreciation and gratification at this genuine manifestation of patriotic interest in the efforts to finance the war. So I am asking the newspapers of the country to indulge me to the extent of advising the senders of the many telegrams and letters which have poured into the department of the Government's appreciation of the loyal impulse and splendid spirit which inspired them."

APPROVES THE PLAN TO BUILD 1,000 SHIPS

Fleet of Wooden Carriers Sanctioned by President—First Vessels Ready by October

WASHINGTON, April 9.—The Shipping Board's program of building a fleet of 1,000 wooden ships of 3,000 or 3,500 tons each to meet the loss of tonnage by submarine warfare, and thus help to defeat the German undersea campaign, has been formally approved by President Wilson. The first ship will be ready within five months. The board will call upon the Treasury for from $10,000,000 to $15,000,000 within the next few days. Fifty million dollars already has been authorized by Congress for the work of the board.

Chairman Denman announced tonight that the board's plans had been virtually completed, that contracts had been let, and that barring an unforeseen hitch, by October the shipyards on the Atlantic and Pacific would be turning out the new vessels at the rate of two or three a day to be leased to private shipping concerns.

On their way to the front, these recruits seem overjoyed at the prospect of fighting for the United States.

"All the News That's Fit to Print."

The New York Times.

THE WEATHER
Fair today: Tuesday unsettled and warmer; probably rain; west winds.

VOL. LXVI...NO. 21,632. ...   NEW YORK, MONDAY, APRIL 16, 1917.—TWENTY PAGES.   ONE CENT In Greater New York.   TWO CENTS New England and Middle States.   THREE CENTS

WILSON URGES NATION TO 'SPEAK, ACT AND SERVE TOGETHER' TO FURNISH SUPPLIES, ESPECIALLY FOOD, AND WIN THE WAR; BRITISH PATROLS ENTER LENS, FIGHTING GERMAN REARGUARD

Proclamation by the President to the People

The White House, April 15, 1917

My Fellow-Countrymen:

The entrance of our own beloved country into the grim and terrible war for democracy and human rights which has shaken the world creates so many problems of national life and action which call for immediate consideration and settlement that I hope you will permit me to address to you a few words of earnest counsel and appeal with regard to them.

We are rapidly putting our navy upon an effective war footing and are about to create and equip a great army, but these are the simplest parts of the great task to which we have addressed ourselves. There is not a single selfish element, so far as I can see, in the cause we are fighting for. We are fighting for what we believe and wish to be the rights of mankind and for the future peace and security of the world. To do this great thing worthily and successfully we must devote ourselves to the service without regard to profit or material advantage and with an energy and intelligence that will rise to the level of the enterprise itself. We must realize to the full how great the task is and how many things, how many kinds and elements of capacity and service and self-sacrifice it involves.

These, then, are the things we must do, and do well, besides fighting—the things without which mere fighting would be fruitless:

We must supply abundant food for ourselves and for our armies and our seamen, not only, but also for a large part of the nations with whom we have now made common cause, in whose support and by whose sides we shall be fighting.

We must supply ships by the hundreds out of our shipyards to carry to the other side of the sea, submarines or no submarines, what will every day be needed there, and abundant materials out of our fields and our mines and our factories with which not only to clothe and equip our own forces on land and sea, but also to clothe and support our people, for whom the gallant fellows under arms can no longer work; to help clothe and equip the armies with which we are co-operating in Europe, and to keep the looms and manufactories there in raw material; coal to keep the fires going in ships at sea and in the furnaces of hundreds of factories across the sea; steel out of which to make arms and ammunition both here and there; rails for worn-out railways back of the fighting fronts; locomotives and rolling stock to take the place of those every day going to pieces; mules, horses, cattle for labor and for military service; everything with which the people of England and France and Italy and Russia have usually supplied themselves, but cannot now afford the men, the materials, or the machinery to make.

It is evident to every thinking man that our industries, on the farms, in the shipyards, in the mines, in the factories, must be made more prolific and more efficient than ever, and that they must be more economically managed and better adapted to the particular requirements of our task than they have been; and what I want to say is that the men and the women who devote their thought and their energy to these things will be serving the country and conducting the fight for peace and freedom just as truly and just as effectively as the men on the battlefield or in the trenches.

The industrial forces of the country, men and women alike, will be a great national, a great international service army—a notable and honored host engaged in the service of the nation and the world, the efficient friends and saviors of free men everywhere. Thousands, nay, hundreds of thousands, of men otherwise liable to military service will of right and of necessity be excused from that service and assigned to the fundamental, sustaining work of the fields and factories and mines, and they will be as much part of the great patriotic forces of the nation as the men under fire.

I take the liberty, therefore, of addressing this word to the farmers of the country and to all who work on the farms: The supreme need of our own nation and of the nations' with which we are co-operating is an abundance of supplies, and especially of foodstuffs. The importance of an adequate food supply, especially for the present year, is superlative. Without abundant food, alike for the armies and the peoples now at war, the whole great enterprise upon which we have embarked will break down and fail. The world's food reserves are low. Not only during the present emergency, but for some time after peace shall have come, both our own people and a large proportion of the people of Europe must rely upon the harvests in America.

Upon the farmers of this country, therefore, in large measure rests the fate of the war and the fate of the nations. May the nation not count upon them to omit no step that will increase the production of their land or that will bring about the most effectual co-operation in the sale and distribution of their products? The time is short. It is of the most imperative importance that everything possible be done, and done immediately, to make sure of large harvests. I call upon young men and old alike and upon the ablebodied boys of the land to accept and act upon this duty—to turn in hosts to the farms and make certain that no pains and no labor is lacking in this great matter.

I particularly appeal to the farmers of the South to plant abundant foodstuffs, as well as cotton. They can show their patriotism in no better or more convincing way than by resisting the great temptation of the present price of cotton and helping, helping upon a great scale, to feed the nation and the peoples everywhere who are fighting for their liberties and for our own. The variety of their crops will be the visible measure of their comprehension of their national duty.

The Government of the United States and the Governments of the several States stand ready to co-operate. They will do everything possible to assist farmers in securing an adequate supply of seed, an adequate force of laborers when they are most needed, at harvest time, and the means of expediting shipments of fertilizers and farm machinery, as well as of the crops themselves when harvested. The course of trade shall be as unhampered as it is possible to make it, and there shall be no unwarranted manipulation of the nation's food supply by those who handle it on its way to the consumer. This is our opportunity to demonstrate the efficiency of a great democracy, and we shall not fall short of it!

This let me say to the middlemen of every sort, whether they are handling our foodstuffs or our raw materials of manufacture or the products of our mills and factories: The eyes of the country will be especially upon you. This is your opportunity for signal service, efficient and disinterested. The country expects you, as it expects all others, to forego unusual profits, to organize and expedite shipments of supplies of every kind, but especially of food, with an eye to the service you are rendering and in the spirit of those who enlist in the ranks, for their people, not for themselves. I shall confidently expect you to deserve and win the confidence of people of every sort and station.

To the men who run the railways of the country, whether they be managers or operative employes, let me say that the railways are the arteries of the nation's life and that upon them rests the immense responsibility of seeing to it that those arteries suffer no obstruction of any kind, no inefficiency or slackened power. To the merchant let me suggest the motto, " Small profits and quick service," and to the shipbuilder the thought that the life of the war depends upon him. The food and the war supplies must be carried across the seas, no matter how many ships are sent to the bottom. The places of those that go down must be supplied, and supplied at once. To the miner let me say that he stands where the farmer does: the work of the world waits on him. If he slackens or fails, armies and statesmen are helpless. He also is enlisted in the great Service Army. The manufacturer does not need to be told, I hope, that the nation looks to him to speed and perfect every process; and I want only to remind his employes that their service is absolutely indispensable and is counted on by every man who loves the country and its liberties.

Let me suggest, also, that every one who creates or cultivates a garden helps, and helps greatly, to solve the problem of the feeding of the nations; and that every housewife who practices strict economy puts herself in the ranks of those who serve the nation. This is the time for America to correct her unpardonable fault of wastefulness and extravagance. Let every man and every woman assume the duty of careful, provident use and expenditure as a public duty, as a dictate of patriotism which no one can now expect ever to be excused or forgiven for ignoring.

In the hope that this statement of the needs of the nation and of the world in this hour of supreme crisis may stimulate those to whom it comes and remind all who need reminder of the solemn duties of a time such as the world has never seen before, I beg that all editors and publishers everywhere will give as prominent publication and as wide circulation as possible to this appeal. I venture to suggest, also, to all advertising agencies that they would perhaps render a very substantial and timely service to the country if they would give it widespread repetition. And I hope that clergymen will not think the theme of it an unworthy or inappropriate subject of comment and homily from their pulpits.

The supreme test of the nation has come. We must all speak, act, and serve together!

WOODROW WILSON.

Volunteers First, Roosevelt's Idea; Troops to France in Two Months

Believes in Universal Obligatory Military Service, But Tells Congress Leaders Such a System Will Be Long in Building —Would Enlist Men Not Liable Under Draft.

Special to The New York Times.

WASHINGTON, April 15. — Colonel Theodore Roosevelt, in a letter to Senator Chamberlain, Chairman of the Senate Military Committee, and to Representative Dent, Chairman of the House Military Committee, heartily supports the Administration Army bill, but urges that it be supplemented with legislation authorizing the raising of from 100,000 to 500,000 volunteers to be sent to the firing line in Europe at the earliest possible moment.

If legislation is enacted authorizing the formation of a volunteer force, Colonel Roosevelt will ask leave to raise for immediate service overseas "with the first expeditionary force," an infantry division of three three-regiment brigades and one divisional brigade of cavalry, together with an artillery brigade, a regiment of engineers, a motorcycle machine-gun regiment, an aero squadron, a signal corps, the supply service and other adjuncts to such a division. Colonel Roosevelt, in his letter to Chairmen Chamberlain and Dent, asserts that he could raise the division and have it ready to begin shipment to France in two or three months, his idea being to have the intensive training in gas work, bomb throwing, bayonet fighting and trench work given in France.

The letter follows:

April 12, 1917

Sir—In accordance with our conversation, I have the honor to submit to you my views in writing.

I most earnestly and heartily support the Administration bill for providing an army raised on the principle of universal obligatory military training and service. I cannot too strongly emphasize my support of the Administration in this matter and my appreciation of the need of introducing this principle as a permanent feature of our national policy. It is the really democratic principle, the only principle fit for a free republic, in which citizenship should be based on equality of both rights and duties, so that universal suffrage and universal service should go hand in hand.

It is along the lines proposed by the Administration that we should inaugurate our permanent military policy and it is only thus that we can carry on the war in proper manner if it should last a year, or two or three years, or over—and no one can foretell how long it will last. But, of course, a great system of this kind, a system entirely new in this country, cannot be immediately inaugurated. Many months, probably at least a year or over, must elapse before the army thus raised would be available for use in Europe in the hard, aggressive fighting campaigns which it is honorably incumbent on us to undertake now that we have entered into the war.

Meanwhile, let us use volunteer forces in connection with a portion of the regular army, in order at the earliest possible moment, within a few months, to put our flag on the firing line. We owe this to humanity. We owe it to the small nations who have suffered such dreadful wrong from Germany. Most of all we owe it to ourselves, to our national honor and self-respect. For the sake of our own souls, for the sake of the memories of the great Americans of the past, we must show that we do not intend to make this merely a dollar war. Let us pay with our bodies for our soul's desire. Let us without one hour's unnecessary delay put the American flag on the battle front in this great world war for democracy and civilization, and for the reign of justice and fair dealing among the nations of mankind.

My proposal is to use the volunteer system, not in the smallest degree as a substitute for, but as the at present necessary supplement to the obligatory system. Certain of the volunteer organizations could be used very soon; they could be put into the fighting within four months. They could, therefore, be used from the beginning as an integral proportion of the expeditionary forces sent abroad; a proportion which would be of constantly increasing size. The volunteers would, therefore, enable us to take an effective part in the war much sooner than would otherwise be the case. They would represent, moreover, pure gain from the military standpoint, for the law would provide—or department regulations could provide—that they should be composed exclusively (save where the Secretary of War might make exceptions) of men who would not be taken under the obligatory service law. There are many hundreds of thousands of men in this country who are of first-class fighting material and available for service within a short time, who would eagerly volunteer for immediate service at the front, but who would not be included among those levied under the obligatory service acts, and who could not be expected to enter the regular army or the militia. My proposal is that we utilize these men who would otherwise remain unutilized; that we utilize them to serve in the fighting line during the many months when otherwise we shall have few or no men in the fighting line; that we utilize them as volunteers because otherwise they would not be utilized at all. To make use of them as proposed in this letter would not mean the deduction of a single man from the forces raised under the obligatory law; they would represent purely the addition of a considerable body of troops available for use almost immediately.

I, therefore, propose that there be added to the proposed law, a section based on Section 12 of the Army act of March 2, 1899. This section provides for raising the 35,000 volunteers, which did most of the work in putting down the Filipino insurrection; slightly modifying the language of this act the proposed section might read as follows: "The President is hereby authorized to raise a force of not more than 100,000 (or 200,000 or later still 500,000) volunteers to be recruited as he may determine from the country at large, and to organize the same as infantry or cavalry regiments, or in other units, and to appoint officers for the same, these officers to be appointed and retained, or reduced, or discharged in accordance with the rules which he may lay down. All enlistments for the volunteer force thus organized shall be for the term of three years, or the duration of the war, unless sooner discharged." These organizations would be intended for overseas service, as was the case with those raised in 1899.

Under this act I should ask leave to raise for immediate service overseas with the first expeditionary force an infantry division of three three-regiment brigades and one divisional brigade of cavalry, together with an artillery brigade, a regiment of engineers, a motor cycle machine gun regiment, an aero squadron, a signal corps, the supply service, &c. I should request the War Department for the detail of, say, two officers for every 1,000 men. I believe that, acting under the direction and with the aid of the department, I could raise the division and have it ready to begin shipment to France in two or three months. My idea would be to have the intensive training in gas work, bomb-throwing, bayonet fighting, and trench work given in France; they would then be sent into the trenches when they were thoroughly prepared.

As for my fitness to command troops in the field, I respectfully refer you to my three immediate field commanders in the Cuban campaign. Lieut. Gen. S. B. M. Young, (retired,) Major Gen. Samuel Sumner, (retired,) and Major Gen. Leonard Wood. In the first fight of the campaign, the Guasimas fight, I commanded first, the right wing, and then the left wing of the regiment. In the second, San Juan fight, I commanded the regiment. I ended the campaign in command of the brigade. The regiment with which I first served as Lieutenant Colonel, and which I afterward commanded as Colonel, was raised, armed, equipped, drilled, mounted, dismounted, kept two weeks on a transport, and put through two victorious, aggressive fights, in which it lost a third of the officers and a fifth of the men, within sixty days, all told.

(Signed) THEODORE ROOSEVELT.

PAINT BRITISH DESPAIR IN FACE OF FAMINE

German Papers Say America's 'Bluff' of Shipping Aid Can't Save England.

Special Cable to The New York Times.

ROTTERDAM, April 15, (Dispatch to The London Daily Mail.)—German papers devote columns to descriptions of the starvation which they say is facing England through the unimagined success of the submarines. The people are officially told that only six submarines have been lost in two months.

Lloyd George's speech to the American Luncheon Club has also been made to serve the purpose of cheering up the population. With remarkable unanimity the German papers discover that the most important part of his speech is his cry for ships, naval experts like Captain Kuhlwetter being directed to prove that the American promise to provide shipping is pure bluff, because the United States does not possess skilled artificers.

Another expert devotes columns in the Rheinische Westfälische Zeitung, in which he says of Lloyd George's speech:

"He feels and knows that the water is up to England's throat, but now his task is to arouse the sinking courage of his own people and allies lest they utterly collapse when they learn the truth."

The American Ambassador's speech is made the subject of such remarks as this:

"So low is England's monarchy sunk that the representative of an allied power dares to put it on a parallel with a republic! Is this not warning for us monarchists to prevent our State from becoming a republic, with an Americanized plutocracy?"

NEW SONG FOR PATRIOTS.

"Defend Our Land" by A. S. Crockett Played at Waldorf Concert.

The Waldorf-Astoria orchestra at its Sunday concert last evening played for the first time in public a patriotic song written and composed by Albert S. Crockett and dedicated "To the Spirit of Americanism." The song is called "Defend Our Land" and was written by Mr. Crockett last Summer when the entry of the United States into the war seemed still a remote possibility. But he believes that in the present emergency the song may be of help in recruiting. The words are as follows:

I.

Whose fathers fought at Lexington
For Liberty and Right;
Whose fathers fled from every sun
That lit Oppression's might:
Awake! the peril's nigh;
Prepare to do or die!
Arouse; unite;
Prepare to fight
For Humanity and Freedom!

II.

If there be traitor on our soil
Who dare our aims oppose;
Who'd strive our nation to embroil
With friends and yield to foes;
Who 'gainst our help-hand turns;
For him the hangman yearns!
Arouse; unite;
Prepare to fight
For Humanity and Freedom!

III.

Who'd bend the knee at tyrant nod,
And yield, a cringing slave:
Him hurl without, for only God
Is Master of the Brave!
Call now on Him for aid;
And, Up, ye undismayed!
Arouse; unite;
Prepare to fight
For Humanity and Freedom!

CHORUS.

We love not the way of war,
But for Justice and Peace we stand;
And from him who both would bar
We'll defend our beloved land!
We love all men; we know not Hate;
But foes assail our Union State!
From Maine's rock coast to the Golden Gate
Raise the cry;
Shout it high;
Americans, defend our land!

"All the News That's Fit to Print."

The New York Times.

THE WEATHER
Fair today; tomorrow overcast, warmer; gentle variable winds.
For full weather report see Page 19.

VOL. LXVI...NO. 21,633. NEW YORK, TUESDAY, APRIL 17, 1917.—TWENTY PAGES.

ONE CENT In Greater New York. | TWO CENTS New England and Middle States. | THREE CENTS Elsewhere

FRENCH PIERCE 25-MILE FRONT, TAKE 10,000 PRISONERS; BRITISH IN SEVEN DAYS HAVE SMASHED 10 GERMAN DIVISIONS; GREAT GENERAL OFFENSIVE OPENS; STRIKES BEGIN IN BERLIN

FRENCH BREAK WHOLE LINE

Capture Important Positions on Front from Soissons to Rheims.

GERMANS FIGHT FIERCELY

Massed Troops and Guns Try in Vain to Hold Back the Attackers.

FRENCH SUCCESS IN ALSACE

Penetrate Enemy's Second Line at Six Places and Capture Some Prisoners.

PARIS, April 16.—General Nivelle, the French Commander in Chief, launched a great offensive today, just a week after the beginning of the battle of Arras, on a front of some twenty-five miles between Soissons and Rheims. The German first line positions along the entire front were captured after desperate fighting and at some places the French captured the second line. Over 10,000 prisoners were taken, together with a large amount of war material not yet enumerated.

The scene of the offensive is the famous line of the Aisne to which the Germans fell back after the battle of the Marne and from which the Allies had not been able to drive them. In expectation of a strong offensive in this region the enemy had massed large numbers of men and many guns on this front, the intense bombardment of the last ten days having given them ample warning that the French were preparing an attack. The Germans fought with great desperation along the whole front, realizing that a successful French advance would isolate the important city of Laon, upon which the Hindenburg line depends, but according to General Nivelle's report tonight, "everywhere the valor of our troops overcame the energetic defense of our adversary."

North of Berry-au-Bac, where the old battle line swings to the southeast toward Rheims, the French made their greatest advance, penetrating to the enemy's second line south of Juvincourt, which they now hold. Here the Germans launched several counterattacks during the day in a supreme effort to retake the positions, but they were cut to pieces under the concentrated fire of the French artillery. Further to the south the French drove the Germans across the Aisne Canal as far as the outskirts of the village of Bermericourt, while they advanced to the banks of the canal at the villages of Loivre and Courcy.

The most difficult task of the attack-

Offensive Now Under Way Along the Whole Line; Ten German Divisions Have Been Smashed by British

BRITISH HEADQUARTERS IN FRANCE, April 16, (via London.)—With the hot flames of war raging along the entire western front, British and French alike, it can be said that each detail of the offensive plans has been worked out at prolonged conferences between General Nivelle and Field Marshal Haig and the War Councils of France and England.

The part to be played by each belligerent has been definitely agreed upon, and a schedule has been arranged as for one great cohesive force. Various tasks have been precisely allotted along the wide-reaching battle lines, and the results thus far attained justify the conclusion that the supreme military test of the war is near at hand.

It was planned that the British should strike from Arras while the French guns were still roaring their preparation for infantry hostilities along a wide front further to the south. The successes gained in the first stages of the British advance have given the French great confidence in the inauguration of their own enterprises.

The whole struggle in the western theatre promises to be a titanic one. The Allies are prepared as never before both in material and personnel, and are co-operating with a smoothness which comes from a complete understanding and thorough appreciation of the work in hand. The Germans have more divisions on the western front than would have been thought possible a year ago, and however much of an "Easterner" Field Marshal von Hindenburg may have been in the past, he will have to devote his entire time and attention to western events for some weeks to come.

Already half a score of Germany's best divisions have been smashed to pieces by the British onslaught and their own unsuccessful counterattacks. The Bavarian divisions were sacrificed first, but the Prussian Guard divisions, thrown in to stem the British flood tide, have been suffering such casualties in the last few days that they will have to be relieved. The Canadians accounted for a large contingent of Grenadiers in the fighting about the Pimple, while yesterday's affair at Lagnicourt took its heaviest toll both in dead and prisoners from five German Guard regiments.

General Battle Will Involve 5,000,000 Men.

The entire line in Belgium, France, and Alsace is about 500 miles long. It has been roughly estimated that 5,000 men a mile are required on an intrenched front. This would give 2,500,000 to each side, involving 5,000,000 men in a general battle along the entire front. The Germans are supposed to have about 1,500,000 men in reserve, the British and French together a much larger number.

ers was on the front of about 18 miles from Soissons to Craonne. Here the Germans had established themselves in strong positions on a high wooded plateau, known as the plateau of Craonne, covered with numerous quarries and wooded districts easy of defense and almost impossible of capture by frontal attack. But here again the French drove forward, capturing the front line positions on the entire front.

French troops also penetrated German positions in Lorraine and Alsace after violent artillery preparation. On the Alsatian plain they reached the enemy's second line at six points, inflicting serious losses and bringing back prisoners and material.

The text of the statement issued this evening reads:

Between St. Quentin and the Oise artillery fighting continued throughout the day. South of the Oise we made new progress on the plateau east of the line of Barisis-Quincy Basse.

Between Soissons and Rheims, after artillery preparation which lasted several days, we attacked this morning the German lines along an extent of about forty kilometers, (twenty-five miles.) A desperate battle was fought along the whole front, where the enemy had grouped very important forces and numerous artillery. Everywhere the valor of our troops overcame the energetic defense of our adversary.

Between Soissons and Craonne the whole German first position fell into our power. East of Craonne our

troops occupied the enemy's second position south of Juvincourt. Further to the south we carried our line as far as the outskirts of Bermericourt and up to the Aisne Canal at Loivre and Courcy.

Violent counterattacks launched several times north of Ville-au-Bois were broken down by our fire with considerable losses to the enemy.

The number of prisoners made by us up to the present exceeds 10,000. We likewise captured important material which has not yet been inventoried.

In Champagne artillery fighting continued actively during the day on the various sectors. The cannonade was intermittent on the rest of the front. The afternoon statement follows:

Between St. Quentin and the Oise we continued to direct a destructive fire at the defenses of the Germans, who replied vigorously in the region of St. Quentin. South of the Oise we made further progress eastward on the plateau between Barisis and Quincy-Basse and occupied several points of support of the enemy. Our patrols are in contact with the German positions on the western edge of the upper forest of Coucy.

The artillery fighting became extremely violent during the night on the front between Soissons and Rheims. In Champagne we easily repulsed two surprise attacks. East of Auberive French patrols brought back prisoners. In Lorraine and in Alsace French detachments, after violent artillery preparation, penetrated the enemy lines at several points. In the forest of Parroy we found numerous German dead in the trenches blown up by our fire. In the Alsatian plain French detachments at six points reached the second German line and inflicted serious losses on the enemy. Prisoners and material were brought back.

ENEMY TRAPPED IN HIS OWN WIRE

Panicstricken Troops at Lagnicourt Slaughtered by the British Guns.

GERMANS TRY TO HOLD LENS

Clinging to Scattered Positions Around City in Face of Heavy Fire.

By PHILIP GIBBS.
Special Cable to THE NEW YORK TIMES.
Copyright, 1917, by The New York Times Company.

WAR CORRESPONDENTS' HEADQUARTERS, April 16.—The enemy is making a determined effort at Lens until his defenses have been strengthened in the Hindenburg switch line along this northern sector from Drocourt to Queant, upon which the British are forcing him to retreat. He has guns behind Hill 70, that knoll of earth tragic in British history during the battle of Loos, when the London and Scottish territorials, followed by the Guards, fought and died in great numbers to take and hold it. It has long been in the enemy's hands, and he is using it now as a pivot upon which he is swinging back in his retreat by Lens.

Last night he made an attack in this neighborhood, and this morning, as I saw from Notre Dame de Lorette, looking down on Loos battlefields and all the town and suburb of Lens, he was flinging over a large number of shells in order to barrage the lines of approach. It was heavy stuff of eight-inch guns and raised great pillars of earth and smoke. The scene upon which I looked was wild and grim. A gale was blowing, and black rain clouds scudded across the sky, blowing the smoke of the shell bursts in long ribbons across the city of mines. The wind howled and the guns roared, and looked very ugly today around that doomed city, which will be in British possession, however long the enemy delays the entry, and that will not be long, I take it. The British troops are now well beyond Lievin and close against the outer defenses of Lens itself on the western side. The hill of Riaumont on the south, where I saw the men attacking last Saturday, is now firmly held by the British and the line is well beyond the northern side of it in the outskirts of Lens and approaching the church.

The enemy in his flight through Lievin left a vast quantity of stores, not only ammunition and timber and other material of war, but officers' private property and kits, including valuable telescopes and field glasses, revolvers, telephones and signal apparatus and a number of very fine top boots, which will be very useful to the British during this wet weather and in this present quagmire of all the fields, where, by the way, I got bogged today so that my message must be short for lack of time. In the regimental headquarters of the Tenth Infantry, the officers seem to have left in a mad rage, unable to carry their furniture away. They smashed it to bits and used the axe to destroy their piano and their beds. Rage will not save them from disaster nor avert the terrors of war which are close about them.

The Lagnicourt Slaughter.

What happened at Lagnicourt yesterday is one of the bloodiest episodes in all this long tale of slaughter. At 4:30, before daybreak, the enemy made a very heavy attack upon the British

The New York Times.

"All the News That's Fit to Print."		THE WEATHER Fair, cool today and Sunday; moderate north winds.

VOL. LXVI...NO. 21.658.   NEW YORK, SATURDAY, MAY 12, 1917.—TWENTY PAGES.

BALFOUR AND VIVIANI WELCOME US AS ALLY IN THE WAR FOR CIVILIZTAION; STIR DINERS TO WILDEST ENTHUSIASM

CITY LEADERS THE HOSTS

Call to Do Our Utmost in the War Loudly Cheered.

CRIES OF "LET TEDDY GO!"

Balfour Says the Very Heart of Civilization Is Trembling in the Balance.

VIVIANI ROUSES THE THRONG

Asserts German Kultur Is All Very Well Until Crossed; Then It Is Like a Beast.

A gathering distinguished as even New York has rarely seen before, more than 1,000 of the leaders of the city's public life, business, art, finance, science, and education, gathered at the Waldorf-Astoria last night at the dinner given by the Mayor's Committee to the British and French commissions. At the high table sat with the Mayor and the leading members of the visiting missions two ex-Presidents of the United States, the Governor of New York, the junior United States Senator, and a group of the most prominent men of the city. On the floor were two former Presidential candidates, Charles E. Hughes and Alton B. Parker, great financiers and business men, and the officers and civilians lower in rank of the British and French commissions.

The diners did more than cheer the Mayor's official welcome and the responses of the visitors; they threw their whole enthusiasm into repeated cheers whenever the demand was voiced for immediate and active prosecution of the war, for the sending of American troops as quickly as possible to assist those of Great Britain and France.

Great Applause for Colonel.

When the guests of honor filed in two by two to take their places at the high table the order of march became somewhat disturbed, and Colonel Roosevelt came in almost at the tail of the procession. When the crowd saw him the cheers for Joffre, Viviani, and Balfour, which had rung out as the leaders of the visiting commissions made their way to their seats, rang out again for the Colonel. The crowd had more ex-

cuse for cheering when the Colonel shook hands with Marshal Joffre, who sat beside him; and it was with difficulty that it was finally stilled.

Every time the Colonel moved after that somebody cheered him. While the dinner was going on he slipped out for a few minutes to talk to the members of the University of California Ambulance Unit, sailing for France, who were dining in another room in the hotel; and there were cheers from a few devotees as he left his seat and as he returned to it.

When the Mayor in enumerating the list of distinguished guests for the visitors mentioned "two ex-Presidents of the United States," there were clamorous cries of "Teddy! Teddy!" from all parts of the hall. The cries continued long and vigorously and toward the end were mingled with cheers for Taft.

And again the diners had a chance to exercise their lungs for their favorite when Mr. Choate, calling for immediate and vigorous aid to the Allies, cried: "Let Teddy go!"

During most of the dinner the Colonel and Marshal Joffre were engaged in a voluble conversation in French, and those on the floor who speculated as to the subject did not have to guess many times to find an answer that satisfied them.

Cheers for General Wood, Too.

Of other Americans the one who received most applause was Major Gen. Leonard Wood, who, when mentioned by Mayor Mitchel in his Who's Who of the high table, was cheered enthusiastically by all the diners. General J. Franklin Bell, U. S. A., who succeeded General Wood in command of the Department of the East, was absent.

The dinner was arranged by a committee headed by Fire Commissioner Robert Adamson, which had the painful

duty of turning down thousands of requests for seats from persons who applied too late. It was held in the grand ballroom, where in 1902 another dinner, which at the time was believed by many people to be the beginning of a new era in American affairs, was given for Prince Henry of Prussia. But the dinner on that occasion was far more sumptuous. Last night, because the committee wanted to give an example of the economies rendered desirable by war conditions, there was a simple menu of five courses, most of them characteristically American—the simplest ever served at a great public function in the history of the Waldorf.

The diners began with cherrystone clams. Then came pepper pot soup, Delaware planked shad, cucumber salad, squab chicken roasted with sweet potatoes, strawberry ice cream and petits fours, and coffee. Champagne and liqueurs were the only drinks served. The meal, designed by Oscar Tschirky, manager of the hotel, was prepared by a French chef, René Anjard, who slipped upstairs after the dinner was over to listen to the address of M. Viviani and get a good look at Marshal Joffre.

Artists Arranged Decorations.

Great American artists collaborated in the preparations. The cover of the menu was designed by Edwin H. Blashfield, who also designed the France-Britannia medallion widely used in the decorations for the reception of the two commissions. The decorations of the dining room, designed by Cass Gilbert and executed by Wadley & Smythe and the C. H. Coster Company, were based on a background of horizon blue, the color of the French field service uniform, hung across the entire wall behind the high table.

Thirteen wreaths and festoons tied with gold ribbons hung from the top of this screen, and in the middle two American flags, with the ensigns of the other allies grouped about them, surmounted the Blashfield medallion, beneath which was a gilt panel emblazoned with the President's famous phrase, "To make the world safe for democracy." A hedge

of laurel rose just behind the guests of honor for the whole length of the wall, with cedar trees rising at either end, and just in front on tall staffs two American flags waved in the breezes from electric fans. The Blashfield medallion, laurel wreaths and American flags were the decorations of the boxes.

One of the features of this remarkable dinner was that it began approximately on time. The guests gathered in the Astor gallery and trooped in under the watchful eye of secret service men only a few minutes after 8, while the Waldorf orchestra under Joseph Knecht played "Columbia, the Gem of the Ocean." Other selections during the evening were "Marche Lorraine," "The British Grenadier," "Sambre et Meuse," "Tipperary," old French songs, "Pinafore," "The American Patrol," with "Dixie," "Hands Across the Sea," and "Hail Columbia"

Those at the Speakers' Table.

Meanwhile the French and British Commissions had left their quarters in the residences of Henry C. Frick and Vincent Astor on upper Fifth Avenue and driven down the bright-lit boulevard between cheering crowds to the Thirty-third Street entrance of the Waldorf. Here, with throngs of eager men and women in evening dress who crowded forward to get a look at the notables held back by lines of policemen and secret service men, they hurried upstairs and marched into the dining room at 8:15 o'clock.

During the dinner Mayor Mitchel presented to Mr. Balfour and M. Viviani gold copies of the medal which has been worn by members of his committee during the visit.

Secret Service men had requested that none of the diners should go up to the high table to talk to the distinguished guests, but this request was ignored. Before the dinner was half over many men had gone up to chat with one or another of the diners. Colonel Roosevelt had many calls from admirers, and Myron T. Herrick, former Ambassador to France, spoke to a number of members of the French Commission with whom he was personally acquainted.

Many Women in Boxes.

The boxes around the hall, seating somewhat less than 400, were filled with women who watched the dinner with great interest and joined in the cheers during the speeches. Mrs. John Purroy Mitchel had the foremost box in the side of the room opposite the guests' table, with Mme. Jusserand and Lady Spring-Rice, wives of the French and British Ambassadors, as her guests.

Others who had boxes were Clive Bayley, the British Consul General; Gaston Liebert, the French Consul General; Mrs. Joseph H. Choate and Miss Choate, with whom sat Mrs. Charles E. Hughes; Mrs. Charles S. Whitman, Mrs. Robert Adamson, Mrs. Arthur Woods and her mother, Mrs. William Pierson Hamilton; Mrs. Cornelius Vanderbilt, Mrs. Edmund Baylies, Mrs. C. R. Alexander, Mrs. Leonard Wood and Mrs. Daniel Guggenheim.

It was at 9:52 that the Mayor rose and called the diners to order. He had a hard time in getting them to stop cheering for him, and when the long roar of applause that greeted his first attempt finally died down somebody called for "Three cheers for our fighting Mayor!" which were given with great enthusiasm.

Then the Mayor asked the audience to drink to the health of the President of the United States. After the toast a verse of "The Star-Spangled Banner" was sung, and then three cheers were given for the President.

There followed a toast to the King of England, a verse of "God Save the King," and three cheers for George V. Then a toast to the President of the French Republic, which was accompanied by a prolonged roar of cheering that was finally quieted to give the audience a chance to sing a verse of "The Marseillaise," and then to give three cheers for the President of France, followed by three more for the rulers of the allied countries.

Copyright Underwood & Underwood, N. Y.
Right Hon. Arthur J. Balfour and Joseph H. Choate.

The New York Times.

"All the News That's Fit to Print."

THE WEATHER
Generally fair today and Sunday; moderate west to variable winds.
For full weather report see Page 18.

VOL. LXVI...NO. 21,665.   NEW YORK, SATURDAY, MAY 19, 1917.—TWENTY PAGES.   ONE CENT In Greater New York. | Elsewhere N. Y. State, N. J., Conn. TWO CENTS | THREE CENTS Other States.

PRESIDENT CALLS THE NATION TO ARMS; DRAFT BILL SIGNED; REGISTRATION ON JUNE 5; REGULARS UNDER PERSHING TO GO TO FRANCE

A Proclamation by the President of the United States

Executive Mansion, Washington, D. C., May 18, 1917.

Whereas, Congress has enacted and the President has on the 18th day of May, one thousand nine hundred and seventeen, approved a law, which contains the following provisions:

Section 5.—That all male persons between the ages of 21 and 30, both inclusive, shall be subject to registration in accordance with regulations to be prescribed by the President: And upon proclamation by the President or other public notice given by him or by his direction stating the time and place of such registration, it shall be the duty of all persons of the designated ages, except officers and enlisted men of the regular army, the navy, and the National Guard and Naval Militia while in the service of the United States, to present themselves for and submit to registration under the provisions of this act: And every such person shall be deemed to have notice of the requirements of this act upon the publication of said proclamation, or other notice as aforesaid, given by the President or by his direction: And any person who shall willfully fail or refuse to present himself for registration or to submit thereto as herein provided, shall be guilty of a misdemeanor and shall, upon conviction in the District Court of the United States having jurisdiction thereof, be punished by imprisonment for not more than one year, and shall thereupon be duly registered: provided that in the call of the docket precedence shall be given, in courts trying the same, to the trial of criminal proceedings under this act; provided, further, that persons shall be subject to registration as herein provided, who shall have attained their twenty-first birthday and who shall not have attained their thirty-first birthday on or before the day set for the registration; and all persons so registered shall be and remain subject to draft into the forces hereby authorized unless excepted or excused therefrom as in this act provided; provided further, that in the case of temporary absence from actual place of legal residence of any person liable to registration as provided herein, such registration may be made by mail under regulations to be prescribed by the President.

Section 6.—That the President is hereby authorized to utilize the service of any or all departments and any or all officers or agents of the United States and of the several States, territories, and the District of Columbia, and subdivisions thereof in the execution of this act, and all officers and agents of the United States and of the several States, territories, and subdivisions thereof, and of the District of Columbia; and all persons designated or appointed under regulations prescribed by the President, whether such appointments are made by the President himself or by the Governor or other officer of any State or territory to perform any duty in the execution of this act, are hereby required to perform such duty as the President shall order or direct, and all such officers and agents and persons so designated or appointed shall hereby have full authority for all acts done by them in the execution of this act by the direction of the President. Correspondence in the execution of this act may be carried in penalty envelopes, bearing the frank of the War Department. Any person charged, as herein provided, with the duty of carrying into effect any of the provisions of this act or the regulations made or directions given thereunder who shall fail or neglect to perform such duty, and any person charged with such duty or having and exercising any authority under said act, regulations, or directions, who shall knowingly make or be a party to the making of any false or incorrect registration, physical examination, exemption, enlistment, enrollment, or muster, and any person who shall make or be a party to the making of any false statement or certificate as to the fitness or liability of himself or any other person for service under the provisions of

this act, or regulations made by the President thereunder, or otherwise evades or aids another to evade the requirements of this act or of said regulations, or who, in any manner, shall fail or neglect fully to perform any duty required of him in the execution of this act, shall, if not subject to military law, be guilty of a misdemeanor, and upon conviction in the District Court of the United States, having jurisdiction thereof, be punished by imprisonment for not more than one year, or, if subject to military law, shall be tried by court-martial and suffer such punishment as a court-martial may direct.

Now, Therefore, I, Woodrow Wilson, President of the United States, do call upon the Governor of each of the several States and Territories, the Board of Commissioners of the District of Columbia, and all officers and agents of the several States and Territories, of the District of Columbia, and of the counties and municipalities therein, to perform certain duties in the execution of the foregoing law, which duties will be communicated to them directly in regulations of even date herewith.

And I do further proclaim and give notice to all persons subject to registration in the several States and in the District of Columbia in accordance with the above law, that the time and place of such registration shall be between 7 A. M. and 7 P. M. on the fifth day of June, 1917, at the registration place in the precinct wherein they have their permanent homes. Those who shall have attained their twenty-first birthday and who shall not have attained their thirty-first birthday on or before the day here named are required to register, excepting only officers and enlisted men of the regular army, the navy, the Marine Corps, and the National Guard and Naval Militia, while in the service of the United States, and officers in the Officers' Reserve Corps and enlisted men in the Enlisted Reserve Corps while in active service. In the territories of Alaska, Hawaii, and Porto Rico a day for registration will be named in a later proclamation.

And I do charge those who through sickness shall be unable to present themselves for registration that they apply on or before the day of registration to the County Clerk of the County where they may be for instructions as to how they may be registered by agent. Those who expect to be absent on the day named from the counties in which they have their permanent homes may register by mail, but their mailed registration cards must reach the places in which they have their permanent homes by the day named herein. They should apply as soon as practicable to the County Clerk of the county wherein they may be for instructions as to how they may accomplish their registration by mail. In case such persons as, through sickness or absence, may be unable to present themselves personally for registration shall be sojourning in cities of over 30,000 population, they shall apply to the City Clerk of the city wherein they may be sojourning rather than to

the Clerk of the County. The Clerks of counties and of cities of over 30,000 population in which numerous applications from the sick and from non-residents are expected are authorized to establish such agencies and to employ and deputize such clerical force as may be necessary to accommodate these applications.

The Power against which we are arrayed has sought to impose its will upon the world by force. To this end it has increased armament until it has changed the face of war. In the sense in which we have been wont to think of armies, there are no armies in this struggle, there are entire nations armed. Thus, the men who remain to till the soil and man the factories are no less a part of the army that is France than the men beneath the battle flags. It must be so with us. It is not an army that we must shape and train for war; it is a nation.

To this end our people must draw close in one compact front against a common foe. But this cannot be if each man pursues a private purpose. All must pursue one purpose. The nation needs all men; but it needs each man, not in the field that will most pleasure him, but in the endeavor that will best serve the common good. Thus, though a sharpshooter pleases to operate a trip-hammer for the forging of great guns and an expert machinist desires to march with the flag, the nation is being served only when the sharpshooter marches and the machinist remains at his levers.

The whole nation must be a team, in which each man shall play the part for which he is best fitted. To this end, Congress has provided that the nation shall be organized for war by selection; that each man shall be classified for service in the place to which it shall best serve the general good to call him.

The significance of this cannot be overstated. It is a new thing in our history and a landmark in our progress. It is a new manner of accepting and vitalizing our duty to give ourselves with thoughtful devotion to the common purpose of us all. It is in no sense a conscription of the unwilling; it is, rather, selection from a nation which has volunteered in mass. It is no more a choosing of those who shall march with the colors than it is a selection of those who shall serve an equally necessary and devoted purpose in the industries that lie behind the battle line.

The day here named is the time upon which all shall present themselves for assignment to their tasks. It is for that reason destined to be remembered as one of the most conspicuous moments in our history. It is nothing less than the day upon which the manhood of the country shall step forward in one solid rank in defense of the ideals to which this nation is consecrated. It is important to those ideals no less than to the pride of this generation in manifesting its devotion to them, that there be no gaps in the ranks.

194

It is essential that the day be approached in thoughtful apprehension of its significance, and that we accord to it the honor and the meaning that it deserves. Our industrial need prescribes that it be not made a technical holiday, but the stern sacrifice that is before us urges that it be carried in all our hearts as a great day of patriotic devotion and obligation, when the duty shall lie upon every man, whether he is himself to be registered or not, to see to it that the name of every male person of the designated ages is written on these lists of honor.

In Witness Whereof, I have hereunto set my hand and caused the seal of the United States to be affixed Done at the City of Washington this 18th day of May in the year of our Lord one thousand nine hundred and seventeen, and of the independence of the United States of America the one hundred and forty-first.

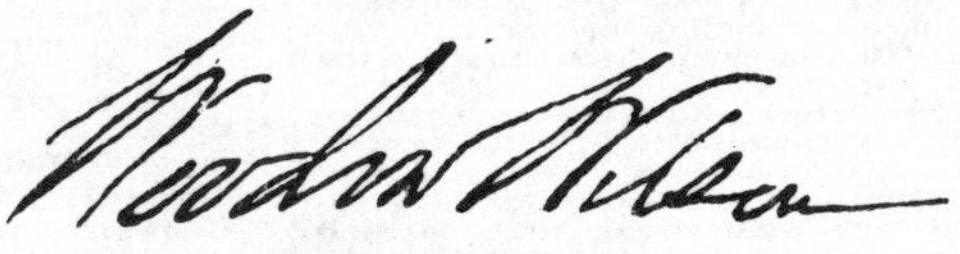

By the President:
ROBERT LANSING, Secretary of State.

PLANS FOR NATIONAL ARMY

First Draft of 500,000 Men to be Divided Into Sixteen Divisions.

MILITIA SIMILARLY PLACED

Arrangement of Concentration Camps Will Be Near Home Regions of Units.

CALLS OUT NATIONAL GUARD

Entire Force to Mobilize and Recruit to War Strength, Beginning on July 15.

Special to The New York Times.

WASHINGTON, May 18.—**President Wilson, tonight at 10 o'clock, issued his proclamation fixing June 5 as the day on which registration is to take place for the national army of 500,000 men to be drafted under authority of the Draft bill, which he signed tonight. On this date all men in the country between the ages of 21 and 30 years, inclusive, will be required to present themselves for registration. Those away from home will register by mail, according to the terms of the proclamation. The registration date for Hawaii, Alaska, and Porto Rico will be announced later.**

The President's proclamation sets forth in detail the plans for registration and was telegraphed tonight by the War Department to all parts of the country so as to have the widest publicity by official posting and publication. It is expected that the registration will occupy about five days. After that those entitled to exemption will be excluded from the draft. About 10,000,000 men between 21 and 30, inclusive, are expected to be registered. After the registration and exemptions have been completed, those declared to be eligible for drafting will have their names placed in jury wheels and 500,000 will be drafted for Federal service in the formation of the new national army.

Plans for the formation of the new army have been completed. It will be divided into sixteen divisions, each to consist of 28,000 men. They will be mobilized in sixteen concentration camps, the names of which soon will be announced, The draft army will be officially known as the National Army, in contradistinction to the regular army and the National Guard army. These National Army divisions will be numbered consecutively from one to sixteen.

New York and Pennsylvania will furnish enough men in the draft to form three National Army divisions, exclusive of what they will furnish for the regular army and the National Guard army. New York and Pennsylvania will each furnish about a division and a half for the National Army. The only other State to furnish as much as a division for the National Army will be Illinois. Seven Pacific Coast States, where the population is not so dense, will furnish the sixteenth National Army division.

Distribution of Divisions.

The distribution of the division, according to the States that will form them, will be as follows:

First—Massachusetts, Maine, Connecticut, Rhode Island, Vermont, and New Hampshire.
Second—Lower New York State and Long Island.
Third—Upper New York State and Northern Pennsylvania.
Fourth—Southern Pennsylvania.
Fifth—Virginia, Maryland, Delaware, New Jersey, and District of Columbia.
Sixth—Tennessee, North Carolina, and South Carolina.
Seventh—Alabama, Georgia, and Florida.
Eighth—Ohio and West Virginia.
Ninth—Indiana and Kentucky.
Tenth—Wisconsin and Michigan.
Eleventh—Illinois.
Twelft—Arkansas, Mississippi, and Louisiana.
Thirteenth—North Dakota, South Dakota, Nebraska, Minnesota, and Iowa.
Fourteenth—Colorado, Kansas, and Missouri.
Fifteenth—Arizona, New Mexico, Texas, and Oklahoma.
Sixteenth—Washington, Oregon, Idaho, Montana, California, Nevada, and Utah.

Calls Out the Guard.

President Wilson also issued orders today for the mobilization of the entire National Guard of the country. Instructions were sent to the Adjutant General of the States to the effect that the National Guard not now in Federal service and enlisted men of the National Guard Reserve would be drafted into the Federal service on various dates, ranging from July 15 to Aug. 5. All National Guard coast artillery will be drafted on July 15. The organizations will be held at their rendezvous for about two weeks and will then be sent to concentration camps in the Southern, Southeastern, and Western Departments for training.

There are now 60,000 National Guardsmen in Federal service. There are more than 100,000 not yet in Federal service. These are to be called into Federal service under the orders issued today. New National Guard units will also be formed and all the guard units will be expanded until 400,000 men have been obtained. This will be designated the National Guard Army, and it will consist of sixteen divisions, to be designated as the fifth to the twentieth, inclusive.

The approximate dates for drafting the National Guard are:

July 15—New York, Pennsylvania, Ohio, West Virginia, Michigan, Wisconsin, Minnesota, Iowa, North Dakota, South Dakota, and Nebraska.

July 25—Maine, New Hampshire, Vermont, Massachusetts, Rhode Island, Connecticut, New Jersey, Delaware, Maryland, District of Columbia, Virginia, North Carolina, South Carolina, Tennessee, Illinois, Montana, Wyoming, Idaho, Washington, and Oregon.

Aug. 5—Indiana, Kentucky, Georgia, Florida, Alabama, Mississippi, Arkansas, Louisiana, Oklahoma, Texas, Missouri, Kansas, Colorado, New Mexico, Arizona, Utah, California.

"All National Guard organizations," said an official War Department announcement tonight, "both in and out of the Federal Service, will be recruited at once to full war strength. The necessary arms, equipment, and clothing for recruits is not at present on hand, but it is hoped all supplies will be available by the time the troops are sent to their concentration camps.

Like the regular army and the national army the National Guard army is to be organized on a divisional basis. New York, Pennsylvania, and Illinois will each supply sufficient guardsmen to form its own army division. The other divisions are to be formed by brigading and other wise amalgamating the units of groups of two or more States. The original National Guard mobilization plan called for the formation of only twelve divisions, numbered from five to sixteen, inclusive. The plan now adopted, which allows for formation of new units and great expansion of the present National Guard force, calls for the formation of sixteen divisions.

These divisions will be formed out of the various troops of the different States as follows:

Fifth—Maine, Massachusetts, Vermont, New Hampshire, Connecticut, and Rhode Island.
Sixth—New York.
Seventh—Pennsylvania.
Eighth—New Jersey, Delaware, Maryland, Virginia, and District of Columbia.
Ninth—Tennessee, North Carolina, and South Carolina.
Tenth—Georgia, Alabama, and Florida.
Eleventh—Michigan and Wisconsin.
Twelfth—Illinois.
Thirteenth—North Dakota, South Dakota, Nebraska, Iowa, and Minnesota.
Fourteenth—Kansas and Missouri.
Fifteenth—Texas and Oklahoma.
Sixteenth—Ohio and West Virginia.
Seventeenth—Kentucky and Indiana.
Eighteenth—Arkansas, Louisiana, and Mississippi.
Nineteenth—California, Nevada, Utah, Colorado, Arizona, and New Mexico.
Twentieth—Washington, Oregon, Idaho, Montana, and Wyoming.

32 Concentration Camps.

It will be necessary to establish thirty-two concentration camps to take care of the thirty-two army divisions to be formed out of the national army and the National Guard army. All camps for the National Guard divisions will be in the Southern, Southeastern, and Western Departments of the army. The plan for the distribution of the National Guard divisions and the National Army divisions in concentration camps was announced today as follows:

Northeastern Department—First National Army Division.

Eastern Department—Second, Third, Fourth, and Fifth National Army Divisions.

Southeastern Department—Sixth, Seventh, and Twelfth National Army Divisions; also the Fifth, Sixth, Seventh, Eighth, Ninth, Tenth, Sixteenth, Seventeenth, and Eighteenth National Guard Divisions.

Southern Department—Fifteenth National Army Division; also the Eleventh, Twelfth, Thirteenth, Fourteenth, and Fifteenth National Guard Divisions.

Western Department—Sixteenth National Army Division; also the Nineteenth and Twentieth National Guard Division.

Central Department—Eighth, Ninth, Tenth, Eleventh, Thirteenth, and Fourteenth National Army Divisions.

Thus it will be seen that all of the National Guard army divisions, with the exception of two, will be trained and sheltered south of Mason and Dixon's line in the Southern and Southeastern Departments. The two exceptions will be the Nineteenth and Twentieth National Guard Divisions, which will be trained in the Western Department of the army.

Big Command for Wood.

Thus it is evident that Major Gen. Leonard Wood, by his transfer from the old Department of the East, with headquarters at New York City, to the newly formed Southeastern Department, with headquarters at Charleston, S. C., on May 1 put him in line to command what is now becoming the most important military division of the country in the number of men to be concentrated into cantonments for training purposes in connection with the formation of the new armies. There will be twelve concentration camps in General Wood's department. Each will shelter an army division of 28,000 men. Three of these will be divisions of the new national draft army, while the other nine will be divisions of the expanded National Guard army.

All of the thirty-two concentration camps have not been selected. They are being chosen by the department commanders. But the location of six of the camps was announced today. These will be at Ayer, Mass.; El Paso, Texas; American Lake, Wash.; Atlanta, Ga.; Augusta, Ga., and Columbia, S.C. Three of them, those at Atlanta, Augusta, and Columbia are in General Wood's Department.

The selection of all cantonment sites is being rushed, and in some instances boards appointed by the department commanders are inspecting possible locations for the purpose of making recommendations to the departmental commanders, who makes the selection. There will be no public hearings, as there was said to be no time for these.

The requisites of a camp site were said to be: Space, good sanitary conditions, such as absence of marshes, with natural advantages for drainage: proximity to lines of transports, a good water supply.

The War Department is assembling vast quantities of supplies for the construction of the thirty-two camps, each of which will be a complete town, with sewerage, water works, lighting systems, streets, &c. The construction of the cantonments will be started immediately after the selection and approval of sites.

WILL NOT SEND ROOSEVELT

Wilson Not to Avail Himself of Volunteer Authority at Present.

COMMENDS THE COLONEL

But Declares the Business at Hand Is Scientific and for Trained Men Only.

SAYS RESPONSIBILITY IS HIS

Sending of Pershing Division Believed to be in Direct Response to France's Call.

Special to The New York Times.

WASHINGTON, May 18.—**Announcement was made at the War Department tonight by Secretary Baker that an expeditionary force of approximately one division of regular troops, under Major General John J. Pershing had been ordered to proceed to France on as early date as practicable. General Pershing and his staff will precede the troops to the fighting area.**

Shortly before this announcement came from Secretary Baker, the White House gave to the press a statement from President Wilson in which he said that he would not avail himself, "at any rate at the present stage of the war," of the authority conferred by the Military Selective Draft act, which he had just approved, to organize volunteer divisions.

While referring in complimentary terms to Colonel Roosevelt's public service and gallantry, the President made it plain that he was entirely out of sympathy with the Roosevelt proposal that volunteers be sent to France without delay.

"Politically, too," said the President, "it would no doubt have a very fine effect and make a profound impression," but he added that "the business now at hand is undramatic, practical, and of scientific directness and precision." The President indicated that he did not regard Colonel Roosevelt as a military expert. He also stressed the point that upon the Executive rested the responsibility for the successful conduct of the war, and that he intended to be influenced by considerations along that line and let everything else wait.

It is apparent from President Wilson's statement that his present state of mind is strongly opposed to sending Colonel Roosevelt or any volunteer force to France.

The official announcement that an expeditionary force of regular troops would be sent to France "at as early date as possible" was handed to newspaper men at the War Department by Major Douglas MacArthur of the General Staff at 9:30 o'clock with the injunctions that it was not to be published through extra editions or otherwise until 10 o'clock. The statement containing this important announcement follows:

"The President has directed an expeditionary force of approximately one division of regular troops under command of Major Gen. John J. Pershing to proceed to France at as early a date as practicable. General Pershing and staff will precede the troops abroad. It is requested that no details or speculations with regard to the mobilization of this command, dates of departure, composition, or other items, be carried by the press, other than the official bulletins given out by the War Department relating thereto."

The President's Statement.

The President's statement regarding Colonel Roosevelt follows:

"I shall not avail myself, at any rate at the present stage of the war, of the authorization conferred by the act to organize volunteer divisions. To do so would seriously interfere with the carrying out of the chief and most immediately important purpose contemplated by this legislation, the prompt creation and early use of an effective army, and would contribute practically nothing to the effective strength of the armies now engaged against Germany.

"I understand that the section of this act which authorizes the creation of volunteer divisions in addition to the draft was added with a view to providing an independent command for Mr. Roosevelt and giving the military authority an opportunity to use his fine vigor and enthusiasm in recruiting forces now at the Western front.

"It would be very agreeable to me to pay Mr. Roosevelt this compliment and the Allies the compliment of sending to their aid one of our most distinguished public men, an ex-President who has rendered many conspicuous public services and proved his gallantry in many striking ways. Politically, too, it would no doubt have a very fine effect and make a profound impression. But this is not the time or the occasion for compliment or for any action not calculated to contribute to the immediate success of the war. The business now in hand is undramatic, practical, and of scientific definiteness and precision. I shall act with regard to it at every step and in every particular under expert and professional advice from both sides of the water.

Need All Trained Officers.

"That advice is that the men most needed are men of the ages contemplated in the draft provision of the present bill, not men of the age and sort contemplated in the section which authorizes the formation of volunteer units, and that for the preliminary training of the men who are to be drafted we shall need all of our experienced officers. Mr. Roosevelt told me, when I had the pleasure of seeing him a few weeks ago, that

regular meeting of the Cabinet this afternoon. The decision to send to Europe a division of regular troops without delay was the outcome of a compromise between the expressed wish of the French Government and the view of the General Staff. The General Staff as a whole was opposed to sending any troops to the fighting areas until the War Department had completed the organization and equipment of the army of regulars, National Guard, and drafted men, amounting approximately to 1,200,000 men of all three classes in the first increment.

The French Government, however, virtually appealed to this Government, at first informally, and later in a way to show that compliance with the appeal was regarded as vital, to send troops to the battle front with the least possible delay. Marshal Joffre made known this desire of France to representatives of American newspapers soon after he reached Washington, and his words were emphasized in the statement furnished to THE NEW YORK TIMES this week by General Pétain, the new Commander in Chief of the French armies in the field. It was obvious from what General Pétain said that what France needed was men; in fact, he said so in as many words.

President Responsive.

To these appeals the President has been responsive, although in taking the action announced tonight, with reference to the Pershing expedition, he went contrary to the ideas of a majority of the members of the General Staff, who contended that an untrained army or a small army would be useless in the trenches. There was a disinclination in some quarters, however, to concur in the opinion of the General Staff that it was desirable to wait a year while the new army was being trained before attempting to send an expedition across the Atlantic. According to the General Staff view the French Government wanted Americans to fill up the gaps in the French ranks.

It was contended by military critics here that the scheme advanced by General Pétain through the columns of THE NEW YORK TIMES did not contemplate having the American volunteers for whom he called serve as a single unit under the Stars and Stripes, but distributed among the French troops under the tricolor of France. The decision of the President announced tonight means that the men of the Pershing expedition will fight under their own flag.

Under the voluntary censorship to which the press has assented, no detail can be given of the formation of the Pershing expedition. It is evident from the formal announcement, however, that its departure for France will not be long delayed.

Until the War Department announcement cleared away doubt, it was supposed that the first expedition would be composed of National Guard organizations as well as regulars. There had been indications that National Guard forces were being prepared for service abroad, but the War Department declined to furnish any information.

General Pershing arrived in Washington last week from El Paso, Texas, where he established his headquarters after his return from command of the expeditionary force sent into Mexico to disband the Villistas. He has been in consultation every day with Secretary Baker and officers of the General Staff, and it was generally understood that he would wish to have associated with him some of the most effective officers of the regular army. He named many of those whom he would desire to have designated for the service, and they were men who cannot possibly be spared from the too small force of officers at our command for the much more pressing and necessary duty of training regular troops to be put into the field in France and Belgium as fast as they can be got ready.

"The first troops sent to France will be taken from the present forces of the regular army, and will be under the command of trained soldiers only.

"The responsibility for the successful conduct of our own part in this great war rests upon me. I could not escape it if I would. I am too much interested in the cause we are fighting for to be interested in anything but success. The issues involved are too immense for me to take into consideration anything whatever except the best, most effective, most immediate means of military action. What these means are I know from the mouths of men who have seen war as it is now conducted, who have no illusions, and to wohm grim matter is a matter of business. I shall centre my attention upon those means and let everything else wait.

"I should be deeply to blame should I do otherwise, whatever the argument of policy for a personal gratification or advantage."

Sending Colonel Roosevelt or any force of volunteers to France was strongly, even bitterly, opposed by the General Satff, and it is supposed that its views were communicated to President Wilson by Secretary Baker. The definite decision not to send Colonel Roosevelt to France or exercise the authority conferred in the President by the Draft bill is believed to have been reached at a way of suggestion as to the effect of adverse action by the President on the desire of Colonel Roosevelt to go to France.

The opinion was expressed tonight that friends of Colonel Roosevelt might take umbrage at some of the comments of the President in his statement on the ground that he was ironical at the Colonel's expense. The reference to the "very fine effect" and "profound impression" that might be made politically by sending the Colonel to Europe was mentioned, as was the statement that "the business now at hand is undramatic."

Pershing Promoted by Roosevelt.

Elsewhere there is a disposition to contend that President Wilson turned a very clever political trick when he combined the selection of General Pershing to command the first American expedition to France with his announcement of his refusal to send Colonel Roosevelt there with a volunteer contingent.

It was recalled in this connection that General Pershing owed his first military boost to Colonel Roosevelt, then President of the United States. General Pershing was a Captain of the regular army, who was making an enviable record in the Philippines insurrection when President Roosevelt promoted him to the grade of Brigadier General, a tremendous jump over many officers senior to Captain Pershing in years and service.

President Roosevelt was severely criticised for this action. It was contended he would be placed in command of the first military expedition sent from this country to the theatre of conflict in Europe.

Mr. Balfour and members of the British War Mission were also of the opinion that American troops should be sent to France without delay. Their reasons, however, were not entirely similar to those advanced by French representatives. It was apparent that the main reason for the anxiety of France to have Americans on the battle front was that stated so frankly by General Pétain: "But what is imperative now is men," he said.

"What France needs most is men—infantry." All that was said by the French representatives in Washington bore out that statement. The British, on the other hand, stressed that the presence of American troops in the trenches would have a marked psychological effect upon the French and British forces in the field, and would cause a corresponding lowering of the morale of the German armies. There is also reason to believe that the British observers here reached the conclusion that America needed something to awaken it to a realization that it was actually engaged in the bloody European conflict, and that nothing would better accomplish this than the sending of an expeditionary force to France. The knowledge that American soldiers were fighting in the trenches would stimulate American enthusiasm, with all that that would mean, in the opinion of some of the British visitors.

The Pershing expedition may be said to have been ordered to Europe for two reasons—to strengthen the French battle line and to produce the desired psychological effect in all the allied countries, including the United States. In these days a division of American troops, consisting of about 28,000 men, is a mere handful in comparison with the enormous armies that have been engaged in the present conflict. But it was felt by the Administration that it would be well to have the Stars and Stripes shown on the battle line and at the same time furnish France with some assistance in carrying out the great offensive in which her armies are engaged in combination with those of Great Britain.

Expect Criticism in Congress.

What effect will be produced in Congress by the refusal of President Wilson to send Colonel Roosevelt to Europe could not be ascertained with any degree of accuracy tonight for the reason the Senators and Representatives interested in the Colonel's cause could not be found. Their course is problematical. But the question as to what was likely to follow a decision by the President not to send Colonel Roosevelt to France has been discussed here with animation in the past several days.

It is not doubted that the President will be criticised by friends of Colonel Roosevelt in the Senate and the House. That the President understood the intent of the Senate and the House was admitted by him in the statement he issued tonight, and after that admission he proceeded to give his reasons for believing it unwise to form a volunteer force or to appoint Colonel Roosevelt to any command.

It has been suggested here within the past few days that if the country should obtain the idea that President Wilson had treated Colonel Roosevelt unfairly it would cause widespread indignation among the American people. But beyond that there has been little in the

ment for publication until he had had time to study the full text of the President's statement.

The decision of the President came with sharply defined force, for this afternoon, after receiving information that the measure was before the President for final action, the Colonel sent a telegram to the White House tendering his services.

"I sent to President Wilson this afternoon a message offering to raise a division at once, or if it seemed desirable to him, two divisions," said the Colonel.

"No, no; not tonight," he replied to requests to make a statement as to what his plans would be with regard to going to France. He would not say whether he would contemplate any plan for offering his services in other capacities. He received an offer of a Major Generalship in the New York National Guard from Governor Whitman.

Earlier in the day Colonel Roosevelt expressed hearty approval of the suggestion of General Pétain, as printed in THE NEW YORK TIMES Wednesday morning, that France have American volunteers at once, to be trained in France by French officers.

"I, of course, emphatically agree with General Pétain that American volunteers should be sent abroad at once," he said, "and if I am allowed to take them over I should welcome the chance to have them given intensive training by the use of French officers in whatever way would most quickly and efficiently produce results."

While the Colonel took interest in the suggestion of General Pétain, it is said that he has been advised that the French and British Governments would be very slow to accept the services of any body of Americans who did not come to the arena of war with the approval of President Wilson.

There, of course, remains open to the Colonel the chance to accept the commission Governor Whitman has offered him, which in due course would bring him face to face with Federal service. At that he would have to be acceptable to the General Staff before he could go to France to fight. Friends of the Colonel say that he is not anxious for rank, but merely wants to have a part in whipping Germany. Incidentally he is 58 years old, and it would have to be a high rank he would hold in order to come under the age limit.

Right up to tonight the Colonel continued to receive offers from well-known men to raise forces for his proposed division. He said today that Adjt. Gen. Barber of New Jersey offered to raise a full regiment in New Jersey, or two battalions. Governor Edge also offered to recruit a regiment. General Barber is an ex-army officer, and served in the Philippines with a volunteer regiment. The Colonel has received offers from members of Congress of several Northwestern States to raise regiments. Offers of two regiments have also come from Tennessee.

Colonel Roosevelt was asked to reply to statements published this week that his was only a paper army.

"I say," he replied, "that I can raise four divisions, two of them at once."

The Colonel probably will hold a meeting in a few days with the men who have been leaders in his plan to raise a volunteer division, after which he is that he had been influenced in doing so by the fact that Captain Pershing was the son-in-law of Senator Francis E. Warren of Wyoming, then Chairman of the Senate Committee on Military Affairs.

The nomination was confirmed by the Senate, and since then General Pershing has given great satisfaction to the War Department. It is asserted in some quarters that Colonel Roosevelt has been placed in a position where he cannot criticise the selection of the commander of the expeditionary force, and by some this is held to be an advantage to President Wilson in any controversy that might arise over the contention that the President has acted unfairly to Colonel Roosevelt and ignored the wish of Congress.

ROOSEVELT SILENT ON WILSON'S ACTION

Refuses to Discuss Plans for Going to France—Had Wired Offer to President.

Special to The New York Times.

OYSTER BAY, May 18.—Colonel Roosevelt was told tonight of President Wilson's decision not to allow the ex-President to take a division of volunteers to France. He showed acute interest, but refused to make any comexpected to make an announcement of his intentions with regard to the war.

"All the News That's Fit to Print."

The New York Times.

THE WEATHER
Fair, warmer today and Thursday; moderate south winds.
For full weather report see Page 21.

VOL. LXVI...NO. 21,690. NEW YORK, WEDNESDAY, JUNE 13, 1917.—TWENTY-TWO PAGES. ONE CENT In Greater New York. | TWO CENTS Elsewhere N. Y. State, N. J., Conn. | THREE CENTS Other States.

CONSTANTINE GIVES UP GREEK THRONE; ALEXANDER, SECOND SON, IS NOW KING; RULER AND HIS HEIR OUSTED BY ALLIES

ANGLO-FRENCH TROOPS LAND

Occupy Corinth and Take Control of the Harvest in Thessaly.

PREMIER HEEDS JONNART

Told Powers' Purpose Is to Re-establish Greek Unity and Protect Allied Army.

EX-KING TO LEAVE COUNTRY

Will Start for Italy, En Route to Switzerland, with the Crown Prince on British Warship.

ATHENS, June 12.—The fall of Constantine I., King of the Hellenes, has come. In response to the demand of the protecting powers—France, Great Britain and Russia—he abdicated today in favor of his second son, Prince Alexander.

This climax in the affairs of Greece was brought about through the agency of the French Senator, M. Jonnart, who has held posts in several French Cabinets and who arrived at Athens only a day or two ago on a special mission as the representative of France, Great Britain and Russia. M. Jonnart had previously visited Saloniki and other points, and he lost no time in getting into conference with the Greek Premier, Alexander Zaimis.

The demands of the powers respecting the abdication of King Constantine also specifically eliminated Crown Prince George as his successor, the Crown Prince being included among those Greeks in official life who were considered strongly pro-German. Both the former King and Prince George, it was announced today by Premier Zaimis, intend to leave the country immediately. It is reported that they will embark on a British warship and proceed to Switzerland by way of Italy.

It is presumed that Prince Alexander will take his kingly duties with full acceptation of the ideas which the protecting powers desire to be put into effect in the Government of Greece during the present war. He is twenty-four years of age and has been free from anti-Entente proclivities.

Appeal to Premier Heeded.

Affairs in Greece, which several times since the outbreak of the war had seemed on the verge of a settlement, recently have taken on such an aspect of uncertainty that it became necessary for the powers to act with decision. M. Jonnart was selected to proceed to Athens for the purpose of laying before the Premier the aims which France, Great Britain, and Russia had with respect to establishing unity or feeling among the Greeks and greater security for the Entente forces engaged in operations in the East. While he informed the Premier that troops had been placed at his disposal, he appealed to that official to use his influence toward a peaceful settlement. The troops, according to M. Jonnart's instructions, were not to land until the King had given his answer.

M. Jonnart called upon Premier Zaimis on Monday morning and demanded in the name of the protecting powers the abdication of King Constantine and the nomination of his successor to the exclusion of the Diaboque. (Crown Prince.)

M. Zaimis recognized the disinterestedness of the powers, whose sole object was to reconstitute the unity of Greece under the Constitution, but he pointed out to M. Jonnart that a decision could only be taken by the King after a meeting of the Crown Council, composed of former Premiers. It was not until 9:30 o'clock this morning that the Premier communicated in a letter to the Commissioner of the allied powers the King's decision to accede to their demands.

Adherents Wanted to Defend King.

Prior to the announcement of the King's decision many Greeks, loyal to the crown, gathered for the protection of the sovereign. On Monday night 2,000 reservists formed a cordon around the palace in his defense, if that should be necessary, and a delegation headed by naval Commander Mavromichaelis was received by Constantine and pledged the devotion of the army and the people to his cause. The King's only reply was an appeal that they should remain calm.

All efforts of agitators to start a manifestation failed, and the army officers announced their intention to obey the order of the Government to take no part in any demonstrations and to maintain peace.

Agitators were still attempting to operate in the streets of Athens tonight, but there were no disorders, and everything leads to the belief that there will be none.

French and British Troops Landed.

Special Cable to THE NEW YORK TIMES.

LONDON, Wednesday, June 13.—An Exchange Telegraph dispatch from Paris says French and British troops have been landed in Thessaly and Corinth.

PARIS, June 12.—The War Office tonight announced the landing of troops in Thessaly in the following bulletin:

The troops charged with control of the harvests in Thessaly have penetrated that province without difficulty as far as the region of Elassona.

A dispatch from the Havas Agency from Athens says:

"M. Jonnart in a conference with Premier Zaimis announced that military forces had been placed at his disposition to establish control of the Isthmus of Corinth and to maintain order in Athens. These forces were landed Monday without incident."

ROYALIST LOST LAST PROP.

Had Told Greeks the United States Would Intervene for King.

Special to The New York Times

WASHINGTON, June 12.—While the State Department is without official confirmation of the Athens report that Constantine, the King of Greece, has abdicated in favor of his second son, Prince Alexander, and will soon leave the country, accompanied by Crown Prince George, the announcement carried in press dispatches came as no surprise to official and diplomatic Washington.

It has been alleged and pretty substantially proved that the Greek King has been in close touch with Berlin by wireless from his headquarters in Greece, and that German submarines have been using Greek islands as a base of submarine operations against Entente shipping with the approval if not the secret connivance of the King.

It is known that a message reached the State Department yesterday which indicated that something was going to happen involving the Greek royal family and that a member of the family probably would become Regent of Greece. If the King has abdicated in favor of his son, it is interpreted here as a last attempt to save the throne to the Constantine dynasty.

As the protectors of Greek independence, the Governments of Great Britain, France, and Russia claim treaty rights to interfere in the internal affairs of Greece if the independence of the kingdom and the liberties of the people are threatened. This right of the Entente is declared to be somewhat similar to the right of the United States under the Platt amendment to intervene in Cuba for the protection of Cuban independence and the preservation of public order.

The entry of the United States Government into the war against Germany placed King Constantine in an isolated and not enviable plight among his own people. The Royalist papers of Greece had been feeding the people with stories that the United States would intervene in Greece in support of the Constantine Government. Since the entry of this country into the war it has been out of the question for this Government to take any course that would strengthen the position of the Greek King as long as his sympathies and actions were favorable to the Teutonic allies.

CAUSES THAT LED TO CRISIS.

Ex-King an Implacable Opponent of Entente's Policy.

Rumors that King Constantine would abdicate have been periodical. There was a meeting of the allied Ministers to Switzerland in the middle of April—at St. Jean de Maurienne—when, it is said, full powers were given France as a negotiator to present this alternative to the King: either he must abdicate in favor of his second son, Alexander, or the Entente Powers would recognize the Venizelos Provisional Government as pertaining to the whole of Greece instead of, as some of them had already done, as a war Government identified only with Saloniki. Immediately all the Governments of the Allies were sounded on this proposition—the United States on April 23. Since then it had been semi-officially stated that France would conduct negotiations at Athens tending to clear up the difficult situation.

A significant dispatch was sent out of Greece to London on May 2. It read:

"The King is steadily losing followers. Fifty-seven officers recently left Athens in one day for Saloniki, and the stream is continuing. Since the Provisional Government declared that the population on any territory seceding hereafter to the National Government will not be mobilized the last plank was knocked from under the King's feet, and it is at least most doubtful if any of the rank and file will be found to stand between him and his fate."

Neither of King Constantine's elder sons is married. Prince George, the Duke of Sparta, and hitherto heir to the throne, was born July 19, 1890. He accompanied his father on his campaigns in the two Balkan wars of 1912-13, and since the Summer of 1915, together with his uncle George, has been engaged in propaganda work in order set the policy of his father right before the Chancelleries of the Entente. Last Winter he was reported to have been in Berlin and Vienna on important missions.

Just prior to the outbreak of the war it was announced that a marriage had been arranged between Prince George and Princess Elizabeth of Rumania. The Princess is the eldest daughter of the present King Ferdinand of Rumania and the grandniece of the late King Carol. Another claimant for her hand—she is now 23—was the Czarovitch of Russia. The Kaiser, it was reported, was prepared to press the claim of his Greek nephew.

Alexander a Venizelist.

His younger brother, Prince Alexander, the new King, is nearly three years his junior, having been born Aug. 1, 1893. He is known to have an unrestrained admiration for Venizelos and is believed to be intensely pro-Entente. A year ago it was reported that he had thrown up his commission as Captain in the first regiment of artillery in order to join Venizelos's volunteers, but was either restrained or was advised by the veteran statesman to remain where he was.

"The difficult situation" between King Constantine and the Allies has developed from three distinct causes: The alleged pro-German attitude of the King, the fact that three of the Entente Powers are guarantors of Greek constitutional liberty, the fact that the Greek-Serbian treaty of March, 1913, which he violated, pledged the support of either power if the other were attacked by Bulgaria.

The King either personally or through his spokesmen has explained his case as follows:

"When the war began the guarantors of Greek integrity insisted that we should remain neutral, although we were then ready to fulfill our destiny in the East. When Bulgaria attacked Serbia we could not carry out the treaty of 1913 for two reasons: Serbia was not only attacked by Bulgaria, but by Austria and Germany, and to attempt to aid Serbia then would have meant for Greece the fate of Belgium."

As to the King's alleged personal pro-Germanism, that arises from the fact

AMERICA'S ENTRY AIDED GREEK COUP

High British Authority Characterizes Its Influence as "a Breeze of Democracy."

THESSALY'S GRAIN SAVED

Failure to Act Now Would Have Given Constantine Supplies to Defy a Blockade.

Special Cable to THE NEW YORK TIMES.

LONDON, Wednesday, June 13.—The announcement of the methods selected by the Allies to deal with King Constantine was not unexpected. Intimation of the action to be taken was given in the House of Commons, and in well-informed quarters it is believed that the situation will be rapidly developed.

THE NEW YORK TIMES correspondent is informed on the highest authority that the entrance of the United States into the war had a direct and important influence in bringing about the present solution of the Greek difficulty. American influence is characterized by the authority in question as a fresh breeze of democracy sweeping out the corners where the autocracies which disregard the claims of their peoples have been sheltering.

Plans for dealing with the situation which King Constantine provoked first began to assume definite shape at the British, French, and Italian conference held in Savoy, when Premier Lloyd George and Paul Painlevé, the French War Minister, found themselves in entire agreement, and the Italian representative was seen to be nearly of the same mind. The execution of the details of the plan was placed in the hands of the French, of course in full collaboration with their allies, and Senator Jonnart was selected to take on the work with whatever support might be necessary from General Sarrail and the Admiral commanding the allied fleets in Greek waters.

Importance of Thessaly.

"Is it not time to depose King Constantine?" was the question asked in

The Daily Chronicle yesterday morning. Lord Robert Cecil had stated in the House of Commons that the Allies were taking steps to prevent Constantine from obtaining control of the Thessalian harvest. Thessaly is the most important grain-growing region of Greece, and its harvest will very soon be reaped. If the grain had passed into Constantine's hands he would have had the wherewithal to defy an allied blockade for a long time to come.

The King always attached extreme importance to keeping the district within the royalist boundaries, and, although it is reputed to include a large proportion of Venizelists among its population, it was left to the King when the Allies agreed on the line between the territory under his Government and that of the Venizelists last year. This was done, presumably, because the alternative then would have been war with King Constantine's still numerous army—a war which the allied army at Saloniki, busied with the Bulgars and threatened by the Germans, had every motive for avoiding, and to which at the time the Venizelists were quite incapable of contributing any.

The new action by the Powers with regard to Constantine was made necessary by the fact that the King did not act straightforwardly and honorably, and the Allies were, therfore, justified in going back on the arrangements previously agreed upon. The King repeatedly broke his pledges. Throughout the whole period his conduct has been crooked and hostile. He has been willing to wound, though half afraid to strike. Yet he did strike at times, when opportunity offered for such a blow as the murder of the allied marines and seamen on Dec. 1 and the more recent comitadji outrages against General Sarrail's army, which were organized from the Greek General Staff, with the complicity of the Greek royal family.

The Daily Chronicle says editorially:

"From the point of view of the allied operations on the Serbian front a good deal may be said for the hastening eventuality, [i. e., the deposition of Constantine.] The Allies have been much urged to hasten it by the Venezilists from a somewhat different point of view. Their object, apart from getting even with the King, is that Greece, under their leadership, should at this eleventh hour of the war make a sort of deathbed repentance and start earning some of that merit on the side of the Allies, which, under the King's leadership, she has for two and one-half years earned assiduously on the other and, as it now appears, the losing side.

"The British championship of nationality will preserve absolutely intact at the end of the war the Greece of 1913, with Crete added; but the territory annexed by the treaty of Bucharest is on a different footing. Greece's default in 1915 to the Serbian treaty stops her from claiming any sanctity for the Bucharest arrangement. It was purely an arrangement of military conquest and could not purport to be made on the basis of nationality. That being so, there is more than one respect in which it may conceivably be reopened. Italy's action at Janina must bring home painfully to Greek opinion the risks which the country ran through following King Constantine's policy."

Thus at the very beginning England had a system which was the cause of incalculable waste in man power. The other day I met an old London cabdriver, an ex-army man, who, at the age of 67, succeeded in getting into the army.

After passing the eyesight test, which was not severely applied, he was put into the army and managed to get through a little sentry duty at home, but when it came to marching in the country he was bowled over and eventually discharged. He gets his old-age pension this Autumn when he reaches the age of 70.

It became manifest as the demand grew for more and more men that there would have to be drastic reforms in the whole conduct of these medical examinations. All previously rejected men were called up for re-examination before newly constituted Medical Boards, attended by four or more doctors, including a specialist. Each man examined came before the doctors, stripped, and was thoroughly overhauled.

AMERICAN KILLED AT FRONT.

Four with Canadian Forces Are Reported Wounded Also.

OTTAWA, June 12.—The casualty list of the Canadian Overseas force, issued today, included the following names of Americans:

Killed—C. W. Riddles, Mystic, Conn.

Wounded—Lieutenant J. M. Stevenson, Marlboro, Mass.; H. C. Leary, Hudson, Mass.; T. Billingsly, Boston; W. L. Perkine, Chester, Ia., (on duty.)

RUMOR MONGERS CAUGHT IN NET OF GOVERNMENT

Twelve, Found by Secret Service, Must Explain Origin of Disturbing Reports.

ENEMY ALIENS RESPONSIBLE

Washington Authorities Determined to Put an End to Widespread Propaganda.

ANTI-DRAFT CONVICTIONS

Verdicts in Case of Two Anarchists the First of Their Kind in America.

The Government has started a roundup of the persons who for several weeks past—in fact, almost from the day that President Wilson signed the declaration of war against Germany—have been circulating rumors through the country that the Navy had met with a great disaster, and that the Navy Department was keeping the facts from the people. Already twelve men suspected of knowing about the origin of these rumors have been located by Federal agents and a demand made upon them to give the Government all the information they possess.

Rumors that American warships had been in battle with the German fleet and that several of the American vessels had been lost with their crews, that a mutiny had taken place on board a battleship of the Atlantic Fleet, while that ship was on the way to a French port, and that the superdreadnought Pennsylvania, flagship of the fleet, had been destroyed, have been circulated in New York, Baltimore, Boston, and other cities.

One of the men who is now being investigated by the Secret Service wrote a letter in which he stated that he had infrommation that there had been a mutiny on board one of the Atlantic fleet battleships, and that in quelling it many bluejackets were wounded and several killed. The Governement was able to locate the man who wrote the letter, and he was taken before the proper authorities yesterday. Whether or not he disclosed the source of his rumor the Government agents declined to say last night.

Another scheme followed by the enemy aliens, believed to be responsible for this propaganda, the purpose of which is to stir up discontent in the naval service, and to cause the people generally to distrust the Government, is to tell these stories to boys in their teens, especially school boys and newsboys, who carry the news to all parts of the city or town in which it is desired to have the report circulated.

For weeks these reports have been coming to the attention fo the Federal authorities, and in each instance the report has been promptly branded as false by Secretary Daniels, but even his vigorous denials failed to stop the rumor-mongers, and the result was the issuance last Saturday of the official statement in which Secretary Daniels said that "the country is being poisoned by rumors of battle and disaster that are absolutely without the slightest foundation in truth" and that reports from officers in command of naval stations, inquiries from newspapers and individuals, letters and telegrams from all parts of the country had led him "to the conclusion that there is an organized conspiracy on foot to alarm and distress the people of the United States."

Another matter which has caused much trouble of late is the willingness of a few liquor dealers to supply soldiers and sailors in uniform with liquor in direct violation of the law recently passed by Congress. On one subway train, early yesterday morning, a citizen reported seeing five sailors and one soldier stupefied with drink.

Similar reports have come from other sources, and saloon keepers who are detected selling intoxicating drink to men in uniform will face prompt arrest and trial in the Federal courts.

Reports of violations of the Military Liquor laws are also coming from various parts of New Jersey. Director of Public Safety Bernard McFeely and Chief of Police Patrick Hayes announced yesterday that evidence had been obtained against six saloonkeepers. One night recently so great was the demand for drink by soldiers that they stood in line to get to bars in River Street. Five of the saloons are in River Street, and the sixth just around the corner. When soldiers and sailors applied at the other places in Hoboken they were refused. The violation was open, but the Hoboken police did not take any steps to close the places because the military authorities threatened, when they took charge of the German piers in Hoboken, to deal summarily with any liquor dealers in the neighborhood who sold to soldiers. The police say they expected the provost guard would act, but it did not.

Director McFeely said he was going to demand that the Federal authorities prosecute under Section 12 of the Army act, which makes it a misdemeanor to sell liquor to men in uniform. The punishment is a thousand dollars fine and a year in prison.

BRITISH ADVANCE AGAIN IN BELGIUM

Sweep Forward on Front of Two Miles and Occupy the Village of Gaspard.

DISORDER IN ENEMY LINES

Haig, Praising Messines Victors, Says Nothing Can Save Germans from Defeat.

LONDON, June 12.—Information from unofficial sources at the British front that the crushing victory at Messines last Thursday, had demoralized the Germans, is borne out by General Haig's report tonight, in which he says the troops pushed forward today on a front of about two miles east and northeast of Messines, occupying the village of Gaspard, one mile northwest of Warneton. The Germans evidently feel back with little resistance as they did yesterday southeast of Messines, where they abandoned seven field guns.

"Although the Germans continue to splash shells about the positions won last week east of Messines Ridge," says The Associated Press correspondent at the front, "they have attempted no further counterattack. On the other hand, the British, having thoroughly consolidatd the new line running due north and south, well east of Oostaverne, are further securing their new ground by pushing patrols well forward. Thus far they have met with comparatively little resistance from the enemy, who appears to be undecided whether to make a further stand or to fall completely back to his Warneton line. The British are pressing toward this town.

"Most of the artillery firing comes from long-range guns. Seven field guns were captured late yesterday. Information reaching the British indicates temporary disorganization of the German forces, or at least nervousness regarding their position between the converging Ypres-Comines Canal and the River Lys."

The text of tonight's communication says:

Our troops gained further ground today east and northeast of Messines on a front of nearly two miles and occupied the hamlet of Gaspard.

We also advanced our line slightly early this morning astride the Souchez River, and captured seventeen prisoners and three machine guns.

The enemy's artillery has shown considerable activity during the day northeast of Gouzeaucourt and north of the Scarpe, and in the neighborhood of Lens and Ypres.

Our airplanes were active yesterday. Although weather conditions were not favorable much useful work was accomplished. One of our machines is missing.

The early statement reads:

We successfully raided the enemy's trenches last night north of Neuve Chapelle and took thirteen prisoners. Hostile raiding parties were repulsed south of Neuve-Chapelle, east of Armentières and north of Ypres. A number of the enemy were killed and we captured a few prisoners.

A dispatch from the Associated Press correspondent at the front says:

"General Haig has issued a special order of the day congratulating General Plumer and the entire Second Army which he commands, and saying that the complete success of their attack last Thursday is 'an earnest of the eventual final victory of the Allied cause.' General Haig emphasizes the fact that the position assaulted was 'one of very great natural strength, on the defenses of which the enemy had labored incessantly for nearly three years,' and says the British casualties for a battle of such magnitude were gratifyingly light.

"The full effect of the victory cannot be estimated yet, but that they will be very great is certain. After detailing the advantage which the Germans had in possessing the ridge, which gave them foreknowledge of and time to prepare for the British attack, General Haig declares that the capture of Messines shows 'nothing can save the enemy from complete defeat, and, brave and tenacious as the German troops are, it is only a question how much longer they can endure the repetition of such blows.'

"The total number of prisoners taken by the Canadians in their record-breaking raid last week was 168, including four officers."

English Cavalry "Decimated."

BERLIN, June 12, (via London.)—English cavalry yesterday advanced against the German lines east of Messines on the Belgian front, but only remnants returned, says the German War Office statement today.

During the month of May the Germans lost seventy-nine airplanes while the Entente Allies lost 262 machines, says the official statement issued today by the German Army Headquarters Staff. The statement says that 114 Entente airplanes fell behind the German lines and 140 British and French machines were forced down within the Entente positions.

The text of the official statement reads:

Army Group of Crown Prince Rupprecht: In Flanders the artillery activity near Ypres and south of the Douve increased during the evening. During the afternoon British cavalry advanced against our lines east of Messines. Only remnants returned. South of Messines the attacking infantry was repulsed by a counterattack.

The firing activity was lively in Artois, especially in the Lens salient and south of the Scarpe Valley. Near Fromelles, Neuve Chappelle, and Arleux, British reconnoitring detachments were repulsed.

Army Group of the German Crown Prince: The French yesterday made five counterattacks against the trenches occupied by us west of Cerny on June 10. All failed with heavy losses either under our fire or in hand-to-hand fighting. Only north of Vailly and on the Winterberg did the artillery duel attain greater intensity, and this was limited in duration. In eastern Champagne, French reconnoitring thrusts near Tahure and Vauquois failed.

Army Group of Duke Albrecht.—There is nothing to report.

In the largely increased aerial activity during the month of May the Flying Corps has achieved great success in the execution of its manifold duties. Among those who especially distinguished themselves, in addition to the battle airmen and the infantry airmen, were those indispensable artillery airmen, who, admirably supplemented by observation officers in captive balloons, directed our fire and observation services.

In the west, the east, and the Balkans we lost 79 airplanes and 9 captive balloons. Of the enemy airplanes shot down 114 were behind our lines, while 148 were seen to fall beyond enemy positions.

The official communication issued by the War Office this evening says:

Southwest of Lens British attacks failed in fighting at close range.

Gun Duels On the French Front.

PARIS, June 12.—Artillery fighting continued throughout the day on the whole French front, of particular violence at the eastern end of the Chemin des Dames and in Western Champagne. Trench raids were carried out at various points, the War Office reports.

The New York Times.

"All the News That's Fit to Print."

THE WEATHER

Probably fair today; Friday thunder storms; moderate west winds.

VOL. LXVI...NO. 21,706.   NEW YORK, THURSDAY, JUNE 28, 1917.—TWENTY-TWO PAGES.

ONE CENT In Greater New York. | TWO CENTS Elsewhere N. Y. State, N. J., Conn. | THREE CENTS Other Makes.

FIRST AMERICAN TROOPS REACH FRANCE, SETTING RECORD FOR QUICK MOVEMENT; FRANTIC CROWDS CHEER THEIR LANDING

GEN. SIBERT IN COMMAND

Force, Arriving in Two Contingents, Moves to Its Camp.

SEAPORT DECKED IN FLAGS

All Troops in Excellent Shape and Enthusiastic Over the Successful Trip.

CONVOYED IN DANGER ZONE

Pershing Will Join Expedition Today—Its Place at the Front Not Known.

A FRENCH SEAPORT, June 27.—The second contingent of American troops arrived and disembarked this morning.

The troops landed amid the frantic cheers of the people, who had gathered for hours before in anticipation of duplicating yesterday's surprise.

Enthusiasm rose to fever pitch when it was learned that the transports and convoys had successfully passed the submarine zone. The port was speedily beflagged in honor of the occasion.

All the troops now arrived were transferred today to a camp not distant from this point, where Major Gen. William L. Sibert is installed. Thence they probably will go soon to a point near the front. All the troops are in excellent shape, enthusiastic over the successful trip and their reception, and eager for action.

Major Gen. Pershing, the American commander, is expected tomorrow.

The harbor is dotted with convoys. The streets are filled with soldiers in khaki and with bluejackets.

Great numbers of trucks are transporting immense supplies to the camp in which the troops are concentrating.

First of the Mighty Army.

WASHINGTON, June 27.—The advance guard of the mighty army the United States is preparing to send against Germany is on French soil tonight. In defiance of the German submarines, thousands of seasoned regulars

125 American Airplane Experts Reach England; Units of Lumbermen Also There to Begin War Work

Special to The New York Times.

WASHINGTON, June 27.—The Aircraft Production Board announced today the safe arrival at a British port of a group of nearly 125 experts, sent from this country to acquire and bring back to the United States all possible information regarding aircraft designing and the manufacture of both engines and planes. In the delegation are men representing legal, manufacturing, designing, engineering, military, and naval experience and training.

It will be the duty of this group to gather and bring to America as soon as possible the latest information regarding European aircraft development, which can then be easily made available for American manufacturers. Arrangements have been made through the allied Governments for placing expert American mechanics in the European aircraft plants in whose products the United States is interested.

The National Advisory Committee for Aeronautics and the Aircraft Production Board has made plans for a permanent exhibit of aircraft materials of all kinds, to be established in Washington for the benefit of army and navy engineers and American manufacturers. A building to house the exhibit is being constructed by the Government south of the Smithsonian Institute.

"The Aircraft Production Board has no illusions as to the size and character of the job before it," a statement issued by the board today, says, "but the whole task is one of industrial organization for quantity production, and in this we Americans are above all other nations fitted by experience and tradition to break records."

LONDON, June 27.—Ten units of American Woodmen sent over by New England States and organizations to turn various forests of the United Kingdom into lumber have arrived on English soil.

The complete equipment of the units caused much surprise and occasioned a great deal of favorable comment. The woodmen not only brought with them the necessary machinery, but were fully equipped in every way, even to lubricating oils. Their arrival found them ready to establish their sawmills and begin work at once. The only necessity for their maintenance is raw food, which their own cooks will prepare.

and marines, trained fighting men with the tan of long service on the Mexican border, or in Haiti or Santo Domingo, still on their faces, have been hastened overseas to fight beside the French, the British, the Belgian, the Russian, the Portuguese, and the Italian troops on the western front.

News of the safe arrival of the troops sent a new thrill through Washington. No formal announcement was made at the War Department. None will be made, probably, until Major Gen. Pershing's official report has been received. Then there may be a statement as to the numbers and composition of the advance guard.

Press dispatches from France, presumably sent forward with the approval of General Pershing's staff, show that Maj. Gen. Sibert, one of the new Major Generals of the army, has been chosen to command the first force sent abroad, under General Pershing as commander in chief of the expedition.

One thing stands out sharply, despite the fact that the size of the task that has been accomplished is not fully revealed as yet. This is that American enterprise has set a new record for the transportation of troops.

Expedition Sets a Record.

Considering the distance to be covered and the fact that all preparations had

to be made after the order came from the White House, the night of May 18, it is practically certain that never before has a military expedition of this size been assembled, conveyed, and landed without mishap in so short a time by any nation. It is a good augury of future achievements. The only rival in magnitude is the movement of British troops to South Africa in the Boer war, and that was made overseas that were unhampered by submarines, mines, or other obstacles.

The American forces will be a net gain to the Allies. It will throw no single burden of supply or equipment upon them. The troops will be fed, clothed, armed, and equipped by the United States. Around them at the camp on French soil tonight are being stored supplies that will keep them going for months.

General Pershing and his staff have been busy for days preparing for the arrival of the men. Despite the enormous difficulties of unpreparedness and submarine dangers that faced them, the plans of the Army General Staff have gone through with clocklike precision.

When the order came to prepare immediately an expeditionary force to go to France, virtually all of the men now across the seas were on the Mexican border. General Pershing himself was at his headquarters in San Antonio.

There were no army transports available in the Atlantic. The vessels that carried the troops were scattered on their usual routes. Army reserve stores were still depleted from the border mobilization. Regiments were below war strength.

Organizing Pershing's Forces.

That was the condition when President Wilson decided that the plea of the French High Commission should be answered and a force of regulars sent at once to France. At this word the War Department began to move. General Pershing was summoned quietly to Washington. His arrival caused some speculation, but at the request of Secretary Baker the newspapers generally refrained from discussion of the matter.

There were a thousand other activities afoot in the department at the time—all the business of preparing for the military registration of 10,000,000, of providing quarters and instructors for nearly 50,000 prospective officers, of finding arms and equipment for millions of troops yet to be organized, of expanding the regular army to full war strength, of preparing and recruiting the National Guard for war.

General Pershing dropped quietly into the department and set up the first headquarters of the American expeditionary forces in a little office, hardly large enough to hold himself and his personal staff. There, with the aid of the General Staff, of Secretary Baker and the Chiefs of the War Department Bureaus, the plans were worked out.

Announcement that the force under General Pershing would be sent was made May 18. There came a day when General Pershing was no longer in the department. Officers of the General Staff suddenly were missing from their desks. No word of this was reported. Then came word from England that Pershing and his officers were there. All was carried through without publicity.

Not a Word of Publicity.

Other matters relating to the expedition were carried out without a word of publicity. The regiments that were to go with General Pershing were all selected before he left and moving toward the sea coast from the border. Other regiments also were moving north, east, and west to the points where they were to be expanded, and the movements of the troops who were to be first were obscured in all this hurrying of troop trains over the land.

Great shipments of war supplies began to assemble at the embarkation ports. A great armada was made ready, supplied, equipped as transports, loaded with men and guns and sent to sea, and all with virtually no mention from the press.

The navy bears its full share in the achievement. From the time the troop ships left their docks and headed toward sea, responsibility for the lives of their thousands of men rested upon the officers and crews of the fighting ships that moved beside them or swept free the sea lanes before them. As they pushed on through the days and nights toward the danger zone where German submarines lay in wait, every precaution that trained minds of the navy could devise was taken. And the news from France today shows that the plans were well laid.

While his troops were embarking or steaming toward their destination, General Pershing and his staff, supplemented by a special corps of General Staff officers, have been busy in France preparing the way for the new army that is to fling itself soon against the German lines. The camp sites have been selected. The details of the final training to be given before the move to the front begins have been worked out, and the question of supply and transportation lines has been studied. Regiments of the national army, composed of railway workers and engineers, will aid in that work. They, too, have been created in a few weeks' time.

Disposition of the Troops.

The War Department has no announcement to make as to General Pershing's disposition of his forces. Presumably that has been left to him to decide in conference with the French General Staff and officials of the British Army.

The reference in the cable dispatches to a duplication of "yesterday's surprise," intimating that there was also a landing yesterday, passed without comment here, but obviously disclosed a landing of a contingent not recorded in yesterday's dispatches.

General Pershing's men will operate under his supreme command, not under that of the French Generalissimo, or of General Haig, the ranking British commander on the western front. No official announcement of the instructions

The fist American troops land in France to the cheers of the French citizens.

given to General Pershing has been made public, but it is definitely understood that his forces will maintain their own separate line of supplies and communications from the United States. The Americans will operate with the British and French, but this co-operation, it is understood, will not in any way affect the independent character of the command.

Elaborate preparations have been made by the Government for handling of the great volume of mail that will pass between the troops of America's expeditionary forces and home. Postmaster General Burleson announced tonight the appointment of Marcus H. Bunn of the department force here as United States Army postal agent in Europe.

Rates on army mail to and from France have been reduced by the department, so that the cost is the same as for mail between points in this country. Branch and mobile post offices will be established in the field for delivery and receipt of mail, the sale of stamps, and the issuance of money orders.

United States postage stamps will alone be valid for the prepayment of postage on mail for the troops. All letters should be addressed to the division, regiment, company, and organization to which the addressee belongs, but designation of the location of the unit will not be permitted.

FRANCE'S EXPENSES MOUNT.

Nearly Two Billion Dollars Needed for Third Quarter of 1917.

PARIS, June 27.—France will require for the third quarter's expenses $1,968,-000,000, or about $43,600,000 more than for the second quarter of 1917, making total appropriations for thirty-eight months of $19,766,400,000.

These are the totals which will be submitted to the Senate tomorrow by M. Millies-Lacroix, General Reporter of the Appropriations Committee. He is authority for the statement that more than 20 per cent. of the appropriations already made have not been disbursed, although they have been allocated. Upward of $1,200,000,000 of the total has been advanced to France's allies.

MOVES TO INSURE MEN SENT TO WAR

Secretary McAdoo Summons Representatives of Life Companies to a Conference.

WOULD SET A PRECEDENT

Federal Bureau May Undertake Task, or Government May Supplement Private Concerns.

Special to The New York Times.

WASHINGTON, D. C., June 27.—Government life insurance for the officers and men of the United States Army and Navy who serve in France will be discussed at a conference of life insurance experts to be held at the office of Secretary McAdoo here July 2.

The Secretary signed a call today on the leading life insurance companies doing business in the United States to send representatives to the meeting. This action was taken to overcome a condition about which there has been much complaint. It has been found practically impossible for men who expect to go to the firing line to get insurance. Old line companies decline to write such risks owing to the hazard due to submarines and the intensive trench fighting that marks the military operations in Europe.

Hitherto there has been only comparative difficulty in getting insurance for officers and men in the regular army or navy. Rates have not been considered unduly high, and but for the inconvenience of the rule that permits must be obtained for service in tropical countries army men have fared reasonably well at the hands of the insurance companies. In addition to the opportunity to take out insurance for the benefit of families of army and navy men there has been for the last ten years the further advantage of the benefit system maintained by the Government which officers and men are entitled, in case of death in the line of duty, to a payment to their designated beneficiaries of an amount equal to half their yearly pay at the time of death. It is not proposed to alter or repeal the benefit law, in arranging new insurance.

"The war risk insurance bureau of the Treasury Department," said Secretary McAdoo, "is insuring the lives of masters, officers, and seamen of the merchant marine of the United States, and the question has arisen as to how insurance on the lives of the officers and enlisted men of the army and navy can be effected most advantageously, through an extension of the powers of the war risk insurance bureau or through the combined agency or co-operation of the life insurance companies of the United States. It is expected that the discussion at the coming conference will prove of great value in determining the wisest policy to be adopted.

"This is a great problem, and it appeals immediately and instinctively to the highest thought and purpose of the country. Certainly everything possible should be done to give protection to those who are dependent upon the men who give their lives for their country, and to ameliorate the rigors and horrors of war. No organized effort has ever been made by any Government to provide this sort of protection and comforting assurance to its fighting men. Why should not America take the lead in this noble and humane action?

"I earnestly hope that as a result of the measures thus intimated a great system of insurance will be devised which will give to every officer, soldier, and sailor in the service of the United States the assurance that some provision is made for the loved ones he leaves behind if he is called upon to make the greatest sacrifice that a patriot can make for his country."

"All the News That's Fit to Print."

The New York Times.

THE WEATHER
Fair today and Sunday; warmer Sunday; moderate southwest winds.
For full weather report see Page 17.

VOL. LXVI...NO. 21,728. ....   NEW YORK, SATURDAY, JULY 21, 1917.—EIGHTEEN PAGES.   ONE CENT In Greater New York. | TWO CENTS Elsewhere N. Y. State, N. J., Conn. | THREE CENTS Other Cities

DRAWING FOR NATION'S DRAFT ARMY ENDS AT 2:18 A. M. AFTER 16½ HOURS; MISSING CITY LISTS CAUSE WORRY

BAKER OPENS CEREMONIES

Blindfolded, He Takes "258" as First Number; One Blank Found.

SOLEMN SCENE IN CAPITOL

Army Officers, Congressmen, and Other Officials Watch the Huge Glass Bowl.

RIGID PRECAUTIONS TAKEN

Triple-Check System Employed and Numbers on Blackboard Are Photographed.

Special to The New York Times.

WASHINGTON, July 21.—In a room in the Senate Office Building the Government yesterday began the greatest lottery in history to select the men who will be called first in the drafting of an army to go to France.

At 2:18 o'clock, sixteen and a half hours after the first number was drawn, the lottery was completed. The 9,000th number was called out at midnight, and thereafter the drawing proceeded rapidly. At 1 o'clock the tellers reached the last thousand capsules. Serial No. 2 was drawn at exactly 2 o'clock, and the last capsule was opened eighteen minutes later.

The final number was 3,217, and it was the 10,499th number drawn. There should have been 10,500, but one capsule, the 10,004th, when opened contained only a blank without any figure on it.

For a while it was undecided whether to mark the 10,004th place " Blank " or to proceed as if there had been no blank and make notes of the fact. The latter course was followed.

The next number drawn after the blank was 5,699, and this received the 10,004th place. The tellers were instructed to note on their tally sheets that a blank had been drawn at this point.

It was hoped that it would turn out that one extra capsule had dropped in containing a blank. But this hope did not materialize. As the drawing closed with the 10,500th place designated as a blank, it will now be necessary to check up the entire list of numbers carefully to locate the number that should have been on the blank.

There were 10,500 capsules in the glass container when Secretary of War Baker drew out the first at 9:49 o'clock yesterday morning. As the Secretary, following a brief address on the dignity and solemnity of the occasion, drew 258 as the first number in all the registration districts throughout the country, a scene of unusual dramatic appeal came to its climax. Mr. Baker was blindfolded and led to the large glass jar. He reached within deliberately, held a capsule in plain view of a distinguished audience and said:

" I have drawn the first number."

The First Number.

A clerk assigned by the War Department opened the capsule and announced " 258." An officer seated at the long table upon which were spread the tally sheets repeated the number, and another clerk walked to a large blackboard at the rear and wrote upon it the figures.

Simultaneously there came the clicking of moving picture cameras and the noise of the shutters in the " still picture " cameras. Dozens of newspaper correspondents, stationed at a long table, rustled copy paper and messengers darted toward waiting telegraph instruments which flashed the first result of the lottery to the country.

Senator Chamberlain of Oregon, likewise blindfolded, drew the second number. He was plainly nervous. His hand was guided at the top of the jar, which was fourteen inches in diameter.

" The second number is 2,522," said the announcer, and again there came the click of cameras, the rustle of copy paper, and the murmur of excited men and women who thronged the committee room.

Members of Congress and high officials of the army attended the start of the drawing. Eight numbers were drawn by officials before the ceremony became routine, with students from various universities acting as the blindfolded withdrawers of the fateful capsules.

THOUSANDS LEFT IN DOUBT

Men Stand in Line All Night Here to Find Numbers.

Hundreds of thousands of New Yorkers subject to military duty under the selective draft law waded through column after column of figures yesterday to discover what their position was as the numbers were drawn. Every edition of the afternoon newspapers was eagerly bought, and crowds about the news ticker machines listened eagerly as the man nearest the tape shouted out the numbers. Meanwhile every newspaper office in the city was a bureau of information to which anxious thousands telephoned to find out if some one young man was among the first few hundred numbers.

A more orderly day New York has never known. Not one unpleasant incident due to the momentous happenings in Washington was reported from any part of the city. The fact that many local exemption boards had failed to finish their alphabetically arranged lists with the serial red numbers caused much irritation, but in no instance did that lead to disorder.

Thousands of men in New York have been unable to find their serial number, and thus have no way of knowing their fate because those boards failed to post the lists yesterday. All day complaints from men who wanted to know why they could not find out what their numbers were reached the offices of the Mayor's Committee on National Defense. Roscoe Conkling, representing the State, and Philip J. McCook, representing the city, assured the complainants that they expected every board in the city to have its public list ready for inspection by noon today.

The thousands who gathered at the headquarters of the exemption boards took the situation seriously, and, in the great majority of cases, in a most patriotic spirit. Men studied the long columns of figures in a matter of fact way, but every now and then some young chap would strike his companion on the shoulder and say: " That's me," or " There's my number." If he found it among the first few hundred one would sometimes hear: " Its France for me." The man who apparently did not relish fighting for his country kept very quiet.

In a few of the congested sections of the city, where the population, to a great extent, is foreign in origin, there was some excitement due to the efforts of men to get into the headquarters and find out their numbers. In a few of these districts the lists of eligibles was sent to the police stations, where Sergeants of Police read out the names and numbers to the waiting crowds.

Mr. Conkling, when asked if there was a chance that some person might tamper with the duplicate, or public, copies of those lists which had not been completed when the drawing of the numbers began in Washington, laid special emphasis on the fact that all cards and lists of men who registered under the Selective Draft act have been protected against any tampering with the numbers since the beginning of the drawing in Washington and for several hours before it began.

" I know absolutely," Mr. Conkling said, " that persons representing this office were on the ground in every district where the duplicating and numbering of cards and the compilation of the serially numbered lists were delayed, and that the lists and cards in every one of these districts were protected."

These volunteers are on their way to Camp Dix in New Jersey for induction into the United States Army.

"All the News That's Fit to Print."

The New York Times.

THE WEATHER

VOL. LXVI...NO. 21,751.   NEW YORK, TUESDAY, JULY 24, 1917.—TWENTY PAGES.   TWO CENTS

KERENSKY MADE DICTATOR OF RUSSIA; COUNCILS, FEARING COUNTER REVOLT, APPEAL TO ARMY TO SAVE COUNTRY

ALARMED BY ARMY'S ROUT

Commanders Give Orders to Fire on Mutinous or Retreating Troops.

LENINITES TO BE SEIZED

Two Executive Committeemen of Council and Admiral of Baltic Fleet Arrested.

WORKMEN BEING DISARMED

Crowds in Petrograd Kill Revolutionists Who Start Shooting Affrays.

PETROGRAD, July 23. — Unlimited power for the re-establishment of public order, both at the front and at home, were voted to the Government of Premier Kerensky today by the Council of Workmen's and Soldiers' Delegates and the Council of Delegates of the Peasants of All Russia at a joint sitting.

The Cabinet is designated as the Government of National Safety.

Orders have been given to fire on deserters and runaways at the front, and warrants have been issued for the arrest of revolutionary agitators wherever they may be. Rear Admiral Verderevski, commander of the Baltic fleet, has been seized for communicating a secret Government telegram to sailors' committees. Lieutenant Dashkevitch and another executive committeeman of the Workmen's and Soldiers' Council have been arrested, the former on the charge of inciting the Peterhof troops to remove the Provisional Government.

The decision of the councils to resort to the extreme measure of conferring supreme and unrestricted power on the Government was reached after a session that lasted throughout the night and was embodied in the following resolution, which was passed by 252 to 37:

Recognizing that the country is menaced by a military débâcle on the front and by anarchy at home it is resolved:

First—That the country and the revolution are endangered;

Second—That the Provisional Government is proclaimed the Government of National Safety;

Third—That unlimited powers are accorded the Government for re-establishing the organization and discipline of the army for a fight to the finish against the enemies of public order and for the realization of the whole program embodied in the governmental program just announced.

There are indications that the Workmen's and Soldiers' Council, after the events of the past week and all circumstances connected therewith, are apprehensive of a counter-revolution. The Central Committee has issued a manifesto calling local organizations of the revolutionary democracy and army to be ready at any moment to rally round their political centres, namely, the Councils of the Workmen's and Soldiers.

The chaotic conditions prevailing on part of the Russian front were disclosed in a telegram sent to Premier Kerensky, the Provisional Government and the Council of Workmen's and Soldiers' Delegates by the Executive Committee and the Commissioner of the Provisional Government with the Second Army, on the southwestern front. The telegram announced the inauguration of stern measures to combat disaffection.

"We unanimously recognize that the situation demands extreme measures and efforts, for everything must be risked to save the revolution from 'catastrophe,' the message reads. "The

Councils Warn Army No Mercy Will Be Shown By the Government to Traitors and Cowards

PETROGRAD, July 23.—The Executive Councils of the All-Russia Workmen's and Soldiers' and Peasants' organizations have issued the following proclamation:

Fellow-Soldiers: One of our armies has wavered, its regiments have fled before the enemy. Part of our front has been broken. Emperor William's hordes, which have moved forward, are bringing with them death and destruction.

Who is responsible for this humiliation? The responsibility rests with those who have spread discord in the army and shaken its discipline, with those who at a time of danger disobeyed the military commands and wasted time in fruitless discussions and disputes.

Many of those who left the line and sought safety in running away paid with their lives for having disobeyed orders. The enemy's fire mowed them down. If this costly lesson has taught you nothing, then there will be no salvation for Russia.

Enough of words. The time has come to act without hesitation. We have acknowledged the Provisional Government. With the Government lies the salvation of the revolution. We have acknowledged its unlimited authority and its unlimited power. Its commands must be law. All those who disobey the commands of the Provisional Government in battle will be regarded as traitors. Toward traitors and cowards no mercy will be shown.

Fellow-soldiers: You want a durable peace. You want your land, your freedom. Then you must know that only by a stubborn struggle will you win peace for Russia and all nations. Yielding before the troops of the German Emperor you lose both your land and your freedom. The conquering, imperialistic Germans will force you again and again to fight for your interests.

Fellow-soldiers at the front: Let there be no traitors or cowards among you. Let not one of you retreat a single step before the foe. Only one way is open for you—the way forward.

Fellow-soldiers in the rear: Be ready to advance to the front for the support of your brothers, abandoned and betrayed, fleeing from their positions in the regiments. Gather all your strength for the struggle for a durable peace, for your land and your freedom. Without wavering, without fear, without disastrous discussions, carry out all military commands. At the time of battle disobedience and wavering are worse than treachery. Your ruin lies in them, the ruin of Russia.

Fellow-soldiers: You are being watched by those who work for Russia and by the whole world. The ruin of the Russian revolution spells ruin for all. Summon up all your manhood, your perseverance and sense of discipline and save the fatherland.

Commander in Chief on the western front and the commander of the Second Army today have given orders to fire on deserters and runaways.

"Let the country know the truth. Let it act without mercy. Let it find enough courage to strike those who by their cowardice are destroying Russia and the revolution.

"Most military units are in a state of complete disorganization. Their spirit for the offensive has utterly disappeared. They no longer listen to orders of their leaders, and they neglect all exhortations of comrades, even replying by threats and shots. Some elements voluntarily evacuate positions without even waiting for the approach of the enemy.

"Cases are on record in which an order given to proceed with all haste to such and such a spot to assist comrades in distress has been discussed for several hours at meeting, and reinforcements consequently have been delayed several hours.

"These troops abandon their positions at the first shots of the enemy. For a distance of several hundred versts long

ENGLAND'S COSTLY MEDICAL BLUNDERS

Aged Volunteers Accepted and Unwilling Youth Rejected Three Years Ago.

"REJECTED" SLIPS SOLD

Many Old Men Drew Pensions After Few Months' Service When Medical Boards Were Reorganized.

By EDMUND YARE.

In the first great rush to the colors in England at the beginning of the war were single men and married men of all ages and varying degrees of physical fitness and domestic responsibilities. The voluntary system was to have a long trial, and eventually to be abandoned and conscription adopted. As a manifestation of the patriotism of a nation it was a triumphant success. It raised an army of 5,000,000 volunteers, which was what no country had done before.

But as a means of obtaining the best of the fighting material in the country in the most economical way it was a great and costly failure.

Vast numbers of unfit were passed into the army, together with elderly men who could not stand the strain of active service in the field, and married men with large families who had to be supported by the State, while a large number of the youth of the country physically fit with no responsibilities were untouched.

The great mistake of those early days was the perfunctory medical examinations. The doctors were overworked and had no time to do their work properly, and there was every inducement to pass the recruits through as quickly as possible.

In some instances the men merely bared their chests and the medical men sometimes sounded the heart and sometimes they did not, and within a minute the man was either passed as perfectly sound or totally rejected. If he was accepted he was sworn in and he joined up almost immediately. If he was rejected he was merely given a slip of paper with the word "rejected" stamped upon it—nothing else, not even his name and address, the signature of the doctor or the recruiting officer, or the date. Subsequently scraps of paper like these changed hands for considerable sums until the authorities were obliged to refuse to recognize the legality of any paper unless it bore the name of the recruiting officer and was properly drawn up and dated and signed.

Doctors Aided Slackers.

These cursory examinations did not have the effect one would have expected of roping in all the fit as well as many of the unfit. The strange thing was that while epileptics, consumptives, the one-eyed, the deaf, even those in advanced stages of heart disease, were certified as fit, an enormous number of men suffering from the most trifling ailments were given certificates of rejection—men who complained of nervous troubles, a varicose vein in the foot, or a mild form of hernia.

There was undoubtedly some bribery and corruption and also some of the more kindly disposed doctors were ready to reject men who did not want to be soldiers, but were anxious to be in a position to refute the accusation of "shirker." Also a great number of the men who were rejected for minor defects, while they may not have been fit for the firing line, were fit enough for labor on the lines of communication, and would have been able to release for the trenches thousands of perfectly fit men who were engaged on this noncombatant work.

files of deserters, armed and unarmed, men in good health and robust, who have lost all shame and feel they can act altogether with impunity, are proceeding to the rear. Frequently entire units desert in this manner."

"All the News That's Fit to Print."

The New York Times.

THE WEATHER
Fair today; fair, cooler tomorrow; light northwesterly winds.

VOL. LXVI...NO. 21,755. ...   NEW YORK, FRIDAY, AUGUST 17, 1917.—TWENTY PAGES.   ONE CENT In Greater New York. | TWO CENTS Elsewhere N.Y. State, N.J. Conn. | THREE CENTS Other States.

ALLIES SWEEP FORWARD IN FLANDERS; WIN LANGEMARCK, BEGIN NEW ADVANCE; 1,800 PRISONERS AND HEAVY GUNS TAKEN

STRIKE ON A 9-MILE FRONT

French On the Left and British Centre Win Much Ground.

RIGHT GAINS, THEN LOSES

MORE FIGHTING NEAR LENS

Canadians Withstand Ten Furious Assaults — Nearly 900 Prisoners Taken There.

LONDON, Aug. 16.—Striking together on a nine-mile front east and northeast of Ypres in Flanders early this morning, British and French troops carried all their objectives except on the right flank, and tonight unofficial advices say that a new advance was ordered this afternoon.

The French, on the left, drove the Germans from the tongue of land between the Yser Canal and the Martjevaart and captured the bridgehead of Dreigrachten.

In the centre Haig's troops captured the village of Langemarck, which has been held strongly by the Germans ever since the allied attack of early this month, and pushed half a mile beyond. The Reuter correspondent at British headquarters reports tonight that fighting is proceeding well beyond the town.

On the right British troops attempted to seize the high ground almost directly east of Ypres, which lies north of the road to Menin. They swept up and gained the ground, but in the face of terrific losses the Germans attacked with great fury, and finally pressed the British back from the terrain they had won.

More than 1,800 prisoners, including thirty-eight officers, already have been counted by the Anglo-French forces. Some German guns have been taken.

In addition to the successes won in the Ypres sector the British have made further progress east of Loos and north of Lens. Severe fighting has been going on there ever since the Canadians won Hill 70 yesterday morning, but the repeated German assaults have been futile.

Official Account of Progress.

The night bulletin of the British War Office gives this account of the day's events:

The allied attacks, delivered early in the morning on a front of nine miles north of the Ypres-Menin road, have been continued during the day in the face of strong enemy resistance.

On the left the French troops, advancing on both sides of the Zuydschoote-Dixmude road, drove the enemy from the tongue of land between the Yser Canal and the Martjevaart and captured the bridgehead of Dreigrachten.

In the centre the British troops rapidly captured their first objectives, and, continuing their advance, carried the village of Langemarck after heavy fighting. They then forced their way forward a distance of half a mile beyond the village and established themselves in the German trench system, which constituted their final objective for the day.

On our right there has been fierce and continuous fighting since the early morning for the possession of the high ground north of the Menin Road. The enemy disputed our advance with determination, counterattacking with large forces. As the result of the counterattacks the enemy succeeded during the afternoon, at great cost, in pressing back our troops in this area from part of the ground won earlier in the day. This evening further enemy counterattacks in this neighborhood were broken up by our artillery fire.

The number of prisoners taken by the Allies in the course of this attack cannot yet be ascertained, but over 1,800, including 58 officers, already have been brought in. A few German guns also were captured.

Our troops made further progress this afternoon east of Loos. The number of troops we captured on this front since the opening of our attack yesterday has now reached a total of 896, including 22 officers.

Throughout yesterday's attack our airplanes co-operated successfully with the artillery and assisted effectively with machine gunfire in repelling the enemy's counterattacks. In the air fighting eleven German airplanes were brought down and four others were driven down out of control. Another was brought down by anti-aircraft fire. Three of our airplanes are missing. Today also our aircraft has done excellent work.

The early bulletin telling of the opening of the attack reads:

At 4:45 o'clock this morning the allied troops again attacked on a wide front east and north of Ypres.

Heavy fighting is taking place, but progress is being made at all points in spite of the stubborn resistance of the enemy.

On the Lens battle front three more counter attacks made by the enemy last night against our positions were repulsed. A hostile concentration in the neighborhood of Cité St. Auguste was broken up by our artillery.

The day report of the French operations as issued by the French War Office reads:

In Belgium, after violent and most thorough artillery preparation, we made an attack at dawn this morning in conjunction with the British army on our right.

With superb spirit our infantry made the assault on the enemy positions on both sides of the road between Steenstraete and Dixmude, capturing all objectives and crossing the Steenbeck. Our troops are making progress on the right bank in contact with our allies.

The Associated Press correspondent on the British front telegraphs describing the situation on the battle line at 4 o'clock this afternoon, stating that no more than a general idea can be given because "a signal was given a few hours ago for an advance." He says:

"From Dreigrachten, which the French occupied with little resistance, southward, the French pushed their positions forward to the edge of the flooded area along the left bank of the St. Jansbeek River, and on the right bank they surged across the Steenbeck, which is a continuation of the St. Jansbeek, and occupied German positions to an extreme depth of about 1,000 yards.

"At the same time the British advanced on the right of the French and occupied considerable territory in the region of St. Julien and Langemarck. Apparently Langemarck Village itself is firmly in the hands of the Allies.

Fighting Is Very Heavy.

"Further south the British had pushed forward at various points as far down the salient as the country west of the Polygon Wood. In all this region heavy fighting was in progress, especially in the vicinity of the Polygon Wood and the neighboring forests.

"At this time it is impossible to give more than a general idea of the events that are transpiring, since a signal was given a few hours ago for an advance.

There is little doubt, however, that the German troops engaged have been dealt a heavy blow, and that the British have made appreciable advances at many points in this difficult territory.

"The preliminary bombardment by the British artillery worked havoc in the German ranks, according to prisoners. All night the heavy guns poured a steady stream of shells into the small forts and the fortified farms in which the Germans had established machine gun squads, and many of their defenses were wiped out or made untenable.

"About Langemarck, where heavy fighting took place, the Seventeenth Reserve Division of the Prussians suffered severely from the bombardment.

"The barrage which the British artillery dropped before the infantry for the advance was perfect. The German guns pounded away valiantly, but their fire was not effective and the British troops suffered little as they pushed forward.

"In the Langemarck region the main difficulty encountered was the mud in the approaches to the town, and into this bog the infantry plunged deep at every step. Not infrequently the soldiers had to extricate a comrade who had sunk to the waist in the morass, but they continued to push forward steadily, facing machine gun fire from hidden redoubts and battling their way past with bombs and rifle fire.

"Thus the British came to Langemarck. There were concrete gunpits about the position in front of the town, which was flooded from the Steenbeck River, but the infantry divided and bombed their way about either side of the town. As they passed to the further side the Germans could be seen running away, and little resistance was offered in the town itself. The fighting still continues beyond Langemarck, according to the latest reports.

French Pushed Ahead Half a Mile.

The French attack began simultaneously with the British advance and the contact between the allied armies was excellent throughout. The French completed the task mapped out for them in about one hour. The extreme depth which they penetrated into the German territory was over 1,000 yards.

The terrain over which the French advanced was most difficult for on their right the Steenbeck River was in flood and on their left they were moving toward an inundated area, and the ground was becoming marshier all the time. The German defenses in this inhospitable zone consisted chiefly of fortified machine gun positions. These, however, were accounted for largely in the preliminary bombardment. The French met little resistance, and the operation was carried out with few casualties.

The movement of heavy guns and equipment on the front in Flanders was especially difficult, due to the marshy terrain.

WILSON EXPECTED TO SOUND ALLIES AFTER STUDYING POPE'S PEACE NOTE; NO HOPE OF ACCEPTANCE IS SEEN

DEEP DISTRUST OF BERLIN

Special to The New York Times.

WASHINGTON, Aug. 16.—The receipt by this Government of the official text of Pope Benedict's peace note has not changed in any way the situation as it is understood to exist in this and other capitals of the nations engaged in fighting the Prussian autocracy.

Nobody is authorized to represent the views of President Wilson and Secretary Lansing, and nothing has been officially disclosed as to the attitude of the Entente Governments toward the Pope's move, but opinion in Washington official circles and among the diplomatic agents of the Entente is generally to the effect that the proposal of the Pope cannot be accepted in the absence of assurance from Germany of willingness to make redress for the wrongs she has committed and to furnish satisfactory guarantees for the future.

It was only today that the State Department received the official text of the Pope's communication, which had been transmitted by the Papal Secretary of State to King George and handed by the London Foreign Office to the American Ambassador to Great Britain, who cabled it to Washington.

Deny Equal Responsibility.

The allied nations, it is gathered, will never be willing to admit that they had an equal responsibility with Austria and Germany for starting the war. One impression that gained supporters today was that the note after all will be an advantage to the Governments at war with Germany in that it will afford them the opportunity to make statements that will clear all misunderstanding as to the fundamental issues of the war and allow them to express with the greatest clearness an outline of the terms upon which they will insist in the adjustment of the issues that are being fought out on the battlefields of Europe.

One rather interesting view expressed in a diplomatic quarter was that every nation that is opposing Germany had some distinct and separate reason for declining to enter into peace negotiations until a clearer insight had been given by Germany herself into the conditions which she would be willing to accept as fundamental to the re-establishment of peace. But in addition, it was said, there were questions of common interest that all the nations making war on Germany would insist on seeing adjusted before peace was agreed upon. The Pope's note, it was suggested, did not pave the way for making Germany declare in advance of a peace conference that she would seek to remedy the evils that have brought so much trouble to the world.

A study of the text of the Pontiff's communication brought expressions of gratification over his desire to see measures taken after the war to minimize future wars.

LONGSHORE WOMEN LOAD BIG VESSELS

Girls in High-Heeled Shoes Climb Rigging and Hop In and Out of Freight Cars.

Clerks at Bush Terminal Drop Typewriters and Take Places at Engine Throttles.

Girls from different clerical departments of the Bush Terminal in Brooklyn gave a demonstration yesterday afternoon of what they can do to take the lighter forms of the longshoremen's work in case the men are called for war duty. There are 70 per cent. of the men working at the terminal who are eligible, and for the last six weeks, off an on, some fifty of the girls have been taking instruction to prepare for emergencies.

Representatives of half a dozen other large concerns were present at the demonstration yesterday to profit by what the terminal people have done in preparing to meet their own needs. Emphasis was given to the possible early need of the girls' work by a message received from Washington while the demonstration was in progress calling out two of the terminal men whose numbers had been chosen.

The young longshorewomen, wearing blue overalls and jumpers and black caps with visors, looked very fit. The shoes were not all in keeping with the costume, for the girls had been called at a moment's notice, and longshoreman costume does not include footwear. White shoes got very much smudged, and high heels were unsatisfactory when the girls hopped out of freight cars they were loading, and climbed rigging, but there were few serious mishaps.

Cleaning lamps is one of the jobs which will fall to the girls, and the first thing one of them undertook yesterday was to wipe out the shade on the searchlight projector, opposite the office at the foot of Forty-third Street, which is for special war use. With a greasy rag hanging from her overalls pocket, she ran up the ladder, unscrewed the lamp, laid it on the low roof of the building from which it was hanging, when, pop! off it went, and smashed on the ground. These lamps are big and expensive, and the watching men were delighted with this demonstration of feminine ability.

Longshorelady Has an Alibi.

"She'll never get another job," cried one.

"There's a day's pay gone already," called another.

"I didn't do a single thing to it. It rolled off itself," said the longshorelady.

Next the girls tackled a big five-ton electric truck. They took to industrial tractors and tractor cranes like ducks to water, and two or three of them in a freight car pulled in big bundles of rattan, while as many more handed them. A slender longshorewoman, hardly five feet, looked very cunning standing with her small feet wide apart to keep her balance on a long, flat trailer, while her companions manipulated the electric control on the big driving car in front.

Once started, the girls were indefatigable. They drove the electric engine which runs in the Bush Terminal plant or rode on the step at the back. They even essayed a trolley car which came along; they ran a big electric elevator and handled small hand trucks; loaded a truck with a big conveyer which piles to a desired height, and finally boarded a big Nova Scotia fishing smack, climbed high into the shrouds and ran out on the big main boom. One of the girls swept up the deck while another tried what she could do at the wheel, which wasn't much on a stationery vessel.

"It wouldn't do to have that girl at the wheel with a drunken mate," said one of the men who was looking on.

One of the few things which the girls did not demonstrate was the comparatively feminine task of bag mending. In the freight that is handled there are frequent breaks which would let out coffee, cocoa beans, flour, and the like. There are special stitches for these on which the girls have already practiced. They will also be able to take charge of the weighing and run the four big time clocks which can register the time of 600 men in less than five minutes.

Washington Text of the Pope's Appeal Translated From Official Copy There

Special to The New York Times.

WASHINGTON, Aug. 16.—The text of the Pope's peace proposal, of which the version issued by the London Foreign Office was printed in a late edition of THE NEW YORK TIMES this morning, was made public by the State Department today as follows, in the form of a translation from the French:

To the Rulers of the Belligerent Peoples:

From the beginning of our Pontificate, in the midst of the horrors of the awful war let loose on Europe, we have had of all things three in mind: to maintain perfect impartiality toward all the belligerents, as becomes him who is the common father and loves all his children with equal affection, continually to endeavor to do them all as much good as possible, without exception of person, without distinction of nationality or religion, as is dictated to us by the universal law of charity as well as by the supreme spiritual charge with which we have been intrusted by Christ; finally, as also required by our mission of peace, to omit nothing, as far as it lay in our power, that could contribute to expedite the end of these calamities by endeavoring to bring the peoples and their rulers to more moderate resolutions, to the serene deliberation of peace, of a "just and lasting" peace.

Whoever has watched our endeavors in these three grievous years that have just elapsed could easily see that, while we remained ever true to our resolution of absolute impartiality and beneficent action, we never ceased to urge the belligerent peoples and Governments again to be brothers, although all that we did to reach this very noble goal was not made public.

About the end of the first year of the war we addressed to the contending nations the most earnest exhortations, and in addition pointed to the path that would lead to a stable peace honorable to all. Unfortunately, our appeal was not heeded, and the war was fiercely carried on for two years more, with all its horrors. It became even more cruel, and spread over land and sea, and even to the air, and desolation and death were seen to fall upon defenseless cities, peaceful villages, and their innocent people.

And now no one can imagine how much the general suffering would increase if other months or, still worse, other years were added to this sanguinary triennium. Is this civilized world to be turned into a field of death, and is Europe, so glorious and flourishing, to rush, as carried by a universal folly, to the abyss and take a hand in its own suicide?

In so distressing a situation, in the presence of so grave a menace, we, who have no personal political aim, who listen to the suggestions or interests of none of the belligerents, but are solely actuated by the sense of our supreme duty as the common father of the faithful, by the solicitations of our children who implore our intervention and peace-bearing word, uttering the very voice of humanity and reason—we again call for peace, and we renew a pressing appeal to those who have in their hands the destinies of the nations. But no longer confining ourselves to general terms, as we were led to do by circumstances in the past, we will now come to more concrete and practical proposals and invite the Governments of both belligerent peoples to arrive at an agreement on the following points, which seem to offer the base of a just and lasting peace, leaving it with them to make them more precise and complete.

First, the fundamental point must be that the material force of arms shall give way to the moral force of right, whence shall proceed a just agreement of all upon the simultaneous and reciprocal decrease of armaments, according to rules and guarantees to be established, in the necessary and sufficient measure for the maintenance of public order in every State; then, taking the place of arms, the institution of arbitration, with its high pacifying function, according to rules to be drawn in concert and under sanctions to be determined against any State which would decline either to refer international questions to arbitration or to accept its awards.

When supremacy of right is thus established, let every obstacle to ways of communication of the peoples be removed by insuring, through rules to be also determined, the true freedom and community of the seas, which, on the one hand, would eliminate any causes of conflict, and, on the other hand, would open to all new sources of prosperity and progress.

As for the damages to be repaid and the cost of the war, we see no other way of solving the question than by setting up the general principle of entire and reciprocal conditions, which would be justified by the immense benefit to be derived from disarmament, all the more as one could not understand that such carnage could go on for mere economic reasons. If certain particular reasons stand against this in certain cases, let them we weighed in justice and equity.

But these specific agreements, with the immense advantages that flow from them, are not possible unless territory now occupied is reciprocally restituted. Therefore, on the part of Germany, there should be total evacuation of Belgium, with guarantees of its entire political, military, and economic independence toward any power whatever; evacuation also of the French territory; on the part of the other belligerents, a similar restitution of the German colonies.

As regards territorial questions, as, for instance, those that are disputed by Italy and Austria, by Germany and France, there is reason to hope that, in consideration of the immense advantages of durable peace with disarmament, the contending parties will examine them in a conciliatory spirit, taking into account, as far as is just and possible, as we have said formerly, the aspirations of the population, and, if occasion arises, adjusting private interests to the general good of the great human society.

The same spirit of equity and justice must guide the examination of the other territorial and political questions, notably those relative to Armenia, the Balkan States, and the territories forming part of the old Kingdom of Poland, for which, in particular, its noble historical traditions and suffering, particularly undergone in the present war, must win, with justice, the sympathies of the nations.

These we believe are the main bases upon which must rest the future reorganization of the peoples. They are such as to make the recurrence of such conflicts impossible and open the way for the solution of the economic question, which is so important for the future and the material welfare of all of the belligerent States. And so, in presenting them to you, who at this tragic hour judge the destinies of the belligerent nations, we indulge a gratifying hope, that they will be accepted and that we shall thus see an early termination of the terrible struggle, which has more and more the appearance of a useless massacre.

Everybody acknowledges, on the other hand, that on both sides the honor of arms is safe. Do not, then, turn a deaf ear to our prayer, accept the international invitation which we extend to you in the name of the Divine Redeemer, Prince of Peace. Bear in mind your very grave responsibility to God and man. On your decision depend the quiet and joy of numberless families, the lives of thousands of young men, the happiness, in a word, of the peoples, for whom it is your imperative duty to secure this boon.

May the Lord inspire you with decisions conformable to His very holy will. May Heaven grant that in winning the applause of your contemporaries you will also earn from the future generations the great title of pacificators.

As for us, closely united in prayer and penitence with all the faithful souls who yearn for peace, we implore for you the divine spirit, enlightenment, and guidance.

Given at the Vatican, Aug. 1, 1917. BENEDICTUS P. M. XV.

The New York Times.

THE WEATHER
Partly cloudy, cooler today; Thursday cloudy; light, variable winds.
For full weather report see Page 19

VOL. LXVI...NO. 21,767. ...   NEW YORK, WEDNESDAY, AUGUST 29, 1917.—TWENTY PAGES.   ONE CENT In Greater New York. | TWO CENTS Elsewhere in N. Y. State, N. J., Conn. | THREE CENTS Other Cities.

PRESIDENT REJECTS THE POPE'S PEACE PLAN; CANNOT TRUST GERMANY'S PRESENT RULERS; HER GREAT PEOPLE MUST FIND THE WAY OUT

AUTOCRACY A PERIL

Secretly Planned to Dominate World, Wilson Declares.

KNOW NO LAW OR MERCY

"Swept Whole Continent Within the Tide of Blood and Now Stands Balked."

CAN GIVE NO GUARANTEES

To Deal with Such a Power Now Would Abandon Russia to Certain Intrigue.

Special to The New York Times.

WASHINGTON, Aug. 28.—President Wilson's response to Pope Benedict's peace proposals is a courteous but firm refusal to have any dealings with the present German autocracy. The text of the President's answer, made public by the State Department tonight, contains a scathing, even bitter, indictment of the Imperial German Government for cruelty, injustice, dishonesty, a bloodthirsty disregard of human rights.

"This power," says the President, "is not the German people. It is the ruthless master of the German people." Until that power has changed, until guarantees from Berlin are "explicitly supported by such conclusive evidence of the will and purpose of the German people themselves as the other peoples of the world would be justified in accepting," the Government of the United States will enter into no negotiations for peace.

There is no mistaking the President's purpose. Peace at this time is impossible in his view. The President expresses appreciation of "the dignity and force of the humane and generous motives" that prompted the Pontiff's offer, but he views it as a suggestion that the nations at war return to the status quo ante bellum, with a settlement of many perplexing problems left to be based on the principle of arbitration, and he feels that no satisfactory basis for such a settlement can be afforded while it is dependent on the promises of "an irresponsible Government."

Sought World Domination.

That irresponsible Government, in the words of the President's indictment, "having secretly planned to dominate the world, proceeded to carry the plan out without regard either to the sacred obligations of treaty or the long-established practices and long-cherished principles of international action and honor, which chose its own time for the war; delivered its blow fiercely and suddenly; stopped at no barrier either of law or of mercy; swept a whole continent within the tide of blood—not the blood of soldiers only, but the blood of innocent women and children also and of the helpless poor; and now stands balked but not defeated, the enemy of four-fifths of the world."

Men who are in the President's confidence have been saying privately that he had set his teeth in the determination to go on with the war until the German autocracy had come to an end. His words confirm all that they have said.

The President's response fairly bristles with indignant denunciation of the German Government. He is careful to make a distinction between the German people and their rulers. He holds out the hope to the German people that they will not be made the subject of revenge on account of the crimes of those who have plunged them into the bloody struggle which has come from the ambition of these men. The object of the war, says the President, is to deliver the free peoples of the world from the menace and the actual power of a vast military establishment controlled by an irresponsible Government.

Contains Message to Russia.

To have peace on the Pope's terms would merely bring a repetition of the conditions that prevailed before the war, in the President's opinion. Germany would recuperate its strength and renew

Moscow Council Cheers President Wilson's Message

LONDON, Aug. 28. — President Wilson's message promising the full support of the United States was read to the National Council at Moscow yesterday. A dispatch to the Exchange Telegraph Company says this was the first and only incident that brought complete agreement in the convention, all the delegates rising and cheering wildly.

its policy, and it would be necessary for the other nations to form a hostile combination against the German people.

In this connection the President sends a message of hope and cheer to the Russians. A return to the ante-bellum conditions, he says, would result in abandoning the new-born Russia to the intrigues and all the malign influences "to which the German Government has of late accustomed the world."

In the form of a question, the President says, in effect, that peace based on a restitution of Germany's power, or on its word of honor to observe treaty obligations, would be impossible. To the German people he holds out the assurance that they will be included, "if they will accept equality and not seek domination," in the peace which he hopes for and in which the American people believe, resting upon the rights of peoples, not the rights of Governments.

The President consistently adheres to previous expressions, such as those contained in his address to the Senate in January, and his statement of America's aims in his note to the warring powers sent in the previous December. He does not again use the expression "peace without victory," but points out that "no proper basis for peace of any kind, least of all for an enduring peace," is to be found in "punitive damages, the dismemberment of empires, the establishment of selfish and exclusive economic leagues." These things, he asserts, "we deem inexpedient and in the end worse than futile." They must be based, he contends, "upon justice and fairness and the common rights of mankind."

In some quarters here there is already a disposition to read into these expressions of the President a criticism of the agreement between the members of the Entente alliance to erect a commercial and economic wall against Germany after the war. It is also argued that the President has shown that he was opposed to any great change in the map of Europe after the war. He has heretofore indicated that he did not favor a peace based on arbitrary territorial disruption and the placing of people of one race under the domination of another race. This policy, however, bears as much on the ambition of Germany, Austria, and Turkey to keep under their control the peoples of alien races as it does upon any notice to the Allies that the United States deprecates any intention on their part to wrest territory from the Central Powers.

It might even be construed to mean that the people of Alsace-Lorraine had the right to expect that their territory would be transferred to French control, that the people of Herzegovina and Bosnia should be released from Austrian domination, and that the people of Trieste should achieve their wish to be under the authority of Italy.

One suggestion heard this evening was that the Government of Austria-Hungary, anxious for peace, might find encouragement to make overtures in the suggestion drawn from the President's note that the United States Government would not be a party to ruthless dismomberment of that empire.

Regard It as the Last Word.

From expressions heard tonight it is evident that the President's response to Pope Benedict has cheered and encouraged those who believe that the war must be carried on until the German autocracy is overthrown. The President, it is asserted, has spoken the last word, and it is useless to bring forward any

No Action by the Pope Pending Peace Replies

By The Associated Press.

PARIS, Aug. 28.—A dispatch to the Intransigeant from Rome says:

"Vatican circles say that Pope Benedict does not intend to issue a second or explanatory note to clear up his peace proposals, as it had been reported he would do, but will wait until he has heard from the belligerents before offering any interpretation of his original communication."

further peace proposals until Germany and her partners are willing to give their people a chance to control their affairs and to furnish guarantees that will prevent a recurrence of the horrors of the present war.

The President's message was sent yesterday. Contrary to expectation, it was addressed directly to Pope Benedict and not through the medium of the British Government, which transmitted it to the United States at the request of the Papal Secretary of State.

WATTERSON COMMENDS NOTE.

No Peace Until Allies Dictate It from Berlin, He Declares.

Henry Watterson, editor of The Louisville Courier-Journal, expressed the strongest commendation of the President's reply to the Pope's peace proposal last night, and suggested that the White House make a flat official statement that no peace ever will be made by this Government with the present rulers of Austria or Germany. He declared that no peace would be made until it was dictated by the Allies sitting in Berlin. Colonel Watterson dictated this opinion of the President's reply to the Pope:

"The President is always lucid with his pen. He writes admirably and succinctly. Nothing is now wanted except an official declaration that we will not make peace with either the Hohenzollerns or the Hapsburgs.

Trieste Civilians Evacuate City as the Armies of Italy Drive On

Special to The New York Times.

WASHINGTON, Aug. 28.—That the fall of Trieste before the Italian advance is threatened is the encouraging news received by the Italian Embassy today from Rome.

The message states that news dispatches from Zurich to the Italian newspaper Corriere d'Italia bring confirmation from Austrian sources that on account of the dangers threatening Trieste the civilian population has been ordered by the military authorities to evacuate the city. The majority of the inhabitants, according to the Corriere's advices, has already departed, and everything of value has been transported to the interior.

ROME, Aug. 28. (British Admiralty, per Wireless Press.)—The Italians made further progress yesterday on the Bainsizza Plateau, on the front north of Gorizia, the War Office announces. The Austrians made violent counterattacks, but failed to recover positions taken by the Italians. The announcement follows:

On the whole battle front there were artillery actions principally yesterday. On the Bainsizza Plateau our troops, continuing their progress, have been in closer contact with the enemy. Vigorous local attacks assured for us some positions which the enemy failed to recapture, although he made violent counterattacks.

Unfavorable atmospheric conditions greatly impeded the activity of our airplanes.

LONDON, Aug. 28.—King George has telegraphed congratulations to King Victor Emmanuel on the achievements of the Italian Army, expressing the opinion that they will exercise a far-reaching effect on the war. The King said he was happy that British guns and monitors contributed to the success of the Italians.

President Wilson's Reply to the Pope

WASHINGTON, D. C., Aug. 27, 1917.

To His Holiness Benedictus XV., Pope:

In acknowledgment of the communication of your Holiness to the belligerent peoples, dated Aug. 1, 1917, the President of the United States requests me to transmit the following reply:

Every heart that has not been blinded and hardened by this terrible war must be touched by this moving appeal of his Holiness the Pope, must feel the dignity and force of the humane and generous motives which prompted it, and must fervently wish that we might take the path of peace he so persuasively points out. But it would be folly to take it if it does not in fact lead to the goal he proposes. Our response must be based upon the stern facts, and upon nothing else. It is not a mere cessation of arms he desires; it is a stable and enduring peace. This agony must not be gone through with again, and it must be a matter of very sober judgment what will insure us against it.

His Holiness in substance proposes that we return to the status quo ante-bellum and that then there be a general condonation, disarmament, and a concert of nations based upon an acceptance of the principle of arbitration; that by a similar concert freedom of the seas be established; and that the territorial claims of France and Italy, the perplexing problems of the Balkan States, and the restitution of Poland be left to such conciliatory adjustments as may be possible in the new temper of such a peace, due regard being paid to the aspirations of the peoples whose political fortunes and affiliations will be involved.

It is manifest that no part of this program can be successfully carried out unless the restitution of the status quo ante furnishes a firm and satisfactory basis for it. The object of this war is to deliver the free peoples of the world from the menace and the actual power of a vast military establishment, controlled by an irresponsible Government, which, having secretly planned to dominate the world, proceeded to carry the plan out without regard either to the sacred obligations of treaty or the long-established practices and long-cherished principles of international action and honor; which chose its own time for the war; delivered its blow fiercely and suddenly; stopped at no barrier, either of law or of mercy; swept a whole continent within the tide of blood—not the blood of soldiers only, but the blood of innocent women and children also and of the helpless poor; and now stands balked, but not defeated, the enemy of four-fifths of the world.

This power is not the German people. It is the ruthless master of the German people. It is no business of ours how that great people came under its control or submitted with temporary zest to the domination of its purpose; but it is our business to see to it that the history of the rest of the world is no longer left to its handling.

To deal with such a power by way of peace upon the plan proposed by his Holiness the Pope would, so far as we can see, involve a recuperation of its strength and a renewal of its policy; would make it necessary to create a permanent hostile combination of nations against the German people, who are its instruments; and would result in abandoning the new-born Russia to the intrigue, the manifold subtle interference, and the certain counter-revolution which would be attempted by all the malign influences to which the German Government has of late accustomed the world.

Can peace be based upon a restitution of its power or upon any word of honor it could pledge in a treaty of settlement and accommodation?

Responsible statesmen must now everywhere see, if they never saw before, that no peace can rest securely upon political or economic restrictions meant to benefit some nations and cripple or embarrass others, upon vindictive action of any sort, or any kind of revenge or deliberate injury. The American people have suffered intolerable wrongs at the hands of the Imperial German Government, but they desire no reprisal upon the German people, who have themselves suffered all things in this war, which they did not choose. They believe that peace should rest upon the rights of peoples, not the rights of Governments—the rights of peoples, great or small, weak or powerful—their equal right to freedom and security and self-government and to a participation upon fair terms in the economic opportunities of the world, the German people, of course, included, if they will accept equality and not seek domination.

The test, therefore, of every plan of peace is this: Is it based upon the faith of all the peoples involved, or merely upon the word of an ambitious and intriguing Government, on the one hand, and of a group of free peoples, on the other? This is a test which goes to the root of the matter; and it is the test which must be applied.

The purposes of the United States in this war are known to the whole world—to every people to whom the truth has been permitted to come. They do not need to be stated again. We seek no material advantage of any kind. We believe that the intolerable wrongs done in this war by the furious and brutal power of the Imperial German Government ought to be repaired, but not at the expense of the sovereignty of any people—rather a vindication of the sovereignty both of those that are weak and of those that are strong. Punitive damages, the dismemberment of empires, the establishment of selfish and exclusive economic leagues, we deem inexpedient, and in the end worse than futile, no proper basis for a peace of any kind, least of all for an enduring peace. That must be based upon justice and fairness and the common rights of mankind.

We cannot take the word of the present rulers of Germany as a guarantee of anything that is to endure unless explicitly supported by such conclusive evidence of the will and purpose of the German people themselves as the other peoples of the world would be justified in accepting. Without such guarantees treaties of settlement, agreements for disarmament, covenants to set up arbitration in the place of force, territorial adjustments, reconstitutions of small nations, if made with the German Government, no man, no nation, could now depend on.

We must await some new evidence of the purposes of the great peoples of the Central Powers. God grant it may be given soon and in a way to restore the confidence of all peoples everywhere in the faith of nations and the possibility of a covenanted peace.

ROBERT LANSING,
Secretary of State of the United States of America.

Recent recruits try to relax in this "lounging and recreation" hut on base. Here new soldiers were encouraged to read, visit with other recruits and write letters home.

The New York Times.

THE WEATHER

Fair today and Tuesday; warmer Tuesday; moderate south winds.

VOL. LXVII...NO. 21,793.   ...   NEW YORK, MONDAY, SEPTEMBER 24, 1917.—TWENTY PAGES.   ONE CENT ... TWO CENTS ... THREE CENTS

DEADLY GERMS AND BOMBS WERE PLANTED BY GERMANS IN RUMANIAN LEGATION WHEN THEY LEFT IT IN AMERICAN HANDS

BUCHAREST PLOTTING BARED

Lansing Shows How Germans Exploited Our Protection There.

PLOT AIMED AT RUMANIA

Anthrax and Glanders Microbes Imported to Poison Cattle of Neutral Neighbor.

FOUND BURIED IN GARDEN

Explosives and Poison Sent from Berlin and Bore Official Seals and Directions.

Special to The New York Times.

WASHINGTON, Sept. 23.—Before the National capital had found time to recover from the amazing story of German intrigue disclosed in the Government's publication this morning of the activities of Count von Bernstorff and Wolf von Igel, a new chapter of German criminality was revealed tonight, when Secretary Lansing made public documentary evidence of a plot of German military and diplomatic agents to use deadly microbes and powerful explosives against Rumania.

The evidence given out by the State Department shows that before Rumania had declared war against Austria-Hungary, and was observing strict neutrality, German official agents clandestinely introduced into Bucharest, the capital of Rumania, packages containing explosives powerful enough to wreck public works and vials containing deadly microbes destined to infect domestic animals and susceptible of provoking terrible epidemics among the human population of the country. The vials contained anthrax microbes and the bacilli of glanders.

The Rumanian Government is satisfied from its evidence that "in time of peace members of the German Legation, covered by their immunity, prepared in concert with the Bulgarian Legation the perpetration on the territory of a neutral and friendly State of plots directed against the safety of this State and against the lives of its subjects."

After its discovery of the plot the Rumanian Government called in William Whiting Andrews, the Chargé d'Affaires of the American Legation at Bucharest, who witnessed the digging up of the boxes of explosives and the packages containing the vials of microbes from the grounds of the German Legation, to which they had been secretly moved from the German Consulate in Bucharest on the eve of Rumania's declaration of war.

The explosives and microbes had been sent into Rumania secretly by German diplomatic couriers and hidden in the Consulate while Rumania was at peace.

Abused Our Protection.

Just before Rumania broke relations they were removed to the Legation. Some of the objects were even taken to the German Legation after the American Legation at Bucharest had taken over the protection of German interests. Dr. Bernhardt, former confidential agent of the German Minister, and servants of the German Legation confessed that this had been done. In this respect the action of Germany's agent was a shameful abuse of the protection which the United States Government was giving to German interests in Bucharest. At the time the United States was at peace with Germany, and had agreed to take charge of Germany's legation in the Rumanian capital.

"The protection of the United States was in this manner shamefully abused and exploited," says the official report of Chargé d'Affaires Andrews to the State Department, made public tonight with the evidence; "in this instance, at least, the German Government cannot have recourse to its usual system of denial."

Some of the German diplomatic or military agents prominent in this plot against the safety of Rumania and the lives of its subjects were Werner von Rheinbaben, Counselor of the German Legation; Rudolph Kruger, Chancellor of the legation, and Colonel von Hammerstein, attached to the German Legation as Military Attaché.

They appear from the evidence to have been assisted by Constantin Kostoff, Delegate of the Bulgarian Railways in Rumania, and Colonel Samargieff, the Bulgarian Military Attaché. Kostoff, the man to whom the packages of explosives figuring in the plot were sent, under the seal of the German Consulate at Kronstadt by secret courier, to be delivered to Colonel von Hammerstein, was two days before Rumania's declaration of war suddenly presented to the Rumanian Ministry of Foreign Affairs in the quality of Attaché to the Bulgarian Legation at Bucharest.

The plot appears to have been frustrated by the extreme vigilance of the Rumanian Government and its action in severing relations with the allied powers of Austria-Hungary. This forced the various German and Bulgarian principals in the plot to leave Rumanian territory. The Rumanian Government had become aware that these packages were being secretly taken to the German Consulate, and that some of them had been shifted to the German Legation, and knew the packages had not been removed. Investigations made after Rumania had entered the war, and while the United States Government was in charge of the premises, bore out the Rumanian Government's suspicions that something was wrong, but it was not until after the boxes of explosives and the microbe vials were exhumed in the presence of the American diplomatic representatives and their contents subjected to laboratory tests, that the character of the plot was ascertained. Eight of the vials were filled with anthrax microbes. A typewritten note in the box containing these vials stated that "each vial is sufficient for 200 head." This same note indicated that the contents of the vials were to be used while Rumania was still at peace, for the note asked the German Legation to "please make a little report on the success obtained therein" and to indicate the results to "Mr. K." There were also six other vials, each containing a yellow liquid which was found on laboratory examination to be the microbes of glanders.

Secretary Lansing made public the official report to the State Department by the American Legation at Bucharest, since removed to Jassy, the new temporary capital of the Rumanians, the official protest made by the Rumanian Minister of Foreign Relations, and various exhibits attached to that protest.

TO OFFER BELGIUM FOR LOST COLONIES AND ALLIED PLEDGE

COPENHAGEN, Sept. 23.—Dr. Michaelis, the German Imperial Chancellor, will discuss the Belgian question and German peace conditions in a speech Thursday, according to the Neuste Nachrichten of Munich.

The Chancellor will declare, the newspaper says, that Germany is ready to re-establish Belgian independence if the Entente Powers agree to restore the German "colonies and to give up "their policy of territorial and economic conquest."

The correspondent at Vienna of the Berliner Tageblatt says:

"The replies of Turkey and Bulgaria will be forwarded to the Pope today. Turkey demands that her territory shall not be violated. Bulgaria demands that her frontiers shall be regulated in accordance with the principles of nationality."

Belgium as a German Pawn.

Special Cable to The New York Times.

THE HAGUE, Sept. 23.—One feature of the German press comment on the Kaiser's reply to the Pope's peace proposal stands out prominently, namely, the unanimity with which the German papers draw a comparison between Germany's conciliatory tone and President Wilson's reply to the Pope. Thus, the Lokal-Anzeiger declares that Germany's reply will encourage the Pope to take further steps, whereas President Wilson's reply made further efforts appear hopeless. The same note is struck by all the annexationist papers, especially those, like the Cologne Volkszeitung, which, in other articles, violently attack the United States.

Thus one object of Germany's note is clear, namely, to encourage American pacifists, especially the Hearst group, in their belief that America alone, anyhow chiefly the American Government, stands in the way of peace. A second object also appears clearly, namely, to endeavor to persuade the French pacifists that England must be forced to disgorge what are termed ill-gotten gains, as the German colonies and Mesopotamia, in order that France may recover the districts now occupied by the Germans and Belgium be restored.

There is nowhere the faintest suggestion that Belgium will be restored as an unconditional preliminary to peace negotiations, although the Germans are perfectly well aware that this is indispensable. They have made the most elaborate attempts to obtain information on this point in Holland for the last two months, and The New York Times correspondent has very good reason to believe that their neutral informants have left them no reasonable doubt regarding the opinion on this point of the whole civilized world.

Germany's actual proposals regarding Belgium as made known to the Papal Nuncio at Munich by Foreign Secretary von Kühlmann are nowhere detailed, although probably they are contained in various semi-official communications. One feature of these requirements is emphasized by the Cologne Volkszeitung, namely, that on the conclusion of hostilities Belgium shall not be restored by American capital. The paper argues at length that the uncompromising attitude recently adopted by the Belgian ex-Minister Derbroqueville is mainly due to the certainty that American capital will be put into Belgium after the war. The paper says such a condition of affairs would be intolerable, as America, England, and France would control trade and industry.

Significantly, a similar point is made by the radical Georg Gothein, one of the three compilers of the Reichstag peace resolution. He declares that German trade via Antwerp must be facilitated immediately on the conclusion of fighting, and says cheap rates must be guaranteed for German goods via that route. The German idea of the restoration of Belgium thus involves the prevention either of economic or political rapprochement with Germany's present enemies and in particular the prevention of Belgium's obtaining capital for her restoration where it would probably be obtainable most readily and with the least selfish motive.

Germans Seize Males in Bruges Between Ages of 14 and 60

HAVRE, Sept. 23.—The German military authorities at Bruges, Belgium, are conscripting forcibly all the boys and men of that city between the ages of 14 and 60 to work in munition factories and shipyards. The rich and the poor, shopkeepers and workmen, all are being taken, only the school teachers, doctors, and priests escaping.

The Germans virtually conducted raids in the city, according to reports received here, seizing men in their homes, in the streets, and in all public places. The Provincial Committee has been ordered by the Germans to release 75 per cent of its staff.

Bruges is the capital of the Province of West Flanders, lying fifty-five miles northwest of Brussels and fourteen miles east of Ostend. the population in 1914 was about 55,000.

"All the News That's
Fit to Print."

The New York Times.

THE WEATHER
Probably rain today; Thursday fair;
fresh northeast winds.
For full weather report see Page 21.

VOL. LXVII...NO. 21,909.　　　　NEW YORK, WEDNESDAY, OCTOBER 10, 1917.—TWENTY-TWO PAGES.　　ONE CENT In Greater New York. | TWO CENTS Within Commuting Distance. | THREE CENTS Elsewhere.

BRITISH AND FRENCH SMASH THROUGH WIDE GERMAN FRONT NORTH OF YPRES; PLOT IN THE GERMAN NAVY FOR PEACE

FRENCH GAIN 1¼ MILES

Advance on 1½-Mile Front, Occupying Mangelaere and Veldhoek.

BRITISH TAKE POELCAPELLE

All Haig's Objectives Gained in Operations Over Ground About 10 Miles in Extent.

FIGHTING IN A SEA OF MUD

Attack Launched at Dawn, with Allied Airplanes Co-operating Effectively in a Clear Sky.

LONDON, Oct. 9.—Attacking early this morning on a wide front, the British and French armies near Ypres made notable advances north and northwest of that city. The former drove the Germans from their last positions in the town of Poelcapelle and pushed on for nearly two miles to the northwest of that place. Field Marshal Sir Douglas Haig reports all his objectives gained and the capture of more than 1,000 prisoners. The French took more than 300 prisoners.

The French troops, operating on the left of the British line, north of Ypres, pierced the German positions to a depth of a mile and a quarter on a front of more than a mile and a half, capturing the villages of St. Jean de Mangelaere and Veldhoek, with numerous blockhouses, and reached the southern edge of Houthulst Wood, about seven miles north of Ypres.

To the south of the main British advance Haig's men pushed northeast from the Gravenstafel ridge to a point about 1,000 yards southwest of the village of Passchendaele, on the heights of the same name. A little further south, between the Ypres-Roulers Railway and the village of Broodseinde, which was already in their hands, the British forced the Germans a considerable distance down the eastern slope of Broodseinde Ridge.

The Germans astride the Ypres-Roulers Railway counterattacked heavily.

Advance Made Through Swamps.

Today's gains, although made under a clear sky, were won by fighting over ground which the recent rains had turned into a swamp.

From Draeibank, the most Western

point on the front of the French offensive, to Reutel, the eastern and southern limit of the hard fighting experienced by the British forces, the length of the irregular battle line is rather more than ten miles.

As a result of today's victory practically all the observatories commanding a view of the great plain of Flanders are now in the possession of the allied forces.

Attack Begins at Dawn.

An Associated Press dispatch from the British front in Belgium says:

"Another big attack was begun at dawn today against the German positions to the east and north of Ypres by both the British and French armies, and had met with great success in the first few hours of the fighting. In many places the allied forces had battled their way forward to a depth of 1,200 yards or more within the enemy territory, and reports from all along a wide front indicated that everything was going in favor of the assaulting troops, despite the exceedingly bad condition of the ground, due to the last few days' rain.

"On the north the French had surged across on the Posbeek and Broenbeek Rivers in the direction of Houthulst Wood, and at an early hour were reported to be fighting around Mangelaere, about 1,500 yards beyond their original front lines. By 8:30 o'clock they had secured several hundred prisoners.

"Further to the South the British had pushed the Germans back to Poelcapelle, and were fighting well in the eastern outskirts of the city around a big brewery. British troops on the Gravenstafel Ridge had carried their drive forward to the Passchendaele Ridge, and were resting about 1,000 yards southwest of the town of Passchendaele.

Force Germans to Lower Ground.

"Between the Ypres-Roulers Railway and the village of Broodseinde the assaulting forces had pushed forward for a considerable distance down the eastern slopes of the Broodseinde Ridge, on the lower ground. East of Ypres, in the zone embracing Reutel and Polderhoek, where there has been such bitter fighting recently, the British were carrying out strong operations, and it was reported that success had been achieved here also.

"Just north of Broodseinde, at Daisy Wood, the Germans were holding out strongly. The British had pushed forward and surrounded the wood, and hot fighting was proceeding. The British also met with strong resistance at Polderhoek Château. They reached this position early in the attack, but were forced to withdraw a little for the moment. At the latest report they had again made an advance.

"A meagre report received just as this dispatch was filed said that the Germans were counterattacking heavily astride the Ypres-Roulers Railway.

"The air service is doing fine work, notwithstanding the gale of wind which is blowing. Six German airplanes which ventured over the British lines at a height of 9,600 feet were engaged in battle by British airmen, and a spectacular fight is proceeding.

"Prisoners were being brought back

in large numbers soon after the fighting began. the battle opened at 5:20 o'clock under a clear sky, but the ground had been turned into a morass in many places by the recent heavy rains. It was especially difficult for operations along the northern section of the attack, where there are so many little rivers which are bordered with marshy ground.

"The gunfire from both the British and French artilleries was terrific at the hour of attack, and the preliminary bombardment had been intense for days. The German artillery was replying weakly this morning at most places."

A Brilliant French Victory.

The Associated Press correspondent with the French armies in Flanders telegraphs as follows:

"Amid one of the most terrific hurricanes of Artillery fire the French army, co-operating in conjunction with the British, early this morning, won a brilliant vicotry, which carried the troops forward to a depth of half a mile along a front about a mile, stretching from Draeibank to Wydendreeft. More than 300 prisoners and a number of cannon and machine guns fell into the hands of the French, and their advance took them to a position where they command the western border of the forest of Houthulst.

"The movement was a pivoting one, as a result, virtually all the observatories dominating the vast Flanders plain are now in the hands of the Allies.

"The attack was preceded by a howling wind storm, accompanied by a drenching rain, which made the ground a quagmire. The correspondent passed over the French side of the battlefield on the evening preceding the attack and found everything and everybody ready for the difficult work of the morrow. But underneath the feet the ground gave way, while the atmosphere resembled a shower bath. No garments could withstand the penetrating qualities of the elements. All around shellholes were filled to their brims with water, and the only protection of the French troops toward the enemy were the drenched sandbags piled up. Here the shelterless troops had passd the day and night awaiting orders to go over.

"At length, soon after 5 o'clock in the morning, definite orders arrived and the troops were glad. They went forward with great rapidity, despite the conditions, circling the shellholes and slipping through the deepest mud. They knew, however, that the success of future operations depended on their efforts today. When they reached their first objective points they found the Germans crowded in nests of craters, which hereabouts form the first lines, the building of trenches in this section of Flanders being impossible owing to the watery soil.

Catch Germans Changing Troops.

"Good luck had made the advance coincide with the period when the Germans were changing the troops occupying their front lines. A German division was just handing over the lines to a fresh division recently arrived from the Russian front. The French, with wonderful dash, were upon them before they realized the situation and killed many of them.

"There was a short respite before the next forward movement was undertaken in co-operatin with the British, who were advancing simultaneously on the French right. Slithering along over the broken and muddy ground, the French troopers made their way quickly toward Mangelaere, which soon fell into their possession.

"The whole scheme of operations for the day had been carried out long before noon. The infantry's advance was greatly assisted by the daring of the aviators, who would not permit the weather conditions, which presented the greatest danger for the airmen, to inter-

fere with the work of recording the artillery preparation. The French aviators ascended and flew low over the German lines, taking capital photographs of the destruction caused by the guns, and then returned in the fearful gale to their bases to turn in their reports. Meanwhile not a single German airplane was seen in the air.

French Consolidating Gains.

"The reult of the day's fighting, in addition to the men and material captured, is that the forest of Houtholst, which comprises five or six miles of thickly wooded ground, is now virtually flanked on both sides. As far as can be learned, the wood contains considerable artillery and large numbers of machine guns, but the Germans must find extraordinary difficulty in keeping them supplied.

"For the moment the French troops are occupied in consolidating the ground won, which, although small in extent, represents an invaluable gain, as it deprives the Germans of their points of observation."

PLOT TO PARALYZE GERMAN FLEET

Reichstag Told of Plan to Compel the Government to End the War.

LAID TO RADICAL SOCIALISTS

COPENHAGEN, Oct. 9.—Vice Admiral von Capelle, German Minister of Marine, announced in the Reichstag today that a plot had been discovered in the navy to for ma committee of delegates on the Russian model and to paralyze the fleet, so as to force the Government to make peace. The guilty parties have been arrested and have received their just deserts, the Minister added.

Admiral von Capelle attempted to link the Radical Socialists with the plot. He said the ringleader had discussed the plot with Deputies Haace and Vogtherr in the Radical Socialist conference room in the Reichstag Building. The Deputies had called attention to the dangerous nature of the plot and had advised the greatest caution, but had agreed to furnish propaganda material.

Socialist Deputies interrupted the speaker with cries of dissent. Deputy David of the Majority Socialists demanded that the Government produce proof and that the Reichstag should suspend judgment in the meantime.

Chancellor Michaelis earlier in the session had referred to the affair, rumors of which evidently had gained public circulation. He declared he could not co-operate with or recognize a party which put itself beyond the pale by activities directed against the Fatherland.

The disclosures in connection with the Radical Socialists, if they are true, came most opportunely to help the Government out of its embarrassment over the interpellation regarding pan-German propaganda. Admiral von Capelle hammered home his statement with a declaration of the necessity for a proper "enlightenment" of the military forces.

"All the News That's Fit to Print."

The New York Times.

THE WEATHER
Fair today; Tuesday probably rain and warmer; moderate west winds.
For full weather report see Page 16.

VOL. LXVII...NO. 21,828. ...   NEW YORK, MONDAY, OCTOBER 29, 1917.—TWENTY PAGES.   ONE CENT In Greater New York. | TWO CENTS Within Commuting Distance. | THREE CENTS Elsewhere.

TEUTONS TAKE GORIZIA, CIVIDALE, 100,000 ITALIANS AND 700 GUNS; FRANCE PLANS TO HELP HER ALLY

ROME CHARGES COWARDICE

Official Bulletin Says Part of Second Army Fled Without Fighting.

TWO ARMIES IN RETREAT

Austro-Germans Are Pressing Forward from the Julian Alps to the Sea.

MONTE SANTO HAS BEEN WON

Invaders Menace Udine, the Railroad Centre of the Rich Region of Friuli.

BERLIN, Oct. 28, (via London.)—The Austrians and Germans have forced their way through the mountains to the plains of Northern Italy, capturing the City of Gorizia, on the Isonzo, and the town of Cividale, which the Italians left in flames.

The War Office, which makes this announcement, says in a statement issued tonight that the number of Italian prisoners taken is 100,000, that 700 guns have been captured, and that the Italian Second and Third Armies are in retreat.

The text of the night report follows:
The Italian Second and Third Armies are in retreat toward the west.

Our pursuit is advancing rapidly from the mountains as far as the sea.

Up to the present 100,000 prisoners and 700 guns have been enumerated.

The Italian front as far as the Adriatic Sea is said to be wavering.

The War Office announcement issued this afternoon says:

Rapid development of the united attack on the Isonzo again brought entire success yesterday. The Italian forces which sought to prevent our divisions from emerging from the mountains were thrown back by powerful thrusts. In the evening German troops forced their way into the burning town of Cividale, the first town in point of position in the plain.

The Italian front as far as the Adriatic Sea is wavering. Our troops are pressing forward on the whole line. Gorizia, the much-disputed town in the Isonzo battles, was taken early this morning by Austro-Hungarian divisions.

The number of prisoners has been increased to more than 80,000 and the number of guns to more than 600.

Monte Santo Won, Vienna Reports.

VIENNA, Saturday, Oct. 27, (via London, Oct. 28; British Admiralty per

Wireless Press.) — Austro - Hungarian General Headquarters today issued the following official statement on the operations in the Italian theatre of war:

The blow directed against the chief Italian front under the personal command of the Emperor-King develops with great force. Our veteran glorious Isonzo troops and German forces, advancing with irresistible thrusts, have won great successes. The brotherhood in arms of the allied troops, welded on numerous battlefields and sealed by the blood of our dead, has proved itself anew in an incomparable manner.

On the Upper Isonzo our Alpine troops have conquered territory and overcome the enemy in the rocky district of Monte Rombon, and elsewhere they have shown tenacious endurance and energy. Southwest of Karfreit Prussian and Silesian troops took by storm the lofty Monte Matajur. There and west of Tolmino the fighting was altogether in Italian territory.

On the Bainsizza Plateau the Italians defended themselves on the once hotly contested Height 652, near Vodice. Monte Santo, so highly celebrated as the prize of victory in the eleventh Isonzo battle, was captured after fighting.

The sons of all districts of Austria-Hungary competed in the joy of attack of two Austro-Hungarian divisions near Canale and east of Bajught, capturing 1,600 prisoners and 200 guns. We stand on the Isonzo north of Gorizia.

The Seventeenth Hungarian Division, which for more than two years held victorious watch on the Lower Isonzo, deprived the enemy by a sudden storming attack of his first line. Italians to the number of 3,500 fell into their hands.

The total number of prisoners captured is 60,000, and we have taken 500 guns and twenty-six airplanes.

TEUTON HORDES PRESS THE ITALIANS

First Stages of Battle Described as the Usual Automatic Initial Success of a Heavy Attack.

PLAIN OF VENICE THE OBJECT

Italians Check Two Columns of the Enemy and Heavily Counterattack One.

By PERCEVAL GIBBON.
Copyright, 1917, by The New York Times Company.

Special Cable to THE NEW YORK TIMES.

WITH THE ITALIAN ARMY, Friday, Oct. 26.—The battle which commenced in the early hours of Wednesday is still in

Path of Austro-German Isonzo Drive.

The arrows indicate the principal points from which the invaders have driven the Italian forces—Gorizia and Cividale, which fell in the course of the operations described in yesterday's bulletins from Berlin; Monte Stol and Monte Majaru, the capture of which was announced in those of Saturday. The heavy double line marks the battle front as it existed before the Teuton drive started.

that initial stage of almost automatic victory for the attacker which follows an assault elaborately organized and strongly manned.

Mackensen's troops, having crossed the Isonzo at numerous points between Auzza, just north of Canale, and Plezzo (Flitch) to the north of Monte Nero, have climbed the high ridge along the right bank of the captured village of Caporetto, and thrust thence along the road toward Natisone Valley as far as Robie. They have occupied our thinly held line in Conca di Plezzo, and caused General Cadorna to fall back to the strongly prepared line, which corresponds roughly with the old frontier in the bend of the Isonzo below Caporetto.

The enemy's purpose is plain. These highlands are intersected by rivers, each running deep in a ravine with its level, winding road alongside it, leading back to the plain of Venice and its cities, and by an advance beyond Caporetto he might also hope to cut off Monte Nero and its garrison of the Alpini.

The last news I have heard from Monte Nero reported that the Alpini were holding out.

The attack which carried the enemy beyond Caporetto was conducted by Germans, of whom at least one army

corps were employed. In the Isonzo Valley they thrust through the poor little village and along a road and developed a subsequent attack northward toward one of many Monte Stols which are scattered through the geography of these parts. Here they were pulled up dead by an unbending Italian defensive.

Another column advancing from the Capornetto Road near Idersko made for Luico and was not only stopped, but violently counterattacked by infantry under the command of a famous General.

The enemy's first assault made aim momentarily master of a portion of the mountain, where numerous Italian batteries still remained, and it was around there and among the guns themselves that hand-to-hand fighting took place, which finally drove the enemy down the hill and left the Italians in possession of every gun upon the Bainsizza Plateau.

The Austrians are in great force, and our aerial reconnaissance reports that the roads and the country in the rear of the enemy are full of troops. What is certain is that the reinforcements include vast forces of artillery.

Along the whole of the active front the firing is intense. German airmen have been active all day. Little towns along the front are visited at almost half-hourly intervals.

The situation is a serious one, in the

sense that Italy has again to put out every effort and to tax every resource. The temperament of the army adapts itself with difficulty to the sense of defeat, however local and temporary.

SEE GRAVE CRISIS IN ITALY'S ROUT

Washington Experts Fear the Possibility of the Conquest of Northern Provinces.

HOPE FOR ALLIED AID

Capital Expects to Hear of Dispatch of French and British Reinforcements.

Special to The New York Times.

WASHINGTON, Oct. 28.--Mackensen's drive through the Austro-Italian mountain passes into the Friulian plains of Northeastern Italy threatens to develop the most critical problem in the European military situation since the battle of the Marne.

Italian military men were confident of the ability of General Cadorna to check the steam-roller advance of Mackensen's men; but the rapid advance of the German forces in great numbers, with apparently large captures of men and guns, the retreat of the Italian forces, first toward their own boundary line, then the surrender of their hard-won positions on the Bainsizza Plateau, the loss of Gorizia, and even of Cividale—the last on Italian soil—have forced the conclusion that the situation for Italy is most desperate, and that unless heroic remedies are applied immediately, much of Northern Italy may pass into the hands of the Germans.

The immediate objective of Mackensen is Udine, the principal rail centre of the Friulian plain, and the most important point between Venice and the Austrian border. With Udine in his possession, it is not doubted here—bearing in mind the manner in which he developed his famous Rumanian campaign—that Mackensen will strike a swift blow at Venice and move westward toward Padua and Verona. The failure of the Italians to check the Germans at the passes was most unfortunate, and may force the Entente Allies to a complete revision of their military plans.

It is difficult for military men to believe, after the high hopes which were developed by General Cadorna's brilliant offensive of last Summer, that such sudden reverses should have come to the Italian arms. The official admissions by the Rome Government of the yielding of important territory, along with tonight's admission that Mackensen's forces have actually invaded Italian soil, show that the situation is most grave from the military point of view, particularly when it is remembered that the brilliant Mackensen, who is managing the German campaign, is the man who overran Rumania with his horde of men carrying out his pincers plan of campaign.

French Cabinet in Council to Devise Aid for Italy

PARIS, Oct. 28.—The Cabinet met this evening to determine upon co-operation of the Allies on the Italian front. President Poincaré presided.

ALLIES GAIN IN FLANDERS

All of Merckem Peninsula, South of Dixmude, Is Now Occupied.

BELGIANS A BIG FACTOR

Cross Morasses and Flooded Areas and Fling Themselves Resistlessly on Foe.

All the Towns in the Area Now Won—British in Raid East of Ypres.

LONDON, Oct. 28.—The allied forces in Flanders have captured the entire Merckem Peninsula, two miles south of Dixmude, following up their successes of yesterday.

The peninsula is a strip of land in which Merckem lies, surrounded by streams or canalized rivers on all sides except to the eastward.

Belgian and French troops were responsible for the success, advancing across morasses with comparatively little hindrance from the foe.

An Associated Press dispatch from the British front gives this view of the value of the gains:

"The story of the highly important victory won by the French and Belgian Armies over the marshlands of Flanders yesterday is the record of a spectacular military operation, which before its completion would have been branded as impossible by the average expert. It is a story of men who battled their way forward over morasses and through water, into which they sank literally to their necks at times, and, with rifle and cold steel, conquered the enemy in a large and vital strip of territory, which includes within its borders such places as Kippe, Merckem, Aschhoope, Verbrandesmis, and Kostermolen.

"The striking feature of the performance lies in the part played by the Belgians in yesterday's drive. When the poilus reached the neighborhood of Luyghem in the afternoon and began their assault on this place, the Belgians, who were watching from their lines across the floods, joined in, and numbers of them, piling into ferries, poled their way to the eastern shore and hurled themselves on the Germans concealed in concrete defences in the region north of Luyghem with such good effect that they quickly mopped up this entire northern tip of the so-called Luyghem Peninsula.

"The territory conquered yesterday is a strip of land about 7,000 yards long and varying in width from 1,500 yards at the narrowest place to 3,000 at the widest. If a line be drawn from a point just north of Langewaede westward almost to Sevekoten, this would constitute the base of the strip."

"From this base it extends in a northwesterly direction, running to its tip, (that is, the Luyghem Peninsula,) up into an inundated area formed on the west by the Yser waterways above Driegrachten, and on the east by the Steenluisvaart River, a large lake known as Le Blankaert and streams flowing southward from this body of water.

The night report of the British War Office says:

During the course of the day operations by French and Belgian forces north of Merckem were successfully carried out. The village of Luyghem was captured this morning by French troops and the whole Merckem Peninsula is now in the hands of the Allies. A further number of prisoners has been captured.

On the battlefront the activity of both artilleries continued. The hostile artillery also has been more active than usual south of Lens.

The afternoon report says:

We improved our positions slightly during the night in the neighborhood of the Ypres-Roulers Railway.

On Friday night Belgian troops carried out a successful raid north of Dixmude, capturing sixteen prisoners and a machine gun. Yesterday morning Belgian troops, acting in conjunction with the French, crossed the inundations and occupied Merckem Peninsula, in the neighborhood of Vyfhuysen.

The Belgian communication issued at Havre today says:

A Belgian detachment operating in conjunction with the French advanced in the Vyfhuysen Peninsula and captured a number of prisoners, as well as considerable material, including three mine sweepers. A patrol crossed Blankaert Lake and brought back a score of prisoners. Our artillery carried out numerous fires of destruction against the enemy batteries and organizations. The enemy replied weakly, except before Dixmude, where our fire caused bomb-fighting, which terminated quickly to our advantage.

Our aviators carried out sixty-one flights, including seventeen for the purpose of ranging the guns, fourteen for protection, and fifteen for pursuit. Two air engagements were fought.

The Belgian communication of yesterday, also made public, reads, in part:

Last night, following an emission of gas in the direction of German trenches in the region of Dixmude, one of our reconnoitring parties caused heavy losses among the enemy and brought back a score of prisoners and one machine gun, blowing up also a shelter from bomb throwers. Today we continued to co-operate directly by our fire with the French offensive in the region of Merckem. A Belgian detachment, after having traversed inundated territory, gained a footing in the enemy works in the region of Luyghem. The reaction of the Germans was feeble. Spirited bomb-fighting in the neighborhood of Dixmude ended to our advantage.

The day report from the French War Office reads:

In Belgium we continued to make progress on our left, at the Laighem Peninsula, and reduced a number of small islands held by the enemy. The number of prisoners taken since yesterday exceeds 200.

On the Aisne front there was intermittent artillery fighting, which was very spirited in the region of Hurtebise. In Champagne we repulsed an enemy attack in the sector of Maisons.

We penetrated a German trench south of Forges Brook, on the left bank of the Meuse, and brought back prisoners.

Elsewhere the night was calm.

The night statement from the French War Office tonight reads:

North of the Aisne there was spirited artillery activity in the region of Pinon-Chavignon and Epine de Chevregny. About 12 o'clock the Germans delivered a strong attack against our positions north of the Froidmont Farm. Our fire drove back the enemy waves, which were broken up with serious losses. About sixty prisoners remained in our hands.

In the Argonne an enemy surprise attack was without result.

The artillery action was quite spirited in the Champagne, in the region of the Monts.

The day was calm everywhere else.

GERMAN AVIATORS DROP POISONED CANDY

PROOF that German aviators make a practice of dropping poisoned candies into the French villages near the western battle front is contained in a letter just received from T. Shaw Bosworth, a member of the editorial staff of THE NEW YORK TIMES, now driving an ambulance for the American Ambulance Corps in the region of Verdun. Mr. Bosworth writes:

"Here's evidence of the latest Boche atrocity—the 'lowest down' thing they've yet pulled off. I have had some difficulty in getting the official copies for THE TIMES. Here are the facts: The copy, signed with the Mayor's stamp, was posted on our official military bulletin board, 15 K. from the lines two days after the date—March 21—which you see at the top and attracted a good deal of attention, as Boche aviators fly over us very frequently. The notice was followed by a second one, in substance the same as the first, on a small sheet of paper and signed by the Mayor. No similar warning to the inhabitants had up to then appeared on the bulletin board, which daily carries the official communique—lately brilliant records of English advances in the north and yesterday the news that fifteen civilians had been killed during a storm of shells sent into Rheims.

"It is said that the bombardment of Rheims is a barometer of the state of mind of the Germans. When things are going well for them they usually leave the town alone, but when anything goes against them they bombard Rheims. America having declared war yesterday, Rheims received something like 5,000 shells, as befitted the occasion.

"That some of the Boches who fly over us may drop poisoned candies, which might be found by some of the children that still remain in the village, strikes us as the last refinement of Prussian barbarism in its death throes. The French don't make announcements like the warning I am sending you with a view to creating an 'effect' in the sense of influencing public opinion against the enemy, so the reason for spreading this warning broadcast is a sound one and has no connection with propaganda.

"Tell the readers of THE TIMES, as best you can, what brand of enemies they have at last chosen to fight."

The following is the literal translation of the notice posted by the Mayor of the village in which is stationed the unit of the American Ambulance Corps with which the writer is serving:

Province of Meuse.
Division of Verdun.
District of Souilly.
Parish of Vadelaincourt.

Republic of France.

NOTICE TO THE INHABITANTS.

The Mayor has been officially warned that poisoned candies have lately been dropped by German aviators in the neighborhood of St. Menehould, (Marne.) This information confirms the fears expressed by the Prefect in his circular of March 21, following similar actions by German aviators behind the English lines: "It is reasonable to believe that the enemy will, at any moment, commit the same indescribable acts at certain points in the Province of Meuse. The population is, therefore, warned for the second time to guard against the danger which may result from this criminal action of our barbarous enemies."

Consequently, in accordance with instructions recently published, any candy found within the borders of the parish must be taken to the Mayor to be sent to the Prefecture, in order to have it analyzed at the military laboratory.

Vadelaincourt, March 30, 1917.

THE MAYOR.

The notice of March 21, posted by the Prefect of the Meuse, read as follows:

REPUBLIC OF FRANCE.

Bar-le-Duc, 21 March, 1917.

Prefecture of the Meuse, First Division.

Candy dropped by the enemy to cause poisoning and disease.

INSTRUCTIONS.

THE PREFECT OF THE MEUSE.

To the Mayors and to the Schoolmasters and Mistresses of the District.

The military authorities have given me a letter of the 9th inst. from the General Commander in Chief, giving notice that German aviators have recently dropped poisoned candy within the English lines.

The text is worded thus:

"German aviators have just dropped candy within the English lines. There would seem to be in this act a first attempt on the part of the enemy to cause outbreaks of poisoning and disease. It therefore seems opportune to put the soldiers and civilians on their guard against eating these candies. It is the duty of those picking them up to send them to the civil or military authorities for analysis. The commanders of the districts in the military zones ought to arrange with the Prefects regarding the instructions to be given to the civilian population."

It is urgently necessary to warn the population of the risks they run in swallowing any candy the origin of which is unknown or suspected. Notices to this effect ought to be placed in all localities.

I have the honor to ask you to be good enough to see that formal instructions are given to parents that any candy found be sent to me at once by the Mayor's Secretary with a note of explanation. I will send it immediately to the military laboratory for analysis.

The Prefect of the Meuse,
AUBERT.

Correspondents at the front alluded to this candy dropping some time ago, but this is the first official proof that the German aviators had adopted the practice.

"All the News That's Fit to Print."

The New York Times.

THE WEATHER
Fair today and tomorrow; moderate northwest to north winds.
Full weather report see Page 21.

VOL. LXVII...NO. 21,839. NEW YORK, FRIDAY, NOVEMBER 9, 1917.—TWENTY-TWO PAGES. ONE CENT In Greater New York. | TWO CENTS Within Commuting Distance. | THREE CENTS Elsewhere.

REVOLUTIONISTS SEIZE PETROGRAD; KERENSKY FLEES; PLEDGE IS GIVEN TO SEEK "AN IMMEDIATE PEACE", ITALIANS AGAIN DRIVEN BACK; LOSE 17,000 MORE MEN

MINISTERS UNDER ARREST

Winter Palace Is Taken After Fierce Defense by Women Soldiers.

FORT'S GUNS TURNED ON IT

Cruiser and Armored Cars Also Brought Into Battle Waged by Searchlight.

TROTZSKY HEADS REVOLT

Giving Land to the Peasants and Calling of Constituent Assembly Promised.

PETROGRAD, Nov. 8.—With the aid of the capital's garrison complete control of Petrograd has been seized by the Maximalists, or Bolsheviki, headed by Nikolai Lenine, the Radical Socialist leader, and Leon Trotzsky, President of the Central Executive Committee of the Petrograd Council of Workmen's and Soldiers' Delegates. Their action has been indorsed by the All-Russia Congress of Workmen's Councils.

A proclamation has been issued declaring that the Revolutionary Government purposes to negotiate an "immediate democratic peace," to turn the land over to the peasantry, and to convoke the Constituent Assembly.

Premier Kerensky has fled. He is variously said to be headed for Moscow and the northern front of the army, and orders for his arrest have been issued. Last night he was reported to be at Luga, eighty-five miles southwest of Petrograd. Several members of his Cabinet have been taken into custod

The Preliminary Parliament is declared dissolved.

Little serious fighting has attended the revolt so far. The Provisional Government troops holding the bridges over the Neva and various other points yesterday were quickly overpowered, save at the Winter Palace, the chief guardians of which were the Women's Battalion. Here last night a battle royal took place for four hours, during which the Bolsheviki brought up armored cars and the cruiser Aurora and turned the guns of the Fort of St. Peter and St. Paul upon the palace before its defenders would surrender.

Prior to the attack the Workmen's and Soldiers' leaders sent the Provisional Government an ultimatum demanding their surrender and allowing twenty minutes' grace. The Government replied indirectly, refusing to recognize the Military Committee.

Vice President Kameneff of the Workmen's and Soldiers' Delegates told The Associated Press today that the object of taking possession of the posts and telegraphs was to thwart any effort the Government might make to call troops to the capital. The Russkia Volia and the Bourse Gazette have been commandeered.

The city today presented a normal aspect. Even the noonday band accompanying the guard of relief under the previous administration continued its function. There were the customary lines in front of the provision stores and children played in the parks and gardens. There was even a notable lessening of the patrols, only a few armed soldiers and sailors moving about the streets

How the Revolt Developed.

The Maximalist movement toward seizing authority, rumors of which had been agitating the public mind ever since the formation of the last Coalition Cabinet, culminated Tuesday night, when, without disorder, Maximalist forces took possession of the Telegraph office and the Petrograd Telegraph Agency.

Orders issued by the Government for the opening of the spans of the bridges across the Neva later were overridden by the Military Committee of the Council of Workmen's and Soldiers' Delegates. Communication was restored after several hours of interruption. Nowhere did the Maximalists meet with serious opposition.

An effort by militiamen to disperse crowds gathered in the Nevski and Letainy Prospekts during the evening provoked a fight in which one man is reported to have been killed. Minor disturbances, some of them accompanied by shooting, occurred in various quarters of the city. A number of persons are reported to have been killed or wounded.

Yesterday morning found patrols of soldiers, sailors, and civilians in the streets maintaining order. Further than a continuation of suppressed excitement, the streets of the city presented no unusual aspects. The shops and banks which had opened for business began closing up about noon.

Shortly after noon a Soviet force occupied the telephone exchange, where a small guard had been stationed for weeks. An effort by Government forces to retake the exchange led to a brief fusillade, by which it is believed a number of casualties was caused. The Maximalists remained in possession of the building.

Toward 5 o'clock in the afternoon the Military Revolutionary Committee issued its proclamation stating that Petrograd was in its hands.

The Petrograd Council of Workmen's and Soldiers' Delegates considers this to be the program of the new authority:

First—The offer of an immediate democratic peace.

Second—The immediate handing over of large proprietarial lands to the peasants.

Third—The transmission of all authority to the Council of Workmen's and Soldiers' Delegates.

Fourth—The honest convocation of a Constitutional Assembly.

The national revolutionary army must not permit uncertain military detachments to leave the front for Petrograd. They should use persuasion, but where this fails they must oppose any such action on the part of these detachments by force without mercy.

The actual order must be read immediately to all military detachments in all arms. The suppression of this order from the rank and file by army organizations is equivalent to a great crime against the revolution and will be punished by all the strength of the revolutionary law.

Soldiers! For peace, for bread, for land, and for the power of the people!

Council Welcomes Lenine.

The Petrogad Council of Workmen's and Soldiers' Delegates held a meeting at which M. Trotzky made his declaration that the Government no longer existed; that some of the Ministers had been arrested, and that the preliminary Parliament had been dissolved. He introduced Nikolai Lenine as "an old comrade whom we welcome back."

Lenine, who was received with prolonged cheers, said:

"Now we have a revolution. The peasants and workmen control the Government. This is only a preliminary step toward a similar revolution everywhere."

He outlined the three problems now before the Russian democracy. First, immediate conclusion of the war, for which purpose the new Government must propose an armistice to the belligerents; second, the handing over of the land to the peasant; third, settlement of the economic crisis.

At the close of the sitting a declaration was read from the representatives of the Democratic Minimalist Party of the Workmen's and Soldiers' Delegates, stating that the party disapproved of the coup d'état and withdrew from the Council of Workmens and Soldiers' Delegates.

Later it was announced that the split in the Council had been healed and that a call had been sent out for a delegate from each 25,000 of the population to express the will of the Russian Army.

The official news agency today made public the following statement:

'The Congress of the Councils of Workmen's and Soldiers' Delegates of all Russia, which opened last evening, issued this morning the three following proclamations:

To All Provincial Councils of Workmen's and Soldiers' and Peasants' Delegates.

All power lies in the Workmen's and Soldiers' Delegates. Government commissaries are relieved of their functions. Presidents of the Workmen's and Soldiers' Delegates are to communicate direct with the revolutionary Government. All members of agricultural committees who have been arrested are to be set at liberty immediately and the commissioners who arrested them are in turn to be arrested.

The second proclamation reads as follows:

The death penalty re-established at the front by Premier Kerensky is abolished and complete freedom for political propaganda has been established at the front. All revolutionary soldiers and officers who have been arrested for complicity in so-called political crimes are to be set at liberty immediately.

"The third proclamation says:

Former Ministers Konovaloff, Kishkin, Terestchenko, Malyanovitch, Nikitin, and others have been arrreted by the Revolutionary committee.

Mr. Kerensky has taken flight and all military bodies have been empowered to take all possible measures to arrest Kerensky and bring him back to Petrograd. All complicity with Kerensky will be dealt with as high treason.

Capture of the Winter Palace.

While the All-Russian Congress of Councils had been deliberating the Government forces, including the Women's Battalion, which had been guarding the Winter Palace had been driven inside in the course of a lively machine-gun and rifle battle, during which the cruiser Aurora, that had been moored in the Neva at the Nicolai Bridge, moved up within range, firing shrapnel, and armored cars swung into action. Then the guns of the Fortress of St. Peter and St. Paul, across the river, opened on the structure.

The palace stood out under the glare of the searchlights of the cruiser and offered a good target for the guns. The defenders held out for four hours, replying as best they could with machine guns and rifles. but at 2 o'clock this morning were compelled to surrender.

'RUSSIA OUT' SPURS SPARTANBURG BOYS

Tired Soldiers Speed Up Drill When They Hear That Petrograd Is Moving for Peace.

ANXIOUS FOR THE FRAY

Two More Brigades to be Made of Skeleton Guard Units and Men from Yaphank.

Special to The New York Times.

CAMP WADSWORTH, Spartanburg, S. C., Nov. 8.—Just before sundown a company from the former Second Infantry was wearily going through close order drill out on the parade ground.

The officers, dust from shoes to hats, were hoarse from shouting commands all afternoon and the men, tired of toting their heavy equipment back and forth, were eager for the word to quit. A couple of men from the 102d United States Engineers with nothing to do until mess idly stood by enjoying the grilling of the infantrymen.

Soon a newsboy selling a Spartanburg afternoon paper ambled along and one of the engineers bought a paper. With one last, satisfied grin at the toiling "dough boys," the ex-Twenty-second man languidly glanced at the first page headlines telling the bad news from Petrograd. As they say in the movies, he registered keen and amazed interest, then discipline was forgotten and the engineer shouted at the laboring company: "Hey, fellows, here's news—Russia is out."

The fagged and dusty company heard the announcement just as they came to a halt. While the Lieutenant drilling the infantrymen indignantly scowled at he excited and offending engineers, there was talking in the ranks. Then the Lieutenant ran the company off into another evolution. He said afterward it was like leading another set of men. The fatigue was gone and until "recall" sounded the company went through the drill freshly and with vim.

Afterward the top Sergeant explained the reason for the change of spirit, thus: "When that guy said that Russia had dropped out, every fellow in the company knew that it was up to the United States to take her place. And, believe me, if you had been doubling over that drill ground for weeks and fairly aching for the welcome word 'Embark,' you'd think any drill was light, too."

A similar sentiment throughout the division was found tonight when the 200 company units were canvassed to find out what the men thought about the news. Everywhere the men were enthusiastic about their chances for quick action. Somewhere in the camp some strategist figured out that if Russia really went out, Germany could throw all the troops now on the Russian front to the Western theatre, and the Allies would have need of reinforcements at once.

This "reliable, inside information" went over the camp like all reports, quickly and thoroughly, and as the newspapermen were assured tonight, the Twenty-seventh being the "best division anywhere," the soldiers became exceedingly optimistic over the outlook.

The New York Times.

"All the News That's Fit to Print."

THE WEATHER
Generally fair today and tomorrow; fresh northeast winds.
For full weather report see Page 21.

VOL. LXVII...NO. 21,843.   NEW YORK, TUESDAY, NOVEMBER 13, 1917.—TWENTY-TWO PAGES.   ONE CENT In Greater New York. | TWO CENTS Within Commuting Distance. | THREE CENTS Elsewhere.

LLOYD GEORGE SEES VICTORY IN UNITY, WITHOUT RUSSIA; WILSON TELLS LABOR VICTORY ALONE SPELLS PEACE; KERENSKY FIGHTING REBELS; ITALY FACING A GREAT BATTLE

PREMIER RECALLS ERRORS

Serbian and Rumanian Disasters Due to Lack of Joint War Direction.

ITALY ENFORCED THE NEED

He Was Ready to Quit if the Allies Had Not Taken This Forward Step Now.

AMERICA TO PARTICIPATE

Russia Also, He Believes--Bonar Law Suggests War Council Will Be Only Advisory.

PARIS, Nov. 12.—At a luncheon given today by Premier Painlevé in honor of David Lloyd George, the British Prime Minister, the latter discussed the plan for centralized direction of the Allies' military efforts. He said in part:

"Unfortunately we did not have time to consult the United States or Russia before creating this council. The Italian disaster necessitated action without delay to repair it. This made it indispensable to commence right now with the powers whose forces may be employed on the Italian front. But, in order to assure the complete success of this great experiment, which I believe is essential to the victory of our cause, it will be necessary that all our great allies be represented in the deliberations. I am persuaded that we shall obtain the consent of these two great countries and their co-operation in the work of the inter-allied council."

Mr. Lloyd George talked of the reasons for not taking the step earlier. He referred to "timidities and susceptibilities" when it came to treating questions on any front not commanded by Generals taking part in the inter-allied consultations. The Allies had committed a great fault, he said, in not assisting Serbia adequately in holding her line. The result was that the Central empires broke the blockade and procured men and supplies from the East, without which Germany would have been unable to maintain the force of her armies.

Reason for Balkan Disasters.

"Why was this unbelievable fault committed?" asked the Premier. "The reply is simple. It was because no one in particular was charged with guarding the Balkan gate. The united front had not become a reality. France and England were absorbed by other problems in other regions. Italy thought only of the Carso. Russia was mounting guard over a frontier of a thousand miles, and, even without that, she could not have passed through to have helped Serbia, because Rumania was neutral.

"It is true that we sent troops to Saloniki to succor Serbia, but, as always, they were sent too late. Half the men who fell in the vain effort to pierce the Western front in September that same year would have saved Serbia, saved the Balkans and completed the blockade of Germany.

"You may say this is an old story. I grant you that it was simply the first chapter of a series that has continued to the present hour; 1915 was the year of the Serbian tragedy; 1916 was the year of the Rumanian tragedy, which was a repetition of the Serbian story almost without change. This is unbelievable, when you think of the consequences to the Allies' cause of the Rumanian defeat. Opulent wheatfields and rich petroleum wells passed to the enemy and Germany was able to escape us.

"Through the harvest of 1917 the siege of the Central Powers was raised once more, and the horrible war was once more prolonged. That would not have happened, had there existed some central authority, charged with meditating upon the problem of the war for the entire theatre of the war."

Was Ready to Drop Responsibility.

After reviewing the Italian campaign the Premier said:

"As far as I am concerned. I had arrived at the conclusion that if nothing was changed I could no longer accept the responsibility for the direction of a war condemned to disaster from lack of unity. Italy's misfortune may still save the alliance, because without it I do not think that even today we would have created a veritable superior council.

"National and professional traditions, questions of prestige and susceptibilities all conspired to render our best decisions vain. No one in particular bore the blame. The guilt was in the natural difficulty of obtaining of so many nations, of so many independent organizations that they should amalgamate all their individual particularities to act together as if they were but one people."

Mr. Lloyd George said later:

"I have spoken today with a frankness that is perhaps brutal. At the risk of being ill understood here and elsewhere, and not, perhaps, without risk of giving a temporary encouragement to the enemy, because now that we have established this council it is for us to see that the unity it represents be a fact and not an appearance.

"The war has been prolonged by particularism. It will be shortened by solidarity. If the effort to organize our united action becomes a reality, a have no doubt as to the issue of the war. The weight of men and material and of moral factors in every sense of the word is on our side. I say it, no matter what may happen to Russia or in Russia. A revolutionary Russia can never be anything but a menace to Hohenzollernism.

"But even if we are obliged to despair of Russia, my faith in the final triumph of the cause of the Allies remains unshakable."

Premier Painlevé in his speech at the luncheon remarked:

"A single front, a single army, a single nation—that is the program requisite for future victory. If after forty months of war, after all the lessons the war has taught us, the Allies were not capable of that sacred international union, then, in spite of their sacrifices, they would not be worthy of victory."

In discussing the manner of accomplishment of this fusion, M. Painlevé said:

"The enemies' alliance realized unity of effort by brutal discipline, one of the peoples among them having mastered the others and rendered them serviceable. But we are free peoples. We do not admit of subjection to other peoples in time of war. That independence is at the same time a source of strength and weakness—of strength because there is a capacity for resistance which is unknown to subject peoples, and of weakness because it renders more difficult co-ordination of military operations. To reconcile this independence with the need for unity of direction which is required to achieve an efficacious war policy will be the work of the Interallied War Committee or of the Superior War Council just created by the Allies."

President Poincaré today received the new Italian Ambassador, Count Bonin-Longare. The President referred to the invasion of Italian territory over which he had traveled recently with the King of Italy, and added:

"Yes, as was said by King Victor Emmanuel in his noble proclamation, any weakness today would be treason. Treason also would be all internal discord and treason would be all discord between the Allies."

RUSH TO AID ITALY, EAGER FOR BATTLE

Heavy Allied Reinforcements Pouring In to Stiffen the Nation's Defense.

HOW FOES BROKE THROUGH

"Fraternizing" Austrians on Isonzo Secretly Replaced by German Shock Divisions.

By CHARLES H. GRASTY.
Copyright, 1917, by The New York Times Company.
Special Cable to THE NEW YORK TIMES.

ROME, Nov. 11.—The greatest battle of history, with more men engaged, and possessing for the world large significance, is preparing in Italy. The Germans, on their side, are pressing the advantage gained by their successes, hoping to keep the Italians demoralized and prevent the recovery of equilibrium while the Italians, reinforced by the French and British, and aided by leaders accustomed to cope with Hun ingenuity and prowess, are seeking to organize resistance at a place and under conditions as favorable as possible.

In point of mere numbers the advantage lies with the Allies, but the Italian Army has suffered a rout which has momentarily destroyed its integrity. The immediate problem of the allied strategists seems to be to maintain an ordered rearguard action, reorganize the scattered units, and stop the contagion of panic that seized on parts of the army, and there are doubtless huge other problems known only to the higher command involving resistance to the Germans in the Trentino and the Cadore.

Reckoning numbers solely, Italy still has 4,000,000 enlisted men, conceding the German claim of half a million killed, wounded, captured, and missing or dispersed, and therefore should meet the invader on better than equal terms. As against the Italian deterioration, Mackensen must suffer the same exhaustion and difficulty from lengthened communication that made von Kluck's defeat possible at the Marne.

It is in guns that the Allies seem weakest. The German drive has already cost them 2,200. But here again comfort may be drawn from the Marne parallel. In that battle the French were vastly inferior to the Germans in artillery. The German advance to the Channel was checked. The French Army did it practically with rifle and bayonet against an enemy intrenched in commanding positions and well supplied with artillery and machine guns.

To carry the parallel further, the same man who struck the blow at the Marne and who was the master strategist at Lorette is helping and planning for the battle of the Venetian plain. He is General Foch, the coolest, most accomplished and audacious strategist of this war.

Arrival of Allied Aid.

Still another encouraging feature is the wholehearted and swift action of France and England. Men and machinery are pouring into Italy in quantities that seemed impossible. I have seen many of the troop trains and the sight stirs one's enthusiasm. Finer soldiers never wore boots. As one said of the Anzacs: "They're in the pink of condition and don't give a damn for anybody."

In train after train of French soldiers every man looks like an Alpine chasseur. The spirit among them is extraordinary. They treat the expedition as a big lark and when a stop is made at a station they are as lively as fox terriers.

The men seem delighted to leave the trenches and get into the open. As for Fritz and his gases and guns and propaganda and smart tricks generally, one bit afraid of him.

England and France appear to have put aside all narrow and petty considerations and to have given Italy of their very best. The handling of the transport has been a remarkable feat. Both French and Italians have perhaps they think they know him and are not formed miracles.

Work of the German Agents.

The German propagandists are working in harmony with Mackensen's advance and are attempting to break the will of the civilian population. They are spreading talk of England's using other nations for her own selfish purposes. They declare that it is England's war and nobody else has any stake in it. Germany alone, they say, stands against England's self-seeking the world over.

Venice has been suddenly invaded by a swarm of German agents who have popped in from nobody knows where and are spreading peace propaganda. These people make unauthorized use of the Pope's name, saying that everything has been arranged by the Vatican for peace and that Italy will be well treated.

This was the method pursued in the preliminary softening of the front of the Second Army. Opposite these troops appeared Austrian troops similarly affected with peace longings and socialistic tendencies. There was general fraternization and an understanding that both sides would refuse to fire on one another.

On the day of the attack these particular Austrian troops had been transferred elsewhere and their places taken by German shock divisions. But the Italian corps kept their fraternal promises and the Germans went right through them.

ITALIANS URGE US TO FIGHT AUSTRIA

Thus, They Say, America Can Render Them the Most Important Service.

COAL AND WHEAT NEXT

Need for Munitions Is Great, but Less Imperative Than for Food and Fuel.

Special Cable to THE NEW YORK TIMES.

PARIS, Nov. 12.—In a previous dispatch I set forth the necessity for American aid to Italy and the principal reasons of the internal weakness in Italy that rendered that aid so imperative. I will now try to indicate how in the opinion of the best informed Italians America's aid can be exercised most usefully.

To begin with, it is moral even more than material help that Italy requires at this juncture. It has been the misfortune of the Entente leaders to have but insufficiently recognized the importance of the moral factors in this war of peoples. It is only recently that they are beginning to understand the vital necessity of informing public opinion and directing it along right lines.

As I showed yesterday, the greater part at least of Italy's present troubles is due to the demoralization of the masses by anti-Italian elements. Obviously, then, the first thing to do is to recreate and strengthen a healthy morale in Italy, and in this America can aid enormously.

A moment's thought will show that the return to Italy of hundreds of thousands of Italian emigrants in the United States, who made what for them are fortunes, must have created an almost fabulous belief in the strength, richness, and importance of America. America's voice would carry weight in Italy superior even to that of the Roman Catholic Church.

What Italy Most Needs.

What, then, is America to say? First and most important, in the opinion of Italians, America must declare her solidarity with Italian aims by declaring war on Austria. No one who has not been recently in Italy can realize the harm done by crafty propaganda whose theme is America's abstention from war with Austria—which, say the propagandists, proves the justness of the Vatican's pacifism by showing that America also is not in sympathy with the war Italy is waging to complete her national unity.

How far that unity is in line with the Vatican's dream of temporal power may be judged by the fact that its heart and centre is Rome—the city which the Popes regard equally as the home pivot of their rule on earth. This question of Rome demarks immediately the vastness of the gulf between the Papal aspirations and those of Italy as a nation. For both parties Rome is a holy palladium whose possession guarantees and typifies everything they hold dear. Yet the Italian Government has in no way tried to hamper or interfere with the Vatican.

If the Vatican would confine its activities to spiritual affairs, no enlightened politician in Italy or France would have a word to say against it, but—and this is hard for American or Englishman to realize—the Roman Catholic Church in Continental Europe has always insisted and still insists on exerting political influence, which by the nature and traditions of the Vatican has always been absolutist and antidemocratic.

America's declaration of war on Austria and of complete solidarity with the Entente would take the strongest weapon from the hands of the anti-Italian elements in Italy. It is hard for Americans to realize the importance of this question.

To take a specific case: Cardinal Gasparri, at the time of the Pope's note and before the arrival of President Wilson's reply, gave an interview to a well known American journalist for publication in America. The whole tenor of the interview was an attempt to prove the exactitude with which the Papal views coincided with the statements and opinions of Wilson. The journalist in question was too well informed to be caught, and sacrificed a good "story" in the national interests.

When I add that the President's reply threw the Vatican literally into consternation it will be understood how fictitious was the parallel Gasparri tried to draw between the viewpoints of the Pope and our President.

This example may give an idea of what capital the Catholic Party can draw from America's failure to declare war on Austria.

Call for an American Mission.

The next most important aid, from the Italian standpoint, is that America should send to Italy an official mission, however small, of prominent men with the twofold obect of giving the Italian people concrete proof of American sympathy and of procuring for America a wider knowledge of the Italian situation. On similar lines the Italians ask that the press relations between the two countries should be strengthened, and that the leading American newspapers should be represented by their own American correspondents rather than by Italians or the use of English services.

As I said in one of my cables from the Italian front, "Is this a gang fight or not?" Are we all in a common war, or is American trying to hunt with the hounds and run with the hare? We loan Italy money, but we cannot send her men—not as a serious military aid—Italians don't ask that—but as a moral demonstration whose value would be incalculable. Our ships transport to Italy wheat or coal or steel, but theoretically at least we have no right to fire on an Austrian submarine until it has actually launched a torpedo that will send the ship, cargo, and American sailors to the bottom.

Her Need of Coal and Wheat.

That brings me to the question of material assistance. It may be summed up in two words—coal and wheat. Italy neds other things—steel and guns, munitions, and rolling stock for railroads—but her need for them is less imperative. On coal and wheat depends the whole economic and physical life of the country—the heart's blood of her industries and the food of her people. In America we think the Italian masses live on spaghetti and macaroni, but they can do without either. Like the French, bread is their staple food and deprived of bread they will weaken under the strain. For the matter of that, spaghetti and macaroni are also prepared from wheat, so that either way you look at it wheat is the paramount necessity.

Unfortunately through a mistaken expectation of a short war, to which I referred in a previous dispatch, the Italian Government neglected to make economic conventions with her Western Allies on terms and at a time that would have enabled her to satisfy her present needs. She looks now to America.

And does America realize what failure to aid her might involve, what result might follow from disaster to Italy?

Remember France's burden has been borne long and is terrible beyond words.

Kaiser at Italian Front with Charles and Ferdinand

AMSTERDAM, Nov. 12.—The German Emperor arrived Sunday at the Italian front, where he met Emperor Charles and King Ferdinand of Bulgaria, according to a Gorizia dispatch. He congratulated Emperor Charles on his escape from drowning.

The Kaiser continued his journey along the front.

PLAN STRICTER BAN ON MUNITION PLANTS

Waterfront Fire Here May Lead to Revision of Rules for Permits.

Government to Insist That Its Own Interests Are Above Those of Employers.

Special to The New York Times.

WASHINGTON, Nov. 12.—The execution of the plan adopted by the Government almost from the beginning of the war to safeguard manufacturing plants engaged on war supplies is being questioned now by owners of warehouses and plants where fires and explosions have occurred under suspicious circumstances suggesting the activity of enemies. The permit system, it is urged, does not work, as plotters are still able to get employment where they can carry on their plans to the risk of large amounts of property and the hazard of human lives.

Government officials who are charged with the execution of the plan of granting permits complain that they have beeen made the target for blame by manufacturers on two counts. They have uniformly found the employers, they say, prone to plead for the retention of old enemy alien employes, and as an employer countersigns the permits obtained from the United States Marshal of the Judicial District where the plant is situated they say they have the right to retain such employes as they desire. For some reason, it was asserted, they have insisted that the special faithfulness of an employe should be considered, and have retained men who would otherwise have been kept out of war plants.

Many such enemy aliens have been in the employ of corporations or firms for years before the war in Europe. Employers cite such cases to back their contention that it would be a hardship to discharge such men, and they are usually emphatic in asking that they receive permits. When fires and explosions have occurred it was said manufacturers in several cases declared that the Government was lax in enforcing the permit plan and that had there been strict enforcement the trouble would not have occurred.

It is likely that in consequence of the New York waterfront fires there will be a more rigid inquiry into the antecedents and character of men vouched for by employers and that permits will not be so easily granted hereafter. The Government has proceeded, it was said, too much on the theory that the judgment of the employers in regard to their men could be relied on and that their own self-interest was sufficient to safeguard the industry. But officials now admit that this view is not conclusive of all contingencies and that a hard and fast exercise of caution is demanded. No new method of protecting munition plants will be employed, but there will be new regulations buttressing the administration of the existing method. The Government will insist on the view that its own interests are paramount and the necessity for the output of munition plants is so great that employers must bend to the rules to be laid down by the Government.

It was said to night that there has never been carried out in this country anything like the precautions taken in English and Canadian war plants. Their uniform practice has been to place barbed wire barriers around their works and employ large and competent forces of watchmen. All employes are subjected to the most rigid test of loyalty, and monitors are kept in the works during all working hours to note any suspicious conduct or any sign of defection that might give rise to trouble. The United States Government has no present intention of going as far as this, but the practical co-operation of employers will be expected, and there will be more thoroughly organized effort hereafter to protect munition manufacturing plants.

TEUTONS CAPTURE 14,000 ITALIANS

Cut Off Retreating Forces in the Upper Piave and Cordevole Valleys.

ADVANCE DOWN THE PIAVE

Are Now Before Feltre, 17 Miles Below Belluno—Checked Elsewhere on River.

BERLIN, Nov. 12, (via London.)—The Austro-German forces in Northern Italy have cut off and captured 14,000 Italian troops—10,000 in the Upper Piave Valley and 4,000 in the Cordévole Valley—according to War Office reports.

The German afternoon statement also says that the invading forces have advanced from Belluno down the Piave and are in front of Feltre.

The text of the afternoon report reads:

The energetic collaboration of Württemberg and Austro-Hungarian mountain troops, near Longarone, barred the way of the enemy retreating in the upper Piave Valley. Ten thousand Italians were compelled to surrender, and numerous guns, material, and war stores were captured.

Our troops, who pressed forward from Belluno down the Piave, are before Feltre.

On the lower Piave there was nothing new to report.

The supplementary report from General Headquarters issued tonight says:

In Cordévole Valley, west of Belluno, 4,000 Italian prisoners were taken.

Italians Fighting on Northern Front.

ROME, Nov. 12.—The Italians have resisted the enemy everywhere on the northern front, along which the Austrians are attempting to outflank the Italian river line, the War Office reports. On the plain there is brisk firing across the Piave River.

An enemy action on the Asiago plateau, on the Trentino front, was a complete failure.

The text of the official statement follows:

From the Stelvio Pass to the Astico River there was no notable event yesterday. On the Asiago Plateau the enemy renewed yesterday afternoon his attack on our lines in the sector of Gallio, Monte Longara, Hill 1074 and Meletta di Gallio. The enemy actions failed completely under our artillery and rifle fire. On the extreme northern part of the front of the attack, where a bitter infantry struggle took place, our men counterattacked and succeeded in capturing some prisoners. On the remainder of the mountainous front, during contact engagements with the enemy vanguards, our advanced troops resisted everywhere.

On the plain across the Piave River brisk firing is reported.

Feltre is a town of about 4,600 inhabitants on a height near the Piave, seventeen miles southwest of Belluno. The town is situated about ten miles north of the Venetian plains. The military operations reported by the Germans in the mountainous region of Feltre have no direct bearing on the Italian line on the lower Piave.

"All the News That's Fit to Print."

The New York Times.

THE WEATHER
Rain, northwest gale by tonight; Friday colder, probably fair.
For full weather report see Page 20.

VOL. LXVII...NO. 21,852.

NEW YORK, THURSDAY, NOVEMBER 22, 1917.—TWENTY-FOUR PAGES.

ONE CENT In Greater New York. | TWO CENTS Within 200 Miles. | THREE CENTS Elsewhere.

HAIG HURLS HIS ARMY AT CAMBRAI, GAINING FIVE MILES; HUNDREDS OF TANKS LEAD DRIVE, CAVALRY CAPTURES GUNS; 8,000 PRISONERS TAKEN, FOE'S LAST DEFENSES REACHED

TANKS INSURE THE VICTORY

Masses of Them Open Way for British Infantry's Charges.

DESTROY WIRE DEFENSES

Giant Machines Screened by Smoke to Baffle the German Gunners.

HAIG HID HIS PREPARATIONS

Moved Tanks and Guns at Night and Few Officers Knew His Real Plans.

First Stage of the Battle.

By PHILIP GIBBS.

Copyright, 1917, by The New York Times Company.

Special Cable to THE NEW YORK TIMES.

WAR CORRESPONDENTS' HEADQUARTERS, Nov. 21.—The enemy yesterday had, I am sure, the surprise of his life on the western front, where, without any warning by ordinary preparations that are made before a battle, without any sign of strength in men and guns behind the British front, without a single shot fired before the attack, and with his great belts of hideously strong wire still intact, the British troops suddenly assaulted him at dawn, led forward by great numbers of tanks, smashed through his wire, passed beyond to his trenches, and penetrated in many places the main Hindenburg line and the Hindenburg support line beyond.

It was not only a surprise to the enemy, but, to be frank, it will be a surprise to all the British officers and men in other parts of the line. To my mind it is the most sensational and dramatic episode of this year's fighting, brilliantly imagined and carried through with the greatest secrecy. Not a whisper of it had reached men like myself, who are always up and down the lines, and since the secret of the tanks themselves, which suddenly made their appearance on the Somme last year, this is, I believe, the best kept secret of the war.

During the last twenty-four hours or so certain uneasy suspicions seem to have been aroused among the German troops immediately in front of the attack, but their higher command did not dream of such a blow. How could the enemy guess, in his wildest nightmare, that a blow would be struck quite suddenly at that Hindenburg line of his —enormously strong in redoubts, tunnels, and trenches—and without any artillery preparation or any sign of gun power behind the British front?

Tanks Secretly Moved at Night.

It is true he had withdrawn many of his guns from this "quiet" part of the front, but unless that wire of his was cut in the usual way by days of bombardment and unless there was artillery action which gives away all secrets, he had every right to believe himself safe—every right though he was wrong. He did not know that during recent nights great numbers of tanks had been crawling along the roads toward Havrincourt and the British lines below Flesquieres Ridge, hiding by day in the copses of this wooded and rolling country beyond Peronne and Bapaume. Indeed he knew little of all that was going on before him under the cover of darkness.

For the Generals and staff officers directing this operation there were hours of anxiety and suspense as the time drew near for the surprise attack. It was a most audacious adventure and depended absolutely on surprise.

Had the secret been kept? It looked as if the enemy suspected something a night or two ago when he raided the British trenches and captured two or three prisoners. Had those men told anything or had they kept the secret like brave men? All was on the hazard of that.

Relied on Wire Defenses.

It was probable that the night sentries had heard the movement of traffic on those quiet, silent nights, the clatter of gun wheels over the rough roads, the rumble of transport behind the lines, but his wire was still uncut and no new batteries revealed themselves, and that was the thing which might lull all his suspicions.

To attack against uncut wire has always been death to the infantry, and every time until this it has been the gun's job to smash the barrier. We know now that whatever suspicions were aroused, a real surprise was scored this morning. The British caught the enemy "on the hop," as men say, and in spite of uneasy moments on Monday night they had no evidence of what was coming to them and no time to prepare against the blow.

Most of the prisoners say that the first thing they knew of the attack was when, out of the mist, they saw the tanks advancing upon them, smashing down their wire, crawling over their trenches and nosing forward with gunfire and machine gun fire slashing from their sides.

The Germans were aghast and dazed. Many hid down in their dugouts and tunnels, and then surrendered. Only the steadiest and bravest of them rushed to the machine guns and got them into action and used their rifles to snipe the British.

British Rushed on Cheering.

Out of the silence which had prevailed behind the British lines a great fire of guns came upon the Germans. They knew they had been caught by an amazing stratagem, and they were full of terror. Behind the tanks, coming forward in platoons, the infantry swarmed, cheering and shouting, trudging through the thistles, while the tanks made a scythe of machine gun fire in front of

them, and thousands of shells went screaming over the Hindenburg lines.

The German artillery made but a feeble answer. Their gun positions were being smothered by the fire of all the British batteries. There were not many German batteries, and the enemy's infantry could get no great help from them. They were caught, German officers knew they had been caught, like rats in a trap. It was their black day.

I think all the British felt the drama of this adventure and had the thrill of it, a thrill which I had believed had departed out of war because of the ferocity of shellfire and the staleness of war's mechanism and formula of attack.

To me it seemed the queerest thing to be on the road again down south, where we had followed the Germans in their retreat in March of this year, and to pass over the Somme once more, to reach the first villages of the old fighting two years ago and then see the great track of that desolate, destroyed country, where the enemy in his retreat blew up every village, cut down trees and laid waste all the countryside.

A few days ago I was looking at Passchendaele in the mist. Could it be real that this morning at dawn I was passing through Peronne with the first pale light of the sky upon its ruins, across wooden bridges and into that square where we came first to look upon the German destruction of a fair little city? Houses were burning when I went in the first time, but only their ashes remained today. It was stranger now after Passchendaele to come back for this other battle, which had come so swiftly and so stealthily.

Shell Craters Were Lacking.

The battle had begun and the British had already gone away to the Hindenburg line when I went forward through the thistles. It was queer to see the absence of mud and shell craters. I walked over to the village of Beaucamp and the front line trenches, from which our men were attacking. Just to the left of me was the brown earth of newly dug assembly trenches. I think they must have been dug in the night.

A little beyond were the white parapets of the Hindenburg line, and beyond that again a few hundred yards the villages of Ribecourt and Flesquieres, toward which our men were fighting.

Behind me were our field batteries and the "heavies" through which I had passed. They were not in hiding but were in full view of the astonished enemy and were making an intense bombardment, so that the air was filled with the scream of shells and with the frightful thumping of fire, so that one's ears were deadened, while the mists of early morning were thrust through with gunflashes.

Having left the salient where it seemed to me we had most of our guns, it was astounding to see so many batteries here. From the ruins of Beaucamp I walked across to Flesquieres Ridge. To the left of me was the wood of Trescault, and higher up Havrincourt Wood and the Château of Havrincourt, which is still standing, though in ruins. Outside the village, where there are roofless houses and standing walls, unlike villages in the Flanders fighting, which have only a stone or two and a stick or two to mark their site, the battle picture was the most wonderful thing I have seen in this war, wonderful because very strange.

The war in South Africa was fought before intense bombardments, as we know them, had been invented, and the fighting must have been like this. The

is rolling, unpitted by those great cavities which mark the Flemish battlefields for miles. It was dotted about with camps, horses, guns, gun-limbers, transport, and all the movement of an army in action.

A number of tanks were on the battlefield "resting" awhile for another advance. The strange gray masses in the pale light of morning were scarcely visible at any distance. I spoke to one of the pilots. "How are you doing?" I asked. "We are giving them merry hell," he said. "It is our day out."

He was thoroughly pleased with himself, and only sorry that his tank was temporarily indisposed. As I stood looking down on the battle, seeing only gunfire and nothing of the infantry in the thistles, though I was very close, I heard the awful sweep of machine-gun fire from the flanks of the tanks. It was answered by machine guns from the enemy redoubts in Lateau Wood, where there was heavy fighting going on, and in Flesquières Village, on the height of the crest in front of where I stood.

It was a very dreadful sound in one steady blast of fire from many of those weapons, from hundreds of them, and broken into by a sharp staccato hammering, like a coffin maker with his tacks, from single machine guns closer to the captured ground. Hardly a shellburst came from the enemy's side, I think. I saw only a dozen big shells burst anywhere near the British batteries, though the fire of shrapnel was greater over the lines of advance— greater, but with nothing like the intensity of the battle up north. It was clear at a glance that the enemy was weak in artillery.

One of the battalions, Royal Fusiliers, gained their objectives without a single casualty. Other battalions of English county regiments had very light losses, and they were mostly from machine gun bullets. At the field dressing station on the southern part of the attack they had only received 200 walking wounded by 11 o'clock in the morning, five hours or so after the battle began. They were very few as battles go now, but I hated to see those poor fellows coming out of the fighting and making their way down in long, long trails to the dressing station. Some of them could hardly hobble, and every few hundred yards had to sit down and rest against a bank of sunken road.

Some of them were helped down by German prisoners, and it was queer to see a Tommy with his arms around the necks of two Germans. German wounded helped down by British men less hurt than they walked in the same way, with their arms around the necks of their enemies, and sometimes English and German soldiers came along together very slowly, arm in arm, like old cronies.

Most of the prisoners on my side of the battlefield were from the 20th Landwehr Division, which had relieved the 54th overnight. They were Brunswick men and oldish fellows. Through fields of thistles came single figures and little groups of wounded, and on the sides of some of the tracks were groups of prisoners with their guards, and on the ground badly wounded men on stretchers waiting for relays of stretcher bearers or ambulances. Some of the ambulance drivers were wonderful, and drove within a few hundred yards of the battle to pick up fallen men.

In spite of their pain and weariness, the wounded always had a cheery word to say. "How is it going?" I asked, and man after man said: "Oh, it's splendid. We're doing grand! The boys are going straight on." One man, a Cockney fellow, wounded in the leg, kept a group of comrades halted for a rest on their way back in roars of

New Line Won by the Great British Drive on Cambrai

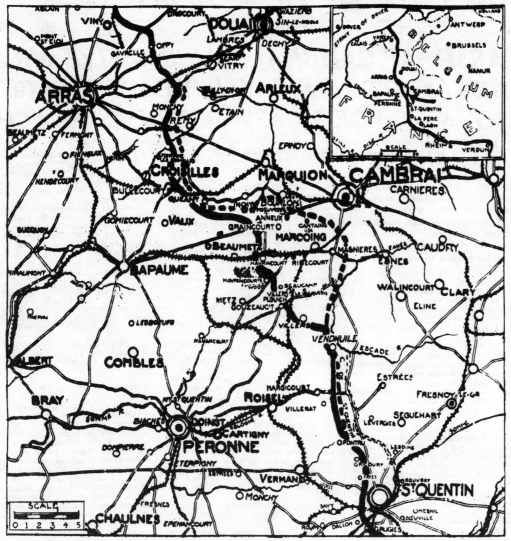

The broken line indicates approximately the position reached by Field Marshal Haig's advance, which began early Tuesday morning and has penetrated at one point (Cantaing) to within less than three miles of Cambrai. The drive at Cambrai imperils the entire Hindenburg line from St. Quentin to the sea. The inserted map shows the general configuration of the western front.

laughter as he described his adventures of the morning and how he was hit by a German sniper who suddenly appeared out of a trench. He used lurid language, but was so comical and honest a fellow that a padre standing near joined in the shouts of laughter, that followed his monologue. This padre and others this morning went very close to the lines with hot coffee and brandy in their flasks to meet the wounded and help them.

One of the wonders of the day was the work of the British airmen. Just after dawn they came flying overhead so low that they seemed to make a breeze over my steel hat, so low that they waved hands to the infantry and shouted cheery words to them as they went through the enemy's lines. In the air the enemy was stone dead this morning. He had been caught napping in the sky as well as on the earth.

In strategy, it seems to me, the battle may prove the best adventure we have had. The enemy was utterly deceived.

HOW THE CAVALRY WENT IN

Dashed After Tanks and Infantry and Charged Enemy Batteries.

TANKS NUMBERED HUNDREDS

Squadrons of Land Battleships Had a General to Command Them.

HIS TERSE ORDER OBEYED

Second Stage of the Battle

By PHILIP GIBBS.

Copyright, 1917, by The New York Times Company.

Special Cable to THE NEW YORK TIMES.

WAR CORRESPONDENTS' HEADQUARTERS IN FRANCE, Wednesday Night, Nov. 21.—In my earlier messages, which were held back for military reasons of the soundest kind, I was able to give only an outline and a beginning of the most striking strategical blow the British have inflicted on the enemy. Now, after hours spent in the area of fighting at Ribecourt and Flesquières Ridge, with the battle in progress to the left, where the great Bois de Bourlon dominates the ground, I am able to give more details about this dramatic adventure of our troops. There is no longer any need for secrecy.

I have already told how we surprised the enemy by the stealthiness of our preparation, by the absence of all shell fire from batteries moved up to new positions in darkness, and by the skillful distribution of bodies of troops in well chosen positions. What I was not able to tell earlier was that a mass of cavalry was also brought up and hidden very close to the enemy's lines, ready to make a sweeping drive should the Hindenburg line be pierced and broken by the advance of the tanks over the great belts of barbed wire and the deep, wide trenches of the strongest lines on the western front.

Yesterday I saw the cavalry in all this country waiting for their orders to saddle up and get their first great chance. I was astounded to see them there and was stirred by a great thrill of excitement, not without some tragic foreboding, because after seeing much of the war on this front and coming straight from Flanders with its terrifying artillery and frightful barrages, it seemed to me incredible that after all cavalry should ride out into the open and round up the enemy. I had seen the Hindenburg lineup by Bullecourt and Quéant and knew the strength of it and the depth of the barbed wire belts that surround it.

Horsemen in Gay Spirits.

The cavalry were in the highest spirits and full of tense expectation. Young cavalry officers galloped past smiling and called out a cheery "Good morning," like men who have good sport ahead. In the folds of land toward the German lines there were thousands of cavalry horses, massed in parks, with their horse artillery limbered up, and ready for their ride.

All through yesterday morning the infantry officers and men taking part in the advance were asked the question, "When are the cavalry going through?" and then I heard the news: "The cavalry are through." With all my heart and soul I wished them luck on the ride.

This morning very early, in the steady rain and wet mist, I saw squadrons of them going into action, and it was the most stirring sight I had seen for many a long day in this war, one which I sometimes thought I should never live to see. They rode past me as I walked along the road through our newly captured ground and across the Hindenburg line. They streamed by at a quick trot and the noise of the horses' hoofs was a strange, rushing sound.

Rain slashed down upon their steel hats, their capes were glistening, and mud was flung up to the horses' flanks, as in long columns they went up and down the rolling country and cantered up the steep track, making a wide curve around two great mine craters in roads which the enemy had blown up in his retreat. It was a wonderful picture to see and remember.

Other squadrons of cavalry had already gone ahead and had been fighting in the open country since midday yesterday after crossing the bridges as Masnières and Marcoing, which the enemy did not have time to destroy. They had done well. One squadron rode down a battery of German guns, and a patrol had ridden into Flesquières Village, when the Germans were still there. Still other bodies of cavalry had swept around German machine-gun emplacements and German villages and drawn many prisoners into their net.

The drama was far beyond the most fantastic imagination. This attack on the Hindenburg lines before Cambrai has never been approached on the western front, and the first act began when the tanks moved forward before dawn toward the long, wide belts of wire, which they had to destroy before the rest could follow.

Order Tanks to Do Their "Damnedest."

These squadrons of tanks were led into action by the General commanding their corps, who carried his flag on his own tank—a most gallant man, full of enthusiasm for his monsters and their brave crews, and determined that this day should be theirs. To every officer and man of the tanks he sent this order of the day before the battle:

"The Tank Corps expects that every tank this day will do its damnedest."

They did. As the pilot of one of them told me, they "Played merry hell." They moved forward in small groups, several hundreds of them, rolled down the German wire, trampled down its lines, and then crossed the deep gulf of the Hindenburg main line, pitching their noses downward as they drew their long bodies over the parapets, rearing up again with their long forward reach of body, and heaving themselves on to the ground beyond.

The German troops knew nothing of the fate that awaited them until out of the gloom of dawn they saw these great numbers of gray inhuman creatures bearing down upon them, crushing down their wire, crossing their impregnable lines, firing fiercely from their flanks, and sweeping the trenches with machine gun bullets.

"All the News That's Fit to Print."

The New York Times.

THE WEATHER
Fair today and Thursday; slight temperature change; west winds.
For full weather report see Page 23.

VOL. LXVII...NO. 21,865. NEW YORK, WEDNESDAY, DECEMBER 5, 1917.—TWENTY-FOUR PAGES. ONE CENT In Greater New York. | TWO CENTS Within Commuting Distance. | THREE CENTS Elsewhere.

PRESIDENT CALLS FOR IMMEDIATE WAR ON AUSTRIA; CONGRESS WOULD INCLUDE BULGARIA AND TURKEY; OUR WATCHWORDS ARE: JUSTICE, REPARATION, SECURITY

WILSON FOR VICTORY FIRST

"We Shall Not Slacken or Be Diverted Until It Is Won."

PACIFISTS TOUCH NO HEART

"May Be Left to Strut Their Uneasy Hour and Be Forgotten," Says President.

FIGHTING TO FREE GERMANY

Throng in the House Stands to Cheer Message—La Follette Remains Seated.

Special to The New York Times.

WASHINGTON, Dec. 4.—With dramatic suddenness, yet with no apparent effort at dramatic effect, President Wilson, addressing in person the Senate and the House of Representatives assembled in joint session today, recommended that "the Congress immediately declare the United States in a state of war with Austro-Hungary."

The legislators and the great crowd of spectators who filled floor and galleries were unprepared for the call for a declaration of war. On the contrary, some preceding parts of the President's address had tended to create the impression that the Vienna Government, although allied with Germany, was entitled to special consideration, to charitable treatment, in the realization that it was a mere tool of the military autocracy at Berlin. Then came the call for action against the Dual Monarchy.

The effect was electrical. Not for a moment was the President left in doubt as to the temper of Congress regarding this recommendation. A thrill went through that audience of men and women who had listened with increasing interest to every word that had come with clear-cut distinctness from the lips of the man, who, more than any other, controls the destinies of the nation at this critical time.

War Call Unexpected.

The assemblage had risen before to heights of patriotic enthusiasm over appealing passages of the President's address. But only a minute prior to the stirring declaration his auditors had heard expressions which brought the too ready interpretation that the hour was not at hand when the United States should undertake to deal in a hostile military way with Germany's chief partner in the war. He had named Austria specifically, along with Serbia and Poland, in mentioning the countries he had in mind when, last January, before America entered the great European conflict, he had declared that the nations of the world "were entitled not only to free pathways upon the sea but also to assured and unmolested access to those pathways."

The disappointment of those—and they were many—who had looked for a stirring denunciation of Austro-Hungarian intrigue and international criminality was short-lived. The temporary elation of the few pacifists who were there dropped like a dead weight in a vacuum.

Prior to the remarkable demonstration of patriotic fervor that followed the President's declaration, his auditors had had ample opportunity to find an outlet for their feelings, for the address was filled with statements that appealed in full measure to love of country and determination to see the sanguinary struggle on the battlefields of Europe to a finish.

An important feature of the address was the reiteration and amplification of the war aims of America: Belgium and Northern France must be delivered from Prussian conquest and Prussian menace, but the peoples of Austria-Hungary, the Balkans and Turkey, "alike in Europe and in Asia," must be freed also from Prussian domination; "we do not wish in any way to impair or rearrange the Austro-Hungarian Empire"; "our attitude and purpose with regard to Germany herself are of a like kind"; "we intend no wrong against the German Empire, no interference with her internal affairs."

Assailed Germans' Masters.

If the German people continued after the war to accept the Government of their present masters, the President said, "it might be impossible to admit them to the partnership of nations which must henceforth guarantee the world's peace," and "it might be impossible also to admit Germany to the free economic intercourse which must inevitably spring out of the other partnerships of a real peace"; "the wrongs, the very deep wrongs, committed in this war will have to be righted."

If the Marquis of Lansdowne can find comfort in the analogy between his own statement of war aims and those of President Wilson, he will be disappointed in the President's attitude toward the other proposal of the British statesman—that a reiteration of war aims shall be used as a basis for peace negotiations. President Wilson is not in sympathy with this program. He left no doubt on that score in his address when he declared that "the German power must be crushed," and emphasized it with such stirring utterances as these:

"Our present and immediate task is to win the war, and nothing shall turn us aside until it is accomplished. We shall regard the war as won only when the German people say to us, through properly accredited representatives, that they are ready to agree to a settlement based upon justice."

The President declared that 'every power and resource we possess, whether of men, of money, or of materials, is being devoted, and will continue to be devoted, to that purpose [winning the war] until it is achieved," and added:

"Those who desire to bring peace about before that purpose is achieved, I counsel to carry their advice elsewhere. We will not entertain it."

These declarations brought cheers from the great crowd assembled in the chamber of the House. But the greatest demonstration came when the President called upon Congress to make war against Austria-Hungary. This satisfied the gathering, and there was no trace of disappointment when immediately thereafter he indicated that, while the logic of the situation that had forced us to put Austria on the same plane as Germany "would lead us also to a declaration of war against Turkey and Bulgaria," these two nations were mere tools of Germany and "do not yet stand in the direct path of our necessary action."

But immediately after the President left the Capitol sentiment began to develop among Senators and Representatives in favor of making war on Bulgaria and Turkey as well as Austria, and an effort to include all three of Germany's allies in the new declaration of war is now afoot.

Crowd Rises with Cheers.

When the President unexpectedly called for war on Austria, a cheer that came from a dozen places at once broke the silence that had been intensified by the sense of disappointment over the feeling he had created that the day of reckoning with the Vienna Government, and particularly with those Austrian subjects in America who were playing Germany's game of intrigue and incendiarism under the very nose of the United States, was not at hand. It was as if the President had carried his auditors through the gamut of patriotic emotions to bring them back to a depressing feeling that their enthusiasm had been wasted, and then had flashed upon them the great thing they wanted and had lost hope of realizing.

That cheer, sharper because scattered, became a mighty shout. More dignified legislators and public officials contented themselves with clapping their hands, but the younger element of the House gave vent to their joy in "yip-yip-yips" and variations of that masculine vocal emotion which in Congress has come to be called "the Rebel yell." As the applause continued, Senators and Representatives, Republicans with Democrats, rose to their feet to emphasize their approval of the welcome words they had just heard the President utter.

Chief Justice White, seated with five other Justices of the United States Supreme Court directly in front of the rostrum where the President stood waiting for the demonstration to subside, rose with the rest and swept the audience behind him with a beaming smile that left no doubt of the satisfaction he felt. Senator Lodge, seated almost directly behind the Chief Justice, returned the smile and nodded understandingly as he beat the palms of his hands together vigorously like a boy at a play.

Women in the galleries waved their handkerchiefs. The "rebel yell" punctuated the more even roar of cheering and the continuous patter of handclapping.

Barring the President, one man on that floor of enthusiastic Americans came in for the greatest share of attention while the demonstration was in progress. He was Robert M. La Follette, Senator from Wisconsin. Around him were men standing, cheering, and otherwise showing their approval of the pronouncement that Germany's most powerful associate was to be declared an enemy of the United States.

La Follette Refuses to Stand.

But La Follette kept his seat, an evident mark of his disapproval of any measure directed against the Teutonic autocracy. The usual smile of defiance that has appeared on the Wisconsin Senator's face when things were going against him was not there. He showed his resentment of the patriotic outburst that raged about him by remaining in his seat while his brother Senators stood. Another who failed to stand was Congressman at Large William Mason of Illinois.

The demonstration compelled the President to suspend his address which he had been reading from small typewritten sheets laid upon the high desk in front of him. Behind him were seated Speaker Clark and Vice President Marshall, presiding officers of the joint session. He stepped aside while the cheering lasted, and waited without show of any elation or other feeling for an opportunity to resume the reading.

Mr. Wilson has seldom or never appeared to better personal advantage since his residence in Washington. The black frock coat which he usually wore when he addressed Congress had given way to a dark cutaway—a morning coat—that fitted closely to his figure and gave him an almost youthful trimness. From behind the lapels of his waistcoat peeped white slips that relieved the sombreness of that garment and the coat. And for the usual black or black-and-white striped cravat there had been substituted a real "creation" in neckwear, with colored figures twisting through it. At least that was the way it looked from the press gallery.

It took the President thirty-three minutes to deliver his address, which was the "annual message" required by the Constitution to be communicated to the Congress at the opening of each December session. He had entered the hall of the House at exactly 12:30 o'clock, the hour fixed for his appearance. Shortly prior to that time the Senate had marched in a body from its end of the Capitol, led by Vice President Marshall, to participate in the joint assemblage. The galleries were then crowded with spectators who were obliged to have special cards of admission for the occasion.

Mrs. Wilson and a party of relatives and friends sat in the "Executive box" in one of the reserved galleries. Most of the members of the Cabinet had seats on the floor. Many distinguished diplomats and Americans also were present.

The President got a rousing welcome when he entered the House. Throughout his address there were enthusiastic outbursts. When he had finished and turned to go, with a bow to the Speaker and the Vice President, the crowd began cheering, which was kept up until he was out of sight. Then the Senate returned to its wing of the Capitol.

WAR DECLARATION READY

Resolution Aligning Austria as Foe Likely to Pass This Week.

MANY WOULD GO FURTHER

Inclined to Declare War on Turkey and Bulgaria Unless Good Reason Is Given.

MESSAGE HIGHLY PRAISED

But Disappointment Keen at Failure to Urge War on All of Germany's Vassals.

Special to The New York Times.

WASHINGTON, Dec. 4.—Immediate action by Congress is to follow President Wilson's demand today for a declaration of war against Austria-Hungary. In both houses the sentiment is unwavering for such a declaration, and it is likely that the country will be arrayed as an enemy of Austria-Hungary by the end of this week.

The House Foreign Affairs Committee

will tomorrow draft a resolution, which is likely to be offered before the day is over, declaring war on Austria-Hungary. The Senate Foreign Relations Committee will not meet until Thursday—the Senate having adjourned today until Friday—when a similar resolution will be prepared.

Representative Flood, Chairman of the House Foreign Affairs Committee, has called his committee to meet at 2 o'clock tomorrow afternoon. He is prepared to report a resolution declaring war against Austria-Hungary. There is no opposition to such a course, but action may be delayed by reason of a strong demand to include Turkey and Bulgaria in such a declaration. Indications are that the latter course will be pursued unless the President furnishes the committee with a compelling reason against the inclusion of Turkey and Bulgaria.

As to Austria-Hungary, nothing remains to be done but make the formal declaration, for only scant opposition is expected to spring up. Senators and Representatives who voted against the declaration of war against Germany were not talking today against the President's pronouncement for throwing down the gage of battle to Austria. An almost complete unanimity of sentiment prevailed as to the logic of putting Austria-Hungary in the enemy alignment.

Omission of Turkey and Bulgaria.

The talk at the Capitol after the President's message bore more upon the Executive's advice against a pronouncement against Turkey and Bulgaria than upon the demand for hostilities against Austria-Hungary. Leaders in both houses, Democrats and Republicans alike, expressed not only frank surprise, but regret that the President had not included Turkey and Bulgaria. They felt that Turkey, as one of the arch allies of Germany, ought to be embraced in any declaration of war, and that no obvious reason existed for leaving out Bulgaria.

Members of the Senate Committee on Foreign Relations and the House Committee on Foreign Affairs unhesitatingly expressed the belief that resolutions putting Turkey and Bulgaria along with Austria-Hungary as enemies of the United States would be offered in both houses and passed. For the United States to declare war against Austria-Hungary and not against Turkey, it was suggested by some, smacked of inconsistency. No disposition was manifest to quarrel with the President in having left Turkey and Bulgaria out of it. The opinion was ventured that the President must have had a sufficient reason for naming Austria-Hungary alone, depending, perhaps, upon Congress to take the initiative with the two other countries.

Senator Stone, Chairman of the Senate Committee on Foreign Relations, said that the committee would draft its resolution against Austria-Hungary on Thursday, and that it would be offered to the Senate the following day.

"All along, since the declaration of war against Germany, I have favored putting Austria-Hungary, Turkey, and Bulgaria in the list of America's enemies," said Senator Stone. "Congress will act quickly in declaring war on Austria-Hungary. I hope similar action will just as speedily be taken against Turkey and Bulgaria. If it develops that there is a diplomatic reason why we should not at this time include Turkey and Bulgaria, Congress naturally will withhold action. Such intimation would come, if there were occasion for it, from the White House. I believe I am safe in saying that, unless Congress hears that it would be unwise to act now, declarations will at once be made against Turkey and Bulgaria."

Senator Lodge, another of the Foreign Relations Committee, said he could not understand why the President did not ask for a declaration against Turkey and Bulgaria along with Austria-Hungary.

"I have always favored declaring war against all of Germany's allies," said Senator Lodge. "It seems to me that Congress ought not to delay in including them all. Congress, after all, has the power to declare war."

A Resolution for War.

Soon after the Senate met, following the President's message, Senator Pittman of Nevada offered a resolution, in behalf of Senator King of Utah, embracing a declaration of war against Austria-Hungary, Turkey, and Bulgaria. It was referred without comment to the Foreign Relations Committee. The resolution follows:

> Joint resolution declaring that a state of war exists between the United States of America and Austria-Hungary, Bulgaria, and Turkey.
>
> *Whereas*, The Congress did upon the 6th day of April, 1917, declare that a state of war exists between the United States of America and the Imperial Government of Germany; and,
>
> *Whereas*, In the course of the war it has become manifest that the Governments of Austria-Hungary, of Bulgaria, and of Turkey have become and are vassals of the Imperial Government of Germany; and,
>
> *Whereas*, The military forces and materials of Austria-Hungary, of Bulgaria, and of Turkey are being exerted and employed by Germany against the United States of America; and,
>
> *Whereas*, The defeat of Austria-Hungary, of Bulgaria, and of Turkey is necessary to a military decision against Germany; now, therefore, be it
>
> *Resolved*, That the state of war exists between the United States of America and the Governments of Austria-Hungary, Bulgaria, and Turkey, and that the United States wage and make war against said Governments as the vassals of the Imperial Government of Germany.

Here are typical expressions on the President's message from members of both houses of Congress:

Admirable and Even Inspiring.

Representative Miller, Minnesota—That part of the President's recommendations to Congress as to measures and methods in carrying on the war with the utmost vigor to complete victory is admirable and even inspiring. The recommendation that we declare war on Austria is armirable. We should have taken that action six months ago. However, I feel strongly that we should go the whole length. We should declare war on Bulgaria and Turkey.

Representative Porter, Pennsylvania—It was a very high-class message. It was a careful statement of the situation, and I approve of his declaration of purpose very heartily. I think it comes at a good time and will have a good effect upon the country.

Speaker Clark—The present anomalous situation with respect to Germany and her allies is perfectly demoralizing. Of course, there ought to be a declaration of war against Austria, and it ought to be against Turkey and Bulgaria, too. It is ridiculous to fight one-half the enemy and not the other half.

Majority Leader Kitchin—The President's message comes nearer reflecting the thought and sentiment of the American people than anything we have heard since the war began.

Minority Leader Gillett—I was very favorably impressed with the message. I think it is the best we have heard from the President, and I am in hearty accord with his views in general. I particularly agree with the decision to declare war against Austria. I only wish he had gone far enough to include Turkey. Bulgaria has not done anything to offend us, but Turkey's course during the war has been so contemptible that I do not think we should hesitate or delay in declaring war against her.

A Powerful Exposition.

Representative Fess, Ohio—It was a powerful exposition, succinctly expressed, and leaves no doubt in the minds of the people of America or other nations of the sort of peace this country will demand. I am especially pleased with the demand for a declaration of war against Austria-Hungary.

Representative Flood, Virginia—It was a splendid message and has my hearty approval. As Chairman of the Foreign Relations Committee of the House, I would have presented today the resolution calling for a declaration of war on Austria but for the early adjournment. I will present such a resolution tomorrow.

Representative Britten, Illinois—I thoroughly approve of the President's recommendation for a declaration of war on Austria. I think that he should have gone a step further and called for a declaration of war on Turkey and Bulgaria.

Representative Longworth, Ohio—It was a very impressive message. I do not quite get the President's distinction as to the necessity of a war on Austria without making war on the other allies of Germany.

Turkey the Outlaw of Nations.

"I am entirely in accord with the President's demand for a declaration of war against Austria-Hungary," said Senator Borah of the Foreign Relations Committee. "For my part, I wish he had included Turkey and Bulgaria in it. The United States to my mind ought to have declared war against Austria-Hungary, Turkey, and Bulgaria at the time we went into the war against Germany.

"The President struck a responsive chord with Congress in his demand for a declaration of war on Austria," said Senator Martin, Democratic floor leader. "I hope Congress includes Turkey and Bulgaria."

Senator Brandegee of Connecticut favored a declaration against Austria-Hungary, Turkey, and Bulgaria, as did Senator Ashurst of Arizona. Hardly a Senator could be found who did not urge the inclusion of Turkey and Bulgaria in the declaration of war.

WHOLE WORLD GOT WILSON'S MESSAGE

Steps Taken for It to Reach Indirectly All of the Enemy Capitals.

SENT ABROAD AS HE SPOKE

35,000 Miles of Telegraph Wires Used as Well as Wireless and Other Means of Transmission.

President Wilson's address to Congress was heralded yesterday throughout the world by the United States Government.

Nearly every known means of communication—express train, telephone, telegraph, wireless, and submarine cable—was utilised in transmitting the address. While an operator in New York was clicking off its text on a transcontinental wire direct to San Francisco, where it was immediately relayed to the Orient, another at his side was sending a Spanish translation to Colon, Panama Canal Zone, from where it radiated throughout the Central and Southern American capitals.

Wireless operators picked the President's words out of the air and relayed them to Caribbean Sea points. Doubtless many ships in these waters knew what was being said in Washington at almost the same time the address was being distributed over telegraphic systems in this country.

It is estimated that approximately 35,000 miles of telegraph and cable wires were called into use in transmitting the message.

George Creel, Chairman of the Committee on Public Information, who directed the sending out of the address, received a copy of it in this city by special courier from Washington early in the day. A corps of typists was put at work in a locked room to make duplicate copies. Meanwhile, in an adjoining room, the address was being translated into French and Spanish. These rooms were guarded as a precaution against the contents of the message becoming public prematurely.

Upon receiving word from Washington that President Wilson had begun delivering the address, shortly after noon, a corps of telegraph and cable operators immediately began their task of wiring the message broadcast—across the United States to San Francisco, there to be relayed to Shanghai and thence to Tokio and Peking; across the Atlantic to London, where it was picked up and resent to the Continent, and down the eastern coast to Panama for transmission to Central and South American points.

At London and Paris the message was placed in the hands of the established commercial and governmental news agencies. From London a French translation was forwarded to Paris. London also served as a relay point to Stockholm, Copenhagen, Christiania, and The Hague. From Stockholm a copy of the message was sent to the American Embassy at Petrograd. London also filed to Algiers and other Northern African points.

From Paris were served Lisbon, Madrid, Rome, and Berne.

New York sent the address to South America, the most southern point being Rio de Janeiro. This cable runs by way of Colon to Chile. Colon relayed to Bogota, Valparaiso, Quito, and Lima, Lima in turn forwarding to La Pas and Valparaiso to Santiago and Buenos Aires.

Colon was the point from which the message radiated throughout Central America.

In the absence of perfected news agencies with extensive connections in Central and South America, copies of the message were placed directly in the hands of American Ministers in these countries for immediate release to newspapers and distributing organizations in their jurisdictions.

Indirectly the address will get to Berlin and other enemy capitals.

WILSON CONVINCING, IS LONDONERS' VIEW

Address to Congress Arrives at Night—Rush to Tickers to Learn of It.

Special Cable to THE NEW YORK TIMES.

LONDON, Wednesday, Dec. 5.—Although President Wilson's address to Congress is understood to have been filed for cabling early in the day, it was 9 o'clock last night before it began to appear on the tickers here. It had been awaited with a tenser interest than I have ever known to be given to a Presidential utterance before.

At one great London political club, when the news spread that President Wilson's speech was coming through on the tape, there was a rush to the machine, and members stood three or four deep spelling out the words as they were ticked off.

Comment under such circumstances for the moment necessarily must be hurried. On one point, however, there was unanimity of opinion. This was that the President had put into words the thoughts that lie deep in the breasts of all who are fighting for freedom and had pointed out clearly and convincingly the essential things that make this war worth while.

The Times in a editorial on Wilson's message, says:

"With this straight forward and logical statement of America's war aims the last hope of the pacifists must founder."

In regard to the President's picture of the German nation, the Times says, it can discover no solid grounds for supposing that it is true.

"For the present," it says, "we must continue to regard the German people as willing accomplices of their rulers."

The Chronicle says:

"In its principle it does not deviate from the previous war utterances of the President, but at a time like the present even reaffirmations may have first-class importance. Nothing could be more emphatic nor in the circumstances of the moment bolder than the President's reassertion of the need of an out-and-out victory over the Prussian autocracy. He literally nails his colors to the mast."

FRANCE ON BREAD RATION.

Allowance of 1 1-3 Pounds a Day for Men Doing Hard Manual Work.

PARIS, Dec. 4.—The bread ration has been officially fixed.

Men employed in hard manual labor are allowed 600 grammes (about 1 1-3 pounds) daily and women 500 grammes. Men employed in light work will be permitted to have 400 grammes and women 300.

All other men and women are to be allowed 200 grammes.

"All the News That's Fit to Print."

The New York Times.

THE WEATHER
Light snow today; cold; Tuesday fair and cold; northwest winds.
For full weather report see Page 19.

VOL. LXVII...NO. 21,877.   NEW YORK, MONDAY, DECEMBER 17, 1917.—TWENTY PAGES.

ARMISTICE IS SIGNED BY BOLSHEVIKI; PEACE NEGOTIATIONS TO BEGIN AT ONCE; TROTZKY THREATENS TO USE GUILLOTINE

TRUCE "PROTECTS" ALLIES

Only Transfers of Troops That Had Begun Can Be Carried Out.

APPEAL MADE TO PEASANTS

With Workmen's Councils, Are Urged Not to Balk Success of Revolution.

WANT EX-CZAR IN CAPITAL

Soldiers Demand That Nicholas and Family Be Imprisoned There or at Kronstadt.

Trotzky Tells Opponents They May Expect Guillotine

PETROGRAD, Dec. 16.—The Executive Committee of the Workmen's and Soldiers' Delegates, by a vote of 150 to 104, today approved a decree declaring the Constitutional Democrats enemies of the people. The Peasants' Congress, by a vote of 360 to 321, denounced the arrest of members of the Constituent Assembly, and called upon the country and the army and navy to defend the Delegates with all their forces.

Leon Trotzky, the Bolshevist Foreign Minister, in an address to his opponents, said today:

"You are perturbed by the mild terror we are applying to our enemies. But know that within a month this terror will take the terrible form of the French revolutionary terror—not the fortress, but the guillotine."

BERLIN, Dec. 16, (via London.)—An armistice agreement between the Bolshevist Government in Russia and the Teutonic allies was signed at Brest-Litovsk yesterday, according to an official communication issued today. The armistice becomes effective at noon Monday and is to remain in force until Jan. 14. A provision in the agreement is that peace negotiations are to begin immediately after the signing of the armistice. The text of the communication follows:

Germans Now "Long for Conciliation"; Foes Urged to Avoid Victor's Heavy Hand

Special Cable to THE NEW YORK TIMES.

THE HAGUE, Dec. 16.—Commenting on Lloyd George's speech, the Lokal-Anzeiger says:

"The British Prime Minister is vying with Wilson in forceful language, and their ideas are so completely identical that it is difficult to tell one from the other. 'Victory first; negotiations afterward,' is their motto; they know no middle way. With us it is just the contrary. Some of us are longing for a middle way of conciliation, and they are anxious that the enemy should not feel the heavy hand of the victor.

"Even the prospect of prolonging the war for years does not frighten Lloyd George. We only ask how long the 'busy minorities' which he deplores so impressively will leave him a free hand in his peculiar bridge-building task. To bait Russia once more he will find very difficult, and Italy will feel her defeat no less intensely because the English Prime Minister has the kindness to call it only a passing misfortune.

"We, too, believe that the present hour is not a happy one for the Entente, and our leading Generals will take care it does not improve in 1918. Then England will probably reconsider the question of a premature peace, and perhaps look at it more closely than Lloyd George has been pleased to do until now."

Calls on Germany to Move Openly for Peace.

AMSTERDAM, Dec. 16.—The Berlin Socialist paper Vorwärts, commenting on the alleged attempt to open preliminary peace discussions between Great Britain and Germany, demands that the Government tell the German people what it intended to communicate to Great Britain.

Attacking secret diplomacy, the paper suggests that both Governments are afraid to take the initiative, lest it be considered a sign of hidden weakness.

"When will it be realized," the paper asks, "that it is a great honor, instead of a disgrace, to strive with the enemy for a means for reconciliation with freedom and self-respect to end this insane human slaughter?"

The Frankfurter Zeitung says:

"Balfour did not say whether Britain was still willing to discuss the question, but there is no apparent reason why there should be a change. It is worth something that Britain formally declares her readiness for such discussion."

An armistice agreement was signed at Brest-Litovsk yesterday by plenipotentiary representatives of the Russian upper army administration on the one hand and those of the upper army administrations of Germany, Austria-Hungary, Bulgaria, and Turkey on the other hand.

The armistice begins at noon, Dec. 17, and remains in force until Jan. 14, 1918. Unless seven days' notice is given it continues in force automatically. It extends to all the land, air, and naval forces of the common fronts.

According to Clause 9 of the treaty, peace negotiations are to begin immediately after the signing of an armistice.

PETROGRAD, Dec. 16.—Announcement was made today by the Bolshevist official news agency that Russia and Germany had agreed upon the terms of an armistice. The Russian delegates constituting the Armistice Committee at Brest-Litovsk advised the Bolshevist authorities at the Smolny Institute that the agreement reached concerning the transfer of troops was to this effect:

"Both sides signing this agreement bind themselves until Dec. 30, 1917, (Jan. 12, 1918,) not to carry on operative military transfers on the front from the Baltic to the Black Sea, except such transfers as were already begun up to the moment of signing this agreement."

Leon Trotzky, the Bolshevist Foreign Minister, declared at a meeting of the Petrograd Council of Soldiers' and Workmen's Delegates last night that peace negotiations would be begun immediately after the armistice had been signed. The Foreign Minister announced that for a time a break in the negotiations seemed imminent because General Hoffmann, the German negotiator, insisted on the right to transfer troops in small units. The German commander finally accepted the Russian formula.

"We can't and won't aid militarism in any way," M. Trotzky said. "This question of transferring troops was most fundamental. I think our formula is

considered by our allies to be satisfactory."

LONDON, Dec. 16.—A Russian Government wireless message received here says:

"Ensign Krylenko, Commander in Chief of the army, in a proclamation addressed to all the army commands on all the fronts and the Military Revolutionary Committee, announces that in consequence of the signing of the armistice, which begins Dec. 17, 'I propose, until receiving the full text of the treaty, to cease all military operations.'"

An official Russian statement received here by wireless from Petrograd says that the following proclamation signed by the Commissaries of Agriculture and War and the Bolshevist Premier Lenine has been addressed to the Executive Committee of the Peasants' Deputies and the Military Council at the front:

"For the sake of closer unification of all the revolutionary forces of the laboring people, which forces are a guarantee for the victorious conclusion of the revolution, we propose to all peasant organizations and sections and to the Workmen's and Soldiers' Delegates that they shall interpose no obstacles, but shall render every possible aid to the work of developing and strengthening the peasant organizations at the front."

A dispatch from Reuter's Petrograd correspondent says that yesterday at about the same time that it was reported that former Emperor Nicholas had escaped, a meeting of the Ismailovsky and Petrogradsky Regiments was passing a resolution demanding the immediate removal of the former ruler "with Alice and family" to Kronstadt or to the St. Peter and St. Paul Fortress for strict confinement and the cancellation of all theatre privileges.

The meetings of almost all units of the Petrograd Garrison have sided with the People's Commissaries and the Workmen's and Soldiers' Delegates against the Constituent Assembly in the form originally intended. Three Cossack regiments quartered in Petrograd have offered to send detachments against General Kaledine.

The newspaper Isvestia, organ of the Workmen's and Soldiers' Delegates, says that the Maximalists, Socialists, and Social Revolutionaries of the Right must be classed with the Right parties and the counter-revolutionaries. Since the ejection of members of the Constituent Assembly from Taurida Palace by armed sailors attempts to meet there have been abandoned. The Bolshevist Red Guards broke up a meeting for the defense of the Constituent Assembly and made forty arrests. Uproarious scenes in the Peasants' Congress have followed clashes between the supporters and opponents of the Constituent Assembly.

The destruction of wine stores in Petrograd continues, accompanied by orgies and shooting.

Kaiser Puts Submarines In Special Department

LONDON, Dec. 16.—An Imperial decree prescribing for the duration of the war the formation of a new section in the German Imperial Navy Department to be called the U-Boat Department has just been published, according to an Amsterdam dispatch to Reuter's, Limited.

The new department deals solely with U-boat affairs, which heretofore have been handled by the dockyards section of the Navy Department.

"All the News That's Fit to Print."

The New York Times.

THE WEATHER

Partly cloudy, much colder today; tomorrow fair, cold; wind northwest

☞For full weather report see Page 21.

VOL. LXVII...NO. 21,885. ... NEW YORK, TUESDAY, DECEMBER 25, 1917.—TWENTY-TWO PAGES. ONE CENT In Greater New York | TWO CENTS Within 200 Miles of New York | THREE CENTS Elsewhere

TEUTONS' PEACE REPLY TO RUSSIA TODAY; KAISER THREATENS TO USE THE 'IRON FIST' AND 'SHINING SWORD' IF PEACE IS SPURNED

EMPEROR ADDRESSES TROOPS

Tells Them God Is Their 'Unconditional and Avowed Ally.'

HAS "VISIBLY PREVAILED"

German Check to British Flanders Drive Is Declared a "Most Gigantic Feat."

PROVES GERMANY'S SPIRIT

He Thanks Verdun Fighters as Helping in Eastern and Italian Victories.

AMSTERDAM, Dec. 24.—Declaring that in God the German people had " an unconditional and avowed ally," Emperor William said at the conclusion of a speech to the Second Army on the French front on Saturday:

" If the enemy does not want peace, then we must bring peace to the world by battering in with the iron fist and shining sword the doors of those who will not have peace."

The Emperor visited the front north of Verdun on Friday, according to a Berlin dispatch, and in an address to the troops thanked them warmly for their efforts.

" But for the calm and heroic warriors on the western front," he said, " the enormous deployment of German forces in the east and in Italy never would have been possible. The fighter in the west has exposed heroically his body so that his brothers on the Dvina and the Isonzo might storm from victory to victory. The fearful battles on the bloody hills around Verdun were not in vain. They created new foundations for the conduct of the war."

In his speech on Saturday the Emperor said:

" It has been a year full of events for the Germany Army and the German Fatherland. Powerful blows have been delivered, and your comrades in the east have been able to bring about great decisions.

" There has been no man, no officer and no General on the whole eastern front, wherever I have spoken to them, who has not frankly admitted that they could not have accomplished what they have if their comrades in the west had not stood to a man.

" The tactical and strategical connection between the battles on the Aisne, in the Champagne, Artois, and Flanders and at Cambrai, and the events in the east and in Italy is so manifest that it is useless to waste words on it.

" With a centralized direction, the German Army works in a centralized manner. In order that we should be able to deliver these offensive blows one portion of the army had to remain on the defensive, hard as this is for the German soldier. Such a defensive battle, however, as has been fought in 1917 is without parallel. A fraction of the German Army accepted the heavy task, covering its comrades in the east unconditionally, and it had the entire Anglo-French Army against itself.

" In long preparation the enemy had collected unheard-of technical means and masses of ammunition and guns in order to make his entry into Brussels over your front, as he proudly announced. The enemy has achieved nothing.

" The most gigantic feat ever accomplished by an army and one without parallel in history was accomplished by the German Army. I do not boast. It is a fact and nothing else. The admiration you have earned shall be your reward and at the same time your pride. Nothing can in any way place in the shade or surpass what you have accomplished, however great and overwhelming it may be.

" The year 1917 with its great battles has proved that the German people has in the Lord of Creation above an unconditional and avowed ally on whom it can absolutely rely. Without Him all would have been in vain.

" Every one of you had to exert every nerve to the utmost. I know that every one of you in the unparalleled drumfire did superhuman deeds. The feeling may have been frequently with you: ' If we only had something behind us; if we only had some relief!' It came as the result of the blow in the east, where it is seen that the storms of war there are at present silenced. God grant that it may be forever.

" Yesterday I saw and spoke to your comrades near Verdun, and there, passing through all minds like the scent of the morning breeze was the thought: ' You are no longer alone.' The great successes and victories of the recent past, the great days of battle in Flanders and before Cambrai, where the first crushing offensive blow delivered upon the arrogant British showed that despite three years of war and suffering our troops still retained their old offensive spirit, have their effect on the entire Fatherland and on the enemy.

" We do not know what is still in store for us, but you have seen how in this last of the four years of war God's

BURNED TO DEATH IN AIR.

Two Aviators at Fort Worth Die When Gasoline Tank Explodes.

FORT WORTH, Texas, Dec. 24.—Two unidentified aviators were burned to death 5,000 feet in the air at Hicks Field tonight. They fell to the earth with the remnant of the airplane a mass of wreckage. It is supposed the gasoline tank exploded.

The bodies were burned beyond identification. One is supposed to be a Lieutenant and the other a cadet in the Royal Flying Corps.

WARNING BY BAKER OF PEACE DRIVE

German Propaganda Must Not Check America's Preparations, Says War Secretary.

BIG RESPONSIBILITY ON US

We Have the "Reserves of Victory" and Must Push Forward.

WASHINGTON, Dec. 24.—Germany's newest peace propaganda, viewed as a forerunner to an offensive in the west undess a German-made peace is accepted by the Allies and the United States, "should not for a moment induce us to slacken our preparations for war," says Secretary Baker in his weekly review of the military situation.

" The Germans realize," continues the statement, " that within a short time our armies will form the principal body of fresh strategic reserves remaining available on the battlefield of Europe.

" Our armies constitute the reserves of victory."

German Arms in Italy.

The review says:

" The Italian theatre once again is the scene of important military activity. The enemy, impatient of the delays which have occurred in bringing about the successful penetration of the Italian plain and the overthrow of the Italian armies, has dispatched further forces to the Italian front, with a view to achieving a decisive result.

" The Germans are endeavoring to follow the precepts of classic strategy and by a successful enveloping movement effect the destruction of the Italian and allied forces.

" It would appear that they are anxious to conclude their Italian adventure in a manner similar to the previous campaigns in Russia, Serbia and Rumania, where, as a result of the strategic envelopments gained at relatively small cost, vast tracts of territory were conquered.

" Enemy pressure continues intense along the entire front. • • • Before proceeding with any operations in the west the Germans hope to drive the Italians back to the Adige, anticipating that such a reverse would have a very disintegrating influence throughout Italy.

" It is apparent that the Germans have not given up all hope of bringing about a social upheaval in Italy, as they did in Russia after their victorious campaigns of 1915.

" No matter how intensive this new subversive propaganda may be, nevertheless we can confidently rely on the fighting morale of the Italian people.

" Along the western front the enemy has continued his harassing raids with a view to keeping the allied forces on the alert. However, none of the engagements recorded in the west were of more than local importance. • • •

Forecasts Peace Propaganda.

" It would appear that as a forerunner to the German offensive heralded to be launched in the west, an intensive peace propaganda is to be initiated.

" Careful examination of the situation reveals that the enemy is again preparing to sue for ' peace before victory.'

" Information from various sources confirms the reports that the Germans would have the world believe that the military situation is such that they are able to dictate the terms of peace. They therefore threaten that unless this dictated peace is accepted by the allied powers and ourselves the German forces now being concentrated on the western front will break through the allied line in the west.

" The various reports of immediate peace proposals by the Germans on seemingly favorable terms should not for a moment induce us to slacken our preparations for war.

" It is only necessary for us to recall that during the Christmas season of last year the Germans put forth very similar peace rumors.

" In considering the general military situation in its true light it must be understood that the Germans realize that within a short time our armies will form the principal body of fresh strategical reserves remaining available for action on the battlefields of Europe. Thus, no matter what superiority in men and guns the enemy may for the time being be able to bring to bear in the west, and even admitting an eventual modification of the allied lines in his favor, nevertheless he knows that, in so far as it is humanly possible to foresee, his effort will inevitably result in merely a local success which can have no determining influence on the final outcome of the war.

" For the first two years of the war, France bore the brunt of battle, while Great Britain was preparing.

" Since the defeat of the German forces in front of Verdun, England and the British dominions have taken over an increasingly large share of the burden of the war.

" Italy has, to the limit of her forces, also assumed a considerable share of this burden.

" When, as a result of the defection of the Russian forces, the weight of Austro-German pressure was directed against Italy, France and England united in coming to the rescue of their ally, and are today aiding the Italian armies.

America's " Reserves of Victory."

" It is our duty, therefore, in looking to the future to realize that if we are to fulfill the pledge we made on entering the war, if we are to fight this war to a successful conclusion, we must assume the full responsibility which rests upon us. We are the freshest in the struggle; we have the reserve man power and the reserve mechanical power.

" Our armies constitute the reserves of victory.

" In Russia, the armistice negotiations having been concluded, peace negotiations are about to be entered upon.

" Reports of the dissatisfaction of a large element of the Russian population, especially in Southern and Central Russia, with the terms of the armistice have led to the formation of an active opposition which, it is believed, will endeavor to resist all attempts to enforce the proposals agreed to by the Lenine Government."

1918

"All the News That's Fit to Print."

The New York Times.

THE WEATHER
Fair today; Thursday snow; diminishing northwest to north winds.
For full weather report see Page 23.

VOL. LXVII...NO. 21,900. ..... NEW YORK, WEDNESDAY, JANUARY 9, 1918.—TWENTY-FOUR PAGES. ONE CENT In Greater New York. | TWO CENTS Within Commuting Distance. | THREE CENTS Elsewhere.

PRESIDENT SPECIFIES TERMS AS BASIS FOR WORLD PEACE; ASKS JUSTICE FOR ALSACE-LORRAINE, APPLAUDS RUSSIA, TELLS GERMANY SHE MAY BE AN EQUAL BUT NOT A MASTER

APPEALS TO GERMAN PEOPLE

Wilson Declares We Must Know for Whom Their Rulers Speak.

READY TO FIGHT TO END

Insists That Principle of Justice to All Nations Is Only Basis for Peace.

DEMANDS FREEDOM OF SEAS

Congress Cheers Utterance as Momentous Declaration of Entente War Aims.

Special to The New York Times.

WASHINGTON, Jan. 8.—The terms upon which Germany may obtain peace were given to the American Congress for the benefit of the whole world by President Wilson today. With scant notice of his coming, notice barely sufficient to enable the Senate and the House to make the necessary arrangements for a joint session, the President appeared at the Capitol, and in an address, brief by comparison to the momentous issues discussed, enumerated the conditions for a cessation of hostilities, the rejection of which will place upon Germany the responsibility for the further bloodshed that must precede the final victory of the allied nations.

President Wilson's address bore a striking resemblance to the speech made last Saturday by Mr. Lloyd George, the British Prime Minister, before the Trade Union Conference on Man Power, in which he specified the war aims and peace conditions of the British Government. The diversions in the President's address from statements of the Prime Minister were for the most part more in the form than in the substance.

But in the opinion of many of those who compared Mr. Wilson's address with the utterances of Mr. Lloyd George the President was more definite in declaring that the wrong done to France through the annexation of Alsace-Lorraine must be righted and he differed from Mr. Lloyd George with regard to the Russian situation in that he held out to the Russian people an offer of assistance from America, and tendered sympathy for the aims that those now in control of the affairs of that perturbed country are seeking to achieve.

Leaves No Doubt of Unity.

By the President's official utterances he has pledged this Government to the achievement of ends that affect Europe more intimately and deeply than the United States. No doubt was left in the minds of those who listened to the President's words that this Government has entered heart and soul into the cause of the Entente Allies, to fight for the objects for which they are fighting, to free Europe from the menace of Prussianism, to take Alsace-Lorraine from German domination, to prevent Russia from becoming part of the German Empire, to see that Italy has restored to her those portions of the Austro-Hungarian Empire that are inhabited by a people who are Italian in heart and blood, to bring all the Polish peoples into a common Government, to restore Belgium, Serbia, and the small nations that have been devastated by Teuton hordes, to their own, to give the separate nationalities of Austria-Hungary, Turkey and the Balkan States the right to govern themselves as separate entities, to have Northern France restored to French control.

And, in addition to these aims, the allied nations, in order to find a peace acceptable to them, must be assured of freedom of the seas, the establishment of an equality of trade conditions among the nations of the world, the reduction of armaments, and an association of nations in a league to enforce peace. There must also be no secret agreements among nations that would threaten again the peace of the world.

Immediately following the delivery of the President's address, there was a disposition manifest to refer to his outline of the conditions which Germany must accept before the war could end as a definition of peace terms. But in the official quarters best qualified to interpret the meaning of the President, it was declared that his statement must be taken as a definition of war aims. The President left no doubt that, unless Germany consented to enter into peace exchanges on the basis of the conditions set forth in his address, the United States and the Allies would fight on until the Central Powers realized that there could be no peace in any other way. "It was an outline of war aims, not a peace address," declared one official.

Terms Clear and Definite.

Never before has President Wilson or any other spokesman for a nation at war with Germany made such a clear and definite exposition of the conditions upon which the war must be fought, or put another way, the conditions upon which peace might be obtained. Until today the President had refrained from making any official expression whatever as to the views of the Washington Government concerning Alsace-Lorraine. Nor had he indicated how the Government felt toward the aspiration of Italy to regain the territory that Austria had obtained through the Treaty of Vienna.

He had refrained also from expression of sentiment concerning the disposition of the German colonies which have been taken from her since the war began. But today he made clear that in these as in other questions that must be adjusted around the peace council table, the United States has an interest as deep as any of the European nations more intimately concerned. In other words, the United States and the Allies are fighting to achieve common objects, and each has assumed its share of helping its partners to gain the ends that more immediately pertain to their welfare and future happiness and stability.

Washington—that is, official and diplomatic Washington—was never more interested by any official utterance since the United States entered the war than by the words spoken by President Wilson in the hall of the House of Representatives today. No statement has come from any Administration source to give closer interpretation of any of his declarations. Those who are anxious to know whether the President delivered his definition of war aims with the knowledge and consent of the Allied Governments, could obtain no satisfaction. Upon this point the State Department had no comment, but there was a very general opinion that exchanges had taken place between Washington, London, Paris, Rome, and possibly Tokio, and an agreement reached along general lines as to what the President should say.

Counseled with Colonel House.

It is believed also that the speech of Mr. Lloyd George was not prepared until its substance or its text had been communicated to the capitals of the other Allies and their views obtained.

The President is supposed to have begun the preparation of today's address last Saturday, the day that Mr. Lloyd George delivered his speech. Colonel E. M. House, the President's unofficial emissary and adviser in war matters, who returned recently from a mission to Europe which resulted in the establishment of an interallied war council, came to Washington on Saturday evening and has been the President's guest since. No inkling was given by the President that he contemplated delivering an address defining the war aims of America. Even some of those who ordinarily would have known of this work were apparently kept in the dark.

The manuscript of the address was sent to the Government Printing Office last night, and copies of it were delivered at the White House this morning. When the Senate and the House assembled Vice President Marshall and Speaker Clark had been notified that the President desired to address the two houses in joint session at 12 o'clock, and the half hour intervening after the hour of assembling was spent in putting through the necessary resolution for the joint meeting and the march of the Senators to the House wing of the Capitol.

The President's statement was generally approved in Congress. Republicans were as enthusiastic as Democrats in indorsing the President's outline of the conditions for world peace. There was an under-current of private criticism over his statement with reference to Alsace-Lorraine on the ground that he was so specific that Germany might find this a stumbling block to peace overtures, but those who voiced this sentiment wished to be understood that they felt that the address was otherwise so commendable that it would be poor taste for them to find cause for dissent in this particular feature.

Republicans Fear Free Trade.

The only real outspoken criticism came from Republicans who saw in one of the war aims specified by the President a declaration that would commit the Allies and their enemies to the establishment of free trade for all the world for a basis of peace. This condition was stated by the President in these words:

"The removal, so far as possible, of all economic barriers and the establishment of an equality of trade conditions among all the nations consenting to the peace and associating themselves for its maintenance."

If this meant an acceptance of the principle of free trade that would permit Germany as well as other nations to dump their products in American ports and bring them into competition with American production the Republicans, it was asserted, would enter a vigorous protest and would not consent to any peace that included such a condition.

Generally, however, Congress gave hearty approval to practically everything that was said by the President.

Cheers for Alsace-Lorraine.

Perhaps the most surprising evidence of responsiveness was given when the President referred to Alsace-Lorraine. He declared that "the wrong done to France by Prussia in 1871 in the matter of Alsace-Lorraine should be righted." Up to that time there had been hearty applause for several of the sentiments and war aims enunciated by Mr. Wilson. But when he referred to Alsace-Lorraine, floor and gallery made known its sympathy with this view in a way that left no doubt of the heartiest indorsement of the thing nearest to the heart of France.

With more feeling than he had shown at any time in the delivery of his address today or in any other important utterance made to the Congress, the President began reading his declaration with reference to the lost French provinces.

"All French territory," he said, "should be freed and the invaded portions restored, and the wrong done to France by Prussia in 1871 in the matter of Alsace-Lorraine—" But here he was obliged to pause. A great shout went up from the Senators and Representatives. The whole Congress came to its feet and continued to express its approval with shouts and handclapping. The galleries, too, rose to the occasion, and soon the House was in a turmoil of enthusiasm that showed the President how deeply the American people were interested in the realization of France's dearest hope.

Demonstration for Russia.

The President had read a page and a half of his address before the enthusiasm, which grew in volume with each successive outburst, was manifested. A reference to Mr. Lloyd George's speech was greeted with a round of hand-clapping. A minute later his expression of sympathy for the Russian people brought a longer demonstration of approval. It was apparent that the President's words struck home when he declared the intention of the Government to assist the Russians in realizing the ideals that they had set forth in their statement of peace terms to the German envoys at Brest-Litovsk. In this connection, it was noted by many Senators and Representatives that the President's expressions differed somewhat from the declaration made by Mr. Lloyd George with reference to Russia.

The view of the British Prime Minister had been interpreted here as meaning that the British Ministry believed that Russia was lost to the Allies, and that no good could be accomplished by any further effort to bring that country back into the war on the side of the Allies. But according to the opinion most prevalent in Washington after the delivery of the President's address, the United States Government will use every endeavor to make the present Russian authority realize that its views are those of America, and that this nation, in fighting on, is seeking to help Russia achieve the aims laid down at Brest-Litovsk. A view rather generally held among Senators and Representatives is that the President delivered his address today partly to encourage Russia to adhere to the principles proposed to the German Peace Commissioners and to understand that America and the other allied Governments would help her in every way.

Means have already been taken by the Government to have copies of the President's address distributed in Russian, and it is felt in official circles that the heads of the Petrograd authority are bound to be impressed by the sympathy with Russian democratic ideals shown in Mr. Wilson's words.

"All the News That's Fit to Print."

The New York Times.

THE WEATHER
Snow today or tonight; Friday fair; moderate shifting winds.
For full weather report see Page 21.

VOL. LXVII...NO. 21,908. ... NEW YORK, THURSDAY, JANUARY 17, 1918.—TWENTY-TWO PAGES. ONE CENT In Greater New York. | TWO CENTS Within Commuting Distance. | THREE CENTS Elsewhere.

SHUT-DOWN OF INDUSTRIES FOR FIVE DAYS; BEGINS FRIDAY; NINE IDLE MONDAYS FOLLOW; WASHINGTON ORDER STARTLES THE COUNTRY

FOOD PRODUCERS EXCEPTED

Order Applies East of the Mississippi and in Minnesota and Louisiana.

CLOSES MUNITION PLANTS

Drastic Move Decided Upon Suddenly After White House Conference.

Garfield Declares Action Was Necessary to Prevent Crisis and Widespread Suffering.

Special to The New York Times.

WASHINGTON, Jan. 16.—The entire industrial fabric of the nation in the territory east of the Mississippi River was made to feel the full force of the coal famine tonight, when, with the approval of President Wilson, a revolutionary order was issued directing all factories with the single exception of those engaged in the production of foodstuffs to suspend for a period of five days beginning Friday morning, and to remain closed on Mondays of each week from Jan. 28 to March 25, inclusive.

This action, admittedly the most drastic adopted by any of the nations at war, was decided upon after a series of conferences between Government officials at which the situation was carefully canvassed and some other less severe solution of the problem sought in vain. Before the announcement was made the facts were laid in detail before President Wilson by H. A. Garfield, the Fuel Administrator, supplemented by the frank statement that " there was no other way."

The order in its final form was even more sweeping than any had predicted, for it had been believed that munition factories at least would be kept in operation if a period of inactivity was fixed for industries not absolutely essential to the war. The only concession made to the war industries, such as the huge steel and munition works, was the promise of a sufficient supply of coal to make it unnecessary for them to permit their plants to " go cold."

Business interests also, aside from those classed as manufactories, will suffer severely during the ten Mondays ending March 25. The huge office buildings of New York and other large cities will be permitted to use only a sufficient supply of fuel to prevent injury to property from freezing or from fire; theatres and other places of amusement and cafés and saloons will not be allowed to use fuel for heating purposes, and only stores where food and drugs are sold will be permitted to continue open as in the past.

The use of oil as well as coal for heating purposes will be denied. Churches and schools are not mentioned in the order, and office buildings used exclusively for Government purposes and for the conduct of State, county, or municipal administrative business will be supplied.

As far as possible it will be the purpose of the Federal Government to have the Mondays set aside as national holidays by the Governors of the various States, so that there will be a general suspension on those days of all industrial business and financial activities. The first five-day period of suspension, with the exception of Monday next, will not be made applicable to any classes with the exception of manufactories.

The order came with an abruptness which left official Washington gasping at the extent to which the Government agencies had exercised their powers and created a decided sensation here.

Fuel Administrator Garfield stood the brunt of the complaints and protests which began to come in as soon as the first outline of the plan was flashed over the wires and he refused to budge an inch from the position he had taken.

A great national emergency, Dr. Garfield said, had brought about the necessity for drastic action, and all of the officials, including the President, the Director General of Railroads, the Secretary of War, and the Secretary of the Navy, had agreed that no other course was possible if a national calamity was to be averted and untold suffering avoided.

Garfield States the Substance of His Order Shutting Down Business

Special to The New York Times.

WASHINGTON, Jan. 16.—Following is the statement issued tonight by H. A. Garfield, Fuel Administrator, regarding the order for fuel conservation:

The order of the United States Fuel Administrator directing the curtailment in consumption of fuel provides substantially as follows:

(1) Until further order of the United States Fuel Administrator, all persons selling fuel in whatever capacity shall give preference to orders for necessary requirements,

(A) Of railroads;

(B) Of domestic consumers, hospitals, charitable institutions and army and navy cantonments;

(C) Of public utilities, telephones, and telegraph plants;

(D) Or ships and vessels for bunker purposes;

(E) Of the United States for strictly Governmental purposes, not including orders from or for factories or plants working on contracts for the United States;

(F) Of municipal, county, or State Governments for necessary public uses;

(G) Of manufacturers of perishable food or of food for necessary immediate consumption.

The order further provides that on Jan. 18, 19, 20, 21, and 22, 1918, no fuel shall be delivered to any person, firm, association, or corporation for any uses or requirements not included in the foregoing list until the requirements included in the list shall have been first delivered.

On Jan. 18, 19, 20, 21, and 22, 1918, and also on each and every Monday beginning Jan. 28, 1918, and continuing up to and including March 25, 1918, no manufacturing plant shall burn fuel or use power derived from fuel for any purpose except—

(A) Such plants as from their nature must be continuously operated seven days each week to avoid serious injury to the plant itself or its contents.

(B) Manufacturers of perishable foods.

(C) Manufacturers of food not perishable and not in immediate demand, who may burn fuel to such extent as is authorized by the Fuel Administrator of the State in which such plant is located or by his representatives authorized therefor, upon application by the United States Food Administrator.

(D) Printers or publishers of daily papers may burn fuel as usual excepting on every Monday from Jan. 21 to March 25, 1918, inclusive, on which days they may burn fuel to such extent as is necessary to issue such editions as such papers customarily issue on important national legal holidays, and where such papers do not issue any editions on a holiday they are permitted to issue one edition on the said Mondays.

(E) Printing establishments which may burn fuel on Jan. 18, 19, 20, and 22 to such extent as is necessary to issue current numbers of magazines and other publications periodically issued.

On each Monday beginning Jan. 21, 1918, and continuing up and including Monday, March 25, 1918, no fuel shall be burned (except to such extent as is essential to prevent injury to property from freezing) for the purpose of supplying heat for:

(A) Any business or professional offices, except offices used by the United States, State, County, or municipal Governments, transportation companies, or which are occupied by banks and trust companies or by physicians or dentists;

(B) Wholesale or retail stores, or any other stores, business houses, or buildings whatever, except that for the purpose of selling food only, for which purposes stores may maintain necessary heat until 12 o'clock noon; and for the purpose of selling drugs and medical supplies only, stores may maintain necessary heat throughout the day and evening;

(C) Theatres, moving picture houses, bowling alleys, billiard rooms, private or public dance halls, or any other place of amusement.

On the above specified Mondays no fuel shall be burned for the purpose of heating rooms or buildings in which liquor is sold on those days.

No fuel shall be burned on any of the foregoing specified Mondays for the purpose of supplying power for the movement of surface, elevated, subway, or suburban cars or trains in excess of the amount used on the Sundays previous thereto.

The order provides that nothing in this order shall be held to forbid the burning of fuel to heat rooms or such portions of buildings as are used in connection with the production or distribution of fuel.

The State Fuel Administrators are authorized by the order to issue orders on special applications for relief, where necessary, to prevent injury to health or destruction of or injury to property by fire or freezing.

The order is effective in all of the territory of the United States east of the Mississippi River, including the whole of the States of Louisiana and Minnesota.

The New York Times.

"All the News That's Fit to Print."

THE WEATHER
Cloudy, colder today; Sunday probably snow; northerly winds.
For full weather report see Page 21.

VOL. LXVII...NO. 21,917. ....   NEW YORK, SATURDAY, JANUARY 26, 1918.—TWENTY-TWO PAGES.   TWO CENTS In Greater New York and Within Connecting Distance. | THREE CENTS Elsewhere.

HERTLING REJECTS WILSON PEACE AIMS; PROPOSES REVISION OF ALLIES' TERMS; CZERNIN WANTS EXCHANGES STARTED

FLAT REFUSAL ON ALSACE

Belgium and Occupied France Held as Pawns, Says Hertling.

POLISH CONTROL ASSERTED

Teutons Alone Propose to Settle Questions Pending with Russia.

WANT THE COLONIES RECAST

Germany Leaves Austria and Turkey to Decide Problems Which Concern Them.

AMSTERDAM, Jan. 25.—In his address before the Reichstag Main Committee yesterday Chancellor von Hertling replied to each of the fourteen points contained in President Wilson's recent address to Congress, giving Germany's position on the points which concerned her alone and specifying the points relating to Austria-Hungary and Turkey, which, he said, would be left for those Governments to deal with. He commented in general terms upon the war aims speech of Premier Lloyd George.

The Chancellor summed up his attitude in his peroration, saying:

"Gentlemen, you have acquainted yourselves with the speech of Premier Lloyd George and the proposals of President Wilson. We now must ask ourselves whether these speeches and proposals breathe a real and earnest wish for peace. They certainly contain certain principles for a general world peace, to which we also assent, and which might form the starting point and aid negotiations.

"When, however, concrete points come into the question, points which for us allies are of decisive importance, their peace will is less observable. Our enemies do not desire to destroy Germany, but they cast covetous eyes on parts of our allies' lands. They speak with respect of Germany's position, but their conception, ever afresh, finds expression as if we were the guilty who must do penance and promise improvement. Thus speaks the victor to the vanquished, he who interprets all our former expressions of a readiness for peace as merely a sign of weakness.

"The leaders of the Entente must first renounce this standpoint and this deception. In order to facilitate this I would like to recall what the position really is. They may take it from me that our military position was never so favorable as it now is. Our highly gifted army leaders face the future with undiminished confidence in victory. Throughout the army, in the officers and the men, lives unbroken the joy of battle.

"I will remind you of the words I spoke Nov. 29 in the Reichstag. Our repeatedly expressed willingness for peace and the spirit of reconciliation revealed by our proposals must not be regarded by the Entente as a license permitting the indefinite lengthening of the war. Should our enemies force us to prolong the war they will have to bear the consequences resulting from it.

"If the leaders of the enemy powers really are inclined toward peace let them revise their program once again, or, as Premier Lloyd George said, proceed to reconsideration.

Will Examine New Proposals.

"If they do that and come forward with fresh proposals, then we will examine them carefully, because our aim is no other than the re-establishment of a lasting general peace. But this lasting general peace is not possible so long as the integrity of the German Empire and the security of her vital interests and the dignity of our Fatherland are not guaranteed. Until that time we must quietly stand by each other and wait.

"As to our purpose, gentlemen, we are all one. [Loud cheering.]

"Regarding methods and moralities, there may be differences of opinion, but let us shelve all those differences. Let us not fight about formulas, which always fall short in the mad course of world events, but above the dividing line of party controversies let us keep our eyes on one mutual aim—the welfare of the Fatherland.

"Let us hold together the Government and the nation, and victory will be ours. A good peace will and must come.

"The German nation bears in an admirable manner the sufferings and the burdens of a war which now is in its fourth year. In connection with these burdens and sufferings I think especially of the sufferings of the small artisans and the lowly paid officials. But you all, men and women, will hold on and see it through.

"With your political knowledge, you do not allow yourselves to be fooled by catch phrases. You know how to distinguish between the realities of life and the promises of dreams.

"Such a nation cannot go under. God is with us and will be with us also in the future." [Loud cheering.]

In opening his address the Chancellor, after referring to the negotiations with the Russians at Brest-Litovsk and saying that he held fast to the hope that a good conclusion would be arrived at, continued:

"Our negotiations with the Ukrainian representatives are in a more favorable position. Here, too, difficulties have yet to be overcome, but the prospects are favorable. We hope shortly to reach conclusions with the Ukrainians which will be in the interest of both parties and also economically advantageous.

"One result, gentlemen, might be recorded as you all know. The Russians last month proposed to issue an invitation to all the belligerents to participate in the negotiations. Russia submitted certain proposals of a very general character. At that time we accepted the proposal to invite the belligerents to take part in the negotiations, on the condition, however, that the invitation should have a definite period for its acceptance.

"At 10 o'clock on the evening of Jan. 4 the period expired. No answer had come, and as a result we were no longer under obligations and had a free hand for separate peace negotiations with Russia. Neither were we longer bound, of course, by the general peace proposals submitted to us by the Russian delegation.

Sees No Peace Hope in Lloyd George.

"Instead of the reply which was expected but which was not forthcoming, two declarations were made by enemy statesmen—Lloyd George's speech and President Wilson's speech. I willingly admit that Mr. Lloyd George altered his tone. He no longer indulges in abuse, and appears desirous of again demonstrating his ability as a negotiator, which I had formerly doubted.

"I cannot go so far, however, as many opinions which have been expressed in neutral countries, which would read in this speech of Mr. Lloyd George a serious desire for peace, and even a friendly disposition. It is true he declares he does not desire to destroy Germany, and never desired to destroy her. He has even words of respect for our political, economic, and cultural position. But other utterances also are not lacking, and the idea continually comes to the surface that he has to pronounce judgment on Germany, charging her with being guilty of all possible crimes.

"That is an attitude with which we can have nothing to do, and in which we can discover no trace of a serious purpose to attain peace. We are to be the guilty ones, over whom the Entente is now sitting in judgment.

"That compels me to give a short review of the situation and the events preceding the war, at the risk of repeating what long ago was said. The establishment of the German Empire in the year 1871 made an end of dismemberment. By the union of its tribes the German Empire in Europe acquired a position corresponding to its economic and cultural achievements and the claims founded thereon.

"Bismarck crowned his work by the alliance with Austria-Hungary. It was purely a defensive alliance, so conceived and willed by the exalted allies from the first. Not even the slightest thought of its misuse for aggressive aims ever occurred in the course of decades. The defensive alliance between Germany and the Danube monarchy, closely connected by old traditions and allied to us by common interest, was to serve especially for maintenance of peace.

OVERTURES TO AMERICA

Austrian Foreign Minister Suggests a Beginning of Negotiations.

HOPE IN WILSON'S SPEECH

Agrees Substantially with the President's Views on Poland's Future.

SAYS STRIKES DELAY PEACE

Compromise Between Germany and Russia Must Be Reached, He Asserts.

BASLE, Switzerland, Jan. 25.—Count Czernin, the Austro-Hungarian Minister of Foreign Affairs, in an address to the Austrian delegations in the Reichsrath, has laid bare for the people of a nation war worn and desirous of peace the stand of the dual monarchy toward the peace aims as stated by President Wilson and David Lloyd George, the British Prime Minister.

While declaring that the Government was in virtual agreement with some of the peace aims of President Wilson, and that the differences which still exist did not appear to be so great that a conversation regarding them would not lead to enlightenment and a rapprochement which might bring together all the allied States in peace negotiations, the dominant note in the address was his plea to the delegations for their support in the crisis, and the making known of the fact that Austria is in straits for food.

The Foreign Minister laid particular stress on the negotiations with Russia, and particularly with the Ukraine. "I wish to use the peace with those Russian States which possess foodstuffs available for export to assist our population," he said.

He declared that if the delegations attacked him and compelled him to conclude an agreement in great haste, "then we shall derive no economic advantage, and our population will have to forego the advantages which they might derive from the conclusion of peace."

If the erroneous impression was created among the enemies of the dual monarchy that it must absolutely conclude peace immediately—a peace at any price—"then we shall not have a single bushel of wheat," the Minister concluded.

He dwelt upon the entire difference between the Brest-Litovsk negotiations and any previously known to history, one of the chief differences being the publicity given to the various phases of the negotiations, the details of which were daily telegraphed throughout the world.

"It is quite natural, in view of the nervousness which prevails all over the globe," Count Czernin said, "that they should produce the effect of electric shocks which agitate public opinion. We are in no doubt as to the inconvenience of this system, but nevertheless we yielded to the Russian Government's desire for publicity because we have nothing to hide. If we had wished to keep to the former secret system that might have created a false impression."

Count Czernin emphasized the fact that to counterbalance this publicity it was necessary for the public, as well as its leaders, to remain calm. The business would be conducted to the end with coolness, he asserted, and would achieve good results if the peoples of the Dual Monarchy supported their responsible Delegates at the conference.

The Foreign Minister went on to say that the basis of the negotiations between Austria-Hungary and what he alluded to as the various recently-created Russian States was peace without annexations or indemnities.

"I shall not abandon this program," he announced, "and those who thought I should allow myself to be led away from the path which I determined upon are bad psychologists. I have never left public opinion in the least doubt as to the path which I am following, and I have never allowed myself to be diverted an inch from this path, either to the right or to the left."

Hertling's Reply to Wilson's Fourteen Peace Demands

WILSON'S TERMS.	HERTLING'S REPLY.
I.—Open covenants of peace, openly arrived at, after which there shall be no private international understandings of any kind, but diplomacy shall proceed always frankly and in the public view.	We are quite ready to accept this proposal and declare publicity of negotiations to be a general political principle.
II.—Absolute freedom of navigation upon the seas, outside territorial waters, alike in peace and in war, except as the seas may be closed in whole or in part by international action for the enforcement of international covenants.	There is here no difference of opinion. The limitation introduced by Mr. Wilson at the end, which I need not quote textually, is not intelligible, appears superfluous, and would therefore best be left out. It would, however, be highly important for the freedom of shipping in future if strongly fortified naval bases on important international routes, such as England has at Gibraltar, Malta, Aden, Hongkong, the Falkland Islands, and many other places, were removed.
III.—The removal, so far as possible, of all economic barriers and the establishment of an equality of trade conditions among all the nations consenting to the peace and associating themselves for its maintenance.	We, too, are in thorough accord with the removal of economic barriers which interfere with trade in superfluous manner. We, too, condemn economic war, which would inevitably bear within it causes of future warlike complications.
IV.—Adequate guarantees given and taken that national armaments will reduce to the lowest point consistent with domestic safety.	As already declared by us, the idea of limitation of armaments is entirely discussable. The financial position of all European States after the war might most effectively promote a satisfactory solution.
V.—Free, open-minded, and absolutely impartial adjustment of all colonial claims, based upon a strict observance of the principle that in determining all such questions of sovereignty the interests of the population concerned must have equal weight with the equitable claims of the Government whose title is to be determined.	Practical realisation of Mr. Wilson's principles in the realm of reality will encounter some difficulties in any case. I believe that for the present it may be left for England, which has the greatest colonial empire, to make what she will of this proposal of her ally. This point of the program also will have to be discussed in due time, on the reconstitution of the world's colonial possessions.
VI.—The evacuation of all Russian territory and such a settlement of all questions affecting Russia as will secure the best and freest co-operation of the other nations of the world in obtaining for her an unhampered and unembarrassed opportunity for the independent determination of her own political development and national policy, and assure her of a sincere welcome into the society of free nations under institutions of her own choosing; and, more than a welcome, assistance also of every kind that she may need and may herself desire. The treatment accorded Russia by her sister nations in the months to come will be the acid test of their good-will, of their comprehension of her needs as distinguished from their own interests, and of their intelligent and unselfish sympathy.	Now that the Entente has refused, within the period agreed upon by Russia and the Quadruple Alliance, to join in the negotiations, I must in the name of the latter decline to allow any subsequent interference. We are dealing therewith questions which concern only Russia and the four allied powers.
VII.—Belgium, the whole world will agree, must be evacuated and restored, without any attempt to limit the sovereignty which she enjoys in common with all other free nations. No other single act will serve as this will serve to restore	My predecessors in office repeatedly declared that at no time did the annexation of Belgium to Germany form a point in the program of German policy. The Belgian question belongs to those questions the details of which are to be settled by negotiation at the peace conference. So long as our opponents have unre-

confidence among the nations in the laws which they have themselves set and determined for the government of their relations with one another. Without this healing act the whole structure and validity of international law is forever impaired.

VIII.—All French territory should be freed and the invaded portions restored, and the wrong done to France by Prussia in 1871 in the matter of Alsace-Lorraine, which has unsettled the peace of the world for nearly fifty years, should be righted, in order that peace may once more be made secure in the interest of all.

IX.—A readjustment of the frontiers of Italy should be effected along clearly recognizable lines of nationality.

X.—The peoples of Austria-Hungary, whose place among the nations we wish to see safeguarded and assured, should be accorded the freest opportunity of autonomous development.

XI.—Rumania, Serbia, and Montenegro should be evacuated; occupied territories restored; Serbia accorded free and secure access to the sea; and the relations of the several Balkan States to one another determined by friendly counsel along historically established lines of allegiance and nationality; and international guarantees of the political and economic independence and territorial integrity of the several Balkan States should be entered into.

XII.—The Turkish portions of the present Ottoman Empire should be assured a secure sovereignty, but the other nationalities which are now under Turkish rule should be assured an undoubted security of life and an absolutely unmolested opportunity of autonomous development, and the Dardanelles should be permanently opened as a free passage to the ships and commerce of all nations under international guarantees.

XIII.—An independent Polish State should be erected which should include the territories inhabited by indisputably Polish populations, which should be assured a free and secure access to the sea, and whose political and economic independence and territorial integrity should be guaranteed by international covenant.

XIV.—A general association of nations must be formed under specific covenants for the purpose of affording mutual guarantees of political independence and territorial integrity to great and small States alike.

servedly taken the standpoint that the integrity of the Allies' territory can offer the only possible basis of peace discussion, I must adhere to the standpoint hitherto always adopted and refuse the removal in advance of the Belgian affair from the entire discussion.

The occupied parts of France are a valued pawn in our hands. Here, too, forcible annexation forms no part of the official German policy. The conditions and methods of procedure of the evacuation, which must take account of Germany's vital interest, are to be agreed upon between Germany and France. I can only again expressly accentuate the fact that there can never be a question of dismemberment of imperial territory.

The questions dealt with by Mr. Wilson under Points 9, 10, and 11 touch both the Italian frontier question and questions of the future development of the Austro-Hungarian monarchy and the future of the Balkan States; questions in which, for the greater part, the interests of our ally, Austria-Hungary, preponderate. Where German interests are concerned, we shall defend them most energetically. But I may leave the answer to Mr. Wilson's proposals on these points in the first place to the Austro-Hungarian Foreign Minister.

The matters touched upon by Mr. Wilson in Point 12 concern our loyal, brave ally, Turkey. I must in nowise forestall her statesmen in their attitude. The integrity of Turkey and the safeguarding of her capital, which is connected closely with the question of the straits, are important and vital interests of the German Empire, also. Our ally can always count upon our energetic support in this matter.

The German Empire and the Austro-Hungarian Monarchy liberated Poland from the Czaristic régime which was crushing her national characteristics. It may thus be left to Germany and Austria-Hungary and Poland to come to an agreement on the future constitution of this country. * * * We are on the road to this goal.

If the idea of a band of nations, as suggested by President Wilson, proves on closer examination really to be conceived in a spirit of complete justice and complete impartiality toward all, then the Imperial Government is gladly ready, when all other pending questions have been settled, to begin the examination of the basis of such a band of nations.

"All the News That's
Fit to Print."

The New York Times.

THE WEATHER
Cloudy, colder today; Sunday probably snow; northerly winds.
For full weather report see Page 21.

VOL. LXVII...NO. 21,929. ...

NEW YORK, THURSDAY, FEBRUARY 7, 1918.—TWENTY-TWO PAGES

TWO CENTS In Greater New York and | THREE CENTS
Within Commuting Distance. | Elsewhere.

TUSCANIA, CARRYING 2,179 U. S. TROOPS, SUNK; 1,912 SURVIVORS LANDED AT IRISH PORTS; WASHINGTON FEARS 260 MEN ARE LOST

SHIP WAS UNDER CONVOY

Anchor Liner Was in Use as an American Transport.

GOES DOWN IN WAR ZONE

War Department Announces Disaster, but Has No Names of the Saved.

NO BIG UNIT WAS ABOARD

Troops Included Scattering Detachments from All Parts of the Country.

Special to The New York Times.

WASHINGTON, Thursday, Feb. 7. —The British steamship Tuscania of the Anchor Line, under charter to the Cunard Line, serving as a transport for American troops, mostly National Guardsmen from Michigan and Wisconsin, has been torpedoed and sunk off the coast of Ireland with loss of life. How many American soldiers went to their deaths through this disaster, the first involving the sinking of a ship carrying American troops to France, is not known. At 1 o'clock this morning the official reports to the War Department and the State Department placed the number of missing at more than 260 out of a total of American troops on board of nearly 2,200. A list of the organizations on the ship appears in another column.

The survivors were landed on the north coast of Ireland at Buncranna, a point about ten miles north of Londonderry, and at Larne, about fifteen miles north of Belfast.

The War Department bulletin issued by the Committee on Public Information at 10.40 last night, was as follows:

The War Department has official advices of the sinking of the steamship Tuscania. The vessel was torpedoed and sunk, and survivors to the number of 1,100, so far as can be ascertained, have landed at Buncranna and Larne, Ireland. There was a total of 2,179 United States troops on this vessel. No names have been reported to the War Department, and

The torpedoed transport Tuscania.

no names of persons surviving have been reported. Additional particulars are promised as soon as received.

At 12:05 this morning the State Department issued the following more reassuring statement:

The latest advice received by the State Department from the Embassy at London in regard to the transport Tuscania is that at 11 P. M. Feb. 6, the latest information was that 1,912 officers and men on the Tuscania had been accounted for out of 2,173.

Taking the War Department figures of 2,179 soldiers on board, those lost number 267. Taking the State Department figures of 2,173 on board, the lost number 261.

It was 10:40 o'clock last night when the Committee on Public Information, in behalf of the War Department, made the announcement that the Tuscania, with 2,179 American soldiers on board, had been torpedoed and sunk. While the dispatch to the War Department did not say so, it was taken for granted that the sinking was done by a German submarine.

President Was at the Theatre.

President Wilson was at Keith's Theatre, enjoying the vaudeville performance at the time of the announcement. With him were Mrs. Wilson and her brother and sister-in-law, Mr. and Mrs. Joseph Bolling. The President did not reach the White House from the theatre, a block away, until 11:40 o'clock, and it was said that he received his first intimation of the disaster when he arrived there. Extra newspapers announcing the loss of the transport had just been issued, but the President did not hear the cry

of the newsboys in his short journey in a motor car to the White House. Even the Secret Service men who were with the President at the theatre did not learn of the disaster until after they had seen the President safely within the White House doors.

Gives Names of Units.

After hours of consultation the War Department early this morning decided to make known to the press the identity of the military units on board the Tuscania. Prior to that time Secretary Baker had declined to give this information, being advised to withhold it by Major Gen. Frank McIntyre, Chief of the Bureau of Insular Affairs and Chief Censor of the War Department, who took the ground that great distress would be caused to many people by an announcement of the list of organizations supposed to be on the transport. What circumstance induced the War Department officials to change their first decision is not known.

Shock to the Capital.

The news of the disaster came to Washington as a great shock. There had been an American transport sunk on her return voyage to this country with comparatively small loss of life among the American soldiers on board, but this was the first occasion when a vessel filled with American troops on their way to the theatre of war had gone to the bottom. Major Frederick Palmer, Chief Censor on the staff of General Pershing, had just concluded a lecture at the National Press Club on his experiences at the front when the

news contained in the bulletin of the Committee on Public Information was circulated in the large assembly room where Major Palmer's lecture was delivered. Major Palmer made the announcement to the audience. Immediately newspaper men began hurrying from the room to the War Department and the Committee on Public Information.

Very few officers were on duty at the War Department, and there was nothing in or about the big granite building to indicate that anything unusual had occurred. The centre of interest was the Committee on Public Information, which occupies two red brick dwellings on Jackson Place, a street bounding Lafayette Square on the west and only a stone's throw from the White House. Here many newspaper men gathered, seeking details of the disaster.

George Creel, Chairman of the committee, went to the War Department and afterward rode in a motor car to the residences of officials, seeking to obtain permission to give out the identity of the units on board the transport. In this effort Mr. Creel was not successful. Just before midnight he explained to the waiting newspapermen who crowded around him that it had been decided that nothing should be given out to indicate what units were on board, but the names of those lost or survivors would be made public as fast as they were received at the War Department.

Secrecy Is Abandoned.

An hour after Mr. Creel had made known the decision of the War Department officials not to publish a list of the units on board of the Tuscania the change of policy was announced and the Committee on Public Information then gave out the names of the organizations which had taken passage on the transport. In his first statement Mr. Creel had said that the decision of the War Department, as it stood shortly before midnight, was that every effort would be made to obtain the names of lost and survivors, and that these would be announced as soon as they were received in Washington.

Mr. Creel was permitted by the War Department to say that the troops on board the Tuscania came from almost every State in the Union, and there was no large contingent from any one State. When the identity of the military units on board the vessel was made known it was seen that most of the contingents were from Michigan and Wisconsin National Guard organizations.

Giving to the press information furnished to him by the War Department in his earlier announcement, Mr. Creel said that most of the men belonged to small units, among them aeronautic and forestry contingents, as well as some National Guardsmen. Officials of the War Department,

Region in Which the Tuscania Was Sunk; Where Survivors Landed.

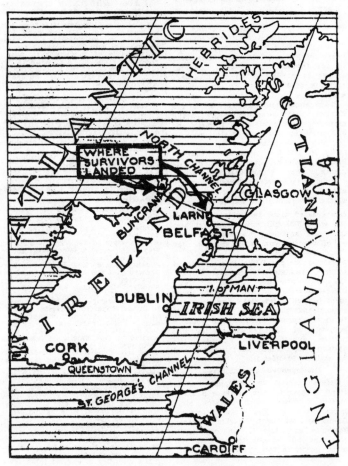

he explained, took the position that if it were disclosed that these troops came from particular States, especially States which had a considerable number of troops in transit, the impression might be created that a great many more troops from two States in particular were involved than was the fact. It is supposed, in the light of the later information given to the press, that the War Department was fearful that should it be disclosed that contingents from Michigan and Wisconsin were on the Tuscania people in those States who had relatives and friends in larger Michigan and Wisconsin organizations would suppose that those in whom they were interested had taken passage on the Tuscania. Representatives of the press were urged not to send to their newspapers until authorized to do so the names of the States which were represented by National Guardsmen on board the torpedoed vessel.

Recruiting of the Foresters.

The War Department did not give out last night the districts from which the three companies of the 20th Engineers, a regiment of foresters, were recruited. These companies were formed in various parts of the country. Only last month the Forest Service of the Department of Agriculture furnished the following bulletin to the press:

Six thousand additional men are wanted at once to bring the Twentieth Engineers (Forest) Regiment up to full strength, according to officials of the Forest Service who have been requested by the War Department to aid in securing the necessary recruits. This is the second Forest regiment formed by the War Department and will be the biggest regiment in the world.

The First Forest Regiment has been

in France for several months busy in cutting and getting out of the French forests timber, lumber, and other material for our army. Some battalions of the Twentieth have also gone across, and others will follow as their equipment and preliminary training are completed. Men who enter this unit are, therefore, assured, the officials say, of early service abroad.

Where Survivors Landed.

Buncrana, at which survivors from the Tuscania were landed, is situated on Lough Swilly, on the northern coast of Ireland, twelve miles from Londonderry. Lough Swilly is a long, narrow bay running in from the Atlantic Ocean.

Larne, at which other survivors were landed from the vessel, is on the northeast coast of Ireland, twenty-three miles from Belfast. It is a North Channel port. The approximate distance by water between the two ports is 100 miles.

Major Gen. Shanks, in charge of the Embarkation Service at New York, did not know of the sinking of the Tuscania until he was told of it by a reported last night. He said he could give no details of the sailing of the Tuscania or who was on her until he had access to records at his office. He referred all inquiries at the War Department in Washington.

13 TRANSPORTS SUNK.

England Lost 8, France and Italy 2 Each, and America 1.

Since the beginning of the war, up to yesterday, twelve transports had been sunk by the Germans. The Tuscania made the thirteenth. Eight transports were British, two French, and two Italian. The largest recorded loss of life on any transport sunk was 970 men, who went down with the Royal Edward of the British transport service on Aug. 14, 1915. The American transport Antilles was sunk by a German submarine

on Oct. 17 of last year on her return trip from France, with a loss of 67 men. The following tabulation shows the record of transports lost:

BRITISH.

Name, Locality, and Date.	Tons.	Loss.
Royal Edward, Aegean Sea, Aug. 14, 1915	11,117	970
Marquette, Aegean Sea, Oct. 20, 1915	7,057	99
Ramazan, Aegean Sea, Sept. 17, 1915	3,477	Large
Wordfield, off Morocco, Nov. 30, 1915	...	7
Russian, Mediterranean Sea, Dec. 14, 1916	...	28
Ibernia, Mediterranean Sea, Jan. 1, 1917	...	153
Cameronian, Mediterranean Sea, June 2, 1917	...	63
Tuscania, Atlantic, Feb. 6, 1918	...	...

FRENCH.

Provence, Mediterranean, Feb. 27, 1916	...	3,100
Chateaurenault, Mediterranean, Dec. 14, 1917	7,898	...

ITALIAN.

Principe Umberto, Adriatic, June 9, 1916	...	Large
Citta di Messina, June 25, '16	3,495	...

UNITED STATES.

Antilles, Atlantic, Oct. 17, '17	...	67

CAPITAL EXPECTED TRANSPORT ATTACK

Secretary Baker Had Information of German Plans on Jan. 27.

NOT LOOKED FOR SO SOON

Decoration of Commander Who Made Voyage to Cape Verde Island Recalled with Interest.

It was announced at Washington on Jan. 27 by Secretary of War Baker that the War Department had information of German plans for carrying on a more intense submarine warfare against American transports. In his official resume for last week Secretary Baker said:

"During the last fortnight enemy submarines have been recalled to home ports to be refitted, and the most powerful submarine offensive hitherto undertaken may be expected to be launched against our lines of communication with France, to interrupt the steady flow of men and munitions for our own armies and food supplies for the Allies.

"During the period under review renewed activity along the entire western front is noted. The region bordering the North Sea has once again become the scene of severe fighting."

The belief that Germany was going to undertake a more vigorous submarine war against American transports was widely held in Washington on information which had been received from Europe. A dispatch to THE NEW YORK TIMES from Washington on Jan. 27 said:

"There are naval officers in Washington who would not be surprised to find Germany this Spring ready to launch new and more powerful attacks against transatlantic routes."

Honor for U-Boat Commander.

Unofficial information came from Amsterdam on Jan. 7 that the German Emperor has conferred the order Pour le Merite on Commander Kophamel on his return from a cruise in a large German submarine to the Cape Verde Islands.

On Jan. 8 a German wireless statement was received in London, saying that Germany had established a new and broader submarine barred zone. It was then announced that the original submarine barred zone had been extended to include the Cape Verde Islands, the Island of Madeira, and part of French Senegal around Dakar. It was announced that the new regulations would become effective Jan. 11. Previously, in November, the barred zone had been extended to take in the Azores.

The real significance of these extensions was not developed at the time, but the announcement of Kophamel's decoration is looked upon as having revealed something of the inner meaning of the establishment of a zone so far from the German submarine bases. All these extensions of the submarine zone are on the principal steamship routes between America and Italy, America and some French ports, Europe and South America, Europe and Africa, and the United States and Africa.

During his voyage Kophamel asserted that he sank an American destroyer and fourteen merchantmen, most of them bound from the United States for Italy and France. It is about 5,000 miles from the Belgian coast to the Cape Verde Islands and back. This is believed to have been the submarine which sank the American destroyer Jacob Jones.

Simultaneously with the announcement that Commander Kophamel had been decorated word reached this country from London that German submarine warfare had gradually taken on a new phase since the beginning of Winter weather, and that submarines of the so-called cruiser type were doing most of the sinkings, while the smaller submarines were confining their activity principally to mine laying. These cruiser submarines are described as carrying two 5.9 guns and sixteen torpedoes, and as being able to keep the seas for six weeks.

On Jan. 15 Secretary McAdoo announced that because of the extension of the war zone by the German Government he had issued an order making mandatory the insurance of masters, officers, and crews of American merchant vessels against loss of life and personal injury by the risks of war and for compensation during detention by an enemy of the United States following capture in the case of vessels engaged in trade on these routes: From all ports to the Cape Verde Islands and ports on the west coast of Africa, north of Sierra Leone, and vice versa."

Secretary McAdoo's order became effective as to vessels leaving American ports on and after Feb. 1 and as to vessels sailing from a foreign port on and after Feb. 15. At the same time he announced that sailing vessels going to and from the same area, their cargoes, freights, and passage moneys would not be insured by the Bureau of War Risk Insurance. This ruling followed one previously made that such insurance on account of sailing vessels through the so-called "war zone" would not be granted by the Bureau.

The announcement of the extension of the German war zone to the Azores, of the decoration of Commander Kophamel, and of the McAdoo rulings attracted virtually no attention at the time they were made. In the opinion of some close students of the submarine situation, however, it was said that the announcement issued by Secretary Baker must be interpreted as meaning that the American Government had information of a reliable character not yet officially disclosed on which the Baker and McAdoo announcements were based.

Both are members of the President's Cabinet. Secretary McAdoo, without disclosing any reasons other than that the war zone had been extended for submarine operations, refused to vessels entering the new war zone the benefits of war risk insurance. In taking this action it was held that he must have had some good reason for believing that Germany intended to operate submarines on a more extensive scale than before across a wider stretch of sea. There was no qualification, either, about Secretary Baker's announcement that "the most powerful submarine offensive hitherto undertaken may be expected to be launched against our lines of communication with France."

Unofficial reports were received recently in Washington from Brazilian, Mexican, and Porto Rican ports that German submarines had been sighted off the coast of Brazil and in the Gulf of Mexico. When these reports were brought to the attention of Secretary Daniels he said that there was no official confirmation of them, and that, so far as the navy knew, there had been no German submarine in American waters since the departure of the U-53.

TUSCANIA CARRIED NO CIVIL PASSENGERS

Recently Lent to America by British Government as Troopship—Not Held Up by Coal Shortage.

The Tuscania was not delayed in New York for lack of coal, according to statements made last night at the offices of the Anchor Line and by J. W. Searles, Deputy Commissioner of the Tidewater Coal Exchange. Mr. Searles said that while supply ships had been forced to wait for coal there had been no holding up of transports and that other demands had been forced to wait upon the bunkering of such ships.

The Tuscania sailed from Pier 56, a Cunard pier. It was more convenient for the troops to be loaded there than at the Anchor Line pier, which is on the East River.

The Tuscania carried no passengers this trip. She had been in regular service until recently, when the British Government lent her to this country for troop transport. She was manned by British officers and crew.

The Tuscania had carried a four-inch gun since October, 1916. She arrived in this port on Oct. 28, 1916, carrying a rapid-fire gun in her stern for the first time.

The liner was chased by a submarine in March, 1917, on a trip from Glasgow to this port. The U-boat appeared on March 12, when the Tuscania was 300 miles west of Fastnet Light, off the Irish coast. The ship took a zig-zag course at sixteen knots and escaped.

British Loss of Ships Held to 15 for the Week

LONDON, Feb. 6.—The Admiralty reports fifteen British merchantmen sunk by mine or submarine in the last week. Of these ten were 1,600 tons or over and five were under 1,600 tons. Four fishing vessels were also sunk.

A dispatch from Rome states that the Italian ship losses by mine or submarine in the week ending Feb. 2 were very light, only one steamer under 1,600 tons being sunk.

The French shipping losses, according to a dispatch from Paris, were two steamers of more than 1,600 tons, and one under that tonnage in the week ending Feb. 2.

The British losses by mine or submarine the last week are approximately the same as the previous week, when nine British merchantmen of more than 1,600 tons and six of lesser tonnage were destroyed.

OFFICER ARRESTED FOR SAILING TALK

Violated Rules by Telling Relative on What Ship He Was Going and When.

WASHINGTON, Feb. 6.—A young army officer who confided to a relative the name of the ship on which he was going overseas and the date of sailing is under arrest, pending an investigation of whether his superiors properly instructed him concerning the requirement of secrecy.

In announcing the arrest tonight the War Department said:

"The War Department authorizes the announcement that a young officer is held in arrest because he divulged to a relative the name of the vessel upon which he was about to start overseas and the schedule date of departure. As a result of this prohibited information, the relative of the young officer, a First Lieutenant, sent a telegram to him at the port of embarkation. This telegram, which was not in cipher, furnished information which, in the hands of the enemy, might have endangered the vessel and all aboard.

"The disclosure of such information by officers and men about to sail is strictly forbidden in General Orders No. 94, War Department, 1917, and warning is again issued that officers and men must not acquaint relatives or friends with details of arrangement for departure. Disciplinary action faces offenders.

"The case of the young officer in arrest in this instance is before the War Department for action, following an investigation at the port of embarkation.

"There is also to be further inquiry to ascertain whether the immediate superior of the officer held in arrest properly instructed this officer as to the requirement of secrecy concerning the names of vessels and sailing dates."

PRESIDENT SEEKS BLANKET POWERS FOR WAR PERIOD

Bill to Give Him Authority to Coordinate and Consolidate All Governmental Activities.

POWER OVER PUBLIC FUNDS

"We Might as Well Abdicate," Say Senators on Hearing Provisions of Bill.

CALLED ANSWER TO CRITICS

Simmons and Martin, Democrats, Would Not Introduce It—Overman Finally Did So.

Special to The New York Times.

WASHINGTON, Feb. 6.—Unrestricted power to the President to "co-ordinate and consolidate" all the governmental activities as a war emergency is contemplated in a bill offered in the Senate late today by Senator Overman of North Carolina, an Administration supporter.

The measure, which came from the President, caused the most profound sensation of the entire legislative session, in which sensations have been frequent. It was criticised tonight as intended to provide assumption of the entire power of Government by the Executive.

Leaders in the Senate, Democrats and Republicans alike, showed anger tonight over the proposal of the President to take over complete authority in the conduct of America's part in the world struggle.

"We might as well abdicate," said several Senators.

The bill was handed to Senator Overman by Postmaster General Burleson, the recognized intermediary between the White House and Congress, at the Capitol early in the afternoon. It r... ..d the wishes of the President, Mr. Burleson said, in his effort to achieve the utmost efficiency in governmental war activity.

Far-Reaching in Scope.

In its scope the bill goes much beyond any other legislation attempted during the war. It outstrips in its delegation of power the authority contemplated in the War Cabinet bill and the measure for a Director of Munitions together.

In fact, Senate leaders said tonight, if the bill were enacted into law the President would be entirely independent of any further legislation in Congress except to ask—or insist—on measures carrying appropriations to conduct the war.

Frank amazement was expressed at the Capitol at the sweeping nature of the measure. Not only would it mean the abdication by Congress of its law-making power, Senators said, but it would carry in effect a wholesale repeal of laws by which Governmental departments or agencies have been established.

Under the measure the President might abolish all the war-making machinery of the Government, including the agencies created since the country entered the war. The bill would empower him to create any new bureaus, agencies, or offices he wanted in the place of those discarded.

Exactly the same bill, it was learned tonight, was given to Senator Martin, the Democratic floor leader, by Postmaster General Burleson or by the President himself a few days ago, with the request that the Virginia Senator offer it in the Senate. Although a staunch supporter of the President in his war policies, Senator Martin expressed the opinion that the bill went too far, and he declined to offer it.

Disapproved by Simmons.

Before making up his mind not to stand sponsor for the measure Senator Martin conferred with Senator Simmons, another firm Administration Democrat from North Carolina. Senator Simmons agreed with Senator Martin that the bill sought to delegate too much power to the President.

Postmaster General Burleson took the measure to Senator Overman during a lull in the war debate and urged him to put the bill in. The North Carolina Senator agreed to do so when told that the President wanted it.

Only a few Senators were in the Chamber when the bill was offered by Senator Overman. Without a word the measure was referred to the Judiciary Committee, which will decide whether it is to be reported out.

PERSHING'S ARMY TO CONSERVE FOOD

Commander Asked by Secretary Baker to Prevent Waste at Mess Tables.

AND RESTRICT FOOD BUYING

Exorbitant Prices Charged to Our Soldiers Raises Cost of Living to French Civilians.

WASHINGTON, Feb. 6.—Food conservation by the American forces in France was suggested to General Pershing today by Secretary Baker. The American commander was asked to consider regulations governing the purchase of foods by soldiers from post exchanges and from the French people and to take up the subject of avoiding food wastes at the table.

The Secretary's cablegram, given out by the Food Administration, reads:

"The importance of the conservation of food and the desirability of avoiding waste among our military forces and the ever increasing difficulty of supplying food products to our allies as well as to our military forces and civilian population, suggests the advisability of propaganda among your forces in the matter of the necessity of food conservation. Action looking to similar result has been taken up in division camps, cantonments and war prison camps in the United States.

"The idea suggests itself of issuing instructions to your command looking not only to the avoidance of waste in messes, but also to a possible regulation of the sale of foodstuffs in post exchanges, Y. M. C. A's, Knights of Columbus, etc. Also the advisability of attempting to regulate the purchase by American soldiers of foodstuffs from the French people.

"Complaints have been made that the French people in selling food products to American soldiers are charging exorbitant prices and thereby increasing the cost of living for the French people. This causes the unnecessary consumption by American soldiers of considerable quantities of food. This, it is believed, adds unnecessarily to the burden of the French food problem. Your recommendations in this matter are requested."

France to Supply Canned Goods.

PARIS, Feb. 6.—An agreement has been concluded between the French and American Governments by which the canned fruit and vegetables required by the American expeditionary forces will be supplied by France. This action was taken after a joint investigation by experts of the United States Army Purchasing Board, and French authorities showed that the normal fruit and vegetable crop in France was sufficient to supply both armies as well as all domestic needs.

The Americans will be required only to import sugar for preserving the fruit, and tinplate for the manufacture of cans. These materials will be sold to the French Government, which will apportion them among private manufacturers.

The American Army Purchasing Board expects that by purchasing canned goods in France there will be a saving of 70 per cent. on the tonnage required for canned goods. The monthly canned food requirement for 25,000 men is estimated at 850 tons. Fifty tons of this represents sugar and tinplate, which will be imported, thus saving 300 tons of shipping space.

For an army of 500,000 men the saving would amount to 6,000 tons monthly. Products for canning will be purchased at reasonable prices to be fixed by the French Government.

The quantity of canned tomatoes consumed by the American soldiers greatly exceeds the proportionate amount used by the other allied armies and the French civilian population. It may be necessary, therefore, to import some tomatoes from Italy. The fruits and vegetables for the American army will be picked and canned by female labor.

DROP LIES TO ITALIANS.

Teuton Airmen Seek to Rouse Disaffection by Leaflets.

Special Cable to THE NEW YORK TIMES.

LONDON, Thursday, Feb. 7.—The Daily Mail correspondent at Italian Headquarters telegraphs:

"German and Austrian airplanes have been very busy lately, dropping leaflets on and behind the lines. These are signed 'The Austro-Hungarian soldiers,' and incite the Italian Army to conclude peace with them, giving the designedly false impression that Bolshevist formations are arising in the Austrian Army.

"Others declare that Italy is the 'latest British colony' with a British censorship in Naples and a commander and military governorship in Rome and that British troops have fired on rioters in Milan. All, of course, are preposterous nonsense."

Hindenburg and Ludendorff Now Established in Belgium

Special Cable to THE NEW YORK TIMES.

AMSTERDAM, Feb. 6.—Hindenburg and Ludendorff have moved their headquarters to Belgium. An interview with German army chiefs recently published in an Austrian journal indicated vaguely that their headquarters were somewhere in the Rhine region. The new locality where they are established is within easy reach of Brussels.

"All the News That's Fit to Print."

The New York Times.

THE WEATHER
Fair today and Tuesday; warmer Tuesday; east to south winds.
For full weather report see Page 17.

VOL. LXVII...NO. 21,954. ....   NEW YORK, MONDAY, MARCH 4, 1918.—EIGHTEEN PAGES.   TWO CENTS In Greater New York and | THREE CENTS Elsewhere

PEACE SIGNED, GERMAN ADVANCE ENDS; RUSSIA FORCED BY NEW TERMS TO CEDE LANDS TAKEN FROM TURKEY IN 3 WARS

TALK USELESS, ENVOYS SAID

Delay Would Only Make Things Worse—Aviator Bombs Petrograd.

ANCIENT BORDER RESTORED

Regions of Batoum, Kars, and Karabagh, in Caucasus, Are Given Up.

RUMANIA'S TURN NOW

Basis of Conditions Fixed by Central Powers Agreed To by King Ferdinand.

Bombs Dropped on Petrograd; Three Killed by German Raider

PETROGRAD, March 3.—A German airman bombed various parts of the city. Three persons were killed and five wounded. The material damage was unimportant.

BERLIN, March 3, (Via London.)—"By reason of the signing of the peace treaty with Russia," says the official communication from headquarters tonight, "military movements in Great Russia have ceased."

PETROGRAD, March 3.—The peace treaty with Germany has been signed.

The following message, addressed to Premier Lénine and Foreign Minister Trotzky, had been received yesterday at the Smolny Institute from the delegation at Brest-Litovsk:

As we anticipated, deliberations on a treaty of peace are absolutely useless, and could only make things worse in comparison with the ultimatum of Feb. 21. They might even assume the character of leading to the presentation of another ultimatum.

In view of this fact, and in consequence of the Germans' refusal to cease military action until peace is signed, we have resolved to sign the treaty without discussing its contents, and leave after we have attached our signatures. We, therefore, have requested a train, expecting to sign today and leave afterward.

The most serious feature of the new

Thousands of Armenians Massacred at Samsun; German Socialists Urged to Curb the Turks

Special Cable to THE NEW YORK TIMES.

THE HAGUE, March 3.—Authentic information received here from Asia Minor direct states that the entire Armenian male population of Samsun, thousands of whom were driven there by the Turks, and including children, has been massacred. This information was brought from Samsun by an official of one of the Central Powers.

The Turks are endeavoring to stir up the Georgians against the Armenians, and it is asserted that appalling massacres have taken place in Georgia also. This is considered a striking commentary on von Hertling's proposals for the future of Armenia.

LONDON March 2.—The Copenhagen correspondent of the Exchange Telegraph Company says that information has been received there that Turkish soldiers have committed new massacres in the district of Armenia which has been deserted by the Russians.

Hjalmar Branting, editor of the Social Demokraten, has telegraphed to the two German Socialist parties to make energetic representations to the German Government, the dispatch adds.

Samsun is a port on the Black Sea, and is the capital of a sanjak in the vilayet of Trebizond. Its normal population is about 13,000.

---

demands compared with those of Feb. 21 is the following:

To detach the regions of Karaband, Kars, and Batoum from Russian territory on the pretext of the right of peoples to self-determination.

AMSTERDAM, March 3.—A dispatch from Brest-Litovsk filed yesterday says that fresh peace negotiations with Russia were opened at a plenary meeting under the chairmanship of Minister von Rosenberg, assistant to the Foreign Secretary.

As regards the regulation of political questions, the Chairman proposed that a common treaty should be concluded between the four Teutonic allies and Russia while economic compacts and legal questions should be dealt with partly in appendices to the main treaty and partly in supplementary treaties for each separate allied power.

The head of the Russian delegation expressed agreement with this plan, whereupon the actual negotiations were begun. The Chairman handed the Russian Chairman the draft of the main political treaty drawn up jointly by the Allies, and gave a detailed explanation of the individual treaty stipulations. The drafts for the economic and legal agreements, with a corresponding explanation, were likewise communicated. The Russian delegation reserved determination of its attitude to the individual points until the material in its entirety is laid before it. The negotiations were continued in the afternoon, and the next plenary sitting was fixed for this (Sunday) morning at 11 o'clock.

According to reports emanating from Poland, Leon Trotzky, the Bolshevist Foreign Minister, did not return to the peace conference at Brest-Litovsk because Germany objected to his continuance as a Russian delegate. It is stated that Trotzky's resignation will be forthcoming as a result.

Semi-official German and Austrian statements received here today set forth claims of forward steps toward peace between the Central Powers and Rumania.

The Berlin dispatch quotes a Bucharest message under today's date declaring that the Rumanians have accepted the basis for negotiations proposed by the Central Powers and will send representatives to deliberate upon the conclusion of peace.

The Vienna dispatch states that word has been received from Bucharest that the negotiations with the Rumanians are progressing favorably.

THE NEW TERRITORY TAKEN.

Restores to Turkey Lands Lost Through Four Wars in 90 Years.

The territorial cessions in Transcaucasia which the Germans have now added to those previously demanded in Eastern Europe destroy the results of four wars waged by Russia against Turkey—1828-29, 1854-5, 1877-8, and the campaigns in Asia Minor of the present war. Batoum, a seaport twenty miles north of the Turkish frontier, has one of the best harbors on the Black Sea, and has been the port of outlet for much of the petroleum and other products of Transcaucasia. The Government of which it was the capital was ceded to Russia after the war of 1878, and eight years later the city was strongly fortified by Russia as a base for future conflicts with Turkey.

The frontier province of which Kars is the capital, lying to the east of Batoum, was also part of the spoils of the war of 1878. Kars itself, a city strongly situated and occupying a strategic position, has been the scene of much bitter fighting in the wars between Turkey and Russia. It was captured in 1828 by the Russian armies, but restored to Turkey upon the conclusion of peace. Again, in the Crimean War, it was taken after a six months' siege, in which the Turkish army was commanded by the English General Williams, but again the treaty of peace forced Russia to give it up.

In the Russo-Turkish war of 1877-8 the Russian Army, after successes in the early Summer of 1877, besieged Kars in June, but after several weeks, during which there was desperate fighting and considerable glory to both sides, the siege was raised following the reinforcement of the Turkish Army. In October, however, the Turks, under Mukhtar Pasha, were defeated, and Kars was again besieged and stormed after a heroic defense on Nov. 11. This time both the town and the surrounding district were allowed to remain in Russian hands.

The region mentioned in the cable dispatches as Karaband is probably that of Karabagh, lying to the north of the Persian border in the southern part of the province of Yelizavetpol. The total area of the territories ceded is apparently about 18,000 to 20,000 square miles, and the population may be somewhat less than 1,000,000. The bulk of the inhabitants of these districts, as of the

New Territory Taken From Russia by Peace Treaty With Germans

The territory in the Caucasus taken from Russia by the treaty of peace is comprised within the heavy black lines shown in the map. As vaguely defined in the news from Petrograd this comprises the regions of Batoum, Kars, and Karaband, presumably Karabagh, (Black Garden.) The ceded territory was wrested from Turkey by Russia in three wars.

lands over the Turkish and Persian frontiers, are Armenians.

In addition to these territories which were in her possession at the outbreak of the war, Russia loses the fruits of a brilliant campaign conducted in Turkish Armenia under the leadership of the Grand Duke Nicholas Nikolaievitch in 1916.

Caucasian Campaign in This War.

Russia's offensive power in the early part of the war was occupied in Europe, and this permitted Turkey, whose troops were at that time preparing under German leadership the attack on the Suez Canal, which failed disastrously in February, 1915, and who had no other occupation than the defense of Mesopotamia against the British expedition from India, to take the initiative in Transcaucasia. While a Turkish raiding force crossed the Persian frontier to support the intrigues of the German diplomats in that country, a strong army set out from the fortress of Erzerum, fifty miles southwest of the Transcaucasian frontier, which was the centre of the strategic defense of Turkish Armenia, and moved against the Russian army in Kars. The operations culminated in a battle fought in December, 1914, at Sarikamysh, just inside the Russian border, in which the Turkish troops were disastrously defeated.

The necessity of defending the Dardanelles and Bagdad kept the Turks from making any further attempt during 1915, and the Russians were too busy on the German and Austrian fronts to make serious advances in Armenia, though a small expeditionary force landed at a Persian port on the Caspian drove the Turks pretty well out of Persia and foiled the machinations of the German agents in that country. The Caucasus front once more became active when the Grand Duke Nicholas was made Viceroy and Commander in Chief after being removed from command in Europe following the great retreat in the Summer and Fall. He spent the early part of the Winter in reorganizing the armies of the Caucasus, and in January, 1916, the Russians made a general advance. They were victorious in a number of battles, and finally, in the middle of February, stormed the forts around Erzerum and captured the city.

This victory, notable in itself, was particularly heartening to the Allies as coming at a time when they had almost forgot the taste of success. The Turkish forces driven out of Erzerum retreated westward toward Erzingan and southwest toward Mush and Bitlis. The Russians were close on their heels in the southern region and occupied Mush and Bitlis early in March. Meanwhile an army landed on the Black Sea coast captured the important port of Trebizond in April, and in July the city of Erzingan, where some of the Turkish armies had rallied, was occupied. Meanwhile a raiding force had been sent into the district of Urumiah, on the Turco-Persian border, and had cleared this of Turks, as well as inflicting losses on the Kurds of the mountains around Rowandiz.

This, however, marked the limit of the Russian advance. The troops were fighting in an extremely difficult country, with no good lines of communication, and had become scattered to a considerable extent in pursuing the Turks. Indeed, before the victory at Erzingan Mush and Bitlis had been retaken by the Turks; and attempts to establish connection with the British army in Mesopotamia failed, aside from the entry into the British camp of a squadron of Cossack raiders.

The failure of munitions caused by reactionary treachery in the Imperial Government, which hampered Brusiloff's offensive in Galicia, was apparently in evidence here, too, and the Grand Duke's armies were compelled to halt on a wide semi-circular front, 100 to 150 miles in Turkish territory. There have been no real military operations on this front since, though occasional reports have come through of the sporadic attempts made by the Turks to regain their lost ground.

As early as last May A. F. Kerensky, then Minister of War, warned the Russians that they were in danger, if the army continued to retrograde in morale, of losing not only Armenia, which he declared they could not return to the mercies of the Turks and Kurds, but also some of the Caucasus. But apparently the troops here retained some of their fighting spirit, for as late as November the Russian troops around Erzingan were holding their own against desultory attacks.

Germany's Former Terms.

The territorial cessions and other terms demanded in Western Europe by the Germans, as made public by the Russian Government on Feb. 23, included the surrender of all of Courland, Poland, and Lithuania, except part of the Province of Grodno. "Russia renounces every claim to intervene in the internal affairs of these regions," said the official German demand as given out by the Russians. "Germany and Austria-Hungary have the intention to define further the fate of these regions, in agreement with their populations."

Livonia and Esthonia were further to be evacuated by the Russians and "occupied by German police until the date when the constitution of the respective countries shall guarantee their social security and political order."

Russia was also to stop her revolutionary crusade against Finland and the Ukraine (the frontiers of this latter country were left conveniently undefined) and to keep her warships in port until the conclusion of peace. But there was hardly a hint of the present demands in Transcaucasia in the clause: "Russia will do all in its power to secure for Turkey the orderly return of its Anatolian frontiers."

Other clauses provided for economic relations very favorable to Germany, and for the abandonment by Russia of "every propaganda and agitation, either on the part of the Government or on the part of persons supported by the Government, against members of the Quadruple Alliance and their political and military institutions, even in territories occupied by the Central Powers." There was added an indemnity, variously reported at $4,000,000,000 and $1,500,000,000.

Forty-eight hours were given for the acceptance of this proposal. A section of the Bolshevist Government wanted to fight, but Lenine forced the decision to surrender, which was announced to the Germans by wireless. At first, however, the Germans refused to recognize this promise, and continued the invasion of Russia with practically no opposition until the last two or three days, when their small advanced detachments were compelled to fall back on the main bodies.

GERMANS, ANGRY AT FAILURE, POUR FIRE ON OUR FRONT

Drop More Than 2,000 Shells on the Trenches in 24 Hours After Repulsed Raid

HAD MAP OF POSITIONS

Complete Details Found on Body of Captain Who Led Foe—Five Groups Assault.

HEROISM OF AMERICANS

WITH THE AMERICAN ARMY IN FRANCE, Saturday, March 2, (Associated Press.)—There has been extraordinary artillery activity along the American sector on the Toul front since yesterday's attack was repulsed. The enemy, apparently angered by his failure, is trying to punish the American troops with a deluge of shells, but not much damage has been done.

Two thousand shells of all calibres were counted along the front from noon yesterday until noon today, while many more fell uncounted. Some ten-inch projectiles battered towns behind the American line.

American infantry and engineers who had been cleaning up the scene of the fight on Friday found some bodies buried. Among them was a surgeon of the Reserve Corps and a stretcher-bearer, who was killed when a shell hit a first aid station. Some of the American missing have been found.

Another German prisoner has been captured in front of the American wire entanglements. He had lain there wounded for many hours before the Americans discovered him and shouted: "Come out." He refused, and a patrol went out and brought him in. One of the German prisoners taken during the fight has since died.

Among the German dead who have been buried were the Lieutenant and Captain leading the attack. The latter was taken from the American wire entanglements. On his body was found a complete plan of the American position.

The map shows how completely the Germans prepare their raids—if, in fact, this was but a simple raid, not having as its ultimate object the retention of a portion of the salient.

The map goes into such detail as to show every machine gun emplacement, every trench, and every depression in the ground within the American lines. At the bottom there is simply a line drawn, labeled: "Our front line." Along this line are five shaded portions, each marked: "Nest."

Four rehearsals were held for the attack, and the troops who made it were specially picked from new arrivals in the sector. They were told that the Americans were in front of them.

Attacked in Five Groups.

After the artillery had nearly leveled our positions the Germans started out from their nests, each of which contained forty infantrymen, one Lieutenant, and three pioneers to precede the infantry and five to follow it. The two groups on our extreme right went around this flank, and the group on the extreme left carried out a similar movement there. The two groups in the center had planned to attack directly, but the American defense changed all the plans. When they were met by the heavy machine gun fire from our lines they saw it would be impossible to gain a footing there, changed their direction and followed the other groups around the flank. The duty of the pioneers preceding the infantry was to clean up any wire that had not been broken by the artillery, while the pioneers who followed carried large quantities of explosives for the purpose of cleaning up the dugouts.

LOOT BRITISH EMBASSY.

Russian Soldiers Break Into It While Official Is Still There.

LONDON, March 3.—The British Embassy was plundered by Russian troops in command of a Colonel immediately after the embassy staff left Petrograd, according to a Petrograd dispatch received by way of Dusseldorf and Amsterdam.

Another report says that the Russian troops broke into the embassy while the British Chargé was still there, and, ignoring his protest, burned some documents and confiscated others. The Chargé, it is understood, made a protest to Leon Trotzky, the Bolshevist Foreign Minister, who replied that the Government could not be held responsible for the outrage.

NEW TYPE BULLETS FOR AIRMEN'S GUNS

Successful Tests Made of Special Cartridges Devised by Ordnance Department.

SOME EXPLODE GAS TANKS

Others Pierce Light Armor or Emit Sparks That Show Range of Firing.

Special to The New York Times.

WASHINGTON, March 3.—Announcement was made by the War Department tonight that the Ordnance Department has developed special types of bullets for use in airplane work in France, and that tests of these missiles indicate that they are fully equal to or surpass those in use abroad. These special types of bullets are intended to pierce the armor of military airplanes. Some of them are of the tracer type and others are incendiary bullets, intended to explode the gasoline tanks of enemy airplanes.

Concerning the development of the new bullet the War Department authorized this announcement:

"The present war brought forth a new kind of ammunition for airplane, for use in the form of special cartridges containing bullets for armor-piercing, tracing, and incendiary purposes. With the progress of the war, the more vital parts of the airplane were protected with light armor, so that it became necessary to introduce the armor-piercing bullet.

"As the gasoline tanks were particularly susceptible to incendiary explosion, it was necessary to procure a bullet containing an inflammable substance, ignited upon discharge, which would carry the spark or flame into the tank upon piercing it.

"As the target, the enemy airplane, was within fighting range for only brief moments at a time and as there were no means of determining the fire effect, as on land, a tracer bullet containing a bright-burning composition which would indicate the path of the bullet in daylight as well as in darkness and thereby allow the aim of the machine gun to be corrected, was introduced. The composition is set on fire upon discharge, and the bullet flies through the air as a bright spark, plainly visible to the machine-gun operator.

"All of these cartridges are of the small rifle calibres—calibre .30 or thereabout. The three-tenths of an inch diameter and short length of this bullet left little space in it for the armor-piercing element or for the tracer or incendiary composition. Nevertheless, combinations of armor-piercing and tracer, and armor-piercing and incendiary bullets have been made.

"The bullets developed by the United States Ordnance Department have been tested on land and from airplanes to see if there is any difference in their performance when fired from a quickly moving airplane in the upper atmosphere and when fired on land. These tests indicate that the United States has developed a class of special cartridges with a performance fully equal to or surpassing that attained abroad."

It was not uncommon for a retreating army to leave behind the more cumbersome of their weapons. In these two photos, American and British troops take advantage of German guns and ammunition to fire on German positions.

"All the News That's Fit to Print."

The New York Times.

THE WEATHER

Fair, warmer today; tomorrow fair, somewhat colder; westerly winds.
For full weather report see Page 21.

VOL. LXVII...NO. 21,962. ....

NEW YORK, TUESDAY, MARCH 12, 1918.—TWENTY-TWO PAGES.

TWO CENTS In Greater New York and Within Commuting Distance. | THREE CENTS Elsewhere.

WILSON PLEDGES OUR AID TO RUSSIA; EXPRESSES SYMPATHY, AND HOPES SHE MAY BE FREED OF GERMAN POWER

MESSAGE TO SOVIET CONGRESS

Consul General at Moscow Will Deliver It to Great Meeting Today.

HELP JUST NOW IMPOSSIBLE

But President Will Lose No Chance to Promote Aim of Complete Independence.

COUNTER-BLOW AT ENEMY

Message Will Offset Attempt to Rouse Fear of Japan's Action in Siberia.

Special to The New York Times.

WASHINGTON, March 11.—President Wilson took steps today to counteract any feeling that might have been aroused in Russia against the Allies. He sent a cable message to the people of Russia through the Soviet Congress, which meets in Moscow tomorrow, expressing the sympathy of the American people toward the Russian people over the manner of their treatment by the invading Germans. While regretting the inability of the United States Government to render direct aid at this time, the President gave assurance to the Russian people that it " will avail itself of every opportunity to secure for Russia once more complete sovereignty and independence in her own affairs and full restoration to her great rôle in the life of Europe and the modern world."

Through this cordial message President Wilson serves notice to the whole world that he still regards Russia as a party to the war against Germany and a co-belligerent of the United States and the other nations engaged in the effort to put an end to German autocratic methods. At the same time he brings to the minds of the Russian people that the allied purpose is remote from any desire to make a conquest of Russian territory.

Although no interpretation of the President's reasons for sending this message is offered in any authoritative quarter, it is obvious that it was the outcome, in part, at least, of a desire to counteract as far as possible the attempt to make it appear that the Japanese proposal to place armed forces in Siberia meant dismemberment of Russian territory at the hands of Japan. The representations made in response to Japan's invitation for a statement of the American view showed that the President was fearful that the presence of Japanese soldiers on Russian soil would lead to anti-Ally feeling among the Russian people. There has been evidence that the attempt to arouse this feeling is being made. Officials in Washington do not doubt that German agents in Russia will spread the report that Japan contemplates seizing Siberian territory and retaining it permanently.

President's Consistent Policy.

From the very beginning of the Russian collapse President Wilson has been insistent that it should be kept plainly before the Russian people that the United States Government was in sympathy with their democratic aims, and did not intend to permit the condition of chaos in which the country found itself to sway the firm friendship of America for Russia. He has voiced this policy before Congress, and to an extent consistent with the circumstances has emphasized it in the American communication to Japan concerning the suggestion of Japanese intervention in Siberia. He has taken occasion to show his lack of sympathy with the declaration of Mr. Lloyd George, the British Prime Minister, indicating that Great Britain expected nothing more from Russia. In these and other ways the President has made it manifest that the United States still has faith in the ability of Russia to " come back."

Today's message is the most pronounced example of the President's attitude toward demoralized and shattered Russia. In a measure it is a more important declaration than the " conversational " note to Japan in response to the invitation for a statement of American views as to the suggestion that Japanese troops should take possession of Eastern Siberia, for it is a public declaration delivered at a time when Russia is agitated over Japan's contemplated action.

It is quite evident to observers that the President wishes to keep before the world in the strongest possible light that he holds consistently to his view that nothing should be done by the allied powers that would seem to be at variance with the purposes of the Russian revolutionaries to gain complete freedom for themselves and recognition of their right of self-determination within the limits of what was once the Russian Empire.

His message to the Congess of the Soviets calls to mind that the danger in Russia results from the German invasion, which suggest that the people of Russia should concentrate their energies against the Teutonic conquerors and not against the Japanese. The President also promises that the United States Government will stand by the Russian people with the purpose of obtaining for them again "complete sovereignty and independence" and restoration of their standing as a first-class power.

This appears to mean that the United States, as a co-belligerent of Japan, will use its influence, should necessity arise, to bring about the withdrawal of Japanese troops from Russian territory and take every other necessary step to preserve the administrative and territorial integrity of Russia.

The President's message to the Congress of the Soviets is in line with his policy of holding before the peoples of the perturbed countries of Europe, including Germany and Austria-Hungary, that the main aim of the United States in the War is to produce a condition which will insure all peoples such a measure of participation in their own government that the autocratic military power which was able to throw the whole world into a bloody conflict will be unable to do its will without popular approval.

Following the practice adopted with the entrance of the United States in war, it is expected that efforts will be made to have the President's message circulated in Germany and Austria-Hungary, so that the peoples of those countries will be reminded that the Untied States has not swerved from its declared sympathy with the democratic ideas that are shared by many liberals of enemy allegiance.

The message appears to put an end to speculation as to whether the President would revise his policy of disapproval toward suggestions that Japanese troops be sent to occupy parts of Siberia. There have been signs that the statements of Lord Robert Cecil, defending British indorsement fo Japan's proposal, have made interested persons here see the situation in a light more favorable to Japanese intervention, but the President's words of sympathy to the Russian people indicate that his attittude has not changed.

AMERICAN TROOPS, TAKING OFFENSIVE, MAKE 3 BIG RAIDS

Sweep Over Foe's First Line in Lorraine and Reach Second, 600 Yards Back.

GUNS CO-OPERATE FINELY

Germans Flee Before Shells, So Prisoners Are Few—French Aid in Two Operations.

SECRETARY BAKER IN PARIS

WITH THE AMERICAN ARMY IN FRANCE, March 10, (Associated Press.)—American troops on the Lorraine sector carried out three raids last night and this morning. They swept past the German first line and penetrated to the enemy's second line, 600 yards back.

Two of the raids, made in co-operation with the French, were started simultaneously, one northwest and one northeast of ——— (deleted,) after intense artillery preparation, lasting four hours, in which the German positions were leveled.

The two forces, each one of ——— (deleted,) with small French forces on their flanks, moved upon the German objectives at midnight behind a creeping barrage, each on a front of 600 yards. When the Americans reached the German first lines the barrage was lifted so as to box in the enemy positions at both points.

The men dropped into the trenches, expecting a hand-to-hand fight, but found that the Germans had fled. Continuing the advance, they went forward 600 yards to the second German line. All the time American machine guns were firing on each flank of the two parties to prevent the enemy from undertaking flanking operations.

One French flanking party found two wounded Germans in a dugout and took them prisoner. The Americans found none.

The Americans remained forty-five minutes in the enemy's lines. They found excellent concrete dugouts, which they blew up, and brought back large quantities of material and valuable papers.

While they were in the German lines the enemy artillery began a vigorous counterbarrage, but it was quickly silenced by American heavy and light artillery, which hurled large quantities of gas shells on the batteries.

An American trench mortar battery, the homes of most of whose men are ——— (deleted) participated in the artillery preparation preceding the raid, helping to level the enemy positions. The artillery, both light and heavy, was manned by soldiers mostly from ——— (deleted).

Soon after these two raids had been completed, the Americans staged another at a point further along the line to the right. They went over the top after artillery preparation of forty-five minutes, in which the enemy's positions were obliterated for the most part.

At this place the dugouts were found to have been constructed principally of logs. Engineers accompanying the raiding party completed the artillery's work of destruction. The American infantrymen who took part in this raid are from ——— (deleted) and the engineers from ——— (deleted).

The raids were carried out skillfully, and but for the fact that the Germans fled more prisoners doubtless would have been taken.

The American gas shells are believed to have caused many casualties among the enemy. No Americans are unaccounted for.

A "Bold Raid," Says Paris.

PARIS, March 12.—Today's report of the War Office includes this statement: " American troops in Lorraine carried out a bold raid into the German lines."

The New York Times.

"All the News That's Fit to Print."

THE WEATHER
Fair today; Sunday fair, warmer; northwest winds, becoming variable. For full weather report see Page 21.

VOL. LXVII...NO. 21,966. ... | NEW YORK, SATURDAY, MARCH 16, 1918.—TWENTY-TWO PAGES. | TWO CENTS In Greater New York | THREE CENTS Within Commuting Distance. Elsewhere.

MOSCOW CONGRESS RATIFIES PEACE; HAD RECEIVED PRESIDENT'S MESSAGE; WASHINGTON SPURS WAR EFFORTS

AMERICA'S TASK GRIMMER

Washington Officials Scout Rumors of an Early Peace

NO ILLUSIONS ON GERMANY

Conquests in the East Destroy the Prospect of Teuton Concessions.

NEW SPIRIT IN WAR TASK

Co-operation with Congress a Sign of Determination, to Fight to Victory.

Allies Will Make No Peace at Russia's Expense, Cecil Says

LONDON, March 15.—Replying to an inquiry as to whether there was any truth in the rumors that proposals had been received from Germany for a peace at the expense of Russia, Lord Robert Cecil, the Minister of Blockade, said in the House of Commons today:

"As far as I know, no such proposals are being considered or will be considered."

Special to The New York Times.

WASHINGTON, March 15.—In some curious way the impression has spread through the country that peace will come soon. Nobody seems able to formulate a reason for this impression, but many persons are satisfied in their own minds, judged by what is said and heard in Washington, to which opinion from all sections drifts naturally, that the end of the war is near.

An American soldier in France writes to his mother that the French are confident that hostilities will cease this year. A report comes to Washington that Wall Street knows that President Wilson is in frequent conference with certain bigwigs (unnamed) preparing the formulae for stopping the conflict. Others assert that they have this or that bit of information which points to an early peace. Most persons infected with the peace germ show their symptoms in some

such expression as "I don't exactly know why, but I feel that the war won't go on much longer."

Sentiments and opinions of this character are exactly contrary to the Washington official view. A new spirit is noticeable here, a spirit of determination that carries with it the banishment of all illusions as to the task that confronts the United States and its co-belligerents.

The final collapse of Russia, the evidence that Germany is bent on conquest wherever it is possible, the knowledge that Austria-Hungary was using diplomatic camouflage in expressing sentiments that appeared to be at variance with Germany's desire to rule the world, the veiled threats of the Prussian autocracy to the Scandinavian nations, have brought to Washington a full realization that the future of democratic institutions depends upon the sword, and not on peace by understanding with Germany on the other side of the peace table.

New Motto Is "Live or Die."

"We have been going on the principle of 'Live and Let Live,'" said one of the foremost men of the Government. "From now on we are going on the principle of 'Live or Die.'"

The new spirit, or rather the old spirit, is exemplified in the decision of Great Britain and the United States to commandeer Dutch ships. In this action, as in others of a similar character contemplated, the two English-speaking nations intend to live up to all the obligations of international law. But while they have satisfied themselves that the seizure is justified by international observance and precedent, including Prussia's seizure of British tonnage in the Franco-Prussian War, they contend that justification is emphasized on the moral ground that the Allies are fighting the battle of small neutral States which must stand their share of sacrifice in the struggle to aid them.

Under the new conditions that have arisen through the triumphal progress of Germany and Austria in Eastern Europe, the Washington Government feels that it is fighting more than ever for the basic principle of President Wilson's policy of protecting small States from the aggression of militaristic powers. "The League to Enforce Peace is now in operation" was the way the situation was expressed by one of those in a position to understand the President's point of view.

The Allies are banded together in the struggle to prevent Germany and her subservient partners from extending their domination over all the peoples who are unable to protect themselves. Russia, Serbia, Rumania, Montenegro, not to speak of Belgium, are feeling the effects of the conqueror's iron rule. It is realized that this condition arises out of the fortunes of war. But in the Washington view the turn of Holland, Denmark, and Norway, and perhaps Switzerland, may come next.

Whatever may have been the feeling among individual members of the Administration that led them to hope for an early peace, there is now a general determination and understanding that the war must go on until victory has come to the allied cause. Washington fully appreciates that hot shot and cold steel are the only arguments that appeal to Germany. The spirit that dominates here savors of the idea that Germany will see peace only when her enemies are victorious.

Spurt in War Preparations.

Lord Northcliffe's residence in America taught him the potent meaning of the expression "pep." If he were in Washington now he would grasp that even greater "pep" is being put into the conduct of the war. Under the impetus of the new order of things, which are partly the outgrowth of the investigation of the Senate Committee on Military Affairs and partly of the knowledge that Germany has thrown aside pretense and is out for conquest, troops are moving to France in greater number, supplies for the Allies are being forwarded in enormous volume, and there has been improvement all along the line in industrial military activity.

A better understanding between the executive and legislative branches of the Government is shown in the invitation to members of the Military Committees of the Senate and House to attend meetings of the War Council. Under General Goethals the supply sections of the army are making long strides. Under General Wheeler the Ordnance Department is overcoming the handicap of delay in furnishing arms and ammunition, and the workers of that department are realizing that they are serving a going instead of a discredited concern.

It is true that doubts are expressed over the optimistic appraisement of the efforts to overcome the submarine menace, but conservative experts continue to insist that before the Summer is over the U-boats will have become a negligible quantity in their competition with destroyers, chasers and new devices for their detection. The production of aircraft by the United States is not all that has been claimed, according to report, but the President is said to be taking a personal interest in this condition, and no effort will be spared to overcome the setbacks.

Allies Realize Firmness Here.

All these things have not been lost on the partners of the United States in the war. They understand that the determination to win is foremost in the minds of those in authority in Washington, and has displaced every dream of an early peace.

Lord Reading, the British Ambassador and head of the British War Mission, has entered into the most cordial relations with the Administration, and the good result of the teamwork is already apparent. M. André Tardieu, the head of the French War Mission, who declined a Cabinet office to return to America, is active in perfecting plans for French-American participation in the war. Count di Cellere, the Italian Ambassador, who is also head of his Government's war mission, is equally active in co-operation.

The action of the Japanese Government in sending Viscount Ishii to the United States as Ambassador is regarded as assurance of even closer understanding between the two Governments. It was Viscount Ishii who, when he came here recently on a special mission, laid his cards on the table before Secretary Lansing, asked that suspicion be forgotten, and entered into the agreement that showed Japanese distrust of Germany and paved the way for cordial relations between Japan and the United States.

VOTE FOR PEACE 453 TO 30

Delegate of Professional Unions Quits Red Party After Ballot.

TEUTONS TO TAKE CONTROL

Commissioners with Veto Power Will Sit on the Russian Ministries.

RUSSIA - UKRAINE PARLEY

Joint Conference Opens at Kiev in Effort to End Hostilities, Vienna Hears.

PETROGRAD, March 14.—The All-Russian Congress of Soviets, meeting at Moscow today, by a vote of 453 to 30 decided to ratify the peace treaty with the Central Powers.

M. Ryazonov, a prominent Bolshevist theorist, representative of all the professional unions, resigned from the Bolshevist Party after the vote.

In view of the repeated violations by both the Germans and the Russians of the line of demarcation fixed for the Pskov front, the Germans have demanded the establishment of a new line ten versts east of the present Russian position. A German official explanation of this change in the line is that it is necessary to strengthen Germany's strategic position.

Germans to Oversee Ministries.

German authorities have announced that German commissions with the power of veto will be appointed to the Russian Ministries to control the fulfillment of the treaty of peace.

The Germans have occupied Razdielnaya, a station on the Odessa railway line, and the evacuation of Odessa and Nicholiev is proceeding.

The German Admiral, Siegert, has been appointed commander of Odessa. Before the occupation of Odessa by the Germans anti-Jewish riots occurred there.

Fresh disorders have occurred in the German fleet off the Aland Islands, according to the Russian military newspaper, Krasnaya Armia.

The Caucasus Government has issued a statement in which it refuses to indorse the Brest-Litovsk peace treaty, which cedes Kars, Batoum, and Ardahan to Turkey, and declares that peace with Turkey can only be signed by the Caucasus Government, which has sent its own delegation to Trebizond to discuss peace.

AMSTERDAM, March 13—(Delayed.) —The opening of peace negotiations at Kiev between Russia and Ukraine is reported in a Vienna dispatch to the Vossische Zeitung of Berlin.

The Ukrainian Rada, the dispatch says, will meet soon to ratify the peace treaty with the Central Powers.

Chaos Likely to Last a Long Time.

WASHINGTON, March 15.—Official expression here today indicated that America and the Allies expect the action of the Moscow Congress to have little direct bearing on the general Russian situation. It apparently was believed that chaotic conditions will continue in Russia for a long time to come, even though the Germans make every effort to re-establish order and to reorganize the country's industrial and agricultural life.

Officials here do not profess to know to what extent Germany plans to use her forces in policing the provinces Russia is compelled to relinquish or how much further German troops may penetrate Russia itself. They were deeply interested in a dispatch from Moscow which said that the Russian factions were declaring freely that peace would be temporary only, and that Russia would gather herself together with a new socialistic army to resist the Germans. The fact that only slightly more than half of the delegates expected to attend the congress were reported as voting also caused comment.

The attitude of the American Government toward any German move for a general peace at the expense of Russia is directly in line with the expression of Lord Robert Cecil in the House of Commons today that even if such a proposal came from Germany it would not be considered.

SAYS GERMANY'S ALLIES SEEK PEACE DISCUSSION

Cable to Washington Tells of Their Representatives Reaching Berne.

Special to The New York Times.

WASHINGTON, March 15.—The following was given to its clients today by a new-gathering agency which devotes itself to foreign news as developed in Washington:

"Official dispatches form an allied foreign office, received here today, disclose an effort made by the allies of Germany to open in Berne a discussion with the Entente Powers on peace terms, and after failing in that quarter to receive any encouragement, the cable states, the representatives of Austria-Hungary, Turkey, and Bulgaria obtained the ear of a representative of the United States.

"A Bulgarian delegate has arrived at Berne with the intention of proceeding to the United States, the advices state, and he Government which dispatched the cable reveals its concern in connection with the enemy machinations. The name of the American official approached in Switzerland was not given, but there is doubt here whether the person was the chargé d'Affaires or Mrs. Norman DeR. Whitehouse, representative of the Committee on Public Information."

The cable says in part:

"Representatives of Turkey have jointed the representatives at Berne of Austria-Hungary and Bulgaria who are attempting to negotiate with the Entente. But they have been made to understand that England will have nothing to do with them. They have sought to get in touch with the Americans, toward whom they display much activity.

"The terms of peace proposed by Turkey and Bulgaria are as follows:

"For Turkey: The integrity of her territory, the abolition of the capitulations and provisions against any foreign intervention in her internal affairs in the future.

"For Bulgaria: She declares that she complies with the principle of non-annexation, but asks for a referendum in the provinces actually occupied by her during this war, so that the populations would be enabled to declare what they want.

"According to certain dispatches, the American representative in Switzerland has communicated with the United States Government, telegraphing opinion."

BRITISH CONFRONT FOE'S BIGGEST ARMY

But Gen. Maurice Voices Growing Doubt About Any Great Stroke Being Near.

BRITISH CONTROL THE AIR

He Forecasts Large Results When Our Full Aviation Power Is Developed in Action.

Special Cable to THE NEW YORK TIMES.

LONDON, March 15.—"Disbelief in an early development of the much talked-of German offensive on the western front is growing owing to the fact that after a period of weather favoring the air work preliminary to an offensive there are still no indications of the opening of operations on a big scale, said General Maurice, Director of British military operations, today.

General Maurice added that the recent aerial activity had been in favor of the British, whose aerial offensive had been steadily extended. The German raids on Paris, made under the guise of reprisals for British raids into German territory, were a clumsy attempt to create friction between the French and British. This was on a par with the German propaganda which sought to depreciate Great Britain's efforts in the war.

"America can now appreciate the fact," continued the General, "that it takes time to create and place new armies in the field. During the period of British preparation France had to bear the brunt of the war.

"Now look around on the various theatres of war and consider the part Great Britain is playing. Over and above its naval contribution, Great Britain's military efforts is greater than could have been anticipated by anybody four years ago. Half the German forces between the North Sea and Switzerland are arrayed against the British front. The German propagandists have slightingly compared the length of the British front with that held by the French, but geographical measurements are not the supreme test of importance.

"At no period of the war have the German forces opposite the British been so great as they are now, either absolutely or relatively."

General Maurice referred to the British assistance to Italy and to the British forces engaged against Turkey and against Bulgaria and to the expedition which was clearing the Germans out of their last colonial possession in East Africa. He emphasized the fact that he drew attention to these matters merely because of the German efforts to create the belief that Great Britain was using her allies and saving her own strength.

In conclusion General Maurice laid special emphasis on the part that America would play in the aerial warfare,

FRENCH RECOVER CHAMPAGNE LOSS

GERMANS ADMIT DEFEAT

PARIS, March 15.—In the Champagne region west of Monte Carnillet French troops have regained trenches which the Germans had occupied since March 1, according to the official War Office statement issued today. The French brought back forty-two prisoners and two machine guns.

The statement adds:

"This morning a surprise attack by the Germans against French positions near Massiges was a complete failure.

"There is nothing important to report on the rest of the front except lively artillery firing in the region of Moncel and in the Violu sector."

Last night's official report of operations reads:

The enemy artillery activity in Champagne, in the region of the Monts; in the Vosges, east of St. Die, and in the region of Hartmanns-Weilerkopf, was less violent.

During the day three German airplanes were destroyed by our pilots. It is confirmed that on March 9 Sub-Lieutenant Madon destroyed two German airplanes. Our aviators in several sorties recently carried out effectual bombardments, dropping 1,800 kilograms of projectiles on railway stations, works and airdromes in the enemy zone.

With A Song On His Lips

A German soldier walking down the main street of Malines singing, "drove his bayonet with both hands through a living child's stomach, lifting the child into the air on his bayonet and carrying it away on his bayonet, and his comrades still singing."

(d4 Bryce Evidence.)

IT IS to prevent such gruesome, degenerate crimes in America that the United States is at war with Germany. To save our wives, daughters and children from a fate far worse than violent death.

The American Defense Society is a patriotic society which is aiding the Government to win the war. It is offsetting filthy German propaganda with the pure sunlight of Americanism.

We Need All Loyal Citizens as Members

We need your aid to carry on effective propaganda work. The officers, trustees and thousands of loyal members of this Society have given their time generously. Now the time has come for other loyal Americans to help. Sit down now. Fill out the coupons and mail them and if you choose send a contribution proportionate to your means.

NOTE:—If you think the atrocity described in this advertisement is a remote incident in a great war, send 75c. for a copy of the paper covered edition of the most startling book of the war, THE CRIMES OF GERMANY. It describes many fiendish crimes of German soldiers. It is illustrated with reproductions some from photographs of mutilated victims, living and dead. Every atrocity could be proved in any civilized court of law by documentary evidence on file in the archives of the British, French and Belgium Governments. THE CRIMES OF GERMANY created a furore in England where millions of copies were printed and distributed among English troops.

AMERICAN DEFENSE SOCIETY, Inc.

National Headquarters—44 East 23rd Street, New York

Serve at the Front or Serve at Home

Hon. President
COL. THEODORE ROOSEVELT, Ex-President of the United States

Hon. Vice-Presidents

HON. DAVID JAYNE HILL, Ex-Ambassador to Germany
HON. ROBERT BACON, Ex-Ambassador to France
HON. PERRY BELMONT, Vice-President, Navy League
HON. CHARLES J. BONAPARTE, Ex-Attorney General U. S.

JOHN GRIER HIBBEN, President, Princeton University
HENRY B. JOY, Ex-President, Lincoln Highway Ass'n.
HON. CHARLES S. FAIRCHILD, Ex-Secretary of the Treasury

Executive Officers
CHARLES STEWART DAVISON, Chairman, Board of Trustees
HENRY C. QUINBY, Chairman, Executive Committee
WILLIAM GUGGENHEIM, Chairman, Publication Committee
ROBERT APPLETON, Treasurer
H. D. CRAIG, Secretary
GEORGE GARNER, Director, Washington News Bureau

You may enroll me as a member of one of the following Committees, and I will render such service as I can to make this activity a success.
German Goods Boycott Committee
Crimes of Germany Committee
German Language Newspaper Committee
German Language in the Schools Committee
Membership Committee
Publication Committee
N. Y. Tms.

Fill In the Coupon —Don't Delay—

JOIN NOW!

And ask ten friends to do the same— It is a patriotic work

American Defense Society, Inc.
4. East 23rd Street, New York Date_____191
Please enroll me as a member of the American Defense Society.
I enclose my check for $1.00—Annual Membership
To the order of ROBERT APPLETON Treasurer
$5.00—Sustaining Membership
10.00—Subscribing Membership
25.00—Contributing Membership
100.00—Life Membership
Certificate of Membership, Society button and Hand Book will be mailed from Headquarters.

Name _____
Street Address _____
City _____ State _____
N. Y. TMS.

This Advertisement designed and executed by the Ethridge Association of Artists.

This advertisement is an example of extreme, anti-German propaganda.

The New York Times.

THE WEATHER
Fair, warmer Sunday; Monday fair; fresh southwest winds.
For full weather report see Page 23.

Section 1

VOL. LXVII...NO. 21,967.   NEW YORK, SUNDAY, MARCH 17, 1918.—120 PAGES, In Nine Parts, Including Picture and Magazine Sections in Rotogravure.   FIVE CENTS In Greater New York | SEVEN CENTS Elsewhere

JAPAN SEEKS CHANCE TO AID RUSSIA; TOKIO PLANS SAFE AND SANE POLICY; WILSON WILL SPEAK SOON ON ISSUE

WOULD LIKE OUR APPROVAL

Japanese Leaders See That Opposition Would Handicap Financially.

WANT TO BRING CHINA IN

Believe Siberian Crisis Offers Chance for Peking Government to Check Revolution.

LESS EXCITEMENT NOW

TOKIO, Thursday, March 14, (Associated Press.)—When a week ago the possibility of Japanese intervention in Siberia became known and a flood of opinion from the Western press poured into Japan, there was considerable excitement, in the belief that speedy mobilization of the army and navy would be ordered.

Extremists pictured airplanes over Tokio and submarines from Vladivostok. The hysterical "Cutz" in the Diet heckled the Government, and the newspapers were filled with contrary views, according to the interests or the imagination of those responsible for the situation.

Presently, however, the tone became quieter, and it appears possible to see more clearly the true Japanese outlook, which is characterized in many quarters as "entirely safe, sane, and loyal."

Today practically the entire responsible press of the capital is advocating intervention in Siberia in co-operation with the Allies and China, not directed against Russia, but as an ally loyal to the Russians, wishing to save the country.

One of the most outspoken papers is the Kokumin Shimbun, owned and edited by Ichiro Tokutomi, who is a close personal friend of the Premier.

Japan realizes, it is authoritatively stated, that if the United States declines its support, the situation will be extremely delicate because financial and material assistance must come from America. Any feeling of distrust or unfriendliness seems to be lacking.

As a matter of fact, a large section of influential men in Japan favor the American viewpoint, while only a few chauvinists jeer at Premier Terauchi

and Foreign Minister Motono as being under American influence.

Leading men, such as Baron Shibusawa, President of the American-Japanese Association, for the commercial section, and Yukio Ozaki, leader of the Constitutional Party, for the "outs," advocate extreme caution. Similarly, many strong supporters of the Administration point out that the hour for action has not yet struck.

They say that first it is absolutely necessary for all of Russia and the rest of the world to understand that Japan is engaged in no chauvinistic adventure, and desires nothing more than to safeguard the Far East, assist the Allies, and, if possible, save Russia from German domination, which means the mailed fist in the Far East.

The Chinese problem is one of the most serious features. It is recognized that this is China's great opportunity, and Japan is urging the leaders in the north and south to settle their differences by a sound compromise, form a capable national Government at Peking, and join Japan and the Allies in guarding the frontiers and helping Russia. Some indications are manifest that this effort may be successful.

Tang Shao-yi, who has held many posts in the Cabinet, was formerly Governor of Mukden Province, and is leader of the National Party of China, is on his way to Japan. Baron Hayashi, the Japanese Minister to China, has returned to Peking, and it is stated that there is reason to believe that by tactful diplomacy the obstacles to the effective co-operation between Japan and China in Siberia may be removed in time to enable both countries to share in the Far Easterners' real participation in the war.

Such an outcome of the present negotiations, resulting in agreement and co-operation between Japan and China, would mean, to the minds of Japanese statesmen, an alliance of vast importance.

Japanese Premier Terauchi

MAY MAKE ADDRESS MONDAY

Expected to Say Teutons' Course Shows They Are Not to be Trusted.

MAY REJECT PEACE TALK

Officials Agree That Czernin's Terms to Rumania Have Belied All His Professions.

JAPAN'S ACTION A PROBLEM

Tokio Has Shown Great Consideration for Our Views, Washington Admits.

Special to The New York Times.
WASHINGTON, March 16.—Conditions in Russia, complicated as they are by the subserviency of the Bolshevist authority to Germany, the civil conflicts in Russian territory, the agitation over the proposal that Japan take measures to protect allied interests in Eastern Russia, expected German aggression or propaganda, and the general state of chaos, economic, political, and military, prevailing in the territory formerly ruled by the Czar, are to be reviewed soon in public by President Wilson, according to an intimation given today.

In what manner the President will make known his position on the Russian situation is not made known, but it is accepted that he will follow the usual course of appearing before Congress in joint session and state the conclusions he has reached as to the attitude the United States should assume in the difficult problem that confronts the allied Governments as the result of the Russian collapse and the acceptance by the Congress of Soviets at Moscow of the harsh German conditions.

One suggestion heard today was that the President might present his views in a public statement, but this was mere surmise, and the more general opinion was that he would address Congress on the subject. It was reported that he was preparing a formal address.

Intimations of the character given today are usually followed quickly by the appearance of the President before the Senate and the House, and it would not be a surprise if he went to the Capitol on Monday.

There is an expectation that the President will take advantage of the opportunity to discuss the effect on peace prospects of the conditions resulting from the Russian collapse and the Teuton occupation of Russian territory.

That he cannot avoid this subject in any consideration of the Russian situation is argued, and the hope is expressed that he will dissect the German and Austrian pretense of a desire for an ending of the war in accordance with the general principles enunciated by President Wilson.

Paralleling this hope is the strong feeling that the President will make his address an occasion for serving notice on the Central Powers that they have again shown that they are unworthy of trust among decent nations and that from now on the war must be waged by the Allies for the one purpose of overcoming the menace of militarism, which can be accomplished only by victory on the battlefield. What Germany and Austria have done to Russia makes Teutonic peace talk hereafter unworthy of the slightest consideration, according to the opinion that prevails generally in Washington.

The effect on the President's feelings of the Soviet's failure to answer in any effective manner his assurance of American sympathy and promise to help was not discussed today in connection with his reported purpose to make a public statement on the Russian situation.

The President has always shown sympathy with the democratic aims of those concerned in the revolution and insisted in an address to Congress that the Allies should not turn the perturbed former subjects of the Czar adrift to be the playthings of Germany and her allies. In this the President has gone contrary to sentiments expressed by Prime Minister Lloyd George, and there is no reason to believe that his policy has undergone any change.

Interest in Japanese Phase.

Much of the interest in the President's expected statement with respect to Russia centres in the Japanese phase of the problem. In this connection it was learned today that exchanges were still in progress between the Japanese and other allied Governments, and that Japan has not undertaken to put in operation her reported plan to invade Siberia with armed forces to maintain order, prevent the seizure of allied property sent to the Russian Government, protect foreigners, and check any attempt at German domination in that part of the Russian possessions.

It is now well recognized that Japan has shown a gratifying consideration for the doubts of the United States as to the wisdom of Japanese intervention in Siberia. Japan has emphasized this consideration through the fact that in her desire to enter Russian territory she has the support of Great Britain, France, and Italy. While it is accepted rather generally that the Japanese Government will decide ultimately to undertake the venture, the feeling is growing that the Government at Tokio is giving careful consideration to the representations of the United States, and if its final views do not accord with the American position, it will be coupled with assurances that will go far toward satisfying those who fear that any occupation of Russian territory by Japan will be permanent.

In this connection it is reported that Great Britain, France, and Italy will join in assurances that the occupation of Eastern Siberia is for no other purpose than to protect the interests of the Allies from the menace that arises from Germany's control of Russian affairs.

FRENCH DEFY GERMAN OFFENSIVE WITH DEFENSES 20 MILES DEEP; SEE THE REAL PERIL IN U-BOATS

See No Use of Talking Peace.

The hope, so strongly expressed nowadays in Washington, that the President will put a damper on further talk of peace is born of sundry considerations. Most Washington officials believe that the aims of the allied Powers can be achieved only by the sword, and that it is useless to appeal to Germany with any other argument. To discuss peace now, it is held, would mean that Germany would be in a position to demand concessions that simply lay the foundation for a resumption of the struggle in the future. But, outside of this, the feeling here is that resumption of peace discussion would help the German cause, and that the sooner the President puts a damper on it the better it will be for all those concerned in making the world safe for democracy.

Just at this time an apparent effort is being made to have it appear that Germany and her partners are ready for a discussion of peace terms. This is a form of German propaganda, designed to impress the workers of the allied countries with the belief that their own Governments are bent on conquest and not on the attainment of the high ideals that caused them to enter the conflict.

The symptoms are the usual ones. The Prussian group is too clever to make itself prominent in the propaganda, so it is following the course of having others put out the feelers that are in evidence. Bulgaria is the "come on" in the present case, and it is thought that there will be no letup in the attempt to show that this one of the Central Powers is weary of the war and anxious to make peace. The attention of the Bulgarian peace agitators is being directed mainly to the United States, which is regarded as fruitful soil, because they think that this Government may be impressed by the argument that Bulgaria loves America too well to engage in hostilities with her.

Inquiry here today brought statements that as far as the United States was concerned no peace suggestion had come from any official quarter, directly or indirectly. The reports that Bulgarian agents had approached or were about to approach American representatives in neutral countries in Europe with peace proposals were not credited in official quarters. It was said that there were many unofficial busybodies who undertook, some from the most worthy motives and others from reasons that suggested collusion with Germany, to agitate the question of peace, but none had any authoritative standing and this Government had paid no attention to them.

Official Washington now accepts Count Czernin's peace terms to Rumania as the Austro-Hungarian Foreign Minister's reply to President Wilson's latest address on peace terms. The conditions he made has convinced persons close to the White House that the Austrian statesman consciously practiced deception in his professed desire for peace, and that his actions prove the valuelessness of his professions and his betrayal of principles.

No one ventures to speak for President Wilson, but the feeling is growing that further discussion of peace at the present time is furthest from the President's mind, and that he realizes that the enemy has employed and is employing propaganda to weaken the morale of the allied countries.

Official reports from diplomats in countries contiguous to Germany state that sentiment in Germany toward peace has greatly changed since the collapse of Russia. The Pan Germanists and militarists in Germany are in the saddle. The tone of the moderate press has been modified, and even the Scheidemann Socialists are now giving support to the Government, their criticism of the direction of the war having been nearly silenced. Germany, it is now believed, is trying to make even the extreme Socialists see that war is profitable by efforts to convince them that the spoils of war acquired by Germany will be permanent.

There was nowhere any inclination to believe that President Wilson would extend formal recognition to the Bolshevist Government.

DEFENSIVE POWER DOUBLED

Multiplication of Trench Systems a Tremendous Factor of Safety.

WELCOMES AN ATTACK

"Let Us Pray for It," Says a General When Asked About the Prospects.

NEED OUR HELP AT SEA

Leaders in France Emphasize Importance of Ship Output to Offset Sinkings.

Tirpitz Again Predicts U-Boats Will Win Victory

LONDON, March 16.—"If we continue the U-boat war without flinching we can secure a peace with England which will insure for Germany's navy a base off the Flemish coast for all time," Admiral von Tirpitz is quoted as declaring in a recent telegram.

The Admiral's message, says the Exchange Telegraph correspondent at Amsterdam, was sent in reply to a telegram from the Director of the new von Tirpitz school at Swinemünde, Germany.

By G. H. PERRIS.

Copyright, 1918, by The New York Times Company.

Special Cable to THE NEW YORK TIMES.

WITH THE FRENCH ARMIES, March 14 (Delayed)—The strange interval continues. We have had four months of unusually favorable weather, and yet the great German offensive continually threatened and still discussed by the German press does not come to pass. This hesitation is significant and encouraging. Whatever we may think of the German Grand Staff, no one suggests that they are slackers, and all their traditions are against leaving their chief adversary in peace to accumulate new strength; and the growth of the Allies' power in the west goes on steadily. Its first purpose is of course defensive.

I spent yesterday in an important part of the front examining the new works that had been established in these quiet months. They cannot be described precisely, but it would not be too much to say that in this period the defensive power of the French armies has been doubled. At the beginning of the war the Allies had no time, and in the middle period they had little inclination, to multiply defense works. Any old ditch served before Ypres, and Verdun was saved not by any kind of fortification, ancient or modern, but by the unconquerable faithfulness of the poilu.

Allies See Victory Only in Defeat of U-Boats, And Look to America for Her Utmost Efforts

By CHARLES H. GRASTY.

Copyright, 1918, by The New York Times Company.

Special Cable to THE NEW YORK TIMES.

PARIS, March 16.—I have received inside information calling renewed attention to the submarine situation. There has been too much optimistic generalizing on this subject. I am urged by expert authorities to point out to America constantly how useless will be all her strength and how utterly hopeless all her plans for defeating Germany unless the submarine is mastered. And it is not mastered yet. For eight months I have been digging out, and by hook or crook getting censors to pass to America, tonnage figures on submarine sinkings. Public appreciation there of the seriousness of this phase of the war has constituted a driving force to increase the effort in building destroyers and shipping. But twice as much tonnage was sunk in 1917 as was built. The year 1918 therefore opened with an accumulated deficit. It is safe to say that if we had twice the tonnage actually possessed by the Allies today we should still be far short of supplying Europe's needs and transporting the American army.

All estimates about the future are vitiated by the element of speculation. After a year of sinking twice the tonnage that was constructed we are still losing more than we are building. Optimists sharpen their pencils and figure on a certainty of construction overtaking the destruction by next June, and then unexpectedly British labor develops some strange distemper that slows down results in the shipyards. I am reliably informed that the hours necessary to produce a given unit have increased since the war in the proportion of eight to thirteen. There are so many possibilities in the submarine field that all estimates should have a liberal margin of safety. The Germans may upset the present naval balance by transferring their Baltic forces, released by the Russian collapse, to the North Sea and the Atlantic, thus crippling the convoy system and increasing the loss by submarines. Or they may make their U-boats larger and more of them. The field of invention is as open to them as it is to us.

The submarine situation should be opened up and dealt with frankly on both sides of the ocean. Much of the trouble now experienced in England with labor and war weariness is due to ill-advised concealment about the submarine. Democracies can fight best when they know the worst. Political coddling produces enfeeblement. For months London has been more concerned about stopping the air raids than beating the submarines. Remissness with the Government is a more potent force than righteous indignation against Germany or the firm resolve to win at all hazards. In a word, we deny in practice the very principle of publicity that we are fighting this war to vindicate and establish.

The leaders here who are bearing the burden of this war are anxious for America to understand and keep steadily in mind that, whatever may happen in any arena, the submarine remains the bulls-eye at which allied effort must be aimed. Assuming that the western front can be held for the time being, as asserted by General Foch and other authorities, Germany can be defeated militarily, despite her eastern conquests, by swift and effective measures against the submarine. Germany's strategy is conceived with a view to diverting popular interest to other and comparatively irrelevant matters, like air raiding, while the silent U-boats cut the allied jugular. With the western line holding intact, the problem chiefly is one of sustaining the life of the European Allies and transporting an American army strong enough to deal the deathblow to Prussia. The extent to which America is relied on for the extinction of the submarine may be judged from the expectation generally entertained that the United States from now on will contribute nearly three-fourths of the new construction. Until now, preliminary preparations have largely absorbed American effort, but henceforth shipping is expected in such quantity from the American yards as to restore normal conditions within six months, and assured transport thereafter.

Those trials at least are things of the past. Never again will it be necessary to defend the front trenches to the death because there are no others ready behind them. Today the centre of France is plowed with trenches, bearded with wire. Fields, dotted with battery emplacements, all scientifically designed to give the most advantageous lines of fire. There is system behind system for a score of miles—I am not speaking figuratively—behind the present front.

I asked a very distinguished soldier the other day what he thought of the prospects of a great enemy attack.

"Let us pray for it," he replied.

There was nothing lighthearted in his tone; the General knew what he was saying. His men would say with him: "Let us pray for it." No pacifist can teach him or them anything about hell or war, but they see a worse hell that it is in their power to refuse, and, having to fight, they know now the advantages of method of defense compared with which the Hindenburg line, so far as we know it, was but a student's essay. Even though the labor may have been in vain, it was their plain duty to take these precautions. Evidently they do not exhaust the program of the Allies.

"All the News That's Fit to Print."

The New York Times.

THE WEATHER

Rain today; tomorrow fair, slightly colder; north to variable winds. For full weather report see Page 23.

VOL. LXVII...NO. 21,972. ...   NEW YORK, FRIDAY, MARCH 22, 1918.—TWENTY-FOUR PAGES.   TWO CENTS In Greater New York and Within Commuting Distance. | THREE CENTS Elsewhere

GERMANS OPEN DRIVE AGAINST BRITISH ON 50-MILE FRONT; MASSED FORCES GAIN GROUND AFTER TERRIFIC SHELLING, BUT HAIG REPORTS THAT THEY WON LITTLE AT HEAVY COST

WOUNDED BACK IN LONDON

Ambulances Ready to Receive Victims of the Big Battle.

HAIG TELLS OF THE DAY

Foe Attacks "With Vigor and Determination" and Penetrates Parts of the Front.

DOVER HEARS THE FIRING

Houses There Shaken by German Fire Along the Cambrai Front—Flashes Seen.

First of the Wounded Arrive in London

LONDON, Friday, March 22.—Long lines of ambulances began forming at the Charing Cross Railway Station early this morning to receive wounded men from Channel port trains.

Scenes not unlike those during the battle of the Somme were enacted, the line of ambulances stretching away from the station for four city blocks.

Only small groups of night workers and railroad employes greeted the first arrivals from the front.

LONDON, March 21.—Field Marshal Haig's report from British headquarters in France tonight describes the German offensive today as comprising an intense bombardment by the artillery and a powerful infantry attack on a front of over fifty miles.

Some British positions were penetrated, but the German losses are declared to have been exceptionally heavy. On no part of the long front of the attack did the Germans attain their objective, it is stated.

The report reads:

At about 8 o'clock this morning, after an intense bombardment of both high explosive and gas shells on our forward positions and back areas, a powerful infantry attack was launched by the enemy on a front of over fifty miles, extending from the River Oise in the neighborhood of La Fère to the Sensée River, about Croiselles.

A hostile artillery demonstration has taken place on a wide front north of La Bassée Canal and in the Ypres sector.

The attack, which for some time past was known to be in course of preparation, has been pressed with great vigor and determination throughout the day.

Victory Must Not and Will Not Fail Us, Says Kaiser; Clear the Way to Peace, Hindenburg Urges

AMSTERDAM, March 21.—"The prize of victory must not and will not fail us—no soft peace, but one which corresponds with Germany's interests," was Emperor William's message to the Schleswig-Holstein Provincial Council, according to a Kiel dispatch. The telegram was sent in reply to a congratulatory message.

"We are at the decisive moment of the war, and one of the greatest moments in German history," said the Emperor in a telegram to the Rhenish Provincial Council, according to a Central News dispatch from Amsterdam.

Field Marshal von Hindenburg has telegraphed to the Posen Provincial Council as follows:

"God willing, we will also overcome the enemy in the west and clear the way to a general peace."

In the course of the fighting the enemy broke through our outpost positions and succeeded in penetrating into our battle positions in certain parts of the front.

The attacks were delivered in large masses, and have been extremely costly to the hostile troops engaged, whose losses have been exceptionally heavy.

Severe fighting continues along the whole front. Large numbers of hostile reinforcing troops have been observed during the day, moving forward behind the enemy's lines.

Several enemy divisions, which had been especially trained for this great attack, have already been identified, including units of the Guards.

Captured maps, depicting the enemy's intentions, show that on no part of the long front of the attack has he attained his objective.

The afternoon statement of the War Office, telling of the beginning of the bombardment, says:

A heavy bombardment was opened by the enemy shortly before dawn this morning against our whole front from the neighborhood of Vendeuil, south of St. Quentin, to the River Scarpe.

A successful raid was carried out by us last night in the neighborhood of St. Quentin. Thirteen prisoners and three machine guns were brought back by our troops. Prisoners also were taken by us in patrol encounters southeast of Messines and in another successful raid carried out by us south of Houthulst Forest.

A raid undertaken by the enemy in the neighborhood of Armentières was repulsed.

A Rumor of German Tanks.

Reuter's correspondent at British Headquarters states that with heavy masses of troops, supported by a great weight of artillery, the Germans appear to have penetrated the British front line at "certain points between the Scarpe and Vendeuil." He adds:

"Our counter measures have not yet developed, therefore it is difficult to define the position. Apparently the enemy's purpose has been to launch converging attacks upon the two flanks of the Flesquieres salient, in the hope of cutting it off.

"There are unconfirmed rumors that the enemy has employed tanks."

The artillery in action on the western front could be distinctly heard at Dover and other towns on the east coast of England. Doors and windows of the houses at Dover, for instance, were continuously shaken by the heavy concussions.

The firing, which was the heaviest that has been heard in that district from such a distance, began at 8 o'clock this morning and lasted at brief intervals until 7 A. M.

At Ramsgate, besides the sound of the cannonading, bright flashes were seen at sea, while the vibration of the explosions shook the windows and dislodged tiles from the roofs.

AIM AT CAMBRAI SALIENT

Concentrated Assaults Made to Pinch British Out of Their Front.

INTENSE STRUGGLE ENSUES

The Battle Spreads North and South and Is Still Continuing with Great Fury.

SHELL STORM OVER LINES

Wide Area Back of the British Front Is Swept by the German Missiles.

BRITISH ARMY HEADQUARTERS IN FRANCE, March 21, (Associated Press.)—The Germans this forenoon launched a heavy attack against the British lines over a wide front in and near the Cambrai sector, and the assault bears all the earmarks of being the beginning of the enemy's much-heralded grand offensive.

The attack was preceded by a heavy bombardment from guns of all calibres, and the duel between the opposing heavy batteries has been rocking the countryside for hours. The front under fire extended from a short distance below the Scarpe River to the British right flank, (from east of Arras to the region of La Fère.)

At the same hour the Germans began a display of artillery activity in the Messines sector. At 4 o'clock they began a bombardment with gas shells along the Fleurbaix-Armentières sector.

The Germans employed gas shells freely, and a constant stream of high velocity shells has been breaking with frightful concussion far back of the British lines.

Five hours after the heavy shelling began the enemy forces hurled themselves on the British front line trenches north of Lagnicourt and Louveral, the latter place lying due west of Boursies, (southwest of Cambrai.)

At the same time other German forces advanced behind a smoke barrage along the ridge running northward from Gouzaucourt. The attack in this region was by no means unexpected by the British, and they had made great preparations to meet the onslaught.

Hard fighting then extended from the point north of Lagnicourt southward to Gauche Wood, just below Gouzaucourt.

The two vast forces were locked in a bitter struggle over this wide front for hours. The bombardment was of a most terrific nature, and finally the infantry drove forward against numerous points in the Cambrai sector.

At last reports sanguinary fighting was in progress as far south as the region of Hargicourt and as far north as Bullecourt.

The early stages of the battle would seem to indicate that the Germans were trying to drive a wedge on both sides of the Cambrai salient and pinch it off. A keen struggle has been proceeding in the neighborhood of Bullecourt and Lagnicourt and south of the salient near Hargicourt and Roussoy.

British Forces Were Ready.

The British forces had been looking for this attack today. Not only have prisoners declared that yesterday or today would mark the beginning of the offensive on this front, but there were abundant signs of an enemy smash against this sector, which was the scene of the last great battle in the British theatre.

That the Germans were as thoroughly prepared as possible was well known, and, as a consequence, the British had taken extensive steps to meet the blow.

It is too early to predict the outcome of the first few hours of the struggle, in which vast forces and every conceivable engine was probably employed. On general principles, however, it may be stated that the great concentration of attacking forces will probably result in the defensive line being pushed back in places. This would merely be history repeating itself.

It is certain, however, that at no period has the British war machine been in such fine condition. Never before has there been higher morale or optimism among the British troops. The general impression on the front is in agreement with that of the Germans—that this is the decisive contest of the war. But on the British side there is no doubt that the decision will eventually be in the Allies' favor.

Germany Staking Everything.

Germany is staking everything on this play, and if the great attack fails to break clear through, it is believed that the Germans will be finished, for they have nothing further to offer, except a gradually weakening defense.

Section
1

"All the News That's
Fit to Print."

The New York Times.

THE WEATHER
Fair Sunday and Monday; slight
temperature change.
☞For full weather report see Page 22.

Section
1

VOL. LXVII...NO. 21,974.   NEW YORK, SUNDAY, MARCH 24, 1918.—108 PAGES, In Nine Parts,   FIVE CENTS

GERMANS SMASH BRITISH FRONT, DRIVE IN FOUR MILES; CLAIM 25,000 PRISONERS; HELD AT SOME POINTS, SAYS HAIG; GUN SAID TO BE 74½ MILES AWAY LANDS SHELLS IN PARIS

SAYS BRITISH ARE BEATEN

Berlin Claims Victory Over "Considerable Part" of Foe's Army.

FIRST BATTLE STAGE ENDED

And German Forces Now Hold Line Northeast of Bapaume, Peronne, and Ham.

MANY TOWNS ARE CAPTURED

Third British Positions Reached or Penetrated at Some Points, It Is Stated.

BERLIN, March 23, (via London.) —"A considerable part of the English Army is beaten," says the official statement this evening from General Headquarters, which announces the end of the first stage of the great battle in France, with victories near Monchy, Cambrai, St. Quentin, and La Fère. It is further stated that the German forces are now on a line northeast of Bapaume, Péronne, and Ham.

The day announcement from headquarters told of successes along the battle front at many points, and stated that 25,000 prisoners, 400 guns, and 300 machine guns had been captured.

Between Fontaine-les-Croisilles and Moeuvres German forces penetrated into the second enemy position and captured Vaulx-Vraucourt and Morchies, (the former about 3½ miles and the latter about 2½ miles behind the former British front.)

The British evacuated their positions in the bend southwest of Cambrai, and were pursued by the Germans through Demicourt, Flesquières, and Ribecourt.

Between Gonnelieu and the Omignon stream the first two British positions were penetrated, and the heights west of Gouzeaucourt, Heudicourt, and Villers-Faucon were captured. The Germans now stand before the third British position.

Between the Omignon stream and

the Somme, after the capture of the first British position, the Germans made their way through Holnon Wood and fought across the heights of Savy and Roupy, penetrating into the third hostile position.

South of the Somme the Germans broke through the hostile lines and in an uninterrupted forward movement drove the enemy over the Crozat Canal toward the west.

A crossing over the Oise west of La Fère was forced by Jaeger battalions, it is added.

Tonight's official statement reads as follows:

The first stage of the great battle in France is ended. We have won the engagements near Monchy, Cambrai, St. Quentin, and La Fère. A considerable part of the English Army is beaten.

We are fighting approximately on a line northeast of Bapaume, Péronne, and Ham.

The day bulletin reads as follows:

Under the command of the Emperor and King, the battle of attack against the British front near Arras, Cambrai, and St. Quentin has been proceeding two days. Yesterday also good progress was made.

Divisions of Crown Prince Rupprecht stormed the heights north and northwest of Croisilles. Between Fontaine-les-Croisilles and Moeuvres they penetrated into the second enemy position and captured the villages, situated there, of Vaulx-Vraucourt and Morchies. Strong British counterattacks failed. Between Gonnelieu and the Omignon stream the first two enemy positions were penetrated. The heights west of Gouzeaucourt, Heudricourt, and Villers-Faucon were captured, and in the Valley of the Cologne stream Roisel and Marquaix were stormed.

The fighting around Epehy heights was bitter. These heights being encircled from the north and south, the enemy was compelled to leave them for our troops.

Between Epehy and Roisel the enemy vainly endeavored by means of strong counterattacks to bring our victoriously advancing troops to a standstill. He was driven back everywhere, with the heaviest losses.

The heights north of Vermand were stormed. We stand before the third enemy position.

Under the effect of this success the enemy evacuated his positions in the bend southwest of Cambrai. We pursued him through Demicourt, Flesquières, and Ribecourt.

Between the Omignon stream and the Somme, corps of the army group of the German Crown Prince, after the capture of the first enemy positions, made their way through Holnon Wood and fought across the heights of Savy and Roupy, penetrating into the third enemy position.

South of the Somme divisions broke through the enemy lines, and in an uninterrupted forward movement drove the enemy over the Crozat Canal toward the west.

Jaeger battalions forced a crossing of the Oise west of La Fère. In company with divisions following, they stormed the heights northwest of the town, which are crowned with the permanent works of La Fère.

The captures so far reported by the army group of Crown Prince Rupprecht are 15,000 prisoners and 250 guns; by the army group of the German Crown Prince, 10,000 prisoners, 150 guns, and 300 machine guns.

Artillery battles continue between the Lys and La Bassée Canal.

Germans' Vast Superiority in Guns Is Backed By Fifty Divisions

One Cannon to Every Twelve Yards of Front—One British Division Fought Six Near St. Quentin—Massed Assailants Mowed Down at Point Blank Range.

By PHILIP GIBBS.

Copyright, 1918, by The New York Times Company.

Special Cable to THE NEW YORK TIMES.

The following are the first dispatches received in this country from any special correspondent at the scene of the battle:

WAR CORRESPONDENTS' HEADQUARTERS, March 22.—The enemy flung the full weight of his great army against the British yesterday. Nearly forty divisions are identified, and it is certain that as many as fifty must be engaged. In proportions of men, the British are much outnumbered, therefore the obstinacy of the resistance of the troops is wonderful.

Nine German divisions were hurled against three British at one part of the line, and eight against two at another.

All the storm troops, including the guards, were in brand-new uniforms. They advanced in dense masses, and never faltered until shattered by the machine-gun fire.

As far as I can find, the enemy introduced no new frightfulness, no

tanks and no specially invented gas, but relied on the power of his artillery and the weight of the infantry assault.

The supporting waves advanced over the bodies of the dead and wounded. The German commanders were ruthless in the sacrifice of life, in the hope of overwhelming the defense by the sheer weight of numbers.

Long-range Guns on the Front.

They had exceeding power in guns. Opposite three of the British divisions they had a thousand, and at most parts of the line one to every twelve or fifteen yards. They had brought a number of long-range guns, probably naval, and their shellfire was scattered as far back as twenty-eight miles behind the lines. During the last hour of the bombardment they poured out gas shells, and continued to send concentrated gas about the British batteries and reserve trenches. The atmosphere was filled with poisonous clouds. With this they failed to achieve success. There were only six cases of gas poisoning this morning in one of the largest casualty clearing stations.

The main object of the enemy's attack on the left of the battle front probably was to bite off the Bullecourt salient and pierce through the three main lines of defense below Croisilles and St. Leger and turn the line, so that he could capture Spin Hill with his old Hindenburg tunnel trench.

The Germans never made ground on the extreme left by the old Hindenburg line. A very gallant division of men drove them back when they attempted to cross No Man's Land, and did not lose a foot of their ground.

A little to the right of them the Bullecourt salient was utterly smothered with fire. No men could hold such a position.

Pushed on in Face of Slaughter.

Fortunately, in all parts of the line such a state of things was foreseen, and the outpost lines had only to fall back upon the battle positions to the rear, where there was a stronger defensive system. When the enemy followed on, bringing forward light artillery with support lines of infantry, the British guns slashed down his ranks and left masses of dead on the field. The British armies all report that they have seen large numbers of German dead heaped amid the débris of the wire and in the open ground.

But still they came on, with most fanatical courage of sacrifice. When the first lines fell, their places were filled by others, and the British guns and machine-gun fire could not kill them fast enough.

At 5:30 in the afternoon the enemy made another attack in massed formation, crowding down the slopes of the Sensée Valley from Cherisy and Fontaine Wood, striking down to the north of Vaulx. The British gunners fired into them with open sights, cutting swaths in the ranks and checking their tide of assault.

When the darkness fell they had not gained anything like the objectives marked out for them, and

The Battle Area in France.

In this map the solid black indicates the battlefront before the German offensive began on Thursday and the broken line to the west shows the approximate position of the combatants yesterday, according to the day report of the German War Office yesterday. It should be said, however, that General Haig reported last night that most of the northern part of the line was still holding.

West and south of St. Quentin, however, the British have lost ground heavily. At some points the fighting front is four miles and more back from where it was on Thursday morning. This is true in the Roisel region, east of Peronne, and also in the district south of St. Quentin, on the Crozat-Somme Canals.

The light broken line running from east of Arras, southwesterly and then easterly around Combles, and southward by Peronne and Roye, shows the position held by Hindenburg before he executed his strategic retreat early last year.

during the night they made no further attempt.

This morning there was fierce fighting round St. Leger, and the British troops took some prisoners and four machine guns.

Intense Assault on Salient.

From Noreuil eastward from Lagnicourt, around the bend of the Cambrai salient, the fighting was of the same intensity and the bombardment was equally terrific, supported by the same numbers of men, advancing in deep formations.

The outpost lines became untenable under the bombardment, and the British were ordered to fall back to battle position behind.

The enemy, by great sacrifices of life, was able to penetrate the first British defensive system in the neighborhood of Lagnicourt, Bouries, and Hargicourt, after which they were held.

A number of tanks made a brilliant counterattack before dark last evening and recaptured some of the ground near Doignies.

The defense of the British everywhere was splendid. An especially heavy attack was made yesterday by six German divisions on one British division south of St. Quentin. In spite of this vast superiority of numbers they were stricken with losses and the attack was checked all day until night, when the enemy, being spent, could make no further effort.

The British line was withdrawn to a strong position behind the canal between St. Quentin and the Oise, where the enemy will be caught in a waste of waters and marshes if he tries to make any further advance.

How the Offensive Began.

Thursday, March 21.—A German offensive against the British front has begun.

At about 5 o'clock this morning the enemy began an intense bombardment of the lines and batteries on a very wide front—something like sixty miles, from the country south of the Scarpe and to the west of Bullecourt in the neighborhood of Croisilles, as far south as the positions between St. Quentin and the British right flank.

After several hours of this hurricane shelling, in which it is probable that a great deal of gas was used with the intention of creating a poison gas atmosphere around the British gunners and forward posts, the German infantry advanced and developed attacks against a number of strategical points on a front of about twenty-five miles between the Scarpe and Hargincourt, ten miles north of St. Quentin. Whether they have attacked still further south I do not yet know.

Among the places against which they seem to have directed their chief efforts are Bullecourt, Lagnecourt, and Noreuil, both west of Cambrai, where they once before penetrated the British lines and were slaughtered

in great numbers; the St. Quentin Ridge, which was on the right of the Cambrai fighting, and the villages of Ronssoy and Hargicourt, south of the Cambrai salient.

It is impossible to say yet how far the enemy will endeavor to follow up the initial movement of his troops over any ground that he may gain in the first rush or with what strength he will press forward his supporting divisions and fling his storm troops into the struggle, but the attack already appears to be on a formidable scale, with a vast amount of artillery and masses of men, and there is reason to believe that it may be, indeed, the beginning of the great offensive, advertised for so long a time and with such ferocious menaces by the German agents in neutral countries.

If so, it is a bid for a decisive victory on the western front, at no matter what sacrifice and with the fullest brutalities of every engine of war gathered together during the months of preparation and liberated entirely for this front by the downfall of Russia.

Today I can give no details of the fighting, but will reserve all attempts to give a clear insight into the situation until my next message, when out of the hurricane of fire, now spreading over sixty miles or more of battlefields, there will come certain knowledge of the fighting.

At the moment there are only scraps of news from one part of the

front and another, unconfirmed rumors, reports of ground given or taken, and vague tidings of men hard pressed but holding out against repeated onslaughts.

It would be a wicked and senseless thing to make use of these uncertain fragments from many sources, and some hours must pass before it becomes clear how much the enemy has gained by his first blow and how much he has failed to gain against heroic resistance of the British troops.

The immediate endeavor of the enemy seems obvious. It is an enlargement of his strategical plan in the attack of Nov. 30 against the lines the British held after the first Cambrai battle, and it covers the same ground on a much wider boundary.

He appears to be assaulting both wings of the salient between the Scarpe and the south end of Flesquières ridge in order to cut off all the intervening ground, which includes Havrincourt Wood and V??? Wood, the line south of Morchies and Beaumetz, and the stretch of country east and southeast of Bapaume, which he abandoned to us in the retreat of last March after the battles of the Somme.

By a rapid turning movement from both wings he would hope to capture many British troops and guns. It is a menace which cannot be taken lightly, and at the present moment Haig's troops are fighting not only for their own lives, but also for the fate of England and all the race.

During the last few weeks I have been along sectors now involved in this battle, and have met the men who are today fighting to hold their lines against the enemy's storm troops under the fury of his fire.

I have described the spirit of those men, their confidence, their splendid faith, their quiet and cheerful courage, their lack of worry until this hour should come, the curious incredulity they had that the enemy would dare to attack them, because of the strength of their positions and of the great British gunfire.

But though many of them were incredulous of a great attack, they had been fully warned and fully trained and were on the alert day and night. By labor that never ceased they wired in their positions with acres of wire and strengthened their defenses and made their gun positions, and wore their gas masks so often and so long that it became a habit with them.

The attack today has been no surprise, for it had been expected every day, though many persons without evidence, the amateur critic and the armchair strategist, have professed to know that it was all a bluff, without the same excuse of courage which made some of the British troops doubtful, though upon them would fall the brunt of it.

It is not a bluff so far as today's battle shows, but appears to be the real thing in all its brutal force. Many thousands of men are engaged in defense and counterattack, and the one thing that is certain is their valor. Whatever may happen, they will fight to the death to safeguard the British lines, and whatever ground the enemy may take in his first assaults will have to be paid for by enormous sacrifice, and held, if held at all, against counterattacks, which the British will make with a most fierce and obstinate spirit.

The heart of all the people of our race must go out to these battalions of boys upon whom our destiny depends, and who now, while I write, are making a wall with their bodies against the evil and the power of the enemy.

FRENCH CAPITAL UNDER FIRE

Ten Killed and Fifteen or More Wounded in Mysterious Bombardment.

62 MILES FROM THE FRONT

Projectiles of 9.5-Inch Calibre Show Rifle Marks and Evidently Came from a Gun.

PUZZLES ORDNANCE CHIEFS

No Cannon So Far Known to Ordnance Experts Can Cover Any Such Range.

PARIS, March 23.—Paris has been under bombardment of long-range guns today, beginning at 8 o'clock this morning Shells of 240 millimeters (about 9.5 inches) have been reaching the capital and its suburbs at intervals of twenty minutes, killing about ten persons and wounding about fifteen. The shortest distance from Paris to the front is over 100 kilometers, (62 miles.)

The news of the bombardment was confirmed by an official announcement this afternoon. At that time it was stated that measures for counterattacking the enemy's cannon were under execution.

The city received its third warning of an air attack within twenty-four hours with unshaken nerves at 9 o'clock tonight. The "all clear" signal was given at 10:20 before the population could learn whether the warning was against an airplane raid or whether the long-distance German cannon had resumed operations. The people were crowding to music halls and theatres, fully confident nothing further would happen, only to be advised to seek the nearest shelter as quickly as possible.

The first daylight air raid on Paris also came today, which was one of perfect sunshine. The people refused to hide in cellars and other subterranean shelters, and, although the subway stations were crowded, the streets always had great crowds in them, watching for an aerial battle or some other stirring incident.

Await "All Clear" Signal.

As the day passed and the "all clear" signal was not given, the feeling grew that something new in the way of a raid was expected, and this was not explained until an official statement was issued saying that the delay was due to the bombardment by long-distance cannon.

The "all clear" was then sounded, and the normal life was resumed. The cable office reopened, to take up accumulated piles of dispatches.

Pieces of the shells on examination were found to bear rifling marks, which proved that they had not been dropped, but had been fired from a gun.

This apparently left a greater mystery than ever, as to where the gun in question was located, the nature of it, and by what method it was being operated.

Another thing which turned the thoughts of the officials at the municipal laboratory to the possibility that a cannon was being used was the regularity with which the bombs fell—one every twenty minutes.

LINES HOLDING IN NORTH

But West of St. Quentin the British Are Swept Back by Massed Foe.

ASSAULTS ARE CONTINUING

Ninety German Divisions Now Reported Engaged—Kaiser's Cavalry Thrown In.

BIG STROKE NEAR LA FERE

Foe Seeks to Break Through Line There — British Take Up Prepared Positions.

LONDON, March 23.—Battle of the most intense character is proceeding along the entire front from the Scarpe River to La Fère, according to the report of Field Marshal Haig tonight.

The British commander says that despite the determined attacks of the Germans, regardless of their losses, the British have held their positions on the northern part of the line.

South and west of St. Quentin, however, Haig's forces have been forced to retire to new positions and are now meeting new assaults by the enemy.

The day report stated that the Germans, by massed attacks, backed by great weight of artillery, had broken through the "defensive system" in this area. Tonight's bulletin tells of the repulse of the foe near Jussy, (lying south of the Somme Canal and about four miles west of the British front previous to the present offensive.)

Heavy Engagements Continue.

Tonight's bulletin reads as follows:

The battle is continuing with the greatest intensity on the whole front south of the Scarpe River.

South and west of St. Quentin our troops have taken up their new positions and we are heavily engaged with the enemy.

During the night strong hostile attacks in the neighborhood of Jussy (south of St. Quentin) were repulsed with great loss to the enemy.

On the northern portion of the battle front the enemy's attacks have been pressed with the utmost determination and regardless of losses.

Our troops have maintained their positions on the greater part of this front after a fierce and prolonged struggle.

Great gallantry has been shown by the troops engaged in the fighting in this area and south thereof. The 19th and 9th Divisions distinguished themselves by the valor of their defense. In one sector alone six hostile attacks, in two of which German cavalry took part, were beaten off by one of our infantry brigades.

The enemy's attacks continue with great violence.

The day report from General Haig, telling of the break in the British defensive system west of St. Quentin, reads:

Heavy fighting continued until late hours last night on the whole battle front. During the afternoon powerful hostile attacks, delivered with great weight of infantry and artillery, broke through our defensive system west of St. Quentin.

Our troops on this part of the battle front are falling back in good order across the devastated area to prepared positions further west.

Our troops on the northern portion of the battle front are holding their positions.

Very heavy fighting with fresh hostile forces is in progress.

SAY GERMANS AIM AT CHANNEL PORTS

London Observers Think Hindenburg's Ultimate Purpose Is Made Plain.

ENGLAND FEELS CONFIDENT

Danger of the Drive at Anglo-French Junction Point Is Understood

LONDON, March 23.—The attention of all England was centred today on the western front. There was no boastfulness, but the feeling was one of supreme confidence and pride in the army which stands on the first line of defense between democracy and autocracy.

While clouds of uncertainty obscure the details of the battle, some relief is felt that Germany has finally shown her hand.

The purpose and method of her long-talked-of blow are now thought to be plain. Hindenburg's objective is undoubtedly the Channel ports, but he purposes to take the first step toward them by breaking through the Allies' line near the junction of the French and British Armies.

The attack thus far has shown no new strategy, but appears to be simply a colossal blow with masses of guns and men, hitherto never used together on any battlefield.

No surprise is felt here that the British line has been forced back. Lines of defense have bent before all great offensives in this war. What the British people look to the army for is that it shall not break.

The newspapers warn against undue optimism, but they point out that the fighting instinct still lives in the British breast, notwithstanding the long years of peace and ignorance of military training, and that when that fighting instinct dies the world will see the death of the British nation.

Since it has developed that this is the heralded German offensive, the most colossal struggle in the world's history, the public and press are unanimously of the opinion that its failure will mean the end of the war. The Times says Germany is evidently resolved to stake all her chances on the western front, and adds:

"She has committed herself to the greatest gamble in history. We believe that she will fail, and it is precisely because the failure of the present attack must react disastrously upon Germany that we derive encouragement from the military position as it is disclosed today."

The Morning Post cautions the nation "to keep a cool head and allow no plausible argumentation upon scanty facts to persuade it to premature conclusions."

The Manchester Guardian says:

"If the Germans persist in attacks and lose they will have lost the war, and the only thing left doubtful will be the magnitude of their defeat."

This newspaper points out that at no point except one would a German victory be strategically decisive, adding:

"That point is south of St. Quentin, where a continuation of the present rate of advance would imperil the position of the French north of the Aisne. Here, then, south of St. Quentin, is the chief danger zone."

The Daily News says:

"Although the allied strength will reach its maximum only as the full force of America's contribution to the war is felt, the opening of the greatest battle the world has known is received with something like relief. * * * The salient fact about the offensive now in progress is that its authors cannot afford to fail. They cannot afford to face a country left, after another Summer of battle, to count its gains and find them no more than a myriad of nameless graves."

The newspapers dwell on the accuracy of the British Intelligence Service in divining the enemy's intentions and foreseeing the points and attack.

"Serious but not alarming" summed up the reception of today's news from the front. It is pointed out that in battles of such dimensions the attacking forces, by the employment of troops regardless of sacrifices, are nearly always enabled to force first line positions.

The Evening News in commenting on the situation refers to the failure of the British report to say anything about prisoners, and adds:

"In the matter of figures, our opponents have been notoriously inexact."

The military expert of The Westminster Gazette says that the Germans began their offensive partly through excessive egotism and also in desperation.

"We have upset the calculations of the enemy's defensive by our ascendancy in the air which, not being temporary, portended a situation likely to become intolerable if by bombing the lines of communication it had not become intolerable already," says this writer. "Were this state of affairs to continue, the morale of the German Army on the defensive would be destroyed. It is not the enemy, it is we who have forced the pace."

Smith-Dorrien Feels No Alarm.

LONDON, Sunday, March 24.—"Nothing we have heard up to the present would lead me to think that anything has happened which could not have been expected. There is no reason to come to the conclusion that things are looking bad," said General Horace Lockwood Smith-Dorrien, in an interview published in the Weekly Dispatch.

The New York Times.

"All the News That's Fit to Print."

THE WEATHER
Fair today and Friday; moderate northwest to north winds.
For full weather report see Page 21.

VOL. LXVII...NO. 21,973.   NEW YORK, THURSDAY, MARCH 28, 1918.—TWENTY-TWO PAGES.   TWO CENTS in Greater New York and | THREE CENTS

BRITISH, REINFORCED, BEAT GERMANS BACK; BERLIN ADMITS PROGRESS IS NOW SLOW; LLOYD GEORGE CALLS FOR AMERICA'S AID

HAIG HOLDS ON THE SOMME

Retakes Two Towns on the North Bank and One on the South.

NEW NORTHERN LINE INTACT

Unsuccessful German Attacks Result in Heavy Losses to the Assailants.

GERMANS TAKE ONE TOWN

Gain Footing in Ablainville, Near Albert—German Reserves Fill Roads.

LONDON, March 27.—In a day of furious fighting all along the front of the German offensive the British troops have checked the enemy with heavy losses and by counterattacks have made several important gains.

British Cavalry in France Win a Brilliant Victory

OTTAWA, March 27.—British cavalry has been in action and has achieved a brilliant victory, according to a dispatch from the Reuter correspondent at British headquarters, received here tonight.

The message said that no details of the action had been given.

The battle was renewed this morning with great violence north and south of the Somme. Near Rozières, south of the river, the Germans delivered a series of fierce attacks, all of which were beaten off with heavy casualties.

Further north the fortunes of battle fluctuated, the British, after a successful defense early in the day, falling back a short distance before a fresh German attack, but later counterattacking and regaining their original positions.

South of Albert, which, as the official report admits, is now held by German troops, the British retook a position and held it in the face of heavy German attacks.

Morlaincourt and Chipilly, villages

British Premier's Message Asking Us to Rush Help

Read by the Earl of Reading at the Lotos Club dinner last night:

We are at the crisis of the war. Attacked by an immense superiority of German troops, our army has been forced to retire. The retirement has been carried out methodically before the pressure of a steady succession of fresh German reserves, which are suffering enormous losses. The situation is being faced with splendid courage and resolution. The dogged pluck of our troops has for the moment checked the ceaseless onrush of the enemy, and the French have now joined in the struggle. But this battle, the greatest and most momentous in the history of the world, is only just beginning. Throughout it the French and British are buoyed with the knowledge that the great Republic of the West will neglect no effort which can hasten its troops and its ships to Europe.

In war time is vital. It is impossible to exaggerate the importance of getting American reinforcements across the Atlantic in the shortest possible space of time.

a little to the north of the Somme, in the angle formed by that river and the Ancre, were recaptured from the Germans in British counterattacks; and immediately to the south of the river Haig's men advanced their lines to the village of Proyart.

Late in the day the Germans, attacking in great strength near Bucquoy and Ablainville, (villages north of Albert,) gained a footing in the latter. At all other points, says Field Marshal Sir Douglas Haig in a bulletin issued tonight, the enemy was beaten off with great loss.

The text of the night statement reads:

The battle was renewed this morning with great violence south and north of the Somme. Intense fighting has taken place during the day from south of Rosières to north of Ablainville (Ablainzevelle).

An unsuccessful attempt made by the enemy last night to drive in our line south of the Somme was followed this morning by a series of heavy attacks in the neighborhood of Rosières and to the south of that place. At Rosières all the enemy's assaults have been beaten off by our troops, who inflicted heavy casualties on the enemy.

Further north our line was maintained through the earlier part of the day in spite of great pressure from large hostile forces.

Later in the day a fresh German attack developed in this area, with the result that our line was taken back a short distance to the west. Later reports show that our coun-

terattacks have again completely restored the situation.

During the day the enemy made a number of determined attacks against our positions between the Somme and the Ancre and north and south of Albert. Fierce fighting has taken place in this sector also.

Part of our position to the south of Albert, into which the enemy at one time forced his way, was regained by us by a counterattack, and a further heavy attack delivered by the enemy at this point during the afternoon was completely repulsed.

Attempts made by the enemy in the course of the day to debouch westward from the town of Albert have been driven back, in each instance with the heaviest casualties.

BERLIN REPORTS SLOW GAIN

Says the British Are Retreating on Both Sides of the Somme.

ALBERT IN GERMAN HANDS

Foe Say They Are Across the Ancre River North and South of the City.

TALE OF BOOTY GROWS

Increased Number of Prisoners Reported — Battling in Flanders and Lorraine.

BERLIN, March 27, (via London.) —"On both banks of the Somme our armies are engaged in a slowly progressing attack," says the German official communication issued this evening.

According to the announcement issued by Army Headquarters early in the day, the British began to retreat early this morning on a wide front on both sides of the Somme. The stubborn resistance of the hostile rearguard was overcome in the sharp pursuit, it was stated.

British and French divisions which were defeated on Monday en-

deavored again yesterday in the pathless crater fields of the Somme battle, the announcement added, to arrest the German advance, but the Germans broke through the enemy's lines.

To the north and south of Albert the Germans won crossings of the Ancre. Albert was captured last evening.

To the south of the Somme, after violent fighting, German forces drove the enemy back by way of Chaulnes and Lihons. Roye was taken by storm, and Noyon was cleared of hostile forces after bloody street fighting, the report said.

The day bulletin reads:

The British began a retreat this morning on a wide front on both sides of the Somme. The stubborn resistance of the hostile rearguard was overcome in the sharp pursuit.

British and French divisions which were defeated on March 25 tried again yesterday in the pathless crater fields of the Somme battle area to arrest our advance. Our attack broke through the enemy's lines.

To the north and south of Albert we won a passage across the Ancre. Albert fell in the evening.

To the south of the Somme after violent fighting we drove back the enemy by way of Chaulnes and Lihons. Roye was taken by storm and Noyon was cleared of the enemy after bloody street fighting.

At many points we have crossed our old positions, held before the Somme battle of 1916, toward the west. The number of prisoners grows and the booty increases.

There were artillery battles in Flanders, before Verdun, and in Lorraine.

Captain Baron von Richthofen has achieved his sixty-ninth and seventieth aerial victories.

In the other theatres there is nothing new.

KAISER GRIEVED BY RUIN.

Tells How Glad He Is That Germany Is Spared Such Things.

AMSTERDAM, March 27.—The Volkszeitung of Cologne says that, according to General von Ludendorff, Emperor William has been deeply impressed by the terrible devastation in the battle area, remarking:

"How glad we should be that our country has been spared such terrible things. Why did we succeed in keeping the fighting beyond our frontiers? Because before the war we always urged the need of armaments. When mankind changes these things also will change, but first mankind must begin to change."

"All the News That's Fit to Print."

The New York Times.

THE WEATHER
Snow or rain, colder today; Thursday probably rain; northeast gales.
☞For full weather report see Page 23.

VOL. LXVII...NO. 21,991. ....   NEW YORK, WEDNESDAY, APRIL 10, 1918.—TWENTY-FOUR PAGES.   TWO CENTS In Greater New York and | THREE CENTS Elsewhere.

ANGRY PROTESTS ROUSED BY LLOYD GEORGE, AS HE ANNOUNCES CONSCRIPTION FOR IRELAND; GERMANS STRIKE HEAVY BLOW IN THE NORTH

SPEECH IN THE COMMONS

Premier Presents Bill for Drafting All Men 18 to 50.

BILL ADMITTED BY 299 TO 80

Irish Members Shouting Defiance and Vowing Never to Submit.

NEW LIGHT ON GREAT DRIVE

British Bravery Retrieved Initial Reverse—Dramatic Aid of Wilson Warmly Acknowledged.

Special Cable to THE NEW YORK TIMES.

LONDON, April 9.—Great Britain was asked this afternoon to place at the disposal of the Government the services of every able-bodied man up to 50 years old, and even in certain cases up to 55. The announcement was made that conscription was to be applied to Ireland.

Crowds gathered at the approaches to the Houses of Parliament, and the benches of the Commons were closely packed with members, who showed deep interest in the questions and the Premier's method of presenting the prime importance of the issues involved. There were no fireworks in his speech, but an earnest insistence on the peril of the moment and the necessity of taking every possible measure to meet it.

The House at question time had shown itself full of life. It rose to every controversial point, and it sent up a deep cheer of welcome as Captain Redmond took the oath on his re-election to his father's old seat. As Mr. Lloyd George began his speech it settled down to listen, and resented fiercely interruptions from pacifist members.

Premier Shows Gravity of Task.

The Premier seemed at first to be restrained by the gravity of the moment. "We have now entered the most critical phase of this terrible war," he began, and he spoke slowly and with constant consultation of his notes. For nearly an hour he reviewed the military situation, and though he expressed his entire confidence in the army and paid a high tribute to the courage, endurance, and skill of soldiers and Generals alike, it was clear that he was impressed by the vastness of the forces against the Allies and the reality of their danger.

Not until he spoke of General Carey and his "brilliant achievement" in stopping the German advance with a scratch corps of signalmen, engineers, and labor battalions did he arouse the enthusiasm of the House in a round of deep cheers.

As the Premier came to discuss the appointment of Foch as generalissimo it was clear that he felt himself to be on delicate ground. He spoke with something like his old animation, smote the box on the table, and looked the House squarely in the face. He was prepared for criticism and got applause, but it was not very cordial.

Irish Create a Storm.

The real surprise came when the Premier announced shortly and decidedly:

"As to Ireland, it is not possible any longer to justify her exclusion from the act."

Like a field of wheat swept by gusts of wind, sharp interruptions burst out. Lloyd George appealed to the United States, more Irish than Ireland, he called it, where all were subject to conscription. "But not by the English," came back a retort by a member, shouted with a stentorian voice.

Cheers burst out in a great volume from all parts of the house except the Irish benches, and they answered with cries of protest. The Premier tried to continue his quiet, dispassionate speech, but Irish members were wound up to fierce excitement. Their quarter of the house was rocking with anger. Lines of members swayed to and fro.

"It is a declaration of war on Ireland," said one.

Quietly the Premier read out what Irish leaders like the late John Redmond had said of the justice of the war, and brought John Dillon, the new leader, to his feet in explanation of words he had used in 1914. But what especially roused the Irish to bitter anger was the Premier's insistence that this was a war in the interest of small nations. They flung back the words in his teeth, and stirred the rest of the House to angry reply, but the Premier, with only one protest that he be permitted to speak, went quietly on to his peroration.

Asquith Counsels Deliberation.

John Devlin wished to move an adjournment to permit the Government to consider the report of the Committee on Conscription of the Irish convention, but gave way to ex-Premier Asquith.

Mr. Asquith spoke calmly and coolly, dwelling on the reality of the crisis. He reserved the right to criticise the Government bill at a time when he had an opportunity to consider its details, and then obtained a sympathetic cheer from the House as he told of the heroism of the British soldiers, as he had just learned it from a letter from a "relative, in fact one of my own sons." As an old Parliamentarian, he advised the Premier not to rush the new bill, but to permit the House plenty of time to digest it.

FOE GAINS NEAR LA BASSEE

Forces Back the British-Portuguese Centre on the River Lys.

BUT BRITISH FLANKS HOLD

Repulse Attacks at Givenchy and Fleurbaix, While Richebourg and Laventie Fall.

FOG AIDS THE ASSAILANTS

Battle, Which Began in the Morning, Still Rages on the 11-Mile Front.

LONDON, April 9.—Beginning with a bombardment of great intensity, German troops this morning delivered heavy attacks upon the British and Portuguese lines from the La Bassée Canal to the neighborhood of Armentières (a distance of about eleven miles.)

The enemy forced back the Portuguese in the centre and the British on the flanks of the line of the River Lys between Estaires and Bac St. Maur.

Richebourcq-St. Vaast, (about a mile south of Neuve Chapelle,) and Laventie, (about two miles northeast of Neuve Chapelle,) were taken by the Germans in the assault.

The British withstood all attacks at Givenchy, (at the southern limit of the German assaults,) and Fleurbaix, at the north, about three miles southeast of Armentières.

The German attack was favored by the thick mist which shrouded the battlefield in the early morning.

Severe fighting continues on the whole of this front, according to Field Marshal Haig's night report.

South of Arras there were only minor engagements today on the British front.

Following is the text of the night bulletin:

This morning, after an intense bombardment of our positions from La Bassée Canal to the neighborhood of Armentières, strong hostile forces attacked the British and Portuguese troops holding this sector of our front. Favored by a thick mist, which made observation impossible, the enemy succeeded in forcing his way into the Allies' positions in the neighborhood of Neuve Chapelle, Fauquissart, and Cardonnerie Farm.

After heavy fighting, lasting throughout the day, the enemy succeeded in forcing back the Portuguese troops in the centre and the British troops on the flanks of the line of the River Lys, between Estaires and Bac St. Maur.

We held our positions on both banks (flanks?) about Givenchy and Fleurbaix. At both these latter places there was heavy fighting, but the enemy was repulsed.

Richebourg-St. Vaast and Laventie have been taken by the enemy.

Severe fighting is continuing on the whole of this front.

South of Arras only minor engagements, in which were secured a few prisoners, have taken place during the day on the British front.

The afternoon official statement reads:

Early this morning the enemy's artillery developed great activity on the front extending from La Bassée Canal to south of Armentières.

Elsewhere on the British front, except for heavy hostile shelling in the neighborhood of Villers-Bretonneux and Mericourt l'Abbé, there was nothing special to report.

Monday's Rain Checked Aviation.

The following official communication dealing with aviation was issued this evening:

With the exception of a few flights at low altitudes, there was no flying Monday, owing to the mist and rain. One hostile balloon was downed. None of our airplanes is missing.

Germans Made Early Gains.

WITH THE BRITISH ARMY IN FRANCE, April 9. (Associated Press.) —Another sector of the British front suddenly developed intense fighting today, when the Germans delivered a heavy attack over approximately an eleven-mile front between Givenchy (near La Bassée) and a point east of Fleurbaix, just below Armentières. A Portuguese sector is included in the line involved.

East of Le Plantin and east of Petillon the enemy appeared to have gained a footing in advanced defenses, according to the latest reports, and a fierce battle was raging all along the sector. Le Plantin is northwest of Givenchy, and Petillon lies to the east of Laventie.

At Givenchy and on the left of the front attacked the Allies apparently are holding their ground in the very heavy fighting, which was reported to be especially bitter east of Festubert. The Portuguese were being supported by British troops.

The attack was preceded by a violent bombardment, which began in the early morning and extended all along the front affected. Bethune, Estaires, and other towns behind the British lines have been heavily shelled.

It is too early to say what relation this new move has with the main German offensive further south. Only time will tell whether it was undertaken as a diversion or whether the enemy has a serious idea of pushing forward here.

GREAT GAS ATTACK BY FOE

More Than 60,000 Poison Shells Rained on British During the Night.

SEVERAL TOWNS UNDER FIRE

Portuguese, Who Hold Part of Line, Sustain Fierce Onslaughts Gallantly.

BATTLE ON FAMOUS GROUND

Germans Hampered by Bad Weather and Bad Terrain for Their Offensive.

By PHILIP GIBBS.
Copyright, 1918, by The New York Times Company.
Special Cable to THE NEW YORK TIMES.

WAR CORRESPONDENTS' HEADQUARTERS IN FRANCE, April 9.—A heavy and determined attack was begun against us this morning a considerable distance north of our recent battles on about eleven miles of front between Armentières and La Bassée Canal. So far as the news comes to us up to this afternoon the enemy apparently has succeeded in driving in parts of the Allies' post lines, while the troops are holding him by Givenchy on the right and about Fleurbaix on the left.

This new attack was preceded by a long, concentrated bombardment, which had gradually been increasing during the last day or two, until it reached great heights of fury last night and early this morning. The

In this photo American soldiers are using "gas flappers" to remove heavy gasses from a trench.

enemy used poison gas in immense quantities, and it may be estimated that during the night he flung over 60,000 gas shells in order to create a wide zone of this evil vapor and stupefy the gunners, transport, and infantry if they were caught without their masks, which is improbable.

His gunfire reached out to many towns and villages behind the allied lines, like Bethune and Armentières, Vermelles and Philosophe, Merville and Estaires, and this did not cease around Armentières until 11:30 this morning, though further south from Fleurbaix his infantry attack was in progress at an early hour, certainly by 8 o'clock, and his barrage lifted in order to let his troops advance.

The strength of his attack is not yet known with any certainty, but three divisions are in that area, including the 44th Reserve and 81st and 11th Ersatz, and it is probable that he has other forces engaged.

Portuguese Troops in Line.

Part of the line was held by Portuguese troops, who for a long time have been between Laventie and Neuve Chapelle, holding positions which were subject to severe raids from time to time. They are now in the thick of this battle, most fiercely beset and fighting gallantly.

It is a battle over the old and famous ground where early in this war there was most deadly strife during the struggle around Neuve Chapelle in March of 1915 and at Festubert. It is ground where the Indian infantry attacked again and again with most gallant courage and where afterward the survivors held the lines through the Spring and Summer, so that the flat fields all around with fringes of willows along narrow canals that intersect all this moist land and the villages behind, like Estaires and Laventie, and places of ruin like La Gorgue and Richebourg and Quinque Rues, will be forever haunted with memories of those dark-dyed men, who to the French peasants seemed like fairy princes and figures out of the Arabian Nights tales. They disappeared long ago through the mists of these flats to other fighting fields in other countries.

Suddenly the enemy has struck, and the centre of strife for the moment has shifted. It is awkward ground for attack and bad weather for such

ground, because the enemy has to advance across dead-flat marshes, cut through and through by an intricate system of canals, which must be all flooded now, after the heavy rain and the shellfire which has broken their banks.

Enemy Checked in Marshes.

All the enemy's efforts this morning do not seem to have carried him far through these marshes, and up to the time I write his storm troops are being held back and shattered by machine-gun fire before Givenchy, outside an outpost in the marshes, a sap, and a place called Picanty, in front of Laventie. If he gets no further,

his venture will be futile except as a demonstration in order to weaken our reserves by further casualties and increase the strain on our main defense.

Meanwhile his own losses must be reaching prodigious figures. Today again many of his men lie dead in those swamps by Neuve Chapelle.

AIRMEN BROKE UP GERMAN ATTACKS

Flew as Low as 68 Feet and Rained Bullets on Infantry Near Montdidier.

BAYLIES, DOWNED, ESCAPED

American Sergeant Fell Almost Into Enemy's Hands, but Got Back Amid Cheers.

From a Staff Correspondent.
Copyright, 1918, by The New York Times Company

Special Cable to THE NEW YORK TIMES.

WITH THE FRENCH ARMIES, April 9.—Although the American infantry is not in action on the Picardy battlefield, the United States has been represented in the air from the outset of the German drive. Many American aviators serving under the French flag have been engaged in battle. A NEW YORK TIMES correspondent met today Sergeant Frank Baylies, from New Bedford, a member of the famous "Ace squadrilla" of storks to which Guynemer belonged.

Soldiers weren't the only fighters that needed protection from poisonous gasses, as shown in this photo of a cavalryman and his horse.

Baylies joined the aviation service last June after two years in Macedonia with the French Red Cross, for which he was decorated with the War Cross with star, became a member of the Stork squadrilla Oct. 1, a few days after Guynemer's death, and has brought down two Germans for which he has been rewarded with two palms on the cross. Shortly after the opening of the German offensive the squadrilla went by air at an hour's notice to Montdidier and took active part in all subsequent operations.

When the town was captured by the enemy the airmen managed to remove all the machines and camions, but several fliers lost the greater part of their personal effects. Baylies was more fortunate.

Throughout the French retirement the airmen co-operated with the infantry and made three patrol flights—averaging from an hour and a half to two hours' duration—daily. As the German attacks were made almost without artillery or airplanes—for whole days no enemy planes were sighted—the fliers devoted themselves to harassing enemy infantry and convoys on the march.

Flew Low for Attacks.

Flying often as low as sixty-eight feet, airmen turned mitrailleuses point-blank on the enemy, who fled headlong or threw themselves flat to escape the stream of bullets. When convoys were attacked, horses plunging madly in death agony threw the whole line into confusion.

At such an altitude the aviator was greatly exposed to the fire of the German infantry, and injury to the motor forced an immediate landing, as the height was insufficient for a long volplane. On March 28 Baylies was thus downed near Mesnil-St. Georges. The young American—he is just 22—gave the following description of his experience:

"I had been annoying Fritz all morning and having a wonderful time when I spotted a body of infantry moving toward Tickish Wood just after luncheon. As I dived upon them over the trees, quickfirers concealed there riddled my machine with bullets. My impetus luckily carried me a little further into a grassy field, just between the two armies, where I landed not too abruptly.

"Unfortunately I was barely fifty feet from the boches and nearly a hundred yards from the French. At this point there were no trenches and both sides fought in the open, the Germans advancing in small groups from thicket to thicket and taking cover wherever possible. As they saw me falling the enemy began firing furiously and a party of five Germans ran out to intercept me. A French Alpine Chasseur shot one dead and an infantry quickfirer drove the rest to cover. Just the same, I never covered a hundred yards faster in my life with bullets buzzing around me like angry wasps.

Dashing French Attack.

"The French cheered in delight when I threw myself down among them unhurt, and I stayed with them till night and saw them make a counterattack that afternoon, when they advanced two kilometres. Though many of them had been fighting several days without rest, they charged forward in splendid style. All were supremely confident that they could beat the boche, and kept saying, 'Wait. You'll soon see the whole lot retreat.'

"Next morning I got another machine and began again as before."

In the last few weeks the Storks have accounted for a great number of Germans officially corroborated and nearly as many whose fall it has been impossible to check up.

GERMANS' GREAT GUN BOMBARDED BY FRENCH

Long-Range Piece Discovered by Airmen—Continual Attacks Hamper Its Handling.

PARIS, April 9.—French aviators have discovered the location of the big gun with which the Germans have been bombarding Paris at long range. Continual bombardment of the spot by French artillery and bombing by airmen have made the handling of the great piece difficult. This explains the intermittent fire of the long-range weapon.

The piece is mounted at Crepy-en-Laonnois, near the road from La Fere to Laon. (The spot is eight miles southeast of La Fere and about seventy-five miles from Paris.)

A reply to Cardinal Farley's message of sympathy in connection with the German long-distance bombardment of a Paris church on Good Friday, in which seventy-five persons were killed, was received yesterday from Cardinal Amette, Archbishop of Paris. The message follows:

"I hasten to thank your eminence and the Catholics of New York for their sympathy, their prayers and the generous resolutions which the sacrilegious deed of Good Friday has inspired them to make. I am confident that the Almighty will heed your vows and prayers in favor of the cause which unites us and which more than ever proves itself to be the cause of justice and of Christian civilization."

DAYS OF BIG ODDS OVER FOR FRENCH

Terrific Casualties Begin to Tell on the Force of German Blows.

LONG "BATTLES OF ARREST"

Germans Paid Ruinous Price for Gains, While French Economized in Men.

By G. H. PERRIS.

Copyright, 1918, by The New York Times Company.

Special Cable to THE NEW YORK TIMES.

WITH THE FRENCH ARMIES, April 8.—Apart from a local attack at Grivesnes, which completely failed on Saturday evening, there has been, up to this morning, no further action on the French front in Santerre. The loss of force in the German offensive is noteworthy, but not at all surprising. An unprecedented mass having been prepared to deliver a swift and crushing blow, enormous losses do not at once arrest it, but everything in such an adventure depends upon rapid success. The original mass, prodigally spent and yet not successful, has lost its freshness, and passed its maximum strength just when the more economical adversary is reaching his maximum. What the latter has lost in ground he has saved in men; and, on the other hand, the enemy, who wanted not these miles of desolate territory, but a final decision, has paid inordinately without getting any nearer the desired result.

For five days his advance, though somewhat behind his ambitious program, was not seriously interrupted. On March 23 a certain General reached the region of Montdidier and began to build a human barrier. On March 27 began what may be called a four days' battle of arrest. Three French divisions had to meet and did meet the onset of fifteen German divisions. There were smaller units that fought one against ten.

Attacked with 150,000 Men.

The main German effort was against the Moreuil-Grivesnes-Montchel line, the object being (with 150,000 men in play there could be no less ambitious aim) to break right through to the south of Amiens and completely separate the French and British Armies. It culminated on the 31st with a suicidal assault by the pick of the Prussian Guards and other chosen divisions at Grivesnes, when a certain gallant Colonel, rifle in hand, directed the barricading of the windows of the château, and with not more than 500 men kept off three or four times as many assailants and had strength enough left at last to sweep those who remained out of the park.

I need not measure again the trivial gain for the enemy of this four days' battle. Perhaps the most significant fact about it is that while, overwhelming as was his original force, the enemy had repeatedly to withdraw and renew his units, not one French unit was relieved in that time. At Mesnil St. Georges one infantry battalion, with some groups of chasseurs, drove off five successive attacks by a whole German division. I might multiply such instances, but space would fail me to make them real with detail.

A pause of four days followed this failure. Then, on April 4, twelve divisions were again launched in the northern part of the same narrow field—10,000 men per mile of front. They won at great cost the ruins of two hamlets and a slice of fields beside them. Three days more have passed without any considerable development. Prisoners say all leave has been stopped in the German armies. Men are not allowed to write home, and official bulletins are no longer read to the troops.

Needn't Struggle Against Odds Now.

What I know from sure sources is that, while General Foch hoards his reserves, not merely to have a mass for manoeuvre in hand when the time is ripe, but to save the manifold wastage of superfluous men in the front lines, the days of struggle against odds have gone by, and that means that the German opportunity has gone, too.

Among the minor actions there are two which deserve mention. The French position on Mont Renaud, near Noyon, has been maintained against repeated attacks preceded by heavy bombardments. I have described this lately. It was a pleasant little hill, with its country house and farm hidden in a clump of trees. Its importance is very slight, for it is overlooked by the hills on the north and northwest, held by the enemy, as well as by the French heights west of Chiry. It is a local observatory, useful for its view over Noyon—that is all; and, German bulletins to the contrary notwithstanding, it has been bravely and continuously kept since the end of last month.

A final word about the position of the armies between St. Gobain Forest and the Oise. Here the German advance left the French in a somewhat dangerous corner, reaching as far north as Deuillet, with the Germans across the river on the west, and in the great forest block on the east. A retirement to the line of the Ailette and the canal running beside it was clearly advisable. The new front was already prepared when the Germans attacked in strength on Saturday afternoon, between Chauny and Barisis. North of the Ailette there remained only light detachments, and these retired after taking toll of their assailants. The front now runs from Renaud across the Oise and up the south bank to near Abbecourt, whence it turns southeast.

AMERICANS TO JOIN IN BIG BATTLE SOON

Assistant Secretary Crowell Announces That They Are Not Yet in the Fighting.

HAVE 1,000 AIRPLANES NOW

Machines Obtained from French and Italians, He States—Expects Long Battle.

WASHINGTON, April 9.—American troops have not yet gone into battle in Picardy, Acting Secretary of War Crowell announced tonight in an address to the National Conference of American Lecturers.

He added, however, that indications were that in the near future General Pershing's men would be actively opposing the Germans in their supreme effort on the western front.

The purpose of the German high command in its thrust, Mr. Crowell said, is to drive a wedge between the British and French armies, roll up the former force to the sea, and capture the Channel ports. No Bavarian or Austrian troops have been employed in the battle, the speaker asserted, the German leaders depending upon the Prussian troops, the flower of their army, to carry through to victory.

"The situation will be serious for a long time," Mr. Crowell declared. "The Germans have been going well, and only heavy rainstorms have prevented them from making further progress."

Turning his attention to the nation's much-discussed airplane program, Mr. Crowell said that there were more than 1,000 qualified American army fliers in France and that 1,000 machines had been procured from the French and Italians.

"When you hear of American soldiers defending themselves from German airplanes with their pistols, you need not believe it," the speaker said.

André Tardieu, French High Commissioner to the United States, addressing the conference this afternoon, said that to crush the German military machine allied unity must extend beyond military commands, that it must be applied to war supplies, to food, and to shipping.

"The first duty is national unity," said M. Tardieu. "Follow your chief. Act like one single man. Forget political struggles. We have done it, you will do it. The second duty is inter-allied unity. It has been effected as far as military command is concerned, but is not enough. The same unity must be truly and practically carried out for all other purposes, such as war supplies, food, shipping. This has not yet been done; it must be done. The third duty is the unity of feeling and understanding as to the conditions of victory."

France has been able to furnish the American forces with artillery, machine guns and airplanes, M. Tardieu said, and thus America has been allowed a sufficient length of time to organise and to start her own production along that line.

In telling of the sacrifices that France has made and is making the High Commissioner said that 1,300,000 French soldiers had been killed in action or died of wounds, and that another 1,000,000 had been maimed, invalided or captured.

PEKING HEARS JAPAN MAKES NEW DEMANDS

Sending of 200,000 Troops Into China to Restore Order Said to be Included.

PEKING, April 4, (Associated Press.) —It is reported in semi-official circles that Japan has proposed to send 200,000 troops to China to co-operate with 200,000 Chinese troops, officered by the Japanese, to restore order throughout China and protect the borders. The alternative is that Japan will dispatch troops to Shantung and Fukien Provinces for the protection of Japanese interests.

It is said also that Japan has submitted a new series of demands to China, including the complete control of China's finances, purchase of 50 per cent. of ammunition to be made in Japan, operation of iron mines and dockyards under Japanese control, and recognition of special Japanese interests in Mongolia, the same as in Manchuria.

The proposal is said to have been submitted by Baron Sakatani, the new financial adviser to China, and Baron Hayashi, Japanese Minister to China, at a conference with the President and Premier Tuan Chi-Jui. It is believed that part of the plan is the reorganisation of China's currency on the basis of a Chino-Japanese financial alliance, which is alleged to be the object of the presence in Peking of Baron Sakatani as the head of a group of leading Japanese bankers.

"All the News That's Fit to Print."

The New York Times.

THE WEATHER
Generally fair today and Sunday; gentle north to northeast winds.
For full weather report see Page 21.

VOL. LXVII...NO. 22,001. ...   NEW YORK, SATURDAY, APRIL 20, 1918.—TWENTY-TWO PAGES.   TWO CENTS In Greater New York and | THREE CENTS

GERMAN ADVANCE IS STOPPED BY APPALLING SLAUGHTER; EXHAUSTED BY THEIR EFFORTS, BUT BRING UP MORE GUNS; ITALIAN ARMY JOINS ALLIES, WILL SOON BE IN BATTLE

ITALIANS FORM RIGHT WING

Orlando Stirs Deputies to Enthusiasm by the Official Announcement.

500,000   MEN   AVAILABLE

Experts Say They Could Be Sent Without Endangering the Home Front.

SPEEDING UP AMERICAN AID

Troops Going Overseas More Rapidly — 2,200,000 Men Under Arms by July.

Special to The New York Times.

WASHINGTON, April 19.—Announcement was made by the Italian Embassy today that Italian troops had been sent to France and would soon be engaged in battle on the French front. In making the announcement the embassy gave out a wireless message which it had received from Rome saying that Italian Premier Orlando had announced the fact at the opening of Parliament. The news that Italian troops were in France came as a surprise only to those who had not for two weeks been aware that the decision had been reached to send Italian reinforcements to France.

This has been done in accordance with the plan of the Entente War Council at Versailles to treat the entire western front as an entity, from the Channel to the Adriatic, and to employ all the energies of the four leading allied nations wherever they may be most needed or best used. This joint use of the British, French, American, and Italian forces under the supreme direction of General Foch has developed a greater flexibility in the use of the troops of these four nations, and is expected from now on to have a most important bearing on plans now being shaped for taking the offensive away from the Germans at the proper moment.

The embassy's announcement today fully confirms the Washington dispatch printed in THE NEW YORK TIMES on April 5, in which it was asserted that Italian troops had been sent to France for use as part of the great interallied army commanded by General Foch. In that dispatch the statement was made that "the reserve army of the Allies, which was decided upon by the Entente War Council at Versailles, is composed of units from the armies of all the allied nations represented along the western front," and also that "it not only embraces many thousands of British and French soldiers, but contains large Italian contingents," besides the American forces placed at the disposal of General Foch when he accepted General Pershing's offer of American men and resources.

GERMAN LOSSES STAGGERING

Massacre Reaches a Height of Horror Rarely Recorded in History.

ASSAULTS IN NORTH WEAK

Attack on Large Scale Abandoned Where French Are Fighting with the British.

BELGIANS FOUGHT WITH JOY

Went Into Battle Singing and Waving Their Helmets to Their Airmen.

By PHILIP GIBBS.

Copyright, 1918, by The New York Times Company.

Special Cable to THE NEW YORK TIMES.

WAR CORRESPONDENTS' HEADQUARTERS, Friday, April 19.—How long is this massacre going on? It is reaching heights of horror which the world has hardly seen in its history. The senselessness of it makes one despair of humanity, for what do these Germans hope to gain out of all this sacrifice, these field-gray men who come swarming upon the British lines wave after wave, gaining ground or not gaining ground, but always leaving a wake of dead and dying and mangled men behind them?

The German High Command is out for victory and domination at all costs, save that of their own skins and blood, but not even the full and brutal victory which they are failing to gain would give any increase of comfort or any forgetfulness of agony to these German soldiers who are sent into that car-

nage. Yet it goes on and will go on until even they revolt from the increasing slaughter.

A Black Day for the Enemy.

It was a black day for the enemy yesterday all along the line of his attack between Robecq and Givenchy, and especially at the southern end by Givenchy itself, where he made desperate efforts to gain British defenses on the high ground there.

In my first account yesterday I described how he flung five hours of bombardment on the British lines—the noise of it and of the answering guns was stupendous when I went up that part of the countryside—and how he then attacked in heavy strength, being repulsed almost everywhere with staggering losses.

At the end of the day all his efforts ended in bloody failure, in spite of the daring and courage of his troops, who sacrificed themselves under the British fire, but were only able to gain a few bits of trench work and one or two outposts below the fortified works at Givenchy, which are quite useless to them for immediate or future use.

It was a big attack, for which they had prepared in a formidable way. After the shock of their repulse by the Lancashire men of the 55th Division, which I described in detail, they increased their strength of heavy artillery by three times bringing up large numbers of howitzers, including eleven-inch monsters.

They were massed in divisions in front of us and determined to smash through in the wake of a tremendous bombardment.

Pluck of British Under Fire.

For five hours, as I said, this storm went on with high explosives and gas, and the devoted British had to suffer this infernal thing, the worst ordeal human beings may be called upon to bear, this standing to

while all the earth upheaved and the was thick with shell splinters.

But when the bombardment had passed and the German infantry came forward the British received them with blasts of machine gun fire, incessant volleys of rifle fire, and a trench mortar bombardment that burst with the deadliest effect among the attacking troops.

This trench mortar barrage of the British was one of the most awful means of slaughter yesterday, especially when the enemy tried to cross La Bassée Canal further north, and in that sector the infantry and gunner officers say more Germans were killed yesterday along the canal bank than on any other day since the fighting in this neighborhood. One battery of trench mortars did most deadly execution until their pits were surrounded, and only two of their crews were able to escape.

The machine gunners fought out in the open after some of their positions had been wiped out by gunfire, caught the enemy waves at fifty yards' range, and mowed them down; but the enemy was not checked for a long time, despite his losses, and when one body fell another came up to fill its place and press on into any gap that had been made by their artillery or their own machine gun sections.

Gap Stopped by Scottish Troops.

There was one such momentary gap between a body of the Black Watch who had been weakened by shellfire and some of their comrades further north, and into this the enemy tried to force a way. Other Scottish troops were in reserve, and when it became clear that a portion of the line was endangered by this turning movement they came forward with grim intent, and by a fierce counterattack swept through the gap and flung back the enemy, so that the position was restored.

Further north some Gloucesters

were fighting the enemy both ways, as once before in history when they fought back to back, thereby winning the honor of wearing their cap badge back and front, which they do to this day. The Germans had worked behind them as well as in front of them, and they were in a tight corner, but did not yield, and finally after hard fighting cleared the ground about them.

Meanwhile further south some Lancashire troops on the canal lost some parts of their front line under an intense bombardment, but still fought on in the open, repulsing every effort to drive them back and smashing the enemy out of their positions so that only remnants of the German outposts clung on until late last night, up to which time there was savage strife on both sides.

Headquarters Staff in Fight.

At one time, I hear, there was fierce hand-to-hand fighting around one of the British battalion headquarters to which the Germans had penetrated, and a gallant and successful defense was made by the servants and staff.

Elsewhere in yesterday's battle Welshmen fought stubbornly and with the greatest gallantry in hours most critical for British success. Along this line they were fighting in small parties, holding on to isolated bits of ground and rallying to counterattack when the enemy got a footing in the forward lines. The battle spread up northward over a wide front, and on another sector of the line some of the English battalions engaged the enemy's masses and destroyed them so utterly that at the end of the day they had gained nothing after terrible casualties on their side.

Part of this fighting was around the farm called Riez du Vinage, where a day or two ago, as I recorded, some British troops made a dashing attack and captured prisoners and machine guns. The attack north of Givenchy was at a different time from that down south It began at 4 o'clock in the morning, took place in half darkness, and was all over by 7 o'clock, when the German troops were beaten and demoralized by the severity of their losses. In Pacant Wood, near by, their assemblies were raked by machine gun fire, and when they left the wood many others fell. One column of assault drove into the hamlet of Riez du Vinage, and the British in those sectors were forced to retire a little, and afterward drew back to another line for a chance to counterattack.

Extraordinary scenes took place on the canal bank when the enemy tried to cross. In the twilight of early dawn a party came out of a wood and tried to get across the water, but was seen by the British machine gunners and shot down.

Then another body of men advanced and carried with them a floating bridge, but when those who were not hit reached the water's edge they found the bridge as fixed did not reach to the other side. Some of them walked on it, expecting perhaps to jump the gap, but were shot off, and other men on the bank also were caught under British fire.

A Corporal went down to the canal

edge and flung hand grenades at the Germans still struggling to fix the bridge, and then a Lieutenant and a few men rushed down and pulled the bridge on to their side of the bank.

Swam to Catch a Pontoon.

Later this young officer saw one of the British pontoons drifting down and swam to it and made it fast beyond the enemy's reach, but in a position so that some of his men ran across and caught the enemy under their fire on his side of the canal.

At 7 o'clock yesterday morning, while a handkerchief was hoisted by the enemy, three hundred of them made signs of surrender. Some of them changed their minds at the last moment and ran away, but 150 gave themselves up, and some of them swam the canal in order to reach our side for this purpose. They were shivering in their wet clothes and in the northeast wind, which lashed over the battle lines yesterday, and they were very miserable men.

Yesterday evening it was decided to recapture the ground which, as I have said, had been left in enemy hands near Riez du Vinage, and this attack succeeded easily this morning. The patrols went out gathering up odd men and small parties of the enemy as prisoners. In this sector they had lost all stomach for fight, having suffered fearful things since they had been in line from the British artillery fire and the defense of the troops. Many of them were hungry, having been six days on two days' rations, and they bemoan the losses of their companies and battalions.

The Fourth Ersatz Division, for instance, was severely mauled in the battles of the first phase of the German offensive, and was then sent further north, where, according to a prisoner's letter, they devoutly hoped for a rest on a quiet sector after their blood bath, but while the letter was still in the man's pocket and while he and his comrades were marching up to Merville, this new battle was being ordered by the German commanders, and these poor wretches were flung in without ing.

They say the harassing fire of the British on the ground and camps in all the country between Armentières and La Bassée was simply fearful and that during the whole long night their transport and working parties, thousands of men, working feverishly on roadmaking with concrete slabs, were slashed to pieces, while there was never any rest or safety for them.

Six German divisions were engaged yesterday. All of them suffered many casualties, so for some time, at least, until they recover from the shock which the British gave them, the heart has been knocked out of them.

Up in the north between Wytschaete and Bailleul, where the French are fighting with the British, there were no further attacks on a big scale after the preparatory efforts to capture Kemmel Hill, which were easily repulsed yesterday. The enemy probably is pausing before striking another blow with full weight by troops specially trained to

hill fighting, like the Jaegers, the 11th Bavarians, and the Alpine Corps from the mountain districts of Germany.

The Alpine troops so far have not indulged their spirits with plunder on a big scale, which is their intention, as revealed in one of their letters.

"We made up our minds," wrote one of them, "to plunder ruthlessly, and that is the beauty of the whole thing. In the Alpine Corps we understand the business."

Meanwhile, in the north the Belgians are justly elated over the brilliant success wherein they attacked and captured 700 of the enemy. According to the account of Belgian officers their gallant troops went into action singing and waving helmets

to salute their flying men who flew low overhead, and every man was uplifted by enthusiasm.

The enemy was hard hit by them. He will get more such knocks from the armies of England, France, and Belgium now barring his path.

AMERICANS IN RAID INFLICT LOSSES

Find Bodies of Several of Foe in Wire Where Our Barrage Had Caught Them.

22 DIED IN CAREY FIGHT

Two American Officers and 20 Enlisted Men Fell in Opposing German Advance.

WITH THE AMERICAN ARMY IN FRANCE, April 19. (Associated Press.)— Thirty American infantrymen, with the same number of French troops, raided the German line on the right bank of the Meuse this morning, inflicting a number of casualties on the enemy.

The Americans found the enemy trenches empty, but saw the bodies of several Germans in the American wire, apparently members of a working party who had been caught in the American barrage.

The enemy laid down a counterbarrage soon after the American barrage started, but all the Americans returned safely to their trenches.

American gunners in France. In one the men await the enemy, in the other, they are in the heat of battle.

"All the News That's Fit to Print."

The New York Times.

THE WEATHER

Showers, cooler today; tomorrow cloudy; south to westerly winds.

VOL. LXVII...NO. 22,011. ... NEW YORK, TUESDAY, APRIL 30, 1918.—TWENTY-FOUR PAGES. TWO CENTS In Greater New York and THREE CENTS Within Commuting Distance Elsewhere

VON ARNIM'S ARMY DISASTROUSLY DEFEATED IN ALL-DAY ASSAULT ON A 15-MILE FRONT; MOWED DOWN IN MASSES, NO GROUND GAINED

FOE'S DEFEAT DISASTROUS

"Great Offensive Troops," Hurled Wave on Wave, Are Cut to Pieces.

MAKE NO GAIN ANYWHERE

Masses of Men Sacrificed by von Arnim in Attempt to Take Chain of Hillocks.

FIRE WITHERS ALL ATTACKS

French Centre and British Wings Hold Firm After Terrific All-Night Bombardment.

By PHILIP GIBBS.

Copyright, 1918, by The New York Times Company.

Special Cable to THE NEW YORK TIMES.

[Supplementary Dispatch from Mr. Gibbs.]

WAR CORRESPONDENTS' HEADQUARTERS, Monday, April 29—Evening.—It becomes clearer every hour that the enemy suffered a disastrous defeat today. Attack after attack was smashed up by the British artillery and infantry, and he has not made a foot of ground on the British front.

The Border Regiment this morning repulsed four heavy assaults on the Kemmel-La Clytte road, where there was extremely hard fighting, and destroyed the enemy each time.

One of the enemy's main thrusts was between Scherpenberg and Mont Rouge, where they made a wedge for a time and captured the crossroads, and it was here that a gallant French counterattack swept them back.

The British had no more than a post or two in Voormezeele this morning, and the enemy was there in greater strength, and sent his storm troops through this place, but was never able to advance against the fire of the English battalions.

Meet Massed Death in Fog.

His losses began yesterday, when his troops were seen massing on the road between Zillebeke and Ypres in a dense fog, through which he attempted to make a surprise attack. This was observed by low-flying planes, and his assembly was shat-

tered by gunfire. After a fierce shelling all night, so tremendous along the whole northern front that the countryside was shaken by its tumult, German troops again assembled in the early morning mist, but were caught once more in the British bombardment.

At 3 o'clock a tremendous barrage was flung down by the German gunners from Ypres to Bailleul, and later they began the battle by launching first an attack between Zillebeke Lake and Meteren. South of Ypres they crossed the Yser Canal by Lock 8, near Voormezeele, which was their direction of attack against the British, while they tried to drive up past Locre against the French on the three hills.

The successful defense has made the day most bloody for many German regiments.

Furious Night Bombardment.

[Mr. Gibbs's Earlier Dispatch.]

WAR CORRESPONDENTS' HEADQUARTERS, Monday, April 29—Afternoon.—There was violent, widespread gunfire all last night from the enemy's batteries from the Belgian front down through Flanders to the districts about Bethune, and this morning the German bombardment was intensified to heights of fury all around Ypres, and upon the British lines near Voormezeele and Vierstraat and against the French front west of Kemmel Hill to the country south of Dranoutre, where the British troops join them again.

Then began, about 6 o'clock this morning, that attack which was the inevitable plan of General Sixte von Arnim after the capture of Kemmel Hill; that is, an attempt in strong force to gain the chain of hillocks running westward below Ypres and

Poperinghe, and known to all of us as familiar landmarks—the Scherpenberg, Mont Rouge, and Mont Noir. These hills, forming the central keep, as it were, in the allied defensive lines south of Ypres, are held by the French and are of great tactical importance at the present moment, so that the enemy covets them and is ready to sacrifice thousands of men to get them.

Plan of the High Command.

In order to turn them if frontal attacks failed against the French, German storm troops—they are now called grosskampf, or great offensive troops—were to break the British lines on the French left between Locre and Voormezeele and on the French right near Merris and Meteren. That obviously was the intention of the German High Command this morning, judging from their direction of assault.

So far they have failed utterly. They failed to break or bend the British wings on the French centre, and they failed to capture the hills, or any one of them, defended by the French divisions.

They have attacked again and again since this morning's dawn, heavy forces of German infantry being sent forward after their first wave against Scherpenberg and Voormezeele, which lies to the east of Dickebusch Lake, but these men have been slaughtered by the French and British fire and make no important progress at any point.

For a time the situation seemed critical at one or two points, and it was reported that the Germans had been storming the slopes of Mont Rouge and Mont Noir, but one of the British airmen flew over those hills

at 200 feet above their crests, and could see no German infantry near them.

Round about Voormezeele, North Country and other English battalions had to sustain determined and furious efforts of Alpine and Bavarian troops to drive through them by weight of numbers, after hours of intense bombardment, but the men held their ground and inflicted severe punishment upon the enemy.

All through the day the German losses have been heavy under field-gun and machine-gun fire, and the British batteries, alongside the French seventy-fives, swept down the enemy's advancing waves and his masses assembled in support at short range.

Counterattack Restores Line.

There is no doubt that the French guarding the three hills have fought with extreme valor and skill. For a brief period the Germans apparently were able to draw near and take some of the ground near Locre, but an immediate counterattack was organized by the French General, and the line of French troops swung forward and swept the enemy back. Further attacks by the Germans north of Ypres and on the Belgian front were repulsed easily, and again the enemy lost many men.

The battle continues, but the first phase of it has been decided in our favor, and it has been another day of sacrifice for the German regiments, who, one by one, as they come up fresh to reinforce their battle line, lose a high percentage of strength in this continuing slaughter. The German High Command still has many divisions untouched, but their turn will come, and if, as today, they are spent without great gain, the enemy's plans of a decisive victory will be thwarted forever.

There is a limit even to German man power, and surely their people will tire of making these fields of France and Flanders the graveyard of their youth. This frenzy must pass from them and from our stricken world when the truth comes home to them at last.

German Official Report Ignores Flanders Repulse, But Tells of Checking Attacks "Against Hangard"

BERLIN, April 29, (via London.)—The announcement from General Headquarters today says:

On the Flanders battlefront from midday on the artillery fire revived.

The booty taken since the storming of Mont Kemmel has increased to over 7,100 prisoners, including 181 officers, 53 guns, and 233 machine guns.

Between La Bassée Canal and the Scarpe, as well as north of the Somme, there has been lively reconnoitring activity on the part of the English.

Strong partial attacks made by the French against Hangard Wood and the village were sanguinarily repulsed.

Forefield engagements occurred at many points on the remainder of the front.

On the eastern bank of the Meuse a thrust into the French trenches brought in some prisoners.

The French forces recaptured part of Hangard and Hangard Wood on Friday.

Berlin Dreams of Fleet Ready To "Take British Army Home"

LONDON, April 29.—A Reuter dispatch from Stockholm says that the Aftonbladet publishes, and one or two other papers repeat, a telegram from Zurich, by way of Berlin, to the effect that "an entire fleet of British transports is waiting in the Channel to take the British Army home in case of need."

On inquiry of the Admiralty, Reuter's Agency was informed that the statement contained in the aforementioned telegram "is absolutely devoid of any foundation whatever."

The New York Times.

"All the News That's Fit to Print."

THE WEATHER
Fair until Sunday, warmer tonight;
diminishing northwest winds.
For full weather report see Page 18.

VOL. LXVII...NO. 22,012. ...   NEW YORK, THURSDAY, MAY 2, 1918.—TWENTY-FOUR PAGES.   TWO CENTS In Greater New York and   THREE CENTS Elsewhere

AMERICANS WIN FIRST FIGHT ON AMIENS FRONT; REPEL FOE WITH LARGE LOSSES ON BOTH SIDES; VON ARNIM REORGANIZING HIS BROKEN FORCES

BRITISH GUARDS SAVED DAY

Fighting Back to Back They-Held Line for 48 Hours, as Ordered.

THEN AUSTRALIANS CAME

First News That Famous Brigade Was in Battle Records Heroic Exploit.

FOE BUSY BURYING DEAD

Broken Divisions Being Replaced by Fresh Troops for Another Assault.

By PHILIP GIBBS.
Copyright, 1918, by The New York Times Company.
Special Cable to THE NEW YORK TIMES.

WAR CORRESPONDENTS' HEADQUARTERS, Wednesday, May 1.—The Germans are very quiet in their lines since they were repulsed so utterly in their attacks against Scherpenberg and the British lines around Ypres. Even their guns were not very active last night, and today they are burying their dead and getting back their wounded, and taking the broken divisions out of the line to replace them with fresh troops for another battle.

I believe that will happen, because now that the enemy has Kemmel Hill his temptation to seize the three hills below is predominant, and there is no doubt that he will again risk the loss of many men to gain these positions. From the political point of view Ypres is also a lure to him, and there would be a great blowing of trumpets in Germany if their troops could capture that city of the salient, which as a name and a ruin is the great shrine of the British Army in this war.

Now that the French are with the British to strengthen the latter's defensive power, which has sustained such furious onslaughts by over 100 German divisions since six weeks ago, the next battle in Flanders may not give the enemy any further ground than the day before yesterday, which was nothing at all, and it is certain, anyhow, that not a yard of it will be yielded until the next waves of German soldiers have paid great ... s of life.

Foe Used Two Mo . Divisions.

In the last battle two additional divisions have now been identified as having been put in against the British front in Flanders, one being the 117th, near Voormezeele, and the other the 3d Guards Division, including the Maikaefer, or Cockchafers, whom the Welsh regiments shattered at Pilkem last year and who have fought against the British in the Cambrai salient.

Last night, when no doubt German reliefs were in progress, the British guns turned loose with shrapnel and high explosives upon the transport and troops crowding the track from Vierstraat to Wytschaete, and this morning the enemy had more dead to bury. So the slaughter goes on.

During a rare day without great news there is an opportunity of writing a few words about some of the British battalions who in the earlier fighting during these recent battles were wonderful in courage and endurance and self-sacrifice, but have not yet appeared in our narratives because for a time it was inadvisable to mention their presence in the battleline. They are battalions of Guards. There is no need for secrecy now, because the enemy met them at close quarters and knows how these men fought, sometimes in small bodies almost to the last man.

The recent history of the Guards begins with the battle of Arras on March 28, when the 56th London one of his comrades was dead or wounded, and for twenty minutes after that—twenty minutes of those forty-eight hours—kept the Germans back with his rifle until he was killed by a bomb.

Bought Each Minute With Blood.

Forty-eight hours is a long time in a war like this. For two days and nights the Irish Guards who had come up to support the Grenadiers and Coldstreamers tried to make a defensive flank, but the enemy worked past their right and attacked them on two sides. The Irish Guards were gaining time. They knew that was all they could do, just drag out the hours by buying each minute with their blood. One man fell and then another; but minutes were gained, and quarters of hours, and hours.

Small parties of them lowered their bayonets and went out among the gray wolves swarming around them, and killed a number of them until they also fell. First one party and then another of these Irish Guards made those bayonet charges against men with machine guns and volleys of rifle fire. They bought time at a high price, but they did not stint themselves nor stop their bidding because of its costliness.

The brigade of Guards here and near Vieux Berquin held out for those forty-eight hours, and some of them were fighting still when the Australians arrived, according to the timetable.

I have told the story briefly and baldly, though every word I have written holds the thread of a noble and tragic episode. One day some soldier of the Guards will write it as he lived through it, and that saving of forty-eight hours outside the forest of Nieppe shall never be forgotten.

OUR MEN BEAT OFF ATTACK

Drive Back Three Assaulting Battalions Near Villers-Bretonneux.

FIERCE HAND-TO-HAND FIGHT

Germans Suffer Heavy Losses, Leaving Behind Many Dead and Five Prisoners.

OUR OWN LOSSES SEVERE

French Applaud the Bravery of Our Soldiers in the Violent Encounter.

WITH THE FRENCH ARMY, May 1, (Associated Press.) — A heavy German attack launched yesterday against the Americans in the vicinity of Villers-Bretonneux was repulsed with heavy losses for the enemy.

The German preliminary bombardment lasted two hours, and then the infantry rushed forward, only to be driven back, leaving large numbers of dead on the ground in front of the American lines.

The German bombardment opened at 5 o'clock in the afternoon and was directed especially against the Americans, who were supported on the north and south by the French. The fire was intense, and at the end of two hours the German commander sent forward three battalions of infantry.

There was hand-to-hand fighting all along the line, as a result of which the enemy was thrust back, his dead and wounded lying on the ground in all directions. Five prisoners remained in American hands.

The struggle, which lasted a considerable time, was extremely violent, and the Americans displayed marked bravery throughout.

It was the first occasion in which the Americans were engaged in the big battle which has been raging since March 21, and their French comrades are full of praise for the manner in which they conducted themselves under trying circumstances, especially in view of the fact that they are fighting at one of the most difficult points on the battlefront.

The American losses were rather severe.

Germans Leave "Souvenirs" To Kill Unwary Americans

WITH THE AMERICAN ARMY IN FRANCE, May 1. (Associated Press.)—Knowing that the Americans are persistent souvenir hunters, the Germans in the Toul sector have been strewing No Man's Land with all sorts of infernal devices.

These consist of electric wires attached to belts, helmets, rifles, and other paraphernalia connecting with concealed bombs.

In a number of instances American soldiers have tripped over these and escaped.

1,000 "Match" the President As He Buys Bond at Theatre

WASHINGTON, May 1.—President Wilson went to a local theatre tonight and formally offered his " buy another bond " $50 subscription to a four-minute speaker. The audience rose and cheered lustily. A landslide of subscriptions followed, more than half of the 2,000 persons present " matching the President," and the total ran over $300,000.

Some one speaking for Francis R. Mayer of New York offered to take $100,000 of bonds if 200 $50 subscriptions were forthcoming. Two hundred subscribers promptly responded, and the $100,000 sale was recorded.

The New York Times.

"All the News That's Fit to Print."

THE WEATHER
Fair, warmer today; Sunday probably showers; wind south.

VOL. LXVII...NO. 22,029.　　　NEW YORK, SATURDAY, MAY 18, 1918.—TWENTY-FOUR PAGES.　　　TWO CENTS In Greater New York and　THREE CENTS

FRENCH COMMAND EXPECTS IMMEDIATE GERMAN BLOW; AMERICAN TROOPS JOIN BRITISH ON LINES IN THE NORTH; GOVERNMENT DISCOVERS GERMAN PLOTTING IN IRELAND

FOE'S DIVISIONS REGROUPED

Large Forces of Picked Troops Massed Behind the Battlefront.

ATTACK ON VIMY FORECAST

But General French Opinion Locates the Main Attempt Between La Bassee and Amiens.

FOCH'S TROOPS WELCOME IT

Say They Have the Germans' Measure and Will Soon Prove It.

By WALTER DURANTY.

Copyright, 1918, by The New York Times Company.
Special Cable to THE NEW YORK TIMES.

WITH THE FRENCH ARMIES, Saturday, May 18, 12:30 A. M.—The blow may fall at any hour now. THE NEW YORK TIMES correspondent was told yesterday that in the last few days there was evidence that the Germans had finished regrouping their divisions with a view to a second great offensive, and, as before, had massed large forces of picked troops some distance behind the front, ready to be transferred by forced marches to a given point at the last possible moment. The present fine weather and moonlight nights favor such an operation, and there are other signs which indicate that the Germans may strike before these lines are in print.

It is still believed that the main attack will be made between La Bassée and the Amiens region. The allied line in Flanders is likely to be assaulted with almost equal force, and another drive may come between Amiens and Noyon, or elsewhere.

One officer, however, advances a slightly different theory.

"I shall not be surprised," he says, "if the boche makes his principal effort against the Vimy Ridge positions, which he regards as the key to the allied line between the sea and Amiens. It would be a terribly costly experiment, but success would hold out great opportunities."

Whenever and wherever the blow falls the Allies are more than ready, and the confidence and morale of the whole French army were never higher. I visited the front line trenches yesterday and talked with men who may be called on at any minute to bear the first brunt of the shock. All say the same thing:

"The sooner the boche comes the sooner it will all be finished. We know we have got his measure and when this attack has been checked we will prove it."

GERMAN GUNFIRE IS INCREASING

Lys Salient and the Hailles Region See Heaviest Shelling—Air Fights Are Numerous.

LONDON, May 17.—Increasing artillery activity by the Germans along the British front is noted by the War Office today in its official communication, but there has been no infantry action of consequence.

The centres of the German gunfire were along the Lys salient, notably near the Pacaut Wood, north of Hinges, (on the southern flank of the salient,) between Hinges and Locon, and from the forest of Nieppe to Meteren, (west of Bailleul.)

There was some raiding on both sides. The British rushed a German post north of Merris (southwest of Bailleul) and killed or drove out the men of the garrison. Another successful raid was carried out during the night near Beaumont-Hamel, (north of Albert.)

On the French front heavy fire was kept up last night in the region of Hailles, (southwest of Hangard.) A successful raid was made by the French southeast of Montdidier.

Field Marshal Haig's report from British Headquarters tonight says:

We carried out a successful raid last night in the neighborhood of Beaumont-Hamel and captured a few prisoners.

This morning a hostile post north of Merris was rushed by our troops. Its garrison was killed or driven out.

On the remainder of the front there is nothing to report beyond artillery activity by both sides.

The day report of the British War Office is as follows:

A hostile raiding party was repulsed last night in the neighborhood of Meyenneville, south of Arras.

There was great artillery activity on both sides during the night in the Pacaut Wood sector north of Hinges.

The hostile artillery also has shown increased activity between Locon and Hinges and from the Forest of Nieppe to Meteren.

The day bulletin of the French War Office says:

During the night there was a violent bombardment in the region of Hailles. Near Mesnil-St. Georges we repulsed a German raid and took prisoners.

South of Canny-sur-Matz (southeast of Montdidier) French detachments penetrated the German lines at two points, bringing back forty prisoners, including an officer.

On the southern bank of the Oise German attacks on small French posts in the sector of Varennes were broken up by our fire.

Elsewhere the night passed in quiet.

The statement, issued by the French War Office tonight, says:

There was only the usual activity by the opposing artilleries along the front north and south of the Avre River.

Our aviation squadrons have been active. On Tuesday night a number of our aviators participated in bombardments of the zone occupied by the enemy. 36,000 kilograms of projectiles being dropped on railway stations, communications, and airdromes at St. Quentin, Jussy, Flavy le Martel, Nesles, and Ham. Munition depots were exploded at Nesles and large fires were observed at Guiscard and Chatelet. The railway station at Nesles was burned.

On the following night 30,000 kilograms were dropped on the same regions and 10,000 kilograms on the regions of Amage, Bucquoy, and Mont Cornet.

On May 16 four enemy airplanes were shot down and three others were gravely damaged.

On the night of May 16 railway stations and German cantonments at Chaulnes, Roye, Nesles, and St. Quentin received 25,000 kilograms of projectiles, and munition depots were destroyed. Fires and explosions were caused at other points.

REPORTS BRITISH REPULSES.

Berlin Also Says a Monitor Shelled Ostend, Killing Civilians.

BERLIN, May 17, (via London.)—The official communication issued today says:

An enemy monitor shelled Ostend, inflicting considerable losses among the population.

During a repulse of a strong English thrust north of the Scarpe and near Beaumont-Hamel, and also during a successful operation we undertook south of Arras, we made some prisoners.

Yesterday eighteen enemy airplanes and one captive balloon were shot down.

Mysterious Shots Fell in Dover; German Supergun Was Suspected

The Bombardment of April 26, When No German Airplanes Could Be Found by the British—Official Denial of the Supergun Theory—France Has a New 22-Inch Gun.

Copyright, 1918, by The New York Times Company.
Special Cable to THE NEW YORK TIMES.

LONDON, May 17.—On inquiry at the Ministry of Information with reference to a report that a German supergun at or near Ostend had been firing shells into Dover, notably on April 26, THE NEW YORK TIMES was informed that the story was absolutely false. General Radcliffe, Director of Military Operations, also stated that the report was without foundation.

The story which reached New York is apparently an elaboration of speculations which were prevalent at the time when the Germans began the long-range shelling of Paris. Dover could not be shelled without London coming to know of it, and there have not been any reports of such a thing having happened, even in circles where Dame Rumor wags her tongue most busily.

The sand dunes of Ostend and the neighborhood do not present favorable situations for emplacing long-range guns, which, it is believed, would speedily be spotted and destroyed by British airmen.

The story that the port of Dover, situated on the southeast coast of England, was believed to have been shelled by a German supergun from Ostend, a distance of about sixty-five miles across the North Sea, was brought to New York by passengers recently arrived from England. It was told by one of these to THE TIMES as follows:

"Belgian spies in the employ of the British Intelligence Department reported on April 5 that a gun of about the same calibre as those set up near Laon and used in the bombardment of Paris had passed through Belgium from the Krupp Works at Essen on April 2, on its way to Ostend. This gun was said to be from 65 to 75 feet long and of 23 centimeters calibre.

"The supposed shelling of Dover occurred at 10 o'clock on Friday night, April 26, and was at first taken for an aerial attack. Fifty British fighting machines went up to drive back the boche aviators, but could not get any trace of them, and an alarm was sent to London that the Germans had dropped three bombs on Dover and proceeded toward the metropolis.

"The first missile fell short of the town of Dover and struck Shakespeare's Cliff, sending some hundreds of tons of chalk into the sea with a deafening report, which roused the people in their beds, and hundreds of them took to the cellars and caves for safety. The second and third missiles were better aimed, passed over the harbor and part of the town, and dropped in a residential street, demolishing two small houses. Those who were living near by said that the 'bomb,' they called it, made a great noise when it exploded, but did not have the destructive force of the bombs that had been previously dropped by airplanes.

Destroyer's Report Aroused Suspicion.

"The officers of the Flying Corps and the Naval Air Force stationed at Dover did not suspect that the missiles were shells fired by a German supergun until early next morning, when a report was received from the commander of a destroyer which had been out scouting during the night off the Belgian coast.

"The aviators on guard duty along the Kentish coast believed that they did not see the planes which were supposed to have attacked Dover, because they were flying at over 15,000 feet and the night was dark. When the alarm reached London the people were still in the theatres, but as it was nearly closing time they were not informed that German raiders had passed Dover. At 11 o'clock, as nothing more had been heard of the German planes at any of the air stations on the road from Dover to London, about seventy miles, the 'All clear' signal was given.

"The newspapers published next morning stated that the alarm had been given on account of the warning received from Dover, which had proved to be incorrect. They did not give any explanation regarding the three missiles dropped on the port, and there has been no mention of the big German gun being placed in position at Ostend.

"On April 14 it was reported in the Paris papers that the Germans had two of the seventy-mile-range guns in Ostend and that they were intended to be used on the English coast when the enemy had succeeded in breaking through to Boulogne or Calais.

"Belgian spies again got through the German lines into Holland at Maastricht on May 1, and said that they had seen the superguns at Ostend, with their shells lying on a concrete platform beside them. The weight of the shells was estimated to be about 200 to 225 pounds each. So far there has been no means of obtaining the weight of the shells fired from the German superguns into Paris, because they have all exploded when they fell and scattered into fragments.

"The British Admiralty declined to give out any particulars concerning the big guns at Ostend or the shelling of Dover on April 26, and the London newspapers were content with calling it the mysterious false alarm."

France Has Greatest Gun in the World.

Another person, who has just arrived from England, reports that the new 22-inch French gun, by far the greatest in the world, has been completed, and the first photograph of one of them is presented herewith. For obvious reasons it is not permitted to describe the gun in detail. It is conjectured that it is one of these guns that has succeeded in silencing the two German superguns located near Laon. Before the German superguns near Laon were put out of commission they are said to have killed in Paris 368 persons, wounded 300, and driven to places of refuge elsewhere in France many thousands of the population of Paris.

Fifteen experimental eighteen-inch rifles have been built by the United States Government for the protection of the Panama Canal. These were the largest hitherto known. It has been reported that the Krupps had made several seventeen-inch guns for the protection of Heligoland. It has been seriously questioned by ordnance experts whether the Germans possess a direct-fire rifle larger than sixteen-inch, although the existence of the seventeen-inch Skoda howitzer is no longer doubted. The long range guns which shelled Dunkirk were found to carry twelve-inch and fifteen-inch shells; those which have shelled Paris from near Laon, a distance of seventy-four miles, nine-inch. The maximum naval gun of the United States and British Navies is the sixteen-inch piece, firing from a floating emplacement a 2,100-pound shell twenty-two miles.

LOOKS TO RUMANIA FOR FOOD.

Berlin Talks of Large Imports of Meat and Cereals to Come.

LONDON, May 16.—Berlin expects to receive 150,000 sheep and 30,000 pigs shortly from Rumania, and 100,000 tons of cereals in July or August.

TOMMIES CHEER OUR MEN

Promptly on Their Arrival in Flanders They Begin Training.

FIRST OF THE RUSH FORCES

They Are Commanded by an American General Who Has Been on the French Line.

DOUBLE PURPOSE SERVED

They Will Back Up Allies Where Needed and Be Fitted Quickly for Front Line.

By EDWIN L. JAMES.

Copyright, 1918, by The New York Times Company.

Special Cable to THE NEW YORK TIMES.

WITH THE AMERICAN ARMY IN FRANCE, May 17.—American troops have taken their place in the British war zone in Northern France. Announcement to this effect was authorized by the American army authorities today.

The presence of American soldiers back of the British lines and of Americans fighting in co-operation with the French in Picardy, together with the Americans holding sectors northwest of Toul and in Lorraine, show that our men will have a chance to participate in heavy fighting whenever the next German drive may come.

There is no reason to doubt that as the American troops arrive, greater numbers will be found at other points on the western battle front.

The scattering of the American troops is not to be taken to cast the slightest doubt on the eventual unification of the American forces in France. Whenever the proper time comes in the opinion of the allied command, the United States troops will have their own organization and play their own rôle, and the glory of our army will be reflected upon the Stars and Stripes, as well as upon the general cause of the Allies.

Brigading Helps in Two Ways.

The assignment of American troops to the British and French armies at this time serves two purposes. Primarily it places fresh troops at points where they are needed, tending to lessen any chance that Germany might win the war this year. A secondary but no less important purpose is that the arrangement will give the American troops invaluable training which they could get in no other way.

There are indications that much of the warfare in future months may be open fighting. It is not easy for the Americans to get training in that kind of warfare except in this region.

Participation of the American units in warfare with the British and French units will also give our officers such training in modern warfare as they could get in no other way.

The great task of the Allies is to block the plans of the Germans to make further advances now. This is a task for America, no less than for England and France, especially since the Kaiser hoped to win the war before our growing weight could be thrown in serious strength against him. Therefore, the chance for Americans to help fight the foe on his chosen battlefield at this time is nothing less than an opportunity to make our rôle the more glorious.

There is something in the service of American fighters with the British and French that is in keeping with the spirit of our whole participation in the war—the spirit of unselfishness.

Grasp Opportunity to Fight.

While America's soldiers might prefer, if possible, to defeat the foe under their own flag, this does not mean at all that they do not seize with the best spirit the opportunity to help defeat him somewhere else, until they can do it as it may suit them best.

Because of the uncertainties of war, it is impossible to say at this time how long the present arrangement will continue. It is safe to say that it will continue as long as there is need for Americans elsewhere more than in their own sectors.

Of course, it is not permitted to state the plans as to the extent of participation of America's fighting men with the armies of the Allies. Moreover, today's plans are likely to be changed before tomorrow.

I am not allowed to tell the size of the American forces in the British war zone or give their identity, save to say that they are large enough to prove of material assistance should the Germans resume the pounding of the British lines.

Cheered by British on Arrival.

WITH THE AMERICAN ARMY IN FRANCE, May 17, (Associated Press.)—Troops of the new American army who have arrived within the British zone in Northern France are completing their training in the area occupied by the troops which are blocking the path of the Germans to the Channel ports. Their commander has already commanded American forces in trenches on the French front.

The British officers and men who are training the new force say that the Americans are of the finest material and are certain to give a most excellent account of themselves when they meet the Germans.

The British troops greeted the Americans not only as comrades in arms, but as warm friends, and the work of instruction is being continued in that spirit. The American forces on arriving were cheered to the skies by the sons of Britain, many of whom bore unmistakable signs of battle. They had not seen the Americans before, but knew they were coming.

The Americans, on the other hand, gained all the more enthusiasm by the heartiness of the greeting which they received from their comrades in arms.

The last stages of training before entering the line were begun by the Americans almost as soon as they reached their destination. From that point they could hear the rumble of the not distant guns.

How long the American troops have been with the British and when the news that they are making their presence felt along the line may be expected cannot be disclosed. It is enough to say that men speaking almost every language, descendants from almost every nationality, are working day and night to fit themselves to enter the line as quickly as possible.

"MORE COMING!" THEY SHOUT.

Americans Hearten the British, Who in Turn Inspire New Arrivals.

By FLOYD P. GIBBONS.

Copyright, 1918, by The Chicago Tribune Company.

PERSHING'S HEADQUARTERS IN FRANCE, May 17.—American fighting men in numbers are now part of the army of Sir Douglas Haig. Behind the Flanders front soldiers of the empire and sons of Uncle Sam occupy positions side by side.

It has put heart into the British ranks to see our khaki-clad columns swing along the roads. It has put snap into our men to march to their places in such worthy company. The veterans of a four years' struggle have gained renewed hope at the sight of this fresh help from the West. The young arrivals in the war zone have gained new inspiration upon meeting men who have "been there."

Daily, it seems, the French ports which have grown as if by magic under the hands of the American engineers, are brimful of troops. Almost as fast as one troop ship can be unloaded and moved away another is warped into her place and soon the gangways are erupting streams of khaki.

"And there's more where we come from," is the shout of our men as they exchange words on the road with the British transport.

"Bring 'em over," replied a wounded Canadian, sticking his head out of an ambulance door. "You know, Yank, we're not stingy about this here war."

Tommy and Sammy have found much in common, but more to exchange. Tommy is taking costly lessons in dice rolling on an army blanket and Sammy is trying to understand how any human being can drink tea for breakfast. Sammy is learning that the use of the broad A does not necessarily mean that the user is putting on dog or "swanking," as Tommy would put it, and on the other hand Tommy is finding out that the American nose is not actually stopped up, but that we talk that way for a special reason.

"Which is," explained Corporal Benny, "so we wont be taken for Englishmen."

These exchanges of customs, manners, and knowledge are not confined to the ranks. Our officers dine at mixed messes where wearers of Sam Browne from every Anglo-Saxon corner of the earth are gathered. The English imperialist rather prides himself upon the fact that among the men in France today, who answered the call of King and country, are representatives from Australia, Canada, New Zealand, Ireland, Wales, Scotland, India, Egypt, and Fiji Islands. This pride received a jolt at one mess where an American Lieutenant advanced the information that his battalion included recent naturalization from twenty-seven different countries, and that eight languages were spoken.

"My word," replied the English "Leftenant," "one must have to be a linguist to give one's commands."

And the chaplain of the High Church of England was dumfounded to learn from an American chaplain that ten different religions were represented in some regiments.

These cosmopolitan troops from the New World have hardly had a spare minute since they left the ships.

"All the News That's Fit to Print."

The New York Times.

THE WEATHER
Fair, warmer today; Sunday cloudy; south to southwest winds.
For full weather report see Page 19

VOL. LXVII...NO. 22,043. .... NEW YORK, SATURDAY, JUNE 1, 1918.—TWENTY PAGES. TWO CENTS in Greater New York and Within Commuting Distance. THREE CENTS

GERMANS REACH THE MARNE IN 8-MILE DRIVE; OUTRUN ARTILLERY, ARE HELD ON THE FLANKS; HINT OF A NEW FORCE AHEAD TO STOP THEM

EXPECT RALLY AT THE MARNE

Its Name a Trumpet Call and the Best of Omens for Defenders.

STRONG ON BOTH FLANKS

Reserves Coming Up Rapidly and a Crisis in the Battle Is Approaching.

BRAVE DEEDS TO GAIN TIME

Three French Battalions, Cut Off in Woods, Dig In and Decide to Fight to the Death.

By G. H. PERRIS.
Copyright, 1918, by The New York Times Company.
Special Cable to THE NEW YORK TIMES.

WITH THE FRENCH ARMIES, Friday, May 31.—It is almost impossible to discuss the situation today without giving some indication that might be useful to the enemy. I shall therefore be very brief, and shall not attempt to explain why I and those who know the real outlook much better still are confident and cheerful. I do not know whether the German people yet understand the truth about the last battle of the Marne or how the repetition of this great name will affect them. To Frenchmen, if there is to be a new battle of the Marne, the name, so far from being a cause of fear, will be a trumpet call and the best of omens.

The Wings Holding.

In contrast with the further advance of the German centre, the French and British forces on the wings are holding firm. The great highroad from Soissons to Château Thierry marks broadly the western limit of the offensive.

On the northern stretch of it there was hard fighting yesterday. In the morning the enemy crossed the road at Hartennes and attacked westward with a number of tanks, but was checked near the hamlet of Tigny.

Further north a well-known French division made, with its traditional spirit, a thrust westward across the road and the little River Crise and reached the village of Noyant. It had to fall back, but here, too, the German advance was arrested.

The Compiègne road is firmly held, and the disparity of forces is being rapidly reduced.

On the other flank of the battlefield the French and British divisions stand across the hills on the other bank of the Ardre, a small tributary of the Vesle, from Brouillet to Thillois, on the northern foothills of the mountain of Rheims, whence the front runs around the ruined city.

This French division is the same that I have already cited for its determined resistance on the first day of the battle. Yesterday it struck out from La Neuvillette along the canal and captured two hummocks, called Castalliers and De Courcy. It was a bold effort, intended to check the enemy rather than in the hope of retaining the position. This indeed proved impossible, but the French were slow to retire, and the lesson will not be lost upon their adversaries.

Decided to Fight to the Death.

The news is gradually coming in of what happened on the front, submerged by the assault of Monday morning. Its most northerly part was the low ground beside the Ailette called the Forest of Pinon, which I described fully last Christmas, when I spent several days with the outposts by which it was held, in conditions somewhat reminiscent of wild West warfare. The nearest trenches were on the hills a mile or two behind, this ground being too marshy to dig in. In the forest blockhouses were then being built, and were laid out while each side raided the other across the frontier on the stream and canal. Nothing then seemed less likely than an attack across such ground, but preparations were being pushed forward with the idea that a few groups of defenders would gather in and around the blockhouses and fight a delaying action, and then, if possible, escape back to the hill trenches.

The event turned out otherwise. When the surviving groups and outposts, amounting in all to three battalions, got together on Monday morning, they decided to intrench themselves and to fight to the death. Carrier pigeons brought notes from them to this effect. The last note received was dated 2 P. M. on Tuesday. The best that can be hoped is that some survive as prisoners.

I think it may be said that there is now no danger of a break through toward any vital objective.

It is not to take the pitiful remains of Rheims and Soissons that the German command has committed itself to this development of its final effort. At both these extremes we have abundant room and better positions; and that is equally true at the centre, where the French are selling dearly every foot they yield. On the south of the Vesle the crisis is passing, and the position has none of the dangers peculiar to the fronts of the Somme and Flanders.

Once more, in General Foch's phrase, "the wave will die upon the beach."

SUGGESTS GERMANS ARE NOW IN RHEIMS

British Staff Statement Also Says the Enemy Reached the Marne on a Ten-Mile Front.

CALLS SITUATION 'SERIOUS'

But Says Germans Are Using Up Effectives and Reserves Will Settle the Struggle.

LONDON, May 31. — A statement given to The Associated Press tonight by a high military authority, expressive of the opinion of the British General Staff of the situation on the western front, says:

"The main German offensive has been directed toward Château Thierry and Dormans. The Germans have reached the right bank of the Marne on a front of ten miles from a point west of Château Thierry to Dormans. They have not captured Château Thierry, but are attacking very heavily here and to the northward.

"They already have captured Soissons, and yesterday they extended their attack northwest to Noyon and forced the French back, so that the line now runs almost straight from Noyon to Soissons.

"Around Rheims the position is still somewhat obscure. Probably the Germans already have entered Rheims.

"The French reported yesterday that the allied line had retired to the south of the canal near Rheims, but this morning there was news that the British were resisting north of the city. The new development is that the German attempt is to extend the attack east of Rheims, where they were reported attacking last night, but no further details have yet been received.

"The Germans have thrown in every resource in an effort to widen the salient in which they find themselves by attacking its flanks, but on the heights to the west of Soissons the French are resisting well, while the British are making a stand south and southwest of Rheims. These efforts thus far have held the German salient to a narrow width.

"The situation is very anxious, not only because the Germans have made such rapid progress, (an advance of twenty-six miles in four days,) but also because they still have such large reserves available to be thrown in at any point.

Thirty Divisions Attacked Seven.

"The Germans' big attack began May 27 with about thirty divisions on a front of thirty-five miles from Bermericourt to Leuilly. This front was held by seven allied divisions, of which three British were on the right and four French on the left.

"After a bombardment of two hours, which appears to have been very effective in cutting our wire, the Germans assaulted. They overran the French front lines. The British held in their second line at first, but eventually were compelled to fall back to conform to the French alignment.

"The Germans advanced very rapidly, crossing the Aisne, although the French had occupied very strong positions here with three divisions commanding the river crossings.

"Since this time the Crown Prince has done the utmost possible with his group of armies to push forward. He has thrown in every reserve division he possesses, with the aim of pushing through to the Marne and cutting the important railway to Chalons.

"Our transport of reserves has worked very well, and there is every reason to hope that Germany will not make any further progress at this point, although the situation must remain anxious as long as they have plenty of reserves available. The immediate future depends on what course the enemy adopts.

Now a Question of Reserves.

"The Crown Prince has used up practically all his own reserves, but could get a few from the army corps to the eastward. But the great bulk of the German reserves are to the north. It remains to be seen whether the enemy will use them to develop a success toward Paris or to pursue his original intention toward Amiens, with the aim of cutting the allied armies in two.

"The Germans have the initiative. The Crown Prince has on his left the army group under General von Gallwitz, and to the left of Gallwitz is the army group under Duke Albrecht. Neither of these army groups has been engaged.

"Some reinforcements for further efforts by the Crown Prince could be obtained from these armies, but the bulk of the German reserves are in Prince Rupprecht's group, to the right of the Crown Prince, and they are very formidable in strength. The enemy may put them in to exploit the success already gained and push in the direction of Paris, or he may continue his effort through Amiens.

"The question has been much discussed during the last few days as to whether this German attack was a surprise to the Allies. It cannot be called a complete surprise, for the fact is that the concentration in the Laon area was well known. But until a day or two before the battle we had no indication that an attack on a big scale was impending. The Germans deserve full credit for maintaining secrecy regarding their plan.

"The main masses of men were brought up to the actual front lines only on the night before the attack, which was preceded by only two hours' bombardment for the purpose of cutting our wire. The Germans are not making the same use of their artillery as heretofore. They are using trench mortars in large numbers for wire cutting.

Germans Skillful in Secrecy.

"The Germans were very skillful in keeping secrecy and in bringing up their troops at night. They had prepared for an attack on this part of the line for a long time, constructing the necessary gun emplacements and assembly places so that our aircraft did not observe any construction of new trenches or emplacements just before the attack. The German use of artillery before the attack was of a different character than heretofore.

"Their guns did not register on definite targets, but selected merely a wide area and shelled it continuously. It always has been difficult for aircraft to obtain definite strategical information. Thus in 1914 airmen found it very hard to detect columns on the road, and much doubt existed as to the actual front covered by the German advance in Belgium.

"Under the conditions which prevailed in the region of the Chemin-des-Dames, an initial success could hardly be prevented. Nor can it be prevented anywhere where there are not adequate reserves immediately avaiable.

Cites Allies' Disadvantages.

"The Allies have these disadvantages: First, they are inferior in numbers; second, they are acting on exterior lines; third, they have many vulnerable points; fourth, north of the Somme they have little foot in which to manoeuvre.

"It is not fair to blame the high command when the Allies have inherently an unfavorable strategic position. If it is said that the high command placed three tired British divisions on an exposed part of the front, it must be remembered that this disposition was made with full agreement of the British Headquarters.

"Questions such as the bases of supply and communication have to be taken into account in the employment of troops. Until fresh reserves of the Germans have been engaged somewhere, the situation must continue anxious.

"On the other hand, the attack of the past week has not been so serious as on some other points in the allied line, because we have more room to manoeuvre and can better afford to fall back.

"Another thing that must always be considered is that the Germans are rapidly using up their effectives. Thus far they probably have employed forty-five divisions in the present attack, of which twenty-nine have been identified."

A previous statement from the same source said:

"Is this the enemy's main attack?

"He probably did not know when he initiated it whether it would prove to be a subsidiary or leading operation. It must be remembered that the enemy has three great geographical objectives as means toward his great objective of destroying the Franco-British Armies—the Channel ports, separation of the allied armies by an attack through Amiens, and an attack on Paris.

"In the present operations he is doing all possible to develop his initial success by attacks both on the centre and on the flanks of the salient. He has achieved considerable success in the centre, but on the flanks the French are holding well on the heights west of Soissons and the British are similarly fighting hard on the heights around Rheims.

Praise for American Exploit.

"No review of the past week would be c[illegible]plete without mention of the fine exploit of the American troops in the capture of Cantigny. It was an extremely well conducted operation, and in view of the fact that the troops were untried it is notable that they not only captured their objective, but held it. It is always much more difficult to consolidate and retain a position than to capture it, and the performance of the Americans shows the very high standard attained, as well as their training, bravery, and fighting qualities."

HOSPITALS BOMBED BEHIND OUR LINES

German Airmen in Wave Formation on Most Pretentious Raid in Picardy.

AMERICAN GIRLS FEARLESS

Nurses Remove the Wounded and Ill—Several Babies Among the Killed and Injured.

WITH THE AMERICAN ARMY IN FRANCE, May 30—(Associated Press.)—German airmen made a pretentious raid on the area behind the American lines in Picardy last night. Bombs were dropped on all sides of one of the largest hospitals in a town many miles to the rear of the front. American and French wounded soldiers were carried to cellars and caves by American nurses and members of the American Red Cross.

Only a few persons were injured by flying glass, as most of the windows in the hospital had been shattered by bombs dropped the previous night. Several private houses were wrecked and a number of civilians, including several babies, were killed and injured.

That the raid was planned on a much larger scale than recent ones over this territory is evidenced from reports made by many Americans in villages over which the raiders passed. The Germans came in wave formation and then scattered widely. One squadron dropped bombs a few hundred feet from an American field hospital, and at the same time one of the long-range guns shelled a village a few hundred yards away.

The first alarm was sounded at 11 o'clock. The dropping of bombs and the firing of many anti-aircraft guns began almost immediately. Later, there was a brief pause after which the raiders returned to remain almost until dawn.

Hospital Windows Shattered.

A new American evacuation hospital had been opened only yesterday in a certain village. A bomb fell in front of it last night and shattered windows, but none of the patients was injured.

In some instances the bombs fell within thirty and forty feet of a hospital building, but, fortunately, there were no direct hits. A French nurse, her mother and two little sisters were killed in a house a short distance from a hospital. Another nurse was standing on the upper floor of the hospital, ministering to patients, when a piece of a bomb pierced her lung.

Five American nurses were in the same hospital. They were Miss Natalie Scott of New Orleans, Miss Helen Spalding of Brooklyn, Miss Mary McCadlish of Atlanta, Miss Blanche Gilbert of Cleveland, and Miss Constance Cook of San Francisco. While the raid was in progress they went about cheering the patients. Although many serious cases of sick and wounded were aggravated because they had to be moved, the nurses had to carry them to the lower floors and the cellar.

"It was an exciting time," said Miss Scott, "but there was no panic. Some of our boys actually slept through it all although their beds were showered with broken glass.

Three Ambulances Caught.

Three ambulances were caught in the raid. Sergeant Wells of San Francisco, who was driving the first ambulance, said:

"Our three ambulances were hurrying to hospitals with patients when a bomb wrecked a building directly in front of us, in a narrow street. Our ambulance was perforated by flying missiles. We were all hurled out, but escaped with a few scratches."

Private Robert A. Bowman of Galveston, who was in the same car, said:

"There was a terrific explosion. The next thing I knew I was lying on the ground. I looked around and heard the patients groaning. I pulled myself together and found the patients uninjured, except for shock. Our ambulance was shot to pieces."

The second car apparently received the full force of the explosion, and was wrecked completely.

Private Roscoe Wiley of Madisonville, Texas, was driving the third car. Sergeant J. W. Nolder of Altoona, Penn., and three patients were with him.

"There was wreckage all around us," said Sergeant Nolder. "Injured civilians in the shattered houses near by were begging for help. We all pitched in as soon as we had recovered from the shock, and assisted in the work of rescue. We had to dig many persons from the débris by the light of small pocket lamps. Meanwhile enemy aircraft were buzzing overhead. The barrage was deafening. Bombs continued to fall. It was worse than anything in the trenches. I would rather have been in No Man's Land."

Funeral Establishment Hit.

In one village a large funeral establishment opposite a hospital was bombed and wrecked. Although the patients in the hospitals were hurriedly covered with blankets and carried off to cellars, there was no panic anywhere.

The Americans and French joked and laughed. One American who participated in the capture of Cantigny said:

"We've got Fritz's goat. We licked the tar out of him when we took Cantigny. Now that some of us are sick or injured and helpless he wants revenge. If murdering the sick and wounded and defenseless women and old men and children is his idea of 'kultur' we must destroy 'kultur' if it takes us a hundred years."

Many villages in the rear of the American line were attacked by the raiders.

This morning, while a Memorial Day service was in progress at a little American cemetery near the Picardy front, German aviators attempted to raid the cemetery. The enemy planes were driven off by anti-aircraft guns.

The ceremony was most picturesque. French civilians—old men, women, and children dressed in white—placed flowers on the graves. Notwithstanding the hum of the German aircraft overhead, the service continued without interruption.

Patients in Burning Ruins.

WITH THE BRITISH ARMY IN FRANCE, May 31, (Associated Press.)—Early on Thursday morning German airmen bombed another hospital—this time a Canadian institution—and exacted a considerable toll of casualties. Among those killed by the explosion or flames was an American medical officer who was administering an anaesthetic to a British officer in the operating room when that part of the hospital was demolished. The raid was made at 12:30 o'clock in the morning.

The hospital attacked was a large one. It had been in existence since the early days of the war, and was marked by huge Red Cross signs. The German airmen, working partly by the light of the moon, dropped four bombs near the hospital, and then, not apparently able to see exactly where they were hitting, lighted a brilliant flare which was let fall to illuminate the surroundings.

As the place was lighted up by this flare, they released another bomb or two, which dropped squarely on a large wing of the hospital. In this wing there were three floors, on the bottom one of which was the operating room. On the story above were the office and patients' room, and above them were members of the hospital personnel. Part of the wing was demolished by the terrific explosion, and many unfortunate people were killed and wounded when the building collapsed and buried them.

Strange to say, those who were on the top floor had better luck than those below them, and several escaped because they fell on top of the débris.

The surgeons were just about to operate on an aviation officer, and the American was standing by with the anaesthetic when the crash came. All those in the room were buried under an avalanche of brick and woodwork. The demolished wing caught fire and burned fiercely, with many victims still pinned in the wreckage.

Rescuers' Desperate Work.

Nothing more awful has occurred in the annals of the hospital service since the war began. Every available person in the neighborhood was called out to assist in the rescue work, and two fire brigades were called in. With the assistance of ladders and other fire apparatus the hospital proper was rapidly emptied of patients and personnel. It was a desperate situation. A roaring furnace represented what was left of the big wing.

Scores of people worked frenziedly at the flaming mass of twisted timbers in their attempts to reach those entombed, and many unconscious forms were carried out by heroic men who risked their lives to reach them. Excellent work on the part of the firemen finally resulted in the fire's being extinguished, but there were still many people, including more than one sister, burned in the ruins. There was no hope that they were alive.

NURSES AND DOCTORS PLUCKY.

New York Girl Among Those Who Stuck to Their Posts.

Special to The New York Times.

CHICAGO, May 31.—Junius B. Wood, correspondent of The Chicago Daily News with the American Army on the French front, in a cablegram to his newspaper today describes the bombing by Germans of American hospitals last Tuesday and says:

"Six American nurses in a city back of the lines heroically stuck to the job of caring for the American wounded, who were in cellars when the town was bombed Tuesday night. Most of the German bombs struck near hospitals, and two French nurses and two babies were struck. The Americans aiding in the rescue were the Misses Helen Spalding of Brooklyn, N. Y.; Mary McCandliss of Atlanta, Ga.; Natalia V. Scott of New Orleans, La.; Blanche Gilbert of Cleveland, Ohio; Constance Cook of San Francisco, Cal., and Mary Hoyt of 310 West Seventy-fifth Street, New York City.

"Some of the ambulances bringing wounded to the hospitals here had narrow escapes from destruction. One ambulance was blown away as if by a cyclone, the only thing remaining being the battered radiator hood.

"While bombs were crashing on all sides ambulances were dashing in, bringing new victims, and the surgeons continued working with the aid of flashlights and candles through the remainder of the night. Major Fred G. Murphy of St. Louis, Captain Charles Farmer of Louisville, Ky.; Lieutenant Joseph McDevitt of New York City, Lieutenant Thomas Hardy of Richmond, Va., and Dr. William Clark of Washington, D. C., were the men who stuck to their work in this hospital."

Wisconsin Aviator Killed.

MILWAUKEE, May 31. — Lieutenant John L. Mitchell, aviator, was killed in action somewhere in France, according to a telegram received by his mother last night.

Lieutenant Mitchell, 25 years old, was a son of the late United States Senator John L. Mitchell of Wisconsin and brother of Colonel William M. Mitchell, in charge of the American Aviation Corps.

The New York Times.

"All the News That's Fit to Print."

THE WEATHER
Fair, slightly cooler today; Sunday fair, diminishing northwest winds.
For full weather report see Page 19.

VOL. LXVII...NO. 22,050.   NEW YORK, SATURDAY, JUNE 8, 1918.—TWENTY PAGES.   TWO CENTS In Greater New York and Jersey City | THREE CENTS Elsewhere.

OUR GALLANT MARINES DRIVE ON 2½ MILES; STORM TWO TOWNS, CAPTURE 300 PRISONERS; RAIDER SINKS ANOTHER NEUTRAL SHIP HERE

NEW ADVANCE BY OUR MEN

Torcy and Bouresches Stormed in a Drive on Six-Mile Front.

ENEMY LOSSES VERY HEAVY

Each Man Get a German, Don't Let Him Get You, Is the Victors' Slogan.

NOTHING STOPS THEIR RUSH

Twenty-five of Them Fight 200 in Torcy — German Dead Three Deep in Places.

WITH THE AMERICAN ARMY IN PICARDY, June 7, (Associated Press.)—As the result of the two attacks by the Americans upon the enemy in the second battle northwest of Château-Thierry yesterday and today, 300 prisoners have been captured and the Americans have extended their line over a front of about six miles to a depth of nearly two and one-half miles.

While the losses of the Americans necessarily have been heavy, owing to the nature of the fighting, the German dead are piled three deep in places.

A number of machine guns have been added to the American booty.

The fighting last night raged with great fierceness for five hours. The Americans captured Bouresches and entered Torcy.

Twenty-five Americans in Torcy engaged and drove out 200 Germans, and then withdrew to the main line on the outskirts of the town.

The importance of the operations of the Americans on the Marne sector may be realized when it is recalled that only the day before the Americans entered the line the Germans advanced about ten kilometers.

The Americans are now holding the Paris road near Le Thiolet for a number of kilometers.

A remarkable story is told of a company of marines, all the officers of which, including the Sergeants, were put out of the fighting. A Corporal then assumed command, and

the men pushed on and obtained their objective.

Private John B. Flocken of Olney, Ill., one of the first men to reach Torcy, said today:

"I never saw such wonderful spirit. Not one of our fellows hesitated in the face of the rain of the machine gun fire, which it seemed impossible to get through. Every German seemed to have a machine gun. They fought like wildcats, but the Americans were too much for them."

Private Carl B. Mills of Visalia, Cal., was in the first wave of Americans to go over the top in Veuilly Wood to smoke out the Germans remaining there. He said that after his unit attained its objective, many of the men went back and filled the ranks of their advancing comrades. All moved like clockwork, he said.

The favorite slogan was, "Each man get a German; don't let a German get you."

The German prisoners taken, many of whom are mere boys, have only been in the line for two days. Some wore the white bands of the Prussian Guard.

Many instances are related of the heroism of the Red Cross workers in braving shells in No Man's Land and gathering in or aiding wounded.

The correspondent today talked with a 19-year-old German prisoner, who was sitting under a tree eating American bread and drinking French wine. He was the object of the curiosity of a crowd. The soldier said that he had been fighting a year and a half, mainly in Russia. He carried a picture of his sweetheart on heavy cardboard, which he said had saved his life from an American bullet.

The youth added that in Germany there was talk of millions of American soldiers, but nobody believed it. He did not know that it was the Americans opposed to the Germans. He thought the troops were British, as they wore English helmets. He added that the German soldiers no longer hoped to reach Paris. All of them were sick of the war, and he was glad that he had been made prisoner.

Graphic stories of last night's fighting were related by wounded Americans today. They said that at one point the Germans crouched behind boulders and opened fire when the Americans were within ten feet of them. One man who participated in an encounter of this kind said:

"Some of us had not slept for four nights, but we were not tired. We took a second lease of life and sprang at those Germans and smothered them. I never saw so many machine guns. Our men did not think of themselves. They only thought of getting Fritz."

A Corporal captured three Germans and was leading them away when twelve others surrendered to him and joined the procession.

Madison Girman of Evansville, Ind., was in Torcy. He said:

"We were not supposed to go there, but the men were so enthusiastic they kept on. They would go to Berlin if their commanders would let them. The only way to stop them is to kill them. The Germans can't make prisoners of us. They tried hard to get some of us, but we fooled them. We turned the machine guns on them and took them prisoner."

WITH THE FRENCH ARMIES IN FRANCE, Evening, June 7, (Associated Press.)—The sharpest fighting continues around the sector of Veuilly-la-Poterie, Bussiares, and Bouresches, where the Americans and French have been attacking shoulder to shoulder for some days,

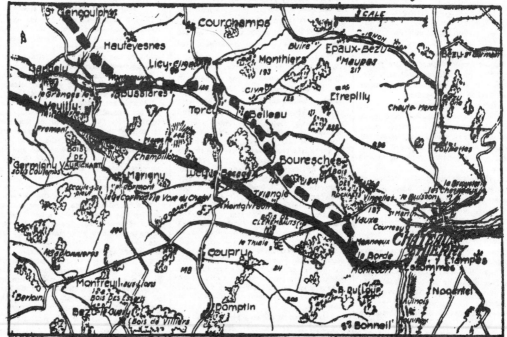

Area Where the Marines Have Won Victory

The solid line represents the approximate position of the American-French forces in this sector before the first attack on the Germans was made Thursday morning. The broken line indicates the present battlefront, so far as it can be gauged by official and unofficial advices.

Apparently the Americans are holding the front from a little east of Veuilly to beyond Bouresches. While Torcy and Bouresches have fallen into American hands, the status of Belleau is in doubt, although Belleau Wood (probably the forest south of the town) has been taken by the Americans.

To the westward the French also have struck hard, having taken Veuilly and Vinly and a little village, north of the latter, to the east of Chezy (about three miles northeast of Veuilly) and a mile and a third west of St. Gengoulph. They are pounding the vertex of the German salient here

254

making almost uninterrupted progress, notwithstanding strong enemy resistance.

The French thi.. morning completed the capture of Vilny, Veuilly-la-Poterie, and the heights southeast of Hautevesnes.

At the same time the Americans were fighting in a wood that contained numerous enemy machine gun emplacements. At the time this dispatch was filed the line was uncertain, but it was evident that progress was being accomplished by the allied troops.

An American Lieutenant went out alone, attacked a German machine gun position, killed the gunners, and brought back the piece.

Drove Germans Headlong from Torcy.

WITH THE AMERICAN FORCES ON THE MARNE, June 7, (Associated Press.)—At daybreak today the United States marines, following up their gains of yesterday, were slowly driving the Germans back in the face of heavy artillery fire, including gas shells. The American artillery was performing magnificently in this operation. Torcy was then being held in the face of repeated counterattacks, while the marines were pushing the enemy through the streets of Bouresches.

Fierce fighting was going on in Belleau Wood, the one point of yesterday's objectives that was not fully attained by the Americans.

The American plan had not included the taking of Torcy, but the marines swept into it late in the day and drove out the Germans. At the same time they pushed their way into Bouresches.

No one who saw the marines in action yesterday and today could fail to agree thoroughly with the exclamation of their commander, himself an army man, when he said:

"I just wish I had an army corps of 'em here."

The artillery fire that preceded the first advance yesterday morning lasted an hour, and was of especial intensity for five minutes preceding the time when the marines went over the top. French and American batteries both took part in the firing, putting down a rolling barrage, and then shifting to the roads behind the German lines.

As the Allies started out, the Prussians who opposed them put up a brisk fight, for their officers were among them, urging them on. The marines dashed into them yelling like Indians and plying bayonet and rifle.

The Americans who advanced in the Belleau Wood region went forward in four waves in open formation. The men in the first wave were armed for the most part with rifles and bombs, while the rear waves were equipped with automatic rifles. With them came squads of machine gunners, lugging their collapsible guns. They crossed the open space and coiled up the slope bent over like gnomes.

The trenches that the marines passed over were clearly visible from below, but they hardly deserved the name, for they were simply lines of little holes, each big enough to hold a man, while barbed wire was lacking there. There was some, however, interlaced among the trees of Belleau Wood, but the marines pushed their way through it.

Out in the open, field artillery officers with glasses were directing the supporting fire, while on the roof of a nearby farmhouse a signal man wigwagged with his red and white flag.

On all sides the guns were flashing, some of them stationed right out in the field, while others were hidden in the woods. Looking down into the valley, only a mile away, the village of Bussaires could be seen on fire. As the correspondent watched the scene the clouds of white shrapnel smoke over the village of Torcy also became brownish and flames appeared in that town.

Following upon their early successes, which inflicted heavy losses on the Germans, a second attack began at 5 P. M. This was undertaken largely because of the splendid showing the marines had made, coupled with the discovery that the morale of the Germans was low, which made the going easier for the fiery soldiers of the Marine Corps.

Get Enemy on the Run.

The second advance was carried out by the same men who attacked in the morning, and who had had no rest. They asked nothing, however, but plenty of ammunition, and hardly ate the food that was brought up to them, so absorbed were they in the task of chasing the enemy as far as possible.

The marines in this new forward sweep took strong ground on either side of Belleau Wood and cleared out the ravine south of Torcy, which linked up the line with Hill 142, which had been taken this morning. This gave them a strong and dominating position for a continuation of their attack.

The marines reached all their objectives set for the first hour within that time limit, and pushed beyond them. Early reports indicated that the Germans were on the run for the time being and surrendering right and left to the Americans.

There was evidence, however, of coming counterattacks, for even before 5 o'clock the roads behind the German lines were filled with troops, guns, and wagons. The American artillery turned on them and created havoc.

During the night the marines reached the outskirts of Bouresches and poured volleys of machine gun fire into the enemy, inflicting terrific casualties. Bayonets were used freely against many of the Germans who attempted to make a stand in the streets.

MARINES WIN NAME OF 'DEVIL HOUNDS'

Germans Promptly Gave It to Them After the First Clash on Western Front.

HARBORD IS IN COMMAND

Temporarily at Head of the Men Who Are Winning New Fame for Their Branch of the Service.

A German writer recently termed the United States marine the greatest fighting man in the world.

"The American marine comes first," said the German; "the Canadian Northwest Police is second, and the Potsdam Guard is third."

The recent fighting in the Château-Thierry sector of the western front is taken as confirmation of the German estimate in at least one particular.

The American marine contingent on the Marne is temporarily under the command of Brig. Gen. James G. Harbord, who is General Pershing's Chief of Staff, and rose from the ranks of the American Army.

General Harbord has exercised command over the marines, it is understood, since the recent relief of Brig. Gen. Charles A. Doyen of the Marine Corps, who has been found physically disqualified for further hard work at the front. General Doyen took the marines to France, and had charge of their training work there in camp and trench. He will soon be succeeded by another prominent general officer of marines, to whom General Harbord will hand over the command of the marines.

General Harbord is a typical example of the American self-made soldier. Born in Illinois, he was graduated from the Kansas State Agricultural College in 1886 and at the age of 20 and enlisted in the army as a private in Company A of the 4th Infantry Jan. 10, 1889. He soon became Corporal, Sergeant, and Quartermaster Sergeant of that company. During the Spanish-American War he was appointed Second Lieutenant of the 5th Cavalry and later served with the 10th, 11th, and 1st Cavalry Regiments. He was a Major when the war in Europe began. He was Lieutenant Colonel when he went to France a year ago as General Pershing's Chief of Staff and has seen fine service in Cuba and the Philippines.

At Marine Headquarters in East Twenty-fourth Street it was said yesterday that no official word identifying the units who were covering themselves with glory "over there" had been transmitted from headquarters in Washington.

"Our boys are doing exactly what we knew they would do," said an enthusiastic officer at the New York headquarters yesterday, "and my only fear is that they will get too enthusiastic and run too far forward. That bunch of ours in France is the finest lot of lads that ever crossed the Atlantic. They are, every one of them, of the 'one in seven' type; that is, for every man we accepted we examined seven. We have been getting reports lately from the fellows in the trenches, and we knew that their time to get a whack at the Hun was coming, and we have been waiting for a week or ten days for the news that they were in it.

"The Huns got their first real impression of what an American marine is several weeks ago, when several companies of our men went after them with a dash and a vim that took Fritz clean off his feet. It was on that occasion that the Germans gave to the American marine his newest nickname, namely 'Teufelhund,' which is good German for 'devil hound.' In that fight we had a big percentage of casualties. Our loss in killed and wounded was over 60 per cent. of the force engaged, but the Germans never got one single marine prisoner."

In a Marine Corps bulletin issued a few days ago the "Teufelhunden" story was told for the first time.

"The German," said the bulletin, "has met and named the fighting American marine. In the past the foe who encountered the prowess of marines received a mingled impression of wildcats and human cyclones and movements as quick as lightning. When Fritz was first introduced to him he uttered one guttural gasp:

"'Teufelhunden.'

"From now on the soldiers of the sea apparently have lost their old-time name of 'Leathernecks' and are to be known as 'Devil Dogs' or 'Devil Hounds.' Take your choice.

Brigadier General James G. Harbord

In Command of Our Marines on the Marne Battlefield.

The New York Times.

VOL. LXVII...NO. 22,057. ...   NEW YORK, SATURDAY, JUNE 15, 1918.—TWENTY PAGES.   TWO CENTS In Greater New York and | THREE CENTS Within Commuting Distance. | Elsewhere.

GERMANS AGAIN BEATEN TO A STANDSTILL; OISE OFFENSIVE ENDS IN A COSTLY REVERSE; FRENCH COUNTERBLOWS TURN THE SCALE

BIG VICTORY WON BY ALLIES

Move Carefully Planned by Hindenburg Met and Completely Nullified.

HIS LAST CHANCE PASSING

Efforts to Weaken Defense to Breaking Point Foiled by American Reinforcements.

GERMAN MORALE SHAKEN

Dashing Counterattacks Bewilder Enemy as He Grasps for Success.

By WALTER DURANTY.

Copyright, 1918, by The New York Times Company.

Special Cable to THE NEW YORK TIMES.

WITH THE FRENCH ARMIES, Friday, June 14.—The fifth day of the battle marked the definite check of the German operations after gains of little importance and prodigious losses. The credit goes in no small degree to the General commanding the army that held the sector, who more that justified his already brilliant reputation.

It is now known that the big French counterattack on the left which he launched on Tuesday was a veritable stroke of genius, as an essential factor of the enemy plan was an immediate advance in that very region with the object of reaching the Aronde Valley so as to turn the French centre and undertake a converging movement upon Complègne.

The complete dislocation of the projected attack and the substantial progress of the French, despite the very heavy forces opposite to them that had been moved up in preparation for it, threw the whole German tactical scheme out of gear. Hindenburg attempted to counter—eight hours after the French advance began—by a powerful diversion between the Aisne and Villers-Cotterets Forest. Here, too, the Germans were checked by the troops in line.

In desperation, strong forces estimated at 30,000 to 40,000 men were flung yesterday against the rewon line from Courcelles to Mery. The result was literally disastrous. The French soldiers, keyed to the highest pitch by the successes of the last forty-eight hours, surpassed their former performances and refused to allow

Americans in Air Raid Beyond Metz Bomb German Towns and Railway; Fight Way Back

WITH THE AMERICAN ARMY IN FRANCE, June 14, (Associated Press.)—The first American bombing squadron to operate behind the front successfully raided the Domgoy-Baroncourt railway at a point northwest of Briey late Wednesday, dropping many bombs. It is believed that several direct hits were made by the five planes participating.

A large number of German Albatross machines attacked the bombers after they had performed their mission and were returning home. Three of the Albatrosses attempted to cut off two of the American bombers, but themselves were attacked by other American planes. The fight continued until the machines reached the battleline, when the Germans retired.

All the American aviators returned safely, though they had been heavily shelled by anti-aircraft batteries.

A second excursion of American bombing planes was made late this afternoon behind the German lines. All returned safely, notwithstanding anti-aircraft fire and after repulsing the attacks of two German airplanes. Five American machines launched seventy-nine bombs, weighing two kilos each, on the railway station and adjoining buildings at Conflans.

WASHINGTON, June 14.—Details of the American aircraft bombing expedition over the enemy lines June 13 were reported by General Pershing tonight in an addition to yesterday's communiqué. Five planes carrying out the attack dropped eighty bombs and returned safely after fighting off three German pursuit machines. The dispatch said:

Bombing expedition reported communiqué June 13 was executed by five of our planes. Eighty bombs were dropped. One was observed to strike a warehouse at the station. Poor visibility prevented effect of others being ascertained, but our aviators believe that all dropped in area where they are likely to have produced useful effect. Our planes were attacked by three German pursuit machines, but all returned safely.

Baroncourt lies about forty-six miles northeast of Verdun. It is possible that Domgoy is a mutilated spelling of Domremy, a village on the railroad near Baroncourt.

the Germans to gain a yard of ground. After eight hours' vain and costly efforts, the attack was abandoned through sheer exhaustion.

As the situation stands today, the Allies have won a great victory in one of the hardest fought battles of the war, and a carefully planned move in Hindenburg's desperate struggle against time has been met and nullified. The Germans have also learned to their cost that the American troops are already to be counted with. The enemy, whose morale is daily weakening under the strain of non-successes and never-ending calls upon his strength, has received a bitter reminder of the American menace, which more than any other factor is responsible for his convulsive striving after a speedy decision.

What will Hindenburg do? Between Noyon and Montdidier the Allies are at the acme of victorious resistance, and hill and plain and forest are carpeted with German dead. Should he once more attempt to shift the battle centre by a drive north of Amiens, he knows that nothing short of complete penetration to the seacoast will avail him now. It is more in keeping with German strategy that, the right jaw of the huge pincers that were to squeeze the allied armies having failed to act, the left will once more be set in movement and a new drive be made between the Ourcq and the Marne, in the direction of Paris.

The Germans may cherish the wild hope of discouraging the Americans by a stunning blow before they are fully accustomed to battle conditions. Certainly the shock if it comes will be very different from the comparatively minor actions in which our divisions so gallantly won their spurs, but the Americans have already shown their resistance by no less determination than the rest of the Allies. "These Americans fight like madmen. They absolutely refuse to surrender," runs a letter found on a captured soldier of the Prussian Guard. With such spirit the future can be faced in complete confidence.

Question of Time and Effectives.

The war situation today is a question of time, space, and effectives. Those are the three factors of equation on whose solution depends the fact of the world. Can the Germans reduce the allied effectives in time to strike a fatal blow before the reinforcements rushed across the Atlantic are ready to turn the scale in the Allies' favor?

Until the present week it needed robust optimism to view the future with confidence. In two great drives the enemy had taken important positions and had inflicted upon the Allies losses that—though perhaps inferior to his own—certainly did not materially reduce his balance of superiority. But the third and latest attempt has been less successful. Not only are the German gains small, but the losses are out of all proportion to those of the Allies.

The time, precious as it is to Germany, is not yet ripe for the decisive stroke that Hindenburg has just attempted to deliver. The allied effectives are still too strong, their resistance still too unflinching. And every week fresh American divisions are pouring into France by tens of thousands.

Problem Before the Enemy.

Can the enemy take the chance of further reducing the allied strength in proportion to his own by operations—hard for the Allies to meet owing to the length of their communications—outside the central battle zone—which may be said to stretch from Amiens to the Marne—from which, even if successful, no results can come that will influence the principal strategic situation? Can he prolong such attacks until the Allies are so weakened that the central "coup de grâce" may be launched with better possibilities of success than now? That is the whole problem to which the coming weeks will give the answer.

Meanwhile the gaps in the allied line are being more than filled by the soldiers of America, to whose superb spirit and physical fitness is being added the battle training they needed. What does it profit Germany if a hundred square miles of ground are won in a strategically unprofitable area? More precious time has been wasted, but the hour for a victorious decision is no nearer. And Germany cannot wait. Letters found on the dead and prisoners show that the home population, faced by three months of starvation, is unimpressed by any victories that are not the victory.

Yet if Hindenburg decides to concentrate his forces for a last despairing drive on Paris the odds are against him. The bloody check the enemy suffered in the last week has weakened his morale and steeled allied resistance. The success of the big French counterstroke points the way to similar operations on a vaster scale, in which the lack of modern war training of the Americans will be not a handicap but an advantage. War of movement requires strong, young, dashing troops, whose accuracy with the rifle is superior to their utilization of grenades. A leader of Foch's quality will not shrink from a bold course. If the enemy cares to put the matter to the supreme test, it may well happen that the American Army will be the big factor in his defeat.

Petain's Masterly Tactics.

June 13.—It has been said that the secret of Petain's rise in three years from the position of Colonel to Commander in Chief of the French armies is his knowledge of when to launch counterattacks. The ability to select the right place and time for a sudden stroke which nullifies the enemy's gains has been the attribute of great Captains throughout history, and is one of the cardinal bases of successful strategy. In that one word, counterattacks, lies the explanation of the triumphant French resistance in the present battle against vastly superior numbers—that and the indomitable courage of the defenders.

The master tactician commanding the army whose sector has been assailed has so imbued his subordinates with his own principles, that there is hardly a position in the whole range of operations that the Germans have not been forced to take two or three times over. For it is not only the counterstroke on a grand scale, like that which has won back nearly all the Germans' gains on the left wing, which counts in a struggle of this kind, where the losses inflicted on the enemy are far more important than a hill or a village saved or abandoned. It is the unexpected change from defense to attack, at the psychological moment, that has maintained the spirit of the French troops and smashed their weakened assailants just as they were thinking their success was assured.

Again and again a tiny band of defenders, holding out in a central redoubt of some unshattered house have been encouraged to supreme resistance by the thought that a counterattack may bring rescue at the eleventh hour. Again and again that counterattack has succeeded, just because the enemy was hampered by their resistance in his midst.

Entered Courcelles by a Ruse.

What happened at Courcelles is typical. The village is situated on a commanding hill. Early Sunday morning, after a short, heavy bombardment, the Germans advanced up the hillside, green with wheat, which is now shoulder high. The expanse presented a splendid "field of fire" for the defenders' machine guns; but the wily boches tied great bunches of grass around their helmets, and crawled unseen through the green cover until the village was almost within their grasp. Then a sudden rush of greatly superior numbers surprised the defending battalion and captured the position. Before they could consolidate their hold, the French countered and retook the village at 9:30 o'clock, capturing 200 men and two officers.

Twice more the enemy attacked that morning, at 10:30 o'clock and a quarter of an hour later. But now the wheat had become trampled and cut by the streams of bullets which bloodily repulsed each assault. Again at 3 o'clock came still a stronger attack.

This time the slaughter of the assailants was such that the enemy adopted new tactics, and leaving Courcelles for the moment, passed on toward Mery and Belloy, whose capture with that of Ressons enabled them to encircle Courcelles on three sides. Only westward there remained a narrow strip of communication between the garrison and their comrades. At 4:30 o'clock Monday morning the enemy attacked, after another violent preparation. The fighting was furious and prolonged, but at 5 o'clock the assailants gave way reluctantly, and it was not until an hour and a half later that the outer defenses were finally cleared.

All morning the Germans tightened their net round the beleaguered stronghold, and in the afternoon attacked three times, at 2:30 o'clock, 7:30, and 10. All attempts failed, though the last penetratd the village, but they were thrown out again by the dash of the French Grenadiers.

On Tuesday a big French counterstroke on the left developed, led by tanks. The huge machines, rolling and pitching through the sloping cornfields with groups of foot soldiers, looked for all the world like battleships in a rough sea with a flotilla of attendant destroyers. Before noon the Courcelles defenders were delivered and the enemy forced back from the ground he had paid thousands of dead to win.

It is but one such incident of many, but I have told it in detail to show just how the French are holding the road to Compiègne. The utmost efforts of the enemy have brought him along the Matz Valley to Melicocq, but he can get no further. Further east the line of resistance has been straightened by the abandonment of Carlepont Wood and Ourscamp Forest.

Back in Old Positions.

The French are back on their old positions of before the Spring of 1915, whose strength has been proved by many a bloody fray. Ourscamp is so low and swampy as to be useless for artillery positions, and even the higher ground on the right is dominated by Saint Mard Wood, which is held by the French.

The new attack on the north of Villers-Cotterets Forest meets with small success. The enemy is fighting desperately, but flesh and blood cannot stand such pressure, and there are signs of weakening. Sometimes French counterstrokes have met but feeble resistance; and, once at least, the enemy voluntarily came forward from his defenses to surrender. The German prisoners appear dispirited, and seem to be realizing that the Allies are too strong for them.

The work of our aviators has had a prodigious effect. Enemy masses are never safe from their nerve-shattering bombs. Night and day, Roye, Lassigny, Montdidier, and the roads leading from these centres to the front, are raked with aerial destruction. French battleplanes—unlike those of the enemy, who scarcely cross the line at all—harass the German infantry incessantly and break up many attacks almost before they are launched.

At one point a German battery of heavy guns was put out of action by the air-bombers—a feat hitherto unparalleled—who flew down intrepidly to drop charges right on the guns themselves.

The Germans are not yet defeated. They may advance still further if they pay the price. But the French have proved that their thunderbolt attack is not irresistible. It can be checked, and when checked—by its very nature—the losses are terrifying. The week's fighting has answered the pessimist's question, "What is to prevent the enemy from repeating these surprise attacks until he is at the gates of Paris?"

'SAYS GERMANS WANT A "STOMACH PEACE"

Artificially Prepared Foods Fail to Make Up Lack—Meatless Weeks for Bavaria.

Copyright, 1918, by The New York Times Company.
Special Cable to THE NEW YORK TIMES.

PARIS, June 14.—"The Germany which is attacking our armies with such fury," writes Pertinax in the Echo de Paris, "is a hungry Germany." In the course of a striking article Pertinax says the peace, which Germany wants before everything else, is a stomach peace. He writes:

"Within four days the German people will be reduced from 200 to 100 grams of flour per head per day (or less than six ounces.) Last Autumn, according to official statements, the German Government estimated there would be a shortage of 2,000,000 tons of flour during this period, but it was hoped to make up the difference from Rumania and the Ukraine. But Rumania has supplied 40,000 tons less within the last ten months than during eight months of last year. The Ukraine, which undertook to supply 1,000,000 tons before July 1, had, down to May 12, in spite of the price having been fixed as high as 1,000 marks a ton, supplied only 30,229 tons.

"The meat ration cannot be increased to supplement the bread shortage, as the cattle, if not diminished in number, have decreased in weight, and bones and skin form much the greater proportion of the total weight of the ration than formerly. The potato harvest has been good, but only sufficient to permit the daily ration of a pound per head per day. Efforts are being made to make up the shortage with artificially prepared foods, such as powdered milk, fruit, and eggs, which, it is claimed, give the same number of calories as bread, but are not satisfying.

"In Austria," says Pertinax, "supplies are still less abundant, and by the admission of the newspapers unequal distribution of foodstuffs is producing great bitterness and racial feeling among the various peoples who make up both empires. If the Germans suffer a military defeat," concludes Pertinax, "all these accumulated sufferings will be useful auxiliaries to the Allies."

LONDON, June 14.—It will be necessary to introduce meatless weeks in Bavaria owing to a serious shortage of food, the Munich Home Secretary has announced, according to a Copenhagen dispatch to the Exchange Telegraph Company.

According to a report from Augsburg, stocks of cattle are much depleted and there is a lack of other important provisions there.

GENEVA, June 14.—The Neueste Nachrichten of Munich, a copy of which has been received here, says that the Tyrol has begun to suffer from famine, both among the civilians and the troops. The Bavarians, therefore, have sent from their food reserves 3,500 tons of potatoes and 80 tons of sauerkraut to the sufferers.

This fact is considered in Geneva as a possible explanation of the virtual inactivity of the Austrian troops on the Italian front.

HUNGER IMPAIRING GERMAN VITALITY

Labor Department Study Shows Disastrous Blunders in Food Administration.

Special to The New York Times.

WASHINGTON, June 14.—Announcement by the Bureau of Statistics of the Department of Labor, of the results of a survey setting forth that Turkey is starving, that Germany and Austria are not starving, but are having a hard struggle to feed themselves; that Hungary is in better shape than either Germany or Austria, and that Bulgaria, so far as food is concerned, is suffering the least of all the countries covered, is based upon a long and careful investigation.

The survey shows that Germany has failed by a wide margin to live up to her reputation for efficiency in her attempts at food administration, having been obliged to reverse her policies in an effort to remedy in part the disastrous results of official blunders. It shows conclusively that the civil populations of Germany and Austria are suffering permanent physical deterioration from lack of proper food, that the death rate from tuberculosis is rapidly increasing, that growing boys and girls are not getting half the nourishment they should have, and that manual laborers are being underfed to about the same extent.

Profiteering, greed, the breakdown of transportation, and faulty organization are set forth as big factors in the food situation of Germany and her allies.

Data which the department obtained concerning the effect of the food shortage upon the public health in Germany cover the period up to the late Spring of 1917, and it is believed, from the fragmentary reports which have since been received, that the situation has gradually become more serious.

The figures obtained show that during March, April, and May, 1917, 1,606 persons in Berlin died of tuberculosis, as compared with 1,032 for the same period in the previous year; that deaths from pneumonia in Berlin for the same periods were respectively 1,000 and 622, and deaths from other diseases of the lungs, including pleurisy, 337 and 190.

Details are given to show that in 1917 children of 7 and 8 years, who required 1,700 calories daily, were provided with about 1,300, and that conditions among older persons were even worse.

Men engaged in light work who required 2,450 calories were receiving about 1,200, and those engaged in heavy work who required from 3,500 to 6,000, according to their labors, received from 1,600 to 1,950. These examples are given not as proof that Germany was starving, but as an indication of the struggle for existence.

In Vienna the figures show that deaths from tuberculosis had jumped from 7,810

in 1915 to 9,651 in 1916, and information is to the effect that conditions since have been even worse.

OISE DRIVE ENDS IN LOSS TO ENEMY

What He Has Gained in Ground More Than Offset by His Casualties.

FAILING STRENGTH SHOWN

But Ambitious Designs Aim at Nothing Less Than Destruction of Allied Armies.

By G. H. PERRIS.
Copyright, 1918, by The New York Times Company.
Special Cable to THE NEW YORK TIMES.

WITH THE FRENCH ARMIES, June 14.—The front has subsided into actions of no more than local importance. The five days' battle west of the Oise has ended for the Germans, after an advance varying from two to six miles, in a very costly reverse, and for the Allies in a brilliant success of good generalship and indomitable spirit in the ranks.

Beside the losses of the enemy, the French loss of the Thiescourt hills and the wooded part of the valley opposite is of little importance. The offensive which was to give a decision against them is far from finished, but in relation to the resistance it encounters it shows a falling, not a rising, gamut of power.

The first push toward Amiens ended in ten days, having entailed upon the Allies the sacrifice of a tract forty miles deep and serious casualties. The following attack in the north lasted about as long, but with much slighter gains. The German success on the Chemin-des-Dames brought the Crown Prince's vanguard to the Marne, twenty-five miles from its starting point, but that it touched much less vital ground is proved by the transfer of its centre of pressure to the Ourcq Valley near Villers-Cotterets.

From these results to those of the present week's fighting there is a marked descent, and this failure occurs in what must be accounted one of the most critical directions the enemy can pursue. The ambitious character of his design is now clear. It is not merely to divide the British from the French army and then destroy one of them, but also by a single series of converging operations to destroy them both.

"All the News That's Fit to Print."

The New York Times.

THE WEATHER
Fair and warmer today; Tuesday, continued warmer; southwest winds
For full weather report see Page 21.

VOL. LXVII...NO. 22,059 .....   NEW YORK, MONDAY, JUNE 17, 1918.—TWENTY-TWO PAGES.   TWO CENTS In Greater New York and | THREE CENTS Within Commuting Distance. | Elsewhere.

AUSTRIANS CROSS THE PIAVE AT TWO POINTS; CLAIM 16,000 PRISONERS, BUT ALLIES GET 3,000; AMERICANS DEFEAT THE GERMANS WITH GAS

ITALIAN ARMY STRIKES BACK

Checks Massed Attacks by Austrians by Strong Counterattacks.

RECOVERS TWO MOUNTAINS

Enemy Detachments That Succeeded in Crossing Piave River Are Being Pressed Hard.

VIENNA CLAIMS WIDE GAINS

British Eject Invaders from Positions They Stormed at Beginning of the Drive.

ROME, June 16.—A battle of great violence, in which large masses of infantry are being used by the Austrians in an attempt to break through the Italian lines, particularly in the eastern sector of the Asiago Plateau, in the Brenta Valley, and on Monte Grappa, and during which they succeeded in crossing the Piave River at two places, is described in the official report from Italian Headquarters today.

Unofficial advices from the front say the objective of the drive across the Piave was Treviso, but that the enemy was pressed back.

The enemy's attacks in the mountains, which were met in the advanced defensive area, at first carried some of the Italian positions there, but later the line was re-established at most points.

The Italian forces are firmly holding the Asiago front. The War Office announcement says they have completely reoccupied their original positions on Asolone and Monte Solarola and are closely pressing he enemy who crossed the Piave.

During their wide offensive the Austrians, after a violent bombardment, attacked the French positions, (between Osteria di Monfenera and Maranzine,) but the very efficacious fire of the French broke down the thrusts. The enemy casualties were heavy, and in addition he left numerous prisoners in the hands of the French.

The battle is in progress along the whole of the front.

Official Version of the Battle.

The text of the official statement reads:

A great battle has been in progress on our front since yesterday.

After artillery preparation, which was exceptionally intense on account of the violence of the fire and the number of guns employed, the enemy has begun his expected offensive by launching large masses of infantry to attack our positions in the eastern sector of Asiago Plateau, at the end of the Brenta Valley and on Monte Grappa, by attempting at several points to force the Piave, and by carrying out heavy local demonstrative action on the remainder of the front.

Our infantry and that of the allied contingents fearlessly bore the tempest of the destructive fire, and, supported by a barrage of their own artillery, which had already prudently anticipated the enemy's preparation with a timely and deadly counter-preparation bombardment, bravely sustained the enemy's onslaught in the advanced defensive area.

On the 150-kilometre front more intensely attacked the powerful storming columns of the enemy occupied in their initial rush forward only a few front line positions in the Monte Di Val Bella region, in the Asolone area, and at the head of the Monte Solarola salient.

Some troops succeeded in passing to the right bank of the Piave River in the Nervesa area and in the Fagare-Musile region.

During the day our troops initiated along all the front, attacked energetic counterattacks, which succeeded in holding back the powerful pressure of the enemy and in regaining a good portion of the positions temporarily yielded, on some of which, however, isolated detachments had with great valor continued to remain at all costs.

The struggle did not diminish in violence during the night, and is continuing fiercely. But our troops are firmly holding the front along the Asiago Plateau, have completely reoccupied their original positions on Asolone and at the Monte Solarola salient, and are very closely pressing the enemy infantry which has passed to the right bank of the Piave.

The number of prisoners so far counted is more than 3,000, including 89 officers.

Our own and the allied airmen are taking a strong part in the battle by bombarding the crossing points on the Piave and by attacking the enemy's massed troops with machine gun fire. Thirty-one enemy airplanes have been brought down.

British Retake Lost Positions.

LONDON, June 16.—The Austrian troops who penetrated the line held by the British on the Italian front have been driven back and the British line has been completely re-established.

This announcement is made tonight in the official statement issued by the War Office on the operations in Italy, the text of which follows:

The pocket in the British front, mentioned in the communiqué of last night, has been cleared of the enemy during the night and the early hours this morning and we are now again established on our original front line. (Four Austrian divisions attacked the British line on Saturday, and on the left penetrated the front to a depth of a thousand yards along an extent of 2,500 yards. There the enemy was held.)

Over 350 prisoners have been counted and we have, in addition, captured two mountain guns and a considerable number of machine guns.

In the early hours of yesterday, when the hostile attack was first launched, invaluable assistance both in infantry and artillery was immediately provided by the Italians on our left, and this assistance was largely responsible for bringing the Austrian infiltration to an immediate halt.

Heavy fighting is continuing in many places along the Piave, on the eastern end of Montebello Heights, and astride the Brenta Valley.

Three additional enemy airplanes were destroyed in air fighting yesterday, seven having previously been reported. The clouds remained low and distant reconnoissances were impossible. The energy of our air service has been mainly confined to attacks on bridges for troops, which the enemy was attempting to throw across the Piave. In these attacks the aviators have been very successful.

CLAIM 16,000 PRISONERS.

Austrians Admit All Gains in the Mountains Were Not Held.

LONDON, June 16, (British Admiralty, per Wireless Press.) — The Austrian official communication received here by wireless tonight says:

Yesterday morning our armies, after artillery fire lasting several hours,

Scene of the Great Drive in Italy

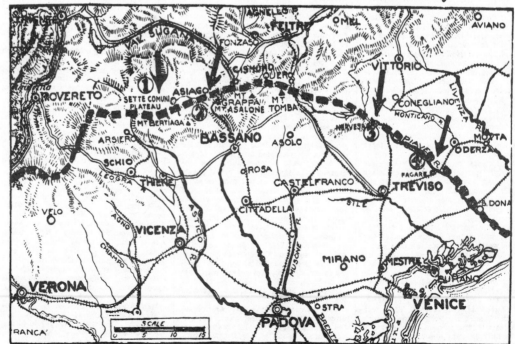

While the Austrian attack extends all along the front, indicated on the map by the broken black line, their principal efforts in the mountains were directed at the Sette Comuni plateau, (1,) and eastern end of the Brenta, from the river to the regions of Monte Asolone and Monte Grappa, (2.) On both of these sectors the attack at first made some progress, but by fierce counterattacks the line was re-established. Along the Piave River the Austrians succeeded in crossing in the vicinity of Nervesa, (3,) and in the Fagara-Musile area, (4,) but the detachments which reached the west bank are being closely pressed, according to the Italian official report.

attacked the Italians and their allies on the Piave and on both sides of the Brenta.

The army group of Field Marshal von Borevic forced crossings at numerous points over the high-flowing Piave. General Wurms's corps, after overcoming a desperate defense near Sandona, took an enemy position on the Piave and on both sides of the Oderzo-Treviso railway on a broad front.

Archduke Joseph's troops by a strong surprise attack took possession of the defensive works on the eastern edge of Montello and penetrated into the highroad.

Cavalry General Prince of Schoenburg was wounded by a shell during the passage of his corps.

The number of prisoners captured on the Piave amounts to 10,000. About fifty guns are reported to have been captured up to the present.

Even the first assault on both sides of the Brenta was successful in breaking down the strong enemy resistance and overcoming all the obstacles of the serrated and wooded mountains. Our troops pressed forward at many points as far as the third enemy positions, as a result of which 6,000 Italians, French, and English fell into their hands and were made prisoners.

The advantages thus gained, we were only able to maintain partially.

East of the Brenta River, Rabero Mountain had to be given up in the face of superior enemy counterattacks, which were supported by a flanking gunfire. On the western slopes of Monte Grappa the Italians stormed in vain our battalions which had firmly established themselves in his front line.

In the wooded zone of the seven communes (Sette Comuni) our regiments encountered an attacking group which had been prepared during previous days and before whose counterthrust a portion of the captured territory was evacuated.

Near Riva, on the sector of Major Duke Maximilian, we wrested from the Italians the Dossa Alto and Adamello regions. Trusted mountain troops stormed Dorno di Cavento, during which 100 prisoners and three enemy guns were brought in.

VIENNA, June 16, (via London.)— Ten thousand Italian, English, and French prisoners have been taken by the Austrians in their great offensive, according to the official communication from headquarters today. The Piave River has been crossed. The statement reads:

Our armies this morning broke into the enemy lines on the plateau of the Seven Communes (Sette Communi) and also crossed the Piave.

Up to midday reports have arrived reporting the capture of over 10,000 Italians, English, and French. The capture in guns is considerable.

"HOLD AT ANY COST," ORDER TO ITALY'S ARMY

Austrians Thought to be Striking for Plains Through the Trentino District.

ITALIAN HEADQUARTERS IN NORTHERN ITALY, June 16, (Associated Press.)—In their attempt to cross the Piave in great force Saturday the Austrians had the City of Treviso as their objective. In getting across the river they paid a tremendous sacrifice before the machine gun fire of the Italian defenders of the western bank. Counterattacks by Italian infantry and heavy Italian artillery fire forced the enemy to retire from most of his gains along the Piave.

An order found in the pockets of prisoners was to the effect that the Austrians were to be at Preganziol, south of Treviso, on Saturday night.

"Hold at any cost" was the word that has been passed to the Italian

troops as the Austrian offensive developed yesterday all along the line of 117 miles with the use of gas and special liquid bombs and every other means of attack to weaken the defenses.

The long comparative silence by the Austrians was broken precisely at 8:05 o'clock in the morning by a violent cannonade, the sounds of which reached the cities of Verona, Vincenza, and Venice, all long distances from the front.

While the exact geographic objectives of the Austrians as yet are conjectural, it seems evident that their earliest attack was heaviest against the positions in the Upper Brenta River Valley, in the Val Sugana region, where the Brenta flows toward Bassano. It is considered possible that Austria is following Field Marshal Conrad von Hötzendorf's old plan of striking at the Italian plains through the Trentino district, of which the first classic move consists in obtaining possession of Val Stagna, Monte Tomba, and Monte Grappa, then following the Brenta River to the plains, and then attacking with three columns westerly along the valleys of the rivers Adige and Astico and also on the Asiago Plateau.

Summing up the situation, it seems to be a renewal of the great battle for Italy's Alps, which was left off last November, with the keys to the mightiest fortresses of Europe held by the Italians, who have spent the entire Winter fortifying with extraordinary care Val Stagna, Monte Grappa, Monte Tomba, and other positions.

The Austrian offensive is particularly vigorous on the sixty-five-mile front from Val Stagna to the sea, with the greatest pressure on the Asiago Plateau, Monte Grappa, and along the Piave River. At many points the Italians forestalled the offensive. Nowhere has there been any surprise of the Italians by the enemy. Deserters and prisoners captured during the last few days all possessed information that the offensive was set for Saturday.

Three Austrian airplanes were brought down over the Piave yesterday by one Italian flier.

LONDON, June 16.—The opening of the latest Austrian offensive in Italy is described by Reuter's correspondent with the British army in Italy. The correspondent's dispatch, dated Saturday afternoon, reads:

The Austrians opened a heavy bombardment at 3 o'clock this morning and attacked the British positions on the Asiago Plateau at 7:30 with a division composed of Austro-Germans and Bosnian troops. The enemy objective, apparently, was to reach eventually a line of hills about the plateau and Cima di Fonte, some four kilometers behind our front. The enemy reached our front lines, but made very little progress. They were repulsed on the right completely, but gained a few hundred yards near the left of our centre.

"Our line, following a shell-like depression in which is the town of Asiago, is irregular in outline and thickly wooded in places. Flat as it looks from our positions, the country is full of hidden folds in the ground and lends itself rather easily to attack by small, isolated detachments. The morning of the attack was more than usually misty, and the bulk of the enemy troops approached along the line of a railway running from Asiago to the little village of Cesuna, which follows a marked depression in the ground.

"In accordance with recent German methods, the attacking troops were rushed up during the night from Val Sugana by motor transport. Heavy as was the preliminary bombardment, gas shells were only sparingly used against our troops. The attack on the British formed only a part of the Austrian plan."

ITALIAN DEPUTIES JOYFUL.

ROME, June 16.—There were scenes of great enthusiasm in the Chamber of Deputies today when the Minister of War, General Zupelli, announced the success of the Italian troops and the repulse of the enemy, despite his numerical superiority, on the greater part of

the front. The whole House rose and applauded.

The War Minister said that the capture of 5,000 prisoners was proof that the Italian troops were truly heroic.

OUR MEN WIN A GAS DUEL

Catch German Reserves with 7,000 Gas Shells After 48-Hour Attack

ON CHATEAU-THIERRY FRONT

Heavy Casualties in Kaiser's Favorite Divisions — Belleau Wood Attack Also Defeated.

TWO OTHER ATTACKS FAIL

One at Xivray and the Other in the New Alsatian Sector Beaten Off.

By EDWIN L. JAMES.
Copyright, 1918, by The New York Times Company.
Special Cable to THE NEW YORK TIMES.

WITH THE AMERICAN ARMY ON THE MARNE, June 16, 4 P. M.— After forty-eight hours of continuous gassing of the American troops, northwest of Château-Thierry, the Germans today called off the attack. They called it off because the Americans had repaid them in their own coin.

On Friday the Germans started heavy gas shelling of our entire sector, and they kept it up all day Saturday. Yesterday the American artillery began to carry out the contemplated retaliation. One thousand gas shells were put down on the German lines, running from Bussiares to Belleau yesterday afternoon. Last night 5,000 gas shells from 75-calibre guns were hurled at the German positions in front of Bouresches and toward Château-Thierry, and this morning 1,000 heavy calibre lethal gas shells were put down on German reserve units in the vicinity of Epaux-Bezu.

Soon after this the German gas shelling stopped and there has been none since up to the time this was written. This experience shows that one way to meet gas attacks is with more gas.

We have evidence that the Germans believed the Americans were not equipped to fire gas shells, and therefore unable to retaliate in kind. They received a lesson they will not soon forget.

Our gas caught his reserves in a valley, which is an excellent place for shelling, and evidence is not lack-

ing that we inflicted very heavy casualties, especially upon the Kaiser's favorite division, the well-known Twenty-eighth.

When America gets to producing gas shells in the quantity the army hopes she will our soldiers intend to give the enemy a large does of his own grim war weapon.

While the Germans have thus far always had the start in the gas warfare, Americans hope for the day when things will be the other way. Should a German clamor for mercy arise, the American gunners will remember some of their comrades who were gassed northwest of Château-Thierry.

Early this morning the Germans launched a strong attack on our positions at the northern end of the Bois de Belleau, and were repulsed with extra heavy losses.

The 1,500 assailants could not get within 500 yards of our positions.

The night was very dark, but by the light of flares after the attack the Americans could see the Germans dragging off their dead.

When daylight came many German bodies were still lying in the field across which the attack was made. Thirty-five were counted in one group.

ALLIED AIRMEN FLY FAR.

GENEVA, June 16.—Allied aviators at the end of last week performed two long distance flying feats on which they averaged 350 miles in an average of four hours' elapsed time, according to a telegram from Milan to the Chronique Italienne of Geneva.

From a base south of Idnice, Italy, a party of aviators went over the Tyrolese Alps to Innsbruck and then to Friedrichshafen, where photographs were taken, showing that new airplane factories are being constructed there. The aviators did not drop any bombs.

OUR AMBULANCES ARRIVE.

ROME, June 16.—Colonel Parsons and other American officials who arrived in Rome with ambulances for the American Army were presented by Ambassador Page to General Giuseppe Zupelli, Minister of War.

The Minister congratulated the Americans on their arrival, which he said was timely owing to the commencement of the Austrian offensive.

ITALIAN MONUMENTS HIT.

The Italian Bureau of Information in New York made public yesterday a dispatch from Rome stating that the Giornale d'Italia had compiled from official data a list of Italian edifices and architectural monuments which had been damaged or destroyed by Austrian aerial bombardment. Many of the acts of vandalism against the ancient churches and palaces of Venice and other Italian towns have apparently been intentional, as the same churches have been singled out time after time as targets for Austrian bombs.

The most important items in the list are as follows:

In 1915 the Church of San Ciriaco at Ancona, the castle and palace Albérotanza at Bari, the castle at Barletta, and the Church of the Scalzi at Venice.

In 1916 the churches of San Apollinare Nuovo at Ravenna, Santa Maria Formosa, San Pietro in Castello, Santi Giovanni e Paolo in Venice, the Abazia at Chiaravalle, and the Church of Santa Corona in Vincenza.

In 1917 the Basilica and Museum at Aquileja, the Episcopio at Udine, the Villa Soderini at Nervesa, and the Tempio Canoviano at Possagno.

In 1918 the Museum and Library at Bassano, as in the Tempio Canoviano at Possagno, the Palazzo Provinciale, and the hospital and the Church of San Nicolo at Treviso.

"All the News That's
Fit to Print."

The New York Times.

THE WEATHER
Showers today; Sunday probably
fair; moderate winds, mostly west.
For full weather report see Page 17.

VOL. LXVII...NO. 22,078.   ...   NEW YORK, SATURDAY, JULY 6, 1918.—EIGHTEEN PAGES.   TWO CENTS in Greater New York and | THREE CENTS

CRYING 'LUSITANIA!' OUR MEN VICTORIOUSLY RUSH ON HAMEL; U. S. TRANSPORT COVINGTON SUNK; SIX OF THE CREW LOST; LLOYD GEORGE OFFERS PEACE TO GERMANY ON WILSON'S TERMS

'LUSITANIA' OUR BATTLE CRY

Americans with Anzacs Went Into Hamel Fight Seeking Vengeance.

NO TENDERNESS TO FOE

One Boy Corporal Slew Seven Germans, Although Thrice Wounded Himself.

ALLIES PRAISE OUR MEN

Some Had Never Been at the Front Nor Seen the Shellfire of Battle.

By PHILIP GIBBS.

Copyright, 1918, by The New York Times Company.
Special Cable to THE NEW YORK TIMES.

WAR CORRESPONDENTS' HEADQUARTERS IN FRANCE, July 5.—After the Australian attack south of the Somme yesterday morning, the enemy, whose guns had been almost silenced during the battle by the intense counter-battery work, shelled some of the new allied positions rather heavily, and in the evening made three counterattacks. These seem to have been directed on the wings and centre of the Australian line, but were feeble and unsuccessful.

Groups of German machine gunners and infantry established themselves within fifty yards of the Australians, who were annoyed by this close approach and decided not to tolerate it. So last night a number of them went out, drove in the German outposts, and brought back another batch of prisoners to the number of something over fifty.

I was unable to mention yesterday one of the most interesting features of this action, and that was the share taken in the fighting by American troops. There were not many of them, compared with the strength of the Australian brigades, but these few companies were eager to go forward to meet the enemy face to face for the first time and prove their fighting quality. They have proved it up to the hilt of that sword, which is in their temper and spirit.

Australian officers with whom I spoke yesterday and today all told me the Americans attacked with astonishing ardor, discipline, and courage. If they had any fault at all, it was over-eagerness to advance, so that they could hardly be restrained from going too rapidly behind the wide belt of the British shellfire as the barrage rolled forward.

Our First Fight on British Front.

It was a historic day for them and for the British. It was the Fourth of July, the day of American independence, when, as I described yesterday, many French villages quite close to the fighting lines were all fluttering with the Tricolor and the Stars and Stripes in honor of their comradeship in arms and symbolizing the hope of peace in the united strength of the armies that now defend her soil.

And it was the first time the American soldiers had fought on the British front. They understood that on their few companies fighting as platoons among the Australians, rested the honor of the United States in this adventure. Their General and his officers addressed them before the battle and called on them to make good.

"You are going in with the Australians" they said, "and those lads always deliver the goods. We expect you to do the same. We shall be very disappointed if you do not fulfill the hopes and belief we have in you."

The American boys listened to these words with a light in their eyes. They were ready to take all the risks to prove their mettle. They were sure of themselves, and were tuned up to a high pitch of nervous intensity at the thought of going into battle for the first time and on the Fourth of July.

Thousands More Wanted to Go.

There were thousands of other American soldiers desperately eager to go with them, though a battle is not a pleasant pastime, but all their training, all their purpose in this war, and their pride in their own regiments lead up to the fighting line, and they wanted to pass the test of it and measure their spirit against its terrors and dangers. In the hearts of these men, new to war, the adventure of battle is greater than its chance of pain or death, and there is the call of the hunter's instinct in them, so they went gladly, strange as it may seem to people who, after four years of war, look only on the tragic side of it.

The Australians had many requests from American companies who were not allowed to share in the battle. "Can't we lend you a hand?" they asked. "Can't we be of any use to you?"

In one case outside of the order of battle their offer was accepted. The Australians took so many prisoners that they found it difficult for the moment to provide a proper escort for them from the forward to the back inclosure.

"Some of your lads might help us to conduct prisoners," said an Australian officer in charge of this work.

They did help. No German prisoners had such a strong and proud escort as that provided by the Americans who had not the luck, as they thought it, to take part in the actual fighting with their comrades who had gone forward with the Australian infantry and the tanks into the smoke clouds and the light of shellfire.

Engulfed in Battle's Roar.

Up there these lads from America were engulfed in the frightful excitement of battle, and found it an easier and less fearful thing than they had thought, because of the utter surprise of the enemy, and the silencing of his guns. More formidable to them was the intensity of the British gunfire which swept the ground in front of them and close to them with a backward blast of shell splinters and an informal tumult of drumfire. They could not tell at first whether it was the British barrage or the enemy's. They seemed to be in the centre of its fury and were surprised to find themselves alive, still moving forward with their comrades and with the dark line of Australians on either side of them.

"The barrage passed like a storm," said an Australian officer, "leaving behind perfect peace." And it was in this peace of the battlefield like the peace of death that the Americans and Australians met groups of men who were the enemy, strange, uncanny creatures, many of them in gas masks and with hands up in submission, knowing that surrender was their only chance of life. Those who showed any fight, like some who used their machine guns to the last, had hardly a thread of a chance.

The Americans were not tenderhearted in that eighty minutes of the advance to the ultimate objective with any of the enemy who tried to bar their way. They went forward with fixed bayonets, shouting the word "Lusitania" as a battlecry.

Again and again the Australians heard that word on American lips, as if there was something in the sound of it strengthening to their souls and terrifying to the enemy. They might well have been terrified—any German who heard that name, for to the American soldiers it is a call for vengeance.

It is a curious fact that with less provocation than the French, who see their own towns destroyed before their eyes and a great belt of ruin across their country and a world of tragedy where their own families are separated from them by the German lines, the American soldiers have come over here with such a stern spirit and with no kind of forgiveness in their hearts for the men who caused all this misery.

Today the young American soldiers who come out of battle wounded tell their experiences, and through them all is the conviction that the Germans are "bad men," and that death is a just punishment for all that they have done.

A Corporal's Story of Combat.

One young Corporal with a most boyish look described in a simple way how before the battle he was placed in charge of twenty-four of his comrades because he had worked hard and done his best to become a good soldier, and how then they had gathered together the night before going into the line and had resolved to inflict as much loss upon the enemy as they could because that was their duty.

Not knowing that they would ever meet again in this life, they then shook hands with each other and the young Corporal placed himself at the head of the platoon and went with them up to the support line and afterward to the front line.

None of them had seen the front-line trench before, as their regiment had come to France only a few weeks ago, and for the first time they saw shellfire, and then, two minutes before the attack, a barrage. It astounded them so that they held their breath, but they kept their nerve.

Germany Can Have Peace on Terms Wilson Stated, Lloyd George Tells American Troops at Front

WITH THE AMERICAN ARMY IN FRANCE, July 5 (Associated Press).—Addressing American troops, after a review, Premier Lloyd George of Great Britain today said:

"Germany can have peace tomorrow with the United States, France, and Great Britain if she will accept the conditions voiced yesterday by President Wilson."

The Prime Minister paid high tribute to the Americans who fought at Chateau-Thierry, saying that they had shown the Kaiser that he had made another mistake in believing that the new American troops were not capable of meeting the trained Germans.

He then sketched the illusions of the German ruler regarding the United States getting into the war and her participation in the war, adding:

"Now that one million Americans have arrived, the Kaiser is beginning to realize that defeat, certain and inevitable, is staring him in the face."

" It was a real Fourth of July celebration," said one boy.

The line of country in front of them to Hamel Village and the trench system beyond was over a little ridge and then into a valley, and then over another small ridge of ground. In the valley they were held up for a few minutes by some barbed wire and machine gun fire, but got forward and did not meet much trouble in Hamel.

It was beyond that in the trench system that the Germans fought hard, though some surrendered without fighting. Two of them ran forward, shouting " Kamerad " to the young American Corporal, who did not understand their meaning and would have killed them but for an officer, who told him not to.

Then a little later he was wounded by a bullet, and as he stumbled to his knees two Germans ran at him with bayonets. He had his finger on the trigger of his rifle, and shot one dead as he came forward. But the other drew near with bayonet lowered.

" Then," said this Corporal, who is not more than a boy in looks, " I knew I had to get up and fight him like a man."

He stood up in spite of his wound, and with his fixed bayonet turned aside a lunge which the German made to kill him, and then swung up his rifle and cracked the man's skull.

One Boy Killed Seven Germans.

Another American Corporal, 21 years of age, was wounded three times, but killed seven Germans, which, as he reckons, is two boches for each wound and one over. He had an astonishing series of episodes in which it was his life or the enemy's. After going through the enemy's wire near Vair Wood, he found himself under fire from a machine gun hidden in a wheat field, and was wounded badly in the thigh with an armor-piercing bullet designed for tanks.

He fell at once, but staggering up again threw a bomb at the German gun crew and killed four of them. One ran and disappeared into a dugout. The American Corporal followed him down and the man turned to leap at him in the darkness, but he killed him with his bayonet.

He went up from the dugout again to the light of day above, and a German soldier wounded him again, but he paid a price for the blow with his own life.

Another German attacked him, wounded him for a third time, and was killed by this lad whose bayonet was so quick.

That made six Germans, and the seventh was a machine gunner whom he shot. By this time the American Corporal was weak and bleeding from his wounds, and while he lay, unable to go further, he hoisted a rag onto his rifle as a signal to the stretcher-bearers, who came and carried him back.

The American companies had very light casualties and are satisfied. They accounted for many of the enemy. They are glad of that in a simple, serious way, and the spirit shown by those American soldiers in action on the British front for the first time seems to me, in spite of their youth, like that of Cromwell's Ironsides, stern and terrible to the enemy, who to them is the enemy of God and mankind.

Didn't Believe Americans Were There.

Before this war is over the German soldiers will come to know and fear that spirit, which is a new revelation on this western front, for our men and the French, fierce as they are in attack, are different in temperament and are inspired by different psychological causes.

As yet the Germans do not know much about the army that is growing in might against them. The prisoners I saw today under guard by Australians had no idea how many American soldiers are in France, and were astonished to meet some of them in this last battle. They believe we exaggerate the numbers grotesquely in order to scare them, and have been utterly deceived by their rulers.

These Germans now in our hands after the brilliant attack by the Australians with these American companies impressed me certainly as being among the best in quality of any men I have yet seen taken on this front. Rhinelanders, Brandenburgers, and Westphalians, they were tall men in the prime of young manhood, and obviously well nourished.

They said themselves to our officers that, though their rations had deteriorated since the early days of the war, and one man spoke with the authority of four years of service, they were not at all bad, as whatever happens about food in Germany the soldiers are provided first with enough to keep up their strength.

They were tired and spent after their battle and lay about on the grass sleeping in every attitude of extreme weariness; but their discipline was still so good, even on our side of the lines, that when an American Sergeant gave an order in their own tongue—he knows it perfectly, having been a student for four years at Carlottenburg—the Feldwebel, or German Sergeant Major, sprang up at attention as though a bell had rung in his ears, and the other men rapidly obeyed the command to fetch their rations.

200 GERMAN PLANES SENT TO OUR FRONT

But Our Air Fighters Face Them Boldly in the Chateau-Thierry Sector.

IN TWO COMBATS YESTERDAY

Four Defeat 8 of Foe—Eight Defeat 15 Others — Two Enemy Machines Downed.

By EDWIN L. JAMES.
Copyright, 1918, by The New York Times Company.
Special Cable to THE NEW YORK TIMES.

WITH THE AMERICAN ARMY ON THE MARNE, July 5.—There are as yet no indications of a new German attack on the American lines northwest of Château-Thierry, but since the American aviators appeared on this sector German pursuit machines have been brought in opposite them in considerable number.

I learn that the enemy now has something more than 200 fighting airplanes on the front opposite the Americans.

Before the arrival of our airmen German observation machines sometimes made a hundred flights daily over this sector, going as far as twenty miles behind the lines.

Since Monday this has all been changed, and the enemy machines, both observation and pursuit, are challenged as they reach the line, and in many cases are met before they arrive there.

Despite the expectations that the Germans might be active on the night of July 4, the only infantry activity on the American front last night was patrolling by our soldiers, who brought in two prisoners.

There was an intermittent exchange of artillery fire, but this was in no wise equal to that of the two preceding nights.

Two German Planes Downed.

WITH THE AMERICAN ARMY IN FRANCE, July 5, (Associated Press.)—Two sharp air combats took place between American and German airmen over the front northwest of Château-Thierry today, and two of the German airplanes were brought down.

Lieutenants Carlisle Rhodes of Terre Haute, S. P. Thompson of Honeoye Falls, N. Y.; Waldo N. Heinrichs of Granville, Ohio, and John Mitchell of Manchester, Mass., engaged in a thrilling battle this morning. One German machine was downed during the combat. It is believed that Lieutenant Heinrichs was the American who sent the enemy airplane to earth.

The four Americans were patrolling five or six kilometers inside the German lines when they encountered six enemy machines. The battle began at an altitude of 4,200 meters, and continued twenty minutes, until the machines had dropped down to 2,200 meters from the earth.

An hour later eight American machines engaged in a battle with fifteen enemy airplanes at a height of 4,700 meters. The combat swayed backward and forward over the German and American lines near Château-Thierry. The German machines were higher than the Americans, but the latter manoeuvred their airplanes admirably.

Suddenly one of the enemy airplanes dived toward the earth and went spinning downward, being chased down by Lieutenants Ralph A. O'Neill of Nogales, Ariz., and J. C. Raible of New York. It is believed that the German airplane was out of control during its plunge.

Another Division Now Faces Us.

In a small patrol encounter last night two Germans were captured and another of the enemy was killed by an American detachment.

This skirmish developed the fact that another new German division is now opposing the Americans in this sector.

This uniquely camouflaged German flighter plane was shot down during a raid on the Marne area of France.

"All the News That's Fit to Print."

The New York Times.

THE WEATHER
Fair today and tomorrow; gentle northwest to north winds.
*For fuji weather report see Page 20.

VOL. LXVII...NO. 22,081. ... NEW YORK, TUESDAY, JULY 9, 1918.—TWENTY-FOUR PAGES. TWO CENTS In Greater New York and | TImee Cwee

GERMANS POISED FOR BLOW AT ALLIES; FRENCH GAIN SOUTH OF AISNE, CAPTURE 347; MOSCOW RISING IS CRUSHED WITH HEAVY LOSS

NEW OFFENSIVE IS NEAR

Abbeville and Chalons, It Is Expected, Will Be Foe's Objectives.

DRIVE ON PARIS TO FOLLOW

660,000 Shock Troops Are Rejuvenated and Ready for Another Blow.

BUT ALLIES REMAIN CALM

Morale of Kaiser's Troops, Already Low, Has Been Shaken by Our Successes.

By EDWIN L. JAMES.

Copyright, 1918, by The New York Times Company.
Special Cable to THE NEW YORK TIMES.

WITH THE AMERICAN ARMY IN FRANCE, July 8.—The next German offensive is at hand. It is now a matter of a few days, or perhaps hours.

The German High Command apparently has the stage set in two places—for a drive against the British, with Abbéville as the grand objective, and for an attack in Champagne, with Chalons as the objective. They may make a stroke at both places at about the same time.

Somewhere back of the German lines are forty-four divisions (660,000 men) of the Kaiser's best troops, his army of manoeuvre, which he uses to make his drives. This highly mobile and well-trained hammer force is now rejuvenated from the effects of the Aisne attacks and ready for another effort.

It takes about forty days for the German High Command to prepare for a drive like that on the Somme. The Kaiser's storm troops who took part in this offensive, beginning on March 21, were withdrawn in detachments, beginning April 17.

The next drive, that on the Aisne, began on May 27, or just forty days afterward. The troops that pushed the advance as far as Château-Thierry were withdrawn, beginning June 6. Counting forty days from June 6 would give July 16. But the effort made on the Aisne was not so great as that on the Somme, and not so many shock troops were used, only three-fourths, it is estimated.

How Time Periods Work Out.

This might mean that a period of thirty days would be required to get ready, which would make the date July 6. If it took thirty-five days, this would mean July 11, or if it took the full forty days, it would mean July 16.

To understand how the Kaiser's army of manoeuvre works, it must be understood that in the German offensives not all the shock troops enter the battle at the outset. One wave which starts is replaced by a second, and so on. Therefore it is not necessary for all forty-four divisions to have completed their forty days' preparation when the drive begins. In the Aisne battle troops came into the line on the fifth day which were known to be in the training area on the first day of the assault on the Chemin des Dames.

These forty-four divisions of the army of manoeuvre are trained a considerable distance back of the line and rushed where the attack is to be made at the last moment after the stage is all set. That is why it is so difficult for the allied command to prevent German gains in the first few days. Many points must be protected, but the enemy makes his assault at one or at most two points. His supply of shock troops is drawn, as needed, on a scientific schedule, from the training area where the advance has been rehearsed.

Great Issues at Stake.

While it is true that the Germans have been good at beating the best allied forecasts, there is little sign of an attack now on the front between Montdidier and Château-Thierry. Beyond a doubt the greatest result for the Kaiser would be to reach Abbéville and cut the British Army off from the French, or to force the British lines to fall back on the Somme and give up the Channel ports. It is also true beyond any doubt that the cost of such an effort would be terrific for the Germans.

Perhaps the next best prize, always omitting Paris, would be Chalons. An offensive in Champagne, reaching Chalons, might force the Allies to fall back to a line from Château-Thierry through Chalons to St. Mihiel. This would give the enemy a new line of railroad communication from Metz through Chalons to Château-Thierry and greatly strengthen this portion of his front. Either of these drives would be easier than a drive at Paris.

It is not to be supposed that the offensive now about to begin will be the Germans' supreme effort. Evidence is not lacking that the German High Command plans a supreme attempt to seize Paris in August. The drive at Chalons or Abbéville, or both, would be for the purpose of obtaining a better position for the August effort. With the British cut off at Abbéville or forced back on the Somme, or with Germans in possession of Chalons, the enemy would be in much stronger position for a stroke at Paris than at the present time, when they hesitate to deepen their salient between Montdidier and Château-Thierry.

Our Successes Among the Enemy.

It would be giving the Germans valuable information to say where they would encounter the Americans. The enemy knows they stand between him and Paris. He has learned that by costly experience.

In considering the German efforts, it must be borne in mind that the American successes northwest of Château-Thierry is a very sore subject for the German High Command. The German people are learning what the Americans have done there, and the knowledge of what we did has also had a bad effect on the morale of the German Army.

Will the Kaiser decide to hurl enough soldiers against the Americans to drive them back, which he can, undoubtedly, if he pays the price?

Will he attempt to show the German people that the Americans are not better than his best German soldiers, when he really means business?

There is nothing more than a moral victory to be gained at this time by a German attack upon our troops northwest of Château-Thierry. A glance at the map shows that the enemy cannot make much of an advance in that region unless on a front much wider than that held by the Americans. To do this would put the Germans in a corner between the Marne and the Ourcq. The Kaiser knows now that to attempt this enterprise would cost him dear.

Holding Troops in Low Spirits.

There is no denying that the morale of the Kaiser's crack troops is good, but it is gratifying to know that he is having trouble in keeping up the morale of the troops which are not used for attack. These form 65 per cent. of the German Army.

An order recently issued by General Ludendorff calls on the officers to stop desertions and calls on the men to stop giving information when captured. Ludendorff says that German desertions are increasing.

The German soldiers, with the emphatic exception of the Prussians, are tiring of the war. Here is an extract from a letter written to his sisters by a German soldier three days ago:

" Here all sorts of things are happening. You cannot imagine them. Of my squad I am the only one left. The others are all dead or wounded, and believe me, my dears, I wish all this nonsense would soon come to an end, for we all have a noseful."

Here is an extract from another letter from a German on the front facing the Americans:

" There is no thought of leave, because we have had such great losses. Half my company has been put out of action because we are now in a very bad position. If this misery would only end."

This is from a third letter, dated June 30:

" Here there is a terrible mixup because we have Americans directly opposite us, and next to them are colored troops, English, and some French. The Frenchmen have already made stone piles out of our place. At night they always come over and try to penetrate our positions.

Got Little Sleep Night or Day.

" I am northwest of Château-Thierry. But as long as my machine gun works they will not get near me. They will have to hop along like frogs in the

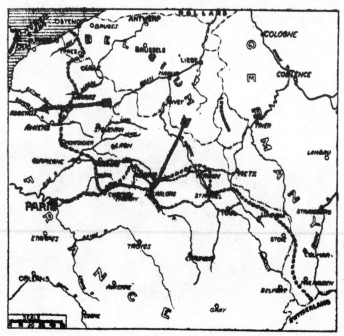

Possible Directions of New German Offensive

grass when the mowing machine approaches. [This German has been captured by the Americans.]

"There is no use thinking of sleep at night. It has now been three weeks since we closed an eye during the night, and during the day it is about the same, which is a colossal hardship.

"It is also difficult to cook, because the houses are all destroyed, and as soon as the Americans see any smoke, their artillery starts an awful racket. Food is scarce, and what we receive from the rolling kitchens is miserable. We do not really know when the end will be to all this."

The weakened morale of the holding troops is important, because with them the German command must hold terrain won by the better shock troops.

The opinion of well-informed experts is that the German Army as a whole is not in a position to make as strong an effort as in March.

STREET BATTLE IN MOSCOW

Heavy Casualties in Quelling the Social Revolutionists.

ENVOY'S SLAYERS SHIELDED

Rebels Seized Part of City, but Were Ousted—Hundreds of Arrests Made.

GERMANS ACCUSE ALLIES

Rumors of March on Moscow as Teutons in Russia Are Heavily Reinforced.

LONDON, July 8.—A formidable counter-revolution was attempted in Moscow on Saturday at the time of the assassination of Count von Mirbach, the German Ambassador, according to dispatches received here today. These dispatches indicate that the outbreak was suppressed with much bloodshed.

The Russian wireless circulated the following, signed by M. Araloff, the chief Moscow commissioner:

"The Social Revolutionists, by fraudulent means, captured for a few hours a small part of Moscow and the Government telegraph office, whence they issued false reports of the suppression of the Soviet in Moscow. I beg to announce that the mutiny was caused by a group of cheeky fools, and was suppressed without difficulty by the Moscow garrison. The mutineers have been arrested, and order has been restored.

"The counter-revolutionary rising in Moscow has been suppressed, and the Social Revolutionaries are making a most ingnominious fight. Orders have been issued to arrest and to disarm all members of the Social Revolutionary detachments and to shoot on the spot all who resist.

"Several hundred participants in the rising have been arrested, among them Vice Chairman Alexandrovich, while special orders have been issued to secure all members of the Executive Committee of the Social Revolutionary party.

"The Red Guards troops continue watchful. The mobilization of our forces must continue, and all Social Revolutionaries must disarm to the last man."

Fierce Fighting in the Streets.

"The Moscow outbreak was a serious counter-revolution," according to a German semi-official Wolff Bureau telegram dialed on Sunday from Moscow, and transmitted to London by the Exchange Telegraph Company's correspondent at Copenhagen. Fighting of great severity took place in the streets between the Bolshevist troops and Social Revolutionaries.

German newspapers are now pointing to General Savinkoff, who was War Minister of the Kerensky Cabinet, as the man behind the von Mirbach plot, which is being gradually developed by the Teuton press into a great anti-German movement backed by all those men whom Germany has found to be hindrances in her plans of aggression in Russia. A Moscow telegram circulated by the Wolff Bureau says:

"Savinkoff is considered to be responsible for the deed. He is, moreover, said to be closely connected with the Czechoslovak and Social Revolutionary movments. His whereabouts is unknown."

The German press is preparing the public for a radical move against Russia as punishment for the Mirbach affair. Exactly what this move will be is not as yet indicated, but Dutch and Scandinavian newspapers hint at a March on Moscow. Dispatches are printed showing that German forces are now about 300 miles west of that city and are being heavily reinforced.

German newspapers give many columns to developments in the Mirbach case, particularly long telegrams from Moscow praising the work that Count von Mirbach did there, and describing the alleged trecherous manner in which the assassins gained entrance to his office by posing as delegates of a commission for combating the social revolutionist movement. It is stated that they fired their revolvers, not only at Count von Mirbach, but also at German Councilor Kiezler and Lieutenant Mullers, who were in the room. Immediately after the firing they jumped out of a window, hurling hand grenades back of them as they jumped. They leaped into a waiting automobile and escaped.

Trying to Put Blame on Allies.

Nikolai Lenine, the Bolshevist Premier, is endeavoring to placate the Germans by appointing an "extraordinary commission of investigation" to probe the death of Count von Mirbach. The commission is headed by "Comrade Peters." A German official account of the assassination concludes:

"The result of a preliminary inquiry permits the assumption that agents in the service of the Entente are implicated in the affair."

As soon as Emperor William heard of the assassination of Count von Mirbach, according to an Exchange Telegraph dispatch from Amsterdam, he ordered Foreign Secretary von Kühlmann to break off negotiations with the Russian delegates in Berlin. A strong guard has been placed before the house of the Bolshevist Ambassador in Berlin, as it is feared that the populace of the capital will inaugurate anti-Russian demonstrations.

The assassination of Count von Mirbach is seen as an event of great importance, which may have far-reaching results, by the newspapers here. The Daily Mail and The Daily Express agree that the assassination may have momentous consequences, and compare it to the murder of Archduke Francis Ferdinand at Sarajevo four years ago. The Express adds:

"German influence (in Russia) can only be established on a solid basis by the maintenance of a great army of occupation. Russia may once more play a part in the war."

Machine Guns Guarded Murderers.

AMSTERDAM, July 8.—According to a Moscow telegram to the Frankfurter Zeitung, the two assassins of Count von Mirbach fled after committing the crime to a building occupied by Social Revolutionists, where they were being defended by machine guns. It is asserted in the advices that the assassination of the Ambassador was to have been the signal for a big revolt under the leadership of the Social Revolutionists, but that this failed to materialize on the scale that had been planned.

The Frankfurter Zeitung says:

"Changes in Russia are imminent. If the Entente's enterprise should lead to the collapse of the present Government, then not much will remain of the peace treaties. Our problems would then become more complicated than ever. Let us hope that in the solution of them the sword will play as little a rôle as possible. Nevertheless, the Central Powers on no account can permit the Entente to find fresh resources in the East."

Comments in the Vossiche Zeitung, the Lokal-Anzeiger, the Norddeutsche Allgemeine Zeitung, and other German newspapers, copies of which have been received here, all tend to absolve the Soviet Government of responsibility for the murder of Count von Mirbach. The papers hint at an intrigue of the Entente Governments to sow distrust between Germany and the Soviet Government.

The Vossische Zeitung expresses the hope that "British over-cleverness has again produced one of those follies which may easily result in the exact opposite of what was intended."

TROTZKY WON'T LET BOURGEOISIE FIGHT

Permits Its Members to Do Only Noncombatant Service in the Soviet Army.

FEARS TO GIVE THEM ARMS

Thinks They Would Use Them Against Government—Ukraine Rebels Well Equipped.

Special Cable to THE NEW YORK TIMES.

PETROGRAD, June 20, (Dispatch to The London Daily Express.)—The latest stage reached by the Bolshevist Utopia reads like a fairy tale or a tidbit of news from nowhere, but in Russia the truth is stranger than fiction.

Trotzky's recent report on the situation of the republic is causing comment and apprehension among all classes of the public. He is again harping on the holy war idea, saying that the safety of the Soviets and the republic depends on general conscription. But according to him it is inadvisable to call the younger members of the bourgeoisie to arms, as, instead of fighting the dark forces of capital and exploitation these, naturally, would want to fight the proletariat.

The fertile Bolshevist mind has found a way out of the dilemma by imposing on the members of the bourgeoisie, old and young, "light" duties for home and domestic defense, such as cleaning out barracks and camps, street scavenging, and digging trenches. The humor of the whole business lies in the announcement that bourgeois units showing more than ordinary zeal will be promoted from fatigue duty to real soldiering in the Socialist Army. Shirkers, conscientious objectors, and those failing to enlist are to be fined from $150 to $30,000, instead of being placed in concentration camps, and the strictest supervision is to be established over drones, parasites, and those not engaged in useful work.

The conundrum, who are bourgeois and who are Socialist, is expected to be solved by a by-law which will leave no loop-hole for Socialist shirkers masquerading as bourgeois in order to evade their military obligations. The Soviet is busy working out suitable designs for the uniforms and equipment for this army. All important artistic societies in Petrograd are competing by invitation of the War Commissariat, and a prize of $250 is offered for the best design, the Government to retain the right to purchase the three best designs, which must be original and artistic as well as simple and democratic.

I learn that while the Soviet is thus engrossed with fashion-plates for the Red Army, the Ukraine peasants, well armed and equipped, numbering some 75,000 and commanded by efficient officers and instructors, are advancing against the Germans at Kiev.

Panic reigns among the bourgeois, who are alarmed because the Germans are refusing to accept open battle, and the withdrawing Germans, who are supposed to have only 20,000 men are frantically requesting reinforcements from the western front. I understand the total number of peasant troops operating against the Germans is 250,000. At Krinitchki, a hamlet in the Ekaterinoslav Government, an actual battle between Ukraine Peasants and Germans resulted in the latter losing 1,000 men, while the peasants lost only 300.

KERENSKY'S METHODS OFFEND PARISIANS

Confers Only with Extreme Socialists and Scorns Bourgeois, Papers Say.

Special Cable to THE NEW YORK TIMES.

PARIS, July 8.—The visit of Kerensky to Paris has not so far proved to be a very striking success. It is generally felt here that the Russian ex-dictater can now only be looked upon as a back number, and French opinion inclines to the view that not much is to be expected from a man who failed so utterly to take advantage of the splendid opportunity offered him a few months ago, when he had all Russia at his call.

The result is that, as The Temps remarks this evening, although Kerensky is here neither Paris nor the nation is showing itself very much excited at his presence. Kerensky has made the mistake, as the Journal points out, of regarding everything in this country that is not revolutionary-socialistic as nonexistent.

"Since he came to Paris," says the paper, "he has consistently referred to the middle classes with a scorn which can scarcely be described. He has made a practice of declining to meet ordinary Republicans and even Socialist-Radicals. He declines to confer with anybody except pure-blooded internationalists. Yet he is supposed to have come here to plead for help from France and her allies in reconstituting Russia as a nation.

"By what fresh aberration does he imagine that the Revolutionary Socialists have the right to speak for France and her allies? Does he think that this method he affects of separating the good grain from the rubbish is consistent with his self-imposed mission? Does he think that this attitude reveals him as an able politician?

"When he sees Wilson will Kerensky explain to him what precautions he has taken in order to avoid meeting all but an infinitesimal minority in our country? Will he adopt the same tactics in America and treat the revolutionary Socialists there as the only people worthy of him? Will he confess that he has been rather coldly received by our Socialist party, which in matters of foreign policy is still inspired by Karl Marx?"

The Temps says that Kerensky's visit could hardly have been less fruitful if he had confined his meetings to non-Socialist Frenchmen. His own chosen Socialist friends have asked him several very awkward questions. Among them, they wanted to know why he allowed the order to be issued which suppressed all discipline and resulted in the practical disbandment of the Russian army. They asked also why he had allowed Lenine to come back to Russia, and to travel from Switzerland in a special train supplied by Germany, and why he did not suppress treason when it became evident that the Bolshevist leaders and German spies were in collusion. Further, he was asked why did he throw Korniloff overboard.

These are questions, says the Temps, that come into the mind of any man speaking of Kerensky, and which he must answer or be discredited. The Temps dismisses Kerensky as a man of words and nothing else, and complains bitterly that although the ex-dictator loudly asserted at Moscow that he would put down indiscipline and treason with fire and sword he subsequently allowed treachery to be accomplished with the result that the only sufferers from fire and sword have been France and her allies.

"All the News That's Fit to Print."

The New York Times.

THE WEATHER
Fair today; tomorrow partly cloudy; gentle winds, mostly south. For full weather report see Page 22.

VOL. LXVII...NO. 22,068.   NEW YORK, TUESDAY, JULY 16, 1918.—TWENTY-FOUR PAGES.   TWO CENTS

AMERICANS DRIVE GERMANS OVER MARNE: TAKE 1,000 PRISONERS AND CHECK BIG DRIVE; GERMAN ATTACK ON A 60-MILE FRONT FAILS

AMERICAN BLOW UPSETS FOE

German Forces Flee When Our Troops Begin Forward Rush.

15,000 DRIVEN ACROSS RIVER

Intense Fighting Continues, with Heavy Guns Roaring Far Into the Night.

ADVANCE COSTLY TO ENEMY

Slaughtered by Our Machine Gunners as They Debouch to Cross Marne on Pontoons.

By EDWIN L. JAMES.
Copyright, 1918, by The New York Times Company.
Special Cable to THE NEW YORK TIMES.

WITH THE AMERICAN ARMY ON THE MARNE, July 15, 6 P. M.—The Germans launched their expected offensive this morning on a front extending from north of Chalons, in the Champagne, westward beyond Château-Thierry.

The enemy's drive fell upon American troops east of Rheims, east of Château-Thierry, and west of Château-Thierry.

After battling for many hours the American troops in a magnificent counterattack threw a whole division of Germans back across the Marne River in the curve of the river west and southwest of Jaulgonne. There are now no Germans across the Marne in front of our troops. At 10 o'clock this morning there were 15,000 of them.

We inflicted heavy losses on the enemy, many of whom were drowned in the swollen stream. We took 600 prisoners.

[Other advices say that the number of prisoners taken is 1,000 to 1,500,

including an entire brigade staff. While the correspondent speaks of a division of Germans being driven back across the Marne, it is evident that he means men to the number of a division. The Germans usually attack with a division to each mile of front, and the front here referred to is from five to seven miles long. The 15,000 Germans who had got across the Marne were the survivors of the large masses who tried to cross on pontoons and were badly cut up in the attempt. It is probable, therefore, that the result of the day's battle on this sector was the defeat by the Americans of a German force of at least five divisions.]

Huge Artillery Preparation.

The offensive in the region of Château-Thierry was preceded by intensive artillery demonstration, beginning at midnight. It was predicted in these dispatches ten days ago that the offensive might start on July 14.

An hour after midnight the whole countryside was lighted up with the flare from thousands of cannon in action. Not only did the enemy heavily bombard the front line, but, evidently using a new long-range gun, he shelled points twenty, twenty-five, and thirty miles behind the line.

By noon today the Germans had crossed the Marne where the river makes a salient northward, with the point at Jaulgonne, and had advanced three and one-half kilometers, [two miles.] This was held partly by Americans and partly by French.

The salient was exposed to fire from three sides. From midnight till 7 o'clock in the morning the German gunners poured thousands upon thousands of their explosive and gas shells into the area, putting down heavy barrages for the purpose of hindering the bringing up of reinforcements.

After seven hours of this shelling, the Germans, at enormous cost in men, pushed forward detachments from the edge of the woods on the north bank of the Marne and started to make attempts to throw pontoon bridges across the river, which was too deep to ford on account of the rains yesterday.

Foiled Three Efforts to Cross.

Three times the American guns balked the enemy's efforts, but finally he was successful, and soon his troops were making their costly way across the bridges.

Germans who were taken prisoners said they had been long trained for this crossing, and their conduct showed it.

This crossing recalls that six days ago our scouts discovered materials for a pontoon bridge on the north side of the river, and later our shellfire destroyed them.

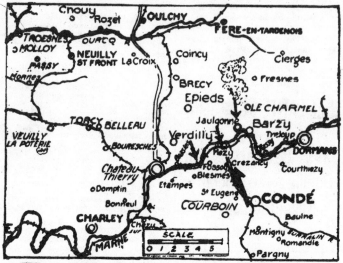

Where the American Victory Was Won

The three arrows at Jaulgonne, Fossoy and Mézy show the principal points where the Germans crossed the Marne and the sector in which American troops counterattacked, driving the enemy back and taking more than 1,000 prisoners.

As the Germans passed across the bridges with a large number of machine guns they went into action. In the face of superior numbers the Americans fell back to the base of the salient made by the river.

At 11:30 o'clock the battleline ran from the base of the salient through a point just north of Crezancy, where our men were firmly holding.

It was difficult in the early hours to get accurate reports from all our forces. However, there was enough information to show that while the Germans were crossing at Jaulgonne the German High Command was directing attacks all along the line to Rheims and east of that city.

While there is fighting west of Château-Thierry, its character shows that the German drive is not now directed that way. The shelling, which started generally at midnight, fell with great violence on the American sector northwest of Château-Thierry. Thousands of high-explosive and gas shells fell in the Bois de Belleau, the Bois de la Roche, and the village of Vaux. This shelling was concentrated on Vaux from 4 to 6 o'clock, after which the Germans launched an attack with two battalions against that town.

The Americans, withdrawing from their front trenches north of the railroad track in front of the town, waited until the attackers were very close, and then opened with a direct and flanking rifle fire. The attacking force was completely demoralized and retired in disorder.

The Americans immediately counterattacked and advanced their lines 750 yards and took twenty-seven

prisoners. No further attacks have yet been made on Vaux.

I have just received a semi-official report that, following the Vaux attack, the American troops advanced on the west side of Hill 204 so far that the Germans expected an attack and evacuated the hill they had paid so much to hold the last three weeks. This is not yet positively confirmed, but I do know that at this moment our guns are pouring high explosives over the German lines of communication to the north of the hill.

So far the Germans have made no attempt to advance directly through Château-Thierry. The four bridges of the city have been blown up and it would mean a great and dangerous effort to cross there, where the artificial channel of the river is deep and machine guns command the northern side of the stream.

More Long-Range Guns in Action.

The Germans in this drive have introduced another novelty. At 3 o'clock this morning shells began to drop on a point thirty miles back of our lines at intervals of five minutes. This means that guns were being used having a range of perhaps thirty-five miles.

This has accomplished small military result thus far, but serves, in the main, only to terrify women and children.

It has been supposed that what the German high command aimed at was to force the allied armies to fall back to almost a straight line from Château-Thierry through Chalons to St. Mihiel, compelling them to yield Verdun.

"All the News That's Fit to Print."

The New York Times.

THE WEATHER
Fair today; Sunday fair, somewhat warmer; gentle shifting winds.

VOL. LXVII...NO. 22,092. ...   NEW YORK, SATURDAY, JULY 20, 1918.—EIGHTEEN PAGES.   TWO CENTS | THREE CENTS | FOUR CENTS

ALLIED DRIVE NETS 17,000 PRISONERS, 360 GUNS; FRENCH AND AMERICANS GAIN BELOW SOISSONS; CRUISER SAN DIEGO SUNK NEAR FIRE ISLAND

BATTLE TO KEEP SOISSONS

Germans Rush Reserves from South to Win Back Vital Plateau.

FAIL AND ALLIES PRESS ON

Advance of Nearly Two Miles Is Made in the Centre of the Long Front.

IMPORTANT HEIGHTS WON

French South of the Marne and Italians North of River Also Make Progress.

LONDON, July 19.—In the face of heavy resistance by the enemy, who threw large reserves into the line, the French and American forces continued their advance today between the Aisne and the Marne.

Ground was gained along the greater part of the front, the progress amounting to about two miles at some points.

Seventeen thousand prisoners have already been taken by the allied troops, and 360 guns, according to the official bulletin of the French War Office tonight.

The stiffest fighting of the day was about the plateau southwest of Soissons, in the Crise River section, which was wrested from the Germans yesterday. The Paris communiqué says only that the allied position was maintained, but unofficial advices state that late this afternoon the Allies began to push ahead again.

Further south the Germans have been pushed back further from the line of Vau Castille-Villers-Helon-Noroy-sur-Ourcq.

Still further south, by dint of hard fighting, the Germans have been driven from the plateau northwest of Bonnes, and have been compelled to cede more ground to the north of Torcy.

French and Italians together have made advances southwest of Rheims.

The Italians have made progress from Pourcy along the Ardre, and have also gained in the Bouilly region.

French troops just to the south have won some ground in the Courton Wood and Roi Wood.

South of the Marne the Germans have been driven from Montvoison and pushed back to Ocuilly.

Germans Hurried Troops North.

WITH THE AMERICAN ARMY BETWEEN THE AISNE AND THE MARNE, July 19, (Associated Press.)—The French and American troops made an advance late this afternoon on the Soissons-Château-Thierry front, averaging about two kilometers (about a mile and a quarter.)

Vicious German machine gun fire southwest of Soissons hampered the advance for only a short period.

In the same section the Germans attempted to use tanks against the Americans, but a hot fire soon compelled the tanks to retreat.

The advance began with a barrage, opening at 5:30 o'clock. Tanks were sent in by the Allies to assist the infantry and machine gunners, and the Germans endeavored to stem the tide with a heavy shellfire.

The advance was one of the best organized the Allies ever attempted, the system working wonderfully well from one end of the line to the other. The machine gun defense of the Germans was feeble and was quickly silenced, the Germans falling back upon their rear defenses.

Southwest of Soissons the Germans repeatedly attempted to reach the Allies' big guns. The German firing continued until long after dark, but the French and American guns responded in kind, and gave full protection to the allied forces as they advanced along the line. Several towns were captured.

Heavy reinforcements were rushed up from the north by the German command in a desperate effort to head off the hard-fighting Allies, whose rapid advance would, if continued, sever the German lines of communications. There are still strong German forces south of the Marne.

The Germans began to make counterattacks yesterday southwest of Soissons, but their effort fell down as soon as the American heavy artillery got into action.

This was one of the fiercest struggles in connection with the offensive, and resulted in the Germans falling back finally under the heavy gunfire of the Americans.

The Americans took several towns in the course of the night. Among these was Vierzy, six miles south of Soissons. Towns to the north and south were also captured in the carrying out of the plan to straighten the entire line on the Soissons-Château-Thierry front. No resistance was encountered at Vierzy or in the neighboring villages.

While the American force engaged in the present battle is small in comparison with the total allied strength, it may be said that it is greater than any participating in a battle since the civil war, and the conduct of the men is eliciting the commendation of the French. They have performed the part assigned to them with steadiness, courage, and skill.

To a large portion of the Americans these four days have been their first real fighting. Reports from along the lines indicate a great deal of clean, open warfare, some spontaneous localized actions being undertaken without a preliminary barrage.

AMERICANS DRIVE WEDGE

Gains to the South May Force the Evacuation of Soissons.

By EDWIN L. JAMES.
Copyright, 1918, by The New York Times Company.
Special Cable to THE NEW YORK TIMES.

WITH THE AMERICAN ARMY, July 19.—The first thirty hours of the Franco-American offensive drove a deep point into the German lines south of Soissons and yielded a net gain of from five to fifteen kilometers on a forty-kilometer front.

Just before dark last night allied aviators saw French cavalry to the northeast of Soissons and scouting parties of Americans on the heights south of the city. French cavalry also penetrated far eastward, returning to make reports of conditions. Aviators reported that late yesterday the Germans began to draw back guns from the woods north of Château-Thierry.

While allied soldiers have been around Soissons, with the Americans holding Belleau, immediately to the south, there has been as yet no fighting direct for Soissons. If the Franco-American forces advance far enough south of the city, the Germans may evacuate it without a fight.

In gaining this terrain, the French and Americans took thousands of prisoners. Thirty-five hundred were credited to the Americans alone. It should be stated that the American forces compose a small proportion of the total allied forces involved in this operation. We have taken many guns and an immense quantity of ammunition.

The whole operation has shown how splendidly the French and Americans can co-operate in such an action. In no case have the Americans lagged behind. The only difficulties have come through their not stopping upon reaching their objectives.

There was a busy scene yesterday back of the battleline. I started out to a certain place to find one of our headquarters. When I got there, I found a lone doughboy, who said that headquarters had been moved ahead. I went there, and they had been moved again. Finally I found headquarters at a place which before the attack started had been in German hands.

As has been told, the attack started without artillery preparation. As the boys started, the artillery laid down a barrage of short duration, and then lifted it to the limit of the range. Our men reached that limit, and we had to stop firing until the horses could be hitched to the guns, which were carried further to the front.

The American attack schedule worked like this—a hundred yards in three minutes, a rest of five minutes, another 100 yards, and a rest of forty minutes. Because the boche was completely surprised and the going was found to be easy, many of our men disregarded the schedule and went on further. The waves which were supposed to overflow one another finally got going all together, and this proved to be not half bad when the Germans launched their counterattacks.

Our Men Take 52 Guns.

The most formidable German counterattack against the Americans was aimed at our troops near Soissons, but just as it started at noon the Americans started a fresh attack further south, which smashed the German counterattack and netted us a gain of three kilometers and several hundred prisoners. In this attack the Americans got fifty-two field guns.

A fleet of tanks did yeoman work, smashing their way through the German wire defenses. In several instances the Americans got ahead of the tanks and cut the wire with pliers.

The front on which our tanks were used was the only spot where the Germans were found to be the least bit expecting our attack. They had heard the tanks coming, and had got ready. However, the resistance was overcome in twenty minutes of fighting.

Many of our troops rushed from distant points to take part in the attack. I know of one unit which got to the detraining point twelve kilometers from the fight, where it was to be met by trucks. The trucks weren't there, and so the boys said, "We will walk!" and they did—into the battle.

The artillery fire against the French and Americans yesterday afternoon and last night was very light, because so many German guns had been captured or forced hurriedly back. Because of the absence of artillery fire, an extraordinarily large proportion of our casualties were only slightly wounded. Back of the lines yesterday for every stretcher case I saw there seemed to be twenty slightly wounded.

Chaplain's Exuberant Bulletin.

In one truck filled with such youngsters was a dignified Chaplain comforting them. When he saw a carload of correspondents, he landed from the truck and shouted:

"The boys are giving Heinie hell up ahead—beaucoup hell!"

There was a wonderful sight in many big woods back of the allied line. The French and Americans were making camp in the shade of mighty trees standing in the straight rows of an artificial forest. It looked like a big picnic far removed from the trench warfare of which the armies have seen so much in France in the last four years. Here they were, camped out in the open, ready to pack up and move Hunward this morning if the call came.

It was certainly more comfortable for the Americans than being cooped up in the dirty little billets where they have been living for the last few months. "This is regular war," was the way one of our lads put it.

I think that the happiest Americans seen in a long time were a half hundred who were stretching barbed wire on trees, making a big corral. Inside it were 2,800 German prisoners. "They're all ours, too," explained a Corporal, who was hammering stakes, speaking with the same sort of pride with which he would have described a big string of fish.

Evidence is abundant that General Foch's little surprise party played havoc with the Crown Prince's drive for Epernay and Châlons. The shock troops known to have been rushing east of Dormans day before yesterday were not heard from today, and the whole German effort east of Château-Thierry slowed down. Events will show what changes have been made in the enemy's plans, but he must realize now that his whole Château-Thierry salient is in peril.

Foch's Plan Not Developed.

A glance at the map shows what many days' advances like those of yesterday will mean to the whole German salient dipping toward the Marne. Perhaps General Foch has not played his whole hand yet. Perhaps the allied drive may have wider effects than the slowing up of the German drive for Châlons and Epernay. The next two weeks may tell.

The allied drive has put new heart into this part of France. People who yesterday were packing up their belongings preparatory to evacuating towns south of the Marne are today unpacking the wagons and moving back into their houses, only stopping long enough to cheer the passing American soldiers. Somehow or other they seem to think that things have changed, seem to think that now the French people will do no more evacuating.

They say that now that the Americans have come the Allies are going to win the war in a hurry. They are right, except for the time element. It is a long, long journey from the Marne to the Rhine, but the Allies know the way. General Foch has a big map, with the roads all marked in red.

GERMANS LOST 60,000 BY CROSSING MARNE

Heavy Casualties, Especially on the American Front, Staggered the Enemy.

HAD TO RUSH IN RESERVES

Crown Prince's Intense Desire to Enter Rheims, Paris Thinks, Caused Offensive.

Copyright, 1918, by The New York Times Company.
Special Cable to THE NEW YORK TIMES.

PARIS, July 18.—It is now clear that the Crown Prince, finding beyond reach all chance of another spectacular advance such as characterized the former German offensives of the present year, has decided on a more or less limited plan of making a desperate effort to secure Rheims and Epernay. From the advertising point of view, nothing would suit the enemy's purpose better than for the heir to the German throne to make a theatrical entry at the head of his troops into the City of Rheims, around which cling traditions of so many great moments in French history for a thousand years past.

The fall of Epernay, which lies only a dozen miles south of the Champagne capital, would almost inevitably involve the evacuation of Rheims and the strong defensive position of the Montagne de Rheims, which lies between the two towns. This accounts clearly for the fact that the enemy yesterday localized all real efforts along the Marne west of Epernay and in the difficult country lying northeast of the same town.

Pincers Fail to Close.

Fears have been expressed that the German effort to pinch out Rheims by closing in to the south may prove successful, but it must be remembered that the jaws of the enemy pincers at Vrigny on the west and Prunay on the east are still nearly fourteen miles apart. Further, the Mountain of Rheims is so strongly held by the French, and they have been so well reinforced in the hilly country north of the Marne, that we are much more likely to hear of a French counteroffensive at this point than anything in the way of serious progress by the enemy.

The danger point for the moment appears to be further south, at Monvoison, which is south of the Marne, and only about seven miles west of Epernay. On this point there appears to be some confusion.

An American communiqué, dated 9 o'clock last night, stated that in the Marne sector the Americans had retaken the south bank of the river, whereas the French communiqué, dated two hours later, asserts that the Germans had been able to set foot in Montvoison. Information gathered here indicates that this village was in German hands more than once yesterday, and it is not clear for the moment in whose possession it remains.

The fact that Vrigny is still strongly held by the French indicates that Rheims is amply protected on the southwest, while the failure yesterday of repeated desperate efforts against Prunay and Les Marquises shows that the French need have no fear as to their ability to hold their line on the Vesle, which runs into Rheims from its source thirty miles to the southeast.

The great drive along a front of fifty miles that was to bring the Germans another stage toward Paris has been whittled down, now that the enemy forces have been beaten in the brilliant defense offered by Gouraud's army in the Champagne, and a great part of von Boehm's army has been fought to a standstill east of Rheims in the obstinate effort to take Rheims and Epernay.

Foe's Losses Enormous.

The German losses south of the Marne, whence they have been driven out by American troops, are proved to have been enormous. All accounts agree in placing the number at 60,000 at the lowest.

In the whole battle the Germans so far have engaged at least sixty divisions, including twenty which were held in support. Owing to his stupefying losses, the enemy had to throw in many of his reserves which he obviously did not expect to have to utilize for some days yet. This heavy loss is regarded here as one of the main reasons for the hesitating tactics which the enemy adopted in the greater part of his line of attack.

Official Reports of Operations

French

Paris, July 19.

Night Report—The battle begun yesterday between the Aisne and the Marne continued all day with extreme violence, the enemy reacting along the whole line with large reserves in an attempt to stay our progress. Despite his efforts we continued our advance over the greater part of the front.

On the left we maintained the plateau southwest of Soissons and in the region of Chaudun. In the centre our advance exceeded three kilometers at certain points along the line of Vaux-Castille, Villers-Helon, and Noroy-sur-Ourcq. On the right our troops occupied, after bitter fighting, the plateau northwest of Monnes and the height north of Courchamps and advanced beyond Torcy.

The number of prisoners counted up to the present exceeds 17,000, including two Colonels, with their Chiefs of Staff. We have captured more than 360 cannon, including one battery of 210's.

Day Report—Between the Aisne and the Marne our troops, surmounting the resistance of the enemy, which was increased by the arrival of new reserves, realized sensible progress at the close of yesterday. The number of prisoners counted is being augmented. The battle continues with violence along the whole front.

West of Rheims and south of the Marne our troops yesterday, by a vigorous attack, retook Montvoisin, and threw the enemy out of the outskirts of Oeuilly.

To the north of the Marne we have made progress in the Roi Wood and the Courton Wood and carried our line a kilometer to the westward. Further north the Italians have taken Moulin d'Ardre and conquered ground in the region of Bouilly.

In the course of these actions the French have captured four cannon, thirty machine guns, and 400 prisoners.

Between Montdidier and Noyon and also in the Woevre region, in raids against the German lines, we captured 100 prisoners.

German

Berlin, July 19. (via London.)

Night Report—On the battlefield between the Aisne and the Marne a fresh attempt by the French to break through our lines failed with heavy losses to the enemy.

Day Report—The battle has blazed up again between the Aisne and the Marne. There the French have begun their long-expected counteroffensive. By the employment of extremely strong squadrons of tanks they succeeded at first in penetrating by surprise into our front infantry and artillery lines at isolated points and in pressing back our line.

Afterwards our line divisions, together with reserves which had been held in readiness, frustrated the enemy from breaking through.

Toward midday French attacks on the line southwest from Soissons to Neuilly and northwest of Château-Thierry were defeated. In the afternoon very strong partial attacks of the enemy on the whole of the front of attack broke down against our new line. Enemy columns, which were endeavoring to reach the battlefield, were the objectives of our successful battle-planes. Our chasing planes shot down thirty-two enemy airplanes.

On the front south of the Marne the French, since their failures of July 16-17, have only directed partial attacks southeast of Mareuil, which were repulsed.

Between the Marne and Rheims and east of Rheims the fighting activity has been confined to local operations. Enemy attacks in the Bois du Roi and on both sides of Pourcy broke down. We have captured prisoners in successful attacks northwest of Trosgnes, on the Suippes, and on both sides of Perthes. The number of prisoners brought in since the 15th exceeds 20,000.

1,187 Officers and Men from the San Diego Saved

WASHINGTON, Saturday, July 20.—This announcement was made at 1 o'clock this morning by the Navy Department:

"The Navy Department early this morning received information that two steamships which are proceeding to port have aboard 1,156 officers and men of the U. S. S. San Diego. These are in addition to the one officer and thirty men previously reported landed. The men are said to be in good condition, and so far as known none was injured."

Although it did not always work this way, both these photos show movement of German prisoners of war from battle fronts to prison camps.

Section 1

"All the News That's Fit to Print."

The New York Times.

THE WEATHER
Fair Sunday and Monday; slight temperature change; shifting winds
For full weather report see Page 18.

Section 1

VOL. LXVII...NO. 22,093.   NEW YORK, SUNDAY, JULY 21, 1918.—92 PAGES, in Nine Parts.   FIVE CENTS In Greater New York | SEVEN CENTS Elsewhere

ALL GERMANS PUSHED BACK OVER THE MARNE; ALLIES GAIN THREE MILES SOUTH OF SOISSONS; NOW HOLD 20,000 PRISONERS AND 400 GUNS

BERLIN ADMITS RETREAT

Says Troops Withdrew Without Being Noticed By the Enemy.

HAD TO RETIRE, SAYS PARIS

Violent Attacks Were Made South of River and Also North —British Aiding Here.

BIG THRUST ON THE OURCQ

French-American Forces Push Ahead Most in Centre—Command Soissons Bridges.

LONDON, July 20.—The German offensive has been broken and the Crown Prince's troops have been thrown back across the Marne River.

The Franco-Americans fighting on the Soissons-Château-Thierry front, up to noon today, had made an average gain of a mile, and an extreme advance, in the centre, of three miles.

The complete collapse of operations south of the Marne, which had previously witnessed a great and decisive defeat of the German invaders early in the war, was announced laconically by a Reuter correspondent at French Headquarters in a dispatch, timed this evening, which said:

"No Germans remain south of the Marne except prisoners and dead."

Official communications from the Paris and Berlin War Offices quickly confirmed the withdrawal, the imminence of which had been indicated by earlier dispatches from correspondents at the front.

These told how the Germans south of the river had suffered a repulse at the hands of the Allies and were retreating toward the river, with French and American troops on their heels. Capture of the Bois de Misy and Port-à-Binsone (one and one-

Germans Try to Excuse Retreat Over the Marne

AMSTERDAM, July 20.—A semi-official statement received here from Berlin says the German Supreme Army Command had several aims in its attack on the southern bank of the Marne, the crossing of which river, it asserts, was unobserved by the Entente Allies. The statement goes so far as to claim that the German objectives have been fully attained.

The first aims of the Marne crossing, the semi-official statement says, were to broaden the basis of attack for a German blow on both sides of Rheims and to attack and to hold strong enemy forces. Furthermore, the attack on the southern bank of the Marne, which was so menacing for the Entente, the statement adds, finally unloosed the long-expected French counteroffensive.

After urging that the counteroffensive has miscarried because a break through has been prevented, the message naively adds:

"The task of the German troops fighting on the southern bank of the Marne was thereby entirely fulfilled and the further holding of the lines there was unnecessary. The German command could now withdraw the troops to the northern bank for fresh important tasks."

half miles west of Oeuilly) was announced early.

German Version of Retreat.

The day bulletin from the German headquarters, in announcing the retirement, says:

"South of the Marne there was moderate firing activity during the day. Southeast of Mareuil enemy partial attacks were repulsed.

"During the night our troops south of the Marne were withdrawn to the north bank of the river without being noticed by the enemy."

The German communication insists that allied thrusts southwest of Soissons and southward along the Aisne-Marne front were repulsed, with heavy losses.

The French official bulletin says that the enemy was compelled to retire from below the Marne by the violent attacks of the allied forces. Its statement concerning the operations in that area reads:

"We have not had long to wait for the result of our victorious counteroffensive.

"The Germans, violently attacked on their right flank and south of the Marne, have been compelled to retreat and recross the river. We hold the whole south bank of the Marne."

The Paris bulletin also reveals that British troops are in action with the French on the front between the Marne and Rheims. Here vigorous attacks were made by the allied forces in co-operation with the drive south of the river, and important ground was gained in the region along the Ardre.

Continuation of the French and American advance between the Aisne and the Marne is chronicled.

Since and including Thursday the allied troops have captured more than 20,000 prisoners and more than 400 guns.

The battle along the Aisne-Marne front, which was renewed late yesterday afternoon, continued with fierceness into the night, the Germans losing better positions to the French, who were fighting uphill. The advance was won foot by foot, owing to the huge reserves thrown in to support the Crown Prince.

On the average the advance of the French and Americans on a twenty-eight-mile front between noon of yesterday and 9 o'clock last night was about a mile.

Today the Allies again took the offensive, and the Germans were compelled to yield gradually on both sides of the deep pocket, of which Soissons and Rheims mark the edges. Meanwhile, life in this pocket was being made miserable for the Germans by long-range guns and airplane bombers.

Up to midafternoon there was no indication in the advices reaching here of the voluntary withdrawal of the Germans from the pocket. The enemy was reported putting up a stubborn resistance everywhere. The French, however, were doing terrible execution on the Germans all along the fifty-mile circumference of the loop.

Late dispatches from the field of the offensive between the Marne and the Aisne this afternoon reported that the allied line ran as follows:

From Belleau northward to the west of Monthiers and on to Sommelans, Mont Chevillon, the Bois de Lud, Geronemil Farm, le Plessier Huleu, Parcy-Tigny, Villemontoire, Berzy le Sec, Courmelles, Montaigne de Paris, Pernant, and Fontenoy.

This indicated that the French had bitten off several square miles of German territory in the vicinity of the Ourcq, about midway between Château-Thierry and Soissons. The French line in this district is thus seven miles in front of that held before the offensive began.

The situation in this section has been obscure for twenty-four hours, and bitter fighting had been going on. The French, however, it is said,

have established their line definitely, and have cleared the Germans out of the rough country thereabouts.

Gains on East Side of Salient.

On the east side of the salient, also, there was activity today. North of the Marne and southwest of Rheims the French captured the town of Marfaux, southeast of Bligny, after heavy fighting, and moved forward west of Pourcy.

On the front east of Rheims the French forces advanced for a distance of 1,000 yards between Souain and Auberive.

FIERCE FIGHTING YESTERDAY

Our Men in a Severe Struggle With the German Reserves.

SUCCESS AS SHOCK TROOPS

Americans, Previously Untried, More Than a Match for the Kaiser's Best.

OVER 6,000 PRISONERS NOW

German Machine Guns Firing Explosive Bullets at Our Men.

By EDWIN L. JAMES.
Copyright, 1918, by The New York Times Company.
Special Cable to THE NEW YORK TIMES.

WITH THE AMERICAN ARMY, July 20.—On the bloody battlefield south of Soissons the American soldiers, along with their comrades of the allied arms, today were matching their strength with the best German warriors.

No one says yet how the battle goes because no one knows yet. We have gained and gained, but the struggle grows in fierceness as both sides throw fresh troops into the maelstrom of death and dust and flying shells out of which may come a result that will have much to do with the end of the war.

The German offensive of July 15 is now turned into a German defensive. Forced back by French and American troops at the start, it was to be expected that when the German high command hurled their shock troops against the French and Americans the progress after the first day would not be so rapid.

Our Men as Shock Troops.

Out of the storm where allied determination, leavened with the new spirit of Americanism, met the famed war machine of the German autocracy has already come one conclusion that augurs well for an allied victory. That is that the backbone of the United States fighting man is a stiff proposition for the Kaiser's warriors.

All the armies class as their best fighters their shock troops. This was a job of shock troops, performed by the Americans, and they have made good.

It was not the brilliant advance of the first day, good as it was, that told the story of the grit of Uncle Sam's fighting lads. It was not the furthest advance that told the real story. That came yesterday, when the new American attacks east of Vierzy and northeast of Chaudon met the German shock troops.

The fighting men were trained for more than a month by Ludendorff to take part in the offensive for Epernay and Châlons. Fresh and in the best of condition and on their tiptoes they were met by our men, who already had been fighting thirty hours.

Then the Germans tried to turn our attack into an advance for themselves. They failed.

Holding Their Gains.

Holding against a murderous machine gun fire, against bombs and bullets from hostile aircraft, against the unquestioned force of the German shock troops, the youthful Americans with their French comrades stood firm, and are so standing as this is written.

The full story of the fast and furious battle cannot yet be told. Word comes one minute that the Germans have a village, and ten minutes later another word comes that the Americans have that village.

Up the roads go trucks of ammunition and down the roads come the ambulances. German shells come groaning over, and in reply one hears a crescendo, oft repeated, which tells that bottled destruction is on its way from the American side.

Down the roads from the front come every now and then a big truckload of slightly wounded Americans, all angry to have been put out of the fight.

The truck halts. A stocky American lad, caked with dust, and with two bullet wounds through the shoulder, asks me for a cigarette, and I ask him what he thinks of it.

"I'll tell you," said he. "I was never in a battle before, and felt kind of squeamish a couple of hours before. I felt squeamish when I went over the top, but as soon as the real fighting started I forgot to be squeamish, and went on until the boche machine gunner got me.

Honest to God, I had rather fight than eat now. I hope the 'doc' lets me back soon."

This lad was a coal miner eight months ago.

The Americans started their second attack at 5 o'clock yesterday morning. They had reached their objectives, a varying number of kilometers eastward, and were consolidating their positions when the shock troops struck them about noon.

Then began the battle, which is still going on with the fiercest struggles.

Against one American unit two German shock divisions were hurled. Against another came the famous Prussian Guards.

The Germans had machine guns mounted on wheels, and had rolled them to the edge of the woods. These guns shot explosive bullets, which are the latest piece of barbarity the German has invented.

One story was told by all the wounded whom I talked with, and that was the great number of machine guns the Germans have. This now appears to be the favorite weapon of the Germans against Americans.

Our Huge Bag of Prisoners.

There is one feature of the battle which stands out—the number of prisoners taken by the Americans. The number placed to our credit south of Soissons is now something more than 6,000.

Two regiments have officially booked more than 2,800 German captives, including sixty-six officers.

Coming down the wooded hill I saw a sight that made me think I had run into the German Army, but when I came near I found only a corral of Germans taken by Americans. There were more than 3,000 in a barbed wire cage, and the dirtiest lot of humans I ever saw, with the exception of the Colonel and some of the officers. There they stood, sat, and squatted in the sunlight. The French officer told me they were the most unclean lot of men he had seen during the war.

These prisoners were mostly holding troops, caught in the French-American surprise, and not belonging to the crack German troops. Unshaven and unkempt in every way, they looked like beasts.

The officers captured were entirely different. The Colonel was of the most natty sort, glistening with many decorations. A Captain with whom I talked used to be a business man with an office in Manhattan and a home in New Jersey. He gave it as his opinion that the war would never end in a military victory, but in bankruptcy for one side or the other. He remarked:

"I am thinking of Germany. I am almost sure the Kaiser cannot win a complete military victory, but nothing is left now but to fight on in the hope of a favorable settlement by negotiation, for if we stop now the taxes will be so heavy for Germany that no one can live. We must fight on until the Allies pay us."

I noticed that all the German gas masks on the shock troops were equipped with a new attachment against the new allied gases.

This large number of captives gives reply to the lie that the American troops take no prisoners.

Clark Williams a Worker.

This is the time to pay tribute to an American, Clark Williams, of New York, former Banking Commissioner. In the shade of a noble old château lay a yardful of American wounded, waiting for attention by the surgeons. There were slightly wounded and seriously wounded, happy wounded and discouraged wounded, and hungry wounded. There I found Mr. Williams representing the Red Cross. He had spent the night getting out from Paris five tons of food, and then sent the trucks back for surgical material. He was directing the helpers to feed the half-famished fighting lads, and was himself carrying cans of bouillon around. His pockets were filled with cigarettes and under his arms were packages of prunes. He was truly a working man.

The army surgeon in charge of the hospital asked that public thanks be given to the American Red Cross and Mr. Williams, whose aid had been invaluable.

I spent yesterday back of the fighting line, in territory that had been German the day before. I had seen some scenes of destruction in France, but these scenes were worse. On one road, for three miles, all the trees had been hit by shells and most of them were cut down.

Here is a village with not a building left standing. Here is another with an untouched church steeple, the only whole thing there. Here American and French shells fell when the attack started, and the German shells had hit as well. Caught between the millstones of war, this strip of country was ground to ruin. The shell holes are so thick you can step from one to another.

Camions with broken wheels had been shoved aside and left. A war-weary Missouri mule, shot in its tracks, had been shoved over an embankment.

Piles and piles of ammunition lay about, which caused an involuntary shrinking when a boche shell came screaming over and landed fifty feet away from the bottled death, throwing streaks of earth and stalks of ripened wheat across the roadway packed with the pageantry of war. There were camions loaded with jaded fighting men, made weary by many miles of jostling over roads worn rough with ceaseless passing, ammunition wagons, their drivers cursing over the endless delays, field kitchens on their important way, cannon going along Hunward, followed by heavily laden caissons, swift autos darting in and out with important looking officers, mule carts, horse carts, and men on foot.

Numberless ambulances, loaded, were going one way and empty ones were going the other, all covered with a thick layer of dust.

When a German Shell Hits.

Here comes a hurtling 210, alighting twenty yards from the roadside, and a horse shies and throws a field kitchen into the ditch, while a much-soiled doughboy cook utters maledictions upon the Kaiser, who started the war, and all his family.

Here a shell strikes a tree and throws its foliage across the procession. It is cleared away in a jiffy, while the raucous horn of a French General's car outdoes the screeching shells.

Back behind it all our guns keep roaring, the earth seeming to shake as some big piece sends a message of cheer to the enemy.

Never was there such a procession and never such a setting. Let me say that never was there such dust. The brown of the doughboys' uniforms and the blue of the poilus look all the same.

On each side of the road runs a ravaged fields of yellow wheat, the color of which is almost matched by nearby woodland.

Now we are in the woods, and the dust is not so bad. America knows no such woods. The trees all stand in rows, and the carpet beneath is marred by no underbrush. All are made to order.

Beneath noble old trees are soldiers and soldiers, wagons and wagons and wagons, war and more war. Here poilus and doughboys are making themselves comfortable for a brief respite before being called on when a shell brings down a tree across a pile of shells where a nest was being built.

All the world knows the fighting man cusses. I didn't understand the cussing of the poilus, but there was no doubt about the doughboys cussing the Hun.

Perhaps they forgot about democracy and autocracy and the rights of small nations, but the expression of their innermost thought showed the band had not forgotten they had something serious against the Hun as they righted the overturned "goulash cannon," the wreck of which had played havoc with the evening meal.

Then out of the woods marched a sturdy line of lads in brown turning northeastward. Their rifles were on their backs and their belts full of ammunition. They marched on to argue it out with the foe.

An Unforgettable Battle.

This battle will never be forgotten by the boys in it. The rapidity of the advance brought, of course, difficulties for the supply trains, which made eating late and often long deferred. It made it hard for the ambulances always to reach the wounded quickly, and right here should be said a word of praise for our ambulance drivers, who all day ran time after time into the jaws of death on their errands of mercy. They laid down their lives as calmly and as willingly as the doughboys with the heated rifles speaking in the midst of the battle.

Say a word for the ammunition train drivers who took their trucks up the road with the shells popping right and left. Remember the doctor who stuck at their posts close to the firing line, many of them famed surgeons who are serving their country for the love of it. Keep in mind the world-renowned surgeon now lying at the point of death with a wound through his chest because he insisted on sticking where he was most needed.

The communiqués tell nothing of what these men do, but they make it possible for eight of every ten of the wounded fighting men to rejoin their comrades at the front.

If there is any one in the world who doubts the stamina of American men, call attention to one unit of our lads who Thursday morning went over the top fifteen minutes after reaching the front line, following an all-night ride in camions. They fought all day Thursday and Thursday night and all day yesterday, and today they are there in line, with no other rest than brief snatches of sleep.

Stretcher bearers tell me that they have picked up hundreds of wounded men with grievous hurts sleeping soundly where they fell. That is the American fighters' spirit. They stop when their job is done.

We were here in the woods when we heard of bitter fighting up ahead. Leaving the car, we started that way. We went through the woods where the shot-down trees lay in tangled profusion, across a wheat field dotted with ugly shell holes, and then into another strip of woods.

Here we began to see the bodies of French and Americans, but mostly those of Germans, sprawled in grotesque attitudes where they had made the supreme sacrifice. It seemed a holy place. It was almost calm here on the wooded hillside where so many men had died and now lay about awaiting burial.

Suddenly a steam hammer sound ahead told us to keep out of machine gun range. Through the trees over a little embankment and then on the other side was a sight never to be forgotten. A German trench position fifty yards in length was seemingly filled with enemy dead. I started counting, got up to seventeen at one end and stopped the grewsome undertaking.

Where Some Americans Fell.

The scene at the other end of the trench told the story that all fighting Americans have now learned. There had been a German machine-gun nest, sheltered by wickerwork, with earth behind. Just in front lay the bodies of three doughboys, part of the platoon that had charged the gun. I knew their comrades had been successful when I saw behind the breastworks the bodies of a German gunner and two helpers, dead from American bullets. All lay where they had fallen in the fight, more than twenty-four hours before.

On beyond the trench position lay dozens of dead Germans, and here and there an American fighter who had finished his work. Then from the top of an embankment I heard a whistle, and saw, a mile ahead, a line of brown backs leap out from the edge of a wood and start across a wheat field. As they went through the ripened grain I heard the machine gun going again from the strip of woods ahead of them. Some fell,

but others kept on, and at last I saw them going into the edge of the wood in skirmish formation. I do not know yet how far they went, but it was in that wood that bitter fighting took place.

I heard a bumping behind us, and there was a Ford ambulance on the exposed road, going to get the boys who had fallen.

A glance over the field of wheat showed the surface shimmering in the Summer breeze, broken here and there by indentations. Some of them were made by shell holes, but they were mostly by falling bodies of fighting men. As we left I could hear machine guns going in that wood.

While this operation was being staged, Americans south of Soissons made advances yesterday afternoon east of Courchamps, capturing three villages and taking some prisoners.

ALLIED GUNS COMMAND RAILWAY JUNCTION

German Supply Line Is Menaced —Bridges at Soissons Also Under Fire.

WITH THE AMERICAN ARMY ON THE AISNE-MARNE FRONT, July 20, (Associated Press.)—Gunfire increased on both sides after daylight today with the continuation of the struggle on this front.

Up to midday the French and Americans had made an average gain of more than a mile along the line of Château-Thierry-Soissons, while another gain of a similar distance had been made south of the Marne and east of Château-Thierry, thus helping to squeeze the bag in which the Germans were.

Information from beyond Château-Thierry indicates the beginning of a movement by the Germans that may develop into an effort by the Crown Prince to extricate his army.

The character of the fighting has been radically altered, and the Germans have been forced more into the open. The trenches run in such a manner as to leave none into which they can fall back, forcing them to depend upon those which they hastily construct.

There was a marked decrease in German aerial activity late today and the big guns were less active. The greater part of the German airplanes appeared to be used in patrolling their own lines.

The battle raged all night and the Germans this morning increased their artillery fire to a degree greater than any attained since Thursday.

The allied guns were much more effective, however, as reports from the aviators and observation balloons on the enemy positions came in. There were numerous bombing raids by the airmen this morning.

The Franco-American forces are continuing the steady pounding of the northern part of the line, near Soissons, although the movement is lacking the dashing advance which characterized the first days of the attack.

The allied guns now command the bridges southeast of Soissons.

The allied advance to the Soissons-Château-Thierry road has brought the Allies within artillery striking distance of the junction of the railroad serving the Germans as a line of communication. The junction is under fire already, and unless the desperate attempt which the Germans are making to hold is successful thousands of the Crown Prince's men may be cut off.

Attempts of the Crown Prince's Generals to rally their forces to meet the movement of the Allies has resulted in such strengthening of the opposition as to indicate that the battle is approaching the point when the armies will soon be locked in a giant struggle.

Both on the northern end of the line and to the south the reinforced Germans are making a desperate effort to hold their positions. The combat to the southward is extending nearer to Château-Thierry.

Already in the course of this offensive one American unit has taken since Thursday 2,889 prisoners, including ninety-one officers.

Another American unit on the northern front has captured 2,261 prisoners, including thirty-two officers.

Among the latter were a Colonel and two Majors, all in one group.

From a hill east of Dommiers, about six kilometers southwest of Soissons, the correspondent saw American troops going into action in the renewal of their forward movement late yesterday afternoon. The advance was well organized and the system worked well from one end of the line to the other.

Under a barrage fire from 75's and 55's, American infantry and machine gunners advanced through ripening grain fields, which had been trampled by the retreating Germans Thursday, and reached their objectives according to schedule, despite the fire of German machine guns. The bombardment of the big German guns was feeble at this point.

The Americans started from a point just west of the Paris-Soissons road, near the shell-shattered village of Missy-aux-Bois, advancing nearly a kilometer before the Germans began to reply with their big guns to the American barrage.

Missy-aux-Bois lies in a valley, and the Americans were advancing up grade toward the east. A few tanks, here and there, preceded the infantrymen. As the Americans progressed, the enemy barrage fire increased.

The hillsides east of Dommiers, over which the Americans advanced, were dotted with dead. The entire region was well within the German lines until after the Franco-American offensive of Thursday. One quickly dug trench had been filled with German bodies. They were machine gunners who had been caught by the terrific fire of the allied artillery. In many places the German dead were in piles, while a trench on the crest of a hill contained more than 100 dead.

The allied advance began at exactly 5:30 o'clock after intense barrage fire along the entire front from Soissons to Château-Thierry. As far as the eye could reach could be seen allied observation balloons, while the sky was specked with allied airplanes, darting in various directions, many returning from over the German lines to make a quick report on observations and the result of the fire of the big guns. From the hillside the smoke and dust, thrown up by the allied shells, could be seen away beyond the advancing Americans.

American troops passing through a ruined French town just recaptured after fierce fighting in the Marne.

"All the News That's Fit to Print."

The New York Times.

THE WEATHER

Showers, northwest wind today; Thursday fair; wind variable.
For full weather report see Page 13.

VOL. LXVII...NO. 22,103.   ...   NEW YORK, WEDNESDAY, JULY 31, 1918.—TWENTY PAGES.   TWO CENTS

ALLIES AGAIN DRIVE FORWARD NEAR FERE; PRUSSIAN GUARDS PUSHED BACK TWO MILES; OUTWITTED AND OUTFOUGHT BY AMERICANS

CENTRAL POWERS FACE DEADLOCK OVER SPOILS

All Four Are Now Involved in Clashes for Which No Solution Is in Sight.

POLISH DISPUTE SHARPER

Austria Firm in Demand to Bring New Kingdom Under Hapsburg Rule.

Ignore German Aims in Caucasus—Inspired Berlin Warning of Threatened Danger.

Special Cable to THE NEW YORK TIMES.

AMSTERDAM, July 30, (Dispatch to The London Daily Express.)—Trouble is admittedly brewing among the Central Powers, first between Germany and Austria over the Polish question, and also between Bulgaria and Turkey regarding the Dobrudja. Every possible solution of both questions has been repeatedly discussed by the four Governments, but no agreement is likely to be reached.

Germany will not hear of the Austrian annexation of Poland in any form whatever, whereas Austria considers the bringing of the "Kingdom" of Poland under the Hapsburg sceptre as a "vital necessity." It was hoped in Germany that once Czernin resigned no more would be heard of the "Austro-Polish" solution of the Polish question, and thus Austria was permitted to annex important Rumanian lands under the pretext of the "safety of her frontiers."

It appears from an inspired article by Emil Zimmermann in yesterday's Berlin Lokal-Anzeiger that Baron Burian is just as anxious as Czernin was about the Austro-Polish solution, over which Austria seems likely to remain most obdurate.

No peaceful solution is in sight regarding the Turkish-Bulgarian Dobrudja and Adrianople difficulties. The feeling is rising high in both Sofia and Constantinople. The Turks are accusing the Bulgarians as being "the Germans of the Balkans," while the Bulgarians are saying equally hasty things about the Turks.

Zimmermann urges the Central Powers not to fight among themselves during the war, for otherwise "what they have so far managed to gain will probably be lost."

BAYONETS ROUTED GUARDS

Our Soldiers Whip the Kaiser's Shock Troops in Man-to-Man Fighting.

EPIC BATTLE FOR SERGY

Village Changed Hands Nine Times, but Is Now Back of American Line.

BROOKLYN BOY'S HEROIC ACT

Hyland Held Street with One Comrade After Rest of Platoon Was Shot Down.

By EDWIN L. JAMES.

Copyright, 1918, by The New York Times Company.
Special Cable to THE NEW YORK TIMES.

WITH THE AMERICAN ARMY ON THE MARNE, July 30.—Sergy changed hands nine times in twenty-four hours. That tells the story of the bitter fighting when the German command threw two fresh Guard divisions against the Americans north of the Ourcq yesterday, in an endeavor to put them back across the stream.

The result may be best told by saying that the Americans are not only on the north side of the Ourcq this morning, but in positions further advanced than when the Crown Prince hurled his violent attacks against our line early yesterday. At least one German Guard division was rendered fightless for some time to come.

Had the Americans not held back these fighting Prussians the French would not have been able to make their advance north of Fère-en-Tardenois, and also on our right.

Germany's Best Shock Troops Beaten

The Prussians and Bavarians now trying to hold back the Americans were brought hurriedly from the rear, where they had been held to make an attack against the English, preparatory to the Crown Prince's grand drive in August.

It should be a source of the greatest pride to America that her youthful soldiers are able to hold their own against the Kaiser's best shock troops, for such the Prussian and Bavarian Guards are.

At Sergy was an American division which met the 4th Prussian Guard Division. The result speaks for itself.

As told in these dispatches yesterday, it was part of the German plan to stand on the north bank of Ourcq and hold the Americans while the withdrawal behind the lines was made more easily. The charge of the Americans across the river on Sunday, in which they took Seringes and Sergy and established themselves, broke up this part of the German plan.

Early yesterday morning the Americans in Sergy were attacked by the 4th Prussian Guard Division, which had arrived only a few hours before from the training area in Lorraine. Overwhelmed by vastly superior numbers, the Americans withdrew before a terrific small artillery and machine-gun fire.

But when the Prussians got into the town the German artillery could no longer shoot into it. That gave a chance for man to man in a hand-to-hand fight, and the Americans grasped the opportunity.

Machine Guns Under the Red Cross.

They rushed back into the village, up against a withering fire from machine guns placed practically in every building. When the charge was at its height, from a building bearing the Red Cross five machine guns spoke with telling effect. But soon the Americans got hand-to-hand with the Prussians. In repayment for the deadly machine-gun work our men got their bayonets into action, and no German has yet been known to stand before a bayonet with an American behind it. In half an hour we had possession of the town.

Down came the German artillery fire again, and we had to retire. Into the village came the Prussians, and when the artillery fire stopped, back went the Americans. Again we drove them out. No sooner had we got into the village, when back came the Prussians. The German airplanes rendered their men great aid, sweeping down close to the ground and raking our lines with machine guns. They also used bombs against us. Neither side would throw gas into Sergy, for fear of injuring their own troops.

The fighting went back and forth all morning. First we had the mauled village, and then the Prussians had it. Both sides made advances from edges of woods and retreated to that shelter. Finally, just after noon, when it was our turn in the village, the American artillery got down a heavy barrage, which caught the Prussian attackers and drove them back. By the time the enemy came again we were too strongly situated for them, and the result of the bloody battle was that we held Sergy.

Bitter Battle at Seringes.

Almost the same story tells the fighting yesterday for Seringes, only the battle was not so fierce and the village changed hands five times instead of nine.

To realize that this fighting was entirely different from the rear-guard actions of last week one has only to consider the hurrying of the Guard divisions, which are shock troops, into the line and the infantry counterattacks, whereas during the six previous days we had machine-gun opposition almost exclusively.

The truth of the matter is that the Germans wanted to hold their line on the north bank of the Ourcq for some days. Sergy and Seringes are strong villages on a series of hills running along the north side of the Ourcq, and evidence taken from prisoners showed that the Americans were supposed to have been held on the southern bank of the stream.

Evidence still points to the probability that the Germans intend to go back to the Vesle and hold there. The desire to hold the northern bank of the Ourcq is to be explained for the same reason.

Fighting to Save Supplies.

The Germans tried to hold the French and Americans in the southern part of the Forest de Ris. A trip through that forest today showed hundreds of tons of ammunition for big German guns, piled six feet high in rows a hundred yards long for some distances. This ammunition had been stored there to be used in the advance on Paris.

It is the belief that in Nesle Woods, north of the Ourcq, the Crown Prince has stored great supplies, and intends to get them out at any cost. Else why did he hurl against the Americans two divisions from the dwindling supply of his reserve divisions? This was done, of course, to stop the Americans, who could not be halted by ordinary German troops.

He succeeded in slowing down the Americans yesterday, but there are Americans in France who have not yet faced the Kaiser's fighters. The Germans have got to go further back, and they know it well. The throwing by the German command of fresh Guard divisions against the Americans is significant, when it is known definitely that it is planning another drive soon, perhaps against the British, for which it will need all available troops.

Lies Told to the Germans.

A captured officer said a regimental commander told his men two days ago that the Germans had hit the British and captured the Channel ports, but that the announcement had not yet been made by Ludendorff. He explained that Germany was still winning the war and that the withdrawal from the Soissons-Rheims sector was only for strategical reasons. The German command promised the German people to hit the British, and wants to make good.

Another significant factor in yesterday's counterattack against the Americans was that the Germans brought a large number of new airplanes, at least sixty, into the sector, and thus gained a temporary air supremacy which enabled the air fighters to do effective work against our troops. Undismayed by superior numbers, for the sixty were in addition to many chase machines the Hun already had, the American fliers went out to meet them, and there were many air fights all day long. British and French aviators also aided us. The Americans last night believed that they had brought down at least six airmen.

Grenades Under the White Flag.

The Germans are trying every art of their kind of warfare against our boys, but the Americans are learning fast. For instance, one squad advanced toward a platoon of Americans yesterday waving a white flag. The Americans let them come about a hundred yards and then cut loose and annihilated them. That they acted rightly was shown by the fact that the white flag had been tied to the handle of a live grenade, and while the Germans appeared at a distance to be weaponless, each was loaded down with deadly grenades.

Another favorite trick is that the German machine gunners, when seeing Americans approach, wait until our lads are close, when they cut loose with a final spurt of bullets, and then step out and cry "Kamerad!" Our men have adopted a rule that any German who shoots a machine gun at a closer range than 200 yards cannot be allowed to surrender.

Considering the good treatment we give the German wounded, their use of the Red Cross flag to shelter machine guns appears particularly dastardly.

If the Germans' withdrawal seems to be a success, it is because they use countless machine guns, of which they appear to have an inexhaustible supply. Our men, seeing what these deadly weapons can do, are very grateful that our army plans will eventually give us a great number of machine guns. Incidentally, the best German machine gun is a Maxim.

Seeing reapers at work today in wheatfields liberated by the allied offensive led me to make inquiries, which revealed that the advance of the Americans alone has freed several million bushels of ripened wheat for the use of the French people.

It happens also that the advance of the American contributed very largely to freeing the main railroad line through Château-Thierry. The Paris-Nancy line is thus freed, and will soon be in operation.

Brooklyn Boy's Story of Heroism.

I struck up a conversation last night with a weary-looking lad back from the front, and he told me a story that ought to be recorded. He is James Hyland of 121 Fort Greene Place, Brooklyn, and he used to be a law clerk. Hyland was a member of a platoon of fifty men who were ordered to go in Sunday morning and hold a certain street.

From a wooded shelter on the northern bank of the Ourcq the platoon went across a sloping field toward Sergy. Caught under the fire of machine guns on the outskirts of the village, they kept on going. Twenty-odd of them reached Sergy and got into a poor shelter, where they were raked by machine guns and snipers. The Lieutenant in command, who is now dead, decided, inasmuch as his orders were to stay there until relieved, that he would stick.

Hyland said that in the windows of a Red Cross building three machine guns kept picking them off. The Americans fired nearly all their ammunition trying vainly to get those guns. Then they rushed them, but had to come back. Foodless and waterless, they stayed there as the long hours dragged on, and the gallant band grew smaller and smaller. All the officers had been killed, and the privates elected commanders, who one by one were shot down.

When relief reached them at 7 o'clock Hyland and one comrade were left of the fifty who had started. Hyland was in command, and the two were shooting their last bullets at the machine gunners up the street they had been told to hold.

I have heard of no instance that better tells the spirit of Americans in this war. They do not know when to quit. In fact the allegation is being made that they do not know well enough the line between proper bravery and recklessness.

OUR MEN DEFY BARRAGE

Rush Through Heaviest Fire; Now at Apex of Allied Advance.

STRUGGLE IS MERCILESS

LONDON, July 30.—French and American troops in the region of Fère-en-Tardenois again thrust their lines forward, despite stiff resistance from the enemy.

The American troops have advanced from Sergy nearly two miles, again defeating the Prussian Guards and Bavarians. This followed a terrific German assault on the American lines, whereby the Germans won Cierges, [southeast of Sergy,] and apparently still hold it.

The French gains were made northeast of Fère and to the eastward of Sergy.

Heavy counterattacks were made by the Germans along almost the entire front to the east, but gained little ground except west of St. Euphraise [southwest of Rheims.]

In this same area the French troops have captured Romigny.

Some advance also has been effected by the Allies in the Ardre Valley, toward the village of Aubilly.

The main advance on the westerly side of the front seems to have been at Grand Rozoy, northwest of Fère-en-Tardenois. The French here are progressing north to the crest of the plateau between the Vesle and the Ourcq. The Germans drove the French out of Bengneux, but it was afterward retaken.

There has been heavy fighting near Buzancy, five miles south of Soissons, and also in Plessier Wood, about five miles further south.

There are now seventy-one German divisions in the Marne salient. Of these, ten belong to the northern army of Crown Prince Rupprecht of Bavaria. Five of these ten have been twice used in attacks.

Our Men Defy Barrage and Advance.

WITH THE AMERICAN ARMY ON THE AISNE-MARNE FRONT, July 30, (Associated Press.) — Through a barrage as deadly as any the Germans have laid down on any sector for months, the American soldiers, comprising men from the Middle West and Eastern States, pushed their line forward a little more today, and tonight it forms the apex of the long allied front between the Marne and the Vesle.

Their progress was somewhat less than two miles, but their operation is regarded as a brilliant one in view of the determined countering by the Germans.

On either side the French also moved forward, while steady pressure was maintained against the east and west flanks.

Information early in the day indicated the withdrawal of the 4th Division of Guards from this front, but it developed that that renowned organization and the Bavarians were still there, and the strong opposition they offered justified their reputation. But their sacrifice was in vain.

The Americans withstood two heavy attacks during the night, and at daylight began their operations, which left them tonight well to the north of Sergy, on the long slopes approaching the heavy woods beyond Nesles, a town directly east of Serignes-et-Nesles, for which the Germans fought bitterly.

The east end of the line swings northeasterly opposite this point, and then drops off sharply in the direction of Cierges and Ronchères. The Ourcq Rivers has been left far behind, the line being pushed forward across the zone to the northwest.

The Germans are holding positions in Nestles forest, from which their guns are shelling ineffectively.

It was late in the day before the whole of Seringes was cleared. The Germans clung to the northern part of the town tenaciously, and used their machine guns murderously.

Neither side used artillery in this particular battle. There was hand-to-hand fighting in the streets, in which the Americans proved the masters, driving the enemy before them.

No Mercy Shown in Battle.

The story of the fight for the possession of Meury Farm, lying directly south of Seringes, will long be remembered in the history of the division. The Germans, on their withdrawal, left behind a strong force of machine gunners and infantry. The Americans moved forward through the yellow wheatfields, which were sprayed and torn by bullets. But they advanced as though on a drill ground.

The American guns laid down a heavy artillery fire, but notwithstanding this many Germans remained when it came to hand-to-hand fighting. In a group of farm buildings the enemy had set up a strong defense. Here the Germans stuck to their guns, and the Americans rushed them and killed the gunners at their post.

It was a little battle, without mercy, and typical of similar engagements along the whole line. The Prussian Guards and Bavarians everywhere fought in accordance with their training, discipline, and traditions, but were outwitted and outfought.

To the north of the farm, up the long slopes leading to the woods, the Americans encountered the fiercest exhibition of Germany's war science. The Germans laid down a barrage which, it was said, was as heavy as had ever been employed. The American guns replied heavily.

The order for the advance came, and the line moved forward across the grain fields directly through the barrage. On a nearby hillside the chief staff officers watched the operation. They saw shells fall, leaving long gaps in the line in some cases, but the troops never halted.

On through the barrage the Americans went into the German positions, attacking fiercely the machine gun and infantry detachments. The barrage died away, the Germans leaving the work of resistance to the men they had failed to protect with their heavy guns.

German Forces Cut Up.

The Germans were "mopped up" and the Americans held their new line, just east of the forest. Not many prisoners were taken, but here and there a few were rounded up and brought in.

Sergeant Louis Loetz of Sioux City contributed fourteen. He attacked eighteen Germans who had become separated from their command, killing four of them and capturing the others.

Heavy execution was done by the Americans. Eight captured Guards said that they were all that remained of a company of eighty-six. Yesterday their number had been reduced to thirty and a Lieutenant. Today the Lieutenant and all but they were killed.

Corporal Chris Berthelsen of Sioux City was among the men of the first wave to cross the Ourcq River on the recent advance. They immediately went after machine guns on a hill on the north bank of the Ourcq.

| "All the News That's Fit to Print." | # The New York Times. | THE WEATHER
Thundershowers, not so warm today; tomorrow fair, light west winds. For full weather report see Page 10. |

VOL. LXVII...NO. 22,112.   NEW·YORK, FRIDAY, AUGUST 9, 1918.—TWENTY PAGES.   TWO CENTS Metropolitan District | THREE CENTS Within 200 Miles. | FOUR CENTS Elsewhere.

HAIG BREAKS FOE'S LINE ON 25-MILE FRONT; GAINS 7 MILES, TAKES 10,000 MEN, 100 GUNS; GERMAN MAN POWER VISIBLY ON THE WANE

ATTACK BEGINS AT DAWN

British and French Push Forward from Near Albert South to Avre.

ADVANCE IS VERY RAPID

Multitude of Tanks Leads the Rush of Allies That Sweeps the Enemy Before It.

HARD DAY AT MORLANCOURT

But the British Thrust to the South Reaches Framerville, Seven Miles Back.

10,000 Prisoners Counted; Enormous Booty Taken

PARIS, Friday, Aug. 9, 4:40 A. M.—The number of prisoners taken by the French and British in Picardy now exceeds 10,000, according to the latest news from the battlefront.

The Allies also have taken an enormous booty in guns and material, says Marcel Hutin in the Echo de Paris.

LONDON, Aug. 8.—Under the command of General Haig, British and French struck a terrific blow early today at the German lines from near Albert south to Braches, on the Avre above Montdidier.

The surprised enemy gave way along nearly the entire front of more than twenty-five miles, and the allied forces made swift progress, headed by a large number of tanks.

Late today, according to General Haig's official report, the allied thrust had extended at the extreme points to Framerville [southeast of Albert,] showing a gain of nearly seven and one-half miles.

North and south of that place, also, a large area had been won by the Allies, whose advance still continued at a late hour.

The general line reached by the allied troops ran from Plessier-Rozainvillers to Beaucourt, to Caix, to Framerville, to Chipilly, and to the west of Morlancourt.

"Tenacity, Audacity, Victory," Petain's Words to His Soldiers

PARIS, Aug. 8.—General Pétain, Commander in Chief of the French Armies, has issued the following order of the day to the French troops:

"Four years of effort, with our stanch allies; four years of trials, stoically endured, begin to bear fruit.

"His fifth attempt in 1918 smashed, the invader retreats, his man power decreases, and his morale wavers, while at your side your American brothers have no sooner landed than they have made a baffled enemy feel the weight of their blows.

"Incessantly placed in the advanced guard of the allied peoples, you have prepared the triumphs of tomorrow.

"Not long ago I said to you: 'Abnegation, patience; your comrades are arriving.'

"Today I say: 'Tenacity, audacity; you shall force victory.'

"Soldiers of France, I salute your banners illuminated with new glory."

In his official bulletin General Haig did not specify the number of prisoners and guns taken, but in the House of Commons tonight Bonar Law made this announcement:

"Up to 3 o'clock this afternoon, on a twenty-kilometer front between Morlancourt and Montdidier, we had reached all our objectives and captured 100 guns and 7,000 prisoners.

"The advance was between four and five miles, and at one point seven miles."

"I do not desire," he continued, "that any one should exaggerate the importance of the achievement. It is quite possible, indeed it may be regarded as probable, that the Germans, on account of previous attacks, had intended to retire. But this attack has come upon them as a complete surprise and has upset whatever plans they had formed."

The attack took the Germans by surprise, as the weather has not been such as would generally be chosen for the commencement of new operations.

It is believed here that the troops engaged by the allied forces are elements of Crown Prince Rupprecht's army. It has long been known that he had reserves concentrated behind the Arras-Amiens-Montdidier front, where it was expected that the Germans would make their next blow.

The moment chosen for the blow is regarded as an opportune one, as it is known that a large number of Rupprecht's reserves were taken by the German Crown Prince to extricate his army from the predicament it had encountered through Marshal Foch's counteroffensive on the Soissons-Rheims salient.

FORMING 'LAST STAND' ARMY

Kaiser Preparing Special Force of 500,000 Men to Defend the Rhine.

KNOWS TIDE HAS TURNED

Best Officers and Soldiers from All His Divisions to be Called to "Old Guard."

FOCH'S RESERVES INTACT

Hindenburg Believed Now to Have Only 20 Fresh Divisions —No Chance for New Drive.

By EDWIN L. JAMES.
Copyright, 1918, by The New York Times Company.
Special Cable to THE NEW YORK TIMES.

WITH THE AMERICAN ARMY, Aug. 8.—From sections of the German Army there are being drawn a certain proportion of officers and the sturdiest soldiers for the formation of a force of half a million men which is to receive special training and have special organization. There are to be no Poles or Alsatians in this army, but only fighters that the Kaiser believes he can trust to the last.

This German force is not to be used as a hammer in any new drive for Paris; it is not to be used for any blow against the British; it is not to be used to "punish" the Americans; but, according to information reaching allied commanders, is being formed for no other purpose than to stand back of the Rhine against an invasion of German soil.

It so happens that any allied approach to the Rhine would be through the Alsace-Lorraine line, on a large part of which American forces stand. It is this force that

the Americans will face when, with the French, we get ready to "take the war to Germany."

Come what may between now and that time, the Kaiser wants to be sure to have the force with which to make the stand for the Fatherland and himself.

Knows Now the Tide Is Turned.

Than the formation of such an army for such a purpose at such a time, when the Kaiser needs all his available forces on the western front, what could better show that the German high command realizes that the tide of war is about to turn, if, indeed, it has not already done so? One may not say that the war is almost won, but one may say that the sun now shines on our side of the fence. Up to three weeks ago, for months the Allies waited to see what the Germans were doing and wondered where they would strike next; now it is the Germans who wonder where the Allies will strike next. The war will continue to be thus.

Far more in value than the terrain won back from the Germans in the last three weeks, is General Foch's action in taking the initiative which, with the help of American troops and the French and British, he will maintain.

Certainly, the sun shines on our side of the fence. For the first time since Russia broke down the Allies now have a numerical superiority of effectives. While for some little time the number of Americans in France has given our side superiority as to actual numbers, the recent fighting has brought into the line and support positions Americans in sufficient numbers, the presence of whom, coupled with the German losses of the last month, places us in a position of superiority of men ready to fight.

It cannot be said that the American Army just now is as good a machine as the German Army, but we have the makings all ready and seasoned. To carry this to a revelation of numbers would not do at this time.

German Morale Failing.

German Army morale is unquestionably weakening, so far as certain elements which make up a large part of the army are concerned. But disregarding that, and, putting all the Germans on an equal plane, when the Germans started their drive on July 15 Hindenburg had some seventy divisions in reserve with which to batter his way to Paris. In the fighting to date, since then, seventy-three German divisions have been identified, of which forty-eight were brought up from the German reserve. Of these forty-eight, sixteen were so decimated that they cannot be used as shock troops for at least four months. Four of these were put out by the Americans—the 5th Guard Division, the 4th Prussian Guard, the 23d, and the 216th.

The Germans now face the problem of building up these divisions with a great scarcity of first-class fighting material.

Hindenburg had to draw very heavily on his reserves, it is thus seen. On the other hand, Foch hardly touched his. Germany now has twenty fresh divisions.

She can use these for her promised drive against the British. But will she? I think she will not; she dare not. Hindenburg dare not take a chance with those twenty divisions. Should he even succeed against the British, he would not have gained a victory, for it would leave him stripped of shock troops to meet another allied attack. Germany will not take that chance.

It will be many weeks before she will have enough shock divisions to stage another drive. While Hindenburg is building up another reserve force Foch will be adding new American divisions to his already strong shock force. This means that Germany would have to have a larger reserve force than at any time this Summer to be able to try a serious drive again. It appears that she may not be able to try another drive this Summer.

This leads to the conclusion that the Allies have more than succeeded in the task which confronted Marshal Foch when he obtained unified command of the allied armies. In boastful terms Germany had announced that by a series of drive after drive she was going to get Paris and win the war this year before America was a telling factor. The general view in the allied camps last March was that if the Allies could hold Germany this year all would be well.

Germany More Than Held.

Germany has been more than held, and there is nothing she can do the rest of this year that Foch need seriously fear. Certainly no one fears what she may do next year, when to the allied forces which held the Germans this year will be added at least 1,500,000 more Americans, against whom the enemy will have no counterpart. Then the war will be taken to Germany, where it belongs.

That the Kaiser knows, and that is why he is forming a new force of 500,000 men, to be his "Old Guard," which will make for him the last stand of Prussian militarism behind the Rhine.

Foch's Reserves Intact.

The Germans now face the problem of building up these divisions with a great scarcity of first-class fighting material.

Hindenburg had to draw very heavily on his reserves, it is thus seen. On the other hand, Foch hardly touched his. Germany now has twenty fresh divisions.

GERMANY LACKING IN MEN AT HOME; ARMY'S EFFECTIVES ALSO DIMINISH

Amsterdam Hears of Discontent Over New Combing Out to Fill Army's Ranks.

SHOCK OVER U-BOAT FAILURE

Depression Caused by Realizing That America Is Shifting the Balance of Power.

By GEORGE RENWICK.

Copyright, 1918, by The New York Times Company.
Special Cable to THE NEW YORK TIMES.

AMSTERDAM, Aug. 8.—I learn that the comb out in Germany, to which I recently referred, is being carried out with the greatest severity. This action is, I am informed, causing much discontent and considerable depression, coming, as it does, after a period in which the German people had been so definitely assured of the vast numerical superiority of their forces in the field.

Some months ago very considerable numbers of business men were released from service in order to look for or carry on business in neutral countries and in various Russian provinces, as well as to begin on an increase of home businesses producing articles for export to those places. The great majority of the persons so released have now been called up again, especially travelers in neutral countries.

To this evidence that Germany is in need of men must be added a decision not to release yet the old classes which were recently promised that they would be sent home at an early date.

Travelers from the Fatherland say that Germany is in an extremely despondent mood, especialy in the Rhineland centres, where a vast number of wounded men have made a very hard impression on the population. A curious thing one gentleman just arrived from Germany tells me is the general discussion heard everywhere regarding the U-boat war. That is much more talked about than the offensives, as it cannot be longer concealed from the people that there are very large American forces now at the front in France. The German man in the street is greatly surprised that the U-boat has obviously done so little—done nothing, indeed—to prevent the allied armies from being so greatly strengthened.

That feeling undoubtedly caused Admiral von Holtzendorff, just before he retired, to endeavor to explain away the U-boat's ill-successes in that direction, and in yesterday's Cologne Gazette a well-known naval writer, Captain von Kühlwetter, warns the people not to go on expecting too much from the submarines.

"England's Grand Fleet still floats today, despite our unparalleled U-boats," he says, "and it bars us from the sea, and will continue to do that so long as no equal power can be placed against it. The U-boat in battle against the Grand Fleet is not a deciding weapon."

Regarding the offensive on the front, the same indifference and fatalism prevails as that referred to in more than one Reichstag speech at the time when the Kühlmann crisis arose.

In the Berliner Tageblatt General von Ardenne prepares the people for a further retreat, which, as I gather from visitors from Germany, is just what the people do expect. The war of movement, he says, is still going on. That means, he adds, that the retirement of the German right wing must not be regarded as concluded. It is likely that one or more defensive positions will be found and then given up after they have served their purpose.

He says it is quite natural that the people were surprised and alarmed by the giving up of positions north of the Ourcq, because "the official communiqués of July 29 and 30 and Aug. 2 stated that on the whole front from Soissons to southwest of Rheims strong enemy attacks were defeated, and one could not therefore quite understand why a retirement from the battlefield should take place."

Ardenne makes a long explantion in his usual style, but cannot disguise the seriousness of the situation. The German offensive, he declares, has suffered a disagreeable interruption, and all the comfort he can give is to say it will be resumed again.

Orders Seized by French Show Heavy Losses Are Worrying German High Command.

GERMAN PARENTS PROTEST

Threats of Resistance in Saxony and Bavaria to Keep Young Boys from Front.

By WALTER DURANTY.

Copyright, 1918, by The New York Times Company.
Special Cable to THE NEW YORK TIMES.

WITH THE FRENCH ARMIES, Aug. 8.—History is again repeating itself. The Allies have followed the second victory of the Marne by a combined attack in the region of the Somme.

At 5 o'clock this morning, after short but extremely violent artillery preparation, the French and British attacked on a twenty-mile front between the river and Montdidier. The latest news shows that the French are progressing favorably. By 8 o'clock the Avre had been crossed south of Moreuil and all the first objectives reached.

Moreuil and Morizel, obstinately defended, were the scene of bitter fighting, but the whole German position on the Avre was threatened by an advance made further north along the Luce Rivulet, east of Hangard, in the direction of Aubecourt and Demuin.

Foch has thus refused to allow the enemy to reconstruct his force of manoeuvre, which, as was said three days ago, was the object of his recent rectifications of front and principal pre-occupation. As Mangin put it, the Crown Prince received a severe knock, and Rupprecht was in the position of a man who, after weakening himself to aid a friend, saw the latter temporarily hors de combat and wondered what on earth was going to happen to himself. Now he knows.

An important feature of the situation is that at present Germany is unquestionably facing a serious crisis of effectives. The class of 1919 has already been used to fill the gaps caused by previous battles, and little of the gradual flow of recuperated wounded is available.

It is known that the enemy leaders made an effort to shorten the instruction of the class of 1920, which ordinarily would not be ready before Autumn, but opposition was strong, and it was stated in Parliament that if the class were taken before its time no one could answer for the consequences. In Saxony and Bavaria especially the project was actually received with threats of resistance.

Seized German orders—evidence a hundredfold more reliable than statement of prisoners—throw a lurid light on the losses of the enemy in the recent battle. One, of July 2, runs:

"It is always desirable to relieve and reconstruct tired and weakened divisions, but in a time like the present this is not always possible."

Another shows that the 82d Regiment of the 22d Division, engaged in the Ardre Valley against Berthelot, was forced to form its three battalions into companies, owing to their terrific losses.

In the 5th Division in the same region the 3d Regiment had some companies entirely eliminated, and an order states that a Captain must transfer his command from one company to another as his own ceases to exist.

The 39th Regiment of the same division was scacely more fortunate. Engaged on July 20, it had lost from 60 to 75 per cent. of its total effectives by the 23d, and the next day the whole division had to be relieved.

RAID AUSTRIAN LINES.

ROME, Aug. 8.—Italian troops drove in an enemy advanced post on the mountain front north of Col del Rosso yesterday, taking prisoners and a machine gun, the War Office announced today. The text of the statement reads:

We drove back an advanced post north of Col del Rosso, capturing prisoners and a machine gun.

The enemy on Tuesday night, after brief artillery fire, attempted to storm our positions on the Cornone. Our artillery and infantry frustrated the attack.

Section
1

"All the News That's
Fit to Print."

The New York Times.

THE WEATHER
Fair Sunday; Monday warmer;
probably fair; east winds.
For full weather report see Page 17.

Section
1

VOL. LXVII...NO. 22,114.   NEW YORK, SUNDAY, AUGUST 11, 1918.—90 PAGES, in Nine Parts.   FIVE CENTS

SOMME SALIENT SMASHED, MONTDIDIER TAKEN; HUTIER'S ARMY FLEES AFTER FOCH'S NEW BLOW; 400 GUNS, MORE THAN 24,000 MEN CAPTURED

DOUBLE STROKE TAKES CITY

French Plunge Forward Six Miles After Capturing Montdidier.

BRITISH GAIN IN THE NORTH

Capture Morlancourt and Chipilly Ridge and Drive Forward on Bray.

FOE THROWN IN CONFUSION

So Shaken by the Swift Allied Strokes That He Cannot Counterattack.

LONDON, Aug. 10.—Throwing his 1st Army against the apex of the German salient southeast of Amiens, Marshal Foch today captured Montdidier, and followed up his success by smashing into the salient for an average depth of six miles on a thirteen-mile front, reaching a line extending from Andechy [seven miles northeast of Montdidier] to Elincourt [ten miles to the southeast.]

The attack on Montdidier, which was made from the north and southeast simultaneously, resulted in the capture of many prisoners and great quantities of material.

The whole allied line from Albert to the southern side of the Montdidier salient has been pushed eastward, reaching its maximum distance in that direction in the neighborhood of Chaulnes, at about the middle point of the fighting front of the last few days.

Between the Ancre and the Somme American troops have co-operated with British, and the two captured Morlancourt and held the village against heavy counterattacks.

The general line reached by the Allies in the Albert-Montdidier sector is described in Field Marshal Haig's night report as running from Lihons to Fresnoy-les-Roye, to Lignières, and Conchy-les-Pots.

The number of German prisoners was estimated in the British official day bulletin at 24,000, but this has been increased, according to the night report.

Allied Casualties Only 6,000.

LONDON, Aug. 10, (Associated Press.)—The advance of the allied armies on the Picardy battlefront continued today. Nowhere, it appears, have the Germans yet been able to organize for any severe counterstroke.

The guns captured by the Allies are now nearly 400 in number.

The total of prisoners is mounting rapidly because of the disorganization of the Germans.

Allied casualties, including all the killed, wounded, and missing, are less than 6,000, or not more than one-fourth of the number of prisoners counted. On the other hand, the German casualties have been very heavy.

The German communications have been so disorganized that thus far only two divisions of reserves have been identified, and these new troops have not been able to make any impression on the advancing Allies.

11 German Divisions Smashed.

Eleven German divisions have been defeated in the fighting of the last three days.

These eleven divisions are now in such condition that they can be of little use to the German command for a long time to come, and probably some can never be re-formed.

The two new divisions which appeared on the front were rushed down the two principal arteries of communication. It is along these arteries, however, that the Allies' forces are strongest, particularly in cavalry and tanks, and these reinforcements were far too few in numbers to stem the onrushing tide.

Retreat Along Whole Front.

WITH THE BRITISH ARMY IN FRANCE, Aug. 10, (Associated Press.)—North of the Ancre the British have firmly established their positions and are pushing out patrols toward Bray.

North of the Somme and also south of it the Germans are showing every sign of a rapid retreat. Most of the shells that came over from their batteries today were of small calibre and fired at extremely long range, showing that the enemy probably was removing his heavier pieces for a further retirement. The allied forces, who everywhere today advanced their lines, moved their artillery along with them.

North of the Somme the Allies, after taking Chipilly Spur, went on, driving the enemy before them.

In their advance south of the Somme the British captured Warvillers, Vrely, Folies, Rosières, and Vauvillers.

It is not easy to delineate the line as it stood this afternoon, for along the whole fighting front the allied forces had thrown screens of tanks, cavalry, and infantry pickets in scattered localities a long distance in advance, preparing the way for further penetration. The actual line, solidly held, could be conservatively described, however, as running:

From Albert, to Meracourt-sur-Somme, to Proyart, west of Chaulnes, and on to Rouvroy; thence east of Bouchoir, east of Faverolles and Piennes, east of Mortemer, and thence to Ricquebourg and Marqueglise.

Numerous tanks and "whippets" assisted the advancing infantry to smother the enemy's resistance.

British tanks have been seen well to the east of Meharicourt [about three miles southwest of Chaulnes.]

The Allies have captured many towns, large quantities of material, and a complete German divisional headquarters and staff. This headquarters was captured at Lihons.

Many more prisoners have been taken during the operations of the last twenty-four hours, among them troops from at least four new divisions that were hurled in north of the Somme.

Apparently, the enemy has rushed in new troops from wherever they could be obtained, for among the prisoners are some from reserve battalions of divisions located far to the north. This would indicate that considerable confusion prevails among Crown Prince Rupprecht's forces as a result of the unexpected allied assaults and their continued success.

The number of prisoners accounted for this morning was close to 25,000.

The enemy continues to destroy his stores of munitions in various localities along the battlefront, as is the practice of a beaten army.

The Germans are now well back toward the Somme, south of Peronne. With this stream at their back and the allied guns and airplanes pouring shells into the crossings over the Somme, the position of the enemy is serious.

Streams of German transports are still going eastward.

ADVANCED 13 MILES IN DAY.

French Infantry on Friday Set Record After Capturing Castel.

LONDON, Aug. 10.—When the French captured Beaufort on Friday, they made an advance of thirteen miles eastward from Castel.

PRESS ENEMY ON THE VESLE

Americans Repulse Repeated Counterattacks and Make Gains.

PREPARED FOR NEXT TASK

That Will Depend on Outcome to North—Taking Vesle-Aisne Terrain Not Essential.

DISCOVER GERMAN TRAPS

Explosives Left Camouflaged in Many Ways and Food and Water Poisoned.

Five of Our Airmen Fight 12 Enemy Machines and Down 2

WITH THE AMERICAN ARMY ON THE VESLE FRONT, Aug. 10, (Associated Press.)—In a battle in the air between twelve German and five American airplanes, Lieutenant Walter Avery of Columbus, Ohio, and Harold Buckley of Agawam, Mass., each brought down a German.

There were no casualties among the Americans.

By EDWIN L. JAMES.
Copyright, 1918, by The New York Times Company.
Special Cable to THE NEW YORK TIMES.

WITH THE AMERICAN ARMY, Aug. 10.—The American troops along the Vesle are keeping up a constant pressure against the enemy, making local but important gains. On the right and the left the French troops are pursuing the same policy.

In the last thirty-six hours the Germans have executed four counterattacks against the Americans between Bazoches and Fismes, using high explosive and gas preparation. All these attacks have been repulsed with losses, and our troops are holding along the Rheims-Soissons road and to the north of it in front of Fismes.

Lively artillery activity on both sides continues night and day.

From the body of a German officer who led one of yesterday's attacks was taken an order showing that the Germans are basing their operations on three lines—first, the line along the Vesle; second, the line along the heights between the Vesle and the Aisne, and third, the line behind the Aisne. The order directed the troops along the Vesle to hold at all costs for the present. Prisoners say they were ordered to hold along the Vesle until the Aisne defenses could be prepared.

Preparing for New Tasks.

Allied plans in this sector are in the making. It is not now essential to our plans to hold the region between the Vesle and the Aisne. Against determined German resistance it would not be worth taking at this stage. But affairs are going to shape themselves so that the Germans will go back of the Aisne when the proper time comes.

It is entirely probable the moves to be made on the Vesle line will be influenced by the outcome of the new allied drive in the region of Amiens. Meanwhile the Americans are steadily bettering their positions north of the Vesle, to be ready for whatever task may be given to them to do.

As our engineers clean up the territory from which the Germans have retreated they continue to find hundreds of infernal machines of all sorts. A favorite brand was to arrange the branches of trees to look .e the camouflage of a door of a dugout; when brushed aside they uld set off mines.

Bombs of great strength have been found in foul rubbish piles, which would naturally be burned. Loose boards were arranged on stairways so that the step of a man would detonate a charge. In a number of instances a large number of big shells have been placed in pockets under roads, arranged so that the weight of a passing camion would explode them.

The most novel infernal device was to arrange barbed wire entanglements so that attacking troops would explode mines. Not only did the Germans leave their infernal machines behind, but poisoned food and water also marked their backward trail.

These methods of warfare fortunately were discovered early, thanks largely to the previous experience of the French fighters, and such effective means have been taken against them that few losses have been caused to the Americans.

Following is a warning bulletin issued to all our soldiers on this front:

"Ruses, traps, and infernal devices employed by the enemy during his retreat — characteristic devices used by the enemy during his retreat between Artois and the Aisne included:

"First, within dugouts strings attached to branches apparently were attached to camouflage the entrance were attached to mines; detonators in charcoal or rubbish heaps; fuses connected with explosive charges fastened in stoves or fireplaces; protruding nails when stepped on exploded mines; shovels, picks, &c.,

apparently stuck at random into a heap of earth, when removed set off a mine; loose board on a step or a stairway when stepped upon set off an explosion.

"Second, along roads—a slight depression caused by the passage of vehicles would explode a detonator in a mine gallery under the road, where 150 or 200 shells were located.

"Three, in barbed wire entanglements—Wires concealed in grass to explode mines.

"Four, Houses—Intact houses remaining among others which have been destroyed should be approached or entered with the utmost circumspection.

"Five, Stables—Mines often are found under bricks or tiles covered with hay or manure. Hay, fodder, &c., should be removed with the utmost caution.

"Six, Poisoned Food—Abandoned food should be carefully inspected and investigated."

It is such instances in this kind of warfare that are teaching the American soldiers rapidly to arrive at a proper estimation of the enemy.

FOE'S COUNTERBLOWS FIERCE.

Repeated Attempts Friday Night to Beat Back Americans and French.

WITH THE AMERICAN ARMY ON THE VESLE FRONT, Aug. 10.—(Associated Press.)—In attempting to dislodge the French and the Americans from positions north of the Vesle River on both sides of Fismes the Germans launched repeated counterattacks, which began just before dark Friday night and continued until Saturday morning. There was desperate fighting in the region of Fismette, where the German attacks were repulsed by the Americans, who were clinging to the outskirts of the village. In the region of Bazoches the Germans made several vicious attacks, but the Allies successfully fought them off.

The Germans began with airplane attacks, the aviators attempting to bomb infantrymen north of the Vesle and bridges over which other troops were passing. French and American anti-aircraft guns beat off the German fliers, however.

Just after dark the Germans launched an artillery attack, which steadily increased in volume until nearly daylight, when the Franco-Americans counterattacked with such force that the Germans were forced to lessen the volume of their fire.

During the night the Germans attacked Fismette three times and once after daylight Saturday.

From the region southeast of Braisne to Fismes, the Franco-Americans put down such a terrific barrage that the Germans were stopped. Saturday morning the Teutons started another attack along the same line, but heavy artillery quickly checked this assault.

The enemy used much gas in attempting to dislodge the Americans from Fismette. Infantrymen plentifully supplied with machine guns also made futile attacks.

The Americans took a few prisoners at Fismette as a result of hand-to-hand encounters. After a second German night attack, the Americans retaliated and penetrated the German lines a short distance. They reached one of the enemy's first-aid field stations and took prisoner several wounded Germans.

The Americans then returned to their semi-circular positions at Fismette and resisted all attempts of the enemy to dislodge them. The Germans put their heaviest artillery into operation Saturday, but the big guns of the Allies returned the fire with interest.

The skies cleared this afternoon, and as a result there was much aerial activity.

SPEED OF ADVANCE SURPRISES LONDON

LONDON, Aug. 10.—Surprise is notably mingled with gratification in the comment of the morning newspapers on the continued advance of the Anglo-French forces in the Somme region.

No offensive in which the British Army has participated, it is remarked, ever made so much progress on the opening day, and although the advance was slower on Friday this, it is contended, was only to be expected.

The full story of Friday's opera-

tions apparently has not yet been told, as bad visibility made it difficult to obtain early news from the fighting front. The employment of a large number of light, fast tanks—the "whippets"—with strong forces of cavalry is regarded as giving entry to a new feature of battle.

The military correspondent of The Times, referring to the remarkable speed developed by the whippets in keeping pace with the cavalry, foresees a future when every heavy infantry company will have a small, light tank, while swarms of airmen will take the place of the cavalry and light infantry.

The extraordinary employment of aircraft in pursuit of the enemy is also remarked. The services they rendered obviously were of the utmost military value, which it is hoped is not out of proportion to the losses. The number of airmen officially reported not returned reached the high figure of fifty. This was mostly due to fire from the ground and is comprehensible in view of the fact that they flew at a height of only a few hundred feet, bombing trains, railway junctions, and bridges. The enemy's losses in the air were forty-eight machines destroyed and seventeen brought down out of control.

The newspapers comment upon the stubborn resistance the Germans are making on both wings of the salient, and the narrowness of this bulge is remarked as an allied disadvantage which it is hoped will be rectified by its enlargement through future operations.

A further success for the Allies is regarded as depending to a large extent upon the fate of the important railway town of Chaulnes. Should Chaulnes fall, says The Times, very large results may follow.

Nowhere is any attempt made to disguise the fact that a great German effort to retrieve the losses is inevitable.

This small version of the tank was developed by the French and nicknamed "whippet" by the British.

"All the News That's Fit to Print."

The New York Times.

THE WEATHER
Fair today; Tuesday partly cloudy; moderate shifting winds.
For full weather report see Page 16.

VOL. LXVII...NO. 22,186. ...   NEW YORK, MONDAY, SEPTEMBER 2, 1918.—SIXTEEN PAGES.   TWO CENTS | THREE CENTS | FOUR CENTS

LENINE REPORTED DEAD; WAS SHOT BY A GIRL; HAIG TAKES PERONNE AND 2,000 PRISONERS; PRESIDENT ASKS THE NATION'S UTMOST EFFORT

LENINE'S ASSASSIN CAUGHT

Official Bolshevist Paper Says She Is Girl of Intellectual Class.

LONDON, Sept. 1.—Nikolai Lenine, the Bolshevist Premier, who was shot twice by an assassin last Friday night at Moscow, has died of his wounds, according to a telegram from Petrograd to the Exchange Telegraph Company by way of Copenhagen.

The latest official news concerning Lenine's condition is in the form of two bulletins by Russian wireless, timed 7:30 and 8:30 Saturday evening respectively. These bulletins described his general condition as good, with immediate danger past, and stated that no complications had arisen.

A medical bulletin issued at 11 o'clock Saturday morning at Petrograd, and received here by Russian wireless service, says Lenine had a disturbed night. The bulletin adds:

"Pulse 112, temperature 37, Centigrade, (98.6 Fahrenheit, normal.) the effusion of blood in the pleura is not increasing.

Condition Serious, Stockholm Hears.
Copyright, 1918, by The New York Times
Special Cable to The New York Times

STOCKHOLM, Sept. 1.—News has been received here of an attempt on the life of Nikolai Lenine. One of the bullets damaged his left lung, and, although Lenine is conscious and seemingly confident, it is feared his condition is more serious than at first supposed. There is internal hemorrhage and his pulse is very weak.

This is not the first attempt on Lenine's life and the fact that there have not been many more is not due to any efficient bodyguard. Rumors have been continually put about that Lenine never moved without guards. This is untrue, both concerning him and Trotzky. Both Trotzky and Lenine laughed at the efforts of their assistants to protect them. Trotzky, for example, more than once, impatiently waiting for a motor, set off on foot until pursued and captured by his secretary.

There is nothing easier than for one to go straight into the National Hotel and into Lenine's private room. Lenine is seldom accompanied by more than his own secretary or his wife, whereas Kerensky never moved, in Moscow conference or Democratic Assembly, unaccompanied by two armed adjutants. Lenine wanders about by himself, sits where he chooses, here or there, even in such conferences as that which ratified the Brest-Litovsk peace, where feeling ran very high, and some such attempt might easily have been expected.

AMSTERDAM, Sept. 1.—The condition of Nikolai Lenine against whose life an attempt was made Friday night, is reported by the Russian newspaper Pravda to be serious, owing to internal hemorrhages, according to a telegram from Moscow. The Pravda says the Premier was shot by a young girl belonging to the intellectual class. She was arrested.

Americans Fight in Belgium; Strongholds Taken by Them

WITH THE BRITISH ARMY IN FLANDERS, Sept. 1, (Associated Press.)—For the first time, American troops fought on Belgian soil today.

They captured Voormezeele and were engaged in the operations elsewhere in the same locality.

LONDON, Sept. 1.—Reuter's correspondent at British Headquarters says he hears the Americans, besides taking Voormezeele, have captured several strong positions between Voormezeele and Ypres.

AUSTRALIANS WIN PERONNE

English Carry Outlying Towns to the North of the City.

Germans Lose Another Hindenburg Line Post and Continue Their Lys Retreat.

LONDON, Sept. 1.—Péronne, the German stronghold at the great bend of the Somme, fell today before the assaults of the Australians, who took two suburbs of the town in the same operation.

Co-operating with the Australians, London troops captured Bouchavesnes [four miles north of Péronne] and Rancourt [five miles], both villages on the road to Bapaume.

More than 2,000 prisoners were taken in these operations.

Further north the British drove the Germans from several villages south of Bapaume.

The struggle astride the Hindenburg line northeast of Bapaume continued with success for the British, who, according to Field Marshal Haig's night report, now hold the bitterly contested ruins of Bullecourt and Hendecourt.

The Germans continue to retreat, and the British to advance, in the Lys salient. Haig's troops are in close pursuit of the enemy, and, having occupied in the last twenty-four hours several villages in a strip of territory about two miles wide, along a considerable part of a twenty-mile front, are fighting on the western borders of Neuve Eglise and Wulverghem. [The latter town is less than two miles west of the famous Messines Ridge.]

The British have reached the suburbs of Lens. Large fires are burning in the neighborhood of Lens and Armentières. These are regarded as an indication of a further German retirement.

AUSTRALIAN DASH DOOMED PERONNE

Number of Prisoners Taken by Antipodeans Exceeds Their Losses Ten Times.

TANKS ASSAILED REDOUBTS

Germans in Their Desperate Need of Reserves Use Cavalrymen as Infantry.

By PHILIP GIBBS.
Copyright, 1918, by The New York Times Company.
Special Cable to The New York Times.

WITH THE BRITISH ARMY, Sept. 1.—Peronne has fallen today in consequence of the Australians' brilliant attack yesterday which resulted in the capture of Mont St. Quentin.

One of the fine features of the capture of Mont St. Quentin was the rapid way in which the Australians moved their guns forward over the Somme and fired at close range on the enemy. This was largely due to the work of their engineers at the river crossings. At one of these they discovered several land mines laid by the Germans with trip wires artfully concealed, but they routed them out and prevented their explosion.

Part of the secret of the light Australian losses in this attack was the quick way in which they dived into the German trenches before clearing them, getting shelter there after they had taken 150 prisoners so that the hail of machine gun bullets passed harmlessly over their heads.

In the fighting from Aug. 26 until yesterday morning they took fully ten times more prisoners than their own total casualties, which must be a record in this war.

The individual gallantry of the men reached the high summit of audacity, as when an Australian Corporal in a recent action one day heard his comrades debating how they could destroy an enemy post which was giving them great trouble and said to them:

"That's all right, I'll take it." He slipped one Mill's bomb in his pocket, crawled through tall corn, jumped into the German trench, felled the first man he saw, and by sheer force of spirit so cowed the garrison of the German post that one officer and thirteen men surrendered to him.

I have narrated how our London lads captured Croisilles a few days ago and went on to Bullecourt, which they took also by grim assault. West Lancashire troops, on their left, had attacked and taken Hendecourt and some of their patrols had entered Riencourt, while on the right of this line of attack some Liverpool and other English troops had entered Ecoust, Dongatte, and Vraucourt.

That was the situation on Thursday and Friday, but under a fierce counterattack this part of our line was hard pressed and not all the ground we had made could be kept. It threatened the enemy's main line of defense in the Drouicart-Quéant line, which he must hold at all costs to safeguard the whole of his Hindenburg line, of which this is a switch, and he sent up a fresh division, the 58th, to strengthen mixed units of the 36th and 12th reserve divisions which had been badly shattered and demoralized.

Fight Dismounted Cavalry.

For the first time also our men came up against dismounted German cavalry, including the 15th Dragoons and men of the 7th Cavalry.

So the boys of London—old London, which on this Sunday evening will be in its best clothes with the church bells ringing and all its pretty girls in the parks, where no shell fire slashes through the trees—were in the thick of it.

Under abominable bombardment in ditches which they had taken by bloody fighting and with machine gun bullets flying like swarms of wasps on all sides of them, they had fought gloriously through the rough miles of enemy ground since the 23d of August, when they went through the line of Boyelles and Becquerelles and broke the Hindenburg line as before in April of last year.

Every day since they had fought the battle, and all the pluck and pride that live in London streets in peace as in war, God knows, have been revealed on this field of ruin, in which each tract between that litter and wreckage of war is a highway of heroes. Bullecourt belongs to London.

Further north the Canadians have been having hard fighting after their first triumphant march with hundreds of prisoners in their wake. South of the Scarpe, by Gemappe and Vis-en-Artois, German resistance has stiffened for the same reason as it did at Bullecourt, because our progress here imperils their whole line of defense. So they have flung up what reserves they can gather and some of the best troops that remain to them, and they are counterattacking and firing every battery they can bring to bear on this ground with ferocious intent.

French Canadians in Thick of It.

French Canadians lately have taken part in some very fierce assaults and been through perilous adventures, but with that great courage which is always theirs when they have to go through hellfire, as at Courcellette, on the Somme, in the old first battles and many times around Lens.

To the Highlanders to the north of them at Pelves and outside Plouvain they pay high tribute, grateful for that strong flank on their left, held by the kilted men through days of ceaseless fire. We have not been making further headway there, and our men have only been asked to hold the ground they won, though that is not a light and joyous thing to do.

Meanwhile on our northern front our battleline is moving again and our men are following up the enemy rear guards, who are covering another program of retirement forced upon the enemy by his enormous losses, which compel him against his pride and will to shorten his line even at the cost of positions of immense importance to him.

His withdrawal from Bailleul has been followed by retirement from Kemmel Hill and positions on the west side of the Ypres-Comines Canal, so that our patrols are reported to be at Vierstraat and Vormizeele and Lindenhoek. His rearguards are fighting stubbornly to hold us back until he has gained the time he needs for his defensive plans, but apparently our troops have hustled him off Ravelsberg Ridge on the east of Bailleul and are driving him through Neuve Eglise.

So after the strange vicissitudes of this year's warfare we are getting back again into that old ground of Flanders, the loss of which for a time was a hard thing to bear because of all the sacrifice of our men through years of fighting and their desperate conquest of the Flanders ridges.

As I have been on the southern end of the line from Bapaume downward to Devil's Wood and the outskirts of Péronne, I haven't yet been up into Flanders to see this new phase, but a warm after thrill comes to us to know that Bailleul, which I have known for years as the capital of our northern armies and saw in April last on fire from hostile shelling, is no longer in enemy hands, and that once again our men are walking over Kemmel Hill, from which we used to watch the enemy's lines and see the sweep of the battle in the salient.

Traps Left to Catch the Unwary.

Kemmel Hill will not be a pleasant place for a walk for some time to come. The enemy doubtless has arranged many devilish devices there, such as trip wires which touch off high explosives. He has been busy with those filthy tricks along many parts of the front, which blow men to death if they touch innocent-looking objects. One of these things had the appearance of a book lying on a shelf, but when moved it set off a bomb to carry a man's hand away. But our engineers were quick to see the trick of wire, and by this time perhaps have searched Kemmel for its secret.

Before going the enemy blew up his ammunition dump and material too heavy to move.

I know some Frenchmen who will be glad that Kemmel is in our hands again, for when we were hardest pressed in April last it was French troops who defended this hill and lost it after tragic fighting.

I met those French troops who held the outer defenses holding their line at Locre with most self-sacrificing courage under a dreadful fire, which they told me was far worse than anything they had seen at Fleury, by Verdun.

Perhaps some of my readers will remember what I wrote about that old French Colonel who was there, that gallant old man who was so proud of his children, as he called them. It will be sweet vengeance to him to know that the Germans have had to creep away from Kemmel again.

The enemy's object is easy to guess, and indeed he has revealed it beyond much doubt. To save his man power, thinned out by frightful losses in this year of his devil's gamble with fate, he is, I believe, retiring to a line north and south of Armentières, hoping perhaps to hold the line of ridges from Wytschaete and Messines, as in the old days when we were in the low country of the Ypres salient.

Looking at the general situation as it exists after yesterday's and today's successes at Péronne, it seems to me we have practically reached the object of the British offensive which began Aug. 8, and has had the result of flinging back the enemy from the ground which he traversed after March 21, when he hurled the full weight of his available forces upon the British front with odds of three to one in the hope of destroying us forever.

In less than four weeks we have almost completely reversed the table of fortune, so that he has been smashed back twenty miles and more and all the country between Amiens and Bapaume and Amiens and Péronne is cleared of his men, except of those who lie dead in the ditches and craters, while north of the Scarpe we have gone further than ever before in this war, and further north still the Germans are forced to withdraw from positions which they gained by enormous sacrifice without our being troubled to fight them.

That is a wonderful chapter of history, and the triumph of it, the marvel of it, is that these victories have been gained very largely by those very troops who sustained the full brunt of the German offensive in March and again in April, when the enemy made his attack in Flanders, and once again were engaged—some of them like the Highland Division—in the French assaults near Rheims.

No troops in the world or in history have been more tried by fire, and never, as far as my knowledge of history goes, have any masses of men struck such a succession of rapid and victorious blows after battling so long in rearguard and holding actions with heavy losses, enormous fatigue, and the mental strain of intense activity and never-ending danger.

Our Australian and Canadian troops were fresher than our English battalions because they had escaped previous battles more than the English, and since then they have done wonders, and we could not have achieved these results without them.

But the greatest glory of human endurance goes to the English and Scottish and Irish battalions who fought in the retreat of March, who fought again in Flanders, who suffered losses which would have broken the spirit of weaker men, and who now in these recent weeks have beaten the enemy fairly and squarely back over the same ground.

During the last day or two the enemy has recovered somewhat, it seems, from the demoralization which overtook his men, and has brought up divisions who are fighting hard to save the reputation of the German Army, but that army as a whole will never recover its prestige or its power, however long they maintain their defensive warfare—and it will be long yet.

This Autumn some 400,000 boys of the 1920 class may fill up gaps in their ranks, and they will be well trained young soldiers capable, no doubt, of hard fighting. But Germany has lost in three weeks so many prisoners and wounded that those new drafts will not give her back the initiative. Everything that follows must be a further decline in her strength and fighting quality, and the knowledge of doom is upon her.

There have been various factors in our success, never to be separated from the courage of our men to whom victory is due, and undoubtedly the tanks have helped most to secure surprise and terror. We have many proofs that the German command recognizes them as a terrible menace. A captured German order reads:

"The enemy only attacks with tanks. If we shoot the tanks to pieces we shall have won the battle." And then it bribes the men to destroy tanks by offers of decorations.

Many other captured documents reveal decline in discipline of the German troops owing to their frightful losses and the weariness of war as well as real demoralization in the fighting line.

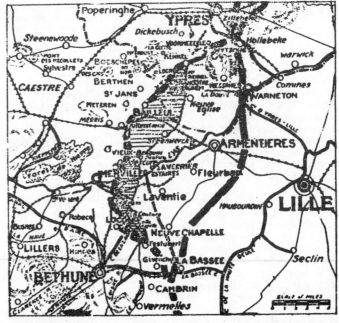

Where Germans Are Retiring on the Lys

The shaded area shows approximately the ground reoccupied in the last twenty-four hours by the British, who are closely pursuing the retreating enemy.

The New York Times.

L. LXVII...NO. 22,140. ....   NEW YORK, FRIDAY, SEPTEMBER 6, 1918.—TWENTY-FOUR PAGES.   TWO CENTS

FRENCH WIN 30 TOWNS IN AILETTE ADVANCE; OUR MEN DRIVE GERMANS ACROSS THE AISNE; BERLIN IS DECLARED IN A STATE OF SIEGE

COUCY IS IN FRENCH HANDS

Its Capture an Added Menace to the Chemin des Dames.

BIG GAINS NORTH OF VESLE

Allies Have Cleared Eight Miles of the Southern Bank of the Aisne.

BRITISH NEARER CAMBRAI

Continued Pressure Improves Their Positions North and South of Peronne.

Will Pursue Foe Implacably, Foch Tells Paris Council

PARIS, Sept. 5.—In a telegram replying to the congratulations of the Paris Municipal Council Marshal Foch, Commander in Chief of the Entente allied forces, thanked the council in his own name and on behalf of the French and allied armies, and added:

"The German rush which menaced Paris and Amiens has been broken. We will continue to pursue the enemy implacably."

LONDON, Sept. 5.—The French armies have today driven the Germans before them in Southern Picardy and, with the co-operation of the Americans, in the territory lying between the Vesle and Aisne Rivers.

In their advance along the whole Ailette front they have occupied more than thirty villages.

The Germans offered considerable resistance at certain points, but failed to check the advance, which in some parts of the line amounted to about seven miles.

Pushing eastward and southward from the Canal du Nord, [the waterway from Noyon to the neighborhood of Nesle, which should not be confused with the canal of the same name running north from Péronne,] the French crossed the Somme Canal at several points, approaching Ham, with its roads leading to St. Quentin and La Fère.

Further south, by their capture of Coucy-le-Château and several neighboring towns, they threaten the

wooded defenses of the Chemin des Dames.

At Landricourt, near the edge of the Coucy forest, they are in possession of a part of their old front as it stood before the German offensive.

North of the Vesle, where Americans have taken part in the advance, the allied line has been pushed to the southern bank of the Aisne on a front of eight miles or more.

Germans North of the Aisne.

WITH THE AMERICAN ARMY ON THE AISNE FRONT, Sept. 5. (Associated Press.)—With the exception of a few machine gun detachments, left to sacrifice themselves in an effort to cover the retreat, the Germans were on the north side of the Aisne tonight.

The American and French troops, who have followed closely on the heels of the enemy since the evacuation of the Vesle Valley began, were still in contact, harassing the rearguard and hastening the movement of the whole force.

Long before nightfall the Americans had worked their way down into the lowlands toward the Aisne, off the plateau, from which they had been able to look over the next valley at the Cathedral towers in Laon, not fifteen miles away.

At that point is located the heart of the present German operations. Laon is a great communication center and must naturally be defended with the utmost determination if the allied forces are to be prevented from driving back to it the German lines from west and south.

The retirement of the Germans to positions north of the Aisne is regarded as only preliminary to their reoccupation of their old lines of defense along the Chemin des Dames. With their recrossing of the Aisne the second phase of the retreat from the Marne is ended.

The Present a Strategic Retreat.

In the first they were driven back mile by mile, and desperate fighting marked almost every bit of the territory yielded. It was entirely different in this case. It was, in fact, a strategic retreat and has cost comparatively little in men and munitions.

So steadily and rapidly was the withdrawal of the Germans carried out that French cavalry was employed today to maintain contact at one or two places, the cavalry also contributing to the locating of machine gun nests.

The Americans were subjected at times to a rather heavy artillery fire, especially while going over the plateau. For about two miles it was necessary for them to advance in the open over high ground plainly visible to the German observers. There was little cover, and both heavy and light artillery swept the zone, but with slight effect and without checking to any degree the forward movement.

Artillery Reduces Machine Guns.

The French and American artillery meanwhile delivered a punitive fire directed against the villages and roads beyond the Aisne and shelled the points where machine gun nests were located. The clearing out of these nests was accomplished more by the artillery in this engagement than in

previous battles. These machine guns had been left by the Germans along a line admirably constructed. The usual overwhelming number of automatics were substituted for men, and these were so placed that never were they so far apart that from some angle a crossfire could not be effectively used.

Some sharp engagements did occur. These were brief, however, the Germans, who were not killed or seriously wounded, withdrawing along little communication trenches into large trenches leading to ravines, through which they escaped. This was not a day for prisoners, the whole number taken being less than twenty.

The movement of the Americans over the plateau was effected without material loss, because, instead of advancing in regular formations, they were filtered into and through the zone, never presenting a satisfactory target. The progress down into the lowlands was similarly carried out.

New Rheims Salient in Peril.

It would be no surprise if the Germans extended their evacuation to the region south of the Aisne which they hold in the direction of Rheims. It is considered possible that had a push been made there, that part, too, would have been included in the gains of the past few days; but it is regarded as inevitable that the Germans will find that the newly made salient is untenable. If they do not withdraw they will be in a serious position, as at any time pressure may be exerted upon them from the south and northwest.

Germans Standing North of the Aisne.

WITH THE FRENCH ARMIES IN THE FIELD, Sept. 5. (Associated Press.)—French reconnoitring parties to the east of Soissons this morning advanced to the River Aisne north of Brenelle and Chassemy. Further east advanced elements reached the Canal Lateral, which runs along the south bank of the Aisne, and are facing the positions on the north bank, from machine guns.

General Mangin's forces, after repulsing two violent counterattacks

German Capital Under Restraint to Check the Growing Unrest

AMSTERDAM, Sept. 5. (Received in New York, Friday, Sept. 6, 3:30 A. M.)—A decree signed by General von Linsingen, commandant of the Brandenburg Province, according to the Cologne Volks-Zeitung, places the city of Berlin and the Province of Brandenburg under "the law relating to a state of siege, which provides for a fine or imprisonment for persons inventing or circulating untrue rumors calculated to disquiet the populace."

A notice accompanying the decree calls attention to the circulation of frivolous and sometimes malevolent and traitorous gossip, exaggerating the transitory success of the enemy and casting doubt upon Germany's power for an economic resistance and depreciating the wonderful achievements of the German troops, who it declares are victoriously withstanding the enemy.

General von Linsingen expresses the hope that this admonition will suffice and that it will not be necessary to enforce the decree. The Volks-Zeitung adds that similar decrees have been issued in Breslau and other cities, all operative immediately.

Geneva Hears Hertling Has Resigned

LONDON, Sept. 6.—Count George F. von Hertling the Imperial German Chancellor, has resigned, giving bad health as the cause of his retirement, according to the Geneva correspondent of The Daily Express, quoting a dispatch received in Geneva from Munich, Bavaria.

launched by Prussian Guards against the Mont des Tombes last evening, made further progress today to the east of Leuilly.

Humbert Crosses the Somme.

General Humbert's men crossed the Somme at Epanancourt during the night, occupying several points on the east bank. Further south the advance continued this morning with greater facility than yesterday between the Oise and the Autrecourt Heights. The passage of the Somme was effected after a series of sharp engagements, in which the German mountain troops contested vigorously every foot of ground.

Hidden among the bulrushes and in the hollows and the dried beds of branches of the river, the Germans were able to use their quickfirers effectively, compelling the pursuers now and again to slow up their progress, in order to turn difficult positions. General Humbert's men built footbridges under the enemy's fire. The first bridges were destroyed, together with their builders, but other men gallantly replaced those killed, and, facing a galling fire, continued until pontoons and footbridges were thrown across the stream.

This work afforded numerous occasions for acts of the greatest heroism. Among these may be mentioned that of a French soldier who, notwithstanding the fact that the river was under the fire of German sharpshooters, undertook the task of swimming to the opposite side of the stream and bringing back a rowboat. During the trip across the soldier dived time after time to escape the enemy bullets, but he braved an even more dangerous fire while rowing back, being an excellent target for the enemy ambushed along the banks of the stream.

Pluckily crossing the stream under fire, the French troops then attacked the enemy in the marshes and weeds and in all sorts of other hiding places on the opposite bank and finally took the positions, which were veritable nests of machine guns, and pushed on toward the Peronne-Ham road. Ham thus is threatened from the north and outflanked on the south.

How far the Germans in the north

are going back voluntarily or in response to pressure is uncertain. Hill 63 is well in British hands, and the village of Ploegsteert has been captured. Lens is still in enemy hands, and there is no indication that the enemy intends to leave it in the immediate future.

The British troops continue to advance east of Neuve Eglise and Wulverghem and southeast of Steenwerck, where another mile has been gained. There has been rather sharp fighting west of Wytschaete, where the British have held the ground gained and added to it. Posts have been established on the embankment of La Bassée Canal.

The German casualties from the British shellfire all along the line have been excessively heavy, especially in the area where they are retiring to the Hindenburg line. More than once within the last two days the British gunners have seen German masses moving and have laid on their guns over open sights, the shells crashing into the enemy formations.

BRITISH GAINED GROUND IN DRIVE ON CAMBRAI

Drive Germans Back on Both Sides of Peronne—Push on in Flanders.

LONDON, Sept. 5.—Field Marshal Haig, continuing his pressure upon the northern part of the Hindenburg line, has made progress on the front north and south of Péronne, driving back the German rearguards.

On the Arras-Cambrai road his patrols, crossing the Canal du Nord south of Marquion, have increased the menace to the Germans in Cambrai. Other slight advances south of this road are reported in the night bulletin.

There has been local fighting at Moeuvres, on the Bapaume-Cambrai road.

The British advance in Flanders continues. The village of Plogsteert, north of Armentières, has been captured, as well as Hill 63, southwest of Messines.

From Neuve Chapelle southward to Givenchy the British have reached the line they held up to the German attack in April, while to the eastward of Givenchy sections of the old German positions have been taken.

More than 16,000 prisoners and more than 100 guns have been taken by the British in the last four days.

ENEMY BEGINNING GENERAL RETREAT

Using Artillery Furiously Merely with Hope of Retarding Allied Pursuit.

By WALTER DURANTY.
Copyright, 1918, by The New York Times Company.
Special Cable to THE NEW YORK TIMES.

WITH THE FRENCH ARMIES, Sept. 5.—General Humbert's army, having bitten off the block which was formed by the angle of the enemy's line between the Somme and the Oise, continued to advance today.

The left of the line of the Somme has been crossed at Epenancourt. Hill 77, the scene of several days' obstinate fighting, has fallen. Our troops have occupied Esmery-Hallon, midway between the canal and the Ham-Guiscard Road. Here our advanced guards are not more than three miles from Ham, and the guns will soon be able to play on the Ham-St. Quentin Railway, which

is the enemy's main means of access to his front in the sector between the rivers. Three hundred prisoners were taken. Further south Humbert's troops at Flavy Meldeux are a thousand yards from the Ham-Berlancourt - Guiscard Road, on which the enemy anticipated he would be able to make a further stand.

As our troops are on the outskirts of Berlancourt and Ham is menaced from the north, it is obvious that further retirement is imposed on the enemy. On the Aisne front Missy has been taken.

Sept. 4.—The Germans are retreating on part of the French battlefront. The British victory, combined with Mangin's dogged pressure, is beginning to produce the inevitable result. All night long the heights behind the Vesle were illuminated with the same fires that preceded the retreat from the Marne.

This morning patrols crossed the river in the belief that the enemy was abandoning his position.

On the Ailette and the Oise front the Germans are working their artillery to the utmost. They know it is impossible to evacuate their vast accumulations of shells—and probably guns also—and are trying vainly to retard the hour of reckoning. Nevertheless, the French continue to progress on the outskirts of the Courcy Forest.

But it is northwest of Noyon that the advance is most considerable. Toward Guiscard a double movement is

being carried out. On the left Humbert's troops are pushing the dispirited boche rearguard eastward from Chevilly toward the highroad, and along the road itself there is a simultaneous push north from the region of Noyon.

Need the Trees They Destroyed.

The enemy must long now for the noble trees that bordered the road cut down in last year's retreat. Time has been wanting to mine the highways, and there is nothing to bar the passage of armored automobiles, whose machine guns and light cannon aid the progress of horsemen spread out fanwise on either flank.

On the French left, Ham is menaced, and the eastward march along the Somme Valley offers possibilities that must fill von Hutier with anxiety regarding the men and material still packed in the Noyon massif, Chauny and positions southward.

"Can the Allies end the war this year?" is a question one is beginning to hear seriously debated.

As was said to your correspondent yesterday, it is less extravagant now to entertain such a hope than on July 14 to anticipate that the enemy would be in the position that they are today. The results already gained by Foch's strategy warrant the highest hopes, and the demoralization and terribly reduced effectives of the enemy—which prevented him from holding the colossal Hindenburg line—render more than precarious such an operation of general retreat as he seems about to be forced to undertake.

Admits "It Is All Over."

As early as 1915 it was declared to THE NEW YORK TIMES correspondent that the key to the German line in France lay east of Arras. At last the opportunity is given to put that conviction into practice. The confusion of the German units, shown by the British identification of troops of eleven different divisions on a front of barely three and a half miles, will be accentuated in the retreat—always the most difficult of military operations.

Nor does the quality of the reserves available hold out a chance of retrieving matters. War-worn recuperated wounded are hurried back, still wearing their bandages, to the battlefield; old, feeble, and disguised factory hands or miners, and boys of just 18 are being thrown into the furnace under well-nigh panic conditions, after a few weeks of insufficient training. A recently captured Captain of the regular army spoke bitterly on the subject to a French officer who interrogated him.

"It's all over," he said. "We will be lucky if we can stave off defeat this year. Some of our men fight well enough, but the majority seem to have lost hope and energy. And where are our old noncoms and officers?"

"If they were all like me," he added naïvely, "we might hold out until Winter gives a breathing space; but the ones we have got seem to know nothing, and only care for their own skins. And this dry season has served you well. Your infernal tanks can pass through places that were marshy this time last year."

Blowing up bridges was a common tactic to slow down the pursuing army. Here, the British are undaunted in their pursuit of retreating German forces.

"All the News That's Fit to Print."

The New York Times.

THE WEATHER
Partly cloudy today; Friday fair; moderate west winds.
☞For full weather report see Page 14.

VOL. LXVII...NO. 22,153.   NEW YORK, THURSDAY, SEPTEMBER 19, 1918.—TWENTY-FOUR PAGES.   TWO CENTS

HAIG AND PETAIN PIERCE HINDENBURG LINE; TAKE 10 TOWNS, 6,000 MEN IN 22-MILE DRIVE; SERBS AND FRENCH DRIVE BULGARS 10 MILES

CLOSING IN ON ST. QUENTIN

British Four Miles from the City. French Are Only Three.

Outer Hindenburg Works Are Officially Reported Captured "in Wide Sectors."

FOE'S RESISTANCE STRONG

Victors' Advance of from 1¼ to 3 Miles Made Under Handicap of Rain.

LONDON, Sept. 18.—In co-ordinated operations on a twenty-two-mile front British and French troops have made notable advances upon the outlying defenses of St. Quentin.

The British attack was launched on a line sixteen miles in extent northwest of the city, and resulted in the capture of more than 6,000 prisoners and the occupation of ten villages and several other important enemy positions, including what Field Marshal Haig describes as "outer defenses of the Hindenburg line in wide sectors."

The advance of the British carried them across the Hindenburg line at two points—Villeret and Gouzeaucourt.

The maximum depth of the British thrust was about three miles. Fresnoy le Petit, the village which marks the nearest approach of the attack to St. Quentin, is only four miles northwest of that city.

The Germans offered a strong resistance, and the allied advance was also made under the handicap of a pouring rain.

Immediately to the right of the British, French troops attacked and pushed their lines forward a mile and a quarter on the six-mile front between Holnon and Essigny le Grand, reaching the western outskirts of Francilly-Selency [three miles west of St. Quentin] and the southern edge of Contescourt [four miles southwest of St. Quentin] in their nearest approaches to the German base.

Tonight's Paris bulletin announces the capture of a few hundred prisoners.

Germans Admit We Defeated Them at St. Mihiel; One Thousand Tanks Did It, They Assert

AMSTERDAM, Sept. 18.—The Frankfurter Zeitung's correspondent telegraphs the following from the west front under date of Monday:

"The Franco-American attack at St. Mihiel is now seen to have been a carefully planned undertaking of considerable magnitude.

"The number of attacking enemy divisions is not yet known for certain, but we know that our losses in prisoners were due to the extensive use by the enemy of tanks. More than 1,000 armored cars of all sizes participated.

"One of our divisions counted in its sector alone sixty large and forty small tanks. Troops who hold out stoutly in their positions are always liable to be surrounded by this mobile arm."

BRITISH REGAIN OLD OUTPOST LINE

Drive Motley Crowd of Germans Out of Villages Lost in March Drive.

NOW FACE BIG GUN FIRE.

Long-Range Weapons Sweep the Ground with Terrific Hail of High Velocities.

By PHILIP GIBBS.
Copyright, 1918, by The New York Times Co.
Special Cable to THE NEW YORK TIMES.

WITH THE BRITISH ARMIES, Sept. 18.—On a front of something like sixteen miles from below Gouzeaucort to Savy Wood, near St. Quentin, an attack was made by English, Scottish, Irish, and Australian troops this morning in co-operation with French battalions on the British right by Holnon Wood.

As I saw myself this morning, a considerable number of prisoners have been taken—about 3,000 were reckoned to be coming back—and the British by stubborn fighting against stiff opposition in some of the enemy's positions made good progress and scaled much of the high ground immediately west of the Hindenburg line.

On this southern part of our front several villages, including Peizières, Epehy, Templeux le Guérard, Lerguier, and Hargicourt have been the scene of fierce conflict, but these places are now in our hands, according to reports I have just received, and from one end of this line of attack to its other boundary the Germans have been forced to yield ground which they were ordered to hold at all costs in order to protect the forward positions of the Hindenburg line.

Our primary object this morning was to gain our old outpost line as it existed before last March, running along a ridge from which spurs strike down to St. Quentin Canal. The enemy had already withdrawn his artillery behind that canal and was relying mainly on long range high velocities to harass our positions and silence our batteries.

Many Long Range Guns Massed.

He is now strong in gun power for protection of the Hindenburg line, and from personal observation I can say he has a most unusual number of these long range guns, and he used them this morning to draw a line of fire across our country. He was, however, holding his outpost line, once ours as I have said, with many of the same troops who had borne the full brunt of our recent battles and suffered exceedingly, so that their spirit had been lowered to gloomy depths, while other divisions less mauled, though by no means unscathed, were being held by the German command to defend the Hindenburg line itself.

This has been the enemy's policy for some time owing to his increasing dearth of men after the allied attacks at so many parts of the line. He gives his troops no rest or support until they are thoroughly worn, when he stiffens them with material of better class. It is a merciless but, from the German point of view, necessary method. Since Aug. 8 our 4th Army, for instance, has engaged thirty-four divisions, twelve of which have been in battle for the second time and two for the third time.

Among those facing our men today were remnants of the 2d Guards Division, whose spirit is at low ebb after their fighting at Mont St. Quentin and Péronne, in which city they were hunted into the ramparts and routed out like rats after a savage defense.

The German Alpine Corps, who were met this morning, are the best class of troops the enemy can now muster, and they fought hard and fiercely at Lincourt and other places outside Péronne, so that, in spite of their losses, trouble was expected from them today.

The Sixth German Cavalry Division, from whom we captured many prisoners in recent days, had proved itself of much value as a dismounted force, notwithstanding the beautiful skyblue coats of the officers and their supercilious pride over their own infantry.

The 201st Division, which has come into line against us for the first time, is made up of men from East Prussia, Baden and Silesia.

The 5th Bavarian, 79th German Division, and 25th are all much tried men. To be fair to all of them, however, I must say that as far as today's fighting goes they put up a brave and stubborn defense, which has only been broken down by the determined efforts of our own men.

Capture of Holnon Village.

Down south, on the right of our line of attack, a preliminary operation was carried out yesterday by British and French troops around Holnon Wood and Savy in order to shorten the distance they wanted to go today, and our troops captured Holnon village while the French advanced half way through Savy Wood. In both cases machine gun nests remained in the village as well as in the wood, with French and British troops ahead, and these were not mopped up in our case until early this morning, while the French had some trouble in clearing their ground of this menace behind them.

No night came before the battle, which was begun at dawn today. It was a night of white magic following a strangely beautiful sunset when the sky was filled with wide wings of flame, and then, when the light faded, with wings of white down, until the stars came out into the pale blue of the sky and the moon rose, flooding all the fields with a milky radiance. There was no wind and the air was warm and the trees stood very still, darkly etched under this starlit heaven. Over the lines shells were bursting and guns firing with a scarlet glow, but behind there was peace and beauty.

Advance Made in Heavy Rain.

At 2 in the morning it began to rain a steady downpour, making the ground soft and sticky, especially where it was cut up by shell craters and chalky trenches, so that it was not good going for the tanks crawling forward from their covers, nor afterward for the men in fighting kit, who had to scramble over that slimy chalk, where there was no grip for feet, and go forward behind the creeping barrage of fire to meet their enemy and his machine guns.

That was unlucky, and the mists of dawn creeping up from the undergrowth of wood, floating in the valleys and hanging low below the rain clouds, prevented aerial observation, and I saw numbers of our planes darting about like swallows, as though distressed by this lack of vision when the battle was in progress below.

Later the weather cleared shortly after dawn, as I went over our old battlefields through the stricken city of Péronne and the villages beyond on a far journey through this land of ruin, where gaunt skeletons of trees are like gallows on the sky line and dawn breaks with its light through monstrous shell holes in houses and walls, and in the first twilight of the day there is a leprous look over all the wild litter of these fields.

We had no long preliminary bombardment before this attack. At 5:20, when our men rose and went away, it was a brief hurricane fire followed by a moving barrage, to which our troops kept close with perfect confidence. Several of them afterward told me that it was a very powerful wall of shellfire and so accurate that no shells burst short to do them harm.

The enemy retaliation by artillery was quick and not outrageously heavy, according to official views, though violent enough in the opinion of the men who had to risk it and were wounded by it. Fortunately, they were beyond its mean point of impact, to use a gunner's phrase, before the full weight of it fell. The losses were light in the first assault, if I might judge from the casualties in the field dressing stations to which our walking wounded came first.

It was significant of the end of open warfare for the time being, now that the enemy is protected by the Hindenburg line, that most of these cases had been hit by shell splinters and not by machine-gun bullets, as in recent fighting. Certainly I have seldom if ever seen so much fire from long range guns as this morning when these high velocities were bursting with high clouds of colored smoke over a wide line of country behind Le Verguier and Hargicourt. It almost amounted to a barrage, which is not generally possible with high velocities.

In the area to which I went, the splendid men of the Australian corps who had been fighting almost continuously since the end of March—when they checked the German advance on Amiens and immediately took the offensive at Hamel and Villers-Bretonnaux, and after that brilliant action began their victorious progress over a long stretch of country from which they drove the enemy to Péronne and out of it and far beyond—told me this morning that things had gone well and that they

Scene of the New Allied Advance on St. Quentin

The area won from the Germans in the combined attack of the British and French on the positions defending the approaches to the city, which is one of the buttresses of the Hindenburg line, is represented by shading.

were satisfied with their morning's work.

The enemy put up a hard fight in some positions, especially at Le Verguier, which he defended by many machine guns, and at Ascension Farm beyond, and Villeret, where there was trouble in throwing him out. This struggle was maintained by groups of machine gunners who sold their lives dearly. But on other parts of the Australian front some of the German infantry started running toward our troops as soon as our barrage fire opened and actually risked its deadly barrier in order to surrender to our Australians before they reached their trenches.

Once a battalion of Australians took 180 prisoners, and at an early hour these troops of ours had well over 500 under escort. I passed batches of them down the tracks through the battlefield, looking over their shoulders at the fire behind them from which they were escaping, and crossing open country in order to avoid their own high velocities. They were muddy and dirty, and some lightly wounded, and I noticed that few wore their big steel helmets, most of the others having discarded them to walk more easily in field caps or without headgear.

They were haggard and worn-looking, and I had a sense of pity for some of these youngsters among them, who were weak and wearing big spectacles and tunics too big for their narrow chests. They were mixed in physique and class, some tall and strapping fellows walking sturdily, others puny and hobbling to keep pace; some with cleancut, healthy faces, others sallow and

sickly and longbrowed and evil-looking.

Some badly wounded Germans were brought down to our advanced dressing station flying its Red Cross flag over the wreckage of the recent battlefield and laid out there on stretchers amidst our own men and attended in turn by the doctors. One German had a bayonet wound, but most of them had been hit by shellfire and were badly mauled.

Down the roads came tall Australians walking sturdily in spite of wounds and muddy after their night in the rain, but splendid to see, as these men always are, because of their strength and individual character. One of them raised a wounded hand to me and said:

"I was going back to Australia in two days' time. This will delay my trip, but it's luck all the same. Life is sweet."

The Australian gunners were moving forward with more batteries and ammunition transport, and little groups of mounted men rode about the field behind the fighting line, making a fine picture as they were silhouetted on the skyline above these wide desolate fields of thistles and rank corn growing amidst shell craters and sandbag emplacements and upheaved gunpits.

Further north, where the English troops are fighting, there was very hard resistance and the enemy struggled for a long time at Templeux le Guérard, where fifty prisoners were taken, and at Ronssoy, where 100 surrendered after a stubborn defense.

At Ephev there was most trouble, and the fire of the German machine guns kept our men at bay so that they tried to get around the village from the north, but even then could not cut it off owing to the sweep of fire from its redoubts. Firing still seems to be in progress there. This was where most resistance was expected by us, for the German Alpine Corps garrisoned the place and, as I have said, they are good troops, who are not likely to yield without a hard fight.

Hargicourt was another storm centre, but our troops are around about it and have made good progress in its neighborhood.

Further north they are reported to be in the beetroot factory south of Villers Guislan.

Turning to the south part of the line, there now seems that Fresnoy has been captured by the British troops, but the position is obscure at Pontru, where other bodies are engaged, and the French on the right have not yet advanced very far after their gallant progress yesterday.

It is too soon yet to sum up the result of the day's fighting, because it is difficult to get exact news, owing to bad observation from the airplanes and the state of the ground, but there is no doubt that, in spite of the strong and obstinate defense of some divisions of Germans, obeying a stern command to hold the British back from approach to the Hindenburg line at whatever price in blood because of the enormous importance of these positions to the fate of the whole German army and the prestige of their race, the British made substantial gains today and the total of prisoners, now about 3,000, is in itself good proof of success. The loss of Moeuvres, which the enemy attacked yesterday after violent gunfire extending from that place to Havrincourt, is unfortunate, but doubtless it will be retaken before long.

Meanwhile, as I end this message, it has begun to rain again. That will not help the British, but one comfort in it is that it may prevent night bombing over their lines. Lately the enemy has been flying giant planes by night—monsters which carry a crew of eight men and bombs containing 2,000 pounds of explosives. During the past week the British have destroyed several of these. They have come crashing down alight and are but heaps of ashes on the earth, but the British have four of their monster bombs, which are thirteen feet long and larger than anything yet seen in aerial warfare.

BRITISH WIPE OUT AN ENTIRE TURKISH ARMY; CAPTURE 18,000 IN 60-MILE DRIVE IN PALESTINE; HAIG STRIKES GERMAN LINE AT FOUR POINTS

TURKS TRAPPED BY CAVALRY

Anglo-Indian Horsemen in Swift Dash Northward Bar Line of Retreat.

OCCUPY TOWN OF NAZARETH

While Hedjaz Arabs East of the Jordan Destroy Railroads and Bridges.

AIRMEN SLAUGHTER FOE

120 Cannon, Besides Airplanes and Vast Transport, Taken by Allenby's Fighters.

LONDON, Sept. 22.—The Turkish Army operating in Palestine between the Jordan and the Mediterranean has been virtually wiped out by the British under General Allenby.

In the rapid sweep forward of the British Army, following the overwhelming of the Turkish defense system north of Jerusalem, 18,000 prisoners have been rounded up so far, large numbers of the enemy have been killed or wounded, and in addition to the capture of 120 guns, booty including four airplanes and a large quantity of uncounted transport has fallen into the hands of the pursuing forces.

Cavalry units have advanced sixty miles from their original positions and occupied Nazareth, El Afule, and Beisan.

The British losses were surprisingly slight considering the importance of the advance.

Turks Cut Off from Escape.

The text of this evening's announcement follows:

By 9 o'clock on Saturday night on our left wing the infantry about Birafur had reached the line Beitdajan-Samaria-Birafur, shepherding the enemy on the west of the Jerusalem-Nablus road into the arms of our cavalry operating southward from Jenin and Beisan.

Other enemy columns vainly attempted to escape into the Jordan Valley in the direction of Jisr-ed-Dameer, which still is held by us.

Swiss Hear Bavarian Prince Shot at Hindenburg In Rage Over Differences, but Missed the Marshal

Special Cable to The New York Times.

ZURICH, Sept. 22.—Many Swiss Socialist journals have heard from indirect sources that serious differences have arisen between South German politicians and the Prussian dictators.

The Central Schweiz Demokrat reports that a Bavarian commander attempted in an access of rage to attack Hindenburg, and German deserters are quoted as saying that a Bavarian Prince tried to shoot Hindenburg, but that the Field Marshal was not wounded.

These reports may be sensational versions of recent stories coming through neutral countries that Crown Prince Rupprecht was at odds with Hindenburg and was trying to dodge responsibility for the check of the July offensive. He is known to have left the Somme front for a time in August on a "vacation."

These columns suffered severely from our aircraft, which constantly harassed them with bombs and machine-gun fire from low altitudes.

In the vicinity of Lake Tiberius our cavalry detachments hold Nazareth and the rail and road passages over the Jordan at Jisr-ed-Dameer.

Already 18,000 prisoners have been captured and 120 guns collected.

The appended statement was issued earlier in the day:

Palestine—By 8 P. M. on Sept. 20 the enemy resistance had collapsed everywhere save on the Turkish left in the Jordan Valley.

Our left wing, having swung around to the east, had reached the line of Bidieh, Baka, and Messudich Junction, and was astride the rail and roads converging at Nabulus.

Our right wing, advancing through difficult country against considerable resistance had reached the line of Khan-Jibeit, one and one-fourth miles northeast of El-Mugheir and Es-Sawieh, and was facing north astride the Jerusalem-Nablus road.

On the north our cavalry, traversing the Field of Armageddon, had occupied Nazareth, Afule, and Beisan, and were collecting the disorganized masses of enemy troops and transport as they arrived from the south. All avenues of escape open to the enemy, except the fords across the Jordan between Beisan and Jisr-ed-Dameer, were thus closed.

East of the Jordan Arab forces of the King of the Hedjaz had effected numerous demolitions on the railways radiating from Derat, several important bridges, including one in the Yurmak Valley, having been destroyed.

Several days must elapse before accurate figures of captures can be given, but already more than 8,000 prisoners, 100 guns, large quantities of both horse and mechanical transports, four airplanes, many locomotives, and much rolling stock have been counted.

Very severe losses have been inflicted on the masses of Turkish troops retreating over the difficult roads by our air services.

A German airplane, later ascertained to have been carrying mails, landed in the midst of our troops at Afule. The pilot, who believed the place still to be in Turkish hands, destroyed the machine and its contents before he could be secured.

TURKS OUTWITTED BY GEN. ALLENBY

Were Apparently Unprepared to Face Hostile Operations on So Large a Scale.

COUNTRY MOST DIFFICULT

British Fought Over Steep Hills and Masses of Boulders Till Foe Was Routed.

By W. T. MASSEY.
Special Cable to The New York Times.

WITH THE BRITISH ARMY IN PALESTINE, Sept. 20.—It is impossible to estimate the vast quantity of captured machine guns, motors, ammunition, stores, and rolling stock which the Turk will find it difficult to replace. On the low ground in the passes a great quantity of transport is immovable because the men had taken the horses to try to escape from the advancing troops, or they had been smashed by aircraft action.

Railway communications have been damaged everywhere, and Arab regulars and Bedouin levies have done invaluable service in cutting the Hedjas Railway north and south of Derat and the line running westward thereof.

Though some of the enemy are putting up vigorous rearguard fights in the hills they cannot stop our progress, but large parties are bewildered at meeting our forces in unexpected places. We continually hear of Turks retiring on positions we occupied several hours previously.

Yesterday Londoners and Indians made a swift march from Wadi Faliak across marshy ground to Tul Keram,

where with the aid of a mounted brigade they rounded up much transport on the move. From Tul Keram the infantry moved to the north of the railway which the Australians destroyed yesterday, and deny this pass to Samaria to the Turks. Other infantry which carried the coastal defenses in one marvelous rush faced east.

The progress in the rough hilly country is rapid, considering the ease with which the mountain tracks could be defended by few machine guns. Some of the troops are approaching Samaria and Sudieh.

Though they first stubbornly resisted, the rearguards of the Turks are now retreating hastily toward El Afule and Beisan, where our cavalry is waiting for them.

The attack near Nablus road, which began the operations, was brilliantly conducted. Welsh, Indian, and Cape Colony battalions all shared in the success. The mixed brigade commenced a most difficult night march on Wednesday over a mountainous country east of the road, getting over the watershed, then clambering down the steep faces of hills where they commence to fall toward the Jordan Valley.

The leading battalion passing over the rocks of the Wadi Samieh took the enemy posts and allowed the second battalion to pass through to the second objectives. These taken, the third battalion went on, driving the enemy from other strong points, then gave way to the fourth battalion, which faced west and carried the important feature El Mugheir with a rush and another hill westward. A Cape company battalion captured a hill northeast and took one gun.

Another brigade operation westward was equally meritorious. It attacked Forfar and Bidston Hills, about a mile and half apart, the southernmost hill being taken from the north, the northernmost from the south. Counterattacks on Bidston were beaten off the last time with the bayonet. The rapid advance brought the brigade to an important hill 6,000 yards east of Trumus Aya.

The operations in this area were over extraordinarily difficult country, made up of steep hills or rapid descents. The ground everywhere was a mass of boulders. Fine leadership of troops in excellent condition accounts for the high proportion of the enemy killed and captured with remarkably few losses on our side. Indeed, the brigade operating on the right took thirty-four officers and over 400 of other ranks prisoners, while the killed and wounded were many.

This morning Irish and Indian troops made a vigorous attack in wild mountainous country west of the Nablus Road and drove out the Turks from their long, strong line around Furkah, which was one of the best prepared systems. Pressing forward, they gained a good deal of ground to the north, considerably narrowing the front along which the enemy was driven from the Plain of Sharon

The New York Times.

"All the News That's Fit to Print."

THE WEATHER
Fair, cooler, wind northwest today; tomorrow fair, wind variable.
For full weather report see Page 23.

VOL. LXVIII...NO. 22,165.   NEW YORK, TUESDAY, OCTOBER 1, 1918.—TWENTY-FOUR PAGES.   TWO CENTS

BULGARIA QUITS THE WAR, TURKEY MAY FOLLOW; HAIG'S MEN IN CAMBRAI, BELGIANS PUSH ON; OUR MEN GAIN GROUND IN HARD FIGHTING

ENVOYS SIGN AT SALONIKI

Agreement Hailed in Entente Capitals as Sealing Teutons' Doom.

OPENS ROAD TO RUMANIA

Rising of the Slavs of Southern Austria Also Expected to Follow.

GERMANS REACH SOFIA

Field Marshal Mackensen Rushes Teuton Troops to Fortify and Defend Nish.

PARIS, Sept. 30.—Bulgaria has surrendered unconditionally to the Allies and hostilities ceased officially at noon, following the signing of an armistice at Saloniki last night. General Franchert d'Esperey, the allied Commander in Chief in Macedonia, signed for the Allies, and the Bulgarian delegates for their Government.

Instructions have been given by the Government to General d'Esperey to proceed immediately to the execution of the conditions of the convention.

The armistice, La Liberté declares editorially, was signed with the full consent of King Ferdinand. It prints a denial of a report that he had taken refuge in Vienna. The King, it declares, has not left Sofia.

The announcment of the signing of the convention followed the return of Premier Clemenceau from the front, where he inspected the troops and had an opportunity of talking with General Pétain and General Pershing on the military situation.

No Political Conditions.

While the nature of the conditions is not announced, an official statement says:

"No diplomatic negotiation is actually in progress with Bulgaria and consequently no political conditions have been laid down for her."

With respect to the conditions of the armistice, it is added: " These conditions have been submitted by General Franchet d'Esperey to the allied Governments, who approved them. They are of purely military character designed to guarantee in a complete manner the security and liberty of the allied army in the Orient and to furnish every guarantee for the development of eventual pourparlers."

Bulgaria to Evacuate Territory Won, Disband Army, and Give Allies Free Passage for War Operations

LONDON, Sept. 30.—The armistice concluded with Bulgaria by the Entente Allies is a purely military convention and contains no provisions of a political character. The terms, speaking generally, are:

Bulgaria agrees to evacuate all the territory she now occupies in Greece and Serbia, to demobilize her army immediately, and surrender all means of transport to the Allies.

Bulgaria also will surrender her boats and control of navigation on the Danube, and concede to the Allies free passage through Bulgaria for the development of military operations.

All Bulgarian arms and ammunition are to be stored under the control of the Allies, to whom is conceded the right to occupy all important strategic points.

The Associated Press learns that the military occupation of Bulgaria will be entrusted to British, French, and Italian forces, and the evacuated portions of Greece and Serbia respectively to Greek and Serbian troops.

The armistice means a complete military surrender, and Bulgaria ceases to be a belligerent.

All questions of territorial rearrangement in the Balkans were purposely omitted from the convention.

The Allies made no stipulation concerning King Ferdinand, his position being considered an internal matter—one for the Bulgarians themselves to deal with.

The armistice will remain in operation until a final general peace is concluded.

While the actual suspension of hostilities immediately followed the signing of the armistice, it is noted that this suspension applies only to Macedonian hostilities against Bulgaria, and that it in no way affects Macedonian hostilities which the allied armies will continue against Austria-Hungary, Turkey, and the German contingents sent to that locality.

The capitulation of Bulgaria, says the Journal des Débats, is the beginning of the end for the Central Powers. Germany will have the greatest difficulty in concentrating forces upon the Belgrade-Nish line in an attempt to save her communications with the Orient, and the Central Powers are incapable of occupying Bulgaria or setting up there a Government to resist the Allies.

"Ferdinand is doomed," it continues, "as his subjects will never pardon this disaster.

"Formerly the Central Powers threatened to dominate the Balkans and the Eastern Mediterranean, but the present Bulgarian débacle finds the Central Powers menaced on all the Balkan fronts. The feeble Austrian garrisons remaining in Serbia after Bulgaria's withdrawal will be annihilated.

"With the capitulation of the Bulgarians the Austrian Slavs will rise against their despotic rulers, and the fate of the Hapsburgs will be accomplished. An uprising in Bosnia and Herzegovina is a necessary sequel to the freeing of Serbia.

"Turkey must follow the example of Bulgaria, and thus the Berlin-Bagdad dream disappears."

Fatal Blow to Turkey

The Temps says that Bulgaria capitulated, knowing that Germany could no longer help her, and she did not wish to see her own country a field of battle. In 1913 Radoslavoff (then Bulgarian Premier) avenged the ambush of General Savoff, (Minister of War in the Radoslavoff Cabinet,) and now the Malinoff-Savoff Cabinet avenges the ambush of Radoslavoff.

" While it is too soon to appreciate the full political consequence of Bulgaria's abandonment of the Central Powers," the newspaper concludes, " yet it is plain that Bulgaria's action gives a fatal blow to Turkey, and, perhaps, renders a service to Austria, as Austria now possesses an excuse for capitulation which previously it wanted."

Take Jonescu, former Minister without portfolio in the Rumanian Cabinet, in a statement made to the Intransigeant today, said that the effect of Bulgaria withdrawing from the war would be considerable in Rumania, where the entire nation hates the Central Powers. M. Jonescu said he was convinced that before the end of the war the Rumanian Army would have once more the opportunity of fighting against the common enemy.

London's View of Collapse.

Special Cable to THE NEW YORK TIMES.

LONDON, Tuesday, Oct. 1.—The exact terms of the Bulgarian armistice have not yet been published, but information shows that they are of a most comprehensive kind. They include demobilization of the Bulgarian Army, the surrender of all arms and ammunition, the evacuation of all foreign territory occupied by the Bulgarians, control by the Allies of railways and of transport on the Danube, and allied occupation of all strategic points, as well as control of ports.

These facilities taken together signify that Bulgaria can stand by the Allies in case of necessary as a theatre of war. The fact that the Bulgars are to be deprived of arms disposes, at least momentarily, of the question whether they could now be enrolled against the Turk. They cease to be belligerents indeed, except with permission of the Allies.

Territorial questions are left to the peace conference, as well as the position of Czar Ferdinand. " If they like their Ferdinand they can keep him," a diplomat remarked today. It is apparent that the introduction of such controversial matters at the present time would be inadvisable, both as impeding military operations and in arousing passions.

In other terms, there is no interference with the internal Government of Bulgaria. The right of self-determination operates here, and such reserve offers an excellent prospect of a peaceful solution of the whole Balkan controversy—at the proper moment. The armistice remains in force until final and general peace is concluded.

Discussing the military effect which the Bulgarian armistice will have upon the German position in the Balkans The Daily Chronicle says it is very unlikely that any of Mackensen's army of ten divisions in Rumania will be employed south of the Danube, since it will be needed to consolidate the Danube line and in order to keep the Rumanians down. The most the Germans can do is utilize such footholds as they possess in Bulgaria.

Their control of the railways and rolling stock, for instance, is to delay the allied advance and deprive the Allies of as many as possible of the immediate Bulgarian resources.

The Chronicle estimates that it will be two months or more before the Bulgarian Army is demobilized and the railways, boats, and territories transferred to the Allies, and that it will be at least that time before a new war front is effectively constituted on the Danube.

The Daily News says it is true that Germany can still communicate with Turkey by the Black Sea, but that is a poor alternative to the corridor through the Balkans. It may safely be assumed therefore that Turkey is for effective purposes out of the war.

" Nor is this all," adds The Daily News. " The re-emergence of Rumania, if only in guerrilla warfare, may be confidently anticipated, and it can hardly be doubted that Austria is privy to the Bulgarian surrender. In any case that country is so eager for peace on any terms that it may be expected to welcome the impetus which Bulgaria has given to the movement which has so long been engineered from Vienna."

The Daily News says there is reason to believe that King Ferdinand has been the chief agent in securing the armistice, and finds significance in the fact that both the King of Saxony and the King of Bavaria have recently been in Sofia, and that Ferdinand himself is now in Vienna.

"These circumstances," it says, "point to very formidable possibilities for Prussia. They suggest that a phase of the war that is imminent may leave the Hohenzollern dynasty isolated with the lesser Kings who have been its more or less unwilling feudatories combined against it in order to save themselves from the disaster that now seems unavoidable. That would be a fitting overture to the final humiliation of the despotism of Potsdam.

"There has been a tendency in this direction ever since the death of Emperor Francis Joseph and the catastrophic happenings of the last two months have now brought it to the surface. Sauve qui peut has become the cry of the little Kings."

REPORTS TURKEY ALSO SEEKS PEACE

The Hague Hears That the Porte Has Already Requested an Armistice.

AUSTRIA'S POSITION GRAVE.

Opening of Communication with Rumania Will Change Situation in Russia.

Copyright, 1918, by The New York Times Company.
Special Cable to THE NEW YORK TIMES.

THE HAGUE, Sept. 30.—THE NEW YORK TIMES correspondent learns from a highly authoritative source that the Turkish Government has already asked for an armistice.

Copyright, 1918, by The New York Times Company.
Special Cable to THE NEW YORK TIMES.

LONDON, Sept. 30.—Although no one here believes overtures from Turkey can now be long delayed, THE NEW YORK TIMES learns tonight that they have not yet been made. Bonar Law's speech, however, makes it plain that her position is hopeless. She is believed to have only one army left—that in the Caucasus—and even this is of no great account, according to the European scale of warfare.

A year ago there were in Constantinople a certain force of German troops and a considerable number of German officers. Most of these, however, have been gradually recalled as the Allies' menace in the west increased, and in any case would have no time to organize resistance. The blow has been too sudden for Turkey to make preparations to meet an attack from the northwest, and with her rail communications cut with Germany, she can have no hope of receiving reinforcements, and especially guns.

However, experts here point out

that there may well be some little delay before Constantinople moves. Turkey has already suffered in the destruction of her Palestine army all the injury the Allies can inflict on her for the moment. It will take the Saloniki force a few days to swing around for an attack on the famous lines of Tchatalja, and the Turks consequently have a little leisure in which to consider what is best to be done.

When the question of how the surrender of Bulgaria is likely to affect Austria is asked, experts differ widely. Most admit that there has been a cleavage between Berlin and Vienna with regard to peace, as is shown by the famous Austrian note, and some now contend that Austria was fully aware of the Bulgarian move before it was made. They would not, therefore, be surprised if she made further efforts to get out from under the approaching collapse of the Quadruple Alliance.

Her power to do so, however, depends upon how far the menace on the western front has forced Germany to relax her military domination of the Dual Monarchy, and that is only one of the extraordinarily complex military problems presented by the Bulgarian surrender. The race to secure Serbia between the Allies and any forces the Central Powers might be able to send there, it was pointed out today to THE NEW YORK TIMES by a high military authority, is likely to be one of immediate developments, and on the result will depend where the new front is to be drawn.

To the Allies, of course, it is the most important to re-establish, if possible, communications with Rumania, which will change entirely the complexion of affairs in Russia, but it is too early yet to say whether it can be accomplished. Germany has a certain number of troops in Southeastern Europe, and if she can show enough strength to hearten Austria it will be some time before the Allies can reap the full effect of their conquest of Bulgaria.

FIERCE FIGHT IN ARGONNE

Americans Push Ahead in the Face of Desperate Resistance.

FOE HEAVILY REINFORCED

Pennsylvanians Save the Day When Violent Counterattack Pierces Front.

NEW LINES CONSOLIDATED

Masses of Artillery Brought Up in the Mud in Preparation for New Advance.

By EDWIN L. JAMES.
Copyright, 1918, by The New York Times Company.
Special Cable to THE NEW YORK TIMES.

WITH THE AMERICAN ARMY, Sept. 30, (9 P. M.)—Back and forth the fighting continued today along the Argonne and Meuse front.

North of Nantillois, near Cierges, and in the vicinity of Apremont, violent counterattacks netted the Germans temporary gains. We ad-

vanced our lines slightly in the Argonne Forest and east of Exermont.

The heaviest fighting occurred when the Germans threw fresh divisions against Kansas and Missouri troops in the vicinity of Apremont and drove a considerable wedge into their line, until Pennsylvania troops attacked the Germans from the east and drove them back with terrific losses.

The weather continues wretched—cold, with rains and wind. The spirit of the youthful American soldiers remains excellent under trying conditions.

American Flanks Advance.

Sept. 29.—Bitter seesaw fighting took place all today on the Argonne and Meuse front. Both the Americans and the Germans gained and lost positions in sanguinary struggles. In addition to rearguard actions by machine guns, high explosives, and gas, our troops faced a series of strong counterattacks by fresh German troops, rushed up from distant parts of the front. The Germans were particularly forceful in the centre of our sector between Montfaucon and the vicinity of Cierges. While the bitter struggle was going on, our left and right succeeded in pushing ahead for good gains.

The Germans evidently are doing everything possible to hinder our advance toward the Kriemhilde Stellung, which is in an unfinished state and is being feverishly worked upon by the boche. After breaking through the Hindenburg system, we crossed the Völker Stellung, and are now slowly but surely nearing the Kriemhilde line, which is the last German organized defense this side of the French-Belgian border. Behind this the Germans have placed heavy forces of artillery and concentrated a number of fresh divisions. Evidently there they intend to try to halt the Americans.

We are struggling against great difficulties of transportation because of the mud and bad roads. This afternoon's weather was too bad for aerial activity.

AMERICANS CLEARING THE ARGONNE FOREST

Germans Bring Up Heavy Reinforcements—Captured Batteries Turned on Foe.

WITH THE AMERICAN ARMY NORTHWEST OF VERDUN, Sept. 30, (Associated Press.)—The gains made by the Americans in the Argonne today include a slight advance in the western part and a more material gain in the eastern fringe of the forest.

In ridding the forest of Germans the Americans have been compelled to contend with hundreds of snipers, many of whom take positions in trees, endeavoring to pick off the advancing soldiers. The Americans encountered snipers in such numbers in one part of the forest that the infantry called for artillery, which quickly ousted the snipers by a barrage.

Two complete batteries started action against the Germans today, the guns and ammunition of both of which were captured from the retreating forces near Cierges. Included in the captured equipment were six 150-millimeter guns and 21 pieces of lighter artillery. As American artillery had not come up when the capture was made, the officers took quick advantage of the situation, and turned the guns on the enemy, using

ammunition which they found in stacks nearby.

To hold his present positions the enemy is bringing up reserves and preparing in other ways for an organized resistance. Great activity behind the German lines is observed, trains and wagons bringing up reserves and supplies simultaneously. The enemy is shelling the American back areas heavily, especially the roads leading to Montfaucon and along the centre of the sector.

Just to the right of the American centre the enemy concentrated heavy and light artillery, and also threw in shock troops.

After only four days of rest German divisions returned to the line Sunday, either for the purpose of counterattacking or supporting those already there.

Observers have noted strong bodies of German infantry moving forward, and a narrow-gauge railroad in this region has been abnormally active.

Activity, though general, was heavier on the left today than in the centre, and along the latter position the artillery fire increased in the early morning hours.

German infantry was reported by aerial observers today to be moving north along the Aisne, beyond Lancon, in the Argonne region. They were first seen by the Americans early in the day, and the French and American heavy artillery started firing all along the river.

The Germans concentrated in the regions of Sommerance and Exermont Monday morning in such numbers that the French and American heavy guns were turned upon these regions in force, pounding them for hours. The observers were unable to report the results of this fire, as mist and rain late today prevented observation.

The American artillery fire increased in volume during the day on the right. That of the enemy decreased slightly, though gas and large shells were used freely against the American front everywhere.

There were violent counterattacks in the neighborhood of Nantillois. Tanks were seen on two portions of the sector, but they were not used except near Apremont because of the bad condition of the terrain. The artillery fire again was heavy along the Montfaucon roads.

Just before midnight it was reported that the Germans had shelled the American field hospital at Bethincourt and had set it on fire.

Reports of the excellent aim of the Franco-American artillerists in the drive are coming in. Upon a hill used by the Germans as an observation post, which became a target for the American gunners, American reconnoitring parties found two German officers dead in a sitting position near peepholes in a dugout. Both had been killed by the concussion of a shell which struck close by. Their observation glasses were not damaged. It was apparent that the men had been killed instantly.

In another instance the Franco-American gunners scored a hit between two German 150-millimeter pieces. Both guns were put out of commission, and three of the gunners were killed. Nearby a direct hit was scored on a .77 gun, of which virtually nothing was left but the barrel.

American infantrymen also found three machine-gun nests where heavy projectiles struck, demolishing the guns and killing five Germans.

At various places in the vicinity of German trenches Germans were found who had been killed while endeavoring to reach dugouts. Their comrades who succeeded in reaching the dugouts remained there until the Americans came up, and then surrendered.

A former New York bartender was captured by the Americans today.

The Germans during the day used tear-gas shells on points five kilometers to the rear of the centre line.

A captured document says that the German decision regarding the court-martialing of American aviators caught dropping propaganda pamphlets has been rescinded, and that in the future only aviators having propaganda in their possession will be dealt with as "special cases."

VICTIMS OF U-BOAT ARRIVE.

AN ATLANTIC PORT, Sept. 30.—Three Canadian officers, Captain W. Mackenzie, Lieutenant W. S. Anderson, and Lieutenant A. E. Coapman, who were on the Canadian Pacific liner Missanabia when she was sunk by a U-boat on Sept. 9 off the English coast, arrived here today with several survivors of the crew on their way home to Canada. The officers said that the Missanabia was struck by two torpedoes on the starboard side, one in the engine room and one further aft, which blew a big hole in her side, through which the sea poured so rapidly that the vessel went down stern first in seven minutes.

The attack was made at 11 o'clock in the morning without warning, and there was a heavy sea running. There were only about sixty passengers on board, the officers said, and there was no difficulty in getting the lifeboats away from the port side.

The New York Times.

"All the News That's Fit to Print."

THE WEATHER
Fair today; tomorrow, fair, warmer; northeast winds.

VOL. LXVIII...NO. 22,172. ... NEW YORK, TUESDAY, OCTOBER 8, 1918.—TWENTY-FOUR PAGES. TWO CENTS

EXPECT WILSON TO REJECT TEUTON OFFERS; NOW CONFERRING WITH ALLIES ON REPLY; BRITISH ARE AGAIN DRIVING TOWARD LILLE; FRENCH GAIN ON AISNE, OUR MEN IN ARGONNE

REPLY MAY BE READY TO-DAY

Allies Expected to Unite Against Armistice or Bargaining.

NO CAPITAL FOR THE FOE

Answer to be in Terms That Cannot Be Turned to Account Against Us.

NATION'S ATTITUDE CLEAR

Senate Debate and Flood of Messages Show Stern Temper of the People.

Special to The New York Times.

WASHINGTON, Oct. 7.—The reply of President Wilson to the Austro-German peace proposals will be a rejection, in the convinced opinion of Washington.

When his answer is delivered the President will act as spokesman, not only for the United States Government, but also for all the nations allied in the fight against the Central Powers.

Exchanges have been in progress today between Washington, London, Paris, Rome, and Havre. The result of this comparison of views will be the presentation of a solid front in opposition to either an armistice or dickering with the Berlin and Vienna governments.

Speaking for himself and this Government alone, the President could have sent forward his reply to Germany early this evening. It is understood the President did not care to make such an answer, but preferred that it should have the augmented force of a combined reply from the Entente. For this reason, it is understood, he has indicated his views in advance to the allied Governments, and is obtaining their decisions before putting his answer in final form to be handed to the neutral diplomats in Washington, through whose Governments the note of rejection will be delivered.

When the President's answer will be forwarded and announced is dependent upon the time required for completing the interchange of views between the allied Governments. At the White House this evening it was thought that the consideration might reach a point where the President's decision can be announced tomorrow.

In any event, the reply will not be long delayed, and there is every incentive, on account of the Liberty Loan, and because of the official desire that the German peace offensive shall in no way act as a damper on American and Entente war activities, for a prompt speaking out of the decision of the President and his Allies in the great war.

Feels the Nation Is Behind Him.

The President is confident that his reply to the Austro-Germanic alliance will go forward with the unanimous support of the nation. Every evidence of this reached the White House from all parts of the nation today. Hundreds of telegrams were received. Regardless of party affiliation, the messages voiced the confident belief that the President would neither grant an armistice nor allow this nation to be drawn into any peace parley with the Central Powers. From all quarters the President was urged not to accept the German requests.

The President's position was further strengthened by the unequivocal stand taken by Senators Lodge, Hitchcock, Nelson, Poindexter, Reed, and others in debate in the United States Senate this afternoon, where the sentiment of the nation was patriotically and unmistakably reflected in every utterance. Not a single voice was raised in favor of yielding to the German manoeuvre, which was characterized as being intended as a trap for the Allies and evidence of a desire by the Central Powers to gain a breathing spell at the expense of the allied forces.

There was also encouragement for the President in summaries of editorials from the American press. According to the information reaching the White House, not a single American paper had taken a stand in favor of acceptance of the Teutonic suggestions.

Cablegrams to the State Department, summarizing the comment of the allied press, showed also that sentiment is just as strong and unanimous among the British, French, Italians, and Belgians against yielding to the German overtures as it is in the United States. It was clearly demonstrated from all points of the allied compass that the sentiment of the nations allied in the war against German militarism is overwhelmingly in favor of going through with the war until Germany is forced into an unconditional surrender, so as to enable the allied powers to dictate their own terms for the sort of peace that will bring security and reassurance to all peoples, and make impossible the recurrence of such a war.

Say Hindenburg Resigned After Row With Kaiser; Told Ruler Retreat Was Necessary, War Was Lost

LONDON, Oct. 7.—Field Marshal von Hindenburg is reported to have resigned as Chief of the German General Staff after a heated interview with the Emperor in which the Field Marshal declared that a retreat on a large scale was impossible to avoid.

The statement comes in a dispatch from the Central News correspondent at Amsterdam, who states that his dispatch is based on reports from the frontier.

[Field Marshal von Hindenburg has been Chief of Staff since Aug. 30, 1916.]

By GEORGE RENWICK
Copyright, 1918, by The New York Times Company.
Special Cable to THE NEW YORK TIMES.

AMSTERDAM, Oct. 6.—Events are following one another with the rapidity that characterized the fateful days at the end of July and beginning of August, 1914. At last the powerful alliance against the right has been forced to look the stern facts in the face.

My information, which I have every reason to believe is correct, is that the supreme army command in Germany had a great deal to do with the astonishing developments in the situation. Hindenburg and Ludendorff are said to have informed the Kaiser and the Government some time ago that they now recognized the military situation as hopeless. This view was impressed upon the Chancellor by Hindenburg himself during his visit to Berlin.

Ever since the great German offensive began to stagger it has been amply demonstrated that it was Germany's last possible effort to impose her peace on the world.

The events since the Germans were hurled back over the Marne have emphatically shown that even the war of defense has become a hopeless and costly struggle, and nothing demonstrates that better than the latest communiqués from the west front.

HAIG STRIKES IN FLANDERS

Advances on a 4-Mile Front North of the Scarpe.

MANY VILLAGES CAPTURED

German Rearguards on the Lens-Cambrai Front Are Cut to Pieces.

FRENCH TAKE BERRY-AU-BAC

Occupy Important Town on Left of Champagne Offensive, Holding Gains on Right.

LONDON, Oct. 7.—Resuming offensive operations north of the Scarpe River, the British today advanced on a four-mile front and captured the villages of Oppy and Biache-St. Vaast [the latter six miles southwest of Douai.]

Haig's troops last night established a post at the crossing of the Scheldt Canal north of Aubencheul-au-Bac [about five miles northwest of Cambrai] and pushed their lines slightly nearer Lille on the west and southwest. By the progress they have made north of Wez Macquart they are about five miles west of the city.

German rearguards who ventured to make a stand in opposing the British pursuit in Flanders were annihilated in every case.

Many explosions were observed today in the coal-mining region northeast of Lens, and fires are raging in Douai and many other towns of this district. Prisoners report that before the torch was applied to Douai the Germans indulged in an orgy of looting.

The French pressure in Champagne continues to yield results. Berry-au-Bac, at the junction of the River Aisne and the Aisne Canal and on the left wing of the general Champagne offensive, was taken today.

On the rest of the Champagne front the French have maintained their gains of yesterday and have even pushed further to the east and north of the Arnes River.

Heavy fighting continues between the French and Germans in the region north of St. Quentin. Repeated German counterattacks on Remaucourt and other positions captured by the French yesterday failed: with the exception of those against Tilloy farm, where the enemy recovered part of his lost ground.

Haig's Review of the Fighting.

Field Marshal Haig's summary of the British operations, as contained in his night bulletin, follows:

In successful local operations this morning we advanced our line on a front of about four miles north of the Scarpe River, capturing the villages of Biache-St. Vaast and Oppy and more than 100 prisoners and a number of machine guns.

Patrol fighting took place also northeast of Epinoy and north of Aubencheul-aux-Bois. We have progressed in both localities.

Following is the text of the British day report:

In local fighting yesterday in the neighborhood of Aubencheul-aux-Bois we captured about 400 prisoners.

Yesterday afternoon one of our patrols in the Oppy sector brought in thirty-four prisoners and four machine guns. During the night we established posts at the canal crossings north of Aubencheul-au-Bac, and also northeast and east of Oppy.

A German post east of Berclau was captured by another of our patrols. We made slight progress north of Wez Macquart.

PERSHING CARRIES ARGONNE HEIGHTS

Drives Germans from Chatel-Chehery and Seizes Commanding Positions on Aire.

FOE FIGHTS DESPERATELY

His Tactics Indicate Determination to Force a Decisive Battle Here.

By EDWIN L. JAMES.

Special Cable to THE NEW YORK TIMES
WITH THE AMERICAN ARMY, Oct. 7, (9 P. M.)—A furious battle has been in progress all day for the possession of the north end forts of the Argonne. The Americans attacked from the east and south this morning. After a day of bitter fighting they have driven the Germans from the heights west of the Aire Valley and commanding the Argonne Forest from our line to the end of the jungle at Grand Pré. These heights include Hills 242, 244, and 269, on the crests of which our troops have dug in. This is the best advance we have made against the Argonne stronghold since the drive of the First American Army started on the morning of Sept. 26.

Our attack this morning was started by the troops on the line from Fleville, five kilometers southward, the troops moving due west. A short time after this attack started, at 6:30, the troops holding the line through the forest attacked northward. We used little artillery preparation, but put down heavy barrages ahead of our men.

This fire, while doing considerable damage to the Germans' communications, did not succeed in cutting the

wire, because the thick woods deflected the shells to a great extent. The heavy wire entanglements had to be cut by the advancing infantry. Tanks, of course, could not be used to attack the forest.

Heavy Mist Aids the Attack.

Our attack was aided by a heavy mist, which enabled us to get upon the German positions before being seen. This precipitated a large amount of hand-to-hand fighting. The mist later developed into a cold rain, which still continues.

It is impossible to exaggerate the difficulties of the task of taking the Argonne Forest, so long regarded as impregnable. The Germans have thousands of steel and concrete positions bristling with machine guns, innumerable trenches running in all directions through the jungles, and many funnel-shaped traps commanded by nests of machine guns. They are fighting with desperation against the Americans, who are determined to wrest their highly prized stronghold from them.

The Germans gave up Châtel-Chéhéry without a strong fight, making their stand on the crest of the heights west of the Aire Valley. Using shell-holes and tree stumps as shields, the Americans wormed their way up the hill and leaping into the German trenches, routed the enemy with heavy losses to him.

Meanwhile, infantry elements had filtered through three ravines and caught the retreating Germans with machine gun fire. We organized our newly won positions on the Aire Heights and pushed down the western slopes of the hills, where we met with varying success. Our troops are being withdrawn tonight to organize the line.

Senate Condemns New Peace Pleas

Unanimous Demand Made in Debate That War Go On Until Foe Is Helpless.

AN ARMISTICE NOW ABSURD

Would Mean Loss of War, Says Lodge, and Peace Should Be Dictated on German Soil.

Special to The New York Times.

WASHINGTON, Oct. 7.—Unequivocal rejection of the present peace overtures of Germany and Austria was urged today in vigorous speeches in the Senate. The unwavering sentiment was expressed that no proposals from the Central Powers could be regarded as sincere until all enemy troops had been withdrawn from conquered territory and the foe had displayed a willingness to accept the terms laid down by President Wilson, with indemnity for wanton war destruction as one of the basic conditions.

The Senate was in no receptive frame of mind over the overtures. Not one Senator who took the floor during the two hours the proposals were discussed advocated any other policy than to pursue the war until the Central Powers indicate a willingness to surrender unconditionally. The view was expressed

that an armistice was issued merely to give the foe a breathing spell, during which he would apply himself to rehabilitating his weakened forces.

The sentiment of the Senate was voiced by Lodge of Massachusetts, Poindexter of Washington, Reed of Missouri, Hitchcock of Nebraska, Ashurst of Arizona, Nelson of Minnesota, McCumber of North Dakota, and others. Relentless prosecution of the war was advocated by every Senator who spoke and endorsed by those who did not participate. When peace terms are considered, it was urged, they ought to be taken up with actual representatives of the German people, and not the Hohenzollern military machine.

CHURCHILL SEES NO PEACE.

Righteous Aims of Allies Not Yet Recognized, He Says.

GLASGOW, Oct. 7.—Winston Spencer Churchill, Minister of Munitions, speaking here today said that he did not believe the righteous war aims of the

Allies at present would receive the required recognition.

Therefore, he was not very sanguine of a speedy termination of the war.

VIENNA PRESS VERY HOPEFUL

AMSTERDAM, Oct. 6. — Dispatches from Vienna show Austrian newspapers to be deeply impressed with the importance of the peace move made by the Central Powers and filled with hope for its success.

The Fremdenblatt, however, has doubts, saying:

"We must reckon with everything and must be armed for all events."

"Never before was it necessary to look forward to coming events with such determination," says the Neue Freie Presse." It is not military necessity which forces the monarchy to make such concessions."

The Abendblatt hopes " President Wilson, whose declarations certainly were seriously meant, will not hesitate to seize the hand that is stretched forth, and show the world that he intends to realize the ideas he has laid before it in his speeches."

The New York Times.

"All the News That's Fit to Print."

THE WEATHER
Fair today; Friday cloudy; slight temperature change; wind south.
☞ For weather report see next to last page.

VOL. LXVIII...NO. 22,188. ...

NEW YORK, THURSDAY, OCTOBER 24, 1918. TWENTY-FOUR PAGES.

TWO CENTS

WILSON HAS BUT ONE WORD—SURRENDER! FOR MILITARY AND AUTOCRATIC GERMANY; SENDS HER APPEALS TO ALLIES, BUT WARNS THAT TRUCE MUST LEAVE HER POWERLESS

CALLS FOR DICTATED PEACE

No Truce Possible That Does Not Destroy Her Power to Renew War.

CLOSES DOOR ON KAISER.

Notifies Germany That King of Prussia Still Rules Throughout the Empire.

FIRST CONSULTED ALLIES.

Note Believed to Represent the Combined Views of All Our Cobelligerents.

Special to The New York Times

WASHINGTON, Oct. 23.—"Not peace negotiations, but surrender."

This is the keynote of President Wilson's reply to the last German note as announced by Secretary of State Lansing at 9 o'clock tonight. It tells Germany that the power of the King of Prussia, who is also the German Kaiser, is still in unimpaired control of the empire, that the nations of the world do not trust even the word of those who have been masters of German policy, that the United States refuses to deal with any but veritable representatives of the German people, and that if our Government "must deal with the military masters and the monarchical autocrats of Germany now it must demand not peace negotiatons but surrender."

With the idea of surrender and a dictated peace strictly in view, the President has decided to take up with the allied Governments the question of an armistice. The terms of this armistice are to be dictated by Marshal Foch, and by Generals Haig, Pétain, Pershing, and Diaz and other military advisers of the allied Governments. These are the men who are to submit the terms of the armistice, and they are not to do so unless they consider an armistice possible from the military point of view.

Analysis of the note makes it plain that the President has brushed aside the matter of peace negotiations, and

that he is dealing with the German overtures on a strictly military basis. Such an analysis will show that his action in taking up the question of an armistice with the allied Governments is strictly with the view of complete surrender by Germany to peace terms, and military guarantees and safeguards to be dictated and imposed by the Allied Powers.

The President's reply to Germany was announced so late tonight that it was difficult to round up the Congressional and diplomatic attitude toward his action. But it soon became apparent that the more the note was studied and analyzed by public men the more they regarded it as a strong and vigorous document and that his action would be fully justified by the rapid progress of events.

As opinion matured it became apparent that the President had dealt with all the German overtures, from the first note to the latest, in a most adroit, subtle, and vigorous fashion and that he had closed the door absolutely to negotiations with any German Government that remains under the control of the Kaiser and his clique.

What the President has done in taking up the question of an armistice with the Allies, and it must be borne always in mind that before this action was taken there were careful exchanges of views with the Allied Governments, has been to suggest to the Allies that the military advisers in the field be asked to fix the terms of the only kind of armistice they consider it possible to make from the military point of view. The President lays down specific rules for the guidance even of these military leaders in the making of this armistice, and there is ground for the statement that before he laid down these rules the Allied Governments were aware of their nature, and had indicated approval of the line of procedure which he adopted.

Means Actual Surrender.

According to the belief here, the character of armistice suggested by the President is one which the German militarists will not accept unless they are ready for unconditional surrender. It is believed that no other interpretation or construction can be placed on the words of the President. The kind of an armistice upon which the President insists, it was pointed out by military men, is an armistice which would involve nothing less than the giving of hostages, the laying down of arms by the German forces, and the virtual reduction of the German Army and Navy as military machines. Confidence in Marshal Foch and the allied military commanders in the field is such that it is not dreamed for a moment that they would recommend any armistice if they deemed it impossible from a military point of view, and that the only kind of an

armistice they would sanction would be one equivalent to absolute surrender. It is not believed that President Wilson thinks for a moment, either, that the men who have been entrusted with the command of the allied armies in the field would yield any other kind of an armistice under the present conditions of allied military superiority.

This is the kind of an armistice that President Wilson suggested to the allied Governments after careful exchange of views with them since the text of the German note was first made public by wireless.

First—One that would leave the United States and the Allies in a position to "enforce" any arrangements that may be entered into.

Second—One that would make a renewal of hostilities on the part of Germany impossible.

Third—One that will fully protect the interests of the people involved.

Fourth—One that will insure to the Governments associated against Germany unrestricted power, not only to safeguard, but also "enforce," the terms of the kind of peace to which the present German Government has indicated its agreement.

Admits of No Misconstruction.

It is believed here there can be no possible misconstruction of these words, and the President is known to be a most careful measurer of the language he employs. If this sort of an armistice is granted, and no other kind is thought possible of being made with the sanction of Marshal Foch and the other allied military advisers, it will involve nothing less than complete surrender by the German military forces to the inevitable involved in the President's decision.

Allies in Full Agreement on Terms for Truce; Naval Terms Held to be of First Importance

LONDON, Oct. 23.—Reuter's Limited learns that the allied governments as a result of continual communications are perfectly acquainted with and agreed upon the terms under which it will be possible to enter into negotiations for an armistice. It should be observed that naval questions have never been dealt with in any negotiations between the United States and Germany, and they are of first importance from the Allies' viewpoint.

"The idea of the freedom of the seas as understood by Germany," says the Reuter dispatch, "is not a matter that any allied Government can accept at all. It would appear that the conditions precedent to an armistice must include the question of sea power, as well as of land power, but hitherto Germany has always limited her remarks to land power.

"America, Great Britain, France and Italy owe so much to sea power in carrying on the war and in national development that they cannot omit consideration of sea power from the discussions concerning the armistice.

"The President never assumed that his conditions would be limited to the evacuation of occupied territories, as the Germans always argued. He put a number of questions to Germany after receiving the first note, as a preliminary to placing the matter before the Allies."

Did Not Await Official Text.

President Wilson's note was completed early today, before he received the official text of the German note. This text was delivered by Frederick Oeder in Charge d'Affaires of Switzerland, this morning. The original German text of the note was presented, with an English translation. This English translation was made in Berlin and not in Washington. It is not as accurate a translation as would have been made in Washington, but as it was sent by the German Government with instructions that it be presented to the Washington Government, there was no alternative for the Swiss Legation than to present the German text and the German Government's own translation of it.

The original German text was not obtainable at the State Department today because it had been sent to the desk of the President. It can be stated without qualification, however, that when the German text is made public it will be found to differ in some material respects from the German official translation of the note into English.

The President had a conference of more than an hour this noon with Secretary Lansing. General March, Chief of Staff, and Secretary Daniels were present most of the time.

One of War's Great Issues.

Edward N. Hurley, Chairman United States Shipping Board, points out how raw materials have grown to be a dominant issue in the war, in The Annalist this week. On news stands: 10 cents; $4.00 a year by mail. Published by The New York Times. Times Square, New York.—Advt.

AMERICANS GAIN IN FIERCE BATTLE ALL ALONG FRONT

Occupy Brieulles and the Bois de Foret, Where the Enemy Held Out a Week.

BANTHEVILLE TAKEN AGAIN

Changes Hands Several Times, but Hill 281, Dominating Clery, Is Captured.

GRAND PRE BATTLE BITTER

Bell Joyeuse and Talma Farms Won by Our Men—Foe Gains and Then Is Hurled Back.

By EDWIN L. JAMES.

Copyright, 1918, by The New York Times Company.

Special Cable to THE NEW YORK TIMES.

WITH THE AMERICAN ARMY IN FRANCE, Oct. 23.—The First American Army scored important successes today in severe fighting along the front north of Verdun.

On the left we again drove the Germans out of Grand Pré and advanced into the woods north of the town. In the centre we again took Bantheville and bettered our positions at several points in that vicinity. On the right we cleared the Germans from Brieulles.

The Germans held stubbornly to all these positions. We met very strong resistance in the region of Grand Pré and our attacks precipitated very heavy fighting in the region of Talma Farm and Bellejoyeuse Farm. In the Bois Trayes a bitter fight, with machine guns on both sides, took place.

Bantheville was again taken by virtue of our positions in the Bois Bantheville.

After our capture of Hills 207, 299, and 281 the enemy position in Brieulles was rendered untenable and our shellfire forced him to evacuate this morning. We sent in patrols in force, who in turn were shelled out by the Germans. Tonight we dominate the town.

Today's advances were the most important we have made in ten days, and our success may indicate that the incessant night and day pressure by Pershing's men has somewhat worn down the German resistance in front of us.

Sky Full of Airplanes.

The day was marked by perhaps the most active aerial warfare we have seen. The sky was filled with machines all day. More than a hundred American bombing machines dropped several tons of bombs on German positions. The Germans retaliated with weak day bombing, but tonight were bombing the back areas of the American forces with vigor. Over one town American pursuit machines went into the air after German bombers.

A battery of the British Field Artillery takes up a position nearer the enemy trenches.

There were many air battles along the front. Four of our Lieutenants—Woolsey, Manning, Humes, and Colson—met four fokkers at a height of 3,800 metres. The Germans accepted the challenge, and in view of thousands of soldiers the four German machines were seen to come down. None of our airmen was hurt.

An idea of what our day bombers are doing may be gained by the statement that two tons of bombs were dropped on Buzancy today. Many fires were started in German depots.

Every foot of the infantry advance today was bitterly contested by the Germans with every tool of war they possessed. They are still fighting under orders to hold the Americans at all costs.

VIENNA TO ASK AGAIN FOR ARMISTICE FIRST

Can't Hurry Reforms, It Is Argued—Would Talk with Czechs at Home, Not Those Abroad.

ZURICH, Thursday, Oct. 24.—Austria's reply to President Wilson, which will soon be sent, will state that Austria is not disposed to enter into negotiations with the Czechoslovaks in Paris, but only with those in Austria, according to the Vienna correspondent of the Frankfurter Zeitung, who is usually well informed.

The note will say further that the reconstruction of the Austrian State cannot be effected so rapidly that an armistice must be dependent upon it, and, now that Emperor Charles's manifesto has opened the way to reforms, the Government sees no obstacle to an armistice.

BASLE, Oct. 23.—President Wilson's reply to the Austrian peace proposals in no way justifies the conclusion that the exchange of views which has been begun is to be interrupted, according to Baron von Hussaŕek, Austrian Premier, speaking before the Vienna House of Lords yesterday, according to advices from that city received here.

"We shall continue all the more our efforts toward peace," he said. "We shall answer the note after carefully examining its contents. We hope that the peace discussions, notwithstanding difficulties, will deliver the world in the near future from the unspeakable misery of war."

Official comment in Vienna on President Wilson's answer expresses a complaint that it does not answer the precise question put forward, and that it is now necessary to ask again the President's attitude toward an armistice and the re-establishment of peace, according to advices received from the Austrian capital. It is added that officials say there is a contradiction in the reasons given by Mr. Wilson in justifying his refusal to enter peace negotiations and his answer to Baron Burian on Sept. 15.

Special to The New York Times.

WASHINGTON, Oct. 23.—An official dispatch from Zurich today stated that according to the Munich Augsburger Abend Zeitung, President Wilson's reply to Austria has caused a new panic on the Vienna Stock Exchange. Bonds of Austrian banks, which had already greatly declined, have undergone a fresh depreciation of 80 to 95 per cent. Industrial bonds have lost 34 to 40 per cent. of their value and the State railways 42 per cent. There is no rise except in the Czech bonds.

BALFOUR AGAINST RETURNING COLONIES

Foreign Secretary Says It Would Be Inimical to British Empire's Safety and Unity.

LONDON, Oct. 23. (via Montreal.)—In no circumstances is it consistent with the safety security, and unity of the British Empire that Germany's colonies should be returned to her, declared A. J. Balfour, the British Foreign Secretary, in a speech at the luncheon of the Australian and New Zealand Club today.

Mr. Balfour said that it was absolutely essential that the communications of the British Empire should remain safe. He was asked if the German colonies were returned what security was there that their original oppressors would not use them as bases for piratical warfare.

The doctrine that the colonies should not be returned, Mr. Balfour asserted, was not selfish and imperialistic. It was one, he said, in which the interests of the world were almost as much concerned as the interests of the empire itself. If the empire was to remain united, he declared, it was absolutely necessary that communication between the various parts should not be at the mercy of an unscrupulous power.

HINDENBURG BACKS UP BERLIN PEACE MOVES

Tells Army He Is Obliged to Stand with Government and Asks Its Support.

WITH THE FRENCH ARMY IN FRANCE, Oct. 23 (Associated Press.)—Field Marshal von Hindenburg, in an order to German officers in the field, referring to negotiations for an armistice, declares he approves the peace moves and is obliged to support the Government. He asks that the confidence reposed in him in the days of success be continued.

The German Crown Prince, in an order to the group of armies under his command, reminds the officers of the responsibility they incur when they lose a position or modify the line in any way without orders. Copies of these documents have fallen into the hands of the French.

"Political events of the past few days," says von Hindenburg, "have produced the most profound impression upon the army, notably upon the officers. It is my duty to support the Government instituted by his Majesty. I approve the steps taken toward peace. The German army has a superiority over all others in that the troops and officers have never engaged in politics. We desire to adhere to that principle. I expect that the confidence that was accorded me in the days of success will be all the stronger now."

The order of the Crown Prince is shorter and almost curt. It says:

"The exchange of diplomatic notes gives me the occasion to recall my order according to which each officer in command engages his responsibility when he loses a position or modifies his lines of resistance without express orders."

Another order which emanates from the German High Command says:

"Diplomatic negotiations with a view to terminating the war have begun. Their conclusion will be all the more favorable in proportion as we succeed in keeping the army well in hand, in holding the ground conquered, and in doing harm to the enemy. These principles should guide the direction of the combat in the days that are to follow."

All these documents were taken from the Fifth Bavarian Division.

"All the News That's Fit to Print."

The New York Times.

THE WEATHER
Fair, slightly cooler today; tomorrow, fair; moderate south winds.
For weather report see last page.

VOL. LXVIII...NO. 22,198.   •••   NEW YORK, TUESDAY, OCTOBER 29, 1918. TWENTY-TWO PAGES.   TWO CENTS

AUSTRIA 'ACCEPTS' ALL OF WILSON'S CONDITIONS, ASKS FOR IMMEDIATE AND SEPARATE PEACE; LONDON AND PARIS SAY GERMANY IS ISOLATED; ITALIANS AND BRITISH TAKE 9,000 AUSTRIANS

VIENNA'S PLEA IS URGENT

Lays Stress on Desire for "Immediate" End of the Conflict.

LOOKS TO WILSON FOR AID.

"Adheres to" President's Viewpoint Regarding the Czechoslovaks and Jugoslavs.

BELIEVED TO ECHO BERLIN.

Washington Thinks Central Empires are Seeking Peace in Full Accord.

WASHINGTON, Oct. 28.—While Germany's latest note to President Wilson was being delivered to the State Department today through the Swiss Legation, cable dispatches from Europe brought the information that the Austro-Hungarian Government had caused another communication to be dispatched to the President, asking that immediate negotiations for peace and an armistice be entered into without awaiting the results of exchanges with Germany.

The Vienna Government asserted that it adhered to the same point of view expressed by the President in his last communication upon the rights of the Austro-Hungarian peoples, especially those of the Czechoslovaks and Jugoslavs, and requested that he begin overtures with the allied Governments with a view to ending immediately the hostilities on all Austro-Hungarian fronts.

The official text of the German note did not differ materially from the unofficial version as received by cable. No official comment was forthcoming, but it is known that no response will be made at present to the communication, which is believed to have been dispatched with the primary purpose of satisfying the German public that their Government was not omitting any opportunity to forward the negotiations for an armistice and peace.

Armistice Question Separate.

Regarding the renewed assurance in the German note that the constitutional structure of the German Government has been and is being changed to democratic lines, it is pointed out that the truth of this statement and the scope of the changes already made or projected, after all, are matters to be dealt with in connection with peace and not in arranging an armistice. A strong indisposition seems evidenced officially to yield to the apparent intent of both the German and Austrian negotiators to combine these two essentially different functions in one phase of the negotiations.

In the case of the Austrian communication, now supposed to be on its way to Washington, through the medium of the Swedish Government, it also was noted that the effort was made to show that Austria had complied with the President's demand for the recognition of the rights of the Czechoslovaks, the Jugoslavs, and other oppressed nationalities in Austria. It does not appear that the complete independence of these people has been guaranteed, and probably sufficient assurance must be had on that point before the Austrian proposals will be transmitted to the Entente Powers for submission to the military experts.

Because of the wide extent of the disaffection in the Dual Empire, developments in that quarter are believed to be fraught with greater possibilities in the way of peace than in Germany. In some official quarters the opinion is freely expressed that Emperor Charles fully realizes that he must submit to any terms which the Entente Powers and America choose to impose, and that at present he is seeking simply to secure the least onerous and humiliating.

He will be obliged to permit the Hungarians to shift for themselves in the peace settlement if they persist in the separatist movement already in full swing, but there are intimations in official quarters that by no such means can the Magyars escape the assumption of full responsibility for their share of the war and for the acts of oppression they have practiced upon the helpless minor nationalities within the confines of Hungary and in the Balkans.

The fact that Austria has anticipated Germany's will all through the various peace moves without visibly exciting any resentment at Berlin is taken to mean that the two are working in perfect harmony.

Austria a Drain on Ally.

Indeed, it has been suggested that in her present disorganized and demoralized condition Austria no longer is an asset, but a distinct drain upon Germany from the military point of view, and consequently that even though intending to continue the war on her own account, Germany would be quite willing to allow Austria to drop out, provided she could be insured against attack from the Entente forces on the south.

Warning against any peace with

Text of the Austrian Note Replying to President Wilson

BASLE, Oct. 28.—The Austro-Hungarian Foreign Minister instructed the Austro-Hungarian Minister at Stockholm yesterday to ask the Swedish Government to send the following note to the Washington Government:

VIENNA, Oct. 28.

In reply to the note of President Wilson of the 19th of this month, addressed to the Austro-Hungarian Government and giving the decision of the President to speak directly with the Austro-Hungarian Government on the question of an armistice and of peace, the Austro-Hungarian Government has the honor to declare that equally with the preceding proclamations of the President, it adheres also to the same point of view contained in the last note upon the rights of the Austro-Hungarian peoples, especially those of the Czechoslovaks and the Jugoslavs.

Consequently, Austria-Hungary accepting all the conditions the President has laid down for the entry into negotiations for an armistice and peace, no obstacle exists, according to the judgment of the Austro-Hungarian Government, to the beginning of these negotiations.

The Austro-Hungarian Government declares itself ready, in consequence, without awaiting the result of other negotiations, to enter into negotiations upon peace between Austria-Hungary and the States in the opposing group and for an immediate armistice upon all Austro-Hungarian fronts.

It asks President Wilson to be so kind as to begin overtures on this subject. ANDRASSY.

Text of President Wilson's Note to Austria-Hungary

Department of State.
WASHINGTON, Oct. 19, 1918.
From the Secretary of State to the Minister of Sweden.

SIR: *I have the honor to acknowledge the receipt of your note of the seventh instant in which you transmit a communication of the Imperial and Royal Government of Austria-Hungary to the President. I am now instructed by the President to request you to be good enough through your Government to convey to the Imperial and Royal Government the following reply:*

The President deems it his duty to say to the Austro-Hungarian Government that he cannot entertain the present suggestions of that Government because of certain events of utmost importance, which, occurring since the delivery of his address of the eighth of January last, have necessarily altered the attitude and responsibility of the Government of the United States. Among the fourteen terms of peace which the President formulated at that time, occurred the following:

X.—The peoples of Austria-Hungary, whose place among the nations we wish to see safeguarded and assured, should be accorded the freest opportunity of autonomous development.

Since that sentence was written and uttered to the Congress of the United States, the Government of the United States has recognized that a state of belligerency exists between the Czechoslovaks and the German and Austro-Hungarian Empires and that the Czechoslovak National Council is a de facto belligerent Government clothed with proper authority to direct the military and political affairs of the Czechoslovaks. It has also recognized in the fullest manner the justice of the nationalistic aspirations of the Jugoslavs for freedom.

The President is, therefore, no longer at liberty to accept the mere "autonomy" of these peoples as a basis of peace, but is obliged to insist that they, and not he, shall be the judges of what action on the part of the Austro-Hungarian Government will satisfy their aspirations and their conception of their rights and destiny as members of the family of nations.

Accept, Sir, the renewed assurances of my highest consideration.
(Signed) ROBERT LANSING.

Austria that would not give the Allies free passage through that country to attack the Germans from the south was sounded here today by Captain Vasile Stoica, now in Washington, who represented the Rumanians of Austria-Hungary in the conference of oppressed nationalities last week at Philadelphia, and who was wounded while fighting against the Austrians and Germans.

Captain Stoica said that if immune from attack from the south the Germans, by withdrawing to the natural defenses of the Rhine in the west, might be able to carry on the war several years, because on this shorter front the allied superiority of forces could not be used to full advantage.

DOOM OF GERMANY SEEN

With Austria Gone, She Cannot Hold Out Long, London Believes.

ALLIES CAN HIT FROM SOUTH

Likely to Harden Terms and Demand Complete Surrender by Deserted Berlin.

PARIS SEES END VERY NEAR

Whole Edifice of Central Alliance Crumbling and Peace Must Come Quickly.

Copyright, 1918, by The New York Times Company.
Special Cable to THE NEW YORK TIMES.

LONDON, Oct. 28.—Suspicion, with which every German move, rightly or wrongly, is regarded here, is absent from the view taken of the Austrian position. While Germany wavers on the brink of surrender, it is said, Austria-Hungary has taken the plunge.

The British Government has received a communication of Count Andrassy's unconditional acceptance of all the conditions upon which President Wilson made the entry into negotiations regarding armistice and peace dependent. Comparisons to the disadvantage of Germany and to the advantage of Austria-Hungary are made between the plain whole-heartedness of the Austro-Hungarian acceptance and the verbal trickeries which possibly exist in the guarded language of the German notes.

Austria-Hungary has followed Bulgaria in complete surrender, a fact which, it is pointed out, is very important, because it completes the isolation of Germany. Germany's reluctance to tread the same path is comprehensible, but that she will inevitably be forced to walk this Via Dolorosa is beyond doubt.

Although the terms of armistice to Austria-Hungary may not repeat in all respects the terms to Bulgaria, it is assumed that, in one case as in the other, provision will be made for the Allies to use the territory and railways of the surrendering country against any associate who continues the war.

Thus the Germans, if they decide on a war of defense, must be prepared to meet invasion of Germany from the Austrian side. They will find the whole Italian Army free to operate against them, while they themselves will lose the co-operation of the Austrian divisions on the west front. At the same time they will be cut in on from Rumania, and to a large extent from the Ukraine, and their supply problems will become insoluble. It is obvious that, without Austria-Hungary, Germany can only hold out for a strictly limited period, that all possibility of her improving her situation disappears, and that the only effect of further resistance on her part will be to render her still weaker after the war.

The action of Vienna in throwing up the sponge seems therefore the beginning of the end. The inevitable deduction is that Germany's claims to treat a purely military question, like the conditions of an armistice, on the basis of equality merit even less consideration than was the case when the President clearly indicated his view that an armistice must be determined on the basis of allied supremacy.

The news of the Austro-Hungarian surrender can only strengthen the determination of the military and naval chiefs of the Allies to exact adequate guarantees that Germany, if granted an armistice, will be in no position to renew hostilities in case the terms of peace ultimately to be put before her do not meet her views as to what constitutes a peace of justice.

While all the world waits on the decisions to be rendered in Paris, it is expected here that an essential feature of the reply which will be made to Germany will be that the German high command shall send emissaries, under a white flag, to learn from Marshal Foch what are his terms of armistice, as Generalissimo of all the allied armies on the western front.

In other words, the next conversation must be on the field of battle between Foch and Hindenburg.

It is felt that only by procedure of this kind can the German people be clearly shown that the initiation of the armistice proposals did not come from the Allies, and that Germany's commanders are suppliants and the Allies victors. Being a military people the Germans will understand such action.

There would, it is believed in the circles from which this information is derived, be manifold dangers in confusing the military situation with political considerations.

The terms of a military armistice are one thing; the conditions of peace are another. Germany's latest note clearly seeks to make her acceptance of armistice terms dependent upon an allied statement of conditions of peace. It is the confident belief here that no opportunity will be given the Junkers of Germany to obtain a cry to rally their countrymen for a last fight.

PARIS AGREES WITH LONDON.

After Austria's Reply Sees Germany Standing Alone.

Copyright, 1918, by The New York Times Company.
Special Cable to THE NEW YORK TIMES.

PARIS, Oct. 28.—It sometimes happens that an inmate of an insane asylum thinks he is a King, puts on a paper crown, and struts in the patients' ward, using the language of royalty. Now comes Andrassy of mad Central Europe, calling himself Minister of Foreign Affairs, and asking an armistice and peace in the name of Austria-Hungary.

But there is no Austria-Hungary. Andrassy himself admits it. In the same note that he claims to speak for the people of what was recently the Dual Monarchy he agrees with President Wilson that the Czechoslavs and Jugoslavs shall be free peoples. But it has been Andrassy's life ambition to be Foreign Minister, and he insists on having his hour among the wreckage—the wreckage of the State of which some cynical diplomat once said it would have to be invented if it did not exist. But the invention has run out, and Austria is no longer needed.

Andrassy's father was one of the signers of the Treaty of Alliance of 1879 between Germany and Austria. In the French republic's opinion the chief interest in the son's note, published this afternoon, is that it is a final, conclusive bit of evidence that the alliance no longer exists, that Germany has lost her last accomplice. What else but complete separation of the Central Powers can Andrassy mean when he says he wants to make a separate peace "without awaiting the results of any other negotiations"?

That is the main point in the Andrassy note. It is accepted here as proof of the greatness of President Wilson's shrewdness in his diplomatic treating with Germany and Austria-Hungary separately.

Andrassy's surprising recognition of the rights of the Czechoslovaks and Jugoslavs reminds Paris of what Napoleon once said of Austria: "She is always too late with an idea."

There is a quickly manufactured joke in Paris tonight. It is to ask: 'Who is this Andrassy?'

Answer: "He is Foreign Minister of Austria-Hungary."

"But there is no Austria-Hungary."

The joke indicates French opinion as to what will be done in the matter. Nobody thinks seriously for a moment that peace suggestions can be entertained from a Government which does not exist, and which practically admits the independence of millions of former subjects it still pretends to speak for.

As to an armistice, that is another question. If the fragments of what was once the Dual Monarchy want to make an unconditional surrender, it is taken for granted that the matter will be left to the military chiefs of the Allies.

A tremendous effect of the Andrassy note on Germany is expected in France. Now that the Hungarian statesman has recognized the rights of the Slavic powers, who knows, asks Paris, but that Solf, or some successor, sooner or later will write a note saying Bavaria ought to be an independent State?

PREDICT QUICK END OF WAR.

Whole Edifice of Central Alliance Crumbling, Paris Believes.

By CHARLES H. GRASTY.

Copyright, 1918, by The New York Times Company.
Special Cable to THE NEW YORK TIMES.

PARIS, Oct. 28.—The Austrian note has been received here as the beginning of the end, and Americans with whom I have talked believe that the whole edifice of the Central Alliance is crumbling.

Turkey's capitulation is probably imminent.

It is reported that Hindenburg resigned Oct. 15. The Germans, it is believed, cannot maintain military resistance in the face of the general civilian collapse, and the impression in Paris tonight is that there will be an early end of the war on the basis of unconditional surrender.

GERMAN PRESS FEARS DEMANDS OF ALLIES

Reichstag Votes to Refrain from Discussing President Wilson's Note.

AMSTERDAM, Oct. 28.—A dispatch from Berlin says that a proposal that President Wilson's note to Germany should not be discussed in the Reichstag was adopted by that body at a meeting held on Friday. The Conservatives and Independent Socialists voted against it.

President Wilson's note was printed textually in the German newspapers on Thursday evening and Friday morning. The Vossische Zeitung of Berlin printed the English text alongside the note in German.

Aside from the Junker organs, which proclaimed the necessity of every man coming to the front for the Emperor and the empire, many papers apparently contemplate without excessive lament the prospective disappearance of the Hohenzollern dynasty. The Emperor's abdication is again strongly rumored to be impending.

It is noteworthy that the Frankfurter Zeitung hints at a coming "sacrifice" with comparative equanimity. Both the Berlin and Frankfort Stock Exchanges showed an improved tendency as a result of President Wilson's note."

Fears are not concealed that the Entente conference at Paris will put forward demands "incompatable with German honor," but the anxiety to know the exact terms of the associated Governments puts everything else in the background.

"Anger and shame are bad counselors," says the Lokal-Anzeiger of Berlin, which is content to leave the decision of the army leaders. It is a significant sign of the times that Prince Charles Max Lichnowsky's pamphlet, blaming the German Government for starting the world war and saying that Great Britain did everything possible to avert it, has been permitted to reappear in Germany.

SAYS TROOPS GET RUM ON GOING INTO BATTLE

But Merely as a Stimulant, Mrs. Blatch Explains—War Will Aid Suffrage.

Mrs. Harriot Stanton Blatch, the suffrage leader, returned yesterday on the American liner Philadelphia from England, where she had been to settle the estate of her late husband, who was an Englishman.

She said that Jane Addams had made a mistake when she stated that the soldiers in France and England were made drunk before going into battle.

"That is not true," Mrs. Blatch added. "It is true that whisky and other stimulants are given to the soldiers to prepare them for the fight in the same way that stimulants are given to horses before a race. The reason for this is that no sane man wants to be killed, or really wants to fight, so he must be spurred on."

Mrs. Blatch said that her nephew, who is an officer in the English Army, told her that the Canadians had a great enmity toward the Prussians; but, like the English, they were friendly with the Bavarians and frequently exchanged rations with them in the trenches. During her visits to the hospitals in England and France Mrs. Blatch said she had become convinced that conscription was a proper thing for every nation.

"I come back," she went on to say, "firmly convinced of the necessity of universal military service, also for a systematic training of women to prepare them to take the places of men in industrial pursuits in time of war. Were there such a system as this in France and England now each of those two nations could place immediately an additional army corps in the field. Clerical work performed by men could be done by women even more intelligently.

"The men of England and France will be ready to grant women suffrage after the war, because it has shown them what woman can do and will do in time of need."

When told that President Wilson had declared himself in favor of women's suffrage Mrs. Blatch smiled grimly and said she hoped the eyes of the All-seeing One would penetrate the polling booths and find out how many of those who gave their promises really did cast their votes for suffrage.

"All the News That's Fit to Print."

The New York Times.

THE WEATHER
Fair, continued cool today and to-morrow; went to northwest winds.
For weather report see next to last page.

VOL. LXVIII...NO. 22,196.　　　　NEW YORK, FRIDAY, NOVEMBER 1, 1918. TWENTY-FOUR PAGES.　　TWO CENTS　　　　　　THREE CENTS　　　FOUR CENTS

REPUBLIC IS PROCLAIMED IN VIENNA, AS PEACE MISSION ENTERS ITALY; TURKEY MAKES FULL SURRENDER

WIDE ANARCHY IN AUSTRIA

Revolutionary Mobs Parade in Capital and Cry 'Down with Hapsburgs.'

RAILROAD TO BERLIN CUT

All Lines Are Disorganized— Bands of Robbers and Deserters Cause Terror.

ARMY IS IN DISSOLUTION.

Soldiers' and Officers' Council
Is Set Up to Govern
in Vienna.

BERNE, Oct. 31, (Associated Press.)—Military insurrections occurred in both Vienna and Budapest Wednesday, according to the Berlin newspapers. The people and troops acclaimed a republic.

The situation is particularly grave at Budapest, where the insurgent troops have machine guns with munitions, and already hold one railroad terminal. Apparently the troops are acting in agreement with the Hungarian National Assembly, but the formation of a Military Committee is reported.

The Berliner Tageblatt's Vienna correspondent says that the movement began in Vienna Thursday [probably Wednesday] morning with manifestations by students and workmen.

The President of the National Assembly, Dingshofer, announced from the steps of the Diet that the Assembly would take over the administration at once. Many oficers

tore the imperial cockade from their hats, and the imperial standard was hauled down from Parliament House.

Afterward it was announced that the Assembly had adopted a note to President Wilson and also a Constitution.

"No one," says the correspondent, "pays any attention to the Government or to the Lammasch Ministry. The retirement of Count Andrassy, the Foreign Minister, is expected momentarily.

"Emperor Charles is reported to be at the Royal Palce in Godollo, fifteen miles northeast of Budapest. It is stated that he was followed by eighteen wagons, conveying furniture and the keys to the palace strong room."

Soldiers Council in Control.

AMSTERDAM, Oct. 31.— The Berlin Tageblatt and Vossische Zeitung say that an all-provisional soldiers and officers' council has been established at Vienna, where people are parading the streets, shouting:

"Down with the Hapsburgs!"

According to reports here, the army is in course of full dissolution.

In Budapest people are shouting for a republic and the soldiers are replacing their imperial cockades by revolutionary colors. Revolutionary troops govern the city.

Anarchy Throughout Monarchy.

LONDON, Oct. 31.—The conditions in the interior of Austria-Hungary virtually preclude a continuance of fighting, according to reports from Continental points, which show that the monarchy faces complete anarchy.

The railways necessary for the maintenance of the military forces of the Dual Monarchy have become utterly disorganized.

All communication between Agram, Fiume, Budapest, and Vienna has been interrupted, and the railway communications between Berlin and Vienna have been cut.

Austrian Peace Mission Now Received by Italy After Being Once Rebuffed; Gen. Weber Heads It

VIENNA, Oct. 31, (via London.)—An Austrian deputation has been permitted to cross the fighting line for preliminary pourparlers with the Italian commander, according to an official announcement issued tonight. The statement reads:

The high command of the armies early Tuesday, by means of a parlementaire, established communication with the Italian Army command. Every effort is to be made for the avoidance of further useless sacrifice of blood, for the cessation of hostilities, and the conclusion of an armistice.

Toward this step, which was animated by the best intentions, the Italian high command at first assumed an attitude of unmistakable refusal, and it was only on the evening of Wednesday that, in accord with the Italian high command, General Weber, accompanied by a deputation, was permitted to cross the fighting line for preliminary pourparlers.

If, therefore, the cruelties of warfare must continue in the Italian theatre of war, the guilt and responsibility will have to be ascribed to the enemy.

LONDON, Oct. 31.—The Austrian commander on the Italian front applied to General Diaz, the Italian commander, for an armistice, the Exchange Telegraph Company stated today. The appliction, it was added, was forwarded to the Versailles Conference.

ITALIAN ARMY HEADQUARTERS, Oct. 30, (Associated Press.) In answer to Austria's announcement that she was ready to evacuate Italian territory, Italy officially replied that the offer had come too late.

It is assumed here that the Italians will endeavor to drive the Austro-Hungarians from Italian soil before an armistice can be signed.

General Diaz has issued this bulletin to his troops:

"Soldiers, forward! In Italy's name we will place the wreath of victory on the tomb of our glorious dead. Forward! Our immortal country calls!"

The above dispatch was evidently sent before the Italian command rescinded the refusal to receive the Austrian deputation for preliminary pourparlers.

A Paris dispatch quotes a Zurich dispatch to the Journal as saying that the Czechoslovaks cut the railroad between Berlin and Vienna near Bodenbach and that German trains can go only as far as Schandau.

This fact explains the comment of the Berlin Vorwärts, quoted in a Basle dispatch:

"The Continental policy of the German Empire has collapsed. The Hamburg-Bagdad line has been reduced to the Hamburg-Bodenbach road."

Disorders prevail through Austria-Hungary in addition to immense confusion. Besides serious outbreaks at Budapest, agitations are spreading everywhere, according to dispatches from neutral papers.

The Berlin Vossiche Zeitung prints a dispatch from Budapest saying that a crowd stormed the military prison and released political and military prisoners. Revolutionary troops seized the eastern railroad terminus and two troop trains, which were about to start for the front. The soldiers in these trains joined the insurgents, who had machine guns and enormous quantitites of arms and ammunition, and plundered the arsenals.

The Berlin correspondent of the Copenhagen National Tidende says that on the Hungarian-Croatian frontier thousands of deserters are committing outrages. Railway trains are being attacked and robbed. Another

dispatch says that Austro-Hungarian soldiers are deserting into Serbia.

In Slavonia several castles are afire and towns are burning.

During demonstrations at Prague American flags were unfurled and diminutive reproductions of the Statue of Liberty were displayed. President Wilson was repeatedly cheered.

The Croatian Parliament at Agram has voted for a total separation of Croatia, Slavonia, and Dalmatia from Hungary, according to a Geneva dispatch to the Paris Matin. The dispatch said that Agram was decked in national colors and that the people were celebrating the passage of the resolution.

According to a private message received at Amsterdam and forwarded by the Central News Agency correspondent, some of the soldiers at Agram did not join the revolutionaries, and sanguinary fighting began there.

A dispatch from Basle reports that the City of Fiume has been abandoned by the Austrian authorities to the Croatian troops and that the town has been decked with the Italian colors.

The commander of the garrison at Fiume initiated the abandonment by informing the Governor that it was impossible to defend the town against attack, as there were no munitions. The Governor thereupon asked instructions from Vienna. He was told to leave the town to the Croatian soldiers, which was done, and the town was soon beflagged with Italian bunting.

Berne advices chronicle disrupting movements in various parts of the Empire.

The Hungarian Diet at a joint meeting yesterday adopted a motion declaring that the constitutional relations between Hungary and Dalmatia, Slovenia and Fiume had ceased to exist, according to the Hungarian Correspondence Bureau.

The motion also declared that the relations between Croatia and Austria had been severed. The constitution of a new independent State, (in Hungary?) was to be determined by a constituent assembly.

Meanwhile, according to an Amsterdam dispatch, grave rioting was renewed in Budapest on Wednesday. Mobs looted the stores and attacked the banks, which limited payments to 100 crowns.

One Berne dispatch says that the troubles in Budapest seem to have been caused by an attempt of Archduke Joseph to impose a military dictatorship. It is thought premature there to try to form an opinion on the events which have taken place.

The same dispatch notes that in addition to Berlin newspapers taking measures to inform the German public of the revolutionary troubles in Hungary, care was taken by the Wolff Bureau, the semi-official news-gathering organization, to transmit the news abroad.

A Zurich dispatch of yesterday states that the rapid advance of the Allies in Serbia was causing the liveliest alarm in Budapest, according to a Vienna dispatch. It was feared that the Jugoslavs would cross the Croatian frontier, join the allied troops and march on Budapest. This was one of the reasons for the persistence with which Count Andrassy asked for an armistice.

The "German National Council" of Austria has by act created the German State of Austria and a note to President Wilson notifying him of this action has been drawn up and approved at a full meeting of the Council. The State claims all the territory of old Austria where the majority of the population is German.

A summary of the contents of the note, which was first drafted by the Executive Committee of the Council, is given by the official Vienna Correspondence Bureau. The newly created State, the note sets forth, according to this summary, demands that its representatives be admitted to participation in the peace negotiations.

The new State recognizes the independence of the Jugoslav and Czechoslovak States. It claims Moravia and Silesia for itself and appeals to President Wilson to give the German nation the right to dispose of itself.

The German Bohemian members of the Reichsrat have formed a provisional constitution and selected Reichenberg as the seat of government, dispatches from Vienna announce. It is reported that Dr. Karl Kramarz will be Premier and Professor T.G. Masaryk Foreign Minister of the new Czechoslovak State and that the new Government will proceed to Prague as soon as an armistice is concluded.

Berlin Recalls Bernstorff to "Advise" on America

BASLE, Switzerland, Oct. 31.—The Frankfurter Zeitung, a copy of which has been received here, says Count von Bernstorff, German Ambassador to Turkey, will arrive in Berlin Friday, having been recalled from the Constantinople Embassy less on account of recent events in Turkey than the necessity to have some one in Berlin especially acquainted with American matters.

The newspaper adds that the Turkish Ambassador in Berlin, Turkish officers in Germany, and two Turkish Princes who were studying in the German capital have been recalled to Turkey.

TURKISH ARMISTICE SIGNED

Equivalent to Unconditional Surrender, Opens Black Sea to Allies.

TOWNSHEND AS MESSENGER

Turks Freed General and He Arranged for Negotiations on Aegean Island.

TIGRIS ARMY CAPTURED

British Take 7,000 Prisoners and Much Material in Mesopotamia.

Terms of the Armistice Which Turkey Had to Sign

Copyright. 1918, The New York Times, Special Cable to THE NEW YORK TIMES.

LONDON, Oct. 31.—An English correspondent writes to THE NEW YORK TIMES about the terms of the armistice with Turkey. He says:

"The armistice, which was signed after three days of parley, was both naval and military in character, General Allenby having been kept closely advised of the proceedings. The armistice is as complete as that of Bulgaria, and gives us absolute military domination over Turkey. The guns and the forts of the Bosporus pass into our temporary possession, and all means of communication, as well as control of Turkish rolling stock. There were a dozen points in the armistice, all concerned with military occupation of the country, and they were in substance conceded by the Turks."

LONDON, Oct. 31.—Turkey has capitulated. The terms are understood to be tantamount to unconditional surrender.

An armistice has been signed at Mudros, on the Island of Lemnos, in the Aegean Sea, it is officially announced from Paris. The armistice took effect at noon.

General Townshend, the British commander captured at Kut-el-Amara, was liberated several days ago by the Turks, Sir George Cave, the Home Secretary, announced in the House of Commons today, in order to inform the British Admiral in command in the Aegean Sea that the Turkish Government asked that negotiations be opened immediately for an armistice.

A reply was sent that if the Turkish Government sent fully accredited plenipotentiaries, Vice Admiral Calthorp, the British commander, was empowered to inform them of the conditions upon which the Allies would agree to stop hostilities and could sign an armistice on these conditions in their behalf.

The Turkish plenipotentiaries arrived at Mudros early this week and an armistice was signed by Admiral Calthorp on behalf of the Allied Governments last night.

Free Passage to Black Sea.

It is impossible as yet to publish the full terms of the armistice, but they include the free passage of the allied fleets through the Bosporus to the Black Sea, the occupation of forts on the Dardanelles and in the Bosporus necessary to secure the passage of the ships, and the immediate repatriation of allied prisoners of war.

On the eve of the armistice, The Daily Express declared that, as a part of the terms of surrender, Turkey would be obliged to deliver up certain persons accused of disregarding the rules of civilized warfare, these individuals to be tried and, if found guilty, punished.

Some uneasiness has been expressed by the newspapers over a report that the Allies were prepared to make a bargain with Turkey by which she would be left in possession of Armenia, in return for a free passage of the Dardanelles, to enable the Allies to deal with the German-controlled Black Sea.

The entire Turkish force opposing the British on the Tigris has been captured, it is officially announced. The prisoners are estimated at 7,000. The text of the official statement reads:

"The hard fighting on the Tigris, which began on Oct. 24, ended on the 30th with the capture of the entire Turkish force opposed to us on that river. The prisoners are estimated at 7,000, with much material."

Ismail Hakki, commanding the Turkish armies in that region, surrendered, with one entire division and the best part of two others, The Evening Standard says.

Turkeys' capitulation followed the defeats suffered by her armies in Palestine and Mesopotamia and the collapse of Bulgaria, which left her open to attack on another frontier, and thus was not unexpected, although the Turk in bargaining is in the habit of waiting for the other side to make an offer.

Turkey's Part in the War.

Turkey entered the war in November, 1914. For her unprovoked bombardment of Sebastopol Russia declared war on her on Nov. 3; France and Great Britain two days later. She is the second of the Central Powers to ask the Allies for an armistice, Bulgaria having unconditionally surrendered Sept. 30.

Military operations began against Turkey on Nov. 5, 1914, and Great Britain annexed the Island of Cyprus. Turkey entered the war a few weeks after the German warships Breslau and Goeben had sought shelter in the Dardanelles, which was at once blockaded by the allied fleet. In April, 1915, allied troops were landed on the Gallipoli Peninsula, but the campaign failed and the allied troops were withdrawn in December of the same year.

The British began a campaign up the Tigris in November, 1914. They advanced to within less than nineteen miles of Bagdad a year later but were defeated and forced to retreat to Kut-el-Amara, where they were later forced to surrender. Early in 1917 the British renewed the offensive in Mesopotamia and have continued it successfully ever since, until now they are within a few miles of Mosul.

Turkey sent armies against the British in Egypt and against the Russians in the Caucasus. The Egyptian campaign failed in February, 1915. That in the Caucasus was driven back by the Russians through Armenia. In Palestine the allied drive under General Allenby resulted recently in the capture of the important base of Aleppo. The Russian campaign in the Caucasus was rendered fruitless by the rise of the Bolsheviki to power.

For several weeks after the United States declared war on Germany, Turkey took no action, but on April 21, 1917, she severed diplomatic relations. There has, however, never been a declaration of war by either country.

Turkey's war activities under the leadership of Germanophile Turks like Enver Pasha have been marked by the severity with which the Turks have treated the subject nationalities in their power. The Turkish Army has many German officers, and the Turkish Navy is controlled by Germans. It was reported several weeks ago that the Germans in Turkey probably would resist if the Turks opened the Dardanelles to the Allies.

FOCH'S TERMS IN BERLIN?

Vossische Zeitung Hears Truce Demands Have Arrived.

LONDON, Oct. 31.—Marshal Foch's armistice terms arrived in Berlin Tuesday night, the Vossische Zeitung of Berlin says it learns, according to an Exchange Telegraph dispatch from Copenhagen.

"All the News That's Fit to Print."

The New York Times.

THE WEATHER
Fair today; Tuesday fair and warmer; fresh south winds.
For weather report see next to last page.

VOL. LXVIII...NO. 22,199. .... NEW YORK, MONDAY, NOVEMBER 4, 1918. TWENTY-FOUR PAGES. TWO CENTS in Greater New York | THREE CENTS Within 200 Miles | FOUR CENTS Elsewhere

AUSTRIA SIGNS ARMISTICE, QUITS WAR TODAY; GERMANY STANDS ALONE, KAISER LOATH TO GO; ITALIANS RECAPTURE TRIESTE AND TRENT; AMERICAN RUSH MENACES GERMAN RETREAT

TRUCE WITH ITALY IS SIGNED

Vienna Announces that Hostilities Against the Allies Have Terminated.

JOY AT PARIS CONFERENCE

News of Surrender Reaches Premiers — Text Will Be Made Public Tomorrow.

TERMS TO AUSTRIA AN INDEX

Conditions Imposed in Surrender Furnish a Forecast of What Germany May Expect.

LONDON, Nov. 3.—An armistice with Austria was signed this afternoon by General Diaz, the Italian Commander in Chief, an official announcement made here, this evening says. The text of the statement reads:

A telephone message has been received from the Prime Minister in Paris saying that news has just come that Austria Hungary, the last of Germany's props, has gone out of the war.

The armistice was signed by General Diaz this afternoon and will come into operation tomorrow at 3 o'clock. The terms will be published Tuesday.

VIENNA, Nov. 3, (via London.)—Army Headquarters today issued the following:

In the Italian theatre of the war our troops have ceased hostilities on the basis of an armistice which has been concluded. The conditions of the armistice will be announced in a later communication.

PARIS, Nov. 3. — Official announcement of the signing of the Austrian armistice reached the Premiers while they were in session in the apartment of Colonel House, President Wilson's personal repre-

Kaiser Decrees His Full Support of Reforms; Believed to Be Trying to Avoid Abdication

AMSTERDAM, Nov. 3, (Associated Press.)—On the occasion of the constitutional amendment coming into force, says an official telegram from Berlin, Emperor William addressed to Prince Maximilian of Baden, the German Imperial Chancellor, a decree indorsing the decisions of the Reichstag and avowing his firm determination to cooperate in their full development. The Emperor's decree reads:

Your Grand Ducal Highness:

I return herewith for immediate publication the bill to amend the Imperial Constitution and the law of March 17, 1879, relative to the representation of the Imperial Chancellor, which has been laid before me for signature.

On the occasion of this step, which is so momentous for the future history of the German people, I have a desire to give expression to my feelings. Prepared for by a series of Government acts, a new order comes into force which transfers the fundamental rights of the Kaiser's person to the people.

Thus comes to a close a period which will stand in honor before the eyes of future generations. Despite all struggles between invested authority and aspiring forces, it has rendered possible to our people that tremendous development which imperishably revealed itself in the wonderful achievements of this war.

In the terrible storms of the four years of war, however, old forms have been broken up, not to leave their ruins behind, but to make a place for new, vital forms.

After the achievements of these times, the German people can claim that no right which may guarantee a free and happy future shall be withheld from them.

The proposals of the allied Governments which are now adopted and extended owe their origin to this conviction. I, however, with my exalted allies, indorse these decisions of Parliament in firm determination, so far as I am concerned, to co-operate in their full development, convinced that I am thereby promoting the weal of the German people.

The Kaiser's office is one of service to the people. May, then, the new order release all the good powers which our people need in order to support the trials which are hanging over the empire and with a firm step win a bright future from the gloom of the present.

Berlin, Oct. 28, 1918. WILHELM, I. R.
(Countersigned.)
Max, Prince of Baden.

Kaiser Resists Abdication Pressure

PARIS, Nov. 3.—" There can be no doubt," says the Temps " that a great struggle is going on around the German Emperor's person between the influences which caused the war and wish to maintain the old régime and the partisans of a new régime, more or less democratic, and of a peace for the purpose of repairing Germany's strength.

" By returning to General Headquarters, Emperor William seemed to show clearly that his supreme desire was not to abdicate. So the Emperor's rescript promises co-operation, not his resignation. But Parliamentary exigencies press upon him, even amid his staff, which exhorts him not to yield. Submission is not sufficient; he is summoned with more or less deference to resign."

sentative, this afternoon, and gave the greatest satisfaction.

The meeting of Premiers and military and naval representatives was a continuance of the sessions previously held. While the discussion was largely informal it went over the whole range of subjects.

The representatives were in full accord on practically all the points treated.

The sessions will continue, as the moment has not yet arrived for the taking of a final decision on some of the most important questions involved.

Premier Lloyd George of Great Britain and Premier Clemenceau of France left the conference together. They exchanged friendly greetings

on the prompt signing of the Austrian armistice and showed in their manner the keen satisfaction they felt regarding the progress of events.

TERMS TO AUSTRIA WARNING TO BERLIN

Disarming of Troops and Occupation of Strategic Points Regarded as Certain.

WASHINGTON, Nov. 3.—Armistice terms which the Austrians have accepted are expected here to furnish a clear index to those which the Supreme War Council at Versailles is preparing for Germany. Consequently their publica-

tion will carry greater significance than otherwise would attach, since the Austrian surrender had been discounted in advance by the internal disintegration of the Dual Monarchy and the collapse of the Austro-Hungarian forces on the Italian front.

Official announcement that the armistice had been signed reached the State Department today. In making this known, officials gave no indication of the terms imposed, nor was there any explanation of why cessation of hostilities had been delayed twenty-four hours or more after the actual signing of the articles of surrender. The generally accepted view, however, seemed to be that it was desired to have virtually all Italian soil freed of enemy troops before the Italian armies were committed to end their attacks upon the routed Austrian forces.

Military men here said the terms which the Supreme War Council had prepared would make it impossible for the Austrians to renew hostilities, probably including the disarming of the enemy troops and occupation of strategic points at Welu. Some of these, namely Trent and Trieste, already have been occupied by Italian and allied forces.

May Attack Through Austria.

Free movement of the allied forces through Austria to attack Germany from the south, should the Supreme War command decide such a stroke necessary in the future, also is expected to be stipulated. Unofficial reports from Vienna to-day said the Germans were preparing for such an attack by feverishly digging trenches on and fortifying the Bavarian frontier.

The defection of Austria leaves Germany stripped of its last ally and most of the military men here, both allied and American, believe that her capitulation will follow soon after the terms from Versailles are submitted.

Exchanges of views between Colonel E. M. House, special representative of the American Government in France, and the Allied Premiers continued at Colonel House's home in Paris and apparently the general terms for Germany are not yet ready for submission to the allied military leaders for consideration with their regard to the military necessities. Colonel House is keeping President Wilson constantly advised as to the progress of events.

Great importance is attached here to the course followed by the allied and American Governments in deferring peace settlements with Austria, Turkey and Bulgaria until Germany also shall surrender or be crushed. This policy is counted upon to prevent any eleventh hour attempt on the part of the Germans to sow seeds of discord among the Allies.

Splitting German Armies.

In view of the general situation, the smashing French and American victories north and west of Verdun are regarded as significant. Unless an armistice interrupts, it is believed the thrust will be pressed home relentlessly to cut the German front in the West in half before there is another halt.

With hardened mountaineers of the Italian Army available for use elsewhere, with the surrender of Austria, some observers look for immediate preparation for the invasion of Germany by way of Alsace-Lorraine. Italian picked troops might be spared at once to join such a campaign, as they would not be needed to carry out operations incidental to the Austrian surrender.

Not only will the whole fighting manpower of allied and American Armies be available now for the task of crushing Germany's defensive front, but to supplement the already vastly superior equipment of those armies in guns, aircraft, and all other war machinery, there is now at the disposal of Marshal Foch all the Bulgarian, Turkish, and Austrian military equipment. To answer such a concentration, Germany has only depleted reserves of men, guns, and munitions.

PERSHING'S DRIVE GOES ON

Main German Supply Line Now in Easy Range of His Guns.

JOIN FRENCH BEYOND WOOD

Our Men and Allies Clear Boult of Enemy, Whose Flight Is Nearly a Rout.

RETIRING EAST OF MEUSE

Germans Have Lost More Than 4,000 Prisoners and Great Quantity of Stores.

By EDWIN L. JAMES.

Copyright, 1918, by The New York Times Company.
Special Cable to THE NEW YORK TIMES.

WITH THE AMERICAN ARMY NORTH OF VERDUN, Nov. 3, 8 P. M.—For the third day the American First Army has continued its sensational advance north of Verdun against the demoralized Third and Fifth German Armies. In some sectors Pershing's men have been pursuing the enemy since dawn without catching up. The German retreat is approaching a rout. The French Fourth Army, on our left, is pushing ahead with fine speed.

It is impossible to give the exact line because the rapidity of our rush prevents the best communication, but at this hour it may be said that from left to right we join with the French near Noirval. Our troops near Brieuleulles-sur-Bar have taken Authe. In the centre we have swept on behind Champy Bois to Bois Belval. We have also taken Aucourt Farm and Beauclair. On the right we have pushed beyond Halles and Montigny.

East of the Meuse great acticity is reported behind the German lines.

To Cut German Railway.

The capture of the heights east of Beauclair, on the west bank of the Meuse, places our line seven miles from the Germans' main railroad line, the Mezières-Sedan-Longuyon system, in the vicinity of Lamouilly, which means that the line will be under range of our 75s as soon as they can be got up. We have hundreds of these accurate little guns available for cutting this line.

It appears that almost all German resistance has been broken by the rush of the American First Army after its four-week pitched battle with the enemy. At dawn this morning we sent out patrols all along the line, who found practically no resistance, and our infantry quickly moved forward in force over a fifteen-mile front. At Barricourt the garrison of Germans showed its teeth, but in a sharp, swift bayonet charge we cleared the town, and then resistance seemed to melt away.

Difficulties of Transport.

On most of the front our advance today was limited only by transportation difficulties and the difficulties of getting up guns.

At 9 o'clock this morning a report came from the right of our centre corps:

"We have taken Barricourt Heights. Going like hell."

That about tells the story of the day's advance.

From a strategical standpoint the day's work gives us a decent front, whereas yesterday it was jagged and appeared somewhat dangerous because the Germans were holding along the west bank of the Meuse on the right and still had a salient in the Forêt de Boult on the left.

On the left we started from Briquenay. Troops which had reached there yesterday after an advance by motor trucks started ahead at the same time as the French on the west side of the forest. The Germans had departed in the night, leaving only a thin covering of rearguards, which could no more stem our advance than the famed broom could hold back ocean waves. By noon we had reached Boult, and sweeping doughboys ate "chow" in Germont.

Joined with the French.

After noon we joined with the French just north of Belleville, which meant that the German forest of Boult salient was gone. By 2:30 o'clock we reached Authe, and last reports gave the location of our troops just south of Brieulles-sur-Bar.

In the centre, leaving Buzancy far behind, we swept ahead between four and six kilometers, taking our time to enable the flanks to catch up. In the sector we had little contact with the enemy all day. Incidentally in this one sector we have taken some 4,000 prisoners. The count for the whole army is not complete at this hour.

On the right our success was surprising because the Germans had orders to hold there, no matter what happened elsewhere. But the Germans here, having the deep and swollen Meuse behind them, seemed to think discretion the better part of valor and got out, leaving only victimized weak rearguards.

Advance on the Meuse.

Halles, specially blessed by Nature as a defense stronghold, was taken before noon. Skirting Bois Halles and Bois Sassey, our infantry went up the west bank of the river and took Montigny. In the vicinity of Brieulles some of our men crossed the river under fire from the east bank.

The German retreat is not made in accordance with plans of the German staff nor even of the armies. The Germans simply are not fighting and are getting out of the way. Order after order of recent dates which has been captured commanded them to hold, no matter what happened. This afternoon we captured a German runner sent post haste from army headquarters to find out why the line had broken. We took three other runners who entered our lines looking for German posts of command.

This gives an idea of the demoralization of the enemy. This demoralization, of course, is resulting in a great amount of material falling into our hands.

Three Miles From Stenay.

Our advance along the west bank of the Meuse brings us three miles from Stenay, which is seriously threatened.

Something seems to have happened to most of the German artillery. Last night the Germans threw some high explosive and gas shells into our lines, but their fire was not even comparable to what they had been doing almost daily for the last four weeks.

Despite the difficulties of mud our artillery is being got up, and guns big and little are shooting at the Germans, although for the most part the range finders can only guess where to shoot.

The American First Army is headed toward Sedan and going fast.

PERSHING SAYS 4,000 HAVE BEEN CAPTURED

Sixty-three Guns and Large Quantities of Material Also Taken Up to Saturday Night.

WASHINGTON, Nov. 2.—General Pershing's communiqué for Sunday says the American First Army continued its attack west of the Meuse and that the operation is progressing satisfactorily. Saturday night's report tells of the First Army's successful advance, overcoming all resistance, and of a ten-mile advance in two days by the Americans fighting south of the River Lys. The statements follow:

"Headquarters American Expeditionary Forces, Nov. 3, (morning):

"This morning the First Army continued its attack west of the Meuse. The operation is developing satisfactorily."

"Headquarters American Expeditionary Forces, Nov. 2, (evening):

"Section A.—A series of raids skillfully carried out by troops of the Second Army in the Woevre resulted in the capture of two officers and sixty-three men. The First Army today continued its successful advance, overcoming all resistance. Among the most important towns taken are Champeigneulle, Belleville Morthomme, Verpel, Sivry-les-Buzancy, Thénorgues, Briquenay, Buzancy, Villers-devant-Dun, and Clery-le-Petit. In spite of bad weather conditions, our aviators, flying at extremely low altitudes, carried out important missions over the Meuse Valley and along the whole front of attack.

"The number of prisoners has risen to more than 4,000 men and 192 officers, among whom are four battalion commanders with their staffs.

"The enemy was forced to abandon large quantities of material of all kinds. An official count shows that sixty-three guns of medium and light calibres and hundreds of machine guns have been captured. A Bavarian battalion of artillery was taken with its personnel, horses, and material complete.

"In the course of the operations in the last two days south of the River Lys our troops acting under the command of the King of the Belgians advanced nearly ten miles, reaching the western bank of the Scheldt and capturing several hundred prisoners.

"Section B—There is nothing to report in this section."

Bavarian Border Fortified in Fear of Allied Attack

COPENHAGEN, Nov. 2.—Austro-Hungarian troops are being withdrawn from the western front and the Germans, fearing the Allies will march through Austria, are digging trenches and erecting fortifications along the Bavarian frontier, according to a Vienna dispatch to the Politiken.

Where Pershing's Men Are Pursuing Enemy

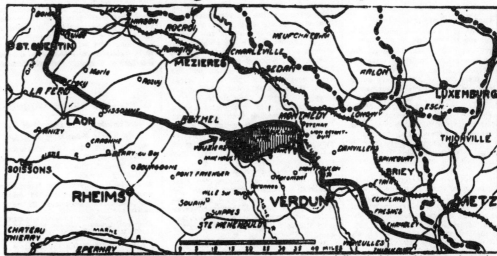

The shaded area indicates the gains of yesterday in the American and French drives which are shown by arrows. The day's advance makes it possible for American artillery to cut the Mézières-Sedan-Montmedy-Metz railway, the Germans' main supply line, which is shown on the map and which is now only seven miles distant at one point.

ALLIES SEIZING GUARANTEES.

That Is an Italian Critic's View of Recent Military Successes.

Copyright, 1918, by The New York Times Company
Special Cable to THE NEW YORK TIMES.

ROME, Nov. 2.—General Corsi, reviewing the general military situation in the Tribuna, says:

"It looks as if the Allies were going to seize those military guarantees necessary to insure the faithful carrying out of the peace conditions for which the Germans are trying to bargain. All the allied armies, from the North Sea to the Tigris, are now advancing against varying resistance. Except on the French and Italian fronts, the operations may be considered as a mere chasing of rearguards.

"The occupation of Aleppo completes the liberation of Syria from the Turkish yoke, besides having great military value, and gives the Allies control of an important railway junction on the Constantinople-Aleppo-Bagdad line.

"In the Balkans, the taking of Alessio and San Giovanni di Medua gives the Allies' left new harbor support, while the revolution in Montenegro threatens the enemy's rear.

"The rest of the Allies, meanwhile, are nearing Hungary, which may lead to important results, when the Hungarians see their country threatened.

"On the Italian front the Allies have advanced against immense difficulties and obtained great success, not so much in the extent of ground taken, as in its tactical value."

ONLY ONE FRONT WITH AUSTRIA OUT

Maurice Sees Shift of Forces to France as Chief Gain from Armistice.

NO BACK-DOOR DRIVE NOW

British Critic Says It Must Be Long Before Allies Can Attack Germany from the South.

By MAJOR GEN. SIR FREDERICK B. MAURICE.

Copyright, 1918, by The New York Times Company.
Special Cable to THE NEW YORK TIMES.

LONDON, Nov. 3.—As was the case in the Napoleonic Wars, the British Army, after passing through a long period of criticism which, if it had been good for its soul, has not always been just or easy to endure, has come into its own and bids fair to end the war in a blaze of glory.

As a nation, we have never appreciated what the making of an army means. Our principle has been, when war has been sprung upon us, to make up for the neglect of preparation in time of peace in a hurry, to provide a commander with men, money and material, and to say to him: "Now, go and win victories." If he does not do this at once, we furnish him with a number of suggestions as to how he should improve the army and carry on the war.

It took Wellington eight years to form and train the army which won victory and drove the French from the Peninsula, and during much of that time he was subjected to very similar criticism to that which has been so freely offered to our commanders during the present war. Any one who cares to turn up Sir Douglas Haig's dispatches will find in every one of them insistence on the vital importance of training and on the need of having men in France in time to train them adequately. Though Sir Douglas Haig has throughout his tenure of command had the greatest difficulties to contend with in this matter, he has in the end overcome them, and we are now seeing the results of his wise policy.

German Defeat Not a Collapse.

I hope I have made it clear in my recent articles that the German Army did not collapse at once as the result of Foch's great counter stroke on July 18. It has, for the most part, been fighting bravely and skillfully, particularly on two vital fronts—that between Douai and St. Quentin leading to the Valley of the Sambre, where the bulk of our army is engaged, and astride the Meuse, where the Americans are fighting. The enemy has not collapsed, but has been beaten in a series of great struggles by the skill and valor of our troops, by superior generalship, and by better staff work. Experience and training are reaping their reward. In France, Bulgaria, Palestine, Mesopotamia, and now in Italy, our troops are showing that the fighting qualities of our race are greater than ever they were.

To Lord Cavan's men in Italy has fallen the honor of making the first breach in the Austrian lines, which now has been so widened that a great victory is within sight. The manoeuvre by which our successes have been won has been among the most interesting of the war.

By the earlier operations of this year the enemy's main reserves had been attracted to the mountain front, and particularly to the Asiago sector, held by the British Army. On Thursday last the enemy's attention was fixed upon this front by the attack which resulted in the capture of the important Monte Sisemol, and our Italian allies kept the enemy under the illusion that our object was an advance into the mountains by extending the front of attack to the Monte Grappa region.

Meanwhile, British troops had been transferred secretly to the Lower Piave, and the Honourable Artillery Company and the Welsh Fusiliers, by a bold and skillful stroke, seized the big Island of Papadopoli, which lies rather north of half way between the points where the Piave enters the plains and the sea.

Always there was the danger that a sudden fall of rain in the mountains might bring the Piave down in flood, and that, as in the case of the last Austrian offensive, the bridges might be swept away and the position of our troops which had crossed be compromised. Indeed, it was actually reported on Monday last that operations had been checked by a rise of the Piave.

Cavan's Bold Stroke on Piave.

This stroke was given the appearance of a local operation, but on Sunday the Tenth Italian Army, strengthened by British troops, transferred rapidly from the Asiago front and placed under command of Lord Cavan, forced their way across the Piave and established themselves on the left bank of the river. This was a bold operation because there was a rise of the Piave, but apparently the delay was only temporary, for our troops have quickly extended their gains.

The position now is that three Italian armies have got across the river, and the Fifth Austrian Army is in grave danger, for behind its centre and left lie the marshes at the mouth of the Livenza, which extend far into the plains, and the lines of retreat open to the enemy between our advance and these marshes are not numerous. His only chance of escaping a considerable disaster appears to be in the immediate and skillful withdrawal of his left flank.

The whole experience of the Austrian Army in this war is that the very diverse elements of which it is composed do not hold well together under the strain of defeat, and the offer of the Austrian Government to break off from Germany and negotiate at once a seperate peace is not likely to inspire their troops to resist to the last. The prospects, therefore, of ending the war against Austria with a really brilliant victory are very bright.

Italian Front Troops for France.

If Austria goes out of the war at once, as now seems to be certain, and Germany decides to continue the struggle, half a dozen Austrian divisions now on the western front will disappear, while the British and French contingents in Italy will at once be available to reinforce the Allies in France, and it may be possible to increase the Italian contingent now fighting with the French Armies. This will mean an important change in our favor in the balance of strength on the main front, and will be the most important military advantage which we shall gain from the collapse of Austria, as whatever the terms of the armistice may be, it must take a very long time before the Allies can be in a position to attack the southern frontiers of Germany through Austria.

AUSTRIANS LEAVE WOUNDED.

Also Abandon Vast Depots of Stores in Their Headlong Flight.

WITH THE ITALIAN FORCES IN NORTHERN ITALY, Nov. 3, (Associated Press.)—The entire Italian front is moving forward. The Italian First Army in its advance on Trente captured enormous quantities of material and innumerable prisoners. Entire regiments are surrendering.

King Victor Emmanuel is visiting the liberated towns. He is being cheered enthusiastically by the inhabitants, old men and women and children surrounding him and relating the tortures they had been enduring during the Austro-Hungarian invasion.

The American Young Men's Christian Association is sending supplies and assistance to the people freed from the enemy.

Yesterday the "day of the dead" was observed along all the fronts, the civil populations visiting the cemeteries to place wreaths and flowers on soldiers' graves.

The battle continues, with the Italians and their allies completing the destruction of Austria's mighty army. It is estimated that 3,000 Austrian cannon will be the total taken by the Italians, in addition to vast quantities of other war material.

The word "strategy" cannot be used in Austria's retreat, which is a pell-mell effort on the part of the various bodies to save themselves. The Austrians are fleeing helter-skelter, fighting in the mountains when obliged to do so. On the plains they are merely putting up rearguard local fights with machine guns, blowing up the bridges as they go along. The long lines of enemy troops on the roads are being pelted with the machine guns of allied airplanes.

The retreat is being hindered by the condition of the roads. For the same reason the Italian advance in some regions is slow. The Austrians are leaving their wounded by the roadside or in houses. Two thousand Austrian wounded were deserted in Feltre without attendance or medicine.

At Vittorio a big petroleum deposit was found, the Austrians not taking the trouble to burn it. Great quantities of telegraph wire also were left undestroyed. At Belluno a large depot of food and material was found by the Italians. The Allies frequently capture long trains of artillery, one train being taken at Razi, near Feltre, it having been abandoned by the retreating Austrians in their haste.

It was on Oct. 29 that the enemy received a mortal blow by a main attack across the River Piave. This permitted the Eighth Army to move to Vittorio and gave the fourth Army room to operate. Then, piece by piece, corps by corps, and division by division the Austrian armies have fallen. When the Italian Fourth Army reached Monte Cismon, at the junction of the Brenta, it gave the Twelfth Army a chance to operate at Feltre, in the Upper Piave Valley, and also permitted the Sixth Army to go into action in the Asiago district.

Between the Fourth and Sixth armies the chief Austrian resistance in Italy was broken. It was in the mountains that the greatest number of cannon was taken.

SAY AUSTRIAN EMPIRE ENDS WITH SURRENDER

Pact of Rome Assures Agreement Between Italy and Jugoslavia, Italians Here Believe.

Special to The New York Times.

WASHINGTON, Nov. 3.—The feeling is emphasized in Italian diplomatic circles here that the surrender of the Austrian armies in the field marks the end of the Austro-Hungarian Empire.

In discussing the situation, a prominent authority on Italian questions held that the Hungarians for some time past had perceived the inevitable failure of the Dual Monarchy, but have moved too late in an effort to protect their own dynastic interests.

"Many of the questions which divided the various national elements under the Austro-Hungarian yoke," he said, "have been settled by these nationalities among themselves. Not one of them looks either to Hungary or to Austria, but to their own independence.

"The most important agreement in this connection is that known as the Pact of Rome, between Italy and the Jugoslavs, by which the solution of the secondary questions of boundaries is voluntarily left to the decision of the general peace conference. Despite the one-sided campaign of discontent, the Pact of Rome remains a formidable document, which assures a full understanding between Italy and Jugoslavia.

"Bohemia is virtually a nation in the fullest sense; Croatia is coming to the fore; Bosnia and Herzegovina certainly will be turned over to Serbia in a short while. The Italians have chosen their time and have dealt Austria-Hungary the death blow.

"The problem of subdividing what was until yesterday the Austro-Hungarian Empire cannot be very easily solved, on account of the uncertainties of the real attitude of the different South Slav nationalities toward a union under the Serbian crown. Italy, through her spokesmen, has repeatedly declared the necessity of averting any discord between the nationalities across the Adriatic and herself, as that would constitute a serious danger to the interests of all the parties concerned and would aid the schemes of the Hapsburg dynasty. Italy has therefore carefully refrained from answering the repeated attacks made against her by ill-advised Jugoslav leaders and has maintained, as she still maintains, that the Pact of Rome is not a scrap of paper, but an act which will determine in the very near future the settlement of the Adriatic question in favor of the aspirations of all the oppressed nationalities opposed to the survival of the Austro-Hungarian Empire, including herself, and herself above all."

MAGYAR REPUBLIC IS PROCLAIMED

Count Karolyi, Released by Emperor from Oath of Fealty, Announces It.

EXPECT ALLIED OCCUPATION

But Leaders Will Ask That the Troops Sent Be Either French or English.

BERNE, Nov. 3.—Count Karolyi, after having obtained a release from his oath of fealty to the Emperor, has proclaimed a republic in Hungary, according to a dispatch to the Bund from Vienna, quoting the Viennese newspaper Die Zeit:

BASLE, Switzerland, Nov. 3, (Associated Press.)—In the course of a meeting of the Executive Committee of the Hungarian National Council at Budapest yesterday Count Karolyi announced that King Charles had freed the Government from its oath of fidelity.

The Government has placed on its program the question whether Hungary shall in the future be a republic or a monarchy.

The Minister of War announced that an order would be given to all soldiers on the Hungarian front, including officers, to lay down their arms and to enter into negotiations with the enemy. If the enemy wished to occupy Hungary, the announcement added, a demand should be made that French or English troops be sent by preference.

The American flag is hoisted in Etrage Mense, France, when these soldiers hear that the last shot of the war has been fired.

These men of the 53rd and 54th Brigades collect and prepare for burial the men killed in the last attack on the Hindenburg Line.

"All the News That's Fit to Print."

The New York Times.

THE WEATHER
Fair, warmer today; tomorrow probably rain by night; wind south. For weather report see last page.

VOL. LXVIII...NO. 22,908. ... NEW YORK, FRIDAY, NOVEMBER 8, 1918. TWENTY-FOUR PAGES. TWO CENTS ... | THREE CENTS ... | FOUR CENTS ...

GERMAN DELEGATES ON THE WAY TO MEET FOCH; FIRING STOPS ON ONE FRONT TO LET THEM PASS; GERMAN NAVY REBELS; OUR MEN TAKE SEDAN; FALSE PEACE REPORT ROUSES ALL AMERICA

ROAD INDICATED TO ENVOYS

Armistice Delegates Due On the French Front Last Night

GERMANS ANNOUNCED TIME

Were to Arrive Between 8 and 10 o'Clock—Marshal Foch Fixed Their Route.

ERZBERGER IS THEIR CHIEF

Order to Cease Firing on That Part of Front Took Effect at 3 o'Clock in Afternoon.

PARIS, Nov. 7, 11 P. M., (Associated Press.)—German Grand Headquarters today requested Allied Grand Headquarters by wireless to permit the passage of the German delegation for armistice negotiations through the lines. The order was given to cease firing on this front at 3 o'clock in the afternoon until further orders.

The German wireless message, asking for an appointment to meet Marshal Foch, says:

"The German Government would congratulate itself in the interests of humanity if the arrival of the German delegation on the Allies' front might bring about a provisional suspension of hostilities."

The message announced that the German plenipotentiaries would arrive at the French outposts on the Chimay-Guise road on Thursday between 8 and 10 o'clock in the evening.

The mission is headed by Mathias Erzberger, Secretary of State and head of the War Press Department, and includes General H. K. A. von Winterfeld, former military attaché at Paris; Count Alfred von Oberndorff, former Minister at Sofia; General von Grunnel and Naval Captain von Salow.

Foch Prescribes Envoys' Route.

LONDON, Nov. 7, (Associated Press.)—Marshal Foch, the Allied Commander in Chief, has notified the German High Command that if the German armistice delegation wishes to meet him it shall advance to the French lines along the Chimay, Fourmies, La Capelle, and Guise roads.

From the French outposts the plenipotentiaries will be conducted to the place decided upon for the interview.

The British Foreign Office this evening stated, according to the Exchange Telegraph Company, that the rumor that an armistice with Germany had been signed was unfounded.

The British naval representative at the armistice negotiations will be Rosslyn Wemyss, First Sea Lord of the Admiralty, it is officially announced.

Earl Curzon, member of the British War Council, it is announced, has gone to the continent on official business.

French Awaited White Flags.

PARIS, Nov. 7, (Associated Press.)—Four German officers bearing white flags, it is officially announced, will probably arrive at the

---

Whole German Fleet Revolts; Mutineers Rule Heligoland

LONDON, Friday, Nov. 8, 12:45 A. M.—Virtually all the German fleet has revolted, according to a dispatch received from The Hague.

The men are complete masters at Kiel, Wilhelmshaven, Heligoland, Borkum and Cuxhaven.

At Kiel the workers have joined the navy men and declared a general strike, says the dispatch.

The greater part of the submarine crews in all the naval harbors have joined the revolt, according to an Exchange Telegraph dispatch from Copenhagen.

Headquarters of Marshal Foch tonight.

The Temps says that the German delegation "charged to conclude an armistice and open negotiations," according to yesterday's official Berlin note, must have arrived at the front, and must soon present itself at Marshal Foch's headquarters.

A considerable crowd gathered around the War Office today, awaiting news of the result of the German application, under a flag of truce, for an armistice, although it is generally believed that several days will pass before a truce can be arranged.

London Papers Correct Error.

Copyright, 1918, by The New York Times Company.
Special Cable to THE NEW YORK TIMES.

LONDON, Nov. 7.—Up to 5 o'clock this afternoon the German Armistice Commission had not reached the French lines.

Evening papers which printed an early report that the armistice had been signed are now getting out special editions apologizing for the error.

UNITED PRESS MEN SENT FALSE CABLE

Armistice Message Signed by President Roy Howard and Simms, Paris Manager.

REACHED CITY AT 11:56 A. M.

News Association Will Not Admit Inaccuracy Despite Repudiation by Washington.

The United Press Association's false cable message announcing that an armistice had been signed by Marshal Foch, the allied Commander in Chief, and the German military and naval envoys was received in the office of the United Press, in the Pulitzer Building, 63 Park Row, at noon yesterday.

W. W. Hawkins, General Manager of the United Press service in this country, said last night that the message was received by the Western Union at 11:56 A. M., and immediately submitted to the censor, who returned it with his "O. K." at 11:59, or three minutes after the message arrived in New York. One minute later it was being flashed into the United Press offices in the Pulitzer Building, and a few minutes later the papers served by the United Press were on the streets with the startling news.

The message as received in the United Press office reads:

Paris.
Unipress, NY.
Urgent. Armistice Allies Germany signed eleven amorning. Hostilities ceased two safternoon. Sedan taken by Americans.
HOWARD. SIMMS.

The signers of the message are Roy W. Howard, the President of the United Press Association, and William Philip Simms, the manager of the Paris office of the service. The message was filed in Paris shortly after 11 A. M., New York time, which was about 4 P. M., French time, or nearly an hour before the time set for the first meeting of Marshal Foch and the German armistice emissaries. The word "urgent" in the message signifies that the highest rate was paid in order to expedite transmission.

Route of the German Delegates Through Foch's Lines

CITY GOES WILD WITH JOY

Supposed Armistice Deliriously Celebrated Here and in Other Cities.

CROWDS PARADE STREETS

Jubilant Throngs Reject All Denials and Tear Up Newspapers Containing Them.

JUDGES CLOSE THE COURTS

Mayor Addresses Crowds at City Hall—Saloons Closed at Night to Check Disorder.

With the nervous tension of the years of war suddenly broken yesterday afternoon by the false report sent out by the United Press Association, a private corporation supplying news to many afternoon newspapers throughout the country, that Germany had signed an armistice with the Allies, all the joyful enthusiasm pent up by New Yorkers through the long ordeal of the business of war and the waiting for peace and victory was wasted on a fake. When the sirens, whistles and bells rose in a resounding clamor, about 1 o'clock in the afternoon, carrying the news of the supposed signing of the armistice and the cessation of hostilities, men and women of all ages, all stations, in every part of the city, with an unspoken accord, suddenly stopped their business and poured out into the streets to join through the afternoon in a delirious carnival of joy which was beyond comparison with anything ever seen in the history of New York.

New York was not the only victim of the deception, for the United Press's false report of the end of the war had been carried throughout the country, and in country villages, small towns, and great cities—most notably, perhaps, in Chicago—there were celebrations as enthusiastic as that of New York.

The afternoon papers which carried the false rumor of peace were snatched off the stands and out of the hands of newsboys by the eager crowd and displayed everywhere, while no attention was paid to those which had stuck to less romantic realities and told only of the steady advance of the allied armies and of the outbreak of revolution in Germany. Not till late in the afternoon, when later editions told the city that the news was false, did the public at large learn that there was anything the matter with the good news, and many people were only angered by the official denial, showing their wrath by tearing up the papers that printed the State Department's correction. Apparently millions of people never learned the truth at all last night. For after thousands of those who had danced in the streets and cheered themselves hoarse in the afternoon had gone home, thousands more—boys who welcomed the release from all inhibitions, hoodlums joyfully seizing any excuse for making a noise, and some who had drunk so much in the afternoon that they neither knew nor cared whether the peace story had any basis of foundation—stayed on the streets; and they were joined after nightfall by other thousands from the homes or from the outlying portions of the city who had seen no papers and still thought that the war was at an end. The crowd knew, anyhow, that the war was virtually over; they had seen German war lords forced aside and new leaders begging for mercy in the name of Germany; the false report unloosed the emotion that had been held in during the weeks of victory.

Despite these new arrivals, it was a different sort of jubilation which filled the night; while the afternoon streets had seen an outburst of popular emotion which was sincere, heartfelt, and profoundly impressive, the night saw much of the city abandoned to aimless mafficking. The police, who had made no attempt to restrain the enthusiasm of the afternoon, perhaps realising that it would have been useless, were alert and occasionally very active after nightfall, and kept a close watch on the throngs to prevent the beginnings of disorder in the greatest mob of New York's history. Saloon keepers throughout the city realising the change in the character of the demonstration, and fearing the possible reaction of the crowds to the eventual realization of the deceit that had called them forth, voluntarily closed their places at 9:30 o'clock.

To the great majority of New Yorkers the news of that to which the whole world had been looking forward for years came almost exactly at 1 o'clock in the afternoon by the blaring of the sirens set up as air raid warnings, combined with the clamor of bells on the City Hall, the borough halls, and the churches, and the rising clamor of hundreds of factory whistles which joined in the noise as soon as the sudden hope stirred by the outbreak of the sirens had been confirmed by telephone calls, or by the appearance on the streets of the first extras bearing the headlines: "Germany Surrenders; the War Is Over."

The clamor, as everybody knew, could at this time mean only one thing; and soon people were pouring into the streets in the residence districts, crowding around the newsstands, and gathering in groups on the corners to shake hands and exchange rather dazed congratulations.

As the tidings spread the clamor grew. Into schoolhouses came teachers, janitors, or pupils with the papers carrying the news, and in almost every room of parochial and public schools the children were told that the war was over, and were not chidden when they responded with a shout of rejoicing. The "Star-Spangled Banner" and the "Marseillaise" were sung, and then there was not much more school. In parochial schools the pupils were led into church to give thanks for the ending of the war, and then dismissed, as were the pupils of many public schools, to go home and tell their parents that it was all over.

The noise grew steadily on the streets as one church bell after another, one factory whistle after another took up the work of adding to the din of celebration. Windows on the street were opened, and old people hung out in the mild Autumn afternoon, waving handkerchiefs and flags and smiling at the younger and more active members of the family who had gone out in the open air to talk it over with the neighbors. The shock and bewilderment with which almost everybody first received the news seemed presently to give place to a desire to help in the making of noise. Automobiles drove through the streets with horns buzzing and hooting, in fire houses the engines were hastily rolled out to the curb and stoked up, and when a full head of steam was on, the whistles were tied down; the sirens and gongs of trucks were worked violently and continuously.

Judges Adjourn the Courts.

Downtown the news came at the noon recess of the courts, and Judges and Justices who heard it at luncheon went back to their courtrooms and with one accord adjourned court for the day, after putting on the record a few words of appreciation of the significance of a date which everybody at that moment thought would go down in history. Police Commissioner Enright had given authority for the blowing of the sirens when he heard what appeared to be confirmation of the news, and Mayor Hylan having ordered the ringing of the bell on the City Hall, appeared on the steps and made a speech.

"Thank God," he said, "that I lived to see this day when the rights of the peoples of the world are recognized, and the world is made safe for democracy and humanity."

The Mayor addressed the crowds in City Hall Park several times during the afternoon, and had announced his intention of leading a parade in the evening before he learned, late in the day, that the report of the end of the war was unconfirmed.

The demonstrations which later in the day tended to centre in the city's chief gathering places—Fifth Avenue, Broadway, Times Square, the chief cross streets, and around City Hall Park, together with 125 Streets, the crossing of 149th Street and Third Avenue, and other centres of the life of New York—really began downtown. In Wall Street and lower Broadway the crowds began to gather first; here first began the flinging out of long rolls of ticker tape or paper from adding machines, followed by the tearing up of sheets of paper and flinging them down on the street in showers like a snowstorm. At the lunch hour Wall Street was already impassable to automobiles, jammed from curb to curb with pedestrians, grouping around soldiers, around orators shouting from improvised pedestals, or around the sellers of flags and novelties who were already capitalizing the end of the war.

In many offices the heads of the firms, as soon as they heard the news, told the office staffs that there would be no more work that day. Where this was not done the effect was the same; everybody decided to take the afternoon off and celebrate. By 3 o'clock office buildings were emptied, and the crowds were on their way uptown, toward Fifth Avenue and Broadway, where the most remarkable demonstrations of the day occurred.

By the middle of the afternoon Fifth Avenue, from Washington Square to the Plaza, was already packed from curb to curb with pedestrians, so closely that automobiles were unable to move for long intervals, and could push forward only a few yards at a time. Presently the traffic police cleared all motor traffic off the avenue, and from that time on till nightfall, when motor cars were once more admitted, Fifth Avenue was given over wholly to the crowds on foot. The only exceptions were at the crossings, where at infrequent intervals lines of cars managed to worm their way across the thoroughfare and into the cross streets through a crowd that unwillingly made way for them; and now and then, at great intervals, a car carrying officers of the United States or the Allies, who had free passage wherever they went and were only halted by the revellers who wanted to shake their hands.

Packed for Three Miles.

From curb to curb the avenue for three miles was packed with the greatest crowd New York has ever seen. Two great streams of traffic moved up and down town, but they were frequently cut into or broken up by the innumerable lines of snake dancers who wriggled their way across the street and up and down. For the moment the whole population of New York was absolutely unrestrained, giving way to its emotions without any consideration of anything but the desire to express what it felt. The city was in the hands of the mob in a way which had never been seen before—more completely than in the days of the draft riots; but it was a different kind of a mob. It could have done anything it wanted to in the afternoon, but it wanted only to celebrate the end of the war. It was a people's jubilation at the victorious ending of a people's war. Some of its manifestations were a bit grotesque, but there was that in it which put considerations of taste on one side; it was the spontaneous expression of what was in the popular heart. And with all the grotesquerie there was no violence, no roughness; nothing but a carnival of enthusiasm and relief.

Sellers of flags, of red, white, and blue streamers, of tin horns, of rattles, had their stocks exhausted in no time; those who were unable to get hold of these things seemed to find it necessary to do something to attract attention, to show that they were not asleep to the general feeling. Men wore their overcoats wrong side out; they solemnly smashed derby hats and set the ruins back on their heads; men put on women's hats and women men's hats, men and women walked about draped in American flags.

From the windows of every building hung enormous flags of America and the Allies, hastily flung out when they were not already flying; and from the windows, as the afternoon went on, came more and more copious showers of torn paper. The rolls of ticker tape and other papers that had served early in the afternoon were soon exhausted, and all kinds of stationery, newspapers, advertising leaflets, waste, and anything that could be torn up and sent fluttering in the air, was flung out. The air was full of it for hours; before long the streets were ankle deep, and the crowds were kicking their way through clouds of paper fluttering about knee high. The Street Cleaning Department helplessly flung up its hands, waiting for nightfall; but long before dusk hundreds of tenants in the lower floors of high buildings had called up Commissioner MacStay and asked him to have his men sweep clean their window sills, which had drifted deep from the paper flung from above. To them the Commissioner could give no direct relief, for he had no window sill cleaners; but he issued notice that if tenants would only sweep the window ledges clean into the streets his men would gather up all that fell there.

Confetti, the ordinarily ballistic staple of times of carnival, was rather infrequent, but was supplied by those impromptu showers of paper from the skies. Just so the horns and whistles and rattles, familiar from New Year's Eve and election night, were few in the afternoon, though more numerous in the evening; but their place was supplied by new methods of noisemaking. To the hooting of automobile horns was added a new noise, produced by the deliberate backfiring of automobile engines. Car after car wormed its way through the crowds, clattering like a machine gun, and, with the popping of blank cartridges fired from revolvers and an occasional salute fired from the cannon of a boat in the river, created a sort of simulated battle scene to remind the revelers of the fighting in France which they thought at last was over.

Cheering in the Crowds.

Early in the day, before the crowds had really begun to gather, the general emotion was expressed only by a joyous smile on the face of every one in the street. Strangers met each other and smiled, and sometimes stopped to shake hands. But soon this was not enough. Cheers began to rise from the crowds; groups here and there sang popular war songs; before long impromptu parades had started everywhere. The workmen from the Standard Shipbuilding Plant in Shooters' Island got off for the day, and just as they stood in their working clothes, they were ferried across the bay in an excursion steamboat and paraded up Broadway and Fifth Avenue to Central Park. Other parades were hastily gathered by labor unions, by schoolboys, by soldiers, sailors, or anybody who felt like starting a parade.

The students of the High School of Commerce, 2,000 strong, marched into Times Square, where they gathered a red-headed sailor with a green draped broom as a baton to act as grand marshal. He associated himself with an extemporized band, consisting of a tin flute, a dishpan, and two tin dishcovers, and with this at its head, the parade moved over eastward via Forty-second Street to Fifth Avenue.

High up in the Knickerbocker Hotel enormous flags of Italy and the United States were flung out of a window, and presently a plump man came out on the balcony above them and waved his arms in joyous elation. A woman in a fur coat came out beside him, and the two lifted up the big flags and swung them back and forth. Presently word spread through the crowd that they were Mr. and Mrs. Enrico Caruso, and the tenor never had a more enthusiastic audience than that which cheered back at him for more than an hour as he danced and cheered on the balcony. Finally the band from the Rialto Theatre came over and played "The Star-Spangled Banner," and Caruso sang it. Then he sang other selections; four or five thousand dollars' worth of melody was flung on the breeze, and most of it was drowned before it reached the pavement by the continuing clamor of horns, drums,

SAYS GERMANS FEAR WILSON'S "JUSTICE"

Neutral Diplomat Just from Germany Asserts Peace or Revolt Must Come.

Copyright, 1918, by The New York Times Company.
Special Cable to THE NEW YORK TIMES.

BERNE, Nov. 7.—A neutral diplomat who has just arrived in Berne from Germany says that both Government circles and the people generally are facing two alternatives, complete acceptance of Wilson's conditions or revolution.

The depression throughout Germany is appalling. People everywhere are exclaiming "We are lost!"

When the neutral diplomat attempted to console certain highly placed Germans by saying that they might depend on Wilson seeing that Germany got justice, one of them replied: "That is exactly what we fear."

They asked the diplomat: "What about Taft's and Roosevelt's manifesto concerning Germany's unconditional surrender?" and he replied: "The Bolsheviki, who are becoming fairly powerful in Germany, hope that the Taft-Roosevelt policy will prevail, as they consider that this would help Bolshevism."

The diplomat believes that the Junkers also prefer the Taft-Roosevelt policy as more likely to be tactless than the Wilson policy. The best Swiss opinion, particularly French-Swiss opinion, favors the Wilson plan because, it is argued, he aims at creating a genuinely liberal party in Germany and preventing the militarists from predominating. By the exercise of tact, judgment, and discretion, the diplomat says, Germany may now be brought uncompromisingly to accept the Wilson conditions.

whistles, and backfiring automobiles. Finally Caruso came out with his arms full of American Beauty roses and poured them down on the crowd looking up from Forty-second Street as a gesture of farewell.

Meanwhile his companions of the Metropolitan Opera House, where a private rehearsal of Verdi's "Forza del Destino" was in progress, were celebrating in their own way. Giulio Gatti Casazza, general manager, brought the news of peace in from Broadway, and there was a general celebration. Just then Geraldine Farrar came in, waving red, white and blue streamers, and she went to the stage and sang "The Star-Spangled Banner," supported by the orchestra, the chorus, the other artists, the stage hands, the house staff, the box office force, and everyone else in sight.

Singing in the Streets.

There was plenty of singing outside. The parades that were sweeping up and down Fifth Avenue and Broadway were all singing. Anybody who wanted to sing on a corner could soon get a crowd to support him. Julie Keley, the French soprano, stood in a window in the Fitzgerald Building, at the corner of Forty-second Street and Broadway and sang "The Star-Spangled Banner" and the "Marseillaise," and everybody who knew the air of the national anthem of France tried to sing it on the streets, whether the words came easily or not.

Bars were crowded everywhere. Men stood four and five deep in front of them, drinking to the restoration of peace and giving vent to their enthusiasm for the victories of the allied armies. For all the drinking, of which there was an enormous amount, there was very little drunkenness visible in the afternoon. The spirit of the day was intoxication enough for anybody.

All the Interborough Rapid Transit Company's employes who were taking the day off had been called back to handle the enormous traffic, and though the congestion was great at the stations, everything moved with satisfactory precision and speed. The telephone company was another sufferer from the prevalent excitement; thousands of calls came in simultaneously from people seeking confirmation of the news, and a staff still reduced by the influenza epidemic had eventually to refuse many of the calls which came in from pay stations.

For all the crowds in Times Square and along Broadway, as well as in City Hall Park, Madison Square, and other gathering places, Fifth Avenue saw the biggest assemblage, because it had been cleared of automobiles. Around the Public Library, naturally, most of the celebration centred; but all the way up and down the avenue the crowds were moving in almost unbroken masses. The balustrades and terraces in front of the Library were massed with people; a Canadian officer stood on the railing and harangued the crowd in words which nobody could hear, but which everybody applauded. And up and down the avenue, under the clouded skies of the late afternoon, poured throngs of flag-waving enthusiasts, shouting and singing.

More soldiers were kissed yesterday in New York than on any other day in its history. Girls sought them out everywhere, and even when a policeman was looking did not hesitate to give expression to their feelings. Members of the armies and navies of our allies were showered with all the expressions of regard that the crowd could think of; and not being debarred, as are American soldiers and sailors, from taking liquor they were literally dragged into barrooms in many cases by crowds of civilians who wanted to express their feelings in the approved manner.

Throngs flocked to the hotels and restaurants for celebratory dinners, and an exceptionally large number of special parties had to be provided for at most places. Even in the hotels hampered by the waiters' strikes unusually large numbers were served; tables were set in the corridors and other usually unoccupied space, and the falsity of the report did not interfere with the merriment of the diners who gathered.

If William Hohenzollern had been in the city yesterday he would have learned something to his advantage. There was no doubt of what New York thought of him. From a third-story window on Forty-second Street an improvised gallows had been thrust out and a dummy hung from the end of a rope. He was crowned with an overturned bucket and labeled "Bad Bill—Gone to Hell."

Stores Shut Up to Celebrate.

Many stores had on their locked doors the mere sign "Closed for Celebration," but many others were marked "Closed for the Kaiser's Funeral," or "Closed on Account of the Death of William Hohnzollern." None of the many parades was complete without the Kaiser's coffin, sometimes draped in black, sometimes surmounted by a burning candle, but always labelled so that there could be no mistake as to what it was. A truckload of enthusiasts that careered through the streets heralded by shrieking horns was draped in black and bore the sign "We Mourn Our Loss—the Kaiser." Another sign read, "Now Is the Time to Hock the Kaiser and Lose the Ticket." One of the banners borne on the Standard Shipbuilders' procession was decorated with a hasty charcoal drawing of a coffin with a German helmet on it, and beside it something that was carefully marked, "One of the Tulips That Karl Rosner Wrote About."

There was only one single sentiment in every mind in New York—except, perhaps, any surviving pro-Germans who may still inhabit the city, and who were prudently silent yesterday. A shopgirl waving a flag purchased from a curbstone pedler said: "The dime that this cost me is the first money I ever spent without missing it." Elderly and dignified citizens were not ashamed to walk through the crowds with tears running down their cheeks. Women paraded with service flags conspicuously draped across their shoulders, and there was a general willingness to make respectful way and hold momentary silence at the passing of one with a black band and gold star.

In front of the Library a motor car containing an Ensign and a naval aviator slowly moved up the avenue through the crowd. A French officer escorting a woman happened to be beside the running board when the car was halted for a moment by a throng in front of it. The officer asked the French couple to ride with them, but when they had taken their seats the crowd insisted on holding back the car long enough to give three cheers for France, and to afford an opportunity for everybody within arm's length to shake hands with any of the officers who could be reached.

It was the same in all the outlying portions of the city. In the Italian colonies of East Harlem and the lower west side, in the Greek colonies along Sixth Avenue, in the Jewish districts of the east side, national flags were carried through the streets beside the Stars and Stripes at the head of long processions, and bonfires, illuminations and the singing of national songs marked the celebration. In front of the offices of a Jewish newspaper 500 persons danced in the street to the music of a band on the fire-escape; men and women embraced each other and cried "Sholem—peace."

In Brooklyn the workers of the Morse Drydock and Repair Company and of shipbuilding companies marched in long parades through the streets to Borough Hall. In Harlem, 125th Street was closed to motor traffic to make way for the biggest crowd Harlem had ever seen. On Riverside Drive huge throngs gathered and were dazzled, in the growing dusk, by the playing of searchlights from the warships in the North River.

From time to time airplanes flew over the city and brought out more cheers from the willing crowds. Churches and synagogues were thronged with worshipers, giving thanks for the victorious ending of the war, and these worshipers thought it not unworthy to come out from the sacred edifices and join in the cheering of the crowds outside.

It was apparent that great as was the afternoon's outpouring of enthusiasts, the night would see an even greater. More parades were in preparation. Mayor Hylan ordered a parade of all city employes to start from the City Hall at 6 o'clock and move up Broadway and Fifth Avenue; the Police Band collected in City Hall Park, and thousands of persons who meant to march in the parade gathered at Fourth and Lafayette Streets ready to join in.

Those who were able to get into communication with newspaper offices learned in the latter part of the afternoon that the report of the ending of the war was as yet unconfirmed, but they were comparatively few. Eventually the later editions of the evening papers carried the news to the crowds, but the newsboys at first were reluctant to sell them. Headlines telling of Germany's surrender had been pasted in shop windows, fixed in the hatbands of marchers, or draped across the fronts of overcoats; nobody wanted to be the bearer of bad news. Even after the papers declaring the peace story a fake were on the streets many newsboys were still crying "Germany surrenders!"

But gradually the news spread among the afternoon crowds; papers were picked off the stands and displayed, and by word of mouth more and more people learned that it was not certain, perhaps not true, that the war was at an end. At first it was hardly credited; the day had been prolific or rumors, and the wildest stories had found someone to repeat them; but they had all been good news. It was said, for example, and in all seriousness, that the reason President Wilson and Secretary Tumulty had cast no votes on election day was because they were at that moment landing in France, their movements having been carefully concealed; and that the President himself had received the surrender of the German armies in the front trenches. For tales of this sort there were ready listeners, but nobody wanted either to tell or to believe that the great news was all a lie.

Yet eventually it spread; the crowds, already thinned by those who had had their fill of jubilation and were going home to dinner, were thinned still more when those willing to accept the bad news had gone home too. There were plenty left to join the newcomers in the night's revelling, but many of the most enthusiastic of the afternoon had gone home. And even the news that the war was still going on created no trouble. With the ordinary good-humored and long-suffering tolerance of an American public, most people merely said: "Aw, another fake. What do you know?"

A good many, by that time, were in the frame of mind where their natural response was "Who cares if it is?" and much long-withheld emotion was blown off in the conviction that even if the war was not over now, it would be soon. But there were others, older people for the most part, who when they found that peace had not yet come, went home in silence, their faces dark, as they thought of the men in khaki who for some time still must face the enemy's machine guns in France.

UNTRUE REPORT STARTS WALL STREET REJOICING

Trading on the Stock Exchange stopped yesterday the moment the ticker announced the false report that an armistice had been signed, but activity on the market began again as soon as the import of the news was realized by the traders. The report was heralded with shouts and cheers that reached the street.

The Governors of the Exchange met and announced that trading would cease at 2:30, half an hour earlier than usual. The total transactions for the day amounted to 1,117,000 shares, of which 829,000 were dealt in after 12 o'clock. The news intensified to an even greater extent the differentiation between the so-called war and peace stocks, which has been going on for several days.

After the close of the stock market the members of the Exchange joined in a jollification. The big war map was draped with the American flag upon which a victory wreath was superimposed, this having been delivered as a result of a hurry order to a downtown florist. Meanwhile the members cast dignity to the winds and cavorted like youngsters, and some took it upon themselves to deliver patriotic speeches with the trading posts as rostrums.

Somewhere and somehow the Consolidated Exchange discovered a band, and this was pressed into service after the close of business and it livened the occasion to a marked degree. When the welcome news of surrender was first received the enthusiasm of the members knew no bounds. The chairman's gong rang with the tidings and American flags appeared in every quarter as if the news had been anticipated.

It was under the folds of Old Glory that the final trading was done. The close saw enthusiasm intensified. Army and navy men joined in the celebration, and there was dancing on the floor and in the gallery, the "welcome sign" being hung out at all the portals inviting the general public to partake in the celebration. At the close the gathering sang "The Star-Spangled Banner."

Scenes of like enthusiasm were enacted at the other Exchanges, the Produce Exchange members venting their approval of the news by hurling the sample bags of oats and trays of other grains about the room.

One of the largest downtown gatherings was at the Sub-Treasury, where under the shadow of the statue of Washington there was a remarkable demonstration of patriotism. Some say it was the Rev. William Wilkinson, the "Bishop of Wall Street," who first called the crowd to the steps of the Sub-Treasury. Throughout the afternoon the constantly changing throng of more than 5,000 persons sang patriotic songs. Sailors and soldiers participated in the celebration.

Until long after dusk the celebration continued. The throngs from the office buildings marched through Broad, Wall, and Nassau Streets and along Broadway, bearing aloft flags that appeared as if by magic and shouting.

From high up in the office buildings, those who were not fortunate enough to get into the processions below showered upon the passing throngs scraps of torn up newspapers, telephone directories, ticker tape, and anything in the way of paper which came handy until it seemed as if great flakes of snow were filling the atmosphere. They swirled and eddied with the currents of wind, swinging up around the spire of Trinity and around the towers of the Singer and Woolworth buildings, finally falling to the street to leave a white covering inches deep.

Probably never before was business on a workday at such a standstill in the financial community. Entire office forces were dismissed in some instances and for the time being nothing mattered except the announcement from one to another of the report that Germany had quit.

Traffic along Broadway almost halted as the afternoon progressed. The surface cars were so hemmed in that it was all but impossible to operate them and the automobiles had little better success.

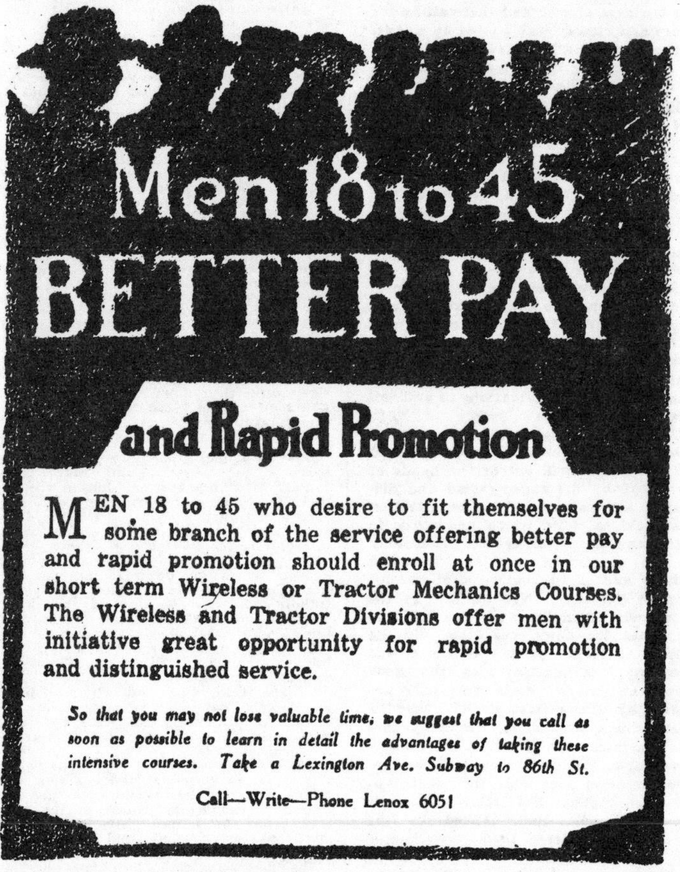

Section
1

"All the News That's Fit to Print."

The New York Times.

THE WEATHER
Fair, slightly colder Sunday; Monday fair; fresh west winds.
☞ For full weather report see Page 22.

Section
1

VOL. LXVIII...NO. 22,906.   NEW YORK, SUNDAY, NOVEMBER 10, 1918.—94 PAGES, In Seven Parts.   FIVE CENTS

KAISER AND CROWN PRINCE ABDICATE; NATION TO CHOOSE NEW GOVERNMENT; MAX IS REGENT; ARMISTICE DELAYED; REVOLT SPREADS ON LAND AND SEA

SOCIALIST AS CHANCELLOR

Prince Max Announces He Will Name Ebert Head of Cabinet.

PLAN NATIONAL ASSEMBLY

This Will Make Provision for the Future Form of German Government.

Copyright, 1918, by The New York Times Company.
Special Cable to THE NEW YORK TIMES.

LONDON, Nov. 9, 4:40 P. M. —Emperor William of Germany has abdicated.

PARIS, Nov. 9.—The abdication of Emperor William is officially announced from Berlin, according to a Havas dispatch from Basle.

LONDON, Nov. 9.—A Havas Agency dispatch from Amsterdam says that Prince Max of Baden has been appointed Regent of the Empire, according to the Berlin newspapers.

A Reuter dispatch, however, says he is yet to be named.

According to a German wireless message received here which announces the Kaiser's abdication, Friedrich Ebert, Vice President of the Social Democratic Party, is to be Imperial Chancellor under the regency, and wide reforms are planned, including the calling of a Constitutional German National Assembly to determine the future good of the nation.

The resignations of the German Ministers of the Interior,

Instruction, Agriculture, and Finance are reported in a telegram from Berlin.

The Prussian Food Controller again requested to be relieved from office, and the resignation of the Prussian Minister of Public Works has been in the hands of the Cabinet some time.

Emperor William had not at a late hour [before his abdication] accepted the resignation of Prince Max of Baden, the Chancellor, according to a Berlin message to Copenhagen. The Emperor, who was kept thoroughly informed by the Chancellor regarding the general situation, the message adds, asked Prince Max to continue holding the office provisionally until the Emperor's final decision was reached.

The Socialists decided not to carry out at the time set their threat to withdraw from the Government if Emperor William had not abdicated by that hour, according to a Berlin dispatch. Instead they extended the time limit, it is stated, "in consideration of an eventual armistice."

Kaiser's Son-in-Law Abdicates.

LONDON, Nov. 9. (British Wireless Service.)—A telegram received at Copenhagen, from Brunswick by way of Berlin, asserts that Emperor William's son-in-law, the Duke of Brunswick, and his successor have abdicated.

The reigning Duke of Brunswick, Ernest Augustus, married the German Kaiser's only daughter, Princess Victoria Louisa, on May 24, 1913. He was then 26 years of age and she was five years younger. The Duke's heir is Prince Ernest Augustus, born on March 12, 1914. Two other sons came during the war—George William, born March 25, 1915, and Frederick, April 18, 1917.

The father of the Duke is the Duke of Cumberland, son of the late King George V. of Hanover and cousin of the late Queen Victoria. The kingdom of Hanover was absorbed by Prussia in 1866.

Text of Decree Announcing Kaiser's Abdication and the Plans for Other Changes in Germany

LONDON, Nov. 9.—A German wireless message received in London this afternoon states:

"The German Imperial Chancellor, Prince Max of Baden, has issued the following decree:

The Kaiser and King has decided to renounce the throne.

The Imperial Chancellor will remain in office until the questions connected with the abdication of the Kaiser, the renouncing by the Crown Prince of the throne of the German Empire and of Prussia, and the setting up of a regency have been settled.

For the regency he intends to appoint Deputy Ebert as Imperial Chancellor, and he proposes that a bill shall be brought in for the establishment of a law providing for the immediate promulgation of general suffrage and for a constitutional German National Assembly, which will settle finally the future form of government of the German nation and of those peoples which might be desirous of coming within the empire.   THE IMPERIAL CHANCELLOR.

Berlin, Nov. 9, 1918.

Chancellor Sees All Hope Gone; Says Germany Is Forced to Yield.

LONDON, Nov. 9, (British Wireless Service.)—Just before Prince Maximilian of Baden offered his resignation as Imperial Chancellor he issued an appeal "To Germans abroad" in which he said:

"In the fifth year, (of hostilities,) abandoned by its allies, the German people could no longer wage war against the increasingly superior forces."

The text of the Chancellor's statement follows:

"In these difficult days the hearts of many among you, my fellow-countrymen, who outside the frontier of the German Fatherland are surrounded by manifestations of malicious joy and hatred, will be heavy. Do not despair of the German people.

"Our soldiers have fought to the last moment as heroically as any army has ever done. The homeland has shown unprecedented strength in suffering and endurance.

"In the fifth year, abandoned by its allies, the German people could no longer wage war against the increasingly superior forces.

"The victory for which many had hoped has not been granted to us. But the German people has won this still greater victory over itself and its belief in the right of might.

"From this victory we shall draw new strength for the hard time which faces us and on which you also can build."

AMSTERDAM, Nov. 7.—Absolute unity is necessary among the German people if they wish to avert unforeseen consequences, says Chancellor Maximilian in an appeal to the German people, which, according to an official dispatch from Berlin, reads as follows:

"For more than four years the German nation, united and calm, has endured the most severe sufferings and sacrifices. If at this decisive hour, when only absolute unity can avert from the entire German people great dangers for its future, internal strength gives way, then the consequences are unforeseeable."

"All the News That's Fit to Print."

The New York Times.

THE WEATHER
Fair today and Tuesday; diminishing northwest winds.
For weather report see last page

VOL. LXVIII...NO. 22,206. .... NEW YORK, MONDAY, NOVEMBER 11, 1918. TWENTY-FOUR PAGES. TWO CENTS

ARMISTICE SIGNED, END OF THE WAR! BERLIN SEIZED BY REVOLUTIONISTS; NEW CHANCELLOR BEGS FOR ORDER; OUSTED KAISER FLEES TO HOLLAND

WAR ENDS AT 6 O'CLOCK THIS MORNING

The State Department in Washington Made the Announcement at 2:45 o'Clock.

ARMISTICE WAS SIGNED IN FRANCE AT MIDNIGHT

Terms Include Withdrawal from Alsace-Lorraine, Disarming and Demobilization of Army and Navy, and Occupation of Strategic Naval and Military Points.

By The Associated Press.

WASHINGTON, Monday, Nov. 11, 2:48 A. M.—The armistice between Germany, on the one hand, and the allied Governments and the United States, on the other, has been signed.

The State Department announced at 2:45 o'clock this morning that Germany had signed.

The department's announcement simply said: "The armistice has been signed."

The world war will end this morning at 6 o'clock, Washington time, 11 o'clock Paris time.

The armistice was signed by the German representatives at midnight.

This announcement was made by the State Department at 2:50 o'clock this morning.

The announcement was made verbally by an officila of the State Department in this form:

"The armistice has been signed. It was signed at 5 o'clock A. M., Paris time, [midnight, New York time,] and hostilities will cease at 11 o'clock this morning, Paris time, [6 o'clock, New York time.]

The terms of the armistice, it was announced, will not be made public until later. Military men here, however, regard it as certain that they include:

Immediate retirement of the German military forces from France, Belgium, and Alsace-Lorraine.

Disarming and demobilization of the German armies.

Occupation by the allied and American forces of such strategic points in Germany as will make impossible a renewal of hostilities.

Delivery of part of the German High Seas Fleet and a certain number of submarines to the allied and American naval forces.

Disarmament of all other German warships under supervision of the allied and American Navies, which will guard them.

Occupation of the principal German naval bases by sea forces of the victorious nations.

Release of allied and American soldiers, sailors, and civilians held prisoners in Germany without such reciprocal action by the associated Governments.

There was no information as to the circumstances under which the armistice was signed, but since the German courier did not reach German military headquarters until 10 o'clock yesterday morning, French time, it was generally assumed here that the German envoys within the French lines had been instructed by wireless to sign the terms.

Forty-seven hours had been required for the courier to reach the German headquarters, and unquestionably several hours were necessary for the examination of the terms and a decision.

It was regarded as possible, however, that the decision may have been made at Berlin and instructions transmitted from there by the new German Government.

Germany had until 11 o'clock this morning, French time, (6 o'clock, Washington time,) to accept. So hostilities will end at the hour set by Marshal Foch for a decision by Germany for peace or for continuation of the war.

The momentous news that the armistice had been signed was telephoned to the White House for transmission to the President a few minutes before it was given to the newspaper correspondents.

Later it was said that there would be no statement from the White House at this time.

SON FLEES WITH EX-KAISER

Hindenburg Also Believed to be Among Those in His Party.

ALL ARE HEAVILY ARMED

Automobiles Bristle with Rifles as Fugitives 'Arrive at Dutch Frontier.

LONDON, Nov. 10.—Both the former German Emperor and his eldest son, Frederick William, crossed the Dutch frontier Sunday morning, according to advices from The Hague. His reported destination is De Steeg, near Utrecht.

The former German Emperor's party, which is believed to include Field Marshal von Hindenburg, arrived at Eysden, [midway between Liége and Maastricht,] on the Dutch frontier, at 7:30 o'clock Sunday morning, according to Daily Mail advices.

Practically the whole German General Staff accompanied the former Emperor, and ten automobiles carried the party. The automobiles were bristling with rifles, and all the fugitives were armed.

The ex-Kaiser was in uniform. He alighted at the Eysden station and paced the platform, smoking a cigarette.

Many photographs were taken by [of?] the members of the Imperial party. On the whole the people were very quiet, but Belgians among them yelled out "En voyage a Paris." (Are you on your way to Paris?)

Chatting with the members of the staff, the former Emperor, the correspondent says, did not look in the least distressed. A few minutes later an imperial train, including restaurant and sleeping cars, ran into the station. Only servants were aboard.

The engine returned to Visé, Belgium, and brought back a second train, in which were a large number of staff officers and others, and also stores of food.

The preparations began for the departure at 10 o'clock this morning, but at 10:40 o'clock the train was still at Eysden. The blinds of the train were all drawn.

The Daily Mail remarks that, if the party arrived in Holland armed, all of them must be interned.

BERLIN TROOPS JOIN REVOLT

Reds Shell Building in Which Officers Vainly Resist.

THRONGS DEMAND REPUBLIC

Revolutionary Flag on Royal Palace — Crown Prince's Palace Also Seized.

GENERAL STRIKE IS BEGUN

LONDON, Nov. 10. — The greater part of Berlin is in control of revolutionists, the former Kaiser has fled to Holland, and Friedrich Ebert, the new Socialist Chancellor, has taken command of the situation. The revolt is spreading throughout Germany with great rapidity.

Dispatches received in London today announce these startling developments. The Workmen's and Soldiers' Council is now administering the municipal government of the German capital.

The War Ministry has submitted, and its acts are valid only when countersigned by a Socialist representative. The official Wolff telegraphic agency has been taken over by the Reds.

The red flag has been hoisted over the royal palace and the Brandenburg Gate. The former Crown Prince's palace is also in possession of the revolutionists.

There was severe fighting in Berlin between 8 and 10 o'clock last night and a violent cannonade was heard from the heart of the city.

Burgomaster and Police Join.

A Copenhagen dispatch states that Dr. Liebknecht, the famous Socialist, who spent many months in prison for antagonizing the German Imperial Government and who was recently released, has issued the following announcement in Berlin in behalf of the Workmen's and Soldiers' Council:

"The Presidency of the police, as well as the Chief Command, is in our hands. Our comrades will be released."

A dispatch from Berne states that the Burgomaster of Berlin has placed himself and his staff at the disposal of the new Government.

Some German newspapers describe the movement as Bolshevism. The people are shouting "Long live the Republic!" and singing the "Marseillaise."

When revolutionary soldiers

With news of the signing of the Armistice, the people of Milan celebrated in the streets.

attempted to enter a building in Berlin in which they supposed that a number of officers were concealed shots were fired from the windows. The Reds then began shelling the building. Many persons were killed and wounded before the officers surrendered.

When the cannonade began the people thought the Reichsbank was being bombarded, and thousands rushed to the square in front of the Crown Prince's palace. It was later determined that other buildings were under fire. Among those killed in the fighting at the "Cockchafer" Barracks was one of the workmen's leaders known as "Comrade" Habersroth.

The Reds, at last reports, were maintaining order.

Berlin was occupied by forces of the Soldiers' and Workmen's Councils on Saturday afternoon, according to a Wolff Bureau report received in Copenhagen. News of Emperor William's abdication was received in the city on that afternoon with general rejoicing, which was tempered by the fear that it had come too late.

Russians Aid in Outbreak.

How far the example of the Russian Bolsheviki influenced the German upheaval is an interesting question. Red flags figured frequently in the various risings and Chancellor Ebert's motor car floats the international emblem.

The shoulder straps were torn from the uniforms of officers in a number of German cities and even the soldiers' insignia were stripped from them. Russian prisoners played a part in the demonstrations in two or three towns.

Delegates of the revolutionary German navy arrived in Berlin on Friday, according to a dispatch from Copenhagen. They conferred for several hours with the Minister of Marine and with members of the Reichstag majority parties.

It is stated that Hugo Haase, a Socialist leader in the Reichstag, has the situation at Hamburg in hand.

It is officially announced from Berlin, according to a Copenhagen dispatch, that the War Ministry has placed itself at the disposal of Chancellor Ebert. This action was for the purpose of assuring the provisioning of the army and assisting in the solution of demobilization problems.

Serious food difficulties are expected in Germany, owing to the stoppage of trains. The Council of the Regency will take the most drastic steps to re-establish order.

In the new German Government there will be only three representatives of the majority parties, namely, Erzberger, Gothein, and Richthofen, says a dispatch from Copenhagen. The other posts will be occupied by Socialists and independents.

Citizens of San Juan, Puerto Rico, carried American flags and danced in the streets to celebrate the signing of the armistice.

NEWS OF ARMISTICE FLASHED TO CITY

Signing of Truce Tidings Wafted Afar by Searchlight on Times Building.

CROWDS GATHER IN STREETS

When the first bulletin of the signing of the armistice, with the acceptance of the terms of the Allies, came into the office of THE NEW YORK TIMES shortly before 3 o'clock this morning orders were given immediately for the lighting up of both The Times Building and The Times Annex, and they remained lighted throughout the rest of the hours of darkness.

A few minutes after the first word had reached the newspaper office the searchlight on the tower of The Times Building played its rays all over the city. It had been put into operation to announce the results of the election on last Tuesday, and the flashing of more momentous news attracted crowds to Times Square.

In such a few minutes that it was almost beyond the belief of persons who have never seen a great city rejoicing over the greatest of former victories and over events of a magnitude to stun the mind, the Square was filled with many hundreds of persons. It was a mystery to all where they came from. Many came out of the subway, others came out of the restaurants, cigar stores, and other places that remain open all night.

This throng was increased by drivers who left their milk wagons, their newspaper wagons, by men on their way to work, by taxicab chauffeurs, by street car conductors, and by many other folk who had heard the tooting of sirens in their neighborhoods and who arose from their beds to find out just what was the latest event of a day that will be marked forever in history.

The display of large bulletins in the windows of The Times Building saying that the armistice had been signed, together with the news in the earlier ditions of the paper that the former German Kaiser had fled from just retribution, moved these many hundreds to full-throated and full-lunged jubilance.

The same bulletins were displayed in the windows of the offices of THE TIMES in other parts of the city, and soon they were the centre of crowds that had forgotten completely that the city had already had one day of celebration over what had been a false report of the event all longed for.

Celebration began all over again, and at that late hour it looked as if the city would outdo its "fake rumor" day, or London's Mafeking Day, and every other day where millions rejoiced.

Police sirens and bells all over the city again took up the Swan Song of the Kaiser, of militarism, and thousands were waked from their slumbers by the din. Hundreds got up from their beds and walked the streets in tousled clothes to get confirmation of the news they had been expecting. Other hundreds saw the flashing of the searchlights from the tower of THE TIMES and telephone calls by the hundreds began to pour into the newspaper office. The invariable question was: "Has the armistice been signed?" and when the question was answered with the affirmative, with the additional information that the Kaiser's right to rule had passed with him in unroyal flight, there were cheers at the other end of the wire.

Among the hundreds around the bulletin boards in Times Square were many sailors and soldiers who had service stripes on their sleeves, some of them having more than one stripe. Many had medals, and many more had scars, scars put upon them by the soldiers of the man whose downfall was reported.

At first these men were unable to comprehend the news. The crowds of civilians were not so slow. They seized the soldiers and sailors and made them prisoners to admiration. The crowd waltzed the soldiers and sailors on their shoulders and bounced them around, pounded them on the backs, cheered them, set them down and tried to force them to make speeches, and then drowned their first words with cheers.

Groans and cries went up from the crowd when the name of William Hohenzollern was mentioned. "Poor Bill! He tried to pinch off the world! He's gone! Bill's dead," one man cried. The man who was taken seriously only a few weeks ago had suddenly become a joke because the allied armies had beaten him so decisively and because he had run away, with his Crown Prince, his General Staff, and a train full of food.

PARIS CONVINCED WAR IS FINISHED

Germans Must and Will Surrender, Is Prevalent Feeling in

Copyright, 1918, by The New York Times Company. Special Cable to THE NEW YORK TIMES.

PARIS, Nov. 10.—Are the Germans manoeuvring for a further military struggle or are they prepared to surrender, no matter what the terms?

That is a question the French people are asking themselves. But putting the question apparently is more for the sake of speculative interest than because of doubt. There is remarkable unanimity in the answer to the effect that Germany must and will surrender.

The thought that is in the air all over Paris is, "The war is finished." You can feel it. You can see it in the faces in the street. It is just as tangible a thing as was the gloom last Spring and Summer, before the beginning of the great victory of July 18.

It is many weeks since things have fallen out of the sky to kill Parisians and damage property. Today things are going up, instead. I mean toy balloons. This is worth mentioning, because, if anything is symbolic of festive cheer, it is the sight of old men and women in the crowds with bunches of red and blue balloons over their shoulders to sell to the children.

There are such crowds today in the Place de la Concorde and the Champs Elysées looking at the hundreds of captured German cannon and gleefully commenting on the coming of a white flag from the armies that were so recently using those same cannon with deadly effect against the allied troops.

There are thousands of these cannon of all kinds and all calibers clustered thickly in the centre of the Place de la Concorde, where the guillotine was set up a little over a century ago, and spreading out in long lines along the Seine, in the Tuileries Gardens and up the Champs Elysées.

There are no rope guards around the captured guns in the Paris streets. Children are allowed to swarm over them, play horse on them, fight imaginary battles, and monkey with the mechanism that raises and lowers the muzzles to their hearts' content.

1919

"All the News That's Fit to Print."

The New York Times.

THE WEATHER
Fair Thursday and probably Friday; moderate west shifting to north winds.
For full weather report see Page 21

VOL. LXVIII...NO. 22,384 ....   NEW YORK, THURSDAY, MAY 8, 1919. THIRTY-TWO PAGES.   TWO CENTS

ON LUSITANIA DAY ALLIES DICTATE A PEACE THAT DESTROYS GERMANY'S MILITARY POWER, EXACTS REPARATION, STRIPS HER OF CONQUESTS

CLEMENCEAU'S STERN WORDS

Tells Germans They Must Now Settle for Cruel Aggressions.

BROCKDORFF ADMITS GUILT

But Brackets Allies' Prolongation of Blockade with Germany's Cruelties in War.

MUST REPLY IN TWO WEEKS

Germans Have That Time for Examination and Interpretation of the Treaty.

VERSAILLES, May 7.—The peace treaty framed by the peace conference was handed to the German plenipotentiaries this afternoon in the great hall of the Trianon Palace Hotel in the presence of delegates of the allied and associated powers which are parties to the compact.

In opening the session of the Peace Congress, Premier Clemenceau, the presiding officer, said:

"Gentlemen, plenipotentiaries of the German Empire: It is neither the time nor the place for superfluous words. You have before you the accredited plenipotentiaries of all the small and great powers united to fight together in the war that has been so cruelly imposed upon them. The time has come when we must settle our account.

"You have asked for peace. We are ready to give you peace. We shall present to you now a book which contains our conditions. You will have every facility to examine these conditions, and the time necessary for it. Everything will be done with the courtesy that is the privilege of civilized nations.

"To give you my thought completely, you will find us ready to give you any explanation you want, but we must say at the same time that this second Treaty of Versailles has cost us too much not to take on our side all the necessary precautions and guarantees that the peace shall be a lasting one.

"I will give you notice of the procedure that has been adopted by the conference for discussion, and if any one has any observations to offer he will have the right to do so. No oral discussion is to take place, and the observations of the German delegation will have to be submitted in writing.

Two Weeks for Examination.

"The German plenipotentiaries will know that they have the maximum period of fifteen days [French idiom for "two weeks"] within which to present in English and French their written observations on the whole of the treaty. Before the expiration of the aforesaid period of fifteen days the German delegates will be entitled to send their reply on particular headings of the treaty, or to ask questions in regard to them.

"After having examined the observations presented within the aforementioned period, the Supreme Council will send their answer in writing to the German delegation and determine the period within which the final worldwide answer must be given by this delegation.

"The President wishes to add that when we receive, after two or three or four or five days, any observations from the German delegation on any point of the treaty we shall not wait until the end of the fifteen days to give our answer. We shall at once proceed in the way indicated by this document."

Paul Dutasta, Secretary General of the Peace Conference, delivered a copy of the treaty to Count von Brockdorff-Rantzau, head of the German delegation.

Count von Brockdorff-Rantzau, speaking in German said:

"Gentlemen: We are deeply impressed with the sublime task which has brought us hither to give a durable peace to the world. We are under no illusion as to the extent of our defeat and the degree of our want of power. We know that the power of the German Army is broken. We know the power of the hatred which we encounter here, and we have heard the passionate demand that the conquerors make us pay as the vanquished, and punish those who are worthy of being punished.

"It is demanded from us that we shall confess ourselves to be the only ones guilty of the war. Such a confession in my mouth would be a lie. We are far from declining any responsibility that this great war of the world has come to pass, and that it was made in the way in which it was made. The attitude of the former German Government at the Hague Peace Conference, its actions and omissions in the tragic twelve days of July, have certainly contributed to the disaster. But we energetically deny that Germany and its people, who were convinced that they were making a war of defense, were alone guilty.

"Nobody will wish to contest that the disaster took its course only in the disastrous moment when the heir-apparent to the throne of Austria-Hungary fell the victim of murderous hands. In the last fifty years the imperialism of all the European States has chronically poisoned the international situation. The policy of retaliation and the policy of expansion and the disregard of the rights of peoples to determine their own destiny have contributed to the illness of Europe, which saw its crisis in the world war.

"Russian mobilization took from the statesmen the possibility of healing, and gave the decision into the hands of the military powers. Public opinion in all the countries of our adversaries is resounding with the crimes which Germany is said to have committed in the war. Here, also, we are ready to confess wrong that may have been done.

"We have not come here to belittle the responsibility of the men who have waged the war politically and economically, or to deny any crimes which may have been committed against the rights of peoples. We repeat the declaration which was made in the German Reichstag at the beginning of the war, that is to say: 'Wrong has been done to Belgium,' and we are willing to repair it.

"But in the manner of making war also Germany is not the only guilty one. Every nation knows of deeds and of people which the best of that nation remember only with regret. I do not want to answer by reproaches to reproaches, but I ask them, when reparation is demanded, not to forget the armistice. It took you six weeks until we got it at last, and six more until we came to know your conditions of peace.

"Crimes in war may not be excusable, but they are committed in the struggle for victory and in the defense of national existence, and passions are aroused which make the conscience of peoples blunt.

Assails the Post-War Blockade.

"The hundreds of thousands of noncombatants who have perished since Nov. 11 by reason of the blockade were killed with cold deliberation after our adversaries had conquered and victory had been assured to them. Think of that when you speak of guilt and of punishment!

"The measure of the guilt of all those who have taken part can only be stated by an impartial inquest before a neutral commission, before which all the principal persons of the tragedy are allowed to speak, and to which all the archives are open. We have demanded such an inquest, and we repeat this demand.

"In this conference also, where we stand before our adversaries alone and without any allies, we are not quite without protection. You yourselves have brought us an ally, namely, the right which is guaranteed by the treaty and by the principles of peace.

"The allied and associated Governments renounced in the time between the 5th of October and the 5th of November, 1918, a peace of violence and have written a peace of justice on their banner. On the 5th of October, 1918, the German Government proposed the principles of the President of the United States of North America as the basis of peace, and on the 5th of November their Secretary of State, Mr. Lansing, declared that the allied and associated powers agreed to this basis, with two definite deviations.

"The principles of President Wilson have thus become binding to both parties to the war—for you as well as for us and also for our former allies. The various principles demand from us severe national and economic sacrifices, but the holy fundamental rights of all peoples are protected by this treaty. The conscience of the world is behind it. There is no nation which might violate it without punishment.

"You will find us ready to examine upon this basis the preliminary peace which you have proposed to us, with a firm intention of rebuilding in co-operation with you that which has been destroyed, and repairing any wrong that may have been committed, principally the wrong to Belgium, and to show to mankind new aims of political and social progress.

"Considering the tremendous quantity of problems which arise, we ought as soon as possible to make an examination of the principal tasks by special commissions of experts, on the basis of the treaty which you have proposed to us. In this it will be our chief task to re-establish the devastated vigor of mankind and of all the people who have taken part by international protection of the life, health, and liberty of the working classes.

"As our next aim, I consider the reconstruction of the territories of Belgium and of Northern France, which have been occupied by us and which have been destroyed by war.

"To do so we have taken upon ourselves the solemn obligation, and we are resolved to execute it to the extent which shall have been agreed upon between us. This task we cannot do without the co-operation of our former adversaries. We cannot accomplish the work without the technical and financial participation of the victorious peoples and you cannot execute it without us.

"Impoverished Europe must desire that the reconstruction shall be fulfilled with the greatest success and with as little expense as is in any way possible. This desire can only be employed. It would be the worst method to go on and have the work done by German prisoners of war. Certainly this work is cheap, but it would cost the world dear if hatred and despair should seize the German people when they considered that their brothers, sons, and fathers who were prisoners were kept so beyond the preliminary peace in their former penal work.

"Without any immediate solution of this question, which has been drawn out too long, we cannot come to a durable peace. Experts of both sides will have to examine how the German people may meet their financial obligations to repair, without succumbing under their heavy burden. A crash would deprive those who have a right to reparation of the advantages to which they have a claim, and would entail irretrievable disorder of the whole European economical system.

"The conquerors, as well as the vanquished peoples, must guard against this menacing danger with its incalculable consequences. There is only one means of banishing it—unlimited acknowledgement of the economic and social solidarity of all the peoples in a free and rising League of Nations.

"Gentlemen, the sublime thought to be derived from the most terrible disaster in the history of mankind is the League of Nations. The greatest progress in the development of mankind has been pronounced, and will make its way. Only if the gates of the League of Nations are thrown open to all who are of good will can the aim be attained, and only then the dead of this war will not have died in vain.

"The German people in their hearts are ready to take upon themselves their heavy burden, if the bases of peace which have been established are not any more shaken.

"The peace which may not be defended in the name of right before the world always calls forth new resistance against it. Nobody will be capable of subscribing to it with good conscience, for it will not be possible of fulfillment. Nobody could be able to take upon himself the guarantee of its execution which ought to lie in its signature.

"We shall examine the document handed to us with good will and in the hope that the final result of our interview may be subscribed to by all of us."

The session closed at 3:51 P. M. Mrs. Wilson was an interested spectator of the ceremonies.

Elaborate preparations were made for the historic occasion both in and outside the building.

Outside there was a small army of gendarmes who formed a barrier against the approach of such persons as were not entitled to enter the room where the momentous scene was to be enacted. Inside everything was in readiness for the meeting between the allied and associated delegates with the German plenipotentiaries, although the early morning hours had witnessed a rearrangement of the great hall, for orders had been received to prepare seats for eighty delegates, instead of the fifty-eight who were expected yesterday. The French functionaries busied themselves with the task of stretching out tables to accommodate the extra guests and laying a new rug to fit the altered dimensions. The increase of the delegations was effected at the cost of space which had been assigned to the press.

MAIN TERMS OF TREATY

Germany to Make First Payment of Five Billions for Damages.

BONDS SECURE LATER SUMS

Army Reduced to 100,000 Men and Navy to 24 Ships, Without U-Boats.

BIG TERRITORIAL LOSSES

Alsace-Lorraine, Danzig, Part of Silesia, and All Colonies Are Taken Away.

PARIS, May 7.—The Treaty of Peace between the twenty-seven allied and associated powers, on the one hand, and Germany, on the other, was handed to the German plenipotentiaries at Versailles today, (the anniversary of the sinking of the Lusitania.)

[The full official summary and maps showing the territorial changes made by the treaty appear on Pages 4, 5, and 6 of today's TIMES.]

It is the longest treaty ever drawn. It totals about 80,000 words, is divided into fifteen main sections, and represents the combined product of over a thousand experts working continually through a series of commissions for three and a half months, since Jan. 18. The treaty is printed in parallel pages of English and French, which are recognized as having equal validity. It does not deal with questions affecting Austria, Bulgaria, and Turkey, except in so far as binding Germany to accept any agreement reached with those former allies.

Following the preamble and deposition of powers come the covenant of the League of Nations as the first section of the treaty. The frontiers of Germany in Europe are defined in the second section. European political clauses are given in the third, and extra-European political classes in the fourth. Next are the military, naval, and air terms as the fifth section, followed by a section on prisoners of war and military graves, and a seventh on responsibilities. Reparations, financial terms, and economic terms are covered in Sections VIII. to X. Then comes the aeronautic section, ports, waterways, and railways section, the labor covenant, the section on guarantees, and the financial clauses.

Must Give Up Big Area.

Germany by the terms of the treaty restores Alsace-Lorraine to France, accepts the internationalization of the Sarre Basin temporarily and of Danzig permanently, agrees to territorial changes toward Belgium and Denmark and in East Prussia, cedes most of Upper Silesia to Poland, and renounces all territorial and political rights outside of Europe, as to her own or her allies' territories, and especially to Morocco, Egypt, Siam, Liberia, and Shantung. She also recognizes the total independence of German Austria, Czechoslovakia, and Poland.

Her army is reduced to 100,000 men, including officers; conscription within her territories is abolished; all forts fifty kilometers east of the Rhine are razed, and all importation, exportation, and nearly all production of war material stopped. Allied occupation of parts of Germany will continue till reparation is made, but will be reduced at the end of each of three five-year periods if Germany is fulfilling her obligations. Any violation by Germany of the conditions as to the zone fifty kilometers east of the Rhine will be regarded as an act of war.

The German Navy is reduced to six battleships, six light cruisers, and twelve torpedo boats, without submarines, and a personnel of not over 15,000. All other vessels must be surrendered or destroyed. Germany is forbidden to build forts controlling the Baltic, must demolish Heligoland, open the Kiel Canal to all nations, and surrender her fourteen submarine cables. She may have no military or naval air forces except 100 unarmed seaplanes until Oct. 1 to detect mines, and may manufacture aviation material for six months.

To Pay for All Damages.

Germany accepts full responsibility for all damages caused to the allied and associated Governments and nationals, agree specifically to reimburse all civilian damages, beginning with an initial payment of 20,000,000,000 marks, (about $5,000,000,000 at pre-war reckoning,) subsequent payments to be secured by bonds to be issued at the discretion of the Reparation Commission. Germany is to pay shipping damage on a ton-for-ton basis by cession of a large part of her merchant, coasting, and river fleets, and by new construction; and to devote her economic resources to the rebuilding of the devastated regions.

She agrees to return to the 1914 most-favored nation tariffs, without discrimination of any sort; to allow allied and associated nationals freedom of transit through her territories, and to accept highly detailed provisions as to pre-war debts, unfair competition, internationalization of roads and rivers, and other economic and financial clauses. She also agrees to the trial of the ex-Kaiser by an international high court for a supreme offense against international morality, and of other nationals for violation of the laws and customs of war, Holland to be asked to extradite the former and Germany being responsible for delivering the latter.

Germany is required to deliver manuscripts and prints equivalent in value to those destroyed in the Louvain Library. She must also return works of church art removed from Belgium to Germany.

The League of Nations is accepted by the allied and associated powers as operative, and by Germany, in principle, but without membership. Similarly, an international labor body is brought into being with a permanent office and an annual convention. A great number of international bodies of different kinds and for different purposes are created, some under the League of Nations, some to execute the Peace Treaty; among the former is the Commission to Govern the Sarre Basin till a plebiscite is held, fifteen years hence; the High Commissioner of Danzig, which is created into a free city under the League, and various commissions for plebiscites in Malmedy, Schleswig, and East Prussia. Among those to carry out the Peace Treaty are the Reparations, Military, Naval, Air, Financial, and Economic Commissions; the International High Court and Military Tribunals to Fix Responsibilities, and a series of bodies for the control of international rivers.

Certain problems are left for solution between the allied and associated powers, notably the details of the disposition of the German fleet and cables, the former German colonies, and the values paid in reparation. Certain other problems, such as the laws of the air and the opium, arms, and liquor traffic, are either agreed to in detail or set for early international action.

FLAWS IN TREATY SEEN BY LONDON

Failure to Dismantle Kiel Forts Excites Some Adverse Comment.

DUBIOUS ABOUT POLAND

Press Comment Highly Diverse—Garvin Thinks Pact Needs Strengthening.

Copyright, 1919, by The New York Times Company. Special Cable to THE NEW YORK TIMES.

LONDON, May 7.—"If anything in this portentous document could raise a smile," said one commentator on the Peace Treaty today, "it would be the arraignment of the Kaiser and the procedure contemplated."

At the same time, it must be noted that some responsible authorities see so many defects in the treaty that it is a question whether in their opinion the bad does not outweigh the good. Perhaps, as a generalization of these views, it may be said some doubt whether the machinery of the League of Nations is good enough to keep the ship on a straight course toward the haven of peace which is Wilson's ideal.

The Chronicle, in a non-committal summary, thinks that the Conference's vacillation on Poland may prove the "Achilles's heel" of the whole treaty.

Curiosity is expressed regarding the distribution of the German shipping under the reparation clauses. There is nothing in the terms as issued to indicate whether a method of division among the Allies has been arranged or has yet to be arranged, or is to be left for the League of Nations.

Reports crediting the United States with obtaining possession of all the German ships left in American ports on the outbreak of the war have given rise to much criticism in British shipping circles, where this method of disposal is regarded as distinctly unfavorable to England, which lost 7,750,000 tons during the war.

Omission from the treaty of a specific demand for the dismantling of the Kiel Canal fortifications attracts some remark, in view of the fact that there is specific mention of Heligoland, but it is pointed out that the naval clauses and the clause affecting Kiel in the ports, waterways, and railways section adequately safeguard this requirement, and that it was therefore unnecessary to stress a point which might be regarded as a precedent governing the Panama Canal.

The terms regulating the cession of German territory to Poland find many critics, particularly in view of existing doubts with regard to the political evolution of the new Poland.

The Manchester Guardian takes the stand that the Peace Conference will be committing a crime if it simply revives the old Polish republic with rule over a large alien population. The present Polish Government is reactionary and intolerant, refusing to recognize the Jews as a national minority, and carrying out against them a program of persecution, exclusion, and discrimination.

The short paragraph in which this important question of Poland is set aside for future settlement by the Field Boundary Commission is regarded by some with disquiet.

Northcliffe's Own Terms Cited.

The reparations terms are expected to provide a bone of contention, which will be applied to the purposes of British domestic politics. One prophet declared that Lord Northcliffe, in view of his own outline of peace terms, would find himself forced to acquiesce in the reparations clauses, but all other opinions obtainable on this point were that, while The London Times might be severely judicial, the rest of the Northcliffe press would impress it on the multitude that the Government's election promises had gone by the board.

On the other hand, an appeal is made in The Evening News today for unity in front of the foe who, until he has signed the treaty, will remain a foe. The News adds: "The treaty is not perfect, but properly used it may become a tolerable instrument of a tolerable peace."

Wilson May Remain in Paris Until the Treaty Is Signed

PARIS, May 7, (Associated Press.)—There is no indication that President Wilson contemplates hastening his return because of the convocation of Congress on May 19, and he will undoubtedly remain here through the period of fifteen days allowed the Germans for consideration of the peace terms, probably until the treaty is signed.

In case the negotiations are prolonged by suggestions advanced by the Germans, it is possible that he may forego the satisfaction of signing the treaty and return home. It is expected that he will send a message to be read in his absence.

The Old World Re-mapped, as Far as the Treaty of Peace With Germany Does It

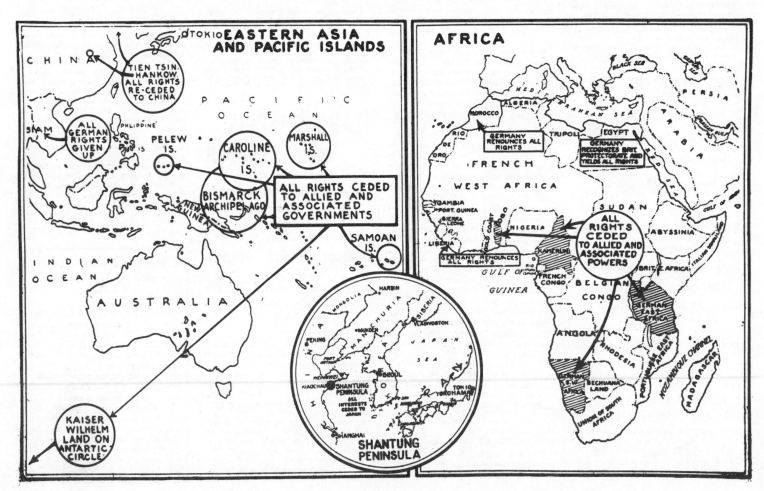

Section 1

"All the News That's Fit to Print."

The New York Times.

THE WEATHER
Fair and continued cool Sunday; fair Monday; moderate winds.
For full weather report see Page 28.

Section 1

VOL. LXVIII...NO. 22,494.　••••　NEW YORK, SUNDAY, JUNE 29, 1919. 122 PAGES, In Nine Parts.　FIVE CENTS

PEACE SIGNED, ENDS THE GREAT WAR; GERMANS DEPART STILL PROTESTING; PROHIBITION TILL TROOPS DISBAND

ENEMY ENVOYS IN TRUCULENT SPIRIT

Say Afterward They Would Not Have Signed Had They Known They Were to Leave First by Different Way.

CHINA REFUSES TO SIGN, SMUTS MAKES PROTEST

These Events Somewhat Cloud the Great Occasion at Versailles—Wilson, Clemenceau, and Lloyd George Receive a Tremendous Ovation.

President Wilson Starts for Home

PARIS, June 28, (Associated Press.)—President Wilson left Paris on his homeward journey tonight. His train started from the Gare des Invalides for Brest at 9:45 P. M.

Mr. Wilson's party was accompanied to Brest by General Leorat and Colonel Lobez, the President's French aids, and also by Stephen Pichon, French Foreign Minister; Georges Leygues, French Minister of Marine, and Captain André Tardieu, a member of the French peace delegation. Ambassador Wallace, General Pershing, Premier Clemenceau, and Colonel House were at the station to say good-bye.

The crowd in the station, numbering upward of a thousand, wildly cheered the departure of the President, who raised his hat to cries of "Vive Wilson." Mrs. Wilson threw kisses to the crowd as the train departed.

The superdreadnought Oklahoma will accompany the George Washington to the United States.

VERSAILLES, June 28, (Associated Press.)—Germany and the allied and associated powers signed the peace terms here today in the same imperial hall where the Germans humbled the French so ignominiously forty-eight years ago.

This formally ended the world war, which lasted just thirty-seven days less than five years. Today, the day of peace, was the fifth anniversary of the murder of Archduke Francis Ferdinand by a Serbian student at Serajevo.

The peace was signed under circumstances which somewhat dimmed the expectations of those who had worked and fought during long years of war and months of negotiations for its achievement.

Absence of the Chinese delegates, who at the last moment were unable to reconcile themselves to the Shantung settlement, struck the first discordant note. A written protest which General Smuts lodged with his signature was another disappointment.

But bulking larger than these was the attitude of Germany and the German plenipotentiaries, which left them, as evident from the expression of M. Clemenceau, still outside of formal reconciliation and made the actual restoration to regular relations and intercourse with the allied

---

Wilson Says Treaty Will Furnish the Charter for a New Order of Affairs in the World

WASHINGTON, June 28.—The following address by President Wilson to the American people on the occasion of the signing of the Peace Treaty was given out here today by Secretary Tumulty:

My Fellow Countrymen: The treaty of peace has been signed. If it is ratified and acted upon in full and sincere execution of its terms it will furnish the charter for a new order of affairs in the world. It is a severe treaty in the duties and penalties it imposes upon Germany; but it is severe only because great wrongs done by Germany are to be righted and repaired; it imposes nothing that Germany cannot do; and she can regain her rightful standing in the world by the prompt and honorable fulfillment of its terms.

And it is much more than a treaty of peace with Germany. It liberates great peoples who have never before been able to find the way to liberty. It ends, once for all, an old and intolerable order under which small groups of selfish men could use the peoples of great empires to serve their ambition for power and dominion. It associates the free Governments of the world in a permanent League in which they are pledged to use their united power to maintain peace by maintaining right and justice.

It makes international law a reality supported by imperative sanctions. It does away with the right of conquest and rejects the policy of annexation and substitutes a new order under which backward nations—populations which have not yet come to political consciousness and peoples who are ready for independence but not yet quite prepared to dispense with protection and guidance—shall no more be subjected to the domination and exploitation of a stronger nation, but shall be put under the friendly direction and afforded the helpful assistance of governments which undertake to be responsible to the opinion of mankind in the execution of their task by accepting the direction of the League of Nations.

It recognizes the inalienable rights of nationality, the rights of minorities and the sanctity of religious belief and practice. It lays the basis for conventions which shall free the commercial intercourse of the world from unjust and vexatious restrictions and for every sort of international co-operation that will serve to cleanse the life of the world and facilitate its common action in beneficent service of every kind. It furnishes guarantees such as were never given or even contemplated for the fair treatment of all who labor at the daily tasks of the world.

It is for this reason that I have spoken of it as a great charter for a new order of affairs. There is ground here for deep satisfaction, universal reassurance, and confident hope.

WOODROW WILSON.

---

nations dependent, not upon the signature of the "preliminaries of peace" today, but upon ratification by the National Assembly.

To M. Clemenceau's warning in his opening remarks that they would be expected, and held, to observe the treaty provisions loyally and completely the German delegates, through Dr. Haniel von Haimhausen, replied after returning to the hotel that had they known that they would be treated on a different status after signing than the allied representatives, as shown by their separate exit before the general body of the conference, they never would have signed.

Under the circumstances the general tone of sentiment in the historic sitting was one rather of relief at the uncontrovertible end of hostilities than of complete satisfaction.

The ceremony had been planned deliberately to be austere, befitting the sufferings of almost five years, and the lack of impressiveness and picturesque color, of which many spectators, who had expected a magnificent State pageant, complained, was a matter of design, not merely omission.

The actual ceremony was far shorter than had been expected, in view of the number of signatures which were to be appended to the treaty and the two accompanying conventions, ending a bare forty-nine minutes after the hour set for the opening.

Premier Clemenceau called the session to order in the Hall of Mirrors at 3:10 P. M.

The signing began when Dr. Hermann Müller and Johannes Bell, the German signatories, affixed their names. Herr Müller signed at 3:12 o'clock and Herr Bell 3:13 o'clock.

President Wilson, the first of the allied delegates, signed a minute later. At 3:49 o'clock the momentous session was over.

The most dramatic moment connected with the signing came unexpectedly and spontaneously at the conclusion of the ceremony, when Premier Clemenceau, President Wilson and Premier Lloyd George descended from the Hall of Mirrors to the terrace at the rear of the palace, where thousands of spectators were massed.

GREAT DEMONSTRATION FOR ALLIED LEADERS.

With the appearance of the three who had dominated the councils of the Allies there began a most remarkable demonstration. With cries of "Vive Clemenceau!" "Vive Wilson!" "Vive Lloyd George!" dense crowds swept forward from all parts of the spacious terrace. In an instant the three were surrounded by struggling, cheering masses of people, fighting among themselves for a chance to get near the statesmen.

It had been planned that all the allied delegates would walk across the terrace after signing, to see the great fountains play, but none of the other plenipotentiaries got further than the door.

President Wilson, M. Clemenceau and Mr. Lloyd George were caught in the living stream which flowed across the great space, and became part of the crowd themselves. Soldiers and bodyguards struggled vainly to clear the way. The people jostled and struggled for a chance to touch the hands of the leaders of the Allies, all the while cheering madly.

Probably the least concerned for their personal safety were the three themselves. They went forward smilingly, as the crowd willed, bowing in response to the ovation, and here and there reaching out to shake an insistent hand as they passed on their way through the château grounds to watch the playing of the fountains—a part of the program which had been planned as a dignified State processional of all the plenipotentiaries

Every available point of vantage in the palace and about the grounds was filled with thousands of people, who, less hardy than their comrades, had not been able to join the procession. No more picturesque setting could have been selected for this drama.

The return of President Wilson, M. Clemenceau, and Lloyd George toward the palace was a repetition of their outward journey of triumph. As they reached the château however, they turned to the left instead of entering. The crowd was in doubt as to what was intended, but followed, cheering tumultuously.

Nearby a closed car was waiting and the three entered this and they drove from the grounds together amid a profusion of flowers which had been thrust through the open window.

All the diplomats and members of their parties who attended the ceremony of treaty signing wore conventional civilian clothes. Outside of this also there was a marked lack of gold lace and pageantry, with few of the fanciful uniforms of the Middle Ages, whose traditions and practices are so sternly condemned in the great, seal-covered document signed today.

One spot of color was made against the sombre background by the French Guards. A few selected members of the Guard were there, resplendent in red-plumed silver helmets and red, white and blue uniforms.

A group of allied Generals, including General Pershing, wore the scarlet sash of the Legion of Honor.

As a contrast with the Franco-German peace session of 1871, held in the same hall, there were present today grizzled French veterans of the Franco-Prussian war. They took the place of the Prussian guardsmen of the previous ceremony, and the Frenchmen today watched the ceremony with grim satisfaction.

The conditions of 1871 were exactly reversed. Today the disciples of Bismarck sat in the seats of the lowly, while the white marble statue of Minerva, Goddess of War, looked on. Overhead, on the frescoed ceiling, were scenes from France's ancient wars.

GERMAN PROTEST AT THE LAST MINUTE.

Three incidents were emphasized by the smoothness with which the ceremony was conducted. The first of these was the failure of the Chinese delegation to sign. The second was the protest submitted by General Jan Christian Smuts, who declared the peace unsatisfactory.

The third, which was unknown to the general public, came from the Germans. When the program for the ceremony was shown to the German delegation, Herr von Haimhausen of the German delegation went to Colonel Henri, French liaison officer, and protested. He said:

"We cannot admit that the German delegates should enter the hall by a different door than the Entente delegates; nor that military honors should be withheld. Had we known there would be such arrangements before, the delegates would not have come."

After a conference with the French Foreign Ministry it was decided, as a compromise, to render military honors as the Germans left. Otherwise the program as originally arranged was not changed.

Secretary Lansing was the first of the American delegation to arrive at the palace, entering the building at 1:45 o'clock.

The Peace Treaty was deposited on the table at 2:10 o'clock by William Martin of the French Foreign Office. It was inclosed in a stamped leather case.

Premier Clemenceau entered the palace at 2:20 o'clock.

Detachments of fifteen soldiers each from the American, British and French forces entered just before 3 o'clock and took their places in embrasures of the windows, overlooking the château park, a few feet from Marshal Foch, seated with the French delegation at the peace table.

The American soldiers who saw the signing of the treaty were all attached to President Wilson's residence. They were: George W. Bender, Baltimore; Stanley Cohek, Chicopee, Mass.; George Bridgewater, Palestine, Texas; Harlan Hayes, Green City, Wis.; J. S. Horton, Lexington, Miss.; William R. Knox, Temple, Okla.; Albert E. Landreth, Portsmouth, Va.; Sergeant Sam Lane, Prosper, Texas; George Laudance, Philadelphia; M. D. Mary, Havre, Mon.; Fred Quantz, Cleveland; Hubert Ridgeway, Mo.; Raymond Riley, Baltimore, and Frank Wilgus, Allentown, Penn.

With the thirty poilus and Tommies they were present as the real "artisans of peace" and stood within the enclosure reserved for plenipotentiaries and high officials of the conference as a visible sign of their rôle in bringing into being a new Europe.

Premier Clemenceau promptly stepped up to the French detachment and shook the hand of each man. The men had been selected from those who bore honorable wounds, and the Premier expressed his pleasure at seeing them there and his regret for the sufferings they had endured for their country.

Delegates of the minor powers made their way with difficulty through the crowd to their places at the table. Officers and civilians lined the walls and filled the aisles.

President Wilson entered the Hall of Mirrors at 2:50 o'clock. All the allied delegates were then seated except the Chinese, who did not attend.

The difficulty of seeing well from many parts of the hall militated against demonstrations on the arrival of the chief personages. Only a few persons saw President Wilson when he came in, and there was but a faint sound of applause for him.

An hour before the signing of the treaty those assembled in the hall had been urged to take their seats, but their eagerness to see the historic ceremony was so keen that they refused to remain seated, and crowded toward the centre of the hall, which is so long that a good view was impossible from a distance. Even with opera glasses, correspondents and others were unable to observe satisfactorily, as the seats were not elevated; consequently there was a general scramble for standing room.

German correspondents were ushered into the hall just before 3 o'clock and took standing room in a window at the rear of the correspondents' section.

When Premier Lloyd George arrived many delegates sought autographs from the members of the Council of Four, and they busied themselves for the next few minutes signing copies of the official program.

At 3 o'clock a hush fell over the hall, and the crowds shouted for the officials, who were standing, to sit down, so as not to block the view. The delegates showed some surprise at the disorder, which did not cease until all the spectators had seated themselves or found places against the walls.

MULLER AND BELL SHOW GREAT COMPOSURE.

At seven minutes past 3 Dr. Müller, German Secretary for Foreign Affairs, and Dr. Bell, Colonial Secretary, were shown into the hall, and quietly took their seats, the other delegates not rising.

They showed composure, and manifested none of the uneasiness which Count von Brockdorff-Rantzau, head of the German peace delegation, displayed when handed the treaty at Versailles.

Dr. Müller and Dr. Bell had driven early to Versailles by automobile from St. Cyr instead of taking the belt line railroad, as did the German delegates who came to receive the terms of peace on May 7. Their credentials had been approved in the morning.

In the allotment of seats in the ceremonial chamber places for the German delegates were on the side of the horseshoe table, where they touched elbows with Japanese plenipotentiaries on their right and the Brazilians on their left. Delegates from Ecuador, Peru, and Liberia faced the Germans across the narrow table.

M. Clemenceau, as President of the Conference, made this address:

"The session is open. The allied and associated powers on one side and the German reich on the other side have come to an agreement on the conditions of peace. The text has been completed, drafted, and the President of the Conference has stated in writing that the text that is about to be signed now is identical with the 200 copies that have been delivered to the German delegation.

"The signatures will be given now and they amount to a solemn undertaking faithfully and loyally to execute the conditions embodied by this treaty of peace. I now invite the delegates of the German reich to sign the treaty."

There was a tense pause for a moment. Then in response to M. Clemenceau's bidding the German delegates rose without a word and, escorted by William Martin, master of ceremonies, moved to the signatory table, where they placed upon the treaty the sign manuals which German Government leaders declared until recently would never be appended to this treaty.

They also signed a protocol covering changes in the document and the Polish undertaking.